JACK THE RIPPER

OTTO PENZLER is the proprietor
of the Mysterious Bookshop in New York City,
founder of the Mysterious Press, a two-time
Edgar winner, and a member of the Baker Street
Irregulars for more than forty years.

**Also edited by Otto Penzler
and published by Head of Zeus**

The Big Book of Christmas Mysteries

Sherlock

Death Sentences

THE ULTIMATE
COMPENDIUM OF
JACK THE
RIPPER
FACT, FICTION,
LEGEND.

SELECTED BY
OTTO PENZLER

HEAD
ZEUS

975312468

A catalogue record for this book is available from the British Library.

ISBN (HB) 9781800240292
ISBN (E) 9781784976231

Typeset by Adrian McLaughlin

Printed and bound in Germany by CPI Books GmbH

Head of Zeus Ltd
5–8 Hardwick Street
London EC1R 4RG
WWW.HEADOFZEUS.COM

FOR ROGER COOPER
*My valued friend, with gratitude
and admiration for his creative guidance*

CONTENTS

Red Jack — An Inspiration

Saucy Jack — Timeless

INTRODUCTION

Otto Penzler

While the world has had no shortage of murderers, with Cain wasting no time in getting humanity started on its bloodstained path, none has imposed himself on the public consciousness as indelibly as Jack the Ripper. Most experts, known in this very specific area of scholarship as Ripperologists, believe that the fiend committed his atrocities during a relatively short period of time in 1888, yet his sobriquet still resonates throughout the world today.

It is reasonable to ask why this remains true after more than a century and a quarter. Certainly, there have been countless other killers whose names have screamed at us in headlines over the years, holding our attention for a while before fading and, mostly, disappearing.

We may remember Adam Lanza now, for having committed the incomprehensible slaughter of twenty children and six adults at a school in Newtown, Connecticut, in 2012, but only devoted scholars of crime will recall Andrew Kehoe, who murdered thirty-eight children and five adults when he blew up a school in Michigan in 1927.

American gangsters such as Al Capone, Bonnie and Clyde, Whitey Bulger, Baby Face Nelson, Machine Gun Kelly, and John Gotti are legendary figures in America but are virtually unknown in the rest of the world. The same is largely true for the icons of the old Western frontier, where Jesse James, Billy the Kid, the Younger brothers, and Doc Holliday became the subject of purple prose newspaper accounts that captivated East Coast readers, leading to dime novels and motion picture portrayals that reimagined vicious thugs as semi-heroic characters. None of these villains sends a chill down the spine, as popular media have sanitized their reputations and deeds.

Equally uninspiring of horror in the present time are British killers such as Fred and Rose West, who are known to have tortured and murdered at least eleven women and girls until they were brought to trial in 1994, their exploits garishly recounted in the news media. Also the merest footnote to the history of serial killers is Dr. Harold Shipman, reputedly the murderer of approximately two hundred and fifty people, mostly his patients, whose wills he forged so that he could inherit their valuables. Some may recall the newspapers' colorful title of the Moors Murderers, but few remember the real names of Ian Brady and Myra Hindley, described at her trial as the Most Evil Woman in Britain. Other names that became famous at one time, mainly because they became the subjects of books or movies, are Burke and Hare, gravediggers who were paid for corpses for medical examination and soon found it easier to kill people than dig them up; Constance Kent, who murdered a child when she was sixteen, a case so notorious in its time (1860) that elements were used by Wilkie Collins in *The Moonstone,* by Charles Dickens in *The Mystery of Edwin Drood,* and in numerous other novels; Peter William Sutcliffe, better known as the Yorkshire Ripper, convicted of murdering thirteen women; and Madeleine Smith, whose trial for poisoning her lover allowed her freedom when the jury returned a verdict of "not proven." She was sensationalized in Wilkie Collins's *The Law and the Lady* and in the 1950 David Lean film *Madeleine*.

Better known in the United States, often because journalists bestowed colorful names on them, are such infamous serial killers as The Hillside Stranglers, Kenneth Bianchi and Angelo Buono; the Son of Sam, David Berko-witz; the Co-ed Killer, Edmund Kemper; the BTK (Bind, Torture, and Kill) Killer, Dennis Rader; the Night Stalker, Richard Ramirez; the Milwaukee Cannibal, Jeffrey Dahmer; the Green River Killer, Gary Ridgway; John Wayne Gacy and Ted Bundy, prolific murderers who somehow eluded colorful titles; and Charles Manson, probably the most fearsome American psychopath of the twentieth century, his crimes splashed along headlines for years, partially because of the unspeakable brutality of the crimes and partially because of the fame and beauty of one of the victims, Sharon Tate.

There is a seemingly limitless number of people who have committed untold numbers of heinous acts throughout the long history of Homo sapiens, a species almost unique in its ability to kill within the species for the sheer pleasure of it. With so many others having murdered in even greater numbers than Jack the Ripper, and some equally brutal (or worse, engaging in unspeakably depraved torture of living victims, a practice almost entirely eschewed by Saucy Jack), why does he continue to maintain his place at the top of the public's radar?

While students of criminology are not unanimous in attributing the number of the Ripper's victims, with five apparently accepted universally, but one, two, three, or four others also credited to him by various scholars, it is generally agreed that all the murders occurred during the autumn of 1888 (again, with outliers claiming at least an additional year at either end). The victims were all prostitutes in London's East End, a ghetto teeming with the poorest segment of the population. The dark, narrow alleyways, often ending in cul-de-sacs, were perfect venues in which to commit an act of violence—or a transaction of a sexual nature, performed by a member of the largest profession of the neighborhood. The noxious fumes of coal stoves and fireplaces, as well as the factories located in the area, combined to provide an almost permanently darkened sky, a smog known as London particular. The women of the night, prowling the streets, looking for partners to pay them enough for a glass of warming gin, were perfect victims, willing—no, eager—to slip off to a darkened corner to quickly ply their trade. Although police patrolled regularly throughout the night, it was seldom the cream of the force, and the odds of them catching a criminal in the act, with visibility frequently limited to two or three feet, were slim.

Since so few cared about the victims of the Ripper's carnage while they were alive, why has their fate continued to resonate today? A likely reason is that he was never caught. Having spread a tsunami of terror for a short time, he disappeared completely, leaving his identity to be theorized, discussed, argued, and written about for decade after decade. It did not hurt his legacy of notoriety that he frequently taunted the police, with the complicity of the local press, by sending letters warning them of forthcoming attacks and daring them to catch him if they can.

The frisson of terror evoked by his name, Jack the Ripper—so much more chilling than merely Jack the Killer or Jack the Stabber—stays in the memory, and on the tongue, so easily. He was written about in such extreme terms, first of course in newspapers, but then in magazine articles and books, that he provided endless fodder for those who became intrigued by him. Theories about his identity were rampant, with clues clutched to advance one theory, while other possible pieces of evidence were ignored if they suggested that someone else was the genuine article. Other Ripperologists rushed to discredit the first theory and advance their own, which suffered the same fate at the hands of still other students of the crimes. Jack the Ripper has now been "proven" to be any one of at least a half-dozen people by various authors and scholars.

This collection has articles describing the area of the atrocities, accounts of the murders, and theories about the identity of Red Jack by some of the world's leading experts on the subject. There also are contemporary reports from newspapers of the day. Taken together, they will provide a reasonably clear picture of the real-life events that inspired so much fiction about the incidents and the demented individual at the heart of them. For the most comprehensive guide to all the facts, if you are interested to read in far greater detail than offered here, I recommend *The Complete Jack the Ripper* by Donald Rumbelow.

The fiction contained in this tome has a wide range. While planned as a volume of crime stories, the almost mythical level at which Jack has been perceived has compelled me to include some of the memorable tales that present him as ageless as his reputation. Many theories about why Jack quit so abruptly have suggested he moved to a different country, or to a different time. It was impossible to resist these stories by several masters of the form.

Finally, proving yet again that Jack the Ripper is as timeless as fear, there are new stories, written especially for this volume by some of today's most distinguished authors—Jeffery Deaver, Loren D. Estleman, Lyndsay Faye, Stephen Hunter, Anne Perry, and Daniel Stashower—and I am grateful to them all for adding to the literature about one of the most singularly vile creatures ever to degrade the planet.

Prepare to be unnerved.

—OTTO PENZLER

The True Story

VICTIMS IN THE NIGHT

David Abrahamsen

As a forensic psychiatrist and psychoanalyst, David Abrahamsen (1903–2002) was called upon to serve as an expert witness at some of the most famous murder cases of the twentieth century, including the Leopold-Loeb "Crime of the Century" trial, the investigations of Lee Harvey Oswald, and the trial of David Berkowitz, known as the "Son of Sam." His interest in the latter led to his book *Confessions of Son of Sam* (1985).

His expertise in criminal psychopathology proved invaluable while working at prisons in New York and Illinois and lecturing at different hospitals, ultimately leading to the publication of fifteen books relating to various elements of the subject, including *Crime and the Human Mind* (1944), *Who Are the Guilty?: A Study of Education and Crime* (1952), *The Psychology of Crime* (1960), *Our Violent Society* (1970), *The Murdering Mind* (1973), and *The Mind of the Accused: A Psychiatrist in the Courtroom* (1983). He also wrote a study of Richard M. Nixon—*Nixon vs. Nixon: An Emotional Tragedy* (1977)—and *Murder and Madness: The Secret Life of Jack the Ripper* (1992), in which he identifies Prince Albert Victor and James Kenneth Stephen as collaborators in the Ripper murders, providing them with credible motives (unlike most of the other suspects who have been advanced over the years), although he supplies no convincing facts to support his hypothesis.

"Victims in the Night" was first published in *Murder and Madness: The Secret Life of Jack the Ripper* (New York, Donald I. Fine, 1992).

> *With life so precarious, and opportunity for the happiness of life so remote, it is inevitable that life shall be cheap . . .*
> JACK LONDON, *THE PEOPLE OF THE ABYSS*

The murders and mutilations of five prostitutes in Whitechapel, in the East End of London, began on the morning of Friday, August 31, 1888. Mary Anne Nichols was found dead, lying in a back street named Buck's Row. Murders connected to theft or rape were common occurrences, and under ordinary circumstances the death of a prostitute would cause no more than a momentary ripple in the dark pool that was the East End. But these circumstances were not ordinary.

First of all, the motive was clearly not robbery, since Nichols had nothing to steal. Second, the violence of her death was chilling. Her throat was severed almost to the vertebrae. Her face was bruised, and both her upper and lower jaws were injured. A deep slash ran across her abdomen. The cuts had ragged edges and some inner organs had been cut out. The murder seemed to have no purpose except as an expression of violence. The police surgeon duly noted the details in his formal report to the London Metropolitan Police.

As an isolated event, the death of Nichols soon subsided in the public consciousness. After all, the Whitechapel of those days was one of the grimmest of all London slums; life there, as Jack London points out, was cheap indeed. One inhabitant of the East End wrote to *The Times* (London) at midcentury:

> *We are Sur, as it may be, livin in a Wilderness, so far as the rest of London knows anything of us, or as the rich and great people care about. We live in muck and filthe. We aint got no privies, no dust bins, no drains, no water splies . . . We al of us suffer, and numbers are ill, and if the colera comes Lord help us . . .*[1]

The writer accurately perceived that the place where he lived was so cut off from the rest of the prospering city that it was almost another country. The East End was the popular name for the area east of the actual City of London, which had grown up around the docks that lined the Thames, the heart of the trade on which the British Empire flourished. Inside this maze of narrow streets and jerry-built houses with totally inadequate sanitary facilities, some ninety thousand people lived in desperate poverty, victims of unemployment, homelessness, overcrowding and disease. The cholera did indeed come, and much worse. High infant mortality was as common as child labor, and prostitution, alcoholism, crime and murder were endemic. Hanging like an evil cloud over the slums was the thick black tarry smoke from factory smokestacks and thousands of coal fires that Charles Dickens describes at the beginning of *Bleak House*: "Smoke lowering down from chimney-pots, making a soft black drizzle, with flakes of soot in it as big as full-grown snow-flakes—gone into mourning, one might imagine, for the death of the sun."[2]

In *The People of the Abyss*—written a little over a decade after the infamous year of 1888—Jack London points out that the personal despair of many East Enders drove them to suicide.

Into this wilderness of poverty, illness and blight some Londoners traveled regularly to buy what could not be bought on more civilized streets—the sexual services of women. In the borough of Whitechapel alone there were ninety thousand people, of whom seventy thousand were women and children, mostly the unemployed poor who lived from hand to mouth. By 1880, there were estimated to be ten thousand prostitutes and three thousand brothels in London. Almost every room, nook, or corridor in Whitechapel, Shadwell, Spitalfields, and adjoining areas was at one time or another used for sexual purposes. Owning a brothel, in fact, was a favored way of investing in a neighborhood. Prostitution was illegal, of course, and many prostitutes were picked up and sent to jail. Men, however, were not harassed, unless they were suspected of performing "unnatural sexual acts" with other men. But the typical English method of dealing with the problem was, in general, to ignore its existence.

---

1   *The Times* (London), circa 1850s.
2   Charles Dickens, *Bleak House,* Bradbury and Evan, London, 1853, p. 1.

The most humane contemporary view of prostitution is found in the writings of the physician William Acton, one of the authors of the Contagious Diseases Act of 1866, which provided that prostitutes in certain areas be subject to periodic medical examination. In his pioneering book on the subject, first published in 1862, Acton writes that "cruel, biting poverty" forces women to become prostitutes:

> Unable to obtain by their labor the means of procuring the bare necessaries of life, they gain, by surrendering their bodies to evil uses, food to sustain and clothes to cover them. Many thousand young women in the metropolis are unable by drudgery that lasts from early morning till late into the night to earn more than from 3s. to 5s. weekly. Many have to eke out their living as best they may on a miserable pittance for less than the least of the sums above-mentioned . . . Urged on by want and toil, encouraged by evil advisors, and exposed to selfish tempters, a large proportion of these girls fall from the path of virtue . . .[3]

The horror and sadness of the Jack the Ripper murders are intensified when we consider the degraded lives of the victims. Scorned by society, these women were defenseless, alienated, and dispossessed. Their lives were narrowly limited to the goal of getting fourpence from a client to buy a shot of gin or a glass of beer, or to rent a bed for the night in a common lodging house. This economic exchange could easily end in syphilis or gonorrhea, or in an unwanted pregnancy that was terminated by an abortion performed under appalling conditions. Life, as they knew it, was dangerous and callous. In the "brute vulgarities" of this world, as Jack London put it, "the bad corrupts the good, and all fester together."[4]

Yet there were some people who felt that the prostitutes' deaths were a kind of moral retribution for the lives they led—essentially, that they got what they deserved. Syphilis was widely regarded as a punishment for sin—why not murder? Hypocrisy, one of the most deadly sins, was nowhere more evident in Victorian society than in the sexual double standard practiced by men. A woman was judged by her effect on men. This was a period when women of one's own class were set on a pedestal and the wife was idealized as the keeper of the sacred flame of home and hearth: kind, gentle, nurturing, and, above all, pure. And, not surprisingly, this produced a view of women as either virgins or whores. Although Victorian men publicly revered women, courted them, catered to them and married them, they secretly sought out prostitutes for sexual release or for taboo sexual pleasures. But there were other, psychological reasons why the Victorian man sought out prostitutes.

First of all, when a man bought the services of a prostitute, he did not have to establish any emotional relationship with her, or any significant relationship at all. The encounter was generally brief and impersonal. He did not have—and usually did not want—to remember her name or face.

---

3   William Acton, *Prostitution, Considered in its Moral, Social, and Sanitary Aspects, in London and other large cities and Garrison Towns, with Proposals for the Control and Prevention of its Attendant Evils*, John Churchill, London 1862, as quoted in Steven Marcus, *The Other Victorians; A Study of Sexuality and Pornography in Mid-Nineteenth-Century En-gland*. Basic Books, New York [1966], p. 7.

4   Jack London, *The People of the Abyss*, Macmillan & Co., New York, 1903, p. 152.

A second reason was the great gulf of class distinction: almost without exception, prostitutes came from the lower classes. Their humble origins and the conditions of squalor in which they lived both excited and revolted the middle-class and aristocratic men who were their patrons. Slumming has always had charms for those who are not condemned to live in poverty, and many Victorian men visited the East End for very different reasons from their wives, who knew it only as a place to set up missions and soup kitchens to save souls and nourish starved bodies.

On the whole there is a general behavior pattern observable among those men who choose prostitutes as their only sexual objects. Such a man is unconsciously attracted to women who are more or less sexually discredited. He identifies with the harlot's lack of fidelity and loyalty. His choice is rooted in his unconscious fixation on his infantile feelings of tenderness for his mother, a crucial point in his sexual development. From his first belief that his mother is sexually pure, he comes to learn that she (like a prostitute) has had sex with a man (his father). The child feels betrayed by her. He fantasizes rescuing her from the father who he feels has defiled her. This leads him later in life to set up a woman as a substitute mother whom he loves, yet despises for her weakness. He ends up seeking out prostitutes, whom he endows with his mother's image.

What drives women to prostitution? Without question, it is a way of obtaining through economic means what a woman has not been able to gain through love, the love from a mother or father, or a substitute. For some women, prostitution seems to offer a means of revenging themselves against weak and passive fathers who never defended them against their mothers' anger and criticism. Other women feel a masochistic identification of sex as sinful or humiliating, as they believe it was for their own mothers. In nineteenth-century Whitechapel, the wretched housing, miserable earnings, and lack of emotional bonds between parents and children inevitably produced strained and callous relationships. Girls moved away from their parents into a situation where the procurer, the pimp, became the father substitute and the madam the mother substitute. The girl's relationship with her abusing father and unloving mother was now played out in the new environment, complete with all the former ambivalent feelings. One must wonder why a woman abused by her mother would become a prostitute and tolerate the madam. The answer is that she hates the madam as she hated her mother, yet is masochistically tied to her.

For most of the Whitechapel prostitutes, their illicit business was a means of scraping by from day to day in a poverty-stricken world. It had desperate and cruel consequences—broken homes and emotional turmoil, sometimes leading to arrest and jail, in addition to the risk of disease, alcoholism, drug addiction, and exposure to crime. Even if a prostitute married or managed to avoid the fate of poverty and disease, her psychological fate remained cloudy at best.

The eternal wish of every woman from childhood onward is to be taken care of by someone who loves her. But few are given such happiness. And the prostitutes of Whitechapel were no exception. For five of them, a horrible death ended their quest.

Falling from the path of virtue had always been dangerous; the story of Mary Anne Nichols shows that it was becoming more so.

Nichols was no young girl, however; she was forty-two years old and an alcoholic. She had had five children and had left her husband about eight years earlier because of her drinking habits. Though separated from her, her husband continued to support her for several years until she moved in with another man. Several times, Nichols had tried to make a fresh start, but her alcoholism always prevailed. At one point she ended up in a workhouse, but was thrown out because she stole some small items—again, the result of her drinking. *The Times* (London) described her life as "intemperate, irregular and vicious."[5] The meaning of "vicious" here is "savage."

On the night of August 30, 1888, Nichols had been drinking steadily at a pub. At about 2:00 A.M., she decided to go out on the streets to raise the price of a bed for the night. She went into Buck's Row, a secluded back alley about a hundred yards from the Jews' Cemetery, close to the Whitechapel Road. At about 3:45 A.M., her body was discovered there by Constable John Neil working his Whitechapel beat. *The Times* (London) described Neil's discovery of the body:

> *With the aid of his lamp he examined the body and saw blood oozing from a wound in the throat. Deceased was lying on her back with her clothes disarranged. [Neil] felt her arm, which was quite warm from the joints upward, while her eyes were wide open.[6]*

She was dressed in a new brown dress, a shabby red overcoat, two flannel petticoats, blue woolen stockings and a straw bonnet, which had fallen from her head and was lying by her side. Her underwear had been removed. Her only possessions were a piece of mirror, a comb, and a handkerchief.

The police surgeon Henry Llewellyn of 152 Whitechapel Road was called to the scene and examined the body at the site. He found no marks of a struggle and no bloody trail as if the body had been dragged. He had the body moved to the mortuary, where he discovered for the first time the mutilation of the abdomen. He concluded that the cuts must have been caused by a moderately sharp, long-bladed knife wielded with violence. Excerpts from his report to the Metropolitan Police the following day, August 31, 1888, are as follows:

> *. . . throat cut nearly severing head from body, abdomen cut open from centre of bottom of ribs along right side, under pelvis to left of stomach, there the wound was jagged: the coating of the stomach was cut in several places and two small stabs on private parts . . .[7]*

Inquiries were made of the neighbors, night watchmen, other prostitutes and friends of Nichols, local tavern owners, coffee-stall keepers, and lodging houses. The police also interrogated three slaughtermen doing night work for a butcher's firm on the next street, but each accounted for himself satisfactorily. Nichols's history "did not disclose the slightest pretext for a motive on the part of her

---

5   *The Times* (London), September 1, 1888.
6   *Ibid.*
7   Report by Henry Llewellyn, Metropolitan Police, London, August 31, 1888.

friends or associates in the common lodging houses," wrote Chief Inspector Donald S. Swanson in his report on the murder.[8]

Early on Saturday, September 8, 1888, London was jolted once again, when the body of another murdered woman was found. Forty-seven-year-old Annie Chapman—also destitute, a prostitute and an alcoholic—was discovered in the back yard of a house on Hanbury Street, Spitalfields, about half a mile from the site of Nichols's murder. This woman had also been hideously mutilated. It was suggested "that the murderer, for some purpose or other, whether from a morbid motive or for the sake of gain, had committed the crime for the purpose of possessing himself of the uterus."[9]

The scene was macabre. Fully dressed, she lay on the ground with her organs exposed like a scientific experiment. The abdominal wall had been cut open and the uterus removed. The vagina, bladder and intestines—still attached to the body—were arranged over her right shoulder. At her feet were her comb and some coins, carefully placed.

On Friday, September 14, 1888, *The Times* (London) described the postmortem of Annie Chapman and stated that, in the coroner's opinion, "there had been no struggle between the murderer and the woman." This was an important finding. Like Nichols, Chapman had died without making any resistance. The coroner also concluded that the murderer "had anatomical knowledge from the way the viscera was removed." In addition, he believed the murder weapon was not an ordinary knife, but "a small amputating knife or a well-ground slaughterman's knife," probably between six and eight inches long.[10]

Annie Chapman was the widow of a veterinarian. They had been separated for several years before his death because of what the police report called "her drunken and immoral ways." However, her husband continued to send her ten shillings a week until he died, at Christmas, 1886. Like Nichols, Chapman was a victim of her alcoholism, which had caused her to lose touch with her family and turn to prostitution. *The Times* (London) on September 27, 1888, reported:

> She had evidently lived an immoral life for some time, and her habits and surroundings had become worse since her means had failed. She no longer visited her relations, and her brother had not seen her for five months, when she borrowed a small sum from him. She lived principally in the common lodging houses in the neighborhood of Spitalfields, where such as she were herded like cattle. She showed signs of great deprivation, as if she had been badly fed.
>
> The glimpse of life in those dens which the evidence in this case disclosed was sufficient to make them feel there was much in the 19th-century civilization of which they had small reason to be proud . . .[11]

On Saturday, September 15, 1888, *The Lancet*, the foremost British medical journal, published an editorial suggesting the theory that the murderer might be

---

8   Report by Chief Inspector Swanson, Metropolitan Police, London, September 2, 1888.
9   *The Lancet*, September 29, 1888, p. 637.
10   *The Times* (London), September 14, 1888.
11   *Ibid.*, September 27, 1888.

a lunatic. But, the writer added, this "appears to us to be by no means at present well established."[12]

The third victim was Elizabeth Stride, forty-five years old, a Swedish prostitute known by the name of "Long Liz." On Sunday, September 30, her body was found at Berner Street, Aldgate, a short distance from Hanbury Street. Although her throat had been cut in the now familiar method, she had not been disemboweled, which suggested that the murderer was interrupted in his work. Did somebody warn him?

Later that same night, the murderer struck again, at Mitre Square, which was only about half a mile from Berner Street, just across the boundary of the City of London. The victim was another prostitute, Catherine Eddowes, who was forty-three. As if in compensation for the murderer's frustration at having had to leave Stride intact, Eddowes's body had been brutally dissected. Her nose was cut off, her abdomen sliced open, and on her right shoulder were placed her left kidney and intestines.

The fact that this murder took place within the City boundaries meant that it was handled by the City Police Department, and these fresh investigators zealously set about gathering evidence. Eddowes's murder, it seems, was the only occasion when a description of the possible assailant was available.

Catherine Eddowes had been trying to make some extra money by picking hops in Kent with her friend John Kelly, who had spent 2s. 6d. of his earnings to buy her a pair of boots. When they returned to London together on Thursday, September 27, however, they had to pawn the boots to get enough money to pay for a night's lodging. The following night they had to part and she spent the night in the Mile End casual ward (a dormitory), while Kelly stayed in a cheap lodging house. By Saturday they had no money left and were unable to find any odd jobs. So at 2:00 P.M., Eddowes left Kelly and went off to Bermondsey to try to borrow money from her daughter. At 8:00 P.M. that evening, she was back in the City, in a drunk and disorderly condition, was arrested by two City policemen and taken to the Bishopsgate Police Station, where she remained until shortly after midnight. During her incarceration, she continued, in the words of Dr. Francis Camps, one of the major authorities on the Ripper story, "singing to herself and asking to be released." His report continued:

> At about 1 A.M. her wish was complied with and she was shooed off into the night. It was a singularly bad piece of luck for her that the instructions of Major Smith, the City Police Commissioner, were not carried out, for he had ordered that every man and woman seen together after midnight must be accounted for and she might have been followed to Mitre Square.[13]

As City Police Commissioner, Major Smith was responsible for all police activity within the City of London, while the Metropolitan Police were under the separate command of General Sir Charles Warren, who had no jurisdiction

---

12 *The Lancet*, September 15, 1888, pp. 533–534.
13 Report by Professor Francis E. Camps, *London Hospital Gazette*, Vol. LXIX, No. 1, April, 1966.

within the City. Both commanders were out in the field that night, and Smith, a more enthusiastic participant than Warren, was intensely frustrated to discover later on that he had been on the heels of the murderer the whole time.

It was a City constable, P.C. Watkins, who found Catherine Eddowes's body. He had passed through the square at 1:30 A.M. and noticed nothing unusual, but when he returned, about fifteen minutes later, his police lantern at once illuminated the body of a woman lying on her back in the corner of the square with her left leg extended and her right leg bent at the knee. Further investigation showed the shocking nature of her wounds, which were subsequently noted by the police surgeon in some pencil drawings made at the scene.

Subsequently, it seemed, the murderer had made his way from Mitre Square across Houndsditch and Middlesex Street to Goulston Street, where a bloodstained rag from Eddowes's apron was found at 2:55 A.M. To confuse the public and the police still more, a chalked message about the Jews—"The Jewes are not the men that will be blamed for nothing"—was found in the passageway at Goulston Street. Neither the rag nor the message had been there half an hour before when the police constable passed through on his beat at 2:20 A.M.

As soon as Major Smith was told of this discovery, he dispatched an inspector with two detectives to photograph the message, but General Warren had arrived in Goulston Street meanwhile and took it upon himself to order the writing rubbed out at once, without waiting for the photographer, on the grounds that he feared it would incite an anti-Jewish riot. We shall hear more later about this mysterious communication about the "Jewes."

While the police doctors, F. G. Brown and George Sequiera, were examining the body in Mitre Square, the murderer apparently left Goulston Street and went north to Dorset Street, where he paused to wash blood off his hands at a public sink. This suggested that he knew the neighborhood, because the sink was set back from the street. Passersby observed the blood shortly afterward.

Eddowes's body was removed to the mortuary. It was stripped and an autopsy carried out, but the body was not identified until Tuesday, October 2, by her friend John Kelly. Ironically, his last words to Eddowes had been a warning to her to be careful of the Ripper; he had been lulled into a false sense of security by the fact that one of his friends had seen her being taken to the police station. It was he who identified her shattered body, finally, by the pawn ticket found in her bonnet for the boots he himself had bought a few days earlier. (Her own husband took two weeks to come forward, having changed his name to avoid being traced by her.)

At the Eddowes inquest in October 1888, a commercial traveler named Joseph Lawende and a J. H. Levy reported having seen a man and a woman talking together at the corner of the court leading to Mitre Square in Duke Street shortly before the murder. The police released the following description: "Thirty years old, five feet nine inches in height, with a small fair moustache, dressed in something like navy serge and with a deerstalker's hat, peak fore and after. He also wore a red handkerchief."[14]

Until 1966, this was the only description given of a man seen close to the scene of the murder. My own research has turned up other and more substantial findings.

14 *Coroner's Inquest: Catherine Eddowes*, No. 135, 1888.

By now the whole of London was in an uproar. Suggestions for catching the murderer poured in from all quarters. A Mr. Blair wrote from Dumfries to suggest the use of decoys:

> Let a number of men—say twelve—be selected, of short stature, and as far as possible of effeminate appearance, but of known courage & tried nerve, dress them as females of the class from whom the victims are selected, arm them with the best and lightest weapons and distribute them over the district haunted by the murderer.
>
> Note, The men would require to be fair actors, and behave in the natural manner of women of that class, further they would require to be shadowed by help, in an unobtrusive way, and the whole scheme would require to be kept absolutely secret, for once let the press get a hint of it, and farewell to any chance of success.[15]

Mr. Blair added that his plan was "based on the theory that the murderer solicits intercourse, and that the woman accompanies him to a quiet spot, where the crime is committed while in the act, so that men who undertook the duty of capturing him would require to have all their wits about them."[16]

A civil servant with the Customs Department became convinced that the murders were the work of Portuguese sailors, because, he said, they had contracted venereal disease from a prostitute and were acting out the "characteristic revengefulness of the Portuguese race." His theory was carefully, if illogically, set forth and Scotland Yard treated it seriously for a while, then concluded the man was "a troublesome faddist."[17]

An engraver wrote to the Yard suggesting that a full pardon be offered to the murderer and that, when he turned himself in, the promise should be ignored: "for once [we should] break our national word of honour for the benefit of the universe."[18]

The fact that the murderer had shown some skill in eviscerating the bodies led the police to suppose that the Ripper might have a medical background, and the police spent much time tracking down "three insane medical students." The police also employed bloodhounds, though to little effect. In the Scotland Yard files I also found a "Secret" memorandum ordering a supply of tricycles for the police to enable them to follow more quickly on the trail of the mysterious assassin who struck with such lightning speed. Local Whitechapel businessmen formed a Vigilance Committee, headed by Mr. George Lusk.[19] A Member of Parliament named Samuel Montagu suggested that a reward be paid for the murderer's capture.[20] Terrified prostitutes continued to ply their trade, however; they had no other means of support.

For forty days following Eddowes's death, nothing happened. It seemed that, temporarily, the violent homicidal impulses of the murderer had become satiated. But on Friday, November 9, a twenty-five-year-old prostitute named Marie Jeanette Kelly was found dead at Miller's Court, Spitalfields, in the vicinity of

---

15 Letter by Mr. Blair to Home Secretary, November 11, 1888.
16 Ibid.
17 Letter to Scotland Yard, October, 1888.
18 Ibid.
19 Memo to Mr. Lusk, Public Record Office, Scotland Yard, October 7, 1888.
20 Daily Chronicle, July 19, 1889.

Hanbury Street. This murder took place in the privacy of Kelly's own room in Miller's Court, and not in the streets. The murderer, therefore, had the safety and leisure to commit the bloodiest butchery of them all.

London policemen who saw Kelly's body never forgot it. She was unrecognizable. Her skin was flayed on the face, upper body and thighs, and the flesh removed on some parts so that only her skeleton remained. The bed and night table had bits of flesh on them. Her nose and ears were cut off and her liver was located at her feet. Her uterus was mutilated. Her amputated breasts and kidneys were carefully placed on a nearby table. A doctor who had viewed the body reported to an American newspaper that the sight of the murdered woman surpassed all his gory experiences.

Once again, those who examined the victim concluded that the murder knife was wielded with some knowledge and practice. At the autopsy it was discovered that Kelly was pregnant.

The Metropolitan Police and Scotland Yard continued their massive investigations, and millions of Londoners became hostages to the night as they waited for Jack the Ripper to be caught. It was a name he had introduced for himself in one of his cocky notes to the authorities and it immediately captured the public's imagination. Everybody had an idea about the identity of the murderer, and it seemed that almost everybody passed on their suggestions to Scotland Yard, which painstakingly investigated each one they thought worthy and filed the others away.

In a memo on October 25, 1888, a police report to the Home Office noted:

> That a crime of this kind should have been committed without any clue being supplied by the criminal is unusual, but that four successive murders should have been committed without our having the slightest clue of any kind is extraordinary, if not unique, in the annals of crime.
>
> The result has been to necessitate our giving attention to innumerable suggestions, such as would in any ordinary case be dismissed unnoticed, and no hint of any kind, which was not obviously absurd, has been neglected. Moreover, the activity of the Police has been to a considerable extent wasted through the exigencies of sensational journalism, and the action of unprincipled persons, who, from various motives, have endeavoured to mislead us.[21]

The Ripper murders stopped just as suddenly as they had started. It was some months before it became apparent that the nightmare was over, but like everything about the case, it was a puzzle to know why. Had the murderer become insane, or fled the country, or had he himself died or been murdered? The guesses were as diverse as the list of people whom the police interrogated about the murders, or on whom public suspicion rested, however briefly.

Whatever the reason, there were no more murders following Kelly's death that bore the Ripper's bloody and unmistakable trademarks. And despite the days and months of dogged work by the police, the case remained unsolved. Eventually, the official files and a mass of papers connected with them passed into the archives of Scotland and New Scotland Yard, some marked with the top

---

21 London Police Report to Home Secretary, October 25, 1888.

confidential notation: "closed until 1993."[22] Despite the British practice not to publish information about a controversial event for at least a century, I obtained permission to release the material in this book. The Jack the Ripper murders became a part of history.

There has always been some dispute about how many women Jack the Ripper killed; the number has varied from five to twelve. But the common features in the five murders presented here, I believe, are conclusive.

All five murders shared certain characteristics. They all took place in an area within one square mile of each other. All were committed between the hours of eleven at night and five in the morning. Each took place on a weekend. The throat of each victim had been severed, and with the exception of Stride, the body carved up and mutilated with a knife. And all of their faces were congested. An article in *The Lancet* which described the circumstances of one of the murders "suggests that the absence of a cry was due to strangulation being the real cause of death, a common practice of sexual murders."[23]

All the women were prostitutes, suggesting a psychologically intimate, if unconscious, connection between the murderer and his victims. They were destitute, vulnerable, and alcoholic. Four out of the five were over forty years old and had borne children. Kelly was pregnant.

The mystery of Jack the Ripper's identity is a major reason for the persistence of the myth. Considering the vast efforts of both police and public, even in those days when investigation was a much more primitive business, it is remarkable that he was never apprehended.

The grotesque murders instilled widespread terror not only throughout London itself, but also across a nation that was already gripped by strong anti-Jewish feelings and fears of radical movements that would lead to political anarchy. Faced with confusion and incredulity over the murders, the police were involved simultaneously in trying to pursue the investigations, reassure frightened citizens, and prevent future attacks.

A divided leadership within the police department exacerbated their difficulties. Individual policemen who remained diligent in their duties were nonetheless hampered in their activities. But weak leadership within the police was far from being the only catalyst of an explosion of social unrest. On the flip side of police ineptitude lay its power structure, designed to protect the upper strata of England's monarchy.

In 1886, two years before the Whitechapel murders, bloody riots and demonstrations had erupted in Pall Mall and Oxford Street. Fueled by continuing mass unemployment, the upheavals continued into the following year, with unemployed workers camping out in the parks and Trafalgar Square on a semipermanent basis. Finally, a confrontation took place on November 13, 1887, in Trafalgar Square between a huge mob of demonstrators and several thousand men from the Metropolitan Police; inevitably, there were injuries and massive arrests, and the day became known as "Bloody Sunday."

The Home Secretary appointed General Charles Warren, a professional soldier,

---

22 Files of Whitechapel Murders, Public Record Office, Scotland Yard, July, 1892.
23 *The Lancet,* September 8, 1888.

as Chief Commissioner of the Metropolitan Police, and it was Warren who handled the confrontation in Trafalgar Square. His success in controlling the riots was rewarded with a knighthood, but his harsh tactics increased public outcry and agitation. Renewed outbursts of dissatisfaction with Warren surfaced during the investigation of the Whitechapel murders.

Warren was not only taken to task for the failure of his men to find the Ripper, but he was also rumored to be a Freemason.[24] In today's society, Freemasonry is considered perfectly respectable, but at that time Freemasons were thought to be potential anarchists because they operated under a clandestine code. It has been subsequently suggested that the rumors themselves were a diversionary tactic masking the involvement in the Whitechapel murders of certain powerful men in the government, and even in the royal family.

There were reasons for Warren's inept handling of the murders. In the first place, he was deprived of full authority to conduct the investigations. Although he had been brought in originally to reorganize the police force, the Metropolitan Police continued to operate under dual supervision. The General was given control only of the operations of the uniformed branch, while the Criminal Investigations Department (CID) remained under the command of a superintendent who dealt directly with the Home Office.[25]

There is considerable mystery as to the extent of Warren's responsibility for the investigation of the Ripper murders. He certainly paid an almost instant visit to the passageway at Goulston Street where the mysterious message had been chalked on the wall: "The Jewes are not the men that will be blamed for nothing."[26]

The inspector in charge of the case appealed to Warren to know what action he should take; Warren told him to erase the message immediately, without waiting for the photographer summoned by Major Smith of the City Police, who was expected within the hour. Warren claimed that the reason for the erasure was to prevent an anti-Jewish riot, and his report to the Home Secretary of November 6, 1888, consists of a lengthy defense of this position:

4 Whitehall Place, S.W.

6th November 1888

Confidential
The Under Secretary of State
The Home Office

Sir,
In reply to your letter of the 5th instant, I enclose a report of the circumstances of the Mitre Square Murder so far as they have come under the notice of the Metropolitan Police, and I now give an account regarding the erasing the writing on the wall in Goulston Street which I have already partially explained to Mr. Matthews verbally.
On the 30th September on hearing of the Berner Street murder, after visiting

---

24 *Ars Quatuor Coronatorum*, Transactions, Lodge No. 2076, Vol. 99, September 1987, Adlaird & Son, The Garden City Press.

25 Geoffrey Trease, *London: A Concise History*, New York, 1975, p. 138.

26 Martin Howells & Keith Skinner, *The Ripper Legacy: The Life and Death of Jack the Ripper*, Sidgwick & Jackson, London, 1987, pp. 16–17.

Commercial Street Station I arrived at Leman Street Station shortly before 5 A.M. and ascertained from Superintendent Arnold all that was known there relative to the two murders.

The most pressing question at that moment was some writing on the wall in Goulston Street evidently written with the intention of inflaming the public mind against the Jews, and which Mr. Arnold with a view to prevent serious disorder proposed to obliterate, and had sent down an Inspector with a sponge for that purpose, telling him to await his arrival.

I considered it desirable that I should decide this matter myself, as it was one involving so great a responsibility whether any action was taken or not.

I accordingly went down to Goulston Street at once before going to the scene of the murder: it was just getting light, the public would be in the streets in a few minutes, in a neighbourhood very much crowded on Sunday mornings by Jewish vendors and Christian purchasers from all parts of London.

There were several Police around the spot when I arrived, both Metropolitan and City.

The writing was on the jamb of the open archway or doorway visible to anybody in the street and could not be covered up without danger of the covering being torn off at once.

A discussion took place whether the writing could be left covered up or otherwise or whether any portion of it could be left for an hour until it could be photographed; but after taking into consideration the excited state of the population in London generally at the time, the strong feeling which had been excited against the Jews, and the fact that in a short time there would be a large concourse of the people in the streets, and having before me the Report that if it was left there the house was likely to be wrecked (in which from my own observation I entirely concurred) I considered it desirable to obliterate the writing at once, having taken a copy of which I enclose a duplicate.

After having been to the scene of the murder, I went on to the City Police Office and informed the Chief Superintendent of the reason why the writing had been obliterated.

I may mention that so great was the feeling with regard to the Jews that on the 13th ulto. the Acting Chief Rabbi wrote to me on the subject of the spelling of the word "Jewes" on account of a newspaper asserting that this was Jewish spelling in the Yiddish dialect. He added "in the present state of excitement it is dangerous to the safety of the poor Jews in the East [End] to allow such an assertion to remain uncontradicted. My community keenly appreciates your humane and vigilant action during this critical time."

It may be realised therefore if the safety of the Jews in Whitechapel could be considered to be jeopardised thirteen days after the murder by the question of the spelling of the word Jews, what might have happened to the Jews in that quarter had that writing been left intact.

I do not hesitate myself to say that if that writing had been left there would have been an onslaught upon the Jews, property would have been wrecked, and lives would probably have been lost; and I was much gratified with the promptitude with which Superintendent Arnold was prepared to act in the matter if I had not been there.

I have no doubt myself whatever that one of the principal objects of the Reward offered by Mr. Montagu was to shew to the world that the Jews were desirous of having the Hanbury Street Murder cleared up, and thus to divert from them the very strong feeling which was then growing up.

 I am, Sir,

Your most obedient Servant,
 (signed) C. Warren[27]

Warren enclosed two identical copies of the following message:

The Jewes are
The men that
Will not
be Blamed
for nothing[28]

There has been some argument about whether the spelling was "Jewes" or "Juwes," the exact position of the word "not" (which differs in the version above from that given earlier), and whether there was significance in the breaks in the message. But it seems clear that the purpose of the message was diabolically cunning—the Ripper intended to throw the police off the scent, linking the message to the murder through the rag from Eddowes's apron; no doubt he also disliked the Jews, and he may well have hoped to incite the sort of anti-Jewish demonstration Warren's swift decision prevented.

In fact, several chief suspects in the murders were Jewish. One, a Polish Jew named John Pizer, was known to be a small-time blackmailer and abuser of prostitutes. He was a boot finisher by trade, and when the police came to question him they found several sharp knives and a leather apron on the premises. Since a leather apron had been found not far from the body of Annie Chapman, he was taken to the police station and jailed on suspicion of her murder. However, the apron turned out to belong to a neighbor on Hanbury Street. Pizer's alibi held up, and the police were forced to release him.

The Jews were particularly unpopular in Whitechapel, where they formed a considerable proportion of the population, and the situation had not been helped by a notorious murder case, some four years earlier, when a Jew named Lipski had been hanged for the murder of his Jewish girlfriend.

Sir Charles Warren considered social liberation in England a critical issue. The Britain of this era was great indeed, rich and authoritative, proud possessor of an Empire on which the sun never set, in which members of a burgeoning middle class could hope to reap rewards, too—although the mansions and great estates were still the privilege of the selected and wealthy few. The British fleet ruled the oceans.

---

27 Report by Charles Warren to Home Secretary, London, November 6, 1888.
28 *Ibid.*

The extravagant lifestyle of the rich was in stark contrast to that of the many slum dwellers who struggled in the wilderness of poverty, alcohol, and illness. In general, members of the aristocratic class lived in an atmosphere of luxury and festivity and appeared to pass their days entirely in entertaining themselves. Very few participated in helping the more unfortunate or were prepared to take on genuine responsibilities. The royal family, in particular, was criticized. Queen Victoria lived almost entirely in retirement at Windsor, in the Highlands, or on the Isle of Wight, while the Prince of Wales, denied by his mother any opportunity to participate in the business of ruling, spent most of his time hunting, going to parties, traveling around Europe, or making triumphal trips through India. People observed, also, that though the Prince had married the beautiful and popular Alexandra, he regularly left her at home while he continued his peripatetic existence, constantly meeting with other attractive women. Such behavior earned him positive dislike in many quarters. His elder son Prince Albert Victor, known as Eddy, was a very unprepossessing heir to the throne and, as we shall hear later, involved in scandals. Even the Princess of Wales's personal popularity could not bring people to think well of her neglectful husband or look forward to Prince Eddy's ascent to the throne.

There were those who agreed with Warren on the social and class inequities. Nevertheless, the General began to feel outcast and isolated. Six months earlier, in March 1888, he had informed the Home Secretary of his intention to resign. The idea of a conspiracy directed by the Freemasons seems extremely questionable; more likely, there may have been some interference by various officials in the murder investigations, including cover-ups and glossing over of possible suspects. It was probably the personality more than the practices of Sir Charles Warren that created controversy and condemnation.

Earlier, Warren appointed as his assistant commissioner a man named Robert Anderson. There were several curious features about Anderson's involvement in the case. The new assistant had arranged to take a vacation in Switzerland and was to begin his duties on his return. The murder of Mary Anne Nichols in Buck's Row took place on August 31, eight days before Anderson was due to leave, and Annie Chapman was murdered on Hanbury Street on September 8, the morning of that eighth day. Despite these dual emergencies, however, Anderson refused to postpone his vacation and departed as planned. Barely a month later, Anderson seemed to be taking credit for the operation by submitting an updated report of the murder investigations to the Home Secretary's Office, though he had had very little to do with its preparation.

As if adding insult to injury, the Home Secretary's Office kept issuing orders directly to Anderson and Warren's other subordinates, rather than routing them through the General himself. This deliberate bypassing of the regular channels caused confusion and resentment throughout the police division and certainly slowed the investigation of the Whitechapel murders. A catch-22 situation evolved in which Warren was severely hampered in his efforts to capture Jack the Ripper while being criticized for not devoting his efforts to the capture of Jack the Ripper.

In the House of Commons on November 12, 1888, Mr. Conybeare rose to question the Home Secretary.

RESIGNATION OF SIR C. WARREN.

Mr. CONYBEARE *asked the Secretary of State for the Home Department whether he could state the exact reason why the late head of the Detective Department in the Metropolitan Police resigned his position; whether it was the fact that Sir C. Warren had now practically the direct control of the Detective Department; and whether, in view of the constant recurrence of atrocious murders, and the failure of the new organisation and methods to detect the murderer, he would consider the propriety of making some change in the arrangements of Scotland-yard. The hon. member also wished to know whether it was true, as reported in the newspapers that afternoon, that Sir C. Warren had tendered his resignation, and that it had been accepted.*

The HOME SECRETARY.—*I have already more than once stated the reason why Mr. Monro resigned. With regard to the remainder of the question, Mr. Anderson is now in direct control of the Criminal Investigation Department, under the superintendence and control, as provided by statute, of the Chief Commissioner. The failure of the police, so far, to detect the person guilty of the Whitechapel murders is due, not to any new reorganisation in the department, but to the extraordinary cunning and secrecy which characterise the commission of the crimes. I have for some time had the question of the whole system of the Criminal Investigation Department under my consideration, with a view to introducing any improvement that may be required. With regard to the last question, I have to inform the hon. member that the Chief Commissioner of Police did on the 8th inst. tender his resignation to her Majesty's Government, and that his resignation has been accepted (loud Opposition cheers).*[29]

Finding the continual erosion of his status intolerable, Warren had in fact tendered his resignation on November 8, and the Home Secretary now confirmed to Mr. Conybeare that it had been accepted, amid loud cheering from the political opposition.

Despite the bifurcated police operations, the CID (now being run by Anderson) fervently pursued all potential clues that might lead them to the murderer. They increased the number of policemen on the case and interrogated an ever-growing number of suspects.

Among those suspected were the seamen whose ships came to London, unloaded their cargo, then left and returned again on a fairly regular basis at the end of each week. The list of crew and cattlemen issued by the Statistical Department of the London Custom House on November 15, 1888, shows that every one of those examined at great length by the police proved to have a watertight alibi.

During their investigations, the department also discussed the idea of offering rewards to those who could help them in their inquiries, but in line with British morality, rewards were felt to be unnecessary, and Mr. Montagu's offer of five hundred pounds was never taken up.

Almost unanimously, the newspapers expressed the outrage of a British public held hostage by fear and panic. The only way of easing the tension was to find the murderer and bring him to justice.

---

29 *The Standard*, November 13, 1888.

THE JACK THE RIPPER MURDERS

Anonymous

The atrocities collectively known as the Jack the Ripper murders did wonders for the newspapers of London, which sold frequent updates to an ever-eager public, issuing new editions at the slightest hint of any scant scrap of new evidence, or (more likely) speculation, gossip, and outright creative fantasy.

Fifty daily newspapers in that overcrowded city vied for the attention of readers, sending out newsboys in droves, screaming out the latest headlines. Each murder was a boon to Fleet Street, and none capitalized on it more than the relatively staid *Times*. Even at the height of the frenzy for greater and greater titillation as reporters struggled to outdo each other with more and more lurid descriptions of the grisly slaughters, *The Times* continued its reportage with adherence to rudimentary journalistic practices of accuracy and as much completeness as possible under the circumstances.

The following narrative provides much of the basic information as it came to light in contemporary accounts published in *The Times*. They were collected and reprinted as a single chapter (one of twenty-eight) in a book edited by Richard Barker (1902–1968) more than a half century later, reflecting the reading public's never-ending interest in Red Jack.

"The Jack the Ripper Murders" accounts were first published in *The Times* (London, August 10–November 22, 1888); they were first collected in *The Fatal Caress*, edited by Richard Barker (New York, Duell, Sloan and Pearce, 1947).

THE FIRST MURDER, APRIL 3

Victim: Emma Elizabeth Smith
[Not reported in The Times.]

THE SECOND MURDER, AUGUST 7

Victim: Martha Tabram
Place: Grove-Yard Buildings

August 10. Yesterday afternoon Mr. G. Collier, Deputy Coroner for the South-Eastern Division of Middlesex, opened an inquiry respecting the death of the woman who was found on Tuesday last with thirty-nine stabs on her body at Grove-Yard Buildings, Whitechapel.

Dr. T. R. Killeen said that he was called to the deceased and found her dead. She had thirty-nine stabs on the body. She had been dead some three hours. The left lung was penetrated in five places, and the right lung was penetrated in two places. The heart, which was rather fatty, was penetrated in one place. The liver was healthy but was penetrated in five places, the spleen was penetrated in two places, and the stomach—which was perfectly healthy—was penetrated in six places. The witness did not think all the wounds were inflicted with the same instrument.

It was one of the most dreadful murders anyone could imagine. The man must have been a perfect savage to inflict such a number of wounds on a defenceless woman in such a way.

THE THIRD MURDER, AUGUST 31

Victim: Mary Ann Nichols
Place: Bucks Row

September 1. Another murder of the foulest kind was committed in the neighbourhood of Whitechapel in the early hours of yesterday morning, but by whom and with what motive is at present a complete mystery. At a quarter to four o'clock Police Constable Neill when in Bucks Row, Whitechapel, came upon the body of a woman lying on a part of the footway, and on stooping to raise her up in the belief that she was drunk, he discovered that her throat was cut almost from ear to ear. She was dead but still warm. He procured assistance and at once sent to the station and for a doctor. Dr. Llewellyn, whose surgery is not above a hundred yards from the spot, was aroused and at a solicitation from a constable, dressed and went at once to the scene. He made a hasty examination and then discovered that besides the gash across the throat the woman had terrible wounds in the abdomen.

The police have no theory with respect to the matter except that a gang of ruffians exists in the neighbourhood which, blackmailing women of the "unfortunate" class, takes vengeance on those who do not find money for them. They base that surmise on the fact that within twelve months two other women have been murdered in the district by almost similar means—one as recently as the 6th of August last—and left in the gutter of the street in the early hours of the morning.

THE FOURTH MURDER, SEPTEMBER 8

Victim: Annie Chapman
Place: Hanbury Street

September 10. Whitechapel and the whole of the East of London have again been thrown into a state of intense excitement by the discovery early on Saturday morning of the body of a woman who had been murdered in a similar way to Mary Ann Nichols at Bucks Row on Friday week. In fact the similarity in the two cases is startling, as the victim of the outrage had her head almost severed from her body and was completely disembowelled. This latest crime, however, even surpasses the others in ferocity.

The scene of the murder, which makes the fourth in the same neighbourhood within the past few weeks, is at the back of the house 29 Hanbury Street, Spitalfields. This street runs from Commercial Street to Bakers Row, the end of which is close to Bucks Row. The house, which is rented by a Mrs. Emilia Richardson, is let out to various lodgers, all of the poorer class. In consequence, the front door is open both day and night, so that no difficulty would be experienced by anyone in gaining admission to the back portion of the premises.

Shortly before six o'clock on Saturday morning John Davis, who lives with his wife at the top portion of No. 29, went down into the backyard, where a horrible sight presented itself to him. Lying close up against the wall, with her head touching the other side of the wall, was the body of a woman. Davis could see that her throat was severed in a terrible manner and that she had other wounds of a nature too shocking to be described. The deceased was lying on her back with her clothes disarranged.

Without nearer approaching the body but telling his wife what he had seen, Davis ran to the Commercial Street Police Station and gave information to Inspector Chandler, who was in charge of the station at the time. That officer, having dispatched a constable for Dr. Phillips, repaired to the house accompanied by several other policemen. The body was still in the same position and there were large clots of blood all round it. It is evident that the murderer thought he had completely cut the head off, as a handkerchief was found wrapped round the neck as though to hold it together. There were spots and stains of blood on the wall. One or more rings seem to have been torn from the middle finger of the left hand. A minute search being made of the yard, a portion of an envelope stained with blood was found. It had the crest of the Sussex Regiment on it and the date "London, August 20," but the address portion—with the exception of the one letter "M"—was torn off. In addition, two pills were also picked up.

The police believe that the murder has been committed by the same person who perpetrated the three previous ones in the district and that only one person is concerned in it. This person might be, is doubtless labouring under some terrible form of insanity, as each of the crimes has been of a most fiendish character, and it is feared that unless he can speedily be captured more outrages of a similar class will be committed.

Inquest on Mary Ann Nichols, September 4–24

Testimony of William Nichols. Nichols, a machinist, stated that the deceased woman was his wife. He had been separated from her for upwards of eight years. The last time he saw her was over three years ago, and he had no idea what she had been doing since that time nor with whom she lived. Deceased was much given to drink. They separated several times, and each time he took her back she got drunk and that was why he had to leave her altogether.

Statement of the Coroner. Referring to the facts in the case before him, the Coroner said the deceased had been identified by her father and her husband to have been Mary Ann Nichols, a married woman with five children and about forty-two years of age. It was pretty clear that she had been living an intemperate, irregular, and vicious life, mostly in the common lodging-houses in that neighbourhood.

On Friday evening, the 31st of August, she was seen by Mrs. Holland—who knew her well—at the corner of Osborn Street and Whitechapel Road, nearly opposite the church. The deceased woman was then much the worse for drink and was staggering against the wall. Her friend endeavoured to persuade her to come home with her, but she declined and was last seen endeavouring to walk eastward down Whitechapel. She said she had had her lodging money three times that day but that she had spent it, that she was going about to get some money to pay her lodgings, and she would soon be back. In less than an hour and a quarter after this she was found dead at a spot rather under three-quarters of a mile distant.

The condition in which the body was found appeared to prove conclusively that the deceased was killed on the exact spot in which she was found. There was not a trace of blood anywhere except at the spot where her neck was lying. That appeared to the coroner sufficient to justify the assumption that the injuries to the throat were inflicted when the woman was on the ground, while the state of her clothing and the absence of any blood about her legs equally proved that the abdominal injuries were inflicted while she was still in the same position.

Nor did there appear any grounds for doubt that, if deceased was killed where she was found, she met her death without cry of any kind. The spot was almost under the windows of Mrs. Green, a light sleeper. It was opposite the bedroom of Mrs. Purkiss, who was awake at the time. Then there were watchmen at various spots within very short distances. Not a sound was heard by any. Nor was there evidence of any struggle. This might have arisen from her intoxication or from being stunned by a blow. It seemed astonishing, at first thought, that the culprit should escape detection, for there must surely have been marks of blood about his person. If, however, blood was principally on his hands, the presence of so many slaughter-houses in the neighbourhood would make the frequenters of that spot familiar with bloodstained clothes and hands, and his appearance might in that way have failed to attract attention while he passed from Bucks Row in the twilight into Whitechapel Road and was lost sight of in the morning's market of traffic.

He himself thought they could not altogether have unnoticed the fact that the death the jury had been investigating was one of four presenting many points of similarity, all of which had occurred within the space of about five months, and all within a very short distance of the place where they were sitting. All four victims were women of middle age; all were married and had lived apart from their husbands in consequence of intemperate habits and were at the time of their death leading irregular lives and eking out a miserable and precarious existence in common lodging-houses. In each case there were abdominal as well as other injuries. In each case the injuries were inflicted after midnight and in places of public resort where it would appear impossible but that almost immediate detection would follow the crime, and in each case the inhuman and dastardly criminals were at large in society.

Emma Elizabeth Smith, who received the injuries in Osborn Street on the early morning of Easter Tuesday, the 3rd of April, survived in the London Hospital for upwards of twenty-four hours and was able to state that she had been followed by some men, robbed and mutilated, and even to describe imperfectly one of them. Martha Tabram was found at 3 A.M. on Tuesday, the 7th of August, on the first-floor landing of Gregory Yard Buildings with thirty-nine puncture wounds on the body. In addition to these and the case under consideration of the jury there was the case of Annie Chapman, still in the hands of another jury. The instruments used in the two earlier cases were dissimilar. In the first it was a blunt instrument such as a walking-stick; in the second some of the wounds were thought to have been made by a dagger. But in the two recent cases the instruments suggested by the medical witnesses were not so different. Dr. Llewellyn said that the injuries on Nichols could have been produced by a very sharp knife, probably with a thin, narrow blade, at least six inches to eight inches in length, probably longer. The similarity of the injuries in the two cases was considerable. There were bruises about the face in both cases, the head was nearly severed from the body in both cases, and those injuries again had in each case been performed with anatomical knowledge. Dr. Llewellyn seemed to incline to the opinion that the abdominal injuries were inflicted first and caused instantaneous death; but if so, it seemed difficult to understand the object of such desperate injuries to the throat or how it came about there was so little bleeding from the severed arteries that the clothing on the upper surface was not stained and the legs not soiled, and that there was very much less bleeding from the abdomen than from the neck. Surely it might well be that, as in the case of Chapman, the dreadful wounds to the throat were first inflicted and the abdominal afterwards. That was a matter of some importance when they came to consider what possible motive there could be for all this ferocity.

Robbery was out of the question, and there was nothing to suggest jealousy. There could not have been any quarrel or it would have been heard. The taking of some of the abdominal viscera from the body of Chapman suggested that they may have been the object of her death. Was it not possible that this may have been the motive in the case they had under consideration? He suggested to the jury as a possibility that the two women might have been murdered by the same man with the same object and that in the case of Nichols the wretch was disturbed before he had accomplished his object, and having failed in the open street, he tried again—within a week of his failure—in a more secluded place. If this was correct, the audacity and daring was equal to its maniacal fanaticism and abhorrent wickedness. But the surmise might or might not be correct.

Inquest on Annie Chapman, September 11–27

Statement of the Coroner. The deceased was a widow forty-seven years of age named Annie Chapman. Her husband was a coachman living at Windsor. For three or four years before his death she had lived apart from her husband, who allowed her ten shillings a week until his death Christmas 1886. She had evidently lived an immoral life for some time, and her habits and surroundings had become worse since her means had failed. She lived principally in the common lodging-houses in the neighbourhood of Spitalfields, where such as she herded like cattle. She showed signs of great deprivation as if she had been badly fed. The glimpse of life in those dens which the evidence in this case disclosed was sufficient to make the jury feel there was much in the nineteenth-century civilization of which they had small reason to be proud; but the jury, who were constantly called together to hear the sad tale of starvation or semi-starvation, of misery, immorality, and wickedness which some of the occupants of the five thousand beds in that district had every week to relate at coroners' inquests, did not require to be reminded what a life in a Spitalfields lodging-house meant.

It was in one of those houses that the older bruises found on the temple and in front of the chest of the deceased were received—in a trumpery quarrel—a week before her death. It was in one of those that she was seen a few hours before her mangled remains were discovered. On the afternoon and evening of Friday, the 7th of September, she spent her time partly in such a place—at 35 Dorset Street—and partly in the Ringers public house, where she spent whatever money she had; so that between one and two o'clock on the morning of Saturday, when the money for the bed was demanded, she was obliged to admit that she was without means and at once turned out into the street to find it. She left there at 1:45 A.M. On her wedding finger she was wearing two or three rings, which appeared to have been palpably of base metal, as the witnesses were all clear about their material and value. They now lost sight of her for about four hours, but at half-past five o'clock Mrs. Long was in Hanbury Street on the way to Spitalfields Market.

Testimony of Elizabeth Long. Mrs. Long stated [that] on Saturday morning the 8th she was passing down Hanbury Street from home and going to Spitalfields Market. It was about 5:30. She was certain of the time as the brewers' clock had just struck that time when she passed 29 Hanbury Street. She saw a man and a woman on the pavement talking. The man's back was turned toward Brick Lane while the woman's was toward Spitalfields Market. They were talking together and were close against the shutters of No. 29. Witness saw the woman's face. She had since seen the deceased in the mortuary and was sure it was the face of the same person. She did not see the man's face except to notice that he was dark. He wore a brown deerstalker hat and she thought he had on a dark coat but was not quite sure. She could not say what the age of the man was, but he looked to be over forty and appeared to be a little taller than the deceased. He appeared to be a foreigner and had a shabby genteel appearance. Witness could hear them talking loudly, and she overheard him say to the deceased, "Will you?" She replied, "Yes." They still stood there as witness passed and she went on to her work without looking back.

Statement of the Coroner Continued. There was nothing to suggest that the deceased was not fully conscious of what she was doing. It was true that she had passed through some stages of intoxication, for although she appeared perfectly sober to her friends who met her in Dover Street at five o'clock the previous evening, she had been drinking afterwards; and when she left the lodging-house shortly after two o'clock the night watchman noticed that she was the worse for drink but not badly so, while the deputy asserts that, though she had been evidently drinking, she could walk straight and it was probably only malt liquor that she had taken—and its effects would pass off quicker than if she had taken spirits. The post mortem showed that while the stomach contained a meal of food, there was no sign of fluid and no appearance of her having taken alcohol.

The deceased, therefore, entered the house in full possession of her faculties although with a different object to her companion's. From the evidence which the condition of the yard afforded and the medical examination disclosed, it appeared that after the two had passed through the passage and opened the swing door at the end, they descended the three steps into the yard. The wretch must have then seized the deceased, perhaps with Judas-like approaches. He seized her by the chin. He pressed her throat, and while thus preventing the slightest cry, he at the same time produced insensibility and suffocation. There was no evidence of any struggle. The clothes were not torn. Even in those preliminaries the wretch seems to have known how to carry out efficiently his nefarious work. The deceased was then lowered to the ground and laid on her back, and although in doing so she may have fallen slightly against the fence, the movement was probably effected with care. Her throat was then cut in two places with savage determination, and the injuries to the abdomen commenced.

All was done with cool impudence and reckless daring; but perhaps nothing was more noticeable than the emptying of her pockets and the arrangement of their contents with business-like precision in order near her feet. The murder seemed, like the Bucks Row case, to have been carried out without an outcry. None of the occupants of the houses by which the spot was surrounded heard anything suspicious. The brute who committed the offence did not even take the trouble to cover up his ghastly work but left the body exposed to the view of the first comer. That accorded but little with the trouble taken with the rings and suggested either that he had at length been disturbed or that as daylight broke a sudden fear suggested the danger of detection that he was running.

There were two things missing. Her rings had been wrenched from her fingers and had not since been found, and the uterus had been taken from the abdomen. The body had not been dissected but the injuries had been made by someone who had considerable anatomical skill and knowledge. There were no meaningless cuts. The organ had been taken by one who knew where to find it, what difficulties he would have to contend against, and how he should use his knife so as to abstract the organ without injury to it. No unskilled person could have known where to find it or have recognized it when it was found. For instance, no mere slaughterer of animals could have carried out these operations. It must have been someone accustomed to the post-mortem room.

The conclusion that the desire was to possess the missing abdominal organ seemed overwhelming. If the object were robbery the injuries to the viscera were meaningless, for death had previously resulted from the loss of blood at the neck. Moreover, when they found an easily accomplished theft of some paltry brass rings and an internal organ taken after at least a quarter of an hour's work and by a skilled person, they were driven to the deduction that the abstraction of the missing portion of abdominal viscera was the object and the theft of the rings was only a thinly veiled blind, an attempt to prevent the real intention being discovered. The amount missing would go into a breakfast cup, and had not the medical examination been of a thorough and searching character it might easily have been left unnoticed that there was any portion of the body which had been taken.

The difficulty in believing that the purport of the murderer was the possession of the missing abdominal organ was natural. It was abhorrent to their feelings to conclude that a life should be taken for so slight an object, but when rightly considered the reasons for most murders were altogether out of proportion to their guilt. It had been suggested that the criminal was a lunatic with morbid feelings. That might or might not be the case, but the object of the murderer appeared palpably shown by the facts and it was not necessary to assume lunacy, for it was clear there was a market for the missing organ. Some months ago an American called on [the sub-curator of the Pathological Museum] and asked him to procure a number of specimens of the organ that was missing in the deceased. He stated his willingness to give £20 a piece for each specimen. He stated that his object was to issue an actual specimen with each copy of a publication on which he was then engaged. He was told that his request was impossible to be complied with, but he still urged his request. He wished them preserved, not in spirits of wine—the usual medium—but glycerine in order to preserve them in a flaccid condition, and he wished them sent to America direct. It was known that this request was repeated to another institution of a similar character. Now was it not possible that the knowledge of this demand might have incited some abandoned wretch to possess himself of a specimen?

FURTHER INVESTIGATION

September 11. Yesterday morning Detective Sergeant Thicke, who has been indefatigable in his inquiries respecting the murder of Annie Chapman, succeeded in capturing a man whom he believed to be "Leather Apron." It will be recollected that this person obtained an evil notoriety during the inquiries respecting this and the recent murders committed in Whitechapel, owing to the startling reports that have been freely circulated by many of the women living in the district as to outrages alleged to have been committed by him. Sergeant Thicke, accompanied by two or three other officers, proceeded to 22 Mulberry Street and knocked at the door. It was opened by a man named Pizer, supposed to be "Leather Apron." Thicke at once took hold of the man, saying, "You are just the man I want." He then charged Pizer with being concerned in the murder of the woman Chapman, and to this he made no reply. The arrested man, who is a boot finisher by trade, was then handed over to other officers and the house was searched. Thicke took possession of five sharp long-bladed knives—which, however, are used by men in Pizer's trade—and also several old hats. With reference to the latter, several women who stated they were acquainted with the prisoner alleged he had been in the habit of wearing different hats. [Pizer] strongly denies that he is known by the name of "Leather Apron."

The following official notice has been circulated throughout the metropolitan police district and all police stations throughout the country: "Description of a man who entered a passage of the house at which the murder was committed of a prostitute at 2 A.M. on the 8th.—Age 37; height, 5 feet, 7 inches; rather dark beard and moustache. Dress—shirt, dark jacket, dark vest and trousers, black scarf, and black felt hat. Spoke with foreign accent."

Great excitement was caused during the afternoon on account of the arrival from Graves-end of a suspect whose appearance resembled in some respects that of "Leather Apron." This man, whose name is William Henry Pigott, was taken into custody on Sunday night at the Pope's Hall public house, Gravesend. Attention was first attracted to Pigott because he had some bloodstains on his clothes. The chief of the local police was communicated with, and a sergeant was sent to the Pope's Head to investigate the case. On approaching the man, who seemed in a somewhat dazed condition, the sergeant saw that one of his hands bore several recently made wounds. Being interrogated as to the cause of this, Pigott made a somewhat rambling statement to the effect that while going down Brick Lane, Whitechapel, at half-past four on Sunday morning, he saw a woman fall in a fit. He stooped to pick her up and she bit his hand. Exasperated at this he struck her, but seeing two policemen coming up he then ran away.

The news of Pigott's arrival, which took place at 12:48, at once spread and in a few seconds the police station was surrounded by an excited crowd anxious to get a glimpse of the supposed murderer. Mrs. Fiddymont, who is responsible for the statement respecting a man resembling "Leather Apron" being at the Prince Albert public house on Saturday, was sent for, as were also other witnesses likely to be able to identify the prisoner. But after a very brief scrutiny it was the unanimous opinion that Pigott was not "Leather Apron."

Intelligent observers who have visited the locality express the utmost astonishment that the murderer could have reached a hiding place after committing such a crime. He must have left the yard in Hanbury Street reeking with blood and yet, if the theory that the murder took place between five and six o'clock be accepted, he must have walked in almost broad daylight along streets comparatively well frequented even at that early hour without his startling appearance attracting the slightest attention. Consideration of this point has led many to the conclusion that the murderer came not from the wretched class from which the inmates of common lodging-houses are drawn. It is at any rate practically certain that the murderer would not have ventured to return to a common lodging-house smeared with blood as he must have been. The police are therefore exhorted not to confine their investigations, as they are accused of doing, to common lodging-houses and other resorts of the criminal and outcast, but to extend their inquiries to the class of householders, exceedingly numerous in the East End of London, who are in the habit of letting furnished lodgings without particular inquiry into the character or antecedents of those who apply for them.

A meeting of the chief local tradesmen was held yesterday, at which an influential committee was appointed consisting of sixteen well-known gentlemen, with Mr. J. Aarons as the secretary. The committee issued last evening a notice stating that they will give a substantial reward for the capture of the murderer or for information leading thereto. The movement has been warmly taken up by the inhabitants and it is thought certain that a large sum will be subscribed within the next few days. The proposal to form district vigilance committees also meets with great popular favour and is assuming practical form. Meetings were held at the various workingmen's clubs and other organizations, political and social, in the district, at most of which the proposed scheme was heartily approved.

September 12. The latest reports as to the search for the murderer are not of a hopeful character. On Monday evening it was stated that John Pizer, the man who was detained on suspicion of being concerned in causing the death of the woman, Annie Chapman, was still in custody at the Leman Street Police Station. Last night it was decided to release him.

September 15. Regarding the man Pigott, who was captured at Gravesend, nothing whatever has been discovered by the detectives in the course of their inquiries which can in any way connect him with the crime of crimes, and his release, at all events, from the custody of the police is expected shortly.

September 20. No further arrest in connection with the Whitechapel murders had been made up to last night and the police are still at fault.

THE FIFTY AND SIXTH MURDERS, SEPTEMBER 30

October 1. In the early hours of yesterday morning two more horrible murders were committed in the East End of London, the victim in both cases belonging, it is believed, to the same unfortunate class. No doubt seems to be entertained by the police that these terrible crimes were the work of the same fiendish hands which committed the outrages which had already made Whitechapel so painfully notorious. The scenes of the two murders just brought to light are within a quarter of an hour's walk of each other, the earlier-discovered crime having been committed in a yard in Berner Street, a low thoroughfare out of the Commercial Road, while the second outrage was perpetrated within the city boundary in Mitre Square, Aldgate.

THE FIFTH MURDER

Victim: Elizabeth Stride
Place: Berner Street

October 1. In the first-mentioned case the body was found in a gateway leading to a factory, and although the murder compared with the other may be regarded as of an almost ordinary character—the unfortunate woman only having her throat cut—little doubt is felt from the position of the corpse that the assassin had intended to mutilate it. He seems, however, to have been interrupted by the arrival of a cart which drew up close to the spot, and it is believed to be possible that he may have escaped behind this vehicle.

The scene of the crime is a narrow court at the entrance to [which] are a pair of large wooden gates, in one of which is a small wicket for use when the gates are closed. At the hour when the murderer accomplished his purpose these gates were open. For a distance of eighteen or twenty feet from the street there is a dead wall on each side of the court, the effect of which is to enshroud the intervening space in absolute darkness after sunset. Further back some light is thrown into the court from the windows of a workmen's club which occupies the whole length of the court on the right, and from a number of cottages occupied mainly by tailors and cigarette makers on the left. At the same time when the murder was committed, however, the lights in all of the dwelling houses in question had been extinguished, while such illumination as came from the club, being from the upper story, would fall on the cottages opposite and would only serve to intensify the gloom of the rest of the court.

At the club—the International Workmen's Educational Club—which is an offshoot of the Socialist League and a rendezvous of a number of foreign residents, it is customary on Saturday night to have friendly discussions on topics of mutual interest and to wind up the evening's entertainment with songs, etc. The proceedings commenced on Saturday about 8:30 with a discussion on the necessity for Socialism among Jews. This was kept up until about eleven o'clock, when a considerable portion of the company left. Between twenty and thirty people remained behind, however, and the usual concert which followed was not concluded when the intelligence was brought in by the steward of the club that a woman had been murdered within a few yards of the house. The people residing in the cottages on the other side of the court were all indoors and most of them in bed by midnight. Several of these persons remember lying awake and listening to the singing in the club, and they also remember the concert coming to an abrupt termination. But during the whole of the time between the hour of their retiring to rest and the moment when the body was discovered, no one heard anything in the nature of a scream or a woman's cry of distress.

Late last night the woman was identified by a sister as Elizabeth Stride, who it seems had resided latterly in Flower and Dean Street. A correspondent—when he was shown the body of the deceased—recognized her by the name of Annie Fitzgerald as having been charged and convicted a great number of times of drunkenness. Whenever so charged she always denied having been drunk and gave as an excuse that she suffered from fits. This statement, although not strictly true in connection with her special visits to the Thames Police Court, was partly correct, for while evidence was being adduced against her she had fallen to the floor of the dock in a fit and had to be carried from the court to the cell in an insensible condition.

Inquest on Elizabeth Stride, October 2–24

Testimony of James Brown. I saw the deceased about a quarter of one on Sunday morning. At that time I was going from my own house to get some supper at the corner of Berner Street and Fairclough Street. As I was going across the road I saw a man and woman standing by the Board School in Fairclough Street. They were standing against the wall. As I passed them I heard the woman say, "No, not tonight, some other night." That made me turn round and I looked at them. I am certain the woman was the deceased. The man had his arm up against the wall and the woman had her back to the wall facing him. I noticed the man had a long coat on, which came very nearly down to his heels. The place where they were standing was rather dark. I then went on and went indoors. I had nearly finished my supper when I heard screams of "Police" and "Murder." That was about a quarter of an hour after I got in. I should say the man was about five feet seven inches in height. He appeared to be stoutish built. Both the man and woman appeared to be sober.

Testimony of William Marshall. On Sunday night I saw the body of [the] deceased in the mortuary. I recognized it as that of a woman I saw on Saturday evening about three doors off from where I am living in Berner Street. That was about a quarter to twelve. She was standing talking to a man. I recognize her both by her face and dress. There was no lamp near and I did not see the face of the man she was talking to. He had on a small black coat and dark trousers. He seemed to me to be a middle-aged man.

CORONER: What sort of a cap was he wearing?

WITNESS: A round cap with a small peak to it—something like what a sailor would wear.

CORONER: What height was he?

WITNESS: About five feet six inches and he was stout. He was decently dressed, and I should say he worked at some light business and had more the appearance of a clerk than anything else.

CORONER: Did you see whether he had any whiskers?

WITNESS: From what I saw of his face I do not think he had. He was not wearing gloves and he had no stick or anything in his hand.

CORONER: What sort of a coat was it?

WITNESS: A cutaway one.

CORONER: Are you sure this is the woman?

WITNESS: Yes, I am. I did not take much notice of them. I was standing at my door and what attracted my attention first was her standing there some time and he was kissing her. I heard the man say to deceased: "You would say anything but your prayers." He was mild speaking and appeared to be an educated man. They went down the street.

Testimony of Police Constable William Smith. Smith said that on Saturday night his beat was past Berner Street.

CORONER: When you were in Berner Street did you see anyone?

SMITH: Yes, a man and a woman.

CORONER: Was the latter anything like the deceased?

WITNESS: Yes, I saw her face. I have seen the deceased in the mortuary and I feel certain it is the same person.

CORONER: Did you see the man who was talking to her?

WITNESS: Yes, I noticed he had a newspaper parcel in his hand. It was about eighteen inches in length and six or eight inches in width. He was about five feet seven inches as near as I could say. He had on a hard felt deerstalker hat of dark colour and dark clothes.

CORONER: What kind of a coat was it?

WITNESS: An overcoat. He wore dark trousers.

CORONER: Can you give any idea as to his age?

WITNESS: About twenty-eight years.

CORONER: Can you give any idea as to what he was?

WITNESS: No, sir, I cannot. He was of respectable appearance. I noticed the woman had a flower in her jacket.

Statement of the Coroner. Unlike other victims in the series of crimes in this neighbourhood—a district teeming with representatives of all nations— [Elizabeth Stride] was not an En-glishwoman. She was born in Sweden in the year 1843, but having resided in this country for upwards of twenty-two years, she could speak English fluently and without much foreign accent. At one time the deceased and her husband kept a coffeehouse in Poplar. At another time she was staying in Devonshire Street, Commercial Road, supporting herself, it was said, by sewing and charring. On and off for the last six years she lived in a common lodging-house in the notorious lane called Flower and Dean Street. She was there known only by the nickname of "Long Liz," and often told a tale, which might have been apocryphal, of her husband and children having gone down with the *Princess Alice.* For the last two years the deceased had been living in Dorset Street, Spitalfields, with Michael Kidney, a waterside labourer belonging to the Army Reserve. But at intervals during that period—amounting altogether to five months—she left him without any apparent reason except a desire to be free from the restraint even of that connection and to obtain greater opportunity for indulging her drinking habits.

[The witness] last saw her alive at the corner of Fairclough Street and Berner Street, saying, "Not tonight but some other night." Within a quarter of an hour her lifeless body was found at a spot only a few yards from where she was last seen alive. It was late and there were few people about, but the place to which the two repaired could not have been selected on account of its being quiet or unfrequented. It had only the merit of darkness. It was the passageway leading into a court where several families resided. Adjoining the passage and court there was a club of Socialists who, having finished their debate, were singing and making merry. The deceased and her companion must have seen the lights of the clubroom and the kitchen and of the printing office. They must have heard the music and dancing, for the windows were open. There were persons in the yard but a short time previous to their arrival. At forty minutes past twelve one of the members of the club named Morris Eagle passed the spot where the deceased drew her last breath, passing through the gateway to the back door which opened into the yard. At one o'clock the body was found by the manager of the club. He did not inspect [it] himself with any care, but blood was flowing from the throat even when Spooner reached the spot some few minutes afterwards.

In this case, as in other similar cases which had occurred in this neighbourhood, no call for assistance was noticed. Although there might have been some noise in the club, it seemed very unlikely that any cry could have been raised without its being heard by some one of those near. The editor of a Socialist paper was quietly at work in a shed down the yard which was used as a printing office. There were several families in the cottages in the court only a few yards distant, and there were twenty persons in the different rooms of the club. But if there was no outcry, how did the deceased meet with her death?

There were no signs of any struggle; the clothes were neither torn nor disturbed. It was true that there were marks over both shoulders, produced by pressure of two hands, but the position of the body suggested either that she was willingly placed or placed herself where she was found. Only the soles of her boots were visible. She was still holding in her hand a packet of cachous, and there was a bunch of flowers still pinned to her dress front. If she had been forcibly placed on the ground, it was difficult to understand how she failed to attract attention, as it was clear from the appearance of the blood on the ground that the throat was not cut until after she was actually on her back. There were no marks of gagging, no bruises on the face, and no trace of any anaesthetic or narcotic in the stomach, while the presence of the cachous in her hand showed that she did not make use of it in self-defence. Possibly the pressure marks may have had a less tragic origin, as Dr. Black says it was difficult to say how recently they were produced.

There was one particular which was not easy to explain. When seen by Dr. Blackwell, her right hand was lying on the chest, smeared inside and out with blood. Dr. Phillips was unable to make any suggestion how the hand became soiled. There was no injury to the hand such as they would expect if it had been raised in self-defence while her throat was being cut. Was it done intentionally by her assassin or accidentally by those who were early on the spot? The evidence afforded no clue. Unfortunately the murderer had disappeared without leaving the slightest trace. Even the cachous were wrapped up in unmarked paper, so that there was nothing to show where they were bought. The cut in the throat might have been effected in such a manner that bloodstains on the hands and clothes of the operator were avoided, while the domestic history of the dead woman suggested the strong probability that her destroyer was a stranger to her.

In the absence of motive, the age and class of woman selected as victim, and the place and time of the crime, there was a similarity between this case and those mysteries which had recently occurred in that neighbourhood. There had been no skilful mutilation as in the cases of Nichols and Chapman, and no unskilful injuries as in the case in Mitre Square—possibly the works of an imitator; but there had been the same skill exhibited in the way in which the victim had been entrapped and the injuries inflicted so as to cause instant death and prevent blood from soiling the operator, and the same daring defiance of immediate detection which—unfortunately for the peace of the inhabitants and trade of the neighbourhood—had hitherto been only too successful.

THE SIXTH MURDER

Victim: Catherine Eddowes
Place: Mitre Square

October 1. The murder in the City was committed in circumstances which show that the assassin, if not suffering from insanity, appears to be free from any fear of interruption while at his dreadful work. Mitre Square is entered from three places—Mitre Street and passages from Duke Street and St. James's Place—through any of which he might have been interrupted by the arrival either of ordinary pedestrians or the police, although the square is lonely at nighttime, being occupied chiefly for business purposes. The constable's beat, moreover, is patrolled in between fifteen and twenty minutes, and within this short space of time, apparently, the murderer and his victim must have arrived and the crime been committed. The deceased was found lying on her back with her head inclined to the left side. Her left leg was extended, the right being bent, and both her arms were extended. The throat was terribly cut; there was a large gash across the face from the nose to the right angle of the cheek, and part of the right ear had been cut off. There were also other indescribable mutilations. It is stated that some anatomical skill seems to have been displayed in the way in which the lower part of the body was mutilated, but the ghastly work appears to have been done more rapidly and roughly than in the cases of the women Nichols and Chapman.

The officer who found the body is positive that it could not have been more than a quarter of an hour before he discovered it. He is timed to "work his beat," as it is called, in from ten to fifteen minutes. The police theory is that the man and woman who had met in Aldgate watched the policeman pass round the square and then entered it for an immoral purpose. The throat of the woman having been cut, the murderer hurriedly proceeded to mutilate the body. Five minutes, some of the doctors think, would have sufficed for the completion of the murderer's work, and he was thus enabled to leave the ground before the return of the policeman on duty. The murderer probably avoided much bloodstaining on account of the woman being on the ground at the time of the outrage, and leaving the square by either of the courts, he would be able to pass quickly away through the many narrow thoroughfares without exciting observation. But one of the most extraordinary incidents in connection with the crime is that not the slightest scream or noise was heard. A watchman is employed at one of the warehouses in the square, and in a direct line but a few yards away a City policeman was sleeping.

A man named Albert Barkert has made the following statement: "I was in the Three Nuns Hotel, Aldgate, on Saturday night when a man got into conversation with me. He asked me questions which now appear to me to have some bearing upon the recent murders. He wanted to know whether I knew what sort of loose women used the public bar at that house, when they usually left the street outside, and where they were in the habit of going. He asked further questions and from his manner seemed to be up to no good purpose. He appeared to be a shabby genteel sort of man and was dressed in black clothes. He wore a black felt hat and carried a black bag. We came out together at closing time—twelve o'clock."

Inquest on Catherine Eddowes, October 5–12

Testimony of Eliza Gold. She recognized the deceased as her sister, whose name was Catherine Eddowes. She was not married but was living with a man named Kelly. Her sister had not been married. Her age last birthday was forty-three, as well as witness could remember. Before she went to live with Kelly she had lived with a man named Conway for some years. She had had two children by him, who were married.

Testimony of John Kelly. He was a labourer and jobbed about the markets. He had seen and recognized the body of the deceased as Catherine Conway. Witness was last with [her] at two o'clock on Saturday afternoon in Houndsditch. She said she was going to see if she could find her daughter Annie in Bermondsey. She promised to be back at four o'clock and no later. She did not return, but witness heard that she was locked up on Saturday night at Bishopsgate. He did not make inquiries about her, feeling sure that she would return on Sunday morning. He had heard that she had been locked up because she had had "a drop to drink."

Testimony of Police Constable Lewis Robinson. Robinson stated that about half-past eight o'clock on the night of the 29th he was on duty in High Street, Aldgate, where he saw a crowd of persons. He then saw a woman who was drunk and who had since been recognized as the deceased. She was lying on the footway. Witness asked if anyone in the crowd knew her or where she lived, but he received no answer. On the arrival of another constable they took her to Bishopsgate Police Station, where she was placed in a cell.

CITY SOLICITOR: Do you recollect whether she was wearing an apron?

WITNESS: Yes, she was.

CITY SOLICITOR: Could you identify it?

WITNESS: I could if I saw the whole of it. —A brown paper parcel was produced, from which two pieces of apron were taken and shown to the witness, who said: To the best of my knowledge and belief that is the apron.

Testimony of Constable George Henry Hutt. On Saturday night at a quarter to ten he took over the prisoners, among whom was the deceased. He visited her several times in the cell until five minutes to one o'clock, when he was directed by Sergeant Byfield to see whether any of the prisoners were fit to be discharged. The deceased was found to be sober and was brought from the cell to the office, and after giving the name of Mary Ann Kelly, she was discharged.

CITY SOLICITOR: It was not witness but Sergeant Byfield who discharged her. She left the station about one o'clock. She said nothing to witness as to where she was going. About two minutes before one o'clock, when bringing her out of the cell, she asked witness the time and he replied, "Too late for you to get any more drink." She then said, "I shall get a d—— fine hiding when I get home." Witness gathered from that that she was going home. He noticed that she was wearing an apron and to the best of his belief the apron shown to the last witness was the one.

Testimony of Joseph Lawende. On the night of the murder he was at the Imperial Club in Duke Street with Joseph Levy and Harry Harris. They were out of the club at half-past one and left the place about five minutes later. They saw a man and a woman standing together at a corner in Church Passage, which led into Mitre Square. The woman was standing with her face toward the man. Witness could not see the woman's face; the man was taller than she. She had on a black jacket and bonnet. He saw her put her hand on the man's chest. Witness had seen some of the clothing at the police station, and he believed the articles were the same that the woman he referred to was wearing.

CORONER: Can you tell us what sort of man it was with whom she was speaking?

WITNESS: He had on a cloth cap with a peak.

CORONER: Unless the jury wish it I have a special reason why no further description of this man should be given now.

The jury assented to [his] wish.

Testimony of Dr. Frederick Gordon Brown.

CITY SOLICITOR: Does the nature of the wounds lead you to any conclusion as to the kind of instrument with which they were inflicted?

WITNESS: With a sharp knife, and it must have been pointed. And from the cut in the abdomen I should say the knife was at least six inches long.

CITY SOLICITOR: Would you consider that the person who inflicted the wounds possessed great anatomical skill?

WITNESS: A good deal of knowledge as to the position of the organs in the abdominal cavity and the way of removing them.

CITY SOLICITOR: Could the organs removed be used for any professional purpose?

WITNESS: They would be of no use for a professional purpose.

CITY SOLICITOR: You have spoken of the extraction of the left kidney. Would it require great skill and knowledge to remove it?

WITNESS: It would require a great deal of knowledge as to its position to remove it. It is easily overlooked. It is covered by a membrane.

CITY SOLICITOR: Would not such a knowledge be likely to be possessed by one accustomed to cutting up animals?

WITNESS: Yes.

CITY SOLICITOR: Can you as a professional man assign any reason for the removal of certain organs from the body?

WITNESS: I cannot.

Testimony of Dr. George William Sequeira.

CITY SOLICITOR: Have you formed any opinion that the murderer had any design with respect to any particular part?

WITNESS: I have formed the opinion that he had no particular design on any particular organ.

CITY SOLICITOR: Judging from the injuries inflicted, do you think he was possessed of great anatomical skill?

WITNESS: No, I do not.

Testimony of Police Constable Alfred Long. Long stated that he was on duty in Goulston Street, Whitechapel, on the morning of the 30th. At about 2:55 he found a portion of an apron (produced as before). There were recent stains of blood on it. It was lying in the passage leading to a staircase of 118 and 119, ordinary model dwelling-houses. Above it on the wall was written in chalk, "The Jews are the men that will not be blamed for nothing." He had previously passed the spot where he found the apron at twenty minutes after two, but it was not there then.

CITY SOLICITOR: Have you not put the word "not" in the wrong place? Is it not "The Jews are not the men that will be blamed for nothing"? Witness repeated the words as he had previously read them.

CITY SOLICITOR: How do you spell "Jews"?

WITNESS: J-e-w-s.

CITY SOLICITOR: Now, was it not on the wall "J-u-w-e-s"? Is it not possible you are wrong?

WITNESS: It may be as to the spelling.

Testimony of Detective Daniel Halse. Witness went to Goulston Street to the spot where the apron had been discovered. He remained there and [Detective] Hunt went to Mr. M'William for instructions to have the writing photographed. Directions were given for that to be done. Some of the Metropolitan Police thought it might cause a riot—if the writing were seen—and an outbreak against the Jews. It was decided to have the writing rubbed out.

CITY SOLICITOR: Did anyone suggest that it would be possible to take out the word "Jews" and leave the rest of the writing there?

WITNESS: I suggested that the top line might be rubbed out, and the Metropolitan Police suggested the word "Juwes." The fear on the part of the Metropolitan Police of a riot was the sole cause of the writing on the wall being rubbed out.

FURTHER REPORTS

October 1. At three o'clock yesterday afternoon a meeting of nearly a thousand persons took place in Victoria Park. After several speeches upon the conduct of the Home Secretary and Sir Charles Warren [Commissioner of Police of the Metropolis], a resolution was unanimously passed that it was high time both officers should resign and make way for some officers who would leave no stone unturned for the purpose of bringing the murderers to justice, instead of allowing them to run riot in a civilized city like London. On Mile-End-Waste during the day four meetings of the same kind were held and similar resolutions passed.

Letter to the Editor of The Times.

> *Sir: I beg to suggest the organization of a small force of plain-clothes constables mounted on bicycles for the rapid and noiseless patrolling of streets and roads by night. Your obedient servant.*

Fred. Wellesley.

October 2. Two communications of an extra-ordinary nature, both signed "Jack the Ripper," have been received by the Central News Agency, the one on Thursday last and the other yesterday morning. The first was a letter bearing the E.C. postmark in which reference was made to the atrocious murders previously committed in the East End, which the writer confessed in a brutally jocular vein to have committed, stating that in the "next job" he did he would "clip the lady's ears off" and send them to the police, and also asking that the letter might be kept back until he had done "a bit more work."

The second communication was a postcard and, as above stated, it was received yesterday morning. It bore the date "London, E., October 1" and was as follows: "I was not coddling, dear old Boss, when I gave you the tip. You'll hear about

Saucy Jacky's work tomorrow. Double event this time. Number One squealed a bit; couldn't finish straight off. Had not time to get ears for police. Thanks for keeping last letter back till I got to work again." The postcard was sent to Scotland Yard. No doubt is entertained that the writer of both communications, whoever he may be, is the same person.

At a late hour last night it was decided by the City Police to offer a reward for the discovery and conviction of the criminal.

At a meeting of the Whitechapel District Board of Works held yesterday evening, Mr. Catmur said he thought that the board as the local authority should express their horror and abhorrence of the crimes which had been perpetrated in the district and that they should address the authorities really responsible. Proceeding, Mr. Catmur spoke of the evil effect which had resulted in the district in the loss of trade. Evening business had become practically extinct in many trades, women finding themselves unable to pass through the streets without an escort.

A correspondent writes: "There are most remarkable coincidences with regard to the times at which all these murders have been committed which demand particular attention. The first and third of the murders, those of Martha [Tabram] and Mrs. Chapman, were committed on exactly the same date of two separate months—namely the 7th of August and September—while the second and fourth murders had the same relative coincidence, both being perpetrated on the last days of August and September. If the same hand carried out these crimes, these facts seem to point to the idea that the criminal was one who had to be absent from the scene of his crimes for regular periods."

Letter to the Editor of The Times.

Sir: With regard to the suggestion that bloodhounds might assist in tracking the East End murderer, as a breeder of bloodhounds and knowing their power, I have little doubt that, had a hound been put upon the scent of the murderer while fresh, it might have done what the police have failed in. There are doubtless owners of bloodhounds willing to lend them if any of the police—which, I fear, is improbable —know how to use them. I am, Sir, your obedient servant.

Percy Lindley.

October 3.

Letter to the Editor of The Times.

Sir: Will you allow me to recommend that all the police boots should be furnished with a noiseless sole and heel, of indiarubber or other material, to prevent the sound of their measured tread being heard at night, which would enable them to get close to a criminal before he would be aware of their approach? Yours faithfully.

L. R. Thomson.

October 4. An American who refuses to give his name or any account of himself was arrested last night on suspicion of being the East End murderer. He is well dressed, rather tall, of slight build, and clean shaven. He accosted a woman in Cable Street, asked her to go with him, and threatened that if she refused he would "rip her up." The woman screamed and the man rushed to a cab. The police gave chase, got upon the cab, seized the man, and took him to Leman Street Police Station, where he asked the inspector in charge, "Are you the boss?"

October 5. Up to half-past one o'clock this morning no arrest had been reported at any City Police station in connection with the East End murders. The American who was arrested on Wednesday evening was released yesterday.

October 6. We are requested to state that Sir Charles Warren has been making inquiries as to the practicability of employing bloodhounds for use in special cases in the streets of London, and having ascertained that dogs can be procured that have been accustomed to work in a town, he is making immediate arrangements for their use in London.

The police authorities of Whitehall have had reproduced in facsimile and published on the walls of London the letter and postcard sent to the Central News Agency. The language of the card and letter is of a brutal character and is full of Americanisms. The handwriting, which is clear and plain—and disguised in part—is that of a person accustomed to write a round hand like that employed by clerks in offices. The exact colour of the ink and the smears of blood are reproduced in the placard, and information is asked in identification of the handwriting. The postcard bears a tolerably clear imprint of a bloody thumb or finger mark.

October 8. Fears were expressed among the police on Saturday that the night would not pass without some startling occurrence, and the most extraordinary precautions were taken in consequence. The parks are specially patrolled and the police, even in the most outlying districts, are keenly alive to the necessities of the situation. Having efficiently provided for the safeguard of other portions of the large area under his jurisdiction, Sir Charles Warren has sent every available man into the East End district. These together with a large body of City detectives are now on duty and will remain in the streets throughout the night.

October 9. It is stated by a news agency that definite instructions have been issued to the police that in the event of any person being found murdered under circumstances similar to those of the recent crimes, they are not to remove the body of the victim but to send notice immediately to a veterinary surgeon in the South-West District, who holds several trained bloodhounds in readiness to be taken to the spot where the body may be found and to be at once put on the scent.

October 10. Sir Charles Warren witnessed a private trial of bloodhounds in one of the London parks at an early hour yesterday morning. The hounds are the property of Mr. Edwin Brough of Wyndgate, who for years past has devoted himself to bloodhound breeding. On the 4th of October [he] was communicated with by the Metropolitan Police as to the utility of employing bloodhounds to track criminals, and negotiations followed which resulted in that gentleman coming to London on Saturday evening, bringing with him two magnificent animals named Champion Barnaby and Burgho. Mr. Brough tried Barnaby and Burgho in Regent's Park at seven o'clock on Monday morning. The ground was thickly coated with hoar-frost but they did their work well, successfully tracking for nearly a mile a young man who was given about fifteen minutes' start. They were again tried in Hyde Park on Monday night. It was of course dark and the dogs were hunted on a leash as would be the case if they were employed in Whitechapel. They were again successful in performing their allotted task, and at seven o'clock yesterday morning a trial took place before Sir Charles Warren. To all appearances the morning was a much better one for scenting purposes than was Monday, though the contrary proved to be the fact. In all, half a dozen runs were made, Sir Charles Warren in two instances acting as the hunted man. The dogs have been purchased by Sir C. Warren for the use of the police in the detection of crime should occasion arise.

October 11.

Letter to the Editor of The Times.

Sir: There is one statement in your otherwise very exact account of the trials of bloodhounds in Hyde Park which I shall be glad to be allowed to correct. My hounds Barnaby and Burgho have not been purchased by Sir Charles Warren for the use of the police. Yours truly.

Edwin Brough.

October 15. In reference to the writing on the walls of a house in Goulston Street, we are requested by Sir Charles Warren to state that his attention having been called to a paragraph in several daily journals mentioning that in the Yiddish dialect the word "Jews" is spelt "Juwes," he has made inquiries on the subject and finds that this is not a fact. He learns that the equivalent in the Judeo-German (Yiddish) jargon is "Yidden."

October 19. Mr. George Lusk of Alderney Road, Globe Road, Mile End, has received several letters purporting to be from the perpetrator of the Whitechapel murders, but believing them to have been the production of some practical joker, he had regarded them as of no consequence. It is stated that a letter delivered shortly after five o'clock on Tuesday evening was accompanied by a cardboard box containing what appeared to be a portion of a kidney. The letter was in the following terms: "From Hell. Mr. Lusk. Sir, I send you half the kidne I took from one woman, prasarved it for you, tother piece I fried and ate it; was very nice. I may send you the bloody knif that took it out if you only wate while longer. (Signed) 'Catch me when you can.' Mr. Lusk."

The receiver was at first disposed to think that another hoax had been perpetrated but eventually decided to take the opinion of the Vigilance Committee. They could of course give no opinions as to whether the kidney was human or not, but they decided to take the contents of the cardboard box to a medical man whose surgery is near. The substance was declared by the assistant to be the half of a human kidney which had been divided longitudinally; but in order to remove any reason for doubt he conveyed it to Dr. Openshaw, who is pathological curator of the London Hospital Museum. The doctor examined it and pronounced it to be a portion of a human kidney—a "ginny" kidney, that is to say one that had belonged to a person who had drunk heavily. He was further of opinion that it was the organ of a woman of about forty-five years of age and that it had been taken from the body within the last three weeks. It will be within public recollection that the left kidney was missing from the woman Eddowes, who was murdered and mutilated in Mitre Square.

It is stated that Sir Charles Warren's bloodhounds were out for practice at Tooting yesterday morning and were lost. Telegrams have been dispatched to all metropolitan police stations stating that if seen anywhere information is to be immediately sent to Scotland Yard.

October 25. During the three days of the week following the Sunday on which the two murders were committed, the following petition to the Queen was freely circulated among the women of the labouring classes of East London: To Our Most Gracious Sovereign Lady Queen Victoria. Madam: We, the women of East London, feel horror at the dreadful sins that have been lately in our midst and grief because of the shame that has befallen the neighbourhood. By the facts which have come out in the inquests, we have learned much of the lives of those of our sisters who have lost a firm hold on goodness and who are living sad and degraded lives. We call on your servants in authority and bid them put the law which already exists in motion to close bad houses within whose walls such wickedness is done, and men and women ruined in body and soul. We are, Madam, your loyal and humble subjects.

October 26.

Letter to the Editor of The Times.

Sir: I have begun to raise a fund, to which I invite contributions from your readers, with a view of powerfully bringing the teachings of Christianity to bear on that corner in Whitechapel which has been disgraced by such hideous crimes. If the Gospel sufficed to change the cannibal inhabitants of the Fiji Islands into a nation of Christian worshippers, it is sufficient—and alone sufficient—to turn the darkest spots in London into the gardens of the Lord. Your obedient servant.

Mary J. Kinnaird.

THE SEVENTH MURDER,
NOVEMBER 9

Victim: Mary Jane Kelly
Place: Dorset Street (Miller's Court)

November 10. During the early hours of yesterday morning another murder of a most revolting and fiendish character took place in Spitalfields. This is the seventh which has occurred in this immediate neighbourhood, and the character of the mutilations leaves very little doubt that the murderer in this instance is the same person who has committed the previous ones, with which the public are fully acquainted.

The scene of this last crime is at No. 26 Dorset Street, which is about two hundred yards distant from [29] Hanbury Street, where the unfortunate woman, Mary Ann Nichols, was so foully murdered. Although the victim, whose name is Mary Jane Kelly, resides at the above number, the entrance to the room she occupied is up a narrow court in which are some half a dozen houses and which is known as Miller's Court; it is entirely separated from the other portion of the house and has an entrance leading into the court. The room is known by the title of No. 13. As an instance of the poverty of the neighbourhood it may be mentioned that nearly the whole of the houses in this street are common lodging-houses, and the one opposite where this murder was enacted has accommodations for some three hundred men and is fully occupied every night.

About twelve months ago Kelly, who was about twenty-four years of age and who was considered a good-looking young woman of fair and fresh-coloured complexion, came to [the owner] with a man named Joseph Kelly [from the inquest it appears that his name was actually Joseph Barnett], who she stated was her husband and who was a porter employed at the Spitalfields Market. They rented a room on the ground floor, the same in which the poor woman was murdered, at a rental of four shillings a week. It had been noticed that the deceased woman was somewhat addicted to drink, but Mr. M'Carthy [the owner] denied any knowledge that she had been leading a loose or immoral life. That this was so, however, there can be no doubt, for about a fortnight ago she had a quarrel with Kelly and—after some blows were exchanged—the man left the house, or rather room, and did not return. Since then the woman has supported herself as best she could, and the police have ascertained that she has been walking the streets.

None of those living in the court or at 26 Dorset Street saw anything of the unfortunate creature after about eight o'clock on Thursday evening, but she was seen in Commercial Street shortly before the closing of the public house and then had the appearance of being the worse for drink. About one o'clock yesterday morning a person living in the court opposite to the room occupied by the murdered woman heard her singing the song "Sweet Violets," but this person is unable to say whether anyone else was with her at that time. Nothing more was seen or heard of her until her dead body was found.

At a quarter of eleven yesterday morning, as the woman was 35 shillings in arrears with her rent, Mr. M'Carthy said to a man employed by him in his shop, John Bowyer, "Go to No. 13 and try and get some rent." Bowyer did as he was directed and on knocking at the door was unable to obtain an answer. He then tried the handle of the door and found that it was locked. On looking through the keyhole he found the key was missing. The lefthand side of the room faced the court and in it were two large windows. Bowyer, knowing that when the man Kelly and the dead woman had their quarrel a pane of glass in one of the windows was broken, went round to the side in question. He put his hand through the aperture and pulled aside the muslin curtain which covered it. On his looking into the room a shocking sight presented itself. He could see the woman lying on the bed, entirely naked, covered with blood, and apparently dead. Without waiting to make a closer examination he ran to his employer and told him he believed the woman Kelly had been murdered. M'Carthy at once went and looked through the broken window, and, satisfying himself that something was wrong, dispatched Bowyer to the Commercial Street Police Station, at the same time enjoining him not to tell any of the neighbours what he had discovered.

Inspector Back, who was in charge of the station at the time, accompanied Bowyer back and on finding that a murder had been committed at once sent for assistance. Dr. Phillips, the divisional surgeon of police, and Superintendent Arnold were also sent for. During this time the door had not been touched. On the arrival of Superintendent Arnold he caused a telegram to be sent direct to Sir Charles Warren, informing him what had happened.

Mr. Arnold, having satisfied himself that the woman was dead, ordered one of the windows to be entirely removed. A horrible and sickening sight then presented itself. The poor woman lay on her back on the bed, entirely naked. Her throat was cut from ear to ear, right down to the spinal column. The ears and nose had been cut clean off. The breasts had also been cleanly cut off and placed on a table which was by the side of the bed. The stomach and abdomen had been ripped open while the face was slashed about so that the features of the poor creature were beyond all recognition. The kidneys and heart had also been removed from the body and placed on the table by the side of the breasts. The liver had likewise been removed and laid on the right thigh. The lower portion of the body and the uterus had been cut out, and these appeared to be missing. The thighs had been cut. A more horrible or sickening sight could not be imagined.

The clothes of the woman were lying by the side of the bed as though they had been taken off and laid down in the ordinary manner. The bedclothes had been turned down, and this was probably done by the murderer after he had cut his victim's throat. There was no appearance of a struggle having taken place, and although a careful search of the room was made, no knife or instrument of any kind was found.

A somewhat important fact has been pointed out which puts a fresh complexion on the theory of the murders. It appears that the cattle boats bringing live freight to London are in the habit of coming into the Thames on Thursdays or Fridays and leave again for the Continent on Sundays or Mondays. It has already been a matter of comment that the recent revolting crimes have been committed at the week's end, and an opinion has been formed among some of the detectives that the murderer is a drover or butcher employed on one of these boats—of which there are many—and that he periodically appears and disappears with one of the steamers. It is pointed out that at the inquests on the previous victims the coroners had expressed the opinion that the knowledge of anatomy possessed by a butcher would have been sufficient to enable him to find and cut out the parts of the body which in several cases were abstracted.

A Mrs. Paumier, a young woman who sells roasted chestnuts at the corner of Widegate Street, a narrow thoroughfare about two minutes' walk from the scene of the murder, told a reporter yesterday afternoon a story which appears to afford a clue to the murderer. She said that about twelve o'clock that morning a man dressed like a gentleman came to her and said, "I suppose you have heard about the murder in Dorset Street?" She replied that she had, whereupon the man grinned and said, "I know more about it than you." He then stared into her face and went down Sandy's Row. When he had got some way off, however, he looked back as if to see whether she was watching him and then vanished. Mrs. Paumier said the man had a black moustache, was about five feet six inches high, and wore a black silk hat, a black coat, and speckled trousers. He also carried a black shiny bag about a foot in depth and a foot and a half in length. Mrs. Paumier stated further that the same man accosted three young women whom she knows on Thursday night, and they chaffed him and asked what he had in the bag, and he replied, "Something that the ladies don't like."

Late yesterday evening a man was arrested near Dorset Street on suspicion of being concerned in the murder. He was taken to Commercial Street Police Station followed by an angry mob and is still detained there. Another man, respectably dressed, wearing a slouch hat and carrying a black bag, was arrested and taken to Leman Street Station. The bag was examined but its contents were perfectly harmless and the man was at once released.

Inquest on Mary Jane Kelly, November 13

Testimony of Joseph Barnett (called Kelly in the first newspaper reports). Deceased occasionally got drunk but generally speaking she was sober when she lived with him. She had told him several times that she was born in Limerick but removed to Wales when quite young. She had married a collier named Davis in Wales when she was sixteen years of age and lived with him until he was killed in an explosion a year or two afterwards. After her husband's death she went to Cardiff with a cousin and came to London about four years ago. She lived in a gay house in the West End for a short time and then went to France with a gentleman, but did not like it and soon returned to London, living in Ratcliff Highway near the gasworks with a man named Morganstone. She afterwards lived with a mason named Joseph Fleming somewhere in Bethnal Green. Deceased told witness all her history while she lived with him. Witness picked her up in Spitalfields on a Friday night and made an appointment to meet her the next day, when they agreed to live together and they had done so ever since.

Testimony of Mary Ann Cox. She last saw deceased alive about a quarter to twelve on Thursday night. Deceased was very much intoxicated at that time and was with a short stout man, shabbily dressed, with a round billycock hat on. He had a can of beer in his hand. He had a blotchy face and a heavy carroty moustache. Witness followed them into the court and said goodnight to the deceased, who replied, "Goodnight, I am going to sing." The door was shut and witness heard the deceased singing, "Only a violet I plucked from mother's grave." Witness went to her room and remained there about a quarter of an hour, and then went out. Deceased was still singing at that time. It was raining and witness returned home at 3:10 A.M., and the light in deceased's room was then out and there was no noise. Witness could not sleep and heard a man go out of the court about a quarter past six. It might have been a policeman for all witness knew.

Testimony of Elizabeth Prater. Mrs. Prater, a married woman living apart from her husband, said she occupied No. 20 room, Miller's Court, her room being just over that occupied by the deceased. If deceased moved about in her room much witness could hear her. Witness lay down on her bed on Thursday night about 1:30 with her clothes on and fell asleep directly. She was disturbed during the night by a kitten in the room. That would be about half-past three or four o'clock. She then distinctly heard in a low tone and in a woman's voice a cry of "Oh! murder." The sound appeared to proceed from the court and near where witness was. She did not take much notice of it, however, as they were continually hearing cries of murder in the court. She did not hear it a second time, neither did she hear a sound of falling, and she dropped off to sleep again and did not wake until five o'clock. Then she got up and went to the Five Bells public house and had some rum.

Testimony of Frederick G. Abberline, Detective Inspector, Scotland Yard. Witness had seen the condition of the room through the window. He examined the room after the door had been forced. From the appearance of the grate it was evident a very large fire had been kept up. The ashes had since been examined and it was evident that portions of a woman's clothing had been burnt. It was his opinion that the clothes had been burnt to enable the murderer to see what he was about. There were portions of a woman's skirt and the rim of a hat in the grate.

FURTHER REPORTS

November 12. Great excitement was caused shortly before ten o'clock last night by the arrest of a man with a blackened face who publicly proclaimed himself to be "Jack the Ripper." This was at the corner of Wentworth Street, Commercial Street, near the scene of the latest crime. Two young men, one a discharged soldier, immediately seized him, and the great crowd—which always on a Sunday night parades this neighbourhood—raised a cry of "Lynch him." Sticks were raised, the man was furiously attacked, and but for the timely arrival of the police he would have been seriously injured. The police took him to Leman Street Station, where the prisoner proved to be a very remarkable person. He refused to give any name but asserted that he was a doctor at St. George's Hospital. He was about thirty-five years of age, five feet seven inches in height, of dark complexion, with dark moustache, and was wearing spectacles. In his pocket he had a double-peaked light-check cap.

November 13. During yesterday several arrests were made, but after a short examination in all cases the persons were set at liberty, as it was felt certain they had no connection with the crime.

As will be seen from our Parliamentary report, Sir Charles Warren tendered his resignation on Thursday last.

November 14. The following statement was made yesterday evening by George Hutchinson, a labourer: "At two o'clock on Friday morning as I passed Thrawl Street, I passed a man standing at the corner of the street, and as I went towards Flower and Dean Street I met the woman Kelly, whom I knew very well having been in her company a number of times. She said, 'Mr. Hutchinson, can you lend me sixpence?' I said I could not. She then walked towards Thrawl Street, saying she must go and look for some money. The man who was standing at the corner of Thrawl Street then came towards her and put his hand on her shoulder and said something to her which I did not hear and they both burst out laughing. He put his hand again on her shoulder and they both walked slowly towards me. I walked on to the corner of Fashion Street near the public house. As they came by me his arm was still on her shoulder. He had a soft felt hat on and this was drawn down somewhat over his eyes. I put down my head to look him in the face and he turned and looked at me very sternly, and they walked across the road to Dorset Street. I followed them across and stood at the corner of Dorset Street. They stood at the corner of Mil-ler's Court for about three minutes. Kelly spoke to the man in a loud voice, saying, 'I have lost my handkerchief.' He pulled a red handkerchief out of his pocket and gave it to Kelly and they both went up the court together. I went to look up the court to see if I could see them but could not. I stood there for three-quarters of an hour to see if they came down again, but they did not and so I went away. My suspicions were aroused by seeing the man so well dressed, but I had no suspicion that he was the murderer.

"The man was about five feet six inches in height, and thirty-four or thirty-five years of age, with dark complexion and dark moustache turned up at the ends. He was wearing a long dark coat trimmed with astrachan, a white collar with black necktie, in which was affixed a horseshoe pin. He looked like a foreigner. I went up the court and stayed there a couple of minutes but did not see any light in the house or hear any noise. I was out last night until three o'clock looking for him. I could swear to the man anywhere. The man I saw carried a small parcel about eight inches long and it had a strap round it. He had it tightly grasped in his left hand. It looked as though it was covered with dark American cloth. He carried in his right hand, which he laid upon the woman's shoulder, a pair of brown kid gloves. He walked very softly. I believe that he lives in the neighbourhood, and I fancied that I saw him in Petticoat Lane on Sunday morning but I was not certain."

November 15. During yesterday several persons were detained by the police on suspicion of being concerned in the Dorset Street murder, but they were after a short detention allowed to go away. During the afternoon a City constable had an uncomfortable walk along the Commercial Road. The officer, who was in mufti and was wearing a low broad-brim hat of rather singular appearance, was quietly walking along the road when suddenly some persons called out that he was "Jack the Ripper." Within a few seconds some hundreds of people surrounded the constable, who tried to evade them by increasing his pace, but the quicker he went the faster the mob followed until he was hemmed in on all sides. The results might have been serious for him had not some constables of the H Division come up, and the man, making known his identity to them, was got away from the mob.

One arrest caused more than usual excitement. A man stared into the face of a woman in the Whitechapel Road and she at once screamed out that he was "Jack the Ripper." The man was immediately surrounded by an excited and threatening crowd, from which he was rescued with some difficulty by the police. He was then taken under a strong escort to the Commercial Street Police Station, followed by an enormous mob of men and women shouting and screaming at him in the most extraordinary manner. At the police station the man proved to be a German unable to speak a word of English. He explained through an interpreter that he arrived in London from Germany on Tuesday and was to leave for America today.

November 22. Considerable excitement was caused throughout the East End yesterday morning by a report that another woman had been brutally murdered and mutilated in a common lodging-house in George Street, Spitalfields, and in consequence of the reticence of the police authorities all sorts of rumours prevailed. Although it was soon ascertained that there had been no murder, it was said that an attempt had been made to murder a woman of the class to which the other unfortunate creatures belonged by cutting her throat, and the excitement in the neighbourhood for some time was intense.

The victim of this last occurrence fortunately is but slightly injured and was at once able to furnish the detectives with a full description of her assailant. Her name is Annie Farmer and she is a woman of about forty years of age who lately resided with her husband but on account of her dissolute habits was separated from him. On Monday night the woman had no money and, being unable to obtain any, walked the streets until about half-past seven yesterday morning. At that time she got into conversation in Commercial Street with a man whom she describes as about thirty-six years old, about five feet six inches in height, with a dark moustache, and wearing a shabby black diagonal suit and hard felt hat. He treated her to several drinks until she became partially intoxicated. At his suggestion they went to the common lodging-house, 19 George Street, and paid the deputy eight pence for a bed. That was about eight o'clock and nothing was heard to cause alarm or suspicion until half-past nine, when screams were heard proceeding from the room occupied by the man and Farmer. Some men who were in the kitchen of the house at the time rushed upstairs and met the woman coming down. She was partially undressed and was bleeding profusely from a wound in the throat. She was asked what was the matter and simply said, "He's done it," at the same time pointing to the door leading into the street. The men rushed outside but saw no one except a man in charge of a horse and cart.

November 23. The man who committed the assault on Annie Farmer on Wednesday morning has not yet been captured. It is now believed that the wound to Farmer's throat was not made with a sharp instrument; also that the quarrel arose between the pair respecting money, as when the woman was at the police station some coins were found concealed in her mouth. The authorities appear to be satisfied that the man has no connection with the recent murders.

KEY TEXTS

Maxim Jakubowski and Nathan Braund

As an editor, author, translator, critic, and expert in several popular fiction categories, Maxim Jakubowski (1944–) has edited more than eighty anthologies in the fields of mystery, science fiction, fantasy, photography, and erotica. After many years in the British publishing world, he left to open Murder One, a bookshop in London that specialized in crime fiction but also sold romance and other categories of fiction; he ran it for more than twenty years before it closed.

Jakubowski was the crime reviewer for *Time Out London* and *The Guardian* and is the literary director of London's Crime Scene Festival, an annual literary and film celebration.

He has also written several short story collections and novels of dark erotica under his own name, and he is one of the suspected (unconfirmed but not denied) authors of many of the explicit Vina Jackson worldwide bestselling novels that followed the *Fifty Shades of Grey* phenomenon.

Nathan Braund (1970–) has been teaching English in such countries as Estonia, Japan, and Oman while pursuing a writing career. His novel *The Broken Boots Guide to Astlavonia* (2012) is the story of a writer who wins a contest with a totally made-up travel article and is sent to a former Soviet state to write its first travel guide. His autobiographical work *The Wrong Way Round to Ewan McGregor* (2013) describes his efforts to get his film script into the hands of the Scottish movie star.

"Key Texts" ("Witness Statements," "Autopsy Reports," and "The 'Ripper Letters'") was first published in *The Mammoth Book of Jack the Ripper*, edited by Maxim Jakubowski and Nathan Braund (London, Robinson Publishing, 1999).

WITNESS STATEMENTS
Elizabeth Long (aka Mrs. Darrell)

Elizabeth Long is a contentious witness, in that her evidence casts into doubt Dr. George Bagster Phillips's statement that Chapman had been dead for two hours when he examined her body at around 6:30 A.M. Those who believe Mrs. Long—and the coroner, Wynne Baxter, was among them—point to the apparently corroborative evidence of Albert Cadosch, who testified that, at 5:30 A.M., he heard a voice in the yard of 29, Hanbury Street saying "No!" as well as something falling against the wooden fence dividing the yards. Those who side with Phillips, allowing for half an hour either way, point out that Long's evidence is vague and inconsistent. Why did she particularly observe the time when she passed No. 29? And if this couple which she observed were of such interest, why did she not turn to see the man's face? She thought he wore a dark coat, but was not quite certain of that . . . She couldn't say what his age was . . . but he looked over forty . . . He appeared to be a little taller than Chapman . . . appeared to be a foreigner . . . Few have pointed out that Cadosch's evidence fits the notion of someone, drunk or otherwise, coming upon the body and lurching into the fence with an ejaculation quite as well as the notion that this was Chapman's last moment, for there must have been other sounds attendant upon the killing— notably the splashing of the blood on such a dry night.

BAXTER: Did you see the man's face?

MRS. LONG: I did not and could not recognize him again. He was, however, dark complexioned, and was wearing a brown deerstalker hat. I think he was wearing a dark coat but cannot be sure.

BAXTER: Was he a man or a boy?

MRS. LONG: Oh, he was a man over forty, as far as I could tell. He seemed to be a little taller than the deceased. He looked to me like a foreigner, as well as I could make out.

BAXTER: Was he a labourer or what?

MRS. LONG: He looked what I should call shabby genteel.

William Marshall

Marshall, a labourer of 64, Berner Street, denied seeing the flower which others reported on Stride's bodice, but that does not mean that he was an unreliable witness. His description of the man's coat and cap tallies with that of PC Smith, while his overall description of the man closely resembles that given by J. Best and John Gardner, who, shortly before 11 P.M., saw Stride leaving the Bricklayer's Arms, Settles Street, with a man about 5 feet 5 inches tall, with a black moustache and weak, sandy eyelashes, and wearing a morning suit and a billycock hat. Gardner corroborated Best's evidence in every regard. Marshall testified that the man he saw had been kissing Stride and that he heard him say, in a mild, educated voice, "You would say anything but your prayers," at which Stride laughed. This is a very natural response to Stride saying (roughly): "Then I'd better say my prayers" (suggestive of a threat).

BAXTER: Did you notice how he was dressed?

MARSHALL: In a black cutaway coat and dark trousers.

BAXTER: Was he young or old?

MARSHALL: Middle-aged he seemed to be.

BAXTER: Was he wearing a hat?

MARSHALL: No, a cap.

BAXTER: What sort of a cap?

MARSHALL: A round cap, with a small peak. It was something like what a sailor would wear.

BAXTER: What height was he?

MARSHALL: About 5 feet 6 inches.

BAXTER: Was he thin or stout?

MARSHALL: Rather stout.

BAXTER: Did he look well dressed?

MARSHALL: Decently dressed.

BAXTER: What class of man did he appear to be?

MARSHALL: I should say he was in business, and did nothing like hard [meaning manual] work.

BAXTER: Not like a dock labourer?

MARSHALL: No.

BAXTER: Nor a sailor?

MARSHALL: No.

BAXTER: Nor a butcher?

MARSHALL: No.

BAXTER: A clerk?

MARSHALL: He had more the appearance of a clerk.

BAXTER: Is that the best suggestion you can make?

MARSHALL: It is.

BAXTER: You did not see his face. Had he any whiskers?

MARSHALL: I cannot say. I do not think he had.

BAXTER: Was he wearing gloves?

MARSHALL: No.

BAXTER: Was he carrying a stick or umbrella in his hands?

MARSHALL: He had nothing in his hands that I am aware of.

Israel Schwartz

He was an immigrant of Hungarian origin, and one of our best witnesses. He testified that he had seen a strange encounter shortly before the murder of Elizabeth Stride. He subsequently gave an interview to the *Star* in which he elaborated his original description. The first man, he said, had been walking "as though partially intoxicated," while the second man, leaving the pub, carried a knife rather than a pipe, with which he threatened Schwartz. It seems plain that Schwartz's evidence was believed by the police, which makes the absence of any account of his giving evidence at the subsequent inquest remarkable.

> 12:45 A.M. *30th Israel Schwartz of 22, Helen Street, Backchurch Lane, stated that at this hour, on turning into Berner Street from Commercial Street and having got as far as the gateway where the murder was committed, he saw a man stop and speak to a woman, who was standing in the gateway. The man tried to pull the woman into the street, but he turned her round and threw her down on the footway and the woman screamed three times, but not very loudly. On crossing to the opposite side of the street, he saw a second man standing lighting his pipe. The man who threw the woman down called out, apparently to the man on the opposite side of the road, "Lipski" and then Schwartz walked away, but finding that he was followed by the second man, he ran so far as the railway arch, but the man did not follow so far.*

Schwartz cannot say whether the two men were together or known to each other. Upon being taken to the mortuary Schwartz identified the body as that of the woman he had seen. He thus describes the first man, who threw the woman down: age, about 30; ht, 5 ft 5 in; comp., fair; hair, dark; small brown moustache, full face, broad shouldered; dress, dark jacket and trousers, black cap with peak, and nothing in his hands. Second man: age, 35; ht., 5 ft 11 in; comp., fresh; hair, light brown; dress, dark overcoat, old black hard felt hat, wide brim; had a clay pipe in his hand.

Joseph Lawende

A commercial traveller in cigarettes of 45, Norfolk Road, Dalston, he left the Imperial Club at 16–17, Duke Street at 1:35 A.M. in company with Harry Harris, a furniture dealer, and Joseph Hyam Levy, a butcher. At the corner of Duke Street and Church Passage, they saw a man and a woman in conversation. Levy and Harris took little notice of the pair, but Lawende was more observant. The description of the man furnished by Lawende but withheld in the following exchange is that of a man of medium build and the look of a sailor. He wore a loose salt-and-pepper jacket, a grey cloth cap and a red or reddish "kingsman" or neckerchief. His age was about 30. He was 5 feet 7 inches or 5 feet 8 inches tall and had a fair complexion and moustache.

LAWENDE: I was at the Imperial Club with Mr. Joseph Levy and Mr. Harry Harris. We could not get home because it was raining. At half past one we left to go out, and left the house about five minutes later. I walked a little further from the others. We saw a man and a woman at the corner of Church Passage, in Duke Street, which leads into Mitre Square.
CORONER (MR. LANGHAM): Were they talking at the time?
LAWENDE: She was standing with her face towards the man. I only saw her back. She had her hand on his chest.
CORONER: What sort of woman was she?
LAWENDE: I could not see her face, but the man was taller than she was.
CORONER: Did you notice how she was dressed?
LAWENDE: I noticed she had a black jacket and black bonnet. I have seen the articles at the police station, and I recognize them as the sort of dress worn by that woman.
CORONER: What sort of woman was she?
LAWENDE: About 5 feet in height.
CORONER: Can you tell us what sort of man this was?
LAWENDE: He had a cloth cap on, with a peak of the same material.
MR. CRAWFORD (SOLICITOR FOR THE POLICE): Unless the jury particularly wish it, I have special reason for not giving details as to the appearance of this man.
JURY: No.
CORONER: You have given a special description of this man to the police?
LAWENDE: Yes.
CORONER: Do you think you would know him again?

LAWENDE: I doubt it, sir.

MR. CRAWFORD: The Club is 16 and 17, Duke Street, about fifteen or sixteen feet from where they were standing at Church Passage. By what did you fix the time?

LAWENDE: By seeing the club clock and my own watch. It was five minutes after the half hour when we came out, and to the best of my belief it was twenty-five to when we saw these persons.

CORONER: Did you hear anything said?

LAWENDE: No, not a word.

CORONER: Did either of them appear in an angry mood?

LAWENDE: No.

CORONER: Was there anything about them or their movements that attracted your attention?

LAWENDE: No, except that Mr. Levy said the court ought to be watched, and I took particular notice of a man and woman talking there.

CORONER: Was her arm on his breast as if she was pushing him away?

LAWENDE: No, they were standing very quietly.

CORONER: You were not curious enough to look back to see where they went?

LAWENDE: No.

George Hutchinson

George Hutchinson was unemployed, and a resident of Victoria Home, Commercial Street. His testimony appears trustworthy, not least because he seems to have known Kelly well. It has been surmised, indeed, that he may have been among Kelly's occasional clients when he could afford her, or may have been, in the slang of the time, "mashed on" her, which would explain his close interest and her request for the loan of sixpence (Hutchinson told journalists that he occasionally gave her a shilling) and, possibly, his subsequent elaboration of his description of the man sighted.

Hutchinson told the press that the man was of respectable Jewish appearance, that he wore a long dark coat with an astrakhan collar and cuffs, a dark jacket and trousers, light waistcoat, dark felt hat turned down in the middle, button boots, gaiters with white buttons, a linen collar, black tie with a horseshoe pin, and a thick gold chain. His age was 34 or 35, his height 5 feet 6 inches. His complexion was fair, his hair and eyelashes dark, his moustache slight and curled up at the ends. He carried a small parcel wrapped in American cloth (a glazed calico or oilcloth). Hutchinson believed he saw this suspect in Petticoat Lane on 11 November. The theatricality of this description—this appears to be a swell or "masher"—grows with each retelling. The "red handkerchief" is a curious motif. Most of the Whitechapel Murderer's victims wore a "kingsman" or neckerchief. Eddowes's, at least, was of red silk. Why did Kelly tell this man that she had lost her handkerchief? Does this imply that he had already given her a significant handkerchief, and why was he so ready to hand her a red handkerchief? Mayhew—admittedly thirty years earlier—writes of a fence who bought stolen silk handkerchieves, paying them ninepence apiece although they might be worth as much as four or five shillings, so this was no insubstantial gift.

The following statement was made at Commercial Street police station by Hutchinson following the conclusion of the Kelly inquest on 12 November.

About 2 A.M. 9th I was coming by Thrawl Street, Commercial Street, and just before I got to Flower and Dean Street, I met the murdered woman Kelly, and she said to me Hutchinson will you lend me sixpence. I said I can't I have spent all my money going down to Romford, she said good morning I must go and find some money. She went away toward Thrawl Street. A man coming in the opposite direction to Kelly, tapped her on the shoulder and said something to her they both burst out laughing. I heard her say alright to him, and the man said you will be alright, for what I have told you: he then placed his right hand around her shoulders. He also had a kind of small parcel in his left hand, with a kind of a strap round it. I stood against the lamp of the Queen's Head Public House, and watched him. They both then came past me and the man hung down his head, with his hat over his eyes. I stooped down and looked him in the face. He looked at me stern. They both went into Dorset Street. I followed them. They both stood at the corner of the court for about three minutes. He said something to her. She said alright my dear come along you will be comfortable. He then placed his arm on her shoulder and [she] gave him a kiss. She said she had lost her handkerchief. He then pulled his handkerchief a red one and gave it to her. They both then went up the Court together. I then went to the court to see if I could see them but I could not. I stood there for about three quarters of an hour to see if they came out. They did not so I went away.

AUTOPSY REPORTS
Mary Ann Nichols

Mary Ann Nichols was the first of the universally accepted "canonical" victims of the Whitechapel Murderer. She was a drab, but had nonetheless retained some vanity. According to her own statement, made on admission to Mitch-am workhouse on 13 February, she was born in Dean Street off Fetter Lane in August 1845. Her father, however, locksmith Edward Walker, declared that she was 42. In 1864, she had married William Nichols and had five children. It appears that William had an affair in or around 1877, and, whether this was cause or effect, it was around this time that Mary Ann's lethal relationship with the gin bottle took over her life.

In 1880, the couple separated, and Mary Ann rapidly became a lodging-house dosser and shilling-shag market dame. On 12 May 1888, she made a last bid for respectability, taking a job as a domestic servant in Rosehill Road, Wandsworth. "They are teetotallers, and very religious," she wrote optimistically of her employers, "so I ought to get on." For all her efforts to convince herself, the lure of the streets, the rowdy companionship, the intoxicating uncertainty of the vagabond life and, above all, the gin, was stronger by far than that of respectability won by solitary service in suburbia. In July, she absconded with clothing to the value of three pounds and ten shillings. We are uncertain where she spent the last five or six nights of her life, though Ellen Holland, her friend and bedfellow, was given the impression that Nichols had been lodging at the White House, a common lodging house in Flower and Dean Street. This, however, is unconfirmed, and Nichols's last days remain a mystery.

On the last night of her life, she reeled into her favoured lodging house at 18, Thrawl Street, where, until the previous week, she had shared a bed with Holland. The deputy turned her out because she did not have the requisite four shillings for her bed. She was good-natured and confident that she would soon have the fee. She drew attention to her new bonnet, saying, "See what a jolly bonnet I've got now." At 2:30 A.M., Holland saw her again, now staggering, at the corner of Brick Lane and Whitechapel High Street. Holland tried to persuade her to return to Thrawl Street, but Nichols informed her that she had earned her "doss money" three times over that day, but had spent it. At 3:40 A.M. or thereabouts, Charles Cross and Robert Paul, carmen, discovered her body at the entrance to the stableyard in Buck's Row. She was dying or newly killed.

The post-mortem report on Mary Ann Nichols by Dr. Rees Ralph Llewellyn demonstrates the killer's savagery and familiarity with the process of killing with the knife. He slashed Nichols's throat with the cutting edge of the blade, whereas anyone who had never killed an animal by this means, or wanting confidence in his knife, would have gouged with the point and ripped in order to be sure at once of achieving his ends and of the victim's silence. It is possible that the killer was interrupted in his work, and might otherwise have extended his exploration of his victim's viscera, but the cuts in the abdomen, though deep, are curiously many and random and want deliberation. The emotive language used by the Star, which helped to establish the legend, bears little relation to Llewellyn's account: "No murder was ever more ferociously or brutally done. The knife, which must have been a long and sharp one, was jabbed into the deceased at the lower part of the abdomen and then drawn upwards not once but twice. The first cut veered to the right, slitting up the groin and passing over the left hip, but the second cut went straight upwards along the centre of the body, and reaching to the breastbone."

Dr. Llewellyn's autopsy report:

Five of the teeth were missing, and there was a slight laceration of the tongue. There was a bruise running along the lower part of the jaw on the right side of the face. That might have been caused by a blow from a fist or pressure from a thumb. There was a circular bruise on the left side of the face, which also might have been inflicted by the pressure of the fingers. On the left side of the neck, about 1 in. below the jaw, there was an incision about 4 in. in length, and ran from a point immediately below the ear. On the same side, but an inch below, and commencing about 1 in. in front of it, was a circular incision, which terminated at a point about 3 in. below the right jaw. That incision completely severed all the tissues down to the vertebrae. The large vessels of the neck on both sides were severed. The incision was about 8 in. in length. The cuts must have been caused by a long-bladed knife, moderately sharp, and used with great violence. No blood was found on the breast, either of the body or clothes. There were no injuries about the body until just about the lower part of the abdomen. Two or three inches from the left side was a wound running in a jagged manner.

The wound was a very deep one, and the tissues were cut through. There were several incisions running across the abdomen. There were also three or four similar cuts running downwards, on the right side, all of which had been caused by a knife which had been used violently and downwards. The injuries were from left to right, and might have been done by a left-handed person. All the injuries had been caused by the same instrument.

Annie Chapman

This autopsy disposes of two myths which should never have come into being. The first is that of the ritualistic ordering of Chapman's rings and a variable number of shiny farthings, at her feet. There were no farthings, and the three brass rings which Chapman habitually wore were not found at the scene of the murder. They may have been removed by the murderer. The second is the notion of the left-handed Ripper, introduced but subsequently rescinded by Dr. Llewellyn at the Nichols inquest. Had there been any doubt with Nichols, there was none here. Chapman was killed as she lay on the ground. As to how she was persuaded or forced to lie on the ground in silence, it is worth referring to Mark Daniel's theory relating to the "two distinct bruises, each the size of a man's thumb, on the forepart of the top of the chest." For difficulties relating to the timing of the murder, and discrepancies between Dr. Phillips's estimate of the time of death and that fixed upon by the coroner, see our comments on the statement of Elizabeth Long.

Chapman's inquest also gave rise to the most pervasive and enduring of all the Ripper myths, that of the Ripper as a surgeon. Only Wynne Baxter, again flying in the face of expert testimony, believed that the Ripper had expert anatomical knowledge, basing his supposition on the discredited notion that the killer had been hunting for uteri to sell to an unknown American (Tumblety?). The Central Officers' Special Report, headed, "Subject: Hanbury Street murder of Annie Chapman" is still more specific than is the autopsy with regard to the killer's want of discrimination in his collecting of organs: "the following parts were missing: part of belly wall including naval [sic], the womb, the upper part of vagina, and greater part of bladder." Ever since Stephen Knight's fanciful and ingenious Final Solution, there has been an attempt to afford significance to the placing of the intestines at one or other shoulder. In fact, the murderer, who plainly wanted to remove the guts in order to obtain unhindered access to the viscera, placed "a flap of the wall of the belly, the whole of the small intestines and attachments" above Chapman's right shoulder, while "two other portions of wall of belly and 'pubes' were placed above left shoulder in a large quantity of blood."

Dr. Phillips's autopsy report, as given before the coroner:

He noticed the same protrusion of the tongue. There was a bruise over the right temple. On the upper eyelid there was a bruise, and there were two distinct bruises, each the size of a man's thumb, on the forepart of the top of the chest. The stiffness of the limbs was now well marked. There was a bruise over the middle part of the bone of the right hand. There was an old scar on the left of the frontal bone. The stiffness was more noticeable on the left side, especially in the fingers, which were partly closed. There was an abrasion over the ring finger, with distinct markings of a ring or rings. The throat had been severed as before described. The incisions into the skin indicated that they had been made from the left side of the neck. There were two distinct clean cuts on the left side of the spine. They were parallel with each other and separated by about half an inch. The muscular structures appeared as though an attempt had been made to separate the bones of the neck. There were various other mutilations of the body, but he was of opinion that they occurred subsequent to the death of the woman, and to the large escape of blood from the division of the neck. At this point Dr. Phillips said that, as from these injuries he was satisfied as to the cause of death, he thought that he had better not go into further details of the mutilations, which could only be painful to the feelings of the jury and the public. The Coroner decided to allow that course to be adopted. Witness, continuing, said,— The cause of death was apparent from the injuries he had described. From these appearances he was of opinion that the breathing was interfered with previous to death, and that death arose from syncope, or failure of the heart's action in consequence of loss of blood caused by severance of the throat . . .

This evidence could only be reproduced in *The Lancet:*

The abdomen had been entirely laid open and the intestines severed from their mesenteric attachments which had been lifted out and placed on the shoulder of the corpse; whilst from the pelvis, the uterus and its appendages with the upper portion of the vagina and the posterior two thirds of the bladder had been entirely removed. Obviously the work was that of an expert—or one, at least, who had such knowledge of anatomical or pathological examinations as to be enabled to secure the pelvic organs with one sweep of the knife.

Elizabeth Stride

There are several oddities about Stride's killing. Several authorities, indeed, are prepared to assert that this was a domestic murder and does not properly belong in the canon. Preferring, however, to rely on contemporary primary sources and experts, we have little doubt, as had the police and the doctors at the time, that Stride was the victim of "the Knife," as the Whitechapel Murderer was known until the publication of the "Jack the Ripper" letters. The most striking common factor, which must have influenced the police at the time, is the killer's technique of compelling the victim to lie down on her back, then slashing, not stabbing, the throat. It may be, as is generally assumed, that Louis Diemschutz, returning home, interrupted the murderer and prevented him from performing his usual mutilations. It may be, however, that he was interrupted rather by Schwartz and the man leaving the pub in Schwartz's testimony, and that Schwartz, then scared off by the other man, witnessed the last seconds of Stride's life. With his victim able to identify him, and with two witnesses to his assault on her, the murderer had to rapidly kill the woman and vanish before the witnesses' return.

The witnesses to Stride's activities before the murder are several, although we know nothing of her movements for five days prior to this. We know that she was in the Queen's Head public house at 6:30 P.M. At 7 P.M., she was back at her lodging house, where she entrusted "a piece of velvet" to Catherine Lane's safekeeping. At 11 P.M., J. Best and John Gardner saw her leaving the Bricklayer's Arms in Settles Street with a "clerkly" young man. At 11:45 P.M., William Marshall saw her with a man in Berner Street. At some time between 11 P.M. and midnight, the unreliable Matthew Packer claims to have sold some grapes to her companion and to have watched them for a full half hour outside Dutfield's Yard. PC William Smith saw her again with a man outside Dutfield's Yard at 12:30 A.M., then we have Schwartz's account and that of James Brown, one of which places Stride outside Dutfield's Yard, the other on Fairclough Street at 12:45 P.M. Diemschutz found her at about 1 A.M., killed mere minutes earlier. Although the weather cleared later, there was heavy rain until 1:30 A.M. One cannot but wonder just why Stride was, apparently, loitering on the streets for so long in these conditions.

Dr. Phillips's autopsy report:

The body was lying on the near side, with the face turned towards the wall, the head up the yard and the feet toward the street. The left arm was extended and there was a packet of cachous in the left hand ... The right arm was over the belly. The back of the hand and wrist had on it clotted blood. The legs were drawn up with the feet close to the wall. The body and face were warm and the hand cold. The legs were quite warm. Deceased had a silk handkerchief round her neck, and it appeared to be slightly torn. I have since ascertained it was cut. This corresponded with the right angle of the jaw. The throat was deeply gashed, and there was an abrasion of the skin about 1½ in. in diameter, apparently stained with blood, under her right brow. At 3 P.M. on Monday at St. George's Mortuary ... Dr. Blackwell and I made a postmortem examination ... Rigor mortis was still thoroughly marked. There was mud on the left side of the face and it was matted in the head ... The body was fairly nourished. Over both shoulders, especially the right, and under the collar-bone and in front of the chest there was a blueish discoloration, which I have watched and have seen on two occasions since. There was a clean-cut incision on the neck. It was 6 in. in length and commenced 2½ in. in a straight line below the angle of the jaw, ½ in. over an undivided muscle, and then becoming deeper, dividing the sheath. The cut was very clean and deviated a little downwards. The artery and other vessels contained in the sheath were all cut through. The cut through the tissues on the right side was more superficial, and tailed off to about 2 in. below the right angle of the jaw. The deep vessels on that side were uninjured. From this it was evident that the haemorrhage was caused through the partial sever-ance of the left carotid artery. Decomposition had commenced in the skin. Dark brown spots were on the anterior surface of the left chin. There was a deformity in the bones of the right leg, which was not straight, but bowed forwards. There was no recent external injury save to the neck. The body being washed more thoroughly I could see some healing sores. The lobe of the left ear was torn as if from the removal or wearing through of an earring, but it was thoroughly healed. On removing the scalp there was no sign of bruising or extravasation of blood . . . The heart was small, the left ventricle firmly contracted, and the right slightly so. There was no clot in the pulmonary artery, but the right ventricle was full of dark clot. The left was firmly contracted so as to be absolutely empty. The stomach was large, and the mucous membrane only congested. It contained partly digested food, apparently consisting of cheese, potato, and farinaceous powder. All the teeth on the left lower jaw were absent . . . Examining her jacket, I found that while there was a small amount on the right side, the left was well plastered with mud . . .

Catherine Eddowes

Eddowes was the fourth of the Whitechapel Murderer's victims, the most savagely mutilated to that date and the subject of the most thorough and detailed autopsy yet surviving. Dr. Brown's precision leaves little room for parsing or construing. He concludes, however, that the murderer possessed anatomical knowledge and surgical skill, basing this assumption upon the notion that the killer set out to extract a kidney, as Wynne Baxter had assumed much the same on the assumption that the killer sought a uterus. It is rather safer to assume, as, it appears, did Sequeira and Sanders (Phillips also attended the postmortem) that, having removed the obtruding intestines and being given liberty to plunder what he could in the crimson cavern of the abdomen, the killer excised stray treasures at will and without prior design. Even Brown concedes, "Such a knowledge might be possessed by someone in the habit of cutting up animals," while Sequeira, asked if the deed had been perpetrated by an expert, was unequivocal; "No," he said, "not by an expert, but by a man who was not altogether ignorant of the use of the knife." With this more temperate verdict we can with assurance concur. The part of the lobe of Eddowes's ear which was cut off may well have been an accidental casualty of the cutting of her throat, especially in that the remainder of the facial mutilations were symmetrical.

Dr. Brown's autopsy report:

The body was on its back, the head turned to left shoulder. The arms by the side of the body as if they had fallen there. Both palms upwards, the fingers slightly bent . . . Left leg extended in a line with the body. The abdomen was exposed. Right leg bent at the thigh and knee . . .

The throat cut across . . .

The intestines were drawn out to a large extent and placed over the right shoulder—they were smeared over with some feculent matter. A piece of about two feet was quite detached from the body and placed between the body and the left arm, apparently by design. The lobe and auricle of the right ear was cut obliquely through.

There was a quantity of clotted blood on the pavement on the left side of the neck round the shoulder and upper part of arm, and fluid blood-coloured serum which had flowed under the neck to the right shoulder, the pavement sloping in that direction.

Body was quite warm. No death stiffening had taken place. She must have been dead most likely within the half hour. We looked for superficial bruises and saw none. No blood on the skin of the abdomen or secretion of any kind on the thighs. No spurting of blood on the bricks or pavement around. No marks of blood below the middle of the body. Several buttons were found in the clotted blood after the body was removed. There was no blood on the front of the clothes. There were no traces of recent connection.

When the body arrived at Golden Lane [mortuary] some of the blood was dispersed through the removal of the body to the mortuary. The clothes were taken off carefully from the body. A piece of deceased's ear dropped from the clothing.

I made a post mortem examination at half past two on Sunday afternoon. Rigor mortis was well marked; body not quite cold. Green discoloration over the abdomen.

After washing the left hand carefully, a bruise the size of a sixpence, recent and red, was discovered on the back of the left hand between the thumb and first finger. A few small bruises on right shin of older date. The hands and arms were bronzed. No bruises on the scalp, the back of the body, or the elbows.

The face was very much mutilated. There was a cut about a quarter of an inch through the lower left eyelid, dividing the structures completely through. The upper eyelid on that side, there was a scratch through the skin on the left upper eyelid, near to the angle of the nose. The right eyelid was cut through to about half an inch.

There was a deep cut over the bridge of the nose, extending from the left border of the nasal bone down near to the angle of the jaw on the right side of the cheek. This cut went into the bone and divided all the structures of the cheek except the mucous membrane of the mouth.

The tip of the nose was quite detached from the nose by an oblique cut from the bottom of the nasal bone to where the wings of the nose join on to the face. A cut from this divided the upper lip and extended through the substance of the gum over the right upper lateral incisor tooth. About half an inch from the top of the nose was another oblique cut. There was a cut on the right angle of the mouth as if the cut of a point of a knife. The cut extended an inch and a half, parallel with lower lip.

There was on each side of cheek a cut which peeled up the skin, forming a triangular flap about an inch and a half.

On the left cheek there were two abrasions of the epithelium . . . under the left ear.

The throat was cut across to the extent of about six or seven inches. A superficial cut commenced about an inch and a half below the lobe below (and about two and a half inches below and behind) the left ear, and extended across the throat to about three inches below the lobe of right ear. The big muscle across the throat was divided through on the left side. The large vessels on the left side of the neck were severed. The larynx was severed below the vocal chord. All the deep structures were severed to the bone, the knife marking intervertebral cartilages. The sheath of the vessels on the right side was just opened. The carotid artery had a fine hole opening. The internal jugular vein was opened an inch and a half—not divided. The blood vessels contained clot. All these injuries were performed by a sharp instrument like a knife, and pointed.

The cause of death was haemorrhage from the left common carotid artery. The death was immediate and the mutilations were inflicted after death.

We examined the abdomen. The front walls were laid open from the breast bone to the pubes. The cut commenced opposite the ensiform cartilage. The incision went upwards, not penetrating the skin that was over the sternum. It then divided the ensiform cartilage. The knife must have cut obliquely at the expense of the front surface of that cartilage.

Behind this, the liver was stabbed as if by the point of a sharp instrument. Below this was another incision into the liver of about two and a half inches, and below this the left lobe of the liver was slit through by a vertical cut. Two cuts were shewn by a jagging of the skin on the left side.

The abdominal walls were divided in the middle line to within a quarter of an inch of the navel. The cut then took a horizontal course for two inches and a half towards right side. It then divided round the navel on the left side, and made a parallel incision to the former horizontal incision, leaving the navel on a tongue of skin. Attached to the navel was two and a half inches of the lower part of the rectus muscle on the left side of the abdomen. The incision then took an oblique direction to the right and was shelving. The incision went down the right side of the vagina and rectum for half an inch behind the rectum.

There was a stab of about an inch on the left groin. This was done by a pointed instrument. Below this was a cut of three inches going through all tissues making a wound of the peritoneum [sic perineum] about the same extent.

An inch below the crease of the thigh was a cut extending from the anterior spine of the ilium obliquely down the inner side of the left thigh and separating the left labium, forming a flap of skin up to the groin. The left rectus muscle was not detached.

There was a flap of skin formed from the right thigh, attaching the right labium, and extending up to the spine of the ilium. The muscles on the right side inserted into the frontal ligaments were cut through.

The skin was retracted through the whole of the cut in the abdomen, but the vessels were not clotted. Nor had there been any appreciable bleeding from the vessels. I draw the conclusion that the cut was made after death, and there would not be much blood on the murderer. The cut was made by someone on right side of body, kneeling below the middle of the body.

I removed the content of the stomach and placed it in a jar for further examination. There seemed very little in it in the way of food or fluid, but from the cut end partly digested farinaceous food escaped.

The intestines had been detached to a large extent from the mesentery. About two feet of the colon was cut away. The sigmoid flexure was invaginated into the rectum very tightly.

Right kidney pale, bloodless, with slight congestion of the base of the pyramids.

There was a cut from the upper part of the slit on the under surface of the liver to the left side, and another cut at right angles to this, which were about an inch and a half deep and two and a half inches long. Liver itself was healthy.

The gall bladder contained bile. The pancreas was cut, but not through, on the left side of the spinal column. Three and a half inches of the lower border of the spleen by half an inch was attached only to the peritoneum.

The peritoneal lining was cut through on the left side and the left kidney carefully taken out and removed. The left renal artery was cut through. I should say that someone who knew the position of the kidney must have done it.

The lining membrane over the uterus was cut through. The womb was cut through horizontally, leaving a stump of three quarters of an inch. The rest of the womb had been taken away with some of the ligaments. The vagina and cervix of the womb was uninjured.

The bladder was healthy and uninjured, and contained three or four ounces of water. There was a tongue-like cut through the anterior wall of the abdominal aorta. The other organs were healthy.

There were no indications of connexion.

I believe the wound in the throat was first inflicted. I believe she must have been lying on the ground.

The wounds on the face and abdomen prove that they were inflicted by a sharp pointed knife, and that in the abdomen by one six inches long.

I believe the perpetrator of the act must have had considerable knowledge of the positions of the organs in the abdominal cavity and the way of removing them. The parts removed would be of no use for any professional purpose. It required a great deal of medical knowledge to have removed the kidney and to know where it was placed. Such a knowledge might be possessed by some one in the habit of cutting up animals.

I think the perpetrator of this act had sufficient time, or he would not have nicked the lower eyelids. It would take at least five minutes.

I cannot assign any reason for the parts being taken away. I feel sure there was no struggle. I believe it was the act of one person.

The throat had been so instantly severed that no noise could have been emitted. I should not expect much blood to have been found on the person who had inflicted these wounds. The wounds could not have been self-inflicted.

My attention was called to the apron. It was the corner of the apron, with a string attached. The blood spots were of recent origin. I have seen the portion of an apron produced by Dr. Phillips and stated to have been found in Goulston Street. It is impossible to say it is human blood. I fitted the piece of apron which had a new piece of material on it which had evidently been sewn on to the piece I have, the seams of the borders of the two actually corresponding. Some blood and, apparently, faecal matter was found on the portion found in Goulston Street. I believe the wounds on the face to have been done to disfigure the corpse.

Mary Jane Kelly

We would have thought that the facts about Mary Jane Kelly's death and mutilation were gruesome enough without further ornamentation. Alas, Ripperology attracts ghouls and romancers and only occasionally serious historians. Entrails, we have been assured, were festooned about the room like Christmas decorations and hung upon the pictures on the walls, Kelly was three months pregnant—and so on ad infinitum and ad nauseam.

The scene in Miller's Court was grotesque, but the gore was restricted to the bed, the wall beside it and the floor beneath it. For the rest, the room was no messier than a butcher's shop, for the murderer had, as ever, most definitively killed before he started his work, slashing Kelly's throat right down to the spinal column, which was notched by the blade. It appears, however, that he was not as humane as was his wont, and that, for a mere second at least, Kelly may have been aware of her impending doom, and raised her arms and the sheet over her head in self-defence. The injuries to the forearms, the chemise which Kelly was wearing (Bond believed that she was naked, but Phillips testified that she was wearing a linen chemise, which is borne out by the photographs), the cut and bloodied sheet, and the locked door of the room all suggest that she may have been asleep until seconds before her death. She had no time to struggle, however, but may have had time to shriek, "Murder!" as heard by Prater and Lewis.

There were further mysteries in Kelly's room. A fierce blaze in the fireplace had melted the solder on the kettle's spout. Subsequent theorists have surmised that this may have happened on another occasion, but it seems highly improbable. The police and doctors at the time were convinced that the fire had been burning at the time of the murder, and it is improbable that the kettle would have been left on the hob without spout or handle. Inspector Abberline believed that the fire had been lit in order to provide light for the murderer's work. It may be so, but there was still a length of unburned candle in the room which must surely have sufficed for a man who had thus far killed in shadow. Initially, the doctors believed that all the body parts were accounted for, but, on Saturday afternoon, Phillips and Dr. Roderick Macdonald returned to sift the ashes from the grate. We now know that the heart at least was missing, but we have no idea whether it was burned or taken away by the murderer. The only identifiable articles in the grate were remnants of women's clothing, said by *The Times* to be a piece of burned velvet and the rim and wirework of a woman's felt hat. Significantly, Walter Dew, who had often seen Kelly "parading" around the area, tells us that Kelly never wore a hat. This gives rise to the improbable supposition that the Ripper, anticipating *Psycho*, lulled his victims by dressing as a woman, and, having on this occasion lingered way into daylight, had to destroy his disguise. But, whatever his motives, clothing of natural fibres smoulders slowly, so what fuel did he use to generate such heat? After all, the kettle was designed to withstand heat, yet the solder had melted. There were two or three chairs in the room, two tables, one by the bedside, a washstand, and a print over the fireplace. The murderer had used none of these, nor did anyone record the increased heat, the light or the sound of a persistent blaze. Prater, who lived directly above, must have heard the fire in the chimney and felt the warmth which it generated. It seems more likely that this was a sudden intense blaze, generated by an inflammable material such as paraffin or alcohol.

The sentimentality attached by now to the Ripper's victims—and, perhaps, the discretion of the police who wished to persuade witnesses to testify—has obscured the nature of "McCarthy's Rents," as this set of Miller's Court rooms were known. John McCarthy must have been aware that Prater and Kelly were "unfortunates," and the fact that he was prepared to allow Kelly to fall nearly thirty shillings behind with the rent suggests that, informally at least, he might have been a "prosser" as well as a landlord, and able to recoup his money with ease.

Dr. Bond's autopsy report:

Position of body

The body was lying naked in the middle of the bed, the shoulders flat, but the axis of the body inclined to the left side of the bed. The head was turned on the left cheek. The left arm was close to the body with the forearm flexed at a right angle & lying across the abdomen. The right arm was slightly abducted from the body & rested on the mattress, the elbow bent & the forearm supine with the fingers clenched. The legs were wide apart, the left thigh at right angles to the trunk & the right forming an obtuse angle with the pubes.

The whole of the surface of the abdomen & thighs was removed & the abdominal Cavity emptied of its viscera. The breasts were cut off, the arms mutilated by several jagged wounds & the face hacked beyond recognition of the features. The tissues of the neck were severed all round down to the bone.

The viscera were found in various parts viz: the uterus & Kidneys with one breast under the head, the other breast by the Rt foot, the Liver between the feet, the intestines by the right side & the spleen by the left side of the body. The flaps removed from the abdomen and things were on a table.

The bed clothing at the right corner was saturated with blood, & on the floor beneath was a pool of blood covering about 2 feet square. The wall by the right side of the bed & in a line with the neck was marked by blood which had struck it in a number of separate splashes.

Postmortem examination

The face was gashed in all directions, the nose, cheeks, eyebrows and ears being partly removed. The lips were blanched & cut by several incisions running obliquely down to the chin. There were also numerous cuts extending irregularly across all the features.

The neck was cut through the skin & other tissues right down to the vertebrae the 5th & 6th being deeply notched. The skin cuts in the front of the neck showed distinct ecchymosis.

The air passage was cut at the lower part of the larynx through the cricoid cartilage.

Both breasts were removed by more or less circular incisions, the muscles down to the ribs being attached to the breasts. The intercostals between the 4th, 5th, & 6th ribs were cut through & the contents of the thorax visible through the openings.

The skin & tissues of the abdomen from the costal arch to the pubes were removed in three large flaps. The right thigh was denuded in front to the bone, the flap of skin, including the external organs of generation & part of the right buttock. The left thigh was stripped of skin, fascia, & muscles as far as the knee.

The left calf showed a long gash through skin & tissues to the deep muscles & reaching from the knee to 5 ins above the ankle.

Both arms & forearms had extensive & jagged wounds.

The right thumb showed a small superficial incision about 1 in long, with extravasation of blood in the skin & there were several abrasions on the back of the hand moreover showing the same condition.

On opening the thorax it was found that the right lung was minimally adherent by old firm adhesions. The lower part of the lung was broken & torn away.

The left lung was intact: it was adherent at the apex & there were a few adhesions over the side. In the substances of the lung were several nodules of consolidation.

The Pericardium was open below & the Heart absent.

In the abdominal cavity was some partly digested food of fish & potatoes & similar food was found in the remains of the stomach attached to the intestines.

Subsequently, Bond wrote a report for Abber-line on all five murders:

I beg to report that I have read the notes of the four Whitechapel Murders, viz:
   1. Buck's Row
   2. Hanbury Street
   3. Berner's [sic] Street
   4. Mitre Square.
I have also made a Post Mortem Examination of the mutilated remains of a woman found yesterday in a small room in Dorset Street—
   1. All five murders were no doubt committed by the same hand. In the first four the throats appear to have been cut from left to right. In the last case owing to the extensive mutilation it is impossible to say in what direction the fatal cut was made, but arterial blood was found on the wall in splashes close to where the woman's head must have been lying.
   2. All the circumstances surrounding the murders lead me to form the opinion that the women must have been lying down when murdered and in every case the throat was first cut.
   3. In the four murders of which I have seen the notes only, I cannot form a very definite opinion as to the time that had elapsed between the murder and the discovering of the body. In one case, that of Berner's [sic] Street, the discovery appears to have been made immediately after the deed—In Buck's Row, Hanbury Street, and Mitre Square three or four hours only could have elapsed. In the Dorset Street Case the body was lying on the bed at the time of my visit, two o'clock, quite naked and mutilated as in the annexed report—
   Rigor Mortis had set in, but increased during the progress of the examination. From this it is difficult to say with any degree of certainty the exact time that had elapsed since death as the period varies from six to twelve hours before rigidity sets in. The body was comparatively cold at 2 o'clock and the remains of a recently taken meal were found in the stomach and scattered about over the intestines. It is, therefore, pretty certain that the woman must have been dead about twelve hours and the partly digested food would indicate that death took place about three or four hours after the food was taken, so 1 or 2 o'clock in the morning would be the probable time of the murder.
   4. In all the cases there appears to be no evidence of struggling and the attacks were probably so sudden and made in such a position that the women could

neither resist nor cry out. In the Dorset Street case the corner of the sheet to the right of the woman's head was much cut and saturated with blood, indicating that the face may have been covered with the sheet at the time of the attack.

5. In the four first cases the murderer must have attacked from the right side of the victim. In the Dorset Street case, he must have attacked in front or from the left, as there would be no room for him between the wall and the part of the bed on which the woman was lying. Again, the blood had flowed down on the right side of the woman and spurted onto the wall.

6. The murderer would not necessarily be splashed or deluged with blood, but his hands and arms must have been covered and parts of his clothing must certainly have been smeared with blood.

7. The mutilations in each case excepting the Berner's [sic] Street one were all of the same character and showed clearly that in all the murders the object was mutilation.

8. In each case the mutilation was inflicted by a person who had no scientific nor anatomical knowledge. In my opinion he does not even possess the technical knowledge of a butcher or horse slaughterer or any person accustomed to cut up dead animals.

9. The instrument must have been a strong knife at least six inches long, very sharp, pointed at the top and about an inch in width. It may have been a clasp knife, a butcher's knife, or a surgeon's knife. I think it was no doubt a straight knife.

10. The murderer must have been a man of physical strength and of great coolness and daring. There is no evidence that he had an accomplice. He must in my opinion be a man subject to periodical attacks of Homicidal and erotic mania. The character of the mutilations indicate that the man may be in a condition sexually that may be called satyriasis. It is of course possible that the Homicidal impulse may have developed from a revengeful or brooding condition of the mind, or that Religious Mania may have been the original disease, but I do not think either hypothesis is likely. The murderer in external appearance is quite likely to be a quiet inoffensive looking man probably middle-aged and neatly and respectably dressed. I think he must be in the habit of wearing a cloak or overcoat or he could hardly have escaped notice in the streets if the blood on his hands or clothes were visible.

11. Assuming the murderer to be such a person as I have just described he would probably be solitary and eccentric in his habits, also he is most likely to be a man without regular occupation, but with some small income or pension. He is possibly living among respectable persons who have some knowledge of his character and habits and who may have grounds for suspicion that he is not quite right in his mind at times. Such persons would probably be unwilling to communicate suspicions to the Police for fear of trouble or notoriety, whereas if there were a prospect of reward it might overcome their scruples.

THE "RIPPER LETTERS"

The police and the authorities in the East End received thousands of letters during the course of the Whitechapel murders: letters helpful, letters suggestive, letters malicious, and letters plain loopy. Everyone, it seems, had a theory as to who the murderer might be (one insistently posited a giant eagle), how he gulled or soothed his victims, what trade he might pursue. From this huge number of documents, two, though almost certainly by a hand unrelated to the killer's, were instrumental in the creation of the legend of Jack the Ripper. One—the "From Hell" letter to George Lusk, accompanying part of a kidney—may well come from the Whitechapel Murderer. The latest discovery, dated 17 September 1888, has just about everything wrong with it and is almost certainly spurious.

The "Dear Boss" letter below was received on 27 September 1888 at the Central News Agency. Originally dismissed as one of many hoaxes, the double murder three days later caused the police to examine the letter a little more closely, particularly when they learned that part of Eddowes's earlobe had been cut from the body (probably, in fact, accidentally in the process of slitting her throat).

Dear Boss,

I keep on hearing the police have caught me but they wont fix me just yet. I have laughed when they look so clever and talk about being on the right track. That joke about Leather Apron gave me real fits. I am down on whores and I shant quit ripping them till I do get buckled. Grand work the last job was. I gave the lady no time to squeal. How can they catch me now. I love my work and want to start again. You will soon hear of me with my funny little games. I saved some of the proper red stuff in a ginger beer bottle over the last job to write with but it went thick like glue and I cant use it. Red ink is fit enough I hope ha.ha. The next job I do I shall clip the ladys ears off and send to the police officers just for jolly wouldn't you. Keep this letter back till I do a bit more work, then give it out straight. My knife's so nice and sharp I want to get to work right away if I get a chance. Good Luck.

Yours truly

Jack the Ripper

Dont mind me giving the trade name

[PS] Wasnt good enough to post this before I got all the red ink off my hands curse it No luck yet. They say I'm a doctor now. ha ha

The "Saucy Jacky" postcard was received on 1 October 1888, again at the Central News Agency. It may be by the same hand as the "Dear Boss" letter, which was published on the same day. Certainly it makes reference both to the earlier letter and to the double event of the previous night. For all that we have improved information technology, however, the post was considerably faster in Victorian London, and a hoaxer could have seen both the details of the letter and the murders in an early edition of the papers.

I wasnt codding dear old Boss when I gave you the tip. You'll hear about Saucy Jackys work tomorrow double event this time number one squealed a bit couldnt finish straight off. Had not time to get ears for police thanks for keeping last letter back till I got to work again.

Jack the Ripper

The "From Hell" letter arrived on 16 October in a three-inch-square cardboard box delivered to George Lusk, president of the Whitechapel Vigilance Committee. Also inside the box was half a human kidney. This letter, with its apparently natural errors (and its indications of Irishness in "Sor" and "presarved"?) has none of the polished, slangy jauntiness of its predecessors, and is plainly in a different hand.

Emily Marsh, whose father traded in hides at 218, Jubilee Street, was minding the shop on 15 October when a man came in and requested Lusk's address, which she read to him from a newspaper. The man was around 45, 6 feet tall, and slim. He had a dark beard and moustache and he spoke with "what was taken to be an Irish accent." Could this have been the sender of the kidney? It may also be worth noting that, in October, Lusk lived in fear of a sinister bearded man watching his house, and even asked for police protection.

From hell.

Mr. Lusk,

Sor

I send you half the Kidne I took from one women, prasarved it for you tother piece I fried and ate it was very nise I may send you the bloody knif that took it out if you only wate a whil longer

signed

Catch me when you can Mishter Lusk

LONDON'S GHASTLY MYSTERY

Anonymous

An unknown reporter in Chicago wrote a feature that was published in New York City's *Daily Graphic* in October 1888 while Jack the Ripper was still active in London's East End. The story quotes Dr. J. G. Kiernan, an alienist (psychologist) and the editor of the *Medical Standard*, who was firmly convinced that the murderer is a cannibal, and warns that insane people on the streets of Chicago are "fully capable of committing Whitechapel murders."

Dr. Kiernan had previously written (in the July 1881 issue of *The Journal of Nervous and Mental Disease*) that quinine can cause insanity. Quinine, he averred, "may give rise to psychoses in hereditarily predisposed individuals." These psychoses, he continued, may present themselves in two forms. The first is a form of acute mania with aural hallucinations; the second is extreme dementia.

Just as he posits that cannibalism is rare among Anglo-Saxons but not uncommon in Russia, Germany, Bohemia, and France, with what may be regarded as scant evidence to support his theory, Dr. Kiernan admits that, apart from his recent discovery of the effects of quinine, he had never heard of a previous case of insanity caused by the medicine.

As a prominent voice in Chicago on numerous subjects, Dr. Kiernan also wrote that forced confessions, acquired from prisoners in "a sweatbox," had no validity, comparing them to the worthless confessions given at the Salem witch trials, and that a rash of deaths among young women attributed to "dying of love" were, in fact, due to poor diet and hygiene. "Cut out the ice cream and the candies: eat sensibly and enough of that which is nourishing and digestible; keep clean," were his nuggets of wisdom.

"London's Ghastly Mystery" was first published in the October 3, 1888, issue of the *Daily Graphic*.

NO CLUE YET OBTAINED
TO THE PERPETRATOR
OF THE MURDERS.

A Chicago Medical Writer's Theory of the Shocking Crime—the Work of a Lunatic of the "Sexual Pervert" Type—His Remedy.

London, October 3.—No further arrests have been made in connection with the Whitechapel murder, and the police have discovered no clues to throw any light on the mystery.

A Chicago Medical Writer's Theory.

Chicago, October 3.—Dr. J. G. Kiernan of this city, editor of the *Medical Standard,* says that the Whitechapel murderer is a cannibal pure and simple. The Doctor added: "The Whitechapel murders are clearly the work of a lunatic of the so-called 'sexual pervert' type, fortunately rare in Anglo-Saxon lands, but not infrequently met with in Russia, Germany, Bohemia, and France. In these lunatics there is return to the animal passions of the lowest cannibalistic savage races. Cannibalism is shown in a thirst for blood, and these animal passions come to the surface when the checks imposed by centuries of civilization are removed by disease or by the defects inherited from degenerate parents. The most noted of these cases was that of Giles Be Rets,[30] the original Blue Beard of the reign of Louis XV, who slaughtered two hundred female children in the same way as the Whitechapel butcher. The mutilations were very similar.

"A number of similar cases are on record in which the murderer devoured the mutilated parts. It was only a few years ago, in 1883, that all Westphalia, in Germany, was roused by several mysterious murders of females of the same type as those of Whitechapel. The vampireism of the middle ages, extending down through the fourteenth, fifteenth, sixteenth, seventeenth, and early nineteenth century, was a phase of this form of insanity.

"As to the remedy," continued Dr. Kiernan, "shut up the harmless, logical lunatics and release fewer so-called 'sane' men by legal procedures from the State insane hospitals and crimes of all types by the insane will cease. No lunatic should be at large unless some reliable person is pecuniarily responsible for his acts. The philanthropists who release 'sane' people from the insane hospitals always decline pecuniary responsibility. There are lunatics now at large in Chicago released as sane from insane hospitals who under certain conditions are fully capable of committing Whitechapel murders."

~

---

30 Gilles de Rais. —Editor.

THE EAST END MURDERS: DETAILED LESSONS

Anonymous

The psychological power of the Ripper murders may be evidenced by the fact that seemingly everyone had something to say on the subject. Politicians, journalists, social activists, doctors, members of the legal community—anyone with a platform from which to offer an opinion— were eager to provide theories and advice.

The most common reason advanced for the heinous crimes was poverty, with a commensurate call for funds to make life in the East End slums better for its inhabitants. The fact that the killer was unknown and, according to the preponderance of theories about his identity, someone wealthy enough that he did not live in the immediate neighborhood and thus was unlikely to carry the burden of impoverishment with him, did not deter those calling for social reform.

Even *The British Medical Journal,* a well-established periodical that had as its two prime objectives the advancement of the medical profession and the dissemination of medical knowledge, felt compelled to weigh in, calling for funds to clean up the area and laying the blame for killings on the general public for its indifference to the plight of the poor, on the municipal authorities for not providing better light and cleaner pavements, and on the police for failing to be stricter on their nightly patrols.

Established on October 3, 1840, as *The Provincial Medical and Surgical Journal,* it later changed its name to *The British Medical Journal* and still publishes under the title *The BMJ*; it is regarded as one of the most prominent medical journals in the world.

"The East End Murders: Detailed Lessons" was first published in the October 6, 1888, issue of *The British Medical Journal.*

The lesson of the Whitechapel murders does not lie on the surface, and, as usually happens, the most important considerations arising out of this series of night tragedies are the least sensational, and those which are most apt to make the least impression on the public mind. The first thought which arises in the average brain, and perhaps the most natural, is that which finds expression in the formula, Whom shall we hang?—an impulse of anger and an effort to ease responsibility by an act of vengeance which gets rid of the idea of reparation.

To deal first with the personal questions involved, we may say that the theory started by the coroner—not altogether without justification on the information conveyed to him—that the work of the assassin was carried out under the impulse of pseudo-scientific mania, is exploded by the first attempt at serious investigation. It is true that inquiries were made at one or two medical schools early last year by a foreign physician, who was spending some time in London, as to the possibility of securing certain parts of the body for the purpose of scientific investigation. No large sum, however, was offered. The person in question was a physician of the highest respectability and exceedingly well accredited to this country by the best authorities in his own, and he left London fully eighteen months ago. There was never any real foundation for the hypothesis, and the information communicated, which was not at all of the nature which the public has been led to believe, was due to the erroneous interpretation by a minor official of a question which he had overheard, and to which a negative reply was given. This theory may be at once dismissed, and is, we believe, no longer entertained even by its author. The discovery of the assassin cannot, we believe, long be delayed. He is undoubtedly insane, and, although insane proclivities of this kind are often concealed with great cunning, and are compatible for a time at least with high intelligence, and the discharge of the ordinary duties of life in a manner which does not excite suspicion, yet the attendant conditions of mind and the ultimate sequence of mental disease do not fail eventually to produce conditions leading to discovery. Judges, statesmen, and lawyers, subject to overwhelming impulses of a cognate kind, have discharged the duties of their various stations for a considerable time, while conscious of an almost overwhelming impulse which they have either concealed or secretly confessed. Ordinarily, the remorse and horror which attend the recognition in lucid intervals of the frightful character of these delusions and impulses lead to early confession and to voluntary precautions taken by such unfortunate persons at the instance of their medical advisers.

The acts of butchery which have so shocked and alarmed our population will probably be found to add another terrible chapter to the records of homicidal insanity. It would, however, be most lamentable if this anxious period of mental disturbances, horror, and grief should pass away, leaving behind it only the records of an unprecedented series of crimes, committed under circumstances of peculiar atrocity. There is a much deeper lesson in the story. We do not echo the vague outcry of blame against highly-placed officials which usually arises under such circumstances. The true lesson of this catastrophe has been written by the Rev. S. A. Barnett, the vicar of Whitechapel, whose life has been well spent in combatting with marvellous success the terrible conditions of social degradation and public indifference of which these murders are in one sense the outcome and the evidence.

What we have to do then as inhabitants of a great city greatly disgraced is to seek out the true causes and apply the true remedy. The main features of all these cases may be summed up in very few words. We have here the heavy fringe of a vast population packed into dark places, festering in ignorance, in dirt, in moral degradation, accustomed to violence and crime, born and bred within touch of habitual immorality and coarse obscenity. That is no news to the inhabitants of London. But the great bulk of the inhabitants content themselves with the consideration that they are not their "brother's keeper"; and so, notwithstanding the vast and successful efforts which Mr. Barnett and men like him have made in rebuilding the habitations of the poor, in cleansing the physical filth of the alleys and courts, in leavening the hideous mass with the ferment of unwearying kindness, brotherly solicitude, and personal service, and in illuminating many of the darkest corners of the East End with gleams of light from the higher life of religion, of reason, of literature, and of recreation, there remains the great residuum untouched and unpurified. But the case is not hopeless; it is not even beyond the means of any considerable number of intelligent, benevolent, and right-minded persons. Even the efforts of single individuals to do away with the abominable system of farming out wretched tenements to the criminal and degraded classes at high rents, without any inquiry or care for the use to which they are put, have produced vast effects.

To Lord Shaftesbury, to the Baroness Burdett-Coutts, to the Rothschilds, to Mr. Peabody, Miss Octavia Hill, Mr. Ruskin, to Mr. Barnett himself and his coadjutors, too numerous to mention and yet far too few to suffice, we owe the sweeping away of nests of crime, filth, and degradation, hotbeds of every social evil, and the substitution of light, cleanliness, purity, and the basis of physical and moral regeneration. No one cognisant of the condition of the East End of London during the last twenty years but must be aware of the enormous physical and moral reformation which has been worked in the habitations and in the minds of the people. But much remains to be done. First, we need to recognise that the remaining centres of crime and of misery and of unspeakable degradation must be swept away, and in their place decent habitations provided under supervision such as that which prevails throughout a large part of Mr. Barnett's parish of Whitechapel, which provides the means of contact with the poor by persons of intelligence, of just aspirations, of kindly sentiments, desirous and capable of holding friendly communion with their poorer neighbours, and of turning it to good purpose. This means, then, the devotion of some considerable sums of money to rebuilding the worst parts of East London, and it means also the assistance of a much larger number of persons added to the not inconsiderable army of workers whose lives have been blessed of late years in the East End by doing good works quietly and with little encouragement, but with vast effect. Their numbers need recruiting by many hundreds, nay, by some thousands; and it is strange indeed if London, with its millions of inhabitants and its untold wealth, cannot be roused now from the apathy which has smitten it to a sense of public duty and individual responsibility. It is more than a scandal, it is a crime, that there should exist, not in the East End only, but in other quarters of London, dark, unlighted places, the known resort of crime and of vice, and which are left, as it were, as a playground for the worst passions, the most bestial impulses; a sort of assumed safety valve on which it would be dangerous to sit. More light then, physical and moral, is the second need; and with this quickening sense of social duty should come, and will come of necessity, a very different interpretation by the police of their duties to the community. It is no secret to many that the lowest neighbourhoods and the darkest spots of some parts of the East End have been habitually patrolled by persons anxious to seek out and to heal some of the worst ulcers of civilisation, and these patrols have been increased in number and in frequency during the last few weeks. The stories which they have to tell are of saddening uniformity—uncontrollable brutality; women turned into the streets, and shivering on the stones at night, fleeing from the execrations and the violence of drunken men; men stabbed and bleeding; tragedies and horrors of public obscenity treated by the police as the ordinary incidents of dark alleys, unlighted courts, and low neighbourhoods. The policeman is only human, and not always, of course, the best specimen of humanity. Obscenity and brutality and violence are to him customary incidents on certain night-beats, and the punishment or the judicial judgment of such conduct mainly the business of the sufferers, so that such offences only require to be dealt with when the sufferer determines to make a charge. When such a charge is made the policeman who has been all night on duty has to appear next morning in court; he loses his rest, he gets no compensation in money and gets no credit, the charge—perhaps for the thirtieth time—of some drunken woman or man, with an act of brutality or of public obscenity, is a piece of mournful routine of which he would fain be relieved. What the neighbourhood tolerates, and what the individual does not insist on resenting, the policeman accordingly passes over in silence, and feels that he ought rather to be congratulated for his tact than condemned for his indifference.

Here, then, are three chief defendants in the indictment which this series of murders opens against London. Ourselves, the great public of London, stand first in the dock, convicted by flagrant and horrible proof of indifference to the physical and moral degradation of our fellow-citizens; convicted of tolerating darkness, filth, crime, and obscenity as ordinary incidents of metropolitan life; standing aside with intellectual apathy, with pockets closely buttoned, and with minds intent on our own pleasures and businesses, and looking on indifferently at the work of the few devoted toilers who have done so much to redeem London from these horrible disgraces. It is for Londoners to respond to Mr. Barnett's appeal for means with which to complete the rebuilding of his parish, and to annihilate the plague spots which still lurk in it. Nor need these contributions be altogether donations in the ordinary sense, since considerable experience has shown that large investments in work of this kind produce a fair and reasonable return for capital.

Next, our municipal authorities stand charged with indifference to the lighting, paving, and cleansing of their streets and courts, and with permitting the inhabitants to carry on a traffic prohibited by law, and one which it lies with them to suppress.

Lastly, the police need to be quickened by a higher sense of public morality, to be strengthened in number, and to be encouraged and commanded to a much stricter exercise of their ordinary duties as patrols. At present, night charges are rather discouraged; the opposite tendency ought henceforth to prevail. But this is a measure of repression which can only be effectual if it be accompanied and preceded by an unwearying and unstinting effort to remove the conditions under which criminal and degraded conditions arise. While earnestly hoping, therefore, that the secret of these assassinations may, as there is some reason to hope, be quickly unravelled, there remains the yet more ardent desire that the lessons taught by these horrors will be enduring, and will have a fruitful effect on the social well-being of the metropolis.

BLOOD MONEY TO WHITECHAPEL

George Bernard Shaw

While the exploits of Jack the Ripper have been regarded by most observers to be the labors of a single person who may be described as either insane or monstrous—possibly both—and a matter to be dealt with by the police and the rest of the justice system, others placed the blame on society as a whole. Numerous articles, essays, and letters to the press vehemently indicted an uncaring populace of the rich and middle class for the atrocities being committed in London's East End.

Among the most eloquent was George Bernard Shaw (1856–1950), the Nobel Laureate playwright, novelist, essayist, and short story writer. As an ardent socialist, he was a prominent member of the Fabian Society, for which he wrote and orated about such of its primary causes as equal rights for women, the elimination of private ownership of land, and the abolition of the exploitation of the working class by the wealthy. As a Fabian, he was one of the founders of Great Britain's Labour Party.

Shaw wrote about sixty plays, most of which focused on his political and social beliefs, attempting to make them more palatable to the general public by making them comedic, but his vast audiences disappointed him by enjoying them for their entertainment value, largely ignoring his polemics. His best-known play is *Pygmalion* (first performed in 1913), which was adapted for a motion picture in 1938, earning him an Oscar for his work on the screenplay. After his death, it found new life as the Broadway musical *My Fair Lady* (1956).

Though Shaw had little to say about Jack the Ripper himself, he used the murders to deliver his message about social injustice, addressed to the editor of *The Star,* even before the final horror was perpetrated.

"Blood Money to Whitechapel" was first published in the September 24, 1888, issue of *The Star.*

Sir,— Will you allow me to make a comment on the success of the Whitechapel murderer in calling attention for a moment to the social question? Less than a year ago the West End press, headed by the *St. James's Gazette, The Times,* and the *Saturday Review,* were literally clamoring for the blood of the people—hounding on Sir Charles Warren to thrash and muzzle the scum who dared to complain that they were starving—heaping insult and reckless calumny on those who interceded for the victims—applauding to the skies the open class bias of those magistrates and judges who zealously did their very worst in the criminal proceedings which followed—behaving, in short, as the proprietary class always does behave when the workers throw it into a frenzy of terror by venturing to show their teeth. Quite lost on these journals and their patrons were indignant remonstrances, argument, speeches, and sacrifices, appeals to history, philosophy, biology, economics, and statistics; references to the reports of inspectors, registrar generals, city missionaries, Parliamentary commissions, and newspapers; collections of evidence by the five senses at every turn; and house-to-house investigations into the condition of the unemployed, all unanswered and unanswerable, and all pointing the same way. The *Saturday Review* was still frankly for hanging the appellants; and *The Times* denounced them as "pests of society." This was still the tone of the class Press as lately as the strike of the Bryant and May girls. Now all is changed. Private enterprise has succeeded where Socialism failed. Whilst we conventional Social Democrats were wasting our time on education, agitation, and organisation, some independent genius has taken the matter in hand, and by simply murdering and disembowelling four women, converted the proprietary press to an inept sort of communism. The moral is a pretty one, and the Insurrectionists, the Dynamitards, the Invincibles, and the extreme left of the Anarchist party will not be slow to draw it. "Humanity, political science, economics, and religion," they will say, "are all rot; the one argument that touches your lady and gentleman is the knife." That is so pleasant for the party of Hope and Perseverance in their toughening struggle with the party of Desperation and Death!

However, these things have to be faced. If the line to be taken is that suggested by the converted West End papers—if the people are still to yield up their wealth to the Clanricarde class, and get what they can back as charity through Lady Bountiful, then the policy for the people is plainly a policy of terror. Every gaol blown up, every window broken, every shop looted, every corpse found disembowelled, means another ten pound note for "ransom." The riots of 1886 brought in £78,000 and a People's Palace; it remains to be seen how much these murders may prove worth to the East End in *panem et circenses*. Indeed, if the habits of duchesses only admitted of their being decoyed into Whitechapel back-yards, a single experiment in slaughterhouse anatomy on an aristocratic victim might fetch in a round half million and save the necessity of sacrificing four women of the people. Such is the stark-naked reality of these abominable bastard Utopias of genteel charity, in which the poor are first to be robbed and then pauperised by way of compensation, in order that the rich man may combine the idle luxury of the protected thief with the unctuous self-satisfaction of the pious philanthropist.

The proper way to recover the rents of London for the people of London is not by charity, which is one of the worst curses of poverty, but by the municipal rate collector, who will no doubt make it sufficiently clear to the monopolists of ground value that he is not merely taking round the hat, and that the State is ready to enforce his demand, if need be. And the money thus obtained must be used by the municipality as the capital of productive industries for the better employment of the poor. I submit that this is at least a less disgusting and immoral method of relieving the East End than the gust of bazaars and blood money which has suggested itself from the West End point of view.

—Yours, &c.,

G. BERNARD SHAW.

WHO WAS JACK THE RIPPER?

Peter Underwood

As the author of more than fifty books, almost all of which were dedicated to ghosts and psychic phenomena, and with more than seventy years' experience investigating paranormal events, Peter Underwood (1923–2014) was named the "King of Ghost Hunters" by Oxford's Ghost Research Foundation.

An early interest for Underwood was Borley Rectory, described by the British press as "the most haunted house in England," and he became the foremost expert on the subject, coming to the conclusion that, indeed, some of the paranormal phenomena were genuine. Having devoted much of his life to the study of apparently supernatural and psychic phenomena as a parapsychologist, he wrote (in *No Common Task: The Autobiography of a Ghost-hunter,* 1983) that he believed 98 percent of reports of ghosts and other unexplainable events were due to such natural causes as misinterpretation, hallucination, pranks (and, although he did not suggest it, alcohol); he was mainly interested in the 2 percent that gave every indication of being genuine.

In addition to his dozens of books about ghosts, Underwood wrote well-researched books on other subjects: *Horror Man: The Fascinating Life and Work of Boris Karloff* (1972), *The Vampire's Bedside Companion: The Amazing World of Vampires in Fact and Fiction* (1975), and *Death in Hollywood* (1992).

"Who Was Jack the Ripper?" was first published in *Jack the Ripper: One Hundred Years of Mystery* by Peter Underwood (London, Blandford Press, 1987).

SUSPECTS NOS. 1, 2, AND 3

Who was Jack the Ripper? A good question and one that it may be possible to answer. But to do so it is necessary to look at all the serious contenders for that title, to look at the people who have reached the conclusions they have reached, and to see whether any of the theories is more likely or more probable than any of the others or whether there is a new suspect who fits the bill better than anyone.

The candidates are numerous and varied. First in the field and quite a strong candidate, still favoured by many people who have studied the murders, is the mad Russian Alexander Pe-dachenko. He was "the greatest and the boldest of all Russian criminal lunatics," claimed William Le Queux, writing sixty-five years ago. In his book, *Things I Know* (1923), Le Queux claimed he had seen a manuscript written by Rasputin entitled *Great Russian Criminals,* which Le Queux had found in the cellars of Rasputin's house. The manuscript was in French.

Here it was stated that Jack the Ripper was Pedachenko, who had worked in maternity hospitals in Russia and was known to have homicidal tendencies. Sent to England by Russia's secret police with the original idea of exposing the weaknesses of the English police, he was said to have lived in Westmoreland Road, Walworth, and stalked Whitechapel by night. He was assisted in his evil schemes by a fellow Russian named Levitski and a seamstress named Winberg. Donald McCormick, one of the more serious and thorough Ripperologists, after exploring most of the plausible theories then under consideration, came down on the side of Dr. Pedachenko as the killer. On his return to Russia Pedachenko is said to have been caught in the act of murdering and mutilating a woman and was committed to a mental hospital where he died in 1908.

There are some difficulties in accepting some of the alleged evidence implicating Pedachenko since, as Colin Wilson has pointed out, Rasputin's own daughter told him that her father could not speak a word of French and there was no basement or cellar in their house. However Prince Serge Belloselski corresponded with William Le Queux, who supplied the Prince with the original French version of part of the Rasputin manuscript, so something of the kind must have existed at some time. Furthermore, in another unpublished manuscript, coeval Dr. Thomas Dutton expounded his experiences over a period of sixty years (he has a lot to say about the alleged handwriting of Jack the Ripper which we shall examine in a later chapter), and Donald McCormick, in an entry in Dr. Dutton's diary for 1924, found an interesting item.

Dutton refers to William Le Queux's book, *Things I Know,* and his theory on the Ripper murders. He says further examination might have established that Pedachenko and Klosowski were doubles. Klosowski was a Pole who had some medical training and was at one time employed in a hairdressing establishment not far from the scene of the murders; he was later known to the police as George Chapman and he is said to have been seen at least once in suspicious circumstances by Inspector Abberline of Scotland Yard. When Chapman was arrested (for poisoning three women) Abberline remarked to the arresting officer that he "had caught the Ripper at last!" Some Ripperologists have suggested that Chapman was motivated by sadism but gave up his Ripper activities when it looked as though he was likely to be arrested and took to poisoning his victims. He was hanged in April, 1903. What Le Queux should also have found out was that Konovalov/Pedachenko worked as a barber-surgeon for a hairdresser named Delhaye in Westmoreland Road, Walworth, in 1888. Donald McCormick found an entry in the *London Post Office Directory* of 1889 listing a William Delhaye, hairdresser, of Westmoreland Road, Walworth.

Donald McCormick also publishes an item from a confidential Russian Secret Police bulletin which contains two unequivocal statements. It refers to "Konovalov, Vassily alias Pedachenko etc.," and it states: "... wanted for the murder of a woman in the Montmartre district of Paris in 1886, for the murder of five women in the East Quarter of London in 1888 and again for the murder of a woman in Petrograd in 1891." The item ends with the sentence: "Known to disguise himself as a woman on occasions and was arrested when in women's clothes in Petrograd before his detention in the asylum where he died."

McCormick ends his book, *The Identity of Jack the Ripper* (1959), by pointing out that, disregarding the Russian evidence against Ko-novalov, there is considerable evidence against him from (according to Dr. Dutton's diaries) a French doctor who says that a Russian surgeon named Konovalov was high on the list of suspects (the same man seems to have been seriously suspected of the murders by Sir Basil Thomson, one time Assistant Commissioner of the Metropolitan Police), and by the French police, following the murders in Paris in 1885–88, and also by Dr. J. F. Williams of St. Saviour's Infirmary, who told Dr. Dutton that a Russian barber-surgeon assisted him occasionally at the Infirmary, and, finally, by the contemporaneous Dr. Thomas Dutton himself who compiled three handwritten volumes of *Chronicles of Crime*. Even more important, damning perhaps, is the fact that Konovalov/Pedachenko knew several of the accepted Ripper victims, including Annie Chapman, Mary Nichols, and Mary Kelly. Dr. Dutton confirmed with Dr. Williams that these, and possibly other Ripper victims, visited the clinic of St. Saviour's.

When he wrote his book Donald McCormick felt, overwhelmingly, after his thorough and time-consuming researches into the Ripper murders, that "all the evidence points to the mysterious Russian doctor as the author of the terrible series of crimes." At the end of 1986—nearly thirty years later—he told me he still believed that the author of the crimes was Dr. Pedachenko. Unfortunately I understand that Dr. Dutton's notebooks have disappeared and Donald McCormick is unable to say what has happened to the lithographed copy of the *Ochrana Gazette* once shown to him by the late Prince Belloselski.

To my mind the evidence that someone such as Dr. Pedachenko committed the murders is quite strong. Certainly Inspector Abberline and his team of seven detectives on the case seem to have thought so at the time, evidenced by the walking stick presented to him at the conclusion of the enquiry with a carved head that may well be based on the suspect's features. This stick is preserved at Bramshill Police Staff College in Hampshire and I am grateful to them for allowing me to examine it and photograph it.

Perhaps the most famous theory, first expounded by Leonard Matters in his book, *The Mystery of Jack the Ripper* (1929), is that the multiple murderer of women in London's East End was a mysterious "Dr. Stanley."

Motive, apart from insanity—which may be a reason but is hardly a motive—has always been the difficulty in deciding who was Jack the Ripper. It is a motive that the police look for in cases of murder but in the Ripper murders of 1888 it was difficult to find one. Colin Wilson, among others, may well be right in assuming that sexual satisfaction, possibly achieved through the act of mutilation, was the motive and it is interesting to note that at none of the inquests was there any mention of sexual assault. It is possible that the victims were forced or persuaded to perform an act of fellatio on the murderer (it was reported that both Mary Nichols and Annie Chapman had front teeth missing) but it is not known whether those performing the post-mortem examinations were looking for or found any traces of male semen in the mouths or upon the mutilated bodies of the victims. Of course at the time of the murders it is unlikely that such evidence would have been made public had it been found. In more recent multiple murders of women medical evidence in this respect has been forthcoming.

But the Dr. Stanley theory does provide a motive. Leonard Matters, an Australian journalist who later became a Labour Member of Parliament, relates that when he was the editor of an English newspaper in Buenos Aires, he came across the "confessions" of "Dr. Stanley" (which he states is a fictitious name). Therein the widowed Dr. Stanley, a former Harley Street surgeon who lived in a luxurious house in Portman Square, had a son who died at the beginning of 1888, having contracted a disease, presumably a venereal disease, from a "high class" prostitute whom he named as Marie Jeannette Kelly. Matters gave the date of the meeting between young Stanley and the prostitute as February 1886 and critics of this theory say it falls down because venereal disease would not kill in two years but in the events related it seems more than likely that the young man, with his promising career ruined and feeling he had nothing to live for, committed suicide.

Determined to avenge the death of his only son Dr. Stanley set out to find the woman who was responsible and to kill her. By means of lengthy exploration and careful questioning he was led to the East End of London. But, so runs the story, he knew he had to be careful; he did not want her warned that he was looking for her. He decided that he would carefully pick out the women of the streets most likely to know her whereabouts but he would be careful how and when he questioned them. Only when he was sure they might be able to help him and only when he was sure he was not overheard would he find out what he could; and then he would silence his informant.

Slowly, very slowly, he began to get nearer to Marie Kelly. "Long Liz" Stride said, yes, she knew the woman Kelly, and within an hour he found the woman known to some of her associates as Kate Kelly, a woman who, all too late, Dr. Stanley found was too old and ugly to have been the young and pretty "high class" Kelly described by his son. And so it proved to be. Catherine Eddowes sometimes called herself Kate Kelly, taking the surname of the man she was currently living with; but before he killed her Dr. Stanley learned that she knew a Mary Kelly, a young and good-looking woman who lived with a man named Joe Barnett in Dorset Street, or rather in Miller's Court off Dorset Street. So Dr. Stanley at last found Marie Jeannette Kelly. For a time he watched her and the room that was her home and when the opportunity was right he went in, ascertained that she was indeed Marie Jeannette Kelly and had known his boy. He told her he had come to avenge the death of his only son: one stifled scream escaped the woman's lips, "Murder!," but such cries were common in that district at that time and no one took any notice. Dr. Stanley killed the woman who had ruined his son and he gave vent to all his anger and frustration with an awful exhibition of fiendish work with his surgeon's knife. After finding and killing Mary Kelly, Dr. Stanley slipped out of Britain and went to live in Buenos Aires.

On his deathbed ten years later he admitted to a friend that he was Jack the Ripper, and Leonard Matters, while admitting that he could "not vouch for its genuineness" conducted no "investigation" himself into the history of the White-chapel murders and became overwhelmingly convinced that this was "the most plausible" of the many theories he had heard of the motives and the identity of Jack the Ripper. Colin Wilson and other Ripperologists have found holes in the story: Mary Kelly, according to the coroner, was not suffering from anything other than alcoholism, although whether he would have made public the fact that she was suffering from a venereal disease is surely debatable. It is suggested that Dr. Stanley should have had no difficulty in finding Mary Kelly within hours, not weeks; little if any medical skill was shown by the mutilations; research has failed to locate any Harley Street surgeon who ceased to practice in 1888 and who died in Buenos Aires and so on. Yet a Mr. A. L. Lee of Torquay told Colin Wilson in April 1972 that his father had worked in the City of London Mortuary in Golden Lane at the time of the murders and his immediate superior was a man named Dr. Cedric Saunders, the City Coroner, who had a very special friend, a Dr. Stanley, who visited the mortuary about once a week. One day Dr. Stanley had said to Dr. Saunders, "The cows have got my son. I'll get even with them!" Very soon afterwards the murders began and Dr. Stanley still visited the mortuary but as soon as the murders stopped, he was never seen again. When Mr. Lee senior asked Dr. Saunders whether Dr. Stanley would be coming again the answer was "No . . . I believe he was Jack the Ripper." In the early 1920s the present Mr. Lee said he had read in a Sunday newspaper that a Dr. Stanley, "believed to have been Jack the Ripper," had died in South America. Whatever the truth of this story it has to be a possibility that there really was a "Dr. Stanley."

Daniel Farson, another Ripperologist, also received a letter from a correspondent which seems to lend some support to the "Dr. Stanley" story. A Mr. Barca of Streatham lived in Buenos Aires for ten years from 1910 to 1920 and while he was there he was told of a bar known as "Sally's Bar" which was frequented by sailors and people of ill-repute. He was given to understand that it was owned by Jack the Ripper and the Sally after whom the bar was named was a young girl he had brought out to South America with him in 1888. After making enough money to live for the rest of her life without working, Sally had returned to Europe and had finally settled in Paris. Dr. Stanley, as we have seen, is supposed to have died in 1920.

On reflection the Dr. Stanley theory has much to commend it and further research might reveal corroborative evidence but until that day the "Dr. Stanley" theory must be regarded as ingenious and possible but unproven. Most Ripperologists seem to regard the story as fiction pure and simple; I'm not so sure.

"Jill the Ripper" is an interesting possibility. It is a theory that the redoubtable Inspector Abberline, who *should* have known as much as anyone about the murders and the murderer, came up with originally, among others. It was after the last murder, that of Mary Kelly, when two women claimed, emphatically, that they had seen Mary Kelly after 8:00 A.M. on the Friday morning when medical evidence seemed to establish that she had been murdered around 3:00 A.M. that Abberline found himself in something of a quandary. One of his sergeants tried to help. "Could they have been mistaken, sir?" Abberline, an experienced officer, felt there was no question of a mistake. Either the women were lying (but why?) or what they said was true. There was too much detail, he felt, for it to be a mistake; they had stuck to their stories in spite of all his endeavours to get them to change them or admit a possible mistake.

Mrs. Caroline Maxwell, wife of a lodging-house keeper, lived at 14 Dorset Street. She had known Mary Kelly for some time, about four months, and although she readily admitted that she had only spoken to the girl about twice she was quite definite that she had seen Mary Kelly on the Friday morning, between eight o'clock and half-past, at the corner of Miller's Court. "I am quite certain it was her," she said, and Mary Kelly had spoken to her! Mrs. Maxwell said it was unusual to see her at that time of the day and she had said as much and invited the girl to "come and have a drop of rum." "But no, she wouldn't have no rum, or nothing," continued Mrs. Maxwell. "Said she just had a pint of ale and it made her proper sick. She looked ill, too, poor soul . . ." Later, when Abberline tried to break her story and catch her out, she said: "Going to call me a liar, are you? . . . Well, I'm quite sure, see. I'd know Mary Kelly anywhere." She said that she saw Mary Kelly again, after she had prepared her husband's breakfast; this time the girl was outside the "Britannia" public house, talking to a man. Told that medical experts said the girl had been dead for five or six hours by that time, Mrs. Maxwell replied: "And how can a doctor tell for sure? You tell me that." She said "of course" Mary recognised her.

Abberline gave up. After all, Mrs. Caroline Maxwell was not the only thorn in his flesh at that time. A tailor also claimed to have seen Mary Kelly at 8:00 A.M., and yet another witness claimed to have seen the girl, who was quite well-known by sight, at 10:00 A.M.; this would be some seven hours after Mary Kelly had been murdered, according to medical evidence.

It was odd if they were all mistaken, thought Abberline, there *must* be an explanation. Could it be that they had seen a woman who looked like Mary Kelly, possibly someone wearing her clothes; and that the woman, when she was spoken to, had *pretended* to be Mary Kelly? Abberline went to see his friend Dr. Dutton and asked him what he thought of the idea that it was perhaps *Jill* the Ripper that they should look for. The more they discussed it, the more the idea seemed a possibility. A man would surely be caught in the police nets that were quickly thrown round the scene of a crime and elsewhere—but a woman? Nobody would have suspected a woman—but *could* a woman have committed the last monstrous murder of Mary Kelly?

The idea was developed and popularised by William Stewart in his book, *Jack the Ripper—A New Theory* (1939). In his Introduction he claims that his enquiries into the mystery extended over a period of several years; that he had consulted every known writing on the subject; made dozens of plans and detailed drawings; and in fact had examined calendars, tide tables and meteorological data, and just about everything bearing "in the least degree" upon the subject. His researches, he claimed, had unearthed many forgotten but important facts and, with the assistance of friends, he had conducted a series of experiments on the spots where the crimes took place. He added that he was an artist and he felt that his knowledge of anatomy ("second only to that of a surgeon"), his life spent in the study of cause and effect, his powers of observation, and a mind trained to "materialise abstruse problems," all helped to equip him for unravelling the mystery of Jack the Ripper. He mentioned too that he had made models of the scenes of some of the murders and they formed the basis for his illustrations in the book. He had also made models of the victims and photographs of them were superimposed on the pictures of the scenes of the crimes.

After pointing out the fact that the coroner at the inquest on Mary Kelly remarked on the unwisdom of making public all the facts which came to the notice of the police, William Stewart writes, in italics: "One of these facts was that the remains of the bonnet and piece of charred velvet were from articles which had never been in the possession of the murdered woman, though some of her clothing was missing" and while it was publicly stated that a further search of the ashes failed to supply any "additional" clues, additional to *what* was never discovered. Stewart then proceeds with the Jill the Ripper theory having prepared his readers by saying he is making an honest attempt to supply a theory which, "unlike *all* which have been advanced hitherto, is tenable."

William Stewart asks what sort of person could have committed such murders and who had advantages which made suspicion for such acts remote and he suggested that, although it is too late now, if at the time the murders were being perpetrated four questions had been asked, the identity of Jack the Ripper might have been a comparatively easy matter to determine:

1) What sort of person could be out at night without exciting the suspicion of the household or neighbours who were keyed up with suspicion on account of the mysterious crimes?
2) What sort of person, heavily bloodstained, could pass through the streets without exciting suspicion?
3) What sort of person could have the elementary anatomical knowledge which was evidenced by the mutilations and the skill to perform them in such a way as to make some people think a doctor was responsible?
4) What sort of murderer could have risked being found by the dead body and yet have a complete and perfect alibi?

William Stewart's answer to all these sane and sensible questions is: a woman who was or had been a midwife. "Not Jack," he says, "but Jill the Ripper can be the only satisfactory answer to the mystery."

In case his readers should consider the idea unthinkable he details other instances of "female ferocity" including Mary Ann Cotton, whose cunning was such that she may well have murdered some twenty people before she was suspected; Mrs. Amelia Dyer, the Reading Baby Farmer, who murdered at least seven infants; and Mrs. Mary Pearcey who murdered Mrs. Phoebe Hogg and also Mrs. Hogg's baby in October, 1890 (almost severing the head from the body). She then wheeled the bodies over one-and-a-half miles through busy streets between five and seven o'clock in the evening. This latter fact makes the Ripper, his crimes, and his escape somewhat less remarkable than one might think at first and leads one to consider whether the Ripper murders, or some of them, may have been committed elsewhere and the bodies conveyed to the places where they were found. This seems likely in several of the murders where the position of the limbs of the body and the condition of the clothing, taking into account the loss of blood, seems difficult to explain otherwise.

Stewart also makes the interesting point that men, when they commit murder, are usually content to kill but a woman is disposed to inflict some further injury on her victim. Moreover, no violence, in the sense that masculine energy had been used, was apparent in the murders attributed to Jack the Ripper. "Mutilation," he says "is the supreme expression of spitefulness and spitefulness is a vice to which female criminals are addicts."

William Stewart contends that it is even possible that Mrs. Pearcey *was* the Ripper, murdering the victims in her room in Priory Street, Camden Town; and this would explain the silence which seemed to surround the killings and even the fact that the bodies were sometimes discovered in comparatively well-frequented places. Stewart adds that she may have confessed her crimes to someone who could not be prosecuted for being an accessory after the fact and this could explain the mysterious message which she inserted in a Continental newspaper the day before her execution, a message that stated: "I have not divulged." Certainly this cryptic message has never been explained. Her defending lawyer, Hutton, said Mrs. Pearcey (who may have once been a midwife) was the most cold-blooded and remarkable murderess he had ever defended and Sir Melville Macnaghten said he had rarely seen a woman of stronger physique and whose nerves were as iron cast as her body.

William Stewart goes to great pains to argue his theory that a midwife or former midwife was the murderer. The knowledge displayed in the performance of the mutilations would be knowledge possessed by a midwife; equally the fact that the mutilations were almost certainly performed by a hand unpractised in surgery but they showed a knowledge and manipulative dexterity that would be possessed by a midwife. Such a person would be a well-known sight; she would have a respectable reputation; she would in all probability have known and be known to her victims and had she been discovered actually bending over the body of one of her victims she had only to say she was passing when she came upon the body and at first thought the dead woman required her professional attention. Her presence anywhere and at any time would not attract undue attention and nor would her clothes if they were bloodstained. Stewart ingeniously points out that at that period a woman's dress, with its voluminous skirts and cloak, could very easily and quickly have been turned inside out and excited no one's interest.

William Stewart argues that his murderess would probably have been content to slash all her victims as she had done to Nichols but when she read newspaper reports of the murder and found that a medical man was thought to be responsible, she decided to mutilate her next victim in a way that suggested the murderer was indeed a doctor. Once this idea had received wide publicity, the possibility of finding the real murderer was considerably lessened, for everyone was looking for a man. Stewart also argues that the neat arrangement of articles from the victim's pocket is a typically feminine impulsive action. He suggests that the final Ripper murder, that of Mary Kelly, made it virtually certain that the perpetrator of the crimes was a woman and a midwife.

Kelly was three months pregnant and this fact does seem to have alerted the authorities to the possibility of "a new line of enquiry" as it was officially put. The murdering midwife, says Stewart, realising that such enquiries might lead to her, fled and took on a new identity elsewhere. Still with the Kelly murder, Stewart suggests that the fierce fire was caused by the murderer burning her own heavily bloodstained clothes; she then dressed in Kelly's clothes and left. This is the explanation for some witnesses thinking they saw Mary Kelly after she was dead; in fact they saw the murderess dressed in Kelly's clothes.

Colin Wilson is among others who have pointed out that Mary Kelly is almost certain to have had no spare clothes (she was desperate for money for the rent and would have sold or pawned anything she could spare) and the murdered woman's clothes lay in a neat pile in the bedroom where the body was found. What could have happened is that the Ripper, having cut Mary's throat, stripped himself naked before inflicting the awful mutilations on Mary's body during the course of which he, or she, could hardly have escaped being heavily bloodstained. Then, having burnt the three-month-old foetus (a fierce fire would have been required to achieve this object and some clothing, bedclothing or even furniture may well have been burnt to build up such a fire), he or she dressed in his or her own clothes and left the scene. It is possible that the murderer brought some clothes for Mary Kelly and after the murder burnt them for fear that he or she might be traced through the sale of the clothes.

This, of course, does not explain altogether the apparent sightings of Mary Kelly by several witnesses after she was almost certainly dead but a possible explanation for this curious occurrence will be suggested in a later chapter. William Stewart's book is a serious early attempt to explain the Ripper murders, although the motive is decidedly weak: he implies that women who practised as midwives were often also abortionists and when these illegal operations were unsuccessful, as not infrequently happened, the mothers would denounce their "helpers" to the police. He says that all the Ripper victims had borne children and it could be that they were women on whom the abortionist had performed unsuccessfully, had been denounced, and was seeking revenge by murdering the women.

In 1955 this theory was revived by an article in the London *Evening News* which told the story of an ex-convict who had been informed by a fellow prisoner in Parkhurst, eighteen years previously, that his informer's wife was the Ripper. Richard Herd, who wrote the article, said that he had to withhold the identities of the people in his article but he had checked the story and established that his informant had served several prison sentences. It was stated that both prisoners were Roman Catholic and the alleged husband of the Ripper wanted to unburden his conscience.

It seemed that he had been married to a nurse and after his last sea-trip as a steward on board a liner he had been picked up by a prostitute. His wife discovered what had happened and she refused to live with him as his wife although they continued to occupy the same house. He obtained a position as a night porter at a hospital and one morning in 1888 when he returned from duty he found a bloodstained knife in the sink, a knife he recognised as a wedding present. A couple of days later he came across a pair of his trousers hanging up to dry but still carrying blood stains. When he asked his wife about the knife and the bloodstained trousers she broke down and confessed that she had been killing prostitutes because one of their kind had seduced her husband and ruined their lives. She was determined to see that as many as possible did not ruin other people's lives. She said she dressed as a sailor when carrying out the murders but always carried her nurse's cloak and bonnet in a bag and after the murders she donned the nurse's outfit to cover her bloodstained clothes and escaped as a nurse on a late errand. The police were looking for a man and never suspected a nurse.

Her husband was inclined to disbelieve her until she told him that her latest victim had been Mary Kelly, the prostitute who had picked him up! When she heard this and learned that a man had been arrested for the murders, she stopped her activities. She had said she would give herself up if the man was actually charged but it never came to that. The story, as presented, is not open to examination and authentication and so, in common with other Jill the Ripper theories, must remain a possible but unproven solution to the Ripper murders.

SUSPECTS NOS. 4, 5, AND 6

A curious solution, and one that may not have received as much attention as it warrants is the idea that the elusive Ripper was Dr. Thomas Neill Cream, the murderer. Interestingly enough he practised as a physician in America and there are Americanisms in some of the alleged communications from Jack the Ripper. Cream's crimes certainly included arson, blackmail, abortion, and murder. He possessed a form of exhibitionism that showed itself in various letters he wrote to the authorities about his crimes.

Cream seems to have killed prostitutes simply to satisfy a sadistic quirk or it may have been revenge for contracting venereal disease from one of them. He killed at least four prostitutes and on the scaffold, on 15 November 1892, he was in the middle of saying, "I am Jack the . . ." when the bolt was drawn and Neill Cream was hanged. But during the whole period when Jack the Ripper was active in Whitechapel, Cream was in prison in the United States, which seems conclusive enough. Yet one wonders whether there was more to that "death confession" than another attempt at exhibitionism.

Edward Marshall Hall, the great criminal advocate, once defended Cream at the Old Bailey, without knowing it at the time. Marshall Hall had been briefed to defend a man for bigamy and when he arrived in court he was taken aback to find a number of young women who all claimed to have been married to the prisoner. The case seemed quite hopeless and Marshall Hall suggested to Cream that his best plan was to plead "Guilty." But the defendant was not in the least inclined to take that course of action. "This is a case of mistaken identity," he claimed. "Communicate with the jail in Sydney, Australia, and you will find that I was there at the time of these alleged marriages and I could not have committed the offences."

Enquiries at Sydney resulted in confirmation of Cream's assertions and he was released. Edward Marjoribanks, in his *Life of Sir Edward Marshall Hall* (1929), writes that his subject "was astonished later when he recognised Cream in court. The mystery was never explained but Marshall Hall's theory was that Neill Cream had a 'double' in the underworld and they went by the same name and used each other's terms of imprisonment as alibis for each other." Could it have been Cream or his double who was in fact Jack the Ripper? The possibility would seem to be there. Billington the executioner was witness to the incident on the scaffold and he swore that he heard Cream utter the confession and there is also evidence to suggest that he confessed to being Jack the Ripper several times to his gaolers. Was it another example of exhibitionism or was it the truth for once, and the man called Cream who was executed in 1892 was not the man who had been in prison in America at the time of the Ripper murders?

The idea that Jack the Ripper was an anonymous Jewish slaughterman has been put forward by Robin Odell in his *Jack the Ripper in Fact and Fiction* (1965). It is a theory that has a lot going for it. Such a man would be "no stranger to the knife"—a phrase used by Dr. Sequiera, one of the doctors who examined the terribly mutilated body of Catherine Eddowes. Shochets or ritual Jewish slaughtermen were trained in anatomy and pathology and their aim was to drain the slaughtered beast of blood. The Jewish population in the East End in the 1880s was quite considerable and there were many shochets (and their assistants) who were adept with their long knives. A quick forward and backward stroke and the throat was cut through to the bone. Death was instantaneous. The shochet would then make an incision in the chest of the animal and examine the lungs and heart; then the abdomen was opened and the internal organs examined for possible defects. Certain internal parts had to be drawn out of the flesh while the animal was still alive to conform with Jewish faith.

Jack the Ripper somehow or other inspired trust in his victims. There was no sign of panic or struggle in any of the murders. The background of the shochet, his social standing and his superior education (a seven-year course was not uncommon) would have placed him above the average East Londoner who, at that time, was poorly educated. Such men were a familiar sight in the area and were easily recognised by their sober dark clothes and black frock coats; the non-Jewish inhabitant would have regarded such a person as a "toff," as indeed some alleged sightings of the Ripper described the man they had seen in the vicinity of the murders. No one would have suspected such a man of chasing prostitutes, nor would such a man have been likely to be questioned by the police.

A shochet would of course know the best way of ensuring that his clothes were not soiled by blood and it may be significant that at least one victim was thought to have been murdered in the lying-down position. Some animals were placed on the ground before being ritually slaughtered by the shochet. So, to sum up, the Ripper seemed to possess some degree of anatomical skill; he cut the throats with a perfected technique, and he knew how to deal with the body immediately after cutting the throat. A Jewish slaughterman would have had knowledge of all these techniques. As far as motive is concerned, it is not unreasonable to suggest a sexual psychopath attributing his murders to the commands of God and it must be regarded as within the bounds of possibility that such a man might have felt some religious justification for killing prostitutes.

Why did the killings cease? Perhaps the psychopath was discovered by his associates, who would not have wished him to be arrested or face any charge by the authorities, for this would have fanned anti-Jewish feeling in the community at the time. He may have been removed or even punished by his own people. Sir Robert Anderson, one-time Assistant Commissioner of the Metropolitan Police, was to write in his memoirs, *The Lighter Side of My Official Life* (1910), that the police believed the Ripper and his associates were Polish Jews and that people of that class would not give up one of their number to Gentiles. He went on to say that the only person who claimed to have had a good view of the murderer had unhesitatingly identified the man but he had absolutely refused to give evidence against him. It is a fact that at one time policemen disguised themselves as slaughtermen during the investigation.

In presenting this theory, Robin Odell points to the four facts that have to be considered in dealing with any suspect.

1) Six prostitutes were murdered in a short space of time in a small area of the East End.
2) The murderer was able to inspire trust in his victims.
3) The killings and mutilations showed some degree of anatomical knowledge.
4) After the murder of Mary Kelly the murders ceased.

Odell points out that of all those most likely to have been the murderer the shochet alone could have possessed the motive, the means, the skill and the opportunity; and it must seem likely that were a Jewish slaughterman responsible, he could have been suspected, even recognised, and silenced by his own kind.

This theory has been dismissed as "insubstantial" and "unconvincing" and "lacking in evidence" by some writers (Stephen Knight, Daniel Farson, and Colin Wilson in particular), but to my mind it is an interesting and plausible theory, convincing in its simplicity. However, Robin Odell's final assertion that the identity of Jack the Ripper is not and never will be absolutely established suggests that he is himself not completely satisfied with the solution and so it must, I feel, be relegated to a "possible" rather than a "probable" solution to the mystery.

A theory that might be said to contain a degree of concrete evidence is that proposed by Daniel Farson in his book, *Jack the Ripper* (1972). He presents and builds up a convincing case for the murderer being Montague John Druitt (1857–88). Alerted by the mention of some "notes" made by Sir Melville Macnaghten (who joined Scotland Yard as an Assistant Chief Constable with the Criminal Investigation Department in 1889, the year after the Whitechapel murders), which mentioned the three chief suspects at the time of the murders, Daniel Farson followed up clues, checked references and, in the best manner of an investigator, came to his conclusions by the weight of the evidence.

Furthermore he reached this conclusion as to the identity of Jack the Ripper nearly twenty years ago and the passing of time has strengthened rather than diminished his conviction. He told me in 1986, as he had told me many years earlier after we had both taken part in a television film, that all the evidence pointed to Druitt. He sincerely believed it was the most likely solution and he doubted whether there would ever be more evidence pointing to anyone else.

Daniel Farson, who lived for a time in the East End of London, made two television films about the Ripper and when, more or less by chance, he discovered the private notes of Sir Melville Macnaghten, he carried out extensive research, some of it in association with an American journalist Tom Cullen, resulting in a degree of circumstantial evidence to support the idea that Druitt was indeed the Ripper.

Macnaghten joined the Yard when stories and memories of personal experiences in the hunt for the Ripper were still talked about by just about everyone in the police force. He became head of the CID in 1903 when, it might be said, the hysteria had lessened and the time had come for reasoned judgement. Certainly, it must surely be accepted, few men were in a better position to state the views of the police regarding the Ripper murders. He did not believe that any witness ever saw the Ripper (except possibly the policeman on his beat near Mitre Square) and he insisted that there was insufficient proof for anyone to be charged although a number of homicidal murderers were at one time and another suspected. Macnaghten lists in his private notes, which Dan Farson saw through the kindness of Macnaghten's daughter, the late Lady Aberconway, the names of three men "against whom the police held very reasonable suspicion." After careful consideration Macnaghten was inclined to exonerate two of them.

The three suspects were Michael Ostrog, a Russian doctor and a homicidal maniac whose movements were never satisfactorily accounted for at the time of the Ripper murders. Ostrog could well have been Dr. Pedachenko, Donald McCormick's prime suspect. Macnaghten's second suspect was Kosmanski, a Polish Jew who resided in the Spitalfields district and who also had "strong homicidal tendencies," coupled with "a great hatred of women." His appearance strongly resembled the man seen by the policeman near Mitre Square. In 1889 Kosmanski was confined to a lunatic asylum; and he too, according to Donald McCormick, could have been his suspect Dr. Pedachenko. At all events Macnaghten came to the conclusion that the evidence against these men was slight and he believed they could be eliminated from enquiries concerning the identity of Jack the Ripper.

Sir Melville Macnaghten's third suspect and the one he finally settled for was M. J. Druitt, "a doctor" aged about forty-one, from a fairly good family, who disappeared at the time of the last murder and whose body was found floating in the Thames on 3 December 1888, or just under four weeks after the murder of Mary Kelly. Macnaghten's notes said the body was thought to have been in the water for about a month and on it was found a season ticket between Blackfriars and London. He adds, "From private information I have little doubt but that his own family suspected this man of being the Whitechapel murderer; it was alleged that he was sexually insane."

So for the first time Daniel Farson was able to name the chief suspect as far as the police were concerned; and who better to know where the most suspicion lay. Dan Farson then set about examining Macnaghten's suspicions and at length discovered the record of the suicide of Montague John Druitt, but he had been thirty-one (not forty-one) and although his body had been recovered on 31 December (not 3) it was not registered until 2 January 1889. In addition the man was not a doctor; he was a barrister. However, Montague's father, William Druitt, his uncle Robert Druitt, and his cousin Lionell Druitt, were all doctors. The death certificate of Montague Druitt states, "Found dead drowned by his own act whilst of unsound mind."

Further research revealed that M. J. Druitt had been born at Wimborne in Dorset where his father had been one of the town's most respected citizens. Montague went to Winchester College where he had a brilliant academic career and ended as Prefect of Chapel. He went on to New College, Oxford, where he did moderately well, taking a Second Class degree in Classical Moderations and a Third in Greats. He left with a BA in 1880 determined to enter the law. He was admitted to the Inner Temple in 1882. After some difficulty in finding the necessary finances (he obtained advances from his father against a legacy) he took his finals and was called to the Bar in 1885. His father died shortly afterwards, leaving an estate worth £16,579, from which Montague did not benefit.

Montague Druitt now rented chambers at 9 King's Bench Walk and joined the Western Circuit and Winchester Sessions but there appears to be no record of his ever accepting a brief of any kind. 1888 finds him working as an assistant teacher at a private school at 9 Eliot Place, Blackheath, although he retained his chambers in King's Bench Walk. As far as is known he was last seen alive on 3 December 1888. In the revised edition of his book Daniel Farson suggests that Montague Druitt may have been murdered by his family.

When Daniel Farson had been preparing a television programme on the Ripper, he received a letter from Australia which he did not regard as being of any great value at the time but later he realised that the writer had referred to a document entitled "The East End Murderer—I Knew Him," said to have been privately printed by a Mr. Fell of Dandenong, and written by a Lionel Druitt (or Drewett)! From a different source Dan Farson learned that Fell had had lodging with him a man named Druitt who claimed to have papers proving the Ripper's identity.

During a visit to Australia in 1961 Daniel Farson made a point of trying to explore the matter further and he located an elderly woman, a Miss Stevens, who remembered Dr. Lionel Druitt. She recalled him practising medicine in 1903 and she remembered a daughter, Dorothy. This was confirmed ten years later when Daniel Farson traced Dr. Peter Druitt, the great-grandson of Robert Druitt; it was also established that Dr. Lionel Druitt died at Mentone, Victoria, in January, 1908.

Back home, Dan Farson discovered that Dr. Lionel Druitt had a surgery of sorts at the Minories in 1879. The Minories, named after the Minoresses or nuns of the order of St. Clare whose convent stood in the street, leads from Aldgate to Tower Green and is a stone's throw from the Whitechapel murder sites. Lionel was four years older than his cousin Montague and Daniel Farson suggests that it is reasonable to assume that Montague, about to leave Oxford, may well have visited his cousin and it is conceivable that he lived at 140 The Minories after his cousin moved to 122 Clapham Road in 1886. It will be recalled by Ripperologists that one of the alleged Ripper letters, the one posted in Liverpool on 29 September 1888, said, "Beware, I shall be at work on the 1st and 2nd inst., in Minories at twelve midnight . . ." and Catherine Eddowes was murdered on 30 September in Mitre Square, one minute's walk from the Minories. After this murder another letter, also sent from Liverpool, said, "What fools the police are. I even give them the name of the street where I am living . . ." but surely this would refer to the address at the top of the letter: Prince William Street, Liverpool, and not the Minories, mentioned in the letter.

Dan Farson now discovered that Montague Druitt's life was more or less in decline after he left Winchester and by 1888 things had begun to go badly wrong. He had been in serious trouble of some kind and had been dismissed from the school in Blackheath; his mother became insane in the July of 1888, a month or so before the murder that is generally considered to be the first Ripper atrocity; and Druitt seems to have feared he was himself going insane (indeed he left a note stating as much). Was this because he had become aware of his unnatural sexual impulses, one wonders; did he realise for the first time that he needed to kill and mutilate to obtain sexual satisfaction? Montague Druitt's body was identified by William Druitt, Montague's brother, a solicitor from Bournemouth. William said the dead man had no other relatives although he knew this to be untrue: could he have been attempting to protect the Druitt family name? Did he suspect—or know—that Montague, his brother, was the Ripper? Remember Sir Melville Macnaghten: "I have little doubt but that his own family suspected the man . . . it was alleged that he was sexually insane." And Daniel Farson seems to have established that Montague Druitt was, if not left-handed (as most people feel the Ripper must have been), ambidextrous. Medical evidence favours this view and furthermore Druitt's background would certainly have provided the opportunity for the limited anatomical knowledge displayed by the Ripper.

Macnaghten, incidentally, was not the only person to think that Montague Druitt was the Ripper. Other people in authority, who might have had access to the same evidence as Macnaghten, came to the same conclusion. Major Arthur Griffiths, Inspector of Prisons, wrote in his *Mysteries of Police and Crime* (1898), "There is every reason to believe that his own friends entertained grave doubts about him . . . he was believed to be insane, or on the borderline of insanity, and he disappeared immediately after the last murder . . . the last day of that year, seven weeks later, his body was found floating in the Thames and was said to have been in the water a month."

Albert Backert of the Whitechapel Vigilance Committee said he was given the same information and the police suggested that the Vigilance Committee and its patrols should be disbanded. Watkin Williams, grandson of Sir Charles Warren, Commissioner of Police at the time of the Ripper murders, said his impression was that his grandfather had believed the murderer to be a sex-maniac who committed suicide after the Miller's Court murder, possibly the young doctor whose body was found in the Thames; Sir John Moylan, Assistant Under Secretary at the Home Office, is on record as having stated: "The murderer, it is now certain, escaped justice by committing suicide at the end of 1888"; Sir Basil Thomson, Assistant Commissioner at Scotland Yard in 1913, said: "He was a man who committed suicide in the Thames at the end of 1888"—and so on. Even as recently as 1971 such an expert in crime in general and the Ripper murders in particular as the late Professor Francis Camps told Dan Farson: "I am sure you have got the answer at last." And Colin Wilson is on record at one time as saying that he thought Druitt was the most likely suspect.

And yet I wonder. Something does not ring true in the Druitt story. The fact that the police may have strongly suspected Druitt; the fact that some of his friends and family suspected him; and the fact that he may have had the opportunity and fills the bill as far as ability is concerned: all this does not mean that he *was* the Ripper. Donald McCormick disposes of Druitt as a suspect to his own satisfaction on the evidence of an unnamed London doctor whose father was at Oxford with Druitt and who says Druitt was definitely at Bournemouth when the first two Ripper crimes were committed—although he played cricket at Blackheath on the morning that Annie Chapman was murdered six hours earlier. (He was not in Bournemouth, at all events, and Blackheath is only half a dozen miles from the East End of London.) To many people there appears to have been a concerted cover-up attempt regarding the identity of the Ripper by the Establishment and such a full-scale operation would hardly have been necessary if the culprit really was the failed barrister Montague John Druitt.

Stephen Knight points out that Macnaghten did not pen his notes until six years after the Whitechapel murders and where did he suddenly come across the name for "nowhere else in the Scotland Yard file is Druitt mentioned, so he was not a suspect at the time of the murders; conveniently he was dead . . ." Furthermore it would seem that Daniel Farson and Tom Cullen saw only *copies* of notes made by Lady Aberconway and in reproducing both the original notes and the copies relied upon by Dan Farson and Tom Cullen it would appear that some of the original intonation and emphasis has been distorted, and actual statements seem to have been inserted. To add to the confusion a grandson of Sir Melville Macnaghten has stated that at one time he owned some of his grandfather's original documents relating to the Ripper crimes, but they seem to have disappeared!

Stephen Knight and Donald Rumbelow assert that Dr. Lionel Druitt was only at an address in the Minories for a few months in 1879 and his permanent London address was in Strathmore Gardens. This must affect the assumption that if Montague Druitt ever visited Lionel it has any bearing on the Ripper murders. In short, Stephen Knight opines that the first half of the case against Montague Druitt is based on a letter that is not produced from a man who cannot be traced and the second half is based on the unsubstantiated testimony of a dead man. Stephen Knight suggests there is no evidence at all to incriminate Montague Druitt; there is no evidence that he was near the scene of the murders, not even that he ever visited the East End, and no evidence is presented to show that Druitt had a motive for the killings.

SUSPECTS AD INFINITUM

Dr. T. E. A. Stowell believed that the Ripper was "Eddy," Duke of Clarence, grandson of Queen Victoria, brother of George V, son of Edward VII and heir to the throne of England. I first heard the story from Nigel Morland, whom I met in the company of Penelope Wallace, Edgar Wallace's only daughter, at the launching of the ill-fated Tallis Books. Morland, who died in April 1986, possessed an extensive library of books on crime and criminology, and a wide circle of influential friends and acquaintances whose knowledge of such subjects was unrivalled. He was able to draw on this information and these people when he came to launch his excellent quarterly, *The Criminologist*; and it was from Nigel Morland that I first heard about Dr. Thomas Stowell CBE and his suspect for the Ripper murders.

During the course of Stowell's article in the November 1970 issue of The Criminologist he remarks on the significant fact that after the murder of Mary Kelly the police definitely relaxed their vigilance. Senior officers and police constables were withdrawn from the area and special patrols were disbanded. It seems certain that the police had some knowledge that convinced them that the Ripper could not strike again. Furthermore the inquest on Mary Kelly was abruptly terminated (whereas the inquests on the other victims had been fairly thorough and in some cases exhaustive), the coroner choosing deliberately to suppress evidence and admitting as much. Stowell believed that within an hour or two of the murder of Catherine Eddowes on 30 September 1888 the Ripper was apprehended, certified insane and incarcerated in a private mental home in the Home Counties. Stowell further believed that the police, perhaps busy with preparations for the London Lord Mayor's Show, afforded the madman the opportunity to escape and return to Whitechapel where he murdered Mary Kelly.

Although he did not name the Duke of Clarence in his article Stowell described his suspect with sufficient detail for some people to be persuaded that it was the Duke whom he had in mind. During a foreign tour Stowell believed the Duke had contracted syphilis, for which he was treated by Sir William Gull, Physician in Ordinary to Queen Victoria, and it has been said that on more than one occasion the illustrious William Gull, a physician at Guy's Hospital, was seen in the neighbourhood of Whitechapel on the night of a Ripper murder. Stowell suggests he was there to certify the murderer insane and put him under restraint. The Duke of Clarence certainly visited a house in Cleveland Street, off Tottenham Court Road, much frequented by aristocrats and prosperous homosexuals.

With the inevitable progress of the venereal affliction the patient lost his ebullience and showed signs of depression and dementia which "in time must inevitably overtake him." His public appearances became fewer and the speeches shorter and then we hear little of him before his death a year or two later after prolonged and careful private nursing.

Stowell asserts that many false trails were laid to throw people off the scent including the idea that the Ripper must be a doctor or a surgeon to have removed the kidneys and pelvic organs of most of his victims: in fact, says Stowell, this is nonsense "for in those days, before the advent of antiseptic and aseptic surgery, the abdomen was almost inaccessible to the surgeon."

Stowell refers to the story, which we will examine in detail in a later chapter, concerning a medium, Lees, who led the police to an impressive mansion in the West End of London, and he speculates as to whether this could have been 74, Brook Street, Grosvenor Square, the home of Sir William and Lady Gull. He adds that Mrs. Acland, Sir William's daughter, told Stowell that she had seen in her father's diary an entry to the effect that he had informed a certain individual that his son was dying of syphilis of the brain. This was in November 1888 and the Duke of Clarence died little more than a year later.

Stowell believed that the Duke's deer-stalking activities provided ample opportunity for him to learn the positions of internal organs and how to remove them; and he pointed out that alleged sightings of the Ripper remarked upon headgear that could well have been a deer-stalker's hat. Stowell believed that Sir William Gull and the authorities could see no point in punishing the culprit, who was not responsible for his actions, and they had no wish to bring shame on the royal family. So the young man was confined in a private mental home but he escaped ("let us remember," says Stowell, "that dangerous lunatics have been known to escape from Broadmoor") and then, after the murder of Mary Kelly, he was restrained and "given such intensive medical care and skilled nursing that he had temporary remissions of his illness and had returned almost to normality until he relapsed and died of broncho-pneumonia a few years later—the usual cause of death in such cases."

Stowell does not excuse the murderer but he cannot conceive "any other humane way of dealing with a sadly afflicted young man and preventing a continuation of the atrocities" and points out that the women he murdered were women of little worth to the community, victims of bad homes, of low mentality, lazy and gin-sodden, adding "it is safe to say that every one of them was infected with one or both of the venereal diseases." These generalisations do not bear examination: Mary Kelly, for one, was not of "low mentality," nor was she "lazy" nor, as far as we know, was she suffering from any venereal disease. Stowell says that at the time of the murders the price for the use of these women's bodies was twopence, when the cost of a bed in a doss-house was fourpence.

Stowell's suspect is perhaps the most astonishing of all the people thought to have been the Ripper. Stowell was a devoted royalist and for years, he claims, he had kept the idea to himself because he did not wish to distress the present Royal Family. After his death, Stowell's son, apparently upset by the scandal, destroyed all the relevant papers. Stowell revealed his utter conviction that the culprit was the Duke of Clarence to Colin Wilson as early as 1960 under the mistaken impression that Colin Wilson had already come to the same conclusion. Stowell claimed he had had access to the private papers of Sir William Gull and therein were claims that the Duke of Clarence had not died in 1892 but was kept in a mental home with "softening of the brain" due to syphilis.

Among the difficulties in accepting the theory that the Ripper was one of the highest in the land is the fact that the Duke of Clarence was in Scotland on 29 and 30 September 1888, when Catherine Eddowes was murdered, and at Sandringham from 3 to 12 November, Mary Kelly being murdered on 9 November. After 12 November the Duke went to Copenhagen to represent his father at the Danish King's accession to the throne. The story, which can probably be best regarded as intriguing speculation, has its adherents but is difficult to prove conclusively without a statement from the Royal Family which is unlikely to be forthcoming, although they have let it be known that they regard the story as ridiculous. Certainly the Duke of Clarence cannot have been "restrained in a mental home" from November 1888 as there is ample evidence that he was alive and appearing in public into the beginning of 1892 when he fell ill with pneumonia the week after he attended the funeral of Prince Victor of Hohenlohe on 4 January and he died ten days later.

After Stowell's death, in November 1970, the theory or something very near it, was revived by Michael Harrison in his biography Clarence (1972). His suspect was not the Duke himself but his friend and probable lover James Stephen, son of Sir James Fitzjames Stephen. After an accident in which he received "a terrible blow on the head" James Stephen suffered painful periods of excitement and depression and "eccentricities of behaviour caused growing anxiety to his family." He died in 1892. Harrison claimed that Stowell's "S" in his writings referred in actual fact to Stephen, James Stephen. Much of what Stowell attributed to the Duke of Clarence applied far better to James Stephen; as far as we know Clarence did not die insane in a mental hospital but Stephen did; Clarence did not resign his commission at the age of twenty-four, Stephen did, and so on. Could Stowell have jumped to the wrong conclusion and assumed Sir William Gull was referring to the Duke of Clarence in his notes when in fact he was referring to James Stephen?

Stowell steadfastly denied during interviews that he was referring to the Duke of Clarence in his Criminologist article and on 9 November 1970 (the eighty-second anniversary of the death of Mary Kelly) a curious letter was published in The Times from Stowell in which he denied he had said or even thought that the Duke of Clarence was the Ripper! Stowell died the same day. However, he certainly told Colin Wilson that he believed the Ripper was the Duke of Clarence.

Even the Prime Minister William Ewart Gladstone has not escaped suspicion. In *Queen Magazine* (September 1970) Graham Norton regards at least some of the Ripper letters as "obviously genuine" for they disclosed aspects of the killings which only the murderer could have known" and he singles out the mention in one communication of "society's pillar":

> *"You should know, as time will show*
> *That I'm society's pillar."*

While this could equally have implied that the Ripper considered he was doing "work" to the benefit of society, Graham Norton looks at the obvious implication. It could not be Queen Victoria herself for a number of reasons and "only one other figure was held in the same veneration as the Queen" and it was on W. E. Gladstone "that the dark shadow of suspicion inevitably falls."

Gladstone had, of course, been mentioned by the Ripper in one of his verses and this could be significant. It is true that pathological criminals often delight in providing hidden clues and savouring their cleverness. Gladstone was certainly fascinated by prostitutes and he was known to be in the area at the time of the murders. Most of those who claimed to see the Ripper said he carried a black bag of distinctive shape, a type of bag that Gladstone was never seen without and that bore his name, a Gladstone bag. Immediately after his honeymoon (a fact which may be significant) in 1840, he began to wander about the streets of London at night, urging "unfortunate" women to reform and repent.

He even involved Mrs. Gladstone in his work of "saving" prostitutes and his critics were well aware of his capacity to "dress up whatever he set his heart upon in the most attractive moral and intellectual clothes." On one occasion Disraeli said of Gladstone: "I don't mind him having the ace of clubs up his sleeve; what I object to is his insistence that the Holy Ghost put it there." He could well have been speaking in 1988 about some other "pillar of society"!

Queen Victoria knew all about Gladstone's admitted nocturnal activities and she suspected much more. She thought him "mad and evil"; and her well-known remark of him addressing her as if she were a public meeting could have stemmed from his defence mechanism; there is little doubt that he was attracted by her undoubted sexuality, and strove to repress it.

Repression seems to have been Gladstone's middle name. His biographer Sir Philip Magnus speaks of his subject "only keeping his daemonic energy in check" by "punishing toil and prayer" while inside the great man there blazed "an unseen volcano . . . the tensions of the age seething in molten fury . . ."

In 1888 Gladstone was seventy-nine but possessing the energy and strength of a much younger man. His method of containing this energy and strength is interesting: he cut down trees and at his Hawarden estate a collection of sharp axes was preserved in the hallway and, as Graham Norton points out, "those that cut down trees also keep a sharp knife to trim the branches." Gladstone fills the bill on a number of counts and he had the physical strength, the cunning, the interest in prostitution, the mental capacity to absorb a little knowledge of anatomy, and he had a mission. One doctor, at the time of the murders, wrote: "the murderer is a homicidal maniac of religious views, who labours under the morbid belief that he has a destiny in the world to fulfil."

None of the Ripper letters were stamped; Gladstone never stamped his letters either. He would hand his post to a servant and, as a Member of Parliament, they would be franked. Clever as Gladstone was, this is an aspect he could easily have overlooked. Even the posting of some of the letters fitted the whereabouts of Gladstone. One, postmarked Kilburn, was sent when Gladstone was at his London home in Dollis Hill (now Gladstone Park), a couple of miles from Kilburn; two others were posted in Liverpool at a time when Gladstone was only a few miles away at Hawarden Castle—and the family business was in Liverpool where Gladstone often had reason to visit. On the other hand I wrote to *Queen Magazine* at the time to say that "careful analysis and examination of the letters reputedly written by the Ripper and Gladstone's handwriting show no similarity whatever and furthermore a number of subtle points, which would be apparent if the writer was disguising his handwriting, are entirely missing. I think there can be no doubt that Gladstone, whatever else he may have done, did not write the letters signed by Jack the Ripper." My letter was dated 26 August 1970.

Gladstone's repeated absences from home "converting" prostitutes was accepted by Mrs. Gladstone and she must have got used to it. Blood was even found on her husband's clothes on occasions, caused, he said, by too much starch in his high collars cutting his neck. After that season of terror in London's East End political matters fully occupied Gladstone and soon his physical strength began to fade. During the last years of his life he was dominated by his wife, "a tool in her hands," and she made sure that nothing would prevent his being universally mourned and ceremonially interred in Westminster Abbey when the time came: death and burial were so very important in Victorian times. So Gladstone became the Grand Old Man but Graham Norton asks whether he was in fact the Grand Old Murderer, Gladstone the Ripper, the terror of the streetwalkers of Whitechapel. It is yet another interesting speculation.

More than one Ripperologist has thought the Ripper may well be a nonentity and there is circumstantial evidence to give some weight to this idea. In the Mary Kelly murder (which may well hold the clue to the whole mystery) it seems likely that the murderer, having sated himself, probably burning his victim's foetus with a necessarily fierce fire helped by gin or other spirit, let himself out of the door and then bolted it on the inside by reaching through the already broken window pane. Why should he do that?

If the murderer had lived some distance from the scene of the murders and had been seen by any of the local people in the vicinity of the murders shortly before the body was found, he would have been merely a vague and unknown individual, but if he were a local man, known by sight in the area, then he could not afford to be seen anywhere in the area of Miller's Court. So to delay discovery of the body he bolted the door.

Weight is added to the idea that the Ripper lived in the East End, and probably quite close to Miller's Court, when the other murders are considered. Hanbury Street is less than a quarter of a mile from Miller's Court; and all the murders took place within an area of a quarter mile. The murderer, by all accounts, must have left Mary Kelly's room about 6:00 A.M.; he must have murdered Annie Chapman about 5:30 A.M. but the other three, Mary Nichols, Elizabeth Stride, and Catherine Eddowes were murdered much earlier, around 3:00 A.M., 1:00 A.M. and 1:45 A.M. respectively.

While prepared to risk being seen in a public place near where a body was found in the open, to be seen in the vicinity—perhaps even leaving the building—of a person murdered in their own room is something quite different. Even the police should have realised that the murderer probably lived in the Whitechapel area, and perhaps they did, for they traced him as far as Dorset Street where he was found to have washed his hands and left behind a piece of linen.

More than one student of the Ripper crimes has suggested that the elusive suspect for the murders came not from the aristocracy or the higher classes but from the lower strata of society. He would have had to have the brains and the control to hold down a steady job, one that might give him cover for his crimes, such as a cab driver. There is much to suggest that Jack the Ripper was a working-class man who knew the Whitechapel district well; he knew also the customs and habits of the East Enders of the day; and, as one Ripperologist puts it, "in all probability he now lies buried in the same cemetery as one of his victims." If the Ripper was a nonentity it is unlikely that much evidence of his existence will be found and even less proof of his guilt. Perhaps, as Donald Rumbelow has suspected, we shall have to wait until the Great Day of Judgement to learn of the Ripper's identity—always assuming that that day ever comes.

Although the name of Frederick Bayley Deeming has been put forward as a contender for the Ripper murders, mainly on his own evidence while in prison awaiting execution for murder, when he claimed to be Jack the Ripper, it is a non-starter as a serious theory. He had murdered his first wife and four children at Rainhill, Liverpool, cementing their bodies underneath the floor of the kitchen fireplace and he had murdered his second wife and hidden her body in a similar fashion in Melbourne, Australia, the police being attracted to his house by a disagreeable smell.

It seems impossible for Deeming to have been Jack the Ripper since he was in prison at the time of the Whitechapel murders but rumours and stories that he was indeed the elusive murderer continued long after his execution in 1892. A plaster death mask was forwarded to New Scotland Yard and for many years it was pointed out to visitors to the famous Black Museum as the death mask of Jack the Ripper.

Chaim Bermant in his book on London's East End, *Point of Arrival* (1975), claims the killer known as Jack the Ripper was in fact a Jewish religious fanatic and he relies largely on the dates on which the murders were committed, linking most of them with Jewish religious festivals but having to go over to "some hours after the close of evening service on the second day of the Jewish New Year" in one instance and admitting that the important Day of Atonement passed without a murder. In addition, curiously, the fourth and fifth murders took place on 30 September, "one of the few days in the holiest of Jewish months to be devoid of any religious significance whatsoever . . ." Although it is suggested that 30 September was chosen deliberately for fear that the pattern might be deduced, it all seems rather to stretch the imagination and the evidence, although there is no doubt that more than one Jew was seriously suspected and twenty years after the murders the then Assistant Commissioner of Police declared: "In stating that he was a Polish Jew I am merely stating a definitely established fact."

Stephen Knight has suggested that Stowell may have been pointing the finger of suspicion at Dr. William Gull instead of the Duke of Clarence or James Stephen but refusing actually to accuse the good doctor for Masonic reasons. Stowell suggested Gull did not die when he is supposed to have done, thereby lending support to three independent claims that Gull was the doctor sent to an asylum under a false name. Stowell told Colin Wilson that in Gull's private papers he had discovered that "S" had not died of pneumonia as he is reported to have done in 1892 but had died later of syphilis; but Gull is said to have died in 1890 so was Stowell really saying: "Sir William Gull did not die in 1890"? Gull was a Freemason with influence; he had suffered from mental trouble which caused him to behave strangely and violently; lies have been woven around his death; he was a strange and unpredictable man; he was seen in Whitechapel on the nights of some of the Ripper murders, and by his own admission he had woken up in his room to find blood on himself. Stephen Knight states that William Gull was stated to be the Ripper by at least six people whose word might be regarded as reliable, including his own daughter Caroline.

The grave, ostensibly of Sir William and Lady Gull, is in the churchyard at Thorpe-le-Soken, Essex. It is a somewhat large grave about which the verger once remarked, without any prompting: "Big enough for three, that grave . . ." If Gull was the doctor committed to an asylum and a bogus funeral was carried out and a coffin filled with stones was lowered into the grave, when Gull did die was he secretly buried beside his wife, making the third in a grave for two?

Further investigation could well prove or disprove whether or not Sir William Gull or James K. Stephen was in reality Jack the Ripper. What does seem difficult to unravel with any degree of certainty is the Stephen Knight theory that the Ripper murders were organised by top government circles of the day to hide a royal scandal, a story that involved Freemasonry: Prime Minister Lord Salisbury (who was *not* a Mason); Sir William Gull, the Queen's physician; Sir Charles Warren, Commissioner of the Metropolitan Police and Sir Robert Anderson, Assistant Police Commissioner. It is a story with an unexpected aftermath and it deserves a section to itself.

NOT "THE FINAL SOLUTION"

In 1976, after several years of research, Stephen Knight, a young Essex journalist, produced a remarkable addition to the ten serious books already published on the Jack the Ripper murders. This was to be the "final solution" (a title thought up by my old friend Ken Thompson, who was at the time in the employ of the publishers Harrap Limited) and a convincing line of deduction led to the novel idea that Jack the Ripper was not one man or even one person but three—two killers and an accomplice. From the "confused skein of truths, half-truths, and lies" woven around the case, Stephen Knight claimed to have at last solved the (then) eighty-odd-year-old mystery and it was confidently predicted that his book would be the last word on the case.

Knight takes as a starting point a story told about the three-times-married painter Walter Richard Sickert (1860–1942). During the course of research for a BBC television series, *The Ripper File,* the producer Paul Bonner and script writer Elwyn Jones began their investigation at New Scotland Yard. Although for years the response of the police to enquiries about the Ripper case (which still come in, to this day) had been, in effect, "The case is closed. We know nothing which has not already been published," the BBC researchers felt there *must* be some information that had not been released and, more by leakage than by direct statement, a curious scrap of information led the researchers on and formed a basis that shaped the course of Knight's book. After much questioning their "impeccable source" at Scotland Yard asked them whether they had had any contact with a man named Sickert, "who has some connection with the artist." The puzzled researchers were told that this man knew of a marriage between the Duke of Clarence, son of King Edward VII and Heir Presumptive to the throne until he died in 1892, and a certain Alice Mary Crook. The clandestine marriage had taken place at "St. Saviour's" and the two witnesses to the marriage were to become victims of the Ripper. Alice Mary Crook died in 1920.

Armed with this information, Ian Sharp, a research assistant who was working on the series, set out to show just how thorough the team were determined to be, but their enquiries at Somerset House and elsewhere failed to locate any marriage certificate or indeed any mention of a woman named Alice Mary Crook. They went back to Scotland Yard and asked for more information about the man Sickert. They were immediately given a London telephone number and when they rang the number they spoke to a man who said his name was Sickert. Without disclosing anything the researchers told Sickert that the BBC was interested in his story as they were doing a series of documentaries and an appointment was made for a personal meeting.

The story that emerged on that and subsequent meetings with Joseph Sickert was to the effect that the whole Ripper episode had its beginnings in Cleveland Street, where Sickert's father, Walter Richard Sickert, had his studio. There was a confectioner and tobacconists' shop nearby in which a certain Annie Elizabeth Crook worked, and another girl who sometimes worked in the shop was named Mary Kelly. It was here that Prince Albert Edward, Duke of Clarence, had met Annie (whose surname was variously rendered as Cook or Crook) on one of his secret visits to the area. They had been married in St. Saviour's Chapel with one witness, Mary Kelly, and there had been a child, Alice Margaret. In 1888 there had been a raid on certain premises in Cleveland Street and two people had been taken away: the Duke of Clarence and Annie, the latter being confined in various establishments and institutions until she finally died, in 1920, insane. Mary Kelly had seen what had happened and she fled to the East End with the child and hid in a convent. She is next heard of on 9 November when she was murdered. The Ripper was hardly mentioned and no hints were given as to his possible identity but the impression was conveyed that more than one person was involved. After a great deal of coaxing and persuasion Joseph Sickert agreed to tell his story on television in the Jack the Ripper series.

In that broadcast, in July 1973, Joseph Sickert, known as "Hobo," said his mother always told him that his grandmother had suffered "terribly" at the hands of the authorities; a servant had died in a terrible way, and he had to be very careful. His father, when Joseph was in his teens, told him in a roundabout way that his grandfather was the Duke of Clarence. Joseph Sickert's father, the artist Walter Sickert, lived at that time at 21 Cleveland Street, an area full of artists and their friends. Prince Edward's mother thought her son should meet artists and painters and she arranged the initial meeting between the Duke of Clarence and Walter Sickert, whose family had been painters to her own Royal Court of Denmark. The Duke and Walter Sickert became friendly and on occasions the Prince would stay with Sickert during his vacations from Cambridge; during these visits he was passed off as Sickert's younger brother. During such a visit the Duke met a very attractive if not beautiful shop girl who sometimes modelled for Sickert, Annie Elizabeth Crook. Prince Eddy fell in love with the girl and when Annie became pregnant a ceremony of marriage was performed at St. Saviour's.

A friend of Annie's was one witness at the wedding, Mary Jane Kelly, Walter Sickert being the other, and when the child was born in a workhouse near Drury Lane, Mary helped to look after the little girl and sometimes accompanied Sickert on visits to France. Things become somewhat confused here but Joseph Sickert thought that suddenly Annie Crook had disappeared, seemingly having moved to the Drury Lane area, but she reappeared from time to time and on one occasion was run down by a carriage and seriously injured. The carriage was being driven by a man named Netley. Annie went to hospital in Fulham and she was kept in confinement there and elsewhere until her death.

Mary Kelly was a Roman Catholic and she was known to the nuns of the convent in nearby Harewood Place. Worried by what seemed to be happening she took the child to a sister convent in the East End. What was happening was that the Royal household and people in high positions were becoming very worried about news getting out that the heir presumptive to the throne had married a Catholic and that there had been a child. In the climate of the time, especially the Irish troubles, revolution was by no means unlikely and it was decided that Mary Kelly, the only real threat (they thought), might have to be silenced. The delicate operation was outlined to Sir William Gull, the Royal physician, and he proposed the association of John Netley, a coachman who regularly drove the Duke of Clarence, although not on the official Palace staff.

For a while all was quiet and, the authorities argued, if Mary Kelly kept quiet and brought up the child as her own, there was no need for anything further to be done but then an untidy attempt at blackmail emanated from somewhere in the East End. It is possible that some gang was behind it but certainly it seemed that four women were involved: Mary Nichols, Annie Chapman, Elizabeth Stride, and Mary Kelly. The authorities decided to act with the help of Sir Robert Anderson,

Assistant Commissioner to the Metropolitan Police, who are only answerable to the Home Office, and Sir William Gull. A plan was devised and carried out; a series of murders that have become known as the work of Jack the Ripper.

Mary Kelly was eventually killed but only after a number of other similar women in the area had also been murdered, people who were suspected of being involved in the blackmail attempt, but also making it look like the work of a madman. The child survived, protected by Walter Sickert and had a son by him; Joseph Sickert claimed to be that son.

There appears to be some circumstantial evidence for this story. In 1888 a rate-book for Cleveland Street shows rates for a basement being paid by an Elizabeth *Cook*. A birth certificate, dated 18 April 1885, exists for a girl Alice Margaret whose mother is given as Ann Elizabeth Crook, confectionary assistant, Cleveland Street; place of birth Marylebone Workhouse; no father's name or occupation appears on the birth certificate. Joseph Sickert possesses a portrait of his mother, painted by Sir William Orpen, and her Christian names are given as Alice Margaret. Around the corner from Cleveland Street there used to be a convent that had close ties with another convent in Providence Row, Dorset Street, fifty yards from Miller's Court. A John Netley did exist, and he was a driver and he was born in 1860 and he was killed in an accident on 26 September 1903. Sir William Gull was one of London's leading physicians and Thomas Stowell, who as far as we know never heard Joseph Sickert's story, said "rumour mongers" picked on Sir William Gull who, as Stowell says, was seen in the neighbourhood of Whitechapel on the nights of some of the murders. Stowell also says the medium Lees led the police to Gull's Park Lane house.

Oddly enough it is a historical fact that Prince Edward, Duke of Clarence, in 1890, wanted to marry a Roman Catholic, the Princess Hélène d'Orleans, daughter of the Comte de Paris, and this brought a sharp comment from the prime minister of the day, Lord Salisbury, who, according to Sir Philip Magnus, the biographer of the Prince's father, Edward VII, warned the Prince that "the anger of the middle and lower classes might endanger the throne if it ever became known that he had even entertained the thought." So it seems that, if the story of the Duke of Clarence marrying a Roman Catholic had come out, it would indeed have caused tremendous repercussions. Yet there is still no hard evidence to connect Gull or anyone else with the Ripper murders. There were a number of alleged sightings of the Ripper and one very detailed one, at the time of the Kelly murder, by George Hutchinson; and yet there is nothing in the police files, or even in the newspapers, to indicate that any enquiries were put in hand to locate the "toff" who was so minutely described. It matters not whether Hutchinson was telling the truth or not, the point is that after at least five very nasty murders a witness provided a very good description and nothing was done about it. There does appear to be an air of cover-up: a good description and nothing done; the inquest on Mary Kelly closed before they had even established the time of death; no serious suspects named in the files—until Sir Melville Macnaghten's notes came to light and the three names there are not mentioned anywhere else in the whole investigation. Could it be that the authorities not only got very near to the Ripper, but that they even knew who he was—but they made sure nobody else found out and "they" keep on making sure no one finds out?

Seeking to establish once and for all everything that was known to the authorities about Cleveland Street and the Duke of Clarence, the BBC team made enquiries at the office of the Director of Public Prosecutions. After being told that there were no names in the Cleveland Street file that were associated with the East End (although how this was known was not revealed) three files were produced. The investigators were convinced that someone had been through the files and some documents had been removed; indeed they were told as much by an official as they left who said, on being told that there were no names of any interest in the files: "You should have seen some of the names in the pages we wouldn't let you see . . ." He would say no more but the conclusion of *The Ripper File* television investigators was that it might well be that somebody at the Director of Public Prosecutions Office is sitting on a file that has the answer to the Ripper murders.

According to Stephen Knight, Jack the Ripper was in reality three people: physician Sir William Gull, coachman John Netley, and either Walter Sickert himself or possibly Sir Robert Anderson. It is alleged that the murderers would locate their victims and in the cases of Mary Nichols, Annie Chapman, Elizabeth Stride, and Catherine Eddowes, they were offered a ride in the carriage. All but Stride were murdered inside the vehicle as Netley drove slowly round the streets. The bodies were then dumped by Netley in the places where they were found. Stride was too drunk to understand what they were saying and as she lurched off the carriage pulled up near her. Netley concealed the vehicle in a dark alleyway and Gull remained inside. Sickert (or Anderson) and Netley trailed Stride to Berner Street and there she was approached and then attacked by Netley as Sickert (or Anderson) kept watch. The deed accomplished, the murderers quietly returned to the coach and drove to Aldgate where they murdered the woman they thought was Mary Kelly. The mistake arose because they had been told that Mary Kelly was in custody at Bishopsgate Police Station for being drunk and disorderly and they knew that she was likely to be released after midnight. The woman they took to be Mary Kelly was in fact Catherine Eddowes. Quickly discovering their mistake the three murderers ran the real Mary Kelly to earth and murdered her in her own room, taking their time and making it look like the final fanatical fling of a madman, for they knew that this would be the last "Ripper" murder.

Joseph Sickert said his father "was induced" to remain silent about the whole affair by fear for his own safety. "He knew more than anyone else about Jack the Ripper, apart from the actual participants in the conspiracy." One day the prime minister, Lord Salisbury, appeared at his studio without warning and without more than a cursory glance he offered Sickert £500 immediately for a painting. At a time when he was lucky if he obtained £3 for a painting Sickert took the money. Although there was no mention of Cleveland Street or the Whitechapel murders, the painter soon realised that he had been given hush-money. He reasoned that nothing would be achieved by fighting the issue and he accepted the bribe and remained silent until many years later when he felt compelled to tell all he knew about the whole affair to his son Joseph; although, Joseph said, his father found himself painting into his pictures cryptic references to the truth behind the Ripper murders, which may have been a way of living with his guilty secret. Alice Margaret had been Walter Sickert's mistress for more than twelve years and she had a son by him, Joseph; Joseph's mother had died in 1950.

Stephen Knight pointed to one or two "facts" that suggested some foundation for what seemed an entertaining but absurd story. Hereditary deafness had afflicted the Sickerts as it had the Royal Family: Princess Alexandra passed on the disability to her son Prince Albert Victor and if he had fathered a child it could well have inherited the affliction. Alice Margaret Crook, the daughter Sickert said was the offspring of the Duke of Clarence, was deaf. In 1902, when she was under the care of the St. Pancras Board of Guardians, she is on record as being "stone deaf" and again in 1905 when she applied for assistance the Relieving Officer of the Westminster Union noted her deafness. Joseph Sickert is almost completely deaf in one ear and his youngest daughter has no hearing at all. A photograph of Alice Margaret, the alleged daughter of Prince Albert Victor, Duke of Clarence, shows a marked similarity to photographs of the Princess Alexandra who may be her grandmother.

Walter Sickert, a strange, compelling, and complicated man, seems also to have been a liar. Stephen Knight says he invented a Ripper story that over many years satisfied his need to talk about the murders and ensured him of being the centre of attraction, a position he loved to occupy. He told the story to Osbert Sitwell and many other people but Sitwell used it in his introduction to an anthology of Sickert's writings. Briefly, Sickert would say that some years after the Ripper murders he took a house in a London suburb and after he had been there some months he asked the old woman who looked after the house whether she knew who had occupied the room before him. At first she had said "No," then, after a pause she had added, "Perhaps Jack the Ripper."

Her story was that the room had been previously occupied by a veterinary student who took to occasionally staying out all night. The old woman and her husband would hear him come home during the early hours and then he would pace up and down his room for an hour or more, until the first editions of the morning papers were available; then he would creep downstairs and run to the corner of the road and buy a paper. He would then return and go to bed. Later there would be evidence in the fireplace that the lodger had burnt the clothing he had been wearing the previous evening. The days would be filled with talk of the terrible murders, all committed in the early hours, but the student never mentioned them. He suffered from consumption and the old couple watched him grow worse and worse. They had their suspicions but it seemed unlikely that this gentle and ailing youth could be responsible for such awful crimes and before they had convinced themselves that they should inform the authorities, the youth's health suddenly took a turn for the worse and his mother, a widow from Bourne-mouth, came and took him away. From that time the murders stopped. The young man died five months later.

This story inspired Marie Belloc-Lowndes to write her best-selling novel, *The Lodger* (New York 1911, London 1913), which in turn inspired two plays, at least five films and a two-act opera. Donald McCormick traces back to Walter Sickert the connection with the Ripper murders, if there is a connection, and Montague John Druitt whom we have already considered as a prime suspect. McCormick tells of tracing a London doctor who knew Sickert and whose father was at

Oxford with Druitt. This doctor maintained that Sickert once told his "lodger" story to Sir Melville Macnaghten at the Garrick Club and Sir Melville took the story seriously because he knew that Druitt had a widowed mother living in Bournemouth. Stephen Knight suggests that McCormick included Druitt's name in his list of suspects as a direct result of hearing Sickert's tale and associating him with the man who was found drowned in the Thames at the end of 1888. Interestingly enough Walter Sickert said from the beginning that Druitt had been a scapegoat in the affair; and there were incidents in Walter Sickert's story that checked out—indeed after sitting on the story for half a century it would be amazing if there were not—but there really is very little in all of it to cause an objective observer to consider it anything other than a story based on real people and real events. Stephen Knight ended up convinced that Sickert himself had assisted in the murders.

Serious consideration of the Sickert/Knight story reveals that there is no hard evidence to link it with the Ripper murders. And what about motive? There *could* have been a threat of revolution and the Royal Family *was* unpopular; indeed Queen Victoria herself seemed to think the monarchy would die with her. Queen Victoria, incidentally, as I have shown in my book *Queen Victoria's Other World* (1986), was much interested in the Ripper murders. At a time when murder was commonplace, especially in the East End of London, the Queen took an active interest in the *first* Ripper murder. Stephen Knight argued that only a person with some inside knowledge can recognise in a single killing the beginning of a series, especially if the second murder has not yet occurred.

There can be no doubt that those in authority could see great danger to the monarchy and the stability of the country at the time of the murders; the Queen herself foresaw an uprising that would end the monarchy if her son married a Roman Catholic. Lord Salisbury, as we have seen, also foresaw great danger, and *if* the Duke of Clarence really had married a Roman Catholic and had a child by her—a child conceived out of wedlock—it *is* possible to see Salisbury and other influential people including the Royal Family regarding the affair as assuming immense and crucial proportions. If he thought the conduct of the Duke was likely to cause chaos and bring about the downfall of the monarchy, Salisbury might well have tried to cover up the affair by arranging the removal of Annie Elizabeth Crook to an institution, with the help and connivance of the Royal physician, Sir William Gull; and if he then discovered that Mary Kelly had escaped and might prove to be a danger, he would then have found himself led into deeper water. All of a sudden it all seems possible.

Nor does it seem to be in serious dispute that there was a cover-up and if there was, this makes nonsense of most of the previous theories concerning Jack the Ripper. If it was a vengeful midwife, a Jewish slaughterman, a mad social reformer, a deranged surgeon, Neill Cream, Montague John Druitt, even James Kenneth Stephen, there would have been no real call for a cover-up—but such action would certainly have been necessary if the murders had been arranged and carried out by those in authority. Without going into detail, a cover-up seems obvious when it is considered that vital evidence was suppressed at some of the Ripper inquests; the course of justice was prevented in the Cleveland Street brothel case; a scapegoat was prepared to safeguard the possibility of having to name the Ripper and to satisfy anyone investigating the case in later years and, without doubt, some documents relating to the case have been withheld from inspection by bona fide investigators, and other documents have been destroyed. And yet, there were criticisms of the Stephen Knight book as soon as it was published and at a time when no one was to know that this Ripper theory would shortly be shown to be little more than a hoax.

In his review of the book in *The Sunday Times* Raymond Mortimer refers to Stephen Knight "embroidering" his research "with many conjections of his own which he takes to be facts." Mortimer continues: "He seems to me a very poor judge of evidence . . ." and "In the hitherto secret files of Scotland Yard Mr. Knight found no mention of Clarence, Gull, Netley, or Sickert. Indeed, apart from Joseph Sickert's boyhood memories of his father's talk, Mr. Knight offers us no evidence whatever to support his 'solution.' Walter Sickert loved tall stories, and must now be chuckling in the Elysian Fields. The whole 'solution' seems to be an obvious mare's nest: and what most surprises me is that a BBC team ever wasted their time on investigating and dramatising a yarn so ill-founded."

This prompted an immediate response from Paul Bonner, the producer of the BBC Jack the Ripper series, in which he pointed out that the Sickert story was accorded only a small part of the BBC series and was, in fact, dismissed from the summary at the end for want of evidence.

But there was worse to come for Stephen Knight. In an article in *The Sunday Times* in June 1978 David May revealed that "the final solution to the Jack the Ripper mystery put forward confidently two years ago is neither final nor a solution, according to the man whose story provided the basis for the claim. Joseph Sickert, who claimed that the Ripper murders of 1888 were organised by top government circles of the day to hide a royal scandal, told *The Sunday Times*: "It was a hoax. I made it all up."

In his book Stephen Knight said at one point, "It all sounded terribly unlikely" but he became convinced that Joseph Sickert believed every word of his father's story, and when Knight's exciting and original researches threw up considerable circumstantial detail that appeared to corroborate Sickert's "unlikely" story, the young author was sure that he had at last solved the mystery of Jack the Ripper.

But now Joseph Sickert said part of his story was nothing but a "whopping fib." The only part he stuck to was the first part pertaining to his father's story concerning his mother's parentage; the part about Jack the Ripper, he now admitted, was pure invention. He said at this time: "As an artist I found it easy to paint Jack the Ripper into the story I had been told about Prince Albert Victor and my grandmother by my father."

Married with three daughters of his own Joseph Sickert said, in 1978, that he had decided to confess because things had got out of hand. He wanted to clear his father's name. When he had made up the story he didn't think it would cause much harm or embarrassment as he thought the story was only going to appear in a local paper. "As far as I am concerned," he is reported as saying, "Jack the Ripper can go back to the Ripperologists." When *The Sunday Times* article appeared Stephen Knight could not be contacted but Simon Scott, Editorial Director at Harrap, who published Stephen Knight's book, tells me that the author did in fact revise the original edition.

The sad story of Stephen Knight continued in 1980 when he was suddenly diagnosed as having a brain tumour and told that he might have only a year to live. After an operation in 1982 he was confident that he was cured and he visited America and wrote other books including *The Brotherhood,* a bestseller about Freemasonry that caused a furore when it was published. In September 1984 he underwent a second operation but died in Scotland in July 1985 aged only thirty-three; and with him died one of the most involved, plausible, and just-possible theories concerning the Ripper murders.

Another kind of Jack the Ripper hoax seems to have been attempted in 1986, according to my friend Dr. Bernard Finch, when a skeleton, some nineteenth-century surgical knives, and pieces of women's clothing were discovered by a builder renovating the cellars of the Old Bull and Bush inn at Hampstead.

Interestingly enough there had long been a tradition in the neighbourhood that Jack the Ripper knew the area and was possibly known to Sir Thomas Spencer Wells (1818–97) who lived in a big house opposite the Old Bull and Bush. He was a famous surgeon after whom the Spencer Wells forceps are named. The house he lived in is no longer standing, having been bombed during the Second World War. Whether there is any foundation for the legend that Jack the Ripper was known to Sir Thomas Spencer Wells, it has to be accepted that the Ripper is likely to have been interested in the man famed for his successful and safe revival of the operation of ovariotomy and whose published works included *Diseases of the Ovaries, Notebook for Cases of Ovarian and other Abdominal Tumours,* and *On Ovarian and Uterine Tumours.*

Newspaper reports suggested that "authorities" thought the skeleton found in the walled-up cellar may be that of none other than Jack the Ripper himself! The bones were found in an old ventilation shaft that was bricked-up sometime in the late nineteenth century.

The landlord of the Old Bull and Bush is reported to have said at the time: "It is impossible to say how the man got into that part of the cellar. He may have been hiding and found he could not get out or he may have become unconscious due to lack of air."

It was also stated in one newspaper report that "one of the main suspects in the unsolved Ripper murders was a medical student living only about a mile from the Old Bull and Bush."

Dr. Bernard Finch, who examined the skeleton, said it belonged to a very strong man who was about five feet ten inches in height. He was right-handed and probably thirty to thirty-five years old, possibly a little younger.

There is a local story that a tunnel linked the public house with the home of Sir Thomas Spencer Wells, who worked in a hospital in the district where Jack the Ripper found his victims. When I spoke to him Dr. Finch told me that efforts were being made to locate this reputed tunnel but he added that he had no doubt whatever the skeleton and the knives and pieces of women's clothing had been placed where they were found by a hoaxer.

For many years, according to Police Sergeant Maurice Link, eerie stories have abounded about the Old Bull and Bush being haunted by the menacing ghost of a man, customers having claimed to see such a figure standing unsmiling at the bar, "looking a bit furtive." Could it be the ghost of Jack the Ripper himself?

TWO *NEW* SUSPECTS

A shadowy figure in the Ripper story who, I had long thought, would well repay study and investigation, is the man whom Bruce Paley, in an issue of the American *True Crime Magazine*, suggests as a possible candidate for the Ripper: Joseph Barnett, the unemployed fish porter and general labourer who lived for nearly two years with the attractive Mary Kelly who was five years his junior . . . Mary Kelly, around whom the whole Jack the Ripper case may well revolve.

By most accounts Barnett thought a great deal of Mary and he did his best, it is said, to persuade her to keep off the streets but the two of them had great difficulty in obtaining sufficient money to live or indeed to make ends meet. There were certainly quarrels in the tiny room they jointly occupied, quarrels that increased with the passing of time and were usually over money or over Mary's liking for gin.

Things seem to have come to a head when Mary Kelly brought home two of her fellow prostitutes in succession, a girl named Julia and Maria Harvey, and calmly suggested they share the conjugal bed. It must be likely that Mary Kelly, in common with many prostitutes before and since her day, had lesbian tendencies and inclinations which, even today, many men of the working class find abhorrent.

Barnett could well have been affected psychologically by the unexpected turn of events and evidently he made his objections all too plain, a violent quarrel ensued with slaps and punches being exchanged, articles being thrown and a window broken. At the end of it all, or perhaps in the middle of it, Barnett moved out and ten days later Mary Kelly was found dead, horribly mutilated, almost certainly by someone who knew their way around and who had been in the room before the night of the murder.

Joseph Barnett was the first person the police suspected of the murder of Mary Kelly: he knew her movements and her habits, he was one of the few people who knew how the bolted door could be opened from outside, he might well have felt he had a motive, and he certainly had the opportunity. A large percentage of murders are committed by people known to the victim and the evidence suggests not that Mary Kelly had met someone and brought them home with her but rather that she was in bed (her clothes were neatly folded by the bed "as though they had been taken off in the ordinary manner") and she was wearing only what was described at the inquest as a "linen undergarment." Medical evidence strongly suggests that she was murdered in a lying-down position and probably in her sleep.

It is likely that Barnett, who is described by most of the people who knew him as a decent enough sort of chap, may well have been a very plausible character. A contemporary drawing of him at the inquest, captioned: "J. Barnett, the friend of the deceased" depicts a cool customer well in control of himself. He certainly convinced the police of his innocence and never seems to have been seriously considered as a suspect again. It is quite remarkable, when you come to look, how little material is to be found about Joseph Barnett in all the books devoted to the murders; he is a shadowy, vague, ordinary, almost likeable figure who gives his evidence in a straightforward manner and then more or less disappears. If he *was* the Ripper not only did he succeed in covering his tracks at the times of the murders but he has been fortunate in that later writers on the murders all seem to have accepted him for what he appeared to be.

It is interesting to note that in Barnett's initial statement, given to Detective Inspector Frederick Abberline only hours after the body of Mary Kelly had been discovered, Barnett stated that "in consequence of not earning sufficient money to give her and her resorting to prostitution, I resolved on leaving her." Three days later he denied this was the reason for his leaving Mary Kelly and somewhat nervously he said he had left her "because she had a woman of bad character there; that was the only reason I left."

It is not disputed that Barnett had employment at Billingsgate Market when he first met Mary Kelly and he was in some sort of a position to support her but later he was often out of work and he had been without any kind of work for several months at the time of the murder of his recent common law wife. When things were difficult Mary Kelly had to procure what little money she could and in the only way she knew how.

It is not difficult to visualise Barnett, perhaps following the murder of Martha Tabram, a local prostitute, in a property near where he had at one time lived with Mary Kelly, conceiving the idea that he might well frighten Mary Kelly off the streets altogether by terrifying her and her fellow prostitutes, since reasoning with her seemed to have no effect.

To some extent Barnett, if that is what he did, was successful. By selecting prostitutes who lived nearby and who were personally known to Mary Kelly (this seems highly likely), Barnett certainly caused Mary Kelly to think twice and even three times about going onto the streets and where and when she did so. There is evidence that Mary Kelly was much interested in the Ripper murders; she encouraged Barnett to buy daily newspapers and if he did not do so, she bought them herself. In addition, as *The Times* reported, she had the habit of going regularly to the Britannia public house in Fish Street Hill, but she had not visited the Britannia for at least a month before her death. Obviously she sought to avoid places and areas likely to be visited by Jack the Ripper; some, at least, of the Ripper victims frequented the Britannia and the public house sent a floral tribute to Mary Kelly's funeral with a card inscribed "From friends using certain public houses in common with the murdered woman."

In the event Mary Kelly certainly met her death at the hands of the killer or killers who became known as Jack the Ripper and afterwards her body was violated far more than any other Ripper victim. The previous four women who had been murdered and whom most Ripperologists accept as Ripper victims, were all in their forties, although they all looked nearer sixty; they were all chronic alcoholics who would almost certainly do absolutely anything and go anywhere for the price of a tipple of gin: Mary was a little more selective. The Ripper murders were marked by increasing savagery which would be consistent with a murderer's attempts to frighten prostitutes (or one prostitute in particular) into staying off the streets. In the case of poor Mary Kelly the murderer spent literally hours dissecting the pregnant body.

It is interesting to try to fathom what was going on in Barnett's mind at the time of the Kelly murder. He must have felt rejected and insulted by her apparent preference for a woman sharing her bed rather than he who was in all probability the father of the child she was carrying. His murder (if he was indeed the murderer) of other prostitutes had not had the desired effect. He was, it seems certain, genuinely fond of Mary Kelly, but now she no longer wanted to have anything to do with him. After he moved out following the violent quarrel, which must have been a painful memory, he had continued to visit Mary, right up to and including the evening of her death and, on his own admission, he gave her money whenever he could. But it was all to no avail. After staying a few days with Mary Kelly one prostitute moved out and Barnett was ready to move back in, but Mary wasn't agreeable. Perhaps she had woken up to the fact that of recent months she had supported Barnett far more than he had supported her; perhaps the fact that she could well be bearing his child was the reason she could no longer bear the sight of him (as a Roman Catholic she would know that she had to have the child; there was no question of an abortion) and then there were his demands on her body. According to Julia Venturney, who lived at number 1, Miller's Court and had known Mary Kelly and Joe Barnett for about four months, Mary Kelly could no longer bear Joe Barnett and was very fond of another man who very often "ill-used her."

Joseph Barnett must have been annoyed and worried. He had murdered three or more prostitutes in an unsuccessful attempt to frighten Mary Kelly off the streets and now she would have nothing to do with him. He must have known she was sick of her way of life and would have liked to go back to Ireland where she was born, or Wales where her parents had moved to, and where they might still be living—but he must have known too that she was virtually starving and was openly talking of suicide.

After Barnett admittedly visited Mary Kelly during the early evening of 8 November, there are witnesses who said they saw Mary with a man later that night and she was "very drunk"; another witness reported seeing a man standing in the street, possibly waiting for someone to come out of Mary Kelly's room. Could this have been Joseph Barnett; or was it a prospective client waiting for her to be free? Perhaps his last meeting with Mary Kelly had been the decisive one for Joseph Barnett. Something may have snapped in his brain. If she would not be his, she would be no one else's, not any more.

When the coast was clear Barnett could have returned to Mary Kelly's room where, by that time, she could well have undressed and retired to bed; he could have let himself in by withdrawing the bolt by means of the broken window. Once at the bedside he may have stripped off his clothes to eliminate the risk of bloodstains and then, transported by frustration and bitter, blinding rage, he could have savagely cut Mary Kelly's throat and then slashed and torn at her body in such a frenzy that something like six hours were needed by people familiar in dealing with corpses to put the body together again.

Even the nature of the shocking atrocities he committed on the body of Mary Kelly have significance in view of his likely psychological state. He cut out her heart; he cut off her breasts; he cut the flesh from her thighs; he ripped out the unborn child from inside her body and burnt it; he pushed one of her hands into her open stomach; he furiously cut her about the face until she was unrecognisable.

Once the hours of fury had passed Joseph Barnett might well have resumed his usual urbane manner: bland, cool, and collected. He could have been sufficiently calm to have identified the body: by the hair and eyes, he said. The police usually look at the family and close friends first in a murder enquiry, "because," as one detective said in 1987 concerning a murder hunt, "that's where we usually find the murderer." The police suspected Joseph Barnett, questioned him for several hours and examined his clothes for bloodstains, but in the end they must have been satisfied, although, as far as we know, he had no alibi other than claiming to be asleep in a lodging house.

After the Kelly murder Barnett was in demand for questioning and interviews and soon he was turned out of his lodgings in Bishopsgate as being a nuisance. He is said to have moved in with his sister in a flat in Portpool Lane, Holborn. He certainly made several statements to newspapers and was a major witness at the inquest where he "laboured under great emotion," "spoke with a stutter" and produced a curious effect by beginning every answer by repeating the last word of every question asked. He was evidently completely engrossed in what was being said to him and in his reply. Nevertheless he must have been relieved to reach the end of his testimony and to be told by the coroner: "You have given your evidence very well indeed."

As an employee from time to time at the enormous Billingsgate fish market, Barnett could easily have acquired the rudimentary anatomical knowledge that some specialists thought the murderer possessed and he must have made a number of friends among the rough and coarse characters there. The "fish fag" of Billingsgate even gained a place in Bailey's Dictionary where "a Billingsgate" is defined as "a scolding, imprudent slut." Here Barnett could easily have picked up a short and sharp knife any time and as easily left it when he had finished with it, where it would have caused no suspicion, even if it was still bloodstained. The knife that killed and mutilated Mary Kelly was never found.

Even the Jack the Ripper letters (as we shall see) reflect what could have been Barnett's anger and purpose. "I am down on whores" . . . "shan't quit ripping them till I do get buckled" (arrested) . . . "my knife is nice and sharp" . . . etc. And there is the rhyme that may have been sent as a joke but could equally have applied to Barnett as to other suspects:

"*I'm not a butcher*
I'm not a Yid
Nor yet a foreign skipper
But I'm your own light-hearted friend
Yours truly Jack the Ripper"

The first letter was signed "Jack the Ripper" and at least one newspaper of the day stated that Joseph Barnett was known to some of his friends as "Jack." Barnett even fits several descriptions of men the police wished to interview and he bears a striking resemblance to the drawing of one suspect reproduced in the Daily Telegraph dated 6 October 1888.

Joseph Barnett lived in many different parts of the East End of London and during a period of four years he seems to have had about ten different addresses. He was therefore fully conversant with the whole area, a necessary acquirement for the murderer, who used this knowledge to get to and from the murder sites easily and quickly to elude capture. Most of those who investigated the Ripper murders thought at the time that the murderer must be resident in the locality.

On 30 September 1888, when the Ripper claimed two victims, Elizabeth Stride and Catherine Eddowes, a bloodstained piece of material, which turned out to be a piece of Catherine Eddowes's apron, was found in a dark courtyard where the murderer had evidently washed his hands only moments before: another indication that he knew his way intimately and well around those mean streets and dark alleyways.

It must also seem likely that the murderer was known to the victims or his presence did not alarm them, for none of them appears to have been sufficiently alarmed at his approach to scream, if of course they were aware of his approach. Joseph Barnett is likely to have been known to the local prostitutes who would know Mary Kelly, with whom he had been living for over a year. He could easily have disarmed them by asking whether they knew the whereabouts of Mary Kelly at that time or some equally innocent question before darting forward and slitting their throats before they could utter a sound.

A lot more research may be called for before Joseph Barnett can be unquestionably identified as Jack the Ripper but he does appear to have answered the description of a prime suspect, to have had the motive, the means, the opportunity, and he was known to be violent.

In December 1986 I noticed a small newspaper report to the effect that John Morrison of Leytonstone, London, had become deeply interested in Mary Kelly (or Marie Jeannette Kelly as she liked to be called), Jack the Ripper's last victim, and he had even arranged for a memorial stone to be erected over her grave. I wrote to him and what follows has been compiled from the information, cuttings, letters, and material that he has been kind enough to send me. He tells me that one room in his home is known as "Jack the Ripper's Headquarters"! It contains a mountain of evidence pertaining to the unsolved Ripper crimes that he has accumulated.

John Morrison, a keen amateur historian, devoted over four years to researching the Ripper murders and in particular the last known victim, Mary Kelly, when he realised that she was buried in a cemetery very near his home. He asked to see the Burial Register and discovered that Mary Kelly lay in grave number 16, Row 67. The Register entry notes: "Marie Jeannette Kelly brought from Shoreditch Mortuary 19 November 1888." The exact place of burial was pointed out to John Morrison who believes that Jack the Ripper was an Irishman named James Kelly who escaped from Broadmoor and murdered his former mistress, Mary Kelly.

James Kelly came originally from Liverpool and John Morrison thinks that Mary Kelly may have also come from the same town; he says the only evidence that she came from Ireland and moved to Wales is contained in the evidence of Joseph Barnett allegedly quoting what Mary Kelly had told him and because of her association with James Kelly and the child she bore or for some other reason it could well be that Mary Kelly did not want her Liverpool connection to become known.

It is a historical fact that James Kelly murdered his wife in Liverpool, was pronounced insane and was committed to Broadmoor Hospital (opened in 1863) a special hospital for the treatment of psychiatric patients of dangerous, violent or criminal propensities. James Kelly escaped from Broadmoor on 28 January 1888, using a pass key made from a corset spring, and *The Guinness Book of Records,* for some years, included his thirty-nine years' freedom as "the longest escape from Broadmoor." It is stated that after an adventurous life in Paris, in New York, and at sea, he returned in April 1927 to ask for re-admission to Broadmoor! After some difficulties this was arranged and he died there in 1929.

In a way John Morrison's long study and absorption with Mary Kelly and the Ripper murders all began when he dreamed that he would find the true name of Jack the Ripper in *The Guinness Book of Records.* It will be noticed that James Kelly was at liberty during the time of the Ripper murders and when similar crimes were reported from Paris and New York: otherwise nothing whatever seems to have been heard of him in all those thirty-nine years. Back in Broadmoor his warders were warned that he apparently suffered from delusions and fantasies, imagining himself to be Jack the Ripper, which he continued to do until his death.

John Morrison says, "Kelly's escape was never made public because the authorities wanted to keep their embarrassment to a minimum. This led, in fact, to the resignation of Commissioner Warren from Scotland Yard in 1888." John Morrison tells me he has "been in contact with leading criminologists who are very interested in his findings and in the fact that he may be the man who exposes the biggest official charade of all time" . . . what he calls "James the Rip-off"!

John Morrison's theory that James Kelly is Jack the Ripper is based on quite a remarkable number of coincidences linking Kelly with facts known about the hitherto unidentified killer. Until other more plausible explanations are forthcoming John Morrison sticks firmly to his conviction as to the identity of Jack the Ripper.

He is convinced that Scotland Yard, the Home Office, and a number of famous people always knew that James Kelly was the Ripper and his researches have all pointed to there being a cover-up in 1888 to "save face" at Scotland Yard and he is certain that this cover-up continues to this day. Broadmoor, he says, is equally embarrassed for in making good his escape Kelly took with him a large hospital pay-roll!

John Morrison tells me that his enquiries have elicited the fact that James Kelly killed his wife for the sake of his lover, Mary Kelly, when he lived in Liverpool. After the trial Mary fled from Liverpool and became a prostitute. All this and a great deal more John Morrison says he has discovered *without* any co-operation from the respective authorities.

When he made enquiries at Broadmoor he was told that no record existed of a James Kelly ever being a patient there; and following enquiries at the Home Office he says the James Kelly entry was withdrawn from *The Guinness Book of Records* and there is no mention of James Kelly in the current issue.

John Morrison has written to people like the Prime Minister asking why James Kelly has been "wiped off" the records at Broadmoor and withdrawn from *The Guiness Book of Records.* In reply the Home Office said it had no knowledge of any request to withdraw the James Kelly entry in the Guinness Book and all official records relating to the Kelly case had been released for public inspection at the Public Records Office at Richmond in Surrey.

John Morrison tells me he wrote to the Records Office and received by way of a reply a statement that any papers relating to the Kelly case "are not yet open to public inspection." He further claims that he has been approached by callers and other people who have appeared to be very upset by his researches; some having even warned him to cease his investigations into the Ripper case.

I have to say here that I contacted Norris McWhirter who edits *The Guinness Book of Records* and whom I happen to have met and in his reply, dated 2 February 1987, he says: "I do not know what gave John Morrison the idea that we deleted the entry on James Kelly on instruction 'by people in high authority.' No such 'instruction' was given to us and indeed we would not have accepted it. The reason why the entry was dropped was because of pressure of space and the fact that Kelly's thirty-nine-year 'absence' was surpassed by the American, Leonard T. Fristoe, who escaped from Nevada State Prison in 1923 and was turned in by his son in 1969, after forty-six years of freedom. The other point of which we took cognisance was that Broadmoor is not strictly a prison but a secure mental hospital, in which the inmates are not deemed to be culpable . . ."

I also wrote to Dr. John R. Hamilton, the Medical Director at Broadmoor, asking for any information about James Kelly. In his reply, dated 6 February 1987, Dr. Hamilton said: "I regret to tell you that for reasons of medical confidentiality (which goes beyond the grave) I am not able to divulge any information . . ." I took the liberty of going back to Dr. Hamilton saying I did not wish to broach medical confidentiality but could he simply tell me the date James Kelly entered Broadmoor; the date he escaped; the date he returned; and the date he died. In his courteous reply Dr. Hamilton told me: "James Kelly was admitted to this hospital on 24 August 1883, escaped on 23 January 1888, returned on 12 February 1927 and died on 17 September 1929."

John Morrison says the diary of the late Mrs. Marie Belloc-Lowndes, a high society socialite who knew several top officials in the late Victorian and Edwardian periods, is a key piece of evidence in supporting his theory. Marie Belloc-Lowndes was the author of the best-known novel based on the Ripper crimes, and John Morrison maintains that her diary shows that seven well-known people, including Winston Churchill, Oscar Wilde, and Queen Victoria, knew about the cover-up by the Government and by Scotland Yard and furthermore they knew the identity of Jack the Ripper.

New Scotland Yard denies there is any substance in these allegations that it has anything to hide in respect of James Kelly and a spokesman said, "It is nonsense to suggest there was ever a cover-up."

John Morrison tells me he is in possession of "concrete documentary evidence" to back his claim to the full and he declares there is "not the slightest margin for error." He says Mary Kelly was the only victim to have heard the name Jack the Ripper, since it only became public knowledge on 2 October 1888 in a letter posted from Liverpool, James Kelly's home town. The other Ripper victims were dead by then. Mary Kelly was the only victim to know about an otherwise "quite respectable" woman named Maria Coroner being sentenced to six months' imprisonment on 6 October 1888 for sending Jack the Ripper hoax letters to the police; she was tried at Bradford. Mary Kelly was the only victim to know that in mid-October 1888 the police were looking for a man with a "Newcastle" accent as the person responsible for sending them hoax Ripper material and Mary Kelly was the only victim to have known the true identity of Jack the Ripper. John Morrison further tells me that in fact the police traced a man they wished to interview to Newcastle but before they could apprehend him, he slipped away by sea. John Morrison says the Central Library at Newcastle have recently informed him that the man in question actually came from Hylton near Sunderland. Mary Kelly, says John Morrison, was the only one of the Ripper victims who could have identified James Kelly. When she saw him she would have known there must have been a cover-up because there was no news of his escape in the newspapers.

John Morrison hopes to publish a book on his findings one day and there is talk of a film or television series. His theories and findings are based on a number of coincidences that do seem to link James Kelly with facts known about the killer and with Mary Kelly with whom John Morrison feels an affinity. He is determined to identify her murderer.

Even a brief run-through of some of these coincidences certainly makes interesting reading as does John Morrison's brief résumé of the Jack the Ripper crimes in 1888. He maintains that James Kelly was a married man living in Liverpool where he meets a pretty girl named Mary. She becomes pregnant and adopts his surname, thus becoming Mary Kelly. In due course she has a little girl; being a Roman Catholic she would never agree to a backstreet abortion. The child was adopted and a man named Daley wrote to John Morrison from Bristol to say that his family had always believed that their great grandmother was the illegitimate child of Mary Kelly. Mr. Daley's grand-parents came from Ireland and all the family are Roman Catholic. He has compiled a family tree and the only unexplained member is the great grandmother.

James Kelly's wife finds out about his affair with Mary and during the course of a quarrel, James murders his wife. He is lodged in the hospital wing of Walton Gaol for the purpose of observation and mental assessment ("this was done in a case of a capital offence whether the sanity of the suspect was in doubt or not"). Kelly, says John Morrison, avoids the gallows and is sent to Broadmoor. In January 1888 he escapes, taking with him all the staff wages. The authorities are naturally embarrassed and a "temporary" cover-up is imposed. Not until the death of Mary Kelly, coupled with the Ripper letters from Liverpool, Kelly's home town, do those authorities see the connection; but by then it is too late to admit to the cover-up.

Sir Charles Warren wants to publicise the whole matter and alert all police forces and the public to the dangers of James Kelly remaining free but the Home Secretary, Henry Matthews, puts a stop to this. Warren is made to sign, for the first time, the Official Secrets Act, and is then dismissed under the guise of resignation.

Matthews reasons that Mary Kelly was the only intended victim so there will be no more Ripper murders and that, after all, he only killed "a load of trash"; it is better James Kelly disappears of his own accord than that the "old lady of Windsor" finds out about his incompetence in the matter, or his own head may roll.

In 1891 police in New York report a series of murders similar to those attributed to Jack the Ripper in London three years earlier and when they ask whether the same man could be responsible they are told by Scotland Yard, "Rubbish—we've got Jack bottled up in London and we'll catch him if he ever kills again." A few months later French police make similar approaches to Scotland Yard following similar murders in Paris: "Rubbish," says Scotland Yard. "We expect to arrest him in London any time now."

In 1927 James Kelly, sleeping rough, down and out, and without any visible means of support, surrenders himself as the escaped madman from Broadmoor. He says he has been at sea most of the time but he has had an "adventurous life" in New York and in Paris.

The government, under Stanley Baldwin, wasted no time in getting Kelly back into Broadmoor, informing the administration and staff that this man suffered with the fantasy that he was Jack the Ripper—but of course he wasn't (John Morrison believes he can prove these conjectures as fact); and because of the nuisance and embarrassment he had caused there should be no possibility of his escaping again; he had better be placed in permanent solitary confinement until further notice or instructions from the Home Office. No such notice ever came and James Kelly died in 1929. On orders from the Home Office he was buried quietly and quickly in an unmarked grave at Crowthorne where he still lies. He was a Roman Catholic and died after receiving the Last Rites.

In 1947, John Morrison says, Mrs. Marie Belloc-Lowndes, not long before she died, asked to see the Catholic priest from Broadmoor Mental Hospital. She had revealed that she believed in communication with the dead and the reality of ghosts, although all this conflicted with her acceptance of the Roman Catholic faith. When, on her deathbed (again according to John Morrison) she was asked why she wrote *The Lodger,* she replied: "Because I would like to think that long after I'm dead it may help someone who is struggling to express himself with regard to the Jack the Ripper crimes."

Mrs. Belloc-Lowndes moved in high circles in her day and John Morrison is convinced that she knew all about the cover-up concerning James Kelly's escape from Broadmoor and that she verified what she knew with the priest who had heard James Kelly's last confession and who received absolution for remaining silent on the subject himself. If Mrs. Belloc-Lowndes—perhaps herself receiving absolution for remaining silent—was buried in a local cemetery it could be that she lies near James Kelly since they were both Roman Catholics and Crow-thorne, in common with most cemeteries, reserves part of the burial ground for Roman Catholics.

John Morrison says he can prove that Mrs. Belloc-Lowndes and Inspector Joseph Chandler, a police officer involved in the Whitechapel murders (as they were known at that time) were great friends and that he told her: "This is not for the newspapers but the man we are seeking in connection with the Whitechapel murders once committed murder in a house in Liverpool. He was found to be insane and placed in a lunatic asylum but he escaped just prior to the commencement of these crimes. I doubt if we will ever catch him, he is such a cunning devil—but you know even if we did we could not hang him, could we?" In *The Lodger* Mrs. Belloc-Lowndes wrote of her "friend from the Yard, Joe Chandler," and her diary, John Morrison says, revealed that he told her about the Liverpool murderer who was responsible for the Whitechapel murders; that the man was committed to an asylum and escaped just prior to the commencement of the London crimes, with the staff wages, and that all this was not made public to save the authorities embarrassment.

In 1927 Mrs. Belloc-Lowndes was helping in the preparation of her book, which was to become a film for the first time. *The Lodger, A Story of the London Fog* with Ivor Novello was the first of four films based on Mrs. Belloc-Lowndes's book and, incidentally, the fifth film to be directed by Alfred Hitchcock. Suddenly, says John Morrison, Mrs. Belloc-Lowndes appeared on the set and insisted that part of the plot be altered. She had just heard that Kelly had surrendered to the authorities and, having achieved what she came to do, she then fled to the United States where she stayed until 1930—the year after James Kelly died. It has to be said that students of the cinema generally accept that the last part of the film differs from the book in order to protect Ivor Novello's matinée idol image; furthermore, feeling certain that the film was *made* in 1926 I asked The British Film Institute whether they could confirm that this was so and they informed me (27 January 1987): "Principal photography on *The Lodger* began at the beginning of May and was completed by early June. The film was trade shown on 14 September 1926 and was released 14 February 1927."

John Morrison believes that for years Mrs. Belloc-Lowndes was obtaining private and unpublished information from various ministers and senior Scotland Yard officials, even up to and including 1939. "Her husband was Obituary Editor for *The Times*; she was at one time a journalist and without doubt was not averse to using bribery anywhere to obtain information." John Morrison says he has seen all this in Mrs. Belloc-Lowndes's own hand.

He tells me that the *Sun* newspaper of 1891 traced Jack the Ripper to Broadmoor and was told not to print the story. He feels that Mary Kelly stands out in the Ripper story in many ways: she was the only Irish National among the Ripper's victims; she was the only Roman Catholic; she was the youngest and the prettiest; she may have been the latest prostitute to come to the area; she was the only victim to be given a decent burial; the only victim whose death caused widespread sympathy; the only pregnant victim; the only one with the same surname as the killer; the only one whose death the killer tried to conceal; she was the only one murdered in Spitalfields and she was the last victim.

It is not altogether true that hers was the only death that caused widespread sympathy: the funeral of Catherine Eddowes (alias Kate Conway, alias Kate Kelly) was quite an affair. Several hundred people saw the coffin, bearing the inscription "Catherine Eddowes died 30 September 1888 aged 43 years," leave the City mortuary escorted by a strong force of police; Catherine Eddowes was followed to her grave by her four sisters and by John Kelly, with whom she had been living. The Mile End Road, and elsewhere along the route, was lined five-deep with spectators. At Ilford Cemetery nearly five hundred people witnessed the actual burial and "great sympathy" was widely expressed. Elizabeth Stride, on the other hand, was certainly buried in all possible haste in a pauper's grave.

John Morrison told me emphatically: "Everything that has ever been said and all the evidence concerning Jack the Ripper fits James Kelly in every respect. My account will eventually be accepted because it is the only account that would stand up in a British Court of Law." This remains to be seen but it is certainly an interesting possibility.

John Morrison has also highlighted for me some strange parallels and incidents in studying James Kelly as Jack the Ripper and the Peter Sutcliffe Ripper murders.

Peter Sutcliffe said he was employed at a cemetery and that there he heard a voice telling him to commit the murders; it seems that it was the cemetery that contains the grave of Maria Coroner, who wrote to the police about the Ripper murders in 1888. Bradford and Newcastle were mentioned in relation to both cases; both Sutcliffe and *James* the Ripper murdered only one victim in "enclosed" premises. They both murdered by night; they were both roughly the same age; they both operated in "red light" districts; they both ended up in Broadmoor; in both cases there was talk of the supernatural; both murdered one woman in Lancashire . . . and so on.

I am not sure how evidential all this, and the researches of John Morrison, will prove to be in seeking to unmask the identity of Jack the Ripper. What it has done for Mary Kelly is to provide her with a memorial stone on her grave in St. Patrick's Roman Catholic Cemetery. Today a marble tombstone, engraved by a local mason, marks the last resting place of the Ripper's last victim. Since he has become interested in Jack the Ripper, John Morrison has become more and more interested in Mary Kelly. She was known to sing to herself, she was known to have been very pretty, and she was a resident of Spitalfields, so he calls her "The Prima Donna of Spitalfields." He has had put on the stone the name that Mary Kelly liked to be called, "Marie Jeannette Kelly" and he has added her age, the date she was murdered and the lines:

> "*Do not stop to stand and stare*
> *Unless to utter fervent prayer.*"

Three years ago John Morrison composed some "simple verses" consisting of six stanzas, which he dedicated to Mary Kelly prior to the erection of her gravestone on 3 December 1986; the two lines on the gravestone come from those verses. Also engraved on the gravestone are the words "Mary Magdalene Intercede," "because Mary Magdalene is the patron saint of prostitutes and she was once herself a woman of easy virtue." By law no grave can be disturbed for a hundred years, and as the expiry date on Mary Kelly's grave grew near John Morrison took steps to be responsible for preserving Mary's memory and looking after her grave—and he has reserved a burial plot for himself nearby.

There is space at the bottom of the headstone for something to be added but only when his suspect is publicly acknowledged will John Morrison arrange for the customary words to be added to Mary Kelly's gravestone: Requiescat in Pace.

MYSTERY SOLVED!

Anonymous

The Irish-born William Greer Harrison (1836–1916) was a prominent businessman in San Francisco who is best-known for being one of the founders of the Bohemian Club. He told the story about the identification of Jack the Ripper as divulged in a conversation with a Dr. Howard, one of a dozen prominent London physicians who interviewed a colleague who apparently had no idea that he had been committing the atrocities.

A preacher and spiritualist named Robert James Lees is said to have played a leading role in the physician's arrest by using his clairvoyant powers to identify the house in London's Mayfair where the murderer lived. The doctors and the clairvoyant persuaded police to take the physician to a private insane asylum in Islington, London, registering him as Thomas Mason. Since "Mason" was unaware of his crimes, allegedly perpetrated while the evil half of his personality was dominant, readers will be reminded of Robert Louis Stevenson's chilling novella, *The Strange Case of Dr. Jekyll and Mr. Hyde,* published two years before the Ripper murders were committed.

The alleged conversation between Harrison and Howard first appeared in the *Fort Wayne Weekly Sentinel* (April 24, 1895) but also in several other newspaper articles across the United States, including the *Fort Wayne Weekly Gazette* (April 25, 1895), the *Williamsport Sunday Grit* (May 12, 1895), the *Hayward Review* in California (May 17, 1895), and *The Brooklyn Daily Eagle* (December 28, 1897).

IDENTITY OF JACK THE RIPPER KNOWN:
THE PERPETRATOR OF THE WHITECHAPEL MURDERS
WAS A LONDON PHYSICIAN OF PROMINENCE.

San Francisco, April 24.

Dr. Howard, a London physician of considerable prominence, was the guest of Wm. Greer Harrison at the Bohemian Club recently. The Englishman told a singular story to his host and vouched for its correctness in every particular. It related to the mystery of Jack the Ripper, which the physician declared was no longer a mystery among the scientific men of London, nor the detectives of Scotland Yard.

He said that the assassin was a medical man of high standing and extensive practice. He was married to a beautiful and amiable wife, and had a family.

Shortly before the beginning of the Whitechapel murders, he developed a peculiar and, to his wife, inexplicable mania, an unnatural pleasure in causing pain. She grew so alarmed that she became afraid of him and locked herself and children up when she saw the mood coming on him. When he recovered from the paroxysms and she spoke to him about it, he laughed at her fears. Then the Whitechapel murders filled London with horror. The suspicions of the wife were aroused, and as one assassination succeeded another, she noted, with heartbreaking dread, that at the periods when these murders were supposed to have been committed, her husband was invariably absent from home.

At last the suspense and fear of the wretched wife became unbearable, and she went to some of her husband's medical friends, stated the case, and asked their advice and assistance. They called the Scotland Yard force to assist them, and by adding one fact to another, a chain of evidence pointing to the doctor as the author of the murders became complete.

The physicians visited the murderer and told him they wished to consult him about the remarkable case. They stated his own case in detail and asked him what should be done under the circumstances. He replied that while the unmistakeable insanity of the person who could commit these crimes would save him from the halter, he should certainly be confined in a lunatic asylum. Then they told him that he himself was the maniac who had committed these fearful acts. He declared the impossibility of the accusation, but confessed that of late years there were gaps in the twenty-four hours of which he positively had no recollection. He said he had awakened in his room as if from a stupor and he found blood upon his boots and stains of blood upon his hands. He also had scratches upon his face and his amputation knives had shown signs of use, though he could not recall having assisted at any operation.

These doctors then assured him there could be no doubt of his identity with the Whitechapel assassinations. They made an exhaustive search of the house, led by the accused, and found ample proofs of murder, and the unhappy man, whose mind at that moment was in its nominally clear condition, begged to be removed from the world as a guilty and dangerous monster. The necessary papers were made out and the irresponsible murderer was committed to an insane asylum. In a month or two he lost all semblance to sanity and is now the most intractable and dangerous confined in the institution.

"FRENCHY" – AMEER BEN ALI

Edwin M. Borchard

As a distinguished legal scholar, dedicated to serious, complex, and innovative issues involving international law, Edwin Montifiore Borchard (1884–1951) may not have been expected to write about Jack the Ripper. However, since one of Borchard's career specialties was advocating for the rights of the innocent, his investigation of a nineteenth-century crime in which a suspect was wrongfully accused is not too far-fetched.

In his book *Convicting the Innocent* (1932), Borchard takes a close look at how an uneducated man was accused of the Ripper murders. The crimes had been so heinous that much of the British public felt that no Englishman could have committed such vicious crimes, thus turning to "foreigners" and, if dark-skinned, so much the better. Ameer Ben Ali made the perfect target but Borchard convincingly makes the case for his innocence.

After working as the Law Librarian at the Law Library of Congress (1911–1916), where he wrote his dissertation, *The Diplomatic Protection of Citizens Abroad, or the Law of International Claims* (1915), Borchard followed with a year as an attorney for National City Bank of New York, then took a job at the Yale Law School, where he was named the Sterling Professor of International Law, a position he held until his death.

"'Frenchy'—Ameer Ben Ali" was original published in *Convicting the Innocent: Sixty-Five Actual Errors of Criminal Justice* (New Haven, CT, Yale University Press, 1932).

On the southeast corner of Catherine Slip and Water Streets, on the Manhattan waterfront of the 1890s, there flourished the East River Hotel, a squalid drinking place and bawdy resort. At nine o'clock on Friday morning, April 24, 1891, the night clerk, Eddie Harrington, made his rounds of the hotel rooms, routing out all those who had not already left. Most of the rooms had been vacated. Room 31, however, was still locked. He rapped lightly—no reply; louder knocks—no reply. Eddie applied his master key to the door. Peering in, he was petrified by the ghastly sight of the mutilated body of "Old Shakespeare," a dissolute woman of sixty, a habitué of the neighbourhood. She was a former actress, and received her nickname because she frequently quoted the Bard's plays when tipsy. Her name was Carrie Brown.

Eddie, greatly excited, rushed to the first floor to spread the news and call for the police, who soon arrived, accompanied by newspaper reporters. The coroner took charge of the body.

An examination of the body showed that the woman had been strangled, atrociously slashed by a filed-down cooking knife, which was found on the floor by the bed—and upon her thigh was cut the sign of the cross. As a murder this was a challenge to Chief Police Inspector Thomas Byrnes, who was justly proud of his record for solving crime mysteries. The cross on the victim's thigh gave the case a special significance. It was the mark of "Jack the Ripper," the notorious London murderer who had baffled Scotland Yard by his nine brutal killings of women in the streets of London from December, 1887, to January, 1891. The New York Police Department had chided the London police about the "Ripper" and boastfully let it be known that if the latter appeared in New York with his evil doings, he would be in the "jug" within thirty-six hours.

On April 25, 1891, the day after the murder, the New York newspapers headlined the arrival of "Jack the Ripper." Inspector Byrnes and his force concentrated upon solving the crime. Investigation showed that "Old Shakespeare" had arrived at the hotel at about eleven o'clock with a male companion half her age, who gave a name which was written down by the clerk as "C. Knick." They were assigned Room 31, to which they repaired with a tin pail of beer. Several of the hotel hang-abouts saw the man and were able to supply descriptions of him—a medium-sized, stocky, blond, seafaring man. This man vanished and was never apprehended. The police combed the water front for him in vain.

Some of "Old Shakespeare's" acquaintances were found, among them Mary Ann Lopez, who had a frequent visitor known in the neighborhood as "Frenchy." Although a decided brunet, Frenchy's general appearance was otherwise not greatly different from the description given of the man who spent the night in Room 31; so Frenchy was arrested, among numerous others, for questioning. He professed not to be able to speak English. Many languages were tried on him until it appeared that he spoke Algerian Arabic—he was an Algerian Frenchman, named Ameer Ben Ali.

On April 25, Frenchy was a suspect. On April 26, the newspapers carried a police statement that he was probably implicated as being a cousin of the murderer. On Wednesday, April 29, the case was still unsettled, with the police apparently at sea. Detective Kilcauley of Jersey City reported to the police that a conductor employed on the New Jersey Central was very sure he had carried the murderer to Easton on his train. All the while, Frenchy was kept in the star cell at the police station.

On April 30, Inspector Byrnes gave several reporters the news that the case against Frenchy was complete, and that the police were convinced that he was the murderer. It was admitted that Frenchy was not "Old Shakespeare's" companion during the fatal night, but it was said that Frenchy had spent the night in Room 33, across the hall from the murder chamber, and that after the other man had left, Frenchy had crept across the hall, robbed his victim and killed her, and then crept back into his own room. As sketched by the Inspector, the evidence against Frenchy consisted of blood drops on the floor of Room 31 (the murder chamber), and in the hall between Rooms 31 and 33 (Frenchy's room); blood marks on both sides of the door of 33, as if the door had been pushed open by bloody fingers and then closed; blood marks on the floor of Room 33, on a chair in that room, on the bed blanket, and on the bedtick (there were no sheets). Blood was said to have been found on Frenchy's socks, and scrapings from his fingernails indicated the presence of blood. His explanations as to how the blood got on him were investigated and found to be false. Some of Carrie Brown's professional sisters said that Frenchy consorted much with "Old Shakespeare" and occupied Room 31 with her only the previous week.

On this same day (April 30), Frenchy, who by this time was called Frenchy No. 1, to distinguish him from other "Frenchies" involved in the case, was arraigned before Judge Martine and was formally committed to jail for the murder. Since the prisoner was unable to employ counsel, Judge Martine appointed Levy, House, and Friend as his counsel. On May 1, Frenchy was removed to the Tombs.

At about this time it was learned that the prisoner had served a vagrancy term in March and April in the Queens County Jail and that two of his fellow prisoners there, David Galloway and Edward Smith, had reported that Frenchy had a knife like the one used in the murder.

On Wednesday, June 24, 1891, Frenchy's trial opened before Recorder Smyth. An interpreter from his own Algerian village had been found in New York. The state was represented by Assistant District Attorneys Wellman and Simms, and the police force by Inspector Byrnes and four officers. In addition to evidence bearing upon the facts as related by the Inspector to reporters on April 30, the prosecutors called many witnesses from the lowest stratum of New York life, to prove that Frenchy had been living a sordid life, and, particularly, that he was accustomed to staying at the East River Hotel and to wandering from room to room at night. On cross-examination, the credibility of these witnesses was thoroughly attacked.

The climax of the trial came on Wednesday, July 1, when District Attorney Nicoll himself took charge of the trial and called Dr. Formand of Philadelphia as an expert witness. Dr. Formand testified that he had made tests of samples of the blood found on the fatal bed in Room 31, in the hallway, on the door to Room 33, inside Room 33, and on Frenchy's socks, and found that they all contained intestinal contents of food elements, all in the same degree of digestion—all exactly identical. This led to the direct inference that all of these bloodstains resulted from blood flowing from the abdominal wound of the deceased. The Doctor stated that he would be willing to risk his life upon the accuracy of his tests. Dr. Austin Flint and Dr. Cyrus Edson corroborated Dr. Formand's testimony, and concluded the case of the state against Frenchy.

On July 2, the defense opened. After calling Constable James R. Hiland of Newtown to prove that when Frenchy was arrested in Queens County, he had no knife, the defense counsel put the defendant on the stand. He was asked about his life history, his eight years of service in the French army, and his movements in this country. Finally he was asked, "Did you kill Carrie Brown?" These words had hardly been translated into Arabic when Frenchy jumped to his feet, lifted his hands over his head, looked skyward, and fairly screamed in Arabic—he appeared to be having hysterics. No one could quiet him. Finally he sank back into his chair exhausted, and the translator gave the gist of Frenchy's plea: "I am innocent, I am innocent, Allah il Allah [God is God]. I am innocent. Allah Akbar [God is great]. I am innocent. O Allah, help me. Allah save me. I implore Allah to help me."

Frenchy made a bad witness, at times appearing to understand English and again pretending not to understand questions even when interpreted into his own tongue. He consistently denied killing "Old Shakespeare," but he became badly tangled up time and again upon cross-examination.

The defense called several medical experts to testify that the substances found in the various blood exhibits did not necessarily all come from the intestine, but that they might have come from other parts of the body. Each of these experts, however, was forced to admit that Dr. Formand was at the top of his profession and that they had high regard for his opinion.

The prosecution added an interesting bit of evidence by showing that Frenchy's tallow candle had been burned for more than an hour in Room 33 on the night of the murder, implying that he had been sitting up for some definite purpose. Testimony was submitted to show that he had left the hotel at five o'clock the following morning, and that he "slinked" out of the door in a guilty manner.

The jury soon returned a verdict of guilty of second-degree murder. The Inspector and the prosecutors were much disappointed; but it was apparent that a compromise had been made by the jury. On July 10, 1891, Ameer Ben Ali was sentenced to Sing Sing for life.

The newspapers and the public had taken great interest in the case. The newspapers reported fully the testimony of each witness and the case was avidly followed by thousands. There was little disapproval of the verdict.

Newspaper men, among them Jacob A. Riis and Charles Edward Russell, who had been assigned to the case from the very beginning, were far from satisfied that this presented a true solution to the murder, and felt that it could never be unraveled until the police had found the man who had gone to Room 31 with "Old Shakespeare." However, the public authorities rested when Frenchy went to Sing Sing to spend the remainder of his days—soon to be transferred to the hospital for the criminally insane at Matteawan.

Persistent rumors drifted back to New York among seafaring men that the murderer had quietly gone to sea, bound for the Far East. These tales could never be substantiated.

At the turn of the century, however, brighter days came to the penniless Frenchy. An application for a pardon on his behalf, based upon new evidence, was submitted to Governor Odell. It was established that just prior to the murder a man answering the description of the murdered woman's companion had been working for several weeks at Cranford, New Jersey, that this man was absent from Cranford on the night of the murder, and that several days thereafter he disappeared entirely. In his abandoned room was found a brass key bearing a tag 31 (the key exactly matched the set of keys at the East River Hotel) and a bloody shirt. From evidence previously adduced, it was quite certain that the murderer had locked the room when he left it. There never was any evidence to connect Frenchy with the key. The principal evidence against Frenchy had been the reported bloody trail between the two rooms, which, even as testified to at the trial, consisted of very small and faint blood marks. There were submitted to Governor Odell numerous affidavits of disinterested persons, described by the Governor as "persons of credit, some of whom had had experience in the investigation of crime," to the effect that these persons had visited the hotel room on the morning following the murder, and prior to the arrival of the coroner, and that after careful examination they had found no blood on the door of either room or in the hallway. It was to be inferred that the bloodstains, found by the police on the second day following the murder, had been made at the time of the visit of the coroner and the crowd of reporters when the body was examined and removed. It was further pointed out that even according to the police testimony there was no blood on or near the lock or knob of the door to the murder chamber which the murderer presumably unlocked, opened, closed, and relocked. This new evidence in the Governor's opinion demolished the case against Frenchy.

The application for executive clemency was based solely upon the ground that Frenchy was innocent. The Governor concluded his report on the case, after reviewing the facts, as follows: "To refuse relief under such circumstances would be plainly a denial of justice, and after a very careful consideration of all the facts I have reached the conclusion that it is clearly my duty to order the prisoner's release."

Frenchy's sentence was commuted on April 16, 1902, and it is understood that the French Government arranged for his transportation back to his native Algerian village.

Frenchy's conviction was apparently due to the zealousness of the New York police in seeking to sustain their boast that the murders which had baffled the London police would not be left unsolved in New York. In Frenchy they found a helpless scapegoat, and there is some ground to believe that the case was worked up against him by insufficient attention to the obvious operative facts. Why no better effort was made to trace the woman's companion or to account for the missing key to Room 31 is not easy to understand. That key was also the key to the mystery. As to the blood spots in the hall and on the door of Room 33, the conclusion seems inescapable that they were not there when Clerk Harrington discovered the murder. How they got there, we shall not venture to say. Let it be assumed that careless visitors dragged the blood around. Nor is it clear how the blood got on Frenchy; there is something very strange about that, which the testimony leaves vague and uncertain. Some of the reporters thought that there was no blood originally on Frenchy, or, if there was any, that it had nothing to do with the murder. The evidence of the experts also seems to have been untrustworthy. In spite of the neatly woven case against Frenchy, the jury evidently had grave doubts, for in such a case a verdict of second-degree murder is not natural. It was manifestly a compromise between a belief in guilt and innocence. Frenchy was also penniless and the assigned counsel could not command the funds to run down the man who had occupied Room 31. The fact that entirely disinterested persons unraveled the mystery attests to the weakness of the prosecution's case and justifies the inference that Allah had apparently not altogether deserted Frenchy.

JACK BE NIMBLE, JACK BE QUICK

A Casual Inquiry into the Theory, Practice —
and Identity — of the Ripper

Stephen Hunter

Best known as a national bestseller for his contemporary thrillers, Stephen Hunter (1946–) has also forged a highly successful career as an author of nonfiction and as a journalist, working as the film critic for *The Baltimore Sun* and *The Washington Post,* winning a Pulitzer Prize for criticism in 2003.

When he set out to leave his comfort zone of narrating the adventures of the Marine sniper Bob "the Nailer" Swagger and similar heroes to write a historical thriller based on the Jack the Ripper murders, he began to do serious research. As a result of those efforts, I, Ripper (2015) has an uncommon authenticity of time, place, language, and society.

The novel also prides itself on the accuracy of the depictions of the murders, both as to what befell the victims and to the locations in which they occurred, with realistic speculations about numerous details of methodology and outside forces.

That research has led to an educated speculation as to the identity of Red Jack. While hundreds of Ripperologists have written convincingly of their own choice for the likely identity of the Ripper, there has been no single name that has been universally accepted by the experts who have devoted years of research and study to Jack. Hunter's exploration of this relentlessly fascinating subject follows—a largely original theory but one supported by convincing pieces of evidence and deduction.

"Jack Be Nimble, Jack Be Quick" was written especially for this collection but was acquired by Ripperologist magazine and published in its August 2015 issue.

Who was Jack the Ripper?

I don't know.

Nobody knows. Two of the best-known theories that claim to be based on forensic science involving DNA (Russell Edwards's and Patricia Cornwell's) are baseless. They disappear into nothingness under the gentlest of scrutiny.

That leaves hundreds of prose essays and books, based on sources, primary or secondary, as forced through a process of applied deduction.

Here's another one, and perhaps it's just as much an epistemological con job of cherry-picked facts arranged along a bias axis as any of them. It represents even less an effort than Edwards's or Cornwell's. I have made no new discoveries, I have done no interviews; I have only traveled to Whitechapel for a week, where I took a Jack the Ripper tour and found it as banal as any tourist attraction. I've had too much beer in the Ten Bells, stood in the vestry at St. Botolph's, the prostitute's church, I've been to all the murder sites—well, I didn't make it to Polly's, because it was too far away from the hotel and I am no longer young. It didn't seem worth it on the last day, as the other four were but dreary pieces of unmarked real estate in a decaying section of London that looked far more like Islamabad than any British city. Polly's promised but more of the same.

In the end, my theory does little but look at and reorganize some classic Jack materials, and it is perhaps illuminated here and there by new insights into methods and means. I think it's a great theory and I will say in its defense it not only identifies a suspect (albeit a well-known one) but it eliminates the other suspects. Additionally, it doesn't turn on some penny-dreadful Freudian reading of someone's psychology. He hated his mum, his da whipped him, he was a sex-deviate from seeing his older sis doing it with the blacksmith in the barn. None of that. I have no idea and not nearly enough imagination to conjure a "motive." My theory is based entirely on suppositions that follow from what was observable about the crimes themselves. It's all drawn from evidence, not bogus insights into the unconscious. In the end, I believe, it proves—at least in the circumstantial sense—that only one man could have and did do the five Whitechapel killings.

First principles. Simplicity. Of each particular thing ask, what is it in itself? What is its nature? What does he do, this man that we seek? Thus: What is the First Thing about Jack? What made Jack Jack? What was the essence of Jack?

It wasn't that he killed five prostitutes or even five women. That had been done before and after and no sordid citation is necessary. It wasn't that London, in 1888 the world's greatest newspaper town with over fifty dailies, boasted a literate, sensation-hungry population of over five million and thus a pool of hungry readers eager for titillation and stimulation, whose maw the press barons fed every morning and night. It wasn't that someone, though probably not Jack, came up with one of the best brand names in history in "Jack the Ripper," an onomatopoeic identifier that penetrated straight to the subconscious like a dart and there struck and stuck forever. (That was the best career move for Jack.) It wasn't the sheer barbarism of what was done to four of the five bodies, bringing to the most civilized city on Earth the lurid imagery seen before only on battlefields and torture chambers. It wasn't that in the end he disappeared, leaving writers high and low, geniuses and charlatans and screwballs and hacks, to write their own endings, however apposite or inapposite to the set up.

It was none of those things, in exactly the same way it was all of them, forming a perfect storm of media, macabre material, folkloric fear, an assault on the modern, and a confirmation of the bestial. But all that was consequence.

*

The fulcrum upon which all of this consequence tipped is often overlooked. It was Marcus Aurelius's and Hannibal Lector's first principle. It was the simple fact that Jack killed quickly and efficiently and silently, a matter, really, of seconds. He never missed his stroke. He never faltered. And afterward—clearly a part of the same attribute of efficiency—he vanished without a trace of a trace. Though his murders took place hard by population concentrations (on residential streets, in the courtyard of a club just after the full blaze of quorum, in a residential square patrolled from two directions every few minutes by bobbies), he got away clean each time. He was as silent as the night, as a cat, as a ninja, as the orang in Poe's "Murders in the Rue Morgue."

Of the five canonical murders we shall closely consider only the first four, which were remarkably similar. The last, of Mary Jane Kelly, on the night of November 9, 1888, took place uncharacteristically indoors. It is a carnival of deviations from the Jack norm. The woman lay abed, on her left side, asleep. The location was her rented room at Miller's Court, off Dorset Street ("London's worst street"), a few blocks from the Ten Bells. She had retired early not having done business, perhaps buzzed from cheap gin (she sang before she fell asleep, a sign of inebriation). He cut her throat on the exposed right side, and she bled out in minutes while he held her down. Many believe that the cut had to be delivered by a left hand, not a right, because he would have used his right to crush her head into the pillow, mooring her for his labor. To account for the discrepancy, some believe he was therefore ambidextrous, having taken four with his right hand and Mary Jane with an equally adroit left. That true ambidexters are quite rare in reality does not seem to faze them.

The other four were all street jobs. The women were so vulnerable to his predation because their profession consisted of leading strange men into the blackness of interior Whitechapel, a maze of alleys and passageways, meandering medieval cow paths now bricked over, and barely lit public squares, locating a secure but hardly private spot, accepting first the thruppence, then a few minutes of vertical rutting. Against a willful, stronger being, a demon from the looks of the carnage, they had no human chance. All were dispatched by deep, strong cuts to the left side of the neck, severing the entwined carotid artery and jugular veins, as performed by a strong right hand. The assumption of death methodology was exsanguination, under the power of the throbbing heart which would continue its mechanical obligation until the brain, issuing its last command, ordered it to shut down. Consciousness would have long since evaporated, in the eight seconds it takes for the brain to empty itself of life-giving, sentience-giving blood. The weapon is thought to be a butcher knife, common to every English kitchen. They died perhaps more quickly than Mary Jane, and in all cases he then did the ghastly things post-mortem that made him so famous. The single exception is Liz Stride, on Berner Street in the courtyard of the International Working Men's Educational Society—sometimes called the Anarchist's Club—where it is thought that he was interrupted by a Mr. Diemschutz, a cheap jewelry peddler, on his pony cart, who arrived at the gateway to the yard after Jack had dispatched the woman but before he began his fun. Somehow, lurking in shadows, Jack got away that night, too.

THE KILLINGS

The question to be answered is alarmingly explicit. It is about methods. Initially, it was believed by most that he approached from the rear, like a commando eliminating a sentry in a movie. With a swift left hand, he reached around to muffle the mouth, stifling any cries, at the same time tipping the chin back to open the throat to cutting. With his right hand, the knife held in fist edge-backward toward flesh, he snaked around the right ear, the face and back to the left ear and then, arm fully encircling and fully extended, pressed the cutting edge against and into the throat, and drew it hard about, severing the artery and vein that were entwined there. As he continued his stroke, his angle to the flesh became difficult and thus the cut became more tenuous.

However, it was noted that in all four cases certain anomalies occurred, so that any discussion of the four women and their victimization must account for them. The first of these is that there was no spatter. Generally, when an artery is nicked or slashed, the pressure from the heart's pumping action forces the flood from the puncture under some propulsion. Thus a pattern of droplets is visible at the crime scene—a later forensic specialty would become the interpretation of these spatter patterns. The laws of hydraulics mean that the smaller the puncture, the farther the spatter will be projected. In none of Jack's four street kills was there any spatter. Why? Second, there was no blood on the front of the victims, that is, upon their dresses, across their bosoms. Instead, the blood coagulated under or to the side of the head, behind and beneath the throat wound. Third—admittedly an inference but surely a sound one—no blood adhered to Jack, as in all cases he exited the scene and re-entered the civilization he had abandoned and although it was late at night, bobbies still patrolled, drunks still cavorted, men still hunted for flesh, and women still sold it, all under a vivid glow from the still-open beer shops and pubs. Yet he was never identified by scarlet splotch so we must assume that he avoided the scarlet splotch.

A solution was soon offered to the lack-of-spatter and the blood-behind-but-not-in-front difficul-ties and it has since become the consensus. Instead of cutting from behind while they were at full verticality with gravity coming into play as the heart pumped, producing copious amounts, he faced them in the dark and, under the guise of offering coin, found a second when they were distracted, and then his left hand lashed out, clamped them about the throat and forced them to the ground. Secured there, pinned and choked, they were helpless as he bent over them and cut with his right hand deep into the left-side neck and its treasure of veins and arteries. The blood, in obedience to gravity, would then flow downward and backward, coming to gather beneath or to the side of the head. It would not mark their chests or his jacket. Under these circumstances, the blood produced would theoretically be appropriate to the blood discovered.

Still, generally, that situation seems quite awkward. He's holding, he's cutting, she's squirming and kicking and writhing, perhaps beating at his pinioning arm, in any event raising a ruckus. Does nobody hear, does nobody notice? It's also hard to believe that he would have brought off this complex physical operation perfectly four times running. It's also hard to believe her dress wouldn't have been much smeared by dirt, abraded by stone, and under it, so too would her flesh. Only one—Annie Chapman, his problem victim—exhibits bruising indicative of some kind of albeit brief struggle.

But more damaging to this claim is that all four were cut completely around the neck, from ear to ear. It's not that such effort was unnecessary, since the first deep cut of vein and artery was sufficient (how would he know?) but the angles of his arms to her body make the transaction extremely awkward. Starting on the left, how does he get his knife all the way around her neck to her far ear? The ground itself offers an impenetrable wall through which he cannot maneuver for better angle. He would have to rotate her or move himself awkwardly to her far right, because the last third of her throat would be in the lee of her head, and he'd find it difficult not merely to cut from that angle but even to reach. That does not say such a cutting was impossible but it certainly makes it seem unlikely and unnatural and unnecessary. Not much notice has been paid to this fact, but it is certainly inconvenient to the on-the-ground fellows.

To explain the lack of spatter, the adherents of this approach suggest the women were already dead by strangulation, thus the heart had stopped beating and nothing propelled the blood into the air. But that opens as many questions as it closes: why would he waste time cutting their throats when they were obviously already dead? It cost time and effort in his fragile public circumstances. Why would the few bruises randomly found on two of the four necks not be coherently organized in the pattern of clenching, choking fingers? Why were no bones broken in the neck? Why would the results be so ambiguous to trained medical examiners? It seems another reason for the lack of spatter and the lack of blood down the front must be found.

There's another limitation to either of these solutions to the how-did-he-cut-them? quandary, not so much for Jack but for anybody trying to understand Jack. It's that neither of them allow much in the way of inference. They imply only the power of the strong over the weak, the tall over the short, the willful over the distracted. Nothing else may be learned from them. No gender may be read into them—a tall, strong woman, a strapping teenage boy, an elderly but determined gentleman, all could equally be suspect—and no other attributes are indicated. We can arrive at no conclusions, much less a next step.

In my rethinking of the four deaths, I put the killer directly in front of and facing the victim. They have arrived at the sex place, in pitch dark—a backyard, a courtyard, a deserted street, an empty square—and now she expects her pay, after some no doubt polite but banal palaver on the walk in. Instead, she gets the blade. It is held in his right hand, but it is not thrust, as none of the women were stabbed when they were alive; nor is it carefully placed for sawing, as the straightness of the cut in three of the four examples suggests that no sawing was done. Instead it arrives at the end of a full-power swing. His arm has flashed out in a crescent and the belly of the blade arrives at speed at the end of a power arc, like the tip of a whip. All muscles of the arm and the right side of the chest propel it, as does, most probably, affiliated hip movement, along the lines of a baseball hitter "stepping into it," which drives the edge to maximum speed. The target is the one inch of neck between the jaw bone and the collar bone. The knife must be held rigidly and furthermore at or very near a ninety-degree angle to the flesh, so that all energy is spent on the penetration of the edge and none on vibration or rebound. The Japanese katana is designed for this type of kill, and, not knowing it, Jack is emulating the killing superiority of that famous weapon.

Driven at such speed, the blade easily cuts epidermis, subcutaneous muscle and tissue, and the carotid highway of blood. That is, it cuts it completely, so the "puncture" is not a nick or a gash or even a rip, it is the diameter of the whole artery itself. That diminishes or at least does not radically increase its pressure, again by the rules of hydraulics. Ergo: no spatter. Instead of spraying or spurting or hose-piping, the thick, oxygenated blood wells, gurgles, even burbles from the interruption, and, following gravity, it runs into the opened cavity itself, but also outside to some degree, down the body, principally (as she is inclining rearward in recoil to the blow) down her back.

Still, the heart would pump for thirty seconds to two minutes, and so much blood being driven outward might not spatter but it surely would not limit itself to her back; it could not be controlled nor predicted. So obviously another mechanism must be in play.

And that is that Jack's cut was so well placed and so efficient that it not only sheared the carotid but the jugular as well as the two are entwined about each other in a sheathing of muscle in the neck. One is artery, one is vein; they course between heart and brain, but in different directions, and it is the jugular that is far more important here. It is the one that moves deoxygenated blood to the heart from the brain.

When it is cut completely, the blood from the brain simply empties from the upper segment into the body cavity, draining consciousness from the victim. However, in the lower of the two segments, still linked to the heart, still under power of the palpitating spasms of the vein, the remaining blood continues its journey. As it moves, it sucks or draws in air behind its path from and through the violently administered new portal. The action is similar to that of the plunger on a syringe as it is raised to draw in liquid medicine for injection. The air, in no small quantities, for it increases as the blood recedes, reaches the heart in four seconds.

This is called an air embolism. It is a catastrophic event. Lodging at the nexus of the four chambers it stops the heart more surely than a .45 bullet dispatched into the same spot. That is what kills—instantaneously upon arrival—all four street victims. That is what stops the heart, stops the pumping, stops the spatter and limits the blood loss merely to smallish amounts that drain when the victim is laid out on the ground.

Jack, meanwhile, oblivious to the heart mechanics that have already concluded his drama, is still cutting. Encountering no planet to halt his progress to the back side of the body, he rotates quickly around her, to catch her, for her raw fall to earth might strike something and make it break or bounce loudly. As he rotates, he draws the knife through her neck. It is not graceful but it is effective and he believes it necessary. Doing so to a woman flat on the ground would have been impossible, without turning her or in other ways disturbing the body and thus spreading the blood puddles. Additionally, cutting an entire circle, particularly that troublesome last third under her far ear, is quite natural in that it flows, it continues an act, it completes the ritual of throat-cutting.

As for his poor victim, her brain suddenly deprived of oxygen, she loses consciousness in four to six seconds but her heart has already stopped beating because of the impediment at its nexus; by that time, he is fully around her and as her knees go, he already grips her intimately, and now he eases her to the ground onto her back, so what blood does flow, flows backward and downward. She probably has no idea what's happened to her, for in the dark, and not paying any attention to anything but her mind's eye where she sees the thruppence and the glass of gin it will subsequently buy, she does not see the flash of the blade but merely feels its sudden impact, like a punch that knocks her backward, then sees lights go off, and then utter dizziness invades her sensibilities and then it's over. Her conscious brain has never noticed that she has been slain.

All the anomalies have been accommodated: No blood has been driven to spatter, none has fallen to the front, none has gotten to him, as his arms and hands are well clear of the ruptured zone.

He gets on with it. But what happens next is of little concern to her or to us: the point is that she has died exactly as he needed her to do so, without fuss or noise, without scream or turbulence, and without a lot of blood spilled, with little of it on him. He has accomplished the first part of the double task that makes Jack Jack.

THE CUT

Let us examine this blow. What does it tell us about Jack, other than the obvious, that he was a murderer and very lucky? Unlike the other possible blows evoked, this one arrives freighted with information and, moreover, it leads somewhere, explicitly.

The first thing it tells us is that Jack had extraordinary eyesight; he saw where others—most others—would not have. He saw in darkness with far more efficiency than a normal fellow. He was able to pin his eyesight exactly on the small part of her anatomy between jawbone and collarbone beneath the ear, for only in riveting it with such intent gaze could he guide his hand to it. As any coach tells any boy, "You've got to keep your eye on the ball," for the coach knows, and Jack knows, that in the visual cue is the access to the brain's inner program that solves angles of deflection, adjusts for movement of target, and encourages such good habits as keeping the head down and following through. Moreover, such vision is really not a skill that can be learned. It is strictly biomechanical. One has it—fighter pilots, .300 hitters, great shooters, for example—or one doesn't, and one can't learn it or pick it up from a mentor. As we shall see, Jack's unusual vision paid other benefits as well.

Second, he has great hand-speed and strength. They are not the same, as a fast man may be weak or a strong man slow. But a gifted man has them both, and he was so gifted he was able to power his hand to extraordinary swiftness as it traced its arc through the Whitechapel night. His strength is manifested in the firmness by which he holds the blade; when he makes contact with the flesh, it is so clamped it does not deviate from the necessary ninety-degree katana cutting angle, the vibrations of its travel through the neck do not loosen it, it does not wobble or yaw, thereby losing velocity and power. It is held so firm that it achieves the maximum efficiency, penetrating as far as its strength can drive it and thereby not nicking or even ripping the carotid and jugular but sundering them totally.

It should also be noted here that vision and hand-strength (as well as suppleness) feature in an attribute of Jack's not usually explained. That is his penchant for removing interior parts of his victims while mutilating them in his post-murder frenzy. His motive for such action remains, shall we say, obscure; nevertheless, it was clearly on his agenda. Many have found the missing parts an indication of surgical or at least medical knowledge. But regardless of the impossibility to understand whether he did or did not know enough with or without a medical education to remove those parts, it is incontrovertible that extremely good eyesight and unusually strong, dexterous hands were absolutely necessary to bring such desecrations off, particularly in the short time frame during which he worked on the bodies. These bits cannot have been easy to see in dark circumstances and manipulating them to achieve their removal demanded strength. His powerful eyes and his strong hands were the key. Again, it's a case of none-but-the-extraordinary need apply.

And since the subject of Jack's organ-snatching has come up, it's a nice spot to address that subject in a larger context. As I stated before it is impossible, in my view, to infer from the evidence whether or not Jack was surgically or medically trained; as well, one cannot conclude that he was a butcher, a veterinarian, a Jewish kosher slaughterer, a samurai, or a Waziri tribal assassin. One can conclude, in fact, nothing. However, one must still conclude that it is indisputable that any education in anatomy was certainly helpful to Jack. Surgeon or not, butcher or not, whatever or not, if he knew the reality of cutting into the body and encountering and overcoming the shock of exposure to blood and the slippery, slithery innards of all mammals, that would go a long way in his chosen profession of murdering, then mutilating, prostitutes. It may have even been what lured him into the game in the first place, and thus acquaintanceship with these intimacies in any form, no matter how vague or incidental, cannot be discounted.

Back to the blow. Implied by the previous attributes, it is finally clear that Jack possesses unusually high hand-eye coordination. He is able to perform complex, even refined, physical movements at speed upon demand. His system—the strength, the accuracy, the sureness—are overall governed by a kind of physical genius by which what he envisions he can perform without much mental effort.

And the final implication here and the facilitator for what has happened before is that Jack is confident. This is not an experiment, it is a destiny. He knows his powers and what must be done to get maximum use of them. He is able to focus on a tiny, poorly (if at all) illuminated, essentially a 1" by 2" rectangle that represents neck and is guarded above by jawbone and below by collarbone, launch a sweeping blow at full strength and strike dead center, four times running. A vulgar comparison would be to a golf swing. It looks so easy; it is so hard. To do such requires great physical skill, but also experience. Clearly he has performed such a strike before, perhaps in moments of urgency, exhaustion, high drama, desperate straits.

THE ESCAPES

Five times he murdered, always in the heart of the city. Though it was late at night, he was never far from concentrations of population. Polly Nichols was sent over on a public street, with bobbies converging on the spot within minutes; sleeping civilians were but feet from him on either side of the street. Annie Chapman was done in the backyard of an apartment house at 29 Hanbury Street, really up against that building. On either side loomed other apartment buildings and in all three buildings people slept, dreamed, dozed, and masturbated, some few of them with windows open. Only one witness, an Albert Cadoche, heard someone say "No," on the other side of the fence at 29 Hanbury and then heard a loud thump against the fence. But no one else heard or suspected a thing until, within an hour or so, enough sun had risen so that an early awakener could see the body. The yard in question was seemingly sealed off by stout five-foot-five-inch fences, requiring him to escape down a hallway to Hanbury Street, itself not far from well-lit Brick Lane. Liz Stride got hers inside the gateway to Dutfield's Yard, just off Berner Street. The yard abutted and had an entrance for the Berner Street ("Anarchist's") club, which was at the time occupied by leftover acolytes from the evening's revolutionary meeting. Moreover, on the other side of the gateway, dwellings housed sleeping workers. Later that same evening, he obliterated Kate Eddowes in Mitre Square, a few hundred feet off Aldgate Road, close by the Whitechapel (Aldgate) Road–Commercial Street intersection, literally in the front yard of one and near to other occupied dwellings, close to a warehouse with an alert night watchman and in a zone well patrolled by and about to be penetrated from two directions by bobbies. Finally, his last and most grotesque crime took place in Mary Jane Kelly's rented room, which lay in the heart of Miller's Court, just down from the Ten Bells and off Dorset Street, and was accessible only by a narrow walkway between buildings which opened to a sort of crevice in the slum architecture. The crevice fronted thirteen apartments on two levels, all of them occupied.

Was he lucky? Certainly; his near misses with bobbies and bystanders, like Mr. Diemschutz, the pony-cartman who entered the open gate to Dutfield's while Jack was beginning his work on Liz Stride, testify to luck, while also advancing the truism that fortune favors the bold. Was he brilliant? There seems to be little evidence of that, for the sites weren't particularly well chosen and if anything they represent not cunning but his confidence that he could improvise his way out of anything. There's no evidence, further, that he planned or reconnoitered them; his locations seem random, presented to him not by logic but by the whimsy of the game he was hunting. He can have done no research or scouting as to the locations and patterns of the bobbies, for he came so close to falling into their net so many times. But he had one thing few killers have, as we have already seen it in play in the killings themselves—that is an uncanny strength, vision, and balance.

At the site of the first murder, that of Polly Nichols on the night of August 31, maps show that not far from the street side location of the crime on Buck's Row, a bridge crossed the wide furrow that contained the East London Railway tracks which had just emerged from their tunnel and ran into the Whitechapel Station on Whitechapel High Street, a block to the east. It would have to be at least twenty-five or thirty feet from Buck's Row to the track beds, too far for a free jump without risk of shattering ankles. Moreover, as photos show, usually high, perhaps six- or seven-foot brick walls guard access to those track beds, forbidding passage to nearly all. Still, it was but seconds from the murder site. A man of power could have climbed over the wall by hoisting himself on sheer arm and chest strength high enough to get a leg up for leverage and by that method, pulled himself over. The leap from the wall atop the bridge would have been suicidal but while no illustrations of the bridge seem to exist, it was the fashion of Victorian bricklayers to embellish. Thus one can presume certain elements of decor—anything from generic bas-relief of heroic or inspirational nature to geometric shapes as simple as rectangles within rectangles or perhaps even an array of round shapes like crop circles—to have been inscribed on the exterior of the bridge walls. Though such cuts would not allow any normal man enough purchase to secure himself, an extraordinary one, gifted with great balance as well as incredible hand-strength, could have eased his way down via the edges of the bas-relief or blooming flower until he hung fully extended from the lower part of the bridge. The drop then is halved, from thirty feet to fifteen feet. Down he goes, breaking his fall with a roll. Then he escapes by moving quickly along the track beds toward the west, and finds another fence or wall over which to disappear, or dips into the deserted (because no trains were running) tunnel and thence reaches a station and hides in the loo until the morning crowds. Because the walls make the track bed all but invisible to the bobbies who arrive in minutes when the body is discovered, they search only on ground level; it never occurs to them (or anybody) that he has descended beneath ground level.

The death of Annie Chapman at 29 Hanbury in the next month provides similar opportunities. The passageway through that building was a known rutting spot for prostitutes, and she presumably took him down it for the act. He talked her—or brutalized her, explaining the lack of neatness at this murder site alone—into continuing through it, which deposited them into the backyard. There, he finished her and had his butcher's fun against the building.

His exit has always been problematic. The yard was on all sides fenced by stout, five-foot-five-inch barriers. Getting over them would have been awkward if not impossible for any save the most gifted man. But for Jack as I see him, a gymnastic vault of some sort, a support of upper body by strong arms and shoulders and a pendulum swing of paralleled legs gets him over in seconds; after the more challenging ordeal at Buck's Row it might have even seemed easy. He perhaps travels from yard to yard in this fashion, sticking close to the buildings so as to be invisible from any upper-story watchers, just a flash to any at ground level. That certainly would have been preferable to an exit back out the 29 Hanbury passageway to Hanbury Street, for he has no idea who is out there and it's on a well-known bobby patrol route. Additionally, late-night sensualists may be using it to cross from Whitechapel High Street to Brick Lane for a commercial hookup, as both were known avenues of temptation. Why would he risk encountering someone that way, giving a witness a good description, perhaps even being apprehended by an alert copper?

But the most compelling evidence of Jack's legerdemain as an escapist comes next, on September 30, the night of the famous double event. This was the killing (of Elizabeth Stride) interrupted by Mr. Diemschutz and his pony, opening the gate to Dutfield's Yard off Berner Street at the inopportune moment after Jack has slain but before he has started to mutilate. Jack almost certainly cottoned to the upcoming interruption when he heard the clip-clop of the pony arriving to the gate as it turned off Berner Street. On that signal, unless he was a fool, he retreated back into the dark yard, finding a place in the shadows to crouch. Meanwhile Mr. Diemschutz noticed something lying at the edge of the building just inside the gate. Climbing down from his cart and then striking a match, he saw that it was a body, screamed when he saw the blood in the light of a match, then hastened past it and entered the club, where a batch of kibitzing leftovers from the night's meeting still remained, to raise an alarm.

Consider Jack's dilemma. He has seen Diemschutz go for help and knows it will soon be there. Alas, his only portal of escape would seem to be that same gate. He would have to race to it, slither by the pony cart which partially blocks the passageway, praying that he does not agitate or cause a ruckus on the part of the horse. He is worried that men will pour out of the club. Even if they don't, and having made it to the gate, he will find himself on Berner Street and from his angle in the yard has no idea who or what awaits him there. Perhaps bobbies swarm in his direction from a nearby station, or the workers are streaming out of the Berner Street Club or lights have gone on and people peer out of windows on Berner across from the club. In any event, it seems a risky passage.

And another factor must be added, that of time. For we know that not forty-five minutes later, having successfully escaped from Dutfield's, Jack has found, killed, and wretchedly mutilated Catherine Eddowes at Mitre Square 1,750 paces (I've counted them) away. So whatever he did, he did swiftly and surely and without second thought.

Was there some kind of tunnel exit? No investigation ever suggested, much less found, one. However, there was, or so it seems to me, another way out—for Jack at least. The one reasonably contemporary photo of Dutfield's in the configuration which Jack found it that night—it was taken in 1900 and is displayed like a trophy in Philip Hutchinson's *The Jack the Ripper Location Photographs*—shows in reality what many maps describe schematically. That is, directly back from the gate to Dutfield's Yard, there's a two-story bungalow containing the Hindley and Co. cabinet factory with a stairway up to a second-story entrance which is fronted by a kind of balcony or porch. The roof is low to the porch and appears to be covered in arched pottery stones, giving much traction. Does no one except me see how easy it would have been for a climber of Jack's natural aptitude, with his strength, balance, and superior night vision, to climb those stairs, go to railing and from railing by his strength hoist himself to roof, and via balance and vision navigate the roof as a kind of stroll to escape? I certainly couldn't do it, and I doubt anyone reading these pages could either, but the Jack I believe defined by his attributes as I have identified them, could do so easily, quickly, and decisively, thus making the meeting with unfortunate Mrs. Eddowes with time to spare.

Of the last two murders, neither offers such obvious candidates for orang-escape as do the first three. However, the two—at Mitre Square and, November 9, 1888, then at Miller's Court—do have in common narrow passages into and out. I do not do so, but one making this argument less responsibly but more wittily could argue that, particularly at Mitre Square, where the coppers were just seconds away, Super Jack could have crab-walked up the narrow passageway—hands braced against one wall, boots against the other, advancing skyward a step at a time—and sustained himself in such a position and in such darkness that he avoided a copper who passed underneath. It's a little too Batman-like to seem feasible, but it is not impossible by any law of physics or strength. Any Hollywood stuntman of the '30s could have done so.

At Miller's Court, entry into the nest of rooms and apartments was also gained by a narrow brick passageway that ran in from Dorset Street, but it had a low roof above it and so I do not contemplate any Batman-gymnastics there. However, the passageway which allows him entrance on the way out offers the same tactical disadvantages of several others: he has no idea who or what awaits at its end, when he reaches Dorset Street that rainy Friday morning. Coppers, pilgrims, a squad of angry unfortunates, a Jewish chicken merchant headed toward Goulston Street poultry market, sharp-eyed workers aimed toward the foundries and mills? All are possible, all, with a good visual ID, could spell doom. Yes, fortune favors the bold but it does not favor the stupid and so he possibly avoided the problem altogether.

Descriptions of Miller's Court as well as maps describe a place best seen as all crammed up with stuff. A lot of small rooms crowd into very little area with the "court" a minimal opening in the structure to give frontage and access to the nest of dwellings. No details survive, but given that, and given the height of only two stories, it does not seem impossible at all that my Jack, wisely shunning the passageway to Dorset Street, might easily find a sequence of handholds—sills, railings, gutter pipes, shutter hinges—by which he boosted himself to roof level and crossed to another building on another street. From that vantage point, he could easily see if witnesses abounded and if so wait until they had left the area and pick a time to descend unseen.

Does this begin to seem silly? Jack as gymnastic superhero, climbing and creeping his way out of tight spots on the fly while bobbies search for him only on ground level. I suppose it does. But at least it goes coherently to one and only one conclusion. That is, whatever he was and whatever he was not, this man we seek was an expression of power, grace, coordination, vision, balance, and most of all, confidence. In other words: he was an athlete.

THE USUAL SUSPECTS

Generally there are between four and seven "classic suspects" as Jack the Ripper. They usually include Aaron Kosminski, Michael Ostrog, George Chapman (also known as Severin Klosowski), Nathan Kaminski, Walter Sickert, and Montague John Druitt. Note, of course, the predominance of immigrants of Polish-Jewish ancestry; clearly, Britons wanted Jack to be an "other," an "outsider," not one of their own fair boys. This bias comes into play frequently in the whole Jack affair. The German-born Sickert is the English artist included by Patricia Cornwell's insistence. It should be obvious but must be stated nevertheless that all save one fails to demonstrate the attributes that I have just delineated.

There are other problems with those candidates as well. I leave to anyone with curiosity to turn to specifics in any of the hundreds of sources ("Casebook: Jack the Ripper," casebook.org, is a superb starting spot). But let me lay out a perhaps larger and less obvious one not mentioned at Casebook. That is that each "theory" justifying each candidate is not really a theory at all. It is instead a new kind of rhetorical gambit which I call an "aggregation of confluence." This technique does not point exactly at one man and explain how his attributes made it possible for him to commit these crimes and at the same time exclude all others. Instead, it examines the external circumstances of the suspect's life and labor to search out facts that prove that he was there then—he was in Whitechapel, or at least London, on each of the nights in the fall of 1888 when the five women were slain. Then, usually, it examines his past for "similar" incidents or tendencies or it examines his future for the same, patches on a little penny-ante Freudian jabber and thus, ipso facto, the Ripper. Would that it were so easy.

Yes, they may well have been there, but that only proves opportunity and neglects to mention that in the immediate London area, there were at least five million other souls, nine hundred thousand of them in the East End, seventy-six thousand in Whitechapel, with the same opportunity. As for mental illness, it is neither here nor there. Any man's life, examined closely enough, yields the occasional theme or practice of irrationality such as odd agitations, peculiarities of dress or habit, feuds in family, church, or workplace, tendencies toward melancholy, perhaps even explosions of ill-tempered (but never close to fatal) violence. From there, confirmation bias takes over and the declaration of guilt is issued. The only criterion appears to be proximity; no attempt is made to identify the attributes the killer must have had and locate them in the suspect pool.

In two widely publicized cases, forensic manipulations are involved. The thriller writer Patricia Cornwell submits in *Portrait of a Killer* that the DNA found on a stamp on a confessional letter sent the London Police was that of the artist Walter Sickert. It helps her case, she thinks, that Sickert was a moody, violent man and he was known to be particularly agitated by Jack. He even painted a picture called *Jack the Ripper's Bedroom,* which hangs in a Manchester museum and sees Jack's figure disassembled into a shimmering series of broken reflections, which she interprets as a representation of a broken, perhaps even shattered, personality. But many artists, probably including Cornwell and me, have broken personalities and we are not serial killers and mutilators, we're just rather annoying people. Moreover, in the end, even accepting the less rigorous mitochondrial DNA—as opposed to nuclear DNA—testing which she used and which only identifies groups, not individuals, she merely places him in the group of people who write crazy letters to the police. Since all gaudy crimes attract hundreds of confessional letters, why should this one be considered any more credible than any of the others? Surely there are thousands more crazy letter writers than serial murderers.

The second case is that of Russell Edwards, whose recent book *Naming Jack the Ripper* claimed that DNA findings identified popular suspect Aaron Kosminski, a Jewish hairdresser in Whitechapel, as the murderer. Again, passing on a discussion of the technical issues of the mitochondrial DNA testing and its much lower reliability than nuclear DNA, let's briefly examine the nuts and bolts of this claim.

It seems specious on its face. Edwards believes that he is in possession of a shawl which Jack carried with him the night he killed Catherine Eddowes in Mitre Square. He makes little of the fact that if so, because it was the night of the double event, Jack would have had this shawl with him during the murder of Elizabeth Stride. He would have had to have it with him over the course of his escape from Dutfield's Yard which may have involved climbing and leaping and jumping. He would have had to have it with him on his 1,750-step walk to Mitre Square, where he met, then murdered, then mutilated Mrs. Eddowes. And . . . *after all the trouble to take it along, he forgot it!* He left it at the scene of the second murder and thus it has both Jack's (i.e., Kosminski's) and Eddowes's (merely and not peer-reviewed) mitochondrial DNA upon it, linking them in the crime.

It gets better. The shawl, as a clue, is taken to the morgue and there it is given as a gift or souvenir to a policeman, whose family owned it until Edwards bought it at auction. Rather hard to believe, because by that time the Jack murders gripped the London and the world imagination so it seems quite unlikely these fellows would have let a clue disappear like that. And it gets even more ridiculous when one realizes that the crime was committed not in London but in the City of London, an administrative oddity of the great city which puts an entirely different municipal government in charge of a patch in the middle of a much bigger municipal government. Thus the shawl, if it exists (it is not recorded in the otherwise well-kept and highly professional City of London files of the crime), fell under the administrative purview of the smaller entity. But the policeman who claimed he received it was from the larger, surrounding entity, namely the London Metropolitan Police. Not only that, he was from an outlying district and had no clear business being in any proximity to the Ripper investigation. The policeman was, in other words, a complete stranger to the men he received the shawl from, not a colleague and constant morgue hanger-on whose friendship with the technicians might carry some weight. And finally and of course, there's no documentation for any of this; it's simply family lore, handed down generation by generation over one hundred–odd years. And of course there was no chain of custody to the shawl recorded, and no quarantine protocols were enforced, so it could have been touched, vomited or sneezed upon, spit on, used to wipe up baby's poos, or anything that cloth is used for in a household. For over a century!

MONTY

Montague John Druitt was born August 15, 1857, in Wimborne, Dorset, to a stable, upper-middle-class family. His father was a doctor as would both a brother and a cousin become, suggesting a household well-fortified in medical reality, not a requisite for Jack suspicion, but not without some weight either. He was well educated, as befits the station of his people, at Winchester and New College, Oxford, from which he graduated with a third class degree in the classics. His time at both establishments was marked by intense involvement in debating societies, where he generally chose denouncing liberals and liberalism as his primary focus. That, of course, is another neither-here-nor-there phenomenon although—thin, I know—one might presume from it a certain emotional intensity of an awkward nature. It could also be argued—now it's getting *really* thin—his conservative politics point to nativism and anti-immigration bias and from that it's an easy leap to an anti-Semitism which evinced itself the night of the double event when Jack may have left what may have been an unfinished anti-Semitic graffito in a doorway.

Anyhow, a photo of the younger Druitt shows a handsome man with cleft chin, strong nose, steady eyes, tight mouth and his hair, abundant, parted after the Victorian fashion, down the middle. He wore no facial hair then. It's the face of a soldier, a barrister, a politician: calm, unflinching, eyes fixed on duty ahead. It's the face of the British Empire in the high Victorian age; nothing in it indicates that he was Jack the Ripper.

He comes to us in that identity via a memorandum from Inspector Melville Macnaghten, chief constable of Scotland Yard, which, in 1894, declared, "From private information I have little doubt that his own family suspected this man of being the Whitechapel murderer; it was alleged that he was sexually insane." He repeated the claim in another file.

None of this is breaking news and will come as a disappointment to someone invested in dramatic discovery. Druitt's guilt or innocence has been argued aggressively for a number of decades, and anyone with an even rudimentary knowledge of the case will recognize his name. In Pick-Jack polls of Ripperologists over the years, he comes in as high as No. 3 and as low as No. 9. Though that in itself is of no consequence, it shows how well and thoroughly he's been examined. Three books (*Autumn of Terror* by Tom Cullen, *Ripper Suspect: The Secret Lives of Montague Druitt* by D. J. Leighton, and *Jack the Ripper* by Daniel Farson) have been written advocating his guilt and a fourth, *Jack the Ripper: Case Solved 1891*, was published in October 2015 by J. J. Hainsworth, an Australian, who picked up his trail in that country, to which many of Druitt's relatives emigrated after his possible involvement became known. Perhaps the Aussie will come up with something that has thus far evaded me: actual evidence.

Druitt's public life and career as an adult was difficult, haunted by failure, loss, severe interior doubt and, killing aside, what was surely bad behavior by Victorian standards. He decided to practice law but also had a passionate pedagogical inclination, and he taught at Mr. George Valentine's School, in

Blackheath, London, a distinguished public institution. He never married. As a solicitor, opinions on his success vary. As a teacher, all commentators understand but variously interpret the fact that he was fired from his part-time teaching post at Valentine's. Though a reason has never been established, some suspect that homosexuality was involved, even child molestation. It is also true that he lost both of his parents within a few years immediately previous to 1888—his father died, his mother was sent to an asylum—and that insanity and a proclivity to suicide ran in the family. His mother died in the asylum and previous relatives had committed suicide; moreover relatives in later years committed suicide.

All these facts are open to interpretation and depending on one's advocacy, they may be used to either bolster or attack the case.

What is not open to controversy is that he was a lifelong athlete, and that alone among the classic suspects he had the physical tools to accomplish the five murders that none of the others came close to possessing. His most public sport was cricket, where opinions vary as to his skills. He was clearly somewhere between average and better than average, his bowling being the strongest part of his game.

"Druitt was granted a spot in the Winchester First Eleven (cricket)," says Casebook, "and was a member of the Kingston Park and Dorset Country Cricket Club. He was noted to have had formidable strength in his arms and wrists, despite his gaunt appearance in surviving photographs. Druitt also became quite talented at Fives, winning the Doubles and Single Five titles at Winchester and Oxford."

His efforts include championships for both Winchester and New College and a post-collegiate career, membership on traveling teams (in cricket clubs well-wired into the English aristocracy) and, as well, a hobby or third job as a "ringer," that is, a bowler for hire who railroaded to villages on the outskirts of London and played in their ardent local leagues.

Many still find puzzling the fact that it can be proven (by newspaper records) that twice he proceeded by trains the day after Jack killings in the fall of 1888 and participated in such matches. To some, this is evidence that he could not be Jack. As it turns out, as many have determined, the physics of the travel—meaning the times of the murders juxtaposed to the times of the train journeys—works out, if barely. As a matter of factuality, yes, he could have committed the crimes and still traveled to and played in the matches.

However the real objection to this possibility is usually psychological. How, many wonder, could a man go from unleashing the most revolting slaughter upon the poor unfortunates and then blithely catch a train, travel, and spend the afternoon bowling for dollars. And at Druitt's level of athletic sophistication, there could be nothing casual about his sports duty; he would have demanded of himself total immersion in the sport, total concentration of the mind and total engagement of his imagination. His paying clients would have accepted no less. How is such a thing possible?

Again, athletic ignorance seems to be at play here, and judgments are being issued by men who've never bowled, batted, caught, jumped, dodged, tackled, or sprinted a second in their lives. My argument—I have minor athletic credentials, including a long-ago state championship—is that not only is such a thing possible, it is probable, even mandatory. My theory of Druitt's illness is that he was what might be called a "remorseful psychotic." Most of the time he knew his impulses were evil, he hated himself for harboring them, he took pleasure in denying them for as long as possible; however, pressure and longing built, will evaporated, fantasy rehearsal became his predominant mind-set, and at a certain point, he could no longer deny them and he committed them in an almost masturbatory frenzy, increasingly barbaric at each outing. The crime scenes certainly support that theory.

Spent as if having ejaculated (though, for the record, he—or rather Jack—left no trace of having done so), he felt crushing remorse. This theme will come into play later, but one can see how his sports offered him an escape from his pain and self-hatred. The match was so all-encompassing a universe that it drove out of his mind images of the red death he had visited upon the unfortunate the night before. One might go so far as to suggest that the date to play was his triggering mechanism, not the moon phase, the weather, the temperature, the kabala, the demands of Masonic ritual, or the Satanist's pentagram. Knowing he had a match, knowing that he would naturally slip into the forgetful, healing bliss that intense sport brings with it, he gave vent to his feelings on the night before.

But cricket is not the vessel that contains the real relationship between his murderer's life and his athletic life. Instead, and I am amazed that no one else has picked up on this, it was his immersion in the game of Fives, or Eton Fives, that most prepared him for his killings.

At this arcane sport he was indeed truly distinguished, one of his country's best. Fives is a wall-ball sport, in which either singly or in two-man teams, players used gloved hands to smack a cork and rubber ball (in size between a golf ball and a baseball) off a three-wall containment and score points by hitting shots their opponents cannot return. The floor isn't just flat as in all other hand- and racket-ball sports, however; at a certain point it is broken down the middle by a two-inch ledge meant to trip and spill the unwary and, oddly to my experience, it also features a blockage on the left side, a sort of cement abutment extending outwards from the left-side court wall about ten inches and rising to about five feet in height, which complicates the angle calculation that lies at the heart of winning strategy, as well as promising the forgetful a brutal comeuppance. The bruise factor in high-level play must be astonishing. (If I had to guess, I'd say the abutment is a relic of the first court, at Eton, which cannot have been a court at all but just a niche in the wall, which the boys put to ingenious athletic use.) The rules are necessarily rigid, and I won't go into them, because I have no idea what they are. My ignorance of them, however, doesn't preclude the observation that the basic shot in Eton Fives, one which Druitt must have mastered and brought off many thousands of times, is almost identical to, and depends upon the same obligations and principles, as the killing stroke he utilized on the Whitechapel streets four times.

The problem to be solved is intercepting a small target with a precise swing, bringing hand to target with full strength and full speed. In one, the hand wears a glove; in the other it grips the knife. In one the target is a moving ball, in the other it is a briefly stationary couple of inches of neck, shielded in tough bone. Whichever, the perpetrator needs superb hand-eye coordination, superb vision, superb body management, superb confidence. He must read the flight of the target, move to position himself appropriately, manage his feet to the most efficient launch position, set his hips, load his arm, and deliver. Then he must keep his head down, his eyes on the target, transfer his weight from one hip to the other as he rotates toward his interception, thus uncoiling a deeper throb of power, guiding the arm in flight while making subtle grip alterations for spin or to keep the knife at right angles to the neck, remaining firm at contact and, another necessity, following through, keeping his head down, and his concentration absolute.

But let us not forget the anomaly of Mary Jane Kelly. Recall that many have argued that he killed her with his left hand, pinning her head to the mattress with his right. That feels most logical given his position vis-à-vis hers. To justify, these acolytes argue for ambidextrousness as the facilitating factor. But is true ambidextrousness really necessary? Jack is not required to pitch both ends of a double-header with separate arms or play a piano concerto for one hand both lefty and righty. His threshold of off-hand usage is merely to administer a deep, straight, powerful cut to a sleeping woman's exposed neck.

The key here again must be Eton Fives. It is an ambidextrous sport, and it requires considerable usage and development of the weak hand to excel, as Monty surely had achieved. It is not a racquet sport, like racquetball or squash but a glove sport, like American handball. Thus there is no backhand, as speeds are too fast and the area too limited for the turn and dip and re-grip and footwork reset of a tennis or racquetball backhand, to say nothing of the fact that no co-equal obverse striking face is available for a return shot from the weak side. The players wear gloves on both hands and when compelled to do so, they will intercept and counterstrike the ball with the weak hand, in order to offer a defensive shot to prolong the point until a winner is possible. Monty must have done this thousands of times.

That means that over time his weak hand became less weak until it was finally not so weak at all. While it almost never achieved the fluency of his right, it was driven by well-developed musculature and guided by deep muscle memory. He had certainly achieved a fair dexterity. More important, he became used to using it as a solution to certain tactical problems. Thus in diverting to his left hand to cut Mary Jane, he was doing nothing particularly new to himself; it must have felt quite natural, so natural that he didn't even note that he was doing it.

Excelling at such a sophisticated sport takes a rare gift. Clearly it was given to Druitt. Clearly—it seems to me—he used it not in search of glory but damnation.

WITNESSES AND DEATH

Though it is not widely known, eight witnesses saw four of the five victims with men a short time before their murders. It was rainy, it was dark, they had no reason to stare and note, they themselves were probably abuzz with gin or stout, they were trying to get laid or had just gotten laid, they were worried about the excuse to be given to their better halves, whatever . . . but still the descriptions are almost remarkably similar. Taken together, the accounts of Elizabeth Darrell, J. Best, John Gardner, William Marshall, Matthew Packer, Constable William Smith, James Brown, Israel Schwartz, Joseph Lawende, and George Hutchinson come up with a composite. They agree that each victim was in the company of a broad-shouldered man in his mid-30s around five feet five inches, with a bowler or some kind of headgear, a heavy or full-length coat and a mustache. That could be three million men in London, particularly when you consider that the average height of a British male in 1888 was about five foot five. But it could also be, quite easily, Monty Druitt, whose height was never described as unusually tall or short and who would thus be around the unremarkable average. Add his late mustache and broad shoulders and athletic mien and the composite, though far from certain, certainly does not exclude him.

There is more, of course. I have been coy about it, but those familiar with the case are fully aware that a short time after the last of the canonical Jack deaths—Mary Jane Kelly's deconstruction on November 9—he killed himself by drowning himself in the Thames. And all know that after the Mary Kelly atrocity, there were no more murders that bore the Jack signature.

It's easy to make too much of this, but at the same time, it certainly fits with the idea of the remorseful psychotic. In my theory, having, in Mary's case, gone beyond the threshold of the barbaric into the realm of the truly insane, he swore to himself he would never do the deed again. But as before, the pressure to do so grew and grew in him, until, a month later—he was last seen alive December 3, 1888—he knew it was a case of killing another or himself. He chose himself, packed stones in his pockets and walked into the river. The body was not found until December 31, 1888, much decomposed.

It's true that most people who commit suicide aren't murderers. It's also true that some of them are. Anti-Druittists point out that there was enough woe in his life to manage to set off a fervor for self-destruction; for example, it was on November 30 that he was dismissed from Valentine's school. That may have been "the reason," but it might also have been the famous straw whose breakage finally brought down the camel. As well, his commission of the murders may have destabilized him so fiercely that his teaching grew erratic and worrisome. The firing may have been a symptom, not a cause. Clearly his mental state was in his mind in his last days. He left a note to his brother, found in his room at Valentine's. "Since Friday, I felt that I was going to be like mother, and the best thing for me was to die."

Friday, of course, was the day of his firing. But the day of Mary Jane Kelly's death was also Friday.

THE CASE

Any explanation of the four street deaths must include justification for three anomalies: the lack of blood spatter, the lack of blood on the chests of the victims and the lack of blood on Jack, as inferred by his escape through crowded streets. Additionally, it must demonstrate speed and silence and a reasonable explanation as to the delivery of the cuts, particularly to the last third of the neck on the victim's right-hand side.

The only anatomical explanation is that while standing and facing each victim, Jack drove his blade with extreme force and coordination horizontally through the neck, totally sundering both carotid and jugular. In severing, rather than piercing, the carotid, the pressurized blood from the heart did not spurt and spatter because it was not subject to passing through an orifice of smaller diameter. By sundering the jugular, the blood in the lower segment of the vein, connected directly to the heart, drew in air as it retreated downward and in four seconds or less, produced a fatal air embolism. That explains why the deaths were so swift and silent. Meanwhile, the killer rotated around the victim's body to his left, drawing the knife around while at the same time supporting her as she sagged backward. Upon completion, he laid her down on her back.

Only Montague John Druitt had the athletic ability to make that stroke four times running, using techniques and bolstered by the extreme confidence acquired on the courts of Eton Fives of which he might be easily considered En-gland's greatest player.

Then there is the matter of the use of his left arm in the murder of Mary Jane Kelly. Fives, being an ambidextrous game, would certainly have taught him supple, strong and precise deployment of that limb, and given the low threshold of precision necessary to make the cut, the game certainly equipped him, alone among the suspects, to use his weak hand to murderous ends.

All five murders represented bold and athletic escapes. No copper ever laid eyes on Jack knowing he was Jack, no whistle was ever blown in response to his presence. All escapes involved climbing, balance, great vision, physical vigor, and great strength. No other suspect comes close to possessing those attributes but Druitt.

The witnesses all put a man of Druitt's body type, age, middle-class wardrobe proclivities, and facial hair in the presence of four of the five women in the minutes before their deaths.

He was known to be under great mental pressure, both from his awareness of his legacy of insanity and from some grotesque reversal at Valentine's School. It may also be that he knew the clapping had to stop soon. He was an athlete, growing older. That can be a terrible pain to bear and it can fill one with rage.

The case is entirely circumstantial—but it is remorseless. Men have hung for far less.

Thanks to Lenne P. Miller, Gary Goldberg, David Fowler, M.D., and David Green.

—STEPHEN HUNTER

COPY MURDERS AND OTHERS

Robin Odell

Although Robin Odell (1935–) has written nearly twenty true crime volumes, his landmark book, *Jack the Ripper in Fact and Fiction* (1965), published more than a half century ago, still ranks among the most important works in the field. He continued his investigations and analysis of Red Jack in *Ripperology: A Study of the World's First Serial Killer and a Literary Phenomenon* (2006), which, despite its hyperbolic subtitle (overlooking, among others, the Countess Elizabeth Báthory, reportedly responsible for the deaths of as many as six hundred fifty girls and young women in the late sixteenth and early seventeenth centuries), won the Gold Medal at the 2007 Independent Publisher Book Awards in the True Crime category and also was nominated for an Edgar. He cowrote with Colin Wilson and J. H. H. Gaute *Jack the Ripper: Summing Up and Verdict* (1987). His most recent book on the subject is *Written and Red: The Jack the Ripper Lectures* (2009), covering more than thirty years of lectures. Among his other works are *The Murderers' Who's Who: Outstanding International Cases from the Literature of Murder in the Last 150 Years,* with J. H. H. Gaute (1979), which won a Special Edgar, *Landmarks in 20th Century Murder* (1995), and *Medical Detectives: The Lives & Cases of Britain's Forensic Five* (2013).

After working as a university laboratory technician and completing his National Service, Odell developed an interest in crime writing and became one of the world's leading authorities on the subject.

"Copy Murders and Others" was first published in *Jack the Ripper in Fact and Fiction* (London, George C. Harrap, 1965).

The murder of Marie Kelly is generally considered to be the last outrage committed by Jack the Ripper, although for many months after there occurred a number of murders which were thought to be attributable to the Whitechapel killer. A number of these have come to be known as "copy murders," and were supposed to have been perpetrated by different murderers, each copying the Ripper's technique.

The first such attempt happened on November 21st, 1888, just thirteen days after the death of Marie Kelly, when a prostitute called Annie Farmer was attacked at a lodging-house in George Street, Whitechapel. The man with whom she was preparing to spend the night tried to cut her throat, but when she screamed he let her go and made off before he could be caught. The police seemed satisfied that the woman's assailant was not the man they were seeking, for his technique certainly seemed amateurish compared with that of the Ripper.

It was some months later, in June 1889, when the next public scare took place. In that month several portions of a human female body were washed up at various points along the river Thames. It was claimed that one of the last portions to be found was wrapped up in a piece of white cloth of the type that medical students used in connection with a certain type of work. The head was never found, but some marks on some of the parts retrieved established the woman's identity. She was a prostitute by the name of Elizabeth Jackson, who had lived in a lodging-house in Chelsea. This incident was known as "The Thames Mystery," and although it bore little relation to the Ripper murders, it was none the less bracketed with them.

In the following month occurred a murder which really led people to believe that Jack the Ripper had taken up the knife again. This killing was stamped with many of the familiar characteristics of the Ripper's methods. At 12:50 A.M. on Wednesday July 17th, 1889, Police Constable Andrews was patrolling in Castle Alley, Whitechapel, a long, dark, and sinister passage no more than a yard wide at one end. Its black depths frequently housed ruffians with criminal intentions. In fact, so many people had been attacked and robbed there that even the local prostitutes feared to use it at night.

Whilst walking the hundred and eighty yards of the passage's length the patrolling policeman came across the body of a woman lying in a doorway. His first thought was that the Ripper had struck again, for the woman's throat was cut and there were gashes across her abdomen.

As in the previous murders, there was the element of luck always on the side of the killer. Police Constable Andrews patrolled the alley every fifteen minutes whilst on his beat, and twenty-five minutes before he discovered the body he had actually eaten his supper at a place nearby.

The police were able to identify the dead woman by the clay pipe which was found underneath the body. She was a local woman, known as "Clay-pipe Alice" on account of her habit of smoking a clay pipe in bed. Her real name was Alice McKenzie, and she lived in Gun Street, Spitalfields. John McCormack, a man with whom "Clay-pipe Alice" had lived, said that she was a respectable woman who earned a living by cleaning for a family in Whitechapel. The police, however, had other ideas as to McKenzie's background. She was known to several constables as an habitual drunkard, and she had frequently been seen soliciting in the Spitalfields area.

In several respects the circumstances of this woman's death fitted the familiar pattern of Jack the Ripper's killings. The type of victim, the area in which the crime had been committed, and the ability to avoid patrolling policemen were all hall-marks of the Ripper. Even the nature of the killing was similar—the cut throat and the abdominal injuries. On this latter question, however, Dr. Bagster Phillips indicated some inconsistencies. McKenzie's throat had been cut with a short blade—in the other crimes a long-bladed knife had been the weapon used; the injuries to the abdomen were no more than superficial and seemed to have been caused by the thumb and fingernails of a hand—in the other murders the abdominal injuries were extensive and effected with a sharp knife. The doctor summed up that in this case the injuries "were not similar to those in other East End murder cases." As to the question of any special skill being shown in inflicting the injuries, the doctor was of the opinion that this particular crime showed nothing more than the ability to deprive someone of life speedily.

The night of February 13th, 1891, brought a return of the fear that East Enders had known three years previously. It was a bitterly cold night that emptied Whitechapel's dingy corners of their huddles of prostitutes and lonely humanity. Police Constable Leeson was patrolling in the neighbourhood of the Mint when he heard the unmistakable shrill of a police whistle. He made off at top speed in the direction that the sound had come from, and he found himself in a place called Swallow Gardens, which was actually a railway arch running from Royal Mint Street to Chambers Street. There Leeson found a colleague, P.C. Thompson, standing with a couple of night-watchmen.

"What's up?" asked Leeson. "Murder," replied Thompson hoarsely. "A Jack the Ripper job." Both constables were inexperienced, and Leeson could see that his colleague was badly shaken. The two men walked to the spot where Thompson had found the body. "The form lying in the roadway was that of a young woman. Her clothing was disarranged, and there could be no doubt that she had been brutally murdered. Apart from the fearful wound in the throat there were other terrible injuries about the lower part of the trunk." So Leeson later described the murder scene.[31]

The woman was still breathing, although speech was impossible and her life was ebbing fast. Leeson recognized her as "Carroty Nell," a woman known to the police on account of her soliciting activities near Tower Hill. In the gutter near the body was a new crêpe hat, although there was another, older hat pinned to the woman's shawl. It was obvious that the murder had not long been committed, but neither policemen nor nearby night-watchmen had seen or heard anything.

More experienced police officers soon arrived at the scene, and a murder hunt began at once. Hundreds of policemen and civilians took part in the search, and small parties of men were organized to scour every alley, passage, and archway. Every house in the district was searched the same night, as the police were of the opinion that the murderer's disappearance into thin air could be accounted for only by his hiding in a nearby house until the coast was clear.

There was something uncanny about the murderer's quick getaway. In addition to P.C. Thompson, who had been patrolling the area in rubber-soled boots a mere stone's throw from the murder spot, there had also been a police constable stationed just fifty yards away in Royal Mint Street. This officer had been on duty all night, and he heard nothing until Thompson blew his whistle on finding the body. It is no wonder that the police felt that the murderer was still in the vicinity, but their searches brought no rewards, although a further precaution was taken in cordoning off the docks. The authorities were leaving nothing to chance, and, perhaps remembering the drover theory, they decided to check on the crews of every vessel leaving the docks.

The dead woman was soon properly identified as Frances Coles of Thrawl Street, Spitalfields, where she was in fact known as "Carroty Nell." Her body was taken to the police station, where it was examined by Dr. Phillips, who by now must have seen some of the worst victims of murder.

---

31 See *Lost London*, by B. Leeson (Stanley Paul, 1934).

Frances Coles was both young and pretty, rare qualities among the women of her class. She was spoken highly of in the places where she had lodged, and was often described as being of a superior type, although her recent behaviour had been anything but high-class.

The police pounced upon the crêpe hat found pinned to Coles's shawl as an important clue. It appeared that Coles had bought a new hat, which she wore straight away, whilst pinning her old one to her shawl until she reached home. But where had she made her purchase? The Spitalfields district was thoroughly combed for the seller of the hat, and perseverance eventually brought results. A shopkeeper was found, and she identified the hat as one that she had sold to Frances Coles the previous afternoon for five shillings. Apparently Coles had tried earlier in the day to buy the hat by making a down payment, with the promise of paying the rest later. The shopkeeper would not accept this arrangement, and told Coles that she would have to pay the full amount if she wanted the hat.

In the afternoon Coles returned, saying that she had found a friend who would lend her the money. The shopkeeper noticed a man standing about outside while Coles was making her purchase, but she was unable to give a clear description of the man, as he kept his back towards the shop. However, she was able to say that he was thick-set, middle-aged, and fairly well dressed. The woman remembered Coles pinning the old hat to her shawl, and on leaving the shop she was joined by the man and they walked off down the street.

The police were obviously keen to question this man, and were about to embark on a full-scale search for him when another issue presented itself. Earlier on the night of the murder a man asking for Frances Coles had called at her lodgings. It was noticed that his hand was bleeding, and by way of explanation he said that some ruffians had set on him and robbed him of all his money. The man stayed with Coles for about an hour, and he was heard to leave at 1 A.M. Thirty minutes later Frances Coles went out on a mission that ended with her death in the gutter at Swallow Gardens.

In addition to this, it appeared that the man returned to Coles's lodgings at 3 A.M. On this occasion he was highly excited and was covered with blood. He told the lodging-house deputy that he wanted lodgings for the night, and explained, "I've been knocked down and robbed in Ratcliff Highway." The deputy would not accept this explanation in view of the fact that the man claimed to have been robbed before his first visit. He refused to give him a bed, and advised him to go to London Hospital for treatment.

The police checked with the authorities at London Hospital to see whether a man covered with blood had asked for treatment. An injured man had sought treatment in the early hours of the morning, but his injuries were not severe enough for him to have been the man the police were seeking. According to the doctors, he was a seafaring man, and after treatment he was allowed to go.

Writing of these events, Leeson said:

There was tremendous excitement now among the police engaged on the case, as it really looked as though they were hot on the trail of the Terror. Next day the excitement spread to the people outside, and big crowds assembled in front of Leman Street Station waiting for the news that Jack the Ripper had been laid by the heels at last.

That night a man was arrested in a Whitechapel public house and taken in for questioning. Whitechapel went mad. The news of the man's arrest spread rapidly, and everyone took it for granted that the Ripper had at last been caught. There was quite a scuffle when the man was taken into the police station, and a crowd stood outside demanding his blood. If the crowd had managed to seize him he would surely have been lynched.

The arrested man gave his name as James Thomas Sadler, and he said that he was a ship's fireman from the S.S. *Fez* in London Docks. He seemed to be ignorant of the murder, but the police were sure he was their man, and he was duly charged with the wilful murder of Frances Coles.

Sadler protested his innocence from the very beginning, but the police badly needed a conviction and public opinion was greatly inflamed. Moreover, the evidence against him was damning. Not only did he admit meeting Frances Coles, but he even said that he had bought her a hat. However, he stated emphatically that after leaving her lodgings at 12:40 A.M. he had not seen her again.

While Sadler was in Holloway Prison stories highly prejudicial to his case were being circulated about him. Some of these tales were so outrageous that questions were asked in the House of Commons, and the Home Secretary spoke of his regret that the newspapers should seek to gratify public curiosity in this way.

With the police and public convinced of his guilt and no one lifting a finger to help him, Sadler, still protesting his innocence, wrote a despairing letter to the Stokers' Union of which he was a member: "What a godsend my case will be to the police if they can only conduct me, innocent as I am, to the bitter end—the scaffold!"

This pathetic eleventh-hour acclamation of innocence was passed on to Mr. Harry Wilson, who agreed to undertake Sadler's defence. Wilson soon discovered that the charges against Sadler were not at all what they seemed to be. To begin with, the circumstances of Coles's death did not altogether match those of the previous victims of the Ripper, and three ship's captains gave references upholding Sadler's character and conduct. This certainly disposed of the scurrilous attacks made on Sadler, painting him as a wild-eyed demon with fits of destructive temper.

But the most telling blow in Sadler's defence was yet to come. Mr. Wilson was able to establish that Sadler *had* been attacked twice on that night, and thus a major deficiency was exposed in the prosecution's case.

The police, however, were reluctant to let their man go, and although they managed to draw out the proceedings, it was plain that there was no longer a case against James Sadler. After the magistrate had consulted with the Attorney-General it was decided that no more evidence could be brought against Sadler, and he was duly discharged.

There was a story that a newspaper took one of its competitors to court over the Sadler affair, claiming damages on the sailor's behalf for articles which had maligned his character. Apparently a sum was awarded to Sadler, and after signing on with a vessel bound for South America he was never seen or heard of again.

Yet another interesting sequel to these events took place when Mr. Wilson was walking down Bow Street a few nights later. He claimed that he was suddenly accosted by a short, thick-set man dressed in black. "Who are you?" asked Wilson. "I am Jack the Ripper," replied the unknown man, adding, "Perhaps there will soon be some more work for you to do, Mr. Wilson." The man made off into the darkness, but Wilson noticed that he was clutching a black bag.

Reluctantly in some instances, the police, Press, and public had to admit that Jack the Ripper still eluded them, and that the man Sadler should never have been arrested on that charge at all. The *Spectator* remarked:

> *It is almost beyond doubt that, black as the evidence against Sadler originally looked, he did not kill the woman; and it is more than possible, it is almost probable, that she was killed by "Jack the Ripper," as the populace have nick-named the systematic murderer of prostitutes in Whitechapel.*

The murder of Frances Coles was the last killing in Britain that could be even remotely attributed to Jack the Ripper. Nevertheless the mysterious Jack has become almost a legend, and certainly a standard by which to measure the enormity of the crime of murder. The names of many murderers since 1888 have been coupled with the Ripper, and as recently as 1961 a murderer in Brooklyn known as "The Mad Strangler" was said by the inspector in charge of the case to be "worse than Jack the Ripper."

After the last Ripper murder in London there came reports of similar murders abroad. From America and Russia came news of such killings during the years 1886 to 1894, and in January 1889 a newspaper in Tunis reported that the Ripper might have been caught there. Apparently the French police had rounded up a number of bandits. Among them was a Briton whose description was said to answer that of a man wanted in connection with the East End murders in London. This man, however, was eventually cleared of suspicion on this count.

From Texas and Jersey City, in the United States, came reports of Ripper-like killings between 1890 and 1892. These led to a careful surveillance of Americans in London, which caused embarrassment to a few visitors and added to the frustration of the police.

The killing of a woman called "Old Shakespeare" in a dock-side hotel in New York in April 1891 again brought the Ripper's name to people's tongues. "Has Jack the Ripper arrived?" asked one New York newspaper. This was a good question, because the New York Police Department had smirked at the inability of Scotland Yard to capture the Ripper, and had said that if the notorious Jack started his games in New York City he would be arrested in a matter of hours.

No doubt with extra diligence, the New York Police Department set about catching Jack the Ripper now that he was operating in their territory. "Old Shakespeare," a drunken wretch, familiar to all the water-front dives, had been strangled and atrociously slashed with a filed-down cooking-knife. Her body had been found lying on the floor of her room in the East River Hotel, and the knife was discovered on the floor by the bed. Some reports remarked that the sign of the cross had been cut upon her thigh. This was given special significance, and even hailed as the mark of Jack the Ripper.

"Old Shakespeare," whose real name was Carrie Brown, had been seen to arrive at the hotel with a man about 11 P.M. on April 25th. The man was described as medium-sized, stocky, blond, and having the appearance of a seaman. A short while later the police arrested a man who filled this description in general terms, and who was known to frequent that neighbourhood. Locally he answered to the name of "Frenchy," and as he could not speak English, it was only with difficulty that the New York police established his identity. He was an Algerian-Frenchman named Ameer Ben Ali.[32] Further investigations followed, and by April 30th the police were convinced of "Frenchy's" guilt. "Frenchy" protested his innocence, and in court his inability to understand English added greatly to the confusion. The jury found "Frenchy" guilty of second-degree murder, and on July 10th, 1891, he was sentenced to prison for life. This was later followed by his admission to a hospital for the criminally insane.

This was not the end of the matter, however, for fresh evidence came to light, and this was to help "Frenchy." It appeared that a man who was known to have been in "Old Shakespeare's" company had been observed in the vicinity just prior to the murder. He was never seen again after the night of the murder, but in his abandoned room the police found a bloodstained shirt and a key which fitted the door of "Old Shakespeare's" room.

On the strength of this new evidence "Frenchy's" sentence was commuted, and he was eventually allowed back to his native Algeria. Clearly the police were satisfied that "Frenchy" was not Jack the Ripper, and the man involved by the new evidence was never traced. In fact, the New York police were experiencing some of the frustrations that had beset London's Metropolitan Police during those terrible months of 1888.

If "Frenchy"—Ameer Ben Ali's name—was only loosely connected with that of Jack the Ripper, there were others who had more serious claims to the mantle of the Whitechapel killer. One of these was George Chapman, who was executed at Wandsworth Prison in 1903 for murdering three women.

There were many facts about Chapman's career that led some people to believe that, apart from the poisonings for which he was executed, he was also responsible for the Whitechapel murders. Chapman was actually of Polish origin, and his real name was Severin Klosowski. He was born in the Polish village of Nargornak in 1865, and there was evidence to indicate that he chose a career in the medical profession. Whether or not he obtained medical degree is a matter of doubt, but he did serve as a hospital assistant or "barber surgeon." In Poland this was a post that was technically known as *Feldscher*, an appointment corresponding to that of a junior surgical assistant.

Klosowski was in Warsaw in 1887, where he met a hairdresser's traveller from London by the name of Wolff Levisohn. Levisohn later saw Klosowski in London about 1888–89 when the Pole was living in Whitechapel. Klosowski obtained work as a hairdresser's assistant in Whitechapel High Street, and it was in this capacity that he again met Levisohn.

---

32 For the information contained here I am indebted to "Frenchy—Ameer Ben Ali," from Dr. Ruth Borchard's *Convicting the Innocent* (Banks-Baldwin Law Publishing Co., Cleveland, Ohio, U.S.A., 1943).

Severin Klosowski made numerous changes of address until he acquired his own shop in Tottenham's High Road. However, this business venture failed, and he took jobs in Shoreditch and then in Leytonstone. On August Bank Holiday 1889 he married a Polish woman, and they lived for a while in Cable Street, Whitechapel. Soon afterwards they went to America together, but in February 1891 Mrs. Klosowski returned to England, leaving her husband in the United States.

Klosowski himself reappeared in London's East End in 1893, and after a while his wife left him altogether. Returning to his hairdressing, Klosowski met a woman named Annie Chapman,[33] and they lived together as man and wife. In fact, Klosowski then adopted the name of George Chapman, but it was not long before Annie Chapman left him. It was then that he set about his murderous ways.

George Chapman, alias Severin Klosowski, murdered three women by antimonial poisoning. His first victim was Mrs. Spink, whom he had met as early as 1895 when he was at Leytonstone. Mrs. Spink, who was separated from her real husband, had private means, and after she "married" Chapman, as Klosowski then called himself, she made several withdrawals from the bank to set him up in a hairdressing business. Mrs. Spink died on Christmas Day two years later.

Chapman next "married" Bessie Taylor, some time between 1898 and 1900. Bessie Taylor had replied to an advertisement for a barmaid that Chapman had inserted in one of the papers. He had by that time acquired a public house, but after living with Chapman for a year or two Bessie Taylor also died.

Maud Marsh, the third victim, also answered an advertisement for a barmaid. She became "married" to Chapman in August 1901, and she died on October 22nd in the following year. Three days after her death Chapman was arrested, and he was duly found guilty of poisoning the three women.

When Chapman was arrested Inspector Abberline, who had featured in the search for the Whitechapel murderer, was said to have remarked to a colleague, "You've got Jack the Ripper at last." Indeed, after Chapman had been convicted of the poisonings the police thought that there was some connection between the poisoner and the Ripper.

The police questioned Chapman's first wife, the Polish woman who had left him, about his nightly habits at the time of the Ripper murders. She said that he was often out as late as 3 and 4 A.M., and she could offer no reason for these absences. The theory gained ground that long before Jack the Ripper killed Marie Kelly he had become aware of the tremendous risks that he was taking. If George Chapman was Jack the Ripper, then the safer and more subtle means of killing that poisoning offered might have suggested itself to him. Furthermore, having changed his technique, he also changed his class of victim.

Other factors supporting the comparison between Chapman and the Ripper were put forward. The description of the man seen with Marie Kelly would have fitted Chapman, and Chapman, with his medical background, could easily have performed the mutilations on the Ripper's victims, which in some cases were said to have demanded skill. Moreover, he was living in the Whitechapel area throughout the period of the murders, and when he went to America the murders in the East End stopped. And whilst Chapman was working in a

---

33 This person should not be confused with the Annie Chapman murdered in Hanbury Street.

barber's shop in Jersey City there were reports of a similar outburst of murders in that locality.

Finally, Chapman passed himself off as an American and frequently used Americanisms in conversation. This it was thought could account for the Americanisms such as "Dear Boss" used in the Ripper's correspondence. This claim, however, was not borne out very faithfully in the letters which Chapman wrote whilst in prison. The following is an example of their style:

> *Believe me, be careful in your life of dangers of other enimis whom are unnow to you. As you see on your own expirence in my case how I was unjustly criticised and falsly Represented. Also you can see I am not Believed. Therefore you see where there is justice. . . .*

This extract seems to bear little resemblance to the letter signed "Jack the Ripper." There were other inconsistencies too, for some of those who had at one time voiced the opinion that the Ripper was a Polish Jew and believed that this tied in with Chapman forgot that the latter was in fact a Roman Catholic. Whilst it must be admitted that there were similar aspects in the careers of the Ripper and George Chapman, it would seem odd that a man could readily change from killing at least six women by ferocious knifing to tamely poisoning three others.

Many people, among them Inspector Abberline, felt that Chapman was the Ripper, in spite of indications to the contrary. This view was certainly held by other police officers, and Inspector A. F. Neil wrote: "We were never able to secure definite proof that Chapman was the Ripper. . . . In any case, it is the most fitting and sensible solution to the possible identity of the murderer in one of the world's greatest crime mysteries."[34]

Lord Carson described Chapman as looking "like some evil beast. I almost expected him to leap over the dock and attack me."[35] No matter how foreboding his appearance, nothing was ever found in Chapman's personal effects which incriminated him as the killer of Whitechapel prostitutes. If he had any such secrets, then he carried them with him to the gallows.

Another celebrated murderer whose name was linked with that of Jack the Ripper was Dr. Neill Cream. Cream was charged in 1892 with the murders of four women. He too was a poisoner, using strychnine to eliminate the street-walkers of Waterloo and Lambeth. Cream's association with the Whitechapel murders stemmed from a report that when actually on the scaffold he shouted, "I am Jack the . . ." just as the bolt was drawn. The truth of this utterance was sworn to by the executioner.

Again there was much about Dr. Neill Cream that would have suited the circumstances of Jack the Ripper's crimes. Cream received a medical training in Canada, and he graduated from McGill University in 1876. He completed his professional training in Edinburgh, where he became a member of the Royal College of Surgeons and Physicians. Dr. Cream returned to Canada and set up in

---

34 *Forty Years of Manhunting,* by A. F. Neil (Jarrolds, 1932).
35 *Carson,* by H. Montgomery Hyde (Heinemann, 1953).

practice in Ontario, but when one of his patients died after an abortion Cream packed his bags and left for the United States.

In Chicago where he next practised medicine he became involved in two cases of suspected abortion, but nothing could be proved against him. Still sailing close to the wind, Cream was involved in a more serious incident in Chicago in 1881. He fatally poisoned the husband of his mistress by putting strychnine in the man's medicine. Cream might well have got away with this, but, being a supreme exhibitionist, he wrote to the coroner and district attorney alleging that a blunder had been made by the druggist who made up the medicine. All that this action achieved was to throw suspicion on Cream himself.

Dr. Cream hastily made off for Canada, but was brought back to the States for trial, where he was convicted of murder. He was sentenced to life imprisonment, but was released in 1891 after serving ten years. Cream arrived in England in October of the same year, and in the course of the next few months murdered four women. Having failed to learn his lesson in America, Cream, after poisoning his first victim, wrote to the coroner offering to provide information which would lead to the murderer's arrest. He signed the letter with a fictitious name and the title of detective.

During the course of his murderous career in London Cream wrote many letters, some of them constituting blackmail. One of these letters caused his undoing, and he was arrested and charged with attempting blackmail. In the meantime the police were able to establish evidence identifying Cream as the Lambeth poisoner.

Nowadays Cream would probably have been found insane, but as it was he paid the supreme penalty. Cream has been described as a sadist, a sexual maniac, and a drug fiend, and one of the suggested motives for his murderous activities was that he took the lives of prostitutes because of having contracted venereal disease. There was no medical evidence to support this, but it was established that Cream suffered from agonizing headaches on account of failings in his sight. This it was thought drove him quite out of his mind at times.

As for Dr. Cream being Jack the Ripper, it seems that if he really did make that utterance on the scaffold, then it must have been his last attempt at the very exhibitionism which had finally betrayed him. For at the time that Whitechapel was under the terror of Jack the Ripper Dr. Neill Cream had been serving a prison sentence in America.

However, Cream's part in the Ripper story does not end here. Some years before Cream was convicted and hanged Sir Edward Marshall Hall, the famous advocate, defended him on a charge of bigamy.[36] Several women claimed to have been "married" to Cream, and Marshall Hall advised his client to plead guilty.

Cream indignantly refused, and protested that he had in fact been in jail in Sydney, Australia, at the time he was supposed to have committed the offences. Cream's description was sent to Australia, and a reply was received confirming that a man of that description had been in prison in Sydney at the time in question. This provided a perfect alibi, and Cream was subsequently released.

The theory was that Cream had a double in the criminal underworld, and they went by the same name, using each other's terms of imprisonment as alibis. It has

---

36 *The Life of Sir Edward Marshall Hall*, by Edward Marjoribanks (Gollancz, 1929).

been suggested that as Cream himself was in prison in America at the time of the Whitechapel murders his double was actually Jack the Ripper and that Cream's last words on the scaffold were aimed at providing his double with a final alibi, this being in the nature of a repayment for the double, whose imprisonment in Australia gave Cream an alibi to escape the charge of bigamy.

This "double" theory is ingenious, but simply leads inquiry round in ever-decreasing circles, and, of course, there is no supporting evidence for making the initial assumption anyway. Actually the idea of Jack the Ripper's double identity arises later in connection with another theory, but such unexplained assertions, though novel, have little application in the serious quest to solve the Ripper mystery.

Mystery, Crime,
Suspense — Stories

IN THE FOURTH WARD

Theodora Benson

Although largely forgotten today, Eleanor Theodora Roby Benson (1906–1968) was once a widely read author of humorous but cynical novels that depicted broken marriages and romances, ruthless selfishness, shattered idealism, and superficial goals of wealth and social position.

Benson's first novel, *Salad Days* (1928), a study of the unfolding of a young girl's character, was dedicated to her friend Betty Askwith, with whom she collaborated on many books. Among Benson's more successful books were *Façade* (1933), in which a Mayfair couple realize their marriage was a mistake, and *Concert Pitch* (1934), about a music hall headliner, his wife, and the colorful vaudevillians in their circle.

Among the best-known books by Benson and Askwith were *Lobster Quadrille* (1930), a novel, and *Foreigners, or the World in a Nutshell* (1936), a humorous, politically incorrect, grossly exaggerated series of biases, clichés, and prejudices, and its sequel, *Muddling Through, or Britain in a Nutshell* (1935), which focused on the British Isles.

If Benson is read today it is for her rather dark short fiction, mainly mysteries and stories of the macabre, some of the best of which are collected in *The Man from the Tunnel and Other Stories* (1950). Her only mystery novel was *Rehearsal for Death* (1954). She also wrote several books on travel and, during World War II, was a ghostwriter of political speeches.

"In the Fourth Ward" was first published in 1930, but I have been unable to find where it originally appeared.

Ben Higgs only told me this story once. This in itself was memorable, because most of his stories, as is generally the case with old seafaring men, he told again and again. The pirates in the South Seas and the five days spent rounding Cape Horn in a blizzard, if I heard of them once I heard of them twenty times.

This tale that he never repeated again (or not to me) came out shortly before he died. I don't think he liked to think about it much; and he was a tough old man. "It was," he said, "the most horrible thing that ever happened to me," and he told it to me on a hot August afternoon, while the sea scarcely moving shimmered blue at our feet, and the stones on the beach were hot beneath our hands, and the whole world seemed wrapped for eternity in stillness and peace.

"It was the first and last time I ever was in New York," he told me. "I was but a boy at the time, along on my second trip, and we sailed aboard the *Isabella C. Paterson* from Liverpool. We had a long voyage, and of course when we reached port I was mad keen to go ashore. New York wasn't the place I've heard it is now, with buildings a hundred storeys high and the streets practically paved with gold, but it was a prospering lively town enough, and as for wickedness—well, I've seen little to touch it and I've seen the back parts of a good few seafaring towns. I went ashore with an older seaman who'd taken a kind of a fancy to me. Middling tall he was, with quick bright dark eyes and a slow gentle voice. He didn't tell us much about himself, he'd been brought up in the country, had started life as a butcher's assistant, and when his old mother died had chucked it up to go to sea. He'd been main fond of her it seemed, had a picture of her inside his sea-chest he'd show me sometimes. He had a picture of his brother too, a nice-looking lad, and one of a pretty girl—but he'd gashed it across with red chalk as though it was wounds. He told me once she'd been his brother's girl; he spoke in such a way that I didn't feel inclined to ask any further questions. But he was very good to me, very very good, and I was only a slip of a boy at the time.

"Well this man, Thomas Goolden his name was, and I, went ashore. To the old Fourth Ward we went, and if there's a wickeder horrider place on the face of the earth Ben Higgs has yet to find it. Kit Burns's rat pit was the first place we visited. Sportsmen's Hall they called it, and there in the middle was a kind of ring with low wooden walls round it. Huge grey half-starved rats were sent against terriers and sometimes against each other, and the terriers didn't always win neither. There was a great tall ruffian with bulging blue eyes in a red bloated face leaning against the wall, and the man next me pointed him out as Snatchem, one of the Slaughter House gang; it was his job to suck the blood from scratches and cuts at the bare knuckle prizefights they used to hold down there. There was also a thin weaselly looking man known as Jack the Rat, and he was Kit Burns's son-in-law, and for ten cents he'd bite the head off a mouse and for a quarter the head off a rat. It turned my stomach rather odd, being only a boy as it were. But Thomas Goolden, who'd ever seemed gentle, was laughing and joking as hard as nails. I mind me he said: 'There's rats *and* rats, Benny. My kind's different—but I like to see their blood too.'

"We'd seen four or five of these rat fights and then we made our way out and went along to another place on Water Street called the Hole-in-the-Wall. And there I met the oddest woman I'm ever like to see. She was six foot at least, as large as a grenadier. She'd a pistol stuck in her belt and a huge bludgeon strapped to her waist. Her skirt was held up with braces, or suspenders as Americans say, above her knee. Galluses they used to call them, so she was known as Gallus Mag. She acted as a kind of chucker-out; when she'd hit a man on the head with her club, she'd fix her teeth in his ear and drag him to the door, all the room cheering and yelling like mad, and if he struggled she'd bite his ear right off. Yes sir, right off, and she'd put it in a jar of pickle she kept back of the bar with all the others she'd collected. It doesn't seem hardly possible, does it? But I saw her do it myself—it made me feel very queer; she was English too. They say she once gave an ear back to its owner years later when they made up a quarrel. Sadie the Goat was the favoured party; a female pirate who'd made men walk the plank. She appreciated getting her ear again and wore it afterwards mounted in a locket.

"Well, we stayed there for a time, spending our money as sailors do. And lucky not to be killed for it. In that very place, the Hole-in-the-Wall, Slobbery Jim and Patsy the Barber, who belonged to the gang called the Daybreak Boys, had fought for over half an hour about how to divide twelve cents they'd murdered a German for. The chuckers-out didn't hinder them, because it was a matter of principle, not just drink, you see, and Slobbery Jim stabbed Patsy the Barber in the throat and trampled him to death with his hob-nail boots. Still, we stood a few drinks and they treated us quite friendly, though they didn't like the English much mostly in New York in those days. And somehow the talk turned on Jack the Ripper and his murders; you'll have heard of them I expect, sir? Well, Byrnes who was Chief of Police in New York at that time, he'd been boasting that if Jack the Ripper had done his murders in New York their police would a' caught him. He wrote in the papers, it was published just before we sailed, that he defied Jack the Ripper to come to the United States. They kept asking us that evening whether we'd caught him yet and saying he wouldn't dare show his face in New York or their police'd have him. It seemed kind of funny that such a group of thugs and criminals should be boasting about their police force, but I s'pose in a way it was what you'd call an indirect compliment to themselves.

"By and by an old hag comes in and that stops the talk about the Ripper. Because they all turns round and calls to her: 'Why there's Shakespeare, come along Shakespeare, give us a piece.' (They were all pretty drunk and so were we by this time.) Well I don't rightly know, sir, but I believe there was a famous actor or play writer or something called Shakespeare; and whether this old girl was any relation of his I can't rightly say—but it seems that she claimed she came of a fine family back over here. (It's funny that both these women I've told you of were English. I dunno if one's exactly proud of it or not—but in a way it sort of made me feel one up on the Yanks.) She would have it too she'd been a famous actress in her day. How it was I can't say but they gave her a bottle of swan gin, and there she stood wrapping her shawl around her and sure enough she began to recite. Maybe 'twas the drink that did it but in any case 'twas wonderful, you'd never have thought that poor bleary-eyed old creature would have had the lungs or the voice to put her stuff over like she did. What she recited I can't remember. There was a lot of it. One bit she said with her voice all deep and shivery made my blood run cold. Something about how she'd given suck and yet how she'd have plucked her breast away and dashed the baby's brain out had she sworn—and something about her voice made you feel she'd have done it too. It was funny, there were all these thieves and murderers, Gallus Mag who I'd seen with my own eyes bite a man's ear off an hour or two agone, and yet they didn't make one shiver like this harmless old crone saying over some kind of fool poetry. And then right at the end she changed her voice and her manner altogether. She went round the circle offering this man a rusty old nail and that man a bit of calico. 'Here's a pansy,' she'd say, or 'here's rosemary, that's for remembrance.' And do you know not one of us laughed? Her voice was like that of a maid as she said it, she was pretending to be half-crazed and God knows in truth she wasn't far off it. But she sounded so young and innocent and pitiful-like, that we stood there like stuck dummies, taking the little scraps of rubbish she offered, and the tears weren't far from all our eyes.

"Only I heard a voice beside me, and it came from Thomas Goolden and it was queer and excited-like and terrible, though he spoke quite low so that it was only me that heard him. 'She's not only mad,' he said, 'she's diseased.'

"I can't tell you much about the rest of that evening, sir, it got a bit blurred as it were. I lost Goolden after the Hole-in-the-Wall and I wandered into John Allen's which was a very famous house on Water Street; a dance-hall and bar and you-know-what-else with cubicles for girls and customers. The girls there wore low black satin bodices and scarlet skirts and stockings, and boots with red tops and bells round their ankles. Very taking it was, and indeed I might have stayed there, but it fell out this way. Allen had been trained for a minister, which is what his three brothers were, and he still had a feeling for it, with a Bible in every cubicle. And quite a popular thing in that vice-house was to have religious sing-songs. They struck up one hymn, and the girl who was sitting on my knee told me it was their favourite, that as luck would have it my mother used to sing. I don't know if you've heard it, sir?—

> "'There is rest for the weary,
> There is rest for you,
> On the other side of Jordan,
> In the sweet fields of Eden,
> Where the Tree of Life is blooming,
> There is rest for you.'

"And what with thinking of my old mother and being so drunk, I came over all soppy and burst into tears and got out somehow.

"Finally I got a bed at the old Fourth Ward Hotel on Catherine and Water Streets. (I found out the name afterwards.) I'm pretty sure they doctored my liquor though I don't know as they needed to, since I was pretty far gone by that time anyway. I woke up with a head such as I never hope to have again and my hands tied behind me in a cellar and a man with a knife creeping towards me. If ever I have nightmares I see that over and over, and I have the feeling of sick terror and I try to get my hands free and I can't. And then I saw the man was Thomas Goolden.

"'Why it's you, Ben,' he said. 'I've been wondering what became of you.'

"And he came up to me and he cut the rope that tied my hands and he helped me up and he showed me a back way out. And just as we got out into the street he gave a chuckle (not very loud but kind of quiet and amused like) and said in his low soft voice as well as I could catch: 'Here's to you, Mr. Byrnes,' and then he disappeared. I got back to the ship as fast as I could. I was sick and sore and shaken, I'd nothing in my pockets, and I'd had enough of New York. I'd been lying in that cellar the best part of eighteen hours I found, and we were to sail the next morning. We did too though we sailed without Thomas Goolden, who never turned up again. But before we left we heard there'd been a terrible murder at the Fourth Ward Hotel, the very one where I'd spent the night. That poor old hag Shakespeare had been carved up as neat as you please, just like a Jack the Ripper murder. They arrested and put in prison a half-wit known as Frenchy, though he swore he was innocent; there were plenty that said he'd been framed and that the Ripper had accepted Byrnes's challenge and come over and the police dursn't own it. All I know is that, when I got out into Water Street that night, there was fresh blood on my hands and wrists; I'd no cut or scratch, and whether it came off the cellar floor or whether it came off the knife that cut my bonds, I don't like to think. But of all the places I've ever been to, New York in those days was the worst, and that was the most horrible thing that ever happened to me."

JACK

Anne Perry

Anne Perry is the pseudonym of Juliet Marion Hulme (1938–), an internationally bestselling author of historical mystery fiction with more than twenty-seven million copies sold. She has produced more than seventy books, most of them classic Victorian-era detective novels about Thomas and Charlotte Pitt or William Monk. In addition, she has written more than a dozen highly successful Christmas-themed novellas, works set during World War I, fantasy novels, young adult books, short stories, and stand-alone novels, and she has edited five anthologies.

The first Perry book was *The Cater Street Hangman* (1979), featuring Thomas Pitt, a Victorian policeman, and his highborn wife, Charlotte, who helps her husband solve mysteries out of boredom. She is of enormous help to him as she is able to gain access to people of a high social rank, which would be extremely difficult for a common police officer to do. There are nearly thirty books in the series, set in the 1880s and 1890s. Intimately familiar with this era, Perry nonetheless has never written about Jack the Ripper, the most infamous villain of the time, until producing this story.

The Monk series, with twenty novels, is set in the 1850s and 1860s. Monk, a private detective, is assisted on his cases by the excitable nurse Hester Latterly. The events in the first Monk book, *The Face of a Stranger* (1990), precede Sherlock Holmes's investigations by a quarter of a century, though Holmes is frequently described as the world's first consulting detective.

After winning an Edgar in 2000 for her short story "Heroes," which was set during World War I, Perry began a series of novels featuring its protagonist, British Army chaplain Joseph Reavely, whose exploits and character were suggested by the author's grandfather; the first book was *No Graves as Yet* (2003).

"Jack" was written especially for this collection and has never been previously published.

It was the last day of September and the mists swirled along the pavement, dimming the streetlamps and muffling the sounds of hooves as the occasional hansom cab went by. Not that there were so many around in the East End of London at two in the morning. Gwen was glad that her husband, Riley, was with her, not that she would ever have been out alone at such an hour! No woman would. Especially this year of 1888, when the man known as Jack the Ripper had killed two women and left them hideously mutilated, not so very far from where they were walking, the four of them, she and Riley, and their good friends Albert and Mary Clandon.

It had been a nice evening, if a little long. But then she had been in no hurry to get home. Home meant being alone with Riley and his temper, his constant fault-finding.

"Nothing like a good bit of beef," Albert was saying with satisfaction. "Do it just right, in the Black Boar, they do."

"Must ask them how they do their Yorkshire pudding," Riley said in agreement. "You should ask them, Gwen," he added. "You could learn a thing or two! God knows, you need to."

There was no answer to give and Gwen had long ago learned not to argue with him. Their two daughters were grown up and gone. Their letters home were one of Gwen's greatest pleasures.

"Did you hear me?" Riley demanded irritably.

"Yes, I heard you," she replied. "And there's no use asking a professional cook what he does, 'cos they don't tell."

"Tried it, have you?" He would not let it go.

There was no point in arguing. It would only make him angrier.

"All got our secrets," Albert said cheerfully. "If every woman could cook like they do, they wouldn't have their trade."

"Just fit to eat would be nice," Riley snapped back.

What could she say to that? She was actually quite a good cook, as well as seamstress, and general manager of the house on a limited budget. But the argument was not really about that at all, and she knew it, even if he pretended otherwise. He simply wanted something to be angry about.

"No excuses?" Riley asked, as if she were deliberately ignoring him.

"It's expensive to have your own cook." Mary observed. "You have to have enough room for her to live with you, for a start." What she was really saying was that Riley did not earn enough to provide for one.

Gwen turned away so Riley could not see her wide smile.

It was a moment before Riley found his answer.

"Shouldn't need one! There's only the two of us in the house. A woman who knows what she's doing ought to manage everything else."

Before he could go on any further they heard footsteps in the fog and they all turned to see the figure looming out of the darkness toward them.

Gwen felt a moment of fear before she recognized the outline of a policeman, and the knots eased out of her.

"Good evening, sir, madam," the warm, agreeable voice said politely. "Bit of a nasty night to be out so late."

"It's all right, Constable," Albert answered calmly. "Been out to dinner. Just stopped a bit long, that's all."

The policeman had been holding his lantern in such a way as to show himself very clearly, so he would not frighten them as a stranger, but now he turned it on them, the men first, then the two women.

"Take that out of my eyes!" Riley said sharply. "We're respectable people going home a bit late, that's all! Do you think if we were out to burgle someone we'd take our wives along?"

"Sergeant Walpole," the policeman introduced himself. "And no, sir, it never occurred to me that you might be burglars. I was making sure you were all safe."

"Why on earth shouldn't we be safe?" Albert asked, but there was a thread of alarm in his voice. Perhaps without doing it intentionally he moved a little closer to Mary.

"There's been another one, sir," Walpole replied quietly. "Dutfield's Yard, sir, just off Berners Street. I don't like to say too much in front of the ladies, but it's even worse than before. You should go home and stay inside. I advise you not to have a newspaper in the house. . . ."

"My wife doesn't read newspapers," Riley said sharply, but now his voice was edged with fear more than anger. Berners Street was just around the corner from where they had eaten such a good meal only an hour or two ago. "Respectable women don't."

"Just so, sir. All the same, I would avoid them if you can. This one is . . ." He hesitated, looking for a word that would convey his urgency to the men without suggesting its real horror to the women. He failed to find it. "Very bad," he finished, his voice hoarse.

Gwen felt cold even through her coat, although perhaps it was only because they had been standing still, and she was tired. The evening had gone on too long and had ended with the terrible news. The Ripper had struck a third time. The first had been the final day of August, the second the 8th of September. Then there had been three weeks without anything, and they had thought it was over. Now the last day of the month and it had happened again. If Sergeant Walpole was right, it was too terrible for him to describe.

There was a moment's silence. They could see nothing beyond the fog, as if the rest of the world had disappeared.

"I do care," Walpole said quietly. "And I'd stay indoors when you can. Goodnight ladies, gentlemen." He turned the lantern off them, and in a few steps he was swallowed up in the night as if he had never existed.

Mary sighed and gave a shiver. "Let's hurry," she said, moving forward toward the next corner, where she and Albert would turn off to go home.

Albert caught up with her and took her arm, calling goodnight over his shoulder.

"Shouldn't have told us," Riley said angrily. "What's he trying to do? Scare us all out of our senses? He'll have half the women in London in hysterics. Fool!"

"Nobody's in hysterics," she retorted, stung at last into response. "Unless it's you! And of course it's women who are frightened. It's women he's killing. He's just advising us not to go out alone after dark. You'd complain enough if he didn't warn us." She wanted to start walking, as fast as she could, but she was far too frightened to risk getting out of his sight. Even a madwoman wouldn't want to be alone in the dark this autumn, not in London.

"Then don't just stand there!" Riley snapped. "Let's go home!" He started to stride out along the pavement.

In the morning, Gwen went out to buy a few necessary groceries.

There was a biting east wind, but it had blown the fog away and she would rather be cold than have the suffocating feeling of being shut in and blind to people perhaps only yards away from her.

It was only when she reached the butcher and had chosen her ham bones—very large and nice looking, excellent for soup—that she saw the newspaper lying on the bench on her way out. The headlines said, "Jack the Ripper strikes again!"

In spite of herself, she stopped and looked at it. The letters were so large and so heavily inked they arrested her attention in spite of common sense telling her she did not want to know.

She read on with a kind of hideous fascination. She could not help it, because Sergeant Walpole had been wrong, completely! It had not been in Dutfields Yard as he had said. It had been in Mitre Square. A woman called Catherine Eddowes had been horribly killed, and her body found at 1:45 in the morning. That was barely quarter of an hour before Sergeant Walpole had spoken to them, if that long! How was it possible he even knew?

The answer was so terrible she could not bear it, and yet neither could she look away. He had been dressed in a police uniform, carrying a bull's-eye lantern like the police carried. Had he just come from slashing that poor woman's throat and then tearing her body apart, opening up her abdomen to lay her entrails on the ground beside her? How was he not covered in blood, drenched in it, soaked? Wouldn't they have seen that, even in the fog?

It couldn't be! His voice was soft, his face gentle. Was that how he got away with it? He looked like a policeman. Maybe he even was one? Of course no one suspected him! She and Riley, all four of them, had stood on the pavement in the fog and spoken to him, just as if he really were a policeman, there to save them, protect them.

"Ma'am, you shouldn't be looking at that!" the butcher's voice was soft and urgent. "One o' my customers must 'ave left it there. 'Ere! Let me take it an' throw it away." He reached across in front of her and picked the paper off the sill.

"It was Catherine Eddowes," she said slowly. "He said it were Lizzie Stride." She gazed at the butcher's mild, troubled face. "That's what he said."

"It were both of 'em, ma'am," the butcher told her. "One off Berners Street an' one in Mitre Square. The first one found at one o'clock, the other at a quarter to two. Both of 'em poor souls cut to pieces like they were animals in a slaughterhouse. He's like something risen out of hell, he is. I'm right sorry that newspaper got left there. I'll see it never 'appens again." He crushed it up in his hands.

"Two . . . both last night?" She could scarcely grasp it, and yet she also felt a kind of relief that it was an ordinary policeman she had met in the street, not the half-human fiend they had come to call Jack the Ripper. Just Sergeant Walpole. She was so overwhelmed with relief that she very nearly let the ham bones slip through her hands onto the floor.

The butcher looked at her with concern. "You all right, ma'am? You like to sit down a bit? I'll fetch you a glass of water."

"That's very kind of you, Mr. Shaw, but I'll be fine." She stood up a little straighter.

"We can't have half of London falling about fainting just 'cos of the newspapers."

She took a deep breath and steadied herself, forcing a smile to the butcher, much to his relief. "Thank you."

He smiled back, nodding in agreement. He thought her a sensible woman, and his respect was in his expression as he returned to behind his counter and got ready for his next customer.

Gwen went on towards the grocer, but the hideous image was still in her mind. Gwen went into the grocery shop and bought tea and sugar, and a pound of butter. The next place she went to was the bakery, for some crumpets. They were fresh and still warm to the touch, even through the paper of the bag they were in. She was just leaving when she met Sergeant Walpole coming in the door.

"Good morning, ma'am," he said cheerfully, as if he were pleased to see her.

"Good morning, Sergeant," she answered, putting on a smile with a bit of effort. "I hope you didn't have to be up all night?"

"I'm afraid so," he said with rueful honesty. "Just going to stop an' have a cup of tea, and a crumpet. Shouldn't have crumpets for breakfast, but after last night I could do with something nice."

"You must be so tired you could sleep on a clothesline," she said with sympathy. She felt a little guilty for the fearful thoughts she had held about him only a few minutes ago. "I don't know how you manage, the things you must see. Nobody should have to . . ." She stopped, knowing she had given herself away.

He shook his head. "You shouldn't 'ave looked, ma'am. I know the newspapers and posters are all over the place, but you'll give yourself nightmares if you looked at them. You've got to believe it all happened quick, or you'll drive yourself daft. We'll catch him."

"You don't have to say that to make me feel better, Sergeant," she told him. "You'll do your best. Enjoy your crumpets. Toast them well and put on plenty of butter."

"I like them with a bit of treacle too," he said with a look on his face as if he could taste them now. "Too sweet, and I dare say it isn't good for you, but sometimes it hits the spot exactly. . . ."

"I must try that," she answered. "Good for you or not, it feels just right."

"And eat it quick, before it goes cold," he added. "I confess, I'll take my boots off in front of the fire, and sit back a bit, before I have to go out again."

"I suppose everybody's on extra shifts now." She looked at him and saw the weariness in his face. He must have little time to sleep, and not much to change his clothes or wash and shave. An hour or two just to eat something really nice, and relax.

"Pretty much," he admitted. "Never known a case like this one." For a moment he allowed his own fear to show through. Then perhaps seeing the sympathy in her face, he blushed. "Sorry, ma'am. Shouldn't be talking like this. It's my job. We've all got to do it right and put a stop to this. Nice to see you, ma'am. Enjoy your crumpets." He stepped aside for her to pass him and leave.

"You too," she replied. Then, conscious of the desire to linger and talk to him, and how wrong it would be, how silly, she hurried along the damp footpath and turned the corner toward her home.

Riley came back from his work at the City Council offices well after dark. His coat was damp across the shoulders and his boots were sodden, as if he had accidentally stepped into a gutter. She had toasted crumpets ready for him, with jam, and a pot of tea. She thought about putting treacle out as well, but decided not to.

He sat down with a sigh as if the day had been difficult. She thought about asking him how he was but could not think of a way of saying it that would sound exactly right. He had told her before, tersely, that his days were all the same and to try and make conversation out of it was foolish. Even if he explained to her, she would not understand. She wondered now if perhaps his work was more difficult than he had allowed her to know. Was she being unfair to him, unsympathetic? Could it be that his bad temper really was at least in part her fault?

She passed him another warm crumpet and smiled at him.

He looked momentarily surprised, but he took it, covered it in butter, then ate it with relish.

"Fresh," he remarked. "Get it in daylight, I hope?"

"Yes, of course."

"Good. Don't go out when you might have to come home as it's getting dark . . . even dusk. Do you understand?"

"I won't," she agreed with some feeling. The hideous pictures in the newspaper were still very clear in her mind, not that she could tell him that, of course.

"And I don't want you visiting Mary anymore, even in daylight," he added. "Not until they catch the Ripper . . . which might be never."

"Don't say that, Riley! Of course they'll catch him!" she protested. "It can't go on forever like this!"

"Maybe. But you'll not visit Mary until he's locked up and then hanged."

She had to argue. Mary was her closest friend. "Mary couldn't have anything to do with him!" she protested. "That's . . . not possible." She had been going to say "ridiculous" then realized how rude it sounded.

He raised his eyebrows high. "Isn't it? Do you know who the Ripper is, then?"

"No, of course I don't!"

"He could be anybody, couldn't he?" he went on. "He doesn't have to be some slavering lunatic anyone could see was mad! He might be a perfectly respectable man who goes about his business all day, just like anyone else. In fact he probably is. That's why we can't catch him." He waved his arm in the air. "He isn't a monster out there! He's a monster inside himself, but to all of us he looks like our neighbors. To some poor woman he probably looks like the man she's been married to for years. Slept beside without a thought of trouble, except maybe he snores, or drops his clothes around for her to pick up."

She stared at him with slow-dawning horror, her tea forgotten. He was not saying this just to frighten her; it was true. Somebody was seeing the man every day, maybe washing his clothes and cooking his meals. To her he was just "Jack" as he had always been. Only to everyone else he was "Jack the Ripper"—a monster so terrifying, whose acts were so dreadful, he was scarcely thought of as human.

But she would know, surely? You would have to know!

He read her thoughts as if she had spoken them aloud.

"Do you know it isn't Albert?" he said, looking at her steadily.

"We've known them for years!" she protested. "That's an awful thing even to think."

"Yes, it is awful," he agreed. "It's an awful thing the Ripper's done, and goes on doing. That policeman told us there was one, but there were two. And I won't tell you what he did to them. But why can't the police catch him, Gwen? I'll tell you why, because they're looking for a maniac, someone wild and haggard, soaked in blood. And he's just an ordinary man, probably wearing a suit and polished boots. I dare say he has nice manners and says 'please' and 'thank you' and 'good morning, ma'am,' like anyone else. Like our polite and helpful policeman the other night. How do we know he wasn't the Ripper himself? What would he have done to you if you'd been out there on the street alone, eh?"

She felt sick at the thought. She had liked Sergeant Walpole, actually rather a lot. But Riley was right, of course. Jack wasn't caught because he looked just like anyone else, except when he struck, and it was too late to run away, maybe too late even to scream.

Riley was looking at her with satisfaction. He could probably see her thoughts written clearly in her face.

"You've known Albert for years," he went on. "But you know the Albert Mary sees. What about the Albert I see? You haven't thought of that, have you?" There was triumph in his eyes.

She was angry because the thought was frightening. "You think you know him better than Mary does?" she challenged.

He gave a short bark of laughter. "For heaven's sake, Gwen! Of course I know him better than Mary does! What does any woman really know about a man? One side of him, one tiny little side."

She did not answer straightaway. She tried to think what she wanted to say to him, and what she dared say. Actually she thought that many women knew a great deal more about the men they had spent their adult lives with than they would be wise to say. When you counted on someone for all you had, you pretended not to see certain things or understand them.

Did the Ripper have a wife, or a sister, or a female servant of any kind? Did she know who he was, what he did, and perhaps because he provided the roof over her head, the clothes on her back, the food on her plate, she protected him?

That was a terrible thought. But life could be terrible at times.

He misunderstood her silence.

"You don't believe me!" he said angrily. "You think you know so much. You look at Albert and see a nice, polite man who speaks to you softly and pays you compliments to make you smile, and you imagine that's who he really is. Sometimes, Gwen, you are so gullible I think you live in a little dream world of your own." He sat up straighter in his chair. "Let me tell you, Albert isn't anything like the man you think he is. He drinks too much . . ."

"I know," she interrupted. "We all know that. But he isn't aggressive, he's just . . . a bit silly."

"A bit silly," he aped her tone. "And what about his affairs? Are they just a bit silly as well? With women off the street? Just like the ones that the Ripper's killed and gutted. Did you know that?"

She was too stunned to argue. That was nothing like the Albert she knew. It was spiteful of Riley to have told her that. She didn't need to know.

"I can see it in your face," he said jubilantly. "You didn't know! And you'd like to disbelieve me, but you can't. You think I made it up? I've seen the black and scarlet garter he keeps as a memento of it. And don't tell me it's Mary's! She never wore anything like that in her life. She hasn't the imagination . . . any more than you have!"

"You like scarlet and black garters?" she asked, her voice trembling.

"I like the sort of women who wear them, yes! Women who can laugh and have a bit of fun. Women who know how to flatter a man and please him, women who are proud of who they are and don't go around with faces like a jug of burnt porridge and a taste to match. You wouldn't know such women if you fell over them."

"And you do?" she asked with sudden spirit. "Fall over them often, do you?" There was an idea stirring in her mind, not that she cared that Riley was praising such people, but that he was trying to make her think that Albert could be the Ripper. It was a horrible, vicious thing to do, as if he were trying to poison her liking for Albert, and hurt Mary as well.

"Don't be stupid," was all he said, standing up from the table and walking out of the room, leaving the door open behind him.

Stupid! Did that mean he did? Or he didn't?

But it started the idea in her mind as to what she would do about it.

It took her two weeks to pluck up her courage, well into the middle of October. The weather grew worse, with the exception of one or two sharp, clear days, but ending earlier and earlier as the nights drew in and winter approached.

The Ripper was still in the news, and of course there were other crimes, some of them appalling. There were reckoned to be sixty-two brothels in Whitechapel alone, with twelve hundred prostitutes on the streets. Violence was not unusual. But these murders stood apart from all others and the words describing them screamed out from the newspapers and the sheets and posters around the city, and in the minds of the people, whether they could read or not.

Riley forbade Gwen from seeing Mary unless it was all four of them out together, most often a good meal, once to the music hall where any joke was good enough, crude or not. The only subject not made fun of was the Ripper. That was the one thing about which no one laughed.

It was because of Riley's spiteful remarks about Albert that Gwen was finally prompted to act. She took the bit of housekeeping money she had saved and went to a shop she had heard of, but had never visited before. She felt conspicuous and knew she would have to buy something else as well, simply to account for being there, if anyone should see her and speak of it.

"I'll have two yards of elastic, please," she began. Then looking around she saw what she had really come for. "And one of those, if you'll be so kind." She pointed to the black lace garter with scarlet ribbons wound through it and tied in a bow with pointed ends.

The girl blinked. "Yes, ma'am. Of course, ma'am. Just the one?"

"Yes please. One will be sufficient."

"Yes, madam. Whatever you say." And still with an air of amazement she wrapped it up, with the elastic, and passed it across the counter, in exchange for the money.

Gwen was a little annoyed that she apparently looked so little the type of woman who would wear such a thing as a lace garter, but then perhaps it was not such an insult after all. It did hint at a trade she would not care to join, even though she knew many did it of necessity.

When she got home she took it out of its paper, stored the elastic in her sewing basket, then went into the bathroom and put on the garter, on her left leg. It looked loud, outlandish. It required more elegant stockings than hers. But it was still fun. And it must look used, not one that came straight from the haberdashery. She added a tiny drop of perfume. Might as well be hanged for a sheep as a lamb.

It was another week before the perfect opportunity arose for it to be publicly displayed. Gwen and Riley were to dine out together at a very well thought of hotel. Gwen even had a new dress for the occasion. In her reticule she placed the garter, looking very slightly worn and definitely carrying a sweet odor of perfume. She knew exactly what she was going to do with it. This was Riley's invitation, so he would be paying the bill.

It was a most pleasant evening. The menu was excellent and both Albert and Riley were in a generous mood, a little boastful perhaps, but not enough to complain of. Other diners seemed to watch them with tolerance.

That was, until it came time to settle the account. The bill was duly presented to Riley, and he put his hand into his pocket to draw out his wallet. With it came a black lace garter with a scarlet ribbon in it.

Mary gave a little shriek and clapped her hand to her mouth. Gwen guessed that she had, after all, seen the one that Albert apparently kept as a souvenir.

"Oh my . . . !" Gwen said loudly, just to make certain everyone's attention was caught. "What is that?" As if anyone couldn't see!

The waiter struggled for words not to offend anyone, and gave up.

Someone stifled a giggle. One or two men swore or muttered about vulgarity and worse.

Riley looked around as if hoping someone might help him. Albert was trying desperately not to laugh. Perhaps he had suffered enough at Riley's teasing to relish this moment.

"Sir . . ." the waiter said at last. "I think . . ."

He was saved from having to say anything more by Gwen reaching across and taking the garter. She stuffed it into one of Riley's outside pockets, wanting to make it perfectly certain that nobody would think it was hers. She did it with a faint air of distaste, holding it between her finger and thumb.

"I think you should pay the bill," she said to Riley.

"Of course I'm going to pay the bill!" he snapped. "What did you think I was going to do?" He pushed the money at the waiter without counting it out.

Gwen raised her eyebrows. "With a scarlet ribboned garter at the dinner table?" she said mildly. "I have no idea! Whose is it?"

Riley blushed fiercely, but he was caught. Any denial would only make it worse.

Albert stifled his laughter and resumed a serious expression again. Mary looked bleak, and a little alarmed, as if she were trying to work out exactly what it meant.

The waiter withdrew with the money, thankful to escape.

Half the people in the dining room were openly staring at Riley. The other half were doing so more surreptitiously, whispering and avoiding his eyes.

"What's the matter with them?" Riley snarled under his breath. "What on earth are they thinking?" He dragged the last word out into silence as he realized exactly what was in their minds: newspaper pictures and terrified imaginations of dead prostitutes, sexually mutilated, blood . . . and a man who came to dinner with a prostitute's garter in his pocket. "Damn them!" he said hoarsely. "Who could . . ." He did not finish the sentence.

Gwen smiled patiently. "Well, Riley, you said yourself, the Ripper could be anyone. Most likely we haven't caught him precisely because he looks just like anyone else, quiet and respectable in the daytime. And very likely his own wife doesn't know for sure."

He stared at her as if he were seeing her for the first time, his eyes wide with incredulity, and then with fear. He looked around the room, and one by one people averted their eyes, some murmuring to the others at their table, some in silence.

Riley stood up, his face still scarlet, and walked out of the room to collect his overcoat and leave.

"I suppose we'd better all go," Gwen rose to her feet. "I'm so sorry."

"Damn stupid thing to do," Albert muttered, but there was a smile of amusement on his mouth and Gwen could guess what he must be thinking. She would have suspected him of having his revenge, if she hadn't put the garter there herself.

They were not home long, perhaps half an hour, when there was a knock at the door, sharp and demanding.

"Ignore it," Riley said tartly. "Just some nosy neighbour come to gawp at us."

The knock was repeated, heavy and hard.

Gwen disregarded Riley and went to answer it, hearing his voice behind her warning her to be careful. She was not afraid. The Ripper had never gone into anyone's home and attacked them.

She opened the door and found Sergeant Walpole on the step, and another uniformed policeman a couple of paces behind him.

"Sorry to trouble you, ma'am," Walpole said gently. "But I need to speak with your husband. I know about the garter, and you understand I can't just let it be."

She felt a chill run through her, leaving her a little shaky. She had meant to frighten Riley and definitely embarrass him, and she had succeeded brilliantly. But she had not intended to raise genuine suspicion with the police. That was entirely different. But if she admitted to buying the garter and putting it in his pocket, on purpose, he would never forgive her. He had seldom actually raised a hand against her, but it had happened. In her imagination, she could still feel the shock and the pain from it. And the fear would always be there.

"Of course," she said hastily. "Please come in."

"Thank you, ma'am," Walpole accepted, and he stepped into the hall, followed immediately by the constable.

Riley appeared at the sitting room door, ready to be angry with Gwen for letting people in at this hour. But when he saw the police, his face went ashen. He backed away and they followed him in, the constable waiting at the door, effectively blocking it.

There was panic in Riley's eyes.

"I expect you know why we're here, sir," Walpole said calmly, but he was watching Riley very closely and his right hand lingered near the truncheon at his belt. "Would you care to explain the very lurid woman's garter that fell out of your pocket this evening at the Albion Hotel?"

"None of your business," Riley said angrily. "A stupid prank. We dined with friends. Albert Clandon has a nasty sense of humor. I know one or two things about him, and he knows I do. He was just getting his own back. Trying to embarrass me."

"Seems he succeeded rather well." Walpole kept a totally straight face. "Are you saying Mr. Clandon put that garter in your pocket, sir?"

Riley saw the trap and sidestepped it. "I don't know, Sergeant. If I'd known, I'd have made damn sure I didn't haul it out at the table, now wouldn't I?"

"Yes, sir. So you're saying someone else put it there, and you weren't aware of it, so it could be anyone. But Mr. Clandon has an odd and rather spiteful sense of humor?"

"Yes, that's right."

Walpole appeared to consider it.

"He has a garter like that himself," Riley went on. "Souvenir of an old affair. I've teased him about it." He took a breath. "Maybe I shouldn't have, in front of his wife. This is probably his way of getting back at me."

"Having you pull that out in front of your wife? Not very funny, in the present circumstance, is it, sir? He had half the clients of the hotel thinking as you were the Ripper."

"Me?" Riley tried to look amazed, as if he had not thought of it himself, but he failed. The fear was clearly too deep.

"Well thank you, sir," Walpole said with a very slight smile. "It will be easy enough to confirm. I'll just have a very stiff word with Mr. Clandon. If he confirms it, that will be the end of the matter."

Riley drew in his breath to protest, and changed his mind. His face was white.

"And if he still has his?" Gwen asked. The moment the words were out of her mouth she wondered if she should have said them. Maybe she would have to admit her part in it. Now she was really afraid. Riley would beat her. This he would never forgive because he was frightened, and others had seen it.

"That would be another matter," Walpole said, looking at her with considerable sympathy.

Should she say that Riley had had it for years? It was new. They might be able to tell that somehow. And it still wouldn't explain why it had been in his pocket tonight, except that she had put it there. No one else had had the chance, except Albert, Mary, or Gwen. The answer had to be that Riley had put it there a while ago, and forgotten it.

"Gwen!" Riley said with a note of desperation. "Tell the sergeant that I was with you when those two women were killed back at the end of last month! You know I couldn't have done anything like that! Go on, tell him."

If she did that she would not only be lying herself, she would be making a liar of Mary as well. Because Mary would tell the truth, that Albert and Riley had gone out for quite a while after dinner.

What would Albert say, if he were asked? And he probably would be.

"Tell them!" Riley's voice was higher, sharper.

"We all had dinner together," she said to Walpole, hating doing it. It was wrong to lie, especially to the police, and on a matter as terrible as this. But it was also wrong not to stand by your husband when he needed you. And it was she who had got him into this trouble by putting the garter in his pocket. He couldn't actually be the Ripper!

Could he?

"So you said when I met you at about two o'clock that morning," Walpole agreed. "And you were together all evening?"

Her mouth was dry. What if it really were Albert? What if that darker side of him that Riley spoke of were something so hideous it ended in the Ripper murders? If they went on, then the next one would be, in a way, her fault.

"Nearly all," she said with a slight stammer. "I wasn't really thinking of the time."

"I see. Thank you, ma'am."

When he was gone, Gwen came back into the sitting room trembling. She was afraid of Riley. She had been afraid of him for a long time. She had never before done anything to earn his anger, except mistakes, sometimes a poor meal, the occasional forgetting of something important. This was different. She had bought the garter and put it where it would embarrass him most.

But he was not the Ripper. Of course he wasn't.

Was he?

No! That was just absurd. Half the women in Whitechapel must have had the thought cross their minds. And maybe one of them was right! Or maybe the one who would have been right had never thought it?

Was that Mary? Could it be?

And was Mary sitting at home now, thinking the same thing of her?

Say nothing, at least for now. She had told Walpole that it could not be Riley. But did he believe her? Maybe he knew she was lying?

Days went by. The nights grew longer and darker. Fog shrouded the streets and on some nights ice made the pavements slick and dangerous. October turned into November.

The police got nowhere in their search for Jack the Ripper.

Then, on the night of November 9th, he struck again. The corpse of Mary Kelly was found at 10:45 in the morning. It was lying on a bed in a room in Mathers Court, off Dorset Street in Spitalfields. It was the most hideously mutilated of them all. A pall of terror hung over London as people hurried through the fog, collars turned up, faces white with fear. It affected everyone.

Sergeant Walpole came to see Gwen and Riley again. He looked exhausted. His face was haggard and there was stubble on his cheeks as if he had had no time to take for even the simplest of things for himself.

He had already been to see Albert Clandon, who had no alibi. Mary had slept soundly and could not say that he had been at home all night. She had a heavy cold, and had gone to bed unusually early, and had not woken during the night.

Neither could Gwen swear that Riley had been home all the hours of darkness. He had not come back from work until after eight. He said he had stopped by for a drink at the Dog and Duck, but had not spoken to anyone he knew.

Walpole nodded and wrote it down on his pad. By the time he left there was nothing more Gwen could do, except blame herself, and wonder with a dark misery at the back of her mind if Riley's lashing out to blame Albert were actually a suspicion in his mind that it could be true.

If it were true, then why? What had Albert confided, or what had Riley seen, and been afraid to interpret, or even had been too loyal a friend to dare think it?

Something had to be done.

Accordingly, the next day she went to visit Mary, early when it was still bright and frosty, no fog. Riley had said she was not to see Mary alone. Was that because he feared Albert was the Ripper? Or just because he liked to order her around, feel that he was in charge? Regardless, she arrived at Mary's house at quarter to eleven.

Mary was delighted to see her. "Come in! Come in!" she pulled the door wide open. "A perfect time for a cup of tea. I have fresh scones. Would you like some?"

"I'd love one, at least," Gwen said with pleasure. She wished this were all as it used to be, before the Ripper terrified half of London out of its wits. They could just have sat and talked, laughed a little, as old friends do. The reality was unspeakable, but the fear of it had withered everything it touched.

They did not bother with the parlor but sat in the kitchen at the table and ate hot scones, rich with butter melting into them, and plum jam on top. For a little while at least, they indulged in old memories.

Of course the real subject had to be broached at last.

"The police were here yesterday," Mary said, the laughter draining out of her face. "I think they suspect Albert, or at the very least, that he knows something about it." She bit her lip. "I know he has his weaknesses, Gwen, but honestly there's no harm in him. I mean . . . not that kind of harm. I know he's had affairs, and I put up with them because it's just his childishness. He wouldn't hurt anyone!" She looked down the tabletop. "He likes a few strange things that I don't. Don't think ill of him, Gwen. It's just the way men are. My ma used to say, *Just let 'em do it, as long as they don't bring it 'ome with 'em.* He's good to me."

Gwen said nothing.

Mary looked up. "He is. He gets silly sometimes, but he don't never make little of me, like your Riley does. And he's never laid a hand on me, I swear."

Gwen found it easy to believe. It all fitted with the Albert she knew.

Mary brushed a tear away with the back of her hand. "But the Ripper's a real person sure enough, and maybe his wife don't think he'd hurt anyone neither. What are we going to do?"

Gwen thought in silence for several moments. Mary had said nothing about the possibility that it could be Riley. But perhaps it didn't need saying. The scarlet garter had come out of his pocket, after all. Did Mary even wonder if Gwen had put it there?

"We're going to find out where they were on the other nights that the Ripper killed," she answered. "If we can prove they were somewhere else, with a witness, that should be enough. Everyone knows they were all killed by the same person, done the same way."

"Right," Mary agreed. "It'll be hard work, but we could do it!"

It was the middle of the second afternoon and the daylight already fading when they collected the last piece of evidence, a question answered by a delivery boy to whom Albert had tipped a generous amount, and the boy had not forgotten him. Albert was safe. Riley was another matter.

But it was late, getting darker, and time they went home. In fact, the streetlights were lit, wreathed in slowly settling fog and it seemed like a long way from the yellow glow of one, through the shadows to the glow of the next. The air was bitter with the choking stillness of the fog.

There were footsteps behind them and they both quickened their pace. Mary slipped on the ice and Gwen held on to her so she did not fall. The footsteps behind were closer, catching them up.

Mary lunged forward as if to run.

Gwen swung around to fight.

"What's the matter with you?" Albert shouted as Gwen started towards him, swinging her string bag with heavy potatoes in it. Riley stood behind him.

"Albert!" Mary cried out in joy. "Oh Albert, you're safe!"

He had no idea what she meant, nor did he care. He threw his arms around her and hugged her.

"Stupid! Stupid!" Riley said under his breath, but he was reasonably civil to Mary. It was only after both Mary and Albert had left and Gwen was alone with him that he changed.

"What on earth do you think you were doing?" he demanded roughly. "It's nearly dark and you're out here alone like some stupid street woman. Do you wonder they get killed. Practically asking for it."

"Nobody asks to get their throats cut and their insides torn out!" she shouted back at him. "And none of them were killed at this time of day. And we were looking to find proof that Albert didn't do it."

"Did you find it?"

"Yes, we did!"

"And me? Did you find that I'm not guilty either?"

"No . . . we didn't."

"Of course you didn't!" he said with a slight hiss to his voice. "You didn't find proof of my innocence, because there isn't any. And do you know why that is, then, Gwendolyn? You're so busy, and clever, can you guess?"

He was so close she could feel his breath on her cheek. The question was too awful to answer. There was total silence, except for the slight sound of water dripping from the eaves somewhere close by. No footsteps. No one would come. Was this what it had been like for the other women, the five dead women who were so hideously disfigured and laid in bloody pieces on the ground?

Riley? Whom she had once loved, and now feared so much. Riley, who had steadily hurt and belittled her all these years. She had been living with a monster, and blind to everything but the petty cruelties, the words that bit and stung, the fear of violence in the air, like the odor of bad drains, getting into everything. And she had not known.

"Frightened, Gwen?" he said softly. "You stupid creature, you should be! You bought that garter, didn't you? You put it in my pocket so it would spill out on the table and embarrass me. You wanted them to think I was Jack!"

She tried to jerk away from him, but he was far too strong. He yanked her back sharply. A hansom cab passed by, its wheels rattling on the cobbles, and he held her closely, up against the wall.

"Don't want to make an exhibition of yourself, now do you? Tell perfect strangers that your husband is Jack the Ripper, now? You wouldn't do that, would you, Gwen?"

Her heart was beating so hard she almost choked getting her breath.

"That'll teach you to make a fool of me with some cheap garter," he said with profound pleasure. "You'll never know, will you? You'll never know where I've been, or what I've done. You stupid cow!" He let her go and started walking swiftly ahead of her, and she had to run to keep up with him.

She had no choice at all. The next day she faced her fears. He was probably not Jack at all, but he might be. She had to know. She could not spend the rest of her life in this terror. As soon as he left in the morning, she began her search. If he were the Ripper, there would be something in the house that would prove it.

She must be quick. If he caught her searching, who knew what he might do?

When she found it she was not at first certain what it meant. It was just notations in bank books in his private desk. They amounted to regular payments of a nice sum, made to Albert Clandon, over the last ten years. Blackmail! For what? What had Riley done that Albert knew about? How did he know?

Simple. They were in it together.

But then why would Riley pay Albert?

If she did nothing, she would be terrified every day and every night for the rest of her life. How many women in London were standing much as she was, with something in their hands, wondering if it meant that their husband, or their son or brother could be the man who had become known as "Jack"? One of them would be right. Would she end up dead too?

She put the papers in her bag and went out into the street. The decision was made.

At the police station, she asked for Sergeant Walpole.

"Have you found something?" he asked gravely.

Could he possibly know already? Then it was Riley! Had Sergeant Walpole suspected all along? Was that why he was sorry for her?

It stung, but it barely touched the coldness of fear inside her.

"Albert knew about it," she told him.

"It looks as if he took money to keep quiet," he agreed. "He helped as a friend. Or perhaps he even understood."

"Understood?" she said incredulously.

She felt Walpole's hand on her arm, strong, but surprisingly gentle. "Ma'am, he's not the Ripper. We've been looking into your husband since the first murder, and we found the truth. He's not the Ripper, but he did lose his temper with a prostitute who stole from him. I dare say he didn't mean to kill her. But even if it was rage rather than deliberate, he'll still go down for it. It'll be bad for a while."

"You mean, he did actually kill somebody?" she said with incredulity, and then belief.

And he said, "I'm afraid so."

"And what'll happen to me? I didn't know . . ."

"It'll be bad for a while," he said softly. "But it'll get better. You'll marry again, someone who'll love you like they should." Then he blushed fiercely and she felt tears of relief run down her cheeks.

"I think that would be nice," she replied.

SPRING-FINGERED JACK

Susan Casper

"Spring-Fingered Jack" is the first horror story written by Susan Casper (1947–), a remarkable achievement for the Philadelphia-born author who had no previous experience writing fiction.

Before turning to writing, she had worked in a record store, a factory that manufactured pants, a supermarket chain, the United States Postal Office, and the Pennsylvania Department of Social Welfare. Married to Gardner Dozois, the noted science fiction writer and editor, she became interested in writing in the same genre and developed a successful career.

She went on to produce several stories in collaboration with Dozois: "Send No Money," "The Stray," and "The Clowns" (on which Jack Dann also collaborated), which were collected in Slow Dancing through Time (1990), which also included her essay, the solo effort "New Kid on the Block." She also collaborated with Dozois to edit a Jack the Ripper–themed anthology, Ripper! (1988).

Casper has written more than two dozen stories for various anthologies, The Magazine of Fantasy and Science Fiction, Whispers, Rod Serling's The Twilight Zone Magazine, Amazing Stories, and Asimov's Science Fiction, for which she also wrote several nonfiction pieces.

"Spring-Fingered Jack" was first published in Fears, edited by Charles L. Grant (New York, Berkley, 1983).

He knew where he was going as soon as he walked into the arcade. He moved past the rows of busy children, blaring computer voices, flashing lights, and ringing bells. He walked past the line of old-fashioned pinball machines, all of them empty, all flashing and calling like outdated mechanical hookers vainly trying to tempt the passing trade.

The machine he wanted was back in the dimly lit corner, and he breathed a sigh of relief to see it unused. Its mutely staring screen was housed in a yellow body, above a row of levers and buttons. On its side, below the coin slot, was a garish purple drawing of a woman dressed in Victorian high fashion. Her large and ornate hat sat slightly askew atop her head, and her neatly piled hair was falling artistically down at the sides. She was screaming, eyes wide, the back of her hand almost covering her lovely mouth. And behind her, sketched in faintest white, was just the suggestion of a lurking figure.

He put his briefcase down beside the machine. With unsteady fingers, he reached for a coin, and fumbled it into the coin slot. The screen flashed to life. A sinister man in a deerstalker waved a crimson-tipped knife and faded away behind a row of buildings. The graphics were excellent, and extremely realistic. The screen filled with rows of dark blue instructions against a light blue field, and he scanned them sketchily, impatient for the game to begin.

He pressed a button and the image changed again, becoming a maze of narrow squalid streets lined with decaying buildings. One lone figure, his, stood squarely centre screen. A woman in Victorian dress, labled Polly, walked toward him. He pushed the lever forward and his man began to move. He remembered to make the man doff his cap; if you didn't, she wouldn't go with you. They fell in step together, and he carefully steered her past the first intersection. Old Montagne Street was a trap for beginners, and one he hadn't fallen into for quite some time. The first one had to be taken to Buck's Row.

Off to one side, a bobby was separating a pair of brawling, ragged women. He had to be careful here, for it cost points if he was spotted. He steered the pair down the appropriate alley, noting with satisfaction that it was deserted.

The heartbeat sound became louder as he maneuvered his figure behind that of the woman, and was joined by the sound of harsh, labored breathing. This part of the game was timed and he would be working against the clock. He lifted a knife from inside his coat. Clapping a hand over "Polly's" mouth, he slashed her throat viciously from ear to ear. Lines of bright red pulsed across the screen, but away from him. Good. He had not been marked by the blood. Now came the hard part. He laid her down and began the disemboweling, carefully cutting her abdomen open almost to the diaphragm, keeping one eye on the clock. He finished with twenty seconds to spare and moved his man triumphantly away from the slowly approaching bobby. Once he had found the public sink to wash in, round one was complete.

Once again his figure was centre screen. This time the approaching figure was "Dark Annie," and he took her to Hanbury Street. But this time he forgot to cover her mouth when he struck, and she screamed, a shrill and terrifying scream. Immediately the screen began to flash a brilliant, painful red, pulsing in time to the ear-splitting blasts of a police whistle. Two bobbies materialized on either side of his figure, and grabbed it firmly by the arms. A hangman's noose flashed on the screen as the funeral march roared from the speaker. The screen went dark.

He stared at the jeering screen, trembling, feeling shaken and sick, and cursed himself bitterly. A real beginner's mistake! He'd been too eager. Angrily, he fed another coin into the slot.

This time, he carefully worked himself all the way to "Kate," piling up bonus points and making no fatal mistake. He was sweating now, and his mouth was dry. His jaws ached with tension. It was really hard to beat the clock on this one, and took intense concentration. He remembered to nick the eyelids, that was essential, and pulling the intestines out and draping them over the right shoulder wasn't too hard, but cutting out the kidney correctly, *that* was a bitch. At last the clock ran out on him, and he had to leave without the kidney, costing himself a slew of points. He was rattled enough to almost run into a bobby as he threaded through the alleys leading out of Mitre Square. The obstacles became increasingly difficult with every successful round completed, and from here on in it became particularly hard, with the clock time shortening, swarms of sightseers, reporters and roving Vigilance Committees to avoid, in addition to a redoubled number of police. He had never yet found the right street for "Black Mary" . . .

A voice called "last game," and a little while later his man got caught again. He slapped the machine in frustration; then straightened his suit and tie and picked up his briefcase. He checked his Rollaflex. Ten-oh-five: it was early yet. The machines winked out in clustered groups as the last stragglers filed through the glass doors. He followed them into the street.

Once outside in the warm night air, he began to think again about the game, to plan his strategy for tomorrow, only peripherally aware of the winos mumbling in doorways, the scantily dressed hookers on the corner. Tawdry neon lights from porno movie houses, "Adult" book stores and flophouse hotels tracked across his eyes like video displays, and his fingers worked imaginary buttons and levers as he pushed through the sleazy, late-night crowds.

He turned into a narrow alley, followed it deep into the shadows, and then stopped and leaned back against the cool, dank bricks. He spun the three dials of the combination lock, each to its proper number, and then opened the briefcase.

The machine: He had thought of it all day at work, thought of it nearly every second as he waited impatiently for 5:00, and now another chance had come and gone, and he *still* had not beaten it. He fumbled among the papers in his briefcase, and pulled out a long, heavy knife.

He would practise tonight, and tomorrow he *would* beat the machine.

~

THE UNCERTAIN HEIRESS

Isak Dinesen

Isak Dinesen is one of the pseudonyms of Karen Christence Dinesen, Baroness Blixen-Finecke (1885–1962). Generally known as Karen Blixen (the other pseudonyms being Osceola, Tania Blixen, and Pierre Andrézel), she is most remembered for her memoir, *Out of Africa* (1937), which recounts her years in Kenya. It is a poignant tale of her beloved farm and coffee plantation; the loss of her longtime lover, the English big-game hunter Denys Finch Hatton; and the erosion of the simple African way of life that she deeply admired. It was lavishly adapted for the screen by producer-director Sydney Pollack, winning seven Academy Awards, including for Best Picture. It starred Robert Redford, Meryl Streep, and Klaus Maria Brandauer, the latter two having been nominated for Best Actress and Best Supporting Actor, respectively.

Born in Rungsted, Denmark, Blixen married her cousin, Baron Bror von Blixen-Finecke, in 1914. They moved to Kenya, where they owned and operated a coffee plantation and became big-game hunters. They were separated in 1921 and divorced four years later. She continued to run the plantation after their separation for another decade, finally forced to give it up due to drought, poor management, and the plummeting price of coffee. Having also lost her lover, who died when his plane crashed in 1931, she returned to Denmark and settled into a life as a writer.

She began writing short stories for Danish magazines in 1905, but her first book, *Seven Gothic Tales*, wasn't published until 1934; it was followed by *Out of Africa*, *Winter's Tales* (1942), *Last Tales* (1957), and the posthumous *Carnival: Entertainments and Posthumous Tales* (1977), *Daguerreotypes, and Other Essays* (1979), and *Letters from Africa, 1914–31* (1981). Her only novel, *The Angelic Avengers* (1944), was written under the Pierre Andrézel byline. Her most famous story is "Babette's Feast," written in 1958 and adapted for a Danish film that won the Academy Award for Best Foreign Language Film in 1988.

"The Uncertain Heiress" was first published in the December 10, 1949, issue of *The Saturday Evening Post*. It was retitled "Uncle Seneca" for its first appearance in book form in *Carnival: Entertainments and Posthumous Tales* (Chicago, University of Chicago Press, 1977).

Melpomene Mulock, the great actor's daughter, got a letter that upset her peace of mind. It was an invitation from her late mother's sister to stay with her for a fortnight at Westcote Manor, her country house.

Melpomene received the invitation on the twenty-eighth of November, 1906, which happened to be a Wednesday. She was accustomed to bills and summonses, but an invitation was a new thing to her. She said to herself, "I shall keep this letter for three days. On Saturday I will show it to father, and he will know how to answer it. Aunt Eulalia has waited eighteen years before writing to me. Now she can wait three days for my answer."

On Thursday she thought, "How could I possibly go to Westcote Manor? Father and I have been poor as long as I remember, and have been proud to be so. I could not bear to live for a whole fortnight in idleness and luxury, with people who have never thought of anything but their own comfort."

On Friday she thought, "How dares Aunt Eulalia invite me? I should betray Father if I accepted her invitation. Her family had no other merit than their wealth, but all the same they despised and rejected him. Should I now accept the belated charity of such hard and heartless people?"

On Saturday she reread the letter, and then slowly put it back in her drawer. For a third question had presented itself to her.

"Why," she asked herself, "does Aunt Eulalia invite me? Can it have anything to do with that young man who picked up my portfolio and offered me his umbrella? I have met him three times since that day, and each time his face has stuck in my mind for a very curious reason: because it was exactly like my own."

She got up and gravely faced the glass. She saw a pale, freckled face with a broad forehead and dark blue eyes, surrounded by glorious red hair.

"His hair," she thought, "was more fair than red, and freckles do look different in a sunburnt face. But his eyes, his nose, and his mouth were precisely like mine. If I were as beautifully dressed as he, I should look as handsome. Can it be that I have a cousin like that? I have heard of my wicked aunt almost every day of my life, but I have never heard of him."

On Sunday morning she felt guilty because she had not carried out her first intention. She brought her father Aunt Eulalia's letter with his breakfast in bed. Felix Mulock read the letter and turned pale; he read it again and turned dark red. He held it out at arm's length.

"So it is time, she thinks," he said with bitter scorn, "that dear Florence's child and her old aunt get to know each other! When I am ill and betrayed by the world, it is time to lure away my child with promises of worldly splendor."

"I shall never leave you, Father," said Melpomene, "and I am not accepting her invitation."

Her father was silent for a moment. "Time!" he repeated slowly. "To this scheming woman's eyes it was time once before. Six years ago, when your mother died, she wrote and claimed that I should hand over my daughter to her. She would give you a home and an education. Imagine what you would have been like today, if for six years you had been petted and coddled, if you had never heard the name of our divine William Shakespeare nor of his humble interpreter, your father!"

Melpomene smiled proudly.

Her father again was silent for a moment, then he put down the letter and looked at her. "Go!" he said. "Accept this invitation, and come back to tell me how you have made them feel that we despise their riches and prefer to starve in our own world of great ideals. Yes," he finished in a mighty outburst, "go, and come back to tell me that you have scorned and humiliated them!"

When Melpomene arrived at the country station, on a deadly still December evening, she was met by a fine carriage and pair. At the big house with the tall, lighted windows a dignified butler took her small box from her.

Aunt Eulalia got up from her chair in front of the sitting-room fire to welcome her niece. She had on a rustling black frock, and she had the very same face, although faded and a little flabby, as the young man with the umbrella, and as the girl herself. She stared at Melpomene, then flung her arms around her and burst into tears.

"My lost Florence," she cried, "have I got you back?"

The room was warm, gently lit, and filled with the scent of hothouse plants. Its deep carpets, silk curtains, and large paintings in heavy gilt frames evidently formed a magic circle round an existence of perfect security, difficult for Melpomene to imagine. Into this room no worry or care, no dunning letters or angry landlord would ever have been admitted. What did the people who lived in it find to think about? Did they think at all?

Melpomene at this moment felt proud of her patched shoes and her old frock. They were her credentials. Here it was she who crossed the doorstep as the stern collector, with all the claims of a higher, wronged world in her hand.

Aunt Eulalia's son, Albert, joined them by the fireside, and the girl saw that he was her old acquaintance of the wind and the rain. He was in perfect harmony with the room, and looked so pleasant in his evening clothes that under other circumstances she would have been happy to know that she resembled him. He shook hands with her in a friendly manner, and blushed a little as he acknowledged their previous meetings.

Melpomene at once felt sure that she owed Albert her invitation. But why had he asked his mother to invite her? He had seen her lonely and tired, in wet clothes. He must have been as amazed at the likeness between them as she had been. He must have followed her and inquired about her. Now he treated her, she thought, as if she were some precious and fragile object which he must be careful not to break.

He made her feel embarrassed, for when she looked at him, it was like looking into a mirror, and when she looked away, she felt his eyes on her face.

Just before dinner an elderly, well-dressed gentleman was introduced to her. They called him Uncle Seneca.

In the evening, before the fire, Aunt Eulalia talked about her dear sister, ten years younger than herself. She had tried to soften the hearts of their angry father and mother when Melpomene's mother had eloped with the actor. When Florence's baby was born, she had wanted to hurry to her bedside, but her husband had forbidden it. Now she did not even remember the exact date of the event.

"I was born," said Melpomene, "on the seventh of August, 1888."

At this, Uncle Seneca turned his bright birdlike eyes at her in a sudden, keen glance.

Melpomene woke up next morning, quite late, under a silk quilt and in a big four-poster, to a day as gray and silent as the last. A maid brought in her dainty breakfast on a silver tray. She had never in her life had breakfast in bed. Now, as she poured out her tea and buttered her hot muffins, she thought of her father, alone in his cold flat, and of the mission on which he had sent her. It might prove more difficult than he had suspected to shock an upholstered and silk-covered world.

During the following week Melpomene often felt as if she had been ordered to strike with a hammer at a featherbed. The whole house folded her in a warm and soft embrace. The old servants did their best to make her as comfortable as possible. And Aunt Eulalia was ever about the rooms, doing her flowers or her needlework, and gazing tenderly at the niece who was so like her dear Florence. Her small flow of chatter ran through all the hours of the day, as if to wash away, quite pleasantly, Melpomene's former existence. She did not question the girl about her father or her home. She dwelt in the past, and described the happy childhood and girlhood which she and her sister had passed in this same house. Or she talked about Albert. No mother had ever had such a good and kind son! Her own sole object in life was to see her dear boy happy.

Albert took his cousin out for drives, to point out views. He told her the names of his horses, and he showed her his dogs, and, to amuse her, every day made them go through the tricks he had taught them.

She smiled ironically at the efforts of her aunt and her cousin. But she began to find it difficult to believe that they were really the schemers and seducers described by her father.

In all the rooms of the house there were portraits of grandparents and great-aunts, and she knew that she had their blood in her veins. She had been amazed to see how much Aunt Eulalia and Albert were like her; now she was panic-stricken to think that she might be like them. She fought down the thought, but it came back. She could not get away from the fact that she had enjoyed flowers in her room and breakfast in bed. She liked Albert's dogs—in particular a little black spaniel.

To strengthen and brace herself she began to talk to her rich relations of her home. She depicted the cold of the rooms, the darkness of the stairs and her late hours of work. She went on in a kind of ecstasy, in the manner of her father himself, as she proudly proclaimed her perfect content in the middle of it all.

Aunt Eulalia listened, her mouth open, and then, all in tears, begged her pardon because she had not come to her rescue before. Albert listened, his lips pressed together, and the next day suggested that she take the black spaniel back with her to London.

Under the circumstances, Melpomene sought refuge with Uncle Seneca. The old gentleman at first had been a little shy with her. Now, whenever she happened to be alone, he peeped out from his own room for a friendly talk. And if he did not speak much, he was a perfect listener.

Melpomene was happier with him than with the others. For he did not feel sorry for her; at times she even thought that he envied her her experiences. He asked her how it felt to be hungry—might the feeling be called a pain? He wanted details of narrow back yards and steep dark stairs, and he took a great interest in rats. He must at some time have bought and studied a map of the poorest quarters of London, for he knew the names of many streets and squares there. Melpomene reflected with dismay that to a rich old bachelor all these things were as fascinating and fantastic as toys in a shop window to a little poor boy in the street.

But she could not be angry with Uncle Seneca himself, for he questioned her and listened to her in the manner of a child. Perhaps, she thought, his eagerness did indeed rise from a nobler motive than curiosity. Sometimes, when she told him about very poor and wretched people, he became restless and his hands trembled a little. "There ought not to be such people," he said.

From Aunt Eulalia, she learned that Uncle Seneca was no blood relation of hers. An old aunt's widower had married again and in his second marriage had had this only son. The boy had been a pretty and talented child, and as a young man had surprised the family by taking up the study of medicine and wanting to become a doctor. But he was a delicate youth, and in the end his family had persuaded him to give up the hard work.

The old man now lived in Aunt Eulalia's house and seldom left it. He did not seem to Melpomene to pay much attention to Albert, but he treated Aunt Eulalia with great respect and consideration. He was, the girl thought, one of those truly chivalrous men with a high ideal of women. "I have had the privilege," he once said, "to be born and brought up, and to have lived my best years, in an epoch when England was ruled by a lady."

He had various small hobbies with which he passed his time: he collected butterflies and was clever at stuffing birds. He also did needlework and would bring his cross-stitch to the fireside. He had a queer little habit of gazing attentively at his own hands. He had inherited a large fortune, which was now increasing year by year, and it was understood that Albert was to be his heir.

But even with Uncle Seneca to support her self-confidence, Melpomene was aware of her false position in the family circle. Within three days she was to return to London. Before that time she must make it clear that she was still a stranger in the house, and still their enemy and their judge.

Two or three times she prepared her speech of denouncement, failed to get it out, and called herself a coward. At last, on Sunday evening, she did her duty.

Aunt Eulalia had dwelt with sadness on the prospect of her departure, and with delight on the prospect of her early return.

"No," said Melpomene suddenly, "no, Aunt Eulalia, I am not coming back. Everything here is sweet and perfect, too sweet and perfect for me. I could not bear to live for my own comfort only."

"Sweet child," said Aunt Eulalia, "you want to live for your father's comfort."

"For his comfort!" Melpomene exclaimed. "Oh, how mistaken you are! It is for his immortality that I want to live!" She was silent for a moment. "I have been suffocating in this house," she went on with heightened color. "To me, it is unnatural and insane to live for the moment, with no thought of futurity."

"Darling Melly," said Aunt Eulalia, "we all have the hope of a better, an everlasting future. And here on earth we wish to live on in our dear children and grandchildren."

"Oh, yes!" Melpomene cried. "You all imagine that better, everlasting future to be exactly like your life here—an easy, carefree existence, one day just like the other, little pleasant talks about nothing, a walk with the dogs. And as to your futurity on earth, I call that a cheap kind of immortality. I myself claim for my father an undying fame! How could I resign myself to the thought that his great creations, as great as any painter's and sculptor's, should all vanish with him?"

"Oh, but we must all," said Aunt Eulalia, "resign ourselves to the idea of mortality."

"No!" cried Melpomene. "No, not at all!" She grew very pale and drew in her breath deeply. "My father," she said very slowly, "has an old friend in London, an Italian and a great sculptor. He has seen father in all his roles, and thinks as highly of them as father himself. They have inspired him with the idea of a memorial which is to preserve father's name for centuries. It is a glorious work of art. On the plinth you see all the figures which father has created, from King Oedipus to the Master Builder. And high above them all stands father himself, in his big cloak, with his splendid hair, and his arm outstretched." There was a long pause. "That," said Melpomene, "is what I live for."

"My poor, precious child," said Aunt Eulalia, "you do not know what you speak about! It is a dream of a person entirely without practical experience! You will never, even if you starve yourself to death, save up enough money for such a thing! Preserve me, the memorial on our family tomb cost three thousand pounds!"

"And what if it cost three thousand pounds?" she cried. "What if it cost six thousand? I am not a person entirely without practical sense, Aunt Eulalia. Father and Signor Benatti have made up a small book with plans and descriptions of the monument; I myself am only to save up the money to get it published. As soon as it is out, everybody in England who has ever seen father on the stage will be happy and proud to contribute. And it is the happiness and pride of my life to work for his undying name."

Again there was a pause.

Melpomene had spoken with her eyes above the heads of her audience; now she looked at them. They all three sat quite still. The faces of Aunt Eulalia and Albert, as often before, expressed mild bewilderment and compassion. But Uncle Seneca listened with profound attention. He looked at his hands.

"A name," he said slowly, "an undying name."

"Uncle Seneca," Melpomene thought, "is the only person here who understands me."

She held her head high as she went up to bed, but she did not sleep well. The sad, concerned faces of Aunt Eulalia and Albert were still before her eyes. She had not succeeded in altering their expression.

Late the next morning when she came down into the hall, she found Albert there.

"Look here," he said, "you talked last night of a memorial for your father. If you had three thousand pounds today, would you spend them on it? And would it make you happy?"

Melpomene looked at him gravely. "Do you mean," she said, "that you would give me three thousand pounds to wipe out your people's guilt toward my father?"

Albert thought her words over. "No," he said, "I cannot honestly say that. I cannot honestly say that I feel called upon to put up a monument for Uncle Felix. But I was wondering whether it would make you happy."

"Make me happy?" said Melpomene slowly. She could not remember that anybody had ever passionately wanted to make her happy.

"Look here," said Albert; "I have wished I could make you happy from that first moment when I met you in the rain. It is a very strange thing. One reads in books about love at first sight, but one never believes that it happens to people in real life. And then it was love at first sight with me myself."

Melpomene felt a great movement of triumph run through her. Albert, young, rich, and handsome, was laying his heart and all his worldly goods at her feet, and within a moment she was going to refuse it all. That would be a finer trophy to carry back to her father than he could ever have dreamed of. The idea stirred her so deeply that she could not find a word to say.

"Look here," said Albert, "I felt at once that you were what people call one's better self. The other girls have all been strangers, somehow, but you were like me. I have had everything and I knew, the instant I saw you, that I should like to give all I have to you, and that only then it might at last be some use to me and give me some fun in life. I should like to see you in pretty clothes, and in a nice room of your own. I should like to see you with a dog of your own. And then I should like you to have your father's monument as well."

As still she did not speak, but only looked at him with clear, bright eyes, he went on.

"As to myself," he said, "I have always been lonely in a way. I have never had a real friend. Now I have got you. I have never believed that I should ever want to marry, and when I told mother that I wanted to marry you, she was so pleased that she wept with joy. I have never believed that I was going to be really happy. It is a very strange thing. Now I should be wonderfully happy if I could make you happy at all."

Melpomene did not speak at once. "No, Albert," she said, "you cannot make me happy. I do not want your pretty clothes; I do not want a room of my own. I am going back to my father tomorrow."

Albert grew very pale; he went to the window and came back again. "I believe," he said, "that you are wrong in going back to your father. I do not believe that you will be happy in London. Look here, Melpomene. I believe that you might come to love me. It is a very strange thing to say—I should never have thought that I would say it to a girl—but I believe that you might come to love me."

Melpomene till now had spoken with self-possession, remembering her program. But when Albert said that she might come to love him, she wavered on her feet, and her throat contracted so that she could not get a word out. To steady herself, in a great effort she called up her father's face. It helped her; after a moment she could speak.

"If I came to love you, Albert," she said very slowly, "I would still not accept a penny from you for father's memorial, for I would know that you did not give it in admiration and repentance. If I loved you at this moment," she went on in a voice that sounded strange to herself, and which indeed seemed to speak all on its own, "I should at this moment vow never to see you again after I have got home tomorrow, and never to open a letter from you until I had in my hand three thousand pounds of my own, for father's monument."

The two young people for a minute remained face to face, both very pale and grave. Then she walked past him and out of the house.

She walked for a long time before she could collect her thoughts sufficiently to realize that she had won her war and fulfilled her mission. That all was well, and that all was over.

At last she stood still; her dizziness had gone; now she felt the cold round her. She had walked so far that she had lost her way, and it was growing dark. She turned and tried to remember the road by which she had come.

She did not recognize it; there were a lot of high fences everywhere, and she had to walk alongside them to find the stiles. Had they all been there on her way out? She suddenly remembered that she had denounced Westcote Manor and all it contained, and wondered if the house had taken her at her word.

At last between the trees of the park she caught sight of lights, and made for them. In the avenue she was surprised to see a figure coming toward her. For a moment it looked very big in the mist, then it grew small. It was Uncle Seneca with a large umbrella in his hand.

He seemed happy to see her. "I was quite worried," he said, "because you did not come back. I thought it was going to snow, so I brought my umbrella."

Melpomene knew how seldom Uncle Seneca went out, and how scared he was of cold weather. She was vaguely touched by his kindness, and at the same time vaguely pained by the memory of how she had once before, long, long ago, been offered an umbrella by a gentleman.

"Eulalia," said Uncle Seneca, "had to go out to see a neighbor. Albert took her in his gig. You and I will have tea by ourselves." They walked up the avenue side by side under the umbrella.

When they came in, tea was ready in front of the fire. The pink-shaded lamps shone on the silver and the china. The gardener must have brought in heliotropes from the hothouse; their scent was strong and sweet in the room.

Uncle Seneca gave two or three little sneezes and looked slightly feverish in the lamplight, as if he might have waited too long in the avenue and have caught a chill on his gallant expedition.

He moved his chair closer to the fire and said, "I forgot to put on my galoshes. Perhaps I really ought to go and change my shoes."

But he did not go. He did not speak for a while either, but gazed at his hands and then smiled at the girl above his teacup. For a long time there was a silence in the room, for Melpomene was too tired and too absorbed in her own thoughts to speak.

"It is an honor and a pleasure," Uncle Seneca began at last, "for an old sedentary person like myself to talk to a young lady who knows the world. People, I suppose, will have been talking to you of almost everything."

"Yes," said Melpomene, who had hardly heard what he said.

"People," he repeated cheerfully, "will have been talking to you of drunkards and opium smokers?"

"Yes," she said again.

"Yes, yes," he said, cheering up more and more. "And of pickpockets and burglars?"

"Yes," she said.

"And of worse than that," he continued, this time a little timidly. "Of creatures sunk still deeper, who really ought not to exist?"

"Yes," said the girl, still in her own thoughts.

"And of murderers?" asked Uncle Seneca.

Something in this queer catechism at last caught Melpomene's attention. She slowly raised her eyes to the old man's face.

"Do you know," he asked, "who Williams was—the man who wiped out two households within a fortnight?"

"Yes, I believe so," said Melpomene.

"Do you know," he inquired again, "who John Lee was—the man who could not be hanged?"

"Yes, I believe so," said Melpomene.

"Do you know," asked Uncle Seneca, "who Jack the Ripper was?"

"Yes," Melpomene answered.

Uncle Seneca gave such a sudden little titter that the girl stared at him. "I beg your pardon," he said. "I did not mean to be rude. It only struck me as a curious thing that you should say that you knew who Jack the Ripper was. For that is the one thing that nobody ever knew."

There was a pause.

"I am Jack the Ripper," said Uncle Seneca. "I was quite struck," he said, "when you told Eulalia that you were born on the seventh of August, 1888. For that was the date of the first of them." He thought the matter over for a moment. "And," he said, "nobody knew. Nobody in all the city of London. Nobody, in fact, in all the world. It is," he continued, "a very strange sensation. You walk down a street full of people. None of them looks at you. And yet every one of them is looking for you." He sneezed again, and blew his nose in a large white handkerchief. "I have never known many people," he went on; "my family was most particular about our circle of acquaintances. But upon that time it might be said that everybody knew me. They gave me a name, 'Jack.' It is a frisky name, a name for a sailor. Friskier than Seneca, do you not think so? And then, 'the Ripper.' Is not that brisk as well . . . smart? I was pleased the first time I heard that this was the name they had given me. I thought it quite bright of them. And nobody knew. . . . You young people nowadays," he remarked thoughtfully, "say 'ripping,' do you not, when something is really pleasant? . . . The second," Uncle Seneca said, after another pause, "was on the last day of the month. The third was a week later. It took a cool hand to come out again to work so quickly, do you not think so? That third one was skillfully done. Some other day, when we have got time, I shall tell you more about that third one.

"There was an odd little circumstance about the matter," he said. "People talked about Jack everywhere, but very few people talked about him to me. My family, I am pretty sure, must have talked a good deal about him, but they never mentioned him to me. They used to put away the papers when they had read them. There were big headlines in the papers those days: Who is Jack the Ripper? Where is Jack the Ripper? I sat and read them by our tea table, which was just like this one here, and I could have answered at any moment, 'Here he is.' In one paper they wrote: 'The great skill points to someone with real anatomical knowledge,' and in another: 'It is possible that after having done the deed Jack put on gloves.' So Jack did."

He sat for a while in silence.

"It all began," he said, "with my dreams. I have always had very vivid, lifelike dreams. Now I began to dream that I did it. I dreamed that I came down a street at night, and that these persons were there and that I did it. Night after night I dreamed it, and I began to walk about in London to find the street. I bought a map to find it. My dreams grew more and more vivid, and in the end I understood that I had to do it."

Again he was silent.

"A name!" Uncle Seneca said, and suddenly looked straight at Melpomene. "You spoke last night of a name. Of a person who ought to have an immortal name to him. Here is an immortal name which, one might say, ought to have a person to it. My family had often teased me because I liked to look into the glass. At that time I looked more frequently than before into the glass, and at the person in it, who looked back at me."

He was perfectly still for a long time. Melpomene, too, sat still; she could not even move her eyes away from his face.

"Your father," Uncle Seneca said, "was indeed a great actor. We went to see him in Macbeth. That was in between the third and the fourth. The bard is always magnificent, of course. Still, he, too, can make mistakes. 'All the perfumes of Arabia will not sweeten this little hand.'" He looked at his hands. "That is a mistake," he said. "They will. I understood you last night," he went on, "although Eulalia and Albert did not. I understand that your father will want his monument. For with him it has never been anything but acting. With him it has never been the real thing. 'As they had seen me with these hangman's hands.' He must have a monument to have his name remembered. It is a strange thing," he said, after a pause, "that I should, late in life, meet a young lady like you, who knows these places of mine and, just like me, has walked down Berners Street. I have been happy to meet you, Miss Melpomene. . . . And nobody knew," he said.

Suddenly his face changed; little nervous twitches ran over it, and his wide-opened eyes sought Melpomene's. "There they are," he said, "back already. I had hoped that we might have had half an hour more to ourselves."

The rumble of wheels was heard on the drive. The front door was opened and voices sounded in the hall.

Melpomene got up from her chair; she went out through the library and slowly mounted the stairs to her room. She lay down on her bed with her face in the pillows. She told the maid who brought the hot water that she had a headache and could not come down for dinner.

Next day she went back to London. Aunt Eulalia embraced and kissed her niece even more tenderly at her departure than she had done at her arrival.

"My darling," she said, "it has been lovely having you here. Now we are looking forward to your return to Westcote Manor."

Albert shook hands with Melpomene in a friendly manner, but with a pale face. Uncle Seneca did not appear. He was in bed with a cold.

In the carriage and in the train, Melpomene kept her mind fixed on her father and her home. When she got back to them, she found the rooms very untidy. The fire had gone out and her father had remained in bed to keep warm.

Felix Mulock had been looking forward to hearing his daughter's report of her visit, and had prepared little biting gibes, in his old manner from Hamlet, with which to accompany it all through. Now he was disappointed that he had to drag the account from her word by word. In the end, he lost patience.

"Well," he cried, "I suppose they have told you they have given me money that you did not know of!"

"No," said Melpomene, "they did not tell me."

"If you had not had all your mother's stubbornness, my girl," he went on with a little bitter laugh, "and of course all those freckles, you might have made Cousin Albert fall in love with you. That would have been a sweet revenge! What a perfect rehabilitation to have the house into which I was never admitted belong to us!"

The idea delighted him. All through the evening he amused himself by depicting in detail his conquest and triumphal occupation of the enemy's camp.

The week that followed on her return seemed very long to Melpomene. The December cold became part of a loneliness that she had never known before. She dared not think of Albert; she dared not think of her father's monument. In fact, she found that she dared not think of anything at all.

One night she woke up with a strange new sensation of happiness and warmth. She sat up in bed, for suddenly she realized that her one place of refuge on earth and her one happiness was in Albert's arms.

The idea overwhelmed her; her whole body ached with it. She did not care for immortal fame. What she longed for, with every drop of her blood, was an easy, carefree existence, one day just like the other, little pleasant talks about nothing, a walk with the dogs.

All through the night she remained sitting up in her small bed in the dark room, her face wet with tears. She felt herself to be a very small figure in all the city of London, in all the world.

"This one little short life," she cried in her heart, "is all that I can be sure of. And I have thrown it away. I have vowed never to see Albert again. I have told him that I would never open a letter from him, so that now he will never, never, write to me."

In this she was wrong. The day before Christmas she received a letter from her cousin.

Albert's letter ran as follows:

Westcote Manor,

22 December, 1906

Dear Cousin Melpomene:

I am afraid that you will be angry with me for writing to you. But you will receive, one of these days, a letter from our old solicitor, Mr. Petri, and it seems to me that I ought to prepare you for it. So I hope that you will forgive me this one time.

I first of all have to tell you that Uncle Seneca has died. He got a bad cold, nobody knows how, for he used to take very good care of himself. It turned into pneumonia; for three days he had high fever and was strangely changed, so that he did not seem to be himself at all. But in the end he passed away quite quietly.

You were very kind to him when you were down here. I think you will be glad to feel that at the end of his life you gave him a pleasant time. He was much upset when he heard that you had gone back to London. All through his fever- ish days he talked of getting up and going after you. But his mind was not clear;

he kept on telling us that he would follow you, and be sure to find you, in some street of which nobody has ever heard the name.

Last Thursday, however, as his temperature went down, he lay for a long time without saying a word, just looking very pleased with himself. In the evening he told us to send for Mr. Petri, and when he arrived, Uncle Seneca informed him that he wanted him to draw up a new will for him.

Mr. Petri will come round to see you next week, and you will hear all about the matter from him. I just want to give you here, before Christmas, the good news that Uncle Seneca has left all his money to you. You will now be able to put up the memorial for your father, of which we talked the last day in the hall. Do not believe that I now mean to hold you to your word from that same talk of ours. You may have changed your mind. But I mean to tell you here that I have not changed mine, and shall never change it.

Mr. Petri will inform you that there is a curious stipulation in Uncle Seneca's will. According to that, you must get your father's monument put up, and you must lay the foundation stone with your own hand. And on this stone, which will, of course, never be seen, because the whole monument will be on the top of it, should be cut the following inscription: IN MEMORY OF *J. T. R.*

I know no more than you what these letters mean, and I can see you smiling quite ironically as you read them here. For one would naturally take them to stand for something romantic, perhaps for the name of a friend or sweetheart. And you will be sure to think Uncle Seneca a lonely old person who cared for nobody, and could never have had a friend, and his whole life too conventional and commonplace for a romance. All the same, since you seemed to like talking with him when you were down here, I suppose you will not mind carrying out what people would call his last wish, nor having his stone to be, so to say, for-ever part of your father's monument.

Until quite lately—in fact, until the time when I met you—I myself should have laughed at the idea of anything romantic ever having happened to Uncle Seneca. I should, in fact, have been quite sure that it had happened only in his own dreams. For he was always extraordinarily keen on his dreams. These last years he did not talk much about anything, but when I was a small boy, he would talk to me for a long time of his dreams and of the things he had done in them.

But when something really romantic and wonderful happens to oneself, one somehow feels that it may have happened to other dull fellows as well. Their dreams, too, may have come true. So now I think it quite possible that Uncle Seneca has meant something to people he has met in life, perhaps to women long since dead.

It is a curious thing that I shall probably miss old Uncle Seneca a good deal more than I ever expected. In fact, I was quite sad today when I remembered his little habit of looking thoughtfully at his own hands.

I should like to write a great deal more to you. But I shall not do so until I hear from you.

Your cousin,

ALBERT ARBUTHNOT

KNUCKLEBONES

Tim Sullivan

The multitalented Timothy Robert Sullivan (1948–) is a polymath with careers as a science fiction writer, actor, screenwriter, and motion picture director.

In addition to scores of short stories, he has written several novels, beginning with three novelizations of the television series *V*, which is set in an America that has been taken over by aliens (some have suggested this may not be fictional). His first original novel, *Destiny's End* (1988), is set on a distant planet and draws on Greek mythology. This was followed by *The Parasite War* (1989), which describes a coterie of humans battling an alien invasion; *The Martian Viking* (1991), which features a human prisoner who escapes from Mars and travels through space and time with, yes, Vikings; and *Lords of Creation* (1992), a fantasy populated by dinosaurs, aliens, and, perhaps most terrifying, a televangelist.

Two of Sullivan's stories were shortlisted for major awards: "Zeke" (1981) was nominated for a Nebula and "The Comedian" (1982) for a Locus.

Sullivan largely stopped writing in the early 1990s to focus on his acting career as he played roles in numerous small-budget science fiction and horror films, perhaps most notably *Camp Blood* (1999) and *Camp Blood 2* (2000), slasher films written and directed by his friend Brad Sykes; both movies went directly to video.

"Knucklebones" was first published in *Ripper!*, edited by Gardner Dozois and Susan Casper (New York, Tom Doherty Associates, 1988).

"Watch this," Maurice Turner said, holding up the tiny guillotine.

The kids who weren't playing basketball gathered around him, curious about what this new kid was up to. Maurice, shorter than most of them, held the guillotine up so that the sun glinted off of it. Even the basketball game stopped for a minute, the guys who were playing wanting to see what was going on as much as the rest of the kids.

"Anybody got a cigarette?" Maurice asked.

Andy McHugh, the biggest kid in the whole school—he had stayed back two grades and was old enough to be an eighth grader, even though he was only in sixth—hooked the ball through the railing chain hoop and walked over to the little crowd gathered around Maurice.

"I got one," Andy said, unrolling a pack of smokes from his T-shirt sleeve. With a swift downward motion, he forced a cigarette's filtertip end out of the crushed cellophane package and offered it to Maurice. "There you go, kid."

"Thanks," Maurice said. Walking to the back wall of the school, he set the toy guillotine down on the highest granite step leading up to the doorway. Then he placed the cigarette in the half-inch-wide hole near the guillotine's base. Maurice waited a few seconds for effect, as he'd seen Doug Henning do on one of the rare occasions his Mom let him watch something on TV besides the religious channel.

Just when they were starting to murmur, he brought the flattened palm of his right hand down hard on the top of the guillotine.

There was a noise like a papercutter, and the cigarette was chopped neatly in half.

Maurice paused again.

"Big deal," a blonde girl said. "All you did was waste Andy's cigarette."

"Oh, yeah?" Maurice stuck his index finger in the hole. "Watch this."

He slammed the top of the guillotine down again.

The girl screamed, and the other kids all started talking excitedly. Maurice withdrew his unharmed finger and waggled it at them.

"Gnarly," Andy McHugh said. "I guess it *was* worth a cigarette."

Maurice grinned and handed him the two pieces. If Andy liked it, then everybody else would too. The blonde girl, who had been watching Andy admiringly during the basketball game, now turned her blue eyes to Maurice. "That was really *rad,*" she said.

Maurice was about to say something back to her when Bobby Feldstein drew his freckled, bespectacled face up to Maurice's. "How does that thing work?"

Annoyed, Maurice nevertheless smiled at him and held up the guillotine. "Here, Bobby," he said, "stick your finger in here and I'll show you."

Bobby pointed his finger at the guillotine, and then hesitated. "How do I know what you're going to do?" he asked.

"Oh, come *on,*" Maurice chided. "Do you think I would have stuck *my* finger in there if it didn't work?"

"I guess not." Bobby smiled nervously, and put his finger through the hole.

Still grinning at Bobby, Maurice whacked the top of the guillotine as hard as he could. There was a wet, chopping sound. Bobby looked puzzled for a minute, and then began to yowl. He pulled his finger free and stared at it in amazement. Between the first and second knuckles was an ugly gash. Blood welled up and ran down his finger, crossing the back of his hand and falling onto the asphalt in bright red drops.

Clutching his hand to his chest, blood soaking into his jacket and shirt, Bobby ran off, screaming.

Maurice noted with satisfaction that nobody was watching Bobby; they were all looking straight at *him* though none of them were making eye contact. They were *scared* of him. Even Andy—who sometimes walked right out into the street, so that cars had to go around him or even stop—looked a little pale. Only the blonde girl looked right into his eyes.

Maurice was pretty sure he would see *her* later.

When he got back from the principal's office, it was time for lunch. Maurice didn't want to eat in the cafeteria, so he started walking away from the school.

"Hey!"

Maurice turned to see the blonde girl running towards him. He waited for her to catch up.

"Are you skipping afternoon classes?" she asked breathlessly.

"No, I'm just walking to the store to get a sandwich."

"Can I come?" the girl asked.

"Sure. Why not."

As they walked down the littered sidewalk, the girl said, "How did you get away with what you did in the schoolyard, anyway?"

"It was easy. I just told the principal it was an accident. She took the guillotine away, but I can get another one."

"Oh, yeah? Where do you get all your bread?"

"My Dad gives it to me." Unless his Mom was around, Maurice thought, but it wouldn't be cool to say that.

"Do you do a lot of errands and stuff for your Dad?"

"Nah." Maurice shrugged. "Here we are."

The store—Popi's—was just a block from the school. Popi was older than Maurice's parents, maybe thirty-five or forty, and he had long dark hair, a beard and rimless glasses. He sold comic books, and also had video games, ice-cream and candy. He would make a hoagie to order for you for three dollars.

"Aren't you worried about being late?" the blonde girl asked.

"Nope."

"Don't you worry about *anything*?" She frowned. "You know, you haven't even asked me my name."

Maurice, leaning against the freezer case, shrugged. "Well, what is it?"

"Mary Jane Toricelli."

Maurice couldn't believe it, but he tried not to show his excitement. "You know something, Mary Jane," he said, "that's a great name."

"Thank you," she replied demurely.

Maurice thought about explaining why he liked her name, but just then Popi brought their hoagies out and waited for Maurice to pay him. By the time they sat down at one of the three metal tables in the place. Maurice had decided against telling her. If she mentioned it to anyone, there could be trouble later.

"I've seen you around school," Maurice lied. He had never noticed her until today, but now God had pointed her out to him.

Mary Jane blushed.

"You're one of the prettiest girls I've seen since my father was stationed here," Maurice said, taking a bite of his hoagie. He hated to say things like that, but it had to be done.

"You're an Army brat, huh?" Mary Jane's eyes widened. She had taken the compliment for granted. "Have you been around the world?"

"Germany, Japan, all over the United States."

"It must be wonderful. I've only been as far as Pittsburgh."

"Never even been to New York City?"

"No." Mary Jane was impressed. Usually she found boys to be tongue-tied. This was the first time she hadn't been the one they talked about. Maurice was really *different*.

They munched on their sandwiches and drank their cherry cokes until it was almost time to go back to school. Mary Jane grabbed Maurice's hand to get a better look at his wristwatch.

"Liquid crystal," Maurice said. He was sickened by her touching him like that. She was a slut, just like the other Mary Jane . . . Mary Jane Kelly.

"Neat." Mary Jane frowned, letting go of his wrist. "But we better get back, or we'll be late."

"Yeah." Maurice wiped his mouth and stood up. He opened the door for Mary Jane and followed her out. On the way back to school, he stopped her by touching her elbow.

"What?" Mary Jane asked.

"Do you like to play jacks?" Maurice said.

"I used to, but most kids our age won't play," said Mary Jane.

"I will."

"Rad!"

"You know the gas patch?" Maurice referred to an abandoned gas works nearby, destined to be torn down by the city.

"Yeah, some kids go there after school to smoke dope."

"Right." Maurice grinned at her, as they continued walking. "What if we go there tomorrow morning, before class?"

"Why there?"

"Oh, just so we can be alone." Maurice smiled his nicest smile. "It'll be our secret."

"My bus usually gets to school a half hour early," Mary Jane said thoughtfully. "I guess it would be all right."

"Great. Don't bring anybody else, though . . . and whatever you do, don't tell anybody."

"Just you and me, huh, Maurice?" Mary Jane blushed.

"Yeah, Mary Jane, just you and me."

They were back at the school now. Mary Jane turned and smiled. "See you there."

"Yeah, see you there." Maurice nodded.

He watched her run to class, hardly able to believe his luck. Mary Jane Toricelli! Almost the same name as Jack the Ripper's fifth and final victim! The only thing he liked about her besides her name was her willingness to go along with him. They always *did* once they saw how much money he had . . . once he got their attention. They *wanted* to be wicked, just like his Mom said . . . just like Saucy Jack had said in the videotape. It wasn't like down south, Mom had told him again and again, where she'd grown up. These Yankee girls were all whores, all white trash, Jews and Catholics. But Maurice had found girls like that when Dad was stationed in Georgia, too. Immoral behaviour was spreading like cancer. These tramps were everywhere nowadays . . . just as they had been a hundred years ago in London.

Today, as then, the Lord's work never ended.

When Maurice got home from school, he found his Dad in the kitchen, starting to cook dinner. It was some kind of stew. Maurice figured he would go up to his room as soon as possible, to make plans for tomorrow. He set the table to hurry things up, so when his Mom got home they could eat right away.

His Mom being out this time of day wasn't unusual. It happened every time they were stationed someplace new. She was probably at the church. The first thing she did whenever they moved to a new place was find a church she liked. He could depend on her being gone a lot, working for some religious group. It made things a lot easier for him to do what he had to do.

"Maybe we can go to a movie after dinner," his Dad said, "if it's not too late."

Ordinarily, Maurice would have jumped at the chance, but not tonight. He had things to do. Leave it to his father to pick the wrong time.

The stew was boiling when Maurice heard the front door open. He saw his Mom in the shadowy hallway, taking off her coat. She hung it up in the closet and came into the kitchen.

"Dinner's ready, Rayette," his Dad said.

His Mom pursed her thin lips and nodded. She sat down at the table. Maurice and his Dad sat down too. They folded their hands and bowed their heads over their bowls. It smelled so good, Maurice could hardly stand it, but he had to wait until the blessing was over.

"Thank you, O Lord, for these thy bountiful gifts . . ." they recited together.

"Maurice," his Mom said as soon as he started eating, "you've got to spend more time on your studies. The Almighty is watching, and He knows when you're not doing your best. Right after supper, go up to your room and do your homework."

"Yes, ma'am." Perfect.

"Dear," his Dad said, "I was thinking about taking Maurice to see a movie this evening."

She glared at him. "Did I hear you correctly, George?" she asked in her prim southern accent. "Do you want this boy to neglect his studies so the two of you can run off and watch some salacious filth?"

"Of course not . . . I just thought . . ."

"Keep your thoughts to yourself, if they're going to be that sinful."

His Dad muttered apologetically, and went back to his stew.

As soon as the dishes were washed, Maurice went up to his room to "study." He bolted the door from the inside. Through the ventilator, he heard his Mom nagging his Dad. That would keep them both busy for a while. It was great to be in his own private place, he thought as he tossed his books on his desk. Except for his bed, the desk was the room's only furnishing. There were no posters on the walls, only one framed reproduction of a painting of Jesus; the Redeemer had blondish-brown hair and he was looking up toward heaven. Maurice always glanced at it when he came in. His Mom had put it in a place that was hard to miss, over the bed, so that it hit you right in the face the minute you walked in the room. He couldn't have any rock star posters or movie posters, even if he'd wanted them. Mom, who had given him the picture of Jesus for his fifth birthday, wouldn't allow it. It was okay, though, because Maurice only cared about those things to the extent that he would be excluded from the company of the other kids if he didn't know a little about them.

His Mom said he could be anything he wanted to be when he grew up, unlike his Dad. His Dad didn't mind just being captain in the Army, but Maurice was expected to do something really great. It didn't seem as if anything he did was quite good enough for his Mom yet, but he was already doing the Lord's work secretly. Trouble was, only the Lord knew about it. That was okay, though, because he hated to stand out, unless he was being cooler than all the other guys, like today with the toy guillotine. What he *really* liked were the things nobody else knew about . . . the things in his collection.

Maurice pushed his bed away from the wall and reached down towards the baseboard. There was a little door down there. He opened it and crawled inside. He had gotten pretty dirty the first time he explored this secret passageway, but in subsequent trips he had swept it out with a whisk broom and removed the dead mice, throwing them down the garbage disposal while his mother was busy praying. When she was praying, Maurice could do just about anything he wanted, and she never knew. It was like she was on another planet. Maurice knew that her heart was in the right place, but all the weeping and wailing in the world wouldn't help clean up the filth on the streets that his Mom always went on about. Maurice had his own ideas about how to deal with sin. Talk and prayer were not enough.

His Dad had told him the secret passageway was designed for ventilation and insulation when the house was built in the nineteenth century. Today they had air conditioning and central heating, of course, so there wasn't any real purpose for it . . . until now.

Maurice wormed his way to the two boxes where he'd hidden his collection. There was a flashlight hanging on a nail there. Maurice lifted it and wrapped its looped strap around his wrist.

He opened one of the boxes.

All of his books, magazines, and newspaper articles on Jack the Ripper were in this one, complete with a police photograph of the Ripper's last victim, Mary Jane Kelly. The name was so much like the name of the girl he'd met today that it seemed incredible.

Remembering the way Mary Jane Toricelli had touched him at lunch, he studied the photograph of her namesake, as he had done hundreds of times before. He savoured the details: the legs, flayed down to the bone; the belly, slit open like a gutted fish, with the hand placed decorously inside the cavity; the breasts, cut off and laid on the table next to the bed; the intestines draped over her shoulder; the other organs, placed next to the breasts; the face, mutilated beyond recognition, a skull-like horror from an old black-and-white monster movie. He had been in love with this image for four of his nine years.

Maurice was only five when Jack came into his life. His parents had just got cable TV, so his Mom could have the religious channel. While they were out, Maurice started to watch a movie showing Jack the Ripper as a minister, a holy man who was doing the Lord's work by cleaning up the filth of Whitechapel's slums. Maurice's Mom had come home before it was over, and Maurice was so engrossed in the movie that he didn't hear her. He thought sure she would punish him, but she didn't. The movie had ended in a church, a shaft of sunlight illuminating the altar, and that was when she walked in. She thought it was a religious programme. Not that it would have mattered, even if she had punished him. The resemblance between Jack the Ripper and Jesus had been burned indelibly into his memory. They both had the same soulful gaze and blondish-brown hair, just like the picture his Mom had nailed onto his bedroom wall. The scene where Jack killed Mary Kelly had reminded Maurice of something his Mom said a lot: "The Lord giveth and the Lord taketh away." Maurice's heart had pounded in excitement as the camera lingered lovingly on Mary Kelly's mutilated corpse. The scene looked a lot like the police photo, one of Maurice's proudest possessions, along with the magazine articles, books, transcripts of the police reports, and the rest of the stuff in this box. But it was the other box that contained his greatest treasures.

Tomorrow morning, he would bring his treasures to school with him.

After his Dad dropped him and his bundle off, Maurice slipped away from the school. It had been tough, talking and acting normal while they drove through the wet, early morning streets, but his Dad hadn't noticed anything unusual. Maurice was a little worried, because he couldn't remember if he had closed the door to his little hideaway before he left the house, but he guessed it didn't matter much. He had more important things to worry about right now, anyhow.

Maurice made his way through the mist to the gas patch, where he waited for Mary Jane in the shadow of a half-destroyed old brick building. That was one of the things he liked about living in this northeastern city: the old buildings, the narrow streets, some of them paved with Belgian block pavement, reminding him of cobblestones. When a fog set in, it could have been London in 1888, the year of Jack the Ripper.

There was a thick fog this morning, rolling down the hill and spilling through the link fence that never kept the kids out. That would help, but Maurice was still nervous. He was always nervous before he did the Creator's work. To calm himself, he looked around carefully, making sure nobody was here, no kids, no old winos sleeping it off behind the brick piles. The building was partially collapsed, one wall fallen into rubble on the inside and overgrown with weeds. Huge black tanks stood just outside the ruined building, empty now but once filled with some kind of gas. Maurice had been here often enough to know that nobody could see you when you were inside, but you could see people coming down the hill that led from Warren Street. Still, he was shaking. This always happened. It wasn't just that he could get caught, and that the police wouldn't understand the importance of what he did. He was acting as God's right arm, and that was something that he had to take seriously. What he was going to do this morning was part of the same righteous quest that the Ripper had undertaken.

Mary Jane was coming now. When he saw her, Maurice's breathing was so fast and ragged that he thought he was going to faint, but he somehow calmed himself as she approached. She was wearing blue jeans and a pair of Ponys, her blonde bangs hanging in her eyes as she negotiated the hillside. She found the hole in the link fence and crawled underneath it, being careful not to get her jeans dirty.

"Maurice?" she said as she stood up.

"Over here," The words sounded funny, as though they came from far away, but he was okay now. He had to be okay, or he would never pull it off. Maurice stepped out of the shadows and waved to her.

Mary Jane smiled and ran over to him. He grabbed her hand and pulled her into the ruins. It was happening, just like all the other times.

"Isn't this place neat?" he said, keeping his voice under control.

She shivered. "Kind of creepy, if you ask me."

"Nobody will bother us here."

"Good." Mary Jane grinned impishly. "Are you gonna try and kiss me?"

Maurice flushed. The idea of kissing her sickened him. She was acting like a slut. He smiled, because she was making it easier. "Maybe," he said. "But first . . . I want to show you something."

"Oh, yeah?"

Maurice beckoned for her to follow him. He led her to a dark corner where he had hidden the bundle, the leather bag wrapped up in his cape. He bent over and picked it up, unravelling the cape and then unfastening the bag's silver clasp.

"What's in the bag?" Mary Jane asked. She stood back while he put on the cape and deerstalker hat, and then asked: "Is it a Hallowe'en costume?"

"Kind of." He turned to her, the cape swirling, the front brim of the deerstalker pulled down over his eyes. "Can you guess who I am?"

"Sherlock Holmes!" Mary Jane said, giggling.

Maurice smiled. "No."

"The King of England?" She laughed out loud.

"No." Maurice showed nothing of his anger.

"I give up. Who, then?"

"I'll tell you later," Maurice said. "First a game of jacks."

Mary Jane looked at him admiringly. She seemed to like having him be the leader. She wasn't like his Mom at all.

"You go first," he said, knowing that she would do exactly as he told her.

"Okay . . . but where are the jacks?"

He held up the black bag. "In here."

Maurice snapped open the clasp and reached inside, feeling around until he found a smaller, plastic bag in there. He pulled it out and dumped the contents on a patch of level ground, between a pile of bricks and the wall. The red, rubber ball and the silver crosses scattered at his feet.

Mary Jane looked at him for a moment before playing. "You're really weird, Maurice," she said. "I like you a lot."

She ran over to him and pecked him on the cheek.

"Play," Maurice said, gritting his teeth. His fear was shrinking now, consumed by a divine fury.

Mary Jane didn't seem to notice his simmering rage. She stooped and picked up the ball. Tentatively, she lifted it and bounced it. "Onesies!" she giggled, picking up a jack. "Twosies!" She bounced it again, her little hands snatching two more jacks off the ground. "Threesies!" This time she managed to pick up three. "Foursies!" Mary Jane moved as quickly as she could, deftly picking up the first three, but the ball fell to the ground on the second bounce, before she could get the last jack.

"Aw." Mary Jane threw down the jacks, stood, and picked up the ball, handing it to Maurice. "Your turn."

"You did real good, Mary Jane," said Maurice. He would go through the motions so that she wouldn't suspect anything. He picked up a ball and studied the random positions of the twelve jacks. Kneeling on the hard ground, he said, "Onesies!"

Maurice only got to threesies, before he failed to get all the jacks.

"Aw, too bad, Maurice," Mary Jane said, trying to sound sympathetic. She eagerly took up the red ball again, but Maurice clutched her elbow.

"Want to know something?" he said.

"What?"

"Know what they used to play jacks with? In olden times?"

"Uh, uh." She shook her head.

"Knucklebones. That's what jacks were called in the old days."

"*Bones?*" Mary Jane was astonished. "What kind of bones?"

"I told you—knucklebones." Maurice let go of her arm and reached into the bag for the scalpel as she knelt to bounce the red ball again. She was into the game. It was time.

Her back was to him now. He pulled her hair back. Before she could cry out, he slid the razor-sharp scalpel blade across the soft flesh of her throat, his hand trembling. The skin resisted and he applied so much pressure his fingers hurt. The knife poked through the skin. Mary Jane made a little moaning sound that turned into a gurgle as he cut. He forgot about everything else as the scalpel separated the flesh. He seemed to be ten feet tall. No, bigger, big as the whole universe. God. Jack the Ripper. From heaven, he looked down at the quaking body beneath him. He savoured the sight for a few seconds and then he pushed her down onto the brick pile, where she flopped like a fish tossed up on shore. When she stopped twitching he bent down and turned her on her back. The blood looked black as it spilled over the bricks in the dim light. Her heart was no longer pumping, so the blood didn't spurt. He didn't have to worry about getting any on his clothes.

Maurice put on his rubber gloves and set to work in imitation of the master, God's chosen, Jack the Ripper. First he dragged the body off the bricks and laid it near the jacks, which he collected. Then he cut open the front of her jacket and blouse. Touching her bare skin excited him, even with the gloves on. He remembered that Jesus had been born unto woman but had resisted the temptations of the flesh.

"Whore!" he cried, shoving the blade into her soft belly. He was stronger now, blessed by the Supreme Being. Using every bit of his strength, he sliced all the way to the crotch, filled with joy, cutting right through her jeans. As soon as he finished the long incision, he set the scalpel down and stuck his fingers inside, pulling the skin apart. The intestines were exposed, coiled inside the girl like a big, meaty Slinky. He reached in and pulled some of them out, juggling them from one hand to the other. They were slippery, steaming in the cool, morning air. The powerful odour of her insides was a vapour, an incense to be smelled only by the Chosen One, Jack the Ripper. He *was* the Ripper now, revelling in his holy work. He had come a long way since the first one he killed, Peggy Nicholson. Her name had been too much of a coincidence to ignore, that was for sure. It was a sign from God. Each time, he had been given such a sign, sometimes just when he felt like giving up on the whole thing. In Georgia there was Carla Edwards, a name close enough to the Ripper's fourth victim Catherine Eddowes, that there could be no mistake. Before her, in Texas, there was Lizzie Streiz, whose name could not have been more like "Long" Liz Stride's, the Ripper's third. And in Japan, another Army brat called Annie Klazewski. (Annie Chapman, Jack's second victim, had been the mistress of a Pole, Klosowski.) Peggy Nicholson's name was almost the same as the Ripper's first, Polly Nichols. Every time, God had given them names similar to the whores Jack had done in. And every time, Maurice got better and better, always finding the ones God wanted him to take.

Before Peggy, he had only killed a kitten, not long after he had seen the movie about Jack. He had petted it out in the back yard until it trusted him. Then he went in and got a big knife from the kitchen drawer and a chicken leg from the fridge. While the little tiger kitty was eating the chicken, Maurice said a prayer and chopped down on the back of its neck as hard as he could. The cat hissed and Maurice cut it some more. It couldn't even scratch him. It couldn't do much of anything after the first chop, just lay there on the flagstone and shake while Maurice sliced it up. It was great.

Something moved behind a brick pile. Maurice snapped to attention, heart pounding in his chest. Had someone sneaked into the gas patch while he was preoccupied? He heard only the sucking of his own laboured breathing, and then a scrabbling noise, the same as before. He caught a glimpse of tiny red eyes in the shadows. A rat.

Relieved, he went back to work, remembering that he couldn't allow his rapture to interfere with what he was doing. He had almost been apprehended in Japan because he was so caught up in the sight and smell and feel of death. He had to be careful. He was getting tired, too, and sweating a lot. This was hard work. Still, the waves of pleasure washed over him as he slashed and sliced.

Mary Jane didn't have large enough breasts to cut off, and besides, there wasn't much time until the bell rang at school. That was always the problem, not enough time. Maybe ten minutes more to work. No time to cut out a kidney, as Jack would have. Maurice had to use his imagination. It was his duty to strike as much terror into the hearts of the sinful as he could.

"I know!" he said. He could actually get some *real* knucklebones. Stretching Mary Jane's limp right arm over the rubble, Maurice placed the left hand palm upward on a brick. He withdrew a blade with a serrated edge from his bag and began to saw.

Pinkish, watery stuff oozed out of the finger. There was no danger of getting it on himself if he was cautious.

Unfortunately, the fingers were harder to cut off than he'd thought they'd be. Maurice had to work even harder to get through the bone, his hands, arms and shoulders ached from his efforts, and he was drenched underneath the heavy cape. He discovered that it was easier, once he'd cut through the skin and sinew, to work the finger joints back and forth until they snapped off.

Each finger took about a minute, so he still had time if he hurried. He broke off eight fingers in all, leaving only the thumbs. Mary Jane looked as if she were wearing red mittens. Staring up at the broken ceiling, unblinking, she was much more beautiful than she had been when she was alive. She would never sin again.

Maurice dropped the fingers one by one into a second plastic bag, taking off the rubber gloves and putting them in with the fingers. He wrapped it all up tidily so that the fingers wouldn't leak onto the medical instruments or the jacks. He wiped the two blades off on Mary Jane's blouse and carefully placed them in their niches inside his medical bag. The two plastic sacks went in on top of the scalpels, with the deerstalker cap laid over them, covering it all. He snapped the silver clasp shut and took off the cape, wrapping it around the leather bag. It just looked like he had taken off a tweed coat and bundled it up because the weather was too warm for it.

"Goodbye, slut," he said, carrying his bundle under his left arm and saluting with his free hand. "May God have mercy on your soul."

Whistling, he walked up the hill towards the school, leaving the remains of Mary Jane Tori-celli to the rats.

Right after lunch, a policewoman came to talk to Maurice's science teacher, Mr. Stubbs. The two adults left the room for a few minutes, and the place erupted in a spitball fight. Maurice joined in so that he wouldn't be conspicuous, while waiting to see what, if anything, Mr. Stubbs would say when he got back.

Mr. Stubbs was gone a long time. Finally, Buddy Hopkins said he was going to find out what was going on. He had to go to the bathroom anyway, so he would check it out.

When he came back, Buddy announced that just about every teacher in the school was gathered in the principal's office along with the policewoman and a black policeman. "This is big stuff," he said.

Shortly after that, Mr. Stubbs returned with the policewoman, holding up his hands for order. Something about the way he looked and sounded stopped the spitballs right away, which was unusual.

"Kids," he said, looking even older and greyer than usual. "There's been an accident."

An *accident*? What was the old fool talking about?

"Officer Cooper is here to ask you a few questions. When she's finished, you can all go home."

There was some sporadic cheering, but that soon stopped as Officer Cooper commanded their attention.

"I have to know if any of you saw a girl named Mary Jane Toricelli this morning, between seven and eight o'clock."

"That would be just before the first bell," Mr. Stubbs interjected.

There was an awkward silence in the classroom, and then a fat girl named Carmen Gifford raised her hand. "I saw her on the bus."

"Did you see her after that?" Officer Cooper asked.

"No."

"When you saw her on the bus, who was she talking to?"

"A couple of girls. She rides with them every morning."

"Are they in this class?"

"No."

"Do you know their names?"

"One of them."

And so it went. Carmen gave Officer Cooper the girl's name, Officer Cooper thanked the kids, and Mr. Stubbs, who really looked nervous and sick, told everybody to go home. Ordinarily, the kids would have been making a lot of noise, happy about getting out of school early, but they were strangely silent now as they filed out to their lockers.

"What's that?" Andy McHugh said as Maurice pulled out the bundle and slammed shut his locker door.

"What?" Maurice said, playing dumb.

"That thing you're holding there, Turner. What is it?"

"Oh, just a coat."

"Looks like a coat your father would wear." Andy kept looking at the bundle. "You got something wrapped up in it?"

"Just some books," Maurice lied.

Andy, who was more than a head taller than Maurice and more than two years older, placed one palm on the lockers on either side of Maurice, hemming him in. "I know you better than that, Moe-rees."

Maurice glared at him. He hated to be called that. Andy was making fun of his southern accent, the only kid in school who still did that.

"The teachers around here might be fooled by you," Andy said. "But I'm not. I know you're nuts."

"Get out of my way, McHugh," Maurice said angrily.

"Chill out, kid," Andy said, stepping back to let him go. "I only want to know what you're up to. Got any more of those chopping things like you had yesterday?"

"No, Mrs. Rainey took it when I was sent to her office." Maurice started walking. "I gotta go."

"You sure you don't have something in there?" Andy demanded.

"Nope. Nothing." Maurice was almost running now, out the front door and into the street, leaving Andy McHugh and his prying questions behind. He ran around the corner, past Popi's and a row of brownstones. When he was quite sure he was rid of Andy, he walked to the stop where kids who were unlucky enough to live in the Army base housing waited for their bus. It was only a little past noon. He would go to the Greyhound station, ditching the stuff he was carrying temporarily in a locker there, and walk the few blocks to the base to see his Dad. Maybe he could get some money out of the old man. It usually worked.

Everything went without a hitch at the bus station, and the guard at the base was so used to seeing him that he didn't even have to show his ID to get through the gate.

He found his Dad in the officers' mess, the bars on his uniform shining brightly, as he drank coffee at a table with a couple of other men. He seemed like a different person than he was at home. Kind of relaxed and important around the other officers. If only they knew what he was *really* like.

"Hello, son," his Dad said, and the others said hello to him too. "What are you doing here on a schoolday afternoon?"

"They let us out early today . . . on account of an accident a girl had."

"Well, that's too bad about the girl." Dad frowned. "But I guess you aren't too unhappy about getting the afternoon off, huh?"

Maurice said nothing. His Dad got out his wallet and gave him twenty dollars. "Catch a bus for downtown and go to that movie we missed last night . . . but don't mention it to your mother."

"Thanks, Dad," Maurice said. "Don't worry. I won't say anything."

His Dad winked, and the other men all laughed. Maurice said goodbye and was off to catch his bus.

*

It had been a pretty good movie, entitled *Maimed,* with plenty of gory violence. It was about a guy who had been mutilated in an accident. When the people responsible got off scot-free by bribing the judge who heard the case, he went around killing them all, saving the judge for last, using chainsaws, buzz-saws, butcher knives, straight razors, and even a Veg-O-Matic. No one under 17 was supposed to get in, but the sleazebag behind the ticket window didn't even look at him, just tore up the ticket and that was it.

It was 3:30 when Maurice emerged, blinking, into the daylight. He was still exhilarated from doing the Lord's work this morning. Unless Mary Jane had told one of the girls on the bus, he was home free. He had the bundle with him, which he had picked up at the Greyhound station after leaving the base. He'd better catch a bus for home right away. If his mother was there when he got in—and not on her prayer planet—he'd catch hell for being late. He wished that he had left the bundle in the locker.

Maurice got off a block from the house. When he got home, he didn't go right in. Instead, he crept up to a window. His mother was turning off the TV, no doubt having just watched *The 700 Club* or one of the other evangelist programmes. She walked toward the back of the house, probably to the kitchen. She might stop him when he came in and demand to see what he was carrying. He had better find some place to hide it.

Around the side of the house, Maurice was surprised to see the car in the driveway. He checked his watch and saw that it was almost 4:30. No, it wasn't that unusual to see his Dad home this early, now that he thought about it. Maurice was the one who was late today. There was no way he was going to get the bundle past both his mother *and* his father.

Maurice tried the car door on the passenger's side. It was unlocked. He opened it as quietly as he could and placed the bundle on the floor of the back seat. Squinting with concentration, he closed it again, barely making a sound. Then he walked back around the front of the house, keeping his head down.

"I'm home," he said as he walked in the front door, deciding to take the bull by the horns.

"We're in the kitchen," his Dad called to him. Maurice didn't like the sound of his voice. "Come on back. We want to talk to you."

Maurice did as he was told, finding them sitting at the kitchen table. His mother was staring at him angrily, and there on the table between her and her husband was a box. Not just any box. The box that had Maurice's Jack the Ripper books and magazines in it.

"What is *this?*" his mother demanded icily.

Maurice shrank before her withering gaze. He *had* left the door to his hideaway ajar, and his Mom had gone snooping in his room and noticed it. She must have made the old man crawl in to see what was in there.

"Answer me!" she screamed. "Answer me in the name of Jesus!"

Maurice's throat felt as if it were filled with marbles. He tried to speak. "It's just . . . just . . ."

"Just *trash,* just the Devil's own *trash!*" She reached into the box, pulled out a magazine and slapped him across the face with it.

Maurice knew better than to say anything now. He was going to get it and get it good, and the less he said the better. Did they suspect what he had done this morning? Would they turn him in?

"Look at this!" his mother raged. She held up a *Playboy* magazine. "Nine years old and he already desires to see the naked flesh of women! Filth in the eyes of God! Whores! Sluts!"

"Look at this, George!" she screamed at her husband, holding up a copy of *Gallery*. "Unadulterated, sinful garbage!"

Suddenly Maurice realized that she was raving about the skin magazines, not about the Ripper material. In her religious fervour, she didn't see what was right under her nose. Maurice couldn't suppress a smirk at this turn of events.

She smacked him with a magazine and then brought it back across the other cheek. "How dare you laugh!"

"I wasn't laughing, Mom," he whined. "I'm sorry, honest."

"Sorry! I'll teach you what sorry means." She turned on her husband. "You've been too permissive, George. How many times have I told you not to spoil this boy?"

"Maybe you're right, Rayette." Maurice's Dad shook his head. "I don't know."

"Well, *I* know." She threw the magazines back into the box. "We'll take these down to the basement and burn them in the furnace."

"*No, Mom!*" The words were out of Maurice's mouth before he could stop them. Maurice knew that he had made a terrible mistake. Her wrath would be all the more terrible now. But what could he do? His collection was the most important thing in the world to him.

"You vile little monster," his mother said coldly. "*Order me* not to destroy this Satanic rubbish, will you?" Her hand shot out like a claw and grabbed hold of his wrist. She began to drag Maurice behind her, her free hand opening the basement door. "Bring that box with you, George."

The wooden stairs creaked under the weight of three people, and Maurice was pulled along so roughly he thought he would fall. But he somehow was still standing when they reached the concrete floor of the basement. His mother flung him away from her, and his back struck the wall, knocking the breath out of his lungs. Maurice wanted to run, but he would never get past them. Their shadows stretched towards him across the concrete floor, cast by the light coming from the kitchen door.

"Punish him," his mother said.

George hesitated. "How?"

"Take your belt off and whup it out of him," she said, her lips curving in a cruel smile.

"Rayette, I don't—"

"Do as I say!" she screamed.

George reluctantly unbuckled his belt and pulled it through the loops with a slithering sound. "Son, I . . ."

"Do it!"

"Bend over, Maurice," his father said.

Having no choice, Maurice did as he was told. At that moment, his mother opened the furnace grating and began to feed the magazines and books to the blue-yellow flames inside.

The belt bit into Maurice's buttocks. It stung so bad he jumped. A second blow descended, and then a third. It really hurt. Maurice didn't think he could take it. Through his tears, he saw his mother looking down at him as she crumpled pages and stuffed them into the furnace, the firelight flickering across her face.

The belt landed a little low, wrapping itself around Maurice's thigh like a snake. Each time his father hit him, it felt as if the fire were burning him, instead of his magazines and books. He screamed.

The beating stopped.

"What are you doing?" his mother demanded. "Whup him some more."

"Rayette," his Dad said imploringly.

"Do as I tell you."

George did as she told him. The stinging tongue of the belt whipped across Maurice's backside again and again. The beating continued until there was no more paper to burn.

"Come here, Maurice," his mother said when it was over.

Maurice, barely able to walk, moved painfully toward her. She reached out and embraced him, tears starting from her own eyes.

"Oh, my poor darling," she said. "It's for your own good. We must drive Satan out of your young soul."

Maurice buried his wet face into her bosom. She rocked him as if he were still a baby, until he stopped crying. Maurice had hated her only a minute ago, but now he knew that he loved his Mom more than anyone on earth. She had punished him because she didn't understand that he was doing God's work, that was all. But she was the one who had taught him that the path of righteousness is strewn with thorns. How he loved her now as she stroked his hair and softly called him her baby.

Maurice was sent to bed without any supper. He lay on his stomach, whimpering, unable to sleep. He wanted to go down and get the bundle out of the car, but he didn't dare to. Fearful that his Dad would be more curious about the bundle after today, he decided he would have to do it in the morning somehow, before Dad drove him to school.

After a sleepless night, Maurice was called down to breakfast. He had tried to creep down earlier, to get outside to the car. But his Mom was already up, on her knees in the living room, praying. There was no way to get past her.

Maurice ate very little cereal this morning. He could actually see the back end of the car through the kitchen window. It was driving him crazy. If they found that bundle, anything might happen. He would never be able to invent a story to fool his mother—she didn't even believe him when he told the truth, usually— and with Mary Jane's knucklebones in that bag, even his Dad would be hard to talk out of doing something really bad to him. He *had* to get out to the car.

His mother didn't speak to him through breakfast, seeming to be lost in thought. The only words his Dad spoke came after they were finished eating, while Mom was washing the breakfast dishes. "Go get your books, Maurice."

Maurice did as he was told, running up to his room and grabbing his school books. Then he ran straight down the stairs and out the front door, shouting that he would wait outside. He came around the side of the house and peeked through the kitchen window. Seeing that his mother was still washing the dishes with her back to him, he looked around for someplace to hide the bundle. If he scooched down really low, he could sneak past the window and stuff it under the back porch steps. His mother would never notice it there, and he could figure out a way to retrieve it when he got home from school. He tried the car door.

It wouldn't open.

But how could that be? . . . Unless his Dad had gone out to the car and locked it last night, it had to open. Maurice felt himself starting to sweat, and he felt kind of itchy, not on his skin but inside. He tried the door again.

It still wouldn't open.

What was he going to do? He couldn't leave the bundle in the car. His Dad would find it sooner or later. His only chance was to smash the window and stash the bundle under the steps fast, before his Dad could get outside to see what was going on. Maurice could say it was an accident. He would probably be punished, but that was better than what would happen if he just stood here.

He looked around for something heavy. There were some rocks out on the strip of grass between the pavement and the street. Maurice put his books down and rushed over to get one. He picked up a big one, grubs and millipedes scurrying out of hiding, some of them crawling on his hands. He didn't care. He *had* to get into that car.

He went back and lifted the rock over his head with both hands, seeing his distorted reflection in the car window. He held it there for an instant, and—

"What are you doing, son?"

Maurice's heart froze. He dropped the rock to the ground with a dull thud. "Nothing, Dad." He looked away from his father's piercing, grey eyes.

"You weren't going to break that window for spite, were you?"

"Of course not," Maurice lied. "I was just pretending I was a Ninja."

His Dad smiled a little. "A Ninja, huh? That's great. Come on, get in the car, or you'll be late for school." he went around to the driver's side. "Look at that," he said, opening the door. "I forgot to lock up the car again. Your mother would kill me if she knew."

Maurice stared at his father, uncomprehending. He tried the door, and it resisted. "This one's locked, Dad."

"No it isn't." His father was putting his keys into the ignition. "It sticks sometimes. Just tug on it a little."

Maurice put both hands on the door handle and pulled hard. The door flew open, nearly knocking him off balance. It had been unlocked all the time!

"What's the matter, Maurice?" his father said. "Get in the car."

Maurice was staring at the open door. At the sound of his father's voice, he snapped out of it and reluctantly got inside. Right behind him, on the floor of the back seat, was the bundle. His father couldn't see it from where he was sitting, but he would find it sooner or later, unless Maurice got it out of there somehow. Maurice slowly buckled his seat belt, desperately trying to think of some way out.

"Son," said his Dad, "I know that boys like to look at pictures of girls without any clothes on. I did it too, when I was your age. But you know how your mother is. If you have any more of those magazines, put them someplace where she'll never find them. Otherwise, she'll make me punish you again, and I don't want to have to do that."

"I'm sorry, Dad." Maurice was disgusted by his Dad's admission. His Mom had been *right* to punish him, for all his parents knew. The old man was *so* weak.

"Well, don't let it happen again."

"I won't, Dad."

They rode on through the mist in silence. When they were within a few blocks of the school, it occurred to Maurice that he might be able to tell his Dad that he needed the bundle for one of his classes. He had to do it. There was no other way to get it now.

"I left something in the back seat yesterday," he said.

"Oh? What's that?"

"It's part of a Hallowe'en costume," Maurice said matter-of-factly, hoping that his Dad wouldn't remember that he had taken the bundle with him yesterday when he was dropped off at the school. "All the kids are making them."

When his father didn't respond, Maurice unbuckled his seat belt, turned around and reached back over the seat. His hands were shaking while he picked up the bundle. He squirmed back into a sitting position with it on his lap.

"It *will* be Hallowe'en in a few days, won't it?" his Dad said.

He bought it! Maurice could hardly believe his luck. He was going to make it now. Once he got to school he could hide it in his locker, and then take it to the bus station later. One thing was for sure, he couldn't bring it home again. Maurice looked down at the tweed cape and tried to keep from laughing out loud.

All of a sudden the car screeched to a halt and Maurice flew forward, striking his head on the dashboard. The bundle fell onto the floor.

His father honked the horn. "That kid almost got herself run over," he said angrily. "Are you all right, son?"

"Yes." Dazed, Maurice looked out the window to see a girl on a bicycle, looking very pale and scared. As his Dad started driving again, she became invisible, lost in the fog.

His Dad looked over at Maurice. "You're sure you're all right?"

Maurice nodded. When he looked down, he saw that the tweed cape no longer covered the black, leather bag. They were both on the floor at his feet, the bag in plain sight.

"What's that?" his father demanded, still driving through the fog, but staring at the bag.

"Nothing . . . just part of the costume."

Something about the way Maurice said that made his Dad suspicious. "Let me see it," he said.

"It's nothing, Dad," Maurice said, panicking. "It's just kid stuff."

"Let me see it, Maurice."

Maurice tried to pick it up. He was getting ready to jump out of the car and run away, but his Dad snatched the bag from his hands and snapped open the silver clasp. "Where did you get this?" he demanded.

"I saved my money." Maurice could feel his heart thudding in his chest. His father seemed to tower over him. "You always taught me to be thrifty."

Glancing sporadically at the road, his Dad pulled out the deerstalker cap and set it on the seat. Then he withdrew the bag of jacks. Next came the surgical instruments.

"Maurice," he said, fingering the scalpel Maurice had used to cut Mary Jane Toricelli's throat, "you could hurt yourself with these. Where did you get them?"

"I send a money order to a mail-order medical supply house," Maurice said, his voice cracking. "I want to become a doctor when I grow up."

But it was too late for lies. Still holding the scalpel in one hand and steering with his elbow, his Dad dumped the rest of the bag's contents onto the seat. His eyes widened when he opened the second plastic sack.

He pulled out the bloody gloves—and the knucklebones tumbled out onto the vinyl car seat.

"For the love of God, Maurice," he said, holding up one of Mary Jane's yellowing fingers, "is this what I think it is?"

Maurice was sobbing now, unable to speak at all.

"Answer me!" his father screamed, dropping the finger in revulsion.

One of the dim shapes passing by loomed out of the fog. His Dad couldn't see it, turned as he was towards Maurice. Maurice started to cry out, to warn his Dad, but then he saw who the car was about to hit and shut his mouth. A tall, lanky figure challenged anyone to dare and try to run him over. Maurice grabbed the wheel and jerked it towards him.

A thump.

"Jesus Christ!" his Dad cried, slamming on the brakes. He opened the door and leaped out of the car, still holding the scalpel. Maurice peered over the dashboard at the unmoving form of Andy McHugh sprawled on the asphalt. A serpent of blood crawled from Andy's head into the gutter and washed down a sewer grating.

Maurice got out of the car, rubbing the bruise on his forehead where he'd struck the dashboard. He called softly, "Dad."

His father turned, his eyes wide, the scalpel still in his hand. People were coming out of the fog, gathering around and staring.

"Hold it right there," a woman shouted.

His Dad turned around and stared straight into the blue barrel of a .38 revolver.

"Don't move!" Officer Cooper commanded him.

Maurice saw his chance, presented to him at this last possible moment when everything seemed so hopeless, by Divine Providence. He grabbed his Dad's wrist.

"Help!" Maurice screamed.

"Let the boy go!" Officer Cooper cried angrily.

His Dad tried to pull his arm away but Maurice held on tight, pretending to struggle, screaming: "He's going to kill me! He's got somebody's fingers in a bag! And knives! He's crazy! He killed Andy!"

"Maurice," his Dad whispered, "what are you doing?" His face was sweating, pale and confused. The blade gleamed in his other hand.

"Help!" Maurice cried. "He's choking me! He's gonna cut my throat!"

"Drop that knife or I'll shoot!" shouted Officer Cooper.

His Dad didn't seem to hear her. He stared at Maurice in disbelief, as if he saw something he'd never imagined before, something out of his wildest nightmares.

Officer Cooper fired twice. His Dad's neat uniform blossomed into bright red flowers in two places, on the chest and belly. Maurice let go of Dad's wrist as he fell. The scalpel clattered to the pavement.

A black policeman, Officer Cooper's partner, ran across the street, his heels clacking sharply on the wet asphalt. He knelt and placed his ear over Maurice's Dad's heart. Officer Cooper was looking through the windshield at the fingers lying on the front seat of the family car.

A few minutes later, an ambulance arrived. Two paramedics worked on Maurice's Dad and Andy for a while. At last they gave up and zipped both of them into shiny body bags, just as three more patrol cars pulled up. The flashing red and blue lights looked very strange in the mist. As he stared at the coloured lights and listened to the crackling of police radios, Maurice felt fingertips gently touch the bruise on his forehead.

He looked up into the tender eyes of Officer Cooper. She smiled at him. "It's going to be all right."

The ambulance carrying his Dad and Andy wheeled into the fog and vanished. Maurice tried to look sad, but it was hard to do, as he thought about what was sure to happen now. They would trace the killings back to all the cities Captain Turner had lived in—American, Japanese, German. Maurice's mother would wail and say that the Devil had gotten into George, and she'd pray even more than she did now. Without Dad around to enforce her will, Maurice would do as he pleased, and some day he would make his Mom see how much he loved her, how he did everything for her as much as for himself.

Someday he would kill for her again. Maurice knew that he would never be caught if he was careful enough, just like the original Jack the Ripper. And, unlike Jack, he wouldn't have to stop after five killings. He would carry on, protected by the All Knowing Spirit, in whose name he had slain the sinful. Nothing could stop him.

He had to agree with Officer Cooper. From now on, it really *was* going to be all right.

∼

A KIND OF MADNESS

Anthony Boucher

The term "Renaissance man" has been overused through the years, but it is entirely reasonable to use that appellation for William Anthony Parker White (1911–1968), better known under the pseudonyms he used for his career as a writer of both mystery and science fiction, Anthony Boucher (rhymes with "voucher") and H. H. Holmes. Under his real name, as well as under his pseudonyms, he established a reputation as a first-rate critic of opera and literature, including general fiction, mystery, and science fiction. He also was an accomplished editor, anthologist, playwright, and eminent translator of French, Spanish, and Portuguese, becoming the first to translate Jorge Luis Borges into English.

He wrote prolifically in the 1940s, producing at least three scripts a week for such popular radio programs as *Sherlock Holmes, The Adventures of Ellery Queen,* and *The Casebook of Gregory Hood.* He also wrote numerous science fiction and fantasy stories, reviewed books in those genres as H. H. Holmes for the *San Francisco Chronicle* and *Chicago Sun-Times,* and produced notable anthologies in the science fiction, fantasy, and mystery genres.

As Boucher, he served as the longtime mystery reviewer of *The New York Times* (1951–1968), with 852 columns to his credit, and *Ellery Queen's Mystery Magazine* (1957–1968). He was one of the founders of the Mystery Writers of America in 1946. The annual World Mystery Convention is familiarly known as the Bouchercon in his honor, and the Anthony Awards are also named for him.

"A Kind of Madness" was originally published in the August 1972 issue of *Ellery Queen's Mystery Magazine.*

In 1888 London was terrified, as no city has been before or since, by Jack the Ripper, who from April through November killed and dissected at least seven prostitutes, without leaving a single clue to his identity.

The chain of murders snapped abruptly. After 1888 Jack never ripped again. Because on July 12, 1889 . . .

He paused on the steps of University College, surrounded by young ladies prattling the questions that were supposed to prove they had paid careful attention to his lecture-demonstration.

The young ladies were, he knew as a biologist, human females; dissection would establish the fact beyond question. But for him womankind was divided into three classes: angels and devils and students. He had never quite forgiven the college for admitting women nine years ago. That these female creatures should irrelevantly possess the same terrible organs that were the arsenal of the devils, the same organs through which the devils could strike lethally at the angels, the very organs which he . . .

He answered the young ladies without hearing either their questions or his answers, detached himself from the bevy, and strolled toward the Euston Road.

For eight months now he had seen neither angel nor devil. The events of 1888 seemed infinitely remote, like a fever remembered after convalescence. It had indeed been a sort of fever of the brain, perhaps even—he smiled gently— a kind of madness. But after his own angel had died of that unspeakable infection which the devil had planted in him—which had affected him so lightly but had penetrated so fatally to those dread organs which render angels vulnerable to devils . . .

He observed, clinically, that he was breathing heavily and that his hand was groping in his pocket—a foolish gesture, since he had not carried the scalpel for eight months. Deliberately he slowed his pace and his breathing. The fever was spent—though surely no sane man could see anything but good in an effort to rid London of its devils.

"Pardon, m'sieur."

The woman was young, no older than his students, but no one would mistake her for a female of University College. Even to his untutored eye her clothes spoke of elegance and chic and, in a word, Paris. Her delicate scent seemed no man-made otto[37] but pure *essence de femme*. Her golden hair framed a piquant face, the nose slightly tilted, the upper lip a trifle full—irregular but delightful.

"Ma'm'selle?" he replied, with courtesy and approbation.

"If m'sieur would be so kind as to help a stranger in your great city . . . I seek an establishment of baggages."

He tried to suppress his smile, but she noticed it, and a response sparkled in her eyes. "Do I say something improper?" she asked almost hopefully.

"Oh, no. Your phrase is quite correct. Most Englishmen, however, would say 'a luggage shop.' "

"Ah, *c'est ça*. 'A luggage shop'—I shall remember me. I am on my first voyage to En-gland, though I have known Englishmen at Paris. I feel like a small child in a world of adults who talk strangely. Though I know"—his gaze was resting on what the French politely call the throat—"I am not shaped like one."

An angel, he was thinking. Beyond doubt an angel, and a delectable one. And this innocently provocative way of speaking made her seem only the more angelic.

He took from her gloved fingers the slip of paper on which was written the address of the "establishment of baggages."

"You are at the wrong end of the Euston Road," he explained. "Permit me to hail a cab for you; it is too far to walk on such a hot day."

"Ah, yes, this is a July of Julys, is it not? One has told me that in England it is never hot, but behold I sweat!"

---

37 A word only Anthony Boucher would use. Originally he wrote "attar"; but he crossed that out and substituted "otto."

He frowned.

"Oh, do I again say something beastly? But it is true: I do sweat." Tiny moist beads outlined her all but invisible blonde mustache.

He relaxed. "As a professor of biology I should be willing to acknowledge the fact that the human female is equipped with sweat glands, even though proper English usage would have it otherwise. Forgive me, my dear child, for frowning at your innocent impropriety."

She hesitated, imitating his frown. Then she looked up, laughed softly, and put her small plump hand on his arm. "As a token of forgiveness, m'sieur, you may buy me an ice before hailing my cab. My name," she added, "is Gaby."

He felt infinitely refreshed. He had been wrong, he saw it now, to abstain so completely from the company of women once his fever had run its course. There was a delight, a solace, in the presence of a woman. Not a student, or a devil, but the true woman: an angel.

Gaby daintily dabbed ice and sweat from her full upper lip and rose from the table. "M'sieur has been most courteous to the stranger within his gates. And now I must seek my luggage shop."

"Mademoiselle Gaby—"

"Hein? Speak up, m'sieur le professeur. Is it that you wish to ask if we shall find each other again?"

"I should indeed be honoured if while you are in London—"

"Merde alors!" She winked at him, and he hoped that he had misunderstood her French. "Do we need such fine phrases? I think we understand ourselves, no? There is a small bistro—a pub, you call it?—near my lodgings. If you wish to meet me there tomorrow evening . . ." She gave him instructions. Speechless, he noted them down.

"You will not be sorry, m'sieur. I think well you will enjoy your little tour of France after your dull English diet."

She held his arm while he hailed a cab. He did not speak except to the cabman. She extended her ungloved hand and he automatically took it. Her fingers dabbled deftly in his palm while her pink tongue peered out for a moment between her lips. Then she was gone.

"And I thought her an angel," he groaned.

His hand fumbled again in his empty pocket.

The shiny new extra-large trunk dominated the bedroom.

Gabrielle Bompard stripped to the skin as soon as the porter had left (more pleased with her wink than with her tip) and perched on the trunk. The metal trim felt refreshingly cold against her flesh.

Michel Eyraud looked up lazily from the bed where he was sprawled. "I never get tired of looking at you, Gaby."

"When you are content just to look," Gaby grinned, "I cut your throat."

"It's hot," said Eyraud.

"I know, and you are an old man. You are old enough to be my father. You are a very wicked lecherous old man, but for old men it is often hot."

Eyraud sprang off the bed, strode over to the trunk, and seized her by her naked shoulders. She laughed in his face. "I was teasing you. It *is* too hot. Even for me. Go lie down and tell me about your day. You got everything?"

Eyraud waved an indolent hand at the table. A coil of rope, a block and tackle, screws, screwdriver . . .

Gaby smiled approvingly. "And I have the trunk, such a nice big one, and this." She reached for her handbag, drew out a red-and-white girdle. "It goes well with my dressing gown. And it is strong." She stretched it and tugged at it, grunting enthusiastically.

Eyraud looked from the girdle to the rope to the pulley to the top of the door leading to the sitting room, then back to the trunk. He nodded.

Gaby stood by the full-length mirror contemplating herself. "That silly bailiff, that Gouffé. Why does he dare to think that Gaby should be interested in him? This Gaby, such as you behold her . . ." She smiled at the mirror and nodded approval.

"I met a man," she said. "An Englishman. Oh, so very stiff and proper. He looks like Phileas Fogg in Jules Verne's *Le Tour du Monde*. He wants me."

"Fogg had money," said Eyraud. "Lots of it."

"So does my professor . . . Michi?"

"Yes?"

Gabrielle pirouetted before the mirror. "Am I an actress?"

"All women are actresses."

"Michi, do not try to be clever. It is not becoming to you. Am I an actress?"

Eyraud lit a French cigarette and tossed the blue pack to Gaby. "You're a performer, an entertainer. You have better legs than any actress in Paris. And if you made old Gouffé think you love him for his fat self . . . Yes, I guess you're an actress."

"Then I know what I want." Gaby's eyelids were half closed. "Michi, I want a rehearsal."

Eyraud looked at the trunk and the block and tackle and the red-and-white girdle. He laughed, heartily and happily.

He found her waiting for him in the pub. The blonde hair picked up the light and gave it back, to form a mocking halo around the pert devil's face.

His fingers reassured him that the scalpel was back where it belonged. He had been so foolish to call "a fever" what was simply his natural rightful temperature. It was his mission in life to rid the world of devils. That was the simple truth. And not all devils had cockney accents and lived in Whitechapel.

"Be welcome, m'sieur le professeur." She curtseyed with impish grace. "You have thirst?"

"No," he grunted.

"Ah, you mean you do not have thirst in the throat. It lies lower, hein?" She giggled, and he wondered how long she had been waiting in the pub. She laid her hand on his arm. The animal heat seared through his sleeve. "I go upstairs. You understand, it is more chic when you do not see me make myself ready. You ascend in a dozen of minutes. It is on the first floor, at the left to the rear."

He left the pub and waited on the street. The night was cool and the fog was beginning to settle down. On just such a night in last August . . . What was her name? He had read it later in *The Times*. Martha Tabor? Tabby? Tabbypussy-devil?

He had nicked his finger on the scalpel. As he sucked the blood he heard a clock strike. He had been waiting almost a half hour; where had the time gone? The devil would be impatient.

The sitting room was dark, but subdued lamplight gleamed from the bedroom. The bed was turned down. Beside it stood a huge trunk.

The devil was wearing a white dressing gown and a red-and-white girdle that emphasized its improbably slender waist. It came toward him and stroked his face with hot fingers and touched its tongue like a branding iron to his chin and ears and at last his lips. His hands closed around its waist.

"Ouf!" gasped the devil. "You may crush *me,* I assure you, m'sieur. I love that. But please to spare my pretty new girdle. Perhaps if I debarrass myself of it . . ." It unclasped the girdle and the dressing gown fell open.

His hand took a firm grip on the scalpel.

The devil moved him toward the door between the two rooms. It festooned the girdle around his neck. "Like that," it said gleefully. "There—doesn't that make you a pretty red-and-white cravat?"

Hand and scalpel came out of his pocket.

And Michel Eyraud, standing in the dark sitting room, fastened the ends of the girdle to the rope running through the block and tackle and gave a powerful jerk.

The rope sprang to the ceiling, the girdle followed it, and the professor's thin neck snapped. The scalpel fell from his dead hand.

The rehearsal had been a complete success.

Just as they planned to do with the bailiff Gouffé, they stripped the body and plundered the wallet. "Not bad," said Eyraud. "Do actresses get paid for rehearsing?"

"This one does," said Gaby. And they dumped the body in the trunk.

Later the clothes would be disposed of in dustbins, the body carried by trunk to some quiet countryside where it might decompose in naked namelessness.

Gaby swore when she stepped on the scalpel. "What the hell is this?" She picked it up. "It's sharp. Do you suppose he was one of those types who like a little blood to heighten their pleasures? I've heard of them but never met one."

Gaby stood pondering, her dressing gown open . . .

The first night, to the misfortune of the bailiff Gouffé, went off as smoothly as the rehearsal. But the performers reckoned without the patience and determination and génie policier of Marie-François Goron, Chief of the Paris Sûreté.

The upshot was, as all aficionados of true crime know, that Eyraud was guillotined, nineteen months after the rehearsal, and Gaby, who kept grinning at the jury, was sentenced to twenty years of hard labour.

When Goron was in London before the trial, he paid his usual courtesy call at Scotland Yard and chatted at length with Inspector Frederick G. Abberline.

"Had one rather like yours recently ourselves," said Abberline. "Naked man, broken neck, left to rot in the countryside. Haven't succeeded in identifying him yet. You were luckier there."

"It is notorious," Goron observed, "that the laboratories of the French police are the best in the world."

"We do very well, thank you," said Abberline distantly.

"Of course." The French visitor was all politeness. "As you did last year in that series of Whitechapel murders."

"I don't know if you're being sarcastic, Mr. Goron, but no police force in the world could have done more than we did in the Ripper case. It was a nightmare with no possible resolution. And unless he strikes again, it's going to go down as one of the greatest unsolved cases in history. Jack the Ripper will never hang."

"Not," said M. Goron, "so long as he confines his attention to the women of London." He hurried to catch the boat train, thinking of Gabrielle Bompard and feeling a certain regret that such a woman was also such a devil.

THE SPARROW AND THE LARK

Lyndsay Faye

It is evident that Lyndsay Faye (1980–) has an affection for research, as all her novels have been set in the nineteenth century and praised for their authenticity.

Faye's trilogy featuring Timothy Wilde, a bartender who became a policeman at the time that New York was creating its police department in 1846—coincidentally the year of the great Irish potato famine—began with *The Gods of Gotham* (2012); it was nominated for an Edgar Award. The second Wilde novel, *Seven for a Secret* (2013), deals with "blackbirders," underworld thugs who kidnap northern Negroes and sell them into slavery in the South. The third, *The Fatal Flame* (2015), puts Wilde on the trail of an arsonist whose secrets might be uncovered by the cryptic murmurings of a starving orphan with a tenuous hold on reality who has been brought to his door by Mercy Underhill, the love of his life.

A lifelong aficionado of Sherlock Holmes, Faye's first book, *Dust and Shadow: An Account of the Ripper Killings by Dr. John H. Watson* (2009), received praise from many sources, including Caleb Carr, who wrote his own pastiche, *The Italian Secretary*, in 2005. Given blessings by the Arthur Conan Doyle Estate, it pits Holmes against Jack the Ripper.

One of the stories that will be included in *The Whole Art of Detection*, a collection of her Holmes stories, "The Case of Colonel Warburton's Madness" was selected for the prestigious *The Best American Mystery Stories 2010*.

"The Sparrow and the Lark" was written especially for this collection and has never been previously published.

I shudder yet when I think of her eyes. Midsummer blue like mine, bright and kindly for most folk, the ones she wanted to pet or admire her. But when she looked my way?

Cold and shallow as winter graves.

It weren't always so betwixt us, this throbbing hate like a poisoned pulse. We was tender for half-moments, specks of time when she was six or so and I around nine, afore the boys arrived to plague us. Afore we begun plaguing each other over them, as girls are wont.

Now I'm dead, there's naught to be done to bridge the rift.

I think back to Caernarfon in Carnarvonshire where we'd kip together on a barley-stuffed pallet in our parents' room, instead of packed like tinned mackerel in t'other bedchamber with our six brothers. All on account we were girls.

We slept too close to Tad and Mam to whisper without a harsh growl or a knock on the pate, for Tad (we always called our father by the Welsh word) were stern with us over the precious few hours of sleep he stole. But we tapped codes into sisterly skin, *Did you eat enough?* and *Search the riverbanks together tomorrow?* and felt as if we shared something sugary and forbidden, secrets that heated the belly like a stolen quaff of Mam's tonic.

All sisters write hidden scripts on eachother's hearts so. Don't they? Even the sisters who rot long afore they're in their graves?

On those friendlier days, in those times, I'd go with Julia Kelly—that's my sister, a spitfire name, and me plain old Mary Jane—down from our crib in Hole in the Wall Street, nearabouts where Tad sweat himself nigh to death in the iron works six days a week, to the river. Well, it *looked* as if 'twere a river. It were Menai, the strait what separated us from Anglesey. I thought as a girl that crossing Menai meant *escape,* and imagining it always made my heart soar high as the gulls.

The word *escape* sent Julia's heart skyward too, only I didn't know it as yet.

As I said, we often went down to the banks to comb for the sort of flotsam children think enchanted. Shiny stones. Driftwood like sorcerers' wands. Water weeds we insisted were mermaids' hair. One day—it were autumn, I remember, because the sun were setting when I glanced up at the brute height of Caernarfon Castle, skies all battered and bloodied in reds and purples and it not yet chimed six unless I'd missed the bells.

There's those as figure otherwise now, in light of violent circumstances, but I don't miss much. Never did. I've ne'er been as clever as Julia, but I know how the world turns, that there's forces that can't be stopped, sure as the sun sets, and her always pulling and stamping to get her own way.

Anyhow, there was egrets about, scavenging as we were but never mussing a single snowy feather, and the bells not chimed yet, and Julia and I searching after some token to hide behind the loose brick by the water pump and keep for ourselves, when my sister froze as if Death had gripped her.

What she'd found wouldn't seem like much to most, I'd wager. Not if they weren't windblown Welsh lasses as often out of shoes as in them. It were half a dredge oyster. They're generally ugly—outside chipped rock, inside a dull grey sheen—but that shell were like a sunrise. One surface smooth and chalky, t'other a sweet gleaming pink like a color we'd dreamt up, the sort you couldn't properly believe unless it were right in front of your nose.

This one must be magic, my sister told me in Gaelic. *We'll hide it in the usual place. It'll bring us both luck that way.*

You found it, I protested. *You can keep it for yourself if you like.*

Talismans could turn their coats if claimed by the wrong party. That much I was sure about even then.

Doesn't matter. If it's yours too, I'll be safe so long as I'm near. It'll keep us together forever.

I still wonder whether she meant that as a blessing or a curse. Or if she suspected I schemed to flee Caernarfon as fast as ever I could. Even afore everything changed.

The day we found the shell were back when we had names, proper names, Mary Jane and Julia—but less than a year later our brothers started up calling us the

Sparrow and the Lark, on account of Julia always warbled whenever a hat was like to drop. My sister sang without knowing it, sang constantly, and her voice were like a berry, bright and sweet at once, and no one in Wales can live with a talent and not attract notice. Our brothers were only rude and selfish over it —*Give us a ditty afore supper, little Lark, or I'll twist your braids clean off*— that sort of rubbish. But brothers aren't so different from the men as come later, are they? So I knew trouble already lurked in the mouse holes and cobblestone cracks, ready to seep out at any moment.

I were granted a voice like a horsehair brush, sounded as if I'd been smoking shag from the cradle, and that were what the boys had latched onto, was the contrast. The way her voice could move a stone to tears and mine scour a copper pot.

I hated Julia first for her voice. As she grew louder, every day I grew quieter, a rough breeze drowned by birdsong.

I pass my hands in their fingerless gloves over a guard rail without touching it, the stink of brine thick as stew in my nostrils. I'm not used to being on this side of the river. Came over early, all the cocks screaming, and since then I've done naught but wander. The Southwark docks are somber this time of year without the reds and yellows and greens peeking from the bushels of the apple vendors. Without the sun's blessing and with the nip of snow in the air. A street seller of tools passes me in the gathering dark, clanking as he goes, hawking knives, cleavers, saws, steels, voice tiredly booming, "Best quality starting at tuppence a blade! First sharpening gratis, new an' used, satisfaction guaranteed!"

Shivering, I settle further into my scarlet shawl, but no one pays me any heed and ne'er do I expect them to. The weary day laborers what search for odd boatyard jobs as my own dear Joe does when he's short on chink glance warily at the knife hawker, scratch at their bristly jaws and head for their homes with tight lips, shuttered looks. The date is November 10th of 1888, and as bad a business as it was before, now nobody can look at a knife the same way any longer. Maybe never will again.

I know I won't.

Crimson dusk is pooling at the sky's edges, bleeding into the Thames, turning the hundreds of ships' masts into stark black spears. The ju-dies will be hurrying indoors soon, whether or not they've earned their billet, though all changed November 9th, and it don't matter a whit anymore whether a girl is indoors or out. Roofs make no difference, nor walls, nor doors.

Nobody's safe.

When I've haunted the riverbank long enough, aimless and cold, I fall into step with a paint-smeared trio of dollymops headed into a public house, trying to puzzle where I can stow soundlessly away, where best to travel, when and whether I should flee the city like a shadow chased by the dawn.

How will I quit London now I've died in it?

When I were eleven, an English lady called Fairbanks whose husband opened a fashionable hotel inside Town Walls grew bored with tea parties and started teaching school to the brightest of Caernarfon's "beggarly" girl children. Julia and I both were accepted after being examined and took lessons with a dozen or so other lasses in Mrs. Fairbanks's parlor, everyone desperate for the smooth pats of her china hands and the tea cakes she'd offer if we excelled. When I gave out in London as I were from well-to-do stock, it were only thanks to Mrs. Fairbanks I was believed, though I lost as many airs and graces later as I'd gained.

Easy earned, easy spent, they say.

My sister could always finish her sums and her catechizations easy as blinking, but I pored over mine, wasted tallow candles over them, and so when the hearth weren't scrubbed or the rugs beaten, I were the one switched for it back at our crib.

I hated Julia second for her wits. She never lifted a finger to help me, though I was the eldest, only tossed her fair head with a false commiserating look, and I begun to see her for what she was. An empty thing, with a heart like a hole, and shovel as much admiration as you liked into the cavity, she'd fault you for shorting her. *It'll keep us together forever,* she'd said that day at Menai about the shell. Then I'd thought she'd wanted a sister, a loyal and true one.

But that weren't it at all.

The dollymops palaver amongst themselves over cups of max at a pub called The Rusted Anchor, swilling carefully as we're wont to do with the first quaff of the night, savoring it, letting the gin coat the tongue. I should know. I perch by the smoking hearth, a shadow within the shadows, watching. Silent.

"They say as she were Jack's particular mistress, and that's why she were gutted so much worse than t'others, like, for he were jealous and it was a love quarrel," the first gushes. She is comely still, dark-haired and rosy with friendly craters in her skin from a bout with the pox.

Not quite right, I think, smiling, *though love did have something to do with it.*

"Oh aye, 'twouldn't do by half to gut an unsuspecting *stranger* so thorough, as any proper gent knows." The second has a shrewish face, witty and knowing, and the trio laugh coarsely.

Truth be told, we all resorted to laughter after the second or third girl died—damned if I can remember which. *But what choice had we?* I think, remembering. 'Twas either laugh or slit your own throat and save Jack the bother, plagued with unholy terror as most were.

Leaning closer, I listen.

The third, a thickset lass, takes a deep swallow of gin and shudders. "I don't see how you can make fun so soon after. She weren't even a cheap whore like us, but a proper ladybird what fell on hard times, so the papers say. And then to make such a bad end! She were once engaged to a *baronet.*"

It's all I can do not to snort. I'd lit out for Southwark, across the river from my neighborhood, as fast as my wits and will could take me, and nary a soul knows me on this side of the water, so I'm not surprised the rumors here are shy of the mark. I'd not wanted to glimpse anyone I'd known *before.* And it's true I were once a proper ladybird, decked in mauve silks and kept like a parrot in a pretty brass cage.

Engaged to a baronet, though? That's a bit thick even for the gutter press.

"You can't *read* the papers, you daft sot, so you're only gossip-mongering, which is shocking wickedness, and you should be ashamed." The shrew-faced one winks drolly as the plump one pouts. "For my money, Mary Jane Kelly weren't any more special than the rest of us. Only more *dead,* or anyways dead in more pieces."

The others howl at this joke, and even I am forced to smile.

I was special though, I think when the mirth passes, my fingers clenching. *I made myself special in spite of Julia, in spite of everything.*

And the Man in the Long Black Coat knew it the moment he spied me.

When I were sixteen, I married a collier by the name of John Davies, the only reason he chose me being that Julia at thirteen weren't fully a woman yet. By then she could sing like an angel and talk like a lady for all that there were holes in her skirts—I knew as well as anyone that it were only time on my side and nothing more. Commonest ally known to womankind, time. Time brings better weather. Turns squalling infants to sturdy helpers or else eliminates them altogether. Kills husbands. Time grants wishes if you're brave enough to snatch at them, when you can see opportunity dangling like a rope down the slick edge of your well.

So I made my move, and John Davies was mine for the taking.

The men simply didn't care which girl was which, I figure. Tad would have been equally chuffed to misplace either daughter since there was eight Kellys to keep in small beer and turnips. John just wanted a warm space to slot himself into of a night. And Julia, every inch of her rosebud breasts and farm boy's hips, sure enough loathed me for getting out first, that endless blue gaze burning as John hugged my shoulders in his bear's grip, promising Tad grandchildren as tall and strong as I'd grown and Tad grunting whilst he poured them another two cups of spruce-scented max.

I hated Julia third for her weakness. She wanted to keep me there all to herself, keep me poor and precocious as she was, nothing but a croaking shadow.

You can't desert me this way, Julia hissed when the men fell to gin and talk of arranging a modest trunk for me to travel away with. *It's not sisterly, Mary Jane. And after me loving John so.*

John *had* sniffed after her right enough, despite her youth, on account of hearing her trilling in the marketplace one Saturday. But that were simply the way of the world now I were marriageable and her only near to it. I couldn't afford to wait.

Every tick-tock clacked at me to *make-haste, make-haste, make-haste.* The sister who'd once wanted to share a shell to keep us both from harm combed her flaxen tresses with a hundred strokes every night, stole precious oats from the larder and scrubbed her face with them, slapped me in a fury when I came home after stepping out with a neighborhood boy if he'd ever so much as cast an eye her way. Our six brothers would quake with laughter and applaud her spirit, Mam shake her head and tell me, *It serves you right for filling out so sudden-like, Mary Jane,* golden-haired and ripe as a fallen plum, though I'd not fallen just yet.

"I heard tell as she was fair as a princess. Everyone is saying so. She were beautiful before . . . before he got to her," the stout dollymop muses.

None of them want to say *left her corpse in tatters all over the room,* and I don't blame them.

"Beautiful, my foot. You're so credible," the snide one scoffs.

"None of us are beautiful anymore, or we'd live better," the raven-haired one agrees, though she's the best of a rather sorry lot.

True enough, I think, recalling the taste of French champagne with the same giddy bliss as I always do. Champagne is dipping your toes in a bath of pure gold. It's pale, pale as hoarfrost, and tingles against the lips just so when the glass is iced. Champagne is the only thing on earth more thrilling than the Man with the Long Black Coat, and I'd not drunk champagne for a long, lonesome time.

"And anyhow," the pockmarked judy continues, "that's only the locals making up fairy tales and the newspapers and the peelers gobbling 'em down like gospel. It's a better story, ain't it? That's our job these days, in these parts, other than getting ourselves ripped—spinning a good yarn. It tickles their fancies better if Mary Kelly's a princess what was killed by a monster, you savvy, and not just a common trull cut up like a dead sow."

"Christ yes," the hatchet-faced girl chuckles, lighting a pipe and crossing her ankles. "Did y'see the way the papers drew Annie Chapman? If I were a dragon, I'd ha' spit her straight out again."

My eyes fall shut.

She's right—it is a better story, I think. *A beautiful girl who grew up in the shadow of Caernarfon Castle met with a monster.*

It's even true, as far as it goes.

You can't marry, Julia growled the day I became engaged to John, bruising my wrist with her little claw. *I won't let you.*

We stood out in the rear yard, the last and sweetest of the sun's rays blocked, as ever, by a feudal relic. The hate rose in me then something fierce, the same hate I always felt when told I'd never make it away from Caernarfon, would always live in the black gloom of that great hideous castle like a giant's prison, in a tiny house on Hole in the Wall Street where our brothers pinched us purple and the leeks we could afford were always wilted and Julia and I would stuff cotton in our ears when Tad shoved Mam's nightdress up and rooted like a great boar in their bed.

The hate I felt whenever I was called sullen and couldn't answer, *That's not true, I'm just a sparrow, and silent when there's a lark nearby to measure me against. That's not the same thing at all.*

'Tis settled, I told her. *In a week's time, I'll be free of this sty.*

It's wickedness and you know it, said Julia, her eyes filling. *Fast, shameful wickedness. I've a trull for a sister, and what am I to do without her?*

Go to the devil, I suggested, *and see if he'll take you for a bride. You'd not refuse, I'd wager.*

Julia turned pale as the pungent froth at low tide. But she didn't care I were marrying—she cared I were marrying *first,* because without shadows to bully, a lamp don't look like much, do it now?

I ne'er looked back after wedding John Davies, nor returned to Caernarfon. But I did raid the secret hiding place behind the brick and keep the shell, that innocent scooped shape, pearl-like and mysterious, and had a hole drilled in it, and carried it about my own neck to keep me safe and remind myself whenever the hate wound round my heart like prickling brambles that I'd won. I got out. I was Mary Jane again and she Julia left behind under the crushing shadow of that terrible heap of rocks, not the Sparrow and the Lark any longer.

Only two things matter in this life: who you are and where. The question is, can you truly change either one? Peel off one skin, don another, and walk away?

It were only two years later when I learnt Julia was right, and her sister Mary Jane was a trull true enough. As common a trull as thighs ever itched when kept too long together.

A fine trick of prophesy, I thought that! Though I'd little enough choice over it. John being blasted to pieces in an explosion at the coal mine and all, them hitting a pocket of poison gas, and me suddenly with no husband, and nothing even left of him to bury, only a few shillings from the overseer and the head of my husband's pickaxe to my name.

What in bloody hell did I want with half a pickaxe?

That were the first time as Julia found me.

I'd sent one letter home, only to say we was situated in South Wales and I'd not time to write nor chink for postage, leaving out the fact I'd discovered that colliers were about as hard worked as African slaves and being Mrs. Davies weren't much other than living in a draughty cottage with a roof of thatched heather which sprouted mould along the eaves. John's hands were gentle enough, but soot-dark no matter how much lye I mixed in the soap. After he'd roll off of me, I'd lie there still tingling, unsatisfied and downright confused over the sensation, exhausted half from drudgery and half tedium. Living an endless loop of toil like a waking sleep. My lot weren't victorious enough to be fit for much correspondence, but I'd given too much away with just the single sheet of foolscap, it seemed, for Julia read of the mining casualties in the paper three years later and turned up alone with a carpetbag.

I were plenty vexed, but not shocked—she were the only Kelly in the house as could read, after all.

"I'm here to help you," she announced in English, smiling. "You needn't worry."

"Aren't you long wed by now?" I replied.

She shook her head, telling the tale, and in every word, I could smell the bitterness on her breath. "Mam fell sick. She needed me. There was twice as much work after you left. And you know what they thought of me back in Caernarfon. And I was that melancholy—oh, Mary Jane, I couldn't breathe for missing you."

Very likely, I thought, but was not flattered.

She reported that two of our brothers had married and thus Mam would now have enough people to do for her. Julia at sixteen was curved and charming, same as I was at three years her senior, only my sister had a voice like a bell with a curse in it. The false smile stayed fixed as she measured what I'd do. But all her neat white teeth were thorns to me, and her eyes pools to drown in.

"You'd best come inside. There's a hare for supper, and nary a soul to share it with," said I pointedly, for she had left out the part about condolences over John being blown to bits.

Of course I knew as she'd only meant to make a final break from Caernarfon, and I a ready excuse—a newly widowed sister taking up with an unmarried sibling, what could be more natural?—but I didn't care one way or t'other what she was after. Within four days I'd done give her the slip and were in huge, hustling Cardiff, where poor dead John's coal had been shipped away all over the globe, without a cent to my name after the train fare nor a soul in the world to claim me as theirs.

It was like going mad. It was like dying. It was like heaven.

When I spread my legs for the first game gent, following some husky words spoken and a fee decided back at his crib, I saw after he'd doffed his gloves that he'd ship's clerk hands, pale and smooth as milk, and I laughed for the pure pleasure of the sight. I weren't always well in Cardiff, caught spells of melancholy and the occasional rotten customer, but I'll always remember how I carried myself like a queen, traded every cent I was worth just to waste the coin on more enjoyment.

I'd never had enjoyment afore, you understand, and found I liked it plenty.

They call it *going bad,* on account of you're servicing blokes what don't love you and ain't about to marry you. But 'twas pretty bad with John Davies, though I was married to him, and all I got in trade for it were more work. When it comes to servicing, I'd fain barter for coin or champagne instead of more work any day, and there's plentiful lasses on the streets who'd not argue with me. The ones who are yet alive to argue at all.

The dollymops are peckish, so they order two pigeon pies between the three of them, hovering over the scran like witches over a cauldron. Some soldiers on leave occupy a table nearby now, clapping one another on the back and hooting and even breaking into raucous song, and they irk me something fierce, as my fellow ladybirds are still discussing me and I've plenty more to learn and noplace better to go as yet. When I move a bit nearer along the narrow communal bench, I fear as they'll spy me, but I might as well be a wisp of steam wafting up from the crusts they're dividing onto tin plates.

"I heard Mary Kelly had a live-in cove called Joe Barnett, but he quit her on account o' her drunkenness," the pretty one says. "They was always moving from crib to crib, for no landlord would have 'em. She got ugly whenever in her cups, so I hear. So he threw her over."

My teeth set. It ain't *news,* I just don't fancy hearing it said.

The sharp-faced one cackles, lifting her cup of max. "I'd prefer a strong drink to a live-in beau any day. What a milksop. I've this to say for Continental types, they don't fault you for taking a drop too many when out carousing, while your stuffed-shirt English variety . . ." She shrugs, sipping.

"Best be wary o' Continentals. Now they say it's an Italian doing it, an opera singer what always played villains onstage and took to it something terrible and caught Cupid's disease from one of us and went mad," the thickset one says as she studies a morsel of what's possibly pigeon.

Covering my mouth with my hand, I chuckle silently into my fraying glove.

You can be driven mad by music sure enough, that I'll warrant you.

The shrewish one licks gravy from her lips. "Twirling his waxed moustaches, unsheathing a great whopping dagger, and laughing maniacally all the while. None of us would find that a bit suspicious. I swear to Christ, you are *such* a ninny. Even a bobby would notice a scoundrel o' *that* caliber."

"It's all very well to stay away from Jews, and foreigners, and butchers, and suspicious characters, but supposing the killer is an *Englishman?*" the brunette laments. "Then how are we to avoid him?"

You won't, I think, and not without certain satisfaction.

The Man with the Long Black Coat is a poised gent whose name I ne'er caught on the few occasions we spoke, but many's the time I saw him about the

'Chapel, and he always made a tiny bow to me, like a shopkeeper or a butler would do, and it always made the laughter bubble up in my throat. He moves like the shadow of a man, your eyes touching him and then glancing off again. A silhouette what ain't there at all. His coat is as deeply black, in fact, as his collar and cuffs are pure white, but he's no aristocrat, only maybe a clerk, for his togs are completed with a quiet black tie, quiet black hat, and quiet black boots. I've nary heard his boots make a single sound, come to think of it.

When first I spoke with him, I were dead drunk in Raven Row, staggering home to Miller's Court on the night after my sister reappeared, and he caught my elbow. He held it—held me—long enough for me to notice. Friendly, caring even. His eyes were colorless in the gloom. He said, "You must be more careful after dark, my dear young lady," and I know how sweet and purring a demon can sound, for I grew up with one.

And the Man with the Long Black Coat is unquestionably an Englishman.

After Cardiff, there were London, and after that were Paris, and Paris is where I discovered champagne.

The dollymops were right: Mary Jane Kelly was a right lush. My neighbors were quoted in the papers, and my landlord, John McCarthy, and all t'other roaches what scuttle about the streets of Whitechapel.

Mary Jane was pretty and well-spoken, but when the drink got in her . . .

When in liquor she was very noisy; otherwise she was a very quiet woman . . .

You scarce saw a pleasanter girl than Mary Jane, save for when . . .

Well, I can explain all that.

After I'd kept enough Cardiff blokes warm to earn another train ticket and a pair of used but well-mended frocks, I went to London in 1884. A practiced hand I were by that time, and not just with my hand, and if I'd been a handsome lass before, by then I was a full-blown rose, and the lads took notice. I said *Paris* and I meant it. Gents carted me off for a fortnight or more to laze about and to eat feasts—fish so fresh they blinked at me, I'd swear it, duck smothered in oranges, bread you didn't have to pick green spots off, and every bite tasted of butter.

And the men themselves! What monocles, what gaits, what togs they had. I'd a handful of regular blokes within a month, and naught would serve them but to buy me new fripperies, put me on a boat, and pretend as I were their wife when they'd business in France. The rings I wore might have been paste right enough, but the men was real as anything, leaving stray hairs and sandalwood cologne and damp patches on the bedsheets.

Chère Marie Jeanette, they would croon as they left me of a morning, *you'll rest peaceful and quiet today, won't you? Promise me?* and I'd sit before the open window with a cigarette and the dregs of the champagne bottle, thinking how like starlight it had tasted, cool and sparkling, as I watched the traffic wend from the lodging houses to the shops and gardens. My voice would feel scraped from use, and I'd mix honey in hot brandy, loll in the ruined linens until the boardinghouse rang the gong calling lodgers to a late breakfast of hot croissants and soft cheese.

Champagne, though . . . in Paris, everyone drank it. Tad and my brothers had ne'er shared their max with me, though Julia and I occasionally stole a taste in the dead of night when we was meant to be using the privy, and we nipped at

Mam's tonics something terrible. I loved gin from the first. I love it now, but I love champagne more than anything. Champagne is nuzzling against the wing of an angel. Gin ain't the same, but I'd every right to chase after the glow that Paris would take on after a few glasses, and Whitechapel needs a sight more help to look romantic than Paris. You're drunk whether you just swallowed liquid diamonds or pure pine bark, and Mary Jane Kelly, I read after dying, was *one of the most decent and nice girls you could meet when sober.*

I'd learnt better than to be sober by that time, thank Christ.

I took my chance in the instant when a bud unfurls, affrighted of my sister's malice, and left Caernarfon a married woman. Cardiff welcomed me as a friendly widow who wanted a shilling or two whenever her mending income ran dry. Then I went from London to Paris with men who thought I sounded like a draught of their favourite cigarette, and that felt like silk against my skin, like a caress, because they paid *extra* for it.

My voice.

They fair bled coin for my voice. They thought it beautiful.

There's neither rhyme nor reason to what men find beautiful. Some want larks, and others sparrows. Some want to make a lass happy, smile when she smiles —and others, as my brothers hinted at so long ago, only care to watch her bleed.

Here is the truth about the Man with the Long Black Coat: if not for champagne, I'd ne'er have took up with him, for I did love Joe Barnett. Love for Joe Barnett felt like eating a great chop running with juices, the sort served alongside roast taters sweet as cream, and after a meal like that you feel *heavy*, though maybe as happy as heavy. Maybe heavier than happy sometimes.

Champagne feels light as a feather, and so did the Man with the Long Black Coat.

"What clues have the police so far?" asks the stout dollymop, pressing her fork into the last crumbs of crust.

"Will you listen to Sherlock Holmes 'ere," the rat-faced one snorts, and we all grin at that, though I again stifle my laughter.

"Clues?" the comely one demands in disbelief just as a serving boy catches her eye. "Oi, there—another round, that's a good lad! Clues, you say? How can a nightmare have clues? This one's not just ripped, she's ripped t' *shreds,* and in her own digs. What are they meant to do, by Jesus? Divine the sick brute's moniker by reading patterns in the blood?"

"There's two things I found out this morning, as might make a difference." The snide one sounds grave for the first time.

"Truly?"

"Truly. Ye'll have heard about the stolen heart, then?"

The others' faces sour with revulsion—even I, who brought the heart's theft about in the first place, feel my belly lurch in protest.

"Aye, though I wish to Christ I'd not. What else?"

"There's a charm or something o' the kind she always wore, 'bout her neck, I heard tell from my cousin what visits the same grocer across the river." She takes a long pull of her pipe. "Fond as anything of the trinket, a seashell I think 'twas."

"And so?"

"And so it's missing too."

At their words, I cannot help but reach up and touch the oyster, feel its smoothness beneath my thumb as I so often have before.

"Give us a hand with this, love, and dry yer eyes. If they'll not miss us like honest good neighbors, they can go straight to hell, says I," Joe announced with strained good cheer.

We stood in a thin rain like workhouse gruel in Brick Lane in March of 1888. None of the judies had yet been gutted, and I'd been with Joe for nearly a year. I shifted my feet, angry at the *squish* of the puddle into my patched boots, angry that both stockings were already sopping. Piled about us were a trunk, a carpetbag, two little wooden crates, and the burlap sack holding the contents of the larder what Joe were thrusting towards me. Taking it, I slipped it over my back and took a pull of max from my flask.

"That's what got us chucked out in the first place, so yer doing us no favors pickling yer guts at six in the morning," Joe said.

He sounded gentle, or maybe just hoarse, because we'd shouted ourselves sick again last night and been sent packing from Brick Lane to sleep rough or find new digs, not so much as a day's notice, and our rent paid through the end of the week and all. I'd have demanded the balance, but a window were broken, how I couldn't recall, though my arm had a rag wrapped about it shielding a cut, and the lemon-sucking landlady told me she'd keep my chink to cover the damages or else whistle for a crusher.

"Don't take on so, Mary," Joe begged again in his Irish lilt, passing me his kerchief.

"I'm not blubbing, I'm bloody *wet*," I sniffed.

I sounded like a stick scraping along a wall, partly thanks to the drink and the shouting, but some of the soreness must have been due to the actual words I'd yelled, I reasoned, because you can't drag every foul name you can recall from your gullet and not bruise it some. Not when the names were lobbed at a steady cove like Joe.

Peering at Joe through the murky rain, I tried to make out what had enraged me the night before. But I ne'er knew what any of my swains had done to set me off come the dawn. Not unless I found marks and knew I'd scratched and yowled just as any cat will when cornered. But Joe wouldn't hit me, not for a king's ransom, so I knew it a useless exercise, like struggling over the harder maths Julia could finish in a quarter of an hour. Sometimes in Paris I'd screamed because they liked it, wanted a touch of spice, and sometimes I'd scream because the bottles were dry or the restaurant closed or the bloke wanted to tie me down.

More often I'd shout to hear myself after being so long a sparrow, I figure now, though it's all very hard to recollect.

That day in 1888 I were twenty-five years old, same age as when I died. By then the better London brothels with the polished windowpanes and pretty door knockers wouldn't have me any longer, on account of I were steady and amiable until I'd took a drop too many. Fair and full-figured as I was, no one took me to Paris any longer, either.

Joe frowned at me, brown whiskers twitching and dripping with moisture. I'd first met Joe Barnett in a pub in Commercial Street, bellowing out a drinking song with his mates what are licensed as porters down Billingsgate Fish Market way. I was low enough to be walking the 'Chapel for custom already, lower than I'd been since Caernarfon, and there Joe stood, broad-chested and still smelling of the sardines he'd delivered, singing in a fine baritone, and he bought six pints that night for *The prettiest girl I've e'er spied in all the East End, and wi' the sweetest smile.* His voice were so tender, and his jokes so bawdy, and he'd good employment, and didn't care I were a dollymop years in the making.

He said as I'd seen life, that times had been hard, and I'd come out the winner yet.

I took digs with him the second time we met for a drink, and Joe said as he'd ne'er felt so lucky. As he spoke those words, in his warmly rumbling way, I touched the pierced shell hanging under my chemise and nigh blinded him with my grin.

When I could manage to stick to beer, I did. When I didn't, I woke up feeling like I'd swallowed a hot poker, and we changed lodgings. George Street, Little Paternoster Street, and now Brick Lane. I'd ne'er thought even I could get myself kicked to the curb of Brick Lane, for Christ's sake. 'Tis wretched cotton flock bedding all lumped into rough canvas, twelve and fifteen to a chamber sometimes, all Irish like Joe, with blushing cheeks and brash jawlines. We'd our own room, complete with rug and basin, but that was over now and to celebrate I took another sip of max.

"Easy, love." Joe sighed, shouldering the pair of crates with the trunk hoisted in his other hand. I took up the carpetbag, balancing its weight with the sack over my shoulder. "Ye'll float away and how will I find ye?"

He weren't wrong—by then I was floating, just a little, and there were tears in my eyes now when before there had been only rain.

"I'm sorry for the things I said," I whispered.

"The gin said them. The gin is a sure enough liar, don't y'know."

"Then I'm sorry the gin is such a harpy. I don't want you to think ill of me."

"I never do, fer I know at heart yer the kindest lass as ever breathed. Just sometimes ye think ill yerself o' perfectly decent folk, afore they've done aught to offend ye, jump to the wrong conclusion without their having meant ye any harm, and that always breaks my heart a little."

Joe shook his head and kissed the top of mine where I stood in the drizzle with neither a hat nor umbrella. He struck off to find us a new crib and I trudged after, watching the sturdy weight of the man beneath his load, placid and dependable as an ox. I wondered whether it were better for us that I didn't savvy what things I was apologizing for, only knew sure as Testament that I'd said them. Supposing I forgot, I couldn't look at Joe's cheap shirt with his back muscles straining and think the bitter words that only meant he wasn't Paris, and wasn't champagne, and not that I didn't love him.

That day, we pawned some handkerchiefs and a few spoons and took a room at number 13 Miller's Court, Whitechapel, by which I might as well say we crawled into a rats' nest. And that afternoon, drowning my sorrows at the Ten Bells Pub, my sister found me for the final time.

Completely by accident, damn London for its small cruelties and damn Julia to hellfire for her sins.

"Maybe the shell necklace were from Kelly's beau, the one as threw her over, and she couldn't bear to look at it anymore and pawned it at the nearest jerryshop," the plump dollymop reflects. When she shakes her head, the firelight catches her across the bridge of her nose and I see she owns kindly hazel eyes. "Dunno why I imagined something like that, it's ever so sad."

"Never in all my days have I seen such a one for nursery stories as you," the cunning one sniffs, pushing her plate away. "Fat lot o' good a bauble like that would do Kelly now, or a beau for that matter. What she wants is a box and a shovel."

"I'd almost think you were glad of another murder if that weren't the awfulest thing I could imagine." I hear tears beginning to form, her throat starting to swell.

" 'Ere now," the dark-haired judy interjects, stricken, "no one's glad of anything of the sort! We're sisters, we ladybirds, in name and in deed, and though they may call our kind *frail* sisters, we're as game as any man jack on these streets, aren't we, and we look out for our own. She meant no harm, only a dark sort o' funning—didn't you?"

"To be sure," the shrewd dollymop says softly, but her lips remain tense. "I only . . . it chips away at you, don't it? Just when you think *I'll have a lucky streak tomorrow,* or *it won't rain,* or *maybe that were the last one to die.* None of it comes true. If I didn't rag you dear silly geese, I'd be crying in my pudding. Ain't this way better?"

"No, for we've no pudding this way," the stout girl mutters, but she's smiling, and all is forgiven as the three rock with laughter.

"Hello, Mary Jane," Julia Kelly said to me tensely. I hadn't seen her enter the pub, but there she stood, dressed much as I was, only her cotton frock were printed with green sprigs and mine were a plain but cheery blue I'd thought perfect for my coloring afore she appeared. "Christ, but you're a sight for sore eyes. You're thinner than I remember. When did we meet last? Cardiff?"

"Paris," I managed, for once Julia had performed the miracle of actually tracking me there, which led to a dreadful row and afterwards a horrid telegram to my brothel madam back in England, sent by my fussy little swain. "Good *God,* what are you doing hereabouts?"

The Ten Bells, with its noisily chatting patrons and sultry gas lights, swam a little. I shifted on my tall barstool, my legs suddenly weak yet restless, like a colt's. I had just fled from Brick Lane that morning, and now there was Joe to consider.

Can I flee Miller's Court the same day? Have we even the chink? What if I—

"I know I just said you had thinned, but it suits you. I meant nothing spiteful by it. You look so well, sister." Julia bit her lip when I held my tongue, as she does whenever being ingratiating. "I've surprised you—you needn't fear I'll be offended. I've got used to your independent streak by now, I hope. And you've surprised me too, this time."

"How did you find me?" I questioned, lungs strapped tight in my chest.

"I didn't!" Julia wore a rust-colored hat freshened with a few dried weeds matching her dress, and I could tell as she'd followed in my footsteps both figuratively and geographically, for never have I spied plainer marks of the London dollymop: her boots were fraying at the toe, ivory apron clean but not pressed, and her white bosoms at as full military attention as were mine. "It's just a wonderful coincidence I thought to try my luck in the 'Chapel. I was over in Stepney for a while, and Rotherhithe, doing odd jobs, a little sewing and washing, but—oh, hullo! How do y'do?"

Setting the fresh ale he'd fetched down before me, Joe Barnett thrust out a calloused hand. We'd revived ourselves with a trip to a public bathhouse after depositing our things at Miller's Court, after I'd put my flask away in the cupboard and vowed to join him in a pint later instead. He looked rugged but happy, the cleft in his chin jutting in a friendly way, his shirt open at the neck revealing a thatch of dark hair, his green eyes twinkling, and I knew disaster were about to strike. It hurt to see my sister's small grip enter Joe's large paw, hurt the way her cornflower eyes travelled from his face down to their fingers touching, all along the length of Joe's strong arm, and Joe never noticing, never suspecting, only grinning like there was sure enough a spree to be had tonight.

I swallowed bile, a familiar flavor.

"Joe, this is my sister, Julia Kelly. Julia, this is my sweetheart, Joseph Barnett."

Joe's head swiveled in happy shock, for it weren't common for me to call him pet names, even when we were sharing a lumpy bed in the endless black cave of the East End. He bowed and kissed my sister's hand.

"Pleased to meet any kin o' my Mary Jane's, I'm sure!"

"Wherever did you find such a specimen, Mary Jane?" Julia breathed in her melodic way.

Joe shifted back to sling an arm about my waist, gesturing for Julia to take the stool I'd been saving for him.

"Oh, my sort are easy to find as blinking, Miss Kelly."

"Do please call me Julia," she cooed, sitting.

"Well, Miss Julia, then." He ducked and planted a loud kiss on my shoulder where my shawl had slipped. "Mary Jane's sister! Aren't ye two like staring into a looking glass, at that! And here I thought my girl never wrote to her family."

"I don't," I said under my breath, knowing Joe were too tickled over Julia's unexpected arrival to hear me.

"What a sight! Does my heart glad to see the pair of ye together, and that's gospel. D'ye live nearabouts?"

Julia's eyes narrowed almost imperceptibly. "I was lodged over Rotherhithe way but lost my crib to a fire—no, no, everyone's safe, thank the Lord. Only I've no home at the moment. I've not found anything yet today that suits. Worse luck. Came here in search of new digs and a clean slate, but now I've had a drop in, I'd not pass up Mary Jane's floor just for tonight, if you can spare the space."

She paused, raising a brow all contrite and abashed like, as if apologizing for the fire. And maybe it had been her fault, God knows—I didn't fancy asking. But didn't my stomach cramp, didn't my heart crumble into dust and cinders there on the beer-sticky floor when I understood that, thanks to my own taste for max, she'd already won the day.

All Joe wanted was for me to prove kindly. How would I look turning away my own sister on the very day I was turned out myself like a whipped cur?

Just sometimes ye think ill yerself o' perfectly decent folk, afore they've done aught to offend ye . . . and that always breaks my heart a little.

"You can kip with us till you get your bearings," I said in a voice the texture of dried husks. "We'll not mind, not for . . . a few days."

Joe slapped us both on the arms, in sky-high spirits despite the row the night previous, despite my losing us yet another living situation. "That's settled! Fer as long as ye like, Miss Julia, our room is yer room. I'd be proud to consider any family o' Mary Jane's dear as my own kin."

Julia smiled wide enough to split her head clean open. So I pictured that, it really happening, her jaw cracked as far as possible, joints creaking, and then *snap* and a loud break as her spine went and then blood, blood enough for the world to drown in, with the split top half of her wretched pate rolling ever so slow along the floor where her carcass fell, the skull trailing meat and brains behind it.

I knew 'twouldn't be a few days. I'd ne'er be rid of her.

Too much had passed between us, too many secrets and small wounds. Knives left in the flesh to fester there.

When Joe and Julia left Miller's Court together arm in arm that night like old chums, happy as larks, to find some fried haddock and chips for the lot of us, I slipped out to a pub fast as thinking, but not afore draining my flask. When I dragged myself home hours later through Raven Row, when the Man with the Long Black Coat kept me from falling and said, *You must be more careful after dark, my dear young lady,* I kissed him instantly with soft lips, lover's lips, kept kissing him until it was more than kissing, and he were in me with my skirts high and one leg hitched over his hip drawing him closer, little throaty gasps coming from the pair of us. His sweet-sounding and mine scorched.

When he moved to pay afterward, I said, *I ain't done it for the coin—I like you,* and walked away staring him in the eye all the while, and he laughed like a man what's spied an old friend in the road at a distance, and that's when I knew for certain I had really *gone bad*.

Julia's stay turned into a week, then a month. We pretended to talk together. Pretended to laugh. Pretended to play at cards. She got me stinking drunk every day when Joe were out working, passed me cup after cup of max whilst only taking half as much for herself. She sang about the house, sang *incessantly,* and Joe joined in harmonies with his gusty tenor. She comforted him when they cleaned my messes and did my share of the housekeeping. She slept with my sweetheart—I know she did, it weren't mere suspicion, for I came home afore they expected me one afternoon, and her collar buttons were all awry, and Joe afterwards looked like a beaten pup.

She told Joe I were a sorry excuse for a sister. She told him she loved him and wanted nothing save his happiness, in a letter what I found at the bottom of his shabby memento case. I said nothing. What could I say apart from *get out*? Thereby proving myself a villain to Joe? There's some as would suggest I could have *refused the gin,* but only them as ne'er tried waking up every livelong morning in Whitechapel.

Finally, Joe left us both after a particular terrible row, one I felt in my neck and my chest for nigh a week after, and there we were—a matched set of sisterly dollymops with no choice but to walk the streets for our keep.

Exactly as I'd planned.

I like catching glimpses of you in the streets, I told the Man with the Long Black Coat the next time we both caught our breaths afterwards, leaning against the brick wall, panting as if we'd streaked across the night like a pair of doomsday comets. *I like knowing you're there, even when I can't see you.*

Why, that's precisely what I like about you, he intoned, and that time he didn't offer me coin, and I thought as that were much better, because it meant he understood.

The dollymops are through with their pies and the streets have quieted, nestling into the comfortable darkness of Southwark, settling like overwrought children. The men what are arriving now bang the door open a mite too hard, order pints a hair too loud. The raven-haired judy yawns and squints into her cup, frowning. I think as they might light out for their doss houses—or for more chink to be earned in the alleys, if any are short—and fear I've lost my entertainment for the night when the hatchet-faced one speaks low, as if she don't want to be heard, and it's all I can do to make out, "Any of us could've already had him, you know."

"Who?" the plump one asks.

"Saucy Jack," the other drawls under her breath.

The pox-scarred ladybird drops her cup, which is thankfully empty, and the thickset one gasps loud enough for one of the soldiers to dart a glance at the bench.

"Leather Apron," she continues, smirking. "The Ripper. *From hell,* that bloke. The mad bugger ain't ripping *all* the time. Sometimes he's like as not sticking his cock someplace to take his mind off his work, same as they all do."

"That's *disgusting.*" The plump one indulges in a full-body shudder and I smirk at the sawdust-strewn floorboards in silence.

"You're the one as said this one might have been a crime of *passion.* Who's to say she didn't have 'im against a water barrel one night, all unawares? What's he like down there, is what I'm keen to know."

"Stop it!"

"See, he can't be the same in bed as he is with a shiv or he'd have been caught long since," the cunning one explains, happily watching her mates squirm on the rough-hewn wood. "We could lay wagers—straight or crooked? Big or small? Rough or cries a bit afterwards? Wants a mouth or an arse or a—"

"I'm leaving this instant if you keep up this filth!" her friend practically shrieks, and then they all dissolve in helpless giggles once more.

"Truly though," the canny one says when they've calmed, "I wonder. And you're mighty squeamish for a pair o' limp-tittied trulls. And I'm curious if Mary Kelly did him any service without knowing. So there."

No, I think with a surge of triumph, *I knew all along.*

Twice I had him before Joe left us, and thrice afterwards, always when I were weaving like a storm-tossed ship back to shore and the Man with the Long Black Coat found me alone somewhere, and he'd tip his quiet black hat in his quiet way, and we'd find a corner where he thrust into me slow and sweet, in some dripping alcove or deep doorway or other, and I ne'er took so much as ha'pence from him.

We didn't say much. But once he passed a thumb under my eye and said softly when it was over, *If you'd let me pay you the first time, all would be different between us. Do you know that, my dear?*

I laughed as I straightened my skirts, and blew him a kiss as I disappeared round the bend of the bitterly cold corridor.

For a moment, I'm seized with longing—I *want* to describe the Man with the Long Black Coat to the dollymops. How he turned us both into fireworks or darkness or both together maybe, yes that's better, because how could you see the one without t'other? But I know I can ne'er explain how it was between us. They say in some parts as fairies still reside in the distant woodlands, and that lovemaking with them would be deadly in its pleasure, for a mortal couldn't channel the magic coursing through 'em, and the fairy would survive the passion whilst the human fried to so much sparkling powder.

What I mean is, whatever the Man with the Long Black Coat is made of—I'm made of the same. Two of a kind. So I don't need to fear him harming me, whilst the dollymops I'm sitting near would ne'er survive.

"We hope we haven't troubled you," the pretty one calls out from a few feet distant on the long community bench. When I glance up, she gives a wee wave, then smiles. "You seem one of our sort right enough, if I'm not being terrible forward, but there you are quiet as a mouse and we've been palavering over that dreadful Miller's Court business. Apologies."

Smiling back, I swallow the last of my fourth cup of gin, shaking my head. I count coins onto the rough grain of the tabletop. I've enough saved for a few days more in London, but I don't want to be here any longer, so I'll have to come by more tonight, in some back alley or another. They're all one to me.

"I were that shaken over it, I've nary a word to say, but you've given no offense," says I. "I promise. I've been quiet since I were a little lass."

"There's a great weight off my mind, then." The shrewish one winks and this time, the wink is directed specially at me. "Take my advice, girls, and don't badger the quiet ones, not if ye want to keep your skins—it's always the quiet ones as win out in the end."

When I last saw the Man with the Long Black Coat, he were striding the opposite way on Commercial Street as I, and I were being jostled by a woman with a basket piled with dirt-caked onions, and the sun had just barely begun to fade, like a skirt hung one too many times from a summer clothesline. We exchanged our usual wordless greeting, and I'd every reason to figure as that were the end of it, thrilling at the notion I might see him under starlight soon enough.

But he held up a hand and dodged across the thoroughfare, neatly proving he does exist after all, as a buggy reined its mount to avoid him and a newsboy's eyes followed his progress. I could not help but smile when he reached the pavement before me, for he added a slight tip of his hat to the bow he'd already accomplished.

"My dear young lady, what luck I caught you, as I don't know your name," said he, a little out of breath.

"What's it to you?" I laughed coquettishly. "I've not a clue as to yours either, and none the worse for it."

"I quite see your point. Sometimes I think it a pity, and sometimes there is rather an air of romance to not knowing, wouldn't you say?"

He half-smiled, and I saw in the daylight and up close that his eyes were amber, like a cat's. That felt far more secret than t'other midnight acts we'd been about.

Dangerous too, dangerous as the edge of a knife at your throat, and a thrill shot through me when I rasped, "Not knowing suits me right down to the ground."

For an eyeblink he looked as if he might laugh. Then he were sucking in a quick breath, saying, "If a man wanted to visit your rooms for a longer appointment than the usual, would you consider it?"

My entire world froze. It were perfect—so much better than I had dared to hope, even. As if I'd just been handed a miracle nestled under spotless glass, aglow on its silver tray, all for me. Blinking, I did my best to focus.

Nearly there, Mary Jane. Nearly through.

"I couldn't say," I answered, deliberate-like. "Does this bloke want to pay me?"

"No," the Man with the Long Black Coat breathed. "It so happens that he doesn't."

I stepped into his space, shoppers and street arabs and immigrants and young mothers and dollymops and every sort of person parting ways around us, the blood pounding in my veins, and slit my eyes at him.

"In that case, I should tell him thirteen Miller's Court at one o'clock tonight," I whispered. "This chap, whoever he is, better be handsome."

"Is that important to you?"

"It might be."

"I am a very poor judge. He is ardent, at least, which I hope might make up for other deficiencies," the Man with the Long Black Coat replied, nodding in his easy fashion as he stepped briskly to the side to resume his course. "I shall deliver the message at once, my dear young lady."

"Thank you for the extra custom, sir."

"Not at all! You have been most accommodating. Any special instructions?"

Half-turning, I flashed him a last quick grin, and it felt like losing a piece of my heart, a little. "Tell him he'd do best not to bring his name."

It only remained for me to find Julia, but that proved laughably easy, as she were lying in wait for me, seated on the steps leading up to our rooms, both a shawl and a thin blanket about her shoulders, smoking a pipe. The smoke will do your voice no good, I had the mad urge to tell her.

But that would have served no purpose whatsoever. I dove straight for the heart of the matter.

"I don't want you here anymore," I said quietly.

Her perched on the staircase and me in the hallway, she were a head or so above me. Julia's eyes had pinched at the edges over the years same as mine had, and they crinkled now as she glared. She took her time in answering, tapping her pipe in her hands, pushing a golden strand of hair away from her brow.

"I'm not going anyplace," she announced, though she stood decisively. "Get used to me."

"*Why?*" I cried.

For therein lay the crux—why should I, the only person in the world what hated Julia with an iron resolve, suffer the keeping of her?

My sister looked startled at my tone, but quickly smoothed her features. "Why not?"

"Go away. Marry someone or other and leave me be."

"Marry who? I like it here."

"I don't like *here* with you *in it*."

"This is what you did to me," she answered, cold as stone. "This is what I'm fit for, Mary. *You. You're* all I'm fit for now. You took the rest away."

"I'd ne'er dream of touching anything of yours."

"Liar. You've taken three things from me at least, I can prove 'em, and that's naught to do with my chances with suitors when we were girls, or my lessons you used to copy out in secret, or my reputation after you hinted I let men court me on the sly afore you left Caernarfon."

I tilted my head, having done all that and then some. One can, after all, accomplish a great deal from the shadows. The Man with the Long Black Coat and I are adepts. Skulking and silence for months, maybe years, but then, oh but *then*—pour the champagne!

"You took John Davies when he said as he'd wait for me to come of age." Julia's voice had turned thick and dark as pitch, a voice calling from a crypt. "That's one definite thing. You took the shell I found, the one I meant to keep us safe *together,* warm and fed *together.* That's another."

Nodding, I scratched at a loose end on the cheap lace trim of my sleeve. *It'll have to be mended.* Her accusations were nothing short of Testament, but 'pon my soul, I don't know what difference she thought they made.

"You said three things. That I took," I urged after a pause.

She stepped down to my level, eyes burning like the sun behind Caernarfon Castle.

"You took yourself away from your sister," she hissed in my ear. "And don't think I'll ever forgive you for it."

Laying a cool palm to her shoulder, I pressed it. Looked at her direct, meaning *listen to me for the last time.*

"I weren't ne'er enough for you." My hand shook, so I smoothed it down her sleeve and then tucked my fingers around my elbows. "Nothing was. It were always you being the best, being noticed—talking, laughing, studying, *singing*. Sucking all the marrow from the room until the bones lay scattered, ever since you were born, and I couldn't help but curse the day. I didn't even exist with you around. Can't you see why there weren't space for me at home, why I had to light out after my own crib, my own *family* once you'd took the one God gave me? Why can't you understand, Julia?"

"You didn't have to *ruin* me in the process, Mary Jane!" she cried, and then shoved her fingers over her trembling lips.

Shifting from foot to foot, I gave her another definite nod whilst I stared at the filthy carpet. We were through here, had been through long ago and far away.

"Joe came round looking for you," I said numbly, like the admission was hard. I cast my eyes up to the invisible door of 13 Miller's Court, studying it as if 'twere a lifeline, and in a way, for me maybe it was. "I think he wants to go away with you. He's drinking with his porter mates closer to Billingsgate, but he'll be back between midnight and one, thereabouts. I think you ought to say yes."

Her blue eyes grew ocean-wide. "You want me to meet Joe here, tonight? You want me to take him for mine?"

"Don't you love him?"

She pursed her lips, considered. "Yes. What do you care for that? I loved John Davies too. After all you've done, why?"

"Because you had the right of it. I owe you tonight," I replied, touching the oyster shell, drawing it out between us. "I'll make myself scarce now, and you'll meet with Joe, and the war will be over for good and all. Those things what I done—copying your sums without asking, taking John Davies though he said he'd wait, telling people you were no better than you should be—you were right. You shouldn't have kept coming after me, but I'm glad you did, truly. I owe you every single second of the rest of your life."

Tears spilled from Julia's eyes. The gap between us closed. We embraced. She said thank you, and goodbye, and I stayed silent, overcome with feeling.

I stepped out into the cold, eyes narrowing at the cutting rays of the dying sun.

Then I went to the pub and set about telling everyone who would listen in strictest confidence—which meant it would spread like wildfire—that Julia were going back to Wales tonight, and that I should be lost without her.

I leave the pub with t'other dollymops, who are now weaving about like lushy mayflies.

"What did you say your name was?" the pretty one asks.

The plump one's arm is about her shoulders. "Yes, do tell us."

"It doesn't matter," I answer, but friendly-like. "Julia will do."

"Christ, ain't that the truth." The shrewish one chuckles. "Can't recall the last time as anybody wanted to know mine. Cheers, Julia . . . see you hereabouts again, I trust."

No, you shan't, I think as I watch them meander away—ribbing each other, stumbling, slapping at each other's bums.

Returning slowly to the Thames, I find a dark corner along the embankment beneath London Bridge and count my store of chink again. Might take a week perhaps, but if I'm careful over food and max and not too particular over where I sleep, I can like as not manage it.

Paris. I can't afford champagne there, but this city isn't for me any longer.

The lights in the boats twinkle in the sullen waters, and the air is icy enough to scrape the skin. I start humming the tune to "A Violet from Mother's Grave," the song the papers say neighbors claim I were singing afore I died so horribly. There's a weight dissolving from my chest, a hollow feeling replacing it, one filled with possibilities, and I watch the slow progression of the cargo ships.

I wonder how the Man with the Long Black Coat is faring. He was angry, I could guess as much after what he done to her, but I wager he shan't be cross for long. Rubbing my thumbnail along the shell at my neck, I wonder what he'll do with her heart. I wonder whether he's been to Paris. Of course I've no address for him, nor name, but anyone can advertise in the Agony Columns, and everyone reads them.

Pulling my red shawl closer about me, I head for the black corridors where the quiet creatures live.

~

THE DECORATOR

Boris Akunin

Perhaps the most distinguished—certainly the most popular—author in Russia today is Grigory Shalvovich Chkhartishvili (1956–), better known under his Boris Akunin nom de plume, whose enormously popular series about the nineteenth-century detective Erast Fandorin has made him a household name. He was nominated in 2000 for the Smirnoff-Booker Prize, also known as the British-sponsored Russian Booker Prize (related to the Man Booker Prize). In the same year, he won the Anti-Booker Prize (with a prize of one dollar more than the Russian Booker Prize) for his Fandorin novel *Coronation, or the Last of the Romanovs*. Also in 2000, Akunin was named the Russian Writer of the Year.

While he is a noted translator and has written under other pseudonyms, it is the Fandorin novels for which Akunin is known in the West. This series of mystery stories began with *The Winter Queen* (1998; English translation in 2003) and has continued with an additional fourteen books, following Fandorin's career from his days as a clerk in the police department to his decision to become a private detective. The most popular mystery fiction in post-Soviet Russia has been the lowest type of pulp hackwork, filled with over-the-top violence, gore, and sex. Akunin set out to write novels in the middle ground between Dostoevsky and this trash, and has succeeded.

Four Fandorin works, *The Winter Queen*, *The Turkish Gambit*, *The State Counsellor*, and "The Decorator," were made into big-budget Russian movies.

"The Decorator" was first published in English in *Special Assignments: The Further Adventures of Erast Fandorin* (London, Weidenfeld & Nicolson, 2007).

CHAPTER 1

A Bad Beginning

Erast Petrovich Fandorin, the Governor-General of Moscow's Deputy for Special Assignments and a state official of the sixth rank, a knight of many Russian and foreign orders, was being violently sick.

The finely moulded but now pale and bluish-tinged features of the Collegiate Counsellor's face were contorted in suffering. One hand, in a white kid glove with silver press-studs, was pressed against his chest, while the other clawed convulsively at the air in an unconvincing attempt by Erast Petrovich to reassure his assistant, as if to say, "Never mind, it's nothing; I shall be fine in a moment."

However, judging from the intensity with which his distress continued, it was anything but nothing.

Fandorin's assistant, Provincial Secretary Anisii Pitirimovich Tulipov, a skinny, unprepossessing young man of twenty-three, had never before had occasion to see his chief in such a pitiful state. Tulipov himself was in fact a little greenish round the gills, but he had resisted the temptation to vomit and was now secretly feeling proud of it. However, this ignoble feeling was merely fleeting, and therefore unworthy of our attention, but the unexpected sensitivity of his adored chief, always so cool-headed and not disposed to excessive displays of feeling, had alarmed Anisii quite seriously.

"G-Go . . ." said Erast Petrovich, squeezing out the word as he wiped his purple lips with one glove. His constant slight stutter, a reminder of a concussion suffered long ago, had been become noticeably stronger as a result of his nervous discomfiture. "G-Go in . . . T-Take . . . -d-detailed . . . notes. Photographs from all angles. And make sure they don't t-t-trample the evidence . . ."

He doubled over again, but this time the extended hand did not tremble—the finger pointed steadfastly at the crooked door of the little planking shed from which only a few moments earlier the Collegiate Counsellor had emerged as pale as a ghost with his legs buckling under him.

Anisii did not wish to go back into that grey semi-darkness, into that sticky smell of blood and offal. But duty was duty.

He filled his chest right up to the top with the damp April air (he didn't want his own stomach to start churning too), crossed himself, and took the plunge.

The little hut was used for storing firewood, but there was hardly any left, because the cold season was already coming to an end. Quite a number of people had gathered inside: an investigator from the Public Prosecutor's Office, detectives from the Criminal Investigation Department, the district superintendent of police, the local police inspector, a forensic medical expert, a photographer, local police constables, and also the yard-keeper Klimuk, first to discover the scene of the monstrous atrocity—that morning he had looked in to get some wood for the stove, seen it there, had a good long yell, and gone running for the police.

There were two oil lamps burning, and shadows flickered gently across the low ceiling. It was quiet, except for a young constable gently sobbing and sniffing in the corner.

"Well now, and what do we have here?" forensic medical expert Egor Willemovich Zakharov purred curiously as he lifted some dark, bluish-crimson, porous object from the floor in a rubber-gloved hand. "I do believe it's the spleen. Yes that's her, the little darling. Excellent. Into the little bag with her, into her little bag. And the womb too, the left kidney, and we'll have the full set, apart from a few odd little bits and pieces . . . What's that there under your boot, Monsieur Tulipov? Not the mesentery, is it?"

Anisii glanced down, started in horror and almost stumbled over the outstretched body of the spinster Stepanida Andreichkina, aged thirty-nine years. This information, together with the nature of her occupation, had been obtained from the yellow prostitute's card left lying neatly on her sundered chest. But there was nothing else neat to be observed in the posthumous appearance of the spinster Andreichkina.

One could assume that even in life her face had not been lovely to behold, but in death it had become nightmarish: it was livid blue, covered with blobs of powder, the eyes had slipped out of their sockets and the mouth was frozen in a soundless scream of horror. What could be seen below the face was even more horrific. Someone had slashed open the poor streetwalker's body from top to bottom and from side to side, extracted all of its contents and laid them out on the ground in a fantastic design. By this time, though, Zakharov had already collected up almost the entire exhibition and put it away in little numbered bags. All that was left was the black patch of blood that had spread without hindrance and little scraps of the dress that had been either hacked or torn to shreds.

Leontii Izhitsin, the district prosecutor's Investigator for Especially Important Cases, squatted down beside the doctor and asked briskly: "Signs of intercourse?"

"That, my darling man, I'll particularise afterwards. I'll compose a little report portraying everything just the way it is, very prettily. In here, as you can see for yourself, we have been cast into the outer darkness."

Like any foreigner with a perfect mastery of the Russian language, Zakharov was fond of peppering his speech with various quaint and whimsical turns of phrase. Despite his perfectly normal surname, the expert was of English extraction. The doctor's father, also a medical man, had come to the kingdom of our late departed sovereign, put down roots and adapted a name that presented difficulty to the Russian ear—Zacharias—to local conditions, making it into "Zakharov": Egor Willemovich had told them all about it on the way there in the cab. You could tell just from looking at him that he wasn't one of us Russians: lanky and heavy-boned, with sandy-coloured hair, a broad mouth with thin lips, and fidgety, constantly shifting that terrible pipe from one corner of his mouth to the other.

The investigator Izhitsin pretended to take an interest, clearly putting on a brave face, as the medical expert twirled yet another lump of tormented flesh between his tenacious fingers and inquired sarcastically: "Well, Mr. Tulipov, is your superior still taking the air? I told you we would have got by perfectly well without any supervision from the Governor's department. This is no picture for over-dainty eyes, but we've already seen everything there is to see."

It was clear enough: Leontii Izhitsin was displeased; he was jealous. It was a serious matter to set Fandorin himself to watch over an investigation. What investigator would have been pleased?

"Stop that, Linkov, you're like a little girl!" Izhitsin growled at the sobbing policeman. "Better get used to it. You're not destined for special assignments; you'll be seeing all sorts of things."

"God forbid I could ever get used to such sights," Senior Constable Pribludko muttered in a half-whisper: he was an old, experienced member of the force, known to Anisii from a case of three years before.

It wasn't the first time he'd worked with Leontii Izhitsin, either—an unpleasant gentleman, nervous and jittery, constantly laughing, with piercing eyes; always neat and tidy—his collars looked as if they were made of alabaster and his cuffs were even whiter—always brushing the specks of dust off his own shoulders; a man with ambitions, carving out a career for himself. Last Epiphany, though, he'd come a cropper with the investigation into the merchant Sitnikov's will. It had been a sensational case, and since it also involved the interests of certain influential individuals to some degree, any delay was unacceptable, so His Excellency Prince Dolgorukoi had asked Erast Petrovich to give the Public Prosecutor's Office a helping hand. But everyone knew the kind of assistance the Chief gave—he'd gone and untangled the entire case in one day. No wonder Izhitsin was furious. He could sense that yet again the victor's laurels would not be his.

"That seems to be all," the investigator declared. "So what now? The corpse goes to the police morgue, at the Bozhedomka Cemetery. Seal the shed, put a constable on guard. Have detectives question everyone living in the vicinity, and make it thorough—anything they've heard or seen that was suspicious. You, Klimuk. The last time you came to collect firewood was some time between ten and eleven, right?" Izhi-tsin asked the yard-keeper. "And death occurred no later than two o'clock in the morning?" (That was to the medical expert Zakharov.) "So what we have to look at is the period from ten in the evening to two in the morning." And then he turned to Klimuk again. "Perhaps you spoke to someone local? Did they tell you anything?"

The yard-keeper (a broad, thick beard, bushy eyebrows, irregular skull, with a distinctive wart in the middle of his forehead, thought Anisii, practising the composition of a verbal portrait) stood there, kneading a cap that could not possibly be any more crumpled.

"No, Your Honour, not at all. I don't understand a thing. I locked the door of the shed and ran to Mr. Pribludko at the station. And they didn't let me out of the station until the bosses arrived. The local folk don't know a thing about it. That is, of course, they can see as lots of police have turned up . . . that the gentlemen of the police force have arrived. But the locals don't know anything about this here horror," said the yard-keeper, with a fearful sideways glance at the corpse.

"We'll check that soon enough," Izhi-tsin said with a laugh. "Right then, detectives, get to work. And you, Mr. Zakharov, take your treasures away, and let's have a full evaluation, according to the book, by midday."

"Will the gentlemen detectives please stay where they are." Fandorin's low voice came from behind Izhitsin. Everybody turned around.

How had the Collegiate Counsellor entered the shed, and when? The door had not even creaked. Even in the semi-darkness it was obvious that Anisii's chief was pale and perturbed, but his voice was steady and he spoke in his usual reserved and courteous manner, a manner that did not encourage any objections.

"Mr. Izhitsin, even the yard-keeper realised that it would not be good to spread gossip about this incident," Fandorin told the investigator in a dry voice. "In fact, I was sent here in order to ensure the very strictest secrecy. No questioning of the locals. And furthermore, I request—in fact I demand—that everyone here present must maintain absolute silence about the circumstances. Explain to the local people that . . . a st-streetwalker has hanged herself, taken her own life, a perfectly ordinary business. If rumours of what has happened here spread around Moscow, every one of you will be subject to official inquiry, and anyone found guilty of divulging information will be severely punished. I'm sorry, gentlemen, but th-those are the instructions that I was given, and there is good reason for them."

At a sign from the doctor the constables were about to take the stretcher standing against the wall and place the corpse on it, but the Collegiate Counsellor raised his hand: "Wait a m-moment. He crouched down beside the dead woman. "What's this here on her cheek?"

Izhitsin, galled by the reprimand he had received, shrugged his narrow shoulders. "A spot of blood; as you may have observed, there's plenty of blood here."

"But not on her face." Erast Petrovich cautiously rubbed the oval spot with his finger—a mark was left on the white kid leather of his glove. Speaking in extreme agitation, or so it seemed to Anissii, his chief muttered: "There's no cut, no bite."

The investigator Izhitsin watched the Collegiate Counsellor's manipulations in bewilderment. The medical expert Zakharov watched with interest.

Fandorin took a magnifying glass out of his pocket, peered from close up at the victim's face and gasped: "The imprint of lips! Good Lord, this is the imprint of lips! There can be no doubt about it!"

"So why make such a fuss over that?" Izhi-tsin asked acidly. "We've got plenty of marks far more horrible than that here." He turned the toe of his shoe towards the open rib-cage and the gaping pit of the belly. "Who knows what ideas a loony might get into his head?"

"Ah, how foul," the Collegiate Counsellor muttered, addressing no one in particular.

He tore off his soiled glove with a rapid movement and threw it aside. He straightened up, closed his eyes and said very quietly: "My God, is it really going to start in Moscow . . . ?"

"What a piece of work is a man! How noble in reason! How infinite in faculties! In form and moving how express and admirable! In action how like an angel! In apprehension how like a god! The beauty of the world! The paragon of animals! And yet, to me, what is this quintessence of dust?" No matter. *What does it matter if the Prince of Denmark, an indolent and blasé creature, has no interest in man? I do! The Bard is half right: there is little angelic in the deeds of men, and it is sacrilege to liken the comprehension of man to that of God, but there is nothing in the world more beautiful than man. And what are action and apprehension but a chimera? Deception and vanity, truly the quintessence of dust? Man is not action, but body. Even the plants that are so pleasing to our eyes, the most sumptuous and intricate of flowers, can in no wise be compared with the magnificent arrangement of the human body. Flowers are primitive and simple, identical within and without, turn the petals whichever way you will. Looking at flowers is boring. How can the avidity of their stems, the primitive geometry of their inflorescences and the crude forms of their stamens rival the purple resilience of muscles, the elasticity of silky-smooth skin, the silvery mother-of-pearl of the stomach, the graceful curves of the intestines and the mysterious asymmetry of the liver?*

How is it possible for the monotonous coloration of a blossoming poppy to match the variety of shades of human blood—from the shrill scarlet of the arterial current to the regal purple of the veins? How can the vulgar shade of the bluebell rival the tender blue pattern of the capillaries, or the autumnal colouring of the maple rival the deep blush of the menstrual discharge! The female body is more elegant and a hundred times more interesting than the male. The function of the female body is not coarse physical labour and destruction, but creation and nurturing. The elastic womb is like a precious pearl oyster. An idea! Some time I must lay open an impregnated womb to expose the maturing pearl within the shell—yes, yes, without fail! Tomorrow! I have been fasting too long already, since Shrovetide. My lips have shrivelled with repeating: "Reanimate my accursed heart through this sacrificial fast!" The Lord is kind and charitable. He will not be angry with me for lacking the strength to hold out six days until the Blessed Resurrection. And after all, the third of April is no ordinary day: it is the anniversary of the Enlightenment. It was the third of April then too. What date it was in the other style is of no importance. The important thing is the music of those words: the third of April.

I have my own fast, and my own Easter. When the fast is broken, let it be in style. No, I will not wait until tomorrow. Today! Yes, yes, lay out a banquet. Not merely to sate myself, but a surfeit. Not for my own sake, but to the glory of God.

For He it was who opened my eyes, who taught me to see and understand true beauty. More than that, to disclose it and reveal it to the world. And to disclose is to create. I am the Creator's apprentice.

How sweet it is to break the fast after a long abstinence. I remember each sweet moment; I know my memory will preserve it all down to the minutest detail, without losing a single sensation of vision, taste, touch, hearing or smell.

I close my eyes and I see it . . .

Late evening. I cannot sleep. Excitement and elation lead me along the dirty streets, across the empty lots, between the crooked houses and the twisted fences. I have not slept for many nights in a row. My chest is constricted, my temples throb. During the day I doze for half an hour or an hour and am woken by terrible visions that I cannot remember when awake.

As I walk along I dream of death, of meeting with Him, but I know that I must not die, it is too soon; my mission has not been completed.

A voice from out of the darkness: "Spare the money for half a bottle." Trembling, hoarse from drinking. I turn my head and see the most wretched and abominable of human beings: a degraded whore, drunk and in tatters, but even so, grotesquely painted with ceruse and lipstick. I turn away in squeamish disgust, but suddenly my heart is pierced by the familiar sharp pity. Poor creature, what have you done to yourself! And this is a woman, the masterpiece of God's art! How could you abuse yourself so, desecrate and degrade the gift of God, abase your precious reproductive system?

Of course, you are not to blame. A soulless, cruel society has dragged you through the mud. But I shall cleanse and save you. My heart is serene and joyful.

Who could have known it would happen? I had no intention of breaking the fast—if I had, my path would not have lain through these pitiful slums, but through the fetid lanes and alleys of Khitrovka or Grachyovka, where abomination and vice make their home. But I am overflowing with magnanimity and generosity, only slightly tainted by my impatient craving.

"I'll soon cheer you up, my darling," I tell her. "Come with me." I am wearing men's clothes, and the witch thinks she has found a buyer for her rotten wares. She laughs hoarsely and shrugs her shoulders coyly: "Where are we going? Listen, *have you got any money? You might at least feed me, or better still buy me a drink." Poor little lost sheep.*

I lead her through the dark courtyard towards the sheds. I tug impatiently on one door, a second—the third is not locked.

The lucky woman breathes her cheap vodka fumes on my neck, and giggles: "Well fancy that! He's taking me to the sheds; he's that impatient."

A stroke of the scalpel, and I open the doors of freedom to her soul.

Liberation does not come without pain; it is like birth. The woman I now love with all my heart is in great pain; she wheezes and chews on the gag in her mouth, and I stroke her head and comfort her—"Be patient." My hands do their work deftly and quickly. I do not need light: my eyes see as well at night as they do during the day.

I lay open the profaned, filthy integument of the body, the soul of my beloved sister soars upwards and I am transfixed by awe before the perfection of God's machinery.

When I lift the hot bread-roll of the heart to my face with a tender smile, it is still trembling, still quivering, like a golden fish fresh from the water, and I kiss the miraculous fish on the parted lips of its aorta.

The place was well chosen, no one interrupts me, and this time the Hymn to Beauty is sung to the end, consummated with a kiss to her cheek. Sleep, sister; your life was revolting and horrible, the sight of you was an offence to the eye, but thanks to me you have become beautiful . . .

Consider that flower again. Its true beauty is not visible in the glade or in the flower-bed, oh no! The rose is regal on the bodice of a dress, the carnation in the buttonhole, the violet in a lovely girl's hair. The flower attains its glory when it has been cut; its true life is inseparable from death. The same is true of the human body. While it is alive, it cannot reveal its delightful arrangement in all its magnificence. I help the body to ascend its throne of glory. I am a gardener.

But no, a gardener merely cuts flowers, while I also create displays of intoxicating beauty from the organs of the body. In England a previously unheard-of profession is becoming fashionable nowadays—the decorator, a specialist in the embellishment and adornment of the home, the shop window, the street at carnival time.

I am not a gardener; I am a decorator.

CHAPTER 2

From Bad to Worse

Holy Week Tuesday, 4 April, midday

Those present at the emergency meeting convened by the Governor-General of Moscow, Prince Vladimir Andreevich Dolgorukoi, were as follows: the Head Police Master and Major-General of the Retinue of His Imperial Majesty, Yurovsky; the Public Prosecutor of the Chamber of Justice of Moscow, State

Counsellor and Usher of the Chamber, Kozlyatnikov; the head of the Criminal Investigation Department of the police, State Counsellor Eichmann; the Governor-General's Deputy for Special Assignments, Collegiate Counsellor Fandorin; and the Investigator for Especially Important Cases of the Public Prosecutor's Office of Moscow, Court Counsellor Izhitsin.

"Oh this weather, this appalling weather, it's vile." These were the words with which the Governor-General opened the proceedings. "It's simply beastly, gentlemen. Overcast, windy, slush and mud everywhere and, worst of all, the River Moscow has overflowed its banks more than usual. I went to the Zamoskvorechie -district—an absolute nightmare. The water's risen three and a half *sazhens*! It's flooded everything up as far as Pyatnitskaya Street. And it's no better on the left bank either. You can't get through Neglinny Lane. Oh, I shall be put to shame, gentlemen. Dolgorukoi will be disgraced in his old age!"

All present began sighing anxiously, and the only one whose face expressed a certain astonishment was the Investigator for Especially Important Cases. The Prince, who possessed exceptionally acute powers of perception, felt that perhaps he ought to explain.

"I see, young man, that you . . . er . . . Glagolev, is it? No, Luzhitsin."

"Izhitsin, Your Excellency," the Public Prosecutor prompted Prince Dolgorukoi, but not loudly enough—in his seventy-ninth year the Viceroy of Moscow (yet another title by which the all-powerful Vladimir Andreevich was known) was hard of hearing.

"Please forgive an old man," said the Governor good-naturedly, spreading his hands. "Well then, Mr. Pizhitsin, I see you are in a state of ignorance . . . Probably your position does not require you to know. But since we are having this meeting . . . well then"—and the Prince's long face with its dangling chestnut-brown moustaches assumed a solemn expression—"at Easter, Russia's first capital city will be blessed by a visit from His Imperial Highness. He will arrive without any pomp or ceremony—to visit and worship at the holy places of Moscow. We have been instructed not to inform the citizens of Moscow in advance, since the visit has been planned as an *impromptu,* so to speak. However, that does not relieve us of responsibility for the standard of his reception and the general condition of the city. For instance, gentlemen, this morning I received a missive from His Eminence Ioannikii, the Metropolitan of Moscow. His Reverence writes to complain that what is going on in the confectionery shops of Moscow before the holy festival of Easter is a downright disgrace: the shop windows and counters are stacked high with boxes of sweets and candy with pictures of the Last Supper, the Way of the Cross, Calvary, and so forth. This is sacrilege, gentlemen! Please be so good, my dear sir," said the Prince, addressing the Head Police Master, "as to issue an order to the police today to the effect that a strict stop must be put to such obscenities. Destroy the boxes, donate their contents to the Foundlings' Hospital. Let the poor orphans have a treat for the holiday. And fine the shopkeepers to make sure they don't get me into any trouble before the Emperor's visit!"

The Governor-General nervously adjusted his curly wig, which had slipped a little to one side, and was about to say something else, but instead began coughing.

An inconspicuous door that led to the inner chambers immediately opened and a skinny old man dashed out from behind it, moving silently in felt overshoes with his knees bent. His bald cranium shone with a blinding brilliance and he had immense sideburns. It was His Excellency's personal valet, Frol Vedishchev. Nobody was surprised by his sudden appearance, and everybody present felt it appropriate to greet the old man with a bow or at least a nod for, despite his humble position, Vedishchev had the reputation in the ancient city of being an influential and in certain respects omnipotent individual.

He rapidly poured drops of some mixture from a small bottle into a silver goblet, gave them to the Prince to drink and disappeared with equal rapidity in the reverse direction without so much as glancing at anyone.

"Shank you, Frol, shank you, my dear," the Governor-General mumbled to his favourite's back, shifted his chin to put his false teeth back in place and carried on without lisping any more. "And so, if Erast Petrovich Fandorin would be so good as to explain the reason for the urgency of this meeting . . . You know perfectly well, my dear friend, that today every minute is precious to me. Well then, what exactly has happened? Have you taken care to make sure that rumours of this vile incident are not spread among the inhabitants of the city? That's all we need on the eve of the Emperor's visit . . ."

Erast Petrovich got to his feet and the eyes of Moscow's supreme guardians of law and order turned to look at the Collegiate Counsellor's pale, resolute face.

"Measures have been taken to maintain secrecy, Your Excellency," Fandorin reported. "Everybody who was involved in the inspection of the scene of the crime has been warned of the responsibility they bear and they have signed an undertaking not to reveal anything. Since the yard-keeper who found the body is an individual with an inclination to intemperate drinking and cannot answer for himself, he has been temporarily placed in a s-special cell at the Department of Gendarmes."

"Good," said the Governor approvingly. "Then what need is there for this meeting? Why did you ask me to bring together the heads of the criminal investigation and police departments? You and Pizhitsin could have decided everything between you?"

Erast Petrovich cast an involuntary glance at the investigator for whom the Governor had invented this amusing new name, but just at the moment the Collegiate Counsellor was not in the mood for jollity.

"Your Excellency, I did not request you to summon the head of the Criminal Investigation Department. This case is so disturbing that it should be classified as a crime of state importance, and in addition to the Public Prosecutor's Office it should be handled by the operations section of the gendarmes under the personal control of the Head Police Master. I would not involve the Criminal Investigation Department at all, there are too many incidental individuals there. That is one."

Fandorin paused significantly. State Counsellor Eichmann started and was about to protest, but Prince Dolgorukoi gestured for him to remain silent.

"It seems I need not have bothered you, my dear fellow," Dolgorukoi said amiably to Eichmann. "Why don't you go and keep up the pressure on your pickpockets and swindlers, so that on Easter Sunday they break their fast at home in Khitrovka and, God forbid, don't show their noses outside. I am relying on you."

Eichmann stood up and bowed without speaking, smiled with just his lips at Erast Petrovich and went out.

The Collegiate Counsellor sighed in the realisation that he had now acquired a lifelong enemy in the person of the head of Moscow's Criminal Investigation Department, but this case really was horrific, and no unnecessary risk could be justified.

"I know you," said the Governor, looking anxiously at his trusted deputy. "If you say 'one,' it means there will be a 'two.' Speak out; don't keep us on tenterhooks."

"I greatly regret, Vladimir Andreevich, that the sovereign's visit will have to be cancelled," Fandorin said in a very low voice, but this time the Prince heard him perfectly.

"How's that—'cancelled'?" he gasped.

The other individuals present reacted more violently to the Collegiate Counsellor's brash announcement.

"You must be out of your mind!" exclaimed Head Police Master Yurovsky.

"It's absolutely incredible!" bleated the Prosecutor.

The Investigator for Especially Important Cases did not dare to say anything out loud, because his rank was too low to permit the taking of such liberties, but he did purse his plump lips as if he were outraged by Fandorin's insane outburst.

"What do you mean—cancelled?" Dolgorukoi repeated in a flat voice.

The door leading to the inner chambers opened slightly, and the valet's face emerged halfway from behind it.

The Governor began speaking with extreme agitation, hurrying so much that he swallowed syllables and even entire words: "Erastpetrovich, it's not the first year . . . you . . . idle words . . . But cancel His Majesty's visit? Why, that's a scandal of unprecedented proportions! You've no idea what effort I . . . For me, for all of us, it's . . ."

Fandorin frowned, wrinkling his high, clear forehead. He knew perfectly well how long Dolgorukoi had manoeuvred and intrigued in order to arrange the Emperor's visit, and how the hostile St. Petersburg "camarilla" had plotted and schemed against it—they had been trying for twenty years to unseat the cunning old Governor from his enviable position! His Majesty's Easter *impromptu* would be a triumph for the Prince, sure testimony to the invincibility of his position. And next year His Excellency had a highly important anniversary: sixty years of service at officer's rank. With an event like that he could even hope for the Order of St. Andrew. How could he suddenly turn around and ask for the trip to be cancelled!

"I understand all th-that, Your Excellency, but if it is not cancelled, things will be even worse. This case of mutilation is not the last." The Collegiate Counsellor's face became more sombre with every word that he spoke. "I am afraid that Jack the Ripper has moved to Moscow."

Once again, as several minutes earlier, Erast Petrovich's declaration provoked a chorus of protests.

"What do you mean—not the last?" the Governor-General asked indignantly.

The Head Police Master and the Public Prosecutor spoke almost with a single voice: "Jack the Ripper?"

Izhitsin gathered his courage and snorted. "Stuff and nonsense!"

"What ripper's that?" Frol Vedishchev croaked from behind his little door in the natural pause that followed.

"Yes, yes, who is this Jack?" His Excellency gazed at his subordinates in obvious displeasure. "Everybody knows; I'm the only one who hasn't been informed. It's always the same with you."

"Your Excellency, he is a famous English murderer who kills streetwalkers in London," the District Prosecutor explained in his pompous fashion.

"If you will permit me, Your Excellency, I will explain in detail."

Erast Petrovich took a notebook out of his pocket and skimmed through several pages.

The Prince cupped one hand round his ear, Vedishchev put on a pair of spectacles with thick lenses and Izhitsin smiled ironically.

"As Your Excellency no doubt remembers, last year I spent several months in England in connection with a case with which you are familiar: the disappearance of the correspondence of Catherine the Great. Indeed, Vladimir Andreevich, you even expressed your dissatisfaction at my extended absence. I stayed in London longer than absolutely necessary because I was following very closely the attempts of the local police to find a monstrous killer who had committed eight brutal murders in the East End in the space of eight months, from April to December. The killer acted in a most audacious fashion. He wrote notes to the police, in which he called himself 'Jack the Ripper' and on one occasion he even sent the commissioner who was in charge of the case half of a kidney that he had cut out of one of his victims."

"Cut out? But what for?" the Prince asked in amazement.

"The Ripper's outrages had a tremendously distressing effect on the public, but not simply because of the murders. In a city as large and ill-favoured as London there is naturally no shortage of crimes, including those that involve bloodshed. But the manner in which the Ripper despatched his victims was genuinely monstrous. He usually cut the poor women's throats and then disembowelled them, like partridges, and laid out their entrails in a kind of nightmarish still life."

"Holy Mother of God!" Vedishchev gasped and crossed himself.

"The abominations you speak of!" the Governor said with feeling: "Well then, did they not catch the villain?"

"No, but since December the distinctive murders have ceased. The police have concluded that the criminal has either committed suicide or . . . left England."

"And what else would he do except come to see us in Moscow?" said the Head Police Master, with a sceptical shake of his head. "But if that is the case, finding and catching an English cut-throat is child's play."

"Why are you so sure that he is English?" Fandorin asked, turning to the general. "All the murders were committed in the slums of London, the home of many immigrants from the continent of Europe, including Russians. Indeed, in the first instance the English police suspected immigrant doctors."

"And why doctors in particular?" Izhitsin asked.

"Because in every case the internal organs were extracted from the victims with great skill, with excellent knowledge of anatomy and also almost certainly with the use of a surgical scalpel. The London police were absolutely convinced that Jack the Ripper was a doctor or a medical student."

Public Prosecutor Kozlyatnikov raised a well-tended white finger and the diamond ring on it glinted.

"But what makes you think that the spinster Andreichkina was killed and mutilated by the Ripper from London? As if we had no murderers of our own? Some son of a bitch got so tanked up on drink he didn't know what he was doing and imagined he was fighting some dragon or other. We have any number of those."

The Collegiate Counsellor sighed and replied patiently: "My dear sir, you've read the report from the forensic medical expert. No one in a drunken fury can dissect so precisely, and use 'a cutting tool of surgical sharpness.' That is one. And also, just as in the East End cases, there are none of the signs of sexual debauchery which are usual in crimes of this kind. That is two. The most sinister point is the imprint of a bloody kiss on the victim's cheek, and that is three. All of the Ripper's victims had that imprint—on the forehead, on the cheek, sometimes on the temple. Inspector Gilson, from whom I learned this detail, was not inclined to attach any importance to it, since the Ripper had plenty of other freakish whims. However, from the limited amount of information that forensic science possesses on maniacal murderers, we know that these fiends attach great significance to ritual. Serial killings with the features of manic behaviour are always based on some kind of 'idea' that prompts the monster into repeatedly killing strangers. While I was in London, I tried to explain to the officers in charge of the investigation that their main task was to guess the maniac's 'idea' and the rest was merely a matter of investigative technique. There can be no doubt at all that the typical features of Jack the Ripper's ritual and that of our Moscow murderer are identical in every respect."

"But even so, it's just too fantastic," said General Yurovsky with a shake of his head. "For Jack the Ripper to disappear from London and turn up in a woodshed on Samotechnaya Street . . . And then, you must agree, cancelling the sovereign's visit just because some prostitute has been killed . . ."

Erast Petrovich's patience was clearly almost exhausted, because he said rather sharply: "Permit me to remind Your Excellency that the case of Jack the Ripper cost the head of London's police his job, and the Home Secretary also lost his position, because they refused for too long to attach any importance to the murders of 'some prostitutes or other.' Even if we assume that we now have our own, home-grown Ivan the Ripper, that does not improve the situation. Once he has tasted blood, he won't stop. Just imagine the situation if the killer hands us another present like today's during the Emperor's visit! And if it comes out that it is not the first such crime? The old capital will have a fine Easter Sunday."

Prince Dolgorukoi crossed himself in fright and General Yurovsky raised a hand to unbutton his gold-embroidered collar.

"It is a genuine miracle that this time we have managed to hush up such a fantastic case." The Collegiate Counsellor ran his fingers over his foppish black moustache, seeming preoccupied. "But have we really managed it?"

A deadly silence fell.

"Do as you wish, Prince," Vedishchev said from behind his door, "but he's right. Write to our father the Tsar. Tell him this and that, and there's been a bit of a muddle. It's to our own detriment, but for the sake of Your Majesty's peace of mind we humbly request you not to come to Moscow."

"Oh, Lord." The Governor's voice trembled pitifully.

Izhitsin stood up and, gazing loyally at his exalted superior, suggested a possible way out: "Your Excellency, could you not refer to the exceptionally high water? As they say, the Lord of Heaven must take the blame for that."

"Well done, Pizhitsin, well done," said the Prince, brightening up. "You have a good head. That's what I shall write. If only the newspapers don't manage to ferret out this business of the mutilation."

Investigator Izhitsin glanced condescendingly at Erast Petrovich and sat down, but not in the same way as before, with half a buttock on a quarter of the stool, but fully at his ease, as an equal among equals.

However, the expression of relief that had appeared on the Prince's face was almost immediately replaced by dismay.

"It won't do any good! The truth will come out anyway. If Erast Petrovich says this won't be the last atrocity, then it won't be. He is rarely mistaken."

Fandorin cast an emphatically quizzical glance at the Governor, as if to say: "Ah, I see, so there are times when I am mistaken!"

At this point the Head Police Master began breathing heavily through his nose, lowered his head guiltily and said in a deep voice: "I don't know if it's the last case or not, but it probably isn't the first. I am to blame, Governor; I didn't attach any importance to it, I did not wish to bother you over trifles. But today's murder looked too provocative altogether, and so I decided to report it to you in view of the Emperor's visit. However, I recall now that in recent times brutal murders of streetwalkers and female vagrants have probably been on the increase. During Shrovetide, I think it was, there was a report of a female beggar found on Seleznevskaya Street with her stomach slashed to ribbons. And before that, at the Sukharev Market, they found a prostitute with her womb cut out. We didn't even investigate the case of the beggar—there was no point—and we decided the prostitute's ponce had mutilated her in a drunken fit. We took the fellow in, but he still hasn't confessed; he's being stubborn."

"Ah, General Yurovsky, how could you?" said the Governor, throwing his hands in the air. "If we had launched an investigation straight away and set Erast Petrovich on the case, perhaps we might have already caught this villain! And we wouldn't have had to cancel His Highness's visit!"

"But Your Excellency, who could have known?—there was no deliberate deception. You know yourself what the city is like, and the people are blackguards; there's something of the kind every single day! I can't bother Your Excellency with every petty incident!" the General said, almost whining in his attempt to justify himself, and he looked round at the Public Prosecutor and the investigator for support, but Kozlyatnikov was gazing sternly at the chief of police and Izhitsin shook his head reproachfully, as if to say: "This is not good."

Collegiate Counsellor Fandorin interrupted the General's lament with a curt question: "Where are the bodies?"

"Where else would they be but at the Bozhedomka? That's where they bury all the dissolutes, idlers, and people without passports. If there are any signs of violence, they take them to the police morgue first, to Egor Zakharov, and after that they ship them over to the cemetery there. That's the procedure."

"We have to carry out an exhumation," Fandorin said, with a grimace of disgust. "And with no delay. Check the records at the morgue to see which female individuals have recently—l-let's say, since the New Year—been brought in with indications of violent death. And exhume them. Check for similarities in the picture of the crime. See if there have been any similar incidents. The ground has not thawed out yet, the c-corpses ought to be perfectly preserved."

The Public Prosecutor nodded: "I'll issue instructions. You deal with this, Izhitsin. And how about you, Erast Petrovich—would you not care to be present? It would be most desirable to have your participation."

Izhitsin grinned sourly—apparently he did not consider the Collegiate Counsellor's participation to be so very desirable.

Fandorin suddenly turned pale—he had remembered his recent shameful attack of nausea. He struggled with himself for a moment, but failed to master his weakness: "I'll assign m-my assistant Tulipov to help Izhitsin. I think that will be adequate."

The heavy job was finished after eight in the evening, by the light of flaming torches.

As a finishing touch, the ink-black sky began pouring down a cold, sticky rain and the landscape of the cemetery, which was bleak in any case, became dismal enough to make you want to fall face down into one of the excavated graves and sleep in the embrace of mother earth—anything not to see those puddles of filth, waterlogged mounds of soil and crooked crosses.

Izhitsin was giving the orders. There were six men digging: two of the constables who had been at the scene of the crime, kept on the investigation in order not to extend the circle of people who knew about the case, two long-serving gendarmes and two of the Bozhedomka gravediggers, without whom they would not have been able to manage the job. First they had thrown the thick, spongy mud aside with their spades and then, when the metal blades struck the unthawed ground, they had taken up their picks. The cemetery's watchman had showed them where to dig.

According to the list, since January of the current year, 1889, the police morgue had taken delivery of fourteen bodies of women bearing signs of "death from stabbing or cutting with a sharp instrument." Now they had extracted the dead women from their wretched little graves and dragged them back into the morgue, where they were being examined by Dr. Zakharov and his assistant Grumov, a consumptive-looking young man with a goatee that looked as if it was glued on and a thin, bleating voice that suited him perfectly.

Anisii Tulipov glanced inside once and decided not to do it again—it was better out in the open air, under the grey April drizzle. However, after an hour or so, chilled and thoroughly damp, and with his sensibilities blunted somewhat, Anisii sought shelter again in the autopsy room and sat on a little bench in the corner. He was discovered there by the watchman Pakhomenko, who felt sorry for him and took him back to his hut to give him tea.

The watchman was a capital fellow with a kind, clean-shaven face and jolly wrinkles radiating from his clear, child-like eyes to his temples. Pakhomenko spoke the language of the people—it was fascinating to listen to, but he put in a lot of Ukrainian words.

"Working in a graveyard, you need a callous heart," he said in his quiet voice, with a compassionate glance at the exhausted Tulipov. "Any folk will grow sick and weary if they're shown their own end every day: Look there, servant of God, you'll be rotting just like that. But the Lord is merciful: he gives the digger calluses on his hand so he won't wear the flesh down to the bone, and them as is faced with human woes, he gives them calluses on their hearts too. So as their hearts won't get worn away. You'll get used to it too, mister. At first I was afraid—green as burdock I was; but here we are, supping our tea and gnawing on our bread. Never mind, you'll get used to it in time. Eat, eat . . ."

Anisii sat for a while with Pakhomenko, who had been around in his time and seen all sorts of things in all sorts of places. He listened to his leisurely yarns— about worshipping at holy places, about good people and bad people—and felt as if he had been thawed out somehow and his will had been strengthened. Now he could go back to the black pits, the rough wood coffins and the grey shrouds.

It was talking to the garrulous watchman and home-grown philosopher that gave Anisii the idea that redeemed his useless presence at the cemetery with interest. It happened like this.

As evening was coming on, some time after six, they carried the last of the fourteen corpses into the morgue. The cheerful Izhitsin, who had prudently dressed for the occasion in hunting boots and rubberised overalls with a hood, called the soaking-wet Anisii over to summarise the results of the exhumation.

In the autopsy room Tulipov gritted his teeth, reinforced the calluses on his heart and it was all right: he walked from one table to the next, looked at the revolting deceased and listened to the expert's summaries.

"They can take these three lovelies back: numbers two, eight, and ten," said Zakharov, pointing casually with his finger. "Our staff have got something confused here. I'm not the one to blame. I only dissect the cases that are under special supervision; otherwise it's Grumov who pokes about inside them. I think he's a bit too fond of the hard stuff, the snake. And when he's drunk, he writes whatever comes into his head in the conclusions."

"What are you saying, Egor Willemo-vich?" Zakharov's goat-bearded assistant protested resentfully. "If I do occasionally indulge in strong drink, it's only a drop, to restore my health and my shattered nerves. Honestly, you should be ashamed."

"Get away with you," the gruff doctor said dismissively to his assistant and continued with his report. "Numbers one, three, seven, twelve, and thirteen are also not in our line either. The classic 'jab in the side' or 'slashed gizzard.' Neat work, no excessive cruelty. Better take them away as well." Egor Willemovich puffed a blast of strong tobacco smoke out of his pipe and lovingly patted a macabre blue woman on her gaping belly. "But I'll keep this Vasilisa the Beautiful and the other four. I have to check how precisely they were carved, how sharp the knife was and so on. At first I'd hazard a guess that numbers four and fourteen were our friend's handiwork. Only he must have been in a hurry, or else someone frightened him off and stopped the fellow from properly finishing off the work he loves." The doctor grinned without parting his teeth, which were gripping the pipe that protruded from them.

Anisii checked the numbers against the list. It all fitted: number four was the beggar Maria Kosaya from Maly Tryokhsvyatsky Lane. Number fourteen was the prostitute Zotova from Svininsky Lane. The same ones that the Head Police Master had mentioned.

For some reason the fearless Izhitsin was not satisfied with the pronouncements of the expert and started to check, almost sticking his nose into the gaping wounds and asking detailed questions. Anisii envied his self-possession and felt ashamed of his own uselessness, but he couldn't think of anything for himself to do.

He went outside into the fresh air, where the diggers were having a smoke

"Well, mister, was it worth all the digging?" asked Pakhomenko. "Or are we going to dig some more?"

"There's no more digging to do," Anisii responded gladly. "We've dug them all up. It's strange, really. In three months in the whole of Moscow only ten streetwalkers were killed. And the newspapers say our city is dangerous."

"Ha! Ten he says," the watchman snorted. "That's just how it looks. They're just the ones with names. But we stack the ones they bring us without names in the ditches?"

Anisii's heart started beating faster. "What ditches?"

"What?" Pakhomenko asked in amazement. "You mean the doctor didn't tell you? Come on, you can look for yourself."

He led Anisii to the far side of the cemetery and showed him a long pit with a thin layer of earth sprinkled over the top.

"That's the April one. Just the beginning. And there's the March one, already filled in." He pointed to a long mound of earth. "And there's the February one, and there's the January one. But before that I can't tell; I wasn't here then. I've only been working here since Epiphany—I came here from the Optinaya Hermitage, from pilgrimage. Before me there was a Kuzma used to work here. I never saw him myself. At Christmas this Kuzma broke his fast with a bottle or two, tumbled into an open grave and broke his neck. That was the death God had waiting for him: You've been watching over graves, servant of God, so now you can die in one. The Lord likes to joke with us in the graveyard. We're like his yard-keepers. The gravedigger Tishka at Srednokrestny——"

"So do they bury a lot of nameless women in the ditches?" Anisii asked, interrupting the talkative fellow. He had completely forgotten his damp boots and the cold.

"Plenty. Just last month it must be nigh on a dozen, or maybe more. A person without a name is like a dog without a collar. Take them to the knacker's yard—it's nobody's concern. Anyone who's lost their name is more like a flea than a human being."

"And have there been any badly cut-up cases among the nameless women?"

The watchman twisted his face into a sad expression. "Who's going to take a proper look at the poor darlings? They're lucky if the sexton from St. John the Warrior rattles off a prayer over them, and sometimes I do, sinner that I am; I sing them 'Eternal Peace.' Oh, people, people . . ."

So much for the Investigator for Especially Important Cases, such a meticulous man, Anisii gloated to himself. Fancy missing something like that. He gestured to the watchman in a way that meant: "Sorry, my friend, this is important," and set off towards the cemetery office at a run.

"Come on, lads," he shouted from a distance. "There's more work to be done! Grab your picks and your shovels and let's get moving!"

Young Linkov was the only one to jump to his feet. Senior Constable Pribludko stayed sitting down, and the gendarmes actually turned away. They'd had enough of swinging picks and knocking themselves out in this unseemly work; the man giving the orders wasn't even their boss, and he wasn't so important anyway. But Tulipov felt he was responsible and he made the men move.

And, as it turned out, it was a good thing he did.

Very late in the evening—in fact it was really night, because it was approaching midnight already—Tulipov was sitting with his chief on Malaya Nikitskaya Street (such a fine outhouse with such fine rooms, with electric lighting and a telephone), eating supper and warming himself up with grog.

The grog was special, made with Japanese sake, red wine, and prunes, prepared according to the oriental recipe of Masahiro Shibata, or Masa, Fandorin's servant. In fact, though, the Japanese did not behave or speak much like a servant. He was unceremonious with Erast Petrovich and did not regard Anisii as an important personage at all. In the line of physical exercise Tulipov was Masa's pupil and Anisii endured no little abuse and mockery from his strict teacher, and sometimes even thrashings disguised as training in Japanese fisticuffs. No matter what trick Anisii invented, no matter how he tried to shirk the practice of this hateful infidel wisdom, there was no way he could argue with his chief. Erast Petrovich had ordered him to master the techniques of ju-jitsu, and he had to do it, even if he was knocked out in the process. Only Tulipov did not make a very good sportsman. He was much more successful at getting himself knocked out.

"You squat hundred time this mornin'?" Masa asked menacingly when Anisii had had a little to eat and turned pink from the grog. "You beat pams on iron stick? Show me pams."

Tulipov hid his palms behind his back, because he was too lazy to pound them against the special metal stick a thousand times a day, and anyway, you know, it was painful. The tough calluses were simply not developing on the edges of Anisii's hands, and Masa abused him seriously for that.

"Have you finished eating? All right, now you can report on business to Erast Petrovich," Angelina told him and took the supper things off the table, leaving just the silver jug with the grog and the mugs.

Angelina was lovely, a real sight for sore eyes. Light-blonde hair woven into a magnificent plait that was arranged in a bun on the back of her head, a clear, white-skinned face, large, serious grey eyes that seemed to radiate some strange light into the world around her. A special woman: you didn't meet many like her. A swan like that would never even glance at a shabby, lop-eared specimen like Tulipov. But Erast Petrovich was a fine partner in every possible respect, and women liked him. During the three years that Tulipov had been his assistant, several passions, each more lovely than the last, had reigned for a while in the outhouse on Malaya Nikitskaya Street before leaving, but there had never been one as simple, bright and serene as Angelina. It would be good if she stayed a bit longer. Or still better—if she stayed for ever.

"Thank you, Angelina Samsonovna," said Anisii, looking at her tall, stately figure as she walked away.

A queen—that was the word for her, even though she came from a simple lower-middle-class background. And the Chief always had queens. There was nothing so surprising about it: that was the kind of man he was.

Angelina Krasheninnikova had appeared in the house on Malaya Nikitskaya Street a year earlier. Erast Petrovich had helped the orphan in a certain difficult business, and afterwards she had clung to him. She obviously wanted to thank him in the best way she could and, apart from her love, she had nothing to give. It was hard now to remember how they had managed without her before. The Collegiate Counsellor's bachelor residence had become cosy and warm, welcoming. Anisii had always liked being here, but now he liked it even more. And with Angelina there, the Chief seemed to have become a bit gentler and simpler somehow. It was good for him.

"All right, Tulipov, now you're well fed and drunk, t-tell me what you and Izhitsin dug up over there."

Erast Petrovich had an unusual, confused expression. His conscience is bothering him, Tulipov realised, for not going to the exhumation and sending me instead. But Anisii was only too happy if he could come in useful once in a blue moon and spare his adored chief unnecessary stress.

After all, he was pampered by the Chief in every way: provided with an apartment at public expense, a decent salary, interesting work. The greatest debt he owed him, one that could never be repaid, was for his sister Sonya, a poor cripple and imbecile. Anisii's heart no longer trembled for her, because while he was at work, Sonya was cared for with affection and fed. Fandorin's maid Palashka loved her and pampered her. Now she had even moved in with the Tulipovs. She would run to her master's house and help Angelina with the housework for an hour or two, then run back to Sonya—Tulipov's apartment was close by, on Granatny Lane.

Anisii began his report calmly, working up to the main point. "Egor Zakharov found clear signs that two of the women had been brutally mutilated after they were dead. The beggar Marya Kosoi, who died in unexplained circumstances on the eleventh of February, had her throat cut and her abdominal cavity slit open; her liver is missing. The woman of easy virtue Alexandra Zotova, who was killed on the fifth of April (it was assumed by her pimp Dzapoev) also had her throat cut and her womb was cut out. Another woman, the gypsy Marfa Zhemchuzhnikova, killed by a person or persons unknown on the tenth of March, is a doubtful case: her throat was not cut, her stomach was slashed open from top to bottom and side to side, but all her organs are in place."

At this point Anisii happened by chance to glance to one side and stopped in confusion. Angelina was standing in the doorway with one hand pressed to her full breasts and looking at him, her eyes wide with terror.

"Good Lord," she said, crossing herself, "what are these terrible things you're saying, Mr. Tulipov?"

The Chief glanced round in annoyance. "Angelina, go to your room. This is not for your ears. Tulipov and I are working."

The beautiful woman left without a murmur and Anisii glanced reproachfully at his chief. You may be right, Erast Petrovich, but you could be a bit gentler. Of course, Angelina Samsonovna is not blue-blooded, she's not your equal, but I swear she'd be more than a match for any noble-born woman. Any other man would make her his lawful wife without thinking twice. And he'd count himself lucky. But he didn't say anything out loud; he didn't dare.

"Signs of sexual intercourse?" the Chief asked intently, paying no attention to Tulipov's facial expression.

"Zakharov had difficulty in determining that. Even though the ground was frozen, some time had still passed. But there's something more important than all that!"

Anisii paused for effect and moved on to the main point. He told Erast Petrovich how on his instructions they had opened up the so-called "ditches"— the common graves for the bodies without names. In all they had inspected more than seventy corpses. On nine of the bodies—and one of them was a man—there had been clear signs of savage abuse. The general picture was similar to today's: someone with a good knowledge of anatomy and access to a surgical instrument had severely mutilated the bodies.

"The most remarkable thing, Chief, is that three of the mutilated bodies were taken from last year's ditches!" Anisii declared, and then modestly added: "I ordered them to dig up the ditches for November and December just to make sure."

Erast Petrovich had listened to his assistant very attentively, but now he suddenly leapt up off his chair: "December, you say, and November! That's incredible!"

"I was indignant about it too. How about our police, eh? A monster like that active all these months in Moscow, and we don't even hear a word about it! If it's a social outcast who gets killed, then it's none of the police's business—they just bury them and forget about them. You know, Chief, in your place I think I'd really give Yurovsky and Eichmann what for."

But the Chief seemed upset about something else. He walked quickly across the room and back again and muttered: "It couldn't have happened in December, let alone in November! He was still in London then!"

Tulipov blinked. He didn't understand what London had to do with anything— Erast Petrovich had not yet acquainted him with his theory about the Ripper.

Fandorin blushed as he recalled the insulted look he had given Prince Dolgorukoi earlier when the Governor had said that his Deputy for Special Assignments was rarely mistaken.

It seemed that Erast Petrovich was sometimes mistaken, and seriously so.

The delightful decision has been realised. Only God's providence could have helped me to implement it so soon.

The whole day was filled with a feeling of rapture and invulnerability— following yesterday's ecstasy.

Rain and slush, there was a lot of work in the afternoon, but I don't feel tired at all. My soul is singing, longing for open space, to wander through the streets and waste plots of the neighbourhood.

Evening again. I am walking along Protopo-povsky Lane towards Kalanchevka Street. There's a woman standing there, a peasant woman, haggling with a cabby.

She doesn't strike a deal, the cabby drives off and she's standing there, shuffling her feet in confusion. I look and see she has a huge, swollen belly. Pregnant, seven months at least. I feel my heart start to race: there it is, it has found me.

I walk closer—everything is right. Exactly the sort I need. Fat, with a dirty face. Her eyebrows and eyelashes have fallen out—she must have syphilis. It is hard to imagine a creature further removed from the concept of Beauty.

I start talking to her. She's come from the village to visit her husband. He's an apprentice in the Arsenal. I say the Arsenal is not far and promise to show her the way. She is not afraid, because today I am a woman. I lead her through the waste lots towards the Immerovsky horticultural establishment. It is dark and deserted there. While we are walking, the woman complains to me about how hard it is to live in the country. I sympathise with her.

I lead her to the river bank and tell her not to be afraid, there is great joy in store for her. She looks at me stupidly. She dies silently. There is only the whistle of the air from her throat and the gurgling of her blood.

I am impatient to lay bare the pearl within and I do not wait until the spasms have ceased.

Alas, a disappointment awaits me. When I open the incised womb with hands trembling in sweet anticipation, I am overcome by disgust. The living embryo is ugly and nothing at all like a pearl. It looks exactly like the little monsters in jars of alcohol in Professor Lints's faculty: a little vampire just like them. It squirms and opens its mousy little mouth. I toss it away in disgust.

The conclusion: man, like a flower, must mature in order to become beautiful. It is clear now why I have never thought children beautiful: they are dwarfs with disproportionately large heads and underdeveloped reproductive systems.

The Moscow detectives have begun to stir—yesterday's decoration has finally made the police aware of my presence here. It's funny; I am more cunning and stronger; they will never unmask me. "What an actor is going to waste," said Nero. That applies to me.

But I throw the body of the woman and her mouse into the pond. There is no point in stirring things up unnecessarily, and the decoration was not satisfactory.

CHAPTER 3

The "smopackadj"

Holy Week Wednesday, 5 April, morning

From first thing in the morning Erast Petrovich locked himself away in his study to think, and Tulipov set out once again for the Bozhedomka—to have the October and September ditches opened up. He had suggested it himself: they had to determine when the Moscow killer had started his activities. The Chief had not objected. "Why not?" he had said; "You go," but he was somewhere miles away, lost in thought—deducing.

It turned out to be dreary work, far worse than the previous day. The corpses that had been buried before the cold weather were severely decomposed and it was more than anyone could bear to look at them, let alone breathe the poisoned air. Anisii did puke a couple of times after all; he couldn't help himself

"You see," he said, with a sickly smile at the watchman, "I still can't grow those calluses . . ."

"There are some as can't never grow them," the watchman replied, shaking his head sympathetically. "It's hardest of all for them to live in this world. But God loves them too. There you are now, mister, take a drop of this liquor of mine . . ."

Anisii sat down on a bench, drank the herbal infusion and chatted for a while with the cemetery philosopher about this and that; listened to his stories; told him about his own life—that mellowed his heart a little—and then it was back to digging the ditch.

Only it was all in vain. They didn't find anything new that was of use to the investigation in the old ditches.

Zakharov said acidly: "A bad head gives the legs no rest, but it would be all right if it were only yours that suffered, Tulipov. Are you not afraid the gendarmes will accidentally tap you on the top of your head with a pick? And I'll write in my report, all in due order: the Provincial Secretary brought about his own death: he stumbled and smashed his bad head against a stone. And Grumov will witness it. We're sick and tired of you and your rotten flesh. Isn't that right, Grumov?"

The consumptive assistant bared his yellow teeth and wiped his bumpy forehead with his soiled shirt. He explained: "Mr. Zakharov is joking." But that was all right: the doctor was a cynical, coarse man. What offended Anisii was having to suffer mockery from the repulsive Izhitsin.

The pompous investigator had rolled up at the cemetery at first light—somehow he'd got wind of Tulipov's operation. At first he'd been alarmed that the investigation was proceeding without him, but then he'd calmed down and turned cocky.

"Perhaps," he said, "you and Fandorin have some other brilliant ideas? Maybe you'd like to dig in the pits while I lead the investigation?"

And the rotten swine left, laughing triumphantly.

In sum, Tulipov returned to Malaya Nikitskaya Street empty-handed. He walked listlessly up on to the porch and rang the electric bell.

Masa opened the door, in a white gymnastic costume with a black belt and a band bearing the word for "diligence" round his forehead. "Hello, Tiuri-san. Le's do renshu."

What—renshu, when he was so tired and upset he could barely even stand?

"I have an urgent report to give the Chief," Anisii said, trying to be cunning, but Masa was not to be fooled.

He jabbed his finger at Tulipov's protruding ears and declared peremptorily: "When you have urgen' repor you have goggrin' eye and red ear, annow eye small and ear aw white. Take off coat, take off shoes, put on trousers and jacket. We goin' run and shout."

Sometimes Angelina would intercede for Anisii—she was the only one who could resist the pressure from the damned Japanese—but the clear-eyed lady of the house was nowhere to be seen, and the oriental tyrant forced poor Tulipov to change into his gymnastics suit right there in the hallway.

They went out into the yard. Jumping from foot to foot on the chilly ground, Anisii waved his hands around, yelled "O-osu" to strengthen his prana and then the humiliation began. Masa jumped up on his shoulders from behind and ordered him to run in circles round the yard. The Japanese was not very tall, but he was stocky and solidly built, and he weighed four and a half *poods* at the very least. Somehow Tulipov managed to run two circles and then began to stumble.

But his tormentor spoke into his ear: "*Gaman! Gaman!*" That was his favourite word. It meant "Patience."

Anisii had enough *gaman* for another half-circle, and then he collapsed. But not without an element of calculation: he collapsed right in front of a large dirty puddle so that this accursed eastern idol would go flying over his head and take a little swim. Masa went flying over the falling man's head all right, but he didn't come down with a splash in the puddle; he just put his hands down into it, then pushed off with his fingers, performed an impossible somersault in the air and landed on his feet on the far side of the watery obstacle.

He shook his round head in despair and said: "Awri, go wash."

Anisii was gone in a flash.

When his assistant reported in the study (after washing off the mud, changing his clothes and brushing his hair), Fandorin listened attentively. The walls were hung with Japanese prints, weapons and gymnastic equipment. Although it was already past midday, the Collegiate Counsellor was still in his dressing gown. He was not disappointed in the least by the lack of any result; in fact he even seemed rather glad. In any case, he did not express any particular surprise.

When his assistant stopped speaking, Erast Petrovich walked across the room, toying with his beloved jade beads and pronounced the phrase that always made Anisii's heart skip a beat: "All right, l-let us think about this."

The Chief clicked a small sphere of green stone and swayed the flaps of his dressing gown.

"Don't think that your little trip to the cemetery has been wasted," he began.

On the one hand it was pleasant to hear this; on the other hand the phrase "little trip" hardly seemed an entirely accurate description of the torture Anisii had suffered that morning.

"To be quite sure, we had to check if there were incidents involving the disembowelling of victims prior to November. When you told me yesterday that two mutilated corpses had been found in the common grave for December and in the November grave, at first I began to doubt my theory about the Ripper moving to Moscow."

Tulipov nodded, since the previous day he had been given a detailed account of the bloody history of the British ogre.

"But today, having reviewed my London notes, I came to the conclusion that this hypothesis should not be abandoned. Would you like to know why?"

Anisii nodded again, knowing perfectly well that just at the moment his job was to keep quiet and not interrupt.

"Then by all means." The Chief picked a notebook up off the table. "The final murder attributed to the notorious Jack took place on the twentieth of December on Poplar High Street. By that time our Moscow Ripper had already delivered plenty of his nightmarish work to the Bozhedomka, which would seem to exclude the possibility that the English and Russian killers might be subsumed in the same person. However, the prostitute Rose Millet, who was killed on Poplar High Street, did not have her throat cut, and there were none of our Jack's usual signs of savagery. The police decided that the murderer had been frightened off by passers-by who were out late. But in the light of yesterday's discovery, I am willing to surmise that the Ripper had absolutely nothing to do with this death. Possibly this Rose Millet was killed by someone else, and the general hysteria that had gripped London following the previous killing led people to ascribe a new murder of a prostitute to the same maniac. Now for the previous murder, committed on the ninth of November."

Fandorin turned over a page.

"This is Jack's work without a doubt. The prostitute Mary Jane Kelly was discovered in her own room on Dorset Street, where she normally received her clients. Her throat had been slit, her breasts had been cut off, the soft tissue on her thighs had been stripped away, her internal organs had been laid out neatly on the bed and her stomach had been cut open—it is conjectured that the killer consumed its contents."

Anisii's stomach began churning again, as it had that morning at the cemetery.

"On her temple she had the bloody imprint of lips that is familiar to us from Andreichkina's corpse."

Erast Petrovich broke off his reasoning at this point, because Angelina had come into the study: in a plain grey dress and black shawl, with locks of blonde hair dangling over her forehead—the fresh wind must have tugged them free. The Chief's lady-friend dressed in various styles, sometimes like a lady, but best of all she liked simple, Russian clothes like the ones she was wearing today.

"Are you working? Am I in the way?" she asked with a tired smile.

Tulipov leapt to his feet and hurried to reply before his chief: "Of course not, Angelina Samsonovna. We're glad to see you."

"Yes, yes," said Fandorin with a nod. "Have you come from the hospital?"

The beautiful woman lifted the shawl off her shoulders and pinned her rebellious hair in place. "It was interesting today. Dr. Bloom taught us how to lance boils. It turns out not to be hard at all."

Anisii knew that Angelina, the kind soul, went to the Shtrobinderovsky Clinic on Mamonov Lane to help relieve the pain of the suffering. At first she had taken them presents and read the Bible to them, but then she had begun to feel that was not enough. She wanted to be of genuine benefit, to learn to be a nurse. Erast Petrovich had tried to dissuade her, but Angelina had insisted on having her own way.

A saintly woman, the kind that was the very foundation of Russia itself: prayer, help for one's neighbour, a loving heart. She might seem to be living in sin, but no impurity could stick to her. And it wasn't her fault that she found herself in the position of an unmarried wife, Anisii thought yet again, feeling angry with his chief.

Fandorin frowned. "You've been lancing boils?"

"Yes," she said with a joyful smile. "For two poor old beggar women. It's Wednesday; they can come without having to pay. Don't worry, Erast Petrovich,

I managed it very well, and the doctor praised me. I can already do a lot of things. And afterwards I read the Book of Job to the old women, for spiritual reinforcement."

"You'd have done better to give them money," Erast Petrovich said in annoyance. "They're not interested in your book or your concern."

Angelina replied: "I did give them money, fifty kopecks each. And I have more need for this care and concern than they do. I'm far too happy living with you, Erast Petrovich. It makes me feel guilty. Happiness is good, but it's a sin to forget about those who are unhappy in your happiness. Help them, look at their sores and remember that your happiness is a gift from God, and not many people in this world are granted it. Why do you think there are so many beggars and cripples around all the palaces and mansions?"

"That's obvious enough: they give more there."

"No, poor people give more than the rich. It's the Lord showing the fortunate people the unfortunate, saying: Remember how much suffering there is in the world and don't try to ignore it."

Erast Petrovich sighed and made no attempt to reply to his mistress. He obviously couldn't think of anything to say. He turned towards Anisii and rattled his beads. "Let's c-carry on. So, I am proceeding on the assumption that Jack the Ripper's last crime in England was the murder of Mary Jane Kelly, committed on the ninth of November, and that he was not involved in the case of the twentieth of December. In the Russian style, the ninth of November is still the end of October, and so Jack the Ripper had enough time to get to Moscow and add a victim of his perverted imagination to the November ditch at Bozhedomka. Agreed?"

Anisii nodded.

"Is it very likely that two maniacs would appear in Europe who act in an absolutely identical fashion, following scenarios that coincide in every detail?"

Anisii shook his head.

"Then the final question, before we get down to business: is the likelihood I have already mentioned so slight that we can concentrate entirely on the basic hypothesis?"

Two nods, so energetic that Tulipov's celebrated ears swayed. Anisii held his breath, knowing that now a miracle would take place before his very eyes: an elegant thesis would emerge, conjured up out of nothing, out of the empty mist, complete with search methods, plan of investigative measures and perhaps even specific suspects.

"Let us sum up. For some reason so far unknown to us, Jack the Ripper has come to Moscow and set about eliminating the local prostitutes and vagrants in a most determined fashion. That is one." The Chief clicked his beads to add conviction to his assertion. "He arrived here in November last year. That is two (click!). He has spent the recent months in the city, or if he has gone away, then not for long. That is three (click!). He is a doctor or he has studied medicine, since he possesses a surgical instrument, knows how to use it and is skilled in anatomical dissection. That is f-four."

A final click, and the Chief put the beads away in the pocket of his dressing gown, which indicated that the investigation had moved on from the theoretical stage to the practical.

"As you can see, Tulipov, the task does not appear so very complicated."

Anisii could not yet see that, and so he refrained from nodding.

"Oh, come now," Erast Petrovich said in surprise. "All that's required is to check everyone who arrived in Russia from England and settled in Moscow during the period that interests us. Not even everybody, in fact—only those who are connected or have at some time been connected with medicine. And th-that's all. You'll be surprised when you see how narrow the range of the search is."

Why indeed, how simple! Moscow was not St. Petersburg; how many medical men could have arrived in the old capital from England in November?"

"So let's start checking the new arrivals registered at all the police stations!" said Anisii, leaping to his feet, ready to get straight down to work. "Only twenty-four inquiries to make! That's where we'll find our friend: in the registers!"

Angelina had missed the beginning of Erast Petrovich's speech, but she had listened to the rest very carefully and she asked a very reasonable question: "What if this murderer of yours didn't register with the police?"

"It's not very likely," the Chief replied. "He's a very thorough individual who has lived in one place for a long time and travels freely across Europe. Why would he take the unnecessary risk of infringing the provisions of the law? After all, he is not a political terrorist, or a fugitive convict, but a maniac. All of a maniac's aggression goes into his 'idea'; he has no strength left over for any other activities. Usually they are quiet, unobtrusive people and you would never think that they c-carry all the torments of hell around inside their heads . . . Please sit down, Tulipov. There's no need to go running off anywhere. What do you think I have been doing all morning, while you were disturbing the dead?" He picked up several sheets of paper, covered in formal clerk's handwriting, off the desk. "I telephoned the district superintendents and asked them to obtain for me the registration details of everyone who arrived in Moscow directly from England or via any intermediary point. To be on the safe side, I asked for November as well as December—just a precaution: what if Rose Millet was killed by our Ripper after all, and your November discovery, on the contrary, turns out to be the work of some indigenous cut-throat? It is hard to reach any firm conclusions on the pathology of a body that has been lying in the ground for five months, even if the ground was frozen. But those two bodies from December—that's a serious matter."

"That makes sense," Anisii agreed. "The November corpse really wasn't exactly . . . Zakharov didn't even want to rummage inside it; he said it was profanation. In November the earth hadn't really frozen yet, so the body had rotted a bit. Oh, I beg your pardon, Angelina Samsonovna!" Tulipov exclaimed, alarmed in case his excessive naturalism had upset her. But apparently his alarm was needless: Angelina had no intention of fainting, and the expression in her grey eyes remained as serious and intent as ever.

"There, you see. But even over two months only thirty-nine people arrived here from En-gland, including, by the way, myself and Angelina Samsonovna. But, with your permission, I won't include the t-two of us in our list." Erast Petrovich smiled. "Of the remainder, twenty-three did not stay in Moscow for long and therefore are of no interest to us. That leaves fourteen, of whom only three have any connection with medicine."

"Aha!" Anisii exclaimed avidly.

"Naturally, the first to attract my attention was the doctor of medicine

George Seville Lindsey. The Department of Gendarmes keeps him under secret surveillance, as it does all foreigners, so making inquiries could not have been any easier. Alas, Mr. Lindsey does not fit the bill. It turned out that before coming to Moscow he spent only one and a half months in his homeland. Before that he was working in India, far from the East End of London. He was offered a position in the Catherine the Great Hospital, and that is why he came here. That leaves two, both Russian. A man and a woman."

"A woman couldn't have done anything like this," Angelina said firmly. "There are all sorts of monsters amongst us women too, but hacking stomachs open with a knife—that takes strength. And we women don't like the sight of blood."

"We are dealing here with a special kind of being, unlike ordinary people," Fandorin objected. "This is not a man and it is not a woman, but something like a third sex or, to put it simply, a monster. We can by no means exclude women. Some of them are physically strong too. Not to mention that at a certain level of skill in the use of a scalpel, no special strength is required. For instance"—he glanced at one of his sheets of paper—"the midwife Elizaveta Nesvitskaya, a spinster twenty-eight years of age, arrived from England via St. Petersburg on the nineteenth of November. An unusual individual. At the age of seventeen she spent two years in prison on political charges and was then exiled by administrative order to a colony in the Arkhangelsk province. She fled the country and graduated from the medical faculty of Edinburgh University. Applied to be allowed to return to her motherland. She returned. Her request for her medical diploma to be accepted as valid is under consideration by the Ministry of Internal Affairs, and in the meantime Nesvitskaya has set herself up as a midwife at the recently opened Morozov Gynaecological Hospital. She is under secret surveillance by the police. According to detectives' reports, although her right to work as a doctor has not yet been confirmed, Nesvit-skaya is receiving patients from among the poor and impecunious. The hospital administration turns a blind eye and secretly even encourages her—no one wishes to waste their time on dealing with the poor. That is the information that we p-possess on Nesvitskaya."

"During the time the Ripper committed his crimes, she was in London—that is one," Tulipov began summarising. "When the crimes were committed in Moscow, she was here—that is two. She possesses medical skills—that is three. From what we know, her personality seems to be unusual and not particularly feminine in its make-up—that is four. Nesvitskaya can certainly not be discounted."

"Precisely. And in addition to that, let us not forget that in the London murders and in the murder of the spinster Andreichkina there are no indications of the sexual molestation which is usual when the maniac is a man."

"And who's the other one?" asked Angelina.

"Ivan Stenich. Thirty years old. A former student of the medical faculty of the Moscow Imperial University. Excluded seven years ago 'for immoral conduct.' God only knows what was meant by that, but it looks as though it might fit our bill all right. He has held several jobs, been treated for psychological illness, travelled around Europe. Arrived in Russia from England on the eleventh of December. Since the New Year he has been working as a male nurse in the Assuage My Sorrows hospital for the insane."

Tulipov slapped his hand on the table: "Damned suspicious!"

"And so, we have t-two suspects. If neither of them is involved, then we shall follow the line suggested by Angelina Samsonovna—that when Jack the Ripper arrived in Moscow he managed to avoid the eyes of the police. And only if we are convinced that this too must be excluded will we then abandon the main hypothesis and start to search for a home-grown Ivan the Ripper who has never been to the East End in his life. Agreed?"

"Yes, but it *is* the same Jack anyway," Anisii declared with conviction. "Everything fits."

"Who do you prefer to deal with, Tulipov—the male nurse or the midwife?" the Chief asked. "I offer you the right to choose as the martyr of the exhumation."

"Since this Stenich works in a mental hospital, I have an excellent excuse for making his acquaintance: Sonya," said Anisii, expressing this apparently perfectly reasonable idea with more vehemence than cold logic required. A man—and one with a history of mental illness at that—appeared a more promising candidate for the Ripper than a runaway revolutionary.

"All right, then," Erast Petrovich said with a smile. "Off you go to Lefortovo, and I'll go to Devichie Polye, to see Nesvitskaya."

In fact, however, Anisii was obliged to deal with both the former student and the midwife, because at that very moment the doorbell rang.

Masa entered and announced: "Post." Then he explained, taking great satisfaction in pronouncing the difficult phrase: "A smopackadj."

The package was indeed small. Written on the grey wrapping paper in a hand that was vigorous but careless and irregular was: "To His Honour Collegiate Counsellor Fandorin in person. Urgent and strictly secret."

Tulipov felt curious, but his chief did not unwrap the package immediately.

"Did the p-postman bring it? There's no address written on it."

"No, a boy. Hand to me and wan away. Should I catchim?" Masa asked in alarm.

"If he ran away, you won't catch him now."

Underneath the wrapping paper there was a small velvet box, tied round with a red satin ribbon. In the box, resting on a napkin, there was a yellow object. For the first moment Anisii thought it was a forest mushroom, a milky cap. He looked closer and gasped.

It was a human ear.

The rumours have spread round Moscow.

Supposedly a werewolf has appeared in the city. If any woman puts her nose outside the door at night, the werewolf is there in a flash. He creeps along so quietly, with his red eye glinting behind the fence, and if you don't say your prayers in time, your Christian soul is done for—he leaps out and the first thing he does is sink his teeth into your throat, and then he tears your belly to shreds and munches and crunches on your insides. And apparently this werewolf has already bitten out countless numbers of women's throats, only the authorities are keeping it a secret from the people, because the Father-Tsar is afraid.

That's what they were saying today at the Sukharev Market.

That is about me, I am the werewolf who is prowling their city. It's funny. My kind don't simply appear in a place, they are sent to bring terrible or joyful news. And I have been sent to you, citizens of Moscow, with joyful news.

Ugly city and ugly people, I will make you beautiful. Not all of you, please forgive me—that would be too much. But many, many.

I love you, with all your hideous abominations and deformities. I only wish you well. I have enough love for all of you. I see Beauty under lice-ridden clothes, under the scabs on an unwashed body, under rashes and eruptions. I am your saviour and your salvatrix. I am your brother and sister, father and mother, husband and wife. I am a woman and I am a man. I am an androgyne, that most beautiful ancestor of humanity, who possessed the characteristics of both sexes. Then the androgynes were divided into two halves, male and female, and people appeared—unhappy, remote from perfection, suffering from loneliness.

I am your missing half. Nothing prevents me from reuniting with those of you whom I choose.

The Lord has given me intelligence, cunning, foresight and invulnerability. Stupid, crude, dull, grey people tried to catch the androgyne in London without even attempting to understand the meaning of the messages he sent to the world.

At first these pitiful attempts amused me. Then a bitter taste rose in my throat.

Perhaps my own land will receive the prophet, I thought. Irrational and mystical Russia, which has still not lost true faith, lured me to itself with its eunuch skoptsy sect, its schismatics, its self-immolations and its ascetics—and it seems to have deceived me. Now the same stupid, crude kind of people, devoid of imagination, are trying to catch the Decorator in Moscow. It amuses me; at night I shudder and shake in silent laughter. No one sees these fits of merriment, and if they did, no doubt they would think there was something wrong with me. Well certainly, if everyone who is not like them is mad; but in that case Christ is also mad, and all the holy saints, and all the insane geniuses of whom they are so proud.

In the daytime I am not different in any way from all the ugly, pitiful people with all their vain concerns. I am a virtuoso of mimicry; they could never guess that I am from a different race.

How can they disdain God's gift—their own bodies? My duty and my calling is to teach them a little about Beauty. I make the ugly beautiful. I do not touch those who are beautiful. They are not an offence against the image of God.

Life is a thrilling, jolly game. Cat and mouse, hide and seek. I hide and I seek. One-two-three-four-five, ready or not, I'm coming.

If you're not hiding, it's not my fault.

CHAPTER 4

Tortoise, Setter, Lioness, Hare

Holy Week Wednesday, 5 April, afternoon

Anisii told Palasha to dress Sonya up in her holiday clothes. His sister, a full-grown adult but mentally retarded, was delighted and began gurgling in joy. For her, the poor imbecile, going on any trip was an event, wherever it was to, and she was particularly fond of visiting the "dot" (in Sonya's language that meant "doctor"). They talked to her patiently for a long time there; they always gave her a sweet or a spice cake; they put a cold metal thing against her chest and pressed her tummy so that it tickled and gazed into her mouth—and Sonya was happy to help by opening it wide enough for them to see everything inside.

They called a cabbie they knew, Nazar Stepanich. As always, at first Sonya was a little bit afraid of the calm horse Mukha, who snorted with her nostrils and jangled her harness, squinting with her bloody eyes at the fat, ungainly woman swaddled in shawls.

They drove from Granatny Lane to the Lefortovo district. Usually they went to a closer place, to Dr. Maxim Khristoforich on Rozhdestvenka Street, to the Mutual Assistance Society; but this time they had to make the journey right across the city.

They had to drive around Trubnaya Street—it was completely flooded. When would the sunshine ever come and dry the ground out? Moscow looked dour and untidy. The houses were grey, the roads were dirty, the people all seemed to be wrapped in rags and hunched up against the wind. But Sonya seemed to like it. Every now and then she nudged her brother in the side with her elbow—"Nisii, Nisii"—and pointed at the rooks in a tree, a water wagon, a drunken apprentice. But she prevented him from thinking. And he had a lot to think about—the severed ear, which the chief was dealing with in person, and his own difficult task.

The Emperor Alexander Society's Assuage My Sorrows Hospital, for the treatment of psychiatric, nervous, and paralytic illnesses, was located on Hospital Square, beyond the River Yauza. He knew that Stenich was working as a male nurse with Dr. Rozenfeld in department five, where they treated the most violent and hopeless cases.

After paying five roubles at the desk, Anisii took his sister to Rozenfeld. He began telling the doctor in detail about what had been happening with Sonya recently: she had begun to wake up crying in the night and twice she had pushed Palasha away, which had never happened before, and she had suddenly got into the habit of toying with a little mirror and staring into it for hours with her little piggy eyes.

It took a long time to tell the doctor everything. A man in a white coat came into the surgery twice. The first time he brought some boiled syringes, then he took the prescription for making up some tincture or other. The doctor spoke to him politely. So he had to be Stenich. Exhausted and pale, with immense eyes, he had grown his straight hair long, but he shaved his beard and moustache, which gave his face an almost medieval look.

Leaving his sister with the doctor to be examined, Anisii went out into the corridor and glanced in through a half-open door with the inscription "Treatment Room." Stenich had his back to him and was mixing up some green stuff in a small bottle. What could Anisii see from the back? Stooped shoulders, a white coat, patches on the back of his boots.

The Chief had taught him that the key to success lay in the first phrase of a conversation. If you could get the conversation going smoothly, then the door would open; you'd find out anything you wanted from the other person. The trick was to make sure you identified their type correctly. There weren't all that many types—according to Erast Petrovich there were exactly sixteen, and there was an approach for each of them.

Oh, if only he didn't get it wrong. He hadn't really mastered this tricky science completely yet. From what they knew about Stenich, and also from visual observation, he was a "tortoise": an unsociable, suspicious type turned in on himself, living in a state of interminable internal monologue.

If that was right, then the correct approach was "to show your belly"—that is, to demonstrate that you are defenceless and not dangerous and then, without even the slightest pause, to make a "breach": to pierce through all the protective layers of alienation and caution, to take the other person by surprise, only without frightening him, God forbid, by being aggressive, or putting him off. You had to interest him, send a signal that seemed to say: You and I are berries from the same field, we speak the same language.

Tulipov mentally crossed himself and had a go. "That was a good look you gave my idiot sister in the surgery just now. I liked it. It showed interest, but without pity. The doctor's just the opposite: he pities her all right, but he's not really all that interested in looking at her. Only the mentally ill don't need pity; they can be happier than we are. That's an interesting subject, all right: a being that looks like us, but is really quite different. And sometimes something might be revealed to an idiot that is a sealed book to us. I expect you think that too, don't you? I could see it in your eyes. You ought to be the doctor, not this Rozenfeld. Are you a student?"

Stenich turned round and blinked. He looked a little taken aback by the breach, but in the right kind of way, without feeling frightened or getting his back up. He answered curtly, in the way a tortoise was supposed to: "I used to be."

The approach had been chosen correctly. Now that the key was in the lock, according to the teachings of the Chief, he should grab it immediately and turn it until it clicked. There was a subtle point here: with a tortoise you had to avoid being too familiar, you mustn't narrow the distance between you, or he'd immediately withdraw into his shell.

"Not a political, are you?" asked Anisii, pretending to be disappointed. "Then I'm a very poor reader of faces: I took you for a man with imagination; I wanted to ask you about my idiot sister . . . These socialists are no good as psychiatrists—they're too carried away with the good of society, but they couldn't give a damn for the individual members of society, especially for imbeciles like my Sonya. Pardon my frankness, I'm a man who likes to speak directly. Goodbye, I'd better go and have a talk with Rozenfeld."

He turned sharply to go away, in the appropriate manner for a "setter" (outspoken, impetuous, with sharply defined likes and dislikes)—the ideal match for a tortoise.

"As you wish," said the male nurse, stung to the quick. "Only I've never concerned myself with the good of society, and I was excluded from the faculty for something quite different."

"Aha!" Tulipov exclaimed, raising one finger triumphantly. "The eye! The eye, it never deceives! I was right about you after all. You live according to your own judgement and follow your own road. It doesn't matter that you're only a medical assistant; I take no notice of titles. Give me a keen, lively man who doesn't judge things by the common standard. I've despaired of taking Sonya round the doctors. All of them just sing the same old tune: oligophrenia, the extreme stage, a hopeless case. But I sense that inside her soul is alive, it can be awakened. Will you not give me a consultation?"

"I'm not a medical assistant either," Stenich replied, apparently touched by this stranger's frankness (and his flattery, of course—a man likes to be flattered). "It's true that Mr. Rozenfeld does use me as a medical assistant, but officially I'm only a male nurse. And I work without pay, as a volunteer. To make amends for my sins."

Ah, so that's it, thought Anisii. That's where the glum look came from, and the resignation. I'll have to adjust my line of approach.

Speaking in the most serious voice he could muster, he said: "You have chosen a good path for the exculpation of your sins. Far better than lighting candles in a church or beating your forehead against the church porch. May God grant you quick relief."

"I don't want it quickly!" Stenich cried with unexpected ardour, and his eyes, which had been dull, were instantly aglow with fire and passion. "Let it be hard, let it be long! That will be the best way, the right way! I . . . I don't talk with people often, I'm very reserved. And I'm used to being alone. But there's something in you that encourages frank talking. I feel like talking . . . Otherwise, I'm on my own all the time; my mind could go again soon."

Anisii was truly amazed by the results of his chief's method! The key had fitted the lock, and fitted it so well that the door had swung open of its own accord. He didn't need to do anything else, just listen and agree with everything.

The pause unsettled the male nurse. "Perhaps you don't have any time?" His voice trembled. "I know you have problems of your own; you can't have time for other people's confessions . . ."

"A man with troubles of his own will understand another person's troubles better," Anisii said jesuitically. "What is eating at your soul? You can tell me. We're strangers; we don't even know each other's name. We'll have a talk and go our separate ways. What sin do you have on your soul?"

For just a moment Anisii dreamed of him dropping to his knees, bursting into sobs and saying: "Forgive me, you good man, I am cursed, I bear the weight of bloody sin, I disembowel women with a scalpel." And that would be it, case closed, and Tulipov would be rewarded by his superiors and, best of all, there'd be a word of praise from the Chief.

But no, Stenich didn't drop to his knees and he said something quite different: "Pride. All my life I've been tormented by it. I took this job, this heavy, dirty work, in order to conquer it. I clean up the foul mess from the mad patients; no job is too disgusting for me. Humiliation and resignation—that's the best medicine for pride."

"So you were excluded from the university for pride?" Anisii said, unable to conceal his disappointment.

"What? Ah, from the university. No, that was something different . . . I'll tell you—why not?—in order to humble my pride." The male nurse blushed violently, turning bright red all the way up to the parting in his hair. "I used to have another sin, a serious one: voluptuousness. I've overcome it now. Life has helped me. But in my young years I was depraved—not so much out of sensuality as out of curiosity. It's even viler, out of curiosity, don't you think?"

Anisii didn't know how to answer that, but it would be interesting to hear about the sin. What if there was a thread leading from this voluptuousness to the murder?

"I don't see any sin at all in sensuality," he said aloud. "Sin is when you hurt your neighbour. But who's hurt by a bit of sensuality, provided of course there's no violence involved?"

Stenich just shook his head. "Ah, you're still young, sir. Have you not heard of the Sadist Circle? How could you?—you probably hadn't even finished grammar school then. It was exactly seven years ago this April . . . But in Moscow not many people know about the case. The rumours spread in medical circles, all right, but not much leaks out of them; it's a matter of *esprit de corps*, sticking together, a common front. Mind you, they threw me out . . ."

"What was that, the saddler's circle?" asked Anisii, pretending to be stupid but remembering that Stenich had been excluded for "immoral behaviour."

Senich laughed grimly. "Not exactly. There were about fifteen of us, wild students in the medical faculty, and two girl students. It was a dark, oppressive time. A year earlier the nihilists had blown up the Tsar-Liberator. We were nihilists too, but without any politics. In those days, for politics we'd have been sentenced to hard labour or worse. But all they did was pack our leader Sotsky off to a penal battalion. With no trial, no fuss, by ministerial decree. Some of the others were transferred to non-medical faculties—pharmacists, chemists, anatomists—they weren't considered worthy of the exalted title of doctor. And some, like me, were simply flung out, if we couldn't find anyone highly placed to intercede for us."

"That's a bit harsh, isn't it?" Tulipov asked with a sympathetic sigh. "What on earth did you get up to?"

"Nowadays I tend to think it wasn't harsh at all. It was exactly right . . . You know, very young men who have chosen the path of medicine sometimes fall into a sort of cynicism. They become firmly convinced that man is not the image of God, but a machine made of joints, bones, nerves and various other bits of stuffing. On the early years of the course it's regarded as daring to take breakfast in the morgue and stand your bottle of beer on the stomach of a 'piece of carrion' that's only just been sewn up. And there are jokes more vulgar than that—I won't tell you about them; they're disgusting. But these are all quite standard pranks: we went further. There were a few among us who had a lot of money, so we had the chance to cut loose. Simple debauchery wasn't enough for us any more. Our leader, the late departed Sotsky, had a fantastic imagination. He didn't come back from the penal battalion; he died there, or he would have carried on even further. We were especially fond of sadistic amusements. We'd find the ugliest streetwalker we could, pay her twenty-five roubles and then mock and torment her. We took it too far . . . Once, in a fifty-kopeck bordello, when we'd had too much to drink, we took an old whore who would do anything for three roubles and worked her so hard she died . . . The incident was hushed up and it never reached the courts. And everything was decided quietly, with no scandal. I was angry at first, because they'd shattered my life—I was studying on a pittance, giving lessons and sending my mother as much as I could . . . But afterwards, years later, I suddenly realised I deserved it."

Anisii screwed up his eyes.

"How do you mean—'suddenly'?"

"It just happened," Stenich replied curtly and sternly. "I saw God."

There's something here, thought Tulipov. Probe here and I'll probably find the "idea" the boss was talking about. How can I turn the conversation to England?

"I expect life has tossed you about quite a lot? Have you not tried seeking happiness abroad?"

"Happiness? No, I haven't looked for that. But I've searched for obscenities in various countries. And found more than enough, may the Lord forgive me." Stenich crossed himself, facing the icon of the Saviour hanging in the corner.

Then Anisii asked in a simple-minded kind of voice: "And have you ever been to England? That's my dream, but I'm obviously never going to get there. Everyone says it's an exceptionally civilised country."

"Strange that you should ask about England," said the repentant sinner, looking at Anisii intently. "You're a strange gentleman altogether. Whatever you ask, it always hits the bull's eye. It was in England that I saw God. Until that moment I was living an unworthy, degrading kind of life. I was sponging off a certain crazy madcap. And then I decided to change everything all at once."

"You said yourself that humiliation is good for conquering pride. So why did you decide to leave a humiliating life? That's not logical."

Anisii had wanted to find out a bit more about Stenich's life in England, but he had committed a crude error: his question had put the tortoise on the defensive, and that was something he ought not to have done under any circumstances.

Stenich instantly withdrew into his shell: "And who are you, to go interpreting the logic of my soul? What am I doing whinging to you like this anyway?"

The male nurse's gaze was suddenly inflamed with hate, his slim fingers began fumbling convulsively at the table. And on the table there happened to be a metal pan with various medical instruments. Anisii remembered that Stenich had been treated for mental illness, and he backed out into the corridor. Stenich wouldn't tell him anything else useful now.

But even so, certain things had been clarified.

Now he had a really long road to travel, from Lefortovo to the opposite extreme of Moscow, Devichie Polye, to the Timofei Morozov Gy-naecological Clinic, financed by the resources of the rich Counsellor of Commerce, at the Moscow Imperial University. With all her disabilities Sonya was still a woman, and some female problems or other were sure to be found. And so the imbecile was to be useful to the inquiry yet again.

Sonya was in an agitated state—the "dot" at Lefortovo had made a strong impression on her.

"Mer tap-tap, knee hop-hop, nofraid, sweety no," she said boisterously, telling her brother about her adventures.

To anybody else, it was a meaningless jumble of sounds, but Anisii understood everything: the doctor had hit her knee with a little hammer, and her knee had jerked, only Sonya hadn't been afraid at all, but the doctor hadn't given her a sweet.

So that she wouldn't prevent him from concentrating, he stopped the cab at the Orphan's Institute and bought a large, poisonous-red sugar cockerel on a stick. Sonya stopped talking. She stuck her tongue out a good two inches and licked, staring around with her pale little eyes. So much had happened today, and she didn't know that there were still a lot of interesting things to come. She'd need a lot of attention in the evening; she'd be too excited to get to sleep for a long time.

They finally arrived. The generous Counsellor of Commerce had built a fine clinic, there was no denying that. The Morozov family had done a lot of good for the city in general. Recently the newspapers had written that Honorary Citizen Madam Morozova had organised working trips abroad for young engineers, in order to improve their practical knowledge. Now anyone who completed the full course at the Moscow Imperial Technical College could take a trip to England if he wanted, or even the United States—provided, of course, that he was Orthodox by faith and Russian by blood. It was a great thing. And here in the gynaecological clinic, consultation and treatment were free for the poor on Mondays and Tuesdays. Wasn't that remarkable?

Today, though, it was Wednesday.

Anisii read the announcement in the reception room: "Consultation with the professor—ten roubles. Appointment with the doctor—five roubles. Appointment with the female doctor Roganova—three roubles."

"A bit on the expensive side," Tulipov complained to the attendant. "My sister's retarded. Won't they take a retarded patient cheaper?"

At first the attendant replied sternly: "It's not allowed. Come back on Monday or Tuesday."

But then he looked at Sonya, standing there with her mouth open, and his heart softened.

"You could go to the obstetrical department, to Lizaveta Nesvitskaya. She's as good as a doctor, even though she's only called a midwife. She charges less, or nothing at all, if she takes pity on someone."

This was excellent. Nesvitskaya was at work.

They walked out of the waiting room and turned into a small garden. As they were approaching the yellow, two-storey building of the obstetrical department, something dramatic happened. A window on the first floor slammed open and there was a loud tinkling of glass. Anisii saw a young woman climb up into the window, wearing just her nightdress, with her long black hair tangled across her shoulders.

"Go away, you torturers," the woman howled. "I hate you. You're trying to kill me!"

She looked down—the storeys in the building were tall and it was a long way to the ground—then she pressed her back against the stone wall and began edging along the parapet in small steps, away from the window. Sonya froze, watching with her mouth hanging open slackly. She'd never seen a wonder like this before.

Immediately several heads appeared at the window and began trying to persuade the black-haired woman not to play the fool and come back.

But it was clear that the woman was distressed. She was swaying, and the parapet was narrow. She was about to fall or jump. The snow below had melted, the earth was bare and covered with stones with some kind of iron rods sticking up out of it. It would be certain death or severe injury.

Tulipov looked to the left and the right. People were gaping, but the expression on all their faces was confusion. What should he do?

"Bring a tarpaulin, or at least a blanket!" he shouted to an orderly, who had come out for a smoke and frozen at the sight, with his small cigar clutched in his teeth. He started and went darting off, but he was unlikely to be in time.

A tall woman pushed her way through the people clustered at the window and climbed determinedly out on to the window sill—a white coat, steel pince-nez, hair pulled into a tight knot at the back of her head.

"Ermolaeva, don't be so stupid!" she shouted in a commanding voice. "Your son's crying; he wants his milk!" And then she set off boldly along the parapet.

"It's not my son!" the dark-haired woman squealed. "It's a foundling! Don't come near me, I'm afraid of you!"

The woman in the white coat took another step and reached out her hand, but Ermolaeva turned away and jumped with a howl.

The spectators gasped—at the very last instant the doctor had managed to grab the crazed woman just below the collar. The night-shirt tore, but it held. The dangling woman's legs were shamefully exposed, and Anisii began blinking rapidly, but immediately felt ashamed of himself—there was no time for that sort of thing now. The doctor grabbed hold of a drainpipe with one hand and held Ermolaeva with the other. Now she'd have to let the other woman go, or come tumbling down with her.

Anisii tore his greatcoat off his shoulders and waved to two men standing nearby. They stretched the coat out as far as it would go, and stood under the dangling woman.

"I can't hold on any longer! My fingers are slipping!" the iron doctor shouted, and at that very moment the black-haired woman fell.

The blow knocked them all down into a heap. Tulipov jumped up and shook his jarred wrists. The woman lay there with her eyes closed, but seemingly alive, and there was no sign of any blood. One of Anisii's helpers, who looked like a shop assistant, sat on the ground and whimpered, clutching his shoulder. Anisii's greatcoat was a sorry sight—it had lost both sleeves and the collar had split—a new greatcoat, he only had it made last autumn: forty-five roubles.

The woman doctor was already there—she must have moved really fast. She squatted down over the unconscious woman, felt her pulse, rubbed her hands and feet: "Alive and unhurt."

To Anisii she said: "Well done for thinking of using your coat."

"What's wrong with her?"

"Puerperal fever. Temporary insanity. Rare, but it happens. What's wrong with you?" she said, turning to the shop assistant. "Put your shoulder out? Come here." She took hold of him with her strong hands and gave a sudden jerk—the shop assistant gave a loud gasp.

A female medical assistant ran up, caught her breath and asked: "Lizaveta Andreevna, what shall we do with Ermolaeva?"

"Put her in the isolation ward—under three blankets; give her an injection of morphine. Let her sleep for while. And be careful not to take your eyes off her." She turned to go.

"I was actually coming to see you, Miss Nesvitskaya," Anisii said, thinking: The Chief was right not to exclude women from suspicion. A mare like this could easily choke you with her bare hands, never mind slicing you up with a scalpel.

"Who are you? What's your business?" The glance through the pince-nez was stern, not feminine at all.

"Tulipov, Provincial Secretary. Look, I've brought an imbecile for a consultation on women's matters. She seems to suffer a lot with her periods. Will you agree to take a look at her?"

Nesvitskaya looked at Sonya and asked briskly: "An imbecile? Does she have a sex life? Are you cohabiting with her?"

"Of course not!" Anisii exclaimed in horror. "She's my sister. She was born like this."

"Can you pay? From those who can afford it I take two roubles for an examination."

"I'll pay, with the greatest of pleasure," Tulipov hastened to reassure her.

"If paying gives you that much pleasure, then why come to me and not to the doctor or the professor? All right, let's go to my surgery."

She set off with rapid, broad strides. Anisii grabbed hold of Sonya's hand and followed her. He worked out his line of behaviour as he went.

There was no doubt about her type: a classic "lioness." The recommended approach was to act embarrassed and to mumble. That made lionesses soften.

The midwife's surgery was small and neat, with nothing superfluous: a gynaecological chair, a table and a chair. There were two brochures on the table: "Problems of hygiene and women's clothing," written by A. N. Sobolev, docent of obstetrics and women's ailments, and "Proceedings of the Society for the Propagation of Practical Knowledge Among Educated Women."

There was an advertisement hanging on the wall:

Ladies' Hygienic Pads
Manufactured from sublimated timber fibre

A very comfortable fastening, with the use of a belt, to be worn by ladies during difficult periods. The price of a dozen pads is one rouble. The price of the belt is from 40 kop. to 1 r. 50 kop.

Egorov's House, Pokrovka Street

Anisii sighed and began to mumble: "You see, the reason I decided to come to you, Miss Nesvitskaya, is . . . well, you see, I've heard that actually you have the highest possible qualifications, although you hold a position that doesn't correspond at all to the learning possessed by such a worthy individual . . . Of course, not that I have anything at all against the title of midwife . . . I didn't mean to belittle or, God forbid, express any doubts, on the contrary in fact . . ."

He thought he'd done really well, and even managed to blush a little, but Nesvitskaya's response astonished him: she took Anisii firmly by the shoulders and turned his face to the light.

"Well now, well now, I know that look around the eyes. Would you be a police spy, then? You've started working with a bit of imagination now, even picked up an imbecile from somewhere. What else do you want from me? Why can't you just leave me in peace? If you're thinking of making something of my illegal practice, then the director knows all about it." She pushed him away in disgust.

Tulipov rubbed his shoulders—she had a fierce grip. Sonya pressed herself against her brother in fright and began to whine; Anisii stroked her hair.

"Don't you be frightened. The lady's only joking, playing games. She's kind, she's a doctor . . . Elizaveta Andreevna, you're mistaken about me. I work in the chancellery of His Excellency the Governor-General. In a very modest position, of course, the lowest of the low, so to speak. Tulipov, Provincial Secretary. I have my identification with me, if you'd like me to show you it. Or is there no need?" He spread his arms timidly and smiled shyly.

Excellent! Nesvitskaya felt ashamed, and that was the very way to get a lioness to talk.

"I'm sorry, I see them everywhere . . . You must understand . . ." She picked up a *papyrosa* from the table with a trembling hand and lit it, but not straight away, only with the third match. So much for the iron doctor.

"I'm sorry I suspected you. My nerves are all shot. And then this Ermolaeva . . . Ah, yes, you saved Ermolaeva, I forgot . . . I must explain myself. I don't know why, but I'd like you to understand . . ."

"The reason you want to explain yourself to me, madame," Anisii answered in his thoughts, "is because you're a lioness, and I'm acting like a hare. Lionesses get on best of all with timid, defenceless little hares. Psychology, Lizaveta Andreevna."

But together with his satisfaction, Tulipov also experienced a certain moral discomfort—he was no police spy, but he was still doing detective work and using his invalid sister as a cover. The doctor had been right.

She smoked the *papyrosa* quickly, in a few puffs, and lit another one.

Anisii waited, fluttering his eyelids pitifully.

"Smoke?" Nesvitskaya pushed the box of *papyrosas* towards him.

Tulipov generally didn't smoke, but lionesses like it when they can order people about, so he took one, inhaled the smoke and started to cough violently.

"Yes, they're a bit strong," the doctor said with a nod. "It's a habit. The tobacco's strong in the North, and in the summer there you can't get by without tobacco—all those mosquitoes and midges."

"So you're from the North?" Anisii asked naively, clumsily shaking the ash off his *papyrosa*.

"No, I was born and brought up in St. Petersburg. Until the age of seventeen I was my mother's little darling. But when I was seventeen, men in blue uniforms came for me in droshkies. They took me away from my mother and put me in a prison cell."

Nesvitskaya spoke in short, abrupt phrases. Her hands weren't trembling any more; her voice had become harsh and her eyes had narrowed in anger—but it wasn't Tulipov she was angry with, that was clear.

Sonya sat down on a chair, slumped against the wall and began sniffing loudly—she was exhausted from all these new impressions.

"What did they arrest you for?" the hare asked in a whisper.

"For knowing a student who had once been in a house where revolutionaries sometimes used to meet," Nesvitskaya said with a bitter laugh. "There had just been another attempt on the life of the Tsar, and so they hauled in absolutely everybody. While they were getting to the bottom of things, I spent two years in solitary confinement. At the age of seventeen. I don't know how I managed not to go insane. Perhaps I did . . . Then they let me out. But to make sure I didn't strike up any inappropriate acquaintances, they sent me into administrative exile—to the village of Zamorenka in the Arkhangelsk province. Under official surveillance. So I have special feelings about blue uniforms."

"And where did you study medicine?" Anisii asked, with a sympathetic shake of his head.

"At first in Zamorenka, in the local hospital. I had to have something to live on, so I took a job as a nurse. And I realised that medicine was the thing for me. It's probably the only thing that makes any sense at all . . . Later I ended up in Scotland and studied in the medical faculty, the first woman in the surgical department—they don't let women get ahead too easily there, either. I made a good surgeon. I have a strong hand; from the very beginning I was never afraid of the sight of blood, and I'm not disgusted by the sight of people's internal organs. They're even quite beautiful in their own sort of way."

Anisii was on the edge of his seat. "And you can operate?"

She smiled condescendingly: "I can perform an amputation, and an abdominal operation, and remove a tumour. And instead of that, for all these months . . ." She gestured angrily.

What "instead of that"? Disembowelling streetwalkers in woodsheds?

Possible motives?

Tulipov slyly examined Nesvitskaya's unattractive, even rather coarse face. A morbid hatred of the female body? Very possible. Reasons? Her own physical unattractiveness and uncertain personal situation, being forced to carry out a midwife's duties, work that she did not like, the daily contemplation of patients whose lives as women had worked out happily. It could be almost anything, even including concealed latent insanity as a result of the injustice she had suffered and solitary confinement at a tender age.

"All right, let's take a look at your sister. I've been talking too long. It's not even like me."

Nesvitskaya removed her pince-nez and wearily rubbed the bridge of her nose with her strong fingers, then for some reason massaged the lobe of her ear; and Anisii's thoughts naturally turned to the sinister ear in the box.

How was the Chief getting on? Had he managed to figure out who had sent the "smopackadj"?

Again it is evening, the blessed darkness concealing me beneath its dusky wing. I am walking along a railway embankment. A strange excitement constricts my chest.

It is surprising how it throws one off balance to see acquaintances from a former life. They have changed, some are even unrecognisable, and as for me, it need hardly be said.

I am troubled by memories. Stupid, unnecessary memories. Everything is different now.

Standing at the crossing, outside the barrier, there is a young girl begging. Twelve or thirteen years old. She is shuddering from the cold, her hands are covered in red goose bumps, her feet are wrapped in some kind of rags. Her face is horrible, simply horrible: suppurating eyes, cracked lips, a runny nose. A miserable, ugly child of humanity.

How can I not pity such a creature? This ugly face can also be made beautiful. And there is really nothing I have to do. It is enough simply to reveal the true Beauty of its gaze.

I follow the girl. The memories are no longer troubling me.

CHAPTER 5

Fellow Students

Holy Week Wednesday, 5 April,
afternoon and evening

After despatching his assistant on his errand, Erast Petrovich prepared himself for some intense thinking. The task appeared to be far from simple. Irrational enlightenment would be very welcome here, and so the right place to begin was with meditation.

The Collegiate Counsellor closed the door of his study, sat down on the carpet with his legs crossed and tried to rid himself of all thoughts of any kind—still his vision, shut off his hearing; sway on the waves of the Great Void from which, as on so many previous occasions, there would come the sound, at first barely audible, and then ever more distinct, and finally almost deafening, of the truth.

Time passed. Then it stopped passing. A cool calm began rising unhurriedly within him, from his belly upwards; the golden mist in front of his eyes grew thicker, but then the huge clock standing in the corner of the room churred and chimed deafeningly: bom-bom-bom-bom-bom!

Fandorin came to himself. Five o'clock already? He checked the time on his Breguet, because the grandfather clock could not be trusted—and he was right: it was twenty minutes fast.

Immersing himself in a meditative state for a second time proved harder. Erast Petrovich recalled that at five o'clock that afternoon he was due to take part in a competition of the Moscow Bicycle Enthusiasts' Club, to support the poor widows and orphans of employees of the military department. Moscow's strongest sportsmen and the bicycle teams of the Grenadier Corps were competing. The Collegiate Counsellor had a good chance of repeating his success of the previous year and taking the main prize.

Alas, there was no time now for sports competitions.

Erast Petrovich drove away the inappropriate thoughts and began staring at the pale-lilac pattern of the wallpaper. Now the mist would thicken again, the petals of the printed irises would tremble, the flowers would begin breathing out their fragrance and satori would come.

Something was hindering him. The mist seemed to be carried away by a wind blowing from somewhere on his left. The severed ear was lying there, in the lacquered box on the table. Lying there, refusing to be forgotten.

Ever since his childhood, Erast Petrovich had been unable to bear the sight of tormented human flesh. He had lived long enough, seen all sorts of horrific things, taken part in wars and yet, strangely enough, he had still not learned to regard with indifference the things that human beings did to their own kind.

Realising that the irises on the wallpaper would not breathe out any scent today, Fandorin heaved a deep sigh. Since he had failed to arouse his intuition, he would have to rely on his reason. He sat down at the table and picked up his magnifying glass.

He began with the wrapping paper. It was just ordinary paper, the kind used to wrap all sorts of things. Nothing to go on there.

Now for the handwriting. The writing was uneven and the letters were large with careless endings to their lines. If you looked closely, there were tiny splashes of ink—the hand had been pressed too hard against the paper. The writer was most probably a man in the prime of life. Possibly unbalanced or intoxicated. But he could not exclude the possibility of a woman with strong emotional and hysterical tendencies. In that regard he had to take into account the flourishes on the Os and the coquettish hooks on the capital Fs.

The most significant point was that they did not teach people to write like that in the handwriting classes in the grammar schools. What he had here was either someone educated at home, which was more typical of female individuals, or someone who had had no regular education at all. However, there was not a single spelling mistake. Hmm. This required a little thought. At least the writing was a clue.

Next—the velvet box. The kind in which they sold expensive cufflinks or brooches. Inside it there was a monogram: "A. Kuznetsov, Kamergersky Way." That was no help. It was a large jeweller's shop, one of the best known in Moscow. He could make inquiries, of course, but they would hardly come to anything—he could assume that they sold at least several dozen boxes of that kind a day.

The satin ribbon was nothing special. Smooth and red—the kind that gypsy women or merchants' daughters liked to tie their plaits with on holidays.

Using his magnifying glass, Erast Petrovich inspected the powder box (from "Cluseret No. 6") with especial interest, holding it by the very edge. He sprinkled it with a white powder like talc, and numerous fingerprints appeared on the smooth lacquered surface. The Collegiate Counsellor carefully and precisely blotted them with a special, extremely thin paper. Fingerprints would not be accepted as evidence in court, but even so they would come in useful.

It was only now that Fandorin turned his attention to the poor ear. Judging from the sprinkling of freckles on both sides of the ear, its owner had been ginger-haired. The lobe had been pierced, and very carelessly: the hole was wide and long. Taking that into account, and also the fact that the skin was badly chapped by cold and wind, he could conclude, firstly, that the former owner of the object in question had worn her hair combed upwards; secondly, that she was not a member of the privileged classes; thirdly, that she had spent a lot of time out in the cold without wearing any hat. The final circumstance was especially noteworthy. It was well known that street girls touted their wares with their heads uncovered even during the cold season. It was one of the signs of their trade.

Biting his lip (he still couldn't manage to regard the ear as an object), Erast Petrovich turned the ear over with a pair of tweezers and began examining the cut. It was even, made with an extremely sharp instrument. Not a single drop of congealed blood. Which meant that when the ear was severed the ginger-haired woman had already been dead for at least several hours.

What was that slight blackening on the cut? What could have caused that? Defrosting, that was what! The body had been in an ice-room—that was why the cut was so perfect: when it had been made the tissues had still not completely thawed out.

A prostitute's body placed in an ice-room? What for? What kind of fastidiousness was this? That kind were always taken straight to the Bozhedomka and buried. If they were put in an ice-room, it was either in the medical-faculty morgue on Trubetskaya Street for educational purposes, or in the forensic morgue at Bozhedomka to help with a police investigation.

And now the most interesting question: who had sent him the ear and why? First—why?

The London murderer had done the same thing the previous year. He had sent Mr. Albert Lusk, the chairman of the committee for the capture of Jack the Ripper, half of a kidney from the mutilated body of Catherine Eddows, which had been found on 30 September.

Erast Petrovich was convinced that this action had had a double meaning for the killer. The first, obvious meaning was a challenge, a demonstration of confidence in his own invulnerability, as if to say: No matter how hard you try, you'll never catch me. But there was probably a second underlying reason too: the typical masochistic desire of maniacs of this kind to be caught and punished: If you protectors of society really are all-powerful and ubiquitous, if Justice is the father and I am his guilty son, then here's the key for you; find me. The London police had not known how to use the key.

Of course, a quite different hypothesis was also possible. The terrible package had not been sent by the killer, but by some cynical joker who regarded the tragic situation as a pretext for a cruel jest. In London the police had also received a scoffing letter, supposedly written by the criminal. The letter had been signed "Jack the Ripper," which was actually where the nickname had come from. The English investigators had concluded that it was a hoax—probably because they had to justify the failure of their efforts to find the sender.

There was no point in complicating his task by making it a double one. At this moment it made no difference whether or not it was the killer who had sent the ear. All he needed to do at this moment was find out who had done it. It was very possible that the person who had severed the ear would turn out to be the Ripper. The Moscow trick with the small package differed from the London case in one substantial respect: the entire British capital had known about the murders in the East End, and in principle anybody at all could have "joked" in that way. But in this case the details of yesterday's atrocity were only known to an extremely limited circle of individuals. How many of them were there? Very few, even if he included intimate friends and relatives.

And so, what details did he know of the person who had sent the "small package"?

It was someone who had not studied in a grammar school, but had still received a good enough education to write the phrase "Collegiate Counsellor" without any mistakes. That was one.

Judging from the box from Kuznetsov's and the powder box from Cluseret, the person involved was not poor. That was two.

This person was not only informed about the murders, but he knew about Fandorin's role in the investigation. That was three.

This person had access to the morgue, which narrowed the circle of suspects still further. That was four.

This person possessed the skills of a surgeon. That was five.

What else was there?

"Masa, a cab. And look lively!"

Zakharov came out of the autopsy room in his leather apron, his black gloves smeared with some brownish sludge. His face was puffy, he looked overhung and the pipe in the corner of his mouth had gone out.

"Ah, the eyes and ears of the Governor-General," he muttered instead of a greeting. "What is it—has somebody else been sliced up?"

"Mr. Zakharov, how many prostitutes' bodies do you have in the ice-room?" Erast Petrovich asked curtly.

The forensic expert shrugged: "On Mr. Izhitsin's orders, they now bring in all the streetwalkers who have come to the end of their walk. In addition to our mutual friend Andreichkina, yesterday and today they've brought in another seven. Why—do you want to have a bit of fun?" Zakharov asked with a debauched grin. "There are some very pretty ones. But probably none to suit your taste. You prefer the giblets, I think?" The pathologist could see perfectly well that Fandorin was not at ease, and he seemed to take pleasure in the fact.

"Show them to me." The Collegiate Counsellor thrust his chin out stolidly, readying himself for the distressing sight.

The first thing that Fandorin saw in the spacious room lit by electric lights was the wooden shelves covered with glass jars with shapeless objects floating in them, and then he looked at the zinc-covered oblong tables. Projecting from one of them, beside the window, was the black neck of a microscope, and beside it a body was lying flat, with Zakharov's assistant working on it.

Erast Petrovich took a quick glance, saw that the body was male and turned away in relief.

"A deep firearms wound to the top of the head, Mr. Zakharov, that's all," the assistant said with a nasal twang, gazing curiously at Erast Petrovich, who was an almost legendary character in and around police circles.

"They brought that one in from Khitrovka," Zakharov explained. "But your little chicks are all over there, in the ice-room." He pushed open a heavy metal door that breathed out a dense, chilly, repulsive stench. A switch clicked and the matte-glass globe on the ceiling lit up.

The doctor pointed. "There are our heroines, on that side," he said to Fandorin, who was feeling numb.

The initial impression was not at all horrific. Ingres's painting *The Turkish Bath*. A solid tangle of naked women's bodies, smooth lines, lazy immobility.

Except that the steam was not hot, but frosty, and for some reason all the odalisques were lying down.

Then the details struck his eyes: the long crimson incisions, the blue patches, the sticky, tangled hair.

The forensic expert patted one of them, who looked like a mermaid, on her blue neck. "Not bad eh? From a brothel. Consumption. In fact, there's only one violent death here: the one over there, with the big breasts; someone stove her head in with a rock. Two of them are suicides. Three of them died of hypothermia—froze to death when they were drunk. They bring them all in, no matter what. Teach a fool to pray and he won't know when to stop. But what's that to me. I don't have to do all that much."

Erast Petrovich leaned down over one woman, thin, with a scattering of freckles on her shoulders and chest. He threw the long ginger hair back from the pitifully contorted, sharp-nosed face. Instead of a right ear the dead woman had a cherry-red hole.

"Well, who's been taking liberties here?" Zakharov asked in surprise and glanced at the tag attached to the woman's foot. "Marfa Sechkina, sixteen years old. Ah, I remember: poisoned herself with phosphorous matches. Came in yesterday afternoon. But she still had both her ears, I remember that very well. So where's her right one got to?"

The Collegiate Counsellor took a powder box out of his right pocket, opened it without speaking and thrust it under the pathologist's nose.

Zakharov took the ear with a steady hand and held it against the cherry-red hole.

"That's it! So what does this mean?"

"That is what I would like you to tell me." Fandorin held a scented handkerchief to his nose, feeling the nausea rising in his throat, and said: "Come on, let's talk out there."

They walked back into the autopsy room which now, despite the presence of the dissected corpse, Erast Petrovich found almost cosy.

"Three qu-questions. Who was here yesterday evening? Who have you told about the investigation and my participation in it? Whose writing is this?"

The Collegiate Counsellor set down the wrapping paper from the "smopackadj" in front of Zakharov. He felt it necessary to add: "I know that you did not write it—I am familiar with your handwriting. However, I trust you appreciate the significance of this correspondence?"

Zakharov turned pale; he had clearly lost any desire to play the clown.

"I'm waiting for an answer, Mr. Zakharov. Shall I repeat the questions?"

The doctor shook his head and squinted at Grumov, who was pulling something greyish-blue out of the corpse's gaping belly with exaggerated zeal. Zakharov gulped and his Adam's apple twitched in his neck.

"Yesterday evening my colleagues from the old faculty called to see me. They were celebrating the anniversary of a certain . . . memorable event. There were seven or eight of them. They drank some medical spirit here, in memory of the old student days . . . It's possible that I might have blurted out something about the investigation—I don't exactly remember. Yesterday was a heavy day, I was tired, and the drink soon went to my head." He stopped.

"The third question," Fandorin reminded him: "whose handwriting is it? And don't lie and tell me you don't know. The handwriting is quite distinctive."

"I'm not in the habit of lying!" Zakharov snapped. "And I recognise the writing. But I'm not a police informer; I'm a former Moscow student. You find out for yourself, without me."

Erast Petrovich said in an unpleasant voice: "You are not only a former student, but a current forensic medical expert, who has taken an oath. Or have you forgotten which investigation we are talking about here?" And then he continued in a very quiet, expressionless voice: "I can, of course, arrange for the handwriting of everyone who studied in the same faculty as you to be checked, but that will take weeks. In that case your honour among your comrades would not suffer, but I would make sure that you were tried and deprived of the right to work in the state service. You've known me for some years already, Zakharov. I always mean what I say."

Zakharov shuddered, and the pipe slid from left to right along the slit of his mouth. "I'm sorry, Mr. Court Counsellor, but I can't. Nobody would ever shake my hand again. Never mind the government service, I wouldn't be able to work in any area of medicine at all. But I'll tell you what . . ." The forensic expert's yellow forehead gathered into wrinkles. "Our revels are continuing this evening. We agreed to meet at seven at Burylin's place. He never completed the course, like many of our company in fact; but we get together from time to time . . . I've just completed a job here; Grumov can finish up everything else. I was just about to have a wash, get changed and go. I have an apartment here. At the public expense, attached to the cemetery office. It's most convenient . . . Well, if you like, I can take you with me to Burylin's place. I don't know if everyone who was here yesterday will come, but the person you're interested in will definitely be there, I'm certain of that . . . I'm sorry, but that's all I can do. A doctor's honour."

It was not easy for the pathologist to speak in such a plaintive manner; he was not accustomed to it, and Erast Petrovich decided to temper justice with mercy and not press him any harder. He merely shook his head in astonishment at the peculiarly elastic ethics of these people's *esprit de corps*: a man could not point out someone he had studied with as a likely killer, but there was no problem in bringing a detective along to a former fellow-student's house.

"You are complicating my task, but very well, let it be so. It's after eight already. Get changed and let's go."

For most of their journey (and it was a long journey, to Yakimanka Street), they rode in silence. Zakharov was as gloomy as a storm cloud and he replied to questions reluctantly, but Fandorin did at least learn something about their host.

He was called Kuzma Savvich Burylin. He was a manufacturer, a millionaire from an old merchant family. His brother, who was many years older, had taken up the eunuch faith of the *skoptsy*. He had "cut off his sin" and lived like a hermit, building up his capital. He had intended to "purge" his younger brother as well, when he reached the age of fourteen, but on the very eve of the "great mystery" the elder brother had died suddenly, and the youth had not only remained completely intact, but inherited an immense fortune. As Zakharov remarked acidly, a retrospective fear and the miraculous preservation of his manhood had marked Kuzma Burylin's life ever since. For the rest of his life he was doomed to demonstrate that he was not a eunuch, and he often went to excess in the process.

"Why did such a rich man join the medical faculty?" asked Fandorin.

"Burylin has studied all sorts of things—both here and abroad. He has a curious and unstable mind. He doesn't need a diploma, so he has never finished any course anywhere, but he was thrown out of the medical faculty."

"What for?"

"There was good cause," the forensic expert replied vaguely. "You'll soon see for yourself what kind of individual he is."

The illuminated entrance to Burylin's house, which faced the river, could be seen from a distance. It was the only house glowing with bright lights of different colours on the dark merchants' embankment, where they went to bed early during Lent and did not use any light unless they needed to. It was a big house, built in the absurd Mauritanian Gothic style: with little pointed turrets, chimeras and gryphons, but at the same time it had a flat roof and a round dome above the conservatory, even a watch-tower shaped like a minaret.

There was a crowd of idle onlookers outside the decorative gates, looking at the gaily illuminated windows and talking among themselves disapprovingly: an obscenity like this on Holy Week Wednesday, during the last week of the forty days of Lent! The muffled whining of gypsy violins drifted out of the house over the silent river, together with the jangling of guitars and jingling of little bells, peals of laughter and an occasional low growling.

They walked in and handed their outer garments to the doormen, and Erast Petrovich was surprised to see that beneath his tightly buttoned black coat, the forensic expert was wearing a white tie and tails.

Zakharov smiled crookedly at his glance of amazement. "Tradition."

They walked up a broad marble staircase. Servants in crimson livery opened tall gilded doors, and Fandorin saw before him a spacious hall, its floor covered with palms, magnolias, and other exotic plants in tubs. It was the latest European fashion—to make your drawing room look like a jungle. "The hanging gardens of Semiramis" it was called. Only the very rich could afford it.

The guests were distributed in leisurely style among the paradisiacal groves. Like Zakharov, everyone was in white tie and tails. Erast Petrovich's dress was dandyish enough—a beige American jacket, a lemon-yellow waistcoat, and a pair of trousers of excellent cut with permanent creases—but in this black-and-white congregation he felt like a Yuletide masker. Zakharov could at least have warned him what kind of clothes he was going to change into.

But then, even if Fandorin had come in tails, he still would not have been able to lose himself among the guests, because there were very few of them—perhaps a dozen. For the most part gentlemen of respectable and even prosperous appearance, although they were not at all old—about thirty, or perhaps a little older. Their faces were flushed from drinking, and some even looked a little confused—evidently for them this kind of merrymaking was not the usual thing. At the far end of the hall Fandorin could see another pair of gilded doors, which were closed, and from behind them he could hear the clatter of dishes and the sounds of a gypsy choir practising. A banquet was evidently in preparation inside.

The newcomers had arrived at the high point of a speech being given by a bald gentleman with a paunch and a gold pince-nez.

"Zenzinov—he was the top student. He's a full professor already," Zakharov whispered, and Fandorin thought he sounded envious.

"...recalling our old pranks from those memorable days. That time, seven years ago, it fell on Holy Week Wednesday too, like today."

For some reason the professor paused for a moment and shook his head bitterly. "As they say: Out with your eye for remembering the past, but if you forget, out with both. And they also say: It will all work out in the end. And it has worked out. We've got old, turned fat and flabby. Thanks to Kuzma for still being such a wild man and occasionally shaking up us boring old disciples of Aesculapius."

At that point everyone began laughing and cackling, turning towards a man who was sitting in an armchair in a stately pose with one leg crossed over the other and drinking wine from an immense goblet. Evidently he was Kuzma Burylin. An intelligent, jaundiced-looking face of the Tatar type—with broad cheekbones and a stubborn chin. His black hair was stuck up in a short French crop.

"It may have worked out for some, but not for everyone," said a man with long hair and a haggard face, who did not look like the others. He was also wearing tails, but they were obviously not his own, and instead of a starched white shirt, he was definitely wearing a false shirt-front. "You got away scot-free, Zenzinov. Of course, you were the faculty favourite. Others weren't so lucky. Tomberg became an alcoholic. They say Stenich went crazy. Sotsky died a convict. Just recently I keep thinking I see him everywhere. Take yesterday, for instance ..."

"Tomberg took to drink. Stenich went crazy, Sotsky died and Zakharov became a police corpse-carver instead of a doctor," their host interrupted the speaker unceremoniously. However, he was looking not at Zakharov but at Erast Petrovich, and with distinct hostility.

"Who's this you've brought with you, Egorka, you English swine? Somehow I don't remember this bright spark as one of our medical brotherhood."

Then the forensic expert, the Judas, demonstratively moved away from the Collegiate Counsellor and declared, as if everything were perfectly normal: "Ah, this, gentlemen, is Erast Petrovich Fandorin, a very well-known individual in certain circles. He works for the Governor-General on especially important criminal cases. He insisted that I bring him here. I could not refuse—he is my superior. In any case, please make him welcome."

The members of the brotherhood began hooting indignantly. Someone leapt out of his chair. Someone else applauded sarcastically.

"What the hell is this!"

"These gentlemen have gone too far this time!"

"He doesn't look much like a detective."

These comments, and similar ones that assailed him from all sides, made Erast Petrovich blench and screw up his eyes. This business was taking an unpleasant turn. Fandorin stared hard at the perfidious forensic expert, but before he could say anything, the master of the house had dashed across to his uninvited guest in a couple of strides and taken him by the shoulders. Kuzma Savvich's grasp proved to be very powerful; there was no way to wriggle out of it.

"In my house there's only one superior: Kuzma Burylin," the millionaire roared. "Nobody comes here without an invitation, especially detectives. And anyone who does come will regret it later."

"Kuzma, do you remember that bit in Count Tolstoy," the long-haired man shouted, "how they tied a constable to a bear and threw them in the river! Let's give this fop a ride too. And it will be good for your Potapich; he's been getting a bit dozy."

Burylin threw his head back and laughed loudly. "Oh, Filka, you delightful soul, that's what I value about you: your imagination. Hey! Bring Potapich here!"

Several of the guests who were not yet completely drunk tried to reason with their hosts, but two burly lackeys had already brought in a shaggy bear in a muzzle from the dining room, leading it on a chain. The bear was growling in annoyance and did not want to come; he kept trying to sit down on the floor, and the lackeys dragged him along, with his claws scraping along the highly polished parquet. A palm in a tub was overturned and went crashing to the floor, scattering lumps of earth.

"This is going too far! Kuzma!" Zenzinov appealed. "After all, we're not boys any longer. You'll have to face the repercussions! In any case, I'm leaving if you don't stop this!"

"He's right," some other reasonable individual chimed in, in support of the professor. "There'll be a scandal, and nobody needs that."

"Well, you can go to the devil then!" Burylin barked. "But remember, you clyster tubes, I've engaged Madam Julie's establishment for the whole night. We'll go without you."

After he said that, the voices of protest immediately fell silent.

Erast Petrovich stood there calmly. He did not say a word and did not make the slightest attempt to free himself. His blue eyes gazed without any expression at the wild merchant.

The master of the house gave brisk instructions to his lackeys. "Turn Potapich's back this way, so he won't maul the detective. Have you brought the rope? And you turn your back this way, you state minion. Afonya, can Potapich swim?"

"Why, of course, Kuzma Savvich. In summer he's very fond of splashing about at the dacha," a lackey with a forelock replied merrily.

"Well then, he can splash about a bit now. The water must be cold, it's only April. Well, why are you being so stubborn!" Burylin shouted at the Collegiate Counsellor. "Turn round!"

He clutched Erast Petrovich's shoulders with all his strength, trying to turn his back to the bear, but Fandorin did not budge an inch, as if he were carved out of stone. Burylin pushed and strained against him. His face turned crimson and the veins stood out on his forehead. Fandorin carried on calmly looking at his host, with just the faintest hint of a mocking smile in the corners of his mouth.

Kuzma Savvich grunted for a little longer but, realising that it looked extremely stupid, he removed his hands and gazed in astonishment at this strange official. The hall went very quiet.

"You're the one I want to see, my dear fellow," said Erast Petrovich, opening his mouth for the first time. "Shall we have a talk?"

He took the manufacturer's wrist between his finger and thumb and strode off rapidly towards the closed doors of the banqueting hall. Fandorin's fingers clearly possessed some special power, because his corpulent host grimaced in pain and minced after the man with black hair and white temples. The lackeys froze on the spot in bewilderment, and the bear slowly sat down on the floor and shook its shaggy head idiotically.

Fandorin looked back from the doorway. "Carry on enjoying yourselves, gentlemen. Meanwhile Kuzma Savvich will explain a few things to me."

The last thing Erast Petrovich noticed before he turned his back to the guests was the intense gaze of forensic medical expert Zakharov.

The table that was laid in the dining hall was a marvel to behold. The Collegiate Counsellor glanced in passing at the piglet dozing blissfully, surrounded by golden rings of pineapple, and the frightening carcass of the sturgeon in jelly, at the fancy towers of the salads, the red claws of the lobsters, and remembered that his unsuccessful meditation had left him without any dinner. Never mind, he comforted himself. Confucius said: "The noble man satisfies himself by abstaining."

In the far corner he could see the scarlet shirts and shawls of the gypsy choir. They saw the master of the house, and the elegant gentleman with a moustache leading him by the hand, and broke off their singing in mid-word. Burylin waved his hand at them in annoyance, as if to say: Stop staring, this is none of your business.

The female soloist, covered in necklaces of coins and ribbons, misunderstood his gesture and began singing in a chesty voice:

He was not her promised one,
He was not her husband . . .

The choir took up the tune in low voices, at only a quarter of full volume.

He brought his little darling
Into the timbered chamber . . .

Erast Petrovich released the millionaire's hand and turned to face him. "I received your package. Should I interpret it as a confession?"

Burylin rubbed his white wrist. He looked at Fandorin curiously. "Well, you really are strong, Mr. Collegiate Counsellor. You wouldn't think so to look at you . . . What package? And a confession to what?"

"You see, you know my rank, although Zakharov didn't mention it today. You severed that ear; nobody else could have done it. You've studied medicine, and you visited Zakharov yesterday with your fellow students. He was certain that whoever else was here today, you would be. Is this your writing?" He showed the manufacturer the wrapping paper from the "smopackadj."

Kuzma Savvich glanced at it and laughed. "Who else's? How did you like my little present? I told them to be sure to deliver it in time for dinner. Didn't choke on your bouillon, did you? No doubt you called a meeting and constructed hypotheses? Yes, I admit it, I like a joke. When the alcohol loosened Egorka Zakharov's tongue yesterday, I played a little prank. Have you heard about Jack the Ripper in London? He played a similar kind of trick on the police there. Egorka had a dead girl lying on the table—ginger-haired she was. I took a scalpel when he wasn't looking. I lopped off her ear, wrapped it in my handkerchief and slipped it in my pocket. His description of you was far too flowery, Mr. Fandorin, you were this and you were that, and you could unravel any tangled thread. Well, Zakharov wasn't lying: you are a curious individual. I like curious individuals, I'm one myself." The millionaire's narrow eyes glinted cunningly. "I tell you what. You forget this little joke of mine—it didn't work anyway—and come along with us. We'll have a right royal time. Let me tell you in secret that I've thought up a most amusing wheeze for my old friends, the little doctors. Everything's all ready at Madam Julie's. Moscow will break its sides laughing when it finds out about it tomorrow. Come along with us, really. You won't be sorry."

At this point the choir suddenly broke off its slow, quiet song and roared out as loud as it could:

Kuzya-Kuzya-Kuzya-Kuzya,
Kuzya-Kuzya-Kuzya-Kuzya,
Kuzya-Kuzya-Kuzya-Kuzya,
Kuzya-Kuzya-Kuzya-Kuzya,
Kuzya, drain your glass!

Burylin merely glanced over his shoulder, and the roaring stopped.

"Do you often go abroad?" Fandorin asked, apropos of nothing.

"This is the palace I often come to," said his host, apparently not surprised by the change of subject. "But I live abroad. I've no need to sit polishing the seat of my pants in the office here—I've got capable managers; they do things without me. In a big business like mine, there's only one thing you need: to understand people. Choose the right people and you can lie back and take it easy, the work does itself."

"Have you been in England recently?"

"I often go to Leeds, and to Sheffield. I have factories there. I drop into the exchange in London. The last time was in December. Why do you ask about England?"

Erast Petrovich lowered his eyelids a little in order to soften the glint in his eyes. He picked a speck of dust off his sleeve and said emphatically: "I am placing you under arrest for mutilating the body of the spinster Sechkina. Only administrative arrest for the time being, but in the morning there will be a warrant from the Public Prosecutor. Your appointed representative must deposit your bail no later than midday tomorrow. You are coming with me, and your guests can all go home. The visit to the bordello is cancelled. It's not good to bring such respectable d-doctors into disgrace like that. And you, Burylin, will enjoy a right royal time in the cells."

As a reward for saving the girl, I was sent a dream last night.

I dreamed I was standing before the Throne of the Lord.

"Sit on my left hand," the Father of Heaven said to me. "Rest, for you bring people joy and release, and that is heavy work. They are foolish, my children.

Their views are inverted: they see black as white and white as black, woe as happiness, and happiness as woe. When in my mercy I summon one of them to Me in their childhood, the others cry and pity the one I have summoned instead of feeling joy for him. When I let one of them live to a hundred years, until his body is weak and his spirit is extinguished as a punishment and a warning to the others, they are not horrified by his terrible fate, but envy it. After a bloody battle, those I have turned away rejoice, even if they have received injuries, while they pity those who have fallen, summoned by Me to appear before My face, and secretly even despise them for their failure. But they are the truly fortunate, for they are already with Me, the unfortunates are those who remain. What am I to do with people, tell Me, you kind soul? How am I to bring them to their senses?" And I felt sorry for the Lord, vainly craving the love of his foolish children.

CHAPTER 6

The Triumph of Pluto

Holy Week Thursday, 6 April

Today it fell to Anisii's lot to work with Izhitsin.

Late the previous evening, after an "analysis" in the course of which it was determined that they now had more suspects than they required, the Chief had walked around the study for a while, clicked his beads and said: "All right, Tulipov. We'll have to sleep on it. You go and rest; you've done more than enough running about for one day."

Anisiii had expected the decision to be: put Stenich, Nesvitskaya, and Burylin under secret observation, check all their movements for the last year, and perhaps also set up some kind of investigative experiment. But no, the unpredictable Chief had come to a different conclusion. In the morning, when Anisii, shivering in the dreary drizzle, arrived at Malaya Nikitskaya Street, Masa handed him a note:

I am disappearing for a while. I shall try to come at this business from the other side. In the meantime, you work with Izhitsin. I am afraid he might botch things up with his excessive zeal. On the other hand, he may not be a very pleasant character, but he is tenacious, and he could just dig something up.

EF

Well, did you ever? And just what "other side" could that be?

The pompous investigator was not easy to find. Anisii phoned the Public Prosecutor's office and they told him: "He was called out by the Department of Gendarmes." He called the Department of Gendarmes and they replied: "He went out on urgent business that can't be discussed over the telephone." The duty officer's voice sounded so excited that Tulipov guessed it had to be another murder. And a quarter of an hour later a messenger arrived from Izhitsin—it was the constable, Linkov. He had called at the Collegiate Counsellor's and not found him in, so he'd come round to Tulipov on Granatny Lane.

Linkov was terribly agitated. "It's an absolute nightmare, Your Honour," he told Anisii. "The brutal murder of a juvenile. It's terrible, terrible . . ." He sniffed and blushed, evidently embarrassed by his own sensitivity.

Anisii looked at the ungainly, scrawny-necked policeman and saw straight through him: literate, sentimental, and no doubt he liked reading books; joined the police out of poverty, only this rough work wasn't for him, the poor lamb. Tulipov would have been the same if not for his fortunate encounter with Erast Petrovich.

"Come on, Linkov," said Anisii, deliberately addressing the constable in a formal, polite tone. "Let's go straight to the morgue; that's where they'll take her anyway."

Deduction is a great thing. His calculation proved to be correct. Anisii had been sitting talking to Pakhomenko in his watchman's hut for no more than half an hour, enjoying a chat about life with the agreeable fellow, when three droshkies drove up to the gates, followed by a blind carriage with no windows, the so-called "corpse-wagon."

Izhitsin and Zakharov got out of the first droshky, a photographer and his assistant got out of the second, two gendarmes and a senior constable got out of the third. No one got out of the carriage. The gendarmes opened its shabby doors with the peeling paint and carried out something short on a stretcher, covered with a tarpaulin.

The medical expert was dour, chewing on his eternal pipe with exceptional bitterness, but the investigator seemed to be in lively spirits, almost even glad about something.

When he caught sight of Anisii, his face dropped: "A-ah, there you are. So you already got wind of this? Is your chief here too?"

But when it turned out that Fandorin was not there and would not be coming, and so far his assistant did not really know anything, Izhitsin's spirits rose again. "Well, now things will really start moving," he told Tulipov, rubbing his hands energetically. "So, it's like this. At dawn today the railway line patrolmen on the Moscow–Brest transfer line discovered the body of a juvenile female vagrant in the bushes close to the Novotikhvinsk level crossing. Zakharov has determined that death occurred no later than midnight. It's not very pretty, I warn you, Tulipov, it was an incredible sight!" Izhitsin gave a brief laugh. "Just imagine it: the belly, naturally, had been completely gutted and the entrails hung all around on the branches, and as for the face . . ."

"What, another bloody kiss?" Anisii exclaimed excitedly.

The investigator burst out laughing and couldn't stop, he was helpless with laughter—obviously it was nerves.

"Oh, you'll be the death of me," he said eventually, wiping away his tears. "Fandorin and you and that kiss of yours. Please forgive my inappropriate merriment. When I show you, you'll understand. Hey, Silakov! Stop! Show him her face!"

The gendarmes put the stretcher down on the ground and turned back the edge of the tarpaulin. Anisii was expecting to see something particularly unpleasant: glassy eyes, a nightmarish grimace, the tongue lolling out of the mouth, but there was none of that. Under the tarpaulin there was some kind of black-

and-red baked pudding with two round blobs: white, with a small dark circle in the centre.

"What is it?" Tulipov asked in surprise, feeling his teeth starting to chatter of their own accord.

"Seems like our joker left her without any face at all," Izhitsin explained with morose humour. "Zakharov says the skin was slit along the hair line and then torn off, like the peel off an orange. There's a kiss for you. And, best of all, now she can't be identified."

Everything was still swimming and swaying in front of Anisii's eyes. The investigator's voice seemed to be coming from somewhere far in the distance.

"Anyway, the secret's out now. Those rogues of patrolmen have blabbed to everyone they could. One of them was taken away in a faint. The rumours were already spreading round Moscow in any case. The Department of Gendarmes is flooded with reports of a killer who's decided to wipe out women completely. This morning they reported everything to St. Petersburg, the whole truth, nothing kept back. The minister himself, Count Tolstoy, is coming. So there you have it. Looks like heads are going to roll. I don't know about you, but I'm quite fond of mine. Your chief can go on playing his game of deduction as long as he likes; he's safe enough, he has protection in high places. But I'll crack this one without deduction, by sheer determination and energy. This is no time for snivelling, I reckon."

Tulipov turned away from the stretcher, gulped to dispel the murky veil that was clouding his eyes, and filled his lungs as full of air as he could. That was better.

Izhitsin couldn't be allowed to get away with that "snivelling," and Anisii said in a flat, expressionless voice: "My chief says determination and energy are good for chopping firewood and digging vegetable patches."

"Exactly, my dear sir." The investigator waved to the gendarmes to carry the body into the morgue. "I'll damn well dig up the whole of blasted Moscow, and if it gets a bit messy, the result will justify it. If I don't get a result, my head's going to roll anyway. Have you been detailed to keep an eye on me, Tulipov? Do that then, but keep your comments to yourself. And if you feel like submitting a complaint, be my guest. I know Count Tolstoy; he appreciates determination and turns a blind eye to minor points of legality if liberties are taken in the interests of the case."

"I have had occasion to hear that sort of thing from policemen, but such views sound rather strange coming from an official of the Public Prosecutor's Office," said Anisii, thinking that was exactly what Erast Petrovich would have told Izhitsin if he had been in Anisii's place.

However, when the investigator simply shrugged off this dignified and restrained reprimand with a gesture of annoyance, Tulipov changed to an official tone of voice: "Would you please stick closer to the point, Mr. Court Counsellor. What is your plan?"

They went into the forensic medical expert's office and sat down at the desk, since Zakharov himself was working on the body in the autopsy theatre.

"Well, all right then," said Izhitsin, giving this man he outranked a superior glance. "So let's put our thinking caps on. Who does our belly-slasher kill? Streetwalkers, vagrants, beggars—that is, women from the lower depths of the city, society's discarded garbage. So now, let's remember where the killings have taken place. Well, there's no way to tell where the nameless bodies in the ditches were brought from. We know well enough that in such cases our Moscow police don't take too much trouble over the paperwork. But on the other hand, we do know where the bodies we dug out of the named graves came from."

Izhitsin opened an exercise book with an oilcloth cover.

"Aha, look! The beggar Marya Kosaya was killed on the eleventh of February on Maly Tryokhsvyatsky Lane, at Sychugin's dosshouse. Her throat was cut, her belly was slit open, her liver is missing. The prostitute Alexandra Zotova was found on the fifth of February in Svininsky Lane, lying in the road. Again with her throat cut and her womb missing. These two are obvious clients."

The investigator walked across to the police map of the city that was hanging on the wall and began jabbing at it with a long, pointed finger: "So, let's take a look. Tuesday's Andreichkina was found just here, on Seleznyovskaya Street. Today's little girl was found by the Novotikhvinsk level crossing, right here. From one crime scene to the other it's no more than a *verst*. And it's the same distance to the Vypolzovo Tatar suburb as well."

"What has the Tatar suburb got to do with anything?" Tulipov asked.

"Later, later," said Izhitsin, with another impatient gesture. "Just hold your horses . . . Now the two old bodies. Maly Tryokhsvyatsky Lane—that's there. And there's Svininsky Lane. All in the same patch. Three hundred, maybe five hundred steps from the synagogue in Spasoglinishchevsky Lane."

"But even closer to Khitrovka," Anisii objected. "Someone gets killed there every day of the week. That's no surprise: it's a hotbed of crime."

"They get killed all right, but not like this! No, Tulipov, this smacks of something more than plain Christian villainy. I can sense a fanatical spirit at work in all these paunchings. An alien spirit. Orthodox folks get up to lots of beastly things, but nothing like this. And don't start with all that nonsense about the London Ripper being Russian and now he's come back for some fun and games in the land of his birth. That's rubbish! If a Russian can travel round cities like London, it means he comes from the cultured classes. And why would an educated man go rummaging in the stinking guts of some Manka Kosaya? Can you picture it?"

Anisii couldn't picture it and he shook his head honestly.

"Well then, you see. It's so obvious. You have to be a crackpot theoretician like your chief to abandon common sense for abstract intellectual postulates. But I, Tulipov, am a practical man."

"But what about the knowledge of anatomy?" Anisii asked, dashing to his chief's defence. "And the professional use of a surgical instrument? Only a doctor could have committed all these outrages!"

Izhitsin smiled triumphantly. "That's where Fandorin is wrong! That hypothesis of his stuck in my throat from the very start. It does-n't hap-pen," he said, hammering home every syllable. "It simply doesn't happen, and that's all there is to it. If a man from respectable society is a pervert, then he'll think up something a bit more subtle than these abominations." The investigator nodded in the direction of the autopsy room. "Remember the Marquis de Sade. Or take that business last year with the notary Schiller—remember that? He got this bint blind drunk, stuck a stick of dynamite up her, you know where, and lit the fuse. An educated man—you can see that straight away; but a monster, of course. But only some low scum is capable of the loathsome abominations we're dealing with here. And as for the knowledge of anatomy and the surgical skill, you'll see that's all very easily explained, you know-alls."

The investigator paused, raised one finger for dramatic effect and whispered: "A butcher! There's someone who knows anatomy as well as any surgeon. Every day of the week he's separating out livers and stomachs and kidneys as neat and tidy as you like, every bit as precise as the late surgeon Pirogov. And a good butcher's knives are as sharp as any scalpel."

Tulipov said nothing. He was shaken. The obnoxious Izhitsin was right! How could they have forgotten about butchers?

Izhitsin was pleased by Anisii's reaction. "And now, about my plan." He went up to the map again. "Seems we have two focal points. The first two bodies were found over here, the last two—over here. What reason the criminal had for changing his area of activity we don't know. Perhaps he decided it was more convenient to commit murder in the north of Moscow than in the central district: waste lots, shrubs and bushes, not so many houses. To be on the safe side, I'm regarding all the butchers who live in either of the regions that interest us as possible suspects. I already have a list." The investigator took out a sheet of paper and put it on the desk in front of Anisii. "Only seventeen names in all. Note the ones that are marked with a six-pointed star or a crescent moon. This is the Tatar suburb, here in Vypolzovo. The Tatars have their own butchers, and real bandits they are. Let me remind you that it's less than a *verst* from the suburb to the shed where Andreichkina was found. It's the same distance to the railway crossing where the little girl's body was found. And here"—the long finger shifted across the map—"in the immediate proximity of Tryokh-svyatsky and Svininsky Lanes, is the synagogue. That's where the kosher meat-carvers are, the filthy Yid butchers who kill the cattle in that barbarous fashion of theirs. Have you ever seen how it's done? Very much like the work of our good friend. Now do you get a whiff of where the case is heading?"

To judge from the pompous investigator's flaring nostrils, it was heading for a sensational trial, serious honours and breathtakingly rapid promotion.

"You're a young man, Tulipov. Your future's in your own hands. You can cling to Fandorin and end up looking stupid. Or you can work for the good of the cause and then I won't forget you. You're a smart lad, an efficient worker. I need helpers like you."

Anisii was about to open his mouth to put the insolent fellow in his place, but Izhitsin was already carrying on with what he was saying: "Of the seven butchers who interest us, four are Tatars and three are Yids. They're at the top of the list of suspects. But to avoid any reproaches of prejudice, I'm arresting the lot. And I'll give them a thorough working over. I have the experience for it, thank God." He smiled rapaciously and rubbed his hands together. "So right then. First of all I'll start by feeding the heathen scum salt beef, because they don't observe the Orthodox fast. They won't eat pork, so I'll order them to be given beef: we respect other people's customs. I'll give the Orthodox butchers a bit of salted herring. I won't give them anything to drink. Or let them sleep either. After they've been in for a night, they'll start howling, and in the morning, to make sure they don't get too bored, I'll call them out by turn and my lads will teach them a lesson with their 'sticks of salami.' Do you know what a 'stick of salami' is?"

Tulipov shook his head, speechless.

"A most excellent little device: a stocking stuffed with wet sand. Leaves no marks, but it makes a great impression, especially applied to the kidneys and other sensitive spots."

"But Mr. Izhitsin, you're a university graduate!" Anisii gasped.

"Exactly, and that's why I know when to stick to the rules and when the interests of society allow the rules to be ignored."

"And what if your theory's wrong and the Ripper isn't a butcher after all?"

"He's a butcher, who else could he be?" Izhitsin said with a shrug. "Well, I've explained things convincingly enough, haven't I?"

"And what if it's not the guilty party that confesses, but the one with the weakest spirit? Then the real murderer will go unpunished!"

By this stage the investigator had become so insolent that he actually slapped Anisii on the shoulder: "I've thought of that too. Of course, it won't look too good if we go and string up some Moshe or Abdul and then in three months or so the police discover another disembowelled whore. But this is a special case, bordering on a crime against the state—the Emperor's visit has been disrupted! And therefore, extreme measures are permissible." Izhitsin clenched his fist so tight that his knuckles cracked. "One of them will go to the gallows, and the rest will be exiled. By administrative order, with no publicity. To cold, deserted places where there aren't too many people to carve up. And even there the police will keep an eye on them."

Anisii was horrified by the determined investigator's "plan," although it was hard to deny the effectiveness of such measures. With a visit from the terrifying Count Tolstoy in the offing, the top brass would probably be frightened enough to approve the initiative, and the lives of a host of innocent people would be trampled into the dust. How could he prevent it? Ah, Erast Petrovich, where are you when you're needed?

Anisii gave a grunt, waggled his celebrated ears, mentally requested his chief's forgiveness for acting without due authority, and told Izhitsin about the previous day's investigative achievements. Just so he wouldn't get too carried away, let him be aware that, apart from his butchers, there were other, more substantial theories.

Leontii Izhitsin listened attentively without interrupting even once. His tense, nervous face first turned crimson, then began to turn pale, and at the end it came out in blotches, and his eyes had a drunken look.

When Tulipov finished, the investigator licked his thick lips with a whitish tongue and slowly repeated: "A nihilist midwife? An insane student? A madcap merchant? Right, right . . ." Izhitsin leapt up off his chair and started running round the room and ruffling up his hair, doing irreparable damage to his perfect parting.

"Excellent!" he exclaimed, halting in front of Anisii. "I'm very glad, Tulipov, that you have decided to collaborate openly with me. What secrets can there be between colleagues, after all; we're all doing the same job!"

Anisii felt a cold tremor run through his heart—he should have kept his mouth shut.

But there was no stopping the investigator now: "All right, let's try it. I'll still arrest the butchers anyway, of course, but let them sit in cells for the time being. First let's get to work on your medicos."

"How do you mean—'get to work'?" Anisii asked in panic, remembering the male nurse and the midwife. "With the 'salami stick'?"

"No; this class of people requires a different approach."

The investigator thought for a moment, nodded to himself and put forward a new plan of action: "Right then, this is what we're going to do. There's a different method for educated people, Tulipov. Education softens a man's soul, makes it more sensitive. If our belly-slasher comes from good society, then he's some kind of werewolf. During the day he's normal, like everyone else, and at night, in his criminal frenzy, it's as if he's possessed. That's where we'll catch him. I'll take the dear people in when they're normal and present them with the werewolf's handiwork. We'll see how their sensitive souls stand up to the sight. I'm sure the guilty party will break down. He'll see by the light of day what his alter ego gets up to and give himself away—he's bound to. That's psychology, Tulipov. Let's hold an investigative experiment."

For some reason Anisii suddenly remembered a story his mother used to tell him when he was a child, keening in the plaintive voice of Petya-Petushka, the cock from the fairy-tale: "The fox carries me off beyond the blue forests, beyond the high mountains, into her deep burrows . . ."

Chief, Erast Petrovich, things are looking bad, very bad.

Anisii did not participate in the preparations for the "investigative experiment." He stayed put in Zakharov's office, and in order not to think about the blunder he had committed, he began reading the newspaper lying on the desk—ploughing through it indiscriminately.

Construction of the Eiffel Tower Completed

Paris. Reuters News Agency informs us that the gigantic and entirely useless structure of iron rods with which the French intend to astound visitors to the Fifteenth World Fair has finally been completed. This dangerous project is causing justified anxiety among the inhabitants of Paris. How can this interminable factory chimney be allowed to tower over Paris, dwarfing all the marvellous monuments of the capital with its ridiculous height? Experienced engineers express concern about whether such a tall and relatively slim structure, erected on a foundation only a third of its own height, is capable of withstanding the pressure of the wind.

A Sword Duel

Rome. The whole of Italy is talking about a sword duel that took place between General Andreotti and Deputy Cavallo. In the speech that he gave last week to veterans of the Battle of Solferino, General Andreotti expressed concern about Jewish dominance of the newspaper and publishing world of Europe. Deputy Cavallo, who is of Jewish origin, felt insulted by this entirely justified assertion and, speaking in parliament, he called the general a "Sicilian ass," as a result of which the duel took place. In the second skirmish Andreotti was slightly wounded in the shoulder by a sword, after which the duel terminated. The opponents shook hands.

Minister's Illness

St. Petersburg. The Minister of Railways, who fell ill with pneumonia a few days ago, is somewhat improved: he has no more chest pains. The patient passed the night comfortably. He is fully conscious and aware of his surroundings.

Anisii even read the advertisements: about a cooling glycerine powder, about a cream for galoshes, about the latest folding beds and nicotine-filtering cigarette holders. Overcome by a strange apathy, he spent a long time studying a picture with the following caption: "The patented smell-free powder-closet using the system of mechanical engineer S. Timokho-vich. Cheap and meets all the requirements of hygiene, can be located in any room in the home. At Adadurov's house near Krasnye Voroty you can observe the powder-closet in action. Can be rented out for dachas."

After that he simply sat there and stared despondently out of the window.

Izhitsin, on the other hand, was a whirlwind of energy. Under his personal supervision they brought additional tables into the autopsy room, so that there were thirteen of them in all. The two gravediggers, the watchman, and the constables carried three identified bodies out of the ice-room on stretchers, one of them the juvenile vagrant. The investigator gave several instructions for the bodies to be laid out this way or that way—he was striving for the maximum visual effect. Anisii simply shuddered when he heard Izhitsin's piercing, commanding tenor through the closed door:

"Where are you moving that table, you dolt! On three sides, I said, on three sides!" Or even worse: "Not like that! Not like that! Open her belly up a bit wider! So what if it is all frozen together; use the spade, the spade! Right, now that's good."

The prisoners were brought shortly after two in the afternoon, each one in a separate droshky with an armed guard.

Through the window Tulipov saw them bring the first one into the morgue—a round-faced man with broad shoulders in a crumpled black tailcoat and a white tie that had slipped to one side—he could assume that he was the manufacturer Burylin, who hadn't managed to get home since being arrested the day before. About ten minutes later they brought Stenich. He was wearing a white coat (he must have come straight from the clinic) and glaring around like a trapped animal. Soon after that they brought in Nesvit-skaya. She walked between two gendarmes with her shoulders held back and her head high. The midwife's face was contorted by an expression of hatred.

The door creaked and Izhitsin came into the office. His face was agitated and flaming red—a genuine theatrical entrepreneur on an opening night.

"For the moment our dear guests are waiting in the front office, under guard," he told Anisii. "Take a look and see if this is all right."

Tulipov stood up listlessly and went into the dissection theatre.

In the middle of the wide room there was an empty space, surrounded on three sides by tables. Lying on each of them was a dead body covered by a tarpaulin. Standing along the walls behind the tables were the gendarmes, the constables, the gravediggers and the watchman: two men for each body. Zakharov was sitting on a chair beside the end table, wearing his perpetual apron and with his eternal pipe in his mouth. The forensic expert's face looked bored, even sleepy. Grumov was loitering behind him and a little to one side, like a wife with her ever-loving in a lower-middle-class photograph, except that he didn't have his hand on Zakharov's shoulder. The assistant had a dejected look—evidently the quiet man wasn't used to such large crowds in this kingdom of silence. The room smelled of disinfectant, but beneath the harsh chemical smell there was a persistent undercurrent: the sweet stench of decomposition.

On a separate, smaller table at one side there was a heap of paper bags. The prudent Izhitsin had provided for anything—somebody might easily be sick.

"I'll be here," said Izhitsin, indicating the spot. "They're here. At my command these seven will take hold of one cover with their right hand and another cover with their left hand, and pull them off. It's a remarkable sight. You'll see it soon for yourself. I'm sure the criminal's nerves won't stand up to it. Or will they?" the investigator asked in sudden alarm, surveying his stage setting sceptically.

"They won't stand up to it," Anisii replied gloomily. "Not one of the three."

His eyes met Pakhomenko's and the watchman gave him a sly wink, as if to say: Don't get upset, lad, remember that callus.

"Bring them in!" Izhitsin barked, turning towards the doors and then, hastily running into the centre of the room, he assumed a pose of stern inflexibility, with his arms crossed on his chest and one foot slightly advanced, his narrow chin jutting forward and his eyebrows knitted together.

They brought in the prisoners. Stenich immediately fixed his eyes on the terrible tarpaulins and tugged his head down into his hunched shoulders. He didn't even seem to notice Anisii and the others. Nesvitskaya, however, was not even slightly interested in the tables. She glanced round everybody there, rested her gaze on Tulipov and laughed contemptuously. Anisii blushed painfully. The captain of industry stood beside the table with the paper bags, leaning on it with one hand, and began turning his head this way and that curiously. Zakharov winked at him and Burylin nodded gently.

"I'm a forthright man," Izhitsin began in a dry, piercing voice, emphasising every word. "So I'm not going to beat about the bush here. In recent months there have been a number of brutal, monstrous murders in Moscow. The investigating authorities know for certain that these crimes were committed by one of you. I'm going to show you something interesting and look into your souls. I'm an old hand at detective work; you won't be able to fool me. So far the killer has only seen his or her own handiwork by night, while in the grip of insanity. But now you can see how lovely it looks by the light of day. All right!"

He waved his hand, and the tarpaulin shrouds seemed to slide to the floor by themselves. Linkov certainly spoiled the effect slightly—he tugged too hard, and the tarpaulin caught on the corpse's head. The dead head fell back on to the wooden surface with a dull thump.

It really was a spectacular sight. Anisii regretted he hadn't turned away in time, but now it was too late. He pressed his back against the wall, took three deep breaths, and it seemed to have passed.

Izhitsin did not look at the bodies. He stared avidly at the suspects, moving his eyes from one to the other in rapid jerks: Stenich, Nesvitskaya, Burylin; Stenich, Nesvitskaya, Burylin. And again, and again.

Anisii noticed that, although Senior Constable Pribludko was standing there motionless and stony-faced, the ends of his waxed moustache were quivering. Linkov was standing there with his eyes squeezed tight shut and his lips were moving—he was obviously praying. The gravediggers had expressions of boredom on their faces—they'd seen just about everything in their rough trade. The watchman was looking at the dead women in sad sympathy. His eyes met Anisii's and he shook his head very slightly, which surely meant: Ah, people, people, why do you do such things to each other? This simple human gesture finally brought Tulipov round. Look at the suspects, he told himself. Follow Izhitsin's example.

The former student and former madman Stenich was standing there cracking the knuckles of his slim fingers, with large beads of sweat on his forehead. Anisii would have sworn it was cold in there. Suspicious? No doubt about it!

But the other former student, Burylin, who had severed the ear, seemed somehow too calm altogether: he had a mocking smile hovering on his face and his eyes were glittering with evil sparks. No, the millionaire was only pretending that it all meant nothing to him—he'd picked up a paper bag from the table and was holding it against his chest. That was called an "involuntary reaction"—the Chief had taught Anisii to take note of them in his very first lesson. A lover of the high life like Burylin could easily develop a thirst for new, intense sensations simply because he was so surfeited.

Now the woman of iron, Nesvitskaya, the former prison inmate, who had learned to love surgical operations in Edinburgh. An exceptional individual—you simply never knew what an individual like that was capable of and what to expect from her. Just look at the way her eyes blazed.

And the "exceptional" individual immediately confirmed that she really was capable of acting unpredictably.

The deathly silence was shattered by her ringing voice: "I know who your target is, Mister Oprichnik," Nesvitskaya shouted at the investigator. "How very convenient. A 'nihilist' in the role of a bloodthirsty monster! Cunning! And especially spicy, because it's a woman, right? Bravo, you'll go a long way! I knew what kind of crimes your pack of dogs is capable of, but this goes far beyond anything I could have imagined!" The female doctor suddenly gasped and clutched at her heart with both hands, as if she'd been struck by sudden inspiration. "Why, it was you! You did it yourselves! I should have realised straight away! It was your executioners who hacked up these poor women—why not? You've got no pity for 'society's garbage'! The fewer of them there are, the simpler it is for you! You scum! Decided to play at Castigo, did you? Kill two birds with one stone, eh? Get rid of a few vagrants and throw the blame on the 'nihilists'! Not very original, but most effective!" She threw her head back and laughed in scornful hatred. Her steel-rimmed pince-nez slid off and dangled on its string.

"Quiet!" Izhitsin howled, evidently afraid that Nesvitskaya's outburst would ruin his psychological investigation. "Be silent immediately! I won't allow you to slander the authorities."

"Murderers! Brutes! Satraps! Provocateurs! Scoundrels! Destroyers of Russia! Vampires!" Nesvitskaya shouted, and it was quite clear that her reserve of insults for the guardians of law and order was extensive and would not soon be exhausted.

"Linkov, Pribludko, shut her mouth!" the investigator shouted, finally losing all patience.

The constables advanced uncertainly on the midwife and took her by the shoulders, but they didn't seem to know how to go about shutting the mouth of a respectable-looking lady.

"Damn you, you animal!" Nesvitskaya howled, looking into Izhitsin's eyes. "You'll die a pitiful death; your own intrigues will kill you!"

She threw up her hand, pointing one finger directly at the pompous investigator's face, and suddenly there was the sound of a shot.

Izhitsin jumped up in the air and bent over, clutching his head. Tulipov blinked: how was it possible to shoot anyone with your finger?

There was a peal of wild laughter. Burylin waved his hands in the air and shook his head, unable to control his fit of crazy merriment. Ah, so that was it. Apparently, while everyone was watching Nesvitskaya, the prankster had quietly blown up a paper bag and then slammed it down against the table.

"Ha-ha-ha!" The captain of industry's smothered laughter soared up to the ceiling in an inhuman howling.

Stenich!

"I can't sta-a-and it!" the male nurse whined. "I can't stand any more! Torturers! Executioners! Why are you tormenting me like this? Why? Lord, why, why?" His totally insane eyes slid across all of their faces and came to a halt, gazing at Zakharov, who was the only person there sitting down—sitting there silently with a crooked smile, his hands thrust into the pockets of his leather apron.

"What are you laughing at, Egor? This is your kingdom, is it? Your kingdom, your witch's coven! You sit on your throne and rule the roost! Triumphant! Pluto, the king of death! And these are your subjects!" He pointed to the mutilated corpses. "In all their grace and beauty!" And then the madman started spouting rubbish that made no sense at all. "Throw me out, unworthy! And you, you, what did you turn out to be worthy of? What are you so proud of? Take a look at yourself! Carrion crow! Corpse-eater! Look at him, all of you, the corpse-eater! And the little assistant? What a fine pair! One crow flies up to another; one crow says unto the other: 'Crow, where can we dine together?'" And he started trembling and burst into peals of hysterical giggling.

The corners of the forensic expert's mouth bent down in a grimace of disapproval. Grumov smiled uncertainly.

A wonderful "experiment," thought Anisii, looking at the investigator clutching his heart, and the suspects: one shouting curses, one laughing, one giggling. Well, damn you all, gentlemen.

Anisii turned and walked out. Phew, how good the fresh air was.

*

He called into his own apartment on Granatny Lane to check on Sonya and have a quick bowl of Palasha's cabbage soup, and then went straight to the Chief's house. What he was most anxious to learn about was what mysterious business Erast Petrovich had been dealing with today.

The walk to Malaya Nikitskaya Street was not very long—only five minutes. Tulipov bounded up on to the familiar porch and pressed the bell-button. There was no one there. Well, he supposed Angelina Samsonovna must be at church or in the hospital, but where was Masa? He felt a sharp stab of alarm: what if, while Anisii was undermining the investigation, the Chief had needed help and sent for his faithful servant?

He wandered back home listlessly. There were kids dashing about in the street and shouting. At least three of the urchins, the wildest, had black hair and slanting eyes. Tulipov shook his head, remembering that Fandorin's valet had the reputation of a sweetheart and a lady-killer among the local cooks, maids and laundrywomen. If things carried on like this, in ten years' time the entire district would be populated with Japanese brats.

He came back again two hours later, after it was already dark. Delighted to see light in the windows of the outhouse, he set off across the yard at a run.

The lady of the house and Masa were at home, but Erast Petrovich was absent, and it turned out that there hadn't been any news from him all day long.

Angelina didn't let her visitor go. She sat him down to drink tea with rum and eat éclairs, one of Anisii's great favourites.

"But it's the fast," Tulipov said uncertainly, breathing in the heavenly aroma of freshly brewed tea, laced with the strong Jamaican drink. "How can I have rum?"

"Oh, Anisii Pitirimovich, you don't observe the fast anyway," Angelina said with a smile. She sat facing him, with her cheek propped on her hand. She didn't drink any tea or eat any éclairs. "The fast should be a reward, not a deprivation. That's the only kind of fast the Lord needs. If your soul doesn't require it, then don't fast, and God be with you. Erast Petrovich doesn't go to church, he doesn't acknowledge the statutes of the Church, and it's all right—there's nothing terrible in that. The important thing is that God lives in his heart. And if a man can know God without the Church, then why coerce him?"

Anisii could hold back no longer, and he blurted out what had been on his mind for so long: "Not all the statutes of the Church should be avoided. Even if it's not important to you, then you can think about the feelings of people close to you. Or else, well, see how it turns out. Angelina Samsonovna, you live according to the law of the Church, you observe all the rites, sin would never even dare come anywhere near you, but in the eyes of society . . . It's not fair, it's hurtful . . ."

He still wasn't able to say it directly and he hesitated, but clever Angelina had already understood him.

"You're talking about us living together without being married?" she asked calmly, as if it were a perfectly ordinary topic of conversation. "Anisii Pitirimovich, you mustn't condemn Erast Petrovich. He has proposed to me twice, all right and proper. I was the one who didn't want it."

Anisii was dumbstruck. "But why not?"

Angelina smiled again, only this time not at Anisii, but at some thoughts of her own. "When you love, you don't think about yourself. And I love Erast Petrovich. Because he's very beautiful."

"Well that's true," said Tulipov with a nod. "A more handsome man would be hard to find."

"That's not what I meant. Bodily beauty is not enduring. Smallpox, or a burn, and it's gone. Last year, when we were living in England, there was a fire in the house next door. Erast Petrovich went in to drag a puppy out of the flames and he got singed. His clothes were burned, and his hair. He had a blister on his cheek, his eyebrows and eyelashes all fell out. He was a really fine sight. His whole face could have been burned away. Only genuine beauty is not in the face. And Erast Petrovich really is beautiful."

Angelina pronounced the last with special feeling, and Anisii understood what she meant.

"But I'm afraid for him. He has been given great strength, and great strength is a great temptation. I ought to be in church now: it's Great Thursday today, the commemoration of the Last Supper; but, sinner that I am, I can't read the prayers that I'm supposed to. I can only pray to our Saviour for him, for Erast Petrovich. May God protect him—against human malice, and even more against soul-destroying pride."

At these words Anisii glanced at the clock and said anxiously: "I must confess I'm more concerned about the human malice. It's after one in the morning and he's still not back. Thank you for the refreshments, Angelina Samsonovna; I'll be going now. If Erast Petrovich shows up, please be sure to send for me."

As he walked home, Tulipov thought about what he'd heard. On Malaya Nikitskaya Street a saucy girl came dashing up to him under one of the gas lamps—a broad ribbon in her black hair, her eyes made up, her cheeks rouged.

"Good evening to you, interesting sir. Would you care to treat a girl to a little vodka or liqueur?" She raised and lowered her painted eyebrows and whispered passionately: "And I'd be very grateful to you, handsome sir. I'd give you a time to remember for the rest of your life . . ."

Tulipov felt an ache somewhere deep inside him. The streetwalker was good-looking—very good-looking, in fact. But since the last time he had given in to temptation, at Shrovetide, Anisii had renounced venal love. He felt awful afterwards, guilty. He ought to marry, but what could he do with Sonya?

Anisii replied with paternal sternness: "You shouldn't be wandering the streets at night. You never know, you might run into some crazy murderer with a knife."

But the saucy girl wasn't bothered in the slightest. "Oh, such concern. I don't reckon I'll get killed. We're watched—the boyfriend keeps an eye on us."

And yes, there on the other side of the street, Anisii could see a silhouette in the shade. Realising he'd been spotted, the ponce came over unhurriedly, at a slovenly stroll. He was a very stylish specimen: beaver-fur cap pulled down over the eyes, fur coat hanging dashingly open, a snow-white muffler covering half his face and white spats as well.

He began speaking with a drawl, and a gold-capped tooth glinted in his mouth. "I beg your pardon, sir. Either take the young lady or be on your way. Don't go wasting a working girl's time."

The girl looked adoringly at her protector, and that angered Tulipov even more than her pimp's insolence.

"Don't you go telling me what to do!" Anisii said angrily. "I'll drag you down to the station in no time."

The ponce turned his head quickly to the left and the right, saw that the street was empty and inquired with an even slower, more menacing drawl: "You sure the dragger won't come unstuck?"

"Ah, so it's like that, is it?" Anisii grabbed the rogue by his collar with one hand, and took his whistle out of his pocket with the other. There was a police constable's post round the corner on Tverskaya Street, and it was only a stone's throw to the gendarme station.

"Run for it, Ineska, I'll handle this!" the gold-toothed scoundrel said.

The girl immediately picked up her skirts and set off as fast as her legs would carry her, and the brazen ponce said in Erast Petrovich's voice: "Stop blowing that thing, Tulipov. You've deafened me."

The constable, Semyon Sychov, ran up, puffing and panting like a horse jangling its harness.

The Chief held out a fifty-kopeck piece to him: "Good man, you're a fast runner."

Semyon Sychov didn't take the money from the suspicious-looking man and glanced quizzically at Anisii.

"Yes, it's all right, Sychov, off you go my friend," Tulipov said in embarrassment. "I'm sorry for bothering you."

Only then did Semyon Sychov take the fifty kopecks, salute in a highly respectful manner and set off back to his post.

"How's Angelina—is she not sleeping?" Erast Petrovich asked, with a glance at the bright windows of the outhouse.

"No, she's waiting for you."

"In that case, if you don't object, let's take a walk and have a little talk."

"Chief, what's this masquerade in aid of? In the note it said you were going to approach things from the other side. What 'other side' is that?"

Fandorin squinted at his assistant in clear disapproval. "You're not thinking too well, Tulipov. 'From the other side' means from the side of the Ripper's victims. I assumed that the women of easy virtue that our character seems to have a particular hatred for might know something we don't. They might have seen someone suspicious, heard something, g-guessed something. So I decided to do a bit of reconnaissance. These people aren't going to open up to a policeman or an official, so I chose the most appropriate camouflage. I must say that I've enjoyed distinct success in the role of a ponce," Erast Petrovich added modestly. "Several fallen creatures have volunteered to transfer to my protection, which has caused dissatisfaction among the competition—Slepen, Kazbek, and Zherebchik."

Anisii was not in the least surprised by his chief's success in the field of procuring—he was a really handsome fellow, and tricked out in full Khitrovka-Grachyovka chic too. Speaking aloud, he asked: "Did you get any results?"

"I have a couple of things," Fandorin replied cheerfully. "Mamselle Ineska, whose charms, I believe, did not leave you entirely indifferent, told me an amusing little story. One evening a month and a half ago, she was approached by a man who said something strange: 'How unhappy you look. Come with me and I'll bring you joy.' But Ineska, being a commonsensical sort of girl, didn't go with him, because as he came up, she saw him hide something behind his back, and that something glinted in the moonlight. And it seems a similar kind of thing happened with another girl, either Glashka or Dashka. There was even blood spilt that time, but she wasn't killed. I'm hoping to find this Glashka-Dashka."

"It must be him, the Ripper!" Anisii exclaimed excitedly. "What does he look like? What does your witness say?"

"That's just the problem: Ineska didn't get a look at him. The man's face was in the shadow, and she only remembered the voice. She says it was soft, quiet and polite. Like a cat purring."

"And his height? His clothes?"

"She doesn't remember. She admits herself that she'd taken a drop too much. But she says he wasn't a gent and he wasn't from Khitrovka either—something in between."

"Aha, that's already something," said Anisii, and he started bending down his fingers. "Firstly, it is a man after all. Secondly, a distinctive voice. Thirdly, from the middle classes."

"That's all nonsense," the Chief said abruptly. "The killer can quite easily change clothes for his n-nocturnal adventures. And the voice is suspicious. What does 'like a cat purring' mean? No, we can't completely exclude a woman."

Tulipov remembered Izhitsin's reasoning. "Yes, and the place! Where did he approach her? In Khitrovka?"

"No, Ineska's a Grachyovka lady, and her zone of influence takes in Trubnaya Square and the surrounding areas. The man approached her on Sukharev Square."

"Sukharev Square fits too," said Anisii, thinking. "That's just ten minutes' walk from the Tatar suburb in Vypolzovo."

"All right, Tulipov, stop." The Chief himself actually stopped walking. "What has the Tatar suburb to do with all this?"

Now it was Anisii's turn to tell his story. He began with the most important thing—Izhitsin's "investigative experiment."

Erast Petrovich listened with his eyes narrowed. He repeated one word: "Custigo?"

"Yes, I think so. That's what Nesvitskaya said. Or something like it. Why, what is it?"

"Probably 'Castigo,' which means 'retribution' in Italian," Fandorin explained. "The Sicilian police founded a s-sort of secret order that used to kill thieves, vagrants, prostitutes, and other inhabitants of society's nether regions. The members of the organisation used to lay the blame for the killings on the local criminal communities and carry out reprisals against them. Well, it's not a bad idea from our midwife. You could probably expect that from Izhitsin."

When Anisii finished telling him about the "experiment," the Chief said gloomily: "Yes, if one of our threesome is the Ripper, it won't be so easy to catch him—or her—now. Forewarned is forearmed."

"Izhitsin said that if none of them gave themselves away during the experiment, he'd order them to be put under open surveillance."

"And what good is that? If there are any clues, they will be destroyed. Every maniac always has something like a collection of souvenirs of sentimental value. Maniacs, Tulipov, are a sentimental tribe. One takes a scrap of clothing from the corpse, another takes something worse. There was one barbaric murderer, who killed six women, who used to collect their navels—he had a fatal weakness for that innocent part of the body. The dried navels become the most important clue. Our own 'surgeon' knows his anatomy, and every time one of the internal organs is missing. I surmise that that the killer takes them away with him for his collection."

"Chief, are you sure the Ripper has to be a doctor?" Anisii asked, and he introduced Erast Petrovich to Izhitsin's butcher theory, and at the same time to his incisive plan.

"So he doesn't believe in the English connection?" Fandorin said in surprise. "But the similarities with the London killings are obvious. No, Tulipov, this was all done by one and the same person. Why would a Moscow butcher go to England?"

"But even so, Izhitsin won't give up his idea, especially now, after his 'investigative experiment' has failed. The poor butchers have been sitting in the lock-up since midnight. He's going to keep them there till tomorrow with no water and not let them sleep. And in the morning he's going to get serious with them."

It was a long time since Anisii had seen the Chief's eyes glint so menacingly.

"Ah, so the plan is already being implemented?" the Collegiate Counsellor hissed through his teeth. "Well then, I'll wager you that someone else will end up without any sleep tonight. And without a job too. Let's go, Tulipov. We'll pay Mr. Pizhitsin a late visit. As far as I recall, he lives in a public-service apartment in the Court Department building. That's nearby, on Vozdvizhenskaya Street. Quick march, Tulipov, forward!"

Anisii was familiar with the two-storey building of the Court Department, where unmarried and seconded officials of the Ministry of Justice were accommodated. It was built in the British style, reddish brown in colour, with a separate entrance to each apartment.

They knocked at the doorman's lodge and he stuck his head out, half-asleep and half-dressed. For a long time he refused to tell his late callers the number of Court Counsellor Izhitsin's flat—Erast Petrovich looked far too suspicious in his picturesque costume. The only thing that saved the situation was Anisii's official cap with a cockade.

The three of them walked up the steps leading to the requisite door. The doorman rang the bell, tugged on his cap and crossed himself. "Leontii Andreevich has a very bad temper," he explained in a whisper. "You gentlemen take responsibility for this."

"We do, we do," Erast Petrovich muttered, examining the door closely. Then he suddenly gave it a gentle push and it yielded without a sound.

"Not locked!" the doorman gasped. "That Zinka, his maid—she's a real dizzy one. Nothing between the ears at all! You never know: we could easily have been burglars or thieves. Nearby here in Kislovsky Lane there was a case recently . . ."

"Sh-sh-sh," Fandorin hissed at him, and raised one finger.

The apartment seemed to have died. They could hear a clock chiming, striking the quarter-hour.

"This is bad, Tulipov, very bad."

Erast Petrovich stepped into the hallway and took an electric torch out of his pocket. An excellent little item, made in America: you pressed a spring, electricity was generated inside the torch and it shot out a beam of light. Anisii wanted to buy himself one like it, but they were very expensive.

The beam roamed across the walls, ran across the floor and stopped.

"Oh, God in Heaven!" the doorman squeaked in a shrill voice. "Zinka!"

In the dark room the circle of light picked out the unnaturally white face of a young woman, with motionless, staring eyes.

"Where's the master's bedroom?" Fandorin asked abruptly, shaking the frozen doorman by the shoulder. "Take me there! Quickly!"

They dashed into the drawing room, from the drawing room into the study and through the study to the bedroom that lay beyond it.

Anybody might have thought that Tulipov had seen more than enough contorted dead faces in the last few days, but this one was more repulsive than anything he'd seen so far.

Leontii Andreevich Izhitsin was lying in bed with his mouth wide open.

The Court Counsellor's eyes were bulging out so incredibly far that they made him look like a toad. The beam of yellow light rushed back and forth, briefly illuminated some dark heaps of something around the pillow and darted away. There was a smell of decay and excrement.

The beam moved back to the terrible face. The circle of electric light narrowed and became brighter, until it illuminated only the top of the dead man's head.

On the forehead there was the dark imprint of a kiss.

It is astounding what miracles my skill can perform. It is hard to imagine a creature more repulsively ugly than that court official. The ugliness of his behaviour, his manners, his speech, and his revolting features was so absolute that for the first time I felt doubt gnawing at my soul: could this scum really be as beautiful on the inside as all the rest of God's children?

And yet I managed to make him beautiful! Of course the male structure is far from a match for the female, but anybody who saw investigator Izhitsin after the work on him was completed would have had to admit that he was much improved in his new form.

He was lucky. It was the reward for his vim and vigour; and for making my heart ache with longing with that absurd spectacle of his. He awoke the longing—and he satisfied it.

I am no longer angry with him; he is forgiven. Even if because of him I have had to bury the trifles that were dear to my heart—the flasks in which I kept the precious mementoes that reminded me of my supreme moments of happiness. The alcohol has been emptied out of the flasks, and now all my mementoes will rot. But there is nothing to be done. It had become dangerous to keep them. The police are circling round me like a flock of crows.

It's an ugly job—sniffing things out, tracking people down. And the people who do it are exceptionally ugly. As if they deliberately choose that kind: with stupid faces and piggy eyes and crimson necks, and Adam's apples that stick out, and protruding ears.

No, that is perhaps unjust. There is one who is ugly to look at, but not entirely beyond redemption. I believe he is even rather likeable.

He has a hard life.

I ought to help the young man. Do another good deed.

CHAPTER 7

A Stenographic Report

Good Friday, 7 April

"... dissatisfaction and alarm. The sovereign is extremely concerned about the terrible, unprecedented atrocities that are being committed in the old capital. The cancellation of the Emperor's visit for the Easter service in the Kremlin is a quite extraordinary event. His Majesty has expressed particular dissatisfaction at the attempt made by the Moscow administration to conceal from the sovereign the series of murders, which, as it now appears, has been going on for many weeks. Even as I was leaving St. Petersburg yesterday evening in order to carry out my investigation, the latest and most monstrous killing of all took place. The killing of the official of the Public Prosecutor's Office who was leading the investigation is an unprecedented occurrence for the entire Russian Empire. And the blood-chilling circumstances of this atrocity throw down a challenge to the very foundations of the legal order. Gentlemen, my cup of patience is overflowing. Foreseeing His Majesty's legitimate indignation, I take the following decision of my own volition and by virtue of the power invested in me . . ."

The rain of words was heavy, slow, intimidating. The speaker surveyed the faces of those present gravely—the tense faces of the Muscovites and the stern faces of those from St. Petersburg.

On the overcast morning of Good Friday an emergency meeting was taking place in Prince Vladimir Andreevich Dolgorukoi's study, in the presence of the Minister of Internal Affairs, Count Tolstoy, and members of his retinue, who had only just arrived from the capital.

This Orthodox champion of the fight against revolutionary devilment had a face that was yellow and puffy; the unhealthy skin sagged in lifeless folds below the cold, piercing eyes; but the voice seemed to be forged of steel—inexorable and imperious.

"... by the power I possess as minister, I hereby dismiss Major-General Yurovsky from his position as the High Police Master of Moscow," the Count rapped out, and a sound halfway between a gasp and a groan ran through the top brass of the Moscow police.

"I cannot dismiss the district Public Prosecutor, who serves under the Ministry of Justice; however, I do emphatically recommend His Excellency to submit his resignation immediately, without waiting to be dismissed by compulsion . . ."

Public Prosecutor Kozlyatnikov turned white and moved his lips soundlessly, and his assistants squirmed on their chairs.

"As for you, Vladmir Andreevich," the minister said, staring steadily at the

Governor-General, who was listening to the menacing speech with his eyebrows knitted together and his hand cupped to his ear, "of course, I dare not give you any advice, but I am authorised to inform you that the sovereign expresses his dissatisfaction with the state of affairs in the city entrusted to your care. I am aware that in connection with your imminent sixtieth anniversary of service at officer's rank, His Highness was intending to award you the highest order of the Russian Empire and present you with a diamond casket decorated with the monogram of the Emperor's name. Well, Your Excellency, the decree has been left unsigned. And when His Majesty is informed of the outrageous crime that was perpetrated last night . . ."

The Count made a rhetorical pause and total silence fell in the study. The Muscovites froze, because the cold breeze of the end of a Great Age had blown through the room. For almost a quarter of a century the old capital had been governed by Vladimir Andreevich Dolgorukoi; the entire cut of Moscow public-service life had long ago been adjusted to fit His Excellency's shoulders, to suit his grasp, which was firm yet did not constrain the comforts of life. And now it looked as if the old warhorse's end was near. The High Police Master and the Public Prosecutor dismissed from their posts without the sanction of the Governor-General of Moscow! Nothing of the kind had ever happened before. It was a sure sign that Vladimir Andreevich himself was spending his final days, or even hours, on his high seat. The toppling of the giant could not help but be reflected in the lives and careers of those present, and therefore the difference between the expressions on the faces of the Muscovites and those on the faces of the Petersburgians became even more marked.

Dolgorukoi took his hand away from his ear, chewed on his lips, fluffed up his moustache and asked: "And when, Your Excellency, will His Majesty be informed of the outrageous crime?"

The minister narrowed his eyes, trying to penetrate the hidden motive underlying this question that appeared so simpleminded at first glance.

He penetrated it, appreciated it, and laughed very quietly: "As usual, from the morning of Good Friday the Emperor immerses himself in prayer, and matters of state, apart from emergencies, are postponed until Sunday. I shall be making my most humble report to His Majesty the day after tomorrow, before the Easter dinner."

The Governor nodded in satisfaction. "The murder of Court Counsellor Izhitsin and his maid, for all the outrageousness of this atrocity, can hardly be characterised as a matter of state emergency. Surely, Minister, you will not be distracting His Imperial Highness from his prayers because of such a wretched matter? That would hardly earn you a pat on the back, I think?" Prince Dolgorukoi asked with the same naive air.

"I will not." The upward curls of the minister's grey moustache twitched slightly in an ironical smile.

The Prince sighed, sat upright, took out a snuff box and thrust a pinch into his nose. "Well, I assure you that before noon on Sunday the case will have been concluded, solved, and the culprit exposed. A . . . a . . . choo!"

A timid hope appeared on the faces of the Muscovites.

"Bless you," Tolstoy said morosely. "But please be so good as to tell me why you are so confident? The investigation is in ruins. The official who was leading it has been killed."

"Here in Moscow, my old chap, highly important investigations are never pursued along one line only," Dolgorukoi declared in a didactic tone of voice. "And for that purpose I have a special deputy, my trusted eyes and ears, who is well known to you: Collegiate Counsellor Fandorin. He is close to catching the criminal and in a very short time he will bring the case to a conclusion. Is that not so, Erast Petrovich?"

The Prince turned grandly towards the Collegiate Counsellor, who was sitting by the wall, and only the sharp gaze of the Deputy for Special Assignments could read the despair and entreaty in the protruding, watery eyes of his superior.

Fandorin got to his feet, paused for a moment, and declared dispassionately: "That is the honest truth, Your Excellency. I actually expect to close the case on Sunday."

The minister peered at him sullenly. "You 'expect'? Would you mind giving me a little more detail? What are your theories, conclusions, proposed measures?"

Erast Petrovich did not even glance at Count Tolstoy, but carried on looking at the Governor-General.

"If Vladimir Andreevich orders me to, I will give a full account of everything. But in the absence of such an order, I prefer to maintain confidentiality. I have reason to suppose that at this stage in the investigation increasing the number of people who are aware of the details could be fatal to the operation."

"What?" the minister exploded. "How dare you? You seem to have forgotten who you are dealing with here!"

The gold epaulettes on shoulders from St. Petersburg trembled in indignation. The gold shoulders of the Muscovites shrank in fright.

"Not at all." And now Fandorin looked at the high official from the capital. "You, Your Excellency, are an adjutant-general of the retinue of His Majesty, the Minister of Internal Affairs and Chief of the Corps of Gendarmes. And I serve in the chancellery of the Governor-General of Moscow and so do not happen to be your subordinate by any of the aforementioned lines. Vladimir Andreevich, is it your wish that I should give a full account to the minister of the state of how affairs stand in the investigation?"

Prince Dolgorukoi gave his subordinate a keen look and evidently decided that he might as well be hung for a sheep as a lamb. "Oh, that will do. My dear minister, my old chap, let him investigate as he thinks best. I vouch for Fandorin with my own head. Meanwhile, would you perhaps like to try a little Moscow breakfast? I have the table already laid."

"Well, your head it is, then," Tolstoy hissed menacingly. "As you will. On Sunday at precisely twelve-thirty, everything will be included in my report in the presence of His Imperial Majesty. Including this." The minister got up and stretched his bloodless lips into a smile. "Well now, Your Excellency, I think we can take a little breakfast."

The important man walked towards the door. As he passed Collegiate Counsellor Fandorin, he seared him with a withering glance. The other officials followed him, avoiding Erast Petrovich by as wide a margin as possible.

"What are you thinking of, my dear fellow?" the Governor whispered, hanging back for a moment with his deputy. "Have you taken leave of your senses? That's Tolstoy himself! He's vengeful and he has a long memory. He'll hound you to death; he'll find the opportunity. And I won't be able to protect you."

Fandorin replied directly into his half-deaf patron's ear, also in a whisper: "If I don't close the case before Sunday, neither you nor I will be here much longer. And as for the Count's vengeful nature, please do not be too concerned. Did you see the colour of his face? He won't be needing that long memory of his. Very soon he will be called to report, not to His Imperial Highness, but to a higher authority, the supreme one."

"We all have to tread that path," said Dolgorukoi, crossing himself devoutly. "We only have two days. You pull out all the stops, my dear chap. You'll manage it, eh?"

"I decided to provoke the wrath of that serious gentleman for a very excusable reason, Tulipov. You and I have no working theory. The murder of Izhitsin and his maid Matiushkina changes the whole picture entirely."

Fandorin and Tulipov were sitting in a room for secret meetings located in one of the remote corners of the Governor-General's residence. The strictest instructions had been given that no one was to disturb the Collegiate Counsellor and his assistant. There were papers lying on the table covered in green velvet, and His Excellency's personal secretary was on continuous duty in the reception room outside the closed door, with a senior adjutant, a gendarme officer and a telephone operator with a direct line to the chancellery of the (now, alas, former) High Police Master, the Department of Gendarmes and the district Public Prosecutor (as yet still current). All official structures had been ordered to afford the Collegiate Counsellor the fullest possible cooperation. The Governor-General had taken the care of the formidable minister on his own shoulders—so that he would get in the way as little as possible.

Frol Vedishchev, Prince Dolgorukoi's valet, tiptoed into the study—he'd brought the samovar. He squatted modestly on the edge of a chair and waved his open hand through the air as if to say: I'm not here, gentlemen detectives; don't waste your precious attention on such small fry.

"Yes," sighed Anisii, "nothing's clear at all. How did he manage to reach Izhitsin?"

"Well that's actually no great puzzle. It happened like this . . ." Erast Petrovich strode across the room and took his beads out of his pocket with an accustomed gesture.

Tulipov and Vedishchev waited with bated breath.

"Last night, some time between half past one and two, someone rang the doorbell of Izhitsin's apartment. The doorbell is connected to the bell in the serv-ant's room. Izhitsin lived with his maid, Zinaida Matiushkina, who cleaned the apartment and his clothes and also, according to the statements of servants in the neighbouring apartments, fulfilled other duties of a more intimate character. However, it would seem that the deceased did not allow her into his bed and they slept separately. Which, by the way, corresponds perfectly to Izhitsin's well-known convictions concerning the 'c-cultured' and 'uncultured' classes. On hearing the ring at the door, Matiushkina threw on her shawl over her nightdress, went out into the entrance hall and opened the door. She was killed on the spot, in the entrance hall, by a blow to the heart with a sharp, narrow blade. Then the killer walked quietly though the drawing room and the study into the master's bedroom. He was asleep, there was no light—that was clear from the candle on the bedside table. The criminal appears to have managed without any light, a f-fact which is quite remarkable in itself, since, as you and I saw, it was absolutely dark in the bedroom. Izhitsin was lying on his back, and with a blow from an extremely sharp blade, the killer severed his trachea and his artery. While the dying man wheezed and clutched at his slit throat (you saw that his hand and the cuffs of his nightshirt were covered in blood), the criminal stood to one side and waited, drumming his fingers on the top of the secretaire."

Anisii thought he was already used to everything, but this was too much, even for him. "Oh come on, Chief, that's too much—the bit about the fingers. You told me yourself that when you're reconstructing a crime you mustn't fantasise."

"God forbid, Tulipov; this no fantasy," Erast Petrovich said with a shrug. "Matiushkina really was a careless maid. There is a layer of dust on the top of the secretaire, and it has been marked by the numerous repeated impacts of fingertips. I checked the prints. They are a little blurred, but in any case they are not from Izhitsin's fingers . . . I shall omit the details of the disembowelment. You saw the result of that procedure."

Anisii shuddered and nodded.

"Let me draw your attention once again to the fact that, during the . . . dissection, the Ripper somehow managed without any light. He obviously possesses the rare gift of being able to see in the dark. The criminal left without hurrying: he washed his hands in the washbasin and cleaned up the marks of his dirty feet in the rooms and the entrance hall with a cloth, and very thoroughly too. In general, he did not hurry. The most annoying thing is that everything indicates that you and I reached Vozdvizhenskaya Street only about a quarter of an hour after the killer left." The Collegiate Counsellor shook his head in vexation. "Those are the facts. Now for the questions and the conclusions. I will start with the questions. Why did the maid open the door to the visitor in the middle of the night? We don't know, but there are several possible answers. Was it someone they knew? If it was, then who knew them—the maid or the master? We don't know the answer. It is possible that the person who rang simply said that they had brought an urgent message. In his line of work Izhitsin must have received telegrams and documents at all times of the day and night, so the maid would not have been surprised. To continue. Why was her body not touched? And—even more interestingly—why was the victim a man, the first in all this time?"

"Not the first," Anisii put in. "Remember, there was a male body in the ditch at Bozhedomka too."

It seemed like a useful and pertinent remark, but the Chief merely nodded "yes, yes," without acknowledging Tulipov's retentive memory.

"And now the conclusions. The maid was not killed for the 'idea.' She was killed simply because, as a witness, she had to be disposed of. And so we have a departure from the 'idea' and the murder of a man—and not just any man, but the man leading the investigation into the Ripper. An energetic, cruel man who would stop short at nothing. This is a dangerous turn in the Ripper's career. He is no longer just a maniac who has been driven insane by some morbid fantasy. He is now prepared to kill for new reasons that were previously alien to him—either out of the fear of exposure or c-confidence in his own impunity."

"A fine business," Vedishchev's voice put in. "Streetwalkers won't be enough for this killer now. The terrible things he'll get up to! And I see you gentlemen detectives don't have a single clue to go on. Vladimir Andreevich and I will obviously be moving out of here. The devil take the state service—we could have a fine life in retirement—but Vladimir Andreevich won't be able to bear retirement. Without any work to do he'll just shrivel up and pine away. What a disaster, what a disaster . . ."

The old man sniffed and wiped away a tear with a big pink handkerchief.

"Since you're here, Frol Grigorievich, sit quietly and don't interrupt," Anisii said sternly. He had never before taken the liberty of talking to Vedishchev in that tone, but the Chief had not finished his conclusions yet; on the contrary, he was only just coming to the most important part, and then Vedishchev had stuck his oar in.

"However, at the same time, the departure from the 'idea' is an encouraging symptom," Fandorin said, immediately confirming his assistant's guess. "It is evidence that we have already got very close to the criminal. It is now absolutely clear that he is someone who is informed about the progress of the investigation. More than that, this person was undoubtedly present at Izhitsin's 'experiment.' It was the investigator's first active move, and vengeance followed immediately. What does this mean? That in some way he himself was not aware of, Izhitsin annoyed or frightened the Ripper. Or inflamed his pathological imagination."

As if in confirmation of this thesis, Erast Petrovich clicked his beads three times in a row.

"Who is he? The three suspects from yesterday are under surveillance, but surveillance is not imprisonment under guard. We need to check whether any of them could have evaded the police agents last night. To continue. We ourselves must personally investigate everybody who was present at yesterday's 'investigative experiment.' How many men were there in the morgue?"

Anisii tried to recall. "Well, how many . . . Me, Izhitsin, Zakharov and his assistant, Stenich, Nesvitskaya, that, what's his name, Burylin, then the constables, the gendarmes, and the men from the cemetery. I suppose about a dozen, or maybe more, if you count everybody."

"Count everybody, absolutely everybody," the Chief instructed him. "Sit down and write a list. The names. Your impressions of each one. A psychological portrait. How they behaved during the 'experiment.' The most minute details."

"Erast Petrovich, I don't know all of their names."

"Then find out. Draw up a complete list for me; our Ripper will be on it. That is your task for today; get on with it. And meanwhile I'll check whether any member of our trio could have made a secret nocturnal outing."

It's good to work with clear, definite instructions, when the task is within your ability and its importance is obvious and beyond all doubt.

From the residence the Governor's swift horses carried Tulipov to the Department of Gendarmes, where he had a talk with Captain Zaitsev, the commander of the mobile patrol company, about the two commandeered gendarmes, asking if he'd noticed anything strange about their characters, about their families and their bad habits. Zaitsev began to get alarmed, but Anisii reassured him. He said it was a top-secret and highly important investigation that required special supervision.

Then he drove to Bozhedomka. He called in to say hello to Zakharov, only it would have been better if he hadn't. The unsociable forensic specialist mumbled something unwelcoming and buried his nose in his papers. Grumov was not there.

Anisii also visited the watchman to find out about the gravediggers. He didn't give the Ukrainian any explanations, and the watchman didn't ask any questions—he was a simple man, but he had a certain understanding and tact.

He went to see the gravediggers too, ostensibly to give them a rouble each as a reward for assisting the investigation. He formed his own judgement about both of them. And that was it. It was time to go home and write out his list for the Chief.

When he finished the extensive document, it was already dark. He read it through, mentally picturing each person on it and trying to figure out if he fitted the role of a maniac or not.

The gendarme sergeant-major Siniukhin: an old trooper, a face of stone, eyes like tin—God only knew what he had in his soul.

Linkov. To look at, he wouldn't hurt a fly, but he made a very strange kind of constable. Morbid dreams, wounded pride, suppressed sensuality—there could be anything.

The gravedigger Tikhin Kulkov was an unpleasant character, with his haggard face and pockmarked jaw. What a face that man had—if you met someone like that in a deserted spot, he'd slit your throat without even blinking.

Stop! He'd slit your throat all right, but how could his gnarled and crooked hands manage a scalpel?

Anisii glanced at his list again and gasped. Beads of sweat stood out on his forehead and his throat went dry. Ah, how could he have been so blind? Why hadn't he realised it before? It was as if his eyes had been blinded by a veil. It all fitted! There was only one person in the entire list who could be the Ripper!

He jumped to his feet and dashed off, just as he was, without his cap or his coat, to see the Chief.

Masa was the only person in the outhouse: Erast Petrovich was out and so was Angelina, praying in the church. Yes, of course, today was Good Friday: that was why the church bells were tolling so sadly—for the procession of the Holy Shroud.

Ah, such bad luck! And there was no time to lose! Today's inquiries at Bozhedomka had been a mistake—he must have guessed everything! But perhaps that was for the best? If he'd guessed, then he'd be feeling anxious now, making moves. He had to be tracked down! Friday was almost over; there was only one day left!

Only one consideration made him doubt the correctness of his inspiration, but there was a telephone in the house on Malaya Nikitskaya Street and that helped him resolve it. In the Meshchanskaya police district, which included Bozhedomka, Provincial Secretary Tulipov was well known and, despite the late hour, the reply to the question that was bothering him was given immediately.

The first thing Anisii felt was sharp disappointment: 31 October—that was too early. The last definite London killing had taken place on 9 November, so his theory didn't hold together. But today Tulipov's head was working quite remarkably well—if only it was always like this—and the catch was easily resolved.

Yes, the body of the prostitute Mary Jane Kelly had been discovered on the morning of 9 November, but by that time Jack the Ripper was already crossing the Channel! That killing, the most revolting of them all, could have been his farewell "gift" to London, committed immediately before his departure for the continent. Anisii could check later to find out what time the night train left over there.

After that the whole thing simply fitted together by itself. If the Ripper left London on the evening of 8 November—that is, on 27 October in the Russian style—then he ought to have arrived in Moscow on precisely the thirty-first!

The mistake he and the Chief had made was that, when they checked the police passport offices, they had limited themselves to December and November and not taken the end of October into consideration. That accursed confusion of the two styles of date had thrown them off the track.

And that was it. The theory fitted down to the last jot and tittle.

He went back home for a moment: to put on something warm, get his "Bulldog" and grab a quick bite of bread and cheese—there was no time to have a real supper.

While he was chewing, he listened to Palasha reading the Easter story from the newspaper to Sonya, syllable by syllable. The imbecile was listening intently, with her mouth half open. But who could tell if she really understood very much?

"In the provincial town of N," Palasha read slowly, with feeling, "last year on the eve of the glorious resurrection of Christ, a criminal escaped from the jail. He waited until all the townsfolk had gone to the churches for matins and crept into the apartment of a certain rich old woman who was respected by all, but who had not gone to the service because she was not well, in order to kill her and rob her."

"Ooh!" said Sonya. My goodness, thought Anisii, she understands. And a year ago she wouldn't have understood a thing; she'd have just dozed off.

"At the very moment when the murderer was about to rush at her with an axe in his hand"—the reader lowered her voice dramatically—"the first stroke of the Easter bell rang out. Filled with an awareness of the solemn holiness of that moment, the old woman addressed the criminal with the Christian greeting: 'Christ is arisen, my good man!' This appeal shook the sinner to the very depths of his soul; it illuminated for him the deep abyss into which he had fallen and worked a sudden moral renewal within him. After several moments of difficult internal struggle, he walked over to exchange an Easter kiss with the old woman and then, breaking into uncontrollable sobbing . . ."

Anisii never learned how the story ended, it was time for him to rush away.

About five minutes after he had dashed off at breakneck speed, there was a knock at the door.

"Oh that crazy man," Palasha said with a sigh; "he's probably forgotten his gun again."

She opened the door and saw that it wasn't him. It was dark outside—she couldn't see the face, but he was taller than Anisii. A quiet, friendly voice said: "Good evening, my dear. Look, I wish to bring you joy."

*

When the essential work had been completed—after the scene of the crime had been inspected, the bodies photographed and taken away, there was nothing left to do. And that was when Erast Petrovich began feeling really bad. The detectives had left and he was sitting alone in the small drawing room of Tulipov's modest apartment, gazing in a torpor at the blotches of blood on the cheerful bright-coloured wallpaper, and still he couldn't stop himself trembling. His head felt as empty as a drum.

An hour earlier Erast Petrovich had returned home and immediately sent Masa to fetch Tulipov. Masa had discovered the bloodbath.

At this moment Fandorin was not thinking of kind, affectionate Palasha, or even meek Sonya Tulipova, who had died a terrible death that could not possibly be justified by God or man. In the grief-stricken Erast Petrovich's head there was one short phrase hammering away over and over again: He won't survive this, he won't survive this, he won't survive this. There was no way that poor Tulipov could ever survive this shock. He would never see the nightmarish picture of the vicious mutilation of his sister's body, never see her round eyes opened wide in amazement; but he knew the Ripper's habits, and he would easily be able to imagine what Sonya's death had been like. And that would be the end of Anisii Tulipov, because no normal man could possibly survive something like that happening to people who were near and dear to him.

Erast Petrovich was in an unfamiliar state quite untypical of him: he could not think what to do.

Masa came in. Snuffling, he dragged in a rolled-up carpet and covered the terrible blotches on the floor, then he set about furiously scraping off the blood-stained wallpaper. That was right, the Collegiate Counsellor thought remotely, but it hardly did any good.

After a while Angelina also arrived. She put her hand on Erast Petrovich's shoulder and said: "Anyone who dies a martyr's death on Good Friday will be in the Kingdom of Heaven, at the side of Christ."

"That is no consolation to me," Fandorin said in a dull voice, without turning his head. "And it will hardly be any consolation to Anisii."

But where was Anisii? It was already the middle of the night, and the boy hadn't slept a single wink last night. Masa said he'd called round without his cap, in a great hurry. He hadn't said anything or left a note.

It didn't matter: the later he turned up, the better.

Fandorin's head was absolutely empty. No surmises, no theories, no plans. A day of intensive work had produced very little. The questioning of the detectives who were keeping Nesvitskaya, Stenich, and Burylin under surveillance, together with his own observations, had confirmed that, with a certain degree of cunning and adroitness, any one of the three could have slipped away and come back unnoticed by the police spies.

Nesvitskaya lived in a student hostel on Trubetskaya Street that had four exits or entrances, and the doors carried on banging until the dawn.

Following his nervous fit, Stenich was holed up in the Assuage My Sorrows clinic, to which the detectives had not been admitted. There was no way to check whether he had been sleeping or wandering round the city with a scalpel.

The situation with Burylin was even worse: his house was immense, with sixty windows on the ground floor, half of them concealed by the trees of the garden. The fence was low. It wasn't a house: it was a sieve, full of holes.

It turned out that any one of them could have killed Izhitsin. And the most terrible thing of all was that Erast Petrovich, convinced of the ineffectiveness of the surveillance, had cancelled it altogether. This evening the three suspects had had complete freedom of action!

"Don't despair, Erast Petrovich," said Angelina. "It's a mortal sin, and you especially have no right. Who else will find the killer, this Satan, if you just give up? There is no one apart from you."

Satan, Fandorin thought listlessly. Ubiquitous, could be anywhere, any time, slip in through any opening. Satan changed faces, adopted any appearance, even that of an angel.

An angel. Angelina.

Freed from the control of his torpid spirit, his brain, so accustomed to forming logical constructions, obligingly joined the links up to form a chain.

It could even be Angelina—why couldn't she be Jack the Ripper?

She had been in England the previous year. That was one.

On the evenings when all the killings had taken place, she had been in the church. Supposedly. That was two.

She was studying medicine in a charitable society and already knew how to do many things. They taught them anatomy there too. That was three.

She was an odd individual, not like other women. Sometimes she would give you a look that made your heart skip a beat—but you couldn't tell what she was thinking about at such moments. That was four.

Palasha would have opened the door for her without thinking twice. That was five.

Erast Petrovich shook his head in annoyance, stilling the idling wheels of his insistent logic machine. His heart absolutely refused to contemplate such a theory, and the Wise One had said: "The noble man does not set the conclusions of reason above the voice of the heart." The worst thing was that Angelina was right: apart from him there was no one else to stop the Ripper, and there was very little time left. Only tomorrow. Think, think.

But his attempts to concentrate on the case were frustrated by that stubborn phrase hammering in his head: He won't survive this, he won't survive this.

The time dragged on. The Collegiate Counsellor ruffled up his hair, sometimes began walking around the room, twice washed his hands and face with cold water. He tried to meditate, but immediately abandoned the attempt—it was quite impossible!

Angelina stood by the wall, holding her elbows in her hands, watching with a sad insistence in her huge grey eyes.

Masa was silent too. He sat on the floor with his legs folded together, his round face motionless, his thick eyelids half-closed.

But at dawn, when the street was wreathed in milky mist, there was the sound of hurrying feet on the porch, a determined shove made the unlocked door squeak open, and a gendarme officer came dashing into the room. It was Smolyaninov, a very capable, brisk young second lieutenant, with black eyes and rosy pink cheeks. "Ah, this is where you are!" Smolyaninov said, glad to see Fandorin. "Everybody's been looking for you. You weren't at home or in the department, or on Tverskaya Street! So I decided to come here, in case you were still at the scene of the murders. Disaster, Erast Petrovich! Tulipov has been wounded. Seriously. He was taken to the Mariinskaya Hospital after midnight. We've been looking for you ever since they informed us; just look how much time has gone by . . . Lieutenant-Colonel Svershinsky went to the hospital immediately and all his adjutants were ordered to search for you. What's going on, eh, Erast Petrovich?"

Report by Provincial Secretary A. P. Tulipov
Personal Assistant to Mr. E. P. Fandorin
Deputy for Special Assignments of His Excellency the Governor-General of Moscow

8 APRIL 1889,

HALF PAST THREE IN THE MORNING

I report to your Honour that yesterday evening, while compiling the list of individuals suspected of committing certain crimes of which you are aware, I realised that it was absolutely obvious that the crimes indicated could only have been committed by one person, to whit, the forensic medical expert Egor Willemovich Zakharov.

He is not simply a doctor, but an anatomical pathologist—that is, cutting out the internal organs from human bodies is his standard, everyday work. That is one.

Constant association with corpses could have induced in him an insuperable revulsion for the whole human race, or else, on the contrary, a perverted adoration of the physiological arrangement of the human organism. That is two.

At one time he was a member of the Sadist Circle of medical students, which testifies to the early development of depraved and cruel inclinations. That is three.

Zakharov lives in a public-service apartment at the police forensic morgue at Bozhedomka. Two of the murders (of the spinster Andreichkina and the unidentified beggar girl) were committed close to this place. That is four.

Zakharov often goes to England to visit his relatives, and he was there last year. The last time he came back from Britain was on 31 October last year (11 November in the European style)—that is, he could quite easily have committed the last of the London murders that was undoubtedly the work of Jack the Ripper. That is five.

Zakharov is informed of the progress of the investigation, and in addition, of all the people involved in the investigation, he is the only one who possesses, surgical skills. That is six.

I could carry on, but it is hard for me to breathe and my thoughts are getting confused . . . I had better tell you about recent events.

After not finding Erast Petrovich at home, I decided there was no time to be lost. The day before I had been at Bozhedomka and spoken with the cemetery workers, which could not have escaped Zakharov's notice. It was reasonable to think that he would feel alarmed and give himself away somehow or other. To be on the safe side I took my gun with me—a Bulldog revolver that Mr. Fandorin gave me as a present on my name day last year. That was a wonderful day, one of the best days in my life. But that has nothing to do with this case.

And so, about Bozhedomka. I got there by cab at ten o'clock in the evening; it was already dark. In the wing where the doctor has his quarters there was a light in one window, and I was glad that Zakharov had not run away. There was not a soul around. A dog started barking—they keep a dog on a chain by the chapel there—but I quickly ran across the yard and pressed myself against the wall. The dog went on barking for a while and then stopped. I put a crate by the wall (the window was high off the ground) and cautiously glanced inside. The lighted window was where Zakharov has his study. Looking in, I saw there were papers on the desk and the lamp was lighted. And he was sitting with his back to me, writing something, then tearing it up and throwing the pieces on the floor. I waited there for a long time, at least an hour, and he kept writing and tearing the paper up, writing and tearing it up. I wondered if I should arrest him. But I didn't have a warrant, and what if he was just writing some nonsense or other, or adding up some accounts? At seventeen minutes past ten (I saw the time on the clock), he stood up and went out of the room. He was gone for a long time. He started clattering something about in the corridor, then it went quiet. I hesitated about climbing inside to take a look at his papers, became agitated and let my guard down. Someone struck me in the back with something hot and I banged my forehead against the window sill as well. And then, as I was turning round, there was another burning blow to my side and one to my arm. I had been looking at the light, so I could not see who was there in the darkness, but I hit out with my left hand as Mr. Masa taught me to do, and with my knee as well. I hit something soft. But I was a poor student for Mr. Masa; I shirked my lessons. So that was where Zakharov had gone to from the study. He must have noticed me. When he started back to avoid my blows, I tried to catch up with him, but after I'd run a little distance, I fell down. I got up and fell down again. I took out my Bulldog and fired three shots into the air. I thought perhaps one of the cemetery workers would come running. I should not have fired. That probably only frightened them. I should have used my whistle. I didn't think of it; I was not feeling well. After that I do not remember very much. I crawled on all fours and kept falling. Outside the fence I lay down to rest and I think I fell asleep. When I woke up, I felt cold—very cold, although I had all my warm things on; I had especially put on a woolly jumper under my coat. I took out my watch and looked at it. It was already after midnight. That's it, I thought, the villain has got away. It was only then I remembered about my whistle. I started blowing it. Soon someone came, I could not see who. They carried me. Until the doctor gave me an injection, I was in a kind of mist. But now it's better, you can see. I'm just ashamed of letting the Ripper get away. If only I had paid more attention to Mr. Masa. I tried to do my best, Erast Petrovich. If only I'd listened to Mr. Masa. If only . . .

POSTSCRIPT

At this point the stenographic recording had to be halted, because the injured man, who spoke in a lively and correct fashion at first, began rambling and soon fell into a state of unconsciousness, from which he never emerged.

Dr. K. I. Möbius was also surprised that Mr. Tulipov had held on for so long with such serious wounds and after losing so much blood. Death occurred at approximately six o'clock in the morning and was recorded in the appropriate manner by Dr. Möbius.

Lieutenant-Colonel of the Gendarmes Corps Sverchinsky
Stenographed and transcribed by Collegiate Registrar Arietti

A terrible night.

And the evening had begun so marvellously. The imbecile turned out wonderfully well in death—a real feast for the eyes. After this masterpiece of decorative art, it was pointless to waste any time on the maid, and I left her as she was. A sin, of course, but in any case there would never have been the same staggering contrast between external ugliness and internal Beauty.

My heart was warmed most of all by the awareness of a good deed accomplished: not only had I shown the youth the true face of Beauty, I had also relieved him of a heavy burden that prevented him from making his own life more comfortable.

And then it all finished so tragically.

The good young man was destroyed by his own ugly trade—sniffing things out, tracking people down. He came to his own death. I am not to blame for that.

I felt sorry for the boy and that led to sloppy work. My hand trembled. The wounds are fatal, there is no doubt about that: I heard the air rush out of a punctured lung, and the second blow must have cut through the left kidney and the descending colon. But he must have suffered a lot before he died. This thought gives me no peace.

I feel ashamed. It is inelegant.

CHAPTER 8

A Busy Day

Holy Week Saturday, 8 April

The investigative group loitered at the gates of the wretched Bozhedomka Cemetery in the wind and the repulsive fine drizzle: Senior Detective Lyalin, three junior detectives, a photographer with a portable American Kodak, the photographer's assistant, and a police dog-handler with the famous sniffer-dog Musya, known to the whole of Moscow, on a lead. The group had been summoned to the scene of the previous night's incident by telephone and given the strictest possible instructions not to do anything until His Honour Mr. Collegiate Counsellor arrived, and they were now following their instructions strictly—doing nothing and shivering in the chilly embrace of the unseasonable April morning. Even Musya, who was so damp that she looked like a reddish-brown mop, was in low spirits. She lay down with her long muzzle on the soaking earth, wiggled her whitish eyebrows dolefully and even whined quietly once or twice, catching the general mood.

Lyalin, an experienced detective and a man who had been around a lot in general, was inclined by nature to scorn the caprices of nature and he wasn't bothered by the long wait. He knew that the Deputy for Special Assignments was in the Mariinskaya Hospital at that moment, where they were washing and dressing the poor wounded body of the servant of God Anisii, in recent times the Provincial Secretary Tulipov. Mr. Fandorin was saying goodbye to his well-loved assistant; he would make the sign of the cross and then dash over to Bozhedomka in no time. It was only a five-minute journey anyway, and he presumed that the Collegiate Counsellor's horses were a cut above the old police nags.

No sooner had Lyalin had this thought than he saw a four-in-hand of handsome trotters with white plumes hurtling towards the wrought-iron gates of the cemetery. The coachman looked like a general, all covered in gold braid, and the carriage was resplendent, with its gleaming wet black lacquer and the Dolgorukoi crest on the doors.

Mr. Fandorin jumped down to the ground, the soft springs swayed, and the carriage drove off to one side. It was evidently going to wait.

The newly arrived Chief was pale-faced and his eyes were burning brighter than usual, but Lyalin's keen eyes failed to discern any other signs of the shocks and sleepless nights that Fandorin had endured. On the contrary, he actually had the impression that the Deputy for Special Assignments' movements were considerably more sprightly and energetic than usual. Lyalin was about to offer his condolences, but then he looked a little more closely at His Honour's compressed lips and changed his mind. Extensive police experience had taught him it was best to avoid snivelling and just get on with the job.

"No one's been in Zakharov's apartment without you, according to instructions received. The employees have been questioned, but none of them has seen the doctor since yesterday evening. They're waiting over there."

Fandorin glanced briefly in the direction of the morgue building, where several men were waiting, shifting from one foot to the other. "I thought I made it clear: don't do anything. All right, let's go."

Out of sorts, Lyalin decided. Which was hardly surprisingly in such sad circumstances. The man was threatened with the ruin of his career and now there was this upsetting business with Tulipov.

The Collegiate Counsellor ran lightly up on to the porch of Zakharov's wing and pushed at the door. It didn't yield—it was locked.

Lyalin shook his head—Dr. Zakharov was a thorough man, very neat and tidy. Even when he was making good his escape he hadn't forgotten to lock the door. A man like that wouldn't leave any stupid tracks or clues.

Without turning round, Fandorin snapped his fingers and the senior detective understood him without any need for words. He took a set of lock-picks out of his pocket, chose one that was the right length for the key, twisted and turned it for a minute or so, and the door opened.

The Chief walked swiftly round all the rooms, throwing out curt instructions as he went; his usual mild stammer had disappeared somehow, as if it had never existed. "Check the clothes in the wardrobe. List them. Determine what is missing . . . Put all the medical instruments, especially the surgical ones, over there, on the table . . . There was a rug in the corridor—see that rectangular mark on the floor. Where has it gone to? Find it! What's this, the study? Collect all the papers. Pay especially close attention to fragments and scraps."

Lyalin looked around and didn't see any scraps. The study appeared to be in absolutely perfect order. The agent was amazed once again by the fugitive doctor's strong nerve. He'd tidied everything up as neatly as if he were expecting guests. What scraps would there be here?

But just then the Collegiate Counsellor bent down and picked up a small, crumpled piece of paper from under a chair. He unfolded it, read it, and handed it to Lyalin.

"Keep it."

There were only three words on the piece of paper: "*longer remain silent.*"

"Start the search," Fandorin ordered and went outside.

Five minutes later, having divided up the sectors of the search among the detectives, Lyalin looked out of the window and saw the Collegiate Counsellor and Musya creeping through the bushes. Branches had been broken off and the ground had been trampled. That must be where the late Tulipov had grappled with the criminal. Lyalin sighed, crossed himself and set about sounding out the walls of the bedroom.

The search did not produce anything of great interest. A pile of letters in English—evidently from Zakharov's relatives: Fandorin glanced through them rapidly, but didn't read them; he only paid attention to the dates. He jotted something down in his notebook, but didn't say anything out loud.

Detective Sysuev distinguished himself by discovering another scrap of paper, a bit bigger than the first, in the study, but its inscription was even less intelligible: "*erations of esprit de corps and sympathy for an old com.*"

For some reason the Collegiate Counsellor found this bit of nonsense interesting. He also looked very closely at the Colt revolver discovered in a drawer of the writing desk. The revolver had been loaded quite recently—there were traces of fresh oil on the drum and the handle. Then why hadn't Zakharov taken it with him, Lyalin wondered? Had he forgotten it, then? Or deliberately left it behind? But why?

Musya disgraced herself. Despite the mire, she went dashing after the scent pretty smartly, but then a massive, shaggy dog came flying out from behind the fence and started barking so fiercely that Musya squatted down on her hind legs and backed away, and after that it proved impossible to shift her from that spot. They put the watchman's dog back on its chain, but Musya had lost all her spirit. Sniffer-dogs are nervous creatures; they have to be in the right mood.

"Which of them is which?" Fandorin asked, pointing through the window at the cemetery employees.

Lyalin began reporting: "The fat one in the cap is the supervisor. He lives outside the cemetery and has nothing to do with the work of the police morgue. Yesterday he left at half past five and he came this morning a quarter of an hour before you arrived. The tall consumptive-looking one is Zakharov's assistant; his name's Grumov. He's just got here from home recently as well. The one with his head lowered is the watchman. The other three are labourers. They dig the graves, mend the fence, take out the rubbish and so on. The watchman and the labourers live here and could have heard something. But we haven't questioned them in detail, since we were told not to."

The Collegiate Counsellor talked with the employees himself. He called them into the building and first of all showed them the Colt: "Do you recognise it?"

The assistant Grumov and the watchman Pakhomenko testified (Lyalin wrote in his notes) that they were familiar with the weapon—they had seen it, or one just like it, in the doctor's apartment. However, the gravedigger Kulkov testified that he had never seen any "revolvert" close up, but the previous month he had gone to watch the "doctur" shooting rooks, and he had done it very tidily: every time he fired, rooks' feathers went flying.

The three shots fired last night by Provincial Secretary Tulipov had been heard by the watchman Pakhomenko and the labourer Khriukin. Kulkov had been in a drunken sleep and the noise had not wakened him.

Those who had heard the shots said they'd been afraid to go outside—how could you tell who might be wandering about in the middle of the night?—and they apparently had not heard any cries for help. Soon afterwards Khriukin had gone back to sleep, but Pakhomenko had stayed awake. He said that shortly after the shooting a door had slammed loudly and someone had walked rapidly towards the gates.

"What, were you listening then?" Fandorin asked the watchman.

"Of course I was," Pakhomenko replied. "There was shooting. And I sleep badly at nights. All sorts of thoughts come into my head. I was tossing and turning until first light. Tell me, *pan* general, has that young lad really passed away? He was so sharp-eyed, and he was kind with simple folk."

The Collegiate Counsellor was known always to be polite and mild-mannered with his subordinates, but today Lyalin could barely recognise him. The Chief gave no reply to the watchman's touching words and showed no interest at all in Pakhomenko's nocturnal thoughts. He swung round sharply and spoke curtly over his shoulder to the witnesses: "You can go. No one is to leave the cemetery. But you, Grumov, be so good as to stay."

Well, he was like a totally different man.

The doctor's assistant blinked in fright as Fandorin asked him: "What was Zakharov doing yesterday evening? In detail, please."

Grumov shrugged and spread his hands guiltily: "I couldn't say. Yesterday Egor Willemovich was badly out of sorts; he kept cursing all the time, and after lunch he told me to go home. So I went. We didn't even say goodbye—he locked himself in his study."

"'After lunch'—what time is that?"

"After three, sir."

"'After three, sir,'" the Collegiate Counsellor repeated, shaking his head for some reason, and clearly losing all interest in the consumptive morgue assistant. "You can go."

Lyalin approached the Collegiate Counsellor and delicately cleared his throat. "I've jotted down a verbal portrait of Zakharov. Would you care to take a look?"

Fandorin didn't even glance at the excellently composed description; he just waved it away. It was rather upsetting to see such a lack of respect for professional zeal.

"That's all," Fandorin said curtly. "There's no need to question anyone else. You, Lyalin, go to the Assuage My Sorrows Hospital in Lefortovo and bring the male nurse Stenich to me on Tverskaya Street. And Sysuev can go to the Yakimanka Embankment and bring the factory-owner Burylin. Urgently."

"But what about the verbal portrait of Zakharov?" Lyalin asked, his voice trembling. "I expect we're going to put him on the wanted list, aren't we?"

"No, we're not," Fandorin replied absent-mindedly, and strode off rapidly towards his wonderful carriage, leaving the experienced detective totally bemused.

Vedishchev was waiting in the Collegiate Counsellor's office on Tverskaya Street. "The final day," Dolgorukoi's "grey cardinal" said sternly instead of saying hello. "We have to find that crazy Englishman. Find him and then report it, all right and proper. Otherwise you know what will happen."

"And how do you come to know about Zakharov, Frol Grigorievich?" Fandorin asked, although he didn't seem particularly surprised.

"Vedishchev knows everything that happens in Moscow."

"We should have included you in the list of suspects, then. You put His Excellency's cupping jars on and even let his blood, don't you? So practising medicine is nothing new to you." The joke, however, was made in a flat voice and it was clear that Fandorin was thinking about something quite different.

"Poor old Anisii, eh?" Vedishchev sighed. "That's really terrible, that is. He was a bright lad, our shorty. He should have gone a long way, from all the signs."

"I wish you would go to your own room, Frol Grigorievich," was the Collegiate Counsellor's reply to that. He was clearly not inclined to indulge in sentimentality today.

The valet knitted his grey eyebrows in a frown of annoyance and changed to an official tone of voice: "I have been ordered to inform Your Honour that the Minister of the Interior left for St. Petersburg this morning in a mood of great dissatisfaction and before he left he was being very threatening. I was also ordered to inquire if the inquiry will soon be closed."

"Soon. Tell His Excellency that I need to carry out just two more interrogations, receive one telegram, and make a little excursion."

"Erast Petrovich, in Christ's name, will you manage it before tomorrow?" Vedishchev asked imploringly. "Or we're all done for."

Fandorin had no time to reply to the question, because there was a knock at the door and the duty adjutant announced: "The prisoners Stenich and Burylin have been delivered. They are being kept in separate rooms, as ordered."

"Bring Stenich in first," Erast Petrovich told the officer, and pointed the valet towards the door with his chin. "This is the first interrogation. That's all, Frol Grigorievich—go, I have no more time."

The old man nodded his bald head submissively and hobbled towards the door. In the doorway he collided with a wild-looking man—skinny and jittery with long hair—but he didn't stare at him. He shuffled off rapidly along the corridor in his felt shoes, turned a corner and unlocked a closet with a key.

But it turned out not to be any ordinary closet: it had a concealed door in the inside corner. Behind the little door there was another small closet. Frol Grigorievich squeezed into it, sat down on a chair with a comfortable cushion on it, silently slid opened a small shutter in the wall and suddenly he was looking though glass at the whole of the secret study, and he could hear Erast Petrovich's slightly muffled voice: "Thank you. For the time being you'll have to stay at the police station. For your own safety."

The valet put on a pair of spectacles with thick lenses and pressed his face up close to the secret opening, but he only saw the back of the man leaving the room. So that was an interrogation, was it?—it hadn't even lasted three minutes. Vedishchev grunted sceptically and waited to see what would come next.

"Send in Burylin," Fandorin ordered the adjutant.

A man with a fat Tatar face and insolent eyes came in. Without waiting to be invited, he sat down on a chair, crossed his legs and began swinging his expensive cane with a gold knob. It was obvious straight away that he was a millionaire.

"Well, are you going to take me to look at offal again?" the millionaire asked merrily. "Only you won't catch me out like that. I have a thick skin. Who was that who went out? Vanka Stenich, wasn't it? Ooh, he turned his face away. As if he'd not had plenty of pickings from Burylin. He rode around Europe on my money, and he lived as my house guest. I felt sorry for him, the poor unfortunate. But he abused my hospitality. Ran away from me to England. Began to despise me— I was dirty and he decided he wanted a clean life. Well, let him go; he's a hopeless man—a genuine psychiatric case. Will you permit me to smoke a small cigar?"

All of the millionaire's questions went unanswered. Instead, Fandorin asked his own question, which Vedishchev didn't understand at all. "At your meeting of fellow-students there was a man with long hair, rather shabby. Who is he?"

But Burylin understood the question and answered it willingly: "Filka Rozen. He was thrown out of the medical faculty with me and Stenich, distinguished himself with honours in the line of immoral behaviour. He works as an assessor in a pawn shop. And he drinks, of course."

"Where can I find him?"

"You won't find him anywhere. Before you came calling, like a fool I gave him five hundred roubles—turned sloppy in my old age, thinking of the old days. Until he's drunk it all to the last kopeck, he won't show up. Maybe he's living it up in some tavern in Moscow, or maybe in Peter, or maybe in Nizhny. That's the kind of character he is."

For some reason this news made Fandorin extremely upset. He even jumped up off his chair, pulled those round green beads on a string out of his pocket and put them back again.

The man with the fat face observed the Collegiate Counsellor's strange behaviour with curiosity. He took out a fat cigar, lit it and scattered the ash on the carpet, the insolent rogue. But he didn't start asking questions; he waited.

"Tell me: why were you, Stenich, and Rozen thrown out of the faculty, while Zakharov was only transferred to the anatomical pathology department?" Fandorin asked after a lengthy pause.

"It depended on who got up to how much mischief," Burylin said with a laugh. "Sotsky, the biggest hothead amongst us, actually got sent to a punitive battalion. I felt sorry for the old dog; he had imagination, even if he was a rogue. I was under threat too, but it was all right: money got me out of it." He winked a wild eye and puffed out cigar smoke. "The girl students, our jolly companions, got it in the neck too—just for belonging to the female sex. They were sent to Siberia, under police surveillance. One became a morphine addict, another married a priest—I made inquiries." The millionaire laughed. "And at that time Zakharka the Englishman wasn't really outstanding in any way—that's why he got off with a lesser punishment. 'He was present and did not stop it'—that's what the verdict said."

Fandorin snapped his fingers as if he had just received a piece of good news that he'd been expecting for ages, but then Burylin took a piece of paper folded into four out of his pocket.

"It's odd that you should ask about Zakharov. This morning I received a very strange note from him, just a moment before your dogs arrived to take me away. A street urchin brought it. Here, read it."

Frol Grigorievich twisted himself right round and flattened his nose against the glass, but there was no point—he couldn't read the letter from a distance. Only it was clear from all the signs that this was a highly important piece of paper. Erast Petrovich's eyes were glued to it.

"I'll give him some money, of course," said the millionaire. "Only there wasn't any special 'old friendship' between the two of us; he's just being sentimental there. And what kind of melodrama is this: 'Please remember me kindly, my brother'? What has he been up to, our Pluto? Did he dine on those girls that were lying on the tables in the morgue the other day?" Burylin threw his head back and laughed, delighted with his joke.

Fandorin was still examining the note. He walked across to the window, lifted the sheet of paper higher, and Vedishchev saw the scrawling, uneven lines of writing.

"Yes, it's such terrible scribble you can hardly even read it," the millionaire said in his deep voice, looking round for somewhere to put the cigar he had finished smoking. "As if it was written in a carriage or with a serious hangover."

He didn't find anywhere. He almost threw it to the floor, but decided not to; he cast a guilty glance at the Collegiate Counsellor's back, wrapped the stub in his handkerchief and put it in his pocket. That's right.

"You can go, Burylin," Erast Petrovich said without turning round. "Until tomorrow you will remain under guard."

The millionaire was highly incensed at that news. "I've had enough; I've already spent one night feeding your police bedbugs! They're vicious beasts, and hungry. The way they threw themselves on an Orthodox believer's body!"

Fandorin wasn't listening. He pressed the bell button. The gendarme officer came in and dragged the rich man towards the door.

"But what about Zakharka?" Burylin shouted. "He'll be calling for the money!"

"That's no concern of yours," said Erast Petrovich, and he asked the officer: "Has the reply to my inquiry arrived from the ministry?"

"Yes, sir."

"Let me have it."

The gendarme brought in some kind of telegram and went back out into the corridor.

The telegram produced a remarkable effect on Fandorin. He read it, threw it on to the desk and then suddenly did something very strange. He clapped his hands very quickly several times, and so loudly that Vedishchev banged his head against the glass in his surprise, and the gendarme, the adjutant, and the secretary stuck their heads in at the door all at once.

"It's all right, gentlemen," Fandorin reassured them. "It's a Japanese exercise for focusing one's thoughts. Please go."

And then even more wonders followed.

When the door closed behind his subordinates, Erast Petrovich suddenly started to get undressed. When he was left in just his underclothes, he took a travelling bag that Vedishchev hadn't noticed before out from under the desk and took a bundle out of the bag. The bundle contained clothes: tight striped trousers with footstraps, a cheap paper shirt-front, a crimson waistcoat and yellow check jacket.

The highly respectable Collegiate Counsellor was transformed into a pushy jerk, the kind that hover around the street girls in the evenings. He stood in front of the mirror, exactly a yard in front of Frol Vedishchev, combed his black hair into a straight parting, plastered it with brilliantine and coloured the grey at his temples. He twisted the ends of his slim moustache upwards and shaped them into two sharp points. (Bohemian wax, Frol Vedishchev guessed—he secured Prince Dolgorukoi's sideburns in exactly the same way, so that they stuck out like eagles' wings.)

Then Fandorin put something into his mouth and grinned, and a gold cap glinted on one tooth. He carried on pulling faces for a while and seemed perfectly content with his appearance.

The Yuletide masker took a small wallet out of the bag, opened it, and Vedishchev saw that it was no ordinary wallet: inside it he could see a small-calibre burnished steel gun barrel and a little drum like the one on a revolver. Fandorin put five shells into the drum, clicked the lid shut and tested the resistance of the lock with his finger—no doubt the lock played the role of a trigger. What will they think of next for killing a man? the valet thought, with a shake of his head. And where are you going dressed like a cheap dandy, Erast Petrovich?

As if he had heard the question, Fandorin turned towards the mirror and put on a beaver-fur cap, tilted at a dashing angle, winked familiarly and said in a low voice: "Frol Grigorievich, light a candle for me at vespers. I won't get by without God's help today."

Ineska was suffering very badly, in body and in spirit—in body, because last night Slepen, her former ponce, had waited for the poor girl outside the City of Paris tavern and given her a thorough beating for betraying him. At least the creep hadn't rearranged her face. But her stomach and sides were battered black and blue—she couldn't even turn over at night; she just lay there shifting about until morning, gasping and feeling sorry for herself. The bruises weren't the worst thing—they'd heal up soon enough, but poor Ineska's little heart was aching so badly she could hardly stand it.

Her boyfriend had disappeared, her fairy-tale prince, the handsome Erastushka; he hadn't shown his sweet face for two days now. And Slepen was as brutal as ever and always making threats. Yesterday she'd had to give her old pimp almost everything she earned, and that was no good; decent girls who stayed faithful didn't do that.

Erastushka had gone missing; that lop-eared short-arse must have handed him over to the police and her pretty dove was sitting in the lock-up in the first Arbat station, the toughest in the whole of Moscow. If only she could send her darling a present, but that Sergeant Kulebyako there was a wild beast. He'd put her inside again, the same as last year, threaten to take away her yellow ticket, and then she'd end up servicing the whole police district for free, down to the last snot-nosed constable. It still made her sick to remember it, even now. Ineska would gladly have accepted that kind of humiliation if she could just help her sweetheart, but after all, Era-stushka wasn't just any boyfriend: he had brains, he was nice and clean, choosy; he wouldn't want to touch Ineska after that. Not that their passion had actually come to anything yet, so to speak; love was only just beginning, but from the very first glance Ineska had taken such a fancy to his lovely blue eyes and white teeth, she'd really fallen for him; terrible it was, worse than with that hairdresser Zhorzhik when she was sixteen, rot his pretty face, the lousy snake—if he hadn't drunk himself to death by now, of course.

Ah, if only he'd show up soon, her sweet honey-bunch. He'd put that vicious bastard Slepen in his place and he'd be sweet and gentle with Ineska, pamper her a bit. She'd found out what he'd told her to, and hidden some money in her garter too—three and a half roubles in silver. He'd be pleased; she had something to greet him and treat him with.

Erastik. It was such a sweet name, like apple jam. Her darling's real name was probably something simpler, but then Ineska hadn't been a Spanish girl all her life either; she'd been born into God's world as Efrosinya, plain simple Froska in the family.

Inessa and Erast—that had a real ring to it, like music it was. If only she could stroll arm-in-arm with him through Grachyovka, so that Sanka Myasnaya, Liudka Kalancha, and especially that Adelaidka could see what a fine fancy-man Ineska had, and turn green with envy.

After that, they'd come to her apertiment. It might be small, but it was clean, and stylish too: pictures from fashion magazines stuck on the walls, a velvet lampshade, and a big, tall mirror; the softest down mattress ever, and lots of pillows, a whole seven of them—Ineska had sewn all the pillowcases herself.

Then, just as she was thinking her very sweetest thoughts, her cherished dream came true. First there was a tactful knock at the door—tap-tap-tap—and then Erastushka came in, in his beaver-fur cap and white muffler, with his wool-cloth coat with the beaver collar, hanging open. You'd never think he was from the Kutuzka jail.

Ineska's little heart just stood still. She leapt up off the bed just as she was, in her cotton nightshirt, with her hair hanging loose, and threw herself on her sweetheart's neck. She only managed to kiss his lips once; then he took hold of her by the shoulders and sat her down at the table. He looked at her sternly.

"Right, tell me," he said.

Ineska understood—those vicious tongues had already been wagging.

She didn't try to deny anything; she wanted everything to be honest between them. "Beat me," she said, "beat me, Erastushka; I'm to blame. Only I'm not all that much to blame—don't you go believing just anyone. Slepen tried to force me" (she was fibbing there, of course, but not so much really) "and I wouldn't give him it, and he gave me a real battering. Here, look."

She pulled up her shirt and showed him the blue, crimson, and yellow patches. So he would feel sorry for her.

But it didn't soften him. Erastushka frowned. "I'll have a word with Slepen afterwards; he won't bother you again. Get back to the point. Did you find who I told you to?—the one who went with that friend of yours and barely came out alive?

"I did, Erastushka, I found her; Glashka's her name. Glashka Beloboka from Pankratievsky Lane. She remembers the bastard all right—he nearly slit her throat open with that knife of his. Glashka still wraps a scarf round her neck, even now."

"Take me to her."

"I will, Erastushka, I'll take you, but let's have a bit of cognac first." She took a bottle she'd been keeping out of the little cupboard, put her bright-coloured Persian shawl on her shoulders and picked up a comb to fluff up her hair and make it all glossy.

"We'll have a drink later. I told you: take me there. Business first."

Ineska sighed, feeling her heart melting: she loved strict men—couldn't help herself. She went over and looked up into his beautiful face, his angry eyes, his curly moustache. "I think my legs are giving are giving way, Erastushka," she whispered faintly.

But today wasn't Ineska's day for kissing and cuddling. There was a sudden crash and a clatter from a blow that almost knocked the door off its hinges, and there was Slepen standing in the doorway, evil drunk, with a vicious grin on his smarmy face. Oh the neighbours, those lousy Grachyovka rats, they'd told on her; they hadn't wasted any time.

"Lovey-doving?" he grinned. "Forgotten about me, the poor orphan, have you?" Then the grin vanished from his rotten mug and his shaggy eyebrows moved together. "I'll talk to you, Ineska, afterwards, you louse. Seems like you didn't learn your lesson. And as for you, mate, come out in the yard and we'll banter."

Ineska rushed to the window—there were two of them in the yard: Slepen's stooges, Khryak and Mogila.

"Don't go!" she shouted. "They'll kill you! Go away, Slepen, I'll make such a racket all Grachyovka'll come running"—and she had already filled her lungs with air to let out a howl; but Erastushka stopped her.

"Don't, Ineska, you heard what he said; let me have a talk with the man."

"Erastik, Mogila carries a sawn-off under his coat," Ineska explained to the dimwit. "They'll shoot you. Shoot you and dump you in the sewer. They've done it before."

But her boyfriend wouldn't listen; he wasn't interested. He took a big wallet out of his pocket, tortoiseshell. " 'Salright," he said. "I'll buy 'em off." And he went out with Slepen, to certain death.

Ineska collapsed face down into the seven pillows and started whimpering—about her malicious fate, about her dream that hadn't come true, about the constant torment.

Out in the yard there were one, two, three, four quick shots, and then someone started howling—not just one person, a whole choir of them.

Ineska stopped whimpering and looked at the icon of the Mother of God in the corner, decorated for Easter with paper flowers and little coloured lamps. "Mother of God," Ineska asked her, "work a miracle for Easter Sunday and let

Erastushka be alive. It's all right if he's wounded; I'll nurse him well. Just let him be alive."

The Heavenly Mediatress took pity on Ineska—the door creaked and Erastik came in. And not even wounded—he was as right as rain, and his lovely scarf hadn't even shifted a bit.

"There, I told you, Ineska; wipe that wet off your face. Slepen won't touch you any more; he can't. I put holes in both his grabbers. And the other two won't forget in a hurry either. Get dressed and take me to this Glashka of yours."

And that dream of Ineska's did come true after all. She went strolling through the whole of Grachyovka on her prince's arm—she deliberately led him the long way round, though it was quicker to get to the Vladimir Road tavern, where Glashka lived, through the yards, across the rubbish tip and through the knacker's yard. Ineska had dressed herself up in her little velvet jacket and batiste blouse, and she'd put on her crêpe-lizette skirt for the first time and even her boots that were only for dry weather—she didn't care. She powdered her face that was puffy from crying and backcombed her fringe. All in all, there was plenty to turn Sanka and Liudka green. It was just a pity they didn't meet Adelaidka; never mind, her girlfriends would give her the picture.

Ineska still couldn't get enough of looking at her darling, she kept looking into his face and chattering away like a magpie: "She has a daughter, Glashka does— a real fright she is. That's what the good folks told me: 'You ask for the Glashka with the ugly daughter.'"

"Ugly? What way is she ugly?"

"She has this birthmark that covers half her face—wine colour; it's a real nightmare. I'd rather put my head in a noose than walk around looking like that. In the next house to us, there was this Nadka used to live there, a tailor's daughter . . ." But before she had time to tell him about Nadka, they'd already reached the Vladimir Road. They walked up the creaking staircase where the rooms were.

Glashka's room was lousy, not a patch on Ineska's apertiment. Glashka was there, putting on her make-up in front of the mirror—she was going out to work the street soon.

"Look, Glafira, I've brought a good man to see you. Tell him what he asks about that evil bastard that cut you," Ineska instructed her, then sat sedately in the corner.

Erastik immediately put a three-rouble note on the table. "That's yours, Glashka, for your trouble. What sort of man was he? What did he look like?"

Glashka was a good-looking girl, though in her strict way Ineska thought she didn't keep herself clean. She didn't even look at the money.

"Everyone knows his kind: crazy," she answered and wiggled her shoulders this way and that.

She stuck the money up her skirt anyway—not that she was that interested, just to be polite. And she stared at Erast that hard, ran her peepers all over him, the shameless hussy, that Ineska's heart started fluttering.

"Men are always interested in me," Glashka said modestly, to start her story. "But that time I was really low. At Shrovetide I got these scabs all over my face, so bad I was scared to look in the mirror. I walked and walked and no one took any interest; I'd have been happy to do it for fifteen kopecks. That one's a big eater"—she nodded towards the curtain, from behind which they could hear the sound of sleepy snuffling. "Plain terrible, it is. And anyway, this one comes up, very polite, he was——"

"That's right, that was the way he came up to me too," Ineska put in, feeling jealous. "And just think, my face was all scratched and battered then too. I had a fight with that bitch Adelaidka. No one would come near me, no matter what I said, but this one comes up all on his own. 'Don't be sad,' he says, 'now I'll give you joy.' Only I didn't do like Glashka did, I didn't go with him, because . . ."

"I heard that already," Erastik interrupted her. "You didn't get a proper sight of him. Keep quiet. Let Glafira talk."

Glashka flashed her eyes, proud-like, at Ineska, and Ineska felt really bad. And it was her own stupid fault, wasn't it?—she'd brought him here herself.

"And he says to me: 'Why such a long face? Come with me,' he says. 'I want to bring you joy.' Well, I was feeling happy enough already. I'm thinking, I'll get a rouble here, or maybe two, I'll buy Matryoshka some bread, and some pies. Oh, I bought them all right, didn't I? . . . had to pay the doctor a fiver afterwards, to have my neck stitched up."

She pointed to her neck, and there, under the powder, was a crimson line, smooth and narrow, like a thread.

"Tell me everything in the right order," Era-stushka told her.

"Well, then, we come in here. He sat me on the bed—this one here—puts one hand on my shoulder and keeps the other behind his back. And he says—his voice is soft, like a woman's—'Do you think,' he says, 'that you're not beautiful?' So I blurts out: 'I'm just fine, the face will heal up all right. It's my daughter that's disfigured for the rest of her life.' He says, 'What daughter's that?' 'Over there,' I say, 'take a look at my little treasure,' and I pulled back the curtain. As soon as he saw my Matryoshka—and she was sleeping then too; she's a sound sleeper, used to anything, she is—he started trembling, like, all over. And he says, 'I'll make her into such a lovely beauty. And it'll make things easier for you too.' I look a bit closer, and I can see he has something in his fist, behind his back, glinting like. Holy Mother, it was a knife! Sort of narrow and short."

"A scalpel?" Erastik asked, using a word they didn't understand.

"Eh?"

He just waved his hand: Come on, tell me more.

"I give him such a clout and I start yelling: 'Help! Murder!' He looked at me, and his face was terrible, all twisted. 'Quiet, you fool! You don't understand your own happiness!' And then he slashes at me! I jumped back, but even so he caught me across the throat. Well then I howled so loud, even Matryoshka woke up. Then she starts in wailing, and she's got a voice like a cat in heat in March. And he just turned and scarpered. And that's the whole adventure. It was the Holy Virgin saved me."

Glashka made the sign of the cross over her forehead and then straight off, before she'd even lowered her hands, she asked: "And you, good sir, you're interested for business, are you, or just in general?" And she fluttered her eyelids, the snake.

But Erast told her, strict-like: "Describe him to me, Glafira. What does he look like, this man?"

"Ordinary. A bit taller than me, shorter than you. He'd be up to here on you." And she drew her finger across the side of Erastushka's head, real slow. Some people have no shame!

"His face is ordinary too. Clean, no moustache or beard. I don't know what else. Show him to me, and I'll recognise him straight away."

"We'll show him to you, we will," Ineska's sweet darling muttered, wrinkling up his clear forehead and trying to figure something out. "So he wanted to make things easier for you?"

"For that kind of help I'd unwind the evil bastard's guts with my bare hands," Glashka said in a calm, convincing voice. "Lord knows, we need the freaks too. Let my Matryoshka live—what's it to him?"

"And from the way he talked, who is he—a gentleman or a working man? How was he dressed?"

"You couldn't tell from his clothes. Could have worked in a shop, or maybe some kind of clerk. But he spoke like a gent. I remembered one thing. When he looked at Matryoshka, he said to himself: 'That's not ringworm, it's a rare nevus matevus.' Nevus matevus—that's what he called my Matryoshka; I remembered that."

"Nevus maternus," Erastik said, putting her right. "In doctor's talk that means 'birth mark.'"

He knows everything, he's so bright.

"Erastik, let's go, eh?" Ineska said, touching her sweetheart's sleeve. "The cognac's still waiting."

"Why go?" that cheeky bitch Glashka piped up. "Since you're already here. I can find some cognac for a special guest, it's Shutov; I've been keeping it for Easter. So what's that your name is, you handsome man?"

Masahiro Shibata was sitting in his room, burning incense sticks and reading sutras in memory of the servant of the state Anisii Tulipov, who had departed this world in such an untimely fashion, his sister Sonya-san and the maid Palashka, whom the Japanese had his own special reasons to mourn.

Masa had arranged the room himself, spending no small amount of time and money on it. The straw mats that covered the floor had been brought on a steamboat all the way from Japan, and they had immediately made the room sunny and golden, and the floor had a jolly spring under your feet, not like stomping across cold, dead parquet made out of stupid oak. There was no furniture at all, but a spacious cupboard with a sliding door had been built into one of the walls, to hold a padded blanket and a pillow, as well as the whole of Masa's wardrobe: a cotton yukata robe, broad white cotton trousers and a similar jacket for rensu, two three-piece suits, for winter and summer, and the beautiful green livery that the Japanese servant respected so very much and only wore on special festive or solemn occasions. On the walls to delight the eye there were coloured lithographs of Tsar Alexander and Emperor Mutsuhito. And hanging in the corner, under the altar shelf, there was a scroll with an ancient wise saying: "Live correctly and regret nothing." Standing on the altar today there was a photograph: Masa and Anisii Tulipov in the Zoological Gardens. It had been taken the previous summer: Masa in his sandy-coloured summer suit and bowler hat, looking serious,

Anisii with his mouth stretched into a smile that reached the ears sticking out from under his cap, and behind them an elephant with ears just the same, except that they were a bit bigger.

Masa was distracted from mournful thoughts on the vanity of the search for harmony and the fragility of the world by the telephone.

Fandorin's servant walked to the entrance hall through the dark, empty rooms—his master was somewhere in the city, looking for the murderer, in order to exact vengeance; his mistress had gone to the church and would probably not be back soon because tonight was the main Russian festival of Easter.

"Harro," Masa said into the round bell mouth. "This is Mista Fandorin's number. Who is speaking?"

"Mr. Fandorin, is that you?" said a metallic voice, distorted by electrical howling. "Erast Petrovich?"

"No, Mista Fandorin not here," Masa said loudly, so that he could be heard above the howling. They had written in the newspapers that new telephones had appeared with an improved system which transmitted speech "without the slightest loss of quality, remarkably loudly and clearly." They ought to buy one. "Prease ring back rater. Would you rike to reave a message?"

"No thank——" The voice had gone from a howl to a rustle. "I'll phone later."

"Prease make yourself wercome," Masa said politely, and hung up.

Things were bad, very bad. This was the third night his master had not slept, and the mistress did not sleep either; she prayed all the time—either in the church or at home, in front of the icon. She had always prayed a lot, but never so much as now. All this would end very badly, although it was hard to see how things could be any worse than they were already.

If only the master would find whoever had killed Tiuri-san and murdered Sonya-san and Palasha. Find him and give his faithful servant a present—give that person to Masa. Not for long, just half an hour. No, an hour would be better . . .

Engrossed in pleasant thoughts, he didn't notice the time passing. The clock struck eleven. Usually the people in the neighbouring houses were already asleep at this time, but today all the windows were lit up. It was a special night. Soon the bells would start chiming all over the city, and then different-coloured lights would explode in the sky, people in the streets would start singing and shouting, and tomorrow there would be a lot of drunks. Easter.

Perhaps he ought to go the church and stand with everyone and listen to the slow bass singing of the Christian bonzes. Anything was better than sitting all alone and waiting, waiting, waiting.

But he didn't have to wait any longer. The door slammed and he heard firm, confident footsteps. His master had returned!

"What, mourning all alone?" his master asked in Japanese, and touched him gently on the shoulder.

Such displays of affection were not their custom, and the surprise broke Masa's reserve; he sobbed and then broke into tears. He didn't wipe the water from his face—let it flow. A man had no reason to be ashamed of crying, as long as it was not from pain or from fear.

The master's eyes were dry and bright. "I haven't got everything I'd like to have," he said. "I thought we'd catch him red-handed. But we can't wait any longer. There's no time. The killer is still in Moscow today, but after a while he could be anywhere in the world. I have indirect evidence: I have a witness who can identify him. That's enough; he won't wriggle out of it."

"You will take me with you?" Masa asked, overjoyed by the good news. "You will?"

"Yes," his master said, with a nod. "He is a dangerous opponent, and I can't take any risks. I might need your help."

The telephone rang again.

"Master, someone phoned before. On secret business. He didn't give his name. He said he would call again."

"Right then, you take the other phone and try to tell if it's the same person or not."

Masa put the metal horn to his ear and prepared to listen.

"Hello. Erast Petrovich Fandorin's number. This is he," the master said.

"Erast Petrovich, is that you?" the voice squeaked. Masa shrugged—he couldn't tell if it was the same person or someone else.

"Yes. With whom am I speaking?"

"This is Zakharov."

"You!" The master's strong fingers clenched into a fist.

"Erast Petrovich, I have to explain things to you. I know everything is against me, but I didn't kill anyone, I swear to you!"

"Then who did?"

"I'll explain everything to you. Only give me your word of honour that you'll come alone, without the police. Otherwise I'll disappear, you'll never see me again, and the killer will go free. Do you give me your word?"

"Yes," the master answered without hesitation.

"I believe you, because I know you to be a man of honour. You have no need to fear: I am not dangerous to you, and I don't have a gun. I just want to be able to explain . . . If you still are concerned, bring your Japanese along, I don't object to that. Only no police."

"How do you know about my Japanese?"

"I know a great deal about you, Erast Petrovich. That's why you are the only one I trust . . . Come immediately, this minute to the Pokrov-skaya Gates. You'll find the Hotel Tsargrad on Rogozhsky Val Street, a grey building with three storeys. You must come within the next hour. Go up to room number fifty-two and wait for me there. Once I'm sure that only the two of you have come, I'll come up and join you. I'll tell you the whole truth, and then you can decide what to do with me. I'll accept any decision you make."

"There will be no police, my word of honour," the master said, and hung up.

"That's it, Masa, that's it," he said, and his face became a little less dead. "He will be caught in the act. Give me some strong green tea. I shan't be sleeping again tonight."

"What weapons shall I prepare?" Masa asked.

"I shall take my revolver; I shan't need anything else. And you take whatever you like. Remember: this man is a monster—strong, quick, and unpredictable." And he added in a quiet voice: "I really have decided to manage without any police."

Masa nodded understandingly. In a matter like this, of course it was better without the police.

I admit that I was wrong: not all detectives are ugly. This one, for instance, is very beautiful.

My heart swoons sweetly as I see him close the ring around me. Hide and seek!

But I can facilitate his enlightenment a little. If I am not mistaken in him, he is an exceptional man. He won't be frightened, but he will appreciate the lesson. I know it will cause him a lot of pain. At first. But later he will thank me himself. Who knows, perhaps we shall become fellow-thinkers and confederates. I think I can sense a kindred spirit. Or perhaps two kindred spirits. His Japanese servant comes from a nation that understands true Beauty. The supreme moment of existence for the inhabitants of those distant islands is to reveal to the world the Beauty of their belly. In Japan, those who die in this beautiful way are honoured as heroes. The sight of steaming entrails does not frighten anyone there.

Yes, there will be three of us, I can sense it.

How weary I am of my solitude. To share the burden between two or even three would be unspeakable happiness. After all, I am not a god; I am only a human being.

Understand me, Mr. Fandorin. Help me.

But first I must open your eyes.

CHAPTER 9

A Bad End to an Unpleasant Story

Easter Sunday, 9 April, night

Clip-clop, clip-clop, the horseshoes clattered merrily over the cobblestones of the street, and the steel springs rustled gently. The Decorator was riding through the Moscow night in festive style, bowling along to the joyful pealing of the Easter bells and the booming of the cannon. There had been illuminated decorations on Tverskaya Street, different-coloured little lanterns, and now on the left, where the Kremlin was, the sky was suffused with all the colours of the rainbow—that was the Easter firework display. The boulevard was crowded. Talking, laughter, sparklers. Muscovites greeting people they knew, kissing, sometimes even the popping of a champagne cork.

And here was the turn on to Malaya Nikit-skaya Street. Here it was deserted, dark, not a soul.

"Stop, my good man, we're here," said the Decorator.

The cabbie jumped down from the coachbox and opened the droshky's door, decorated with paper garlands. He doffed his cap and uttered the holy words: "Christ is risen."

"Truly He is risen," the Decorator replied with feeling, throwing back the veil, and kissed the good Christian on his stubbly cheek. The tip was an entire rouble. Such was the bright holiness of this hour.

"Thank you, lady," the cabby said with a bow, touched more by the kiss than by the rouble.

The Decorator's heart was serene and at peace.

The infallible instinct that had never deceived told him that this was a great night, when all the misfortunes and petty failures would be left behind. Happiness lay very close ahead. Everything would be good, very good.

Ah what a tour de force had been conceived this time. As a true master of his trade, Mr. Fandorin could not fail to appreciate it. He would grieve, he would weep—after all, we are all only human—but afterwards he would think about what had happened and understand; he was sure to understand. After all, he was an intelligent man and he seemed capable of seeing Beauty.

The hope of new life, of recognition and understanding, warmed the Decorator's foolish, trusting heart. It is hard to bear the cross of a great mission alone. Even Christ's cross had been supported by Simon's shoulder.

Fandorin and his Japanese were dashing at top speed on their way to Rogozhsky Val Street. They would waste time finding room number fifty-two and waiting there. And if the Collegiate Counsellor should suspect anything, he would not find a telephone in the third-class Hotel Tsargrad.

The Decorator had time. There was no need to hurry.

The woman the Collegiate Counsellor loved was devout. She was in the church now, but the service in the nearby Church of the Resurrection would soon be over, and at midnight the woman would certainly come home—to set the table with the Easter feast and wait for her man.

Decorative gates with a crown, the yard beyond them, and then the dark windows of the outhouse. Here.

Throwing back the flimsy veil, the Decorator looked around and slipped in through the wrought-iron gate.

It would take a moment or two to fiddle with the door of the outhouse, but that was an easy job for such agile, talented fingers. The lock clicked, the hinges creaked, and the Decorator was already in the dark entrance hall.

No need to wait for such well-accustomed eyes to adjust to the darkness: it was no hindrance to them. The Decorator walked quickly round all the rooms.

In the drawing room there was a momentary fright caused by the deafening chime of a huge clock in the shape of Big Ben. Was it really that late? Confused, the Decorator checked the time with a neat lady's wristwatch—no, Big Ben was fast, it was still a quarter to the hour.

The place for the sacred ritual still had to be chosen.

The Decorator was on top form today, soaring on the wings of inspiration—why not right here in the drawing room, on the dinner table?

It would be like this: Mr. Fandorin would come in from the entrance hall, turn on the electric light, and see the delightful sight.

That was decided then. Now where did they keep their tablecloth?

The Decorator rummaged in the linen cupboard, selected a snow-white lace cloth and put it on the broad table with its dull gleam of polished wood.

Yes, that would be beautiful. Wasn't that a Meissen dinner service in the sideboard? The fine china plates could be laid out round the edge of the table and the treasures could be laid on them as they were extracted. It would be the finest decoration ever created.

So, the design had been completed.

The Decorator went into the entrance hall, stood by the window and waited, filled with joyful anticipation and holy ecstasy.

The yard was suddenly bright—the moon had come out. A sign, a clear sign! It had been overcast and gloomy for so many weeks, but now a veil seemed to have been lifted from God's world. What a clear, starry sky! This was truly a bright and holy Easter night. The Decorator made the sign of the cross three times.

She was here!

A few quick blinks of the eyelashes to brush away the tears of ecstasy.

She was here. A short figure wearing a broad coat and hat came in unhurriedly through the gate. When she approached the door, it was clearly a hat of mourning, with . . . with a black gauze veil. Ah, yes, that was for the boy, Anisii Tulipov. Don't grieve, my dear, he and the members of his household are already with the Lord. They are happy there. And you too will be happy, only be patient a little longer.

"Christ is risen." The Decorator greeted her in a quiet, clear voice. "Don't be frightened, my dear. I have come to bring you joy."

The woman, however, did not appear to be frightened. She did not cry out or try to run away. On the contrary, she took a step forwards. The moon lit up the entrance hall with an intense, even glow, and the eyes behind the veil glinted.

"Why are we standing here like two Moslem women in yashmaks?" the Decorator joked. "Let's show our faces." The Decorator's veil was thrown back, revealing an affectionate smile, a smile from the heart. "And let's not be formal with each other. We're going to get to know each other very well. We shall be closer than sisters. Come now, let me look at your pretty face. I know you are beautiful, but I shall help you to become even more so."

The Decorator reached out one hand, but the woman did not jump back; she waited. Mr. Fandorin had a good woman, calm and acquiescent. The Decorator had always liked women like that. It would be bad if she spoiled everything with a scream of horror and an expression of fear in her eyes. She would die instantly, with no pain or fright. That would be the Decorator's gift to her.

One hand drew the scalpel out of the little case that was attached to the Decorator's belt at the back; with the other he threw back the fine gauze from the face of the fortunate woman.

The face revealed was broad and perfectly round, with slanting eyes. What kind of witchcraft was this? But there was no time to make any sense of it, because something in the entrance hall clicked and suddenly it was flooded with blindingly bright light, unbearable after the darkness.

With sensitive eyes screwed tightly shut against the pain, the Decorator heard a voice speaking through the darkness: "I'll give you joy right now, Pakhomenko. Or would you prefer me to call you by your former name, Mr. Sotsky?"

Opening his eyes slightly, the Decorator saw the Japanese servant standing in front of him, fixing him with an unblinking stare. The Decorator did not turn round. Why should he turn round, when it was already clear that Mr. Fandorin was behind him, probably holding a revolver in his hand? The cunning Collegiate

Counsellor had not gone to the Hotel Tsargrad. He had not believed that Zakharov was guilty. Satan himself must have whispered the truth to Fandorin.

Eloi, Eloi, lama sabacthani? Or perhaps You have not abandoned me, but are testing the strength of my spirit?

Then let us test it.

Fandorin would not fire, because his bullet would go straight through the Decorator and hit the Japanese.

Thrust the scalpel into the short man's belly. Briefly, just below the diaphragm. Then, in a single movement, swing the Japanese round by his shoulders, shield himself with him and push him towards Fandorin. The door was only two quick bounds away, and then they would see who could run faster. Not even the fierce wolfhounds of Kherson had been able to catch convict number 3576. He'd manage to get away from Mr. Collegiate Counsellor somehow.

Help me, O Lord!

His right hand flew forward as fast as an uncoiling spring, but the sharp blade cut nothing but air—the Japanese jumped backwards with unbelievable ease and struck the Decorator's wrist with the edge of his hand; the scalpel went flying to the floor with a sad tinkling sound, and the Asiatic froze on the spot again, holding his arms out slightly from his sides.

Instinct made the Decorator turn round. He saw the barrel of a revolver. Fandorin was holding the gun low, by his hip. If he fired from there, the bullet would take the top of the Decorator's skull off and not touch the Japanese. That changed things.

"And the joy I will bring you is this," Fandorin continued in the same level voice, as if the conversation had never been interrupted. "I spare you the arrest, the investigation, the trial, and the inevitable verdict. You will be shot while being detained."

He has abandoned me. He truly has abandoned me, thought the Decorator, but this thought did not sadden him for long; it was displaced by a sudden joy. No, He has not abandoned me! He has decided to be merciful to me and is calling me, taking me to Himself! Release me now, O Lord.

The front door creaked open and a desperate woman's voice said: "Erast, you mustn't!"

The Decorator came back from the celestial heights that had been about to open to him, down to earth. He turned round curiously and in the doorway he saw a very beautiful, stately woman in a black mourning dress and a black hat with a veil. The woman had a lilac shawl on her shoulders; in one hand she was holding a package of pashka Easter dessert and in the other a garland of paper roses.

"Angelina, why did you come back?" the Collegiate Counsellor said angrily. "I asked you to stay in the Hotel Metropole tonight!"

A beautiful woman. She would hardly have been much more beautiful on the table, soaking in her own juices, with the petals of her body open. Only just a little bit.

"I felt something in my heart," the beautiful woman told Fandorin, wringing her hands. "Erast Petrovich, don't kill him; don't take the sin on your soul. Your soul will bend under the weight of it and snap."

This was interesting. Now what would the Collegiate Counsellor say?

His cool composure had vanished without a trace; he was looking at the beautiful woman in angry confusion. The Japanese had been taken aback too: he was shaking his shaven head either at his master or his mistress with a very stupid expression.

Well, this is a family matter; we won't intrude. They can sort things out without our help.

In two quick bounds the Decorator had rounded the Japanese, and then it was five steps to the door and freedom—and Fandorin couldn't fire because the woman was too close. Goodbye, gentlemen!

A shapely leg in a black felt boot struck the Decorator across the ankle, and the Decorator was sent sprawling, with his forehead flying towards the doorpost.

A blow. Darkness.

Everything was ready for the trial to begin.

The unconscious accused was sitting in an armchair in a woman's dress, but without any hat. He had an impressive purple bump coming up on his forehead.

The court bailiff, Masa, was standing beside him with his arms crossed on his chest.

Erast Petrovich had appointed Angelina as the judge and taken the role of prosecutor on himself.

But first there was an argument.

"I can't judge anyone," said Angelina. "The Emperor has judges for that; let them decide if he is guilty or not. Let them pronounce sentence."

"What s-sentence?" Fandorin asked with a bitter laugh. He had started to stammer again after the criminal had been detained—in fact even more than before, as if he were trying to make up for lost time. "Who needs a scandalous t-trial like that? They'll be only too glad to declare Sotsky insane and put him in a madhouse, from which he will quite definitely escape. No bars will hold a man like this. I was going to kill him, in the way one kills a mad dog, b-but you stopped me. Now decide his fate yourself, since you interfered. You know what this monster has done."

"What if it's not him? Are you quite incapable of making a mistake?" Angelina protested passionately.

"I'll prove to you that he, and no one else, is the murderer. That's why I'm the prosecutor. You judge f-fairly. I couldn't find a more merciful judge for him in the whole wide world. And if you don't want to be his judge, then go to the Metropole and don't get in my way."

"No, I won't go away," she said; "let there be a trial. But in a trial there's a counsel for the defence. Who's going to defend him?"

"I assure you that this gentleman will not allow anyone else to take on the role of counsel for the defence. He knows how to stand up for himself. Let's begin."

Erast Petrovich nodded to Masa, and the valet stuck a bottle of smelling salts under the nose of the man in the chair.

The man in the woman's dress jerked his head and fluttered his eyelashes. The eyes were dull at first, then they turned a bright sky-blue colour and acquired intelligence. The soft features were illuminated by a good-natured smile.

"Your name and title?" Fandorin said sternly, trespassing somewhat on the prerogatives of the chairman of the court.

The seated man examined the scene around him. "Have you decided to play out a trial? Very well, why not. Name and title? Sotsky . . . former nobleman, former student, former convict number 3576. And now—nobody."

"Do you admit that you are guilty of committing a number of murders?" Erast Petrovich began reading from a notepad, pausing after each name: "The prostitute Emma Elizabeth Smith on the third of April 1888 on Osborne Street in London; the prostitute Martha Tabram on the seventh of August 1888 near George Yard in London; the prostitute Mary Ann Nichols on the thirty-first of August 1888 on Back Row in London; the prostitute Ann Chapman on the eighth of September 1888 on Hanbury Street in London; the prostitute Elizabeth Stride on the thirtieth of September 1888 in Berner Street in London; the prostitute Catherine Eddowes also on the thirtieth of September 1888 on Mitre Square in London; the prostitute Mary Jane Kelly on the ninth of November 1888 on Dorset Street in London; the prostitute Rose Millet on the twentieth of December 1888 on Poplar High Street in London; the prostitute Alexandra Zotova on the fifth of February 1889 in Svininsky Lane in Moscow; the beggar Marya Kosaya on the eleventh of February 1889 in Maly Tryokhsvyatsky Lane in Moscow; the prostitute Stepanida Andreichkina on the night of the third of April on Seleznyovsky Lane in Moscow; an unidentified beggar girl on the fifth of April 1889 near the Novotikhvinsk level crossing in Moscow; Court Counsellor Leontii Izhitsin and his maid Zinaida Matiushkina on the night of the fifth of April 1889 on Vozdvizhenskaya Street in Moscow; the spinster Sophia Tulipova and her nurse Pelageya Makarova on the seventh of April 1889 on Granatny Lane in Moscow; the Provincial Secretary Anisii Tulipov and the doctor Egor Zakharov on the night of the seventh of April at the Bozhedomka Cemetery in Moscow—in all eighteen people, eight of whom were killed by you in England and ten in Russia. And those are only the victims of which the investigation has certain knowledge. I repeat the question: do you admit that you are guilty of committing these crimes?"

Fandorin's voice seemed to have been strengthened by reading out the long list. It had become loud and resonant, as if the Collegiate Counsellor were speaking to a full courtroom. The stammer had also disappeared in some mysterious fashion.

"Well, that, my dear Erast Petrovich, depends on the evidence," the accused replied amiably, apparently delighted with the proposed game. "Well, let's say that I don't admit it. I'm really looking forward to hearing the opening address from the prosecution. Purely out of curiosity. Since you've decided to postpone my extermination."

"Well then, listen," Fandorin replied sternly. He turned over the page of his notepad and continued speaking, addressing himself to Pakhomenko-Sotsky, but looking at Angelina most of the time.

"First, the prehistory. In 1882 there was a scandal in Moscow that involved medical students and students from the Higher Courses for Women. You were the leader, the evil genius of this depraved circle and, because of that, you were the only member of it who was severely punished: you were sentenced to four years in a convict battalion—without any trial, in order to avoid publicity. You cruelly tormented unfortunate prostitutes who had no right of redress, and fate repaid you with equal cruelty. You were sent to the Kherson military prison, which is said to be more terrible than hard labour in Siberia. The year before last, following an investigation into a case of the abuse of power, the senior administrators of the punishment battalion were put on trial. But by then you were already far away . . ."

Erast Petrovich hesitated and then continued after a brief pause: "I am the prosecutor and I am not obliged to seek excuses for you, but I cannot pass over in silence the fact that the final transformation of a wanton youth into a ravenous, bloodthirsty beast was facilitated by society itself. The contrast between student life and the hell of a military prison would drive absolutely anyone insane. During the first year there you killed a man in self-defence. The military court acknowledged the mitigating circumstances, but it increased your sentence to eight years and when you were sent to the guardhouse, they put shackles on you and subjected you to a long period of solitary confinement. No doubt it was owing to the inhuman conditions in which you were kept that you turned into an inhuman monster. No, Sotsky, you did not break, you did not lose your mind, you did not try to kill yourself. In order to survive, you became a different creature, with only an external resemblance to a human being. In 1886 your family, who had turned their backs on you long before, were informed that convict Sotsky had drowned in the Dnieper during an attempted escape. I sent an inquiry to the Department of Military Justice, asking if the fugitive's body had been found. They replied that it had not. That was the answer I had been expecting. The prison administration had simply concealed the fact of your successful escape. A very common business."

The accused listened to Fandorin with lively interest, neither confirming what he said nor denying it.

"Tell me, my dear prosecutor: what was it that made you start raking through the case of the long-forgotten Sotsky? Forgive me for interrupting you, but this is an informal court, although I presume the verdict will be binding and not subject to appeal."

"Two of the individuals who were included in the list of suspects had been your accomplices in the case of the Sadist Circle, and they mentioned your name. It turned out that forensic medical expert Zakharov, who was involved in the inquiry, had also belonged to the group. I realised straight away that the criminal could only be receiving news of the inquiry from Zakharov, and I was going to take a closer look at the people around him, but first I took the wrong path and suspected the factory-owner Burylin. Everything fitted very well."

"And why didn't you suspect Zakharov himself?" Sotsky asked, in a voice that sounded almost offended. "After all, everything pointed to him, and I did everything I could to help things along."

"No, I couldn't think that Zakharov was the murderer. He besmirched his name less than the others in the Sadist Circle case; he was only a passive observer of your cruel amusements. And in addition, Zakharov was frankly and aggressively cynical and that kind of character is not typical of maniacal killers. But these are circumstantial points; the main thing is that last year Zakharov only stayed in England for a month and a half, and he was in Moscow when most of the London murders took place. I checked that at the very beginning and immediately excluded him from the list of suspects. He could not have been Jack the Ripper."

"You and your Jack the Ripper," said Sotsky, with an irritated twitch of his shoulder. "Well, let us suppose that while Zakharov was staying with relatives in England he read a lot in the newspapers about the Ripper and decided to continue his work in Moscow. I noticed just now that you count the number of victims in a strange manner. Investigator Izhitsin came to a different conclusion. He put thirteen corpses on the table, and you only accuse me of ten killings in Moscow. And that's including those who died after the 'investigative experiment'; otherwise there would only be four. Your numbers don't add up somewhere, Mr. Prosecutor."

"On the contrary," said Erast Petrovich, not even slightly perturbed by this unexpected outburst. "Of the thirteen bodies exhumed with signs of mutilation, four had been brought directly from the scene of the crime: Zotova, Marya Kosaya, Andreichkina, and the unidentified girl, and you had also not managed to process two of your February victims according to your special method—clearly, someone must have frightened you off. The other nine bodies, the most horribly mutilated of all, were extracted from anonymous graves. The Moscow police are, of course, far from perfect, but it is impossible to imagine that no one paid any attention to bodies that had been mutilated in such a monstrous fashion. Here in Russia many people are murdered, but more simply, without all these fantasies. When they found Andreichkina slashed to pieces, look what an uproar it caused immediately. The Governor-General was informed straight away, and His Excellency assigned his Deputy for Special Assignments to investigate. I can say without bragging that the Prince only assigns me to cases that are of exceptional importance. And here we have almost ten mutilated bodies and nobody has made any fuss? Impossible."

"Somehow I don't understand," said Angelina, speaking for the first time since the trial had begun. "Who did such things to these poor people?"

Erast Petrovich was clearly delighted by her question—the stubborn silence of the "judge" had rendered the examination of the evidence meaningless.

"The earliest bodies were exhumed from the November ditch. However, that does not mean that Jack the Ripper had already arrived in Moscow in November."

"Of course not!" said the accused, interrupting Fandorin. "As far as I recall, the latest London murder was committed on Christmas Eve. I don't know if you will be able to prove to our charming judge that I am guilty of the Moscow murders, but you certainly won't be able to make me into Jack the Ripper."

An icy, disdainful smile slid across Erast Petrovich's face, and he became stern and sombre again. "I understand the meaning of your remark perfectly well. You cannot wriggle out of the Moscow murders. The more of them there are, the more monstrous and outrageous they are, the better for you—you are more likely to be declared insane. But for Jack's crimes the En-glish would be certain to demand your extradition, and Russian justice would be only too delighted to be rid of such a bothersome madman. If you go to En-gland, where things are done openly, nothing will be hushed up in our Russian fashion. You would swing from the gallows there, my dear sir. Don't you want to?" Fandorin's voice shifted down an octave, as if his own throat had been caught in a noose. "Don't even hope that you can leave your career in London behind you. The apparent mismatch of the dates is easily explained. 'Watchman Pakhomenko' appeared at the Bozhedomka Cemetery shortly after the New Year. I assume that Zakharov got you the job for old times' sake. Most likely you met in London during his most recent visit. Of course, Zakharov did not know about your new amusements. He simply thought that you had escaped from prison. How could he refuse to help an old comrade whom life had treated so harshly? Well?"

Sotsky did not reply; he merely shrugged one shoulder as if to say: I'm listening, go on.

"Did things get too hot for you in London? Were the police getting too close? All right. You moved to your native country. I don't know what passport you used to cross the border, but you turned up in Moscow as a simple Ukrainian peasant, one of those godly wandering pilgrims, of whom there are so many in Russia. That's why there is no information about your arrival from abroad in the police records. You lived at the cemetery for a while, settled in, took a look around. Zakharov obviously felt sorry for you; he gave you protection and money. You went for quite a long time without killing anybody—more than a month. Possibly you were intending to start a new life. But you weren't strong enough. After the excitement in London, ordinary life had become impossible for you. This peculiarity of the maniacal mind is well known to criminal science. Once someone has tasted blood, he can't stop. At first you took the opportunity offered by your job to hack up bodies from the graves; it was winter, so the bodies buried since the end of November had not begun to decompose. You tried a man's body once, but you didn't like it. It didn't match your 'idea' somehow. By the way, what is your idea? Can you not tolerate sinful, ugly women? 'I want to give you joy,' 'I will help to make you more beautiful'—do you use a scalpel to save fallen women from their ugliness? Is that the reason for the bloody kiss?"

The accused said nothing. His face became solemn and remote, the bright blue of his eyes dimmed as he half-closed his eyelids.

"And then lifeless bodies weren't good enough any longer. You made several attempts which, fortunately, were unsuccessful, and committed two murders. Or was it more?" Fandorin suddenly shouted out, rushing at the accused, shaking him so hard by the shoulders that his head almost flew off.

"Answer me?"

"Erast!" Angelina shouted. "Stop it!"

The Collegiate Counsellor started away from the seated man, took two hasty steps backwards and hid his hands behind his back, struggling to control his agitation. The Ripper, not frightened at all by Erast Petrovich's outburst, sat without moving, staring at Fandorin with an expression of calm superiority.

"What can you understand?" the full, fleshy lips whispered almost inaudibly.

Erast Petrovich frowned in frustration, tossed a lock of black hair back off his forehead and continued his interrupted speech: "On the evening of the third of April, a year after the first London murder, you killed the spinster An-dreichkina and mutilated her body. A day later the juvenile beggar became your victim. After that, events moved very quickly. Izhitsin's 'experiment' triggered a paroxysm of excitation which you discharged by killing and disembowelling Izhitsin himself, at the same time murdering his entirely innocent maid. From that moment on, you deviate from your 'idea' and you kill in order to cover your tracks and avoid retribution. When you realised that the circle was closing in, you decided it would be more convenient to shift the blame onto your friend and protector Zakharov. Especially since the forensic specialist had begun to suspect you—he must have put a few facts together, or else he knew something that I don't. In any case, on Friday evening Zakharov was writing a letter addressed to the investigators, in which he intended to expose you. He kept tearing it up and starting again. His assistant Grumov said that Zakharov locked himself in his office shortly after three, so he was struggling with his conscience until the evening, struggling with the understandable, but in the present instance entirely inappropriate, feelings of honour and *esprit de corps,* as well as simple compassion for a comrade whom life had treated harshly. You took the letter and collected all the torn pieces. But there were two scraps that you failed to notice. On one it said '*longer remain silent*' and on the other '*erations of esprit de corps and sympathy for an old com.*' The meaning is obvious: Zakharov was writing that that he could no longer remain silent, and attempting to justify harbouring a murderer by referring to considerations of *esprit de corps* and sympathy for an old comrade. That was the moment when I was finally convinced that the killer had to be sought among Zakharov's former fellow students. Since it was a matter of 'sympathy,' then it had to be one of those whose lives had gone badly. That excluded the millionaire Burylin. There were only three left: Stenich, the alcoholic Rozen, and Sotsky, whose name kept coming up in the stories that the former 'sadists' told me. He was supposed to be dead, but that had to be verified."

"Erast Petrovich, why are you certain that this doctor, Zakharov, has been killed?" Angelina asked.

"Because he has disappeared, although he had no need to," replied Erast Petrovich. "Zakharov is not guilty of the murders and he had believed that he was sheltering a fugitive convict, not a bloody killer. But when he realised who he had been sheltering, he was frightened. He kept a loaded revolver beside his bed. He was afraid of you, Sotsky. After the murders in Granatny Lane you returned to the cemetery and saw Tulipov observing Zakharov's office. The guard dog did not bark at you; he knows you very well. Tulipov was absorbed in his observation work and failed to notice you. You realised that suspicion had fallen on Zakharov and decided to exploit the fact. In the report he dictated just before he died, Tulipov states that shortly after ten Zakharov went out of his study and there was some sort of clattering in the corridor. Obviously the murder took place at that very moment. You entered the house silently and waited for Zakharov to come out into the corridor for something. And that is why the rug disappeared from the corridor. It must have had bloodstains on it, so you removed it. When you were finished with Zakharov, you crept outside and attacked Tulipov from behind, inflicting mortal wounds and leaving him to bleed to death. I presume you saw him get up, stagger to the gates, and then collapse again. You were afraid to go and finish him, because you knew that he had a weapon, and in any case you knew that his wounds were fatal. Without wasting any time, you dragged Zakharov's body out and buried it in the cemetery. I even know exactly where. You threw it into the April ditch for unidentified bodies and sprinkled earth over it. By the way, do you know how you gave yourself away?"

Sotsky started, and the calm, resigned expression was replaced once again by curiosity, but only for a few moments. Then the invisible curtain came down again, erasing all trace of living feeling.

"When I talked to you yesterday morning, you said you hadn't slept all night, that you had heard the shots, and then the door slamming and the sound of footsteps. That was supposed to make me think that Zakharov was alive and had gone into hiding. But in fact it made me think something else. If the watchman Pakhomenko's ears were sharp enough to hear footsteps from a distance, why could he not hear the blasts that Tulipov gave on his whistle when he came round? The answer is obvious: at that moment you were not in your hut; you were some distance away from the spot—for instance, at the far end of the cemetery, where the April ditch happens to be. That is one. If Zakharov had been the killer, he could not have gone out through the gates, because Tulipov was lying there wounded and had still not come round. The killer would certainly have finished him off. That is two. So now I had confirmation that Zakharov, who I already knew could not be the London maniac, was not involved in Tulipov's death. If he had nonetheless disappeared, it meant that he had been killed. If you lied about the circumstances of his disappearance, it meant that you were involved in it. And I remembered that both murders that were committed according to the 'idea,' the prostitute Andreichkina and the young beggar, were committed within fifteen minutes' walking distance of the Bozhedomka Cemetery—it was the late investigator Izhitsin who first noticed that, although he drew the wrong conclusions from it. Once I put these facts together with the fragments of phrases from the letter, I was almost certain that the 'old comrade' with whom Zakharov sympathised and whom he did not wish to give away was you. Because of your job you were involved in the exhumation of the bodies and you knew a lot about how the investigation was developing. That is one. You were present at the 'investigative experiment.' That is two. You had access to the graves and the ditches. That is three. You knew Tulipov—in fact you were almost friends. That is four. In the list of those present at the experiment drawn up before he died, you are described as follows."

Erast Petrovich walked across to the table, picked up a sheet of paper and read from it: "Pakhomenko, the cemetery watchman. I don't know his first name and patronymic, the labourers call him 'Pakhom.' Age uncertain: between thirty and fifty. Above average height, strongly built. Round, gentle face, without a moustache or beard. Ukrainian accent. I have had several conversations with him on various subjects. I have listened to the story of his life (he was a wandering pilgrim and has seen a lot of things) and told him about myself. He is intelligent, observant, religious, and kind. He has assisted me greatly in the investigation. Perhaps the only one of them whose innocence could not possibly be in the slightest doubt."

"A nice boy," the accused said, touched, and his words made the Collegiate Counsellor's face twitch, while the dispassionate court guard whispered something harsh and hissing in Japanese.

Even Angelina shuddered as she looked at the man in the chair.

"You made use of Tulipov's revelations on Friday when you entered his apartment and committed a double murder," Erast Petrovich continued after a brief pause. "And as for my . . . domestic circumstances, they are known to many people, and Zakharov could have told you about them. So today or, in fact, yesterday morning already, I had only one suspect left: you. But I still had a few things to do. Firstly, establish what Sotsky looked like, secondly, ascertain whether he really was dead and, finally, find witnesses who could identify you. Stenich described Sotsky to me as he was seven years ago. You have probably changed greatly in seven years, but height, the colour of the eyes, and the shape of the nose are not subject to change, and all of those features matched. A telegram from the Department of Military Justice which included the details of Sotsky's time in prison and his supposedly unsuccessful attempt to escape, made it clear that the convict could quite well still be alive. My greatest difficulty was with witnesses. I had high hopes of the former 'sadist' Filipp Rozen. When he spoke about Sotsky in my presence, he used a strange phrase that stuck in my memory. 'He's dead, but I keep thinking I see him everywhere. Take yesterday . . .' He never finished the phrase—someone interrupted him. But on that 'yesterday,' that is, on the fourth of April, Rozen was with Zakharov and the others at the cemetery. I wondered if he might have seen the watchman Pakhomenko there and spotted a resemblance to his old friend. Unfortunately, I wasn't able to locate Rozen. But I did find a prostitute you tried to kill seven weeks ago at Shrovetide. She remembered you very well and she can identify you. At that stage I could have arrested you; there were enough solid clues. That is what I would have done if you yourself had not gone on the offensive. Then I realised that there is only one way to stop someone like you . . ."

Sotsky appeared not to notice the threat behind these words. At least, he did not show the slightest sign of alarm—on the contrary, he smiled absent-mindedly at his own thoughts.

"Ah yes, and there was the note that was sent to Burylin," Fandorin remembered. "A rather clumsy move. The note was really intended for me, was it not? The investigators had to be convinced that Zakharov was alive and in hiding. You even tried to imitate certain distinctive features of Zakharov's handwriting, but you only reinforced my conviction that the suspect was not an illiterate watchman but an educated man who knew Zakharov well and was acquainted with Burylin. That is—Sotsky. Your telephone call when you took advantage of the technical shortcomings of the telephone to pretend to be Zakharov could not deceive me either. I have had occasion to use that trick myself. Your intention was also quite clear. You always act according to the same monstrous logic: if you find someone interesting, you kill those who are most dear to him. That was what you did in Tulipov's case. That was what you wanted to do with the daughter of the prostitute who had somehow attracted your perverted attention. You mentioned my Japanese servant very specifically—you clearly wanted him to come with me. Why? Why, of course, so that Angelina Samsonovna would be left at home alone. I would rather not think about the fate that you had in mind for her. I might not be able to restrain myself and . . ."

Fandorin broke off and swung round sharply to face Angelina: "What is your verdict? Is he guilty or not?"

Pale and trembling, Angelina said in a quiet but firm voice: "Now let him speak. Let him justify himself if he can."

Sotsky said nothing, still smiling absent-mindedly. A minute passed, and then another, and just when it began to seem that the defence would not address the court at all, the lips of the accused moved and the words poured out—clear, measured, dignified words, as if it were not this man in fancy dress with a woman's face who was speaking, but some higher power with a superior knowledge of truth and justice.

"I do not need to justify anything to anyone. And I have only one judge—our Heavenly Father, who knows my motives and my innermost thoughts. I have always been a special case. Even when I was a child, I knew that I was special, not like everybody else. I was consumed by irresistible curiosity, I wanted to understand everything in the wonderful structure of God's world, to test everything, to try everything. I have always loved people, and they felt that and were drawn to me. I would have made a great healer, because nature gave me the talent to understand the sources of pain and suffering, and understanding is equivalent to salvation—every doctor knows that. The one thing I could not stand was ugliness; I saw it as an offence to God's work—ugliness enraged me and drove me into a fury. One day, in a fit of such fury, I was unable to stop myself in time. An ugly old whore, whose very appearance was sacrilege against the name of the Lord, according to the way that I thought then, died as I was beating her with my cane. I did not fall into that fury under the influence of sadistic sensuality, as my judges imagined—no, it was the holy wrath of a soul imbued through and through with Beauty. From society's point of view it was just one more unfortunate accident—gilded youth has always got up to worse things than that. But I was not one of their privileged favourites, and they made an example of me to frighten the others. The only one, out of all of us! Now I understand that God had decided to choose me, I *am* the only one. But that is hard to understand at the age of twenty-four. I was not ready. For an educated man of sensitive feelings, the horrors of prison—no, a hundred times worse than that, the horrors of disciplinary confinement—are impossible to describe. I was subjected to cruel humiliation, I was the most abused and defenceless person in the entire barracks. I was tortured, subjected to rape, forced to walk around in a woman's dress. But I could feel some great power gradually maturing within me. It had been present within my being from the very beginning, and now it was putting out shoots and reaching up to the sun, like a fresh stalk breaking up through the earth in the spring. And one day I felt that I was ready. Fear left me and it has never returned. I killed my chief tormentor—killed him in front of everyone, grabbed hold of his ears with my hands and beat his half-shaved head against a wall. I was put in shackles and kept in the punishment cell for seven months. But I did not weaken or fall into consumptive despair. Every day I became stronger and more confident; my eyes learned to penetrate the darkness. Everyone was afraid of me—the guards, the officers, the other convicts. Even the rats left my cell. Every day I strained to understand what this important thing was that was knocking at the door of my soul and not being admitted. Everything around me was ugly and repulsive. I loved Beauty more than anything else in the world, and in my world there was absolutely none. So that this would not drive me insane, I remembered lectures from university and drew the structure of the human body on the earth floor with a chip of wood. Everything in it was rational, harmonious, and beautiful. That was where Beauty was, that was where God was. In time God began to speak to me, and I realised that He was sending down my mysterious power. I escaped from the jail. My strength and stamina knew no bounds. Even the wolfhounds that were specially trained to hunt men could not catch me, the bullets did not hit me. I swam along the river at first, then across the estuary for many hours, until I was picked up by Turkish smugglers. I wandered around the Balkans and Europe. I was put in prison several times, but the prisons were easy to escape from, much easier than the Kherson fortress. Eventually I found a good job. In Whitechapel in London. In a slaughterhouse. I butchered the carcasses. My knowledge of surgery came in useful then. I was well respected and earned a lot; I saved money. But something was maturing within me again, as I looked at the beautiful displays of the rennet bags, the livers, the washed intestines for making sausages, the kidneys, the lungs. All this offal was put into bright, gay packaging and sent to the butchers' shops. Why does man show himself so little respect? I thought; surely the belly of the stupid cow, intended for the processing of coarse grass, is not more worthy of respect than our internal apparatus, created in the likeness of God? My enlightenment came a year ago, on the third of April. I was walking home from the evening shift. On a deserted street, where not a single lamp was lit, a repulsive hag approached me and suggested I should take her into one of the gateways. When I politely declined, she moved very close to me, searing my face with her filthy breath, and began shouting coarse obscenities. What a mockery of the image of God, I thought. What were all her internal organs working for day and night? Why was the tireless heart pumping the precious blood? Why were the myriads of cells in her organism being born, dying, and being renewed again? What for? And I felt an irresistible urge to transform ugliness into Beauty, to look into the true essence of this creature who was so unattractive on the outside. I had my butcher's knife hanging on my belt. Later I bought a whole set of excellent scalpels, but that first time an ordinary butcher's instrument was enough. The result far surpassed all my expectations. The hideous woman was transformed! In front of my eyes she became beautiful! And I was awestruck at such obvious evidence of a miracle from God."

The man in the chair shed a tear. He tried to continue, but just waved his arm and did not say another word.

"Is that enough for you?" Fandorin asked. "Do you declare him guilty?"

"Yes," Angelina whispered, and crossed herself. "He is guilty of all these atrocities."

"You can see for yourself that he cannot be allowed to live. He brings death and grief. He must be exterminated."

Angelina started. "No, Erast Petrovich. He is insane. He needs treatment. I don't know if it will work, but it has to be tried."

"No, he isn't insane," Erast Petrovich replied with conviction. "He is cunning and calculating; he possesses a will of iron and he is exceptionally enterprising. What you see before you is not a madman, but a monster. Some people are born with a hump or a harelip. But there are others whose deformity is not visible to the naked eye. That kind of deformity is the most terrible kind. He is only a man in appearance, but in reality he lacks the most important, the most distinctive feature of a human being. He lacks that invisible, vital string that dwells in the human soul, sounding to tell a man if he has acted well or badly. It is still present even in the most inveterate villain. Its note may be weak, perhaps almost inaudible, but it still sounds. In the depths of his soul a man always knows the worth of his actions, if he has listened to that string even once in his life. You know what Sotsky has done, you heard what he said, you can see what he is like. He does not have the slightest idea that this string exists; his deeds are prompted by a completely different voice. In olden times they would have called him a servant of the devil. I put it more simply: he is not human. He does not repent of anything. And he cannot be stopped by ordinary means. He will not go to the gallows, and the walls of an insane asylum will not hold him. It will start all over again."

"Erast Petrovich, you said that the En-glish will demand his extradition," Angelina exclaimed pitifully, as if she were clutching at her final straw. "Let them kill him, only not you!"

Fandorin shook his head. "The handover is a long process. He'll escape—from prison, from a convoy, from a train, from a ship. I cannot take that risk."

"You have no trust in God," she said sadly, hanging her head. "God knows how and when to put an end to evil deeds."

"I don't know about God. And I cannot be an impartial observer. In my view, that is the worst sin of all. No more, Angelina, I've decided."

Erast Petrovich spoke to Masa in Japanese: "Take him out into the yard."

"Master, you have never killed an unarmed man before," his servant replied agitatedly in the same language. "You will suffer. And the mistress will be angry. I will do it myself."

"That will not change anything. And the fact that he is unarmed makes no difference. To hold a duel would be mere showmanship. I should kill him just as easily even if he were armed. Let us do without any cheap theatrics."

When Masa and Fandorin took the condemned man by the elbows to lead him out into the yard, Angelina cried out: "Erast, for my sake, for our sake!"

The Decorator glanced back with a smile: "My lady, you are a picture of beauty, but I assure you that on the table, surrounded by china plates, you would be even more beautiful."

Angelina squeezed her eyes shut and put her hands over her ears, but she still heard the sound of the shot in the yard—dry and short, almost indistinguishable against the roaring of the firecrackers and the rockets flying into the starry sky.

Erast Petrovich came back alone. He stood in the doorway and wiped the sweat from his brow. His teeth chattered as he said: "Do you know what he whispered? 'Oh Lord, what happiness.' "

They stayed like that for a long time: Angelina sitting with her eyes closed, the tears flowing out from under her eyelids; Fandorin wanting to go to her, but afraid.

Finally she stood up. She walked up to him, put her arms round him and kissed him passionately several times—on the forehead, on the eyes, on the lips.

"I'm going away, Erast Petrovich; remember me kindly."

"Angelina . . ." The Court Counsellor's face, already pale, turned ashen grey. "Surely not because of that vampire, that monster . . ."

"I'm a hindrance to you; I divert you from your own path," she interrupted, not listening to him. "The sisters have been asking me to join them for a long time now, at the Boris and Gleb Convent. It is what I should have done from the very beginning, when my father passed away. And I have grown weak with you. I wanted a holiday. But that is what holidays are like: they don't last for long. I shall watch over you from a distance. And pray to God for you. Follow the promptings of your own soul, and if something goes wrong, don't be afraid: I will make amends through prayer."

"You can't go into a c-convent," Fandorin said rapidly, almost incoherently. "You're not like them; you're so vital and passionate. You won't be able to stand it. And without you, I won't be able to go on."

"You will; you're strong. It's hard for you with me. It will be easier without me . . . And as for me being vital and passionate the sisters are just the same. God has no need of cold people. Forgive me, goodbye. I have known for a long time we should not be together."

Erast Petrovich stood in silent confusion, sensing that there were no arguments that could make her alter her decision. And Angelina was silent too, gently stroking his cheek and his grey temple.

Out of the night, from the dark streets, so out of tune with this farewell, there came the incessant pealing of the Easter bells.

"It's all right, Erast Petrovich," said Angelina. "It's all right. Do you hear? Christ is risen."

GUARDIAN ANGEL

Gwendolyn Frame

Gwendolyn Frame is the pseudonym of an American graphic designer who has published two books, both short story collections featuring Sherlock Holmes. The first, *At the Mercy of the Mind: A Journey into the Depths of Sherlock Holmes* (2011), contains one hundred short-short stories, including tales of Holmes's infancy, childhood, and teenage years; stories involving Professor Moriarty; depictions of events from the days leading up to Reichenbach Falls to the Great Hiatus, to Holmes's return; pieces involving the Baker Street Irregulars; and tales of World War I.

Her second book, *Sherlock Holmes: Have Yourself a Chaotic Little Christmas* (2012), is a response to a Christmas advent challenge in which the author wrote stories prompted by fellow Sherlockians, including tales featuring graveyard picnics, vampires, Mycroft, Professor Moriarty, the twelve days of Christmas, and, of course, Jack the Ripper.

Frame prefers to retain her anonymity, saying only that she is a prolific writer about Holmes, but that "most of her work is unfinished and clamoring for her attention."

"Guardian Angel" was first published in *Sherlock Holmes: Have Yourself a Chaotic Little Christmas* (London, MX Publishing, 2012).

She did not *walk* so much as she *flitted* from lighted window to lamppost to lighted window. No lamp could pierce far into a London Particular, but she took what help she could get. Jemima had begged her to stay the night, but Mary wanted—needed—to get home.

For Jemima's sake, she could *visit* Whitechapel, but she drew the line at staying the night.

She picked up her old skirts as she trod through a small stream on the kerb, forcing herself not to think about *what* she was stepping in. Whenever she came here to visit her old friend, she wore old, ragged clothes so as to blend in with the inhabitants of London's most notorious district. Were she to wear clothes marking her out as a member of the middle class, she had no doubt that she would be assaulted, whether for her money or for other things.

John sighed as he clasped his Gladstone closed and turned to bid his patient farewell. There wasn't a blessed thing to be seen out the window. He loathed Particulars—the damp chill seeped past cloth and skin and settled into the damaged bones in his left shoulder and right thigh. From a purely practical standpoint, London was a foolish place for an injured war veteran to make a home, and yet, after seven years, he could not dream of leaving.

He opened the door and stepped out into the atmospheric pea soup.

Mary heard footsteps behind her for a mere four seconds before she was pulled back by her arm. She screamed and whirled on her attacker, her free hand reaching for the derringer John insisted she carry on her at all times. The man—he was a man, but she could tell nothing beyond that—reached for her left arm as he twisted her right one. Screaming again (*dear God in heaven, let someone hear!*), she tried to aim the gun at the man.

His hand wrapped around her left wrist, and they struggled for the derringer. Mary squeezed the trigger.

The little bullet went wide and might have struck a lamppost—she couldn't be sure. His hand constricted around her wrist, and she cried out in pain. He pulled her to him with her captive arm and, irresistibly, twisted her left arm around behind her to join the other. She screamed again as she was jerked back against him, the pain in her arms white-hot and blinding and leaving her unable to struggle.

"Now, now, my pretty," her attacker whispered in her ear. "Just you relax now."

She whimpered in pain, hot tears rolling down her face.

"Ah, you are a spirited one, aren't you? Just relax, and this shall be quick."

He began to drag her away, and she found she could toss in his grip. "No! No! No! No . . ." But he was much stronger, and she soon felt the cold iron of a lamppost against her back as her arms were pulled around it.

"Shh, shh." She could just make out the glint of the man's teeth, feeling rather than seeing his grin as he bound her forearms roughly to the post. "I'm not worried about being overheard, mind you, thanks to this rum fog, but I don't see the sense in putting up a fuss."

"Let me go!" Mary half-screamed, half-sobbed, jerking away from her captor. "Let me go!"

"Shh, dearie, shh. None of that, now, or I shall have to be rough with you, see?"

Her arms bound securely to the post, he sidled around in front of her and put his hands on his hips, whistling in surprise. "Well, now, seems I caught me a lady." She caught the flash of his teeth again. "And here I thought I was getting me a dollymop."

"Don't, please, don't," Mary pleaded. "I can give you money—anything. Just please don't—"

But her pleas were muffled by lips forcefully covering her own, eliciting whimpers deep in her throat. Then his body was pressed up against hers once more, sending thrills of terror through her. She writhed beneath him, but he pressed her tightly against the lamppost, his lips still locked around hers and his hands busy with her clothes.

Father in Heaven, if ever You loved me, help me now!

John was trudging a bit less than gamely through the fog when he heard a wail that stopped him and chilled him to the bone. He knew that kind of wail. Then the woman—for female the voice was—screamed.

He took off running, adrenaline compensating for the debilitating ache spreading through his bad leg. He drew his revolver as the woman screamed again, and he would have sworn the voice sounded familiar. *Please, dear Lord, let me arrive on time.*

He ran straight into someone, bowling them over. The person swore and shoved him away, and John just noticed that the person, a man, was only half-clothed. He took only a split-second to see that, because his gaze was immediately drawn to the figure sagging against a lamppost, bound and even less clothed than the man, blouse, jacket, and skirt hanging in rags about her.

She looked up, and her expression of terror changed instantly to one of shocked relief. *"John!"*

Good heavens . . . *"Mary."*

With a snarl, the man at his feet leapt up and tackled him. Mary screamed again. Broader than his assailant, John stumbled but stood his ground, attempting to bring his Adams to bear. Metal gleamed dully in the lamplight, and John saw white as his bad shoulder erupted in a blaze of agony.

"JOHN!"

He squeezed the trigger, the shot shattering the air around them. The other man howled and staggered back towards Mary, the metal gleaming again. Desperate fury driving him, John leapt at the other man. Mary screamed again as they fell into the road.

They struggled for the gun, and John felt the other's finger tighten around the trigger. The revolver went off, knocking them both down again, but the shot went wide, mercifully missing not only John but Mary as well. Then the man was struggling just to get out of John's grip. Both men were strong, but both were hurt, and John felt the man break free. He staggered after the man, but he was gone, vanished into the fog that had disgorged him.

Panting, John turned to Mary . . . And fervently wished that he could have killed that . . . that monster . . .

A scarlet line ran from Mary's right collarbone down her upper arm. John's rugby tackle must have knocked the knife off-course, keeping it from slashing across her throat.

The Ripper.

"Mary," he pushed out in a croak as he returned to her and fished out his knife to cut her loose.

"John!" she sobbed. "Oh, thank God you were here!"

"Shh, Mary, you are going to be all right," he soothed as he worked at the ropes. "Why on earth were you here, and dressed like this?"

"F-friend," Mary choked out. "Lives here. C-clothes to k-keep me from b-being a t-target . . ."

John understood that much, but why the *devil* was she out *alone* in White-chapel at night in the middle of a Particular? "Mary, haven't you been reading the papers? The stories about the Ripper? That he targets prostitutes in Whitechapel?" He didn't mean to sound harsh, but the aftershock and the horror of the thing put an edge in his voice sharp enough to cut a person on.

"D-didn't th-think . . ." She broke down completely, and John could not fault her at all for it. He shuddered convulsively to think of what *would* have happened had he not arrived in time.

The newspapers would have had another sensational episode to report, Scotland Yard another murder on their hands, and the Ripper another tally to his bloody score. Mrs. Forrester would have lost a daughter, the Forrester children not so much a governess as an older sister, and John the only woman he had ever really loved.

A terrible little part of his mind wondered if Holmes would have even cared.

Of course, he would not have cared, a nasty voice hissed.

He bloody well would *have, John Hamish Watson,* retorted another voice, *and he would have because he cares about* you, *no matter the depths to which he sinks.*

The last of the rope fell away, allowing Mary to sink gratefully into his embrace. "Oh, John," she sobbed.

He wrapped her shawl around her partially exposed torso before carefully lifting her into his arms, mindful of his injured shoulder. It screamed in protest, but he ignored it, taking one step forward, then another. He knew he could ignore it only for so long—they had to get to a better part of town, and quickly.

Mary felt as if she was drowning in shame. She was ashamed of her foolishness, ashamed that her fiancé must see her exposed, ashamed that he had to rescue her at all, ashamed that she could not stop herself from sobbing like a little girl. And yet . . .

And yet she saw the grim determination in John's tense features, and she suddenly felt as if she was in the presence of a guardian angel.

It was late in the morning when at last Watson returned home from his work in Whitechapel. Holmes had a greeting poised upon his lips when Watson staggered through the sitting room door, clothes torn, mudded, and blood-soaked, the stain radiating from his bad shoulder. "My dear Watson!" Holmes cried, leaping to his feet from the settee.

Watson looked up from returning his revolver to his desk, fatigue, residual anger, and pain dimming his hazel eyes and turning them cognac brown. "Holmes," he began, his voice as dull as his eyes. "I beg you not to deduce what has happened."

"Watson, you are asking the impossible," Holmes murmured. *You have been in a fight in Whitechapel—I know that mud—and you were not the only injured party. You smell of disinfectant—there was a victim; you were defending them. That jagged hole in your clothes was clearly made by a knife.*

Even Lestrade could have put the clues together, though Holmes did not dare to do so aloud.

"Holmes. Please." Those expressive eyes were certainly a force to be reckoned with; Holmes merely sighed and shook his head.

"At least tell me that you've had the shoulder tended to."

"Yes." The relief in Watson's voice was profound.

"Very well, old man." Holmes forced levity into his tone, for the doctor's sake. "I do hope that you plan on going to bed soon; you look dreadful."

Watson shook his head in turn and shot Holmes a grateful smile before leaving the room. Holmes frowned contemplatively and turned to retrieve his cherrywood from the pipe rack. Scotland Yard had not yet approached him regarding the Ripper Case—Lestrade and Gregson, despite multiple protests, were not allowed to investigate, either. The powers that be apparently deemed Inspectors Abberline, Moore, and Andrews to be enough to handle the case. Ha. Their incompetence was not even amusing. But . . .

But Watson had now been dragged into this sordid affair.

And not only dragged, but stabbed, right in the shoulder that had cast him out of the army in the first place.

Holmes puffed furiously at his pipe, his hand clenching around the bowl. Whatever this monster called himself—Saucy Jack, Jack the Ripper—he would not continue his reign of terror for long. He was about to find out just how very great a mistake it was to injure the man Sherlock Holmes called "friend."

IN THE SLAUGHTERYARD

Anonymous

As awful as the dark streets of Whitechapel were, as filthy and foul-smelling as the worst alley in the East End, as frightening as a fog so thick that it was impossible to know whose footsteps were approaching from behind, all paled when compared with the premises of Melmoth Brothers and the grotesque business that it conducted. It is here, described as a devil's kitchen by a patrolling constable, that cat food is made from an assortment of disgusting ingredients, and glue is made from dead horses, sending a stench into the night air that can be handled only by those with the strongest stomachs.

It is to this abattoir that a member of the Adventurers' Club ventures during the scourge of Jack the Ripper and, after a close call outside its gates, relishes telling the tale to the other members of the club. It is one adventure in a very rare book that claims to have been written by six different anonymous authors but is almost certainly the work of a single person who is able to wonderfully capture the essence of hopelessly dark and chilling places.

"In the Slaughteryard" was first published in The Adventures of the Adventurers' Club: A Shocker in Six Shocks, by Five Men and a Woman, etc. (London, Gardner & Co., 1890). One can only wonder what the "etc." in the byline represents.

"You seem to have had a lively time of it, Jeaffreson; at all events you've got something to show for *your* night's adventure," said the President of the Adventurers' Club, pointing to the bandaged hand of Mr. Horace Jeaffreson.

"Yes," replied that gentleman, "I've got something to remember last night by; but I've got something more to show than this bandaged hand that you all stare at so curiously." And then Horace Jeaffreson rose, drew himself up to his full height of six feet one, and exhibited the left side of his closely-buttoned, well-fitting frock-coat. "I should like you to notice that," he said, pointing to a straight, clean cut in the cloth, just on a level with the region of the heart. "When you've heard what I've got to tell, you'll acknowledge that I had a pretty narrow squeak of it last night; three inches more, and it would have been all up with H. J. I don't regret it a bit, because I believe that I have been the means of ridding the world of a monster. Time alone will prove whether my supposition is correct," and then Mr. Horace Jeaffreson shuddered. "Before I begin the history of my adventures, there are two objects that I must submit to your inspection; they are in that little parcel that I have laid upon the mantelpiece. Perhaps as my left hand is disabled, you won't mind undoing the parcel, Mr. President."

He laid a long, narrow parcel upon the table, and the President proceeded to open it. The contents consisted of a policeman's truncheon—branded H 1839— and a long, narrow-bladed, double-edged knife, having an ebony handle, which was cut in criss-cross ridges. There were stains of blood upon the truncheon, and the knife appeared to have been dipped in a red transparent varnish, of the nature of which there could be no doubt.

"Those are the exhibits," said Horace Jeaffreson. "The slit in my coat, my wounded hand, that truncheon, and that bloodstained knife, and a copy of the morning paper, are all the proofs I have to give you that my adventure of last night was not a hideous nightmare dream, or a wildly improbable yarn.

"I must confess that when I placed my forefinger haphazard upon the map last night, and found that fate had given me Whitechapel as my hunting-ground, I was considerably disgusted. I left this place bound for the heart of sordid London, the home of vice, of misery, and crime. Until last night I knew nothing whatever about the East End of London. I've never been bitten with the desire to do even the smallest bit of 'slumming.' I'm sorry enough for the poor. I'd do all I can to help them in the way of subscribing, and that sort of thing, you know; but actual poverty in the flesh I confess to fighting shy of—it's a weakness I own, but, so to say, poverty, crass poverty, offends my nostrils. I'm not a snob, but that's the truth. However, I was in for it; I had got to pass the night in Whitechapel for the sake of what might turn up. A good deal turned up, and a good deal more than I had bargained for.

"'Shall I wait for you, sir?' said the cabman, as he pulled up his hansom at the corner of Osborne Street. 'I'm game to wait, sir, if you won't be long.'

"But I dismissed him. 'I shall be here for several hours, my man,' I said.

"'You know best, sir,' said the cabman: 'everyone to his taste. You'd better keep yer weather-eye open, sir, anyhow; for the side streets ain't over and above safe about here. If I were you, sir, I'd get a "copper" to show me round.' And then the man thanked me for a liberal fare, and flicking his horse, drove off.

"But I had come to Whitechapel to seek adventure, something was bound to turn up, and, as a modern Don Quixote, I determined to take my chance alone; for it wasn't under the protecting wing of a member of the Force that I was likely to come across any very stirring novelty.

"I wandered about the dirty, badly-lighted streets, and I marvelled at the teeming hundreds who thronged the principal thoroughfares. I don't think that ever in my life before I had seen so many hungry, hopeless-looking, anxious-looking people crowded together. They all seemed to be hurrying either to the public-house or from the public-house. Nobody offered to molest me. I'm a fairly big man, and with the exception of having my pockets attempted some half-dozen times, I met with no annoyance of any kind. As twelve o'clock struck an extraordinary change came over the neighbourhood; the doors of the public-houses were closed, and, save in the larger thoroughfares, the whole miserable quarter seemed to become suddenly silent and deserted. I had succeeded in losing myself at least half a dozen times; but go where I would, turn where I might, two things struck me— first, the extraordinary number of policemen about; second, the frightened way in which men and women, particularly the homeless wanderers of the night, of both sexes, regarded me. Belated wayfarers would step aside out of my path, and stare at me, as though with dread. Some, more timorous than the rest, would even cross the road at my approach; or, avoiding me, start off at a run or at a shambling trot. It puzzled me at first. Why on earth should the poverty-stricken rabble, who had the misfortune to live in this wretched neighbourhood, be afraid of a man, or appear to be afraid of a man, who had a decent coat to his back?

"The side streets, as I say, were almost absolutely deserted, save for infrequent policemen who gave me good-night, or gazed at me suspiciously. I was wandering aimlessly along, when my curiosity was suddenly aroused by a powerful, acrid, and peculiar odour. 'Without doubt,' said I to myself, 'that is the nastiest stench it has ever been my misfortune to smell in the whole course of my life.' 'Stench' is a Johnsonian word, and very expressive; it's the only word to convey any idea of the nastiness of the mixed odours which assailed my nostrils. 'I will follow my nose,' I said to myself, and I turned down a narrow lane, a short lane, lit by a single gas-lamp. 'It gets worse and worse,' I thought, 'and it can't be far off, whatever it is.' It was so bad that I actually had to hold my nose.

"At that moment I ran into the arms of a policeman, who appeared to spring suddenly out of the earth.

"'I'm sure I beg your pardon,' I said to the man.

"'Don't mention it, sir,' replied the policeman briskly and there was something of a countryman's drawl in the young man's voice. 'Been and lost yourself, sir, I suppose?' he continued.

"'Well, not exactly,' I replied. 'The fact is, I wandered down here to see where the smell came from.'

"'You've come to the right shop, sir,' said the policeman, with a smile; 'it's a regular devil's kitchen they've got going on down here, it's just a knacker's, sir, that's what it is; and they make glue, and size, and cat's-meat, and patent manure. It isn't a trade that most people would hanker for,' said the young policeman with a smile. 'They are in a very large way of business, sir, are Melmoth Brothers; it might be worth your while, sir, to take a look round; you'll find the night-watchman inside, sir, and he'd be pleased to show you over the place for a trifle; and it's worth seeing is Melmoth Brothers.'

"'I'll take your advice, and have a look at the place,' I answered. 'There seems to be a great number of police about tonight, my man,' I said.

"'Well, yes, sir,' replied the constable, 'you see the scare down here gets worse and worse; and the people here are just afraid of their own shadows after midnight; the wonder to my mind is, sir, that we haven't dropped on to him long ago.'

"Then all at once it dawned upon me why it was that men and women had turned aside from me in fear; then I saw why it was that the place seemed a perfect ants' nest of police. The great scare was at its height: the last atrocity had been committed only four days before.

"'Why, bless my heart, sir,' cried the young policeman confidentially, 'one might come upon him red-handed at any moment. I only wish it was my luck to come across him, sir,' he added. 'Lor' bless ye, sir,' the young policeman went on, 'he'll be a pulling it off just once too often, one of these nights.'

"'Well, I suppose he helps to keep you awake,' I said with a smile, for want of something better to say.

"'Keep me awake, sir!' said the man solemnly; 'I don't suppose there's a single constable in the whole H Division as thinks of aught else. Why, sir, he haunts me like; and do you know, sir'—and the man's voice suddenly dropped to a very low whisper—'I do think as how I saw him'; and then he gave a sigh. 'I was standing, sir, just where I was when I popped out on you, a hiding-up like; it was more than a month ago, and there was a woman standing crying, leaning on that very post, sir, by Melmoth Brothers' gate, with just a thin ragged shawl, sir, drawn over her head. She was down upon her luck, I suppose, you see, sir—and there was a heavyish fog on at the time—when stealing up out of the fog behind where the poor thing was standing, sir, sobbing and crying for all the world just like a hungry child, I saw something brown noiselessly stealing up towards the woman; she had her back to it, sir—and she never moved. I could just make out the stooping figure of a man, who came swiftly forward with noiseless footsteps, crouching along in the deep shadow of yonder wall. I rubbed my eyes to see if I was awake or dreaming; and, as the crouching figure rapidly advanced, I saw that it was a man in a long close-fitting brown coat of common tweed. He'd got a black billycock jammed down over his eyes, and a red cotton comforter that hid his face; and in his left hand, which he held behind him, sir, was something that now and again glittered in the light of that lamp up there. I loosed my truncheon, sir, and I stood back as quiet as a mouse, for I guessed who I'd got to deal with. Whoever he was, he meant murder, and that was clear—murder and worse. All of a sudden, sir, he turned and ran back into the fog, and I after him as hard as I could pelt; and then he disappeared just as if he'd sunk through the earth. I blew my whistle, sir, and I reported what I'd seen at the station, and the superintendent—he just reprimanded me, that's what he did.

"' "1839, I don't believe a word of it," said he; and he didn't.

"'But I *did* see him, sir, all the same; and if I get the chance,' said the man bitterly, 'I'll put my mark on him.'

"'Well, policeman,' I said, 'I hope you may, for your sake,' and then I forced a shilling on him. 'I'll go and have a look round at Melmoth Brothers' place,' I said. I gave the young policeman good night, and I crossed the road and walked through the open gateway into a large yard, from whence proceeded the atrocious odour that poisoned the neighbourhood.

"The place was on a slope, it was paved with small round stones, and was triangular in shape; a high wall at the end by which I had entered formed the base of the triangle, and one side of the narrow lane in which I had left the young policeman. There was a sort of shed or shelter of corrugated iron running along this wall, and under the shed I could indistinctly see the figures of horses and other animals, evidently secured, in a long row. All down one side of the boundary wall of the great yard which sloped from the lane towards the point of the triangle, I saw a number of furnace doors, five and twenty of them at least; they appeared to be let into a long low wall of masonry of the most solid description, and they presented an extraordinary appearance, giving one the idea of the hulk of a mysterious ship, burnt well-nigh to the water's edge, through whose closed ports the fire, which was slowly consuming her, might be plainly seen. The curious similitude to a burning hulk was rendered still more striking by the fact that, above the low wall in which the furnace doors were set, there was a heavy cloud of dense white steam which hung suspended above what seemed like the burning hull of the great phantom ship. There wasn't a breath of air last night, you know, to stir that reeking cloud of fetid steam; and the young summer moon shone down upon it bright and clear, making the heaped piles of steaming vapour look like great clouds of fleecy whiteness. The place was silent as the grave itself, save for a soft bubbling sound as of some thick fluid that perpetually boiled and simmered, and the occasional movement of one of the tethered animals. The wall opposite the row of furnaces, which formed the other side of the triangle, had a number of stout iron rings set in it some four feet apart, and looked, for all the world, like some old wharf from which the sea had long ago receded. At the apex of the triangle, where the walls nearly met, were a pair of heavy double doors of wood, which were well-nigh covered with stains and splashes of dazzling whiteness; and the ground in front of them was stained white too, as though milk, or whitewash, had been spilled, for several feet.

"There were great wooden blocks and huge benches standing about in the great paved yard; and I noted a couple of solid gallowslike structures, from each of which depended an iron pulley, holding a chain and a great iron hook. I noted, too, as a strange thing, that though the ground was paved with rounded stones—and, as you know, it was a dry night and early summer—yet in many places there were puddles of dark mud, and the ground there was wet and slippery.

"But what struck me as the strangest thing of all in this weird and dreadful place, were the numerous horses lying about in every direction, apparently sleeping soundly; but as I stared at them, brilliantly lighted up as they were by the rays of the clear bright moon, I saw that they were not sleeping beasts at all—that they were not old and worn-out animals calmly sleeping in happy ignorance of the fate that waited them on the morrow—but by their strange stiffened and gruesome attitudes, I perceived that the creatures were already dead.

"I'm no longer a child, I have no illusions, and I am not easily frightened; but I felt a terrible sense of oppression come over me in this dreadful place. I began to feel as a little one feels when he is thrust, for the first time in his life, into a dark room by a thoughtless nurse. But I had come out of curiosity to see the place; I had expressed my intention of doing so to Constable 1839 of the H Division; so I made up my mind to go through with it. I would see what there was to be seen, I would learn something about the mysterious trade of Melmoth Brothers; and as a preliminary I proceeded to light my briar-root, so as, if possible, to get rid to some extent of the numerous diabolical smells of the place by the fragrant odour of Murray's mixture.

"And then, when I had lighted my pipe, I was startled by a hoarse voice which suddenly croaked out—'Make yourself at home, guv'nor; don't you stand on no sort o' ceremony, for you look a gentleman, you does; a real gentleman, a chap what always has the price of a pint in his pocket, and wouldn't grudge the loan of a bit of baccy to a pore old chap as is down on his luck.'

"I turned to the place from whence the voice proceeded. It was a strange-looking creature that had addressed me. He was an old man with a pointed grey beard, who sat upon a bench of massive timber covered with dreadful stains. The bright moon lighted up his face, and I could see his features as clearly as though I saw them by the light of day. He was clad in a long linen jerkin of coarse stuff, reaching nearly to his heels; but its colour was no longer white—the garment was red, reddened by awful smears and splashes from head to foot. The figure wore a pair of heavy jack-boots, with wooden soles, nigh upon an inch thick, to which the uppers were riveted with nails of copper; those great boots of his made me sick to look at them. But the strangest thing of all in the dreadful costume of the grim figure was the head-dress, which was a close-fitting wig of knitted grey wool; very similar, in appearance at all events, to the undress wig worn by the Lord High Chancellor of England—that wig, that once sacred wig, which Mr. George Grossmith has taught us to look upon with that familiarity which breeds contempt. The wig was tied beneath the pointed beard by a string. I noted that round the figure's waist was a leathern strap, from which hung a sort of black pouch; from the top of this projected, so as to be ready to his hand, the hafts of several knives of divers sorts and sizes. The face was lean, haggard, and wrinkled; fierce ferrety eyes sparkled beneath long shaggy grey eyebrows; and the toothless jaws of the old man and his pointed grey beard seemed to wage convulsively as in suppressed amusement. And then Macaulay's lines ran through my mind—

> "'To the mouth of some dark lair,
> Where growling low, a fierce old bear
> Lies amidst bones and blood.'

"'Haw-haw! guv'nor,' he said, 'you might think as I was one o' these murderers. I ain't the kind of cove as a young woman would care to meet of a summer night, nor any sort of night for the matter of that, am I? Haw-haw! But the houses is closed, guv'nor, worse luck; and I'm dreadful dry.'

"'You talk as if you'd been drinking, my man,' I said.

"'That's where you're wrong, guv'nor. Why, bless me if I've touched a drop of drink for six mortal days; but tomorrow's pay-day, and tomorrow night, guv'nor—tomorrow night I'll make up for it. And so you've come to look round, eh? You're the fust swell as I ever seed in this here blooming yard as had the pluck.'

"And then I began to question him about the details of the hideous business of Melmoth Brothers.

"'They brings 'em in, guv'nor, mostly irregular,' said the old man; 'they brings 'em in dead, and chucks 'em down anywhere, just as you see; and they brings 'em in alive, and we ties 'em up and feeds 'em proper, and gives 'em water, according to the Act; and then we just turns 'em into size and glue, or various special lines, or cat's-meat, or patent manure, or superphosphate, as the case may be. We boils 'em all down within twenty-four hours. Haw-haw!' cried the dreadful old man in almost fiendish glee. 'There ain't much left of 'em when we've done with 'em, except the smell. Haw-haw! Why, bless ye, there's nigh on half a dozen cab ranks a simmering in them there boilers,' and he pointed to the furnace fires.

"And then the old man led me past the great row of furnace doors, and down the yard to the very end; and then we reached the two low wooden gates which stood at the lower end of the sloping yard. He pushed back one of the splashed and whitened doors with a great iron fork, and propped it open; then he flung open the door of the end furnace, which threw a lurid light into a low vaulted brickwork chamber within. I saw that the floor of the chamber consisted of a vast leaden cistern, and that some fluid, on whose surface was a thick white scum, filled it, and gave forth a strangely acrid and, at the same time, pungent, odour.

"'This 'ere,' said the old man, 'is where we make the superphosphate; there's several tons of the strongest vitriol in this here place; we filled up fresh today, guv'nor. If I was to shove you into that there vat, you'd just melt up for all the world like a lump of sugar in a glass of hot toddy; and you'd come out superphosphate, guv'nor, when they drors the vat. Haw-haw! Seein's believin', they say; just you look here. This here barrer's full of fresh horses' bones; they've ben biled nigh on two days. They're bones, you see, real bones, without a bit of flesh on them. You just stand back, guv'nor, lest you get splashed and spiles yer clothes. Haw-haw!'

"I did as I was bid. And then the old man suddenly shot the barrow full of white bones into the steaming vat.

"'There, guv'nor,' he said, with another diabolical laugh, as the fluid in the cistern of the great arched chamber hissed and bubbled. 'They *wos* bones; they're superphosphate by this time. There ain't no more to show ye, guv'nor,' said the old man with a leer, as he stretched out his hand.

"I placed a half-crown in it.

"'I knowed ye was a gentleman,' he said. 'It's a hot night, guv'nor, and I'm dreadful droughty; but I do know where a drink's to be had at any hour, when you've got the ready, and I'll be off to get one.'

"'You've forgotten to shut the furnace door, my man,' I said.

"'Thank ye, guv'nor, but I did it a purpose; the boiler above it's to be drored tomorrow.'

"'Aren't you afraid that if you leave the place something may be stolen?'

"'Lor, guv'nor,' said the old man with a laugh, 'you're the fust as has showed his nose inside of Melmoth Brothers' premises after dark, except the chaps as works here. Haw-haw! they durstn't, guv'nor, come into this place; they calls it the Devil's Cookshop hereabouts,' and taking the iron fork up, the whitened wooden door swung back into its place, and hid the mass of seething vitriol from my view.

"Then, without a word, the old man in his heavy wooden-soled boots clattered out of the place, leaving me alone upon the premises of Melmoth Brothers.

"For several minutes I stood and gazed around me upon the strange weird scene of horror, when suddenly I heard a sound in the lane without, a sound as of a half-stifled shriek of agony. I hurried out into the lane at once. I looked up and down it, and fancied that I saw a dark brown shadow suddenly disappear within an archway. I walked hurriedly towards the archway. There was nothing. And now I heard a low voice cry in choking accents, 'Help!' Then there was a groan. At that instant I stumbled over something which lay half in half out of the entrance of a court. It was the body of a man. I stooped over him—it was the young policeman. I recognized his face instantly.

"'I'm glad you've come, sir,' said the poor fellow, in failing accents. 'He's put the hat on me, sir. He stabbed me from behind, and I'm choking, sir. But I saw him plain this time; it *was* him, sir, the man with the brown tweed coat and the red comforter. Don't you move, sir,' said the dying man, in a still lower whisper;

'*I see him, sir,* I see him now, stooping and peeping round the archway. If you move, sir, he'll twig you and he'll slope. Oh, God!' sobbed the poor young constable, and he gave a shudder. He was dead.

"Still leaning over the body of the dead man, I tried to collect my thoughts, for, my friends, I don't mind confessing to you, for the first time in my life, since I was a child, I was really afraid. An awful deadly fear—a fear of I knew not what—had come upon me. I trembled in every limb, my hair grew wet with sweat, and I could hear—yes, I could hear—the actual beating of my own heart, as though it were a sledge-hammer. I was alone—alone and unarmed, two hours after midnight, in this dreadful place, with—well, I had no doubt with whom. No, not unarmed. I placed my hand upon the truncheon-case of the dead man. I gripped that truncheon, which is now lying upon the table, and in an instant my courage came back to me. Then, still stooping over the body of the murdered man, I slowly—very slowly—turned my head. There was the man, the murderer, the wretch who had been so accurately described to me, the crouching figure in the brown tweed coat, with the red cotton comforter loosely wound round his neck. In his left hand there was something long and bright and keen that glittered in the soft moonlight of the silent summer night.

"And I saw his face, his dreadful face, the face that will haunt me to my dying day.

"It wasn't a bit like the descriptions. Mr. Stewart Cumberland's vision of 'The Man' differed in every possible particular from the being whom I watched from under the dark shadow of the entry of the court, as he stood glaring at me in the moonlight, like a hungry tiger prepared to spring. The man had long, crisp-looking locks of tangled hair, which hung on either side of his face. There was no difficulty in studying him: the features were clearly, even brilliantly illuminated, both by the bright moonlight and by the one street-lamp, which chanced to be above his head; even the humidity of his fierce black eyes and of his cruel teeth was plainly apparent; there wasn't a single detail of the dreadful face that escaped me.

"I'm not going to describe it, it was too awful, and words would fail me. I'll tell you why I'll not describe it in a moment.

"Have you ever seen a horse with a very tight bearing-rein on? Of course you have. Well, just as the horse throws his head about in uneasy torture, and champing his bit flings forth great flecks of foam, so did the man I was watching—watching with the hunter's eye, watching as a wild and noxious beast that I was hoping anon to slay—so did his jaws, I say, champ and gnash and mumble savagely and throw forth great flecks of white froth. The creature literally foamed at the mouth, for this dreadful thirst for blood was evidently, as yet, unsatiated. The eyes were those of a madman, or of a hunted beast driven to bay. I have no doubt, no shadow of doubt, in my own mind, that he—the man in the brown coat—was a savage maniac, a person wholly irresponsible for his actions.

"And now I'll tell you why I'm not going to describe that dreadful face of his, because, as I have told you, words would fail me. Give free rein to your fancy, let your imagination loose, and they will fail to convey to your mind one tittle of the loathsome horror of those features. The face was scarred in every direction—the mouth——

"Bah! I need say no more, the man was a leper. I have been in the Southern Seas, and I know—I know what a leper is like.

"But I hadn't much time for meditation. I was alone with the dead man and his murderer: as likely as not, if the man in the brown coat should escape me, *I* might be accused of the crime; the very fact of my being possessed of the dead man's truncheon would be looked on as a damning proof. Gripping the truncheon I rushed out upon the living horror. I would have shouted for assistance, but, why I cannot tell, my voice died away as to a whisper within my breast. It wasn't fear for I rushed upon him fully determined to either take or slay the dreadful thing that wore the ghastly semblance of a man. I rushed upon him, I say, and struck furiously at him with the heavy staff. But he eluded me.

"Noiselessly and swiftly, without even breaking the silence of the night, just as a snake slinks into its hole, the creature dived suddenly beneath my arm, and with an activity that astounded me, passed as though he were without substance (for I heard no sound of footfalls) through the great open gates which formed the entry to the premises of Melmoth Brothers. As he passed under my outstretched arm he must have stabbed through my thin overcoat, and as you see," said Horace Jeaffreson, pointing to the cut in his frock-coat, "an inch or two more, and H. J. wouldn't have been among you to eat his breakfast and spin his yarn. The slash in the overcoat I wore last night, my friends, has a trace of bloodstains on it—but it was not *my* blood.

"'Now,' thought I, 'I've got him'; his very flight filled me with determination, and I resolved to take him alive if possible, for I felt that he was delivered into my hand, and I was determined that he should not escape me; rather than that, I would knock him on the head with as little compunction as I would kill a mad dog.

"As these thoughts passed through my mind, I sped after the murderer of the unfortunate policeman. I gained upon him rapidly, I was within three yards of him, when we reached the middle of the great knackers' yard; and then he attempted to dodge me round a sort of huge chopping-block which stood there.

"'If you don't surrender, by God I'll kill you,' I shouted.

"He never answered me, he only mowed and gibbered as he fled, threatening me at the same time with the knife which he held in his hand.

"I vaulted the block, and flung myself upon him; and I struck at him savagely and caught him across the forehead with the truncheon; and suddenly uttering a sort of cry as of an animal in pain, he stabbed me through the hand and turned and fled once more, I after him. At the moment I didn't even know that I had been stabbed. I gained upon him, but he reached the bottom of the yard, and turned in front of the low whitened doors and stopped and stood at bay—crouching, knife in hand, in the strong light thrown out by the open furnace door, as though about to spring. Blood was streaming over his face from the wound I had given him upon his forehead, and it half blinded him; and ever and anon he tried to clear his eyes of it with the cuff of his right hand. His face and figure glowed red and unearthly in the firelight.

"I wasn't afraid of him now; I advanced on him.

"Suddenly he sprang forward. I stepped back and hit him over the knuckles of his raised left hand, in which glittered the knife you see upon that table. I struck with all my might, and the knife fell from his nerveless grasp.

"He rushed back with wonderful agility. The white and rotting doors rolled open on their hinges. I saw him fall backwards with a splash into the mass of froth now coloured by the firelight with a pinky glow.

"He disappeared.

"And then, horror of horrors, I saw the dreadful form rise once more, and cling for an instant to the low edge of the great leaden tank, and make its one last struggle for existence; and then it sank beneath the fuming waves, never to rise again.

"That's all I have to tell. I picked up the knife and secured it, with the truncheon, about my person, as best I could.

"I'm glad that I avenged the death of the poor fellow whom I only knew as 1839 H. I shall be happier still if, as I believe, through my humble instrumentality, the awful outrages at the East End of London have ended.

"I got to my chambers in the Albany by three in the morning, then I sent for the nearest doctor to dress my hand. It's not a serious cut, but I had bled like a pig.

"I bought the morning paper on my way here; it gives the details of the murder of Constable 1839 of the H Division by an unknown hand; and it mentions that the murderer appears to have possessed himself of the truncheon of his victim. You see he was stabbed through the great vessels of the lungs.

"I have no further remarks to make, except that I don't believe we shall hear any more of Jack the Ripper. Of one thing I am perfectly certain, that I shall not visit Whitechapel again in a hurry."

~

THE LODGER

Marie Belloc Lowndes

A prolific author of historical, romantic, and crime fiction and plays, Marie Adelaide Belloc Lowndes (1868–1947) based most of her work on historical events. Her most notable story, "The Lodger," draws heavily on the Jack the Ripper murders of 1888. In 1913, two years after it was published as a short story that became enormously popular and created extraordinary attention, it was expanded into a full-length novel that has remained in print for more than a century.

In this classic suspense tale, Mr. Sleuth, a gentle man and a gentleman, takes rooms in Mr. and Mrs. Bunting's lodging house. Inexplicably, Mrs. Bunting becomes more and more terrified of him as the series of brutal Ripper murders continues to horrify London.

Marie Belloc was a member of a distinguished family. She was the daughter of the French barrister Louis Belloc and the English activist Bessie Rayner Parkes. Her brother was the famous writer Hilaire Belloc; her great-great-grandfather was Joseph Priestley, the chemist who discovered oxygen; her grandmother Louise Swanton Belloc was the translator of Harriet Beecher Stowe's *Uncle Tom's Cabin* (1852) in France; and her husband, Frederic Sawrey Lowndes, was a distinguished journalist for the London *Times*.

Although Lowndes was highly successful across several genres, only her short story "The Lodger" and the novel that it inspired are widely read today.

"The Lodger" was first published in the January 1911 issue of *McClure's Magazine*.

"There he is at last, and I'm glad of it, Ellen. 'Tain't a night you would wish a dog to be out in."

Mr. Bunting's voice was full of unmistakable relief. He was close to the fire, sitting back in a deep leather armchair—a clean-shaven, dapper man, still in outward appearance what he had been so long, and now no longer was—a self-respecting butler.

"You needn't feel so nervous about him; Mr. Sleuth can look out for himself, all right." Mrs. Bunting spoke in a dry, rather tart tone. She was less emotional, better balanced, than was her husband. On her the marks of past servitude were less apparent, but they were there all the same—especially in her neat black stuff dress and scrupulously clean, plain collar and cuffs. Mrs. Bunting, as a single woman, had been for long years what is known as a useful maid.

"I can't think why he wants to go out in such weather. He did it in last week's fog, too," Bunting went on complainingly.

"Well, it's none of your business—now, is it?"

"No; that's true enough. Still, 'twould be a very bad thing for us if anything happened to him. This lodger's the first bit of luck we've had for a very long time."

Mrs. Bunting made no answer to this remark. It was too obviously true to be worth answering. Also she was listening—following in imagination her lodger's quick, singularly quiet—"stealthy," she called it to herself—progress through the dark, fog-filled hall and up the staircase.

"It isn't safe for decent folk to be out in such weather—not unless they have something to do that won't wait till tomorrow." Bunting had at last turned round. He was now looking straight into his wife's narrow, colorless face; he was an obstinate man, and liked to prove himself right. "I read you out the accidents in *Lloyd's* yesterday—shocking, they were, and all brought about by the fog! And then, that 'orrid monster at his work again—"

"Monster?" repeated Mrs. Bunting absently. She was trying to hear the lodger's footsteps overhead; but her husband went on as if there had been no interruption:

"It wouldn't be very pleasant to run up against such a party as that in the fog, eh?"

"What stuff you do talk!" she said sharply; and then she got up suddenly. Her husband's remark had disturbed her. She hated to think of such things as the terrible series of murders that were just then horrifying and exciting the nether world of London. Though she enjoyed pathos and sentiment,—Mrs. Bunting would listen with mild amusement to the details of a breach-of-promise action— she shrank from stories of either immorality or physical violence.

Mrs. Bunting got up from the straight-backed chair on which she had been sitting. It would soon be time for supper.

She moved about the sitting-room, flecking off an imperceptible touch of dust here, straightening a piece of furniture there.

Bunting looked around once or twice. He would have liked to ask Ellen to leave off fidgeting, but he was mild and fond of peace, so he refrained. However, she soon gave over what irritated him of her own accord.

But even then Mrs. Bunting did not at once go down to the cold kitchen, where everything was in readiness for her simple cooking. Instead, she opened the door leading into the bedroom behind, and there, closing the door quietly, stepped back into the darkness and stood motionless, listening.

At first she heard nothing, but gradually there came the sound of someone moving about in the room just overhead; try as she might, however, it was impossible for her to guess what her lodger was doing. At last she heard him open the door leading out to the landing. That meant that he would spend the rest of the evening in the rather cheerless room above the drawing-room floor—oddly enough, he liked sitting there best, though the only warmth obtainable was from a gas-stove fed by a shilling-in-the-slot arrangement.

It was indeed true that Mr. Sleuth had brought the Buntings luck, for at the time he had taken their rooms it had been touch and go with them.

After having each separately led the sheltered, impersonal, and, above all, the financially easy existence that is the compensation life offers to those men and women who deliberately take upon themselves the yoke of domestic service, these two, butler and useful maid, had suddenly, in middle age, determined to join their fortunes and savings.

Bunting was a widower; he had one pretty daughter, a girl of seventeen, who now lived, as had been the case ever since the death of her mother, with a prosperous aunt. His second wife had been reared in the Foundling Hospital, but she had gradually worked her way up into the higher ranks of the servant class and as a useful maid she had saved quite a tidy sum of money.

Unluckily, misfortune had dogged Mr. and Mrs. Bunting from the very first. The seaside place where they had begun by taking a lodging-house became the scene of an epidemic. Then had followed a business experiment which had proved disastrous. But before going back into service, either together or separately, they had made up their minds to make one last effort, and, with the little money that remained to them, they had taken over the lease of a small house in the Marylebone Road.

Bunting, whose appearance was very good, had retained a connection with old employers and their friends, so he occasionally got a good job as waiter. During this last month his jobs had perceptibly increased in number and in profit; Mrs. Bunting was not superstitious, but it seemed that in this matter, as in everything else, Mr. Sleuth, their new lodger, had brought them luck.

As she stood there, still listening intently in the darkness of the bedroom, she told herself, not for the first time, what Mr. Sleuth's departure would mean to her and Bunting. It would almost certainly mean ruin.

Luckily, the lodger seemed entirely pleased both with the rooms and with his landlady. There was really no reason why he should ever leave such nice lodgings. Mrs. Bunting shook off her vague sense of apprehension and unease. She turned round, took a step forward, and, feeling for the handle of the door giving into the passage, she opened it, and went down with light, firm steps into the kitchen.

She lit the gas and put a frying-pan on the stove, and then once more her mind reverted, as if in spite of herself, to her lodger, and there came back to Mrs. Bunting, very vividly, the memory of all that had happened the day Mr. Sleuth had taken her rooms.

The date of this excellent lodger's coming had been the twenty-ninth of December, and the time late afternoon. She and Bunting had been sitting, gloomily enough, over their small banked-up fire. They had dined in the middle of the day—he on a couple of sausages, she on a little cold ham. They were utterly out of heart, each trying to pluck up courage to tell the other that it was no use trying any more. The two had also had a little tiff on that dreary afternoon. A newspaper-seller had come yelling down the Marylebone Road, shouting out, "'Orrible murder in Whitechapel!" and just because Bunting had an old uncle living in the East End he had gone and bought a paper, and at a time, too, when every penny, nay, every half-penny, had its full value! Mrs. Bunting remembered the circumstances because that murder in Whitechapel had been the first of these terrible crimes—there had been four since—which she would never allow Bunting to discuss in her presence, and yet which had of late begun to interest curiously, uncomfortably, even her refined mind.

But, to return to the lodger. It was then, on that dreary afternoon, that suddenly there had come to the front door a tremulous, uncertain double knock.

Bunting ought to have got up, but he had gone on reading the paper; and so Mrs. Bunting, with the woman's greater courage, had gone out into the passage, turned up the gas, and opened the door to see who it could be. She remembered, as if it were yesterday instead of nigh on a month ago, Mr. Sleuth's peculiar appearance. Tall, dark, lanky, an old-fashioned top hat concealing his high bald forehead, he had stood there, an odd figure of a man, blinking at her.

"I believe—is it not a fact that you let lodgings?" he had asked in a hesitating, whistling voice, a voice that she had known in a moment to be that of an educated man—of a gentleman. As he had stepped into the hall, she had noticed that in his right hand he held a narrow bag—a quite new bag of strong brown leather.

Everything had been settled in less than a quarter of an hour. Mr. Sleuth had at once "taken" to the drawing-room floor, and then, as Mrs. Bunting eagerly lit the gas in the front room above, he had looked around him and said, rubbing his hands with a nervous movement, "Capital—capital! This is just what I've been looking for!"

The sink had specially pleased him—the sink and the gas-stove. "This is quite first-rate!" he had exclaimed, "for I make all sorts of experiments. I am, you must understand, Mrs.—er—Bunting, a man of science." Then he had sat down—suddenly. "I'm very tired," he had said in a low tone, "very tired indeed! I have been walking about all day."

From the very first the lodger's manner had been odd, sometimes distant and abrupt, and then, for no reason at all that she could see, confidential and plaintively confiding. But Mrs. Bunting was aware that eccentricity has always been a perquisite, as it were the special luxury, of the well born and well educated. Scholars and such-like are never quite like other people.

And then, this particular gentleman had proved himself so eminently satisfactory as to the one thing that really matters to those who let lodgings. "My name is Sleuth," he said. "S-l-e-u-t-h. Think of a hound, Mrs. Bunting, and you'll never forget my name. I could give you references," he had added, giving her, as she now remembered, a funny sidewise look, "but I prefer to dispense with them. How much did you say? Twenty-three shillings a week, with attendance? Yes, that will suit me perfectly; and I'll begin by paying my first month's rent in advance. Now, four times twenty-three shillings is"—he looked at Mrs. Bunting, and for the first time he smiled, a queer, wry smile—"ninety-two shillings."

He had taken a handful of sovereigns out of his pocket and put them down on the table. "Look here," he had said, "there's five pounds; and you can keep the change, for I shall want you to do a little shopping for me tomorrow."

After he had been in the house about an hour, the bell had rung, and the new lodger had asked Mrs. Bunting if she could oblige him with the loan of a Bible. She brought up to him her best Bible, the one that had been given to her as a wedding present by a lady with whose mother she had lived for several years. This Bible and one other book, of which the odd name was *Cruden's Concordance*, formed Mr. Sleuth's only reading; he spent hours each day poring over the Old Testament and over the volume which Mrs. Bunting had at last decided to be a queer kind of index to the Book.

However, to return to the lodger's first arrival. He had had no luggage with him, barring the small brown bag, but very soon parcels had begun to arrive addressed to Mr. Sleuth, and it was then that Mrs. Bunting first became curious. These parcels were full of clothes; but it was quite clear to the landlady's feminine eye that none of those clothes had been made for Mr. Sleuth. They were, in fact, second-hand clothes, bought at good second-hand places, each marked, when marked at all, with a different name. And the really extraordinary thing was that occasionally a complete suit disappeared—became, as it were, obliterated from the lodger's wardrobe.

As for the bag he had brought with him, Mrs. Bunting had never caught sight of it again. And this also was certainly very strange.

Mrs. Bunting thought a great deal about that bag. She often wondered what had been in it; not a nightshirt and comb and brush, as she had at first supposed, for Mr. Sleuth had asked her to go out and buy him a brush and comb and tooth-brush the morning after his arrival. That fact was specially impressed on her memory, for at the little shop, a barber's, where she had purchased the brush and comb, the foreigner who had served her had insisted on telling her some of the horrible details of the murder that had taken place the day before in Whitechapel, and it had upset her very much.

As to where the bag was now, it was probably locked up in the lower part of a chiffonnier in the front sitting-room. Mr. Sleuth evidently always carried the key of the little cupboard on his person, for Mrs. Bunting, though she looked well for it, had never been able to find it.

And yet, never was there a more confiding or trusting gentleman. The first four days that he had been with them he had allowed his money—the considerable sum of one hundred and eighty-four pounds in gold—to lie about wrapped up in pieces of paper on his dressing-table. This was a very foolish, indeed a wrong thing to do, as she had allowed herself respectfully to point out to him; but as only answer he had laughed, a loud, discordant shout of laughter.

Mr. Sleuth had many other odd ways; but Mrs. Bunting, a true woman in spite of her prim manner and love of order, had an infinite patience with masculine vagaries.

On the first morning of Mr. Sleuth's stay in the Buntings' house, while Mrs. Bunting was out buying things for him, the new lodger had turned most of the pictures and photographs hanging in his sitting-room with their faces to the wall! But this queer action on Mr. Sleuth's part had not surprised Mrs. Bunting as much as it might have done; it recalled an incident of her long-past youth—something that had happened a matter of twenty years ago, at a time when Mrs. Bunting, then the still youthful Ellen Cottrell, had been maid to an old lady. The old lady had a favorite nephew, a bright, jolly young gentleman who had been learning to paint animals in Paris; and it was he who had had the impudence, early one summer morning, to turn to the wall six beautiful engravings of paintings done by the famous Mr. Landseer! The old lady thought the world of these pictures, but her nephew, as the only excuse for the extraordinary thing he had done, had observed that "they put his eye out."

Mr. Sleuth's excuse had been much the same; for, when Mrs. Bunting had come into his sitting-room and found all her pictures, or at any rate all those of her pictures that happened to be portraits of ladies, with their faces to the wall, he had offered as only explanation, "Those women's eyes follow me about."

Mrs. Bunting had gradually become aware that Mr. Sleuth had a fear and dislike of women. When she was "doing" the staircase and landing, she often heard him reading bits of the Bible aloud to himself, and in the majority of instances the texts he chose contained uncomplimentary reference to her own sex. Only today she had stopped and listened while he uttered threateningly the awful words, "A strange woman is a narrow pit. She also lieth in wait as for a prey, and increaseth the transgressors among men." There had been a pause, and then had come, in a high singsong, "Her house is the way to hell, going down to the chambers of death." It had made Mrs. Bunting feel quite queer.

The lodger's daily habits were also peculiar. He stayed in bed all the morning, and sometimes part of the afternoon, and he never went out before the street lamps were alight. Then, there was his dislike of an open fire; he generally sat in the top front room, and while there he always used the large gas-stove, not only for his experiments, which he carried on at night, but also in the daytime, for warmth.

But there! Where was the use of worrying about the lodger's funny ways? Of course, Mr. Sleuth was eccentric; if he hadn't been "just a leetle 'touched' upstairs"—as Bunting had once described it—he wouldn't be their lodger now; he would be living in a quite different sort of way with some of his relations, or with a friend of his own class.

Mrs. Bunting, while these thoughts galloped disconnectedly through her brain, went on with her cooking, doing everything with a certain delicate and cleanly precision.

While in the middle of making the toast on which was to be poured some melted cheese, she suddenly heard a noise, or rather a series of noises. Shuffling, hesitating steps were creaking down the house above. She looked up and listened. Surely Mr. Sleuth was not going out again into the cold, foggy night? But no; for the sounds did not continue down the passage leading to the front door.

The heavy steps were coming slowly down the kitchen stairs. Nearer and nearer came the thudding sounds, and Mrs. Bunting's heart began to beat as if in response. She put out the gas-stove, unheedful of the fact that the cheese would stiffen and spoil in the cold air; and then she turned and faced the door. There was a fumbling at the handle, and a moment later the door opened and revealed, as she had known it would, her lodger.

Mr. Sleuth was clad in a plaid dressing-gown, and in his hand was a candle. When he saw the lit-up kitchen, and the woman standing in it, he looked inexplicably taken aback, almost aghast.

"Yes, sir? What can I do for you, sir? I hope you didn't ring, sir?" Mrs. Bunting did not come forward to meet her lodger; instead, she held her ground in front of the stove. Mr. Sleuth had no business to come down like this into her kitchen.

"No, I—I didn't ring," he stammered; "I didn't know you were down here, Mrs. Bunting. Please excuse my costume. The truth is, my gas-stove has gone wrong, or, rather, that shilling-in-the-slot arrangement has done so. I came down to see if *you* had a gas-stove. I am going to ask leave to use it to-night for an experiment I want to make."

Mrs. Bunting felt troubled—oddly, unnaturally troubled. Why couldn't the lodger's experiment wait till tomorrow? "Oh, certainly, sir; but you will find it very cold down here." She looked round her dubiously.

"It seems most pleasantly warm," he observed, "warm and cozy after my cold room upstairs."

"Won't you let me make you a fire?" Mrs. Bunting's housewifely instincts were roused. "Do let me make you a fire in your bedroom, sir; I'm sure you ought to have one there these cold nights."

"By no means—I mean, I would prefer not. I do not like an open fire, Mrs. Bunting." He frowned, and still stood, a strange-looking figure, just inside the kitchen door.

"Do you want to use this stove now, sir? Is there anything I can do to help you?"

"No, not now—thank you all the same, Mrs. Bunting. I shall come down later, altogether later—probably after you and your husband have gone to bed. But I should be much obliged if you would see that the gas people come tomorrow and put my stove in order."

"Perhaps Bunting could put it right for you sir. I'll ask him to go up."

"No, no—I don't want anything of that sort done tonight. Besides, he couldn't put it right. The cause of the trouble is quite simple. The machine is choked up with shillings: a foolish plan, so I have always felt it to be."

Mr. Sleuth spoke very pettishly, with far more heat than he was wont to speak; but Mrs. Bunting sympathized with him. She had always suspected those slot-machines to be as dishonest as if they were human. It was dreadful, the way they swallowed up the shillings!

As if he were divining her thoughts, Mr. Sleuth, walking forward, stared up at the kitchen slot-machine. "Is it nearly full?" he asked abruptly. "I expect my experiment will take some time, Mrs. Bunting."

"Oh, no, sir; there's plenty of room for shillings there still. We don't use our stove as much as you do yours, sir. I'm never in the kitchen a minute longer than I can help in this cold weather."

And then, with him preceding her, Mrs. Bunting and her lodger made a low progress to the ground floor. There Mr. Sleuth courteously bade his landlady good night, and proceeded upstairs to his own apartments.

Mrs. Bunting again went down into her kitchen, again she lit the stove, and again she cooked the toasted cheese. But she felt unnerved, afraid of she knew not what. The place seemed to her alive with alien presences, and once she caught herself listening, which was absurd, for of course she could not hope to hear what her lodger was doing two, if not three, flights upstairs. She had never been able to discover what Mr. Sleuth's experiments really were; all she knew was that they required a very high degree of heat.

The Buntings went to bed early that night. But Mrs. Bunting intended to stay awake. She wanted to know at what hour of the night her lodger would come down into the kitchen, and, above all, she was anxious as to how long he would stay there. But she had had a long day, and presently she fell asleep.

The church clock hard by struck two in the morning, and suddenly Mrs. Bunting awoke. She felt sharply annoyed with herself. How could she have dropped off like that? Mr. Sleuth must have been down and up again hours ago.

Then, gradually, she became aware of a faint acrid odor; elusive, almost intangible, it yet seemed to encompass her and the snoring man by her side almost as a vapor might have done.

Mrs. Bunting sat up in bed and sniffed; and then, in spite of the cold, she quietly crept out of the nice, warm bedclothes and crawled along to the bottom of the bed. There Mr. Sleuth's landlady did a very curious thing; she leaned over the brass rail and put her face close to the hinge of the door. Yes, it was from there that this strange, horrible odor was coming; the smell must be very strong in the passage. Mrs. Bunting thought she knew now what became of these suits of clothes of Mr. Sleuth's that disappeared.

As she crept back, shivering, under the bedclothes, she longed to give her sleeping husband a good shake, and in fancy she heard herself saying: "Bunting, get up! There is something strange going on downstairs that we ought to know about."

But Mr. Sleuth's landlady, as she lay by her husband's side, listening with painful intentness, knew very well that she would do nothing of the sort. The lodger had a right to destroy his clothes by burning if the fancy took him. What if he did make a certain amount of mess, a certain amount of smell, in her nice kitchen? Was he not—was he not such a good lodger! If they did anything to upset him, where could they ever hope to get another like him?

Three o'clock struck before Mrs. Bunting heard slow, heavy steps creaking up her kitchen stairs. But Mr. Sleuth did not go straight up to his own quarters, as she expected him to do. Instead, he went to the front door, and opening it, put it on the chain. At the end of ten minutes or so he closed the front door, and by that time Mrs. Bunting had divined why the lodger had behaved in this strange fashion—it must have been to get the strong acrid smell of burning wool out of the passage. But Mrs. Bunting felt as if she herself would never get rid of the horrible odor. She felt herself to be all smell.

At last the unhappy woman fell into a deep, troubled sleep; and then she dreamed a most terrible and unnatural dream; hoarse voices seemed to be shouting in her ear, "'Orrible murder off the Edgeware Road!" Then three words, indistinctly uttered, followed by "—at his work again! Awful details!"

Even in her dream Mrs. Bunting felt angered and impatient; she knew so well why she was being disturbed by this horrid nightmare. It was because of Bunting—Bunting, who insisted on talking to her of those frightful murders, in which only morbid, vulgar-minded people took any interest. Why, even now, in her dream, she could hear her husband speaking to her about it.

"Ellen,"—so she heard Bunting say in her ear,—"Ellen, my dear, I am just going to get up to get a paper. It's after seven o'clock."

Mrs. Bunting sat up in bed. The shouting, nay, worse, the sound of tramping, hurrying feet smote on her ears. It had been no nightmare, then, but something infinitely worse—reality. Why couldn't Bunting have lain quietly in bed awhile longer, and let his poor wife go on dreaming? The most awful dream would have been easier to bear than this awakening.

She heard her husband go to the front door, and, as he bought the paper, exchange a few excited words with the newspaper boy. Then he came back and began silently moving about the room.

"Well!" she cried. "Why don't you tell me about it?"

"I thought you'd rather not hear."

"Of course I like to know what happens close to our own front door!" she snapped out.

And then he read out a piece of the newspaper—only a few lines, after all—telling in brief, unemotional language that the body of woman, apparently done to death in a peculiarly atrocious fashion some hours before, had been found in a passage leading to a disused warehouse off the Marylebone Road.

"It serves that sort of hussy right!" was Mrs. Bunting's only comment.

When Mrs. Bunting went down into the kitchen, everything there looked just as she had left it, and there was no trace of the acrid smell she had expected to find there. Instead, the cavernous whitewashed room was full of fog, and she noticed that, though the shutters were bolted and barred as she had left them, the windows behind them had been widely opened to the air. She, of course, had left them shut.

She stooped and flung open the oven door of her gas-stove. Yes, it was as she had expected; a fierce heat had been generated there since she had last used the oven and a mass of black, gluey soot had fallen through to the stone floor below.

Mrs. Bunting took the ham and eggs that she had bought the previous day for her own and Bunting's breakfast, and broiled them over the gas-ring in their sitting-room. Her husband watched her in surprised silence. She had never done such a thing before.

"I couldn't stay down there," she said, "it was so cold and foggy. I thought I'd make breakfast up here, just for to-day."

"Yes," he said kindly; "that's quite right, Ellen. I think you've done quite right, my dear."

But, when it came to the point, his wife could not eat any of the nice breakfast she had got ready; she only had another cup of tea.

"Are you ill?" Bunting asked solicitously.

"No," she said shortly; "of course I'm not ill. Don't be silly! The thought of that horrible thing happening so close by has upset me. Just hark to them, now!"

Through their closed windows penetrated the sound of scurrying feet and loud, ribald laughter. A crowd, nay, a mob, hastened to and from the scene of the murder.

Mrs. Bunting made her husband lock the front gate. "I don't want any of those ghouls in here!" she exclaimed angrily. And then, "What a lot of idle people there must be in the world," she said.

The coming and going went on all day. Mrs. Bunting stayed indoors; Bunting went out. After all, the ex-butler was human—it was natural that he should feel thrilled and excited. All their neighbors were the same. His wife wasn't reasonable about such things. She quarreled with him when he didn't tell her anything, and yet he was sure she would have been angry with him if he had said very much about it.

The lodger's bell rang about two o'clock, and Mrs. Bunting prepared the simple luncheon that was also his breakfast. As she rested the tray a minute on the drawing-room floor landing, she heard Mr. Sleuth's high, quavering voice reading aloud the words:

"She saith to him, Stolen waters are sweet, and bread eaten in secret is pleasant. But he knoweth not that the dead are there; and that her guests are in the depths of hell."

The landlady turned the handle of the door and walked in with the tray. Mr. Sleuth was sitting close by the window, and Mrs. Bunting's Bible lay open before him. As she came in he hastily closed the Bible and looked down at the crowd walking along the Marylebone Road.

"There seem a great many people out today," he observed, without looking round.

"Yes, sir, there do." Mrs. Bunting said nothing more, and offered no other explanation; and the lodger, as he at last turned to his landlady, smiled pleasantly. He had acquired a great liking and respect for this well-behaved, taciturn woman; she was the first person for whom he had felt any such feeling for many years past.

He took a half sovereign out of his waistcoat pocket; Mrs. Bunting noticed that it was not the same waistcoat Mr. Sleuth had been wearing the day before. "Will you please accept this half sovereign for the use of your kitchen last night?" he said. "I made as little mess as I could, but I was carrying on a rather elaborate experiment."

She held out her hand, hesitated, and then took the coin.

As she walked down the stairs, the winter sun, a yellow ball hanging in the smoky sky, glinted in on Mrs. Bunting, and lent blood-red gleams, or so it seemed to her, to the piece of gold she was holding in her hand.

It was a very cold night—so cold, so windy, so snowladen the atmosphere, that every one who could do so stayed indoors. Bunting, however, was on his way home from what had proved a very pleasant job; he had been acting as waiter at a young lady's birthday party, and a remarkable piece of luck had come his way. The young lady had come into a fortune that day, and she had had the gracious, the surprising thought of presenting each of the hired waiters with a sovereign.

This birthday treat had put him in mind of another birthday. His daughter Daisy would be eighteen the following Saturday. Why shouldn't he send her a postal order for half a sovereign, so that she might come up and spend her birthday in London?

Having Daisy for three or four days would cheer up Ellen. Mr. Bunting, slackening his footsteps, began to think with puzzled concern of how queer his wife had seemed lately. She had become so nervous, so "jumpy," that he didn't know what to make of her sometimes. She had never been a really good-tempered woman,—your capable, self-respecting woman seldom is,—but she had never been like what she was now. Of late she sometimes got quite hysterical; he had let fall a sharp word to her the other day, and she had sat down on a chair, thrown her black apron over her face, and burst out sobbing violently.

During the last ten days Ellen had taken to talking in her sleep. "No, no, no!" she had cried out, only the night before. "It isn't true! I won't have it said! It's a lie!" And there had been a wail of horrible fear and revolt in her usually quiet, mincing voice. Yes, it would certainly be a good thing for her to have Daisy's company for a bit. Whew! It *was* cold; and Bunting had stupidly forgotten his gloves. He put his hands in his pockets to keep them warm.

Suddenly he became aware that Mr. Sleuth, the lodger who seemed to have "turned their luck," as it were, was walking along on the opposite side of the solitary street.

Mr. Sleuth's tall, thin figure was rather bowed, his head bent toward the ground. His right arm was thrust into his long Inverness cape; the other occasionally sawed the air, doubtless in order to help him keep warm. He was walking rather quickly. It was clear that he had not yet become aware of the proximity of his landlord.

Bunting felt pleased to see his lodger; it increased his feeling of general satisfaction. Strange, was it not, that that odd, peculiar-looking figure should have made all the difference to his (Bunting's) and Mrs. Bunting's happiness and comfort in life?

Naturally, Bunting saw far less of the lodger than did Mrs. Bunting. Their gentleman had made it very clear that he did not like either the husband or wife to come up to his rooms without being definitely asked to do so, and Bunting had been up there only once since Mr. Sleuth's arrival five weeks before. This seemed to be a good opportunity for a little genial conversation.

Bunting, still an active man for his years, crossed the road, and, stepping briskly forward, tried to overtake Mr. Sleuth; but the more he hurried, the more the other hastened, and that without even turning to see whose steps he heard echoing behind him on the now freezing pavement.

Mr. Sleuth's own footsteps were quite inaudible—an odd circumstance, when you came to think of it, as Bunting did think of it later, lying awake by Ellen's side in the pitch-darkness. What it meant was, of course, that the lodger had rubber soles on his shoes.

The two men, the pursued and the pursuer, at last turned into the Marylebone Road. They were now within a hundred yards of home; and so, plucking up courage, Bunting called out, his voice echoing freshly on the still air:

"Mr. Sleuth, sir! Mr. Sleuth!"

The lodger stopped and turned round. He had been walking so quickly, and he was in so poor a physical condition, that the sweat was pouring down his face.

"Ah! So it's you, Mr. Bunting? I heard footsteps behind me, and I hurried on. I wish I'd known that it was only you; there are so many queer characters about at night in London."

"Not on a night like this, sir. Only honest folk who have business out of doors would be out such a night as this. It *is* cold, sir!" And then into Bunting's slow and honest mind there suddenly crept the query as to what Mr. Sleuth's own business out could be on this cold, bitter night.

"Cold?" the lodger repeated. "I can't say that I find it cold, Mr. Bunting. When the snow falls the air always becomes milder."

"Yes, sir; but tonight there's such a sharp east wind. Why, it freezes the very marrow in one's bones!"

Bunting noticed that Mr. Sleuth kept his distance in a rather strange way: he walked at the edge of the pavement, leaving the rest of it, on the wall side, to his landlord.

"I lost my way," he said abruptly. "I've been over Primrose Hill to see a friend of mine, and then, coming back, I lost my way."

Bunting could well believe that, for when he had first noticed Mr. Sleuth he was coming from the east, and not, as he should have done if walking home from Primrose Hill, from the north.

They had now reached the little gate that gave on to the shabby, paved court in front of the house. Mr. Sleuth was walking up the flagged path, when, with a "By your leave, sir," the ex-butler, stepping aside, slipped in front of his lodger, in order to open the front door for him.

As he passed by Mr. Sleuth, the back of Bunting's bare left hand brushed lightly against the long Inverness cape the other man was wearing, and, to his surprise, the stretch of cloth against which his hand lay for a moment was not only damp, damp from the flakes of snow that had settled upon it, but wet—wet and gluey. Bunting thrust his left hand into his pocket; it was with the other that he placed the key in the lock of the door.

The two men passed into the hall together. The house seemed blackly dark in comparison with the lighted-up road outside; and then, quite suddenly, there came over Bunting a feeling of mortal terror, an instinctive knowledge that some terrible and immediate danger was near him. A voice—the voice of his first wife, the long-dead girl to whom his mind so seldom reverted nowadays—uttered in his ear the words, "Take care!"

"I'm afraid, Mr. Bunting, that you must have felt something dirty, foul, on my coat? It's too long a story to tell you now, but I brushed up against a dead animal—a dead rabbit lying across a bench on Primrose Hill."

Mr. Sleuth spoke in a very quiet voice, almost in a whisper.

"No, sir; no, I didn't notice nothing. I scarcely touched you, sir." It seemed as if a power outside himself compelled Bunting to utter these lying words. "And now, sir, I'll be saying good night to you," he added.

He waited until the lodger had gone upstairs, and then he turned into his own sitting-room. There he sat down, for he felt very queer. He did not draw his left hand out of his pocket till he heard the other man moving about in the room above. Then he lit the gas and held up his left hand; he put it close to his face. It was flecked, streaked with blood.

He took off his boots, and then, very quietly, he went into the room where his wife lay asleep. Stealthily he walked across to the toilet-table, and dipped his hand into the water-jug.

The next morning Mr. Sleuth's landlord awoke with a start; he felt curiously heavy about the limbs and tired about the eyes.

Drawing his watch from under his pillow, he saw that it was nearly nine o'clock. He and Ellen had overslept. Without waking her, he got out of bed and pulled up the blind. It was snowing heavily, and, as is the way when it snows, even in London, it was strangely, curiously still.

After he had dressed he went out into the passage. A newspaper and a letter were lying on the mat. Fancy having slept through the postman's knock! He picked them both up and went into the sitting-room; then he carefully shut the door behind him, and, tossing the letter aside, spread the newspaper wide open on the table and bent over it.

As Bunting at last looked up and straightened himself, a look of inexpressible relief shone upon his stolid face. The item of news he had felt certain would be there, printed in big type on the middle sheet, was not there.

He folded the paper and laid it on a chair, and then eagerly took up his letter.

> DEAR FATHER [*it ran*]: *I hope this finds you as well as it leaves me. Mrs. Puddle's youngest child has got scarlet fever, and aunt thinks I had better come away at once, just to stay with you for a few days. Please tell Ellen I won't give her no trouble.*
>
> *Your loving daughter,*
> *Daisy.*

Bunting felt amazingly light-hearted; and, as he walked into the next room, he smiled broadly.

"Ellen," he cried out, "here's news! Daisy's coming today. There's scarlet fever in their house, and Martha thinks she had better come away for a few days. She'll be here for her birthday!"

Mrs. Bunting listened in silence; she did not even open her eyes. "I can't have the girl here just now," she said shortly: "I've got just as much as I can manage to do."

But Bunting felt pugnacious, and so cheerful as to be almost light-headed. Deep down in his heart he looked back to last night with a feeling of shame and self-rebuke. Whatever had made such horrible thoughts and suspicions come into his head?

"Of course Daisy will come here," he said shortly. "If it comes to that, she'll be able to help you with the work, and she'll brisk us both up a bit."

Rather to his surprise, Mrs. Bunting said nothing in answer to this, and he changed the subject abruptly. "The lodger and me came in together last night," he observed. "He's certainly a funny kind of gentleman. It wasn't the sort of night one would choose to go for a walk over Primrose Hill, and yet that was what he had been doing—so he said."

It stopped snowing about ten o'clock, and the morning wore itself away.

Just as twelve was striking, a four-wheeler drew up to the gate. It was Daisy—pink-cheeked, excited, laughing-eyed Daisy, a sight to gladden any father's heart. "Aunt said I was to have a cab if the weather was bad," she said.

There was a bit of a wrangle over the fare. King's Cross, as all the world knows, is nothing like two miles from the Marylebone Road, but the man clamored for one-and-sixpence, and hinted darkly that he had done the young lady a favor in bringing her at all.

While he and Bunting were having words, Daisy, leaving them to it, walked up the path to the door where her stepmother was awaiting her.

Suddenly there fell loud shouts on the still air. They sounded strangely eerie, breaking sharply across the muffled, snowy air.

"What's that?" said Bunting, with a look of startled fear. "Why, whatever's that?"

The cabman lowered his voice: "Them are crying out that 'orrible affair at King's Cross. He's done for two of 'em this time! That's what I meant when I said I might have got a better fare; I wouldn't say anything before Missy there, but folk 'ave been coming from all over London—like a fire; plenty of toffs, too. But there—there's nothing to see now!"

"What! Another woman murdered last night?" Bunting felt and looked convulsed with horror.

The cabman stared at him, surprised. "Two of 'em, I tell yer—within a few yards of one another. He 'ave got a nerve—"

"Have they caught him?" asked Bunting perfunctorily.

"Lord, no! They'll never catch 'im! It must 'ave happened hours and hours ago—they was both stone-cold. One each end of an archway. That's why they didn't see 'em before."

The hoarse cries were coming nearer and nearer—two news-venders trying to outshout each other.

" 'Orrible discovery near King's Cross!" they yelled exultantly. And as Bunting, with his daughter's bag in his hand, hurried up the path and passed through his front door, the words pursued him like a dreadful threat.

Angrily he shut out the hoarse, insistent cries. No, he had no wish to buy a paper. That kind of crime wasn't fit reading for a young girl, such a girl as was his Daisy, brought up as carefully as if she had been a young lady by her strict Methody aunt.

As he stood in his little hall, trying to feel "all right" again, he could hear Daisy's voice—high, voluble, excited—giving her stepmother a long account of the scarlet-fever case to which she owed her presence in London. But, as Bunting pushed open the door of the sitting-room, there came a note of sharp alarm in his daughter's voice, and he heard her say: "Why Ellen! Whatever is the matter? You do look bad!" and his wife's muffled answer: "Open the window—do."

Rushing across the room, Bunting pushed up the sash. The newspaper-sellers were now just outside the house. "Horrible discovery near King's Cross—a clue to the murderer!" they yelled. And then, helplessly, Mrs. Bunting began to laugh. She laughed and laughed and laughed, rocking herself to and fro as if in an ecstasy of mirth.

"Why, father, whatever's the matter with her?" Daisy looked quite scared.

"She's in 'sterics—that's what it is," he said shortly. "I'll just get the water-jug. Wait a minute."

Bunting felt very put out, and yet glad, too, for this queer seizure of Ellen's almost made him forget the sick terror with which he had been possessed a moment before. That he and his wife should be obsessed by the same fear, the same terror, never crossed his simple, slow-working mind.

The lodger's bell rang. That, or the threat of the water-jug, had a magical effect on Mrs. Bunting. She rose to her feet, still trembling, but composed.

As Mrs. Bunting went upstairs she felt her legs trembling under her, and put out a shaking hand to clutch at the bannister for support. She waited a few minutes on the landing, and then knocked at the door of her lodger's parlor.

But Mr. Sleuth's voice answered her from the bedroom. "I'm not well," he called out querulously; "I think I caught a chill going out to see a friend last night. I'd be obliged if you'll bring me up a cup of tea and put it outside my door, Mrs. Bunting."

"Very well, sir."

Mrs. Bunting went downstairs and made her lodger a cup of tea over the gas-ring, Bunting watching her the while in heavy silence.

During their midday dinner the husband and wife had a little discussion as to where Daisy should sleep. It had already been settled that a bed should be made up for her in the sitting-room, but Bunting saw reason to change this plan. As the two women were clearing away the dishes, he looked up and said shortly: "I think 'twould be better if Daisy were to sleep with you, Ellen, and I were to sleep in the sitting-room."

Ellen acquiesced quietly.

Daisy was a good-natured girl; she liked London, and wanted to make herself useful to her stepmother. "I'll wash up; don't you bother to come downstairs," she said.

Bunting began to walk up and down the room. His wife gave him a furtive glance; she wondered what he was thinking about.

"Didn't you get a paper?" she said at last.

"There's the paper," he said crossly, "the paper we always do take in, the *Telegraph*." His look challenged her to a further question.

"I thought they was shouting something in the street—I mean just before I was took bad."

But he made no answer; instead, he went to the top of the staircase and called out sharply: "Daisy! Daisy, child, are you there?"

"Yes, father," she answered from below.

"Better come upstairs out of that cold kitchen."

He came back into the sitting-room again.

"Ellen, is the lodger in? I haven't heard him moving about. I don't want Daisy to be mixed up with him."

"Mr. Sleuth is not well today," his wife answered; "he is remaining in bed a bit. Daisy needn't have anything to do with him. She'll have her work cut out looking after things down here. That's where I want her to help me."

"Agreed," he said.

When it grew dark, Bunting went out and bought an evening paper. He read it out of doors in the biting cold, standing beneath a street lamp. He wanted to see what was the clue to the murderer.

The clue proved to be a very slender one—merely the imprint in the snowy slush of a half-worn rubber sole; and it was, of course, by no means certain that the sole belonged to the boot or shoe of the murderer of the two doomed women who had met so swift and awful a death in the arch near King's Cross station. The paper's special investigator pointed out that there were thousands of such soles being worn in London. Bunting found comfort in that obvious fact. He felt grateful to the special investigator for having stated it so clearly.

As he approached his house, he heard curious sounds coming from the inner side of the low wall that shut off the courtyard from the pavement. Under ordinary circumstances Bunting would have gone at once to drive whoever was there out into the roadway. Now he stayed outside, sick with suspense and anxiety. Was it possible that their place was being watched—already?

But it was only Mr. Sleuth. To Bunting's astonishment, the lodger suddenly stepped forward from behind the wall on to the flagged path. He was carrying a brown-paper parcel, and, as he walked along, the new boots he was wearing creaked and the tap-tap of wooden heels rang out on the stones.

Bunting, still hidden outside the gate, suddenly understood what his lodger had been doing on the other side of the wall. Mr. Sleuth had been out to buy himself a pair of boots, and had gone inside the gate to put them on, placing his old footgear in the paper in which the new boots had been wrapped.

Bunting waited until Mr. Sleuth had let himself into the house; then he also walked up the flagged pathway, and put his latch-key in the door.

In the next three days each of Bunting's waking hours held its meed of aching fear and suspense. From his point of view, almost any alternative would be preferable to that which to most people would have seemed the only one open to him. He told himself that it would be ruin for him and for his Ellen to be mixed up publicly in such a terrible affair. It would track them to their dying day.

Bunting was also always debating within himself as to whether he should tell Ellen of his frightful suspicion. He could not believe that what had become so plain to himself could long be concealed from all the world, and yet he did not credit his wife with the same intelligence. He did not even notice that, although she waited on Mr. Sleuth as assiduously as ever, Mrs. Bunting never mentioned the lodger.

Mr. Sleuth, meanwhile, kept upstairs; he had given up going out altogether. He still felt, so he assured his landlady, far from well.

Daisy was another complication, the more so that the girl, whom her father longed to send away and whom he would hardly let out of his sight, showed herself inconveniently inquisitive concerning the lodger.

"Whatever does he do with himself all day?" she asked her stepmother.

"Well, just now he's reading the Bible," Mrs. Bunting had answered, very shortly and dryly.

"Well, I never! That's a funny thing for a gentleman to do!" Such had been Daisy's pert remark, and her stepmother had snubbed her well for it.

Daisy's eighteenth birthday dawned uneventfully. Her father gave her what he had always promised she should have on her eighteenth birthday—a watch. It was a pretty little silver watch, which Bunting had bought second-hand on the last day he had been happy; it seemed a long time ago now.

Mrs. Bunting thought a silver watch a very extravagant present, but she had always had the good sense not to interfere between her husband and his child. Besides, her mind was now full of other things. She was beginning to fear that Bunting suspected something, and she was filled with watchful anxiety and unease. What if he were to do anything silly—mix them up with the police, for instance? It certainly would be ruination to them both. But there—one never knew, with men! Her husband, however, kept his own counsel absolutely.

Daisy's birthday was on Saturday. In the middle of the morning Ellen and Daisy went down into the kitchen. Bunting didn't like the feeling that there was only one flight of stairs between Mr. Sleuth and himself, so he quietly slipped out of the house and went to buy himself an ounce of tobacco.

In the last four days Bunting had avoided his usual haunts. But today the unfortunate man had a curious longing for human companionship—companionship, that is, other than that of Ellen and Daisy. This feeling led him into a small, populous thoroughfare hard by the Edgeware Road. There were more people there than usual, for the housewives of the neighborhood were doing their marketing for Sunday.

Bunting passed the time of day with the tobacconist, and the two fell into desultory talk. To the ex-butler's surprise, the man said nothing at all to him on the subject of which all the neighborhood must still be talking.

And then, quite suddenly, while still standing by the counter, and before he had paid for the packet of tobacco he held in his hand, Bunting, through the open door, saw, with horrified surprise, that his wife was standing outside a green-grocer's shop just opposite. Muttering a word of apology, he rushed out of the shop and across the road.

"Ellen!" he gasped hoarsely. "You've never gone and left my little girl alone in the house?"

Mrs. Bunting's face went chalky white. "I thought you were indoors," she said. "You *were* indoors. Whatever made you come out for, without first making sure I was there?"

Bunting made no answer; but, as they stared at each other in exasperated silence, *each knew that the other knew.*

They turned and scurried down the street.

"Don't run," he said suddenly; "we shall get there just as quickly if we walk fast. People are noticing you, Ellen. Don't run."

He spoke breathlessly, but it was breathlessness induced by fear and excitement, not by the quick pace at which they were walking.

At last they reached their own gate. Bunting pushed past in front of his wife. After all, Daisy was his child—Ellen couldn't know how he was feeling. He made the path almost in one leap, and fumbled for a moment with his latch-key. The door opened.

"Daisy!" he called out in a wailing voice. "Daisy, my dear, where are you?"

"Here I am, father; what is it?"

"She's all right!" Bunting turned his gray face to his wife. "She's all right, Ellen!" Then he waited a moment, leaning against the wall of the passage. "It did give me a turn," he said; and then, warningly, "Don't frighten the girl, Ellen."

Daisy was standing before the fire in the sitting-room, admiring herself in the glass. "Oh, father," she said, without turning round, "I've seen the lodger! He's quite a nice gentleman—though, to be sure, he does look a cure! He came down to ask Ellen for something, and we had quite a nice little chat. I told him it was my birthday, and he asked me to go to Madame Tussaud's with him this afternoon." She laughed a little self-consciously. "Of course I could see he was 'centric, and then at first he spoke so funnily. 'And who be you?' he says, threatening-like. And I says to him, 'I'm Mr. Bunting's daughter, sir.' 'Then you're a very fortunate girl'—that's what he said, Ellen—'to 'ave such a nice stepmother as you've got. That's why,' he says, 'you look such a good innocent girl.' And then he quoted a bit of the prayer-book at me. 'Keep innocency,' he says, wagging his head at me. Lor'! It made me feel as if I was with aunt again."

"I won't have you going out with the lodger—that's flat." He was wiping his forehead with one hand, while with the other he mechanically squeezed the little packet of tobacco, for which, as he now remembered, he had forgotten to pay.

Daisy pouted. "Oh, father, I think you might let me have a treat on my birthday! I told him Saturday wasn't a very good day—at least, so I'd heard—for Madame Tussaud's. Then he said we could go early, while the fine folk are still having their dinners. He wants you to come, too." She turned to her stepmother, then giggled happily. "The lodger has a wonderful fancy for you, Ellen; if I was father, I'd feel quite jealous!"

Her last words were cut across by a loud knock on the door. Bunting and his wife looked at each other apprehensively.

Both felt a curious thrill of relief when they saw that it was only Mr. Sleuth— Mr. Sleuth dressed to go out: the tall hat he had worn when he first came to them was in his hand, and he was wearing a heavy overcoat.

"I saw you had come in,"—he addressed Mrs. Bunting in his high, whistling, hesitating voice,—"and so I've come down to ask if you and Miss Bunting will come to Madame Tussaud's now. I have never seen these famous waxworks, though I've heard of the place all my life."

As Bunting forced himself to look fixedly at his lodger, a sudden doubt, bringing with it a sense of immeasurable relief, came to him. Surely it was inconceivable that this gentle, mild-mannered gentleman could be the monster of cruelty and cunning that Bunting had but a moment ago believed him to be!

"You're very kind, sir, I'm sure." He tried to catch his wife's eye, but Mrs. Bunting was looking away, staring into vacancy. She still, of course, wore the bonnet and cloak in which she had just been out to do her marketing. Daisy was already putting on her hat and coat.

Madame Tussaud's had hitherto held pleasant memories for Mrs. Bunting. In the days when she and Bunting were courting they often spent part of their "afternoon out" there. The butler had an acquaintance, a man named Hopkins, who was one of the waxworks' staff, and this man had sometimes given him passes for "self and lady." But this was the first time Mrs. Bunting had been inside the place since she had come to live almost next door, as it were, to the big building.

The ill-sorted trio walked up the great staircase and into the first gallery; and there Mr. Sleuth suddenly stopped short. The presence of those curious, still figures, suggesting death in life, seemed to surprise and affright him.

Daisy took quick advantage of the lodger's hesitation and unease.

"Oh, Ellen," she cried, "do let us begin by going into the Chamber of Horrors! I've never been in there. Aunt made father promise he wouldn't take me, the only time I've ever been here. But now that I'm eighteen I can do just as I like; besides, aunt will never know!"

Mr. Sleuth looked down at her.

"Yes," he said, "let us go into the Chamber of Horrors; that's a good idea, Miss Bunting."

They turned into the great room in which the Napoleonic relics are kept, and which leads into the curious, vaultlike chamber where waxen effigies of dead criminals stand grouped in wooden docks. Mrs. Bunting was at once disturbed and relieved to see her husband's old acquaintance, Mr. Hopkins, in charge of the turnstile admitting the public to the Chamber of Horrors.

"Well, you *are* a stranger," the man observed genially. "I do believe this is the very first time I've seen you in here, Mrs. Bunting, since you married!"

"Yes," she said; "that is so. And this is my husband's daughter, Daisy; I expect you've heard of her, Mr. Hopkins. And this"—she hesitated a moment—"is our lodger, Mr. Sleuth."

But Mr. Sleuth frowned and shuffled away. Daisy, leaving her stepmother's side, joined him.

Mrs. Bunting put down three sixpences.

"Wait a minute," said Hopkins; "you can't go into the Chamber of Horrors just yet. But you won't have to wait more than four or five minutes, Mrs. Bunting. It's this way, you see; our boss is in there, showing a party round." He lowered his voice. "It's Sir John Burney—I suppose you know who Sir John Burney is?"

"No," she answered indifferently; "I don't know that I ever heard of him." She felt slightly—oh, very slightly—uneasy about Daisy. She would like her stepdaughter to keep well within sight and sound. Mr. Sleuth was taking the girl to the other end of the room.

"Well, I hope you never *will* know him—not in any personal sense, Mrs. Bunting." The man chuckled. "He's the Head Commissioner of Police—that's what Sir John Burney is. One of the gentlemen he's showing round our place is the Paris Prefect of Police, whose job is on all fours, so to speak, with Sir John's. The Frenchy has brought his daughter with him, and there are several other ladies. Ladies always like 'orrors, Mrs. Bunting; that's our experience here. 'Oh, take me to the Chamber of 'Orrors!'—that's what they say the minute they gets into the building."

A group of people, all talking and laughing together, were advancing from within toward the turnstile.

Mrs. Bunting stared at them nervously. She wondered which of them was the gentleman with whom Mr. Hopkins had hoped she would never be brought into personal contact. She quickly picked him out. He was a tall, powerful, nice-looking gentleman with a commanding manner. Just now he was smiling down into the face of a young lady. "Monsieur Barberoux is quite right," he was saying; "the English law is too kind to the criminal, especially to the murderer. If we conducted our trials in the French fashion, the place we have just left would be very much fuller than it is today! A man of whose guilt we are absolutely assured is oftener than not acquitted, and then the public taunt us with 'another undiscovered crime'!"

"D'you mean, Sir John, that murderers sometimes escape scot-free? Take the man who has been committing all those awful murders this last month. Of course, I don't know much about it, for father won't let me read about it, but I can't help being interested!" Her girlish voice rang out, and Mrs. Bunting heard every word distinctly.

The party gathered round, listening eagerly to hear what the Head Commissioner would say next.

"Yes." He spoke very deliberately. "I think we may say—now, don't give me away to a newspaper fellow, Miss Rose—that we do know perfectly well who the murderer in question is—"

Several of those standing near by uttered expressions of surprise and incredulity.

"Then why don't you catch him?" cried the girl indignantly.

"I didn't say we know *where* he is; I only said we know *who* he is; or, rather, perhaps I ought to say that we have a very strong suspicion of his identity."

Sir John's French colleague looked up quickly. "The Hamburg and Liverpool man?" he said interrogatively.

The other nodded. "Yes; I suppose you've had the case turned up?"

Then, speaking very quickly, as if he wished to dismiss the subject from his own mind and from that of his auditors, he went on:

"Two murders of the kind were committed eight years ago—one in Hamburg, the other just afterward in Liverpool, and there were certain peculiarities connected with the crimes which made it clear they were committed by the same hand. The perpetrator was caught, fortunately for us red-handed, just as he was leaving the house of his victim, for in Liverpool the murder was committed in a house. I myself saw the unhappy man—I say unhappy, for there is no doubt at all that he was mad,"—he hesitated, and added in a lower tone—"suffering from an acute form of religious mania. I myself saw him, at some length. But now comes the really interesting point. Just a month ago this criminal lunatic, as we must regard him, made his escape from the asylum where he was confined. He arranged the whole thing with extraordinary cunning and intelligence, and we should probably have caught him long ago were it not that he managed, when on his way out of the place, to annex a considerable sum of money in gold with which the wages of the staff were about to be paid."

The Frenchman again spoke. "Why have you not circulated a description?" he asked.

"We did that at once,"—Sir John Burney smiled a little grimly,—"but only among our own people. We dare not circulate the man's description among the general public. You see, we may be mistaken, after all."

"That is not very probable!" The Frenchman smiled a satirical little smile.

A moment later the party were walking in Indian file through the turnstile, Sir John Burney leading the way.

Mrs. Bunting looked straight before her. Even had she wished to do so, she had neither time nor power to warn her lodger of his danger.

Daisy and her companion were now coming down the room, bearing straight for the Head Commissioner of Police. In another moment Mr. Sleuth and Sir John Burney would be face to face.

Suddenly Mr. Sleuth swerved to one side. A terrible change came over his pale, narrow face; it became discomposed, livid with rage and terror.

But, to Mrs. Bunting's relief,—yes, to her inexpressible relief,—Sir John Burney and his friends swept on. They passed by Mr. Sleuth unconcernedly, unaware, or so it seemed to her, that there was anyone else in the room but themselves.

"Hurry up, Mrs. Bunting," said the turnstile-keeper; "you and your friends will have the place all to yourselves." From an official he had become a man, and it was the man in Mr. Hopkins that gallantly addressed pretty Daisy Bunting. "It seems strange that a young lady like you should want to go in and see all those 'orrible frights," he said jestingly.

"Mrs. Bunting, may I trouble you to come over here for a moment?" The words were hissed rather than spoken by Mr. Sleuth's lips.

His landlady took a doubtful step forward.

"A last word with you, Mrs. Bunting." The lodger's face was still distorted with fear and passion. "Do you think to escape the consequences of your hideous treachery? I trusted you, Mrs. Bunting, and you betrayed me! But I am protected by a higher power, for I still have work to do. Your end will be bitter as wormwood and sharp as a two-edged sword. Your feet shall go down to death, and your steps take hold on hell." Even while Mr. Sleuth was uttering these strange, dreadful words, he was looking around, his eyes glancing this way and that, seeking a way of escape.

At last his eyes became fixed on a small placard placed about a curtain. "Emergency Exit" was written there. Leaving his landlady's side, he walked over to the turnstile. He fumbled in his pocket for a moment, and then touched the man on the arm. "I feel ill," he said, speaking very rapidly; "very ill indeed! It's the atmosphere of this place. I want you to let me out by the quickest way. It would be a pity for me to faint here—especially with ladies about." His left hand shot out and placed what he had been fumbling for in his pocket on the other's bare palm. "I see there's an emergency exit over there. Would it be possible for me to get out that way?"

"Well, yes, sir; I think so." The man hesitated; he felt a slight, a very slight, feeling of misgiving. He looked at Daisy, flushed and smiling, happy and unconcerned, and then at Mrs. Bunting. She was very pale; but surely her lodger's sudden seizure was enough to make her feel worried. Hopkins felt the half sovereign pleasantly tickling his palm. The Prefect of Police had given him only half a crown—mean, shabby foreigner!

"Yes, I can let you out that way," he said at last, "and perhaps when you're standing out in the air on the iron balcony you'll feel better. But then, you know, sir, you'll have to come round to the front if you want to come in again, for those emergency doors only open outward."

"Yes, yes," said Mr. Sleuth hurriedly; "I quite understand! If I feel better I'll come in by the front way, and pay another shilling—that's only fair."

"You needn't do that if you'll just explain what happened here."

The man went and pulled the curtain aside, and put his shoulder against the door. It burst open, and the light for a moment blinded Mr. Sleuth. He passed his hand over his eyes.

"Thank you," he said; "thank you. I shall get all right here."

Five days later Bunting identified the body of a man found drowned in the Regent's Canal as that of his late lodger; and, the morning following, a gardener working in the Regent's Park found a newspaper in which were wrapped, together with a half-worn pair of rubber-soled shoes, two surgical knives. This fact was not chronicled in any newspaper; but a very pretty and picturesque paragraph went the round of the press, about the same time, concerning a small box filled with sovereigns which had been forwarded anonymously to the Governor of the Foundling Hospital.

Mr. and Mrs. Bunting are now in the service of an old lady, by whom they are feared as well as respected, and whom they make very comfortable.

THE LODGER

Marie Belloc Lowndes

When Marie Adelaide Belloc Lowndes (1868–1947) saw the stir her short story "The Lodger" created, she set about expanding it to a full-length book, two years after the story made its first appearance in *McClure's Magazine* (January 1911).

This very early depiction of the Ripper atrocities intrigued a variety of filmmakers, the first of whom was Alfred Hitchcock, who made *The Lodger*, a 1927 film subtitled *A Story of the London Fog*. In this version, the stranger in the upstairs room, played by silent-film star Ivor Novello, is quite different from the man in Lowndes's story and novel, quiet and reclusive but charming enough to win the heart of the film's heroine.

Novello played the eccentric lodger again in the 1932 film *The Lodger* (released in the United States with the understated title of *The Phantom Fiend*). Directed by Maurice Elvey, it also starred Elizabeth Allan and Jack Hawkins. Perhaps the most familiar version of *The Lodger* is the highly regarded 1944 film with a star-studded cast of Laird Cregar, Merle Oberon, George Sanders, Sir Cedric Hardwicke, and Sara Allgood; it was directed by John Bráhm. A close remake of this film, released in 1953, is *Man in the Attic*, starring Jack Palance, Constance Smith, Byron Palmer, and Rhys Williams; it was directed by Hugo Fregonese. Proving its endurance, *The Lodger* was filmed again in 2009, with a script by David Ondaatje, who also directed. It forgettably starred Alfred Molina, Rachael Leigh Cook, and Hope Davis.

The Lodger has had several stage adaptations, the most notable being *Who Is He?*, written by Horace Annesley Vachell, which made its debut in London's Haymarket Theatre on December 9, 1915, starring Henry Ainley; it ran for one hundred fifty-seven performances. When it crossed the Atlantic to open in New York on January 8, 1917, it reverted to the title of the novel. The director and star was Lionel Atwill, who went on to a long career as a screen villain.

The Lodger was first published in 1913 (London, Methuen & Co.).

> "*Lover and friend hast thou put far from me, and mine acquaintance into darkness.*"
>
> PSALM LXXXVIII. 18

CHAPTER I

Robert Bunting and Ellen his wife sat before their dully burning, carefully banked-up fire.

The room, especially when it be known that it was part of a house standing in a grimy, if not exactly sordid, London thoroughfare, was exceptionally clean and well-cared-for. A casual stranger, more particularly one of a superior class to their own, on suddenly opening the door of that sitting-room, would have thought that Mr. and Mrs. Bunting presented a very pleasant, cosy picture of comfortable married life. Bunting, who was leaning back in a deep leather arm-chair, was clean-shaven and dapper, still in appearance what he had been for many years of his life—a self-respecting man-servant.

On his wife, now sitting up in an uncomfortable straight-backed chair, the marks of past servitude were less apparent; but they were there all the same—in her neat black stuff dress, and in her scrupulously clean, plain collar and cuffs. Mrs. Bunting, as a single woman, had been what is known as a useful maid.

But peculiarly true of average English life is the time-worn English proverb as to appearances being deceitful. Mr. and Mrs. Bunting were sitting in a very nice room and in their time—how long ago it now seemed! —both husband and wife had been proud of their carefully chosen belongings. Everything in the room was strong and substantial, and each article of furniture had been bought at a well-conducted auction held in a private house.

Thus the red damask curtains which now shut out the fog-laden, drizzling atmosphere of the Marylebone Road, had cost a mere song, and yet they might have been warranted to last another thirty years. A great bargain also had been the excellent Axminster carpet which covered the floor; as, again, the arm-chair in which Bunting now sat forward, staring into the dull, small fire. In fact, that arm-chair had been an extravagance of Mrs. Bunting. She had wanted her husband to be comfortable after the day's work was done, and she had paid thirty-seven shillings for the chair. Only yesterday Bunting had tried to find a purchaser for it, but the man who had come to look at it, guessing their cruel necessities, had only offered them twelve shillings and sixpence for it; so for the present they were keeping their arm-chair.

But man and woman want something more than mere material comfort, much as that is valued by the Buntings of this world. So, on the walls of the sitting-room, hung neatly framed if now rather faded photographs—photographs of Mr. and Mrs. Bunting's various former employers, and of the pretty country houses in which they had separately lived during the long years they had spent in a not unhappy servitude.

But appearances were not only deceitful, they were more than usually deceitful with regard to these unfortunate people. In spite of their good furniture—that substantial outward sign of respectability which is the last thing which wise folk who fall into trouble try to dispose of—they were almost at the end of their tether. Already they had learnt to go hungry, and they were beginning to learn to go cold. Tobacco, the last thing the sober man foregoes among his comforts, had been given up some time ago by Bunting. And even Mrs. Bunting—prim, prudent, careful woman as she was in her way—had realised what this must mean to him. So well, indeed, had she understood that some days back she had crept out and bought him a packet of Virginia.

Bunting had been touched—touched as he had not been for years by any woman's thought and love for him. Painful tears had forced themselves into his eyes, and husband and wife had both felt, in their odd, unemotional way, moved to the heart.

Fortunately he never guessed—how could he have guessed, with his slow, normal, rather dull mind?—that his poor Ellen had since more than once bitterly regretted that fourpence-ha'penny, for they were now very near the soundless depths which divide those who dwell on the safe tableland of security—those, that is, who are sure of making a respectable, if not a happy, living—and the submerged multitude who, through some lack in themselves, or owing to the conditions under which our strange civilisation has become organised, struggle rudderless till they die in workhouse, hospital, or prison.

Had the Buntings been in a class lower than their own, had they belonged to the great company of human beings technically known to so many of us as "the poor," there would have been friendly neighbours ready to help them, and the same would have been the case had they belonged to the class of smug, well-meaning, if unimaginative, folk whom they had spent so much of their lives in serving.

There was only one person in the world who might possibly be brought to help them. That was an aunt of Bunting's first wife. With this woman, the widow of a man who had been well-to-do, lived Daisy, Bunting's only child by his first wife, and during the last long two days he had been trying to make up his mind to write to the old lady, and that though he suspected that she would almost certainly retort with a cruel, sharp rebuff.

As to their few acquaintances, former fellow-servants, and so on, they had gradually fallen out of touch with them. There was but one friend who often came to see them in their deep trouble. This was a young fellow named Chandler, under whose grandfather Bunting had been footman years and years ago. Joe Chandler had never gone into service; he was attached to the police; in fact, not to put too fine a point upon it, young Chandler was a detective.

When they had first taken the house which had brought them, so they both thought, such bad luck, Bunting had encouraged the young chap to come often, for his tales were well worth listening to—quite exciting at times. But now poor Bunting didn't want to hear that sort of stories—stories of people being cleverly "nabbed," or stupidly allowed to escape the fate they always, from Chandler's point of view, richly deserved.

But Joe still came very faithfully once or twice a week, so timing his calls that neither host nor hostess need press food upon him—nay, more, he had done that which showed him to have a good and feeling heart. He had offered his father's old acquaintance a loan, and Bunting, at last, had taken 30s. Very little of that money now remained: Bunting still could jingle a few coppers in his pocket, and Mrs. Bunting had 2s. 9d.; that, and the rent they would have to pay in five weeks, was all they had left. Everything of the light, portable sort that would fetch money had been sold. Mrs. Bunting had a fierce horror of the pawnshop. She had never put her feet in such a place, and she declared she never would—she would rather starve first.

But she had said nothing when there had occurred the gradual disappearance of various little possessions she knew that Bunting valued, notably of the old-fashioned gold watch-chain which had been given to him after the death of his first master, a master he had nursed faithfully and kindly through a long and terrible illness. There had also vanished a twisted gold tie-pin, and a large mourning ring, both gifts of former employers.

When people are living near that deep pit which divides the secure from the insecure—when they see themselves creeping closer and closer to its dread edge—they are apt, however loquacious by nature, to fall into long silences. Bunting had always been a talker, but now he talked no more. Neither did Mrs. Bunting, but then she had always been a silent woman, and that was perhaps one reason why Bunting had felt drawn to her from the very first moment he had seen her.

It had fallen out in this way. A lady had just engaged him as butler, and he had been shown, by the man whose place he was to take, into the dining-room. There, to use his own expression, he had discovered Ellen Green, carefully pouring out the glass of port wine which her then mistress always drank at 11:30 every morning. And as he, the new butler, had seen her engaged in this task, as he had watched her carefully stopper the decanter and put it back into the old wine-cooler, he had said to himself, "That is the woman for me!"

But now her stillness, her—her dumbness—had got on the unfortunate man's nerves. He no longer felt like going into the various little shops close by, patronised by him in more prosperous days, and Mrs. Bunting also went afield to make the slender purchases which still had to be made every day or two, if they were to be saved from actually starving to death.

Suddenly, across the stillness of the dark November evening there came the muffled sounds of hurrying feet and of loud, shrill shouting outside—boys crying the late afternoon editions of the evening papers.

Bunting turned uneasily in his chair. The giving up of a daily paper had been, after his tobacco, his bitterest deprivation. And the paper was an older habit than the tobacco, for servants are great readers of newspapers.

As the shouts came through the closed windows and the thick damask curtains, Bunting felt a sudden sense of mind hunger fall upon him.

It was a shame—a damned shame—that he shouldn't know what was happening in the world outside! Only criminals are kept from hearing news of what is going on beyond their prison walls. And those shouts, those hoarse, sharp cries must portend that something really exciting had happened, something warranted to make a man forget for the moment his own intimate, gnawing troubles.

He got up, and going towards the nearest window strained his ears to listen. There fell on them, emerging now and again from the confused babel of hoarse shouts, the one clear word "Murder!"

Slowly Bunting's brain pieced the loud, indistinct cries into some sort of connected order. Yes, that was it—"Horrible Murder! Murder at St. Pancras!" Bunting remembered vaguely another murder which had been committed near St. Pancras—that of an old lady by her servant-maid. It had happened a great many years ago, but was still vividly remembered, as of special and natural interest, among the class to which he had belonged.

The newsboys—for there were more than one of them, a rather unusual thing in the Marylebone Road—were coming nearer and nearer; now they had adopted another cry, but he could not quite catch what they were crying. They were still shouting hoarsely, excitedly, but he could only hear a word or two now and then. Suddenly "The Avenger! The Avenger at his work again!" broke on his ear.

During the last fortnight four very curious and brutal murders had been committed in London and within a comparatively small area.

The first had aroused no special interest—even the second had only been awarded, in the paper Bunting was still then taking in, quite a small paragraph.

Then had come the third—and with that a wave of keen excitement, for pinned to the dress of the victim—a drunken woman—had been found a three-cornered piece of paper, on which was written, in red ink, and in printed characters, the words,

"The Avenger"

It was then realised, not only by those whose business it is to investigate such terrible happenings, but also by the vast world of men and women who take an intelligent interest in such sinister mysteries, that the same miscreant had committed all three crimes; and before that extraordinary fact had had time to soak well into the public mind there took place yet another murder, and again the murderer had been to special pains to make it clear that some obscure and terrible lust for vengeance possessed him.

Now everyone was talking of The Avenger and his crimes! Even the man who left their ha'porth of milk at the door each morning had spoken to Bunting about them that very day.

Bunting came back to the fire and looked down at his wife with mild excitement. Then, seeing her pale, apathetic face, her look of weary, mournful absorption, a wave of irritation swept through him. He felt he could have shaken her!

Ellen had hardly taken the trouble to listen when he, Bunting, had come back to bed that morning, and told her what the milkman had said. In fact, she had been quite nasty about it, intimating that she didn't like hearing about such horrid things.

It was a curious fact that though Mrs. Bunting enjoyed tales of pathos and sentiment, and would listen with frigid amusement to the details of a breach of promise action, she shrank from stories of immorality or of physical violence. In the old, happy days, when they could afford to buy a paper, aye, and more than one paper daily, Bunting had often had to choke down his interest in some exciting "case" or "mystery" which was affording him pleasant mental relaxation, because any allusion to it sharply angered Ellen.

But now he was at once too dull and too miserable to care how she felt.

Walking away from the window he took a slow, uncertain step towards the door; when there he turned half round, and there came over his close-shaven, round face the rather sly, pleading look with which a child about to do something naughty glances at its parent.

But Mrs. Bunting remained quite still; her thin, narrow shoulders just showed above the back of the chair on which she was sitting, bolt upright, staring before her as if into vacancy.

Bunting turned round, opened the door, and quickly he went out into the dark hall—they had given up lighting the gas there some time ago—and opened the front door. . . .

Walking down the small flagged path outside, he flung open the iron gate which gave on to the damp pavement. But there he hesitated. The coppers in his pocket seemed to have shrunk in number, and he remembered ruefully how far Ellen could make even four pennies go.

Then a boy ran up to him with a sheaf of evening papers, and Bunting, being sorely tempted—fell. "Give me a *Sun*," he said roughly, "*Sun* or *Echo*!"

But the boy, scarcely stopping to take breath, shook his head. "Only penny papers left," he gasped. "What'll yer 'ave, sir?"

With an eagerness which was mingled with shame, Bunting drew a penny out of his pocket and took a paper—it was the *Evening Standard*—from the boy's hand.

Then, very slowly, he shut the gate and walked back through the raw, cold air, up the flagged path, shivering yet full of eager, joyful anticipation.

Thanks to that penny he had just spent so recklessly he would pass a happy hour, taken, for once, out of his anxious, despondent, miserable self. It irritated him shrewdly to know that these moments of respite from carking care would not be shared with his poor wife, with careworn, troubled Ellen.

A hot wave of unease, almost of remorse, swept over Bunting. Ellen would never have spent that penny on herself—he knew that well enough—and if it hadn't been so cold, so foggy, so—so drizzly, he would have gone out again through the gate and stood under the street lamp to take his pleasure. He dreaded with a nervous dread the glance of Ellen's cold, reproving light-blue eye. That glance would tell him that he had had no business to waste a penny on a paper, and that well he knew it!

Suddenly the door in front of him opened, and he heard a familiar voice saying crossly, yet anxiously, "What on earth are you doing out there, Bunting? Come in—do! You'll catch your death of cold! I don't want to have you ill on my hands as well as everything else!" Mrs. Bunting rarely uttered so many words at once nowadays.

He walked in through the front door of his cheerless house. "I went out to get a paper," he said sullenly.

After all, he was master. He had as much right to spend the money as she had; for the matter of that the money on which they were now both living had been lent, nay, pressed on him—not on Ellen—by that decent young chap, Joe Chandler. And he, Bunting, had done all he could; he had pawned everything he could pawn, while Ellen, so he resentfully noticed, still wore her wedding ring.

He stepped past her heavily, and though she said nothing, he knew she grudged him his coming joy. Then, full of rage with her and contempt for himself, and giving himself the luxury of a mild, a very mild, oath—Ellen had very early made it clear she would have no swearing in her presence—he lit the hall gas full-flare.

"How can we hope to get lodgers if they can't even see the card?" he shouted angrily.

And there was truth in what he said, for now that he had lit the gas, the oblong card, though not the word "Apartments" printed on it, could be plainly seen outlined against the old-fashioned fanlight above the front door.

Bunting went into the sitting-room, silently followed by his wife, and then, sitting down in his nice arm-chair, he poked the little banked-up fire. It was the first time Bunting had poked the fire for many a long day, and this exertion of marital authority made him feel better. A man has to assert himself sometimes, and he, Bunting, had not asserted himself enough lately.

A little colour came into Mrs. Bunting's pale face. She was not used to be flouted in this way. For Bunting, when not thoroughly upset, was the mildest of men.

She began moving about the room, flicking off an imperceptible touch of dust here, straightening a piece of furniture there.

But her hands trembled—they trembled with excitement, with self-pity, with anger. A penny? It was dreadful—dreadful to have to worry about a penny! But they had come to the point when one has to worry about pennies. Strange that her husband didn't realise that.

Bunting looked round once or twice; he would have liked to ask Ellen to leave off fidgeting, but he was fond of peace, and perhaps, by now, a little bit ashamed of himself, so he refrained from remark, and she soon gave over what irritated him of her own accord.

But Mrs. Bunting did not come and sit down as her husband would have liked her to do. The sight of him, absorbed in his paper as he was, irritated her, and made her long to get away from him. Opening the door which separated the sitting-room from the bedroom behind, and—shutting out the aggravating vision of Bunting sitting comfortably by the now brightly burning fire, with the *Evening Standard* spread out before him—she sat down in the cold darkness, and pressed her hands against her temples.

Never, never had she felt so hopeless, so—so broken as now. Where was the good of having been an upright, conscientious, self-respecting woman all her life long, if it only led to this utter, degrading poverty and wretchedness? She and Bunting were just past the age which gentlefolk think proper in a married couple seeking to enter service together, unless, that is, the wife happens to be a professed cook. A cook and a butler can always get a nice situation. But Mrs. Bunting was no cook. She could do all right the simple things any lodger she might get would require, but that was all.

Lodgers? How foolish she had been to think of taking lodgers! For it had been her doing. Bunting had been like butter in her hands.

Yet they had begun well, with a lodging-house in a seaside place. There they had prospered, not as they had hoped to do, but still pretty well; and then had come an epidemic of scarlet fever, and that had meant ruin for them, and for dozens, nay, hundreds, of other luckless people. Then had followed a business experiment which had proved even more disastrous, and which had left them in debt—in debt to an extent they could never hope to repay, to a good-natured former employer.

After that, instead of going back to service, as they might have done, perhaps, either together or separately, they had made up their minds to make one last effort, and they had taken over, with the trifle of money that remained to them, the lease of this house in the Marylebone Road.

In former days, when they had each been leading the sheltered, impersonal, and, above all, financially easy existence which is the compensation life offers to those men and women who deliberately take upon themselves the yoke of domestic service, they had both lived in houses overlooking Regent's Park. It had seemed a wise plan to settle in the same neighbourhood, the more so that Bunting, who had a good appearance, had retained the kind of connection which enables a man to get a job now and again as waiter at private parties.

But life moves quickly, jaggedly, for people like the Buntings. Two of his former masters had moved to another part of London, and a caterer in Baker Street whom he had known went bankrupt.

And now? Well, just now Bunting could not have taken a job had one been offered him, for he had pawned his dress clothes. He had not asked his wife's permission to do this, as so good a husband ought to have done. He had just gone out and done it. And she had not had the heart to say anything; nay, it was with part of the money that he had handed her silently the evening he did it that she had bought that last packet of tobacco.

And then, as Mrs. Bunting sat there thinking these painful thoughts, there suddenly came to the front door the sound of a loud, tremulous, uncertain double knock.

CHAPTER II

Mrs. Bunting jumped nervously to her feet. She stood for a moment listening in the darkness, a darkness made the blacker by the line of light under the door behind which sat Bunting reading his paper.

And then it came again, that loud, tremulous, uncertain double knock; not a knock, so the listener told herself, that boded any good. Would-be lodgers gave sharp, quick, bold, confident raps. No; this must be some kind of beggar. The queerest people came at all hours, and asked—whining or threatening— for money.

Mrs. Bunting had had some sinister experiences with men and women— especially women—drawn from that nameless, mysterious class made up of the human flotsam and jetsam which drifts about every great city. But since she had taken to leaving the gas in the passage unlit at night she had been very little troubled with that kind of visitors, those human bats which are attracted by any kind of light, but leave alone those who live in darkness.

She opened the door of the sitting-room. It was Bunting's place to go to the front door, but she knew far better than he did how to deal with difficult or obtrusive callers. Still, somehow, she would have liked him to go to-night. But Bunting sat on, absorbed in his newspaper; all he did at the sound of the bedroom door opening was to look up and say, "Didn't you hear a knock?"

Without answering his question she went out into the hall.

Slowly she opened the front door.

On the top of the three steps which led up to the door, there stood the long, lanky figure of a man, clad in an Inverness cape and an old-fashioned top hat. He waited for a few seconds blinking at her, perhaps dazzled by the light of the gas in the passage. Mrs. Bunting's trained perception told her at once that this man, odd as he looked, was a gentleman, belonging by birth to the class with whom her former employment had brought her in contact.

"Is it not a fact that you let lodgings?" he asked, and there was something shrill, unbalanced, hesitating, in his voice.

"Yes, sir," she said uncertainly—it was a long, long time since anyone had come after their lodgings, anyone, that is, that they could think of taking into their respectable house.

Instinctively she stepped a little to one side, and the stranger walked past her, and so into the hall.

And then, for the first time, Mrs. Bunting noticed that he held a narrow bag in his left hand. It was quite a new bag, made of strong brown leather.

"I am looking for some quiet rooms," he said; then he repeated the words, "quiet rooms," in a dreamy, absent way, and as he uttered them he looked nervously round him.

Then his sallow face brightened, for the hall had been carefully furnished, and was very clean.

There was a neat hat-and-umbrella stand, and the stranger's weary feet fell soft on a good, serviceable dark-red drugget, which matched in colour the flock-paper on the walls.

A very superior lodging-house this, and evidently a superior lodging-house keeper.

"You'd find my rooms quite quiet, sir," she said gently. "And just now I have four to let. The house is empty, save for my husband and me, sir."

Mrs. Bunting spoke in a civil, passionless voice. It seemed too good to be true, this sudden coming of a possible lodger, and of a lodger who spoke in the pleasant, courteous way and voice which recalled to the poor woman her happy, far-off days of youth and of security.

"That sounds very suitable," he said. "Four rooms? Well, perhaps I ought only to take two rooms, but, still, I should like to see all four before I make my choice."

How fortunate, how very fortunate it was that Bunting had lit the gas! But for that circumstance this gentleman would have passed them by.

She turned towards the staircase, quite forgetting in her agitation that the front door was still open; and it was the stranger whom she already in her mind described as "the lodger," who turned and rather quickly walked down the passage and shut it.

"Oh, thank you, sir!" she exclaimed. "I'm sorry you should have had the trouble."

For a moment their eyes met. "It's not safe to leave a front door open in London," he said, rather sharply. "I hope you do not often do that. It would be so easy for anyone to slip in."

Mrs. Bunting felt rather upset. The stranger had still spoken courteously, but he was evidently very much put out.

"I assure you, sir, I never leave my front door open," she answered hastily. "You needn't be at all afraid of that!"

And then, through the closed door of the sitting-room, came the sound of Bunting coughing—it was just a little, hard cough, but Mrs. Bunting's future lodger started violently.

"Who's that?" he said, putting out a hand and clutching her arm. "Whatever was that?"

"Only my husband, sir. He went out to buy a paper a few minutes ago, and the cold just caught him, I suppose."

"Your husband——?" he looked at her intently, suspiciously. "What—what, may I ask, is your husband's occupation?"

Mrs. Bunting drew herself up. The question as to Bunting's occupation was no one's business but theirs. Still, it wouldn't do for her to show offence. "He goes out waiting," she said stiffly. "He was a gentleman's servant, sir. He could, of course, valet you should you require him to do so."

And then she turned and led the way up the steep, narrow staircase.

At the top of the first flight of stairs was what Mrs. Bunting, to herself, called the drawing-room floor. It consisted of a sitting-room in front, and a bedroom behind.

She opened the door of the sitting-room and quickly lit the chandelier.

This front room was pleasant enough, though perhaps a little over-encumbered with furniture. Covering the floor was a green carpet simulating moss; four chairs were placed round the table which occupied the exact middle of the apartment, and in the corner, opposite the door giving on to the landing, was a roomy, old-fashioned chiffonnier.

On the dark-green walls hung a series of eight engravings, portraits of early Victorian belles, clad in lace and tarletan ball dresses, clipped from an old Book of Beauty. Mrs. Bunting was very fond of these pictures; she thought they gave the drawing-room a note of elegance and refinement.

As she hurriedly turned up the gas she was glad, glad indeed, that she had summoned up sufficient energy, two days ago, to give the room a thorough turn-out.

It had remained for a long time in the state in which it had been left by its last dishonest, dirty occupants when they had been scared into going away by Bunting's rough threats of the police. But now it was in apple-pie order, with one paramount exception, of which Mrs. Bunting was painfully aware. There were no white curtains to the windows, but that omission could soon be remedied if this gentleman really took the lodgings.

But what was this——? The stranger was looking round him rather dubiously. "This is rather—rather too grand for me," he said at last. "I should like to see your other rooms, Mrs.—er——"

"——Bunting," she said softly. "Bunting, sir."

And as she spoke the dark, heavy load of care again came down and settled on her sad, burdened heart. Perhaps she had been mistaken, after all—or rather, she had not been mistaken in one sense, but perhaps this gentleman was a poor gentleman—too poor, that is, to afford the rent of more than one room, say eight or ten shillings a week; eight or ten shillings a week would be very little use to her and Bunting, though better than nothing at all.

"Will you just look at the bedroom, sir?"

"No," he said, "no. I think I should like to see what you have farther up the house, Mrs.——," and then, as if making a prodigious mental effort, he brought out her name, "Bunting," with a kind of gasp.

The two top rooms were, of course, immediately above the drawing-room floor. But they looked poor and mean, owing to the fact that they were bare of any kind of ornament. Very little trouble had been taken over their arrangement; in fact, they had been left in much the same condition as that in which the Buntings had found them.

For the matter of that, it is difficult to make a nice, genteel sitting-room out of an apartment of which the principal features are a sink and a big gas stove. The gas stove, of an obsolete pattern, was fed by a tiresome, shilling-in-the-slot arrangement. It had been the property of the people from whom the Buntings had taken over the lease of the house, who, knowing it to be of no monetary value, had thrown it in among the humble fittings they had left behind.

What furniture there was in the room was substantial and clean, as everything belonging to Mrs. Bunting was bound to be, but it was a bare, uncomfortable-looking place, and the landlady now felt sorry that she had done nothing to make it appear more attractive.

To her surprise, however, her companion's dark, sensitive, hatchet-shaped face became irradiated with satisfaction. "Capital! Capital!" he exclaimed, for the first time putting down the bag he held at his feet, and rubbing his long, thin hands together with a quick, nervous movement.

"This is just what I have been looking for." He walked with long, eager strides towards the gas stove. "First-rate—quite first-rate! Exactly what I wanted to find! You must understand, Mrs.—er—Bunting, that I am a man of science. I make, that is, all sorts of experiments, and I often require the—ah, well, the presence of great heat."

He shot out a hand, which she noticed shook a little, towards the stove. "This, too, will be useful—exceedingly useful, to me," and he touched the edge of the stone sink with a lingering, caressing touch.

He threw his head back and passed his hand over his high, bare forehead; then, moving towards a chair, he sat down—wearily. "I'm tired," he muttered in a low voice, "tired—tired! I've been walking about all day, Mrs. Bunting, and I could find nothing to sit down upon. They do not put benches for tired men in the London streets. They do so on the Continent. In some ways they are far more humane on the Continent than they are in England, Mrs. Bunting."

"Indeed, sir," she said civilly; and then, after a nervous glance, she asked the question of which the answer would mean so much to her, "Then you mean to take my rooms, sir?"

"This room, certainly," he said, looking round. "This room is exactly what I have been looking for, and longing for, the last few days"; and then hastily he added, "I mean this kind of place is what I have always wanted to possess, Mrs. Bunting. You would be surprised if you knew how difficult it is to get anything of the sort. But now my weary search has ended, and that is a relief—a very, very great relief to me!"

He stood up and looked round him with a dreamy, abstracted air. And then, "Where's my bag?" he asked suddenly, and there came a note of sharp, angry fear in his voice. He glared at the quiet woman standing before him, and for a moment Mrs. Bunting felt a tremor of fright shoot through her. It seemed a pity that Bunting was so far away, right down the house.

But Mrs. Bunting was aware that eccentricity has always been a perquisite, as it were the special luxury, of the well-born and of the well-educated. Scholars, as she well knew, are never quite like other people, and her new lodger was undoubtedly a scholar. "Surely I had a bag when I came in?" he said in a scared, troubled voice.

"Here it is, sir," she said soothingly, and, stooping, picked it up and handed it to him. And as she did so she noticed that the bag was not at all heavy; it was evidently by no means full.

He took it eagerly from her. "I beg your pardon," he muttered. "But there is something in that bag which is very precious to me—something I procured with infinite difficulty, and which I could never get again without running into great danger, Mrs. Bunting. That must be the excuse for my late agitation."

"About terms, sir?" she said a little timidly, returning to the subject which meant so much, so very much to her.

"About terms?" he echoed. And then there came a pause. "My name is Sleuth," he said suddenly,—"S-l-e-u-t-h. Think of a hound, Mrs. Bunting, and you'll never forget my name. I could provide you with a reference——" (he gave her what she described to herself as a funny, sideways look), "but I should prefer you to dispense with that, if you don't mind. I am quite willing to pay you—well, shall we say a month in advance?"

A spot of red shot into Mrs. Bunting's cheeks. She felt sick with relief—nay, with a joy which was almost pain. She had not known till that moment how hungry she was—how eager for a good meal. "That would be all right, sir," she murmured.

"And what are you going to charge me?" There had come a kindly, almost a friendly note into his voice. "With attendance, mind! I shall expect you to give me attendance, and I need hardly ask if you can cook, Mrs. Bunting?"

"Oh, yes, sir," she said. "I am a plain cook. What would you say to twenty-five shillings a week, sir?" She looked at him deprecatingly, and as he did not answer she went on falteringly, "You see, sir, it may seem a good deal, but you would have the best of attendance and careful cooking—and my husband, sir—he would be pleased to valet you."

"I shouldn't want anything of that sort done for me," said Mr. Sleuth hastily. "I prefer looking after my own clothes. I am used to waiting on myself. But, Mrs. Bunting, I have a great dislike to sharing lodgings——"

She interrupted eagerly, "I could let you have the use of the two floors for the same price—that is, until we get another lodger. I shouldn't like you to sleep in the back room up here, sir. It's such a poor little room. You could do as you say, sir—do your work and your experiments up here, and then have your meals in the drawing-room."

"Yes," he said hesitatingly, "that sounds a good plan. And if I offered you two pounds, or two guineas? Might I then rely on your not taking another lodger?"

"Yes," she said quietly. "I'd be very glad only to have you to wait on, sir."

"I suppose you have a key to the door of this room, Mrs. Bunting? I don't like to be disturbed while I'm working."

He waited a moment, and then said again, rather urgently, "I suppose you have a key to this door, Mrs. Bunting?"

"Oh, yes, sir, there's a key—a very nice little key. The people who lived here before had a new kind of lock put on to the door." She went over, and throwing the door open, showed him that a round disc had been fitted above the old keyhole.

He nodded his head, and then, after standing silent a little, as if absorbed in thought, "Forty-two shillings a week? Yes, that will suit me perfectly. And I'll begin now by paying my first month's rent in advance. Now, four times forty-two shillings is"—he jerked his head back and stared at his new landlady; for the first time he smiled, a queer, wry smile—"why, just eight pounds eight shillings, Mrs. Bunting!"

He thrust his hand through into an inner pocket of his long cape-like coat and took out a handful of sovereigns. Then he began putting these down in a row on the bare wooden table which stood in the centre of the room. "Here's five—six—seven—eight—nine—ten pounds. You'd better keep the odd change, Mrs. Bunting, for I shall want you to do some shopping for me to-morrow morning. I met with a misfortune to-day." But the new lodger did not speak as if his misfortune, whatever it was, weighed on his spirits.

"Indeed, sir. I'm sorry to hear that." Mrs. Bunting's heart was going thump—thump—thump. She felt extraordinarily moved, dizzy with relief and joy.

"Yes, a very great misfortune! I lost my luggage, the few things I managed to bring away with me." His voice dropped suddenly. "I shouldn't have said that," he muttered. "I was a fool to say that!" Then, more loudly, "Someone said to me, 'You can't go into a lodging-house without any luggage. They wouldn't take you in.' But *you* have taken me in, Mrs. Bunting, and I'm grateful for—for the kind way you have met me——" He looked at her feelingly, appealingly, and Mrs. Bunting was touched. She was beginning to feel very kindly towards her new lodger.

"I hope I know a gentleman when I see one," she said, with a break in her staid voice.

"I shall have to see about getting some clothes to-morrow, Mrs. Bunting." Again he looked at her appealingly.

"I expect you'd like to wash your hands now, sir. And would you tell me what you'd like for supper? We haven't much in the house."

"Oh, anything'll do," he said hastily. "I don't want you to go out for me. It's a cold, foggy, wet night, Mrs. Bunting. If you have a little bread-and-butter and a cup of milk I shall be quite satisfied."

"I have a nice sausage," she said hesitatingly.

It was a very nice sausage, and she had bought it that same morning for Bunting's supper; as to herself, she had been going to content herself with a little bread and cheese. But now—wonderful, almost, intoxicating thought—she could send Bunting out to get anything they both liked. The ten sovereigns lay in her hand full of comfort and good cheer.

"A sausage? No, I fear that will hardly do. I never touch flesh meat," he said; "it is a long, long time since I tasted a sausage, Mrs. Bunting."

"Is it indeed, sir?" She hesitated a moment, then asked stiffly, "And will you be requiring any beer, or wine, sir?"

A strange, wild look of lowering wrath suddenly filled Mr. Sleuth's pale face.

"Certainly not. I thought I had made that quite clear, Mrs. Bunting. I had hoped to hear that you were an abstainer——"

"So I am, sir, lifelong. And so's Bunting been since we married." She might have said, had she been a woman given to make such confidences, that she had made Bunting abstain very early in their acquaintance. That he had given in about that had been the thing that first made her believe that he was sincere in all the nonsense that he talked to her, in those far-away days of his courting. Glad she was now that he had taken the pledge as a younger man; but for that nothing would have kept him from the drink during the bad times they had gone through.

And then, going downstairs, she showed Mr. Sleuth the nice bedroom which opened out of the drawing-room. It was a replica of Mrs. Bunting's own room just underneath, excepting that everything up here had cost just a little more, and was therefore rather better in quality.

The new lodger looked round him with such a strange expression of content and peace stealing over his worn face. "A haven of rest," he muttered; and then, "'He bringeth them to their desired haven.' Beautiful words, Mrs. Bunting."

"Yes, sir."

Mrs. Bunting felt a little startled. It was the first time anyone had quoted the Bible to her for many a long day. But it seemed to set the seal, as it were, on Mr. Sleuth's respectability.

What a comfort it was, too, that she had to deal with only one lodger, and that a gentleman, instead of with a married couple! Very peculiar married couples had drifted in and out of Mr. and Mrs. Bunting's lodgings, not only here, in London, but at the seaside. . . .

How unlucky they had been, to be sure! Since they had come to London not a single pair of lodgers had been even moderately respectable and kindly. The last lot had belonged to that horrible underworld of men and women who, having, as the phrase goes, seen better days, now only keep their heads above water with the help of petty fraud.

"I'll bring you up some hot water in a minute, sir, and some clean towels," she said, going to the door.

And then Mr. Sleuth turned quickly round. "Mrs. Bunting"—and as he spoke he stammered a little—"I—I don't want you to interpret the word attendance too liberally. You need not run yourself off your feet for me. I'm accustomed to look after myself."

And, queerly, uncomfortably, she felt herself dismissed—even a little snubbed. "All right, sir," she said. "I'll only just let you know when I've your supper ready."

CHAPTER III

But what was a little snub compared with the intense relief and joy of going down and telling Bunting of the great piece of good fortune which had fallen their way?

Staid Mrs. Bunting seemed to make but one leap down the steep stairs. In the hall, however, she pulled herself together, and tried to still her agitation. She had always disliked and despised any show of emotion; she called such betrayal of feeling "making a fuss."

Opening the door of their sitting-room, she stood for a moment looking at her husband's bent back, and she realised, with a pang of pain, how the last few weeks had aged him.

Bunting suddenly looked round, and, seeing his wife, stood up. He put the paper he had been holding down on to the table: "Well," he said, "well, who was it, Ellen?"

He felt rather ashamed of himself; it was he who ought to have answered the door and done all that parleying of which he had heard murmurs.

And then in a moment his wife's hand shot out, and the ten sovereigns fell in a little clinking heap on the table.

"Look there!" she whispered, with an excited, tearful quiver in her voice. "Look there, Bunting!"

And Bunting did look there, but with a troubled, frowning gaze.

He was not quick-witted, but at once he jumped to the conclusion that his wife had just had in a furniture dealer, and that this ten pounds represented all their nice furniture upstairs. If that were so, then it was the beginning of the end. That furniture in the first-floor front had cost—Ellen had reminded him of the fact bitterly only yesterday—seventeen pounds nine shillings, and every single item had been a bargain. It was too bad that she had only got ten pounds for it.

Yet he hadn't the heart to reproach her.

He did not speak as he looked across at her, and meeting that troubled, rebuking glance, she guessed what it was that he thought had happened.

"We've a new lodger!" she cried. "And—and, Bunting? He's quite the gentleman! He actually offered to pay four weeks in advance, at two guineas a week."

"No, never!"

Bunting moved quickly round the table, and together they stood there, fascinated by the little heap of gold. "But there's ten sovereigns here," he said suddenly.

"Yes, the gentleman said I'd have to buy some things for him to-morrow. And, oh, Bunting, he's so well spoken, I really felt that—I really felt that——" and then Mrs. Bunting, taking a step or two sideways, sat down, and throwing her little black apron over her face burst into gasping sobs.

Bunting patted her back timidly. "Ellen?" he said, much moved by her agitation, "Ellen? Don't take on so, my dear——"

"I won't," she sobbed, "I—I won't! I'm a fool—I know I am! But, oh, I didn't think we was ever going to have any luck again!"

And then she told him—or rather tried to tell him—what the lodger was like. Mrs. Bunting was no hand at talking, but one thing she did impress on her husband's mind, namely, that Mr. Sleuth was eccentric, as so many clever people are eccentric—that is, in a harmless way—and that he must be humoured.

"He says he doesn't want to be waited on much," she said at last, wiping her eyes, "but I can see he will want a good bit of looking after, all the same, poor gentleman."

And just as the words left her mouth there came the unfamiliar sound of a loud ring. It was that of the drawing-room bell being pulled again and again.

Bunting looked at his wife eagerly. "I think I'd better go up, eh, Ellen?" he said. He felt quite anxious to see their new lodger. For the matter of that, it would be a relief to be doing something again.

"Yes," she answered, "you go up! Don't keep him waiting! I wonder what it is he wants? I said I'd let him know when his supper was ready."

A moment later Bunting came down again. There was an odd smile on his face. "Whatever d'you think he wanted?" he whispered mysteriously. And as she said nothing, he went on, "He's asked me for the loan of a Bible!"

"Well, I don't see anything so out of the way in that," she said hastily, " 'specially if he don't feel well. I'll take it up to him."

And, then, going to a small table which stood between the two windows, Mrs. Bunting took off it a large Bible, which had been given to her as a wedding present by a married lady with whose mother she had lived for several years.

"He said it would do quite well when you take up his supper," said Bunting; and, then, "Ellen? He's a queer-looking cove—not like any gentleman *I* ever had to do with."

"He *is* a gentleman," said Mrs. Bunting rather fiercely.

"Oh, yes, that's all right." But still he looked at her doubtfully. "I asked him if he'd like me to just put away his clothes. But, Ellen, he said he hadn't got any clothes!"

"No more he hasn't," she spoke quickly, defensively. "He had the misfortune to lose his luggage. He's one dishonest folk 'ud take advantage of."

"Yes, one can see that with half an eye," Bunting agreed.

And then there was silence for a few moments, while Mrs. Bunting put down on a little bit of paper the things she wanted her husband to go out and buy for her. She handed him the list, together with a sovereign. "Be as quick as you can," she said, "for I feel a bit hungry. I'll be going down now to see about Mr. Sleuth's supper. He only wants a glass of milk and two eggs. I'm glad I've never fallen to bad eggs!"

"Sleuth," echoed Bunting, staring at her. "What a queer name! How d'you spell it—S-l-u-t-h?"

"No," she shot out, "S-l-e-u-t-h."

"Oh," he said doubtfully.

"He said, 'Think of a hound and you'll never forget my name,' " and Mrs. Bunting smiled.

When he got to the door, Bunting turned round: "We'll now be able to pay young Chandler back some o' that thirty shillings. I *am* glad."

She nodded; her heart, as the saying is, too full for words.

And then each went about his and her business—Bunting out into the drenching fog, his wife down to her cold kitchen.

The lodger's tray was soon ready; everything upon it nicely and daintily arranged. Mrs. Bunting knew how to wait upon a gentleman.

Just as the landlady was going up the kitchen stair, she suddenly remembered Mr. Sleuth's request for a Bible. Putting the tray down in the hall, she went into her sitting-room and took up the Book; but when back in the hall she hesitated a moment as to whether it was worth while to make two journeys. But, no, she thought she could manage; clasping the large, heavy volume under her arm, and taking up the tray, she walked slowly up the staircase.

But a great surprise awaited her; in fact, when Mr. Sleuth's landlady opened the door of the drawing-room she very nearly dropped the tray. She actually did drop the Bible, and it fell with a heavy thud to the ground.

The new lodger had turned all those nice framed engravings of the early Victorian beauties, of which Mrs. Bunting had been so proud, with their faces to the wall!

For a moment she was really too surprised to speak. Putting the tray down on the table, she stooped and picked up the Book. It troubled her that the Bible should have fallen to the ground; but really she hadn't been able to help it—it was a mercy that the tray hadn't fallen, too.

Mr. Sleuth got up. "I—I have taken the liberty to arrange the room as I should wish it to be," he said awkwardly. "You see, Mrs.—er—Bunting, I felt as I sat here that these women's eyes followed me about. It was a most unpleasant sensation, and gave me quite an eerie feeling."

The landlady was now laying a small tablecloth over half of the table. She made no answer to her lodger's remark, for the good reason that she did not know what to say.

Her silence seemed to distress Mr. Sleuth. After what seemed a long pause, he spoke again.

"I prefer bare walls, Mrs. Bunting," he spoke with some agitation. "As a matter of fact, I have been used to seeing bare walls about me for a long time."

And then, at last, his landlady answered him, in a composed, soothing voice, which somehow did him good to hear. "I quite understand, sir. And when Bunting comes in he shall take the pictures all down. We have plenty of space in our own rooms for them."

"Thank you—thank you very much."

Mr. Sleuth appeared greatly relieved.

"And I have brought you up my Bible, sir. I understood you wanted the loan of it?"

Mr. Sleuth stared at her as if dazed for a moment; and then, rousing himself, he said, "Yes, yes, I do. There is no reading like the Book. There is something there which suits every state of mind, aye, and of body too——"

"Very true, sir." And then Mrs. Bunting, having laid out what really looked a very appetising little meal, turned round and quietly shut the door.

She went down straight into her sitting-room and waited there for Bunting, instead of going to the kitchen to clear up. And as she did so there came to her a comfortable recollection, an incident of her long-past youth, in the days when she, then Ellen Green, had maided a dear old lady.

The old lady had a favourite nephew—a bright, jolly young gentleman, who was learning to paint animals in Paris. And one morning Mr. Algernon—that was his rather peculiar Christian name—had had the impudence to turn to the wall six beautiful engravings of paintings done by the famous Mr. Landseer!

Mrs. Bunting remembered all the circumstances as if they had only occurred yesterday, and yet she had not thought of them for years.

It was quite early; she had come down—for in those days maids weren't thought so much of as they are now, and she slept with the upper housemaid, and it was the upper housemaid's duty to be down very early—and there, in the dining-room, she had found Mr. Algernon engaged in turning each engraving to the wall! Now, his aunt thought all the world of those pictures, and Ellen had felt quite concerned, for it doesn't do for a young gentleman to put himself wrong with a kind aunt.

"Oh, sir," she had exclaimed in dismay, "whatever are you doing?" And even now she could almost hear his merry voice, as he had answered, "I am doing my duty, fair Helen"—he had always called her "fair Helen" when no one was listening. "How can I draw ordinary animals when I see these half-human monsters staring at me all the time I am having my breakfast, my lunch, and my dinner?" That was what Mr. Algernon had said in his own saucy way, and that was what he repeated in a more serious, respectful manner to his aunt, when that dear old lady had come downstairs. In fact, he had declared, quite soberly, that the beautiful animals painted by Mr. Landseer put his eye out!

But his aunt had been very much annoyed—in fact, she had made him turn the pictures all back again; and as long as he stayed there he just had to put up with what he called "those half-human monsters."

Mrs. Bunting, sitting there, thinking the matter of Mr. Sleuth's odd behaviour over, was glad to recall that funny incident of her long-gone youth. It seemed to prove that her new lodger was not so strange as he appeared to be. Still, when Bunting came in, she did not tell him the queer thing which had happened. She told herself that she would be quite able to manage the taking down of the pictures in the drawing-room herself.

But before getting ready their own supper, Mr. Sleuth's landlady went upstairs to clear away, and when on the staircase she heard the sound of—was it talking, in the drawing-room? Startled, she waited a moment on the landing outside the drawing-room door, then she realised that it was only the lodger reading aloud to himself.

There was something very awful in the words which rose and fell on her listening ears:

"A strange woman is a narrow gate. She also lieth in wait as for a prey, and increaseth the transgressors among men."

She remained where she was, her hand on the handle of the door, and again there broke on her shrinking ears that curious, high, sing-song voice, "Her house is the way to hell, going down to the chambers of death."

It made the listener feel quite queer. But at last she summoned up courage, knocked, and walked in.

"I'd better clear away, sir, had I not?" she said.

And Mr. Sleuth nodded.

Then he got up and closed the Book. "I think I'll go to bed now," he said. "I am very, very tired. I've had a long and a very weary day, Mrs. Bunting."

After he had disappeared into the back room, Mrs. Bunting climbed up on a chair and unhooked the pictures which had so offended Mr. Sleuth. Each left an unsightly mark on the wall—but that, after all, could not be helped.

Treading softly, so that Bunting should not hear her, she carried them down, two by two, and stood them behind her bed.

CHAPTER IV

Mrs. Bunting woke up the next morning feeling happier than she had felt for a very, very long time.

For just one moment she could not think why she felt so different—and then she suddenly remembered.

How comfortable it was to know that upstairs, just over her head, lay, in the well-found bed she had bought with such satisfaction at an auction held in a Baker Street house, a lodger who was paying two guineas a week! Something seemed to tell her that Mr. Sleuth would be "a permanency." In any case, it wouldn't be her fault if he wasn't. As to his—his queerness, well, there's always something funny in everybody.

But after she had got up, and as the morning wore itself away, Mrs. Bunting grew a little anxious, for there came no sound at all from the new lodger's rooms.

At twelve, however, the drawing-room bell rang.

Mrs. Bunting hurried upstairs. She was painfully anxious to please and satisfy Mr. Sleuth. His coming had only been in the nick of time to save them from horrible disaster.

She found her lodger up, and fully dressed. He was sitting at the round table which occupied the middle of the sitting-room, and his landlady's large Bible lay open before him.

As Mrs. Bunting came in, he looked up, and she was troubled to see how tired and worn he seemed.

"You did not happen," he asked, "to have a Concordance, Mrs. Bunting?"

She shook her head; she had no idea what a Concordance could be, but she was quite sure that she had nothing of the sort about.

And then her new lodger proceeded to tell her what it was he desired her to buy for him. She had supposed the bag he had brought with him to contain certain little necessaries of civilised life—such articles, for instance, as a comb and brush, a set of razors, a tooth-brush, to say nothing of a couple of nightshirts—but no, that was evidently not so, for Mr. Sleuth required all these things to be bought now.

After having cooked him a nice breakfast, Mrs. Bunting hurried out to purchase the things of which he was in urgent need.

How pleasant it was to feel that there was money in her purse again—not only someone else's money, but money she was now in the very act of earning so agreeably.

Mrs. Bunting first made her way to a little barber's shop close by. It was there she purchased the brush and comb and the razors. It was a funny, rather smelly little place, and she hurried as much as she could, the more so that the foreigner who served her insisted on telling her some of the strange, peculiar details of this Avenger murder which had taken place forty-eight hours before, and in which Bunting took such a morbid interest.

The conversation upset Mrs. Bunting. She didn't want to think of anything painful or disagreeable on such a day as this.

Then she came back and showed the lodger her various purchases. Mr. Sleuth was pleased with everything, and thanked her most courteously. But when she suggested doing his bedroom he frowned, and looked quite put out.

"Please wait till this evening," he said hastily. "It is my custom to stay at home all day. I only care to walk about the streets when the lights are lit. You must bear with me, Mrs. Bunting, if I seem a little, just a little, unlike the lodgers you have been accustomed to. And I must ask you to understand that I must not be disturbed when thinking out my problems——" He broke off short, sighed, then added solemnly, "for mine are the great problems of life and death."

And Mrs. Bunting willingly fell in with his wishes. In spite of her prim manner and love of order, Mr. Sleuth's landlady was a true woman—she had, that is, an infinite patience with masculine vagaries and oddities.

When she was downstairs again, Mr. Sleuth's landlady met with a surprise; but it was quite a pleasant surprise. While she had been upstairs, talking to the lodger, Bunting's young friend, Joe Chandler, the detective, had come in, and as she walked into the sitting-room she saw that her husband was pushing half a sovereign across the table towards Joe.

Joe Chandler's fair, good-natured face was full of satisfaction: not at seeing his money again, mark you, but at the news Bunting had evidently been telling him—that news of the sudden wonderful change in their fortunes, the coming of an ideal lodger.

"Mr. Sleuth don't want me to do his bedroom till he's gone out!" she exclaimed. And then she sat down for a bit of a rest.

It was a comfort to know that the lodger was eating his good breakfast, and there was no need to think of him for the present. In a few minutes she would be going down to make her own and Bunting's dinner, and she told Joe Chandler that he might as well stop and have a bite with them.

Her heart warmed to the young man, for Mrs. Bunting was in a mood which seldom surprised her—a mood to be pleased with anything and everything. Nay, more. When Bunting began to ask Joe Chandler about the last of those awful Avenger murders, she even listened with a certain languid interest to all he had to say.

In the morning paper which Bunting had begun taking again that very day three columns were devoted to the extraordinary mystery which was now beginning to be the one topic of talk all over London, West and East, North and South. Bunting had read out little bits about it while they ate their breakfast, and in spite of herself Mrs. Bunting had felt thrilled and excited.

"They do say," observed Bunting cautiously, "They do say, Joe, that the police have a clue they won't say nothing about?" He looked expectantly at his visitor. To Bunting the fact that Chandler was attached to the detective section of the Metropolitan Police invested the young man with a kind of sinister glory—especially just now, when these awful and mysterious crimes were amazing and terrifying the town.

"Them who says that says wrong," answered Chandler slowly, and a look of unease, of resentment, came over his fair, stolid face. " 'Twould make a good bit of difference to me if the Yard had a clue."

And then Mrs. Bunting interposed. "Why that, Joe?" she said, smiling indulgently; the young man's keenness about his work pleased her. And in his slow, sure way Joe Chandler was very keen, and took his job very seriously. He put his whole heart and mind into it.

"Well, 'tis this way," he explained. "From to-day I'm on this business myself. You see, Mrs. Bunting, the Yard's nettled—that's what it is, and we're all on our mettle—that we are. I was right down sorry for the poor chap who was on point duty in the street where the last one happened——"

"No!" said Bunting incredulously. "You don't mean there was a policeman there, within a few yards!"

That fact hadn't been recorded in his newspaper.

Chandler nodded. "That's exactly what I do mean, Mr. Bunting! The man is near off his head, so I'm told. He did hear a yell, so he says, but he took no notice—there are a good few yells in that part o' London, as you can guess. People always quarrelling and rowing at one another in such low parts."

"Have you seen the bits of grey paper on which the monster writes his name?" inquired Bunting eagerly.

Public imagination had been much stirred by the account of those three-cornered pieces of grey paper, pinned to the victims' skirts, on which was roughly written in red ink and in printed characters the words "The Avenger."

His round, fat face was full of questioning eagerness. He put his elbows on the table, and stared across expectantly at the young man.

"Yes, I have," said Joe briefly.

"A funny kind of visiting card, eh!" Bunting laughed; the notion struck him as downright comic.

But Mrs. Bunting coloured. "It isn't a thing to make a joke about," she said reprovingly.

And Chandler backed her up. "No, indeed," he said feelingly. "I'll never forget what I've been made to see over this job. And as for that grey bit of paper, Mr. Bunting—or, rather, those grey bits of paper"—he corrected himself hastily—"you know they've three of them now at the Yard—well, they gives me the horrors!"

And then he jumped up. "That reminds me that I oughtn't to be wasting my time in pleasant company——"

"Won't you stay and have a bit of dinner?" said Mrs. Bunting solicitously.

But the detective shook his head. "No," he said, "I had a bite before I came out. Our job's a queer kind of job, as you know. A lot's left to our discretion, so to speak, but it don't leave us much time for lazing about, I can tell you."

When he reached the door he turned round, and with elaborate carelessness he inquired, "Any chance of Miss Daisy coming to London again soon?"

Bunting shook his head, but his face brightened. He was very, very fond of his only child; the pity was he saw her so seldom. "No," he said, "I'm afraid not, Joe. Old Aunt, as we calls the old lady, keeps Daisy pretty tightly tied to her apron-string. She was quite put about that week the child was up with us last June."

"Indeed? Well, so long!"

After his wife had let their friend out, Bunting said cheerfully, "Joe seems to like our Daisy, eh, Ellen?"

But Mrs. Bunting shook her head scornfully. She did not exactly dislike the girl, though she did not hold with the way Bunting's daughter was being managed by that old aunt of hers—an idle, good-for-nothing way, very different from the fashion in which she herself had been trained at the Foundling, for Mrs. Bunting as a little child had known no other home, no other family, than those provided by good Captain Coram.

"Joe Chandler's too sensible a young chap to be thinking of girls yet awhile," she said tartly.

"No doubt you're right," Bunting agreed. "Times be changed. In my young days chaps always had time for that. 'Twas just a notion that came into my head, hearing him asking, anxious-like, after her."

About five o'clock, after the street lamps were well alight, Mr. Sleuth went out, and that same evening there came two parcels addressed to his landlady. These parcels contained clothes. But it was quite clear to Mrs. Bunting's eyes that they were not new clothes. In fact, they had evidently been bought in some good second-hand clothes-shop. A funny thing for a real gentleman like Mr. Sleuth to do! It proved that he had given up all hope of getting back his lost luggage.

When the lodger had gone out he had not taken his bag with him, of that Mrs. Bunting was positive. And yet, though she searched high and low for it, she could not find the place where Mr. Sleuth kept it. And at last, had it not been that she was a very clear-headed woman, with a good memory, she would have been disposed to think that the bag had never existed, save in her imagination.

But no, she could not tell herself that! She remembered exactly how it had looked when Mr. Sleuth had first stood, a strange, queer-looking figure of a man, on her doorstep.

She further remembered how he had put the bag down on the floor of the top front room, and then, forgetting what he had done, how he had asked her eagerly, in a tone of angry fear, where the bag was—only to find it safely lodged at his feet!

As time went on Mrs. Bunting thought a great deal about that bag, for, strange and amazing fact, she never saw Mr. Sleuth's bag again. But, of course, she soon formed a theory as to its whereabouts. The brown leather bag which had formed Mr. Sleuth's only luggage the afternoon of his arrival was almost certainly locked up in the lower part of the drawing-room chiffonnier. Mr. Sleuth evidently always carried the key of the little corner cupboard about his person; Mrs. Bunting had also had a good hunt for that key, but, as was the case with the bag, the key disappeared, and she never saw either the one or the other again.

CHAPTER V

How quietly, how uneventfully, how pleasantly, sped the next few days. Already life was settling down into a groove. Waiting on Mr. Sleuth was just what Mrs. Bunting could manage to do easily, and without tiring herself.

It had at once become clear that the lodger preferred to be waited on only by one person, and that person his landlady. He gave her very little trouble. Indeed, it did her good having to wait on the lodger; it even did her good that he was not like other gentlemen; for the fact occupied her mind, and in a way it amused her. The more so that whatever his oddities Mr. Sleuth had none of those tiresome, disagreeable ways with which landladies are only too familiar, and which seem peculiar only to those human beings who also happen to be lodgers. To take but one point: Mr. Sleuth did not ask to be called unduly early. Bunting and his Ellen had fallen into the way of lying rather late in the morning, and it was a great comfort not to have to turn out to make the lodger a cup of tea at seven, or even half-past seven. Mr. Sleuth seldom required anything before eleven.

But odd he certainly was.

The second evening he had been with them Mr. Sleuth had brought in a book of which the queer name was *Cruden's Concordance*. That and the Bible— Mrs. Bunting had soon discovered that there was a relation between the two books—seemed to be the lodger's only reading. He spent hours each day, generally after he had eaten the breakfast which also served for luncheon, poring over the Old Testament and over that strange kind of index to the Book.

As for the delicate and yet the all-important question of money, Mr. Sleuth was everything—everything that the most exacting landlady could have wished. Never had there been a more confiding or trusting gentleman. On the very first day he had been with them he had allowed his money—the considerable sum of one hundred and eighty-four sovereigns—to lie about wrapped up in little pieces of rather dirty newspaper on his dressing-table. That had quite upset Mrs. Bunting. She had allowed herself respectfully to point out to him that what he was doing was foolish, indeed wrong. But as his only answer he had laughed, and she had been startled when the loud, unusual, and discordant sound had issued from his thin lips.

"I know those I can trust," he had answered, stuttering rather, as was his way when moved. "And—and I assure you, Mrs. Bunting, that I hardly have to speak to a human being—especially to a woman" (and he had drawn in his breath with a hissing sound) "before I know exactly what manner of person is before me."

It hadn't taken the landlady very long to find out that her lodger had a queer kind of fear and dislike of women. When she was doing the staircase and landings she would often hear Mr. Sleuth reading aloud to himself passages in the Bible that were very uncomplimentary to her sex. But Mrs. Bunting had no very great opinion of her sister woman, so that didn't put her out. Besides, where one's lodger is concerned, a dislike of women is better than—well, than the other thing.

In any case, where would have been the good of worrying about the lodger's funny ways? Of course, Mr. Sleuth was eccentric. If he hadn't been, as Bunting funnily styled it, "just a leetle touched upstairs," he wouldn't be here, living this strange, solitary life in lodgings. He would be living in quite a different sort of way with some of his relatives, or with a friend of his own class.

There came a time when Mrs. Bunting, looking back—as even the least imaginative of us are apt to look back to any part of our own past lives which becomes for any reason poignantly memorable—wondered how soon it was that she had discovered that her lodger was given to creeping out of the house at a time when almost all living things prefer to sleep.

She brought herself to believe—but I am inclined to doubt whether she was right in so believing—that the first time she became aware of this strange nocturnal habit of Mr. Sleuth's happened to be during the night which preceded the day on which she had observed a very curious circumstance. This very curious circumstance was the complete disappearance of one of Mr. Sleuth's three suits of clothes.

It always passes my comprehension how people can remember, over any length of time, not every moment of certain happenings, for that is natural enough, but the day, the hour, the minute when these happenings took place! Much as she thought about it afterwards, even Mrs. Bunting never quite made up her mind whether it was during the fifth or the sixth night of Mr. Sleuth's stay under her roof that she became aware that he had gone out at two in the morning and had only come in at five.

But that there did come such a night is certain—as certain as is the fact that her discovery coincided with various occurrences which were destined to remain retrospectively memorable.

It was intensely dark, intensely quiet—the darkest, quietest hour of the night, when suddenly Mrs. Bunting was awakened from a deep, dreamless sleep by sounds at once unexpected and familiar. She knew at once what those sounds were. They were those made by Mr. Sleuth, first coming down the stairs, and walking on tiptoe—she was sure it was on tiptoe—past her door, and finally softly shutting the front door behind him.

Try as she would, Mrs. Bunting found it quite impossible to go to sleep again. There she lay wide awake, afraid to move lest Bunting should waken up too, till she heard Mr. Sleuth, three hours later, creep back into the house and so up to bed.

Then, and not till then, she slept again. But in the morning she felt very tired, so tired indeed, that she had been very glad when Bunting good-naturedly suggested that he should go out and do their little bit of marketing.

The worthy couple had very soon discovered that in the matter of catering it was not altogether an easy matter to satisfy Mr. Sleuth, and that though he always tried to appear pleased. This perfect lodger had one serious fault from the point of view of those who keep lodgings. Strange to say, he was a vegetarian. He would not eat meat in any form. He sometimes, however, condescended to a chicken, and when he did so condescend he generously intimated that Mr. and Mrs. Bunting were welcome to a share in it.

Now to-day—this day of which the happenings were to linger in Mrs. Bunting's mind so very long, and to remain so very vivid, it had been arranged that Mr. Sleuth was to have some fish for his lunch, while what he left was to be "done up" to serve for his simple supper.

Knowing that Bunting would be out for at least an hour, for he was a gregarious soul, and liked to have a gossip in the shops he frequented, Mrs. Bunting rose and dressed in a leisurely manner; then she went and "did" her front sitting-room.

She felt languid and dull, as one is apt to feel after a broken night, and it was a comfort to her to know that Mr. Sleuth was not likely to ring before twelve.

But long before twelve a loud ring suddenly clanged through the quiet house. She knew it for the front door bell.

Mrs. Bunting frowned. No doubt the ring betokened one of those tiresome people who come round for old bottles and such-like fal-lals.

She went slowly, reluctantly to the door. And then her face cleared, for it was that good young chap, Joe Chandler, who stood waiting outside.

He was breathing a little hard, as if he had walked over-quickly through the moist, foggy air.

"Why, Joe?" said Mrs. Bunting wonderingly. "Come in—do! Bunting's out, but he won't be very long now. You've been quite a stranger these last few days."

"Well, you know why, Mrs. Bunting——"

She stared at him for a moment, wondering what he could mean. Then, suddenly she remembered. Why, of course, Joe was on a big job just now—the job of trying to catch The Avenger! Her husband had alluded to the fact again and again when reading out to her little bits from the halfpenny evening paper he was taking again.

She led the way to the sitting-room. It was a good thing Bunting had insisted on lighting the fire before he went out, for now the room was nice and warm—and it was just horrible outside. She had felt a chill go right through her as she had stood, even for that second, at the front door.

And she hadn't been alone to feel it, for, "I say, it *is* jolly to be in here, out of that awful cold!" exclaimed Chandler, sitting down heavily in Bunting's easy chair.

And then Mrs. Bunting bethought herself that the young man was tired, as well as cold. He was pale, almost pallid under his usual healthy, tanned complexion—the complexion of the man who lives much out of doors.

"Wouldn't you like me just to make you a cup of tea?" she said solicitously.

"Well, to tell truth, I should be right down thankful for one, Mrs. Bunting!" Then he looked round, and again he said her name, "Mrs. Bunting——?"

He spoke in so odd, so thick a tone that she turned quickly. "Yes, what is it, Joe?" she asked. And then, in sudden terror, "You've never come to tell me that anything's happened to Bunting? He's not had an accident?"

"Goodness, no! Whatever made you think that? But—but, Mrs. Bunting, there's been another of them!"

His voice dropped almost to a whisper. He was staring at her with unhappy, it seemed to her terror-filled, eyes.

"Another of them?" She looked at him, bewildered—at a loss. And then what he meant flashed across her—"another of them" meant another of these strange, mysterious, awful murders.

But her relief for the moment was so great—for she really had thought for a second that he had come to give her ill news of Bunting—that the feeling that she did experience on hearing this piece of news was actually pleasurable, though she would have been much shocked had that fact been brought to her notice.

Almost in spite of herself, Mrs. Bunting had become keenly interested in the amazing series of crimes which was occupying the imagination of the whole of London's nether-world. Even her refined mind had busied itself for the last two or three days with the strange problem so frequently presented to it by Bunting—for Bunting, now that they were no longer worried, took an open, unashamed, intense interest in "The Avenger" and his doings.

She took the kettle off the gas-ring. "It's a pity Bunting isn't here," she said, drawing in her breath. "He'd a-liked so much to hear you tell all about it, Joe."

As she spoke she was pouring boiling water into a little teapot.

But Chandler said nothing, and she turned and glanced at him. "Why, you do look bad!" she exclaimed.

And, indeed, the young fellow did look bad—very bad indeed.

"I can't help it," he said, with a kind of gasp. "It was your saying that about my telling you all about it that made me turn queer. You see, this time I was one of the first there, and it fairly turned me sick—that it did. Oh, it was too awful, Mrs. Bunting! Don't talk of it."

He began gulping down the hot tea before it was well made.

She looked at him with sympathetic interest. "Why, Joe," she said, "I never would have thought, with all the horrible sights you see, that anything could upset you like that."

"This isn't like anything there's ever been before," he said. "And then—then—oh, Mrs. Bunting, 'twas I that discovered the piece of paper this time."

"Then it *is* true," she cried eagerly. "It *is* The Avenger's bit of paper! Bunting always said it was. He never believed in that practical joker."

"I did," said Chandler reluctantly. "You see, there are some queer fellows even—even—" (he lowered his voice, and looked round him as if the walls had ears)—"even in the Force, Mrs. Bunting, and these murders have fair got on our nerves."

"No, never!" she said. "D'you think that a bobby might do a thing like that?"

He nodded impatiently, as if the question wasn't worth answering. Then, "It was all along of that bit of paper and my finding it while the poor soul was still warm"—he shuddered—"that brought me out West this morning. One of our bosses lives close by, in Prince Albert Terrace, and I had to go and tell him all about it. They never offered me a bit or a sup—I think they might have done that, don't you, Mrs. Bunting?"

"Yes," she said absently. "Yes, I do think so."

"But, there, I don't know that I ought to say that," went on Chandler. "He had me up in his dressing-room, and was very considerate-like to me while I was telling him."

"Have a bit of something now?" she said suddenly.

"Oh, no, I couldn't eat anything," he said hastily. "I don't feel as if I could ever eat anything any more."

"That'll only make you ill." Mrs. Bunting spoke rather crossly, for she was a sensible woman. And to please her he took a bite out of the slice of bread-and-butter she had cut for him.

"I expect you're right," he said. "And I've a goodish heavy day in front of me. Been up since four, too——"

"Four?" she said. "Was it then they found——" she hesitated a moment, and then said, "it?"

He nodded. "It was just a chance I was near by. If I'd been half a minute sooner either I or the officer who found her must have knocked up against that—that monster. But two or three people do think they saw him slinking away."

"What was he like?" she asked curiously.

"Well, that's hard to answer. You see, there was such an awful fog. But there's one thing they all agree about. He was carrying a bag——"

"A bag?" repeated Mrs. Bunting, in a low voice. "Whatever sort of bag might it have been, Joe?"

There had come across her—just right in her middle, like—such a strange sensation, a curious kind of tremor, or fluttering.

She was at a loss to account for it.

"Just a hand-bag," said Joe Chandler vaguely. "A woman I spoke to—cross-examining her, like—who was positive she had seen him, said, 'Just a tall, thin shadow—that's what he was, a tall, thin shadow of a man—with a bag.'"

"With a bag?" repeated Mrs. Bunting absently. "How very strange and peculiar——"

"Why, no, not strange at all. He has to carry the thing he does the deed with in something, Mrs. Bunting. We've always wondered how he hid it. They generally throws the knife or fire-arms away, you know."

"Do they, indeed?" Mrs. Bunting still spoke in that absent, wondering way. She was thinking that she really must try and see what the lodger had done with his bag. It was possible—in fact, when one came to think of it, it was very probable—that he had just lost it, being so forgetful a gentleman, on one of the days he had gone out, as she knew he was fond of doing, into the Regent's Park.

"There'll be a description circulated in an hour or two," went on Chandler. "Perhaps that'll help catch him. There isn't a London man or woman, I don't suppose, who wouldn't give a good bit to lay that chap by the heels. Well, I suppose I must be going now."

"Won't you wait a bit longer for Bunting?" she said hesitatingly.

"No, I can't do that. But I'll come in, maybe, either this evening or to-morrow, and tell you any more that's happened. Thanks kindly for the tea. It's made a man of me, Mrs. Bunting."

"Well, you've had enough to unman you, Joe."

"Aye, that I have," he said heavily.

A few minutes later Bunting did come in, and he and his wife had quite a little tiff—the first tiff they had had since Mr. Sleuth became their lodger.

It fell out this way. When he heard who had been there, Bunting was angry that Mrs. Bunting hadn't got more details of the horrible occurrence which had taken place that morning out of Chandler.

"You don't mean to say, Ellen, that you can't even tell me where it happened?" he said indignantly. "I suppose you put Chandler off—that's what you did! Why, whatever did he come here for, excepting to tell us all about it?"

"He came to have something to eat and drink," snapped out Mrs. Bunting. "That's what the poor lad came for, if you wants to know. He could hardly speak of it at all—he felt so bad. In fact, he didn't say a word about it until he'd come right into the room and sat down. He told me quite enough!"

"Didn't he tell you if the piece of paper on which the murderer had written his name was square or three-cornered?" demanded Bunting.

"No; he did not. And that isn't the sort of thing I should have cared to ask him."

"The more fool you!" And then he stopped abruptly. The newsboys were coming down the Marylebone Road, shouting out the awful discovery which had been made that morning—that of The Avenger's fifth murder.

Bunting went out to buy a paper, and his wife took the things he had brought in down to the kitchen.

The noise the newspaper-sellers made outside had evidently wakened Mr. Sleuth, for his landlady hadn't been in the kitchen ten minutes before his bell rang.

CHAPTER VI

Mr. Sleuth's bell rang again.

Mr. Sleuth's breakfast was quite ready, but for the first time since he had been her lodger Mrs. Bunting did not answer the summons at once. But when there came the second imperative tinkle—for electric bells had not been fitted into that old-fashioned house—she made up her mind to go upstairs.

As she emerged into the hall from the kitchen stairway, Bunting, sitting comfortably in their parlour, heard his wife stepping heavily under the load of the well-laden tray.

"Wait a minute!" he called out. "I'll help you, Ellen," and he came out and took the tray from her.

She said nothing, and together they proceeded up to the drawing-room floor landing.

There she stopped him. "Here," she whispered quickly, "you give me that, Bunting. The lodger won't like your going in to him." And then, as he obeyed her, and was about to turn downstairs again, she added in a rather acid tone, "You might open the door for me, at any rate! How can I manage to do it with this here heavy tray on my hands?"

She spoke in a queer, jerky way, and Bunting felt surprised—rather put out. Ellen wasn't exactly what you'd call a lively, jolly woman, but when things were going well—as now—she was generally equable enough. He supposed she was still resentful of the way he had spoken to her about young Chandler and the new Avenger murder.

However, he was always for peace, so he opened the drawing-room door, and as soon as he had started going downstairs Mrs. Bunting walked into the room.

And then at once there came over her the queerest feeling of relief, of lightness of heart.

As usual, the lodger was sitting at his old place, reading the Bible.

Somehow—she could not have told you why, she would not willingly have told herself—she had expected to see Mr. Sleuth *looking different*. But no, he appeared to be exactly the same—in fact, as he glanced up at her a pleasanter smile than usual lighted up his thin, pallid face.

"Well, Mrs. Bunting," he said genially, "I overslept myself this morning, but I feel all the better for the rest."

"I'm glad of that, sir," she answered, in a low voice. "One of the ladies I once lived with used to say, 'Rest is an old-fashioned remedy, but it's the best remedy of all.' "

Mr. Sleuth himself removed the Bible and *Cruden's Concordance* off the table out of her way, and then he stood watching his landlady laying the cloth.

Suddenly he spoke again. He was not often so talkative in the morning. "I think, Mrs. Bunting, that there was someone with you outside the door just now?"

"Yes, sir. Bunting helped me up with the tray."

"I'm afraid I give you a good deal of trouble," he said hesitatingly.

But she answered quickly, "Oh, no, sir! Not at all, sir! I was only saying yesterday that we've never had a lodger that gave us as little trouble as you do, sir."

"I'm glad of that. I am aware that my habits are somewhat peculiar."

He looked at her fixedly, as if expecting her to give some sort of denial to this observation. But Mrs. Bunting was an honest and truthful woman. It never occurred to her to question his statement. Mr. Sleuth's habits *were* somewhat peculiar. Take that going out at night, or rather in the early morning, for instance?

So she remained silent.

After she had laid the lodger's breakfast on the table she prepared to leave the room. "I suppose I'm not to do your room till you goes out, sir?"

And Mr. Sleuth looked up sharply. "No, no!" he said. "I never want my room done when I am engaged in studying the Scriptures, Mrs. Bunting. But I am not going out to-day. I shall be carrying out a somewhat elaborate experiment—upstairs. If I go out at all"—he waited a moment, and again he looked at her fixedly—"I shall wait till night-time to do so." And then, coming back to the matter in hand, he added hastily, "Perhaps you could do my room when I go upstairs, about five o'clock—if that time is convenient to you, that is?"

"Oh, yes, sir! That'll do nicely!"

Mrs. Bunting went downstairs, and as she did so she took herself wordlessly, ruthlessly to task, but she did not face—even in her inmost heart—the strange terrors and tremors which had so shaken her. She only repeated to herself again and again, "I've got upset—that's what I've done," and then she spoke aloud, "I must get myself a dose at the chemist's next time I'm out. That's what I must do."

And just as she murmured the word "do," there came a loud double knock on the front door.

It was only the postman's knock, but the postman was an unfamiliar visitor in that house, and Mrs. Bunting started violently. She was nervous, that's what was the matter with her,—so she told herself angrily. No doubt this was a letter for Mr. Sleuth; the lodger must have relations and acquaintances somewhere in the world. All gentlefolk have. But when she picked the small envelope off the hall floor, she saw it was a letter from Daisy, her husband's daughter.

"Bunting!" she called out sharply. "Here's a letter for you."

She opened the door of their sitting-room and looked in.

Yes, there was her husband, sitting back comfortably in his easy chair, reading a paper. And as she saw his broad, rather rounded back, Mrs. Bunting felt a sudden thrill of sharp irritation. There he was, doing nothing—in fact, doing worse than nothing—wasting his time reading all about those horrid crimes.

She sighed—a long, unconscious sigh. Bunting was getting into idle ways, bad ways for a man of his years. But how could she prevent it? He had been such an active, conscientious sort of man when they had first made acquaintance. . . .

She also could remember, even more clearly than Bunting did himself, that first meeting of theirs in the dining-room of No. 90 Cumberland Terrace. As she had stood there, pouring out her mistress's glass of port wine, she had not been too much absorbed in her task to have a good out-of-her-eye look at the spruce, nice, respectable-looking fellow who was standing over by the window. How superior he had appeared even then to the man she already hoped he would succeed as butler!

To-day, perhaps because she was not feeling quite herself, the past rose before her very vividly, and a lump came into her throat.

Putting the letter addressed to her husband on the table, she closed the door softly, and went down into the kitchen; there were various little things to put away and clean up, as well as their dinner to cook. And all the time she was down there she fixed her mind obstinately, determinedly on Bunting and on the problem of Bunting. She wondered what she'd better do to get him into good ways again.

Thanks to Mr. Sleuth, their outlook was now moderately bright. A week ago everything had seemed utterly hopeless. It seemed as if nothing could save them from disaster. But everything was now changed!

Perhaps it would be well for her to go and see the new proprietor of that registry office, in Baker Street, which had lately changed hands. It would be a good thing for Bunting to get even an occasional job—for the matter of that he could now take up a fairly regular thing in the way of waiting. Mrs. Bunting knew that it isn't easy to get a man out of idle ways once he has acquired those ways.

When, at last, she went upstairs again she felt a little ashamed of what she had been thinking, for Bunting had laid the cloth, and laid it very nicely, too, and brought up their two chairs to the table.

"Ellen?" he cried eagerly, "here's news! Daisy's coming to-morrow! There's scarlet fever in their house. Old Aunt thinks she'd better come away for a few days. So, you see, she'll be here for her birthday. Eighteen, that's what she be on the nineteenth! It do make me feel old—that it do!"

Mrs. Bunting put down the tray. "I can't have the girl here just now," she said shortly. "I've just as much to do as I can manage. The lodger gives me more trouble than you seem to think for."

"Rubbish!" he said sharply. "I'll help you with the lodger. It's your own fault you haven't had help with him before. Of course, Daisy must come here. Whatever other place could the girl go to?"

Bunting felt pugnacious—so cheerful as to be almost light-hearted. But as he looked across at his wife his feeling of satisfaction vanished. Ellen's face was pinched and drawn to-day; she looked ill—ill and horribly tired. It was very aggravating of her to go and behave like this—just when they were beginning to get on nicely again.

"For the matter of that," he said suddenly, "Daisy'll be able to help you with the work, Ellen, and she'll brisk us both up a bit."

Mrs. Bunting made no answer. She sat down heavily at the table. And then she said languidly, "You might as well show me the girl's letter."

He handed it across to her, and she read it slowly to herself.

"DEAR FATHER (it ran) —I hope this finds you as well as it leaves me. Mrs. Puddle's youngest has got scarlet fever, and Aunt thinks I had better come away at once, just to stay with you for a few days. Please tell Ellen I won't give her no trouble. I'll start at ten if I don't hear nothing. —Your loving daughter,

"Daisy."

"Yes, I suppose Daisy will have to come here," said Mrs. Bunting slowly. "It'll do her good to have a bit of work to do for once in her life."

And with that ungraciously worded permission Bunting had to content himself.

*

Quietly the rest of that eventful day sped by. When dusk fell Mr. Sleuth's landlady heard him go upstairs to the top floor. She remembered that this was the signal for her to go and do his room.

He was a tidy man, was the lodger; he did not throw his things about as so many gentlemen do, leaving them all over the place. No, he kept everything scrupulously tidy. His clothes, and the various articles Mrs. Bunting had bought for him during the first two days he had been there, were carefully arranged in the chest of drawers. He had lately purchased a pair of boots. Those he had arrived in were peculiar-looking footgear, buff leather shoes with rubber soles, and he had told his landlady on that very first day that he never wished them to go down to be cleaned.

A funny idea—a funny habit that, of going out for a walk after midnight in weather so cold and foggy that all other folk were glad to be at home, snug in bed. But then Mr. Sleuth himself admitted that he was a funny sort of gentleman.

After she had done his bedroom the landlady went into the sitting-room and gave it a good dusting. This room was not kept quite as nice as she would have liked it to be. Mrs. Bunting longed to give the drawing-room something of a good turn out; but Mr. Sleuth disliked her to be moving about in it when he himself was in his bedroom; and when up he sat there almost all the time. Delighted as he had seemed to be with the top room, he only used it when making his mysterious experiments, and never during the day-time.

And now, this afternoon, she looked at the rosewood chiffonnier with longing eyes—she even gave that pretty little piece of furniture a slight shake. If only the doors would fly open, as the locked doors of old cupboards sometimes do, even after they have been securely fastened, how pleased she would be, how much more comfortable somehow she would feel!

But the chiffonnier refused to give up its secret.

About eight o'clock on that same evening Joe Chandler came in, just for a few minutes' chat. He had recovered from his agitation of the morning, but he was full of eager excitement, and Mrs. Bunting listened in silence, intensely interested in spite of herself, while he and Bunting talked.

"Yes," he said, "I'm as right as a trivet now! I've had a good rest—laid down all this afternoon. You see, the Yard thinks there's going to be something on to-night. He's always done them in pairs."

"So he has," exclaimed Bunting wonderingly. "So he has! Now, I never thought o' that. Then you think, Joe, that the monster'll be on the job again to-night?"

Chandler nodded. "Yes. And I think there's a very good chance of his being caught, too——"

"I suppose there'll be a lot on the watch to-night, eh?"

"I should think there will be! How many of our men d'you think there'll be on night duty to-night, Mr. Bunting?"

Bunting shook his head. "I don't know," he said helplessly.

"I mean extra," suggested Chandler, in an encouraging voice.

"A thousand?" ventured Bunting.

"Five thousand, Mr. Bunting."

"Never!" exclaimed Bunting, amazed.

And even Mrs. Bunting echoed "Never!" incredulously.

"Yes, that there will. You see, the Boss has got his monkey up!" Chandler drew a folded-up newspaper out of his coat pocket. "Just listen to this:

> "'The police have reluctantly to admit that they have no clue to the perpetrators of these horrible crimes, and we cannot feel any surprise at the information that a popular attack has been organised on the Chief Commissioner of the Metropolitan Police. There is even talk of an indignation mass meeting.'

"What d'you think of that? That's not a pleasant thing for a gentleman as is doing his best to read, eh?"

"Well, it does seem queer that the police can't catch him, now doesn't it?" said Bunting argumentatively.

"I don't think it's queer at all," said young Chandler crossly. "Now you just listen again! Here's a bit of the truth for once—in a newspaper." And slowly he read out:

> "'The detection of crime in London now resembles a game of blind man's buff, in which the detective has his hands tied and his eyes bandaged. Thus is he turned loose to hunt the murderer through the slums of a great city.'"

"Whatever does that mean?" said Bunting. "Your hands aren't tied, and your eyes aren't bandaged, Joe?"

"It's metaphorical-like that it's intended, Mr. Bunting. We haven't got the same facilities—no, not a quarter of them—that the French 'tecs have."

And then, for the first time, Mrs. Bunting spoke: "What was that word, Joe—'perpetrators'? I mean that first bit you read out."

"Yes," he said, turning to her eagerly.

"Then do they think there's more than one of them?" she said, and a look of relief came over her thin face.

"There's some of our chaps thinks it's a gang," said Chandler. "They say it can't be the work of one man."

"What do *you* think, Joe?"

"Well, Mrs. Bunting, I don't know what to think. I'm fair puzzled."

He got up. "Don't you come to the door. I'll shut it all right. So long! See you to-morrow, perhaps." As he had done the other evening, Mr. and Mrs. Bunting's visitor stopped at the door. "Any news of Miss Daisy?" he asked casually.

"Yes; she's coming to-morrow," said her father. "They've got scarlet fever at her place. So Old Aunt thinks she'd better clear out."

The husband and wife went to bed early that night, but Mrs. Bunting found she could not sleep. She lay wide awake, hearing the hours, the half-hours, the quarters chime out from the belfry of the old church close by.

And then, just as she was dozing off—it must have been about one o'clock—she heard the sound she had half unconsciously been expecting to hear, that of the lodger's stealthy footsteps coming down the stairs just outside her room.

He crept along the passage and let himself out, very, very quietly. . . .

But though she tried to keep awake, Mrs. Bunting did not hear him come in again, for she soon fell into a heavy sleep.

Oddly enough, she was the first to wake the next morning; odder still, it was she, not Bunting, who jumped out of bed, and going out into the passage, picked up the newspaper which had just been pushed through the letter-box.

But having picked it up, Mrs. Bunting did not go back at once into her bedroom. Instead she lit the gas in the passage, and leaning up against the wall to steady herself, for she was trembling with cold and fatigue, she opened the paper.

Yes, there was the heading she sought:

"The Avenger Murders"

But, oh, how glad she was to see the words that followed:

"Up to the time of going to press there is little new to report concerning the extraordinary series of crimes which are amazing, and, indeed, staggering not only London, but the whole civilised world, and which would seem to be the work of some woman-hating teetotal fanatic. Since yesterday morning, when the last of these dastardly murders was committed, no reliable clue to the perpetrator, or perpetrators, has been obtained, though several arrests were made in the course of the day. In every case, however, those arrested were able to prove a satisfactory alibi."

And then, a little lower down:

"The excitement grows and grows. It is not too much to say that even a stranger to London would know that something very unusual was in the air. As for the place where the murder was committed last night——"

"Last night!" thought Mrs. Bunting, startled; and then she realised that "last night," in this connection, meant the night before last.

She began the sentence again:

"As for the place where the murder was committed last night, all approaches to it were still blocked up to a late hour by hundreds of onlookers, though, of course, nothing now remains in the way of traces of the tragedy."

Slowly and carefully Mrs. Bunting folded the paper up again in its original creases, and then she stooped and put it back down on the mat where she had found it. She then turned out the gas, and going back into bed she lay down by her still sleeping husband.

"Anything the matter?" Bunting murmured, and stirred uneasily. "Anything the matter, Ellen?"

She answered in a whisper, a whisper thrilling with a strange gladness, "No, nothing, Bunting—nothing the matter! Go to sleep again, my dear."

They got up an hour later, both in a happy, cheerful mood. Bunting rejoiced at the thought of his daughter's coming, and even Daisy's stepmother told herself that it would be pleasant having the girl about the house to help her a bit.

About ten o'clock Bunting went out to do some shopping. He brought back with him a nice little bit of pork for Daisy's dinner, and three mince-pies. He even remembered to get some apples for the sauce.

CHAPTER VII

Just as twelve was striking a four-wheeler drew up to the gate.

It brought Daisy—pink-cheeked, excited, laughing-eyed Daisy—a sight to gladden any father's heart.

"Old Aunt said I was to have a cab if the weather was bad," she cried out joyously.

There was a bit of a wrangle over the fare. King's Cross, as all the world knows, is nothing like two miles from the Marylebone Road, but the man clamoured for one and sixpence, and hinted darkly that he had done the young lady a favour in bringing her at all.

While he and Bunting were having words, Daisy, leaving them to it, walked up the flagged path to the door where her stepmother was awaiting her.

As they were exchanging a rather frigid kiss, indeed, 'twas a mere peck on Mrs. Bunting's part, there fell, with startling suddenness, loud cries on the still, cold air. Long-drawn and wailing, they sounded strangely sad as they rose and fell across the distant roar of traffic in the Edgware Road.

"What's that?" exclaimed Bunting wonderingly. "Why, whatever's that?"

The cabman lowered his voice. "Them's 'a-crying out that 'orrible affair at King's Cross. He's done for two of 'em this time! That's what I meant when I said I might 'a got a better fare. I wouldn't say nothink before little missy there, but folk 'ave been coming from all over London the last five or six hours; plenty of toffs, too—but there, there's nothing to see now!"

"What? Another woman murdered last night?"

Bunting felt tremendously thrilled. What had the five thousand constables been about to let such a dreadful thing happen?

The cabman stared at him, surprised. "Two of 'em, I tell yer—within a few yards of one another. He 'ave got a nerve—— But, of course, they was drunk. He *'ave* got a down on the drink!"

"Have they caught him?" asked Bunting perfunctorily.

"Lord, no! They'll never catch 'im! It must 'ave happened hours and hours ago—they was both stone cold. One each end of a little passage what ain't used no more. That's why they didn't find 'em before."

The hoarse cries were coming nearer and nearer—two news vendors trying to outshout each other.

" 'Orrible discovery near King's Cross!" they yelled exultingly. "The Avenger again!"

And Bunting, with his daughter's large straw hold-all in his hand, ran forward into the roadway and recklessly gave a boy a penny for a halfpenny paper.

He felt very much moved and excited. Somehow his acquaintance with young

Joe Chandler made these murders seem a personal affair. He hoped that Chandler would come in soon and tell them all about it, as he had done yesterday morning when he, Bunting, had unluckily been out.

As he walked back into the little hall, he heard Daisy's voice—high, voluble, excited—giving her stepmother a long account of the scarlet fever case, and how at first Old Aunt's neighbours had thought it was not scarlet fever at all, but just nettlerash.

But as Bunting pushed open the door of the sitting-room, there came a note of sharp alarm in his daughter's voice, and he heard her cry, "Why, Ellen, whatever *is* the matter? You *do* look bad!" and his wife's muffled answer, "Open the window—do."

"'Orrible discovery near King's Cross—a clue at last!" yelled the newspaper-boys triumphantly.

And then, helplessly, Mrs. Bunting began to laugh. She laughed, and laughed, and laughed, rocking herself to and fro as if in an ecstasy of mirth.

"Why, father, whatever's the matter with her?"

Daisy looked quite scared.

"She's in 'sterics—that's what it is," he said shortly. "I'll just get the water-jug. Wait a minute!"

Bunting felt very put out. Ellen was ridiculous—that's what she was, to be so easily upset.

The lodger's bell suddenly pealed through the quiet house. Either that sound, or maybe the threat of the water-jug, had a magical effect on Mrs. Bunting. She rose to her feet, still shaking all over, but mentally composed.

"I'll go up," she said a little chokingly. "As for you, child, just run down into the kitchen. You'll find a piece of pork roasting in the oven. You might start paring the apples for the sauce."

As Mrs. Bunting went upstairs her legs felt as if they were made of cotton wool. She put out a trembling hand, and clutched at the banister for support. But soon, making a great effort over herself, she began to feel more steady; and after waiting for a few moments on the landing, she knocked at the door of the drawing-room.

Mr. Sleuth's voice answered her from the bedroom. "I'm not well," he called out querulously; "I think I've caught a chill. I should be obliged if you would kindly bring me up a cup of tea, and put it outside my door, Mrs. Bunting."

"Very well, sir."

Mrs. Bunting turned and went downstairs. She still felt queer and giddy, so instead of going into the kitchen, she made the lodger his cup of tea over her sitting-room gas-ring.

During their midday dinner the husband and wife had a little discussion as to where Daisy should sleep. It had been settled that a bed should be made up for her in the top back room, but Mrs. Bunting saw reason to change this plan. "I think 'twould be better if Daisy were to sleep with me, Bunting, and you was to sleep upstairs."

Bunting felt and looked rather surprised, but he acquiesced. Ellen was probably right; the girl would be rather lonely up there, and, after all, they didn't know much about the lodger, though he seemed a respectable gentleman enough.

Daisy was a good-natured girl; she liked London, and wanted to make herself useful to her stepmother. "I'll wash up; don't you bother to come downstairs," she said cheerfully.

Bunting began to walk up and down the room. His wife gave him a furtive glance; she wondered what he was thinking about.

"Didn't you get a paper?" she said at last.

"Yes, of course I did," he answered hastily. "But I've put it away. I thought you'd rather not look at it, as you're that nervous."

Again she glanced at him quickly, furtively, but he seemed just as usual—he evidently meant just what he said and no more.

"I thought they was shouting something in the street—I mean just before I was took bad."

It was now Bunting's turn to stare at his wife quickly and rather furtively. He had felt sure that her sudden attack of queerness, of hysterics—call it what you might—had been due to the shouting outside. She was not the only woman in London who had got the Avenger murders on her nerves. His morning paper said quite a lot of women were afraid to go out alone. Was it possible that the curious way she had been taken just now had had nothing to do with the shouts and excitement outside?

"Don't you know what it was they were calling out?" he asked slowly.

Mrs. Bunting looked across at him. She would have given a very great deal to be able to lie, to pretend that she did not know what those dreadful cries had portended. But when it came to the point she found she could not do so.

"Yes," she said dully. "I heard a word here and there. There's been another murder, hasn't there?"

"Two other murders," he said soberly.

"Two? That's worse news!" She turned so pale—a sallow greenish-white—that Bunting thought she was again going queer.

"Ellen?" he said warningly. "Ellen, now do have a care! I can't think what's come over you about these murders. Turn your mind away from them, do! We needn't talk about them—not so much, that is——"

"But I wants to talk about them," cried Mrs. Bunting hysterically.

The husband and wife were standing, one each side of the table, the man with his back to the fire, the woman with her back to the door.

Bunting, staring across at his wife, felt sadly perplexed and disturbed. She really did seem ill; even her slight, spare figure looked shrunk. For the first time, so he told himself ruefully, Ellen was beginning to look her full age. Her slender hands—she had kept the pretty, soft white hands of the woman who has never done rough work—grasped the edge of the table with a convulsive movement.

Bunting didn't at all like the look of her. "Oh, dear," he said to himself, "I do hope Ellen isn't going to be ill! That would be a to-do just now."

"Tell me about it," she commanded, in a low voice. "Can't you see I'm waiting to hear? Be quick now, Bunting!"

"There isn't very much to tell," he said reluctantly. "There's precious little in this paper, anyway. But the cabman what brought Daisy told me——"

"Well?"

"What I said just now. There's two of 'em this time, and they'd both been drinking heavily, poor creatures."

"Was it where the others was done?" she asked looking at her husband fearfully.

"No," he said awkwardly. "No, it wasn't, Ellen. It was a good bit farther West—in fact, not so very far from here. Near King's Cross—that's how the cabman knew about it, you see. They seems to have been done in a passage which isn't used no more." And then, as he thought his wife's eyes were beginning to look rather funny, he added hastily. "There, that's enough for the present! We shall soon be hearing a lot more about it from Joe Chandler. He's pretty sure to come in some time to-day."

"Then the five thousand constables weren't no use?" said Mrs. Bunting slowly. She had relaxed her grip of the table, and was standing more upright.

"No use at all," said Bunting briefly. "He *is* artful, and no mistake about it. But wait a minute——" he turned and took up the paper which he had laid aside, on a chair. "Yes, they says here that they has a clue."

"A clue, Bunting?" Mrs. Bunting spoke in a soft, weak, die-away voice, and again, stooping somewhat, she grasped the edge of the table.

But her husband was not noticing her now. He was holding the paper close up to his eyes, and he read from it, in a tone of considerable satisfaction:

"'It is gratifying to be able to state that the police at last believe they are in possession of a clue which will lead to the arrest of the——'"

and then Bunting dropped the paper and rushed round the table.

His wife, with a curious sighing moan, had slipped down on to the floor, taking with her the tablecloth as she went. She lay there in what appeared to be a dead faint. And Bunting, scared out of his wits, opened the door and screamed out, "Daisy! Daisy! Come up, child. Ellen's took bad again."

And Daisy, hurrying in, showed an amount of sense and resource which even at this anxious moment roused her fond father's admiration.

"Get a wet sponge, Dad—quick!" she cried, "a sponge,—and, if you've got such a thing, a drop o' brandy. I'll see after her!" And then, after he had got the little medicine flask, "I can't think what's wrong with Ellen," said Daisy wonderingly. "She seemed quite all right when I first came in. She was listening, interested-like, to what I was telling her, and then, suddenly—well, you saw how she was took, father? 'Taint like Ellen this, is it now?"

"No," he whispered. "No, 'taint. But you see, child, we've been going through a pretty bad time—worse nor I should ever have let you know of, my dear. Ellen's just feeling it now—that's what it is. She didn't say nothing, for Ellen's a good plucked one, but it's told on her—it's told on her!"

And then Mrs. Bunting, sitting up, slowly opened her eyes, and instinctively put her hand up to her head to see if her hair was all right.

She hadn't really been quite "off." It would have been better for her if she had. She had simply had an awful feeling that she couldn't stand up—more, that she must fall down. Bunting's words touched a most unwonted chord in the poor woman's heart, and the eyes which she opened were full of tears. She had not thought her husband knew how she had suffered during those weeks of starving and waiting.

But she had a morbid dislike of any betrayal of sentiment. To her such betrayal betokened "foolishness," and so all she said was, "There's no need to make a fuss! I only turned over a little queer. I never was right off, Daisy."

Pettishly she pushed away the glass in which Bunting had hurriedly poured a little brandy. "I wouldn't touch such stuff—no, not if I was dying!" she exclaimed.

Putting out a languid hand, she pulled herself up, with the help of the table, on to her feet. "Go down again to the kitchen, child"; but there was a sob, a kind of tremor in her voice.

"You haven't been eating properly, Ellen—that's what's the matter with you," said Bunting suddenly. "Now I come to think of it, you haven't eat half enough these last two days. I always did say—in old days many a time I told you—that a woman couldn't live on air. But there, you never believed me!"

Daisy stood looking from one to the other, a shadow over her bright, pretty face. "I'd no idea you'd had such a bad time, father," she said feelingly. "Why didn't you let me know about it? I might have got something out of Old Aunt."

"We didn't want anything of that sort," said her stepmother hastily. "But of course—well, I expect I'm still feeling the worry now. I don't seem able to forget it. Those days of waiting, of—of——" she restrained herself; another moment and the word "starving" would have left her lips.

"But everything's all right now," said Bunting eagerly, "all right, thanks to Mr. Sleuth, that is."

"Yes," repeated his wife, in a low, strange tone of voice. "Yes, we're all right now, and as you say, Bunting, it's all along of Mr. Sleuth."

She walked across to a chair and sat down on it. "I'm just a little tottery still," she muttered.

And Daisy, looking at her, turned to her father and said in a whisper, but not so low but that Mrs. Bunting heard her, "Don't you think Ellen ought to see a doctor, father? He might give her something that would pull her round."

"I won't see no doctor!" said Mrs. Bunting with sudden emphasis. "I saw enough of doctors in my last place. Thirty-eight doctors in ten months did my poor missis have. Just determined on having 'em she was! Did they save her? No! She died just the same! Maybe a bit sooner."

"She was a freak, was your last mistress, Ellen," began Bunting aggressively.

Ellen had insisted on staying on in that place till her poor mistress died. They might have been married some months before they were married but for that fact. Bunting had always resented it.

His wife smiled wanly. "We won't have no words about that," she said, and again she spoke in a softer, kindlier tone than usual. "Daisy? If you won't go down to the kitchen again, then I must"—she turned to her stepdaughter, and the girl flew out of the room.

"I think the child grows prettier every minute," said Bunting fondly.

"Folks are too apt to forget that beauty is but skin deep," said his wife. She was beginning to feel better. "But still, I do agree, Bunting, that Daisy's well enough. And she seems more willing, too."

"I say, we mustn't forget the lodger's dinner," Bunting spoke uneasily. "It's a bit of fish to-day, isn't it? Hadn't I better just tell Daisy to see to it, and then I can take it up to him, as you're not feeling quite the thing, Ellen?"

"I'm quite well enough to take up Mr. Sleuth's luncheon," she said quickly. It irritated her to hear her husband speak of the lodger's dinner. They had dinner in the middle of the day, but Mr. Sleuth had luncheon. However odd he might be, Mrs. Bunting never forgot her lodger was a gentleman.

"After all, he likes me to wait on him, doesn't he? I can manage all right. Don't you worry," she added, after a long pause.

CHAPTER VIII

Perhaps because his luncheon was served to him a good deal later than usual, Mr. Sleuth ate his nice piece of steamed sole upstairs with far heartier an appetite than his landlady had eaten her nice slice of roast pork downstairs.

"I hope you're feeling a little better, sir," Mrs. Bunting had forced herself to say when she first took in his tray.

And he had answered plaintively, querulously, "No, I can't say I feel well to-day, Mrs. Bunting. I am tired—very tired. And as I lay in bed I seemed to hear so many sounds—so much crying and shouting. I trust the Marylebone Road is not going to become a noisy thoroughfare, Mrs. Bunting?"

"Oh, no, sir, I don't think that. We're generally reckoned very quiet indeed, sir."

She waited a moment—try as she would, she could not allude to what those unwonted shouts and noises had betokened. "I expect you've got a chill, sir," she said suddenly. "If I was you, I shouldn't go out this afternoon; I'd just stay quietly indoors. There's a lot of rough people about——" Perhaps there was an undercurrent of warning, of painful pleading, in her toneless voice which penetrated in some way to the brain of the lodger, for Mr. Sleuth looked up, and an uneasy, watchful look came into his luminous grey eyes.

"I'm sorry to hear that, Mrs. Bunting. But I think I'll take your advice. That is, I will stay quietly at home. I am never at a loss to know what to do with myself so long as I can study the Book of Books."

"Then you're not afraid about your eyes, sir?" said Mrs. Bunting curiously. Somehow she was beginning to feel better. It comforted her to be up here, talking to Mr. Sleuth, instead of thinking about him downstairs. It seemed to banish the terror which filled her soul—aye, and her body, too—at other times. When she was with him Mr. Sleuth was so gentle, so reasonable, so—so grateful.

Poor kindly, solitary Mr. Sleuth! This kind of gentleman surely wouldn't hurt a fly, let alone a human being. Eccentric—so much must be admitted. But Mrs. Bunting had seen a good deal of eccentric folk, eccentric women rather than eccentric men, in her long career as a useful maid.

Being at ordinary times an exceptionally sensible, well-balanced woman, she had never, in old days, allowed her mind to dwell on certain things she had learnt as to the aberrations of which human nature is capable—even well-born, well-nurtured, gentle human nature—as exemplified in some of the households where she had served. It would, indeed, be unfortunate if she now became morbid or—or hysterical.

So it was in a sharp, cheerful voice, almost the voice in which she had talked during the first few days of Mr. Sleuth's stay in her house, that she exclaimed,

"Well, sir, I'll be up again to clear away in about half an hour. And if you'll forgive me for saying so, I hope you will stay in and have a rest to-day. Nasty, muggy weather—that's what it is! If there's any little thing you want, me or Bunting can go out and get it."

It must have been about four o'clock when there came a ring at the front door.

The three were sitting chatting together, for Daisy had washed up—she really was saving her stepmother a good bit of trouble—and the girl was now amusing her elders by a funny account of Old Aunt's pernickety ways.

"Whoever can that be?" said Bunting, looking up. "It's too early for Joe Chandler, surely."

"I'll go," said his wife, hurriedly jumping up from her chair. "I'll go! We don't want no strangers in here."

And as she stepped down the short bit of passage she said to herself, "A clue? What clue?"

But when she opened the front door a glad sigh of relief broke from her. "Why, Joe? We never thought 'twas you! But you're very welcome, I'm sure. Come in."

And Chandler came in, a rather sheepish look on his good-looking, fair young face.

"I thought maybe that Mr. Bunting would like to know——" he began, in a loud, cheerful voice, and Mrs. Bunting hurriedly checked him. She didn't want the lodger upstairs to hear what young Chandler might be going to say.

"Don't talk so loud," she said a little sharply. "The lodger is not very well to-day. He's had a cold," she added hastily, "and during the last two or three days he hasn't been able to go out."

She wondered at her temerity, her—her hypocrisy, and that moment, those few words, marked an epoch in Ellen Bunting's life. It was the first time she had told a bold and deliberate lie. She was one of those women—there are many, many such—to whom there is a whole world of difference between the suppression of the truth and the utterance of an untruth.

But Chandler paid no heed to her remarks. "Has Miss Daisy arrived?" he asked, in a lower voice.

She nodded. And then he went through into the room where the father and daughter were sitting.

"Well?" said Bunting, starting up. "Well, Joe? Now you can tell us all about that mysterious clue! I suppose it'd be too good news to expect you to tell us they've caught him?"

"No fear of such good news as that yet awhile. If they'd caught him," said Joe ruefully, "well, I don't suppose I should be here, Mr. Bunting. But the Yard are circulating a description at last. And—well, they've found his weapon!"

"No?" cried Bunting excitedly. "You don't say so! Whatever sort of a thing is it? And are they sure 'tis his?"

"Well, 'tain't sure, but it seems to be likely."

Mrs. Bunting had slipped into the room and shut the door behind her. But she was still standing with her back against the door, looking at the group in front of her. None of them were thinking of her—she thanked God for that! She could hear everything that was said without joining in the talk and excitement.

"Listen to this!" cried Joe Chandler exultantly. " 'Tain't given out yet—not for the public, that is—but we was all given it by eight o'clock this morning. Quick work that, eh?" He read out:

"Wanted"

"A man, of age approximately 28, slight in figure, height approximately 5 ft. 8 in. Complexion dark. No beard or whiskers. Wearing a black diagonal coat, hard felt hat, high white collar, and tie. Carried a newspaper parcel. Very respectable appearance."

Mrs. Bunting walked forward. She gave a long, fluttering sigh of unutterable relief.

"There's the chap!" said Joe Chandler triumphantly. "And now, Miss Daisy"—he turned to her jokingly, but there was a funny little tremor in his frank, cheerful-sounding voice—"if you knows of any nice, likely young fellow that answers to that description—well, you've only got to walk in and earn your reward of five hundred pounds."

"Five hundred pounds!" cried Daisy and her father simultaneously.

"Yes. That's what the Lord Mayor offered yesterday. Some private bloke—nothing official about it. But we of the Yard is barred from taking that reward, worse luck. And it's too bad, for we has all the trouble, after all!"

"Just hand that bit of paper over, will you?" said Bunting. "I'd like to con it over to myself."

Chandler threw over the bit of flimsy.

A moment later Bunting looked up and handed it back. "Well, it's clear enough, isn't it?"

"Yes. And there's hundreds—nay, thousands—of young fellows that might be a description of," said Chandler sarcastically. "As a pal of mine said this morning, 'There isn't a chap will like to carry a newspaper parcel after this.' And it won't do to have a respectable appearance—eh?"

Daisy's voice rang out in merry, pealing laughter. She greatly appreciated Mr. Chandler's witticism.

"Why on earth didn't the people who saw him try and catch him?" asked Bunting suddenly.

And Mrs. Bunting broke in, in a lower voice, "Yes, Joe—that seems odd, don't it?"

Joe Chandler coughed. "Well, it's this way," he said. "No one person did see all that. The man who's described here is just made up from the description of two different folk who *think* they saw him. You see, the murders must have taken place—well, now, let me see—perhaps at two o'clock this last time. Two o'clock—that's the idea. Well, at such a time as that not many people are about, especially on a foggy night. Yes, one woman declares she saw a young chap walking away from the spot where 'twas done; and another one—but that was a good bit later—says The Avenger passed by her. It's mostly her they're following in this 'ere description. And then the boss who has charge of that sort of thing looked up what other people had said—I mean when the other crimes was committed. That's how he made up this 'Wanted.' "

"Then The Avenger may be quite a different sort of man?" said Bunting slowly, disappointedly.

"Well, of course he *may* be. But, no; I think that description fits him all right," said Chandler; but he also spoke in a hesitating voice.

"You was saying, Joe, that they found a weapon?" observed Bunting insinuatingly.

He was glad that Ellen allowed the discussion to go on—in fact, that she even seemed to take an intelligent interest in it. She had come up close to them, and now looked quite her old self again.

"Yes. They believe they've found the weapon what he does his awful deeds with," said Chandler. "At any rate, within a hundred yards of that little dark passage where they found the bodies—one at each end, that was—there was discovered this morning a very peculiar kind o' knife—'keen as a razor, pointed as a dagger'—that's the exact words the boss used when he was describing it to a lot of us. He seemed to think a lot more of that clue than of the other—I mean than of the description people gave of the chap who walked quickly by with a newspaper parcel. But now there's a pretty job in front of us. Every shop where they sell or might a' sold, such a thing as that knife, including every eating-house in the East End, has got to be called at!"

"Whatever for?" asked Daisy.

"Why, with an idea of finding out if anyone saw such a knife fooling about there any time, and, if so, in whose possession it was at the time. But, Mr. Bunting"—Chandler's voice changed; it became businesslike, official—"they're not going to say anything about that—not in the newspapers—till to-morrow, so don't you go and tell anybody. You see, we don't want to frighten the fellow off. If he knew they'd got his knife—well, he might just make himself scarce, and they don't want that! If it's discovered that any knife of that kind was sold, say a month ago, to some customer whose ways are known, then—then——"

"What'll happen then?" said Mrs. Bunting, coming nearer.

"Well, then, nothing'll be put about it in the papers at all," said Chandler deliberately. "The only objec' of letting the public know about it would be if nothink was found—I mean if the search of the shops, and so on, was no good. Then, of course, we must try and find out someone—some private person-like, who's watched that knife in the criminal's possession. It's there the reward—the five hundred pounds will come in."

"Oh, I'd give anything to see that knife!" exclaimed Daisy, clasping her hands together.

"You cruel, bloodthirsty girl!" cried her stepmother passionately.

They all looked round at her, surprised.

"Come, come, Ellen!" said Bunting reprovingly.

"Well, it *is* a horrible idea!" said his wife sullenly. "To go and sell a fellow-being for five hundred pounds."

But Daisy was offended. "Of course I'd like to see it!" she cried defiantly. "I never said nothing about the reward. That was Mr. Chandler said that! I only said I'd like to see the knife."

Chandler looked at her soothingly. "Well, the day may come when you *will* s ee it," he said slowly.

A great idea had come into his mind.

"No! What makes you think that?"

"If they catches him, and if you comes along with me to see our Black Museum at the Yard, you'll certainly see the knife, Miss Daisy. They keeps all them kind of things there. So if, as I say, this weapon *should* lead to the conviction of The Avenger—well, then, that knife 'ull be there, and you'll see it!"

"The Black Museum? Why, whatever do they have a museum in your place for?" asked Daisy wonderingly. "I thought there was only the British Museum——"

And then even Mrs. Bunting, as well as Bunting and Chandler, laughed aloud.

"You are a goosey girl!" said her father fondly. "Why, there's a lot of museums in London; the town's thick with 'em. Ask Ellen there. She and me used to go to them kind of places when we was courting—if the weather was bad."

"But our museum's the one that would interest Miss Daisy," broke in Chandler eagerly. "It's a regular Chamber of 'Orrors!"

"Why, Joe, you never told us about that place before," said Bunting excitedly. "D'you really mean that there's a museum where they keeps all sorts of things connected with crimes? Things like knives murders have been committed with?"

"Knives?" cried Joe, pleased at having become the centre of attention, for Daisy had also fixed her blue eyes on him, and even Mrs. Bunting looked at him expectantly. "Much more than knives, Mr. Bunting! Why, they've got there, in little bottles, the real poison what people have been done away with."

"And can you go there whenever you like?" asked Daisy wonderingly. She had not realised before what extraordinary and agreeable privileges are attached to the position of a detective member of the London Police Force.

"Well, I suppose I *could*——" Joe smiled. "Anyway I can certainly get leave to take a friend there." He looked meaningly at Daisy, and Daisy looked eagerly at him.

But would Ellen ever let her go out by herself with Mr. Chandler? Ellen was so prim, so—so irritatingly proper. But what was this father was saying? "D'you really mean that, Joe?"

"Yes, o' course I do!"

"Well, then, look here! If it isn't asking too much of a favour, I should like to go along there with you very much one day. I don't want to wait till The Avenger's caught"—Bunting smiled broadly. "I'd be quite content as it is with what there is in that museum o' yours. Ellen, there"—he looked across at his wife—"don't agree with me about such things. Yet I don't think I'm a bloodthirsty man! But I'm just terribly interested in all that sort of thing—always have been. I used to positively envy the butler in that Balham Mystery!"

Again a look passed between Daisy and the young man—it was a look which contained and carried a great many things backwards and forwards, such as— "Now, isn't it funny that your father should want to go to such a place? But still, I can't help it if he does want to go, so we must put up with his company, though it would have been much nicer for us to go just by our two selves." And then Daisy's look answered quite as plainly, though perhaps Joe didn't read her glance quite as clearly as she had read his: "Yes, it *is* tiresome. But father means well; and 'twill be very pleasant going there, even if he does come too."

"Well, what d'you say to the day after to-morrow, Mr. Bunting? I'd call for you here about—shall we say half-past two?—and just take you and Miss Daisy down to the Yard. 'Twouldn't take very long; we could go all the way by bus, right down to Westminster Bridge." He looked round at his hostess: "Wouldn't you join us, Mrs. Bunting? 'Tis truly a wonderful interesting place."

But his hostess shook her head decidedly. " 'Twould turn me sick," she exclaimed, "to see the bottle of poison what had done away with the life of some poor creature! And as for knives——!" A look of real horror, of startled fear, crept over her pale face.

"There, there!" said Bunting hastily. "Live and let live—that's what I always say. Ellen ain't on in this turn. She can just stay at home and mind the cat,—I beg his pardon, I mean the lodger!"

"I won't have Mr. Sleuth laughed at," said Mrs. Bunting darkly. "But there! I'm sure it's very kind of you, Joe, to think of giving Bunting and Daisy such a rare treat"—she spoke sarcastically, but none of the three who heard her understood that.

CHAPTER IX

The moment she passed through the great arched door which admits the stranger to that portion of New Scotland Yard where throbs the heart of that great organism which fights the forces of civilised crime, Daisy Bunting felt that she had indeed become free of the Kingdom of Romance. Even the lift in which the three of them were whirled up to one of the upper floors of the huge building was to the girl a new and delightful experience. Daisy had always lived a simple, quiet life in the little country town where dwelt Old Aunt, and this was the first time a lift had come her way.

With a touch of personal pride in the vast building, Joe Chandler marched his friends down a wide, airy corridor.

Daisy clung to her father's arm, a little bewildered, a little oppressed by her good fortune. Her happy young voice was stilled by the awe she felt at the wonderful place where she found herself, and by the glimpses she caught of great rooms full of busy, silent men engaged in unravelling—or so she supposed—the mysteries of crime.

They were passing a half-open door when Chandler suddenly stopped short. "Look in there," he said, in a low voice, addressing the father rather than the daughter, "that's the Finger-Print Room. We've records here of over two hundred thousand men's and women's finger-tips! I expect you know, Mr. Bunting, as how, once we've got the print of a man's five finger-tips, well, he's done for—if he ever does anything else, that is. Once we've got that bit of him registered he can't never escape us—no, not if he tries ever so. But though there's nigh on a quarter of a million records in there, yet it don't take—well, not half an hour, for them to tell whether any particular man has ever been convicted before! Wonderful thought, ain't it?"

"Wonderful!" said Bunting, drawing a deep breath. And then a troubled look came over his stolid face. "Wonderful, but also a very fearful thought for the poor wretches as has got their finger-prints in there, Joe."

Joe laughed. "Agreed!" he said. "And the cleverer ones knows that only too well. Why, not long ago, one man who knew his record was here safe, managed to slash about his fingers something awful, just so as to make a blurred impression—you takes my meaning? But there, at the end of six weeks the skin grew all right again, and in exactly the same little creases as before!"

"Poor devil!" said Bunting under his breath, and a cloud even came over Daisy's bright, eager face.

They were now going along a narrower passage, and then again they came to a half-open door, leading into a room far smaller than that of the Finger-Print Identification Room.

"If you'll glance in there," said Joe briefly, "you'll see how we finds out all about any man whose finger-tips has given him away, so to speak. It's here we keeps an account of what he's done, his previous convictions, and so on. His finger-tips are where I told you, and his record in there—just connected by a number."

"Wonderful!" said Bunting, drawing in his breath.

But Daisy was longing to get on—to get to the Black Museum. All this that Joe and her father were saying was quite unreal to her, and, for the matter of that, not worth taking the trouble to understand. However, she had not long to wait.

A broad-shouldered, pleasant-looking young fellow, who seemed on very friendly terms with Joe Chandler, came forward suddenly, and, unlocking a commonplace-looking door, ushered the little party of three through into the Black Museum.

For a moment there came across Daisy a feeling of keen disappointment and surprise. This big, light room simply reminded her of what they called the Science Room in the public library of the town where she lived with Old Aunt. Here, as there, the centre was taken up with plain glass cases fixed at a height from the floor which enabled their contents to be looked at closely.

She walked forward and peered into the case nearest the door. The exhibits shown there were mostly small, shabby-looking little things, the sort of things one might turn out of an old rubbish cupboard in an untidy house—old medicine bottles, a soiled neckerchief, what looked like a child's broken lantern, even a box of pills. . . .

As for the walls, they were covered with the queerest-looking objects; bits of old iron, odd-looking things made of wood and leather, and so on.

It was really rather disappointing.

Then Daisy Bunting gradually became aware that, standing on a shelf just below the first of the broad, spacious windows which made the great room look so light and shadowless, was a row of life-size white plaster heads, each head slightly inclined to the right. There were about a dozen of these, not more—and they had such odd, staring, helpless, *real*-looking faces.

"Whatever's those?" asked Bunting in a low voice.

Daisy clung a thought closer to her father's arm. Even she guessed that these strange, pathetic, staring faces were the death-masks of those men and women who had fulfilled the awful law which ordains that the murderer shall be, in his turn, done to death.

"All hanged!" said the guardian of the Black Museum briefly. "Casts taken after death."

Bunting smiled nervously. "They don't look dead somehow. They looks more as if they were listening," he said.

"That's the fault of Jack Ketch," said the man facetiously. "It's his idea—that of knotting his patient's necktie under the left ear! That's what he does to each of the gentlemen to whom he has to act valet on just one occasion only. It makes them lean just a bit to one side. You look here——?"

Daisy and her father came a little closer, and the speaker pointed with his finger to a little dent imprinted on the left side of each neck; running from this indentation was a curious little furrow, well ridged above, showing how tightly Jack Ketch's necktie had been drawn when its wearer was hurried through the gates of eternity.

"They looks foolish-like, rather than terrified, or—or hurt," said Bunting wonderingly.

He was extraordinarily moved and fascinated by those dumb, staring faces.

But young Chandler exclaimed in a cheerful, matter-of-fact voice, "Well, a man would look foolish at such a time as that, with all his plans brought to naught—and knowing he's only got a second to live—now wouldn't he?"

"Yes, I suppose he would," said Bunting slowly.

Daisy had gone a little pale. The sinister, breathless atmosphere of the place was beginning to tell on her. She now began to understand that the shabby little objects lying there in the glass case close to her were each and all links in the chain of evidence which, in almost every case, had brought some guilty man or woman to the gallows.

"We had a yellow gentleman here the other day," observed the guardian suddenly; "one of those Brahmins—so they calls themselves. Well, you'd 'a been quite surprised to see how that heathen took on! He declared—what was the word he used?"—he turned to Chandler.

"He said that each of these things, with the exception of the casts, mind you—queer to say, he left them out—exuded evil, that was the word he used! Exuded—squeezed out it means. He said that being here made him feel very bad. And 'twasn't all nonsense either. He turned quite green under his yellow skin, and we had to shove him out quick. He didn't feel better till he'd got right to the other end of the passage!"

"There now! Who'd ever think of that?" said Bunting. "I should say that man 'ud got something on his conscience, wouldn't you?"

"Well, I needn't stay now," said Joe's good-natured friend. "You show your friends round, Chandler. You knows the place nearly as well as I do, don't you?"

He smiled at Joe's visitors, as if to say good-bye, but it seemed that he could not tear himself away after all.

"Look here," he said to Bunting. "In this here little case are the tools of Charles Peace. I expect you've heard of him."

"I should think I have!" cried Bunting eagerly.

"Many gents as comes here thinks this case the most interesting of all. Peace was such a wonderful man! A great inventor they say he would have been, had he been put in the way of it. Here's his ladder; you see it folds up quite compactly, and makes a nice little bundle—just like a bundle of old sticks any man might have been seen carrying about London in those days without attracting any attention. Why, it probably helped him to look like an honest working man time and time again, for on being arrested he declared most solemnly he'd always carried that ladder openly under his arm."

"The daring of that!" cried Bunting.

"Yes, and when the ladder was opened out it could reach from the ground to the second storey of any old house. And, oh! how clever he was! Just open one section, and you see the other sections open automatically; so Peace could stand on the ground and force the thing quietly up to any window he wished to reach. Then he'd go away again, having done his job, with a mere bundle of old wood under his arm! My word, he was artful! I wonder if you've heard the tale of how Peace once lost a finger. Well, he guessed the constables were instructed to look out for a man missing a finger; so what did he do?"

"Put on a false finger," suggested Bunting.

"No, indeed! Peace made up his mind just to do without a hand altogether. Here's his false stump; you see, it's made of wood—wood and black felt? Well, that just held his hand nicely. Why, we considers that one of the most ingenious contrivances in the whole museum."

Meanwhile, Daisy had let go her hold of her father. With Chandler in delighted attendance, she had moved away to the farther end of the great room, and now she was bending over yet another glass case. "Whatever are those little bottles for?" she asked wonderingly.

There were five small phials, filled with varying quantities of cloudy liquids.

"They're full of poison, Miss Daisy, that's what they are. There's enough arsenic in that little whack o' brandy to do for you and me—aye, and for your father as well, I should say."

"Then chemists shouldn't sell such stuff," said Daisy, smiling. Poison was so remote from herself, that the sight of these little bottles only brought a pleasant thrill.

"No more they don't. That was sneaked out of a flypaper, that was. Lady said she wanted a cosmetic for her complexion, but what she was really going for was flypapers for to do away with her husband. She'd got a bit tired of him, I suspect."

"Perhaps he was a horrid man, and deserved to be done away with," said Daisy. The idea struck them both as so very comic that they began to laugh aloud in unison.

"Did you ever hear what a certain Mrs. Pearce did?" asked Chandler, becoming suddenly serious.

"Oh, yes," said Daisy, and she shuddered a little. "That was the wicked, wicked woman what killed a pretty little baby and its mother. They've got her in Madame Tussaud's. But Ellen, she won't let me go to the Chamber of Horrors. She wouldn't let father take me there last time I was in London. Cruel of her, I called it. But somehow I don't feel as if I wanted to go there now, after having been here!"

"Well," said Chandler slowly, "we've a case full of relics of Mrs. Pearce. But the pram the bodies were found in, that's at Madame Tussaud's—at least so they claim, I can't say. Now here's something just as curious, and not near so dreadful. See that man's jacket there?"

"Yes," said Daisy falteringly. She was beginning to feel oppressed, frightened. She no longer wondered that the Indian gentleman had been taken queer.

"A burglar shot a man dead who'd disturbed him, and by mistake he went and left that jacket behind him. Our people noticed that one of the buttons was broken in two. Well, that don't seem much of a clue, does it, Miss Daisy? Will you believe me when I tells you that that other bit of button was discovered, and that it hanged the fellow? And 'twas the more wonderful because all three buttons was different!"

Daisy stared wonderingly down at the little broken button which had hung a man. "And whatever's that?" she asked, pointing to a piece of dirty-looking stuff.

"Well," said Chandler reluctantly, "that's rather a horrible thing—that is. That's a bit o' shirt that was buried with a woman—buried in the ground, I mean—after her husband had cut her up and tried to burn her. 'Twas that bit o' shirt that brought him to the gallows."

"I considers your museum's a very horrid place!" said Daisy pettishly, turning away.

She longed to be out in the passage again, away from this brightly lighted, cheerful-looking, sinister room.

But her father was now absorbed in the case containing various types of infernal machines. "Beautiful little works of art some of them are," said his guide eagerly, and Bunting could not but agree.

"Come along—do, father!" said Daisy quickly. "I've seen about enough now. If I was to stay in here much longer it 'ud give me the horrors. I don't want to have no nightmares to-night. It's dreadful to think there are so many wicked people in the world. Why, we might knock up against some murderer any minute without knowing it, mightn't we?"

"Not you, Miss Daisy," said Chandler smilingly. "I don't suppose you'll ever come across even a common swindler, let alone anyone who's committed a murder—not one in a million does that. Why, even I have never had anything to do with a proper murder case!"

But Bunting was in no hurry. He was thoroughly enjoying every moment of the time. Just now he was studying intently the various photographs which hung on the walls of the Black Museum; especially was he pleased to see those connected with a famous and still mysterious case which had taken place not long before in Scotland, and in which the servant of the man who died had played a considerable part—not in elucidating, but in obscuring, the mystery.

"I suppose a good many murderers get off?" he said musingly.

And Joe Chandler's friend nodded. "I should think they did!" he exclaimed. "There's no such thing as justice here in England. 'Tis odds on the murderer every time. 'Tisn't one in ten that come to the end he should do—to the gallows, that is."

"And what d'you think about what's going on now—I mean about those Avenger murders?"

Bunting lowered his voice, but Daisy and Chandler were already moving towards the door.

"I don't believe he'll ever be caught," said the other confidentially. "In some ways 'tis a lot more of a job to catch a madman than 'tis to run down just an ordinary criminal. And, of course—leastways to my thinking—The Avenger *is* a madman—one of the cunning, quiet sort. Have you heard about the letter?" his voice dropped lower.

"No," said Bunting, staring eagerly at him. "What letter d'you mean?"

"Well, there's a letter—it'll be in this museum some day—which came just before that last double event. 'Twas signed 'The Avenger,' in just the same printed characters as on that bit of paper he always leaves behind him. Mind you, it don't follow that it actually *was* The Avenger what sent that letter here, but it looks uncommonly like it, and I know that the Boss attaches quite a lot of importance to it."

"And where was it posted?" asked Bunting. "That might be a bit of a clue, you know."

"Oh, no," said the other. "They always goes a very long way to post anything—criminals do. It stands to reason they would. But this particular one was put in at the Edgware Road Post Office."

"What? Close to us?" said Bunting. "Goodness! How dreadful!"

"Any of us might knock up against him any minute. I don't suppose The Avenger's in any way peculiar-looking—in fact, we know he ain't."

"Then you think that woman as says she saw him *did* meet him?" asked Bunting hesitatingly.

"Our description was made up from what she said," answered the other cautiously. "But, there, you can't tell! In a case like that it's groping—groping in the dark all the time—and it's just a lucky accident if it comes out right in the end. Of course, it's upsetting us all very much here. You can't wonder at that!"

"No, indeed," said Bunting quickly. "I give you my word, I've hardly thought of anything else for the last month."

Daisy had disappeared, and when her father joined her in the passage she was listening, with downcast eyes, to what Joe Chandler was saying.

He was telling her about his real home, of the place where his mother lived, at Richmond—that it was a nice little house, close to the park. He was asking her whether she could manage to come out there one afternoon, explaining that his mother would give them both tea, and how nice it would be.

"I don't see why Ellen shouldn't let me," the girl said rebelliously. "But she's that old-fashioned and pernickety is Ellen—a regular old maid! And, you see, Mr. Chandler, when I'm staying with them, father don't like for me to do anything that Ellen don't approve of. But she's got quite fond of you, so perhaps if you ask her——?" She looked at him, and he nodded sagely.

"Don't you be afraid," he said confidently. "I'll get round Mrs. Bunting. But, Miss Daisy"—he grew very red—"I'd just like to ask you a question—no offence meant——"

"Yes?" said Daisy a little breathlessly. "There's father close to us, Mr. Chandler. Tell me quick; what is it?"

"Well, I take it, by what you said just now, that you've never walked out with any young fellow?"

Daisy hesitated a moment, then a very pretty dimple came into her cheek. "No," she said sadly. "No, Mr. Chandler, that I have not." In a burst of candour she added, "You see, I never had the chance!"

And Joe Chandler smiled, well pleased.

CHAPTER X

By what she regarded as a fortunate chance, Mrs. Bunting found herself for close on an hour quite alone in the house during her husband's and Daisy's jaunt with young Chandler.

Mr. Sleuth did not often go out in the daytime, but on this particular afternoon, after he had finished his tea, when dusk was falling, he suddenly observed that he wanted a new suit of clothes, and his landlady eagerly acquiesced in his going out to purchase it.

As soon as he had left the house, she went quickly up to the drawing-room floor. Now had come her opportunity of giving the two rooms a good dusting; but Mrs. Bunting knew well, deep in her heart, that it was not so much the dusting of Mr. Sleuth's sitting-room she wanted to do—as to engage in a vague search for—she hardly knew for what.

During the years she had been in service Mrs. Bunting had always had a deep, wordless contempt for those of her fellow-servants who read their employers' private letters, and who furtively peeped into desks and cupboards in the hope, more vague than positive, of discovering family skeletons.

But now, with regard to Mr. Sleuth, she was ready, aye, eager, to do herself what she had once so scorned others for doing.

Beginning with the bedroom, she started on a methodical search. He was a very tidy gentleman was the lodger, and his few things, under-garments, and so on, were in apple-pie order. She had early undertaken, much to his satisfaction, to do the very little bit of washing he required done, with her own and Bunting's. Luckily he wore soft shirts.

At one time Mrs. Bunting had always had a woman in to help her with this tiresome weekly job, but lately she had grown quite clever at it herself. The only things she had to send out were Bunting's shirts. Everything else she managed to do herself.

From the chest of drawers she now turned her attention to the dressing-table.

Mr. Sleuth did not take his money with him when he went out, he generally left it in one of the drawers below the old-fashioned looking-glass. And now, in a perfunctory way, his landlady pulled out the little drawer, but she did not touch what was lying there; she only glanced at the heap of sovereigns and a few bits of silver. The lodger had taken just enough money with him to buy the clothes he required. He had consulted her as to how much they would cost, making no secret of why he was going out, and the fact had vaguely comforted Mrs. Bunting.

Now she lifted the toilet-cover, and even rolled up the carpet a little way, but no, there was nothing there, not so much as a scrap of paper. And at last, when more or less giving up the search, as she came and went between the two rooms, leaving the connecting door wide open, her mind became full of uneasy speculation and wonder as to the lodger's past life.

Odd Mr. Sleuth must surely always have been, but odd in a sensible sort of way, having on the whole the same moral ideals of conduct as have other people of his class. He was queer about the drink—one might say almost crazy on the subject—but there, as to that, he wasn't the only one! She, Ellen Bunting, had once lived with a lady who was just like that, who was quite crazed, that is, on the question of drink and drunkards——

She looked round the neat drawing-room with vague dissatisfaction. There was only one place where anything could be kept concealed—that place was the substantial if small mahogany chiffonnier. And then an idea suddenly came to Mrs. Bunting, one she had never thought of before.

After listening intently for a moment, lest something should suddenly bring Mr. Sleuth home earlier than she expected, she went to the corner where the chiffonnier stood, and, exerting the whole of her not very great physical strength, she tipped forward the heavy piece of furniture.

As she did so, she heard a queer rumbling sound,—something rolling about on the second shelf, something which had not been there before Mr. Sleuth's arrival. Slowly, laboriously, she tipped the chiffonnier backwards and forwards—once, twice, thrice—satisfied, yet strangely troubled in her mind, for she now felt sure that the bag of which the disappearance had so surprised her was there, safely locked away by its owner.

Suddenly a very uncomfortable thought came to Mrs. Bunting's mind. She hoped Mr. Sleuth would not notice that his bag had shifted inside the cupboard. A moment later, with sharp dismay, Mr. Sleuth's landlady realised that the fact that she had moved the chiffonnier must become known to her lodger, for a thin trickle of some dark-coloured liquid was oozing out through the bottom of the little cupboard door.

She stooped down and touched the stuff. It showed red, bright red, on her finger.

Mrs. Bunting grew chalky white, then recovered herself quickly. In fact the colour rushed into her face, and she grew hot all over.

It was only a bottle of red ink she had upset—that was all! How could she have thought it was anything else?

It was the more silly of her—so she told herself in scornful condemnation—because she knew that the lodger used red ink. Certain pages of *Cruden's Concordance* were covered with notes written in Mr. Sleuth's peculiar upright handwriting. In fact, in some places you couldn't see the margin, so closely covered was it with remarks and notes of interrogation.

Mr. Sleuth had foolishly placed his bottle of red ink in the chiffonnier— that was what her poor, foolish gentleman had done, and it was owing to her inquisitiveness, her restless wish to know things she would be none the better, none the happier, for knowing, that this accident had taken place. . . .

She mopped up with her duster the few drops of ink which had fallen on the green carpet and then, still feeling, as she angrily told herself, foolishly upset, she went once more into the back room.

It was curious that Mr. Sleuth possessed no notepaper. She would have expected him to have made that one of his first purchases—the more so that paper is so very cheap, especially that rather dirty-looking grey Silurian paper. Mrs. Bunting had once lived with a lady who always used two kinds of notepaper, white for her friends and equals, grey for those whom she called "common people." She, Ellen Green, as she then was, had always resented the fact. Strange she should remember it now, stranger in a way because that employer of hers had not been a real lady, and Mr. Sleuth, whatever his peculiarities, was, in every sense of the word, a real gentleman. Somehow Mrs. Bunting felt sure that if he had bought any notepaper it would have been white—white and probably cream-laid—not grey and cheap.

Again she opened the drawer of the old-fashioned wardrobe and lifted up the few pieces of underclothing Mr. Sleuth now possessed.

But there was nothing there—nothing, that is, hidden away. When one came to think of it, there seemed something strange in the notion of leaving all one's money where anyone could take it, and in locking up such a valueless thing as a cheap sham leather bag, to say nothing of a bottle of ink.

Mrs. Bunting once more opened out each of the tiny drawers below the looking-glass, each delicately fashioned of fine old mahogany. Mr. Sleuth kept his money in the centre drawer.

The glass had only cost seven-and-sixpence, and, after the auction, a dealer had come and offered her first fifteen shillings, and then a guinea for it. Not long ago, in Baker Street, she had seen a looking-glass which was the very spit of this one, labelled "Chippendale, Antique, £2 15s. od."

There lay Mr. Sleuth's money—the sovereigns, as the landlady well knew, would each and all gradually pass into her and Bunting's possession, honestly earned by them no doubt, but unattainable—in fact unearnable—excepting in connection with the present owner of those dully shining gold sovereigns.

At last she went downstairs to await Mr. Sleuth's return.

When she heard the key turn in the door, she came out into the passage.

"I'm sorry to say I've had an accident, sir," she said a little breathlessly. "Taking advantage of your being out, I went up to dust the drawing-room, and while I was trying to get behind the chiffonnier it tilted. I'm afraid, sir, that a bottle of ink that was inside may have got broken, for just a few drops oozed out, sir. But I hope there's no harm done. I wiped it up as well as I could, seeing that the doors of the chiffonnier are locked."

Mr. Sleuth stared at her with a wild, almost a terrified, glance. But Mrs. Bunting stood her ground. She felt far less afraid now than she had felt before he came in. Then she had been so frightened that she had nearly gone out of the house, on to the pavement, for company.

"Of course I had no idea, sir, that you kept any ink in there."

She spoke as if she were on the defensive, and the lodger's brow cleared.

"I was aware you used ink, sir," Mrs. Bunting went on, "for I have seen you marking that book of yours—I mean the book you read together with the Bible. Would you like me to go out and get you another bottle, sir?"

"No," said Mr. Sleuth. "No, I thank you. I will at once proceed upstairs and see what damage has been done. When I require you I shall ring."

He shuffled past her, and five minutes later the drawing-room bell did ring.

At once, from the door, Mrs. Bunting saw that the chiffonnier was wide open, and that the shelves were empty save for the bottle of red ink which had turned over and now lay in a red pool of its own making on the lower shelf.

"I'm afraid it will have stained the wood, Mrs. Bunting. Perhaps I was ill-advised to keep my ink in there."

"Oh, no, sir! That doesn't matter at all. Only a drop or two fell out on to the carpet, and they don't show, as you see, sir, for it's a dark corner. Shall I take the bottle away? I may as well."

Mr. Sleuth hesitated. "No," he said, after a long pause, "I think not, Mrs. Bunting. For the very little I require it the ink remaining in the bottle will do quite well, especially if I add a little water, or better still, a little tea, to what already remains in the bottle. I only require it to mark up passages which happen to be of peculiar interest in my Concordance—a work, Mrs. Bunting, which I should have taken great pleasure in compiling myself had not this—ah—this gentleman called Cruden, been before me."

Not only Bunting, but Daisy also, thought Ellen far pleasanter in her manner than usual that evening. She listened to all they had to say about their interesting visit to the Black Museum, and did not snub either of them—no, not even when Bunting told of the dreadful, haunting, silly-looking death-masks taken from the hanged.

But a few minutes after that, when her husband suddenly asked her a question, Mrs. Bunting answered at random. It was clear she had not heard the last few words he had been saying.

"A penny for your thoughts!" he said jocularly.

But she shook her head.

Daisy slipped out of the room, and, five minutes later, came back dressed up in a blue-and-white check silk gown.

"My!" said her father. "You do look fine, Daisy. I've never seen you wearing that before."

"And a rare figure of fun she looks in it!" observed Mrs. Bunting sarcastically. And then, "I suppose this dressing up means that you're expecting someone. I should have thought both of you must have seen enough of young Chandler for one day. I wonder when that young chap does his work—that I do! He never seems too busy to come and waste an hour or two here."

But that was the only nasty thing Ellen said all that evening. And even Daisy noticed that her stepmother seemed dazed and unlike herself. She went about her cooking and the various little things she had to do even more silently than was her wont.

Yet under that still, almost sullen, manner, how fierce was the storm of dread, of sombre, anguish, and, yes, of sick suspense, which shook her soul, and which so far affected her poor, ailing body that often she felt as if she could not force herself to accomplish her simple round of daily work.

After they had finished supper Bunting went out and bought a penny evening paper, but as he came in he announced, with a rather rueful smile, that he had read so much of that nasty little print this last week or two that his eyes hurt him.

"Let me read aloud a bit to you, father," said Daisy eagerly, and he handed her the paper.

Scarcely had Daisy opened her lips when a loud ring and a knock echoed through the house.

CHAPTER XI

It was only Joe. Somehow, even Bunting called him "Joe" now, and no longer "Chandler," as he had mostly used to do.

Mrs. Bunting had opened the front door only a very little way. She wasn't going to have any strangers pushing in past her.

To her sharpened, suffering senses her house had become a citadel which must be defended; aye, even if the besiegers were a mighty horde *with right on their side*. And she was always expecting that first single spy who would herald the battalion against whom her only weapon would be her woman's wit and cunning.

But when she saw who stood there smiling at her, the muscles of her face relaxed, and it lost the tense, anxious, almost agonised look it assumed the moment she turned her back on her husband and stepdaughter.

"Why, Joe," she whispered, for she had left the door open behind her, and Daisy had already begun to read aloud, as her father had bidden her. "Come in, do! It's fairly cold to-night."

A glance at his face had shown her that there was no fresh news.

Joe Chandler walked in, past her, into the little hall. Cold? Well, he didn't feel cold, for he had walked quickly to be the sooner where he was now.

Nine days had gone by since that last terrible occurrence, the double murder which had been committed early in the morning of the day Daisy had arrived in London. And though the thousands of men belonging to the Metropolitan Police—to say nothing of the smaller, more alert body of detectives attached to the Force—were keenly on the alert, not one but had begun to feel that there was nothing to be alert about. Familiarity, even with horror, breeds contempt.

But with the public it was far otherwise. Each day something happened to revive and keep alive the mingled horror and interest this strange, enigmatic series of crimes had evoked. Even the more sober organs of the Press went on attacking, with gathering severity and indignation, the Commissioner of Police; and at the huge demonstration held in Victoria Park two days before violent speeches had also been made against the Home Secretary.

But just now Joe Chandler wanted to forget all that. The little house in the Marylebone Road had become to him an enchanted isle of dreams, to which his thoughts were ever turning when he had a moment to spare from what had grown to be a wearisome, because an unsatisfactory, job. He secretly agreed with one of his pals who had exclaimed, and that within twenty-four hours of the last double crime, "Why, 'twould be easier to find a needle in a rick o' hay than this——bloke!"

And if that had been true then, how much truer it was now—after nine long, empty days had gone by?

Quickly he divested himself of his great-coat, muffler, and low hat. Then he put his finger on his lip, and motioned smilingly to Mrs. Bunting to wait a moment.

From where he stood in the hall the father and daughter made a pleasant little picture of contented domesticity. Joe Chandler's honest heart swelled at the sight.

Daisy, wearing the blue-and-white check silk dress about which her stepmother and she had had words, sat on a low stool on the left side of the fire, while Bunting, leaning back in his own comfortable arm-chair, was listening, his hand to his ear, in an attitude—as it was the first time she had caught him doing it, the fact brought a pang to Mrs. Bunting—which showed that age was beginning to creep over the listener.

One of Daisy's duties as companion to her great-aunt was that of reading the newspaper aloud, and she prided herself on her accomplishment.

Just as Joe had put his finger on his lip Daisy had been asking, "Shall I read this, father?" And Bunting had answered quickly, "Aye, do, my dear."

He was absorbed in what he was hearing, and, on seeing Joe at the door, he had only just nodded his head. The young man was becoming so frequent a visitor as to be almost one of themselves.

Daisy read out:

"The Avenger: A——"

And then she stopped short, for the next word puzzled her greatly. Bravely, however, she went on. "A the-o-ry."

"Go in—do!" whispered Mrs. Bunting to her visitor. "Why should we stay out here in the cold? It's ridic'lous."

"I don't want to interrupt Miss Daisy," whispered Chandler back, rather hoarsely.

"Well, you'll hear it all the better in the room. Don't think she'll stop because of you, bless you! There's nothing shy about our Daisy!"

The young man resented the tart, short tone. "Poor little girl!" he said to himself tenderly. "That's what it is having a stepmother, instead of a proper mother." But he obeyed Mrs. Bunting, and then he was pleased he had done so, for Daisy looked up, and a bright blush came over her pretty face.

"Joe begs you won't stop yet awhile. Go on with your reading," commanded Mrs. Bunting quickly. "Now, Joe, you can go and sit over there, close to Daisy, and then you won't miss a word."

There was a sarcastic inflection in her voice, even Chandler noticed that, but he obeyed her with alacrity, and crossing the room he went and sat on a chair just behind Daisy. From there he could note with reverent delight the charming way her fair hair grew upwards from the nape of her slender neck.

"The Avenger: A The-o-ry"

began Daisy again, clearing her throat.

> "DEAR SIR—*I have a suggestion to put forward for which I think there is a great deal to be said. It seems to me very probable that The Avenger—to give him the name by which he apparently wishes to be known—comprises in his own person the peculiarities of Jekyll and Hyde, Mr. Louis Stevenson's now famous hero.*
>
> *"The culprit, according to my point of view, is a quiet, pleasant-looking gentleman who lives somewhere in the West End of London. He has, however, a tragedy in his past life. He is the husband of a dipsomaniac wife. She is, of course, under care, and is never mentioned in the house where he lives, maybe with his widowed mother and perhaps a maiden sister. They notice that he has become gloomy and brooding of late, but he lives his usual life, occupying himself each day with some harmless hobby. On foggy nights, once the quiet household is plunged in sleep, he creeps out of the house, maybe between one and two o'clock, and swiftly makes his way straight to what has become The Avenger's*

murder area. Picking out a likely victim, he approaches her with Judas-like gen-
tleness, and having committed his awful crime, goes quietly home again. After a
good bath and breakfast, he turns up happy, once more the quiet individual who
is an excellent son, a kind brother, esteemed and even beloved by a large circle of
friends and acquaintances. Meantime, the police are searching about the scene
of the tragedy for what they regard as the usual type of criminal lunatic.

"I give this theory, Sir, for what it is worth, but I confess that I am amazed
the police have so wholly confined their inquiries to the part of London where
these murders have been actually committed. I am quite sure from all that has
come out—and we must remember that full information is never given to the
newspapers—The Avenger should be sought for in the West, and not in the East
End of London.—Believe me to remain, Sir, yours very truly———"

Again Daisy hesitated, and then with an effort she brought out the word "Gab-o-ri-you," said she.

"What a funny name!" said Bunting wonderingly.

And then Joe broke in: "That's the name of a French chap what wrote detective stories," he said. "Pretty good, some of them are, too!"

"Then this Gaboriyou has come over to study these Avenger murders, I take it?" said Bunting.

"Oh, no," Joe spoke with confidence. "Whoever's written that silly letter just signed that name for fun."

"It *is* a silly letter," Mrs. Bunting had broken in resentfully. "I wonder a respectable paper prints such rubbish."

"Fancy if The Avenger did turn out to be a gentleman," cried Daisy, in an awestruck voice. "There'd be a how-to-do!"

"There may be something in the notion," said her father thoughtfully. "After all, the monster must be *somewhere*. This very minute he must be somewhere a-hiding of himself."

"Of course he's somewhere," said Mrs. Bunting scornfully.

She had just heard Mr. Sleuth moving overhead. 'Twould soon be time for the lodger's supper.

She hurried on: "But what I do say is that—that—*he* has nothing to do with the West End. Why, they say it's a sailor from the Docks—that's a good bit more likely, I take it. But there, I'm fair sick of the whole subject! We talk of nothing else in this house. The Avenger this—The Avenger that———"

"I expect Joe has something to tell us new to-night," said Bunting cheerfully. "Well, Joe, is there anything new?"

"I say, father, just listen to this!" Daisy broke in excitedly. She read out:

"Bloodhounds to be
Seriously Considered"

"Bloodhounds?" repeated Mrs. Bunting, and there was terror in her tone. "Why bloodhounds? That do seem to me a most horrible idea!"

Bunting looked across at her, mildly astonished. "Why, 'twould be a very good idea, if 'twas possible to have bloodhounds in a town. But, there, how can that be done in London, full of butchers' shops, to say nothing of slaughter-yards and other places o' that sort?"

But Daisy went on, and to her stepmother's shrinking ear there seemed a horrible thrill of delight, of gloating pleasure, in her fresh young voice.

"Hark to this," she said:

"A man who had committed a murder in a lonely wood near Blackburn was traced by the help of a bloodhound, and thanks to the sagacious instincts of the animal, the miscreant was finally convicted and hanged."

"La, now! Who'd ever have thought of such a thing?" Bunting exclaimed, in admiration. "The newspapers do have some useful hints in sometimes, Joe."

But young Chandler shook his head. "Bloodhounds ain't no use," he said; "no use at all! If the Yard was to listen to all the suggestions that the last few days have brought in—well, all I can say is our work *would* be cut out for us—not but what it's cut out for us now, if it comes to that!" He sighed ruefully. He was beginning to feel very tired; if only he could stay in this pleasant, cosy room listening to Daisy Bunting reading on and on for ever, instead of having to go out, as he would presently have to do, into the cold and foggy night!

Joe Chandler was fast becoming very sick of his new job. There was a lot of unpleasantness attached to the business, too. Why, even in the house where he lived, and in the little cook-shop where he habitually took his meals, the people round him had taken to taunt him with the remissness of the police. More than that. One of his pals, a man he'd always looked up to, because the young fellow had the gift of the gab, had actually been among those who had spoken at the big demonstration in Victoria Park, making a violent speech, not only against the Commissioner of the Metropolitan Police, but also against the Home Secretary.

But Daisy, like most people who believe themselves blessed with the possession of an accomplishment, had no mind to leave off reading just yet.

"Here's another notion!" she exclaimed. "Another letter, father!"

"Pardon to Accomplices."

"Dear Sir—During the last day or two several of the more intelligent of my acquaintances have suggested that The Avenger, whoever he may be, must be known to a certain number of persons. It is impossible that the perpetrator of such deeds, however nomad he may be in his habits——"

"Now I wonder what 'nomad' can be?" Daisy interrupted herself, and looked round at her little audience.

"I've always declared the fellow had all his senses about him," observed Bunting confidently.

Daisy went on, quite satisfied:

"——however nomad he may be in his habits, must have some habitat where his ways are known to at least one person. Now the person who knows the terrible secret is evidently withholding information in expectation of a reward,

or maybe because, being an accessory after the fact, he or she is now afraid of the consequences. My suggestion, Sir, is that the Home Secretary promise a free pardon. The more so that only thus can this miscreant be brought to justice. Unless he be caught red-handed in the act, it will be exceedingly difficult to trace the crime committed to any individual, for English law looks very askance at circumstantial evidence."

"There's something worth listening to in that letter," said Joe, leaning forward.

Now he was almost touching Daisy, and he smiled involuntarily as she turned her gay, pretty little face the better to hear what he was saying.

"Yes, Mr. Chandler?" she said interrogatively.

"Well, d'you remember that fellow what killed an old gentleman in a railway carriage? He took refuge with someone—a woman his mother had known, and she kept him hidden for quite a long time. But at last she gave him up, and she got a big reward, too!"

"I don't think I'd like to give anybody up for a reward," said Bunting, in his slow, dogmatic way.

"Oh, yes, you would, Mr. Bunting," said Chandler confidently. "You'd only be doing what it's the plain duty of everyone—everyone, that is, who's a good citizen. And you'd be getting something for doing it, which is more than most people gets as does their duty."

"A man as gives up someone for a reward is no better than a common informer," went on Bunting obstinately. "And no man 'ud care to be called that! It's different for you, Joe," he added hastily. "It's your job to catch those who've done anything wrong. And a man'd be a fool who'd take refuge-like with you. He'd be walking into the lion's mouth——" Bunting laughed.

And then Daisy broke in coquettishly: "If I'd done anything I wouldn't mind going for help to Mr. Chandler," she said.

And Joe, with eyes kindling, cried, "No. And if you did you needn't be afraid I'd give *you* up, Miss Daisy!"

And then, to their amazement, there suddenly broke from Mrs. Bunting, sitting with bowed head over the table, an exclamation of impatience and anger, and, it seemed to those listening, of pain.

"Why, Ellen, don't you feel well?" asked Bunting quickly.

"Just a spasm, a sharp stitch in my side, like," answered the poor woman heavily. "It's over now. Don't mind me."

"But I don't believe—no, that I don't—that there's anybody in the world who knows who The Avenger is," went on Chandler quickly. "It stands to reason that anybody'd give him up—in their own interest, if not in anyone else's. Who'd shelter such a creature? Why, 'twould be dangerous to have him in the house along with one!"

"Then it's your idea that he's not responsible for the wicked things he does?" Mrs. Bunting raised her head, and looked over at Chandler with eager, anxious eyes.

"I'd be sorry to think he wasn't responsible enough to hang!" said Chandler deliberately. "After all the trouble he's been giving us, too!"

"Hanging'd be too good for that chap," said Bunting.

"Not if he's not responsible," said his wife sharply. "I never heard of anything so cruel—that I never did! If the man's a madman, he ought to be in an asylum—that's where he ought to be."

"Hark to her now!" Bunting looked at his Ellen with amusement. "Contrary isn't the word for her! But there, I've noticed the last few days that she seemed to be taking that monster's part. That's what comes of being a born total abstainer."

Mrs. Bunting had got up from her chair. "What nonsense you do talk!" she said angrily. "Not but what it's a good thing if these murders *have* emptied the public-houses of women for a bit. England's drink is England's shame—I'll never depart from that! Now, Daisy, child, get up, do! Put down that paper. We've heard quite enough. You can be laying the cloth while I goes down to the kitchen."

"Yes, you mustn't be forgetting the lodger's supper," called out Bunting. "Mr. Sleuth don't always ring——" he turned to Chandler. "For one thing, he's often out about this time."

"Not often—just now and again, when he wants to buy something," snapped out Mrs. Bunting. "But I hadn't forgot his supper. He never do want it before eight o'clock."

"Let me take up the lodger's supper, Ellen," Daisy's eager voice broke in. She had got up in obedience to her stepmother, and was now laying the cloth.

"Certainly not! I told you he only wanted me to wait on him. You have your work cut out looking after things down here—that's where I wants you to help me."

Chandler also got up. Somehow he didn't like to be doing nothing while Daisy was so busy. "Yes," he said, looking across at Mrs. Bunting, "I'd forgotten about your lodger. Going on all right, eh?"

"Never knew so quiet and well-behaved a gentleman," said Bunting. "He turned our luck, did Mr. Sleuth."

His wife left the room, and after she had gone Daisy laughed. "You'll hardly believe it, Mr. Chandler, but I've never seen this wonderful lodger. Ellen keeps him to herself, that she does. If I was father I'd be jealous!"

Both men laughed. Ellen? No, the idea was too funny.

CHAPTER XII

"All I can say is, I think Daisy ought to go. One can't always do just what one wants to do—not in this world, at any rate!"

Mrs. Bunting did not seem to be addressing anyone in particular, though both her husband and her stepdaughter were in the room. She was standing by the table, staring straight before her, and as she spoke she avoided looking at either Bunting or Daisy. There was in her voice a tone of cross decision, of thin finality, with which they were both acquainted, and to which each listener knew the other would have to bow.

There was silence for a moment, then Daisy broke out passionately, "I don't see why I should go if I don't want to!" she cried. "You'll allow I've been useful to you, Ellen? 'Tisn't even as if you was quite well——"

"I am quite well—perfectly well!" snapped out Mrs. Bunting, and she turned her pale, drawn face, and looked angrily at her stepdaughter.

" 'Tain't often I has a chance of being with you and father." There were tears in Daisy's voice, and Bunting glanced deprecatingly at his wife.

An invitation had come to Daisy—an invitation from her own dead mother's sister, who was housekeeper in a big house in Belgrave Square. "The family" had gone away for the Christmas holidays, and Aunt Margaret—Daisy was her godchild—had begged that her niece might come and spend two or three days with her.

But the girl had already had more than one taste of what life was like in the great gloomy basement of 100 Belgrave Square. Aunt Margaret was one of those old-fashioned servants for whom the modern employer is always sighing. While "the family" were away it was her joy—she regarded it as a privilege—to wash sixty-seven pieces of very valuable china contained in two cabinets in the drawing-room; she also slept in every bed by turns, to keep them all well aired. These were the two duties with which she intended her young niece to assist her, and Daisy's soul sickened at the prospect.

But the matter had to be settled at once. The letter had come an hour ago, containing a stamped telegraph form, and Aunt Margaret was not one to be trifled with.

Since breakfast the three had talked of nothing else, and from the very first Mrs. Bunting had said that Daisy ought to go—that there was no doubt about it, that it did not admit of discussion. But discuss it they all did, and for once Bunting stood up to his wife. But that, as was natural, only made his Ellen harder and more set on her own view.

"What the child says is true," he observed. "It isn't as if you was quite well. You've been took bad twice in the last few days—you can't deny of it, Ellen. Why shouldn't I just take a bus and go over and see Margaret? I'd tell her just how it is. She'd understand, bless you!"

"I won't have you doing nothing of the sort!" cried Mrs. Bunting, speaking almost as passionately as her stepdaughter had done. "Haven't I a right to be ill, haven't I a right to be took bad, aye, and to feel all right again—same as other people?"

Daisy turned round and clasped her hands. "Oh, Ellen!" she cried; "do say that you can't spare me! I don't want to go across to that horrid old dungeon of a place."

"Do as you like," said Mrs. Bunting sullenly. "I'm fair tired of you both! There'll come a day, Daisy, when you'll know, like me, that money is the main thing that matters in this world; and when your Aunt Margaret's left her savings to somebody else just because you wouldn't spend a few days with her this Christmas, then you'll know what it's like to go without—you'll know what a fool you were, and that nothing can't alter it any more!"

And then, with victory actually in her grasp, poor Daisy saw it snatched from her.

"Ellen is right," Bunting said heavily. "Money does matter—a terrible deal—though I never thought to hear Ellen say 'twas the only thing that mattered. But 'twould be foolish—very, very foolish, my girl, to offend your Aunt Margaret. It'll only be two days after all—two days isn't a very long time."

But Daisy did not hear her father's last words. She had already rushed from the room, and gone down to the kitchen to hide her childish tears of disappointment—the childish tears which came because she was beginning to be a woman, with a woman's natural instinct for building her own human nest.

Aunt Margaret was not one to tolerate the comings of any strange young man, and she had a peculiar dislike to the police.

"Who'd ever have thought she'd have minded as much as that!" Bunting looked across at Ellen deprecatingly; already his heart was misgiving him.

"It's plain enough why she's become so fond of us all of a sudden," said Mrs. Bunting sarcastically. And as her husband stared at her uncomprehendingly, she added, in a tantalising tone, "as plain as the nose on your face, my man."

"What d'you mean?" he said. "I daresay I'm a bit slow, Ellen, but I really don't know what you'd be at?"

"Don't you remember telling me before Daisy came here that Joe Chandler had become sweet on her last summer? I thought it only foolishness then, but I've come round to your view—that's all."

Bunting nodded his head slowly. Yes, Joe had got into the way of coming very often, and there had been the expedition to that gruesome Scotland Yard museum, but somehow he, Bunting, had been so interested in the Avenger murders that he hadn't thought of Joe in any other connection—not this time, at any rate.

"And do you think Daisy likes him?" There was an unwonted tone of excitement, of tenderness, in Bunting's voice.

His wife looked over at him; and a thin smile, not an unkindly smile by any means, lit up her pale face. "I've never been one to prophesy," she answered deliberately. "But this I don't mind telling you, Bunting—Daisy'll have plenty o' time to get tired of Joe Chandler before they two are dead. Mark my words!"

"Well, she might do worse," said Bunting ruminatingly. "He's as steady as God makes them, and he's already earning thirty-two shillings a week. But I wonder how Old Aunt'd like the notion? I don't see her parting with Daisy before she must."

"I wouldn't let no old aunt interfere with me about such a thing as that!" cried Mrs. Bunting. "No, not for millions of gold!" And Bunting looked at her in silent wonder. Ellen was singing a very different tune now to what she'd sung a few minutes ago, when she was so keen about the girl going to Belgrave Square.

"If she still seems upset while she's having her dinner," said his wife suddenly, "well, you just wait till I've gone out for something, and then you just say to her, 'Absence makes the heart grow fonder'—just that, and nothing more! She'll take it from you. And I shouldn't be surprised if it comforted her quite a lot."

"For the matter of that, there's no reason why Joe Chandler shouldn't go over and see her there," said Bunting hesitatingly.

"Oh, yes, there is," said Mrs. Bunting, smiling shrewdly. "Plenty of reason. Daisy'll be a very foolish girl if she allows her aunt to know any of her secrets. I've only seen that woman once, but I know exactly the sort Margaret is. She's just waiting for Old Aunt to drop off, and then she'll want to have Daisy herself—to wait on her, like. She'd turn quite nasty if she thought there was a young fellow what stood in her way."

She glanced at the clock, the pretty little eight-day clock which had been a wedding present from a kind friend of her last mistress. It had mysteriously disappeared during their time of trouble, and had as mysteriously reappeared three or four days after Mr. Sleuth's arrival.

"I've time to go out with that telegram," she said briskly—somehow she felt better, different to what she had done the last few days—"and then it'll be done. It's no good having more words about it, and I expect we should have plenty more words if I wait till the child comes upstairs again."

She did not speak unkindly, and Bunting looked at her rather wonderingly. Ellen very seldom spoke of Daisy as "the child"—in fact, he could only remember her having done so once before, and that was a long time ago. They had been talking over their future life together, and she had said, very solemnly, "Bunting, I promise I will do my duty—as much as lies in my power, that is—by the child."

But Ellen had not had much opportunity of doing her duty by Daisy. As not infrequently happens with the duties that we are willing to do, that particular duty had been taken over by someone else who had no mind to let it go.

"What shall I do if Mr. Sleuth rings?" asked Bunting, rather nervously. It was the first time since the lodger had come to them that Ellen had offered to go out in the morning.

She hesitated. In her anxiety to have the matter of Daisy settled, she had forgotten Mr. Sleuth. Strange that she should have done so—strange, and, to herself, very comfortable and pleasant.

"Oh, well, you can just go up and knock at the door and say I'll be back in a few minutes—that I had to go out with a message. He's quite a reasonable gentleman."

She went into the back room to put on her bonnet and thick jacket, for it was very cold—getting colder every minute.

As she stood, buttoning her gloves—she wouldn't have gone out untidy for the world—Bunting suddenly came across to her. "Give us a kiss, old girl," he said. And his wife turned up her face.

"One 'ud think it was catching!" she said, but there was a lilt in her voice.

"So it is," Bunting briefly answered. "Didn't that old cook get married just after us? She'd never 'a thought of it if it hadn't been for you!"

But once she was out, walking along the damp, uneven pavement, Mr. Sleuth revenged himself for his landlady's temporary forgetfulness.

During the last two days the lodger had been queer, odder than usual, unlike himself, or, rather, very much as he had been some ten days ago, just before that double murder had taken place. . . .

The night before, while Daisy was telling all about the dreadful place to which Joe Chandler had taken her and her father, Mrs. Bunting had heard Mr. Sleuth moving about overhead, restlessly walking up and down his sitting-room. And later, when she took up his supper, she had listened a moment outside the door, while he read aloud some of the texts his soul delighted in—terrible texts telling of the grim joys attendant on revenge.

Mrs. Bunting was so absorbed in her thoughts, so possessed with the curious personality of her lodger, that she did not look where she was going, and suddenly a young woman bumped up against her.

She started violently and looked round, dazed, as the young person muttered a word of apology; then she again fell into deep thought.

It was a good thing Daisy was going away for a few days; it made the problem of Mr. Sleuth and his queer ways less disturbing. She, Ellen, was sorry she had spoken so sharp-like to the girl, but after all it wasn't wonderful that she had been snappy. This last night she had hardly slept at all. Instead, she had lain awake listening—and there is nothing so tiring as to lie awake listening for a sound that never comes.

The house had remained so still you could have heard a pin drop. Mr. Sleuth, lying snug in his nice warm bed upstairs, had not stirred. Had he stirred his land-lady was bound to have heard him, for his bed was, as we know, just above hers. No, during those long hours of darkness Daisy's light, regular breathing was all that had fallen on Mrs. Bunting's ears.

And then her mind switched off Mr. Sleuth. She made a determined effort to expel him, to toss him, as it were, out of her thoughts. . . .

It seemed strange that The Avenger had stayed his hand, for, as Joe had said only last evening, it was full time that he should again turn that awful, mysterious searchlight of his on himself. Mrs. Bunting always visioned The Avenger as a black shadow in the centre of a bright blinding light—but the shadow had no form or definite substance. Sometimes he looked like one thing, sometimes like another. . . .

Mrs. Bunting had now come to the corner which led up the street where there was a Post Office. But instead of turning sharp to the left she stopped short for a minute.

There had suddenly come over her a feeling of horrible self-rebuke and even self-loathing. It was dreadful that she, of all women, should have longed to hear that another murder had been committed last night!

Yet such was the shameful fact. She had listened all through breakfast hoping to hear the dread news being shouted outside; yes, and more or less during the long discussion which had followed on the receipt of Margaret's letter she had been hoping—hoping against hope—that those dreadful triumphant shouts of the newspaper-sellers still might come echoing down the Marylebone Road. And yet, hypocrite that she was, she had reproved Bunting when he had expressed, not disappointment exactly—but, well, surprise, that nothing had happened last night.

Now her mind switched off to Joe Chandler. Strange to think how afraid she had been of that young man! She was no longer afraid of him, or hardly at all. He was dotty—that's what was the matter with him, dotty with love for rosy-cheeked, blue-eyed little Daisy. Anything might now go on, right under Joe Chandler's very nose—but, bless you, he'd never see it!

Last summer, when this affair, this nonsense of young Chandler and Daisy had begun, she had had very little patience with it all. In fact, the memory of the way Joe had gone on then, the tiresome way he would be always dropping in, had been one reason (though not the most important reason of all) why she had felt so terribly put about at the idea of the girl coming again. But now? Well, now she had become quite tolerant, quite kindly—at any rate as far as Joe Chandler was concerned.

She wondered why.

Still, 'twouldn't do Joe a bit of harm not to see the girl for a couple of days. In fact, 'twould be a very good thing, for then he'd think of Daisy—think of her to the exclusion of all else. Absence does make the heart grow fonder—at first, at any rate. Mrs. Bunting was well aware of that. During the long course of hers and Bunting's mild courting, they'd been separated for about three months, and it was that three months which had made up her mind for her. She had got so used to Bunting that she couldn't do without him, and she had felt—oddest fact of all—acutely, miserably jealous. But she hadn't let him know that—no fear!

Of course, Joe mustn't neglect his job—that would never do. But what a good thing it was, after all, that he wasn't like some of those detective chaps that are written about in stories—the sort of chaps that know everything, see everything, guess everything—even when there isn't anything to see, or know, or guess!

Why, to take only one little fact—Joe Chandler had never shown the slightest curiosity about their lodger. . . .

Mrs. Bunting pulled herself together with a start, and hurried quickly on. Bunting would begin to wonder what had happened to her.

She went into the Post Office and handed the form to the young woman without a word. Margaret, a sensible woman, who was accustomed to manage other people's affairs, had even written out the words: "Will be with you to tea. —Daisy."

It was a comfort to have the thing settled once for all. If anything horrible was going to happen in the next two or three days—it was just as well Daisy shouldn't be at home. Not that there was any *real* danger that anything would happen,—Mrs. Bunting felt sure of that.

By this time she was out in the street again, and she began mentally counting up the number of murders The Avenger had committed. Nine, or was it ten? Surely by now The Avenger must be avenged? Surely by now, if—as that writer in the newspaper had suggested—he was a quiet, blameless gentleman living in the West End, whatever vengeance he had to wreak, must be satisfied?

She began hurrying homewards; it wouldn't do for the lodger to ring before she had got back. Bunting would never know how to manage Mr. Sleuth, especially if Mr. Sleuth was in one of his queer moods.

Mrs. Bunting put the key into the front door lock and passed into the house. Then her heart stood still with fear and terror. There came the sound of voices—of voices she thought she did not know—in the sitting-room.

She opened the door, and then drew a long breath. It was only Joe Chandler— Joe, Daisy, and Bunting, talking together. They stopped rather guiltily as she came in, but not before she had heard Chandler utter the words: "That don't mean nothing! I'll just run out and send another saying you won't come, Miss Daisy."

And then the strangest smile came over Mrs. Bunting's face. There had fallen on her ear the still distant, but unmistakable, shouts which betokened that something *had* happened last night—something which made it worth while for the newspaper-sellers to come crying down the Marylebone Road.

"Well?" she said a little breathlessly. "Well, Joe? I suppose you've brought us news? I suppose there's been another?"

He looked at her, surprised. "No, that there hasn't, Mrs. Bunting—not as far as I know, that is. Oh, you're thinking of those newspaper chaps? They've got to cry out something," he grinned. "You wouldn't 'a thought folk was so bloodthirsty. They're just shouting out that there's been an arrest; but we don't take no stock of that. It's a Scotchman what gave himself up last night at Dorking. He'd been drinking, and was a-pitying of himself. Why, since this business began, there's been about twenty arrests, but they've all come to nothing."

"Why, Ellen, you looks quite sad, quite disappointed," said Bunting jokingly. "Come to think of it, it's high time The Avenger *was* at work again." He laughed as he made his grim joke. Then turned to young Chandler: "Well, *you'll* be glad when it's all over, my lad."

"Glad in a way," said Chandler unwillingly. "But one 'ud have liked to have caught him. One doesn't like to know such a creature's at large, now, does one?"

Mrs. Bunting had taken off her bonnet and jacket. "I must just go and see about Mr. Sleuth's breakfast," she said in a weary, dispirited voice, and left them there.

She felt disappointed, and very, very depressed. As to the plot which had been hatching when she came in, that had no chance of success; Bunting would never dare let Daisy send out another telegram contradicting the first. Besides, Daisy's stepmother shrewdly suspected that by now the girl herself wouldn't care to do such a thing. Daisy had plenty of sense tucked away somewhere in her pretty little head. If it ever became her fate to live as a married woman in London, it would be best to stay on the right side of Aunt Margaret.

And when she came into her kitchen the stepmother's heart became very soft, for Daisy had got everything beautifully ready. In fact, there was nothing to do but to boil Mr. Sleuth's two eggs. Feeling suddenly more cheerful than she had felt of late, Mrs. Bunting took the tray upstairs.

"As it was rather late, I didn't wait for you to ring, sir," she said.

And the lodger looked up from the table where, as usual, he was studying with painful, almost agonising intentness, the Book. "Quite right, Mrs. Bunting—quite right! I have been pondering over the command, 'Work while it is yet light.'"

"Yes, sir?" she said, and a queer, cold feeling stole over her heart. "Yes, sir?"

"'The spirit is willing, but the flesh—the flesh is weak,'" said Mr. Sleuth, with a heavy sigh.

"You studies too hard, and too long—that's what's ailing you, sir," said Mr. Sleuth's landlady suddenly.

When Mrs. Bunting went down again she found that a great deal had been settled in her absence; among other things, that Joe Chandler was going to escort Miss Daisy across to Belgrave Square. He could carry Daisy's modest bag, and if they wanted to ride instead of walk, why, they could take the bus from Baker Street Station to Victoria—that would land them very near Belgrave Square.

But Daisy seemed quite willing to walk; she hadn't had a walk, she declared, for a long, long time—and then she blushed rosy red, and even her stepmother had to admit to herself that Daisy was very nice-looking, not at all the sort of girl who ought to be allowed to go about the London streets by herself.

CHAPTER XIII

Daisy's father and stepmother stood side by side at the front door, watching the girl and young Chandler walk off into the darkness.

A yellow pall of fog had suddenly descended on London, and Joe had come a full half-hour before they expected him, explaining, rather lamely, that it was the fog which had brought him so soon.

"If we was to have waited much longer, perhaps, 'twouldn't have been possible to walk a yard," he explained, and they had accepted, silently, his explanation.

"I hope it's quite safe sending her off like that?"

Bunting looked deprecatingly at his wife. She had already told him more than once that he was too fussy about Daisy, that about his daughter he was like an old hen with her last chicken.

"She's safer than she would be with you or me. She couldn't have a smarter young fellow to look after her."

"It'll be awful thick at Hyde Park Corner," said Bunting. "It's always worse there than anywhere else. If I was Joe I'd 'a taken her by the Underground Railway to Victoria—that 'ud been the best way, considering the weather 'tis."

"They don't think anything of the weather, bless you!" said his wife. "They'll walk and walk as long as there's a glimmer left for 'em to steer by. Daisy's just been pining to have a walk with that young chap. I wonder you didn't notice how disappointed they both were when you was so set on going along with them to that horrid place."

"D'you really mean that, Ellen?" Bunting looked upset. "I understood Joe to say he liked my company."

"Oh, did you?" said Mrs. Bunting dryly. "I expect he liked it just about as much as we liked the company of that old cook who would go out with us when *we* was courting. It always was a wonder to me how that woman could force herself upon two people who didn't want her."

"But I'm Daisy's father, and an old friend of Chandler," said Bunting remonstratingly. "I'm quite different from that cook. She was nothing to us, and we was nothing to her."

"She'd have liked to be something to you, I make no doubt," observed his Ellen, shaking her head, and her husband smiled, a little foolishly.

By this time they were back in their nice, cosy sitting-room, and a feeling of not altogether unpleasant lassitude stole over Mrs. Bunting. It was a comfort to have Daisy out of her way for a bit. The girl, in some ways, was very wide awake and inquisitive, and she had early betrayed what her stepmother thought to be a very unseemly and silly curiosity concerning the lodger. "You might just let me have one peep at him, Ellen?" she had pleaded, only that morning. But Ellen had shaken her head. "No, that I won't! He's a very quiet gentleman; but he knows exactly what he likes, and he don't like anyone but me waiting on him. Why, even your father's hardly seen him."

But that, naturally, had only increased Daisy's desire to view Mr. Sleuth.

There was another reason why Mrs. Bunting was glad that her stepdaughter had gone away for two days. During her absence young Chandler was far less likely to haunt them in the way he had taken to doing lately, the more so that, in spite of what she had said to her husband, Mrs. Bunting felt sure that Daisy would ask Joe Chandler to call at Belgrave Square. 'Twouldn't be human nature—at any rate, not girlish human nature—not to do so, even if Joe's coming did anger Aunt Margaret.

Yes, it was pretty safe that with Daisy away they, the Buntings, would be rid of that young chap for a bit, and that would be a good thing.

When Daisy wasn't there to occupy the whole of his attention, Mrs. Bunting felt queerly afraid of Chandler. After all, he was a detective—it was his job to be always nosing about, trying to find out things. And, though she couldn't fairly say to herself that he had done much of that sort of thing in her house, he might start doing it any minute. And then—then—where would she, and—and Mr. Sleuth, be?

She thought of the bottle of red ink—of the leather bag which must be hidden somewhere—and her heart almost stopped beating. Those were the sort of things which, in the stories Bunting was so fond of reading, always led to the detection of famous criminals. . . .

Mr. Sleuth's bell for tea rang that afternoon far earlier than usual. The fog had probably misled him, and made him think it later than it was.

When she went up, "I would like a cup of tea now, and just one piece of bread-and-butter," the lodger said wearily. "I don't feel like having anything else this afternoon."

"It's a horrible day," Mrs. Bunting observed, in a cheerier voice than usual. "No wonder you don't feel hungry, sir. And then it isn't so very long since you had your dinner, is it?"

"No," he said absently. "No, it isn't, Mrs. Bunting."

She went down, made the tea, and brought it up again. And then, as she came into the room, she uttered an exclamation of sharp dismay.

Mr. Sleuth was dressed for going out. He was wearing his long Inverness cloak, and his queer old high hat lay on the table, ready for him to put on.

"You're never going out this afternoon, sir?" she asked falteringly. "Why, the fog's awful; you can't see a yard ahead of you!"

Unknown to herself, Mrs. Bunting's voice had risen almost to a scream. She moved back, still holding the tray, and stood between the door and her lodger, as if she meant to bar his way—to erect between Mr. Sleuth and the dark, foggy world outside a living barrier.

"The weather never affects me at all," he said sullenly; and he looked at her with so wild and pleading a look in his eyes that, slowly, reluctantly, she moved aside. As she did so she noticed for the first time that Mr. Sleuth held something in his right hand. It was the key of the chiffonnier cupboard. He had been on his way there when her coming in had disturbed him.

"It's very kind of you to be so concerned about me," he stammered, "but—but, Mrs. Bunting, you must excuse me if I say that I do not welcome such solicitude. I prefer to be left alone. I—I cannot stay in your house if I feel that my comings and goings are watched—spied upon."

She pulled herself together. "No one spies upon you, sir," she said, with considerable dignity. "I've done my best to satisfy you——"

"You have—you have!" he spoke in a distressed, apologetic tone. "But you spoke just now as if you were trying to prevent my doing what I wish to do—indeed, what I have to do. For years I have been misunderstood—persecuted"—he waited a moment, then in a hollow voice added the one word, "tortured! Do not tell me that you are going to add yourself to the number of my tormentors, Mrs. Bunting?"

She stared at him helplessly. "Don't you be afraid I'll ever be that, sir. I only spoke as I did because—well, sir, because I thought it really wasn't safe for a gentleman to go out this afternoon. Why, there's hardly anyone about, though we're so near Christmas."

He walked across to the window and looked out. "The fog is clearing some-what, Mrs. Bunting," but there was no relief in his voice, rather was there disappointment and dread.

Plucking up courage, she followed him. Yes, Mr. Sleuth was right. The fog was lifting—rolling off in that sudden, mysterious way in which local fogs sometimes do lift in London.

He turned sharply from the window. "Our conversation has made me forget an important thing, Mrs. Bunting. I should be glad if you would just leave out a glass of milk and some bread-and-butter for me this evening. I shall not require supper when I come in, for after my walk I shall probably go straight upstairs to carry through a very difficult experiment."

"Very good, sir." And then Mrs. Bunting left the lodger.

But when she found herself downstairs in the fog-laden hall, for it had drifted in as she and her husband had stood at the door seeing Daisy off, instead of going in to Bunting she did a very odd thing—a thing she had never thought of doing in her life before. She pressed her hot forehead against the cool bit of looking-glass set into the hat-and-umbrella stand. "I don't know what to do!" she moaned to herself, and then, "I can't bear it! I can't bear it!"

But though she felt that her secret suspense and trouble was becoming intolerable, the one way in which she could have ended her misery never occurred to Mrs. Bunting.

In the long history of crime it has very, very seldom happened that a woman has betrayed one who has taken refuge with her. The timorous and cautious woman has not infrequently hunted a human being fleeing from his pursuer from her door, but she has not revealed the fact that he was ever there. In fact, it may almost be said that such betrayal has never taken place unless the betrayer has been actuated by love of gain, or by a longing for revenge. So far, perhaps because she is subject rather than citizen, her duty as a component part of civilised society weighs but lightly on woman's shoulders.

And then—and then, in a sort of way, Mrs. Bunting had become attached to Mr. Sleuth. A wan smile would sometimes light up his sad face when he saw her come in with one of his meals, and when this happened Mrs. Bunting felt pleased—pleased and vaguely touched. In between those—those dreadful events outside, which filled her with such suspicion, such anguish and such suspense, she never felt any fear, only pity, for Mr. Sleuth.

Often and often, when lying wide awake at night, she turned over the strange problem in her mind. After all, the lodger must have lived *somewhere* during his forty-odd years of life. She did not even know if Mr. Sleuth had any brothers or sisters; friends she knew he had none. But, however odd and eccentric he was, he had evidently, or so she supposed, led a quiet, undistinguished kind of life, till—till now.

What had made him alter all of a sudden—if, that is, he had altered? That was what Mrs. Bunting was always debating fitfully with herself; and, what was more, and very terribly, to the point, having altered, why should he not in time go back to what he evidently had been—that is, a blameless, quiet gentleman?

If only he would! If only he would!

As she stood in the hall, cooling her hot forehead, all these thoughts, these hopes and fears, jostled at lightning speed through her brain.

She remembered what young Chandler had said the other day—that there had never been, in the history of the world, so strange a murderer as The Avenger had proved himself to be.

She and Bunting, aye, and little Daisy too, had hung, fascinated, on Joe's words, as he had told them of other famous series of murders which had taken place in the past, not only in England, but abroad—especially abroad.

One woman, whom all the people round her believed to be a kind, respectable soul, had poisoned no fewer than fifteen people in order to get their insurance money. Then there had been the terrible tale of an apparently respectable, contented innkeeper and his wife, who, living at the entrance to a wood, killed all those humble travellers who took shelter under their roof, simply for their clothes, and any valuables they possessed. But in all those stories the murderer or murderers always had a very strong motive, the motive being, in almost every case, a wicked lust for gold.

At last, after having passed her handkerchief over her forehead, she went into the room where Bunting was sitting smoking his pipe.

"The fog's lifting a bit," she said in an ill-assured voice. "I hope that by this time Daisy and that Joe Chandler are right out of it."

But the other shook his head silently. "No such luck!" he said briefly. "You don't know what it's like in Hyde Park, Ellen. I expect 'twill soon be just as heavy here as 'twas half an hour ago!"

She wandered over to the window, and pulled the curtain back. "Quite a lot of people have come out, anyway," she observed.

"There's a fine Christmas show in the Edgware Road. I was thinking of asking if you wouldn't like to go along there with me."

"No," she said dully. "I'm quite content to stay at home."

She was listening—listening for the sounds which would betoken that the lodger was coming downstairs.

At last she heard the cautious, stuffless tread of his rubber-soled shoes shuffling along the hall. But Bunting only woke to the fact when the front door shut to.

"That's never Mr. Sleuth going out?" He turned on his wife, startled. "Why, the poor gentleman'll come to harm—that he will! One has to be wide awake on an evening like this. I hope he hasn't taken any of his money out with him."

" 'Tisn't the first time Mr. Sleuth's been out in a fog," said Mrs. Bunting sombrely.

Somehow she couldn't help uttering these over-true words. And then she turned, eager and half frightened, to see how Bunting had taken what she said.

But he looked quite placid, as if he had hardly heard her. "We don't get the good old fogs we used to get—not what people used to call 'London particulars.' I expect the lodger feels like Mrs. Crowley—I've often told you about her, Ellen?"

Mrs. Bunting nodded.

Mrs. Crowley had been one of Bunting's ladies, one of those he had liked best—a cheerful, jolly lady, who used often to give her servants what she called a treat. It was seldom the kind of treat they would have chosen for themselves, but still they appreciated her kind thought.

"Mrs. Crowley used to say," went on Bunting, in his slow, dogmatic way, "that she never minded how bad the weather was in London, so long as it was London and not the country. Mr. Crowley, he liked the country best, but Mrs. Crowley always felt dull-like there. Fog never kept her from going out—no, that it didn't. She wasn't a bit afraid. But"—he turned round and looked at his wife—"I am a bit surprised at Mr. Sleuth. I should have thought him a timid kind of gentleman——"

He waited a moment, and she felt forced to answer him.

"I wouldn't exactly call him timid," she said, in a low voice, "but he is very quiet, certainly. That's why he dislikes going out when there are a lot of people bustling about the streets. I don't suppose he'll be out long."

She hoped with all her soul that Mr. Sleuth would be in very soon—that he would be daunted by the now increasing gloom.

Somehow she did not feel she could sit still for very long. She got up, and went over to the farthest window.

The fog had lifted, certainly. She could see the lamp-lights on the other side of the Marylebone Road, glimmering redly; and shadowy figures were hurrying past, mostly making their way towards the Edgware Road, to see the Christmas shops.

At last, to his wife's relief, Bunting got up too. He went over to the cupboard where he kept his little store of books, and took one out.

"I think I'll read a bit," he said. "Seems a long time since I've looked at a book. The papers was so jolly interesting for a bit, but now there's nothing in 'em."

His wife remained silent. She knew what he meant. A good many days had gone by since the last two Avenger murders, and the papers had very little to say about them that they hadn't said in different language a dozen times before.

She went into her bedroom and came back with a bit of plain sewing.

Mrs. Bunting was fond of sewing, and Bunting liked to see her so engaged. Since Mr. Sleuth had come to be their lodger she had not had much time for that sort of work.

It was funny how quiet the house was without either Daisy, or—or the lodger, in it.

At last she let her needle remain idle, and the bit of cambric slipped down on her knee, while she listened, longingly, for Mr. Sleuth's return home.

And as the minutes sped by she fell to wondering with a painful wonder if she would ever see her lodger again, for, from what she knew of Mr. Sleuth, Mrs. Bunting felt sure that if he got into any kind of—well, trouble outside, he would never betray where he had lived during the last few weeks.

No, in such a case the lodger would disappear in as sudden a way as he had come. And Bunting would never suspect, would never know, until, perhaps—God, what a horrible thought!—a picture published in some newspaper might bring a certain dreadful fact to Bunting's knowledge.

But if that happened—if that unthinkably awful thing came to pass, she made up her mind, here and now, never to say anything. She also would pretend to be amazed, shocked, unutterably horrified at the astounding revelation.

CHAPTER XIV

"There he is at last, and I'm glad of it, Ellen. 'Tain't a night you would wish a dog to be out in."

Bunting's voice was full of relief, but he did not turn round and look at his wife as he spoke; instead, he continued to read the evening paper he held in his hand.

He was still close to the fire, sitting back comfortably in his nice arm-chair. He looked very well—well and ruddy. Mrs. Bunting stared across at him with a touch of sharp envy, nay, more, of resentment. And this was very curious, for she was, in her own dry way, very fond of Bunting.

"You needn't feel so nervous about him; Mr. Sleuth can look out for himself all right."

Bunting laid the paper he had been reading down on his knee. "I can't think why he wanted to go out in such weather," he said impatiently.

"Well, it's none of your business, Bunting, now, is it?"

"No, that's true enough. Still, 'twould be a very bad thing for us if anything happened to him. This lodger's the first bit of luck we've had for a terrible long time, Ellen."

Mrs. Bunting moved a little impatiently in her high chair. She remained silent for a moment. What Bunting had said was too obvious to be worth answering. Also she was listening, following in imagination her lodger's quick, singularly quiet progress—"stealthy" she called it to herself—through the fog-filled, lamp-lit hall. Yes, now he was going up the staircase. What was that Bunting was saying——?

"It isn't safe for decent folk to be out in such weather—no, that it ain't, not unless they have something to do that won't wait till to-morrow." The speaker was looking straight into his wife's narrow, colourless face. Bunting was an obstinate man, and liked to prove himself right. "I've a good mind to speak to him about it, that I have! He ought to be told that it isn't safe—not for the sort of man he is—to be wandering about the streets at night. I read you out the accidents in *Lloyd's*—shocking, they were, and all brought about by the fog! And then, that horrid monster 'ull soon be at his work again——"

"Monster?" repeated Mrs. Bunting absently.

She was trying to hear the lodger's footsteps overhead. She was very curious to know whether he had gone into his nice sitting-room, or straight upstairs, to that cold experiment-room, as he now always called it.

But her husband went on as if he had not heard her, and she gave up trying to listen to what was going on above.

"It wouldn't be very pleasant to run up against such a party as that in the fog, eh, Ellen?" He spoke as if the notion had a certain pleasant thrill in it after all.

"What stuff you do talk!" said Mrs. Bunting sharply. And then she got up. Her husband's remarks had disturbed her. Why couldn't they talk of something pleasant when they did have a quiet bit of time together?

Bunting looked down again at his paper, and she moved quietly about the room. Very soon it would be time for supper, and to-night she was going to cook her husband a nice piece of toasted cheese. That fortunate man, as she was fond of telling him, with mingled contempt and envy, had the digestion of an ostrich, and yet he was rather fanciful, as gentlemen's servants who have lived in good places often are.

Yes, Bunting was very lucky in the matter of his digestion. Mrs. Bunting prided herself on having a nice mind, and she would never have allowed an unrefined word—such a word as "stomach," for instance, to say nothing of an even plainer term—to pass her lips, except, of course, to a doctor in a sick-room.

Mr. Sleuth's landlady did not go down at once into her cold kitchen; instead, with a sudden furtive movement, she opened the door leading into her bedroom, and then, closing the door quietly, stepped back into the darkness, and stood motionless, listening.

At first she heard nothing, but gradually there stole on her listening ears the sound of someone moving softly about in the room just overhead, that is, in Mr. Sleuth's bedroom. But, try as she might, it was impossible for her to guess what the lodger was doing.

At last she heard him open the door leading out on the little landing. She could hear the stairs creaking. That meant, no doubt, that Mr. Sleuth would pass the rest of the evening in the cheerless room above. He hadn't spent any time up there for quite a long while—in fact, not for nearly ten days. 'Twas odd he chose to-night, when it was so foggy, to carry out an experiment.

She groped her way to a chair and sat down. She felt very tired—strangely tired, as if she had gone through some great physical exertion.

Yes, it was true that Mr. Sleuth had brought her and Bunting luck, and it was wrong, very wrong, of her ever to forget that.

As she sat there she also reminded herself, and not for the first time, what the lodger's departure would mean. It would almost certainly mean ruin; just as his staying meant all sorts of good things, of which physical comfort was the least. If Mr. Sleuth stayed on with them, as he showed every intention of doing, it meant respectability, and, above all, security.

Mrs. Bunting thought of Mr. Sleuth's money. He never received a letter, and yet he must have some kind of income—so much was clear. She supposed he went and drew his money, in sovereigns, out of a bank as he required it.

Her mind swung round, consciously, deliberately, away from Mr. Sleuth.

The Avenger? What a strange name! Again she assured herself that there would come a time when The Avenger, whoever he was, must feel satiated; when he would feel himself to be, so to speak, avenged.

To go back to Mr. Sleuth; it was lucky that the lodger seemed so pleased, not only with the rooms, but with his landlord and landlady—indeed, there was no real reason why Mr. Sleuth should ever wish to leave such nice lodgings.

Mrs. Bunting suddenly stood up. She made a strong effort, and shook off her awful sense of apprehension and unease. Feeling for the handle of the door giving into the passage she turned it, and then, with light, firm steps, she went down into the kitchen.

When they had first taken the house, the basement had been made by her care, if not into a pleasant, then, at any rate, into a very clean place. She had had it whitewashed, and against the still white walls the gas-stove loomed up, a great square of black iron and bright steel. It was a large gas-stove, the kind for which one pays four shillings a quarter rent to the gas company, and here, in the kitchen, there was no foolish shilling-in-the-slot arrangement. Mrs. Bunting was too shrewd a woman to have anything to do with that kind of business. There was a proper gas-meter, and she paid for what she consumed after she had consumed it.

Putting her candle down on the well-scrubbed wooden table, she turned up the gas-jet, and blew out the candle.

Then, lighting one of the gas-rings, she put a frying-pan on the stove, and once more her mind reverted, as if in spite of herself, to Mr. Sleuth. Never had there been a more confiding or trusting gentleman than the lodger, and yet in some ways he was so secret, so—so peculiar.

She thought of the bag—that bag which had rumbled about so queerly in the chiffonnier. Something seemed to tell her that to-night the lodger had taken that bag out with him.

And then she thrust away the thought of the bag almost violently from her mind, and went back to the more agreeable thought of Mr. Sleuth's income, and of how little trouble he gave. Of course, the lodger was eccentric, otherwise he wouldn't be their lodger at all—he would be living in quite a different sort of way with some of his relations, or with a friend in his own class.

While these thoughts galloped disconnectedly through her mind, Mrs. Bunting went on with her cooking, preparing the cheese, cutting it up into little shreds, carefully measuring out the butter, doing everything, as was always her way, with a certain delicate and cleanly precision.

And then, while in the middle of toasting the bread on which was to be poured the melted cheese, she suddenly heard sounds which startled her, made her feel uncomfortable.

Shuffling, hesitating steps were creaking down the house.

She looked up and listened.

Surely the lodger was not going out again into the cold and foggy night—going out, as he had done the other evening, for a second time? But no; the sounds she heard, the sounds of now familiar footsteps, did not continue down the passage leading to the front door.

Instead—— Why, what was this she heard now? She began to listen so intently that the bread she was holding at the end of the toasting-fork grew quite black. With a start she became aware that this was so, and she frowned, vexed with herself. That came of not attending to one's work.

Mr. Sleuth was evidently about to do what he had never yet done. He was coming down into the kitchen.

Nearer and nearer came the thudding sounds, treading heavily on the kitchen stairs, and Mrs. Bunting's heart began to beat, as if in response. She put out the flame of the gas-ring, unheedful of the fact that the cheese would stiffen and spoil in the cold air.

Then she turned and faced the door.

There came a fumbling at the handle, and a moment later the door opened, and revealed, as she had at once known and feared it would do, the lodger.

Mr. Sleuth looked even odder than usual. He was clad in a plaid dressing-gown, which she had never seen him wear before, though she knew that he had purchased it not long after his arrival. In his hand was a lighted candle.

When he saw the kitchen all lighted up, and the woman standing in it, the lodger looked inexplicably taken aback, almost aghast.

"Yes, sir? What can I do for you, sir? I hope you didn't ring, sir?"

Mrs. Bunting held her ground in front of the stove. Mr. Sleuth had no business to come like this into her kitchen, and she intended to let him know that such was her view.

"No, I—I didn't ring," he stammered awkwardly. "The truth is, I didn't know you were here, Mrs. Bunting. Please excuse my costume. My gas-stove has gone wrong, or, rather, that shilling-in-the-slot arrangement has done so. So I came down to see if you had a gas-stove. I am going to ask you to allow me to use it to-night for an important experiment I wish to make."

Mrs. Bunting's heart was beating quickly—quickly. She felt horribly troubled, unnaturally so. Why couldn't Mr. Sleuth's experiment wait till the morning? She stared at him dubiously, but there was that in his face that made her at once afraid and pitiful. It was a wild, eager, imploring look.

"Oh, certainly, sir; but you will find it very cold down here."

"It seems most pleasantly warm," he observed, his voice full of relief, "warm and cosy, after my cold room upstairs."

Warm and cosy? Mrs. Bunting stared at him in amazement. Nay, even that cheerless room at the top of the house must be far warmer and more cosy than this cold underground kitchen could possibly be.

"I'll make you a fire, sir. We never use the grate, but it's in perfect order, for the first thing I did after I came into the house was to have the chimney swept. It was terribly dirty. It might have set the house on fire." Mrs. Bunting's house-wifely instincts were roused. "For the matter of that, you ought to have a fire in your bedroom this cold night."

"By no means—I would prefer not. I certainly do not want a fire there. I dislike an open fire, Mrs. Bunting. I thought I had told you as much."

Mr. Sleuth frowned. He stood there, a strange-looking figure, his candle still alight, just inside the kitchen door.

"I shan't be very long, sir. Just about a quarter of an hour. You could come down then. I'll have everything quite tidy for you. Is there anything I can do to help you?"

"I do not require the use of your kitchen yet—thank you all the same, Mrs. Bunting. I shall come down later—altogether later—after you and your husband have gone to bed. But I should be much obliged if you would see that the gas people come to-morrow and put my stove in order. It might be done while I am out. That the shilling-in-the-slot machine should go wrong is very unpleasant. It has upset me greatly."

"Perhaps Bunting could put it right for you, sir. For the matter of that, I could ask him to go up now."

"No, no, I don't want anything of that sort done to-night. Besides, he couldn't put it right. I am something of an expert, Mrs. Bunting, and I have done all I could. The cause of the trouble is quite simple. The machine is choked up with shillings; a very foolish plan, so I always felt it to be."

Mr. Sleuth spoke pettishly, with far more heat than he was wont to speak, but Mrs. Bunting sympathised with him in this matter. She had always suspected that those slot machines were as dishonest as if they were human. It was dreadful, the way they swallowed up the shillings! She had had one once, so she knew.

And as if he were divining her thoughts, Mr. Sleuth walked forward and stared at the stove. "Then you haven't got a slot machine?" he said wonderingly. "I'm very glad of that, for I expect my experiment will take some time. But, of course, I shall pay you something for the use of the stove, Mrs. Bunting."

"Oh, no, sir, I wouldn't think of charging you anything for that. We don't use our stove very much, you know, sir. I'm never in the kitchen a minute longer than I can help this cold weather."

Mrs. Bunting was beginning to feel better. When she was actually in Mr. Sleuth's presence her morbid fears would be lulled, perhaps because his manner almost invariably was gentle and very quiet. But still there came over her an eerie feeling, as, with him preceding her, they made a slow progress to the ground floor.

Once there, the lodger courteously bade his landlady good-night, and proceeded upstairs to his own apartments.

Mrs. Bunting returned to the kitchen. Again she lighted the stove; but she felt unnerved, afraid of she knew not what. As she was cooking the cheese, she tried to concentrate her mind on what she was doing, and on the whole she succeeded. But another part of her mind seemed to be working independently, asking her insistent questions.

The place seemed to her alive with alien presences, and once she caught herself listening—which was absurd, for, of course, she could not hope to hear what Mr. Sleuth was doing two, if not three, flights upstairs. She wondered in what the lodger's experiments consisted. It was odd that she had never been able to discover what it was he really did with that big gas-stove. All she knew was that he used a very high degree of heat.

CHAPTER XV

The Buntings went to bed early that night. But Mrs. Bunting made up her mind to keep awake. She was set upon knowing at what hour of the night the lodger would come down into her kitchen to carry through his experiment, and, above all, she was anxious to know how long he would stay there.

But she had had a long and a very anxious day, and presently she fell asleep.

The church clock hard by struck two, and suddenly Mrs. Bunting awoke. She felt put out, sharply annoyed with herself. How could she have dropped off like that? Mr. Sleuth must have been down and up again hours ago!

Then, gradually, she became aware that there was a faint acrid odour in the room. Elusive, intangible, it yet seemed to encompass her and the snoring man by her side, almost as a vapour might have done.

Mrs. Bunting sat up in bed and sniffed; and then, in spite of the cold, she quietly crept out of her nice, warm bedclothes, and crawled along to the bottom of the bed. When there, Mr. Sleuth's landlady did a very curious thing; she leaned over the brass rail and put her face close to the hinge of the door giving into the hall. Yes, it was from here that this strange, horrible odour was coming; the smell must be very strong in the passage.

As, shivering, she crept back under the bedclothes, she longed to give her sleeping husband a good shake, and in fancy she heard herself saying, "Bunting, get up! There's something strange and dreadful going on downstairs which we ought to know about."

But as she lay there, by her husband's side, listening with painful intentness for the slightest sound, she knew very well that she would do nothing of the sort.

What if the lodger did make a certain amount of mess—a certain amount of smell—in her nice clean kitchen? Was he not—was he not an almost perfect lodger? If they did anything to upset him, where could they ever hope to get another like him?

Three o'clock struck before Mrs. Bunting heard slow, heavy steps creaking up the kitchen stairs. But Mr. Sleuth did not go straight up to his own quarters, as she had expected him to do. Instead, he went to the front door, and, opening it, put on the chain. Then he came past her door, and she thought—but could not be sure—that he sat down on the stairs.

At the end of ten minutes or so she heard him go down the passage again. Very softly he closed the front door. By then she had divined why the lodger had behaved in this funny fashion. He wanted to get the strong, acrid smell of burning—was it of burning wool?—out of the house.

But Mrs. Bunting, lying there in the darkness, listening to the lodger creeping upstairs, felt as if she herself would never get rid of the horrible odour.

Mrs. Bunting felt herself to be all smell.

At last the unhappy woman fell into a deep, troubled sleep; and then she dreamed a most terrible and unnatural dream. Hoarse voices seemed to be shouting in her ear: "The Avenger close here! The Avenger close here!" " 'Orrible murder off the Edgware Road!" "The Avenger at his work again!"

And even in her dream Mrs. Bunting felt angered—angered and impatient. She knew so well why she was being disturbed by this horrid nightmare! It was because of Bunting—Bunting, who could think and talk of nothing else than those frightful murders, in which only morbid and vulgar-minded people took any interest.

Why, even now, in her dream, she could hear her husband speaking to her about it:

"Ellen"—so she heard Bunting murmur in her ear—"Ellen, my dear, I'm just going to get up to get a paper. It's after seven o'clock."

The shouting—nay, worse, the sound of tramping, hurrying feet smote on her shrinking ears. Pushing back her hair off her forehead with both hands, she sat up and listened.

It had been no nightmare, then, but something infinitely worse—reality.

Why couldn't Bunting have lain quiet abed for awhile longer, and let his poor wife go on dreaming? The most awful dream would have been easier to bear than this awakening.

She heard her husband go to the front door, and, as he bought the paper, exchange a few excited words with the newspaper-seller. Then he came back. There was a pause, and she heard him lighting the gas-ring in the sitting-room.

Bunting always made his wife a cup of tea in the morning. He had promised to do this when they first married, and he had never yet broken his word. It was a very little thing and a very usual thing, no doubt, for a kind husband to do, but this morning the knowledge that he was doing it brought tears to Mrs. Bunting's pale blue eyes. This morning he seemed to be rather longer than usual over the job.

When, at last, he came in with the little tray, Bunting found his wife lying with her face to the wall.

"Here's your tea, Ellen," he said, and there was a thrill of eager, nay happy, excitement in his voice.

She turned herself round and sat up. "Well?" she asked. "Well? Why don't you tell me about it?"

"I thought you was asleep," he stammered out. "I thought, Ellen, you never heard nothing."

"How could I have slept through all that din? Of course I heard. Why don't you tell me?"

"I've hardly had time to glance at the paper myself," he said slowly.

"You was reading it just now," she said severely, "for I heard the rustling. You begun reading it before you lit the gas-ring. Don't tell me! What was that they was shouting about the Edgware Road?"

"Well," said Bunting, "as you *do* know, I may as well tell you. The Avenger's moving West—that's what he's doing. Last time 'twas King's Cross—now 'tis the Edgware Road. I said he'd come our way, and he *has* come our way!"

"You just go and get me that paper," she commanded. "I wants to see for myself."

Bunting went into the next room; then he came back and handed her silently the odd-looking, thin little sheet.

"Why, whatever's this?" she asked. "This ain't our paper!"

"'Course not," he answered, a trifle crossly. "It's a special early edition of the *Sun*, just because of The Avenger. Here's the bit about it"—he showed her the exact spot. But she would have found it, even by the comparatively bad light of the gas-jet now flaring over the dressing-table, for the news was printed in large, clear characters:—

"*Once more the murder fiend who chooses to call himself The Avenger has escaped detection. While the whole attention of the police, and of the great army of amateur detectives who are taking an interest in this strange series of atrocious crimes, were concentrating their attention round the East End and King's Cross, he moved swiftly and silently Westward. And, choosing a time when the Edgware Road is at its busiest and most thronged, did another human being to death with lightning-like quickness and savagery.*

"*Within fifty yards of the deserted warehouse yard where he had lured his victim to destruction were passing up and down scores of happy, busy people, intent on their Christmas shopping. Into that cheerful throng he must have plunged within a moment of committing his atrocious crime. And it was only owing to the merest accident that the body was discovered as soon as it was— that is, just after midnight.*

"*Dr. Dowtray, who was called to the spot at once, is of opinion that the woman had been dead at least three hours, if not four. It was at first thought— we were going to say, hoped—that this murder had nothing to do with the series*

which is now puzzling and horrifying the whole of the civilised world. But no—
pinned on the edge of the dead woman's dress was the usual now familiar trian-
gular piece of grey paper—the grimmest visiting card ever designed by the wit of
man! And this time The Avenger has surpassed himself as regards his audacity
and daring—so cold in its maniacal fanaticism and abhorrent wickedness."

All the time that Mrs. Bunting was reading with slow, painful intentness, her husband was looking at her, longing, yet afraid, to burst out with a new idea which he was burning to confide even to his Ellen's unsympathetic ears.

At last, when she had quite finished, she looked up defiantly.

"Haven't you anything better to do than to stare at me like that?" she said irritably. "Murder or no murder, I've got to get up! Go away—do!"

And Bunting went off into the next room.

After he had gone, his wife lay back and closed her eyes.

She tried to think of nothing. Nay, more—so strong, so determined was her will that for a few moments she actually did think of nothing. She felt terribly tired and weak, brain and body both quiescent, as does a person who is recovering from a long, wearing illness.

Presently detached, puerile thoughts drifted across the surface of her mind like little clouds across a summer sky. She wondered if those horrid newspaper men were allowed to shout in Belgrave Square; she wondered if, in that case, Margaret, who was so unlike her brother-in-law, would get up and buy a paper. But no. Margaret was not one to leave her nice warm bed for such a silly reason as that.

Was it to-morrow Daisy was coming back? Yes—to-morrow, not to-day. Well, that was a comfort, at any rate. What amusing things Daisy would be able to tell about her visit to Margaret! The girl had an excellent gift of mimicry. And Margaret, with her precise, funny ways, her perpetual talk about "the family," lent herself to the cruel gift.

And then Mrs. Bunting's mind—her poor, weak, tired mind—wandered off to young Chandler. A funny thing love was, when you came to think of it—which she, Ellen Bunting, didn't often do. There was Joe, a likely young fellow, seeing a lot of young women, and pretty young women, too,—quite as pretty as Daisy, and ten times more artful,—and yet there! He passed them all by, had done so ever since last summer, though you might be sure that they, artful minxes, by no manner of means passed him by,—without giving them a thought! As Daisy wasn't here, he would probably keep away to-day. There was comfort in that thought, too.

And then Mrs. Bunting sat up, and memory returned in a dreadful turgid flood. If Joe *did* come in, she must nerve herself to bear all that—that talk there'd be about The Avenger between him and Bunting.

Slowly she dragged herself out of bed, feeling exactly as if she had just recovered from an illness which had left her very weak, very, very tired in body and soul.

She stood for a moment listening—listening, and shivering, for it was very cold. Considering how early it still was, there seemed a lot of coming and going in the Marylebone Road. She could hear the unaccustomed sounds through her closed door and the tightly fastened windows of the sitting-room. There must be a regular crowd of men and women, on foot and in cabs, hurrying to the scene of The Avenger's last extraordinary crime. . . .

She heard the sudden thud made by their usual morning paper falling from the letter-box on to the floor of the hall, and a moment later came the sound of Bunting quickly, quietly going out and getting it. She visualised him coming back, and sitting down with a sigh of satisfaction by the newly-lit fire.

Languidly she began dressing herself to the accompaniment of distant tramping and of noise of passing traffic, which increased in volume and in sound as the moments slipped by.

When Mrs. Bunting went down into her kitchen everything looked just as she had left it, and there was no trace of the acrid smell she had expected to find there. Instead, the cavernous, whitewashed room was full of fog, but she noticed that, though the shutters were bolted and barred as she had left them, the windows behind them had been widely opened to the air. She had left them shut.

Making a "spill" out of a twist of newspaper—she had been taught the art as a girl by one of her old mistresses—she stooped and flung open the oven-door of her gas-stove. Yes, it was as she had expected; a fierce heat had been generated there since she had last used the oven, and through to the stone floor below had fallen a mass of black, gluey soot.

Mrs. Bunting took the ham and eggs that she had bought the previous day for her own and Bunting's breakfast upstairs, and broiled them over the gas-ring in their sitting-room. Her husband watched her in surprised silence. She had never done such a thing before.

"I couldn't stay down there," she said; "it was so cold and foggy. I thought I'd make breakfast up here, just for to-day."

"Yes," he said kindly; "that's quite right, Ellen. I think you've done quite right, my dear."

But, when it came to the point, his wife could not eat any of the nice breakfast she had got ready; she only had another cup of tea.

"I'm afraid you're ill, Ellen?" Bunting asked solicitously.

"No," she said shortly; "I'm not ill at all. Don't be silly! The thought of that horrible thing happening so close by has upset me, and put me off my food. Just hark to them now!"

Through their closed windows penetrated the sound of scurrying feet and loud, ribald laughter. What a crowd, nay, what a mob, must be hastening busily to and from the spot where there was now nothing to be seen!

Mrs. Bunting made her husband lock the front gate. "I don't want any of those ghouls in here!" she exclaimed angrily. And then, "What a lot of idle people there are in the world!" she said.

CHAPTER XVI

Bunting began moving about the room restlessly. He would go to the window; stand there awhile staring out at the people hurrying past; then, coming back to the fireplace, sit down.

But he could not stay long quiet. After a glance at his paper, up he would rise from his chair, and go to the window again.

"I wish you'd stay still," his wife said at last. And then, a few minutes later, "Hadn't you better put your hat and coat on and go out?" she exclaimed.

And Bunting, with a rather shamed expression, did put on his hat and coat and go out.

As he did so he told himself that, after all, he was but human; it was natural that he should be thrilled and excited by the dreadful, extraordinary thing which had just happened close by. Ellen wasn't reasonable about such things. How queer and disagreeable she had been that very morning—angry with him because he had gone out to hear what all the row was about, and even more angry when he had come back and said nothing, because he thought it would annoy her to hear about it!

Meanwhile, Mrs. Bunting forced herself to go down again into the kitchen, and as she went through into the low, whitewashed place, a tremor of fear, of quick terror, came over her. She turned and did what she had never in her life done before, and what she had never heard of anyone else doing in a kitchen. She bolted the door.

But, having done this, finding herself at last alone, shut off from everybody, she was still beset by a strange, uncanny dread. She felt as if she were locked in with an invisible presence, which mocked and jeered, reproached and threatened her, by turns.

Why had she allowed, nay encouraged, Daisy to go away for two days? Daisy, at any rate, was company—kind, young, unsuspecting company. With Daisy she could be her old sharp self. It was such a comfort to be with someone to whom she not only need, but ought to, say nothing. When with Bunting she was pursued by a sick feeling of guilt, of shame. She was the man's wedded wife—in his stolid way he was very kind to her, and yet she was keeping from him something he certainly had a right to know.

Not for worlds, however, would she have told Bunting of her dreadful suspicion—nay, of her almost certainty.

At last she went across to the door and unlocked it. Then she went upstairs and turned out her bedroom. That made her feel a little better.

She longed for Bunting to return, and yet in a way she was relieved by his absence. She would have liked to feel him near by, and yet she welcomed anything that took her husband out of the house.

And as Mrs. Bunting swept and dusted, trying to put her whole mind into what she was doing, she was asking herself all the time what was going on upstairs. . . .

What a good rest the lodger was having! But there, that was only natural. Mr. Sleuth, as she well knew, had been up a long time last night, or rather this morning.

Suddenly, the drawing-room bell rang. But Mr. Sleuth's landlady did not go up, as she generally did, before getting ready the simple meal which was the lodger's luncheon and breakfast combined. Instead, she went downstairs again and hurriedly prepared the lodger's food.

Then, very slowly, with her heart beating queerly, she walked up, and just outside the sitting-room—for she felt sure that Mr. Sleuth had got up, that he was there already, waiting for her—she rested the tray on the top of the banisters and listened. For a few moments she heard nothing; then through the door came the high, quavering voice with which she had become so familiar:

" 'She saith to him, stolen waters are sweet, and bread eaten in secret is pleasant. But he knoweth not that the dead are there, and that her guests are in the depths of hell.' "

There was a long pause. Mrs. Bunting could hear the leaves of her Bible being turned over, eagerly, busily; and then again Mr. Sleuth broke out, this time in a softer voice:

" 'She hath cast down many wounded from her; yea, many strong men have been slain by her.' " And in a softer, lower, plaintive tone came the words: " 'I applied my heart to know, and to search, and to seek out wisdom and the reason of things, and to know the wickedness of folly, even of foolishness and madness.' "

And as she stood there listening, a feeling of keen distress, of spiritual oppression, came over Mrs. Bunting. For the first time in her life she visioned the infinite mystery, the sadness and strangeness, of human life.

Poor Mr. Sleuth—poor unhappy, distraught Mr. Sleuth! An overwhelming pity blotted out for a moment the fear, aye, and the loathing, she had been feeling for her lodger.

She knocked at the door, and then she took up her tray.

"Come in, Mrs. Bunting." Mr. Sleuth's voice sounded feebler, more toneless than usual.

She turned the handle of the door and walked in.

The lodger was not sitting in his usual place; he had taken the little round table on which his candle generally rested when he read in bed, out of his bedroom, and placed it over by the drawing-room window. On it were placed, open, the Bible and the Concordance. But as his landlady came in, Mr. Sleuth hastily closed the Bible, and began staring dreamily out of the window, down at the sordid, hurrying crowd of men and women which now swept along the Marylebone Road.

"There seem a great many people out to-day," he observed, without looking round.

"Yes, sir, there do."

Mrs. Bunting began busying herself with laying the cloth and putting out the breakfast-lunch, and as she did so she was seized with a mortal, instinctive terror of the man sitting there.

At last Mr. Sleuth got up and turned round. She forced herself to look at him. How tired, how worn, he looked, and—how strange!

Walking towards the table on which lay his meal, he rubbed his hands together with a nervous gesture—it was a gesture he only made when something had pleased, nay, satisfied him. Mrs. Bunting, looking at him, remembered that he had rubbed his hands together thus when he had first seen the room upstairs, and realised that it contained a large gas-stove and a convenient sink.

What Mr. Sleuth was doing now also reminded her in an odd way of a play she had once seen—a play to which a young man had taken her when she was a girl, unnumbered years ago, and which had thrilled and fascinated her. "Out, out, damned spot!" that was what the tall, fierce, beautiful lady who had played the part of a queen had said, twisting her hands together just as the lodger was doing now.

"It's a fine day," said Mr. Sleuth, sitting down and unfolding his napkin. "The fog has cleared. I do not know if you will agree with me, Mrs. Bunting, but I always feel brighter when the sun is shining, as it is now, at any rate, trying to shine." He looked at her inquiringly, but Mrs. Bunting could not speak. She only nodded. However, that did not affect Mr. Sleuth adversely.

He had acquired a great liking and respect for this well-balanced, taciturn woman. She was the first woman for whom he had experienced any such feeling for many years past.

He looked down at the still-covered dish, and shook his head. "I don't feel as if I could eat very much to-day," he said plaintively. And then he suddenly took a half-sovereign out of his waistcoat pocket.

Already Mrs. Bunting had noticed that it was not the same waistcoat Mr. Sleuth had been wearing the day before.

"Mrs. Bunting, may I ask you to come here?"

And after a moment of hesitation his landlady obeyed him.

"Will you please accept this little gift for the use you kindly allowed me to make of your kitchen last night?" he said quietly. "I tried to make as little mess as I could, Mrs. Bunting, but—well, the truth is I was carrying out a very elaborate experiment——"

Mrs. Bunting held out her hand, she hesitated, and then she took the coin. The fingers which for a moment brushed lightly against her palm were icy cold—cold and clammy. Mr. Sleuth was evidently not well.

As she walked down the stairs, the winter sun, a scarlet ball hanging in the smoky sky, glinted in on Mr. Sleuth's landlady, and threw blood-red gleams, or so it seemed to her, on to the piece of gold she was holding in her hand.

The day went by, as other days had gone by in that quiet household, but, of course, there was far greater animation outside the little house than was usually the case.

Perhaps because the sun was shining for the first time for some days, the whole of London seemed to be making holiday in that part of the town.

When Bunting at last came back, his wife listened silently while he told her of the extraordinary excitement reigning everywhere. And then, after he had been talking a long while, she suddenly shot a strange look at him.

"I suppose you went to see the place?" she said.

And guiltily he acknowledged that he had done so.

"Well?"

"Well, there wasn't anything much to see—not now. But, oh, Ellen, the daring of him! Why, Ellen, if the poor soul had had time to cry out—which they don't believe she had—it's impossible someone wouldn't 'a heard her. They say that if he goes on doing it like that—in the afternoon, like—he never *will* be caught. He must have just got mixed up with all the other people within ten seconds of what he'd done!"

During the afternoon Bunting bought papers recklessly—in fact, he must have spent the best part of six-pence. But in spite of all the supposed and suggested clues, there was nothing—nothing at all new to read, less, in fact, than ever before.

The police, it was clear, were quite at a loss, and Mrs. Bunting began to feel curiously better, less tired, less ill, less—less terrified than she had felt through the morning.

And then something happened which broke with dramatic suddenness the quietude of the day.

They had had their tea, and Bunting was reading the last of the papers he had run out to buy, when suddenly there came a loud, thundering, double knock at the door.

Mrs. Bunting looked up, startled. "Why, whoever can that be?" she said.

But as Bunting got up she added quickly, "You just sit down again. I'll go myself. Sounds like someone after lodgings. I'll soon send them to the right-about!"

And then she left the room, but not before there had come another loud double knock.

Mrs. Bunting opened the front door. In a moment she saw that the person who stood there was a stranger to her. He was a big, dark man, with fierce, black moustaches. And somehow—she could not have told you why—he suggested a policeman to Mrs. Bunting's mind.

This notion of hers was confirmed by the very first words he uttered. For, "I'm here to execute a warrant!" he exclaimed in a theatrical, hollow tone.

With a weak cry of protest Mrs. Bunting suddenly threw out her arms as if to bar the way; she turned deadly white—but then, in an instant, the supposed stranger's laugh rang out, with a loud, jovial, familiar sound!

"There now, Mrs. Bunting! I never thought I'd take you in as well as all that!"

It was Joe Chandler—Joe Chandler dressed up, as she knew he sometimes, not very often, did dress up in the course of his work.

Mrs. Bunting began laughing—laughing helplessly, hysterically, just as she had done on the morning of Daisy's arrival, when the newspaper-sellers had come shouting down the Marylebone Road.

"What's all this about?" Bunting came out.

Young Chandler ruefully shut the front door. "I didn't mean to upset her like this," he said, looking foolish; " 'twas just my silly nonsense, Mr. Bunting." And together they helped her into the sitting-room.

But, once there, poor Mrs. Bunting went on worse than ever; she threw her black apron over her face, and began to sob hysterically.

"I made sure she'd know who I was when I spoke," went on the young fellow apologetically. "But, there now, I *have* upset her. I *am* sorry!"

"It don't matter!" she exclaimed, throwing the apron off her face, but the tears were still streaming from her eyes as she sobbed and laughed by turns. "Don't matter one little bit, Joe! 'Twas stupid of me to be so taken aback. But, there, that murder that's happened close by, it's just upset me—upset me altogether to-day."

"Enough to upset anyone—that was," acknowledged the young man ruefully. "I've only come in for a minute, like. I haven't no right to come when I'm on duty like this——"

Joe Chandler was looking longingly at what remains of the meal were still on the table.

"You can take a minute just to have a bite and a sup," said Bunting hospitably; "and then you can tell us any news there is, Joe. We're right in the middle of everything now, ain't we?" He spoke with evident enjoyment, almost pride, in the gruesome fact.

Joe nodded. Already his mouth was full of bread-and-butter. He waited a moment, and then: "Well I have got one piece of news—not that I suppose it'll interest *you* very much."

They both looked at him—Mrs. Bunting suddenly calm, though her breast still heaved from time to time.

"Our Boss has resigned!" said Joe Chandler slowly, impressively.

"No! Not the Commissioner o' Police?" exclaimed Bunting.

"Yes, he has. He just can't bear what's said about us any longer—and I don't wonder! He done his best, and so's we all. The public have just gone daft—in the West End, that is, to-day. As for the papers, well, they're something cruel—that's what they are. And the ridiculous ideas they print! You'd never believe the things they asks us to do—and quite serious-like."

"What d'you mean?" questioned Mrs. Bunting. She really wanted to know.

"Well, the *Courier* declares that there ought to be a house-to-house investigation—all over London. Just think of it! Everybody to let the police go all over their house, from garret to kitchen, just to see if The Avenger isn't concealed there. Dotty, I calls it! Why, 'twould take us months and months just to do that one job in a town like London."

"I'd like to see them dare come into my house!" said Mrs. Bunting angrily.

"It's all along of them blarsted papers that The Avenger went to work a different way this time," said Chandler slowly.

Bunting had pushed a tin of sardines towards his guest, and was eagerly listening. "How d'you mean?" he asked. "I don't take your meaning, Joe."

"Well, you see, it's this way. The newspapers was always saying how extra-ordinary it was that The Avenger chose such a peculiar time to do his deeds—I mean, the time when no one's about the streets. Now, doesn't it stand to reason that the fellow, reading all that, and seeing the sense of it, said to himself, 'I'll go on another tack this time'? Just listen to this!" He pulled a strip of paper, part of a column cut from a newspaper, out of his pocket:

> ### "An ex-Lord Mayor of London
> ### on The Avenger
>
> "'Will the murderer be caught? Yes,' replied Sir John, 'he will certainly be caught—probably when he commits his next crime. A whole army of blood-hounds, metaphorical and literal, will be on his track the moment he draws blood again. With the whole community against him, he cannot escape, especially when it be remembered that he chooses the quietest hour in the twenty-four to commit his crimes.
>
> "'Londoners are now in such a state of nerves—if I may use the expression, in such a state of funk—that every passer-by, however innocent, is looked at with suspicion by his neighbour if his avocation happens to take him abroad between the hours of one and three in the morning.'

"I'd like to gag that ex-Lord Mayor!" concluded Joe Chandler wrathfully.

Just then the lodger's bell rang.

"Let me go up, my dear," said Bunting.

His wife still looked pale and shaken by the fright she had had.

"No, no," she said hastily. "You stop down here, and talk to Joe. I'll look after Mr. Sleuth. He may be wanting his supper just a bit earlier than usual to-day."

Slowly, painfully, again feeling as if her legs were made of cotton wool, she dragged herself up to the first floor, knocked at the door, and then went in.

"You did ring, sir?" she said, in her quiet, respectful way.

And Mr. Sleuth looked up.

She thought—but, as she reminded herself afterwards, it might have been just her idea, and nothing else—that for the first time the lodger looked frightened—frightened and cowed.

"I heard a noise downstairs," he said fretfully, "and I wanted to know what it was all about. As I told you, Mrs. Bunting, when I first took these rooms, quiet is essential to me."

"It was just a friend of ours, sir. I'm sorry you were disturbed. Would you like the knocker taken off to-morrow? Bunting'll be pleased to do it if you don't like to hear the sound of the knocks."

"Oh, no, I wouldn't put you to such trouble as that." Mr. Sleuth looked quite relieved. "Just a friend of yours, was it, Mrs. Bunting? He made a great deal of noise."

"Just a young fellow," she said apologetically. "The son of one of Bunting's old friends. He often comes here, sir; but he never did give such a great big double knock as that before. I'll speak to him about it."

"Oh, no, Mrs. Bunting. I would really prefer you did nothing of the kind. It was just a passing annoyance—nothing more."

She waited a moment. How strange that Mr. Sleuth said nothing of the hoarse cries which had made of the road outside a perfect Bedlam every hour or two throughout that day. But no, Mr. Sleuth made no allusion to what might well have disturbed any quiet gentleman at his reading.

"I thought maybe you'd like to have supper a little earlier to-night, sir?"

"Just when you like, Mrs. Bunting—just when it's convenient. I do not wish to put you out in any way."

She felt herself dismissed, and going out quietly, closed the door.

As she did so, she heard the front door banging to. She sighed—Joe Chandler was really a very noisy young fellow.

CHAPTER XVII

Mrs. Bunting slept well the night following that during which the lodger had been engaged in making his mysterious experiments in her kitchen. She was so tired, so utterly exhausted, that sleep came to her the moment she laid her head upon her pillow.

Perhaps that was why she rose so early the next morning. Hardly giving herself time to swallow the tea Bunting had made and brought her, she got up and dressed.

She had suddenly come to the conclusion that the hall and staircase required a thorough "doing down," and she did not even wait till they had eaten their breakfast before beginning her labours. It made Bunting feel quite uncomfortable. As he sat by the fire reading his morning paper—the paper which was again of such absorbing interest—he called out, "There's no need for so much hurry, Ellen. Daisy'll be back to-day. Why don't you wait till she's come home to help you?"

But from the hall where she was busy dusting, sweeping, polishing, his wife's voice came back: "Girls ain't no good at this sort of work. Don't you worry about me. I feel as if I'd enjoy doing an extra bit of cleaning to-day. I don't like to feel as anyone could come in and see my place dirty."

"No fear of that!" Bunting chuckled. And then a new thought struck him: "Ain't you afraid of waking the lodger?" he called out.

"Mr. Sleuth slept most of yesterday, and all last night," she answered quickly. "As it is, I study him over-much; it's a long, long time since I've done this staircase down."

All the time she was engaged in doing the hall, Mrs. Bunting left the sitting-room door wide open.

That was a queer thing of her to do, but Bunting didn't like to get up and shut her out, as it were. Still, try as he would, he couldn't read with any comfort while all that noise was going on. He had never known Ellen make such a lot of noise before. Once or twice he looked up and frowned rather crossly.

There came a sudden silence, and he was startled to see that Ellen was standing in the doorway, staring at him, doing nothing.

"Come in," he said, "do! Ain't you finished yet?"

"I was only resting a minute," she said. "You don't tell me nothing. I'd like to know if there's anything—I mean anything new—in the paper this morning."

She spoke in a muffled voice, almost as if she were ashamed of her unusual curiosity; and her look of fatigue, of pallor, made Bunting suddenly uneasy. "Come in—do!" he repeated sharply. "You've done quite enough—and before breakfast, too. 'Tain't necessary. Come in and shut that door."

He spoke authoritatively, and his wife, for a wonder, obeyed him.

She came in, and did what she had never done before—brought the broom with her, and put it up against the wall in the corner.

Then she sat down.

"I think I'll make breakfast up here," she said. "I—I feel cold, Bunting." And her husband stared at her surprised, for drops of perspiration were glistening on her forehead.

He got up. "All right. I'll go down and bring the eggs up. Don't you worry. For the matter of that, I can cook them downstairs if you like."

"No," she said obstinately. "I'd rather do my own work. You just bring them up here—that'll be all right. To-morrow morning we'll have Daisy to help see to things."

"Come over here and sit down comfortable in my chair," he suggested kindly. "You never do take any bit of rest, Ellen. I never see'd such a woman!"

And again she got up and meekly obeyed him, walking across the room with languid steps.

He watched her, anxiously, uncomfortably.

She took up the newspaper he had just laid down, and Bunting took two steps towards her.

"I'll show you the most interesting bit," he said eagerly. "It's the piece headed, 'Our Special Investigator.' You see, they've started a special investigator of their own, and he's got hold of a lot of little facts the police seem to have overlooked. The man who writes all that—I mean the Special Investigator—was a famous 'tec in his time, and he's just come back out of his retirement o' purpose to do this bit of work for the paper. You read what he says—I shouldn't be a bit surprised if he ends by getting that reward! One can see he just loves the work of tracking people down."

"There's nothing to be proud of in such a job," said his wife listlessly.

"He'll have something to be proud of if he catches The Avenger!" cried Bunting. He was too keen about this affair to be put off by Ellen's contradictory remarks. "You just notice that bit about the rubber soles. Now, no one's thought o' that. I'll just tell Chandler—he don't seem to me to be half awake, that young man don't."

"He's quite wide awake enough without you saying things to him! How about those eggs, Bunting? I feel quite ready for my breakfast, even if you don't——"

Mrs. Bunting now spoke in what her husband sometimes secretly described to himself as "Ellen's snarling voice."

He turned away and left the room, feeling oddly troubled. There was something queer about her, and he couldn't make it out. He didn't mind it when she spoke sharply and nastily to him. He was used to that. But now she was so up and down; so different from what she used to be! In old days she had always been the same, but now a man never knew where to have her.

And as he went downstairs he pondered uneasily over his wife's changed ways and manner.

Take the question of his easy chair. A very small matter, no doubt, but he had never known Ellen sit in that chair—no, not even once, for a minute, since it had been purchased by her as a present for him.

They had been so happy, so happy, and so—so restful, during that first week after Mr. Sleuth had come to them. Perhaps it was the sudden, dramatic change from agonising anxiety to peace and security which had been too much for Ellen—yes, that was what was the matter with her, that and the universal excitement about these Avenger murders, which were shaking the nerves of all London. Even Bunting, unobservant as he was, had come to realise that his wife took a morbid interest in these terrible happenings. And it was the more queer of her to do so that at first she refused to discuss them, and said openly that she was utterly uninterested in murder or crime of any sort.

He, Bunting, had always had a mild pleasure in such things. In his time he had been a great reader of detective tales, and even now he thought there was no pleasanter reading. It was that which had first drawn him to Joe Chandler, and made him welcome the young chap as cordially as he had done when they first came to London.

But though Ellen had tolerated, she had never encouraged, that sort of talk between the two men. More than once she had exclaimed reproachfully: "To hear you two, one would think there was no nice, respectable, quiet people left in the world!"

But now all that was changed. She was as keen as anyone could be to hear the latest details of an Avenger crime. True, she took her own view of any theory suggested. But there! Ellen always had had her own notions about everything under the sun. Ellen was a woman who thought for herself—a clever woman, not an everyday woman by any manner of means.

While these thoughts were going disconnectedly through his mind, Bunting was breaking four eggs into a basin. He was going to give Ellen a nice little surprise—to cook an omelette as a French chef had once taught him to do, years and years ago. He didn't know how she would take his doing such a thing after what she had said; but never mind, she would enjoy the omelette when done. Ellen hadn't been eating her food properly of late.

And when he went up again, his wife, to his relief, and, it must be admitted, to his surprise, took it very well. She had not even noticed how long he had been downstairs, for she had been reading with intense, painful care the column that the great daily paper they took in had allotted to the one-time famous detective.

According to this Special Investigator's own account, he had discovered all sorts of things that had escaped the eye of the police and of the official detectives. For instance, owing, he admitted, to a fortunate chance, he had been at the place where the two last murders had been committed very soon after the double crime had been discovered—in fact, within half an hour, and he had found, or so he felt sure, on the slippery, wet pavement imprints of the murderer's right foot.

The paper reproduced the impression of a half-worn rubber sole. At the same time, he also admitted—for the Special Investigator was very honest, and he had a good bit of space to fill in the enterprising paper which had engaged him to probe the awful mystery—that there were thousands of rubber soles being worn in London. . . .

And when she came to that statement Mrs. Bunting looked up, and there came a wan smile over her thin, closely-shut lips. It was quite true—that about rubber soles; there *were* thousands of rubber soles being worn just now. She felt grateful to the Special Investigator for having stated the fact so clearly.

The column ended up with the words:

"*And to-day will take place the inquest on the double crime of ten days ago. To my mind it would be well if a preliminary public inquiry could be held at once. Say, on the very day the discovery of a fresh murder is made. In that way alone would it be possible to weigh and sift the evidence offered by members of the general public. For when a week or more has elapsed, and these same people have been examined and cross-examined in private by the police, their impressions have had time to become blurred and hopelessly confused. On that last occasion but one there seems no doubt that several people, at any rate two women and one man, actually saw the murderer hurrying from the scene of his atrocious double crime—this being so, to-day's investigation may be of the highest value and importance. To-morrow I hope to give an account of the impression made on me by the inquest, and by any statements made during its course.*"

Even when her husband had come in with the tray Mrs. Bunting had gone on reading, only lifting up her eyes for a moment. At last he said rather crossly,

"Put down that paper, Ellen, this minute! The omelette I've cooked for you will be just like leather if you don't eat it."

But once his wife had eaten her breakfast—and, to Bunting's mortification, she left more than half the nice omelette untouched—she took the paper up again. She turned over the big sheets, until she found, at the foot of one of the ten columns devoted to The Avenger and his crimes, the information she wanted, and then uttered an exclamation under her breath.

What Mrs. Bunting had been looking for—what at last she had found—was the time and place of the inquest which was to be held that day. The hour named was a rather odd time—two o'clock in the afternoon, but, from Mrs. Bunting's point of view, it was most convenient.

By two o'clock, nay, by half-past one, the lodger would have had his lunch; by hurrying matters a little she and Bunting would have had their dinner, and—and Daisy wasn't coming home till tea-time.

She got up out of her husband's chair. "I think you're right," she said, in a quick, hoarse tone. "I mean about me seeing a doctor, Bunting. I think I will go and see a doctor this very afternoon."

"Wouldn't you like me to go with you?" he asked.

"No, that I wouldn't. In fact, I wouldn't go at all if you was to go with me."

"All right," he said vexedly. "Please yourself, my dear; you know best."

"I should think I did know best where my own health is concerned."

Even Bunting was incensed by this lack of gratitude. "'Twas I said, long ago, you ought to go and see the doctor; 'twas you said you wouldn't!" he exclaimed pugnaciously.

"Well, I've never said you was never right, have I? At any rate, I'm going."

"Have you a pain anywhere?" He stared at her with a look of real solicitude on his fat, phlegmatic face.

Somehow Ellen didn't look right, standing there opposite him. Her shoulders seemed to have shrunk; even her cheeks had fallen in a little. She had never looked so bad—not even when they had been half starving, and dreadfully, dreadfully worried.

"Yes," she said briefly, "I've a pain in my head, at the back of my neck. It doesn't often leave me; it gets worse when anything upsets me, like I was upset last night by Joe Chandler."

"He was a silly ass to come and do a thing like that!" said Bunting crossly. "I'd a good mind to tell him so, too. But I must say, Ellen, I wonder he took you in—he didn't me!"

"Well, you had no chance he should—you knew who it was," she said slowly.

And Bunting remained silent, for Ellen was right. Joe Chandler had already spoken when he, Bunting, came out into the hall, and saw their cleverly disguised visitor.

"Those big black moustaches," he went on complainingly, "and that black wig—why, 'twas too ridic'lous—that's what I call it!"

"Not to anyone who didn't know Joe," she said sharply.

"Well, I don't know. He didn't look like a real man—nohow. If he's a wise lad, he won't let our Daisy ever see him looking like that!" and Bunting laughed, a comfortable laugh.

He had thought a good deal about Daisy and young Chandler the last two days, and, on the whole, he was well pleased. It was a dull, unnatural life the girl was leading with Old Aunt. And Joe was earning good money. They wouldn't have long to wait, these two young people, as a beau and his girl often have to wait, as he, Bunting, and Daisy's mother had had to do, for ever so long before they could be married. No, there was no reason why they shouldn't be spliced quite soon—if so the fancy took them. And Bunting had very little doubt that so the fancy would take Joe, at any rate.

But there was plenty of time. Daisy wouldn't be eighteen till the week after next. They might wait till she was twenty. By that time Old Aunt might be dead, and Daisy might have come into quite a tidy little bit of money.

"What are you smiling at?" said his wife sharply.

And he shook himself. "I—smiling? At nothing that I knows of." Then he waited a moment. "Well, if you will know, Ellen, I was just thinking of Daisy and that young chap Joe Chandler. He *is* gone on her, ain't he?"

"Gone?" And then Mrs. Bunting laughed, a queer, odd, not unkindly laugh. "Gone, Bunting?" she repeated. "Why, he's out o' sight—right out o' sight!"

Then hesitatingly, and looking narrowly at her husband, she went on, twisting a bit of her black apron with her fingers as she spoke:—"I suppose he'll be going over this afternoon to fetch her? Or—or d'you think he'll have to be at that inquest, Bunting?"

"Inquest? What inquest?" He looked at her puzzled.

"Why, the inquest on them bodies found in the passage near by King's Cross."

"Oh, no; he'd have no call to be at the inquest. For the matter o' that, I know he's going over to fetch Daisy. He said so last night—just when you went up to the lodger."

"That's just as well." Mrs. Bunting spoke with considerable satisfaction. "Otherwise I suppose you'd ha' had to go. I wouldn't like the house left—not with us out of it. Mr. Sleuth *would* be upset if there came a ring at the door."

"Oh, I won't leave the house, don't you be afraid, Ellen—not while you're out."

"Not even if I'm out a good while, Bunting."

"No fear. Of course, you'll be a long time if it's your idea to see that doctor at Ealing?"

He looked at her questioningly, and Mrs. Bunting nodded. Somehow nodding didn't seem as bad as speaking a lie.

CHAPTER XVIII

Any ordeal is far less terrifying, far easier to meet with courage, when it is repeated, than is even a milder experience which is entirely novel.

Mrs. Bunting had already attended an inquest, in the character of a witness, and it was one of the few happenings of her life which was sharply etched against the somewhat blurred screen of her memory.

In a country house where the then Ellen Green had been staying for a fortnight with her elderly mistress, there had occurred one of those sudden, pitiful tragedies which occasionally destroy the serenity, the apparent decorum, of a large, respectable household.

The under-housemaid, a pretty, happy-natured girl, had drowned herself for love of the footman, who had given his sweetheart cause for bitter jealousy. The girl had chosen to speak of her troubles to the strange lady's maid rather than to her own fellow-servants, and it was during the conversation the two women had had together that the girl had threatened to take her own life.

As Mrs. Bunting put on her outdoor clothes, preparatory to going out, she recalled very clearly all the details of that dreadful affair, and of the part she herself had unwillingly played in it.

She visualised the country inn where the inquest on that poor, unfortunate creature had been held.

The butler had escorted her from the Hall, for he also was to give evidence, and as they came up there had been a look of cheerful animation about the inn yard; people coming and going, many women as well as men, village folk, among whom the dead girl's fate had aroused a great deal of interest, and the kind of horror which those who live on a dull countryside welcome rather than avoid.

Everyone there had been particularly nice and polite to her, to Ellen Green; there had been a time of waiting in a room upstairs in the old inn, and the witnesses had been accommodated, not only with chairs, but with cake and wine.

She remembered how she had dreaded being a witness, how she had felt as if she would like to run away from her nice, easy place, rather than have to get up and tell the little that she knew of the sad business.

But it had not been so very dreadful after all. The coroner had been a kindly-spoken gentleman; in fact he had complimented her on the clear, sensible way she had given her evidence concerning the exact words the unhappy girl had used.

One thing Ellen Green had said, in answer to a question put by an inquisitive juryman, had raised a laugh in the crowded, low-ceilinged room. "Ought not Miss Ellen Green," so the man had asked, "to have told someone of the girl's threat? If she had done so, might not the girl have been prevented from throwing herself into the lake?" And she, the witness, had answered, with some asperity—for by that time the coroner's kind manner had put her at her ease—that she had not attached any importance to what the girl had threatened to do, never believing that any young woman could be so silly as to drown herself for love!

Vaguely Mrs. Bunting supposed that the inquest at which she was going to be present this afternoon would be like that country inquest of long ago.

It had been no mere perfunctory inquiry; she remembered very well how little by little that pleasant-spoken gentleman, the coroner, had got the whole truth out—the story, that is, of how that horrid footman, whom she, Ellen Green, had disliked from the first minute she had set eyes on him, had taken up with another young woman. It had been supposed that this fact would not be elicited by the coroner; but it had been, quietly, remorselessly; more, the dead girl's letters had been read out—piteous, queerly expressed letters, full of wild love and bitter, threatening jealousy. And the jury had censured the young man most severely; she remembered the look on his face when the people, shrinking back, had made a passage for him to slink out of the crowded room.

Come to think of it now, it was strange she had never told Bunting that long-ago tale. It had occurred years before she knew him, and somehow nothing had ever happened to make her tell him about it.

She wondered whether Bunting had ever been to an inquest. She longed to ask him. But if she asked him now, this minute, he might guess where she was thinking of going.

And then, while still moving about her bedroom, she shook her head—no, no, Bunting would never guess such a thing; he would never, never suspect her of telling him a lie.

Stop—had she told a lie? She did mean to go to the doctor after the inquest was finished—if there was time, that is. She wondered uneasily how long such an inquiry was likely to last. In this case, as so very little had been discovered, the proceedings would surely be very formal—formal and therefore short.

She herself had one quite definite object—that of hearing the evidence of those who believed they had seen the murderer leaving the spot where his victims lay weltering in their still flowing blood. She was filled with a painful, secret, and, yes, eager curiosity to hear how those who were so positive about the matter would describe the appearance of The Avenger. After all, a lot of people must have seen him, for, as Bunting had said only the day before to young Chandler, The Avenger was not a ghost; he was a living man with some kind of hiding-place where he was known, and where he spent his time between his awful crimes.

As she came back to the sitting-room, her extreme pallor struck her husband.

"Why, Ellen," he said, "it *is* time you went to the doctor. You looks just as if you was going to a funeral. I'll come along with you as far as the station. You're going by train, ain't you? Not by bus, eh? It's a very long way to Ealing, you know."

"There you go! Breaking your solemn promise to me the very first minute!" But somehow she did not speak unkindly, only fretfully and sadly.

And Bunting hung his head. "Why, to be sure I'd gone and clean forgot the lodger! But will you be all right, Ellen? Why not wait till to-morrow, and take Daisy with you?"

"I like doing my own business in my own way, and not in someone else's way!" she snapped out; and then more gently, for Bunting really looked concerned, and she did feel very far from well, "I'll be all right, old man. Don't you worry about me!"

As she turned to go across to the door, she drew the black shawl she had put over her long jacket more closely round her.

She felt ashamed, deeply ashamed, of deceiving so kind a husband. And yet, what could she do? How could she share her dreadful burden with poor Bunting? Why, 'twould be enough to make a man go daft. Even she often felt as if she could stand it no longer—as if she would give the world to tell someone—anyone—what it was that she suspected, what deep in her heart she so feared to be the truth.

But, unknown to herself, the fresh outside air, fog-laden though it was, soon began to do her good. She had gone out far too little the last few days, for she had had a nervous terror of leaving the house unprotected, as also a great unwillingness to allow Bunting to come into contact with the lodger.

When she reached the Underground station she stopped short. There were two ways of getting to St. Pancras—she could go by bus, or she could go by train. She decided on the latter. But before turning into the station her eyes strayed over the bills of the early afternoon papers lying on the ground.

Two words,

"The Avenger,"

stared up at her in varying type.

Drawing her black shawl yet a little closer about her shoulders, Mrs. Bunting looked down at the placards. She did not feel inclined to buy a paper, as many of the people round her were doing. Her eyes were smarting, even now, from their unaccustomed following of the close print in the paper Bunting took in.

Slowly she turned, at last, into the Underground station.

And now a piece of extraordinary good fortune befell Mrs. Bunting.

The third-class carriage in which she took her place happened to be empty, save for the presence of a police inspector. And once they were well away she summoned up courage, and asked him the question she knew she would have to ask of someone within the next few minutes.

"Can you tell me," she said, in a low voice, "where death inquests are held"—she moistened her lips, waited a moment, and then concluded—"in the neighbourhood of King's Cross?"

The man turned and looked at her attentively. She did not look at all the sort of Londoner who goes to an inquest—there are many such—just for the fun of the thing. Approvingly, for he was a widower, he noted her neat black coat and skirt, and the plain Princess bonnet which framed her pale, refined face.

"I'm going to the Coroner's Court myself," he said good-naturedly. "So you can come along of me. You see there's that big Avenger inquest going on to-day, so I think they'll have had to make other arrangements for—hum, hum—ordinary cases." And as she looked at him dumbly, he went on, "There'll be a mighty crowd of people at The Avenger inquest—a lot of ticket folk to be accommodated, to say nothing of the public."

"That's the inquest I'm going to," faltered Mrs. Bunting. She could scarcely get the words out. She realised with acute discomfort, yes, and shame, how strange, how untoward, was that which she was going to do. Fancy a respectable woman wanting to attend a murder inquest!

During the last few days all her perceptions had become sharpened by suspense and fear. She realised now, as she looked into the stolid face of her unknown friend, how she herself would have regarded any woman who wanted to attend such an inquiry from a simple, morbid feeling of curiosity. And yet—and yet that was just what she was about to do herself.

"I've got a reason for wanting to go there," she murmured. It was a comfort to unburden herself this little way even to a stranger.

"Ah!" he said reflectively. "A—a relative connected with one of the two victims' husbands, I presume?"

And Mrs. Bunting bent her head.

"Going to give evidence?" he asked casually, and then he turned and looked at Mrs. Bunting with far more attention than he had yet done.

"Oh, no!" There was a world of horror, of fear in the speaker's voice.

And the inspector felt concerned and sorry. "Hadn't seen her for quite a long time, I suppose?"

"Never had seen her. I'm from the country." Something impelled Mrs. Bunting to say these words. But she hastily corrected herself, "At least, I was."

"Will *he* be there?"

She looked at him dumbly; not in the least knowing to whom he was alluding.

"I mean the husband," went on the inspector hastily. "I felt sorry for the last poor chap—I mean the husband of the last one—he seemed so awfully miserable. You see, she'd been a good wife and a good mother till she took to the drink."

"It always is so," breathed out Mrs. Bunting.

"Aye." He waited a moment. "D'you know anyone about the court?" he asked. She shook her head.

"Well, don't you worry. I'll take you in along o' me. You'd never get in by yourself."

They got out; and oh, the comfort of being in some one's charge, of having a determined man in uniform to look after one! And yet even now there was to Mrs. Bunting something dream-like, unsubstantial about the whole business.

"If he knew—if he only knew what I know!" she kept saying over and over again to herself as she walked lightly by the big, burly form of the police inspector.

"'Tisn't far—not three minutes," he said suddenly. "Am I walking too quick for you, ma'am?"

"No, not at all. I'm a quick walker."

And then suddenly they turned a corner and came on a mass of people, a densely packed crowd of men and women, staring at a mean-looking little door sunk into a high wall.

"Better take my arm," the inspector suggested. "Make way there! Make way!" he cried authoritatively; and he swept her through the serried ranks which parted at the sound of his voice, at the sight of his uniform.

"Lucky you met me," he said, smiling. "You'd never have got through alone. And 'tain't a nice crowd, not by any manner of means."

The small door opened just a little way, and they found themselves on a narrow stone-flagged path, leading into a square yard. A few men were out there, smoking.

Before preceding her into the building which rose at the back of the yard, Mrs. Bunting's kind new friend took out his watch. "There's another twenty minutes before they'll begin," he said. "There's the mortuary"—he pointed with his thumb to a low room built out to the right of the court. "Would you like to go in and see them?" he whispered.

"Oh, no!" she cried, in a tone of extreme horror. And he looked down at her with sympathy, and with increased respect. She was a nice, respectable woman, she was. She had not come here imbued with any morbid, horrible curiosity, but because she thought it her duty to do so. He suspected her of being sister-in-law to one of The Avenger's victims.

They walked through into a big room or hall, now full of men talking in subdued yet eager, animated tones.

"I think you'd better sit down here," he said considerately, and, leading her to one of the benches that stood out from the whitewashed walls—"unless you'd rather be with the witnesses, that is."

But again she said, "Oh, no!" And then, with an effort, "Oughtn't I to go into the court now, if it's likely to be so full?"

"Don't you worry," he said kindly. "I'll see you get a proper place. I must leave you now for a minute, but I'll come back in good time and look after you."

She raised the thick veil she had pulled down over her face while they were going through that sinister, wolfish-looking crowd outside, and looked about her.

Many of the gentlemen—they mostly wore tall hats and good overcoats—standing round and about her looked vaguely familiar. She picked out one at once. He was a famous journalist, whose shrewd, animated face was familiar to her owing to the fact that it was widely advertised in connection with a preparation for the hair—a preparation which in happier, more prosperous days Bunting had had great faith in, and used, or so he always said, with great benefit to himself. This gentleman was the centre of an eager circle; half a dozen men were talking to him, listening deferentially when he spoke, and each of these men, so Mrs. Bunting realised, was a Somebody.

How strange, how amazing, to reflect that from all parts of London, from their doubtless important avocations, one unseen, mysterious beckoner had brought all these men here together, to this sordid place, on this bitterly cold, dreary day. Here they were, all thinking of, talking of, evoking one unknown, mysterious personality—that of the shadowy and yet terribly real human being who chose to call himself The Avenger. And somewhere, not so very far away from them all, The Avenger was keeping these clever, astute, highly trained minds—aye, and bodies, too—at bay.

Even Mrs. Bunting, sitting here unnoticed, realised the irony of her presence among them.

CHAPTER XIX

It seemed to Mrs. Bunting that she had been sitting there a long time—it was really about a quarter of an hour—when her official friend came back.

"Better come along now," he whispered; "it'll begin soon."

She followed him out into a passage, up a row of steep stone steps, and so into the Coroner's Court.

The court was a big, well-lighted room, in some ways not unlike a chapel, the more so that a kind of gallery ran half-way round, a gallery evidently set aside for the general public, for it was now crammed to its utmost capacity.

Mrs. Bunting glanced timidly towards the serried row of faces. Had it not been for her good fortune in meeting the man she was now following, it was there that she would have had to try and make her way. And she would have failed. Those people had rushed in the moment the doors were opened, pushing, fighting their way in a way she could never have pushed or fought.

There were just a few women among them, set, determined-looking women, belonging to every class, but made one by their love of sensation and their power of forcing their way in where they wanted to be. But the women were few; the great majority of those standing there were men—men who were also representative of every class of Londoner.

The centre of the court was like an arena; it was sunk two or three steps below the surrounding gallery. Just now it was comparatively clear of people, save for the benches on which sat the men who were to compose the jury. Some way from these men, huddled together in a kind of big pew, stood seven people—three women and four men.

"D'you see the witnesses?" whispered the inspector, pointing these out to her. He supposed her to know one of them with familiar knowledge, but, if that were so, she made no sign.

Between the windows, facing the whole room, was a kind of little platform, on which stood a desk and an arm-chair. Mrs. Bunting guessed rightly that it was there the coroner would sit. And to the left of the platform was the witness-stand, also raised considerably above the jury.

Amazingly different, and far, far more grim and awe-inspiring than the scene of the inquest which had taken place so long ago, on that bright April day, in the village inn. There the coroner had sat on the same level as the jury, and the witnesses had simply stepped forward one by one, and taken their place before him.

Looking round her fearfully, Mrs. Bunting thought she would surely die if ever *she* were exposed to the ordeal of standing in that curious box-like stand, and she stared across at the bench where sat the seven witnesses with a feeling of sincere pity in her heart.

But even she soon realised that her pity was wasted. Each woman witness looked eager, excited, and animated; well pleased to be the centre of attention and attraction to the general public. It was plain each was enjoying her part of important, if humble, actress in the thrilling drama which was now absorbing the attention of all London—it might almost be said of the whole world.

Looking at these women, Mrs. Bunting wondered vaguely which was which. Was it that rather draggle-tailed-looking young person who had certainly, or almost certainly, seen The Avenger within ten seconds of the double crime being committed? The woman who, aroused by one of his victims' cry of terror, had rushed to her window and seen the murderer's shadowy form pass swiftly by in the fog?

Yet another woman, so Mrs. Bunting now remembered, had given a most circumstantial account of what The Avenger looked like, for he, it was supposed, had actually brushed by her as he passed.

Those two women now before her had been interrogated and cross-examined again and again, not only by the police, but by representatives of every newspaper in London. It was from what they had both said—unluckily their accounts materially differed—that that official description of The Avenger had been worked up—that which described him as being a good-looking, respectable young fellow of twenty-eight, carrying a newspaper parcel. . . .

As for the third woman, she was doubtless an acquaintance, a boon companion of the dead.

Mrs. Bunting looked away from the witnesses, and focused her gaze on another unfamiliar sight. Specially prominent, running indeed through the whole length of the shut-in space, that is, from the coroner's high dais right across to the opening in the wooden barrier, was an ink-splashed table at which, when she had first taken her place, there had been sitting three men busily sketching; but now every seat at the table was occupied by tired, intelligent-looking men, each with a notebook, or with some loose sheets of paper, before him.

"Them's the reporters," whispered her friend. "They don't like coming till the last minute, for they has to be the last to go. At an ordinary inquest there are only two—maybe three—attending, but now every paper in the kingdom has pretty well applied for a pass to that reporters' table."

He looked consideringly down into the well of the court. "Now let me see what I can do for you——"

Then he beckoned to the coroner's officer: "Perhaps you could put this lady just over there, in a corner by herself? Related to a relation of the deceased, but doesn't want to be——" He whispered a word or two, and the other nodded sympathetically, and looked at Mrs. Bunting with interest. "I'll put her just here," he muttered. "There's no one coming there to-day. You see, there are only seven witnesses—sometimes we have a lot more than that."

And he kindly put her on a now empty bench opposite to where the seven witnesses stood and sat with their eager, set faces, ready—aye, more than ready— to play their part.

For a moment every eye in the court was focused on Mrs. Bunting, but soon those who had stared so hungrily, so intently, at her, realised that she had nothing to do with the case. She was evidently there as a spectator, and, more fortunate than most, she had a "friend at court," and so was able to sit comfortably, instead of having to stand in the crowd.

But she was not long left in isolation. Very soon some of the important-looking gentlemen she had seen downstairs came into the court, and were ushered over to her seat, while two or three among them, including the famous writer whose face was so familiar that it almost seemed to Mrs. Bunting like that of a kindly acquaintance, were accommodated at the reporters' table.

"Gentlemen, the Coroner."

The jury stood up, shuffling their feet, and then sat down again; over the spectators there fell a sudden silence.

And then what immediately followed recalled to Mrs. Bunting, for the first time, that informal little country inquest of long ago.

First came the "Oyez! Oyez!" the old Norman-French summons to all whose business it is to attend a solemn inquiry into the death—sudden, unexplained, terrible—of a fellow-being.

The jury—there were fourteen of them—all stood up again. They raised their hands and solemnly chanted together the curious words of their oath.

Then came a quick, informal exchange of sentences 'twixt the coroner and his officer.

Yes, everything was in order. The jury had viewed the bodies—he quickly corrected himself—the body, for, technically speaking, the inquest just about to be held only concerned one body.

And then, amid a silence so absolute that the slightest rustle could be heard through the court, the coroner—a clever-looking gentleman, though not so old as Mrs. Bunting thought he ought to have been to occupy so important a position on so important a day—gave a little history, as it were, of the terrible and mysterious Avenger crimes.

He spoke very clearly, warming to his work as he went on.

He told them that he had been present at the inquest held on one of The Avenger's former victims. "I only went through professional curiosity," he threw in by way of parenthesis, "little thinking, gentlemen, that the inquest on one of these unhappy creatures would ever be held in my court."

On and on he went, though he had, in truth, but little to say, and though that little was known to every one of his listeners.

Mrs. Bunting heard one of the older gentlemen sitting near her whisper to another: "Drawing it out all he can; that's what he's doing. Having the time of his life, evidently!" And then the other whispered back, so low that she could only just catch the words, "Aye, aye. But he's a good chap—I knew his father; we were at school together. Takes his job very seriously, you know—he does to-day, at any rate."

She was listening intently, waiting for a word, a sentence, which would relieve her hidden terrors, or, on the other hand, confirm them. But the word, the sentence, was never uttered.

And yet, at the very end of his long peroration, the coroner did throw out a hint which might mean anything—or nothing.

"I am glad to say that we hope to obtain such evidence to-day as will in time lead to the apprehension of the miscreant who has committed, and is still committing, these terrible crimes."

Mrs. Bunting stared uneasily up into the coroner's firm, determined-looking face. What did he mean by that? Was there any new evidence—evidence of which Joe Chandler, for instance, was ignorant? And, as if in answer to the unspoken question, her heart gave a sudden leap, for a big, burly man had taken his place in the witness-box—a policeman who had not been sitting with the other witnesses.

But soon her uneasy terror became stilled. This witness was simply the constable who had found the first body. In quick, business-like tones he described exactly what had happened to him on that cold, foggy morning ten days ago. He was shown a plan, and he marked it slowly, carefully, with a thick finger. That was the exact place—no, he was making a mistake—that was the place where the other body had lain. He explained apologetically that he had got rather mixed up between the two bodies—that of Johanna Cobbett and Sophy Hurtle.

And then the coroner intervened authoritatively: "For the purpose of this inquiry," he said, "we must, I think, for a moment, consider the two murders together."

After that, the witness went on far more comfortably; and as he proceeded, in a quick monotone, the full and deadly horror of The Avenger's acts came over Mrs. Bunting in a great seething flood of sick fear and—and, yes, remorse.

Up to now she had given very little thought—if, indeed, any thought—to the drink-sodden victims of The Avenger. It was he who had filled her thoughts,—

he and those who were trying to track him down. But now? Now she felt sick and sorry she had come here to-day. She wondered if she would ever be able to get the vision the policeman's words had conjured up out of her mind—out of her memory.

And then there came an eager stir of excitement and of attention throughout the whole court, for the policeman had stepped down out of the witness-box, and one of the women witnesses was being conducted to his place.

Mrs. Bunting looked with interest and sympathy at the woman, remembering how she herself had trembled with fear, trembled as that poor, bedraggled, common-looking person was trembling now. The woman had looked so cheerful, so—so well pleased with herself till a minute ago, but now she had become very pale, and she looked round her as a hunted animal might have done.

But the coroner was very kind, very soothing and gentle in his manner, just as that other coroner had been when dealing with Ellen Green at the inquest on that poor drowned girl.

After the witness had repeated in a toneless voice the solemn words of the oath, she began to be taken, step by step, through her story. At once Mrs. Bunting realised that this was the woman who claimed to have seen The Avenger from her bedroom window. Gaining confidence as she went on, the witness described how she had heard a long-drawn, stifled screech, and, aroused from deep sleep, had instinctively jumped out of bed and rushed to her window.

The coroner looked down at something lying on his desk. "Let me see! Here is the plan. Yes—I think I understand that the house in which you are lodging exactly faces the alley where the two crimes were committed?"

And there arose a quick, futile discussion. The house did not face the alley, but the window of the witness's bedroom faced the alley.

"A distinction without a difference," said the coroner testily. "And now tell us as clearly and quickly as you can what you saw when you looked out."

There fell a dead silence on the crowded court. And then the woman broke out, speaking more volubly and firmly than she had yet done. "I saw 'im!" she cried. "I shall never forget it—no, not till my dying day!" And she looked round defiantly.

Mrs. Bunting suddenly remembered a chat one of the newspaper men had had with a person who slept under this woman's room. That person had unkindly said she felt sure that Lizzie Cole had not got up that night—that she had made up the whole story. She, the speaker, slept lightly, and that night had been tending a sick child. Accordingly, she would have heard if there had been either the scream described by Lizzie Cole, or the sound of Lizzie Cole jumping out of bed.

"We quite understand that you think you saw the"—the coroner hesitated—"the individual who had just perpetrated these terrible crimes. But what we want to have from you is a description of him. In spite of the foggy atmosphere about which all are agreed, you say you saw him distinctly, walking along for some yards below your window. Now, please, try and tell us what he was like."

The woman began twisting and untwisting the corner of a coloured handkerchief she held in her hand.

"Let us begin at the beginning," said the coroner patiently. "What sort of a hat was this man wearing when you saw him hurrying from the passage?"

"It was just a black 'at," said the witness at last, in a husky, rather anxious tone.

"Yes—just a black hat. And a coat—were you able to see what sort of a coat he was wearing?"

" 'E 'adn't got no coat," she said decidedly. "No coat at all! I remembers that very perticulerly. I thought it queer, as it was so cold—everybody as can wears some sort o' coat this weather!"

A juryman who had been looking at a strip of newspaper, and apparently not attending at all to what the witness was saying, here jumped up and put out his hand.

"Yes?" the coroner turned to him.

"I just want to say that this 'ere witness—if her name is Lizzie Cole, began by saying The Avenger was wearing a coat—a big, heavy coat. I've got it here, in this bit of paper."

"I never said so!" cried the woman passionately. "I was made to say all those things by the young man what came to me from the *Evening Sun*. Just put in what 'e liked in 'is paper, 'e did—not what I said at all!"

At this there was some laughter, quickly suppressed.

"In future," said the coroner severely, addressing the juryman, who had now sat down again, "you must ask any question you wish to ask through your foreman, and please wait till I have concluded my examination of the witness."

But this interruption, this—this accusation, had utterly upset the witness. She began contradicting herself hopelessly. The man she had seen hurrying by in the semi-darkness below was tall—no, he was short. He was thin—no, he was a stoutish young man. And as to whether he was carrying anything, there was quite an acrimonious discussion.

Most positively, most confidently, the witness declared that she had seen a newspaper parcel under his arm; it had bulged out at the back—so she declared. But it was proved, very gently and firmly, that she had said nothing of the kind to the gentleman from Scotland Yard who had taken down her first account—in fact, to him she had declared confidently that the man had carried nothing— nothing at all; that she had seen his arms swinging up and down.

One fact—if fact it could be called—the coroner did elicit. Lizzie Cole suddenly volunteered the statement that as he had passed her window he had looked up at her. This was quite a new statement.

"He looked up at you?" repeated the coroner. "You said nothing of that in your examination."

"I said nothink because I was scared—nigh scared to death!"

"If you could really see his countenance, for we know the night was dark and foggy, will you please tell me what he was like?"

But the coroner was speaking casually, his hand straying over his desk; not a creature in that court now believed the woman's story.

"Dark!" she answered dramatically. "Dark, almost black! If you can take my meaning, with a sort of nigger look."

And then there was a titter. Even the jury smiled. And sharply the coroner bade Lizzie Cole stand down.

Far more credence was given to the evidence of the next witness.

This was an older, quieter-looking woman, decently dressed in black. Being the wife of a night watchman whose work lay in a big warehouse situated about a hundred yards from the alley or passage where the crimes had taken place, she had gone out to take her husband some food he always had at one in the morning. And a man had passed her, breathing hard and walking very quickly. Her attention had been drawn to him because she very seldom met anyone at that hour, and because he had such an odd, peculiar look and manner.

Mrs. Bunting, listening attentively, realised that it was very much from what this witness had said that the official description of The Avenger had been composed—that description which had brought such comfort to her, Ellen Bunting's, soul.

This witness spoke quietly, confidently, and her account of the newspaper parcel the man was carrying was perfectly clear and positive.

"It was a neat parcel," she said, "done up with string."

She had thought it an odd thing for a respectably dressed young man to carry such a parcel—that was what had made her notice it. But when pressed, she had to admit that it had been a very foggy night—so foggy that she herself had been afraid of losing her way, though every step was familiar.

When the third woman went into the box, and with sighs and tears told of her acquaintance with one of the deceased, with Johanna Cobbett, there was a stir of sympathetic attention. But she had nothing to say throwing any light on the investigation, save that she admitted reluctantly that "Anny" would have been such a nice, respectable young woman if it hadn't been for the drink.

Her examination was shortened as much as possible; and so was that of the next witness, the husband of Johanna Cobbett. He was a very respectable-looking man, a foreman in a big business house at Croydon. He seemed to feel his position most acutely. He hadn't seen his wife for two years; he hadn't had news of her for six months. Before she took to drink she had been an admirable wife, and—and yes, mother.

Yet another painful few minutes, to anyone who had a heart, or imagination to understand, was spent when the father of the murdered woman was in the box. He had had later news of his unfortunate daughter than her husband had had, but of course he could throw no light at all on her murder or murderer.

A barman, who had served both the women with drink just before the public-house closed for the night, was handled rather roughly. He had stepped with a jaunty air into the box, and came out of it looking cast down, uneasy.

And then there took place a very dramatic, because an utterly unexpected, incident. It was one of which the evening papers made the utmost, much to Mrs. Bunting's indignation. But neither coroner nor jury—and they, after all, were the people who mattered—thought a great deal of it.

There had come a pause in the proceedings. All seven witnesses had been heard, and a gentleman near Mrs. Bunting whispered, "They are now going to call Dr. Gaunt. He's been in every big murder case for the last thirty years. He's sure to have something interesting to say. It was really to hear him *I* came."

But before Dr. Gaunt had time even to get up from the seat with which he had been accommodated close to the coroner, there came a stir among the general public, or, rather, among those spectators who stood near the low wooden door which separated the official part of the court from the gallery.

The coroner's officer, with an apologetic air, approached the coroner, and handed him up an envelope. And again in an instant, there fell absolute silence on the court.

Looking rather annoyed, the coroner opened the envelope. He glanced down the sheet of notepaper it contained. Then he looked up.

"Mr.——" then he glanced down again. "Mr.—ah—Mr.—is it Cannot?" he said doubtfully, "may come forward."

There ran a titter through the spectators, and the coroner frowned.

A neat, jaunty-looking old gentleman, in a nice fur-lined overcoat, with a fresh, red face and white side-whiskers, was conducted from the place where he had been standing among the general public, to the witness-box.

"This is somewhat out of order, Mr.—er—Cannot," said the coroner severely. "You should have sent me this note before the proceedings began. This gentleman," he said, addressing the jury, "informs me that he has something of the utmost importance to reveal in connection with our investigation."

"I have remained silent—I have locked what I knew within my own breast"— began Mr. Cannot, in a quavering voice, "because I am so afraid of the Press! I knew if I said anything, even to the police, that my house would be besieged by reporters and newspaper men. . . . I have a delicate wife, Mr. Coroner. Such a state of things—the state of things I imagine—might cause her death—indeed, I hope she will never read a report of these proceedings. Fortunately, she has an excellent trained nurse——"

"You will now take the oath," said the coroner sharply. He already regretted having allowed this absurd person to have his say.

Mr. Cannot took the oath with a gravity and decorum which had been lacking in most of those who had preceded him.

"I will address myself to the jury," he began.

"You will do nothing of the sort," broke in the coroner. "Now, please attend to me. You assert in your letter that you know who is the—the——"

"The Avenger," put in Mr. Cannot promptly.

"The perpetrator of these crimes. You further declare that you met him on the very night he committed the murder we are now investigating?"

"I do so declare," said Mr. Cannot confidently. "Though in the best of health myself,"—he beamed round the court, a now amused, attentive court—"it is my fate to be surrounded by sick people, to have only ailing friends. I have to trouble you with my private affairs, Mr. Coroner, in order to explain why I happened to be out at so undue an hour as one o'clock in the morning——"

Again a titter ran through the court. Even the jury broke into broad smiles.

"Yes," went on the witness solemnly, "I was with a sick friend—in fact, I may say a dying friend, for since then he has passed away. I will not reveal my exact dwelling-place; you, sir, have it on my notepaper. It is not necessary to reveal it, but you will understand me when I say that in order to come home I had to pass through a portion of the Regent's Park; and it was there—to be exact, about the middle of Prince's Terrace—when a very peculiar-looking individual stopped and accosted me."

Mrs. Bunting's hand shot up to her breast. A feeling of deadly fear took possession of her.

"I mustn't faint," she said to herself hurriedly. "I mustn't faint! Whatever's the matter with me?" She took out her bottle of smelling-salts, and gave it a good, long sniff.

"He was a grim, gaunt man, was this stranger, Mr. Coroner, with a very odd-looking face. I should say an educated man—in common parlance, a gentleman. What drew my special attention to him was that he was talking aloud to himself—in fact, he seemed to be repeating poetry. I give you my word, I had no thought of The Avenger, no thought at all. To tell you the truth, I thought this gentleman was a poor escaped lunatic, a man who'd got away from his keeper. The Regent's Park, sir, as I need hardly tell you, is a most quiet and soothing neighbourhood——"

And then a member of the general public gave a loud guffaw.

"I appeal to you, sir," the old gentleman suddenly cried out, "to protect me from this unseemly levity! I have not come here with any other object than that of doing my duty as a citizen!"

"I must ask you to keep to what is strictly relevant," said the coroner stiffly. "Time is going on, and I have another important witness to call—a medical witness. Kindly tell me, as shortly as possible, what made you suppose that this stranger could possibly be—" with an effort he brought out for the first time since the proceedings began, the words, "The Avenger?"

"I am coming to that!" said Mr. Cannot hastily. "I am coming to that! Bear with me a little longer, Mr. Coroner. It was a foggy night, but not as foggy as it became later. And just when we were passing one another, I and this man, who was talking aloud to himself—he, instead of going on, stopped and turned towards me. That made me feel queer and uncomfortable, the more so that there was a very wild, mad look on his face. I said to him, as soothingly as possible, 'A very foggy night, sir.' And he said, 'Yes—yes, it is a foggy night, a night fit for the commission of dark and salutary deeds.' A very strange phrase, sir, that—'dark and salutary deeds.'" He looked at the coroner expectantly——

"Well? Well, Mr. Cannot? Was that all? Did you see this person go off in the direction of—of King's Cross, for instance?"

"No." Mr. Cannot reluctantly shook his head. "No, I must honestly say I did not. He walked along a certain way by my side, and then he crossed the road and was lost in the fog."

"That will do," said the coroner. He spoke more kindly. "I thank you, Mr. Cannot, for coming here and giving us what you evidently consider important information."

Mr. Cannot bowed, a funny, little, old-fashioned bow, and again some of those present tittered rather foolishly.

As he was stepping down from the witness-box, he turned and looked up at the coroner, opening his lips as he did so. There was a murmur of talking going on, but Mrs. Bunting, at any rate, heard quite distinctly what it was that he said:

"One thing I have forgotten, sir, which may be of importance. The man carried a bag—a rather light-coloured leather bag, in his left hand. It was such a bag, sir, as might well contain a long-handled knife."

Mrs. Bunting looked at the reporters' table. She remembered suddenly that she had told Bunting about the disappearance of Mr. Sleuth's bag. And then a feeling of intense thankfulness came over her; not a single reporter at the long, ink-stained table had put down that last remark of Mr. Cannot. In fact, not one of them had heard it.

Again the last witness put up his hand to command attention. And then silence did fall on the court.

"One word more," he said in a quavering voice. "May I ask to be accommodated with a seat for the rest of the proceedings? I see there is some room left on the witnesses' bench." And, without waiting for permission, he nimbly stepped across and sat down.

Mrs. Bunting looked up, startled. Her friend, the inspector, was bending over her.

"Perhaps you'd like to come along now," he said urgently. "I don't suppose you want to hear the medical evidence. It's always painful for a female to hear that. And there'll be an awful rush when the inquest's over. I could get you away quietly now."

She rose, and, pulling her veil down over her pale face, followed him obediently.

Down the stone staircase they went, and through the big, now empty, room downstairs.

"I'll let you out the back way," he said. "I expect you're tired, ma'am, and will like to get home to a cup o' tea."

"I don't know how to thank you!" There were tears in her eyes. She was trembling with excitement and emotion. "You *have* been good to me."

"Oh, that's nothing," he said a little awkwardly. "I expect you went through a pretty bad time, didn't you?"

"Will they be having that old gentleman again?" she spoke in a whisper, and looked up at him with a pleading, agonised look.

"Good Lord, no! Crazy old fool! We're troubled with a lot of those sort of people, you know, ma'am, and they often do have funny names, too. You see, that sort is busy all their lives in the City, or what not; then they retires when they gets about sixty, and they're fit to hang themselves with dullness. Why, there's hundreds of lunies of the sort to be met in London. You can't go about at night and not meet 'em. Plenty of 'em!"

"Then you don't think there was anything in what he said?" she ventured.

"In what that old gent said? Goodness—no!" he laughed good-naturedly. "But I'll tell you what I *do* think. If it wasn't for the time that had gone by, I should believe that the second witness *had* seen that crafty devil—" he lowered his voice. "But, there, Dr. Gaunt declares most positively—so did two other medical gentlemen—that the poor creatures had been dead hours when they was found. Medical gentlemen are always very positive about their evidence. They have to be—otherwise who'd believe 'em? If we'd time I could tell you of a case in which—well, 'twas all because of Dr. Gaunt that the murderer escaped. We all knew perfectly well the man we caught did it, but he was able to prove an alibi as to the time Dr. Gaunt *said* the poor soul was killed."

CHAPTER XX

It was not late even now, for the inquest had begun very punctually, but Mrs. Bunting felt that no power on earth should force her to go to Ealing. She felt quite tired out, and as if she could think of nothing.

Pacing along very slowly, as if she were an old, old woman, she began listlessly turning her steps towards home. Somehow she felt that it would do her more good to stay out in the air than take the train. Also she would thus put off the moment—the moment to which she looked forward with dread and dislike—when she would have to invent a circumstantial story as to what she had said to the doctor, and what the doctor had said to her.

Like most men and women of his class, Bunting took a great interest in other people's ailments, the more interest that he was himself so remarkably healthy. He would feel quite injured if Ellen didn't tell him everything that had happened; everything, that is, that the doctor had told her.

As she walked swiftly along, at every corner, or so it seemed to her, and outside every public-house, stood eager boys selling the latest edition of the afternoon papers to equally eager buyers. "Avenger Inquest!" they shouted exultantly. "All the latest evidence!" At one place, where there were a row of contents-bills pinned to the pavement by stones, she stopped and looked down. "Opening of the Avenger Inquest. What is he really like? Full description." On yet another ran the ironic query: "Avenger Inquest. Do you know him?"

And as that facetious question stared up at her in huge print, Mrs. Bunting turned sick—so sick and faint that she did what she had never done before in her life—she pushed her way into a public-house, and, putting two pennies down on the counter, asked for, and received, a glass of cold water.

As she walked along the now gas-lit streets, she found her mind dwelling persistently—not on the inquest at which she had been present, not even on The Avenger, but on his victims.

Shudderingly, she visualised the two cold bodies lying in the mortuary. She seemed also to see that third body, which, though cold, must yet be warmer than the other two, for at this time yesterday The Avenger's last victim had been alive, poor soul—alive and, according to a companion of hers whom the papers had already interviewed, particularly merry and bright.

Hitherto Mrs. Bunting had been spared in any real sense a vision of The Avenger's victims. Now they haunted her, and she wondered wearily if this fresh horror was to be added to the terrible fear which encompassed her night and day.

As she came within sight of home, her spirit suddenly lightened. The narrow, drab-coloured little house, flanked each side by others exactly like it in every single particular, save that their front yards were not so well kept, looked as if it could, aye, and would, keep any secret closely hidden.

For a moment, at any rate, The Avenger's victims receded from her mind. She thought of them no more. All her thoughts were concentrated on Bunting—Bunting and Mr. Sleuth. She wondered what had happened during her absence—whether the lodger had rung his bell, and, if so, how he had got on with Bunting, and Bunting with him?

She walked up the little flagged path wearily, and yet with a pleasant feeling of home-coming. And then she saw that Bunting must have been watching for her behind the now closely drawn curtains, for before she could either knock or ring he had opened the door.

"I was getting quite anxious about you," he exclaimed. "Come in, Ellen, quick!

You must be fair perished a day like now—and you out so little as you are. Well? I hope you found the doctor all right?" He looked at her with affectionate anxiety.

And then there came a sudden, happy thought to Mrs. Bunting. "No," she said slowly, "Doctor Evans wasn't in. I waited, and waited, and waited, but he never came in at all. 'Twas my own fault," she added quickly. Even at such a moment as this she told herself that though she had, in a sort of way, a kind of right to lie to her husband, she had no right to slander the doctor who had been so kind to her years ago. "I ought to have sent him a card yesterday night," she said. "Of course, I was a fool to go all that way, just on chance of finding a doctor in. It stands to reason they've got to go out to people at all times of day."

"I hope they gave you a cup of tea?" he said.

And again she hesitated, debating a point with herself: if the doctor had a decent sort of servant, of course, she, Ellen Bunting, would have been offered a cup of tea, especially if she explained she'd known him a long time.

She compromised. "I was offered some," she said, in a weak, tired voice. "But there, Bunting, I didn't feel as if I wanted it. I'd be very grateful for a cup now— if you'd just make it for me over the ring."

"'Course I will," he said eagerly. "You just come in and sit down, my dear. Don't trouble to take your things off now—wait till you've had tea."

And she obeyed him. "Where's Daisy?" she asked suddenly. "I thought the girl would be back by the time I got home."

"She ain't coming home to-day"—there was an odd, sly, smiling look on Bunting's face.

"Did she send a telegram?" asked Mrs. Bunting.

"No. Young Chandler's just come in and told me. He's been over there and,— would you believe it, Ellen?—he's managed to make friends with Margaret. Wonderful what love will do, ain't it? He went over there just to help Daisy carry her bag back, you know, and then Margaret told him that her lady had sent her some money to go to the play, and she actually asked Joe to go with them this evening—she and Daisy—to the pantomime. Did you ever hear o' such a thing?"

"Very nice for them, I'm sure," said Mrs. Bunting absently. But she was pleased—pleased to have her mind taken off herself. "Then when *is* that girl coming home?" she asked patiently.

"Well, it appears that Chandler's got to-morrow morning off too—this evening and to-morrow morning. He'll be on duty all night, but he proposes to go over and bring Daisy back in time for early dinner. Will that suit you, Ellen?"

"Yes. That'll be all right," she said. "I don't grudge the girl her bit of pleasure. One's only young once. By the way, did the lodger ring while I was out?"

Bunting turned round from the gas-ring, which he was watching to see the kettle boil. "No," he said. "Come to think of it, it's rather a funny thing, but the truth is, Ellen, I never gave Mr. Sleuth a thought. You see, Chandler came in and was telling me all about Margaret, laughing-like, and then something else happened while you was out, Ellen."

"Something else happened?" she said in a startled voice. Getting up from her chair she came towards her husband: "What happened? Who came?"

"Just a message for me, asking if I could go to-night to wait at a young lady's birthday party. In Hanover Terrace it is. A waiter—one of them nasty Swiss fellows as works for nothing—fell out just at the last minute, and so they *had* to send for me."

His honest face shone with triumph. The man who had taken over his old friend's business in Baker Street had hitherto behaved very badly to Bunting, and that though Bunting had been on the books for ever so long, and had always given every satisfaction. But this new man had never employed him—no, not once.

"I hope you didn't make yourself too cheap?" said his wife jealously.

"No, that I didn't! I hum'd and haw'd a lot; and I could see the fellow was quite worried—in fact, at the end he offered me half-a-crown more. So I graciously consented!"

Husband and wife laughed more merrily than they had done for a long time.

"You won't mind being alone here? I don't count the lodger—he's no good— —" Bunting looked at her anxiously. He was only prompted to ask the question because lately Ellen had been so queer, so unlike herself. Otherwise it never would have occurred to him that she could be afraid of being alone in the house. She had often been so in the days when he got more jobs.

She stared at him, a little suspiciously. "I be afraid?" she echoed. "Certainly not. Why should I be? I've never been afraid before. What d'you exactly mean by that, Bunting?"

"Oh, nothing. I only thought you might feel funny-like, all alone on this ground floor. You was so upset yesterday when that young fool Chandler came, dressed up, to the door."

"I shouldn't have been frightened if he'd just been an ordinary stranger," she said shortly. "He said something silly to me—just in keeping with his character-like, and it upset me. Besides, I feel better now."

As she was sipping gratefully her cup of tea, there came a noise outside, the shouts of newspaper-sellers.

"I'll just run out," said Bunting apologetically, "and see what happened at that inquest to-day. Besides, they may have a clue about the horrible affair last night. Chandler was full of it—when he wasn't talking about Daisy and Margaret, that is. He's on to-night, luckily not till twelve o'clock; plenty of time to escort the two of 'em back after the play. Besides, he said he'll put them into a cab and blow the expense, if the panto' goes on too long for him to take 'em home."

"On to-night?" repeated Mrs. Bunting. "Whatever for?"

"Well, you see, The Avenger's always done 'em in couples, so to speak. They've got an idea that he'll have a try again to-night. However, even so, Joe's only on from midnight till five o'clock. Then he'll go and turn in a bit before going off to fetch Daisy. Fine thing to be young, ain't it, Ellen?"

"I can't believe that he'd go out on such a night as this!"

"What *do* you mean?" said Bunting, staring at her. Ellen had spoken so oddly, as if to herself, and in so fierce and passionate a tone.

"What do I mean?" she repeated—and a great fear clutched at her heart. What had she said? She had been thinking aloud.

"Why, by saying he won't go out. Of course, he has to go out. Besides, he'll have been to the play as it is. 'Twould be a pretty thing if the police didn't go out, just because it was cold!"

"I—I was thinking of The Avenger," said Mrs. Bunting. She looked at her husband fixedly. Somehow she had felt impelled to utter those true words.

"He don't take no heed of heat nor cold," said Bunting sombrely. "I take it the man's dead to all human feeling—saving, of course, revenge."

"So that's your idea about him, is it?" She looked across at her husband. Somehow this dangerous, this perilous conversation between them attracted her strangely. She felt as if she must go on with it. "D'you think he was the man that woman said she saw? That young man what passed her with a newspaper parcel?"

"Let me see," he said slowly. "I thought that 'twas from the bedroom window a woman saw him?"

"No, no. I mean the *other* woman, what was taking her husband's breakfast to him in the warehouse. She was far the most respectable-looking woman of the two," said Mrs. Bunting impatiently.

And then, seeing her husband's look of utter, blank astonishment, she felt a thrill of unreasoning terror. She must have gone suddenly mad to have said what she did! Hurriedly she got up from her chair. "There, now," she said; "here I am gossiping all about nothing when I ought to be seeing about the lodger's supper. It was someone in the train talked to me about that person as thinks she saw The Avenger."

Without waiting for an answer, she went into her bedroom, lit the gas, and shut the door. A moment later she heard Bunting go out to buy the paper they had both forgotten during their dangerous discussion.

As she slowly, languidly took off her nice, warm coat and shawl, Mrs. Bunting found herself shivering. It was dreadfully cold, quite unnaturally cold even for the time of year.

She looked longingly towards the fireplace. It was now concealed by the washhand-stand, but how pleasant it would be to drag that stand aside and light a bit of fire, especially as Bunting was going to be out to-night. He would have to put on his dress clothes, and she didn't like his dressing in the sitting-room. It didn't suit her ideas that he should do so. How if she did light the fire here, in their bedroom? It would be nice for her to have a bit of fire to cheer her up after he had gone.

Mrs. Bunting knew only too well that she would have very little sleep the coming night. She looked over, with shuddering distaste, at her nice, soft bed. There she would lie, on that couch of little ease, listening—listening. . . .

She went down to the kitchen. Everything was ready for Mr. Sleuth's supper, for she had made all her preparations before going out so as not to have to hurry back before it suited her to do so.

Leaning the tray for a moment on the top of the banisters, she listened. Even in that nice warm drawing-room, and with a good fire, how cold the lodger must feel sitting studying at the table! But unwonted sounds were coming through the door. Mr. Sleuth was moving restlessly about the room, not sitting reading, as was his wont at this time of the evening.

She knocked, and then waited a moment.

There came the sound of a sharp click, that of the key turning in the lock of the chiffonnier cupboard—or so Mr. Sleuth's landlady could have sworn.

There was a pause—she knocked again.

"Come in," said Mr. Sleuth loudly, and she opened the door and carried in the tray.

"You are a little earlier than usual, are you not, Mrs. Bunting?" he said, with a touch of irritation in his voice.

"I don't think so, sir, but I've been out. Perhaps I lost count of the time. I thought you'd like your breakfast early, as you had dinner rather sooner than usual."

"Breakfast? Did you say breakfast, Mrs. Bunting?"

"I beg your pardon, sir, I'm sure! I meant supper."

He looked at her fixedly. It seemed to Mrs. Bunting that there was a terrible questioning look in his dark, sunken eyes.

"Aren't you well?" he said slowly. "You don't look well, Mrs. Bunting."

"No, sir," she said. "I'm not well. I went over to see a doctor this afternoon, to Ealing, sir."

"I hope he did you good, Mrs. Bunting"—the lodger's voice had become softer, kinder in quality.

"It always does me good to see the doctor," said Mrs. Bunting evasively.

And then a very odd smile lit up Mr. Sleuth's face. "Doctors are a maligned body of men," he said. "I'm glad to hear you speak well of them. They do their best, Mrs. Bunting. Being human they are liable to err, but I assure you they do their best."

"That I'm sure they do, sir"—she spoke heartily, sincerely. Doctors had always treated her most kindly, and even generously.

And then, having laid the cloth, and put the lodger's one hot dish upon it, she went towards the door.

"Wouldn't you like me to bring up another scuttleful of coals, sir? It's bitterly cold—getting colder every minute. A fearful night to have to go out in——" she looked at him deprecatingly.

And then Mr. Sleuth did something which startled her very much. Pushing his chair back, he jumped up and drew himself to his full height.

"What d'you mean?" he stammered. "Why did you say that, Mrs. Bunting?"

She stared at him, fascinated, affrighted. Again there came an awful questioning look over his face.

"I was thinking of Bunting, sir. He's got a job to-night. He's going to act as waiter at a young lady's birthday party. I was thinking it's a pity he has to turn out, and in his thin clothes, too"—she brought out her words jerkily.

Mr. Sleuth seemed somewhat reassured, and again he sat down. "Ah!" he said. "Dear me—I'm sorry to hear that! I hope your husband will not catch cold, Mrs. Bunting."

And then she shut the door, and went downstairs.

Without telling Bunting what she meant to do, she dragged the heavy washhand-stand away from the chimneypiece, and lighted the fire.

Then in some triumph she called Bunting in.

"Time for you to dress," she cried out cheerfully, "and I've got a little bit of fire for you to dress by."

As he exclaimed at her extravagance, "Well, 'twill be pleasant for me, too; keep me company-like while you're out; and make the room nice and warm when you come in. You'll be fair perished, even walking that short way," she said.

And then, while her husband was dressing, Mrs. Bunting went upstairs and cleared away Mr. Sleuth's supper.

The lodger said no word while she was so engaged—no word at all.

He was sitting away from the table, rather an unusual thing for him to do, and staring into the fire, his hands on his knees.

Mr. Sleuth looked lonely, very, very lonely and forlorn. Somehow, a great rush of pity, as well as of horror, came over Mrs. Bunting's heart. He was such a—a— she searched for a word in her mind, but could only find the word "gentle"—he was such a nice, gentle gentleman, was Mr. Sleuth. Lately he had again taken to leaving his money about, as he had done the first day or two, and with some concern his landlady had seen that the store had diminished a good deal. A very simple calculation had made her realise that almost the whole of that missing money had come her way, or, at any rate, had passed through her hands.

Mr. Sleuth never stinted himself as to food, or stinted them, his landlord and his landlady, as to what he had said he would pay. And Mrs. Bunting's conscience pricked her a little, for he hardly ever used that room upstairs—that room for which he had paid extra so generously. If Bunting got another job or two through that nasty man in Baker Street,—and now that the ice had been broken between them it was very probable that he would do so, for he was a very well-trained, experienced waiter—then she thought she would tell Mr. Sleuth that she no longer wanted him to pay as much as he was now doing.

She looked anxiously, deprecatingly, at his long, bent back.

"Good-night, sir," she said at last.

Mr. Sleuth turned round. His face looked sad and worn.

"I hope you'll sleep well, sir."

"Yes, I'm sure I shall sleep well. But perhaps I shall take a little turn first. Such is my way, Mrs. Bunting; after I have been studying all day I require a little exercise."

"Oh, I wouldn't go out to-night," she said deprecatingly. " 'Tisn't fit for anyone to be out in the bitter cold."

"And yet—and yet"—he looked at her attentively—"there will probably be many people out in the streets to-night."

"A many more than usual, I fear, sir."

"Indeed?" said Mr. Sleuth quickly. "Is it not a strange thing, Mrs. Bunting, that people who have all day in which to amuse themselves should carry their revels far into the night?"

"Oh, I wasn't thinking of revellers, sir; I was thinking"—she hesitated, then, with a gasping effort Mrs. Bunting brought out the words, "of the police."

"The police?" He put up his right hand and stroked his chin two or three times with a nervous gesture. "But what is man—what is man's puny power or strength against that of God, or even of those over whose feet God has set a guard?"

Mr. Sleuth looked at his landlady with a kind of triumph lighting up his face, and Mrs. Bunting felt a shuddering sense of relief. Then she had not offended her lodger? She had not made him angry by that, that—was it a hint she had meant to convey to him?

"Very true, sir," she said respectfully. "But Providence means us to take care o' ourselves too." And then she closed the door behind her and went downstairs.

But Mr. Sleuth's landlady did not go on, down to the kitchen. She came into her sitting-room, and, careless of what Bunting would think the next morning, put the tray with the remains of the lodger's meal on her table. Having done that, and having turned out the gas in the passage and the sitting-room, she went into her bedroom and closed the door.

The fire was burning brightly and clearly. She told herself that she did not need any other light to undress by.

But once she was in bed Mrs. Bunting turned restless. She tossed this way and that, full of discomfort and unease. Perhaps it was the unaccustomed firelight dancing on the walls, making queer shadows all round her, which kept her so wide awake.

She lay thinking and listening—listening and thinking. It even occurred to her to do the one thing that might have quieted her excited brain—to get a book, one of those detective stories of which Bunting had a slender store in the next room, and then, lighting the gas, to sit up and read.

No, Mrs. Bunting had always been told it was very wrong to read in bed, and she was not in a mood just now to begin doing anything that she had been told was wrong. . . .

What was it made the flames of the fire shoot up, shoot down, in that queer way? But, watching it for awhile, she did at last doze off a bit.

And then—and then Mrs. Bunting woke with a sudden thumping of her heart. Woke to see that the fire was almost out—woke to hear a quarter to twelve chime out—woke at last to the sound she had been listening for before she fell asleep—the sound of Mr. Sleuth, wearing his rubber-soled shoes, creeping downstairs, along the passage, and so out, very, very quietly by the front door.

CHAPTER XXI

It was a very cold night—so cold, so windy, so snow-laden was the atmosphere, that everyone who could do so stayed indoors.

Bunting, however, was now on his way home from what had proved a really pleasant job. A remarkable piece of luck had come his way this evening, all the more welcome because it was quite unexpected! The young lady at whose birthday party he had been present in capacity of waiter had come into a fortune that day, and she had had the gracious, the surprising, thought of presenting each of the hired waiters with a sovereign!

This gift, which had been accompanied by a few kind words, had gone to Bunting's heart. It had confirmed him in his Conservative principles; only gentlefolk ever behaved in that way; quiet, old-fashioned, respectable gentlefolk, the sort of people of whom those nasty Radicals know nothing and care less!

But the ex-butler was not as happy as he should have been. Slackening his footsteps, he began to think with puzzled concern of how queer his wife had seemed lately. Ellen had become so nervous, so "jumpy," that he didn't know what to make of her sometimes. She had never been really good-tempered—

your capable, self-respecting woman seldom is—but she had never been like what she was now. And she didn't get better as the days went on; in fact she got worse. Of late she had been quite hysterical, and for no reason at all! Take that little practical joke of young Joe Chandler. Ellen knew quite well he often had to go about in some kind of disguise, and yet how she had gone on, quite foolish-like—not at all as one would have expected her to do.

There was another queer thing about her which disturbed him in more senses than one. During the last three weeks or so Ellen had taken to talking in her sleep. "No, no, no!" she had cried out, only the night before. "It isn't true—I won't have it said—it's a lie!" And there had been a wail of horrible fear and revolt in her usually quiet, mincing voice.

Whew! it *was* cold; and he had stupidly forgotten his gloves.

He put his hands in his pockets to keep them warm, and began walking more quickly.

As he tramped steadily along, the ex-butler suddenly caught sight of his lodger walking along the opposite side of the solitary street—one of those short streets leading off the broad road which encircles Regent's Park.

Well! This was a funny time o' night to be taking a stroll for pleasure, like!

Glancing across, Bunting noticed that Mr. Sleuth's tall, thin figure was rather bowed, and that his head was bent toward the ground. His left arm was thrust into his long Inverness cape, and so was quite hidden, but the other side of the cape bulged out, as if the lodger were carrying a bag or parcel in the hand which hung down straight.

Mr. Sleuth was walking rather quickly, and as he walked he talked aloud, which, as Bunting knew, is not unusual with gentlemen who live much alone. It was clear that he had not yet become aware of the proximity of his landlord.

Bunting told himself that Ellen was right. Their lodger was certainly a most eccentric, peculiar person. Strange, was it not, that that odd, luny-like gentleman should have made all the difference to his, Bunting's, and Mrs. Bunting's happiness and comfort in life?

Again glancing across at Mr. Sleuth, he reminded himself, not for the first time, of this perfect lodger's one fault—his odd dislike to meat, and to what Bunting vaguely called to himself, sensible food.

But there, you can't have everything! The more so that the lodger was not one of those crazy vegetarians who won't eat eggs and cheese. No, he was reasonable in this, as in everything else connected with his dealings with the Buntings.

As we know, Bunting saw far less of the lodger than did his wife. Indeed, he had been upstairs only three or four times since Mr. Sleuth had been with them, and when his landlord had had occasion to wait on him the lodger had remained silent. Indeed, their gentleman had made it very clear that he did not like either the husband or wife to come up to his rooms without being definitely asked to do so.

Now, surely, would be a good opportunity for a little genial conversation? Bunting felt pleased to see his lodger; it increased his general comfortable sense of satisfaction.

So it was that the ex-butler, still an active man for his years, crossed over the road, and, stepping briskly forward, began trying to overtake Mr. Sleuth. But the more he hurried along, the more the other hastened, and that without ever turning round to see whose steps he could hear echoing behind him on the now freezing pavement.

Mr. Sleuth's own footsteps were quite inaudible—an odd circumstance, when you came to think of it—as Bunting did think of it later, lying awake by Mrs. Bunting's side in the pitch darkness. What it meant, of course, was that the lodger had rubber soles on his shoes. Now Bunting had never had a pair of rubber-soled shoes sent down to him to clean. He had always supposed the lodger had only one pair of outdoor boots.

The two men—the pursued and the pursuer—at last turned into the Marylebone Road; they were now within a few hundred yards of home. Plucking up courage, Bunting called out, his voice echoing freshly on the still air:

"Mr. Sleuth, sir? Mr. Sleuth!"

The lodger stopped and turned round.

He had been walking so quickly, and he was in so poor a physical condition, that the sweat was pouring down his face.

"Ah! So it's you, Mr. Bunting? I heard footsteps behind me, and I hurried on. I wish I'd known that it was you; there are so many queer characters about at night in London."

"Not on a night like this, sir. Only honest folk who have business out of doors would be out such a night as this. It *is* cold, sir!"

And then into Bunting's slow and honest mind there suddenly crept the query as to what on earth Mr. Sleuth's own business out could be on this bitter night.

"Cold?" the lodger repeated; he was panting a little, and his words came out sharp and quick through his thin lips. "I can't say that I find it cold, Mr. Bunting. When the snow falls, the air always becomes milder."

"Yes, sir; but to-night there's such a sharp east wind. Why, it freezes the very marrow in one's bones! Still, there's nothing like walking in cold weather to make one warm, as you seem to have found, sir."

Bunting noticed that Mr. Sleuth kept his distance in a rather strange way; he walked at the edge of the pavement, leaving the rest of it, on the wall side, to his landlord.

"I lost my way," he said abruptly. "I've been over Primrose Hill to see a friend of mine, a man with whom I studied when I was a lad, and then, coming back, I lost my way."

Now they had come right up to the little gate which opened on the shabby, paved court in front of the house—that gate which now was never locked.

Mr. Sleuth, pushing suddenly forward, began walking up the flagged path, when, with a "By your leave, sir," the ex-butler, stepping aside, slipped in front of his lodger, in order to open the front door for him.

As he passed by Mr. Sleuth, the back of Bunting's bare left hand brushed lightly against the long Inverness cape the lodger was wearing, and, to Bunting's surprise, the stretch of cloth against which his hand lay for a moment was not only damp, damp may-be from stray flakes of snow which had settled upon it, but wet—wet and gluey.

Bunting thrust his left hand into his pocket; it was with the other that he placed the key in the lock of the door.

The two men passed into the hall together.

The house seemed blackly dark in comparison with the lighted-up road outside, and as he groped forward, closely followed by the lodger, there came over Bunting a sudden, reeling sensation of mortal terror, an instinctive, assailing knowledge of frightful immediate danger.

A stuffless voice—the voice of his first wife, the long-dead girl to whom his mind so seldom reverted nowadays—uttered into his ear the words, "Take care!"

And then the lodger spoke. His voice was harsh and grating, though not loud.

"I'm afraid, Mr. Bunting, that you must have felt something dirty, foul, on my coat? It's too long a story to tell you now, but I brushed up against a dead animal, a creature to whose misery some thoughtful soul had put an end, lying across a bench on Primrose Hill."

"No, sir, no. I didn't notice nothing. I scarcely touched you, sir."

It seemed as if a power outside himself compelled Bunting to utter these lying words. "And now, sir, I'll be saying good-night to you," he said.

Stepping back he pressed with all the strength that was in him against the wall, and let the other pass him.

There was a pause, and then—"Good-night," returned Mr. Sleuth, in a hollow voice.

Bunting waited until the lodger had gone upstairs, and then, lighting the gas, he sat down there, in the hall. Mr. Sleuth's landlord felt very queer—queer and sick.

He did not draw his left hand out of his pocket till he heard Mr. Sleuth shut the bedroom door upstairs. Then he held up his left hand and looked at it curiously; it was flecked, streaked with pale reddish blood.

Taking off his boots, he crept into the room where his wife lay asleep. Stealthily he walked across to the wash-hand-stand, and dipped a hand into the water-jug.

"Whatever are you doing? What on earth are you doing?" came a voice from the bed, and Bunting started guiltily.

"I'm just washing my hands."

"Indeed, you're doing nothing of the sort! I never heard of such a thing—putting your hand into the water in which I was going to wash my face to-morrow morning!"

"I'm very sorry, Ellen," he said meekly; "I meant to throw it away. You don't suppose I would have let you wash in dirty water, do you?"

She said no more, but, as he began undressing himself, Mrs. Bunting lay staring at him in a way that made her husband feel even more uncomfortable than he was already.

At last he got into bed. He wanted to break the oppressive silence by telling Ellen about the sovereign the young lady had given him, but that sovereign now seemed to Bunting of no more account than if it had been a farthing he had picked up in the road outside.

Once more his wife spoke, and he gave so great a start that it shook the bed.

"I suppose that you don't know that you've left the light burning in the hall, wasting our good money?" she observed tartly.

He got up painfully and opened the door into the passage. It was as she had said; the gas was flaring away, wasting their good money—or, rather, Mr. Sleuth's good money. Since he had come to be their lodger they had not had to touch their rent money.

Bunting turned out the light and groped his way back to the room, and so to bed. Without speaking again to each other, both husband and wife lay awake till dawn.

The next morning Mr. Sleuth's landlord awoke with a start; he felt curiously heavy about the limbs, and tired about the eyes.

Drawing his watch from under his pillow, he saw that it was seven o'clock. Without waking his wife, he got out of bed and pulled the blind a little to one side. It was snowing heavily, and, as is the way when it snows, even in London, everything was strangely, curiously still.

After he had dressed he went out into the passage. As he had at once dreaded and hoped, their newspaper was already lying on the mat. It was probably the sound of its being pushed through the letter-box which had waked him from his unrestful sleep.

He picked the paper up and went into the sitting-room; then, shutting the door behind him carefully, he spread the newspaper wide open on the table, and bent over it.

As Bunting at last looked up and straightened himself, an expression of intense relief shone upon his stolid face. The item of news he had felt certain would be printed in big type on the middle sheet was not there.

CHAPTER XXII

Feeling amazingly light-hearted, almost light-headed, Bunting lit the gas-ring to make his wife her morning cup of tea.

While he was doing it, he suddenly heard her call out:

"Bunting!" she cried weakly. "Bunting!"

Quickly he hurried in response to her call. "Yes," he said. "What is it, my dear? I won't be a minute with your tea." And he smiled broadly, rather foolishly.

She sat up and looked at him, a dazed expression on her face.

"What are you grinning at?" she asked suspiciously.

"I've had a wonderful piece of luck," he explained. "But you was so cross last night that I simply didn't dare tell you about it."

"Well, tell me now," she said in a low voice.

"I had a sovereign given me by the young lady. You see, it was her birthday party, Ellen, and she'd come into a nice bit of money, and she gave each of us waiters a sovereign."

Mrs. Bunting made no comment. Instead, she lay back and closed her eyes.

"What time d'you expect Daisy?" she asked languidly. "You didn't say what time Joe was going to fetch her, when we was talking about it yesterday."

"Didn't I? Well, I expect they'll be in to dinner."

"I wonder how long that old aunt of hers expects us to keep her?" said Mrs. Bunting thoughtfully.

All the cheer died out of Bunting's round face. He became sullen and angry.

It would be a pretty thing if he couldn't have his own daughter for a bit—especially now that they were doing so well!

"Daisy'll stay here just as long as she can," he said shortly. "It's too bad of you, Ellen, to talk like that! She helps you all she can; and she brisks us both up ever so much. Besides, 'twould be cruel—cruel to take the girl away just now, just as she and that young chap are making friends-like. One would suppose that even you would see the justice o' that!"

But Mrs. Bunting made no answer.

Bunting went off, back into the sitting-room. The water was boiling now, so he made the tea; and then, as he brought the little tray in, his heart softened. Ellen did look really ill—ill and wizened. He wondered if she had a pain about which she wasn't saying anything. She had never been one to grouse about herself.

"The lodger and me came in together last night," he observed genially. "He's certainly a funny kind of gentleman. It wasn't the sort of night one would have chosen to go out for a walk, now was it? And yet he must 'a been out a long time if what he said was true."

"I don't wonder a quiet gentleman like Mr. Sleuth hates the crowded streets," she said slowly. "They gets worse every day—that they do! But go along now; I want to get up."

He went back into their sitting-room, and, having laid the fire and put a match to it, he sat down comfortably with his newspaper.

Deep down in his heart Bunting looked back to this last night with a feeling of shame and self-rebuke. Whatever had made such horrible thoughts and suspicions as had possessed him suddenly come into his head? And just because of a trifling thing like that blood. No doubt Mr. Sleuth's nose had bled—that was what had happened; though, come to think of it, he *had* mentioned brushing up against a dead animal.

Perhaps Ellen was right after all. It didn't do for one to be always thinking of dreadful subjects, of murders and such-like. It made one go dotty—that's what it did.

And just as he was telling himself that, there came to the door a loud knock, the peculiar rat-tat-tat of a telegraph boy. But before he had time to get across the room, let alone to the front door, Ellen had rushed through the room, clad only in a petticoat and shawl.

"I'll go," she cried breathlessly. "I'll go, Bunting; don't you trouble."

He stared at her, surprised, and followed her into the hall.

She put out a hand, and hiding herself behind the door, took the telegram from the invisible boy. "You needn't wait," she said. "If there's an answer we'll send it out ourselves." Then she tore the envelope open—"Oh!" she said with a gasp of relief. "It's only from Joe Chandler, to say he can't go over to fetch Daisy this morning. Then you'll have to go."

She walked back into their sitting-room. "There!" she said. "There it is, Bunting. You just read it."

"Am on duty this morning. Cannot fetch Miss Daisy as arranged.—Chandler."

"I wonder why he's on duty?" said Bunting slowly, uncomfortably. "I thought

Joe's hours was as regular as clockwork—that nothing could make any difference to them. However, there it is. I suppose it'll do all right if I start about eleven o'clock? It may have left off snowing by then. I don't feel like going out again just now. I'm pretty tired this morning."

"You start about twelve," said his wife quickly. "That'll give plenty of time."

The morning went on quietly, uneventfully. Bunting received a letter from Old Aunt saying Daisy must come back next Monday, a little under a week from now. Mr. Sleuth slept soundly, or, at any rate, he made no sign of being awake; and though Mrs. Bunting often stopped to listen, while she was doing her room, there came no sounds at all from overhead.

Scarcely aware that it was so, both Bunting and his wife felt more cheerful than they had done for a long time. They had quite a pleasant little chat when Mrs. Bunting came and sat down for a bit, before going down to prepare Mr. Sleuth's breakfast.

"Daisy will be surprised to see you—not to say disappointed!" she observed, and she could not help laughing a little to herself at the thought.

And when, at eleven, Bunting got up to go, she made him stay on a little longer. "There's no such great hurry as that," she said good-temperedly. "It'll do quite well if you're there by half-past twelve. I'll get dinner ready myself. Daisy needn't help with that. I expect Margaret has worked her pretty hard."

But at last there came the moment when Bunting had to start, and his wife went with him to the front door.

It was still snowing, less heavily, but still snowing. There were very few people coming and going, and only just a few cabs and carts dragging cautiously along through the slush.

Mrs. Bunting was still in the kitchen when there came a ring and a knock at the door—a now very familiar ring and knock. "Joe thinks Daisy's home again by now!" she said, smiling to herself.

Before the door was well open, she heard Chandler's voice. "Don't be scared this time, Mrs. Bunting!" But though not exactly scared, she did give a gasp of surprise. For there stood Joe, made up to represent a public-house loafer; and he looked the part to perfection, with his hair combed down raggedly over his forehead, his seedy-looking, ill-fitting, dirty clothes, and greenish-black pot hat.

"I haven't a minute," he said a little breathlessly. "But I thought I'd just run in to know if Miss Daisy was safe home again. You got my telegram all right? I couldn't send no other kind of message."

"She's not back yet. Her father hasn't been gone long after her." Then, struck by a look in his eyes, "Joe, what's the matter?" she asked quickly.

There came a thrill of suspense in her voice, her face grew drawn, while what little colour there was in it receded, leaving it very pale.

"Well," he said. "Well, Mrs. Bunting, I've no business to say anything about it —but I *will* tell *you*!"

He walked in and shut the door of the sitting-room carefully behind him. "There's been another of 'em!" he whispered. "But this time no one is to know anything about it—not for the present, I mean," he corrected himself hastily. "The Yard thinks we've got a clue—and a good clue, too, this time."

"But where—and how?" faltered Mrs. Bunting.

"Well, 'twas just a bit of luck being able to keep it dark for the present"—he still spoke in that stifled, hoarse whisper. "The poor soul was found dead on a bench on Primrose Hill. And just by chance 'twas one of our fellows saw the body first. He was on his way home, over Hampstead way. He knew where he'd be able to get an ambulance quick, and he made a very clever, secret job of it. I 'spect he'll get promotion for that!"

"What about the clue?" asked Mrs. Bunting, with dry lips. "You said there was a clue?"

"Well, I don't rightly understand about the clue myself. All I knows is it's got something to do with a public-house, 'The Hammer and Tongs,' which isn't far off there. They feels sure The Avenger was in the bar just on closing-time."

And then Mrs. Bunting sat down. She felt better now. It was natural the police should suspect a public-house loafer. "Then that's why you wasn't able to go and fetch Daisy, I suppose?"

He nodded. "Mum's the word, Mrs. Bunting! It'll all be in the last editions of the evening newspapers—it can't be kep' out. There'd be too much of a row if 'twas!"

"Are you going off to that public-house now?" she asked.

"Yes, I am. I've got a awk'ard job—to try and worm something out of the barmaid."

"Something out of the barmaid?" repeated Mrs. Bunting nervously. "Why, whatever for?"

He came and stood close to her. "They think 'twas a gentleman," he whispered.

"A gentleman?"

Mrs. Bunting stared at Chandler with a scared expression. "Whatever makes them think such a silly thing as that?"

"Well, just before closing-time a very peculiar-looking gent, with a leather bag in his hand, went into the bar and asked for a glass of milk. And what d'you think he did? Paid for it with a sovereign! He wouldn't take no change—just made the girl a present of it! That's why the young woman what served him seems quite unwilling to give him away. She won't tell now what he was like. She doesn't know what he's wanted for, and we don't want her to know just yet. That's one reason why nothing's being said public about it. But there! I really must be going now. My time'll be up at three o'clock. I thought of coming in on the way back, and asking you for a cup o' tea, Mrs. Bunting."

"Do," she said. "Do, Joe. You'll be welcome," but there was no welcome in her tired voice.

She let him go alone to the door, and then she went down to her kitchen, and began cooking Mr. Sleuth's breakfast.

The lodger would be sure to ring soon; and then any minute Bunting and Daisy might be home, and they'd want something, too. Margaret always had breakfast, even when "the family" were away, unnaturally early.

As she bustled about Mrs. Bunting tried to empty her mind of all thought. But it is very difficult to do that when one is in a state of torturing uncertainty. She had not dared to ask Chandler what they supposed that man who had gone into the public-house was really like. It was fortunate, indeed, that the lodger and that inquisitive young chap had never met face to face.

At last Mr. Sleuth's bell rang—a quiet little tinkle. But when she went up with his breakfast the lodger was not in his sitting-room.

Supposing him to be still in his bedroom, Mrs. Bunting put the cloth on the table, and then she heard the sound of his footsteps coming down the stairs, and her quick ears detected the slight whirring sound which showed that the gasstove was alight. Mr. Sleuth had already lit the stove; that meant that he would carry out some elaborate experiment this afternoon.

"Still snowing?" he said doubtfully. "How very, very quiet and still London is when under snow, Mrs. Bunting. I have never known it quite as quiet as this morning. Not a sound, outside or in. A very pleasant change from the shouting which sometimes goes on in the Marylebone Road."

"Yes," she said dully. "It's awful quiet to-day—too quiet to my thinking. 'Tain't natural-like."

The outside gate swung to, making a noisy clatter in the still air.

"Is that someone coming in here?" asked Mr. Sleuth, drawing a quick, hissing breath. "Perhaps you will oblige me by going to the window and telling me who it is, Mrs. Bunting?"

And his landlady obeyed him.

"It's only Bunting, sir—Bunting and his daughter."

"Oh! Is that all?"

Mr. Sleuth hurried after her, and she shrank back a little. She had never been quite so near to the lodger before, save on that first day when she had been showing him her rooms.

Side by side they stood, looking out of the window. And, as if aware that someone was standing there, Daisy turned her bright face up towards the window and smiled at her stepmother, and at the lodger, whose face she could only dimly discern.

"A very sweet-looking young girl," said Mr. Sleuth thoughtfully. And then he quoted a little bit of poetry, and this took Mrs. Bunting very much aback.

"Wordsworth," he murmured dreamily. "A poet too little read nowadays, Mrs. Bunting; but one with a beautiful feeling for nature, for youth, for innocence."

"Indeed, sir?" Mrs. Bunting stepped back a little. "Your breakfast will be getting cold, sir, if you don't have it now."

He went back to the table, obediently, and sat down as a child rebuked might have done.

And then his landlady left him.

"Well?" said Bunting cheerily. "Everything went off quite all right. And Daisy's a lucky girl—that she is! Her Aunt Margaret gave her five shillings."

But Daisy did not look as pleased as her father thought she ought to do.

"I hope nothing's happened to Mr. Chandler," she said a little disconsolately. "The very last words he said to me last night was that he'd be there at ten o'clock. I got quite fidgety as the time went on and he didn't come."

"He's been here," said Mrs. Bunting slowly.

"Been here?" cried her husband. "Then why on earth didn't he go and fetch Daisy, if he'd time to come here?"

"He was on the way to his job," his wife answered. "You run along, child, downstairs. Now that you *are* here you can make yourself useful."

And Daisy reluctantly obeyed. She wondered what it was her stepmother didn't want her to hear.

"I've something to tell you, Bunting."

"Yes?" He looked across uneasily. "Yes, Ellen?"

"There's been another o' those murders. But the police don't want anyone to know about it—not yet. That's why Joe couldn't go over and fetch Daisy. They're all on duty again."

Bunting put out his hand and clutched hold of the edge of the mantelpiece. He had gone very red, but his wife was far too much concerned with her own feelings and sensations to notice it.

There was a long silence between them. Then he spoke, making a great effort to appear unconcerned.

"And where did it happen?" he asked. "Close to the other one?"

She hesitated, then: "I don't know. He didn't say. But hush!" she added quickly. "Here's Daisy! Don't let's talk of that horror in front of her-like. Besides, I promised Chandler I'd be mum."

And he acquiesced.

"You can be laying the cloth, child, while I go up and clear away the lodger's breakfast." Without waiting for an answer, she hurried upstairs.

Mr. Sleuth had left the greater part of the nice lemon sole untouched. "I don't feel well to-day," he said fretfully. "And, Mrs. Bunting? I should be much obliged if your husband would lend me that paper I saw in his hand. I do not often care to look at the public prints, but I should like to do so now."

She flew downstairs. "Bunting," she said a little breathlessly, "the lodger would like you just to lend him the *Sun*."

Bunting handed it over to her. "I've read it through," he observed. "You can tell him that I don't want it back again."

On her way up she glanced down at the pink sheet. Occupying a third of the space was an irregular drawing, and under it was written, in rather large characters:

> "We are glad to be able to present our readers with an authentic reproduction of the footprint of the half-worn rubber sole which was almost certainly worn by The Avenger when he committed his double murder ten days ago."

She went into the sitting-room. To her relief it was empty.

"Kindly put the paper down on the table," came Mr. Sleuth's muffled voice from the upper landing.

She did so. "Yes, sir. And Bunting don't want the paper back again, sir. He says he's read it." And then she hurried out of the room.

CHAPTER XXIII

All afternoon it went on snowing; and the three of them sat there, listening and waiting—Bunting and his wife hardly knew for what; Daisy for the knock which would herald Joe Chandler.

And about four there came the now familiar sound.

Mrs. Bunting hurried out into the passage, and as she opened the front door she whispered, "We haven't said anything to Daisy yet. Young girls can't keep secrets."

Chandler nodded comprehendingly. He now looked the low character he had assumed to the life, for he was blue with cold, disheartened, and tired out.

Daisy gave a little cry of shocked surprise, of amusement, of welcome, when she saw how cleverly he was disguised.

"I never!" she exclaimed. "What a difference it do make, to be sure! Why, you looks quite horrid, Mr. Chandler."

And, somehow, that little speech of hers amused her father so much that he quite cheered up. Bunting had been very dull and quiet all that afternoon.

"It won't take me ten minutes to make myself respectable again," said the young man rather ruefully.

His host and hostess, looking at him eagerly, furtively, both came to the conclusion that he had been unsuccessful,—that he had failed, that is, in getting any information worth having. And though, in a sense, they all had a pleasant tea together, there was an air of constraint, even of discomfort, over the little party.

Bunting felt it hard that he couldn't ask the questions that were trembling on his lips; he would have felt it hard any time during the last month to refrain from knowing anything Joe could tell him, but now it seemed almost intolerable to be in this queer kind of half-suspense. There was one important fact he longed to know, and at last came his opportunity of doing so, for Joe Chandler rose to leave, and this time it was Bunting who followed him out into the hall.

"Where did it happen?" he whispered. "Just tell me that, Joe?"

"Primrose Hill," said the other briefly. "You'll know all about it in a minute or two, for it'll be all in the last editions of the evening papers. That's what's been arranged."

"No arrest, I suppose?"

Chandler shook his head despondently. "No," he said, "I'm inclined to think the Yard was on a wrong tack altogether this time. But one can only do one's best. I don't know if Mrs. Bunting told you I'd got to question a barmaid about a man who was in her place just before closing-time. Well, she's said all she knew, and it's as clear as daylight to me that the eccentric old gent she talks about was only a harmless luny. He gave her a sovereign just because she told him she was a teetotaller!" He laughed ruefully.

Even Bunting was diverted at the notion. "Well, that's a queer thing for a barmaid to be!" he exclaimed.

"She's niece to the people what keeps the public," explained Chandler; and then he went out of the front door with a cheerful "So long!"

When Bunting went back into the sitting-room Daisy had disappeared. She had gone downstairs with the tray. "Where's my girl?" he said irritably.

"She's just taken the tray downstairs."

He went out to the top of the kitchen stairs, and called out sharply, "Daisy! Daisy, child! Are you down there?"

"Yes, father," came her eager, happy voice.

"Better come up out of that cold kitchen."

He turned and came back to his wife. "Ellen, is the lodger in? I haven't heard him moving about. Now mind what I says, please! I don't want Daisy to be mixed up with him."

"Mr. Sleuth don't seem very well to-day," answered Mrs. Bunting quietly. " 'Tain't likely I should let Daisy have anything to do with him. Why, she's never even seen him. 'Tain't likely I should allow her to begin waiting on him now."

But though she was surprised and a little irritated by the tone in which Bunting had spoken, no glimmer of the truth illumined her mind. So accustomed had she become to bearing alone the burden of her awful secret, that it would have required far more than a cross word or two, far more than the fact that Bunting looked ill and tired, for her to have come to suspect that her secret was now shared by another, and that other her husband.

Again and again the poor soul had agonised and trembled at the thought of her house being invaded by the police, but that was only because she had always credited the police with supernatural powers of detection. That they should come to know the awful fact she kept hidden in her breast would have seemed to her, on the whole, a natural thing, but that Bunting should even dimly suspect it appeared beyond the range of possibility.

And yet even Daisy noticed a change in her father. He sat cowering over the fire—saying nothing, doing nothing.

"Why, father, ain't you well?" the girl asked more than once.

And, looking up, he would answer, "Yes, I'm well enough, my girl, but I feels cold. It's awful cold. I never did feel anything like the cold we've got just now."

At eight the now familiar shouts and cries began again outside.

"The Avenger again!" "Another horrible crime!" "Extra speshul edition!"— such were the shouts, the exultant yells, hurled through the clear, cold air. They fell, like bombs, into the quiet room.

Both Bunting and his wife remained silent, but Daisy's cheeks grew pink with excitement, and her eye sparkled.

"Hark, father! Hark, Ellen! D'you hear that?" she exclaimed childishly, and even clapped her hands. "I do wish Mr. Chandler had been here. He *would* 'a been startled!"

"Don't, Daisy!" and Bunting frowned.

Then, getting up, he stretched himself. "It's fair getting on my mind," he said, "these horrible things happening. I'd like to get right away from London, just as far as I could—that I would!"

"Up to John-o'-Groat's?" said Daisy, laughing. And then, "Why, father, ain't you going out to get a paper?"

"Yes, I suppose I must."

Slowly he went out of the room, and, lingering a moment in the hall, he put on his greatcoat and hat. Then he opened the front door, and walked down the flagged path. Opening the iron gate, he stepped out on the pavement, then crossed the road to where the newspaper-boys now stood.

The boy nearest to him only had the *Sun*—a late edition of the paper he had already read. It annoyed Bunting to give a penny for a ha'penny rag of which he already knew the main contents. But there was nothing else to do.

Standing under a lamp-post, he opened out the newspaper. It was bitingly cold; that, perhaps, was why his hand shook as he looked down at the big headlines. For Bunting had been very unfair to the enterprise of the editor of his favourite evening paper. This special edition was full of new matter—new matter concerning The Avenger.

First, in huge type right across the page, was the brief statement that The Avenger had now committed his ninth crime, and that he had chosen quite a new locality, namely, the lonely stretch of rising ground known to Londoners as Primrose Hill.

"The police," so Bunting read, *"are very reserved as to the circumstances which led to the finding of the body of The Avenger's latest victim. But we have reason to believe that they possess several really important clues, and that one of them is concerned with the half-worn rubber sole of which we are the first to reproduce an outline to-day. (See over page.)"*

And Bunting, turning the sheet round about, saw the irregular outline he had already seen in the early edition of the *Sun,* that purporting to be a facsimile of the imprint left by The Avenger's rubber sole.

He stared down at the rough outline which took up so much of the space which should have been devoted to reading matter with a queer, sinking feeling of terrified alarm. Again and again criminals had been tracked by the marks their boots or shoes had made at or near the scenes of their misdoings.

Practically the only job Bunting did in his own house of a menial kind was the cleaning of the boots and shoes. He had already visualised early this very afternoon the little row with which he dealt each morning—first came his wife's strong, serviceable boots, then his own two pairs, a good deal patched and mended, and next to his own Mr. Sleuth's strong, hardly worn, and expensive buttoned boots. Of late a dear little coquettish high-heeled pair of outdoor shoes with thin, paperlike soles, bought by Daisy for her trip to London, had ended the row. The girl had worn these thin shoes persistently, in defiance of Ellen's reproof and advice, and he, Bunting, had only once had to clean her more sensible country pair, and that only because the others had become wet through the day he and she had accompanied young Chandler to Scotland Yard.

Slowly he returned across the road. Somehow the thought of going in again, of hearing his wife's sarcastic comments, of parrying Daisy's eager questions, had become intolerable. So he walked slowly, trying to put off the evil moment when he would have to tell them what was in his paper.

The lamp under which he had stood reading was not exactly opposite the house. It was rather to the right of it. And when, having crossed over the roadway, he walked along the pavement towards his own gate, he heard odd, shuffling sounds coming from the inner side of the low wall which shut off his little courtyard from the pavement.

Now, under ordinary circumstances Bunting would have rushed forward to drive out whoever was there. He and his wife had often had trouble, before the cold weather began, with vagrants seeking shelter there. But to-night he stayed outside, listening intently, sick with suspense and fear.

Was it possible that their place was being watched—already? He thought it only too likely. Bunting, like Mrs. Bunting, credited the police with almost supernatural powers, especially since he had paid that visit to Scotland Yard.

But to Bunting's amazement, and, yes, relief, it was his lodger who suddenly loomed up in the dim light.

Mr. Sleuth must have been stooping down, for his tall, lank form had been quite concealed till he stepped forward from behind the low wall on to the flagged path leading to the front door.

The lodger was carrying a brown paper parcel, and, as he walked along, the new boots he was wearing creaked, and the tap-tap of hard nail-studded heels rang out on the flag-stones of the narrow path.

Bunting, still standing outside the gate, suddenly knew what it was his lodger had been doing on the other side of the low wall. Mr. Sleuth had evidently been out to buy himself another pair of new boots, and then he had gone inside the gate and had put them on, placing his old footgear in the paper in which the new pair had been wrapped.

The ex-butler waited—waited quite a long time, not only until Mr. Sleuth had let himself into the house, but till the lodger had had time to get well away, upstairs.

Then he also walked up the flagged pathway, and put his latchkey in the door. He lingered as long over the job of hanging his hat and coat up in the hall as he dared, in fact till his wife called out to him. Then he went in, and throwing the paper down on the table, he said sullenly: "There it is! You can see it all for yourself—not that there's very much to see," and groped his way to the fire.

His wife looked at him in sharp alarm. "Whatever have you done to yourself?" she exclaimed. "You're ill—that's what it is, Bunting. You got a chill last night!"

"I told you I'd got a chill," he muttered. "'Twasn't last night, though; 'twas going out this morning, coming back in the bus. Margaret keeps that housekeeper's room o' hers like a hothouse—that's what she does. 'Twas going out from there into the biting wind, that's what did for me. It must be awful to stand about in such weather; 'tis a wonder to me how that young fellow, Joe Chandler, can stand the life—being out in all weathers like he is."

Bunting spoke at random, his one anxiety being to get away from what was in the paper, which now lay, neglected, on the table.

"Those that keep out o' doors all day never do come to no harm," said his wife testily. "But if you felt so bad, whatever was you out so long for, Bunting? I thought you'd gone away somewhere! D'you mean you only went to get the paper?"

"I just stopped for a second to look at it under the lamp," he muttered apologetically.

"That was a silly thing to do!"

"Perhaps it was," he admitted meekly.

Daisy had taken up the paper. "Well, they don't say much," she said disappointedly. "Hardly anything at all! But perhaps Mr. Chandler'll be in soon again. If so, he'll tell us more about it."

"A young girl like you oughtn't to want to know anything about murders," said her stepmother severely. "Joe won't think any the better of you for your inquisitiveness about such things. If I was you, Daisy, I shouldn't say nothing about it if he does come in—which I fair tell you I hope he won't. I've seen enough of that young chap to-day."

"He didn't come in for long—not to-day," said Daisy, her lip trembling.

"I can tell you one thing that'll surprise you, my dear"—Mrs. Bunting looked significantly at her stepdaughter. She also wanted to get away from that dread news—which yet was no news.

"Yes?" said Daisy, rather defiantly. "What is it, Ellen?"

"Maybe you'll be surprised to hear that Joe did come in this morning. He knew all about that affair then, but he particular asked that you shouldn't be told anything about it."

"Never!" cried Daisy, much mortified.

"Yes," went on her stepmother ruthlessly. "You just ask your father over there if it isn't true."

"'Tain't a healthy thing to speak overmuch about such happenings," said Bunting heavily.

"If I was Joe," went on Mrs. Bunting, quickly pursuing her advantage, "I shouldn't want to talk about such horrid things when I comes in to have a quiet chat with friends. But the minute he comes in that poor young chap is set upon—mostly, I admit, by your father," she looked at her husband severely. "But you does your share, too, Daisy! You asks him this, you asks him that—he's fair puzzled sometimes. It don't do to to be so inquisitive."

And perhaps because of this little sermon on Mrs. Bunting's part, when young Chandler did come in again that evening, very little was said of the new Avenger murder.

Bunting made no reference to it at all, and though Daisy said a word, it was but a word. And Joe Chandler thought he had never spent a pleasanter evening in his life—for it was he and Daisy who talked all the time, their elders remaining for the most part silent.

Daisy told of all that she had done with Aunt Margaret. She described the long, dull hours and the queer jobs her aunt set her to do—the washing up of all the fine drawing-room china in a big basin lined with flannel, and how terrified she (Daisy) had been lest there should come even one teeny little chip to any of it. Then she went on to relate some of the funny things Aunt Margaret had told her about "the family."

There came a really comic tale, which hugely interested and delighted Chandler. This was of how Aunt Margaret's lady had been taken in by an impostor—an impostor who had come up, just as she was stepping out of her carriage, and pretended to have a fit on the doorstep. Aunt Margaret's lady, being a soft one, had insisted on the man coming into the hall, where he had been given all kinds of restoratives. When the man had at last gone off, it was found that he had "wolfed" young master's best walking-stick, one with a fine tortoise-shell top to it. Thus had Aunt Margaret proved to her lady that the man had been shamming, and her lady had been very angry—near had a fit herself!

"There's a lot of that about," said Chandler, laughing. "Incorrigible rogues and vagabonds—that's what those sort of people are!"

And then he, in his turn, told an elaborate tale of an exceptionally clever swindler whom he himself had brought to book. He was very proud of that job, it had formed a white stone in his career as a detective. And even Mrs. Bunting was quite interested to hear about it.

Chandler was still sitting there when Mr. Sleuth's bell rang. For awhile no one stirred; then Bunting looked questioningly at his wife.

"Did you hear that?" he said. "I think, Ellen, that was the lodger's bell."

She got up, without alacrity, and went upstairs.

"I rang," said Mr. Sleuth weakly, "to tell you I don't require any supper to-night, Mrs. Bunting. Only a glass of milk, with a lump of sugar in it. That is all I require—nothing more. I feel very, very far from well"—and he had a hunted, plaintive expression on his face. "And then I thought your husband would like his paper back again, Mrs. Bunting."

Mrs. Bunting, looking at him fixedly, with a sad intensity of gaze of which she was quite unconscious, answered, "Oh, no, sir! Bunting don't require that paper now. He read it all through." Something impelled her to add, ruthlessly, "He's got another paper by now, sir. You may have heard them come shouting outside. Would you like me to bring you up that other paper, sir?"

And Mr. Sleuth shook his head. "No," he said querulously. "I much regret now having asked for the one paper I did read, for it disturbed me, Mrs. Bunting. There was nothing of any value in it—there never is in any public print. I gave up reading newspapers years ago, and I much regret that I broke through my rule to-day."

As if to indicate to her that he did not wish for any more conversation, the lodger then did what he had never done before in his landlady's presence. He went over to the fireplace and deliberately turned his back on her.

She went down and brought up the glass of milk and the lump of sugar he had asked for.

Now he was in his usual place, sitting at the table, studying the Book.

When Mrs. Bunting went back to the others they were chatting merrily. She did not notice that the merriment was confined to the two young people.

"Well?" said Daisy pertly. "How about the lodger, Ellen? Is he all right?"

"Yes," she said stiffly. "Of course he is!"

"He must feel pretty dull sitting up there all by himself—awful lonely-like, I call it," said the girl.

But her stepmother remained silent.

"Whatever does he do with himself all day?" persisted Daisy.

"Just now he's reading the Bible," Mrs. Bunting answered, shortly and dryly.

"Well, I never! That's a funny thing for a gentleman to do!"

And Joe, alone of her three listeners, laughed—a long hearty peal of amusement.

"There's nothing to laugh at," said Mrs. Bunting sharply. "I should feel ashamed of being caught laughing at anything connected with the Bible."

And poor Joe became suddenly quite serious. This was the first time that Mrs. Bunting had ever spoken really nastily to him, and he answered very humbly, "I beg pardon. I know I oughtn't to have laughed at anything to do with the Bible, but you see, Miss Daisy said it so funny-like, and, by all accounts, your lodger must be a queer card, Mrs. Bunting."

"He's no queerer than many people I could mention," she said quickly; and with these enigmatic words she got up, and left the room.

CHAPTER XXIV

Each hour of the days that followed held for Bunting its full meed of aching fear and suspense.

The unhappy man was ever debating within himself what course he should pursue, and, according to his mood and to the state of his mind at any particular moment, he would waver between various widely-differing lines of action.

He told himself again and again, and with fretful unease, that the most awful thing about it all was that *he wasn't sure.* If only he could have been *sure,* he might have made up his mind exactly what it was he ought to do.

But when telling himself this he was deceiving himself, and he was vaguely conscious of the fact; for, from Bunting's point of view, almost any alternative would have been preferable to that which to some, nay, perhaps to most, householders would have seemed the only thing to do, namely, to go to the police. But Londoners of Bunting's class have an uneasy fear of the law. To his mind it would be ruin for him and for his Ellen to be mixed up publicly in such a terrible affair. No one concerned in the business would give them and their future a thought, but it would track them to their dying day, and, above all, it would make it quite impossible for them ever to get again into a good joint situation. It was that for which Bunting, in his secret soul, now longed with all his heart.

No, some other way than going to the police must be found—and he racked his slow brain to find it.

The worst of it was that every hour that went by made his future course more difficult and more delicate, and increased the awful weight on his conscience.

If only he really knew! If only he could feel quite sure! And then he would tell himself that, after all, he had very little to go upon; only suspicion—suspicion, and a secret, horrible certainty that his suspicion was justified.

And so at last Bunting began to long for a solution which he knew to be indefensible from every point of view; he began to hope, that is, in the depths of his heart, that the lodger would again go out one evening on his horrible business and be caught—red-handed.

But far from going out on any business, horrible or other, Mr. Sleuth now never went out at all. He kept upstairs, and often spent quite a considerable part of his day in bed. He still felt, so he assured Mrs. Bunting, very far from well. He had never thrown off the chill he had caught on that bitter night he and his landlord had met on their several ways home.

Joe Chandler, too, had become a terrible complication to Daisy's father. The detective spent every waking hour that he was not on duty with the Buntings; and Bunting, who at one time had liked him so well and so cordially, now became mortally afraid of him.

But though the young man talked of little else than The Avenger, and though on one evening he described at immense length the eccentric-looking gent who had given the barmaid a sovereign, picturing Mr. Sleuth with such awful accuracy that both Bunting and Mrs. Bunting secretly and separately turned sick when they listened to him, he never showed the slightest interest in their lodger.

At last there came a morning when Bunting and Chandler held a strange conversation about The Avenger. The young fellow had come in earlier than usual, and just as he arrived Mrs. Bunting and Daisy were starting out to do some shopping. The girl would fain have stopped behind, but her stepmother had given her a very peculiar, disagreeable look, daring her, so to speak, to be so forward, and Daisy had gone on with a flushed, angry look on her pretty face.

And then, as young Chandler stepped through into the sitting-room, it suddenly struck Bunting that the young man looked unlike himself—indeed, to the ex-butler's apprehension there was something almost threatening in Chandler's attitude.

"I want a word with you, Mr. Bunting," he began abruptly, falteringly. "And I'm glad to have the chance now that Mrs. Bunting and Miss Daisy are out."

Bunting braced himself to hear the awful words—the accusation of having sheltered a murderer, the monster whom all the world was seeking, under his roof. And then he remembered a phrase, a horrible legal phrase—"Accessory after the fact." Yes, he had been that, there wasn't any doubt about it!

"Yes?" he said. "What is it, Joe?" and then the unfortunate man sat down in his chair. "Yes?" he said again uncertainly; for young Chandler had now advanced to the table, he was looking at Bunting fixedly—the other thought threateningly. "Well, out with it, Joe! Don't keep me in suspense."

And then a slight smile broke over the young man's face. "I don't think what I've got to say can take you by surprise, Mr. Bunting."

And Bunting wagged his head in a way that might mean anything—yes or no, as the case might be.

The two men looked at one another for what seemed a very, very long time to the elder of them. And then, making a great effort, Joe Chandler brought out the words, "Well, I suppose you know what it is I want to talk about. I'm sure Mrs. Bunting would, from a look or two she's lately cast on me. It's your daughter—it's Miss Daisy."

And then Bunting gave a kind of cry, 'twixt a sob and a laugh. "My girl?" he cried. "Good Lord, Joe! Is that all you wants to talk about? Why, you fair frightened me—that you did!"

And, indeed, the relief was so great that the room swam round as he stared across it at his daughter's lover, that lover who was also the embodiment of that now awful thing to him, the law. He smiled, rather foolishly, at his visitor; and Chandler felt a sharp wave of irritation, of impatience sweep over his good-natured soul. Daisy's father was an old stupid—that's what *he* was.

And then Bunting grew serious. The room ceased to go round. "As far as I'm concerned," he said, with a good deal of solemnity, even a little dignity, "you have my blessing, Joe. You're a very likely young chap, and I had a true respect for your father."

"Yes," said Chandler, "that's very kind of you, Mr. Bunting. But how about her—her herself?"

Bunting stared at him. It pleased him to think that Daisy hadn't given herself away, as Ellen was always hinting the girl was doing.

"I can't answer for Daisy," he said heavily. "You'll have to ask her yourself—that's not a job any other man can do for you, my lad."

"I never gets a chance. I never sees her, not by our two selves," said Chandler, with some heat. "You don't seem to understand, Mr. Bunting, that I never do see

Miss Daisy alone," he repeated. "I hear now that she's going away Monday, and I've only once had the chance of a walk with her. Mrs. Bunting's very particular, not to say pernickety in her ideas, Mr. Bunting——"

"That's a fault on the right side, that is—with a young girl," said Bunting thoughtfully.

And Chandler nodded. He quite agreed that as regarded other young chaps Mrs. Bunting could not be too particular.

"She's been brought up like a lady, my Daisy has," went on Bunting, with some pride. "That Old Aunt of hers hardly lets her out of her sight."

"I was coming to the old aunt," said Chandler heavily. "Mrs. Bunting she talks as if your daughter was going to stay with that old woman the whole of her natural life—now is that right? That's what I wants to ask you, Mr. Bunting,— is that right?"

"I'll say a word to Ellen, don't you fear," said Bunting abstractedly.

His mind had wandered off, away from Daisy and this nice young chap, to his now constant, anxious preoccupation. "You come along to-morrow," he said, "and I'll see you gets your walk with Daisy. It's only right you and she should have a chance of seeing one another without old folk being by; else how's the girl to tell whether she likes you or not! For the matter of that, you hardly knows her, Joe——" He looked at the young man consideringly.

Chandler shook his head impatiently. "I knows her quite as well as I wants to know her," he said. "I made up my mind the very first time I see'd her, Mr. Bunting."

"No! Did you really?" said Bunting. "Well, come to think of it, I did so with her mother; aye, and years after, with Ellen, too. But I hope *you'll* never want no second, Chandler."

"God forbid!" said the young man under his breath. And then he asked, rather longingly, "D'you think they'll be out long now, Mr. Bunting?"

And Bunting woke up to a due sense of hospitality. "Sit down, sit down, do!" he said hastily. "I don't believe they'll be very long. They've only got a little bit of shopping to do."

And then, in a changed, in a cringing, nervous tone, he asked, "And how about your job, Joe? Nothing new, I take it? I suppose you're all just waiting for *the next time*?"

"Aye—that's about the figure of it." Chandler's voice had also changed; it was now sombre, menacing. "We're fair tired of it—beginning to wonder when it'll end, that we are!"

"Do you ever try and make to yourself a picture of what the master's like?" asked Bunting. Somehow, he felt he must ask that.

"Yes," said Joe slowly. "I've a sort of notion—a savage, fierce-looking devil, the chap must be. It's that description that was circulated put us wrong. I don't believe it was the man that knocked up against that woman in the fog—no, not one bit I don't. But I wavers, I can't quite make up my mind. Sometimes I think it's a sailor—the foreigner they talks about, that goes away for eight or nine days in between, to Holland maybe, or to France. Then, again, I says to myself that it's a butcher, a man from the Central Market. Whoever it is, it's someone used to killing, that's flat."

"Then it don't seem to you possible——?" (Bunting got up and walked over to the window.) "You don't take any stock, I suppose, in that idea some of the papers put out, that the man is"—then he hesitated and brought out, with a gasp—"a gentleman?"

Chandler looked at him, surprised. "No," he said deliberately. "I've made up my mind that's quite a wrong tack, though I knows that some of our fellows—big pots, too—are quite sure that the fellow what gave the girl the sovereign is the man we're looking for. You see, Mr. Bunting, if that's the fact—well, it stands to reason the fellow's an escaped lunatic; and if he's an escaped lunatic he's got a keeper, and they'd be raising a hue and cry after him; now, wouldn't they?"

"You don't think," went on Bunting, lowering his voice, "that he could be just staying somewhere, lodging-like?"

"D'you mean that The Avenger may be a toff, staying in some West End hotel, Mr. Bunting? Well, things almost as funny as that 'ud be have come to pass." He smiled as if the notion was a funny one.

"Yes, something o' that sort," muttered Bunting.

"Well, if your idea's correct, Mr. Bunting——"

"I never said 'twas my idea," said Bunting, all in a hurry.

"Well, if that idea's correct then, 'twill make our task more difficult than ever. Why, 'twould be looking for a needle in a field of hay, Mr. Bunting! But there! I don't think it's anything quite so unlikely as that—not myself I don't." He hesitated. "There's some of us"—he lowered his voice—"that hopes he'll betake himself off—The Avenger, I mean—to another big city, to Manchester or to Edinburgh. There'd be plenty of work for him to do there," and Chandler chuckled at his own grim joke.

And then, to both men's secret relief, for Bunting was now mortally afraid of this discussion concerning The Avenger and his doings, they heard Mrs. Bunting's key in the lock.

Daisy blushed rosy-red with pleasure when she saw that young Chandler was still there. She had feared that when they got home he would be gone, the more so that Ellen, just as if she was doing it on purpose, had lingered aggravatingly long over each small purchase.

"Here's Joe come to ask if he can take Daisy out for a walk," blurted out Bunting.

"My mother says as how she'd like you to come to tea, over at Richmond," said Chandler awkwardly. "I just come in to see whether we could fix it up, Miss Daisy."

And Daisy looked imploringly at her stepmother.

"D'you mean now—this minute?" asked Mrs. Bunting tartly.

"No, o' course not"—Bunting broke in hastily. "How you do go on, Ellen!"

"What day did your mother mention would be convenient to her?" asked Mrs. Bunting, looking at the young man satirically.

Chandler hesitated. His mother had not mentioned any special day—in fact, his mother had shown a surprising lack of anxiety to see Daisy at all. But he had talked her round.

"How about Saturday?" suggested Bunting. "That's Daisy's birthday. 'Twould be a birthday treat for her to go to Richmond, and she's going back to Old Aunt on Monday."

"I can't go Saturday," said Chandler disconsolately. "I'm on duty Saturday."

"Well, then, let it be Sunday," said Bunting firmly. And his wife looked at him surprised; he seldom asserted himself so much in her presence.

"What do you say, Miss Daisy?" said Chandler.

"Sunday would be very nice," said Daisy demurely. And then, as the young man took up his hat, and as her stepmother did not stir, Daisy ventured to go out into the hall with him for a minute.

Chandler shut the door behind them, and so was spared the hearing of Mrs. Bunting's whispered remark: "When I was a young woman folk didn't gallivant about on Sunday; those who was courting used to go to church together, decent-like——"

CHAPTER XXV

Daisy's eighteenth birthday dawned uneventfully. Her father gave her what he had always promised she should have on her eighteenth birthday—a watch. It was a pretty little silver watch, which Bunting had bought second-hand on the last day he had been happy—it seemed a long, long time ago now.

Mrs. Bunting thought a silver watch a very extravagant present, but she was far too wretched, far too absorbed in her own thoughts, to trouble much about it. Besides, in such matters she had generally had the good sense not to interfere between her husband and his child.

In the middle of the birthday morning Bunting went out to buy himself some more tobacco. He had never smoked so much as in the last four days, excepting, perhaps, the week that had followed on his leaving service. Smoking a pipe had then held all the exquisite pleasure which we are told attaches itself to the eating of forbidden fruit.

His tobacco had now become his only relaxation; it acted on his nerves as an opiate, soothing his fears and helping him to think. But he had been overdoing it, and it was that which now made him feel so "jumpy," so he assured himself, when he found himself starting at any casual sound outside, or even when his wife spoke to him suddenly.

Just now Ellen and Daisy were down in the kitchen, and Bunting didn't quite like the sensation of knowing that there was only one pair of stairs between Mr. Sleuth and himself. So he quietly slipped out of the house without telling Ellen that he was going out.

In the last four days Bunting had avoided his usual haunts; above all, he had avoided even passing the time of day to his acquaintances and neighbours. He feared, with a great fear, that they would talk to him of a subject which, because it filled his mind to the exclusion of all else, might make him betray the knowledge—no, not knowledge, rather the—the suspicion—that dwelt within him.

But to-day the unfortunate man had a curious, instinctive longing for human companionship—companionship, that is, other than that of his wife and of his daughter.

This longing for a change of company finally led him into a small, populous thoroughfare hard by the Edgware Road. There were more people there than usual just now, for the housewives of the neighbourhood were doing their Saturday marketing for Sunday. The ex-butler turned into a small old-fashioned shop where he generally bought his tobacco.

Bunting passed the time of day with the tobacconist, and the two fell into desultory talk, but to his customer's relief and surprise the man made no allusion to the subject of which all the neighbourhood must still be talking.

And then, quite suddenly, while still standing by the counter, and before he had paid for the packet of tobacco he held in his hand, Bunting, through the open door, saw with horrified surprise that Ellen, his wife, was standing, alone, outside a greengrocer's shop just opposite.

Muttering a word of apology, he rushed out of the shop and across the road.

"Ellen!" he gasped hoarsely, "you've never gone and left my little girl alone in the house with the lodger?"

Mrs. Bunting's face went yellow with fear. "I thought you was indoors," she cried. "You *was* indoors! Whatever made you come out for, without first making sure I'd stay in?"

Bunting made no answer; but, as they stared at each other in exasperated silence, each now knew that the other knew.

They turned and scurried down the crowded street.

"Don't run," he said suddenly; "we shall get there just as quickly if we walk fast. People are noticing you, Ellen. Don't run."

He spoke breathlessly, but it was breathlessness induced by fear and by excitement, not by the quick pace at which they were walking.

At last they reached their own gate, and Bunting pushed past in front of his wife.

After all, Daisy was his child; Ellen couldn't know how he was feeling.

He seemed to take the path in one leap, then fumbled for a moment with his latchkey.

Opening wide the door, "Daisy!" he called out, in a wailing voice, "Daisy, my dear! where are you?"

"Here I am, father. What is it?"

"She's all right——" Bunting turned a grey face to his wife. "She's all right, Ellen."

He waited a moment, leaning against the wall of the passage. "It did give me a turn," he said, and then, warningly, "Don't frighten the girl, Ellen."

Daisy was standing before the fire in their sitting-room, admiring herself in the glass.

"Oh, father," she exclaimed, without turning round, "I've seen the lodger! He's quite a nice gentleman, though, to be sure, he does look a cure. He rang his bell, but I didn't like to go up; and so he came down to ask Ellen for something. We had quite a nice little chat—that we did. I told him it was my birthday, and he asked me and Ellen to go to Madame Tussaud's with him this afternoon." She laughed, a little self-consciously. "Of course, I could see he was 'centric, and then at first he spoke so funnily. 'And who be you?' he says, threatening-like. And I says to him, 'I'm Mr. Bunting's daughter, sir.' 'Then you're a very fortunate girl'—that's what he says, Ellen—'to 'ave such a nice stepmother as you've got. That's why,' he says, 'you look such a good, innocent girl.' And then he quoted a bit of the Prayer Book. 'Keep innocency,' he says, wagging his head at me. Lor'! It made me feel as if I was with Old Aunt again."

"I won't have you going out with the lodger—that's flat."

Bunting spoke in a muffled, angry tone. He was wiping his forehead with one hand, while with the other he mechanically squeezed the little packet of tobacco, for which, as he now remembered, he had forgotten to pay.

Daisy pouted. "Oh, father, I think you might let me have a treat on my birthday! I told him that Saturday wasn't a very good day—at least, so I'd heard—for Madame Tussaud's. Then he said we could go early, while the fine folk are still having their dinners." She turned to her stepmother, then giggled happily. "He particularly said you was to come, too. The lodger has a wonderful fancy for you, Ellen; if I was father, I'd feel quite jealous!"

Her last words were cut across by a tap-tap on the door.

Bunting and his wife looked at each other apprehensively. Was it possible that, in their agitation, they had left the front door open, and that *someone,* some merciless myrmidon of the law, had crept in behind them?

Both felt a curious thrill of satisfaction when they saw that it was only Mr. Sleuth—Mr. Sleuth dressed for going out; the tall hat he had worn when he had first come to them was in his hand, but he was wearing a coat instead of his Inverness cape.

"I heard you come in"—he addressed Mrs. Bunting in his high, whistling, hesitating voice—"and so I've come down to ask you if you and Miss Bunting will come to Madame Tussaud's now. I have never seen those famous waxworks, though I've heard of the place all my life."

As Bunting forced himself to look fixedly at his lodger, a sudden doubt, bringing with it a sense of immeasurable relief, came to Mr. Sleuth's landlord.

Surely it was inconceivable that this gentle, mild-mannered gentleman could be the monster of cruelty and cunning that Bunting had now for the terrible space of four days believed him to be!

He it was who answered, "You're very kind, I'm sure, sir."

He tried to catch his wife's eye, but Mrs. Bunting was looking away, staring into vacancy. She still, of course, wore the bonnet and cloak in which she had just been out to do her marketing. Daisy was already putting on her hat and coat.

"Well?" said Mr. Sleuth. Then Mrs. Bunting turned, and it seemed to his landlady that he was looking at her threateningly. "Well?"

"Yes, sir. We'll come in a minute," she said dully.

CHAPTER XXVI

Madame Tussaud's had hitherto held pleasant memories for Mrs. Bunting. In the days when she and Bunting were courting they often spent there part of their afternoon out.

The butler had an acquaintance, a man named Hopkins, who was one of the waxworks staff, and this man had sometimes given him passes for "self and lady." But this was the first time Mrs. Bunting had been inside the place since she had come to live almost next door, as it were, to the big building.

They walked in silence to the familiar entrance, and then, after the ill-assorted trio had gone up the great staircase and into the first gallery, Mr. Sleuth suddenly stopped short. The presence of those curious, still, waxen figures which suggest so strangely death in life, seemed to surprise and affright him.

Daisy took quick advantage of the lodger's hesitation and unease.

"Oh, Ellen," she cried, "do let us begin by going into the Chamber of Horrors! I've never been in there. Old Aunt made father promise he wouldn't take me the only time I've ever been here. But now that I'm eighteen I can do just as I like; besides, Old Aunt will never know."

Mr. Sleuth looked down at her, and a smile passed for a moment over his worn, gaunt face.

"Yes," he said, "let us go into the Chamber of Horrors; that's a good idea, Miss Bunting. I've always wanted to see the Chamber of Horrors."

They turned into the great room in which the Napoleonic relics were then kept, and which led into the curious, vault-like chamber where waxen effigies of dead criminals stand grouped in wooden docks.

Mrs. Bunting was at once disturbed and relieved to see her husband's old acquaintance, Mr. Hopkins, in charge of the turnstile admitting the public to the Chamber of Horrors.

"Well, you *are* a stranger," the man observed genially. "I do believe that this is the very first time I've seen you in here, Mrs. Bunting, since you was married!"

"Yes," she said, "that is so. And this is my husband's daughter, Daisy; I expect you've heard of her, Mr. Hopkins. And this"—she hesitated a moment—"is our lodger, Mr. Sleuth."

But Mr. Sleuth frowned and shuffled away. Daisy, leaving her stepmother's side, joined him.

Two, as all the world knows, is company, three is none.

Mrs. Bunting put down three sixpences.

"Wait a minute," said Hopkins; "you can't go into the Chamber of Horrors just yet. But you won't have to wait more than four or five minutes, Mrs. Bunting. It's this way, you see; our boss is in there, showing a party round." He lowered his voice. "It's Sir John Burney—I suppose you know who Sir John Burney is?"

"No," she answered indifferently, "I don't know that I ever heard of him."

She felt slightly—oh, very slightly—uneasy about Daisy. She would have liked her stepdaughter to keep well within sight and sound, but Mr. Sleuth was now taking the girl down to the other end of the room.

"Well, I hope you never *will* know him—not in any personal sense, Mrs. Bunting." The man chuckled. "He's the Commissioner of Police—the new one—that's what Sir John Burney is. One of the gentlemen he's showing round our place is the Paris Police boss—whose job is on all fours, so to speak, with Sir John's. The Frenchy has brought his daughter with him, and there are several other ladies. Ladies always likes horrors, Mrs. Bunting; that's our experience here. 'Oh, take me to the Chamber of Horrors'—that's what they say the minute they gets into this here building!"

Mrs. Bunting looked at him thoughtfully. It occurred to Mr. Hopkins that she was very wan and tired; she used to look better in the old days, when she was still in service, before Bunting married her.

"Yes," she said; "that's just what my stepdaughter said just now. 'Oh, take me to the Chamber of Horrors'—that's exactly what she did say when we got upstairs."

A group of people, all talking and laughing together, were advancing, from within the wooden barrier, toward the turnstile.

Mrs. Bunting stared at them nervously. She wondered which of them was the gentleman with whom Mr. Hopkins had hoped she would never be brought into personal contact; she thought she could pick him out among the others. He was a tall, powerful, handsome gentleman, with a military appearance.

Just now he was smiling down into the face of a young lady. "Monsieur Barberoux is quite right," he was saying in a loud, cheerful voice, "our English law is too kind to the criminal, especially to the murderer. If we conducted our trials in the French fashion, the place we have just left would be very much fuller than it is to-day. A man of whose guilt we are absolutely assured is oftener than not acquitted, and then the public taunt us with 'another undiscovered crime!'"

"D'you mean, Sir John, that murderers sometimes escape scot-free? Take the man who has been committing all these awful murders this last month? I suppose there's no doubt *he'll* be hanged—if he's ever caught, that is!"

Her girlish voice rang out, and Mrs. Bunting could hear every word that was said.

The whole party gathered round, listening eagerly.

"Well, no." He spoke very deliberately. "I doubt if that particular murderer ever will be hanged——"

"You mean that you'll never catch him?" the girl spoke with a touch of airy impertinence in her clear voice.

"I think we shall end by catching him—because"—he waited a moment, then added in a lower voice—"now don't give me away to a newspaper fellow, Miss Rose—because now I think we do know who the murderer in question is——"

Several of those standing near by uttered expressions of surprise and incredulity.

"Then why don't you catch him?" cried the girl indignantly.

"I didn't say we knew *where* he was; I only said we knew who he was, or, rather, perhaps I ought to say that I personally have a very strong suspicion of his identity."

Sir John's French colleague looked up quickly. "De Leipsic and Liverpool man?" he said interrogatively.

The other nodded. "Yes, I suppose you've had the case turned up?"

Then, speaking very quickly, as if he wished to dismiss the subject from his own mind, and from that of his auditors, he went on:

"Four murders of the kind were committed eight years ago—two in Leipsic, the others, just afterwards, in Liverpool,—and there were certain peculiarities connected with the crimes which made it clear they were committed by the same hand. The perpetrator was caught, fortunately for us, red-handed, just as he was leaving the house of his last victim, for in Liverpool the murder was committed in a house. I myself saw the unhappy man—I say unhappy, for there is no doubt at all that he was mad"—he hesitated, and added in a lower tone—"suffering from an acute form of religious mania. I myself saw him, as I say, at some length.

But now comes the really interesting point. I have just been informed that a month ago this criminal lunatic, as we must of course regard him, made his escape from the asylum where he was confined. He arranged the whole thing with extraordinary cunning and intelligence, and we should probably have caught him long ago, were it not that he managed, when on his way out of the place, to annex a considerable sum of money in gold, with which the wages of the asylum staff were about to be paid. It is owing to that fact that his escape was, very wrongly, concealed——"

He stopped abruptly, as if sorry he had said so much, and a moment later the party were walking in Indian file through the turnstile, Sir John Burney leading the way.

Mrs. Bunting looked straight before her. She felt—so she expressed it to her husband later—as if she had been turned to stone.

Even had she wished to do so, she had neither the time nor the power to warn her lodger of his danger, for Daisy and her companion were now coming down the room, bearing straight for the Commissioner of Police.

In another moment Mrs. Bunting's lodger and Sir John Burney were face to face.

Mr. Sleuth swerved to one side; there came a terrible change over his pale, narrow face; it became discomposed, livid with rage and terror.

But, to Mrs. Bunting's relief—yes, to her inexpressible relief—Sir John Burney and his friends swept on. They passed Mr. Sleuth and the girl by his side, unaware, or so it seemed to her, that there was anyone else in the room but themselves.

"Hurry up, Mrs. Bunting," said the turnstile-keeper; "you and your friends will have the place all to yourselves for a bit." From an official he had become a man, and it was the man in Mr. Hopkins that gallantly addressed pretty Daisy Bunting: "It seems strange that a young lady like you should want to go in and see all those 'orrible frights," he said jestingly. . . .

"Mrs. Bunting, may I trouble you to come over here for a moment?"

The words were hissed rather than spoken by Mr. Sleuth's lips.

His landlady took a doubtful step towards him.

"A last word with you, Mrs. Bunting." The lodger's face was still distorted with fear and passion. "Do not think to escape the consequences of your hideous treachery. I trusted you, Mrs. Bunting, and you betrayed me! But I am protected by a higher power, for I still have much to do." Then, his voice sinking to a whisper, he hissed out, "Your end will be bitter as wormwood and sharp as a two-edged sword. Your feet shall go down to death, and your steps take hold on hell."

Even while Mr. Sleuth was muttering these strange, dreadful words, he was looking round, glancing this way and that, seeking a way of escape.

At last his eyes became fixed on a small placard placed above a curtain. "Emergency Exit" was written there. Mrs. Bunting thought he was going to make a dash for the place; but Mr. Sleuth did something very different. Leaving his landlady's side, he walked over to the turnstile. He fumbled in his pocket for a moment, and then touched the man on the arm. "I feel ill," he said, speaking very rapidly; "very ill indeed! It is the atmosphere of this place. I want you to let me out by the quickest way. It would be a pity for me to faint here—especially with ladies about."

His left hand shot out and placed what he had been fumbling for in his pocket on the other's bare palm. "I see there's an emergency exit over there. Would it be possible for me to get out that way?"

"Well, yes, sir; I think so."

The man hesitated; he felt a slight, a very slight, feeling of misgiving. He looked at Daisy, flushed and smiling, happy and unconcerned, and then at Mrs. Bunting. She was very pale; but surely her lodger's sudden seizure was enough to make her feel worried. Hopkins felt the half-sovereign pleasantly tickling his palm. The Paris Prefect of Police had given him only half-a-crown—mean, shabby foreigner!

"Yes, sir; I can let you out that way," he said at last, "and p'raps when you're standing out in the air, on the iron balcony, you'll feel better. But then, you know, sir, you'll have to come round to the front if you wants to come in again, for those emergency doors only open outward."

"Yes, yes," said Mr. Sleuth hurriedly. "I quite understand! If I feel better I'll come in by the front way, and pay another shilling—that's only fair."

"You needn't do that if you'll just explain what happened here."

The man went and pulled the curtain aside, and put his shoulder against the door. It burst open, and the light, for a moment, blinded Mr. Sleuth.

He passed his hand over his eyes. "Thank you," he muttered, "thank you. I shall get all right out there."

An iron stairway led down into a small stable yard, of which the door opened into a side street.

Mr. Sleuth looked round once more; he really did feel very ill—ill and dazed. How pleasant it would be to take a flying leap over the balcony railing and find rest, eternal rest, below.

But no—he thrust the thought, the temptation, from him. Again a convulsive look of rage came over his face. He had remembered his landlady. How could the woman whom he had treated so generously have betrayed him to his arch-enemy?—to the official, that is, who had entered into a conspiracy years ago to have him confined—him, an absolutely sane man with a great avenging work to do in the world—in a lunatic asylum.

He stepped out into the open air, and the curtain, falling-to behind him, blotted out the tall, thin figure from the little group of people who had watched him disappear.

Even Daisy felt a little scared. "He did look bad, didn't he, now?" She turned appealingly to Mr. Hopkins.

"Yes, that he did, poor gentleman—your lodger, too?" He looked sympathetically at Mrs. Bunting.

She moistened her lips with her tongue. "Yes," she repeated dully, "my lodger."

CHAPTER XXVII

In vain Mr. Hopkins invited Mrs. Bunting and her pretty stepdaughter to step through into the Chamber of Horrors. "I think we ought to go straight home," said Mr. Sleuth's landlady decidedly. And Daisy meekly assented. Somehow the girl felt confused, a little scared by the lodger's sudden disappearance. Perhaps this unwonted feeling of hers was induced by the look of stunned surprise and, yes, pain, on her stepmother's face.

Slowly they made their way out of the building, and when they got home it was Daisy who described the strange way Mr. Sleuth had been taken.

"I don't suppose he'll be long before he comes home," said Bunting heavily, and he cast an anxious, furtive look at his wife. She looked as if stricken in a vital part; he saw from her face that there was something wrong—very wrong indeed.

The hours dragged on. All three felt moody and ill at ease. Daisy knew there was no chance that young Chandler would come in to-day.

About six o'clock Mrs. Bunting went upstairs. She lit the gas in Mr. Sleuth's sitting-room and looked about her with a fearful glance. Somehow everything seemed to speak to her of the lodger. There lay her Bible and his Concordance, side by side on the table, exactly as he had left them when he had come downstairs and suggested that ill-starred expedition to his landlord's daughter.

She took a few steps forward, listening the while anxiously for the familiar sound of the click in the door which would tell her that the lodger had come back, and then she went over to the window and looked out.

What a cold night for a man to be wandering about, homeless, friendless, and, as she suspected with a pang, with but very little money on him!

Turning abruptly, she went into the lodger's bedroom and opened the drawer of the looking-glass.

Yes, there lay the much-diminished heap of sovereigns. If only he had taken his money out with him! She wondered painfully whether he had enough on his person to secure a good night's lodging, and then suddenly she remembered that which brought relief to her mind. The lodger had given something to that Hopkins fellow—either a sovereign or half a sovereign, she wasn't sure which.

The memory of Mr. Sleuth's cruel words to her, of his threat, did not disturb her overmuch. It had been a mistake—all a mistake. Far from betraying Mr. Sleuth, she had sheltered him—kept his awful secret as she could not have kept it had she known, or even dimly suspected, the horrible fact with which Sir John Burney's words had made her acquainted; namely, that Mr. Sleuth was victim of no temporary aberration, but that he was, and had been for years, a madman, a homicidal maniac.

In her ears there still rang the Frenchman's half careless yet confident question, "De Leipsic and Liverpool man?"

Following a sudden impulse, she went back into the sitting-room, and taking a black-headed pin out of her bodice stuck it amid the leaves of the Bible. Then she opened the Book, and looked at the page the pin had marked:—

"My tabernacle is spoiled and all my cords are broken. . . . There is none to stretch forth my tent any more and to set up my curtains."

At last, leaving the Bible open, Mrs. Bunting went downstairs, and as she opened the door of her sitting-room Daisy came towards her stepmother.

"I'll go down and start getting the lodger's supper ready for you," said the girl good-naturedly. "He's certain to come in when he gets hungry. But he did look upset, didn't he, Ellen? Right down bad—that he did!"

Mrs. Bunting made no answer; she simply stepped aside to allow Daisy to go down.

"Mr. Sleuth won't never come back no more," she said sombrely, and then she felt both glad and angry at the extraordinary change which came over her husband's face. Yet, perversely, that look of relief, of right-down joy, chiefly angered her, and tempted her to add, "That's to say, I don't suppose he will."

And Bunting's face altered again; the old, anxious, depressed look, the look it had worn the last few days, returned.

"What makes you think he mayn't come back?" he muttered.

"Too long to tell you now," she said. "Wait till the child's gone to bed."

And Bunting had to restrain his curiosity.

And then, when at last Daisy had gone off to the back room where she now slept with her stepmother, Mrs. Bunting beckoned to her husband to follow her upstairs.

Before doing so he went down the passage and put the chain on the door. And about this they had a few sharp whispered words.

"You're never going to shut him out?" she expostulated angrily, beneath her breath.

"I'm not going to leave Daisy down here with that man perhaps walking in any minute."

"Mr. Sleuth won't hurt Daisy, bless you! Much more likely to hurt me," and she gave a half sob.

Bunting stared at her. "What do you mean?" he said roughly. "Come upstairs and tell me what you mean."

And then, in what had been the lodger's sitting-room, Mrs. Bunting told her husband exactly what it was that had happened.

He listened in heavy silence.

"So you see," she said at last, "you see, Bunting, that 'twas me that was right after all. The lodger was never responsible for his actions. I never thought he was, for my part."

And Bunting stared at her ruminatingly. "Depends on what you call responsible——" he began argumentatively.

But she would have none of that. "I heard the gentleman say myself that he was a lunatic," she said fiercely. And then, dropping her voice, "A religious maniac—that's what he called him."

"Well, he never seemed so to me," said Bunting stoutly. "He simply seemed to me 'centric—that's all he did. Not a bit madder than many I could tell you of." He was walking round the room restlessly, but he stopped short at last. "And what d'you think we ought to do now?"

Mrs. Bunting shook her head impatiently. "I don't think we ought to do nothing," she said. "Why should we?"

And then again he began walking round the room in an aimless fashion that irritated her.

"If only I could put out a bit of supper for him somewhere where he would get it! And his money, too? I hate to feel it's in there."

"Don't you make any mistake—he'll come back for that," said Bunting, with decision.

But Mrs. Bunting shook her head. She knew better.

"Now," she said, "you go off up to bed. It's no use us sitting up any longer."

And Bunting acquiesced.

She ran down and got him a bedroom candle—there was no gas in the little back bedroom upstairs. And then she watched him go slowly up.

Suddenly he turned and came down again. "Ellen," he said, in an urgent whisper, "if I was you I'd take the chain off the door, and I'd lock myself in—that's what I'm going to do. Then he can sneak in and take his dirty money away."

Mrs. Bunting neither nodded nor shook her head. Slowly she went downstairs, and there she carried out half of Bunting's advice. She took, that is, the chain off the front door. But she did not go to bed, neither did she lock herself in. She sat up all night, waiting.

At half-past seven she made herself a cup of tea, and then she went into her bedroom.

Daisy opened her eyes.

"Why, Ellen," she said, "I suppose I was that tired, and slept so sound, that I never heard you come to bed or get up—funny, wasn't it?"

"Young people don't sleep as light as do old folk," Mrs. Bunting said sententiously.

"Did the lodger come in after all? I suppose he's upstairs now?"

Mrs. Bunting shook her head. "It looks as if 'twould be a fine day for you down at Richmond," she observed in a kindly tone.

And Daisy smiled, a very happy, confident little smile.

That evening Mrs. Bunting forced herself to tell young Chandler that their lodger had, so to speak, disappeared. She and Bunting had thought carefully over what they would say, and so well did they carry out their programme, or, what is more likely, so full was young Chandler of the long happy day he and Daisy had spent together, that he took their news very calmly.

"Gone away, has he?" he observed casually. "Well, I hope he paid up all right?"

"Oh, yes, yes," said Mrs. Bunting hastily. "No trouble of that sort."

And Bunting said shamefacedly, "Aye, aye, the lodger was quite an honest gentleman, Joe. But I feel worried about him. He was such a poor, gentle chap—not the sort o' man one likes to think of as wandering about by himself."

"You always said he was 'centric," said Joe thoughtfully.

"Yes, he was that," said Bunting slowly. "Regular right-down queer. Leetle touched, you know, under the thatch," and, as he tapped his head significantly, both young people burst out laughing.

"Would you like a description of him circulated?" asked Joe good-naturedly.

Mr. and Mrs. Bunting looked at one another.

"No, I don't think so. Not yet awhile at any rate. 'Twould upset him awfully, you see."

And Joe acquiesced. "You'd be surprised at the number o' people who disappears and are never heard of again——" he said cheerfully. And then he got up, very reluctantly.

Daisy, making no bones about it this time, followed him out into the passage, and shut the sitting-room door behind her.

When she came back she walked over to where her father was sitting in his easy chair, and standing behind him she put her arms round his neck.

Then she bent down her head. "Father," she said, "I've a bit of news for you!"

"Yes, my dear?"

"Father, I'm engaged! Aren't you surprised?"

"Well, what do *you* think?" said Bunting fondly. Then he turned round and, catching hold of her head, gave her a good, hearty kiss.

"What'll Old Aunt say, I wonder?" he whispered.

"Don't you worry about Old Aunt," exclaimed his wife suddenly. "I'll manage Old Aunt! I'll go down and see her. She and I have always got on pretty comfortable together, as you knows well, Daisy."

"Yes," said Daisy a little wonderingly. "I know you have, Ellen."

Mr. Sleuth never came back, and at last, after many days and many nights had gone by, Mrs. Bunting left off listening for the click of the lock which she at once hoped and feared would herald her lodger's return.

As suddenly and as mysteriously as they had begun the "Avenger" murders stopped, but there came a morning in the early spring when a gardener, working in the Regent's Park, found a newspaper in which was wrapped, together with a half-worn pair of rubber-soled shoes, a long, peculiarly shaped knife. The fact, though of considerable interest to the police, was not chronicled in any newspaper, but about the same time a picturesque little paragraph went the round of the press concerning a small boxful of sovereigns which had been anonymously forwarded to the Governors of the Foundling Hospital.

Meanwhile Mrs. Bunting had been as good as her word about "Old Aunt," and that lady had received the wonderful news concerning Daisy in a more philosophical spirit than her great-niece had expected her to do. She only observed that it was odd to reflect that if gentlefolks leave a house in charge of the police a burglary is pretty sure to follow—a remark which Daisy resented much more than did her Joe.

Mr. Bunting and his Ellen are now in the service of an old lady, by whom they are feared as well as respected, and whom they make very comfortable.

∿

THE SINS OF THE FATHERS

Scott Baker

Although born in Chicago, Scott MacMartin Baker (1947–) was a longtime adult resident of Paris; after twenty years, he returned to the United States and now lives in California. His talent as a writer and master of the French language gave him the opportunity to cowrite the screenplay for *Litan* (1982), which won the Critics Award at the Avoriaz Fantastic Film Festival.

His first novel, *Symbiote's Crown* (1978), was science fiction and won the French Prix Apollo Award; most of his later work has been dark fantasy or horror. His story "Still Life with Scorpion" won the World Fantasy Award for Best Short Fiction in 1985; three of his other stories have been nominated for the same honor.

His best-known work is *Nightchild* (1979, revised in 1983), a supernatural novel in which the protagonist is brought to serve as sustenance for a coterie of vampires but is found to be a vampire himself. A benevolent figure, he succeeds in bringing together humanity and the outcast alien race of vampires. The revised version of the novel begins a trilogy known as the Ashlu Cycle that also includes *Firedance* (1986) and *Drink the Fire from the Flames* (1987).

Baker's other horror novels are *Dhampire* (1982), which later was so heavily revised that it was published as a new novel, *Ancestral Hungers* (1995), and *Webs* (1989), a complex tale that involved supernatural spiders.

"The Sins of the Fathers" was first published in *Ripper!*, edited by Gardner Dozois and Susan Casper (New York, Tom Doherty Associates, 1988).

Emma was awakened by a muffled rattling sound, like a tram going by some streets away. She opened her eyes, saw a vague blur in white wheeling a table made of steel tubes and black plastic trays past her. The table gleamed with knives and scissors and other sharp, hard metal things she couldn't distinguish. She reached out, groped for her glasses with a hand so weak and heavy she could barely move it, though at least they'd taken the tubes out of her arms, but she couldn't find them, she couldn't even find the table they should have been on, just to the right of her bed, and for a moment she thought she was back in the operating room, they were going to have to cut into her again, open up her womb and scrape out more of the cancer that was eating her from within, like some monstrous cannibal foetus.

"I've got your glasses on the table right here, Mrs. Blackwell."

She recognized the voice, turned her head, managed to make out another blur who must have been that young doctor who had always been so patient with her. He was standing just to the left of her bed. She liked to think her own father might have been like Dr. Knight once, when he was still young and freshly ordained and studying medicine so he could become a medical missionary in Africa. Before he'd given that all up for her mother and become just another small-town doctor to support her, and she had destroyed him.

"Dr. Knight?"

"Yes. Here, let me help you."

He held out her glasses. Her hands were trembling so badly she dropped them, but Dr. Knight just picked them up and handed them to her again, let her try a second time without making any attempt to do it for her, allowing her to preserve her dignity. This time she managed to get them on. Dr. Knight came into focus, broad-faced and reassuring. Behind him she could see someone dark-skinned in a white uniform, the young Porto Rican nurse who'd been so kind to her when the pain got too bad. She had a push-table with her, but now that Emma had her glasses on she could see that the things gleaming on it were just knives and forks, glassware. Her dinner. She wasn't back in surgery after all.

But the room still wasn't right. The walls were white, not yellow, and she could see a sort of partition down at the far end, the kind they used for separating patients who had to share a room. "This isn't my room," she said.

"We've put you in another room for a while, where we can keep a better watch on you until we're sure you're ready to go back," the doctor said. "How are you feeling?"

"Better?" She hated the way her voice quavered, made a question out of it. "How should I be feeling?"

"Better." She thought he nodded. "All you need is some rest and then in a few days you can go back home."

"All I ever do is rest. Anyway, I don't have a home anymore. I live here, in the other wing."

"Of course. What I meant was, go back to your room, and your friends."

The nurse—Maria? Conchita? Emma was ashamed that she couldn't remember her name—came forward with a needle, gave her a shot.

"Here. This will help you sleep." So the dinner hadn't been for her after all.

Emma had wanted to be a nurse too, when she was a girl, so she could help her father. She'd always read everything she could find in the papers about Florence Nightingale, and once, about a year after they'd moved to London, she had even managed to sneak out of their rooms over the Britannia Tavern, where her father kept her locked up during the day while he ministered to the beggars and lunatics at the Lambeth Workhouse, to go hear her speak, though Father had found out and thrashed her for it afterward.

Father had never approved of women spending their lives outside the home like that, no matter how much good they thought they were doing. There had been a time when he'd believed her mother was the exception, that it would be all right for her because she was working with him . . . until 1887, when Emma had been twelve, and her mother had abandoned them both to run off to Cleveland with that lawyer with the red face and ginger-coloured moustache, the one who'd always been trying to get her father to become a Freemason and come to his lodge meetings.

Father had started drinking heavily after Mother left, putting himself in a drunken stu-pour every night, until the day when he'd suddenly realized that everything that had happened since he'd met her mother, all his pain, had had a *purpose,* that it had been no detour after all but had instead been pointing him towards his ultimate ministry. She remembered when he'd told her that God had destined him, not to bring the faith to the savages in Africa, as he'd once thought, but to combat Freemasonry. And so he'd sold his practice and brought Emma to England, where he was convinced Freemasonry had its stronghold, to establish his ministry in Whitechapel—there to work with the poor and shiftless, the drunkards and the whores, heal their bodies with his medicines and surgeon's knives while bringing their souls to Christ and saving them from the insidious temptations of the Freemasonry that he was certain had already corrupted the British ruling classes and their puppet Church of England.

For the first year it hadn't been too bad. She'd help him sometimes during the day with his patients at the work-houses, or passing out tracts in the streets. She wanted to be with him all the time, prove to him that she wasn't like her mother, that he would always be able to depend on her. But he'd been too proud to admit how weak he was, that he could ever need help from someone, even after he'd started drinking again. On days when he couldn't keep himself sober she'd wait for him all day alone, with nothing to do after she finished cleaning their rooms but read his tracts and medical books over and over again, until it was so late at night that she finally knew once again that he wasn't going to be coming back, and that she would be forced out into the streets looking for him once again . . . to find him, when she found him at all, drunk in some tavern, buying drinks for squat, diseased whores with rotten teeth, and calling them all by her mother's name.

She'd drag him back to their rooms then—she'd been strong, and bigger than any of the sickly English girls she saw on the streets, even if she was only thirteen—and put him to bed, watch over him, only to have him wake up the next morning hating himself, so sick with self-loathing at the memory of the women and the way he'd been pawing them, what he'd done with them, that he'd stagger over to the wash-bowl and vomit convulsively until there was nothing left in his stomach. And even then he'd keep trying to retch up more, as if he could tear the memory of his weakness out of his entrails and vomit it up with the gin and half-digested food. He had hated Emma, too, whenever she found him and brought him back still sober enough to be able to remember the next morning how she'd dragged him away from the whores he'd been too weak to resist, hated her for witnessing his humiliation and forcing him to remember himself as he really was.

He would beat her then, forbid her to ever go back into any of those taverns looking for him again, tell her she'd end up contaminated and diseased like the whores if she did. That had been when he'd started saying that she couldn't come with him and help him during the day anymore. He'd even begun talking about sending her away, back to some girl's school in Illinois where she would be protected. But he didn't have any money left, it all went for the gin and the whores, and so he would lock her up when he went out, though she'd taken the key from him and had a copy made once when he was too drunk to know what she was doing.

Yet he still spent his days unselfishly, trying to heal those poor souls who were too poverty-stricken and ignorant for any other doctor to interest himself in them, trying to bring them to Christ. Trying, too, to save them from the Freemasonry that he had come to England to combat, but which seemingly had vanished, though he knew that it must still be there, hidden from him where he would never be able to confront it directly—in Parliament, Buckingham Palace, the gentlemen's private clubs to which he would never be admitted. He knew that it was Freemasonry that was behind the squalour and misery all around him, that the men and women of Whitechapel were kept ignorant and corrupted and sodden with cheap gin so that their sons could provide cheap labour for the docks and the rich Freemasons' mills and factories, so that their destitute and debased daughters would have no choice but to offer themselves as whores to those richer and more powerful than themselves, to take their turn as replacements for their mothers, grown old and repulsive before their time.

Then the whores had started dying, and Inspector Abberline had come to question Father about their deaths in his polite, soft-spoken voice, not suspecting for even a moment that Father might himself be the Whitechapel Fiend . . . just hoping that with all the time he spent ministering to the worst of Whitechapel's human refuse, he might know something about somebody who could have done it, or have heard or noticed something suspicious. And then—

No. She couldn't allow herself to think about that. She tried to remember what had happened later, all the happy years afterwards, when she'd gone back to Illinois to live with her uncle on his farm and had met Nathan at that tent meeting outside Naperville, how happy she'd been with him, how good her life had been from then on . . . but the shot the nurse had given her was making it impossible for her to lock the memories back into the little sealed room where she'd kept them for so many years. She couldn't shut out the way her father had looked when she'd found him hanging from the rafter, with his tongue protruding and his face all swollen as if with rage, but *white*, dead white, not the red it had always been when he was drinking. She remembered her impotent, helpless fury, how she'd burned the note he'd left for the police telling them that *he* was the Whitechapel murderer, and that he'd ended his life as the only way to stop himself from killing again, but that he was not committing the sin of suicide: he was a surgeon performing an ablation on himself, cutting a diseased element out of society before its corruption could spread any further.

She'd climbed up on the chair he'd used, taken one of his scalpels from his bag and tried to cut him down. But he'd fallen on her when she tried to catch him, knocking her off the chair so that she'd been pinned there on the floor beneath him, with his dry, swollen tongue pressed against her cheek and his dead popping eyes staring blindly into hers, and she'd screamed and screamed and screamed, but nobody had come to help her . . .

The injection must have finally put her asleep then, because when she opened her eyes again she was back in her own room and her son Teddy was there, his silhouette recognizable like his father's, though Teddy was portlier and more pompous than Nathan had ever been. Nathan had always had his own unique dignity—that had been what had impressed her so much about him, even when she first met him and he'd been only twenty years old. His natural dignity, and his kindness. Not like Teddy, who looked like exactly what he was: a moderately honest, moderately selfish, moderately successful businessman.

"Hello, Mother."

"Hello, Teddy." He was Nathan's son, her only child; she wished she could have felt something more than duty towards him. "Did you bring Mary with you?"

"Here I am, Grandmother."

"Mary?" She could make her granddaughter out now, a vague blur half-hidden behind her son. She tried to sit up.

"Let me help you, Mother."

Emma had always been a strong woman, had always hated to accept anything from anybody, but she was still too weak from the operation to refuse.

"Get me my glasses, Teddy," she told him when they'd managed to get her propped up in place. "They're over there, on the bedside table. Just far enough away so I can't get to them myself."

She managed to stop him before he could actually push them onto her face, made him let her do it herself. Her hands seemed steadier now than when Dr. Knight had helped her put her glasses on. One glance at Teddy was enough to convince her that he was no different than ever—he just got a little stouter, a little jowlier and redder-faced every year—but Mary was growing up so fast it was always a shock to see how much she'd changed since her last visit.

Mary was twelve, just as Emma herself had been when her father had taken her to London. But where Emma had been tall and broad-shouldered for her day, more like girls were nowadays, Mary was slight and slender, as though Mary were the nineteenth-century girl and Emma had been the twentieth-century one. They all looked so much stronger and healthier today, yet their lives were so much easier, so much safer, despite all the nonsense people said about crime and violence and how it wasn't safe to walk the streets at night.

Father had loved Mother more than anything in the world, with the same all-consuming love Nathan and Emma had later had for each other. He would have given up anything for Mother, but she had been a cold, grasping woman who had never returned his love, and when she had left him and destroyed him, he had tried to devote himself to helping others, though he had failed at that, too. Yet unlovable, even contemptible, though Teddy was in so many ways, Mary would still have a better life with him than Emma had ever had with her own father, for all that she loved her father in ways no one could ever love Teddy. Mary would never have to live through anything like Whitechapel, Father's hopeless spiral down into degradation and death.

"We're all sinners, Emma," Nathan had told her soon after he'd met her at that tent meeting in Naperville, where he'd so impressed her with the power and the purity he radiated when he came forward to give his testimony, call on them all to give themselves up to Christ. "One reason you're so strong is because you know who and what you are. When you commit a sin, you don't waste your strength denying it ever happened, or pretending that you're better than you are and had some perfectly good excuse. You admit you were wrong and try to do something to make things better afterwards." And that was true, truer than even Nathan had ever known: she had never lied to herself, never told herself something was somebody else's fault when the blame was hers. That was why she had outlived everyone she had known when she was young, why she was still alive to provide Mary with the strength and love that Teddy would never be able to give her.

"Do you know what day it is, Grandmother?"

She squinted at the calendar. October 29th.

"Of course. It's my birthday."

"Right, Mother," Theodore said, smiling fatuously. "And we've got a telegram of congratulations for you from President Johnson."

"President Johnson? I thought his name was . . ." She couldn't remember. "Some Irish name."

"That was President Kennedy, Mother. The one who was assassinated two years ago. Lyndon Johnson's president now."

"Anyway, you have to be a hundred years old before the President sends you a telegram."

"They send them to you when you're ninety now, too. Do you want me to read it to you?"

"Not now. Just put it there, by the bed." She turned to look at Mary, dismissing him, and smiled at her. "When you're an old lady like me you'll find it's a lot easier to remember things that happened when you were a little girl than things that happened just a year or two ago. How are you doing, Mary?"

"All right." But she wasn't all right, that was obvious, now that Emma peered at her more closely and saw the rigid way she was standing with her face closed and wooden, her hands clenched. Something was wrong. Something secret, that she didn't dare talk about in front of Teddy.

"Teddy, could you go get me a glass of water? No. Get me a Coca-Cola. Two Coca-Colas, one for me and one for Mary. They must have a machine here somewhere."

He just gaped at her.

"Well, what are you waiting for?"

"Mother, you never drink Coca-Cola!"

"How would you know? I feel like one. At my age I may die tomorrow and this will be the last chance I'll ever get to drink a Coca-Cola. Anyway, I'm sure Mary could use one. Couldn't you, Mary?"

"Yes, Grandmother."

"I just don't know if it's good for you."

"Then go ask a nurse. If she says I can't have it, just bring one back for Mary and get me whatever she says I *can* drink. But get going, *now*."

She waited until Teddy was gone, then held out her hand to Mary. Mary took it.

"What is it, Mary? I can tell something's wrong."

Mary nodded.

"Is it school? A boyfriend?"

Mary shook her head.

"Drugs, then, something like that?"

"Grandmother! Of course not!"

"Then what is it? I'm your grandmother, and I love you. You can tell me. Even if you can't tell your father."

"It's Dad. He's—you know his secretary, Miss McCullen? The one with the red hair and the tight sweaters you said made her look like a prostitute?"

"What about her?"

"I hate her! Dad's sleeping with her. He always comes home late and sometimes he doesn't come home at all, he just stays with her all night. He said he's going to leave Mother. He's going to get a divorce and marry her!"

"That's right." Emma looked up, startled. Teddy was standing in the doorway, holding two bottles of Coke.

"I hadn't planned on telling you yet, Mother. Not on your birthday, and not with Mary here like this. But as long as you had to find out, I might as well confirm things for you. I'm going to divorce Jean and marry Sharon."

"Jean's always been a good wife to you."

She tried to keep herself calm, not feel anything, stave off the rage building within her, the old, cold rage she had thought her years with Nathan had exorcised forever.

"Yes, a perfectly good wife! She cleans, she sews, she takes Mary to church on Sunday, she goes to every PTA meeting. This isn't Victorian England, Mother. You think that's what I want out of life?"

For an instant Emma was thirteen years old again, back in Millers Court, the narrow alley where she was waiting hidden in the shadows, clutching the long knife from her father's bag as she watched Father with the whore they called Kelly, the young one who would have looked almost like her mother, if the depravity her mother had kept hidden behind her modest façade had instead been blazoned across her face for the whole world to see. Kelly was leaning back against the wall with her skirts lifted and her legs spread, taunting Father on, and he was swearing at her even as he undid his trousers and let them fall, half squatted and pushed himself clumsily into her, shouting at her all the while that she was evil, she was filth, and calling her Margaret, calling her by *Mother's* name. But Kelly only laughed at him, told him that was *why* he wanted her, wasn't it, because she *was* filthy, she was a whore, *that* was what he wanted, not some nice clean-smelling little wife who would never take her clothes off for him except under the bedclothes in the dark with the curtains and shades drawn. And all the while Emma forced herself to watch, waiting for him to finish and pay the whore and stumble away, blind with self-loathing, so that she could use the knife, rip Kelly open and cut her father's seed out of the whore's diseased womb.

And then she was trapped back in the present, shaking with the same impotent rage she had felt when Kelly called out to a passing man just as Father was finally staggering off, forcing Emma to follow as Kelly took the other man back to the warmth of the room—though the chill November street had been good enough for her with Father—then wait outside until he too left, and Kelly was alone again. But now Emma was ninety years old, and lying in a hospital bed with a cancer in her withered womb that was killing her more slowly, but just as certainly, as she had killed any of the whores who had tried to fatten themselves on her father's weakness, who had used that weakness to humiliate and degrade him . . . and she was as helpless to do anything now as she had been to save him in the end.

"Not now, Teddy," she managed to make herself say. "Not with Mary here. Come back some other time. Tomorrow. We'll talk about it then."

"You're sick, Mother, so I'll let you rest. And I'll come back without Mary, because that's what you want. But not because I think she needs to be shielded from any of this. She needs to understand what's going on, and it doesn't make much difference to me if she hears it with you here or on her own."

"Teddy, just go now. Take Mary home and leave me alone. Please leave me alone."

Nathan would have told her to forgive them, sympathize with them, and try to understand them, in the hope that with time she could bring them to see the error of their ways. She had never told Nathan what had *really* happened with her father, never thought it was fair to burden him with the crimes that were *her* responsibility and hers alone, but he had always known far more than she had ever told him, had perhaps even guessed most of the rest.

"Whatever you did, you did for love," he had told her once, "and for that God will forgive you."

Nathan had loved her anyway, had healed her broken life with his love, his loyalty, his devotion. He had lent her his strength and his vision of God's mercy, so different from anything her father had taught her, and together they had been whole in a way she could never have been on her own. But she was alone now, Nathan was dead and buried, and she had only his memory to guide her, help her keep her rage under control. Yet even if she *could* have been strong and generous and forgiving the way Nathan would have wanted her to be, she was still old and dying, and there would never be enough time for her to bring Teddy to see that what that woman was making him do was wrong.

Still, she had always known Teddy for what he was. She could have probably borne seeing Teddy leave Jean, watch their marriage trail off into another 1960s adultery and divorce, with nothing more than any other mother's anguished regrets, the sympathy she would feel for Jean. But Mary was different. Mary was pure, loving, she had Nathan's love and sweetness and generosity, so like her own father's but without the weakness, and Emma loved Mary the way she had loved Father, totally, without reservation, without concern for herself.

Nothing could be allowed to sully Mary. Nothing. But Emma knew she wouldn't be around to help Mary heal the wounds that would be left by a broken home, a father who would desert Mary just as Emma's own mother had deserted Emma and her father. Even with Nathan's memory preaching tolerance and forgiveness, Teddy's Miss McClure was lucky that Emma was old and bed-ridden and dying.

No. That was insanity. Worse than insanity: stupidity. This was the 1960s, the era of scientific detective work, the FBI, fingerprints. They even had psychics like that Dutch man, whatever his name was, telling the police how to find murderers who had been too smart to leave any normal clues. Even if she'd been as strong as the girl she'd once been, there was no way she could kill someone and hope to get away with it again, no hope she could keep it a secret from Mary, or ever make her understand, and the knowledge that her beloved grandmother was a murderer would destroy Mary far more certainly than any outside taint Emma could shield her from.

As it had perhaps destroyed Father. Emma had never known if he had really believed the note he had left for the police, if he had really thought he had killed them all in fits of drunken insanity, or whether he had realized what she had done for him, and had sacrificed himself to save her.

A coward's sacrifice, if that's what it had been. If he'd just controlled himself, stopped drinking, refused to give in to temptation—but no. He'd been too weak, he'd preferred the cheap heroism of a quick, easy death to living out his life in sobriety, bearing his responsibility and his pain for himself. He would never have been able to have borne his guilt, as Emma had borne her own all these years, knowing she was damned, knowing, too, that that was no excuse, that there had been no point of no return after which suicide or any other sin would have been meaningless and permissible because you were already doomed to the torments of Hell anyway. Knowing, too, that she would do it again if she thought it would save him.

But there was no way to save Mary from the Miss McClures of the world. There were too many of them, they were everywhere today in their short skirts and high heels, almost naked on the beaches, selling their bodies like whores in movies and on billboards and in magazines so companies could sell toothpaste and deodorants and underclothes, and if something happened to *this* Miss McClure, Teddy would just find another to take her place.

Emma was helpless, too weak to strike, tear out the evil and destroy it before it could spread any further, even if that had been possible. As helpless as the surgeons who kept opening her up, cutting out a little more of the cancer suppurating in her diseased womb, but who were unable to keep it from extending its tentacles to her liver and lungs, through her bloodstream, spreading farther and farther throughout her body, like some tree of evil taking root in her every organ and cell . . . until soon she would be only a mass of diseased corruption. Like the world had become, the evil that had once been confined to the ghettos and slums now spreading with ever-increasing speed throughout the seemingly healthy tissue of society, so that the whole thing was rotten and tainted with filth beneath its shining healthy surface, eaten away from within.

She was too weak and helpless to do anything, there was nothing anyone could have done, but that night she started spitting out all the sleeping pills the nurses gave her, and hiding them in the little purse with the jet beads on it they let her keep in her bedside table's drawer, though she never needed to use the few dollars she kept there to buy anything anymore, or ever went anywhere anymore except when they put her in her wheelchair and covered her with blankets and wheeled her out into the garden with the others, to bask in the sun like wrinkled, senile toads and lizards.

But even with the dull pain that never really went away, and the nights she spent sleepless, worrying about Mary or lost in the past, a little of her strength was coming back.

"I'm never going to get better, am I?" she asked Dr. Knight. "I mean, better enough to go home, even for a while."

"No."

"How much longer do I have?"

He shrugged. "There's no way we can tell you. At least another month or two,

531

THE SINS OF THE FATHERS

possibly a year, maybe even more. A lot of it depends on how much longer you want to hang on, and on how hard you're willing to fight."

She had five sleeping pills saved up before Teddy came back to see her, alone this time.

"I don't love her, and she doesn't love me, Mother. We'd both be better off divorced."

She could tell he was lying, like she could *always* tell when he was lying to her. Trying to justify himself, pretend he was innocent, just another helpless and blameless victim of circumstances, when it was all *his* fault, his and that woman's, flaunting her body at him every day at the office like a cheap whore, and him too selfish and spineless to resist her or think about his responsibilities to his wife and daughter when all he cared about was getting *her* into bed, or maybe up on his desk after everyone else at the office had gone home—

"Mother!" To her horror she realized that she'd been mumbling her thoughts out loud, that he'd heard it all. "That's insane! You don't know what you're talking about! That's the exact kind of stupid puritan bullshit that's always kept me from telling you about any of this. Because I knew you wouldn't even try to understand."

Emma caught her breath, tried to start over.

"Jean has always been faithful to you. Why can't you be faithful to her?"

"Because Jean isn't what I want! Any more than you were what Father wanted."

"What do you mean by that?"

"What do you think I mean? You think that all he was doing away from home all day, every day, that he was just working up that half-hour sermon he was going to preach over the radio? That it took him all day to set things up, prepare himself, meditate on mankind's ills and needs? Hell, he just walked in there about ten minutes before he was due to start broadcasting and made it up as he went along."

"I don't believe you."

"He used to take me down there with him sometimes, didn't he?"

"Yes."

"And where do you think he spent the *rest* of that time, when you thought he was preparing his sermons?"

"You're lying. Nathan was never like that."

"With *women*, that's where! *Whores*—isn't that what you used to call them, when you were warning me about spending my time with loose women, how they'd tempt me and subvert me and poison my life? Give me diseases?"

"Teddy—"

"Don't start telling *me* all about your father and his holy mission to England and how he hung himself to keep himself from being tempted anymore, because I don't care! He hung himself because he was a crazy drunk, not because of anything some woman did to him. And nobody poisoned my life! I've been seeing women all my life, but only because *I* wanted to, not because I was too weak to fight off some sleazy prostitute's honeyed temptations."

"He took you *with* him? When he went to see those women?"

"A few times. I mean, not up to see them, no, but I'd wait in the park or at some lunch counter for him, and he knew I knew what he was doing. I saw one of them once, a real pretty blonde woman, when she met him at the door."

"Teddy, stop. Please stop." She put up a hand, trying to ward his words off, but he wasn't listening, wasn't even looking at her, he just went on.

"I never told you before because I knew you'd never understand. I didn't want to hurt you, just like Father never wanted to hurt you. The only reason I'm saying it now is to get you to stop trying to tell me I'm committing some sort of horrible sin, just because I love Sharon and I want to get divorced so I can marry her!"

"What do you want me to do?" She found she was suddenly calm, glacial. Nothing he could say could touch her anymore.

"Stop lecturing me about right and wrong all the time. Stop telling me what I should and shouldn't do. I'm not a child anymore. Just leave me alone."

"And that's all?"

"No, that's not all. Stop poisoning Mary's mind against me and Sharon."

"So now *I'm* the one poisoning people's minds?"

"You know what I mean! Sharon's going to be Mary's new mother, and she's going to have to learn to live with her."

"What about Jean?"

"Jean and I have already worked it out. I'll take Mary for the first year, until Jean can find a job and then we'll split her. She'll be spending the school year with Jean and her summers with me and Sharon."

"Jean *agreed* to all this?"

"She agreed. A lot of it was her idea. She's as sick of me as I am of her, Mother."

"Did you ask Mary about this?"

"She's just a kid. She'll do what we think is best for her."

"Whether I like it or not."

"Whether *either* of you likes it or not." He paused, seemed suddenly embarrassed. "Look, Mother, I'm sorry, I don't want things to be like this with you. I shouldn't have gotten mad like that, told you that about Father. He really loved you. It wasn't true, what I said, he never did anything like that. I was just so mad I didn't know what I was saying. You never did anything to deserve that. I'm sorry."

He hesitated again, looking pleadingly at her, waiting for her to tell him it was all right, she forgave him, he was a good boy after all, so that they could pretend together that he'd never said anything. So that she could lie to herself and go back to believing that Nathan had always been the good and glorious and godly man whose strength she'd built her life upon and whose memory had sustained her all these years, instead of just another hypocrite like all the others.

She stared at her son, despising him for his abject cowardice, his spineless, irresponsible cruelty, as she'd never despised anyone before in her life, not Kelly or Annie Chapman or any of the others.

"Look," he said, "you've got the wrong idea about Sharon, anyway. Maybe you'll understand when you get to know her better. She's not like you think she is."

"Maybe not."

"I'll bring her with me next time I come."

"I just want to see Mary."

"I can't allow that. Not without Sharon and me there, until I'm sure you won't just make things harder for her than they already are."

"Do you want my promise that I won't 'poison her mind' against you?"

"I want you to see how things *really* are between me and Sharon first. Then when you understand, maybe you can see Mary on her own."

She lay awake that night wondering what could have happened to make Nathan change, make him into something as abject and contemptible as Teddy. Worse than Teddy, because where Teddy was just a fool, he had never claimed to be anything he wasn't, while Nathan had *known* what he was doing, had lied about it for years, preaching God's love on the radio every day after committing adultery with his whores, while she waited for him at home, so proud of him, so grateful.

She had thought that Nathan was so much stronger and more loving than Father, when all he had been was a bigger hypocrite, living out his life of sin and luxury with the greatest of ease, lying, corrupting his son. She had always thought that Teddy's cowardice was due to his own lack of character, or perhaps to some taint that had come down to him through her from her own mother or father, but maybe he had only been too dutiful and uncritical a son, too eager to imitate the man she herself had tried to model her life after.

All the little details she had dismissed as nonsense for so many years, forced herself to explain away and forget, were coming back to her: the nights he'd been kept late at the studio, all the phone calls from women that he said were from his listeners, people who needed counselling and help so he could bring them to Christ. The retreats he went on every few months without her, so he could be alone with God. And she knew that she *must* have known somewhere, must have chosen to be blind and comfortable despite all her pride in never lying to herself.

But Nathan *had* been a good man when she had met him and fallen in love with him, she was still certain of that, every bit as good a man as she had gone on believing him to be. She had loved and cherished him, never complained back in the beginning when things were hard or when there wasn't enough money to pay the bills, tried to free him from day-to-day worries so he could devote himself entirely to doing the Lord's work. What had gone wrong, what could have made him into what he had become?

Perhaps if she'd been less blind, less complacent and confident and proud, she would have seen what was happening in time to stop it.

Two days later, when the attendant who was supposed to be pushing her wheelchair back in from the garden left her alone for a few minutes outside the geriatric wing's infirmary to go answer a phone call, she managed to wheel herself in and steal a scalpel, then get back out and into place before he returned. Maybe if she killed herself and left a note for Teddy, there would be some way to use her death to put pressure on Teddy, make him feel so guilty he would give up his idea of abandoning Jean and Mary.

But to do that, she would have to abandon Mary herself. She felt confused, nothing made any sense; she didn't know what she could *do* with the scalpel, what good it could possibly do, but it made her feel a little less helpless to know it was there, hidden between the pages of a magazine in the drawer by her bed.

When Teddy showed up with his Miss McClure, Emma could see that she'd tried to dress less provocatively than usual, in discreet beiges and browns, low heels, but even so her sweater was too tight, emphasizing her enormous, cow-like breasts, and her skirt was just a little too short for the dignified effect she was trying to achieve, as if she couldn't bear not to show off her too-long legs in their sheer nylons. Her lips were covered with blood-red lipstick and she stank of perfume: musk, like some animal in heat.

Teddy made some excuse about checking with the doctor, said he'd be back in a few moments, and left them there alone together. Cowardly as always.

She seemed ill at ease. "Ted said you wanted to see me. He thought it was a good idea for us to get to know each other better."

Emma just looked at her.

"Look, I know you don't like me. Ted told me what you said. About how you think I've been flaunting my body at your son so I can steal him away from his loyal, dutiful, wonderful, devoted, but unfortunately just a bit mousy Christian little wife. Right?"

"Well, isn't that what you've been doing?"

"No! Ted and me, it's not like that at all. We want to get married, spend the rest of our lives together. Have children of our own. If he likes my body, that's his business, his business and mine, not yours or anyone else's. And as for that wife of his— You always approved of her, didn't you? Thought she was the perfect wife and mother, exactly what your son and granddaughter needed, right?"

"And you're telling me she isn't like that at all?"

"That's exactly what I'm telling you! Sure, I'm a loudmouth and she's demure, and she's had a lot more education than I have, and she's a real whiz at church rummage sales and all that. So what?"

"And what do you have to offer that she doesn't?"

"I'm in love with Ted and she *isn't*. That's all. She's in love with being somebody's wife, having a nice house and a nice car and having people call her Mrs. Blackwell. But she doesn't care about *Ted*. She could be Mrs. Anybody, and as long as she had the house and car she wouldn't care who that Mr. Anybody was."

She went on and on, talking about how much she loved Ted, how much Ted loved her, but Emma was no longer listening. She was just another victim like all the others, too weak and stupid to resist the corrupton that had sunk its root into her, was devouring her from within and would eventually destroy her immortal soul, too blind to see it for the cancer it really was. There was no hope for any of them.

Exactly half an hour after Ted left them alone, he returned. They must have planned it out, decided on how much time it would take his Miss McClure to lay out her true love and devotion for Teddy for Emma to see, give her her maximum chance to convince the old lady. It was *all right* to abandon Mary, destroy her home and her faith and her hopes for a future any better than they themselves had had, because they were going to do it for *love*. Like Father in the alley with Kelly, shouting Emma's mother's name as Kelly taunted him on. All for love.

But Emma knew more about love than any of them, and she loved Mary. She had sacrificed her immortal soul for love of her father, though her love had not been enough to save him; she had dedicated her life to her love for Nathan, though she had not been strong or wise enough to save him, either. This was her last chance. She could not let herself fail again.

The next time Ted returned, he had Jean and Mary with him. Jean was subdued, quiet, talking about how things were all going to work out for the best. The time on her own would give her a chance to decide what she was going to do with her life, and though it might be hard for Mary at first, Jean was sure she would be happy with her father until Jean was well enough established that Mary could come live with her. And anyway she was sure that Sharon would be a very good mother to Mary, and grow to love her the same way Jean did. It was all said in a subdued monotone, rehearsed and passionless, and, listening to her, it came to Emma that Teddy's Miss McClure was right after all. Jean never had loved Teddy, had probably never even felt much more for *Mary* than she had for Teddy: perhaps a sense of duty, of her responsibilities as a wife and mother, a respectable woman living a respectable life in a respectable way and expecting a respectable recompense in return. Nothing more.

Mary sat there, listening, not saying anything, her face closed and tight and desperately blank, while Jean and Teddy talked about her as if she weren't there, in the same tones of voice they probably used when they were talking about dividing up the furniture. As if none of them were really there, and they were all already dead, just ghosts reciting speeches that might have meant something to them when they had still been alive, but that were now only empty words echoing over and over again in a void, long after even the memory of the fact that they had once meant something had faded and was gone.

She remembered the night her own mother had gone, how she had just stood there, silent, watching her pack while the carriage waited for her out front, then staring out after her as she drove away. How Father had come back from his lodge meeting to find Mother gone, and Emma had had to tell him about watching her pack, but couldn't tell him where she'd gone or why or for how long, couldn't tell him anything because Mother hadn't told *her* anything, hadn't even left a note. How she'd had to sit there with Father, holding his hand and watching him cry, and there'd been nothing she could do to make it any better, to save him. She would have done anything for him, but there was nothing he needed that had been hers to give.

And then, finally, she knew what it was she had to do, how her whole life had been leading up to this, everything, her father, Nathan, even the cancer devouring her from within. Everything.

Her father had failed his vision. She must not fail hers.

But it was a month before they allowed Mary to take a bus out from town to come see her on her own.

"Mary, do you remember that other time your father came here with you, when he went out and got us two Coca-Colas?"

"Of course, Grandmother. That was when he told you he was leaving Mother."

"I never got a chance to drink that Coca-Cola with you. Do you think you could ask the nurse on duty where the machine was and get us two more bottles?"

"All right, Grandmother."

"Then get me my purse. It's in that drawer."

Mary handed her the purse. Emma took two quarters out, handed them to her. "Here. Hurry back."

She was back five minutes later with the two bottles.

"Here they are, Grandmother."

"Do you think you can go get us some cups? I know that girls like you can drink things straight from the bottle, but I'm from another generation, and I need a cup. There should be some cups down by the water machine at the nurse's station at the end of the hall."

As soon as Mary was gone, Emma slipped one of the green-and-red capsules into her bottle, watched anxiously until it dissolved. She took a cautious sip, but the capsules weren't bitter like the pain pills they gave her, and she couldn't taste anything. She put eight more capsules into the bottle, watched them as they dissolved.

They were almost gone, with only a few mushy fragments of the capsule shells left swirling around at the bottom, by the time Mary returned.

"Mary, can I ask you another favour? I know I must be a bother, constantly asking you favours like this—"

"Not at all, Grandmother."

"Could you help me sit up? And then come up here"—she patted the left side of the bed beside her with the flat of her hand—"and sit here next to me while we drink our Coca-Colas together? Just like we were friends the same age, instead of you being polite to your old grandmother?"

"We are friends, Grandmother."

"Good. I love you very much, Mary."

The pills were completely gone by the time Mary crawled up onto the bed beside her. They drank their Coca-Colas together while Emma listened to Mary and asked her questions, not just about Teddy and Jean and Miss McCullen, but about everything Mary felt and believed and cared about, trying to take this last chance to get to know everything she would ever know about her. And all the while she told Mary how much she loved her, and that she knew how hard things were for her now, but if she just had faith they would turn out all right in the end.

When Mary finally slipped down to sleep beside Emma, still holding her hand, she looked so beautiful, so calm and peaceful and innocent, that Emma wanted more than anything else she could imagine just to let her lie there in peace forever like that, just lie there and never wake up. But she knew that that was hopeless, that even if the nine sleeping pills in Mary's Coca-Cola were enough to give a girl her size a fatal overdose, the hospital staff would still just discover her and pump out her stomach and bring her back, to have her purity tainted and destroyed as Nathan's and her father's had been, as her own had been when her mother abandoned them.

The knife was ready, hidden beneath a magazine, and she knew how to use it. She had done it before, and though that had been more than seventy-five years ago, it was not the kind of thing you could ever forget, no matter how hard you tried. Coming up behind that drunken whore in that passage off Mitre Square and grabbing her scarf with her left hand, the scalpel already ready in her right as she yanked the whore back, slashed her across the throat—

A nurse she didn't recognize poked her head in through the door, saw Mary sleeping by Emma's side, her hand clasped in Emma's. Emma put her other hand to her lips, whispered, "Shhhh!" and the nurse smiled back at her, gent-ly closed the door behind her as she left so as to leave the two of them undisturbed.

Emma disengaged her hand gently from Mary's, picked up the scalpel, gripped it as tightly as she could. The motions, the gestures, would be the same as they had been all those other times, with all those other women, yet everything would be different. She had killed the others out of hatred and rage: that had been why it hadn't been enough to just slash their throats and watch the blood come spurting out as they died, why she'd had to hack and mutilate them afterwards, humiliate and degrade them in their deaths for the way they had humiliated and degraded her father in his life. But this time what she had to do she would do with love, and Mary's soul would soar free of the filth and corruption that would otherwise be her inevitable fate, ascend directly to Heaven, to that paradise of purity and innocent joy that was all that Emma had ever wanted for herself and those she loved, and that she had always known she herself would never see.

DON'T FEAR THE RIPPER

Holly West

Holly West (1968–) is the author of the Mistress of Fortune series, set in seventeenth-century London and featuring Lady Isabel Wilde, a mistress to King Charles II. Wilde is an amateur detective who secretly works at night as a psychic, soothsayer, and fortune-teller under the alias Mistress Ruby.

The first book in the series, *Mistress of Fortune* (2014), is based on the real-life murder of Sir Edmund Berry Godfrey, a magistrate whose body was found in a drainage ditch in 1678. The crime, a sensation in its time, helped to create an anti-Catholic uproar; the murderer was never identified. The crime also served as the basis for a lengthy examination of the circumstances by the mystery writer John Dickson Carr titled *The Murder of Sir Edmund Godfrey* (1936), his sole book-length work of true crime. *Mistress of Fortune* was nominated for the Rosebud Award for Best First Novel at Left Coast Crime in 2015.

The second book in the series, *Mistress of Lies* (2014), introduces a beggar girl claiming to be the twelve-year-old daughter of Isabel's brother, believed to have died of the plague. The girl, however, claims that he was murdered and is seeking help from her aunt.

West has also written hard-boiled stories for such publications as *Feeding Kate: A Crime Fiction Anthology* (2012), *Needle: A Magazine of Noir*, and *Shotgun Honey Presents: Both Barrels* (2012).

"Don't Fear the Ripper" was originally published in *Protectors 2: Heroes*, edited by Thomas Pluck (Middletown, DE, Goombah Gumbo Press, 2015).

31 August 1888

The young woman lay sideways atop a rickety metal bed. Her thin cotton shift stuck to her skin, adhered by the sweat of brutal exertion. Beyond that, she was naked, her legs spread open and bent at the knees as she heaved herself forward. She screamed from the pain.

"Hush, now, Mrs. Levy," Caroline Farmer, the midwife, said. "You mustn't yell; it'll only tire you out."

Mr. Levy, as young and inexperienced as his wife, paced from one end of the room to the other. It now seemed ridiculous to Caroline that she'd hesitated to go with him when he'd arrived on her doorstep twenty-four hours earlier, begging for help. Having grown up in the East End, most of her neighbors were well known to her. She kept a running tally of the women who were expecting and called on each of them regularly, knowing that she was their only source of medical knowledge beyond the superstitious clap-trap passed down through generations.

But Mr. Levy was a stranger and she didn't fancy going out into the night with him, especially with the recent murder in Whitechapel. One month prior, Martha Tabram's body was found in a nearby stairwell, stabbed thirty-nine times. Though the district was rife with all manner of criminal goings-on, no one could recall so savage a killing.

Mr. Levy had insisted. "Please, come quick, ma'am," he said. "My wife is dying, I'm certain of it."

"Is she bleeding?" Caroline asked. "Unconscious?"

"Anyone screaming so loudly must be near death."

She nearly smiled. She'd seen this many times before—a young man on the edge of fatherhood, terrified by the powerful forces of labor overtaking his wife. Caroline took up her bag of medical tools, which felt unusually light in her hand. The one she'd used for years, given to her by her mother who'd trained her, had recently been stolen and all of her implements with it. She had yet to replace many of them.

When she arrived at their home, she found his wife was alone and writhing on the bed, her waters already broken.

"Where's your womenfolk?" she asked.

"My wife's mother intended on birthing the baby," he said. "But she died two weeks ago. We've got no one."

"I'll need your help then."

He'd been a worthy assistant, for a man. But the night had been endless, the day eternal, and still, there was no baby.

"Something must be wrong, how could it take so long?" he'd asked several times.

"This is her first child, Mr. Levy. It takes time. Only God can say with certainty when a baby will arrive."

Caroline and Mr. Levy spent the hours ministering to the laboring woman's needs, massaging her feet and lower back, doing what they could to make her comfortable.

Now, finally, the baby was coming. Caroline alerted Mr. Levy. "Hold up her legs!"

The woman hunched forward, straining hard. Caroline counted to ten. "Very good, Mrs. Levy, you may rest," she said. "It shan't be long now."

When at last the baby slid from his mother's body, he was silent and still; his skin tinged a bluish-gray color. Judging by his small size, he'd come early, but Caroline reckoned he'd survive. She turned him onto his stomach, resting him against her splayed palm while she tapped his back. All at once he let out a lusty cry and his nervous parents wept with relief.

"His name is Louis," Mr. Levy said. "After my father."

It was nearing four in the morning when Caroline made her way home along Buck's Row, content with the knowledge that she'd delivered another life into the world. She couldn't know the child's destiny, but his parents appeared to love him and she hoped he'd thrive in spite of his simple origins in London's East End.

On the far side of the street, a school dominated the landscape and just in front of it, a crowd had gathered. Recognizing several of her neighbors standing on their tiptoes as they tried to see what happened, she hurried over and caught the attention of her friends, Emily Holland and Mary Kelly. Emily was crying.

"What is it?" Caroline said, grabbing Emily's hand.

"Polly's been murdered!" Mary said.

Caroline caught her breath. "Are you certain it's Polly?"

Emily nodded. "I saw her for myself. Oh Lord, forgive me, I should've never let her go out alone last night!"

Caroline squeezed through the bystanders to where Polly's body lay. In the darkness, she could surmise little about the condition of her remains, but noticed her skirts were raised up around her waist, leaving her bottom half exposed.

"You must let me see to this woman," she said to the bobby standing guard. She knew most of the men who patrolled the area but had never seen this one before. The name "Stubbs" was displayed on his uniform jacket.

"Go on and join the others, missus," he growled. "This ain't no penny show."

"I'm a midwife, Constable Stubbs. I know her. She's—she's my patient."

There was some truth to this, though she'd never delivered Polly of a child. Mary, Emily, and Polly were prostitutes, and frequently visited Caroline for ailments suffered as a consequence of their profession.

"Like I said, move along. We're waiting on the *real* doctor."

Frustrated, Caroline returned to her friends. "You must tell me what you know," she said.

"The lodging house deputy turned her away when she couldn't pay the four-pence for her bed last night," Emily said. "You know Polly. I saw her at about half past two this morning and she told me she'd earned her doss money three times over but spent it all on drink. I begged her to come home with me but she'd have none of it. Said it wouldn't be long till she was back."

"Did anyone see her after that?"

"Not that I know. To think, I might've been the last one to see her alive!"

"Except for the killer," Mary said.

"Oh Mary," Emily said. "Don't say such things!"

The doctor arrived with a second police constable, PC Neil, who'd patrolled the beat for several years. The crowd clamored around the body, hoping for a glimpse of something titillating while Caroline pushed her way forward, wanting to hear what the doctor had to say.

"Get these people out of here," the doctor hissed. As the PCs proceeded to disperse the group, he knelt down and felt one of Polly's legs. "Still warm," he said, to no one in particular. "Couldn't be dead for more than half an hour."

PC Stubbs grabbed Caroline's arm, pulling her back. "You again? Thought I told you to leave."

"And I told *you* that Polly Nichols was my friend. I want to know what happened to her."

"You'll find out when you read the newspapers, same as everyone else. If you don't vacate the area we'll take you in to the station."

She made a final appeal to PC Neil, who knew her reputation in the neighborhood.

"Sorry, Mrs. Farmer," he said. "You'd better do as PC Stubbs says."

Just as Caroline decided it was in her best interest to go home, an inspector had come to take a description of Polly's corpse. As she stepped away from the scene, she heard him say, "My God, doctor. This woman's been disemboweled."

After Polly's killing, there was much speculation about who'd committed the Whitechapel Murders.

Emily and Mary were adamant that Leather Apron, an obscure character who'd long extorted money from area prostitutes and other vulnerable citizens, was the killer. The name alone was enough to inspire fear throughout the East End, yet nobody seemed to know exactly who he was, or if he even existed. Nevertheless, the gangs that claimed to work for this bogeyman had only to utter his name in order to get results.

Caroline was skeptical. "Why would Leather Apron suddenly come out of the shadows and start killing after all these years?"

"Maybe Martha and Polly owed him money and they couldn't pay?" Mary replied.

"Wouldn't he just send one of his thugs to break their fingers, same as usual?"

Then, in the wee hours of 8 September, Annie Chapman's body was found on Hanbury Street, her throat and abdomen carved open and her intestines pulled out. The killer had removed her womb, taking it with him as a macabre souvenir.

A freshly laundered leather apron was found near her corpse.

The newspapers' disclosure of the leather apron served only to stir the already simmering pot of anti-immigrant sentiment in Whitechapel, heating it to a full boil in the days after her murder. Obviously, the culprit was a Jew—no Englishman could be responsible for such barbaric crimes. Or so thought the British populace.

Caroline, who'd brought many Jewish and immigrant babies into the world, couldn't bring herself to believe that a person's nationality had any bearing on whether they were capable of such savagery. Until someone came up with real evidence pointing to a Jew as the killer, she would look elsewhere for the culprit.

There were other theories, of course. The suspicion that the killer was a member of the medical profession, or at least had knowledge of anatomy, troubled Caroline the most. She hadn't known Annie Chapman, but upon reading the details of her slaying in the evening newspaper, her eyes welled up. How could someone who'd sworn their oath to take care of others betray it in such a horrifying way?

A fierce protective instinct rose within her. These women might've been sinners, but none of them deserved such a brutal punishment. Poverty turned souls desperate and the East End had more than its share of both. Too many of its inhabitants starved in the streets, reduced to selling their flesh in order to secure shelter for the night. Martha, Polly, and Annie were but a few.

In her work, she saw the penalties wrought by prostitution daily: unwanted pregnancy, venereal disease, and assault. Now, murder. She vowed to do something.

In the early morning hours of 30 September, Caroline received word that Ruth Graves was ready to have her baby.

She set off toward their address in Fairclough Street, not getting very far before a woman's voice broke through the quiet night air. The sound, something between a gasp and a scream, chilled her, and she stopped walking. There was a whisper of movement as a murky figure slipped behind the large wooden gate at the entrance to Dutfield's Yard. She dashed over, and, finding the gate unlocked, she entered the yard, tripping over something in the darkness. She fumbled in her pocket for a match and lit it.

A woman lay on her side, facing the wall. She'd been slashed across the neck. The blood, still pulsing, poured out onto the ground beneath her. Caroline felt her wrist for a heartbeat. Nothing. The match burnt down, flickering out, and she lit a second one, holding it up to inspect the rest of the yard. It appeared empty, but she couldn't escape the peculiar feeling that someone was watching her.

She thought she'd seen someone creeping through the gate and *into* the yard, but had she been mistaken? Had he actually been escaping?

The clop of hooves and wheels crunching across the ground commanded her attention. A cart driver had entered the yard, his pony shying to the right.

"You, there!" he shouted, struggling with the reins. "What have you done?"

The match burned Caroline's fingers and she tossed it to the side. "She's dead," she said. "Stay here with her while I find a bobby."

"How am I to know you didn't do this yourself?"

"Wait or don't wait, I'm going. There's no time to spare!"

She ran into the street, ignoring the driver's protests. She spotted a bobby in the distance, walking in the opposite direction. She started after him and, in her haste, nearly collided with PC Stubbs as he rounded the corner.

"Watch it!" he said.

"There's been another murder," she said, pointing. "Over in Dutfield's Yard."

He broke into a run and she followed him. By this time, a crowd had gathered, their lanterns illuminating the scene. There was so much blood that Caroline couldn't imagine there was a drop left in the poor woman.

"I've seen her about," one man said. "Name is Liz Stride."

"Back away, everyone," PC Stubbs said, removing his own lantern from his belt. At his first sight of Liz Stride's damaged body, he shook his head and cursed. He turned to Caroline. "What did you see?"

"I heard a noise—I went to see to it and found her here. I thought I saw someone entering the yard but it was too dark to know for sure. She was already dead when I arrived."

"You're certain of that?"

"Yes." Knowing she could do nothing more for Liz Stride, she continued, "I'm on my way to a birth. If I'm no longer needed here, I'll be on my way."

"You'll do no such thing. You're a witness and you'll remain here until someone can transport you to the station."

"But, sir, they're waiting on me."

His only response was to put her in handcuffs.

As PC Stubbs pulled Caroline toward the Bishopsgate Police Station, the jailor, PC Hutt, was just releasing another inmate, a woman named Catherine Eddowes. "Good night, ol' Cock," she said, waving over her shoulder.

"Pull to it, Kate," he replied, then turned his attention to PC Stubbs. "What 'ave we 'ere?"

"There's been another Whitechapel murder," Stubbs said. "Found this one at the scene, acting suspicious."

"Suspicious?" Caroline said. "I only wanted to help!"

"Put her in a cell to wait for Inspector Abberline."

"Can you at least remove these handcuffs?" Caroline asked.

Stubbs looked to Hutt for guidance and he nodded. Stubbs removed the hand-cuffs, leaving her wrists sore.

PC Hutt led her to one of the two empty cells located in the far corner of the station. She sat on the hard bench and thought about the baby that was coming. Without her, there'd be no one to deliver it. She hoped that Inspector Abberline would arrive soon so that she could report what she'd seen and be off.

When he finally did come, there were two men with him. To her surprise, he carried a carpetbag in his hands. Caroline recognized it immediately.

"My bag!"

Abberline raised an eyebrow. "We'll get to that later, Mrs. Farmer. These are Inspectors Reid and Drake. We understand that you witnessed the murder of Elizabeth Stride earlier this evening."

"I didn't see it happen," she said. "I was on my way to a confinement and heard what sounded like a scream. I went to see about it and found a woman's body."

"Did you know who she was?"

"No. Only later did I hear someone say her name was Liz Stride."

"A cart driver, Mr. Diemschutz, claims he came into the yard and found you touching the body. Do you have an explanation?"

"I was feeling her wrist for a heartbeat."

"How would you know to do that?"

"I'm a midwife. In fact, I'm needed at a birth this very moment. I've told you everything I know—please dismiss me so that I may see to my patient."

Inspector Abberline raised her bag up. "Where do you think we found this, Mrs. Farmer?"

"I don't know. I'm only glad to have it back."

"When was it last in your possession?"

She thought for a moment. "It was stolen from my person at the beginning of August. I haven't seen it since then."

"You're sure of that?"

"Quite. I reported the theft to this very station."

"Will you see about that?" Abberline asked Inspector Reid. He returned his attention to Caroline. "We found the bag at the scene of Annie Chapman's murder. Have you any guess as to how it got there?"

"I've no earthly idea," she said.

"Is it possible that *you* left it behind?"

She was suddenly apprehensive. How guilty she must appear from his perspective! Not only had she been at the scenes of two of the murders, as a midwife, she had medical knowledge, especially as it pertained to women. And her profession required her to be out on the streets at all hours of the day and night, alongside the prostitutes, criminals, and God knew who else. If her clothing should sometimes have blood on it, it was easily explained—it happened often in the execution of her duties.

Her unease turned to fear as she realized that the murderer himself must've been the thief who stole her medical bag. Had he used the very same tools to kill that she had used to minister to his victims?

Inspector Reid returned to his place beside Abberline. "There's no record of the theft," he said.

"I did not kill these women!" she said. "My life's work is to assist them, to protect them!" Her voice grew quiet. "It's the only thing I'm fit to do."

A great commotion ensued, interrupting Caroline.

"Come quick, Inspector," PC Hutt shouted. "There's been another woman murdered."

Catherine Eddowes, the woman Caroline had seen leaving the police station, had been slaughtered in Mitre Square.

Just days after the murders of Elizabeth Stride and Catherine Eddowes, the killer began his taunts, sending the first letter to Scotland Yard:

I keep on hearing the police have caught me but they wont fix me just yet. I have laughed when they look so clever and talk about being on the right track. That joke about Leather Apron gave me real fits. I am down on whores and I shant quit ripping them till I do get buckled. Grand work the last job was. I gave the lady no time to squeal. How can they catch me now. I love my work and want to start again.

He'd signed it Jack the Ripper.

Given that Catherine Eddowes's murder had occurred while Caroline was incarcerated—an ironclad alibi if ever there was one—the authorities conceded that she wasn't the culprit. They took their time about releasing her, however, waiting until mid-afternoon the following day. She traveled immediately to the Graves' residence, praying that she wasn't too late.

Mr. Graves himself opened the door, looking haggard. It appeared he'd had an even worse night than Caroline had.

"Mr. Graves," she said. "I'm sorry for the delay. I'm here to check on your wife and child."

"We've no need for you now," he said, his eyes tired and devoid of emotion. "The baby is dead."

He closed the door in her face.

The morning newspapers reported her arrest and subsequent release, but the damage was done. Her reputation was ruined. The people who'd known her since childhood, whose own children she'd helped bring into the world, crossed the street when they saw her coming. Mothers with babies due refused to admit her when she came to check on them. The prostitutes she'd advised and treated, often at no charge, wouldn't so much as say hello to her. Only Mary and Emily remained loyal friends.

Caroline didn't fear the Ripper. She despised him. He'd taken everything from her—including her cherished medical bag—and had likely tried to frame her for his murders. The only thing that stood between her and the hangman's noose was the Ripper's own folly when he'd murdered Catherine Eddowes while she'd been in jail.

With these most recent killings, she became even more determined. If she couldn't aid and protect the neighborhood's women as a midwife, she would do it by putting an end to this ogre's killing spree.

*

Alas, her initial investigation attempts proved unsuccessful. In the first, she app-roached two women standing on a street corner, both well worn and obviously destitute.

"Pardon me," Caroline asked. "But I wonder if either of you know a man named John Gardener?" It was reported that a man by this name had been one of the last people to see Elizabeth Stride alive.

The fatter of the two women replied, "If you're looking for a man to pay your doss, you'll have to find one on your own, like the rest of us."

"A woman named Elizabeth Stride was murdered a fortnight ago. Did you know her?"

"She asks a lot of questions, doesn't she, Bessie?" the thin one said. "Why d'ye think that is?"

"Liz was a friend," Caroline said. "I want to know how she died."

"A friend, eh?" Bessie said. "If that's the case, you're the only one she ever had."

"You knew her?"

The thin one said, "Everyone knew Long Liz. She made sure of it."

"How do you mean?"

"She was the most hateful woman I've ever met," Bessie said. "If you were a 'friend,' as you say, you'd a known that."

"Bessie!" said her friend. "Don't speak ill of the dead."

"I don't care if she is dead. She was nothing but a common thief. D'ye know she stole my dear mum's pearl brooch? I never did get it back—she probably sold it on so she could drink herself silly."

"You can't prove it."

"Why're you defending her? She was awful and you know it better than anyone. She stole your bloke!"

"I'm better off without him. She did me a favor on that score, she did."

So Liz Stride had been a thief, Caroline thought. Could that have gotten her killed? Could it have gotten them all killed?

"Has she had rows with anybody recently?" Caroline asked.

"You mean like with anyone who might've killed her?" Bessie said. "I ain't no snitch, am I?"

"Even if it might save another?"

She laughed, her round belly bouncing like a child's rubber ball. "You think one of us whores is out here killing our own, is that it? That's a good one, that is."

"Did you know any of the other victims?"

She gave Caroline a hard look. "Wait a minute," she said, her jaw set. "You're that midwife the police suspected of being the Ripper. What're you doing, trying to start trouble? Looking for someone else to blame so you can save your own hide?"

On another such evening, Caroline outfitted herself in one of her dead husband's suits, piling her hair up into a bowler and rubbing coal along her jaw to mimic beard stubble. She went out, looking for women who might attract the Ripper's attention. It was no difficult task; streetwalkers lurked everywhere, beckoning. One gravel-voiced slattern grabbed her by the arm as she passed, startling her.

"Aye, sir, would ye be liking a bit of company?" she said. She appeared to be forty or so, and quite in need of a good washing up. Her eyes were heavy-lidded with drunkenness and she stunk of gin.

"Indeed, I would," Caroline said, her voice pitched low.

"C'mon then," the woman said. "I know a nice private place where we can spend some time together."

She led Caroline to a darkened stairwell. She gathered her skirts and started to pull them up.

"Oh no, there'll be no need for that," Caroline said. "I only want to talk."

"Bah! I've no time for it." She started to walk away.

"Wait," Caroline said. "I'll pay you. How much?"

The woman looked at her with suspicion. "Fivepence will do."

Three was the going rate, but Caroline handed over the requested coins with no argument. The woman placed them somewhere amid the folds of her abundant cleavage and said, "What d'ye want then?"

"Do you know anything about the Ripper murders?"

The woman's eyes grew wide. "Why should I know anything about the murders? I mind me own business and it's a good thing I do."

"Did you know any of the victims?"

"I'd seen 'em about. Didn't know 'em to talk to 'em."

"Do you know anyone who might've witnessed something? Seen anything suspicious?"

"Why're you so interested in the killings? What're you, a bobby?"

"Nothing like that—"

Realization crossed the woman's face like a shadow, immediately replaced by an expression of pure fear. "Dear God, you're him, aren't you?"

The woman screamed and tried to run, but Caroline was quicker. She grabbed her arm and covered her mouth. "For the love of God, be quiet or the whole of Whitechapel will hear. I'm a—I'm a newspaperman, looking for a story."

The woman seemed to accept this and Caroline loosened her grip. As soon as she did, the woman broke away and ran, yelling, "It's him! It's the Ripper!"

Caroline made it home that night, managing to avoid another arrest. But if she were to catch Jack the Ripper, there seemed only one way to do it. She'd have to lure him out herself.

Caroline assessed her appearance in the mirror. It hadn't been difficult to disguise herself as a common East End whore—all it took was a filthy dress and a slovenly manner. She added a black bonnet and veil to help conceal her face and concluded that she looked the part.

She'd studied every available detail of the Ripper killings—the newspapers reveled in publishing every gruesome detail. In each case, the manner of death was strangulation. He throttled his victims first, waiting until after they died to sever their throats and mutilate their bodies. With this in mind, she practiced defending herself against such an attack.

It had been several weeks since he'd killed Liz Stride and Catherine Eddowes, leading some to believe he'd finished his scourge. But the last letter, sent to the president of the Whitechapel Vigilance Committee two weeks after their deaths, was the most shocking of all. With it, the Ripper had included a human kidney.

To Caroline, this vile package indicated he'd no intention of halting the killings and it made her more determined than ever to find him.

Armed with a scalpel taken from her makeshift tool bag, she wandered the streets, trying to draw the Ripper out. It was easier to conceal than a kitchen knife, and if necessary, easier to use.

A man on the opposite side of the street called to her. "Is that bonny Ida I see over there?"

Caroline smiled. "It's not Ida you see, sir, but Nellie."

"C'mon over then, sweet Nellie, and give us a kiss."

She laughed and continued on her way, turning up Whitechapel High Street. It was well lit here, illuminated by the interior lamps of the public houses, gin shops, penny show houses, and coffee stalls. Street performers offered every sort of entertainment, from singing waifs to wiry acrobats. It was difficult to imagine a killer in the midst of such frivolity.

She walked to the White Hart Pub, intending to stop for a quick drink and a rest. This end of the street was engulfed in darkness, and as she entered George's Yard to access the pub's front door, someone came up behind her.

He grabbed her to him, holding her tightly against his body with one arm and cupping her mouth with the other. Within seconds, he dragged her to the darkest corner of the passage and wrapped a scarf around her neck. Though she'd rehearsed this moment many times, she hadn't known how powerless her panic would render her.

He twisted the scarf tighter. Light-headed now, she just had the strength to pull the scalpel from her pocket and drag it as deeply as she could along the back of his gloved hand. He gasped and flinched, loosening his grip. She lashed out again, digging the blade in even deeper this time. He backed away and she spun around, swinging it across his face.

He howled in pain and ran off toward the passage's other end. She got her first solid glimpse of him and saw that he wore a police constable's uniform.

"Murder!" she cried softly, for the assault had made her hoarse. "Murder!"

She scrambled after him, knowing there was little chance she'd catch him. After a few steps, she turned back toward Whitechapel High Street to find help.

Then, she stopped short. The man who'd attacked her had been a constable, or at least dressed as one. For all she knew, she'd end up reporting the crime to the very man who'd committed it. Having survived one attack, she had no desire to face another. And having already been a suspect in the Ripper killings herself, she didn't dare go to police headquarters for assistance.

She trudged home, frightened and sore. When she stripped off her coat, she found a torn piece of the scarf he'd used caught on one of the buttons. His effort to kill her had left bruises on her neck.

She spent a sleepless night, wondering at the revelation that Jack the Ripper was either a police constable himself or posing as one. Either way, it was a brilliant ruse—the uniform allowed him to walk the streets at night, concealed as a trusted public official, all the while searching for potential victims.

The following morning, she was still in bed when Emily came pounding at her door.

"Caroline! Caroline!"

She opened the door and found her friend in a mess of tears. "Heavens, Emily, what's happened?"

"It's Mary," Emily choked. "She's been—dear Lord, Caroline—the Ripper killed her."

The significance of Emily's words sunk in as Caroline realized the truth. Mary's death was her fault. If she'd reported the Ripper's attack last night, the police might've laid chase and caught him before he did this to Mary.

Oh, dear Mary, I'm so sorry.

Caroline steeled herself as the facts of Mary Kelly's slaying emerged. She couldn't allow herself to succumb to grief and guilt, for it would help no one. Instead, she focused her attention on the only thing that mattered: finding the Ripper and avenging Mary. Avenging all of them.

The details were almost too much to bear. Mary's head was severed and placed beneath one of her arms. Her ears and nose were cut off. He'd disemboweled her body and tore the flesh from her thighs. Some of her organs, including her heart, were missing. He'd ripped the skin off of her forehead and cheeks and pushed one of her hands into her stomach.

But the most important detail of all was the photo printed in *The Star* two days after Mary's death: a torn scarf was found on the bed beside the body. Caroline recognized it, for she still had the other half in her possession.

George Hutchinson, a mutual acquaintance of Mary and Caroline, seemed to have been the last person to see her alive. Two days after Mary's murder, Caroline went to see him.

"I already told the police all this," he complained. "Why's it so important I tell it to you?"

"Mr. Hutchinson, I know how fond you were of Mary. I was, too. I can't rest until I know what happened to her."

"She asked me to lend her sixpence and I didn't have it. She said she'd have to get it some other way then and I let her go off. If I'd a known what was gonna happen I woulda stole it for her myself."

"Mary was deep in debt. Your sixpence wouldn't have changed anything."

"Maybe not. But I had a feeling something bad was set to happen. She met a man on the next corner and I followed them back to a lodging house. I waited outside for half an hour or more but when no one came out, I left."

"What time was this?"

"About two o'clock, I'd say."

"The inquest revealed that Mary died around four," Caroline said. "Unless you stayed with her all night, you probably couldn't have helped."

He nodded, but didn't seem convinced.

"Do you remember what the man looked like?"

Mr. Hutchinson described a stocky man of average height, quite unlike the person who'd attacked her.

"And did you see any bobbies about?" she asked.

"I suppose I did, but since nothing untoward had happened at that point, I didn't think to say anything."

Before she left, she assured Mr. Hutchinson: "You mustn't blame yourself for Mary's death. There's nothing more you could've done. Let that knowledge bring you peace."

She wished she could believe the words for herself.

On her way home she stopped at a fruit cart to buy an apple for lunch. After she handed the merchant her coin, she turned around and saw PC Neil on the opposite side of the street. He might've been the last bobby in Whitechapel she still trusted, but nevertheless, she had no wish to speak to him. She was about to turn and walk the other direction when she noticed the bandage affixed to his cheek.

No, she thought. It's only by chance. He can't be the Ripper.

PC Neil headed toward her and as he got closer, the truth became apparent. He was the right size and build. He'd been at or near the scene of all the murders. He wore a bandage in the very place she'd wounded her attacker. PC Neil, a bobby who'd ever only showed her kindness, was the man who'd tried to kill her. Which meant, likely as not, he was also Jack the Ripper.

She stood still, wanting to flee but unable to move. Her previous determination to destroy the Ripper now seemed brash and foolhardy. Faced with him now, she gave him the brightest smile she could muster. "Goodness, constable, what on earth happened?"

She searched his eyes for anything that might suggest him capable of the Ripper's savagery, but saw nothing but benevolence. Had she been mistaken? Could the wound on his face be only a coincidence?

He raised his hand and touched the bandage. "It's nothing to concern yourself with, Mrs. Farmer. Just a nasty scuffle last night. All in the line of duty, you know."

"It's weeping through the bandage. Have you seen a doctor?"

"Certainly there's no need for that."

She took a deep breath, trying to bolster her courage. "An infection can be quite serious," she said. "I live just around the corner and have medical supplies at my disposal. If you like, I'll clean it up for you."

"Very well, perhaps you're right. That's very kind of you."

Though it was a short distance, the walk home seemed endless. Along the way, she formulated her plan, understanding the risk. If she failed at her task, he would kill her. If she succeeded, she could be arrested.

She unlocked the door and invited him inside. "Sit down," she said, indicating a chair at the kitchen table. "I'll just go get my bag."

She moved casually in spite of her racing heart. Did he realize that she'd been the one he attacked before moving on to Mary Kelly? Was she playing into his hands instead of the other way around? Thankfully, she kept her bag close at hand in case of emergency; it took only a few steps to fetch it, enabling her to keep her eye on him.

"It must've been a terrible fight," she said, crossing back over to where he sat.

"Working the East End is no easy thing," he said. "But that should come as no surprise to you."

She took out a clean cloth and a bottle of carbolic acid. Using her surgical scissors, she carefully cut the tape away from his face, revealing the wound. She'd cut more deeply than she'd thought, dangerously close to his eye. A half an inch higher and she might've blinded him.

She fought to keep her hands steady as she poured a quantity of carbolic acid onto the cloth and raised it to his cut.

"This might sting," she said.

He winced at the first contact, then relaxed somewhat as she continued dabbing the wound. He settled himself, allowing her ministrations to soothe him. Then, all at once, his hand shot up and grabbed her wrist.

"Stop," he said.

She held her breath. "Did I—did I hurt you?"

"No. It's just that—I'm sorry. It's been many months since I've been touched so tenderly. My wife died in July."

She took shallow breaths as she tried to make sense of his words. July. That was just before the Ripper killings started. Was that what had set him off? Simple grief?

"I'm very sorry for your loss," she said, her voice weak. "My husband died four years ago."

"Then you know how it feels, don't you?" He looked at her now, his eyes showing neither kindness nor sorrow. Just emptiness.

No, she thought. I don't know how it feels. Because I would never turn to violence in order to heal my broken heart, no matter the circumstances.

"I'm nearly done here. I just need to prepare a fresh bandage." She used the bag to conceal her hands while she poured chloroform onto the torn scarf. In one swift motion, she pressed it over his nose and mouth.

"I believe this belongs to you," she said, holding his head against her breast tightly as he struggled. "This is for every one of those women you killed. You will die here, Jack the Ripper, and no one will ever know your true name. That's what the letters were all about, weren't they? Notoriety. Infamy. You'll die an anonymous wretch, but the names of your victims will be known forever."

When he lost consciousness, she eased him off of the chair to the floor, rolling him onto his side. She placed a bucket next to him and, using the scalpel, she slit his wrist deep enough to sever the artery. Before she could contain it, it sprayed across her face and onto the wall.

Swallowing back her bile, she cut his second wrist and let him bleed out into the bucket. Within minutes, the ripper known as Jack was dead.

The next day, the newspapers and broadsheets reported the suicide of PC Thomas Neil of Division H of the Metropolitan Police:

PC Neil was distraught due to the death of his wife in July.

East End gossip spread that the constable's wife killed herself when she'd learned he'd given her a venereal disease, rendering her unable to bear children. It seemed that PC Neil enjoyed the company of many of the prostitutes working his beat in Whitechapel, suffering the consequences and inflicting them upon his poor wife. Killing the women he held responsible for his loss was his recourse.

Emily had helped Caroline to drag the Ripper's body out to the street and stage the suicide scene. These women, who'd been friends for so many years, swore on the soul of their dear departed Mary that no one would ever know their secret.

THE MYSTERIOUS CARD UNVEILED

Cleveland Moffett

American dramatist, journalist, novelist, and short story writer Cleveland Moffett (1863–1926) made several major contributions to the mystery genre, notably the neglected novel *Through the Wall* (1909), which is a Haycraft-Queen Cornerstone; *True Detective Stories from the Archives of the Pinkertons* (1897), alleged real-life accounts that are almost as fictionalized as those written by Allan, Frank, and Myron Pinkerton years earlier; *The Bishop's Purse* (1913), coauthored with Oliver Herford, a humorous tale of robbery and impersonation set in England; and *The Seine Mystery* (1924), about an American journalist in Paris who does amateur sleuthing.

Moffett spent many years in Europe as a correspondent for several newspapers and, even after he returned to live permanently in the United States, set many of his stories abroad, mostly in France. He lived his last years in Paris and died there.

His most famous story, and one of the two most famous riddle stories of all time (along with Frank Stockton's "The Lady, or the Tiger?"), is "The Mysterious Card," which has no connection to Jack the Ripper. It is the story of an American in Paris surreptitiously given a card by a beautiful young woman on which are some words in French, a language he doesn't read. When he tries to discern their meaning, the people to whom he shows the card are so repulsed that they want nothing to do with him. Hotel managers and proprietors throw him out, his wife labels him a monster and divorces him, and his closest friends desert him. He is arrested and forced to leave France. Back in New York, he sees the mysterious lady in a carriage, succeeds in meeting her, and learns that she is dying. She recognizes him and murmurs, "I gave you the card because I wanted you to . . . to . . . ," and dies.

It was first published in *The Black Cat* magazine in 1895, and was followed the next year by "The Mysterious Card Unveiled." The enterprising Boston publisher Small, Maynard, and Company put both stories together in 1912 with a gimmick: the second part was sealed and the purchaser was promised a refund if the book was returned to the bookseller with its seal unbroken.

"The Mysterious Card Unveiled" was first published in the August 1896 issue of *The Black Cat* magazine.

No physician was ever more scrupulous than I have been, during my thirty years of practice, in observing the code of professional secrecy; and it is only for grave reasons, partly in the interests of medical science, largely as a warning to intelligent people, that I place upon record the following statements.

One morning a gentleman called at my offices to consult me about some nervous trouble. From the moment I saw him, the man made a deep impression on me, not so much by the pallor and worn look of his face as by a certain intense sadness in his eyes, as if all hope had gone out of his life. I wrote a prescription for him, and advised him to try the benefits of an ocean voyage. He seemed to shiver at the idea, and said that he had been abroad too much, already.

As he handed me my fee, my eye fell upon the palm of his hand, and I saw there, plainly marked on the Mount of Saturn, a cross surrounded by two circles. I should explain that for the greater part of my life I have been a constant and enthusiastic student of palmistry. During my travels in the Orient, after taking my degree, I spent months studying this fascinating art at the best sources of information in the world. I have read everything published on palmistry in every known language, and my library on the subject is perhaps the most complete in existence. In my time I have examined at least fourteen thousand palms, and taken casts of many of the more interesting of them. But I had never seen such a palm as this; at least, never but once, and the horror of the case was so great that I shudder even now when I call it to mind.

"Pardon me," I said, keeping the patient's hand in mine, "would you let me look at your palm?"

I tried to speak indifferently, as if the matter were of small consequence, and for some moments I bent over the hand in silence. Then taking a magnifying glass from my desk, I looked at it still more closely. I was not mistaken; here was indeed the sinister double circle on Saturn's mount, with the cross inside,—a marking so rare as to portend some stupendous destiny of good or evil, more probably the latter.

I saw that man was uneasy under my scrutiny, and, presently, with some hesitation, as if mustering courage, he asked: "Is there anything remarkable about my hand?"

"Yes," I said, "there is. Tell me, did not something very unusual, something very horrible, happen to you about ten or eleven years ago?"

I saw by the way the man started that I had struck near the mark, and, studying the stream of fine lines that crossed his lifeline from the Mount of Venus, I added: "Were you not in some foreign country at the time?"

The man's face blanched, but he only looked at me steadily out of those mournful eyes. Now I took his other hand, and compared the two, line by line, mount by mount, noting the short square fingers, the heavy thumb, with amazing willpower in its upper joint, and gazing again and again at that ominous sign on Saturn.

"Your life has been strangely unhappy, your years have been clouded by some evil influence."

"My God," he said weakly, sinking into a chair, "how can you know these things?"

"It is easy to know what one sees," I said, and tried to draw him out about his past, but the words seemed to stick in his throat.

"I will come back and talk to you again," he said, and he went away without giving me his name or any revelation of his life.

Several times he called during subsequent weeks, and gradually seemed to take on a measure of confidence in my presence. He would talk freely of his physical condition, which seemed to cause him much anxiety. He even insisted upon my making the most careful examination of all his organs, especially of his eyes which, he said, had troubled him at various times. Upon making the usual tests, I found that he was suffering from a most uncommon form of color blindness, that seemed to vary in its manifestations, and to be connected with certain hallucinations or abnormal mental states which recurred periodically, and about which I had great difficulty in persuading him to speak. At each visit I took occasion to study his hand anew, and each reading of the palm gave me stronger conviction that here was a life mystery that would abundantly repay any pains taken in unraveling it.

While I was in this state of mind, consumed with a desire to know more of my unhappy acquaintance and yet not daring to press him with questions, there came a tragic happening that revealed to me with startling suddenness the secret I was bent on knowing. One night, very late,—in fact it was about four o'clock in the morning,—I received an urgent summons to the bedside of a man who had been shot. As I bent over him I saw that it was my friend, and for the first time I realized that he was a man of wealth and position, for he lived in a beautifully furnished house filled with art treasures and looked after by a retinue of servants. From one of these I learned that he was Richard Burwell, one of New York's most respected citizens—in fact, one of her best-known philanthropists, a man who for years had devoted his life and fortune to good works among the poor.

But what most excited my surprise was the presence in the house of two officers, who informed me that Mr. Burwell was under arrest, charged with murder. The officers assured me that it was only out of deference to his well-known standing in the community that the prisoner had been allowed the privilege of receiving medical treatment in his own home; their orders were peremptory to keep him under close surveillance.

Giving no time to further questionings, I at once proceeded to examine the injured man, and found that he was suffering from a bullet wound in the back at about the height of the fifth rib. On probing for the bullet, I found that it had lodged near the heart, and decided that it would be exceedingly dangerous to try to remove it immediately. So I contented myself with administering a sleeping potion.

As soon as I was free to leave Burwell's bedside I returned to the officers and obtained from them details of what had happened. A woman's body had been found a few hours before, shockingly mutilated, on Water Street, one of the dark ways in the swarming region along the river front. It had been found at about two o'clock in the morning by some printers from the office of the *Courier des Etats Unis,* who, in coming from their work, had heard cries of distress and hurried to the rescue. As they drew near they saw a man spring away from something huddled on the sidewalk, and plunge into the shadows of the night, running from them at full speed.

Suspecting at once that here was the mysterious assassin so long vainly sought for many similar crimes, they dashed after the fleeing man, who darted right and left through the maze of dark streets, giving out little cries like a squirrel as he ran. Seeing that they were losing ground, one of the printers fired at the fleeing shadow, his shot being followed by a scream of pain, and hurrying up they found a man writhing on the ground. The man was Richard Burwell.

The news that my sad-faced friend had been implicated in such a revolting occurrence shocked me inexpressibly, and I was greatly relieved the next day to learn from the papers that a most unfortunate mistake had been made. The evidence given before the coroner's jury was such as to abundantly exonerate Burwell from all shadow of guilt. The man's own testimony, taken at his bedside, was in itself almost conclusive in his favor. When asked to explain his presence so late at night in such a part of the city, Burwell stated that he had spent the evening at the Florence Mission, where he had made an address to some unfortunates gathered there, and that later he had gone with a young missionary worker to visit a woman living on Frankfort Street, who was dying of consumption. This statement was borne out by the missionary worker himself, who testified that Burwell had been most tender in his ministrations to the poor woman and had not left her until death had relieved her sufferings.

Another point which made it plain that the printers had mistaken their man in the darkness, was the statement made by all of them that, as they came running up, they had overheard some words spoken by the murderer, and that these words were in their own language, French. Now it was shown conclusively that Burwell did not know the French language, that indeed he had not even an elementary knowledge of it.

Another point in his favor was a discovery made at the spot where the body was found. Some profane and ribald words, also in French, had been scrawled in chalk on the door and doorsill, being in the nature of a coarse defiance to the police to find the assassin, and experts in handwriting who were called testified unanimously that Burwell, who wrote a refined, scholarly hand, could never have formed those misshapen words.

Furthermore, at the time of his arrest no evidence was found on the clothes or person of Burwell, nothing in the nature of bruises or bloodstains that would tend to implicate him in the crime. The outcome of the matter was that he was honorably discharged by the coroner's jury, who were unanimous in declaring him innocent, and who brought in a verdict that the unfortunate woman had come to her death at the hand of some person or persons unknown.

On visiting my patient late on the afternoon of the second day I saw that his case was very grave, and I at once instructed the nurses and attendants to prepare for an operation. The man's life depended upon my being able to extract the bullet, and the chance of doing this was very small. Mr. Burwell realized that his condition was critical, and, beckoning me to him, told me that he wished to make a statement he felt might be his last. He spoke with agitation which was increased by an unforeseen happening. For just then a servant entered the room and whispered to me that there was a gentleman downstairs who insisted upon seeing me, and who urged business of great importance. This message the sick man overheard, and, lifting himself with an effort, he said excitedly: "Tell me, is he a tall man with glasses?"

The servant hesitated.

"I knew it; you cannot deceive me; that man will haunt me to my grave. Send him away, doctor; I beg of you not to see him."

Humoring my patient, I sent word to the stranger that I could not see him, but in an undertone, instructed the servant to say that the man might call at my office the next morning. Then, turning to Burwell, I begged him to compose himself and save his strength for the ordeal awaiting him.

"No, no," he said, "I need my strength now to tell you what you must know to find the truth. You are the only man who has understood that there has been some terrible influence at work in my life. You are the only man competent to study out what that influence is, and I have made provision in my will that you shall do so after I am gone. I know that you will heed my wishes?"

The intense sadness of his eyes made my heart sink; I could only grip his hand and remain silent.

"Thank you. I was sure I might count on your devotion. Now, tell me, doctor, you have examined me carefully, have you not?"

I nodded.

"In every way known to medical science?"

I nodded again.

"And have you found anything wrong with me,—I mean, besides this bullet, anything abnormal?"

"As I have told you, your eyesight is defective; I should like to examine your eyes more thoroughly when you are better."

"I shall never be better; besides it isn't my eyes; I mean myself, my soul,—you haven't found anything wrong there?"

"Certainly not; the whole city knows the beauty of your character and your life."

"Tut, tut; the city knows nothing. For ten years I have lived so much with the poor that people have almost forgotten my previous active life when I was busy with money-making and happy in my home. But there is a man out West, whose head is white and whose heart is heavy, who has not forgotten, and there is a woman in London, a silent, lonely woman, who has not forgotten. The man was my partner, poor Jack Evelyth; the woman was my wife. How can a man be so cursed, doctor, that his love and friendship bring only misery to those who share it? How can it be that one who has in his heart only good thoughts can be constantly under the shadow of evil? This charge of murder is only one of several cases in my life where, through no fault of mine, the shadow of guilt has been cast upon me.

"Years ago, when my wife and I were perfectly happy, a child was born to us, and a few months later, when it was only a tender, helpless little thing that its mother loved with all her heart, it was strangled in its cradle, and we never knew who strangled it, for the deed was done one night when there was absolutely no one in the house but my wife and myself. There was no doubt about the crime, for there on the tiny neck were the finger marks where some cruel hand had closed until life went.

"Then a few years later, when my partner and I were on the eve of fortune, our advance was set back by the robbery of our safe. Some one opened it in the night, some one who knew the combination, for it was the work of no burglar, and yet there were only two persons in the world who knew that combination, my partner and myself. I tried to be brave when these things happened, but as my life went on it seemed more and more as if some curse were on me.

"Eleven years ago I went abroad with my wife and daughter. Business took me to Paris, and I left the ladies in London, expecting to have them join me in a few days. But they never did join me, for the curse was on me still, and before I had been forty-eight hours in the French capital something happened that completed the wreck of my life. It doesn't seem possible, does it, that a simple white card with some words scrawled on it in purple ink could effect a man's undoing? And yet that was my fate. The card was given me by a beautiful woman with eyes like stars. She is dead long ago, and why she wished to harm me I never knew. You must find that out.

"You see I did not know the language of the country, and, wishing to have the words translated,—surely that was natural enough,—I showed the card to others. But no one would tell me what it meant. And, worse than that, wherever I showed it, and to whatever person, there evil came upon me quickly. I was driven from one hotel after another; an old acquaintance turned his back on me; I was arrested and thrown into prison; I was ordered to leave the country."

The sick man paused for a moment in his weakness, but with an effort forced himself to continue:—

"When I went back to London, sure of comfort in the love of my wife, she too, on seeing the card, drove me from her with cruel words. And when finally, in deepest despair, I returned to New York, dear old Jack, the friend of a lifetime, broke with me when I showed him what was written. What the words were I do not know, and suppose no one will ever know, for the ink has faded these many years. You will find the card in my safe with other papers. But I want you, when I am gone, to find out the mystery of my life; and—and—about my fortune, that must be held until you have decided. There is no one who needs my money as much as the poor in this city, and I have bequeathed it to them unless—"

In an agony of mind, Mr. Burwell struggled to go on, I soothing and encouraging him.

"Unless you find what I am afraid to think, but—but—yes, I must say it,—that I have not been a good man, as the world thinks, but have—O doctor, if you find that I have unknowingly harmed any human being, I want that person, or these persons to have my fortune. Promise that."

Seeing the wild light in Burwell's eyes, and the fever that was burning him, I gave the promise asked of me, and the sick man sank back calmer.

A little later, the nurse and attendants came for the operation. As they were about to administer the ether, Burwell pushed them from him, and insisted on having brought to his bedside an iron box from the safe.

"The card is here," he said, laying his trembling hand upon the box, "you will remember your promise!"

Those were his last words, for he did not survive the operation.

Early the next morning I received this message: "The stranger of yesterday begs to see you," and presently a gentleman of fine presence and strength of face, a tall, dark-complexioned man wearing glasses, was shown into the room.

"Mr. Burwell is dead, is he not?" were his first words.

"Who told you?"

"No one told me, but I know it, and I thank God for it."

There was something in the stranger's intense earnestness that convinced me of his right to speak thus, and I listened attentively.

"That you may have confidence in the statement I am about to make, I will first tell you who I am," and he handed me a card that caused me to lift my eyes in wonder, for it bore a very great name, that of one of Europe's most famous savants.

"You have done me much honor, sir," I said with respectful inclination.

"On the contrary you will oblige me by considering me in your debt, and by never revealing my connection with this wretched man. I am moved to speak partly from considerations of human justice, largely in the interest of medical science. It is right for me to tell you, doctor, that your patient was beyond question the Water Street assassin."

"Impossible!" I cried.

"You will not say so when I have finished my story, which takes me back to Paris, to the time, eleven years ago, when this man was making his first visit to the French capital."

"The mysterious card!" I exclaimed.

"Ah, he has told you of his experience, but not of what befell the night before, when he first met my sister."

"Your sister?"

"Yes, it was she who gave him the card, and, in trying to befriend him, made him suffer. She was in ill health at the time, so much so that we had left our native India for extended journeyings. Alas! we delayed too long, for my sister died in New York, only a few weeks later, and I honestly believe her taking off was hastened by anxiety inspired by this man."

"Strange," I murmured, "how the life of a simple New York merchant could become entangled with that of a great lady of the East."

"Yet so it was. You must know that my sister's condition was due mainly to an over fondness for certain occult investigations, from which I had vainly tried to dissuade her. She had once befriended some adepts, who, in return, had taught her things about the souls she had better have left unlearned. At various times while with her I had seen strange things happen, but I never realized what unearthly powers were in her until that night in Paris. We were returning from a drive in the Bois; it was about ten o'clock, and the city lay beautiful around us as Paris looks on a perfect summer's night. Suddenly my sister gave a cry of pain and put her hand to her heart. Then, changing from French to the language of our country, she explained to me quickly that something frightful was taking place there, where she pointed her finger across the river, that we must go to the place at once—the driver must lash his horses—every second was precious.

"So affected was I by her intense conviction, and such confidence had I in my sister's wisdom, that I did not oppose her, but told the man to drive as she directed. The carriage fairly flew across the bridge, down the Boulevard St. Germain, then to the left, threading its way through the narrow streets that lie along the Seine. This way and that, straight ahead here, a turn there, she directing our course, never hesitating, as if drawn by some unseen power, and always urging the driver on to greater speed. Finally, we came to a black-mouthed, evil-looking alley, so narrow and roughly paved that the carriage could scarcely advance.

"'Come on!' my sister cried, springing to the ground; 'we will go on foot, we are nearly there. Thank God, we may yet be in time.'

"No one was in sight as we hurried along the dark alley, and scarcely a light was visible, but presently a smothered scream broke the silence, and, touching my arm, my sister exclaimed:—

"'There, draw your weapon, quick, and take the man at any cost!'

"So swiftly did everything happen after that that I hardly know my actions, but a few minutes later I held pinioned in my arms a man whose blows and writhings had been all in vain; for you must know that much exercise in the jungle had made me strong of limb. As soon as I had made the fellow fast I looked down and found moaning on the ground a poor woman, who explained with tears and broken words that the man had been in the very act of strangling her. Searching him I found a long-bladed knife of curious shape, and keen as a razor, which had been brought for what horrible purpose you may perhaps divine.

"Imagine my surprise, on dragging the man back to the carriage, to find, instead of the ruffianly assassin I expected, a gentleman as far as could be judged from face and manner. Fine eyes, white hands, careful speech, all the signs of refinement, and the dress of a man of means.

"'How can this be?' I said to my sister in our own tongue as we drove away, I holding my prisoner on the opposite seat where he sat silent.

"'It is a *kulos*-man,' she said, shivering, 'It is a fiend-soul. There are a few such in the whole world, perhaps two or three in all.'

"'But he has a good face.'

"'You have not seen his real face yet; I will show it to you, presently.'

"In the strangeness of these happenings and the still greater strangeness of my sister's words, I had all but lost the power of wonder. So we sat without further word until the carriage stopped at the little chateau we had taken near the Parc Monteau.

"I could never properly describe what happened that night; my knowledge of these things is too limited. I simply obeyed my sister in all that she directed, and kept my eyes on this man as no hawk ever watched its prey. She began by questioning him, speaking in a kindly tone which I could ill understand. He seemed embarrassed, dazed, and professed to have no knowledge of what had occurred, or how he had come where we found him. To all my inquiries as to the woman or the crime he shook his head blankly, and thus aroused my wrath.

"'Be not angry with him, brother; he is not lying, it is the other soul.'

"She asked him about his name and country, and he replied without hesitation that he was Richard Burwell, a merchant from New York, just arrived in Paris, traveling for pleasure in Europe with his wife and daughter. This seemed reasonable, for the man spoke English, and, strangely enough, seemed to have no knowledge of French, although we both remembered hearing him speak French to the woman.

"'There is no doubt,' my sister said, 'It is indeed a *kulos*-man; It knows that I am here, that I am Its master. Look, look!' she cried sharply, at the same time putting her eyes so close to the man's face that their fierce light seemed to burn into him. What power she exercised I do not know, nor whether some words she spoke, unintelligible to me, had to do with what followed, but instantly there came over this man, this pleasant-looking, respectable American citizen, such a change as is not made by death worms gnawing in a grave. Now there was a fiend groveling at her feet, a foul, sin-stained fiend.

"'Now you see the demon-soul,' said my sister. 'Watch It writhe and struggle; it has served me well, brother, sayest thou not so, the lore I gained from our wise men?'

"The horror of what followed chilled my blood; nor would I trust my memory were it not that there remained and still remains plain proof of all that I affirm. This hideous creature, dwarfed, crouching, devoid of all resemblance to the man we had but now beheld, chattering to us in curious old-time French, poured out such horrid blasphemy as would have blanched the cheek of Satan, and made recital of such evil deeds as never mortal ear gave heed to. And as she willed my sister checked It or allowed It to go on. What it all meant was more than I could tell. To me it seemed as if these tales of wickedness had no connection with our modern life, or with the world around us, and so I judged presently from what my sister said.

"'Speak of the later time, since thou wast in this clay.'

"Then I perceived that the creature came to things of which I knew: It spoke of New York, of a wife, a child, a friend. It told of strangling the child, of robbing the friend; and was going on to tell God knows what other horrid deeds when my sister stopped It.

"'Stand as thou didst in killing the little babe, stand, stand!' and once more she spoke some words unknown to me. Instantly the demon sprang forward, and, bending Its clawlike hands, clutched them around some little throat that was not there,—but I could see it in my mind. And the look on Its face was a blackest glimpse of hell.

"'And now stand as thou didst in robbing the friend, stand, stand'; and again came the unknown words, and again the fiend obeyed.

"'These we will take for future use,' said my sister. And bidding me watch the creature carefully until she should return, she left the room, and, after none too short an absence, returned bearing a black box that was an apparatus for photography, and something more besides,—some newer, stranger kind of photography that she had learned. Then, on a strangely fashioned card, a transparent white card, composed of many layers of finest Oriental paper, she took the pictures of the creature in those two creeping poses. And when it all was done, the card seemed as white as before, and empty of all meaning until one held it up and examined it intently. Then the pictures showed. And between the two there was a third picture, which somehow seemed to show, at the same time, two faces in one, two souls, my sister said, the kindly visaged man we first had seen, and then the fiend.

"Now my sister asked for pen and ink and I gave her my pocket pen which was filled with purple ink. Handing this to the *kulos*-man she bade him write under the first picture: 'Thus I killed my babe.' And under the second picture: 'Thus I robbed my friend.' And under the third, the one that was between the other two: 'This is the soul of Richard Burwell.' An odd thing about this writing was that it was in the same old French the creature had used in speech, and yet Burwell knew no French.

"My sister was about to finish with the creature when a new idea took her, and she said, looking at It as before:—'Of all thy crimes which one is the worst? Speak, I command thee!'

"Then the fiend told how once It had killed every soul in a house of holy women and buried the bodies in a cellar under a heavy door.

"'Where was the house?'

"'At No. 19 Rue Picpus, next to the old graveyard.'

"'And when was this?'

"Here the fiend seemed to break into fierce rebellion, writhing on the floor with hideous contortions, and pouring forth words that meant nothing to me, but seemed to reach my sister's understanding, for she interrupted from time to time, with quick, stern words that finally brought It to subjection.

"'Enough,' she said, 'I know all,' and then she spoke some words again, her eyes fixed as before, and the reverse change came. Before us stood once more the honest-looking, fine-appearing gentleman, Richard Burwell, of New York.

"'Excuse me, madame,' he said, awkwardly, but with deference; 'I must have dozed a little. I am not myself to-night.'

"'No,' said my sister, 'you have not been yourself to-night.'

"A little later I accompanied the man to the Continental Hotel, where he was stopping, and, returning to my sister, I talked with her until late into the night. I was alarmed to see that she was wrought to a nervous tension that augured ill for her health. I urged her to sleep, but she would not.

"'No,' she said, 'think of the awful responsibility that rests upon me.' And then she went on with her strange theories and explanations, of which I understood only that here was a power for evil more terrible than a pestilence, menacing all humanity.

"'Once in many cycles it happens,' she said, 'that a *kulos*-soul pushes itself within the body of a new-born child, when the pure soul waiting to enter is delayed. Then the two live together through that life, and this hideous principle of evil has a chance upon the earth. It is my will, as I feel it my duty, to see this poor man again. The chances are that he will never know us, for the shock of this night to his normal soul is so great as to wipe out memory.'

"The next evening, about the same hour, my sister insisted that I should go with her to the *Folies Bergère*, a concert garden, none too well frequented, and when I remonstrated, she said: 'I must go,—It is there,' and the words sent a shiver through me.

"We drove to this place, and passing into the garden, presently discovered Richard Burwell seated at a little table, enjoying the scene of pleasure, which was plainly new to him. My sister hesitated a moment what to do, and then, leaving my arm, she advanced to the table and dropped before Burwell's eyes the card she had prepared. A moment later, with a look of pity on her beautiful face, she rejoined me and we went away. It was plain he did not know us."

To so much of the savant's strange recital I had listened with absorbed interest, though without a word, but now I burst in with questions.

"What was your sister's idea in giving Burwell the card?" I asked.

"It was in the hope that she might make the man understand his terrible condition, that is, teach the pure soul to know its loathsome companion."

"And did her effort succeed?"

"Alas! it did not; my sister's purpose was defeated by the man's inability to see the pictures that were plain to every other eye. It is impossible for the *kulos*-man to know his own degradation."

"And yet this man has for years been leading a most exemplary life?"

My visitor shook his head. "I grant you there has been improvement, due largely to experiments I have conducted upon him according to my sister's wishes. But the fiend-soul was never driven out. It grieves me to tell you, doctor, that not only was this man the Water Street assassin, but he was the mysterious murderer, the long-sought-for mutilator of women, whose red crimes have baffled the police of Europe and America for the past ten years."

"You know this," said I starting up, "and yet did not denounce him?"

"It would have been impossible to prove such a charge, and besides, I had made oath to my sister that I would use the man only for these soul-experiments. What are his crimes compared with the great secret of knowledge I am now able to give the world?"

"A secret of knowledge?"

"Yes," said the savant, with intense earnestness, "I may tell you now, doctor, what the whole world will know, ere long, that it is possible to compel every living person to reveal the innermost secrets of his or her life, so long as memory remains, for memory is only the power of producing in the brain material pictures that may be projected externally by the thought rays and made to impress themselves upon the photographic plate, precisely as ordinary pictures do."

"You mean," I exclaimed, "that you can photograph the two principles of good and evil that exist in us?"

"Exactly that. The great truth of a dual soul existence, that was dimly apprehended by one of your Western novelists, has been demonstrated by me in the laboratory with my camera. It is my purpose, at the proper time, to entrust this precious knowledge to a chosen few who will perpetuate it and use it worthily."

"Wonderful, wonderful!" I cried, "and now tell me, if you will, about the house on the Rue Picpus. Did you ever visit the place?"

"We did, and found that no buildings had stood there for fifty years, so we did not pursue the search."[38]

"And the writing on the card, have you any memory of it, for Burwell told me that the words have faded?"

"I have something better than that; I have a photograph of both card and

---

38 Years later, some workmen in Paris, making excavations in the Rue Picpus, came upon a heavy door buried under a mass of debris, under an old cemetery. On lifting the door they found a vault-like chamber in which were a number of female skeletons, and graven on the walls were blasphemous words written in French, which experts declared dated from fully two hundred years before. They also declared this handwriting identical with that found on the door at the Water Street murder in New York. Thus we may deduce a theory of fiend reincarnation; for it would seem clear, almost to the point of demonstration, that this murder of the seventeenth century was the work of the same evil soul that killed the poor woman on Water Street towards the end of the nineteenth century.

writing, which my sister was careful to take. I had a notion that the ink in my pocket pen would fade, for it was a poor affair. This photograph I will bring you tomorrow."

"Bring it to Burwell's house," I said.

The next morning the stranger called as agreed upon.

"Here is the photograph of the card," he said.

"And here is the original card," I answered, breaking the seal of the envelope I had taken from Burwell's iron box. "I have waited for your arrival to look at it. Yes, the writing has indeed vanished; the card seems quite blank."

"Not when you hold it this way," said the stranger, and as he tipped the card I saw such a horrid revelation as I can never forget. In an instant I realized how the shock of seeing that card had been too great for the soul of wife or friend to bear. In these pictures was the secret of a cursed life. The resemblance to Burwell was unmistakable, the proof against him was overwhelming. In looking upon that piece of pasteboard the wife had seen a crime which the mother could never forgive, the partner had seen a crime which the friend could never forgive. Think of a loved face suddenly melting before your eyes into a grinning skull, then into a mass of putrefaction, then into the ugliest fiend of hell, leering at you, distorted with all the marks of vice and shame. That is what I saw, that is what they had seen!

"Let us lay these two cards in the coffin," said my companion impressively, "we have done what we could."

Eager to be rid of the hateful piece of pasteboard (for who could say that the curse was not still clinging about it?), I took the strange man's arm, and together we advanced into the adjoining room where the body lay. I had seen Burwell as he breathed his last, and knew that there had been a peaceful look on his face as he died. But now, as we laid the two white cards on the still breast, the savant suddenly touched my arm, and pointing to the dead man's face, now frightfully distorted, whispered:—"See, even in death It followed him. Let us close the coffin quickly."

∼

JACK BE QUICK

Barbara Paul

There are any number of reasons for people to begin writing fiction. For teacher Barbara Jeanne Paul (1931–), she claimed that she simply could not stand the notion of reading another undergraduate paper.

Her early novels were science fiction, beginning with *An Exercise for Madmen* (1978), followed by three more in the next three years, plus an outlier *Star Trek* novel, *The Three-Minute Universe,* in 1988, by which time she had become established as a successful mystery writer.

Her first mystery novel, *The Fourth Wall* (1979), reflected her affection for the theater. Her second, *Liars and Tyrants and People Who Turn Blue* (1980), combined science fiction with mystery. She asserts that she wrote *Your Eyelids Are Growing Heavy* (1981), about a woman who deduces that she has been hypnotized when a large piece of her life vanishes from her memory, in two weeks as a test to determine how fast a novel could be produced. Paul wrote three historical novels featuring the great opera singer Enrico Caruso: *A Cadenza for Caruso* (1984), *Prima Donna at Large* (1985), and *A Chorus of Detectives* (1987). Her series protagonist, Marian Larch of the New York Police Department, starred in seven novels, beginning with *The Renewable Virgin* (1984). Paul's 1985 novel *Kill Fee* was the inspiration for the 1990 made-for-television movie *Murder C.O.D.,* in which a Chicago cop is being blackmailed for having an extramarital affair. When he and his wife move to Portland, Oregon, the blackmailer follows. It starred Patrick Duffy and William Devane.

"Jack Be Quick" was first published in *Solved!,* edited by Ed Gorman and Martin H. Greenberg (New York, Carroll & Graf, 1991).

30 SEPTEMBER 1888, ST. JUDE'S VICARAGE, WHITECHAPEL.

He took two, this time, and within the same hour, Inspector Abberline told us. The first victim was found this morning less than an hour after midnight, in a small court off Berner Street. The second woman was killed in Mitre Square forty-five minutes later. He did his hideous deed and escaped undetected, as he always does. Inspector Abberline believes he was interrupted in Berner Street, because he did not . . . do to that woman what he'd done to his other victims. My husband threw the Inspector a warning look, not wanting me exposed to such distressing matters more than necessary. "But the second woman was severely mutilated," Inspector Abberline concluded, offering no details. "He finished in Mitre Square what he'd begun in Berner Street."

My husband and I knew nothing of the double murder, not having left the vicarage all day. When no one appeared for morning services, Edward was angry. Customarily we can count on a Sunday congregation of a dozen or so; we should have suspected something was amiss. "Do you know who the women were, Inspector?" I asked.

"One of them," he said. "His Mitre Square victim was named Catherine Eddowes. We have yet to establish the identity of the Berner Street victim."

Inspector Abberline looked exhausted; I poured him another cup of tea. He undoubtedly would have preferred something stronger, but Edward permitted no spirits in the house, not even sherry. I waited until the Inspector had taken a sip before I put my next question to him. "Did he cut out Catherine Eddowes's womb the way he did Annie Chapman's?"

Edward looked shocked that I should know about that, but the police investigator was beyond shock. "Yes, Mrs. Wickham, he did. But this time he did not take it away with him."

It was one of the many concerns that baffled and horrified me about the series of grisly murders haunting London. Annie Chapman's disemboweled body had been found in Hanbury Street three weeks earlier; all the entrails had been piled above her shoulder except the womb. Why had he stolen her womb? "And the intestines?"

"Heaped over the left shoulder, as before."

Edward cleared his throat. "This Eddowes woman . . . she was a prostitute?"

Inspector Abberline said she was. "And I have no doubt that the Berner Street victim will prove to have been on the game as well. That's the only common ground among his victims—they were all prostitutes."

"Evil combating evil," Edward said with a shake of his head. "When will it end?"

Inspector Abberline put down his cup. "The end, alas, is not yet in sight. We are still conducting door-to-door searches, and the populace is beginning to panic. We have our hands full dispersing the mobs."

"Mobs?" Edward asked. "Has there been trouble?"

"I regret to say there has. Everyone is so desperate to find someone to blame . . ." The Inspector allowed the unfinished sentence to linger a moment. "Earlier today a constable was chasing a petty thief through the streets, and someone who saw them called out, 'It's the Ripper!' Several men joined in the chase, and then others, as the word spread that it was the Ripper the constable was pursuing. That mob was thirsting for blood—nothing less than a lynching would have satisfied them. The thief and the constable ended up barricading themselves in a building together until help could arrive."

Edward shook his head sadly. "The world has gone mad."

"It's why I have come to you, Vicar," Inspector Abberline said. "You can help calm them down. You could speak to them, persuade them to compose themselves. Your presence in the streets will offer a measure of reassurance."

"Of course," Edward said quickly. "Shall we leave now? I'll get my coat."

The Inspector turned to me. "Mrs. Wickham, thank you for the tea. Now we must be going." I saw both men to the door.

The Inspector did not know he had interrupted a disagreement between my husband and me, one that was recurring with increasing frequency of late. But I had no wish to revive the dispute when Edward returned; the shadow of these two new murders lay like a shroud over all other concerns. I retired to my sewing closet, where I tried to calm my spirit through prayer. One could not think dispassionately of this unknown man wandering the streets of London's East End, a man who hated women so profoundly that he cut away those parts of the bodies that proclaimed his victims to be female. I tried to pray for *him*, lost soul that he is; God forgive me, I could not.

1 OCTOBER 1888, ST. JUDE'S VICARAGE.

Early the next morning the fog lay so thick about the vicarage that the street gaslights were still on. They performed their usual efficient function of lighting the *tops* of the poles; looking down from our bedroom window, I could not see the street below.

Following our morning reading from the Scriptures, Edward called my attention to an additional passage. "Since you are aware of what the Ripper does to his victims, Beatrice, it will be to your benefit to hear this. Attend. 'Let the breast be torn open and the heart and vitals be taken from hence and thrown over the shoulder.'"

A moment of nausea overtook me. "The same way Annie Chapman and the others were killed."

"Exactly," Edward said with a hint of triumph in his voice. "Those are Solomon's words, ordering the execution of three murderers. I wonder if anyone has pointed this passage out to Inspector Abberline? It could be of assistance in ascertaining the rationale behind these murders, perhaps revealing something of the killer's mental disposition . . ." He continued in this speculative vein for a while longer.

I was folding linen as I listened. When he paused for breath, I asked Edward about his chambray shirt. "I've not seen it these two weeks."

"Eh? It will turn up. I'm certain you have put it away somewhere."

I was equally certain I had not. Then, with some trepidation, I reintroduced the subject of our disagreement the night before. "Edward, would you be willing to reconsider your position concerning charitable donations? If parishioners can't turn to their church for help—"

"Allow me to interrupt you, my dear," he said. "I am convinced that suffering *cannot* be reduced by indiscriminately passing out money but only through the realistic appraisal of each man's problems. So long as the lower classes depend upon charity to see them through hard times, they will never learn thrift and the most propitious manner of spending what money they have."

Edward's "realistic appraisal" of individual problems always ended the same way, with little lectures on how to economize. "But surely in cases of extreme hardship," I said, "a small donation would not be detrimental to their future well-being."

"Ah, but how are we to determine who are those in true need? They will tell any lie to get their hands on a few coins which they promptly spend on hard drink. And then they threaten us when those coins are not forthcoming! This is the legacy my predecessor at St. Jude's has left us, this expectancy that the church *owes* them charity!"

That was true; the vicarage had been stoned more than once when Edward had turned petitioners away. "But the children, Edward—surely we can help the children! They are not to blame for their parents' wastrel ways."

Edward sat down next to me and took my hand. "You have a soft heart and a generous nature, Beatrice, and I venerate those qualities in you. Your natural instinct for charity is one of your most admirable traits." He smiled sadly. "Nevertheless, how will these poor, desperate creatures ever learn to care for their own children if we do it for them? And there is this. Has it not occurred to you that God may be testing *us*? How simple it would be, to hand out a few coins and convince ourselves we have done our Christian duty! No, Beatrice, God is asking more of us than that. We must hold firm in our resolve."

I acquiesced, seeing no chance of prevailing against such unshakable certitude that God's will was dictating our course of action. Furthermore, Edward Wickham was my husband and I owed him obedience, even when my heart was troubled and filled with uncertainty. It was his decision to make, not mine.

"Do not expect me until teatime," Edward said as he rose and went to fetch his greatcoat. "Mr. Lusk has asked me to attend a meeting of the Whitechapel Vigilance Committee, and I then have my regular calls to make. Best you not go out today, my dear, at least until Inspector Abberline has these riots under control." Edward's duties were keeping him away from the vicarage more and more. He sometimes would return in the early hours of the morning, melancholy and exhausted from trying to help a man find night work or from locating shelter for a homeless widow and her children. At times he seemed not to remember where he'd been; I was concerned for his health and his spirit.

The fog was beginning to lift by the time he departed, but I still could not see very far—except in my mind's eye. If one were to proceed down Commercial Street and then follow Aldgate to Leadenhall and Cornhill on to the point where six roads meet at a statue of the Duke of Wellington, one would find oneself in front of the imposing Royal Exchange, its rich interior murals and Turkish floor paving a proper setting for the transactions undertaken there. Across Threadneedle Street, the Bank of England, with its windowless lower storeys, and the rocklike Stock Exchange both raise their impressive façades. Then one could turn to the opposite direction and behold several other banking establishments clustered around Mansion House, the Lord Mayor's residence. It still dumbfounds me to realize that the wealth of the nation is concentrated there, in so small an area . . . all within walking distance of the worst slums in the nation.

Do wealthy bankers ever spare a thought for the *appalling* poverty of Whitechapel and Spitalfields? The people living within the boundaries of St. Jude's parish are crowded like animals into a labyrinth of courts and alleys, none of which intersect major streets. The crumbling, hazardous buildings fronting the courts house complete families in each room, sometimes numbering as many as a dozen people; in such circumstances, incest is common . . . and, some say, inevitable. The buildings reek from the liquid sewage accumulated in the basements, while the courts themselves stink of garbage that attracts vermin, dogs, and other scavengers. Often one standing pipe in the courtyard serves as the sole source of water for all the inhabitants of three or four buildings, an outdoor pipe that freezes with unremitting regularity during the winter. Once Edward and I were called out in the middle of the night to succor a woman suffering from scarlet fever; we found her in a foul-smelling single room with three children and four pigs. Her husband, a cabman, had committed suicide the month before; and it wasn't until we were leaving that we discovered one of the children had been lying there dead for thirteen days.

The common lodging houses are even worse—filthy and infested and reservoirs of disease. In such doss houses a bed can be rented for fourpence for the night, strangers often sharing a bed because neither has the full price alone. There is no such thing as privacy, since the beds are lined up in crowded rows in the manner of dormitories. Beds are rented indiscriminately to men and women alike; consequently many of the doss houses are in truth brothels, and even those that are not have no compunction about renting a bed to a prostitute when she brings a paying customer with her. Inspector Abberline once told us the police estimate there are twelve hundred prostitutes in Whitechapel alone, fertile hunting grounds for the man who pleasures himself with the butchering of ladies of the night.

Ever since the Ripper began stalking the East End, Edward has been campaigning for more police to patrol the back alleys and for better street lighting. The problem is that Whitechapel is so poor it cannot afford the rates to pay for these needed improvements. If there is to be help, it must come from outside. Therefore I have undertaken a campaign of my own. Every day I write to philanthropists, charitable establishments, government officials. I petition every personage of authority and good will with whose name I am conversant, pleading the cause of the *children* of Whitechapel, especially those ragged, dirty street arabs who sleep wherever they can, eat whatever they can scavenge or steal, and perform every unspeakable act demanded of them in exchange for a coin they can call their own.

12 OCTOBER 1888, GOLDEN LANE MORTUARY, CITY OF LONDON.

Today I did something I have never done before: I willfully disobeyed my husband. Edward had forbidden me to attend the inquest of Catherine Eddowes, saying I should not expose myself to such unsavory disclosures as were bound to be made. Also, he said it was unseemly for the vicar's wife to venture abroad unaccompanied, a dictum that impresses me as more appropriately belonging to another time and place. I waited until Edward left the vicarage and then hurried on my way. My path took me past one of the larger slaughterhouses in the area; with my handkerchief covering my mouth and nose to keep out the stench, I had to cross the road to avoid the blood and urine flooding the pavement. Once I had left Whitechapel, however, the way was unencumbered.

Outside the Golden Lane Mortuary I was pleased to encounter Inspector Abberline; he was surprised to see me there and immediately offered himself as my protector. "Is the Reverend Mr. Wickham not with you?"

"He has business in Shoreditch," I answered truthfully, not adding that Edward found inquests distasteful and would not have attended in any event.

"This crowd could turn ugly, Mrs. Wickham," Inspector Abberline said. "Let me see if I can obtain us two chairs near the door."

That he did, with the result that I had to stretch in a most unladylike manner to see over other people's heads. "Inspector," I said, "have you learned the identity of the other woman who was killed the same night as Catherine Eddowes?"

"Yes, it was Elizabeth Stride—Long Liz, they called her. About forty-five years of age and homely as sin, if you'll pardon my speaking ill of the dead. They were all unattractive, all the Ripper's victims. One thing is certain, he didn't choose them for their beauty."

"Elizabeth Stride was a prostitute?"

"That she was, Mrs. Wickham, I'm sorry to say. She had nine children some-where, and a husband, until he could tolerate her drunkenness no longer and turned her out. A woman with a nice big family like that and a husband who supported them—what reasons could she have had to turn to drink?"

I could think of nine or ten. "What about Catherine Eddowes? Did she have children too?"

Inspector Abberline rubbed the side of his nose. "Well, she had a daughter, that much we know. We haven't located her yet, though."

The inquest was ready to begin. The small room was crowded, with observers standing along the walls and even outside in the passageway. The presiding coroner called the first witness, the police constable who found Catherine Eddowes's body.

The remarkable point to emerge from the constable's testimony was that his patrol took him through Mitre Square, where he'd found the body, every fourteen or fifteen minutes. The Ripper had only fifteen minutes to inflict so much damage? How swift he was, how sure of what he was doing!

It came out during the inquest that the Eddowes woman had been strangled before her killer had cut her throat, thus explaining why she had not cried out. In response to my whispered question, Inspector Abberline said yes, the other victims had also been strangled first. When the physicians present at the post mortem testified, they were agreed that the killer had sound anatomical knowledge but they were not in accord as to the extent of his actual skill in removing the organs. Their reports of what had been done to the body were disturbing; I grew slightly faint during the description of how the flaps of the abdomen had been peeled back to expose the intestines.

Inspector Abberline's sworn statement was succinct and free of speculation; he testified as to the course of action pursued by the police following the discovery of the body. There were other witnesses, people who had encountered Catherine Eddowes on the night she was killed. At one time she had been seen speaking to a middle-aged man wearing a black coat of good quality which was now slightly shabby; it was the same description that had emerged during the investigation of one of the Ripper's earlier murders. But at the end of it all we were no nearer to knowing the Ripper's identity than ever; the verdict was "Willful murder by some person unknown."

I refused Inspector Abberline's offer to have one of his assistants escort me home. "That makes six women he's killed now, this Ripper," I said. "You need all of your men for your investigation."

The Inspector rubbed the side of his nose, a mannerism I was coming to recognize indicated uncertainty. "As a matter of fact, Mrs. Wickham, I am of the opinion that only four were killed by the same man. You are thinking of the woman murdered near St. Jude's Church? And the one on Osborn Street?" He shook his head. "Not the Ripper's work, I'm convinced of it."

"What makes you think so, Inspector?"

"Because while those two women did have their throats cut, they weren't cut in the same manner as the later victims'. There is viciousness in the way the Ripper slashes his victims' throats . . . he is left-handed, we know, and he slashes twice, once each way. The cuts are deep, brutal . . . he almost took Annie Chapman's head off. No, Polly Nichols was his first victim, then Chapman. And now this double murder, Elizabeth Stride and Catherine Eddowes. Those four are all the work of the same man."

I shuddered. "Did the four women know one another?"

"Not that we can determine," Inspector Abberline replied. "Evidently they had nothing in common except the fact that they were all four prostitutes."

More questions occurred to me, but I had detained the Inspector long enough. I bade him farewell and started back to St. Jude's, a long walk from Golden Lane. The daylight was beginning to fail, but I had no money for a hansom cab. I pulled my shawl tight about my shoulders and hurried my step, not wishing to be caught out of doors after dark. It was my husband's opinion that since the Ripper killed only prostitutes, respectable married women had nothing to fear. It was my opinion that my husband put altogether too much faith in the Ripper's ability to tell the difference.

I was almost home when a most unhappy incident ensued. A distraught woman approached me on Middlesex Street, carrying what looked like a bundle of rags which she thrust into my arms. Inside the rags was a dead baby. I cried out and almost dropped the cold little body.

"All he needed were a bit o' milk," the mother said, tears running down her cheeks.

"Oh, I am so sorry!" I gasped helplessly. The poor woman looked half-starved herself.

"They said it was no use a-sending to the church," she sobbed, "for you didn't never give nothing though you spoke kind."

I was so ashamed I had to lower my head. Even then I didn't have tuppence in my pocket to give her. I slipped off my shawl and wrapped it around the tiny corpse. "Bury him in this."

She mumbled something as she took the bundle from me and staggered away. She would prepare to bury her child in the shawl, but at the last moment she would snatch back the shawl's warmth for herself. She would cry over her dead baby as she did it, but she would do it. I prayed that she would do it.

16 OCTOBER 1888, ST. JUDE'S VICARAGE.

This morning I paid an out-of-work bricklayer fourpence to clean out our fireplaces. In the big fireplace in the kitchen, he made a surprising discovery: soot-blackened buttons from my husband's missing chambray shirt turned up.

When later I asked Edward why he had burned his best shirt, he looked at me in utter astonishment and demanded to know why I had burned it. Yet we two are the only ones living at the vicarage.

22 OCTOBER 1888, SPITALFIELDS MARKET.

The chemist regretfully informed me that the price of arsenic had risen, so of necessity I purchased less than the usual quantity, hoping Edward would find the diminished volume sufficient. Keeping the vicarage free of rats was costly. When first we took up residence at St. Jude's, we believed the rats were coming from the warehouses further along Commercial Street; but then we came to understand that every structure in Whitechapel was plagued with vermin. As fast as one killed them, others appeared to take their place.

A newspaper posted outside an alehouse caught my eye; I had made it a point to read every word published about the Ripper. The only new thing was that all efforts to locate the family of Catherine Eddowes, the Ripper's last victim, had failed. A front-page editorial demanded the resignation of the Commissioner of Police and various other men in authority. Three weeks had passed since the Ripper had taken two victims on the same night, and the police still had no helpful clues and no idea of who the Ripper was or when he would strike next. That he would strike again, no one doubted; that the police could protect the women of Whitechapel, no one believed.

In the next street I came upon a posted bill requesting anyone with information concerning the identity of the murderer to step forward and convey that information to the police. The request saddened me; the police could not have formulated a clearer admission of failure.

25 OCTOBER 1888, ST. JUDE'S VICARAGE.

Edward is ill. When he had not appeared at the vicarage by teatime yesterday, I began to worry. I spent an anxious evening awaiting his return; it was well after midnight before I heard his key in the lock.

He looked like a stranger. His eyes were glistening and his clothes in disarray; his usual proud bearing had degenerated into a stoop, his shoulders hunched as if he were cold. The moment he caught sight of me he began berating me for failing to purchase the arsenic he needed to kill the rats; it was only when I led him to the pantry where he himself had spread the noxious powder around the rat holes did his reprimands cease. His skin was hot and dry, and with difficulty I persuaded him into bed.

But sleep would not come. I sat by the bed and watched him thrashing among the covers, throwing off the cool cloth I had placed on his forehead. Edward kept waving his hands as if trying to fend someone off; what nightmares was he seeing behind those closed lids? In his delirium he began to cry out. At first the words were not clear, but then I understood my husband to be saying, "Whores! Whores! All whores!"

When by two in the morning his fever had not broken, I knew I had to seek help. I wrapped my cloak about me and set forth, not permitting myself to dwell on what could be hiding in the shadows. I do not like admitting it, but I was terrified; nothing less than Edward's illness could have driven me into the streets of Whitechapel at night. But I reached my destination with nothing untoward happening; I roused Dr. Phelps from a sound sleep and rode back to the vicarage with him in his carriage.

When Dr. Phelps bent over the bed, Edward's eyes flew open; he seized the doctor's upper arm in a grip that made the man wince. "They must be stopped!" my husband whispered hoarsely. "They . . . must be stopped!"

"We will stop them," Dr. Phelps replied gent-ly and eased Edward's hand away. Edward's eyes closed and his body resumed its thrashing.

The doctor's examination was brief. "The fever is making him hallucinate," he told me. "Sleep is the best cure, followed by a period of bed rest." He took a small vial from his bag and asked me to bring a glass of water. He tapped a few drops of liquid into the water, which he then poured into Edward's mouth as I held his head.

"What did you give him?" I asked.

"Laudanum, to make him sleep. I will leave the vial with you." Dr. Phelps rubbed his right arm where Edward had gripped him. "Strange, I do not recall Mr. Wickham as being left-handed."

"He is ambidextrous. This fever . . . will he recover?"

"The next few hours will tell. Give him more laudanum only if he awakes in this same disturbed condition, and then only one drop in a glass of water. I will be back later to see how he is."

When Dr. Phelps had gone, I replaced the cool cloth on Edward's forehead and resumed my seat by the bed. Edward did seem calmer now, the wild thrashing at an end and only the occasional twitching of the hands betraying his inner turmoil. By dawn he was in a deep sleep and seemed less feverish.

My spirit was too disturbed to permit me to sleep. I decided to busy myself with household chores. Edward's black greatcoat was in need of a good brushing, so that came first. It was then that I discovered the rust-colored stains on the cuffs; they did not look fresh, but I could not be certain. Removing them was a delicate matter. The coat had seen better days and the cloth would not withstand vigorous handling. But eventually I got the worst of the stains out and hung the coat in the armoire.

Then I knelt by the bedroom window and prayed. I asked God to vanquish the dark suspicions that had begun to cloud my mind.

Whitechapel had changed Edward. Since he had accepted the appointment to St. Jude's, he had become more distant, more aloof. He had always been a reserved man, speaking rarely of himself and never of his past. I knew nothing of his childhood, only that he had been born in London; he had always discouraged my inquiring about the years before we met. If my parents had still been living when Edward first began to pay court, they would never have permitted me to entertain a man with no background, no family, and no connections. But by then I had passed what was generally agreed to be a marriageable age, and I was enchanted by the appearance out of nowhere of a gentleman of compatible spirit who desired me to spend my life with him. All I knew of Edward was that he was a little older than most new curates were, suggesting that he had started in some other profession, or had at least studied for one, before joining the clergy. Our twelve years together had been peaceful ones, and I had never regretted my choice.

But try as he might to disguise the fact, Edward's perspective had grown harsher during our tenure in Whitechapel. Sadly, he held no respect for the people whose needs he was here to minister to. I once heard him say to a fellow vicar, "The lower classes render no useful service. They create no wealth—more often they destroy it. They degrade whatever they touch, and as individuals are most probably incapable of improvement. Thrift and good management mean nothing to them. I resist terming them hopeless, but perhaps that is what they are." The Edward Wickham I married would never have spoken so.

"Beatrice."

I glanced toward the bed; Edward was awake and watching me. I rose from my knees and went to his side. "How do you feel, Edward?"

"Weak, as if I've lost a lot of blood." He looked confused. "Am I ill?"

I explained about the fever. "Dr. Phelps says you need a great deal of rest."

"Dr. Phelps? He was here?" Edward remembered nothing of the doctor's visit. Nor did he remember where he'd been the night before or even coming home. "This is frightening," he said shakily. His speech was slurred, an effect of the laudanum. "Hours of my life missing and no memory of them?"

"We will worry about that later. Right now you must try to sleep some more."

"Sleep . . . yes." I sat and held his hand until he drifted off again.

When he awoke a second time a few hours later, I brought him a bowl of broth, which he consumed with reawakening appetite. My husband was clearly on the mend; he was considering getting out of bed when Dr. Phelps stopped by.

The doctor was pleased with Edward's progress. "Spend the rest of the day resting," he said, "and then tomorrow you may be allowed up. You must be careful not to overtax yourself or the fever may recur."

Edward put up a show of protesting, but I think he was secretly relieved that nothing was required of him except that he lie in bed all day. I escorted the doctor to the door.

"Make sure he eats," he said to me. "He needs to rebuild his strength."

I said I'd see to it. Then I hesitated; I could not go on without knowing. "Dr. Phelps, did anything happen last night?"

"I beg your pardon?"

He didn't know what I meant. "Did the Ripper strike again?"

Dr. Phelps smiled. "I am happy to say he did not. Perhaps we've seen an end of these dreadful killings, hmm?"

My relief was so great it was all I could do not to burst into tears. When the doctor had gone, I again fell to my knees and prayed, this time asking God to forgive me for entertaining such treacherous thoughts about my own husband.

1 NOVEMBER 1888, LEMAN STREET POLICE STATION, WHITECHAPEL.

It was with a light heart that I left the vicarage this bright, crisp Tuesday morning. My husband was recovered from his recent indisposition and busy with his daily duties. I had received two encouraging replies to my petitions for charitable assistance for Whitechapel's children. And London had survived the entire month of October without another Ripper killing.

I was on my way to post two letters, my responses to the philanthropists who seemed inclined to listen to my plea. In my letters I had pointed out that over half the children born in Whitechapel die before they reach the age of five. The ones that do not die are mentally and physically underdeveloped; many of them that are taken into pauper schools are adjudged abnormally dull if not actual mental defectives. Children frequently arrive at school crying from hunger and then collapse at their benches. In winter they are too cold to think about learning their letters or doing their sums. The schools themselves are shamefully mismanaged and the children sometimes mistreated; there are school directors who pocket most of the budget and hire out the children to sweatshop owners as cheap labor.

What I proposed was the establishment of a boarding school for the children of Whitechapel, a place where the young would be provided with hygienic living conditions, wholesome food to eat, and warm clothing to wear—all before they ever set foot in a classroom. Then when their physical needs had been attended to, they would be given proper educational and moral instruction. The school was to be administered by an honest and conscientious director who could be depended upon never to exploit the downtrodden. All this would cost a great deal of money.

My letters went into the post accompanied by a silent prayer. I was then in Leman Street, not far from the police station. I stopped in and asked if Inspector Abberline was there.

He was; he greeted me warmly and offered me a chair. After inquiring after my husband's health, he sat back and looked at me expectantly.

Now that I was there, I felt a tinge of embarrassment. "It is presumptuous of me, I know," I said, "but may I make a suggestion? Concerning the Ripper, I mean. You've undoubtedly thought of every possible approach, but . . ." I didn't finish my sentence because he was laughing.

"Forgive me, Mrs. Wickham," he said, still smiling. "I would like to show you something." He went into another room and returned shortly carrying a large box filled with papers. "These are letters," he explained, "from concerned citizens like yourself. Each one offers a plan for capturing the Ripper. And we have two more boxes just like this one."

I flushed and rose to leave. "Then I'll not impose—"

"Please, Mrs. Wickham, take your seat. We read every letter that comes to us and give serious consideration to every suggestion made. I show you the box only to convince you we welcome suggestions."

I resumed my seat, not fully convinced but nevertheless encouraged by the Inspector's courtesy. "Very well." I tried to gather my thoughts. "The Ripper's first victim, you are convinced, was Polly Nichols?"

"Correct. Buck's Row, the last day of August."

"The *Illustrated Times* said that she was forty-two years old and separated from her husband, to whom she had borne five children. The cause of their separation was her propensity for strong drink. Mr. Nichols made his wife an allowance, according to the *Times,* until he learned of her prostitution—at which time he discontinued all pecuniary assistance. Is this account essentially correct?"

"Yes, it is."

"The Ripper's next victim was Annie Chapman, about forty, who was murdered early in September?"

"The night of the eighth," Inspector Abberline said, "although her body wasn't found until six the next morning. She was killed on Hanbury Street, less than half a mile from the Buck's Row site of Polly Nichols's murder."

I nodded. "Annie Chapman also ended on the streets because of drunkenness. She learned her husband had died only when her allowance stopped. When she tried to find her two children, she discovered they had been separated and sent to different schools, one of them abroad."

Inspector Abberline raised an eyebrow. "How did you ascertain that, Mrs. Wickham?"

"One of our parishioners knew her," I said. "Next came the double murder of Elizabeth Stride and Catherine Eddowes, during the small hours of the thirtieth of September. Berner Street and Mitre Square, a fifteen-minute walk from each other. The Stride woman was Swedish by birth and claimed to be a widow, but I have heard that may not be true. She was a notorious inebriate, according to one of the constables patrolling Fairclough Street, and she may simply have been ashamed to admit her husband would not allow her near the children—the *nine* children. Is this also correct?"

The Inspector was looking bemused. "It is."

"Of Catherine Eddowes I know very little. But the *Times* said she had spent the night before her death locked up in the Cloak Lane Police Station, because she'd been found lying drunk in the street somewhere in Aldgate. And you yourself told me she had a daughter. Did she also have a husband, Inspector?"

He nodded slowly. "A man named Conway. We've been unable to trace him."

The same pattern in each case. "You've said on more than one occasion that the four victims had only their prostitution in common. But in truth, Inspector, they had a great deal in common. They were all in their forties. They were all lacking in beauty. They had all been married. They all lost their homes through a weakness for the bottle." I took a breath. "And they were all mothers."

Inspector Abberline looked at me quizzically.

"They were all mothers *who abandoned their children*."

He considered it. "You think the Ripper had been abandoned?"

"Is it not possible? Or perhaps he too had a wife he turned out because of drunkenness. I don't know where he fits into the pattern. But consider. The nature of the murders makes it quite clear that these women are not just killed the way the unfortunate victim of a highwayman is killed—the women are being *punished*." I was uncomfortable speaking of such matters, but speak I must. "The manner of their deaths, one might say, is a grotesque version of the way they earned their livings."

The Inspector was also uncomfortable. "They were not raped, Mrs. Wickham."

"But of course they were, Inspector," I said softly. "They were raped with a knife."

I had embarrassed him. "We should not be speaking of this," he said, further chagrined at seeming to rebuke the vicar's wife. "These are not matters that concern you."

"All I ask is that you consider what I have said."

"Oh, I can promise you that," he answered wryly, and I believed him. "I do have some encouraging news," he continued, desirous of changing the subject. "We have been given more men to patrol the streets—more than have ever before been concentrated in one section of London! The next time the Ripper strikes, we'll be ready for him."

"Then you think he will strike again."

"I fear so. He's not done yet."

It was the same opinion that was held by everyone else, but it was more ominous coming from the mouth of a police investigator. I thanked Inspector Abberline for his time and left.

The one thing that had long troubled me about the investigation of the Ripper murders was the refusal of the investigators to acknowledge that there was anything carnal about these violent acts. The killings were the work of a madman, the police and the newspapers agreed . . . as if that explained everything. But unless Inspector Abberline and the rest of those in authority could see the fierce hatred of women that drove the Ripper, I despaired of his ever being caught.

10 NOVEMBER 1888, MILLER'S COURT, SPITALFIELDS.

At three in the morning, I was still fully dressed, awaiting Edward's return to the vicarage. It had been hours since I'd made my last excuse to myself for his absence; his duties frequently kept him out late, but never this late. I was trying to decide whether I should go to Dr. Phelps for help when a frantic knocking started at the door.

It was a young market porter named Macklin who occasionally attended services at St. Jude's, and he was in a frantic state. "It's the missus," he gasped. " 'Er time is come and the midwife's too drunk to stand up. Will you come?"

I said I would. "Let me get a few things." I was distracted, wanting to send him away; but this was the Macklins' first child and I couldn't turn down his plea for help.

We hurried off in the direction of Spitalfields; the couple had recently rented a room in a slum building facing on Miller's Court. I knew the area slightly. Edward and I had once been called to a doss house there to minister to a dying man. That was the first time I'd ever been inside one of the common lodging houses; it was a big place, over three hundred beds and every one of them rented for the night.

Miller's Court was right across the street from the doss house. As we went into the courtyard, a girl of about twelve unfolded herself from the doorway where she had been huddled and tugged at my skirt. "Fourpence for a doss, lady?"

"Get out of 'ere!" Macklin yelled. "Go on!"

"Just a moment," I stopped him. I asked the girl if she had no home to go to.

"Mam turned me out," the girl answered sullenly. "Says don't come back 'til light."

I understood; frequently the women here put their children out on the street while they rented their room for immoral purposes. "I have no money," I told the girl, "but you may come inside."

"Not in my room, she don't!" Macklin shouted.

"She can be of help, Mr. Macklin," I said firmly.

He gave in ungraciously. The girl, who said her name was Rose Howe, followed us inside. Straightaway I started to sneeze; the air was filled with particles of fur. Someone in the building worked at plucking hair from dogs, rabbits, and perhaps even rats for sale to a furrier. There were other odors as well; the building held at least one fish that had not been caught yesterday. I could smell paste, from drying matchboxes, most likely. It was all rather overpowering.

Macklin led us up a flight of stairs from which the banisters had been removed —for firewood, no doubt. Vermin-infested wallpaper was hanging in strips above our heads. Macklin opened a door upon a small room where his wife lay in labor. Mrs. Macklin was still a girl herself, only a few years older than Rose Howe. She was lying on a straw mattress, undoubtedly infested with fleas, on a broken-down bedstead. A few boxes were stacked against one wall; the only other piece of furniture was a plank laid across two stacks of bricks. I sent Macklin down to fill a bucket from the water pipe in the courtyard, and then I put Rose Howe to washing some rags I found in a corner.

It was a long labor. Rose curled up on the floor and went to sleep. Macklin wandered out for a few pints.

Day had broken before the baby came. Macklin was back, sobriety returning with each cry of pain from his young wife. Since it was daylight, Rose Howe could have returned to her own room but instead stayed and helped; she stood like a rock, letting Mrs. Macklin grip her thin wrists during the final bearing-down. The baby was under-sized; but as I cleared out her mouth and nose, she voiced a howl that announced her arrival to the world in no uncertain terms. I watched a smile light the faces of both girls as Rose cleaned the baby and placed her in her mother's arms. Then Rose held the cord as I tied it off with thread in two places and cut it through with my sewing scissors.

Macklin was a true loving husband. "Don't you worry none, love," he said to his wife. "Next 'un'll be a boy."

I told Rose Howe I'd finish cleaning up and for her to go home. Then I told Macklin to bring his daughter to St. Jude's for christening. When at last I was ready to leave, the morning sun was high in the sky.

To my surprise the small courtyard was crowded with people, one of whom was a police constable. I tried to work my way through to the street, but no one would yield a passage for me; I'm not certain they even knew I was there. They were all trying to peer through the broken window of a ground-floor room. "Constable?" I called out. "What has happened here?"

He knew me; he blocked the window with his body and said, "You don't want to look in there, Mrs. Wickham."

A fist of ice closed around my heart; the constable's facial expression already told me, but I had to ask nonetheless. I swallowed and said, "Is it the Ripper?"

He nodded slowly. "It appears so, ma'am. I've sent for Inspector Abberline— you there, stand back!" Then, to me again: "He's not ever killed indoors afore. This is new for him."

I was having trouble catching my breath. "That means . . . he didn't have to be quick this time. That means he could take as much time as he liked."

The constable was clenching and unclenching his jaw. "Yes'm. He took his time."

Oh dear God. "Who is she, do you know?"

"The rent-collector found her. Here, Thomas, what's her name again?"

A small, frightened-looking man spoke up. "Mary . . . Mary Kelly. Three months behind in 'er rent, she was. I thought she was hidin' from me."

The constable scowled. "So you broke the window to try to get in?"

" 'Ere, now, that winder's been broke these past six weeks! I pulled out the bit o' rag she'd stuffed in the hole so I could reach through and push back the curtain—just like you done, guv'ner, when you wanted to see in!" The rent-collector had more to say, but his words were drowned out by the growing noise of the crowd, which by now had so multiplied in its numbers that it overflowed from Miller's Court into a passageway leading to the street. A few women were sobbing, one of them close to screaming.

Inspector Abberline arrived with two other men, all three of them looking grim. The Inspector immediately tried the door and found it locked. "Break out the rest of the window," he ordered. "The rest of you, stand back. Mrs. Wickham, what are you doing here? Break in the window, I say!"

One of his men broke out the rest of the glass and crawled over the sill. We heard a brief, muffled cry, and then the door was opened from the inside. Inspector Abberline and his other man pushed into the room . . . and the latter abruptly rushed back out again, retching. The constable hastened to his aid, and without stopping to think about it, I stepped into the room.

What was left of Mary Kelly was lying on a cot next to a small table. Her throat had been cut so savagely that her head was nearly severed. Her left shoulder had been chopped through so that her arm remained attached to the body only by a flap of skin. Her face had been slashed and disfigured, and her nose had been hacked away . . . and carefully laid on the small table beside the cot. Her breasts had been sliced off and placed on the same table. The skin had been peeled from her forehead; her thighs had also been stripped of their skin. The legs themselves had been spread in an indecent posture and then slashed to the bone. And Mary Kelly's abdomen had been ripped open, and between her feet lay one of her internal organs . . . possibly the liver. On the table lay a piece of the victim's brown plaid woolen petticoat half-wrapped around still another organ. The missing skin had been carefully mounded on the table next to the other body parts, as if the Ripper were rebuilding his victim. But this time the killer had not piled the intestines above his victim's shoulder as he'd done before; this time, he had taken them away with him. Then as a final embellishment, he had pushed Mary Kelly's right hand into her ripped-open stomach.

Have you punished her enough, Jack? Don't you want to hurt her some more?

I felt a hand grip my arm and steer me firmly outside. "You shouldn't be in here, Mrs. Wickham," Inspector Abberline said. He left me leaning against the wall of the building as he went back inside; a hand touched my shoulder and Thomas the rent-collector said, "There's a place to sit, over 'ere." He led me to an upended wooden crate, where I sank down gratefully. I sat with my head bent over my knees for some time before I could collect myself enough to utter a prayer for Mary Kelly's soul.

Inspector Abberline's men were asking questions of everyone in the crowd. When one of them approached me, I explained I'd never known Mary Kelly and was here only because of the birth of the Macklin baby in the same building. The Inspector himself came over and commanded me to go home; I was not inclined to dispute the order.

"It appears this latest victim does not fit your pattern," the Inspector said as I was leaving. "Mary Kelly was a prostitute, but she was still in her early twenties. And from what we've learned so far, she had no husband and no children."

So the last victim had been neither middle-aged, nor married, nor a mother. It was impossible to tell whether poor Mary Kelly had been homely or not. But the Ripper had clearly chosen a woman this time who was markedly different from his earlier victims, deviating from his customary pattern. I wondered what it meant; had some change taken place in his warped, evil mind? Had he progressed one step deeper into madness?

I thought about that on the way home from Miller's Court. I thought about that, and about Edward.

10 NOVEMBER 1888, ST. JUDE'S VICARAGE.

It was almost noon by the time I reached the vicarage. Edward was there, fast asleep. Normally he never slept during the day, but the small vial of laudanum Dr. Phelps had left was on the bedside table; Edward had drugged himself into a state of oblivion.

I picked up his clothes from the floor where he'd dropped them and went over every piece carefully; not a drop of blood anywhere. But the butchering of Mary Kelly had taken place indoors; the butcher could simply have removed his clothing before beginning his "work." Next I checked all the fireplaces, but none of them had been used to burn anything. It *could* be happenstance, I told myself. I didn't know how long Edward had been blacking out; it was probably not as singular as it seemed that one of his spells should coincide with a Ripper slaying. That's what I told myself.

The night had exhausted me. I had no appetite but a cup of fresh tea would be welcome. I was on my way to the kitchen when a knock at the door stopped me. It was the constable I'd spoken to at Miller's Court.

He handed me an envelope. "Inspector Abberline said to give you this." He touched his cap and was gone.

I went to stand by the window where the light was better. Inside the envelope was a hastily scrawled note.

My dear Mrs. Wickham,

   Further information has come to light that makes it appear that your theory of a pattern in the Ripper murders may not be erroneous after all. Although Mary Kelly currently had no husband, she had at one time been married. At the age of sixteen she wed a collier who died less than a year later. During her widowhood she found a series of men to support her for brief periods until she ended on the streets. And she was given to strong drink, as the other four victims were. But the most cogent revelation is the fact that Mary Kelly was pregnant. That would explain why she was so much younger than the Ripper's earlier victims: he was stopping her before she could abandon her children.

Yrs,
Frederick Abberline

So. Last night the Ripper had taken two lives instead of one, assuring that a fertile young woman would never bear children to suffer the risk of being forsaken. It was not in the Ripper's nature to consider that his victims had themselves been abandoned in their time of need. Polly Nichols, Annie Chapman, Elizabeth Stride, and Catherine Eddowes had all taken to drink for reasons no one would ever know and had subsequently been turned out of their homes. And now there was Mary Kelly, widowed while little more than a child and with no livelihood—undoubtedly she lacked the education and resources to support herself honorably. Polly, Annie, Elizabeth, Catherine, and Mary . . . they had all led immoral and degraded lives, every one of them. But in not even one instance had it been a matter of choice.

I put Inspector Abberline's note in a drawer in the writing table and returned to the kitchen; I'd need to start a fire to make the tea. The wood box had recently been filled, necessitating my moving the larger pieces to get at the twigs underneath. Something else was underneath as well. I pulled out a long strip of brown plaid wool cloth with brown stains on it. Brown plaid wool. Mary Kelly's petticoat. Mary Kelly's blood.

The room began to whirl. There it was. No more making of excuses. No more denying the truth. I was married to the Ripper.

For twelve years Edward had kept the odious secret of his abnormal inner being, hiding behind a mask of gentility and even godliness. He had kept his secret well. But no more. The masquerade was ended. I sank to my knees and prayed for guidance. More than anything in the world I wanted to send for Inspector Abberline and have him take away the monster who was sleeping upstairs. But if the laudanum-induced sleep had the same effect this time as when he was ill, Edward would awake as his familiar rational self. If I could speak to him, make him understand what he'd done, give him the opportunity to surrender voluntarily to the police, surely that would be the most charitable act I could perform under these hideous circumstances. If Edward were to have any chance at all for redemption, he must beg both God and man for forgiveness.

With shaking hands I tucked the strip of cloth away in my pocket and forced myself to concentrate on the routine of making tea. The big kettle was already out; but when I went to fill it with water, it felt heavy. I lifted the lid and found myself looking at a pile of human intestines.

I did not faint . . . most probably because I was past all feeling by then. I tried to think. The piece of cloth Edward could have used to wipe off the knife; then he would have put the cloth in the wood box with the intention of burning it later. But why wait? And the viscera in the teakettle . . . was I meant to find that? Was this Edward's way of asking for help? And where was the knife? Systematically I began to look for it; but after nearly two hours' intensive search, I found nothing.

He could have disposed of the knife on his way home. He could have hidden it in the church. He could have it under his pillow.

I went into the front parlor and forced myself to sit down. I was frightened; I didn't want to stay under the same roof with him, I didn't want to fight for his soul. Did he even have a soul anymore? The Edward Wickham I had lain beside every night for twelve years was a counterfeit person, one whose carefully fabricated personality and demeanor had been devised to control and constrain the demon imprisoned inside. The deception had worked well until we came to Whitechapel, when the constraints began to weaken and the demon escaped. What had caused the change—was it the place itself? The constant presence of prostitutes in the streets? It was beyond my comprehension.

The stresses of the past twenty-four hours eventually proved too much for me; my head fell forward, and I slept.

Edward's hand on my shoulder awoke me. I started, and gazed at him with apprehension; but his face showed only gentle concern. "Is something wrong, Beatrice? Why are you sleeping in the afternoon?"

I pressed my fingertips against my eyes. "I did not sleep last night. The Macklin baby was born early this morning."

"Ah! Both mother and child doing well, I trust? I hope you impressed upon young Macklin the importance of an early christening. But Beatrice, the next time you are called out, I would be most grateful if you could find a way to send me word. When you had not returned by midnight, I began to grow worried."

That was the first falsehood Edward had ever told me that I could recognize as such; it was I who had been waiting for him at midnight. His face was so open, so seemingly free of guile . . . did he honestly have no memory of the night before, or was he simply exceptionally skilled in the art of deception? I stood up and began to pace. "Edward, we must talk about last night . . . about what you did last night."

His eyebrow shot up. "I?"

I couldn't look at him. "I found her intestines in the teakettle. Mary Kelly's intestines."

"Intestines?" I could hear the distaste in his voice. "What is this, Beatrice? And who is Mary Kelly?"

"She's the woman you killed last night!" I cried. "Surely you knew her name!" I turned to confront him . . . and saw a look of such loathing on his face that I took a step back. "Oh!" I gasped involuntarily. "Please don't . . ." Edward? Jack?

The look disappeared immediately—he knew, he knew what he was doing! "I killed someone last night, you say?" he asked, his rational manner quickly restored. "And then I put her intestines . . . in the teakettle? Why don't you show me, Beatrice?"

Distrustful of his suggestion, I nevertheless led the way to the kitchen. As I'd half expected, the teakettle was empty and spotlessly clean. With a heavy heart I pulled the piece of brown plaid cloth out of my pocket. "But here is something you neglected to destroy."

He scowled. "A dirty rag?"

"Oh, Edward, stop professing you know nothing of this! It is a strip from Mary Kelly's petticoat, as you well realize! Edward, you must go to the police. Confess all, make your peace with God. No one else can stop your nocturnal expeditions—you must stop yourself! Go to Inspector Abberline."

He held out one hand. "Give me the rag," he said expressionlessly.

"Think of your soul, Edward! This is your one chance for salvation! You *must* confess!"

"The rag, Beatrice."

"I cannot! Edward, do you not understand? You are accursed—your own actions have damned you! You must go down on your knees and beg for forgiveness!"

Edward lowered his hand. "You are ill, my dear. This delusion of yours that I am the Ripper—that is the crux of your accusation, is it not? This distraction is most unbefitting the wife of the vicar of St. Jude's. I cannot tolerate the thought that before long you may be found raving in the street. We will pray together, we will ask God to send you self-control."

I thought I understood what that meant. "Very well . . . if you will not turn yourself over to the police, there is only one alternate course of action open to you. You must kill yourself."

"Beatrice!" He was shocked. "Suicide is a *sin*!"

His reaction was so absurd that I had to choke down a hysterical laugh. But it made me understand that further pleading would be fruitless. He was hopelessly insane; I would never be able to reach him.

Edward was shaking his head. "I am most disturbed, Beatrice. This dementia of yours is more profound than I realized. I must tell you I am unsure of my capacity to care for you while you are subject to delusions. Perhaps an institution is the rightful solution."

I was stunned. "You would put me in an asylum?"

He sighed. "Where else will we find physicians qualified to treat dementia? But if you cannot control these delusions of yours, I see no other recourse. You must pray, Beatrice, you must pray for the ability to discipline your thoughts."

He *could* have me locked away; he could have me locked away and then continue unimpeded with his ghastly killings, never having to worry about a wife who noticed too much. It was a moment before I could speak. "I will do as you say, Edward. I will pray."

"Excellent! I will pray with you. But first—the rag, please."

Slowly, reluctantly, I handed him the strip of Mary Kelly's petticoat. Edward took a fireplace match and struck it, and the evidence linking him to murder dissolved into thin black smoke that spiraled up the chimney. Then we prayed; we asked God to give me the mental and spiritual willpower I lacked.

Following that act of hypocrisy, Edward suggested that I prepare our tea; I put the big teakettle aside and used my smaller one. Talk during tea was about several church duties Edward still needed to perform. I spoke only when spoken to and was careful to give no offense. I did everything I could to assure my husband that I deferred to his authority.

Shortly before six Edward announced he was expected at a meeting of the Whitechapel Vigilance Committee. I waited until he was out of sight and went first to the cupboard for a table knife and then to the writing table for a sheet of foolscap. Then I stepped into the pantry and began to scrape up as much of the arsenic from the rat holes as I could.

23 FEBRUARY 1892, WHITECHAPEL CHARITABLE INSTITUTE FOR INDIGENT CHILDREN.

Inspector Abberline sat in my office, nodding approval at everything he'd seen. "It's difficult to believe," he said, "that these are the same thin and dirty children who only months ago used to sleep in doorways and under wooden crates. You have worked wonders, Mrs. Wickham. The board of trustees could not have found a better director. Are the children learning to read and write? *Can* they learn?"

"Some can," I answered. "Others are slower. The youngest are the quickest, it seems. I have great hopes for them."

"I wonder if they understand how fortunate they are. What a pity the Reverend Mr. Wickham didn't live to see this. He would have been so pleased with what you've accomplished."

"Yes." Would he have? Edward always believed the poor should care for their own.

The Inspector was still thinking of my late husband. "I had an aunt who succumbed to gastric fever," he said. "Dreadful way to die, dreadful." He suddenly realized I might not care to be reminded of the painful method of Edward's passing. "I do beg your pardon—that was thoughtless of me."

I told him not to be concerned. "I am reconciled to his death now, as much as I can ever be. My life is here now, in the school, and it is a most rewarding way to spend my days."

He smiled. "I can see you are in your element." Then he sobered. "I came not only to see your school but also to tell you something." He leaned forward in his chair. "The file on the Ripper is officially closed. It's been more than two years since his last murder. For whatever reason he stopped, he *did* stop. That particular reign of terror is over. The case is closed."

My heart lifted. Keeping up my end of the conversation, I asked, "Why do you think he stopped, Inspector?"

He rubbed the side of his nose. "He stopped either because he's dead or because he's locked up somewhere, in an asylum or perhaps in prison for some other crime. Forgive my bluntness, Mrs. Wickham, but I earnestly hope it is the former. Inmates have been known to escape from asylums and prisons."

"I understand. Do you think the file will ever be reopened?"

"Not for one hundred years. Once a murder case is marked closed, the files are sealed and the date is written on the outside when they can be made public. It will be a full century before anyone looks at those papers again."

It couldn't be more official than that; the case was indeed closed. "A century . . . why so long a time?"

"Well, the hundred-year rule was put into effect to guarantee the anonymity of all those making confidential statements to the police during the course of the investigation. It's best that way. Now no one will be prying into our reports on the Ripper until the year 1992. It is over."

"Thank Heaven for that."

"Amen."

Inspector Abberline chatted a little longer and then took his leave. I strolled through the halls of my school, a former church building adapted to its present needs. I stopped in one of the classrooms. Some of the children were paying attention to the teacher, others were daydreaming, a few were drawing pictures. Just like children everywhere.

Not all the children who pass through here will be helped; some will go on to better themselves, but others will slide back into the life of the streets. I can save none of them. I must not add arrogance to my other offenses by assuming the role of deliverer; God does not entrust the work of salvation to one such as I. But I am permitted to offer the children a chance, to give them the opportunity to lift themselves above the life of squalor and crime that is all they have ever known. I do most earnestly thank God for granting me this privilege.

Periodically I return to Miller's Court. I go there not because it is the site of Edward's final murder, but because it is where I last saw Rose Howe, the young girl who helped me deliver the Macklin baby. There is a place for Rose in my school. I have not found her yet, but I will keep searching.

My life belongs to the children of Whitechapel now. My prayers are for them; those prayers are the only ones of mine ever likely to be answered. When I do pray for myself, it is always and only to ask for an easier place in Hell.

A MATTER OF BLOOD

Jeffery Deaver

One of the most prominent and consistently excellent suspense writers in the world, Jeffery Deaver (1950–) was born outside Chicago and received his journalism degree from the University of Missouri. He became a newspaperman, after which he received his law degree from Fordham University and practiced for several years. A poet, he wrote his own songs and performed them across the country.

He is the author of more than two dozen novels and four short story collections. His works have been translated into twenty-five languages and are perennial bestsellers in America and elsewhere. Among his many honors are six nominations for Edgar Awards (twice for Best Paperback Original, four times for Best Short Story), three Ellery Queen Reader's Awards for Best Short Story of the Year, the 2001 W. H. Smith Thumping Good Read Award for *The Empty Chair,* and the 2004 Ian Fleming Steel Dagger Award from the (British) Crime Writers' Association for *Garden of Beasts*; he also won a Dagger for best short story. In 2009, he was the guest editor of *The Best American Mystery Stories.*

He has written about a dozen stand-alone novels but is most famous for his series about Lincoln Rhyme, the brilliant quadriplegic detective who made his debut in *The Bone Collector* (1997), which was released by Universal in 1999 and starred Denzel Washington and Angelina Jolie. Other Rhyme novels are *The Coffin Dancer* (1998), *The Empty Chair* (2000), *The Stone Monkey* (2002), *The Vanished Man* (2003), *The Twelfth Card* (2005), *The Cold Moon* (2006), and *The Steel Kiss* (2016). His non-series novel *A Maiden's Grave* (1995) was adapted for an HBO movie titled *Dead Silence* (1997) and starred James Garner and Marlee Matlin. His suspense novel *The Devil's Teardrop* (1999) became a 2010 made-for-television movie of the same name.

"A Matter of Blood" was written especially for this collection and has never previously been published.

ONE

Thursday, 8 November 1888

The man in the leather waistcoat left his rooms and began his short walk to a news vendor on Aldgate High Street.

The early morning air chilled the slim man, save for when he passed through one of the bands of sun slipping through gaps between the low buildings here in the East End. The neighborhood was, however, as congested as a hive, and those moments of warmth were few.

At the vendor he bought a number of newspapers and, venturing to a dismal shop, purchased some bread, pickles, and cheese. He then walked south and east, eyeing the crowds around him with some suspicion, in a circuitous route that eventually led him back to his rooms, a not unpleasant living space on the short, dark, and, fortunately, quite private Somerset Street. Entering and locking the door, he hung his jacket and unbuttoned his waistcoat. Then he made a cup of tea and sat at the unsteady table to read the news of the day.

When he found no reports of developments that might alarm him, he located his scissors and clipped some articles, as souvenirs. These he arranged into a stack that he set on a second table, beside a much larger collection of stories, sliced from the *Daily News,* the *Standard,* the *London Journal,* the *Police News,* and the *Manchester Guardian,* as well as some smaller papers from around the British Isles, and from America, the Continent, Australia, and even one from Singapore.

Prominent among them was perhaps his favorite news account from a London broadsheet:

Ghastly Murder
in the East End
Dreadful Mutilation of a Woman

This headline and the accompanying article were not what so pleased him, though. No, what was deliciously agreeable was a small graphic box contiguous to that news account—an advertisement:

Warner's
SAFE
Kidney and Liver Cure

The irony of the juxtaposition was not lost on the man in the leather waistcoat, whose given name was Jacques.

Sipping his tea, Jacques fished his pocket watch from the brown waistcoat and regarded the time.

He was disappointed to see that it was still many hours till nightfall. His impatience swelled. But he was a man who could contain his urges and so, he told himself, he would simply have to wait. Better to be smart.

He unwrapped his cheese and opened the jar of pickles. Then he began to slice the bread with a knife that was, to him, dreadfully dull.

Erasmus Nathan Wentworth used a brass tool to scrape clean his pipe and refill it with tobacco imported from America, cherrywood-tinged. After tamping it, he lit the bowl and drew the relaxing smoke into his mouth. Let the vaporous ghost escape ceilingward.

The hour was 10 A.M. and he was sitting in his dim office at Metropolitan Police headquarters. His facility was on Great Scotland Yard, not Whitehall Place—in one of the buildings into which the organization had just expanded from the private residence that had housed the police for more than five decades.

His eyes settled on the front page of a newspaper, the Daily Advertiser.

BLOODY SUNDAY!
TWO THOUSAND POLICE CLASH
WITH SOCIAL DEMOCRATIC FEDERATION
AND IRISH NATIONAL LEAGUE
THREE DEAD, HUNDREDS INJURED

The incident had happened one year ago and Wentworth had received a commendation for attempting to calm the rampaging officers. He had also received threats upon his life for the very same heroics—from constables who were not pleased to have their antics censured. But Scotland Yard periodically went through paroxysms of crisis, during which the old and the corrupt were winnowed out—like so much chaff. Wentworth kept the newspaper, which his wife had mounted in a gold-painted frame, as a reminder to all that policemen were stewards of the people; they were not overlords, they were not criminals.

He had, however, only to look upon the landscape of sheaves on his desk to be reminded: I am hardly a very good steward at the present moment.

Wentworth, accordingly, thought: And where might you be, Jack? And more to the point, *who* might you be?

It had been more than one month since the Whitechapel killer had so viciously murdered victims three and four, who, like the first two, were unfortunates—prostitutes—in that harsh, hardworking part of East London. Elizabeth Stride and Catherine Eddowes had been killed on the same day. Miss Stride's body was found in Dutfield's Yard, off Berner Street. Miss Eddowes's corpse was discovered in Mitre Square. Unlike the other three victims, whose bodies were horrifically mutilated, Miss Stride had suffered a "mere" (the press reported, with some disappointment, Wentworth assessed) slash to the left side of her neck. There was some speculation that she had been the victim of another murderer, not Saucy Jacky, but Wentworth thought not. His examination of the wound told him that it was most likely caused by the same blade—and passersby had caused him to flee before the dissection could begin.

Detective Inspector Wentworth was one of dozens of officers within the Metropolitan Police's Criminal Investigation Division working full- or part-time to identify and apprehend the Whitechapel murderer. He, along with Frederick Abberline, was based here in the Central Office. Others were in H Division, Whitechapel. In addition, detective inspectors from the City Police were also assisting. And to stir the stew even more vigorously, a private organization—the Whitechapel Vigilance Committee—was prowling the streets of East London, causing trouble with false leads (and unwarranted assaults) more than providing assistance.

Looking at the photographs of the savaged victims (save Miss Stride's intact corpse), however, Wentworth could hardly blame the citizenry for their concern.

Somewhere in this city of four million souls was a demented human being bent on performing the most heinous acts imaginable . . . and Wentworth and his fellow law enforcers were unable to stop him.

He rose and put another log on the fire. He was a lean man, eleven stone, and tall—five foot ten. He was adversely affected by the cold, and today was particularly damp and chill, despite a bold sun. His office was hardly insulated from the elements. He had been told by his Chief Inspector that the Metropolitan

Police would be moving to the Victoria Embankment into a much more fitting building, but that would not be for two to three years.

Just as he settled into his chair once more a figure appeared in his doorway, a constable, a flaxen-haired man, young (although to Wentworth, well into his fourth decade, the newcomers were younger every year). He said, "Two men have arrived to see you, sir."

He was not expecting anyone. Perhaps, he hoped, it was some intelligence that would bear on the Whitechapel affair—some *useful* intelligence; Scotland Yard daily received dispatches and personal accounts from those purporting to have information about Jack's identity, his motive, his whereabouts, his ancestry, his relations, and any number of other bizarre revelations (such as one sworn statement that the killer transmogrified from wolf to human, at will).

The two men entered. Both were dressed well and were close to Wentworth in age, though perhaps a few years older. One walked in a stilted fashion, assisted by a modest wooden cane.

They sat.

"Detective Inspector Wentworth, I am Henry Gladbrook," said the taller of the two, who turned to the man with the infirmity. "And this is Doctor Richard Adams. May we smoke? Or I alone, I should say. The good doctor here does not partake."

The doctor gave a good-natured laugh. "Had enough smoke in Kandahar to last me all my years—that is, from our Martini-Henrys and the muskets of Ayub Khan. Assorted cannon too, of course."

Wentworth lifted his pipe and puffed. "Please, sir."

Gladbrook removed a battered case from his breast pocket and extracted a cigar. He scratched a match to flame and inhaled. "Now, I'll get right to the matter at hand. And I do hope you will forgive my forthrightness."

"Certainly."

"I am a personal advisor to Lord Ashton, who is—"

Wentworth nodded. "An advisor to Her Majesty the Queen." This was well known.

"Her Majesty has had a word with Lord Ashton and he with me. Hence my appearance here today. *Our* appearance, I should say."

"Pray continue, Mr. Gladbrook."

"I will say, Detective Inspector, that you are held in high regard in the Palace."

This was so? He had not thought it to be the case.

"The Bloody Sunday riot, of course. And you've been instrumental in concluding a number of investigations. The Bedford murders, the Leeds Station robbery, the Yates abductions. To name but a few." He exhaled and the cigar smoke joined the pipe's. "But it's my duty to tell you that Her Majesty is displeased one matter has gone unresolved for as long as it has."

This, however, was *not* news. Or at least Went-worth could easily have conjectured the nature of her concern. Indeed, he had been one of the CID officers who worked on a possible lead to the killer that Queen Victoria herself had suggested: that Jack was from the Continent, a worker familiar with butchery, arriving on one of the cattle boats that docked every week in the East End. That strand of investigation, however, was not successful.

"No one is more troubled than I, sir. And I would be pleased if you could tell Lord Ashton and perhaps Her Majesty herself that the officers on the case are working round the clock to see this fellow brought to justice."

"Please, Detective Inspector, rest assured that there is no enmity toward you in particular in the Palace or Halls of Parliament or on Whitehall. But it is believed that we must find a resolution to this matter forthwith. Hence my visit here—in the company of Dr. Adams. Whose presence you must surely be wondering about."

"In truth, yes."

"Are you familiar with the character Sherlock Holmes?"

"I am not."

"He's the creation of a British writer who has written a novel for a general audience about the solving of a crime. This Holmes, a resident of London, is a consulting detective. The novel is *A Study in Scarlet* and it was published last year in *Beeton's Christmas Annual.*" Wentworth was familiar with the publication. Popular stories, many serials. The sort of magazine that Dickens might have published one of his tales in. When his son and daughter, now grown, were young, Wentworth would read to them from such publications and they and his wife delighted to hear him attempt the various voices of the characters, asserting that he was as good as Charles Kean himself.

"The book is quite enjoyable and I understand the author, a fellow named Doyle, is planning more fiction featuring this Holmes. I bring him up because his specialty is using deductive reasoning from obscure facts to come to a conclusion. I know officers such as yourself do that quite frequently."

"It is part of the detection process, yes, sir."

"And that is exactly what my colleague, Dr. Adams, is well known for—in medical circles. But perhaps I'll let him explain."

"Yes, assuredly. Inspector, I am a lecturer at the Royal College of Physicians and maintain a private practice as well. One of my specialties, as Mr. Gladbrook stated, is to use deduction to ascertain the cause of a rare or hitherto unseen malady and determine what might be the best way to treat it: surgery, medicine, relocation to a different climate, and so forth. Your villains are human beings; mine are foreign bodies, pathogens—what we are now calling 'germs'—and other, sometimes obscure, phenomena that threaten lives. Mr. Gladbrook pays me far too great a compliment to compare me to this Holmes. Whom you really must read, sir."

"I will do." Wentworth added, "When time permits."

The doctor continued, "I understand from Mr. Gladbrook that a police surgeon provided some insights into the killings."

"Yes, Thomas Bond. His opinion was that the murderer had no special skills as a surgeon and no particular knowledge of anatomy. The dissection after the murders—three of them—was haphazard at best. Mr. Bond suggests certain insights into the killer's nature—a solitary man and one motivated by erotic mania, that is, satisfaction from the killings. I will say that I myself was not swayed by his way of thinking. I believe the killer's motive is, as yet, unknowable."

"I am not, Inspector, a doctor of the mind. I am a doctor of the body. Physiology—the function of the body. And morphology—its structure. I have considerable experience with the effects of trauma upon the human corpus. Treating, as I did, soldiers in the Second Afghan War. Even if this fellow has no particular medical skills, there may be something about what he has visited upon the victims that might tell us something about him. I am here in all humility. I have no experience with crime or investigations. But I stand ready to help."

Wentworth reflected: More to the point, the Palace stands ready to *force* me to allow you to help.

Still, he was not dismayed by the men's appearance. "Well, Doctor, I can't see that anything untoward would come of your assistance. Indeed, after these difficult weeks, I would welcome a new perspective. Are you free now?"

"I am."

"Then I suggest that you come around to the room where the evidence and our notes and photographs are assembled. You will see things that do not feature in the press accounts. We are circumspect in regard to what is released."

Adams glanced toward Gladbrook and nodded. The Palace's advisor said to Wentworth, "Excellent. I will report to Lord Ashton the outcome of this meeting. Good-day now."

The three men rose and hands were shaken once more. At the door, Gladbrook turned. "Inspector, one question has occurred to me. It has been more than a month since the most recent killings. Do you think there is a chance that Jack has decided to cease the carnage? Or even more felicitously, has himself been murdered?"

Wentworth glanced at his desk, on which sat one of the photographs of a corpse dismembered by Jack the Ripper. "With a man like this, sir, I have little doubt it is merely a matter of time until the madness comes over him again."

Together the two men strode through the warren of offices and hallways until they descended into what had been a cellar. The dingy room they entered was damp and chill and one of the largest in the building.

Wentworth recalled Police Commissioner Warren's first visit here. A young constable had said to the imposing man, " 'Ere's the room where we're conducting the Ripper investigation, sir. You might say it is in the *bowels* of the building." And offered a laugh.

The constable was now assigned to Tongue, a small—very small—town in the Scottish Highlands.

Wentworth jotted some instructions to one of the junior inspectors, as the doctor hung his greatcoat on a hook and, assisted by his cane, made his way to a large table, filled with documents and a few objects taken from the rooms of the victims or, if they'd been discovered outside, the street or alleyways surrounding the bodies.

The inspector joined him.

"The last killing was when?" Adams asked.

"Thirtieth September."

"Yes, the double murders."

"That is correct."

Adams walked slowly up and down the room, examining the pictures, the diagrams, the objects of evidence. He read the missives that supposedly had been sent by the killer.

"The correspondence he sent is real?"

"We believe so. Some contain information that only the real murderer would have knowledge of. And the handwriting seems to match, so that all three were inscribed by the same man."

The killer or someone purporting to be the killer had sent two letters and a taunting postcard. The first, with the salutation "Dear Boss," was signed with the name Jack the Ripper. The valediction on the other was "Saucy Jacky."

"Yet the grammar and spelling," the doctor pointed out, "are not consistent. And one contains serious errors."

"We believe that is done intentionally to throw us off."

"So he's perhaps not a slavering madman, as the press suggests."

"I think not. He's clever."

"Now, tell me everything you can about the murders."

For a quarter of an hour the inspector discoursed on the now exhaustingly familiar details of the killings. Then he pointed out articles of clothing of the victims, weapons located in the vicinity of the poor women that might have been used in the killing, statements by witnesses.

"We have learned to be skeptical, though. The damned press is paying such sums that people who were in Glasgow or Leeds on the nights of the killings are claiming to have seen the actual slaughter."

Adams returned to the photographs and diagrams of the scenes where the four women were killed.

"Tell me, Doctor, do you ascertain anything from what we have here that might aid us?"

"I think he is a slight man. And not particularly strong. This ligature here? I know from post-mortem work that this is not difficult to cut through."

He was pointing to a partially dismembered arm.

"But as you can see, he had to readjust his grip on the cutting tool several times. There were two or three false starts. And the angle suggests he was not towering over the body when he cut."

Wentworth could indeed see that this was the case. He was impressed by the doctor's deduction.

"And the victims were all dead before he began his butchery."

"Yes, our surgeon concluded the same."

The surgeon had fallen silent as he regarded the pictures once more. Without looking up he said, "I see here that organs have been removed. I recall from the press that he took certain organs with him."

"That is right."

"And he claimed to have eaten part of one."

"So he said, when he mailed back a portion of a kidney. Purportedly from Catherine Eddowes."

Adams tapped a photograph. "Do you happen to have the garments of the victims?"

The inspector walked to a wooden box and removed two dresses, a blouse, a shawl, a bodice, a skirt, and several petticoats, all of varying hues but with one thing in common: they were stained dark brown with dried blood. Adams took them and examined each carefully. Wentworth was curious but said nothing. He was intrigued to watch the doctor's narrowed eyes study the garments with the intensity of a wolf choosing from the flock. The doctor then, curiously, lifted piece after piece to his nose and smelled. He gave a brief smile. "I think, Wentworth, that I do indeed have an insight."

"What, Doctor?"

"I noted from the photo stains on one victim's clothing that were not dark enough to be blood. I wondered what they were and now I've come to a conclusion."

"What are they?"

Adams continued, "In my profession, of course, we are not always successful. I am familiar with medicines to treat patients. I am also familiar with those chemicals we use to preserve organs and samples from the bodies we are not able to save. If I'm not mistaken, this stain . . . You see it?"

"Indeed."

"Is from a type of preserving fluid that is rarely found anymore. A crude form of ethanol. The smell is quite distinctive."

"Which he would use to preserve the flesh he takes with him."

"Yes . . . And that fact, by the way, suggests that he is *not* a cannibal; that, I believe, was intended to shock. He would not dine on anything that was steeped in Fitzgerald's Preserving Fluid. That would be as lethal as one of his knives. Indeed, that's why it is little used. It's exceedingly inexpensive but the fumes have made many an undertaker or surgeon's assistant pass out. Now, you believe your killer inhabits essentially the East End."

"We think it likely."

"There are a half-dozen chemists or funeral parlor provisioners who still sell the liquid. I think it worth our while to pay them visits and enquire about recent purchasers."

"Good. The hour's late but we must begin our search immediately."

"Now?" Adams asked. The day had vanished and it was now close to 6 P.M. "They'll be closed."

"Then we shall wake those who sleep above or behind their shops. And send other officers to rouse the ones who live elsewhere."

The inspector whom Wentworth had sent on assignment earlier now appeared in the doorway and nodded to his superior. Wentworth joined him and read the piece of foolscap the man proffered. He nodded and slipped it into his pocket, then turned again to Adams.

The doctor gave a faint laugh. "Inspector, may I enquire? You said 'we' must begin our search. Myself, too?"

"Indeed. You are in a position to ask questions about the preservative, and perhaps other matters, that I am not."

"This is rather far afield from the surgical suite," the doctor said, though Wentworth noted his eyes gleamed. "But I'm game to play detective. If for no other reason than to live up to Mr. Gladbrook's characterization of me as this famous Sherlock Holmes." Then Adams frowned. "One question occurs to me, Inspector."

"And what might that be, sir?"

"You have no idea what this fellow Jack looks like, his age, his station in life, his race?"

"Some unreliable witness accounts not worth tuppence."

Adams smiled. "Did you not worry that I or Mr. Gladbrook might not be the killer, or perhaps the both of us, come here to win your confidence, lead you to some alley and dispatch you like a sacrificial lamb?"

"Of course I did," Wentworth said.

The doctor at first seemed to think he was making a joke and smiled. The expression soon leveled, as Wentworth extracted from his pocket the sheet of paper that had just been delivered to him.

"My associate has just spent the past several hours looking into that very question. And he has verified that you and Mr. Gladbrook were accounted for on the early morning hours of 31 August, 8 September, and 30 September. I had him interview those intimate with Lord Ashton too and he, as well, could not be our Jack. As to *his* employer"—Wentworth's voice fell to a whisper—"I'm satisfied with taking it as a matter of faith that Her Majesty is a most unlikely suspect. Don't you agree?" Without waiting for an answer, he said, "So, shall we get on the trail of our killer, Doctor? I myself feel a certain urgency in this matter."

Seven P.M. of a dank and grim evening. The sun was long gone, and mist and fog had coalesced over the East End of London.

But Jacques LaFleur felt a warmth deep within him.

Ah, there she is. Yes, yes, yes.

Jacques had had his eye on this one for some time.

Something about the way she sauntered, about the way she sang Irish songs as she walked unsteadily, drunk, down the street. About the way she would glower and launch her spittle-flecked temper at those who caused offense, real or imagined, on the pavement.

Jacques now saw her walking on the opposite side of the street. Not slim, not fat. More comely than the others, although that didn't matter to him in any way. What mattered was what was inside her. He laughed to himself.

The woman, wearing a brown brocade dress and decked with a shawl, and—as always—no hat, strolled along Chicksand Street. She paused, engaged a man in conversation. Their words ended and she continued on her way.

Jacques had a pet name for her: she was his Little Heart. This, because she seemed like someone a boy—like Jacques in his youth—would form a youthful but deep affection for.

He walked in the same direction as she did, remaining, though, across the road. For a time he was lost in thought. Jacques had experienced an arduous journey to arrive here—both in London and at the level of satisfaction he had now achieved. Growing up a milliner's son in Oldham, outside Manchester, he had not distinguished himself in that workaday city. This had perplexed him. True, he was not a pretty youth, nor a handsome young man, nor a talented student, nor driven at commerce; he was, though, sharp and charming and he could never fathom why he was not held in higher regard. This concerned him and angered him, and resentfully he left the region of his birth and traveled to London.

Initially the fair-haired Jacques fared no better than in the north, securing fitful employment in menial labor. This stoked his anger, and he regarded those in better circumstances with eyes he'd been told burned like a tiger's. Carting sacks of coffee and tea for an importer and staves for a cooper and skeins for a weaver, sweeping sawdust at a butcher's shop, shoveling coal for Hogg's Foundry... the list, and the jobs, interminable, and his life as bland as blancmange. Even the occasional girl, for pay or charm, did little to stimulate.

Until one day an urge led—no, forced—him to step across a line.

From good to bad, from legal to not.

A drunken gentleman—by his clothes, of means—had stumbled and fallen on a deserted street in the East End. He'd come to the district for the principal vice men of means traveled here from the western part of the city. He'd finished his business at a bawdy house up the road, and was now seeking a hansom to take him back to the bosom of his wife and children. Jacques suspected he could honestly say to his woman that he had not dallied—because surely he was so drunk he wouldn't remember having done so.

Jacques had relieved him of his wallet and gold watch and a small revolver (which told him that if he were to continue along these lines, he would have to remember to be very, very careful).

From that day forth, Jacques had a new calling.

That included being a mutcher—when he stole from drunks—and a mug-hunter (or the new parlance, a "mugger") when he stole from someone else.

Burglary was always good, too.

This life suited him indeed. The old Jacques was gone, the new one reborn. Yes, there was a bit of a diversion to Newgate Prison, but that was behind him now and he was sitting pretty. More content than he'd ever been.

He now turned his attention back to the cold streets before him.

Will tonight be the night for us, Little Heart?

Oh, Jacques hoped so, he prayed so.

Ah, but now, what was this? One man stopped his Little Heart. A portly man in a fine jacket and bowler hat. They began a conversation. He was not, of course, asking for the most expedient route to St. Paul's.

He watched as words continued to be exchanged and business negotiated.

No matter. He certainly felt the urge. But Jacques LaFleur was someone who had learned that patience was the only virtue worth embracing.

TWO

Friday, 9 November, 1 A.M.

For hour upon hour, Wentworth and Adams made their way around the East End, enquiring among chemists about purchases of Fitzgerald's Preserving Fluid.

Midnight had come and gone, and the men were incurring abuse from both the cold and the shopkeepers whom they awakened, some offering oaths liberally.

Finally, his bones were so cold that Wentworth decided he had reached the boundary. He would interview one more chemist and then flee to the bosom of his home and wife. Dr. Adams, too, was showing signs of fatigue and ill effects from the chill; his limp was more pronounced than earlier.

But it was fortunate he chose to awaken the owner of Merry's Chemists, because it was there that at last they found a lead to Jack the Ripper.

The owner, a huge, glowering man with a shabby greatcoat over his white—

better said, dirty *gray*—nightshirt, had a lined face, muscles like a docker's, and a balding pate with a half-dozen hairs striving for heaven from his shiny scalp.

The man listened to Wentworth's appeal and then, to the surprise of both the inspector and, it seemed, the doctor, said in a growling baritone, "Think I know 'oo you mean, Inspector."

"The person who bought some Fitzgerald's?"

"Right you are."

"You have the name of this fellow?"

"No. Only came in once, I think. Recent."

"Around thirtieth September?"

"Could've been. Easy could've been."

The doctor and the officer regarded each other. "What'd he look like?"

"Lor', I can hardly remember now, can I? Get lots o' customers here. Normal fellow, I recall. Moustache?" He frowned. "Can't recall that one, guv'nor."

Wentworth sighed. "Pale, dark?"

"He was a white man, not African. I don't think."

He doesn't think? Wentworth thought cynically. Witnesses were useless as often as not.

"Accent?"

"What'sat, governor?"

"Did he seem foreign?"

"Oh, you mean like from Prussia or China?"

"Anywhere."

"Not 'at I can say."

"Describe him, if you would, Mr. Merry."

"Slightly built, shorter'n you," he said to the inspector. "Weasely face." Merry thought for a moment. "Though I never seen a weasel up close, 'ave I?"

"Wearing?"

"Greatcoat. Brown."

"Did he seem to be a man of means?"

" 'Ow would I know, governor? Smelled of some flower. Lavender. If that 'elps you."

"Did he have any knowledge of medicine?"

" 'E come in, paid 'is coin, and left."

Meaning no, Wentworth assumed.

Adams held up his hands, which were nicked and stained from his work as a surgeon, presumably. "You surely saw his hands when he handed the money over."

"I suppose I did."

"Were they like mine?"

"No. They was like a lady's 'ands, they was. What's this boy wanted for?" Finally some animation in the dull, hostile eyes. "Is 'e Saucy Jacky? 'E is, ain't 'e?"

"Was he alone?"

"Yes, 'e was."

"What happened after he paid?"

"Not a thing, Inspector. 'E just left—after 'e give me the address."

"What?" Wentworth asked, aghast.

"I didn't mention that?"

Witnesses . . .

Merry continued, "Fitzgerald's only come in five-gallon jars. He 'ad someplace to be, so I 'ad me boy deliver it that night. Yes, yes, yes. Let me see." The massive chemist dug through a jumble of documents and scraps of paper.

"'Ere we go." He handed over a sheet to Wentworth, who displayed it to Adams. It was an address on Anthony Street, about a quarter-mile away, an even shabbier district of the East End than where they stood.

Wentworth thanked him. Adams said, "One question, Mr. Merry. Did he ask you for Fitzgerald's specifically?"

"No," Merry offered. "Just wanted some preserver."

"And you sold him Fitzgerald's but charged him for better-quality fluid?"

The chemist's eyes evaded theirs. "And if I did, governor? Man's got to look out for 'imself, don't 'e?"

"No, no, Mr. Merry. Take no offense. I am merely thinking that your tactic of scamming the fellow may be the single most important fact in getting London's worst murderer in recent years in darbies and onto the gallows."

"Blimey. That right?" He beamed.

Wentworth said, "Let's pray that's the case."

Their hopes of finding the killer from the chemist's intelligence, however, were not immediately fulfilled.

The two men hurried on foot to the address on Anthony Street that the hulking chemist had given them. Wentworth peered through a broken window of the warehouse, his police whistle in hand—a Hudson, the latest version, with the pea inside, which could almost split the eardrum of anyone nearby and would summon colleagues from a quarter-mile away.

But he slipped it back in his pocket and shook his head. While Saucy Jacky might very well have taken delivery of the Fitzgerald's Preserving Fluid in this warehouse, the small, decrepit facility was empty.

The inspector kicked in the door and they entered. He found an oil lamp, which he lit. The two men examined the place. In truth, it contained very little: broken-down boxes, staves, nails and bolts, bottles discarded by the unfortunates and homeless who had succumbed to the scourge of alcohol, a man's boot, a jacket, old newspapers and periodicals, scattered receipts, and bills of lading.

And in the corner, the jar of Fitzgerald's.

"Well, this is perhaps his den," Wentworth said. "But he doesn't live here, obviously. He must have used this venue to prepare for some of the assaults. This is roughly midway between them." Much had been made of the location of the killings; lines drawn between them created, some said, a mystical symbol; this was, to Went-worth, nonsense and distracted from the true course of the investigation.

Wentworth panned the lantern over the floor and the men observed that someone had, in fact, been here recently. The dust had been disturbed by footsteps—one man's only, it seemed.

Adams examined the marks. He followed the steps into the corner. "Here!" He was smelling a rag he'd found. "More Fitzgerald's!" The doctor's eyes were wide. "And, Wentworth. It's damp still. He has been here today!"

The inspector's face, he was sure, revealed the dismay he was feeling. "So perhaps he's out on the hunt as we speak. But where, where?"

"We too must keep hunting!" Adams renewed his search of the dim quarters. The inspector joined him.

It was fifteen minutes later that Wentworth made a discovery. "Doctor! Here!" He lifted a scrap of newspaper on which was written in pencil an address. It was on Barker's Row. About ten streets away.

"But did the villain himself write it?" Wentworth mused.

"Does the handwriting look familiar?"

"It might. I cannot say."

Adams lifted the paper to his nose and said, "Look at these finger marks. They are redolent of Fitzgerald's fluid. I would say, yes, this could very well be the address of his next victim."

"Come, Doctor. We must hurry." Outside, Wentworth oriented himself. "This way!" He sprinted to a nearby police signal box, those booths, first established in Glasgow, where police could use a telephone to communicate with Division headquarters—here that would be H Division, Whitechapel, on Leman Street. (The kiosks were also topped with a blue beacon to summon patrolling officers to the box to receive communiqués from their superiors.)

As Adams joined him, moving more slowly because of his wounded leg, Wentworth rang headquarters and reported that constables should proceed to the address on Barker's Row immediately; the Whitechapel killer might be there, murdering another victim. He was assured an alarm would be raised and officers would be en route soon.

Wentworth put the mouthpiece down and stepped to the street with Adams beside him, looking for a hansom, of which none were to be found in this luckless portion of the city.

Now, at last, at 2:30 A.M., his Little Heart was alone.

She had finished with her customer and had recently been in the company of various men and women on the street. Carousing. Trying, it seemed, to borrow some money. Harsh words had passed when she'd apparently been denied the coin she asked for. Then she repaired to a friend's boarding room—troubling Jacques that she might be bedding down for the night. But apparently the stop was merely for a drink or two. She left the place ten minutes later. Walking unsteadily down the deserted street, she began singing in a not unpleasant voice. An Irish ballad. "The Parting Glass."

Jacques smiled to himself, amused that she had picked this particular song, one of farewell.

The street was not entirely deserted, even at this early hour, but Jacques would not let the opportunity pass. Too many days had gone by without a truly satisfying reward. He needed this. And immediately.

He approached, smiling.

"Evening, m'lady."

"I'd say morning now." She was coy. Buxom, and more comely up close than from a distance. Her age was in the middle twenties, he estimated. He gauged her accent to be Welsh.

"Right you are."

She looked him over, fore to aft. He was scrubbed and buffed and assembled with few wrinkles. His waistcoat was dabbed clean. He could see her eyes relax. Most men in this part of the city did not come in quite this pleasant bundle. And, more to the point, someone as charming and well-spoken as he could hardly be the Ripper. His appearance, and the LaFleur charm, had worked their magic on the others, too.

"Isn't the inclement night they'd been thinking it might be," he said, looking up at the sky.

"No, sir, it isn't." She was drunk. That would make his efforts easier. "But then I always wonder who 'they' is, don't I? 'They' say the queen is bloody cross at France. 'They' say the price of coal is going up. Who the hell is 'they'?"

He could not help but smile.

"I'm Henri," he said.

"Marie Jeanette."

He took her gloved hand and kissed it. "If I may be so bold."

A drunken laugh.

"I've an hour free," he said.

"Do you now, governor? Are you French? You said En-*ree*. Not Henry. You don't sound French. I lived there for a time, didn't I?"

Jacques said, "I'm not. But *they* say that I have the charm of a Frenchman."

She laughed once more. "What would *they* say about your purse?"

"That there's some coin in it."

"Lord, it's late. I'm tired. Tuppence upright?"

Jacques frowned. "On a night like this? It's inclement enough. Let's retire inside. A nice warm bed."

"Ach, I'm a tired one, aren't I?"

"Would a florin rouse you?"

Her eyes grew wide. "Two bleeding shillings? Let me see it!"

He dug into his pocket and showed the coin, a Jubilee from last year, Victoria's stern face looking to the left.

"Lor'."

The general rate for unfortunates in the East End was five pence (two for the upright, which she'd suggested, standing in the alley).

He handed it over. She slipped the coin into her purse.

Then she added, "I have a room, small, small. And shabby, perhaps too much so for a gentleman like yourself."

"I'm sure it will be lovely."

In fact, he knew it wasn't lovely at all. For he had already had a look at it himself. He extended his arm. She hooked hers through it. He said, "Lead on, my lady."

They turned and started along the pavement. She whispered, "You know what *they* say? You're in for a good ride tonight."

Jacques smiled, though he didn't feel like smiling. He was thinking about what lay ahead. About the reward. And that was not a matter about which to smile.

Michelangelo, after all, didn't smile when he presented to the admiring crowds in Rome God and Adam gracing the Sistine Chapel high above their heads.

*

"Where the devil are the constables?" Wentworth muttered as the hansom reined to a stop before the address on Barker's Row, where he hoped the Whitechapel killer was at that very moment.

He and Adams leapt out, the inspector tossing coins to the cabby. They looked about, and located the building whose address they had found in the warehouse on Anthony Street.

"Ah, there's one now." Wentworth waved at a tall, slim, uniformed officer, one of the forty-four sergeants attached to H Division.

Wentworth identified himself.

"Sir."

"Where are the others?"

"On their way, sir. A half-dozen constables."

"Tap for more, don't whistle. We don't want to give away our presence."

"The Whitechapel killer's inside?"

"Tap, man, tap!"

Scotland Yard supervisors carried a staff, like a walking stick, which could be used as a truncheon or a horse prod but was more often used to strike the ground, sending a distinctive sound that could be heard many streets away; it meant that any officers nearby should hurry to the tapper's assistance.

The sergeant did this now.

Adams said, "I don't think we can wait, Inspector. He might've heard the hansom pull up."

"Yes, yes. Let's go. Doctor, you stay here."

It was then that two other constables approached, running. They pulled up, breathing heavily, and Wentworth summoned one to join him and the sergeant and told the other to remain with Adams.

The three police officers burst through the door of the two-story flat, the young constable with his truncheon at the ready.

Ten minutes later Wentworth walked down the stairs of the dingy structure and onto the pavement, preceding the uniformed officers—now five of them—who had responded to the alarm.

He glanced at Adams and said through grim lips, "Whatever his interest in this place, if indeed he was interested at all, there is no indication he was ever here. All four rooms—and a suite of two—are occupied by ordinary citizens: pensioners and working people. No one has ever seen a stranger, much less anyone suspicious or who might be a killer. And there is no rear door, so even if he were here, you two would have seen him as he tried to pass us on the way out."

The inspector gazed about him, at the streets gauzed by smoke and fog. "Well, it was a reasonable chance. That is the nature of police work, of course. Most seeming trails to your villain are dead ends. But that cannot stop you from pursuing them all. And we have men watching the warehouse on Anthony Street and will have some here, as well, so perhaps we will have him in irons soon. My, the hour is late. I propose we retire for the evening."

"Yes, I must be getting home."

"And I to my wife." The inspector dismissed the constables, setting a watch from an alley nearby.

As they walked to a wider avenue, in search of hansoms, the inspector said, "By the way, Doctor."

"Yes?"

"Though we did not find our prey, we've made good strides. Thanks to you."

Adams considered this for a moment and said, "I think the success has been due to both of us. We make, dare I say, a good partnership."

"That we do, Doctor. Now, you can come round tomorrow at, say, noon?"

"I will be there, sir. Goodnight to you."

The reunion of Erasmus Wentworth and Dr. Richard Adams later that day was, however, delayed because of circumstances neither man had envisioned.

Though it was not at the address on Barker's Row, the Ripper had indeed struck once more, killing his fifth victim.

At about 1 P.M. Friday, Wentworth arrived via police carriage at a residence in Spitalfields. He nodded to the half-dozen constables and inspectors present and proceeded as directed to Mil-ler's Court, through a covered passageway off Dorset Street. Outside Number 13, he greeted Superintendent Thomas Arnold of H Division, a striking man in full beard, and another superior officer, balding, white-haired Robert Anderson, from Central Office, who had run the Ripper investigation (until he took an unfortunate trip to the Continent at the time two of the victims were killed and was thus replaced, following his vilification in the press).

"Where is she?" Wentworth asked in a subdued voice.

"Inside there," Arnold said, nodding up the dark corridor. Wentworth started in the direction indicated. He paused as Anderson said, "Steel yourself, Inspector."

Wentworth regarded him and then continued to the designated door. Inside he found other officers standing outside a twelve-foot-square room, smoky and hot, despite the chill of the day. The place was furnished with a bed and a few other pieces of furniture, but Wentworth paid little mind to the appointments—or his coworkers.

His attention was solely on the human being—or what remained of a human being—in repose on the bed. The three Ripper victims who had been mutilated did not compare to this carnage. This woman had been savaged beyond recognition. Her breasts and a number of internal organs had been sliced free of the body and rearranged. Much of the skin had been flayed.

The heart was missing altogether.

It was clear what the Ripper needed the Fitzgerald's Preserving Fluid for.

"Ah, Wentworth." This from Frederick Abberline, Inspector First Class. His office was just up the hall from Wentworth's.

"Another." Wentworth sighed.

"Indeed."

"What carnage. Who is, *was,* she?"

"Mary Kelly, twenty-five. She preferred the name Marie Jeanette."

"An unfortunate?" Wentworth asked.

"Yes. Worked most of her life on the streets."

Wentworth glanced at a print, *The Fisherman's Widow,* hanging above the fireplace, in which embers of what seemed to be smoldering cloth still glowed.

Abberline followed the direction of his gaze. "We believe it took him an hour and a half to two hours to complete his surgery, if you will. He wanted more light and had only her clothes to burn."

"What was the time?"

"Between two thirty and eight this morning, the surgeon estimates. But we'll know better after the inquest. Her landlord sent his man around about a quarter to eleven for the rent and he discovered her."

"Witnesses?"

"Several. But some observations seem suspicious, if not wholly unreliable."

A shadow appeared in the doorway, cutting off the glare from Miller's Court. "Inspector."

"Ah." Wentworth turned to see Dr. Richard Adams. His eyes were on the victim.

"Well."

"Come in, Doctor, please."

Introductions were made and Wentworth described Adams's role, and explained further about finding the chemist who had sold the preserving fluid and where that discovery led. "I have constables watching that shop, the warehouse we discovered, and the flat, but they've reported no reappearance."

"Well done," Abberline said. "We appreciate any assistance you might provide, Doctor. I'll stand outside and let you examine the corpse." He left the two men alone.

"A prostitute, like the others?"

"Yes. Doctor, do you think this is the work of the same man? The carnage is much more severe."

Adams looked over the corpse.

"I have no doubt. The thrusts and sawing patterns suggest as much. I think the madness that comes over him varies—one night he is content to be more . . . deliberate, you might say. This? His fit possessed him to utterly destroy the poor creature. God only knows why."

Adams frowned. "The heart?"

"Missing."

"May I?" Adams asked, nodding toward the body.

"Of course."

The doctor stepped forward, leaned down, and regarded the wounds. Using a handkerchief, he lifted the victim's right hand and examined it. There was a knife gash on the palm. He manipulated the appendage and then replaced it. He did the same with her feet. Then he studied the body cavities.

Finally he stepped back and looked down at the Ripper's handiwork as a whole.

"Any conclusions?"

Adams shrugged. "I may have. The scars suggest the use of a new instrument. I will need to look into it more. Perhaps we can stop by a surgical supply company."

"Yes, we will do." The inspector looked down upon the body. "Why, Jack? Why do you do this?"

Adams said, "I'm afraid the doctor within me is flummoxed, Inspector. The religious man, however, has an answer."

"And what that might be?"

"It's the hand of Satan."

"Ah, but we will have a difficult time bringing *him* before the Queen's Bench. So let us continue on our secular investigation."

Inspector Wentworth returned home at close to 8 P.M.

The bad morning had turned into a worse afternoon and evening. His superiors clamored for answers, citizens demanded a suspect, and the reporters cried for details.

He was unable to provide satisfaction to any one of those needy assemblies.

Wentworth washed in the bathroom and returned downstairs. He sat at the dining table and struggled to put his cares aside—all the while wondering where Saucy Jacky might be at this very moment.

Still, he put a smile on his face and nodded as the maid set dishes before Wentworth and his wife. He looked up at the slim young servant. "Thank you, Jenny. You have prepared quite the sumptuous repast, as you always do."

"Thank you, Inspector."

Supper was lamb and potatoes, a small dish of haddock, and grilled tomato.

Edith Wentworth, a handsome woman of Wentworth's age, gave the girl a coy look. "And Mr. Hendrick's son slipped some buns into the package of bread today. And he winked at her."

"Ma'am."

Wentworth turned to the blushing Cockney girl. "You could do worse than to marry into a baker's family, Jenny."

Edith said, "And he's a nice boy and good looking too, Ras. You remember him?"

In fact, Wentworth had no idea who the young man was. But his wife had a keen eye and he knew she had passed an accurate judgment on the potential suitor.

He added, "And a hard worker, for sure. Though he won't be forced to work the hours of a detective inspector. He will get home to you in the evenings." This was said with a glance toward his wife.

"Please, sir. I hardly know the boy." The housekeeper's fiery face was, however, smiling.

The girl retired and Wentworth and his wife ate, speaking of her visit to their daughter-in-law in Islington and a new millinery shop that had opened up the road. She reminded Wentworth that they had committed to a trip to Leeds, where they would join friends on a river boat that weekend.

He began to say, I shall try with all my heart . . . But the word took him right back to the horrific murder of Mary Kelly, who had been robbed of that very organ.

"I will try, my dear."

"I know of the new killing. I understand. It's him?"

"Yes, there's little doubt."

"Are you any closer to finding who it might be? The papers are full of speculation."

"All of it spurious. He's quite the elusive one. Most criminals make the error of *trying* to be clever, though in fact they aren't, and that approach trips them up. This fellow we're after is either indeed clever or, not being so, makes no attempt to try. And thus he blunders his way along, engaging in behaviors that don't give rise to clear evidence or witnesses."

"Lucky, then."

"Lucky in part, yes. The fact that there is no motive—other than butchery itself—for the killings is perhaps the most arduous obstacle." He lowered his voice—Jenny could be nearby. "There is no apparent sexual activity. He does not rob them. He's claimed, if the *Dear Boss* letter he sent be truly his, that he wants to kill prostitutes, but even the most fervent moralists would never cause such carnage because of an unfortunate's profession. For heaven's sake, that part of the city is infested with such poverty that I'm sure if my circumstances placed me in such a locale, I too would turn to crime to put bread in the mouths of my family." He sipped from a water glass, his tongue locating the chipped spot to avoid it. Then sighed. "If we knew why, we could then find who. But, sadly, his purpose remains a mystery.

"Although I will tell you we have had some assistance from an unlikely source." He told her about the famous doctor who was assisting them. "Brilliant fellow. Made a connection, thanks to his medical skills, to where the killer might have stayed for a time. Nothing came of it but I've stationed men nearby to see if he returns." He lowered his voice. "He came at the recommendation of the Palace. Her Majesty's advisor himself."

"No, Ras!" Edith was delighted at this news.

"Yes." Then he gave a dark smile. "Rather at the *insistence* of the Palace. That this fellow remains free is putting the royals and the government in a rather bad light not only here but on the Continent. Even in America too."

"It is a difficult time for Her Majesty," Edith pointed out.

This was certainly the truth. There was the incident of Abdul Karim, the Munshi, an Indian Muslim who was an important clerk to Victoria and much favored by her—to the horror of her family and retainers. Then just months earlier the beautiful Princess Alix, sixteen, the queen's granddaughter, had faced death from a horse-riding incident. Then there were the perennial problems of the socialists, the Irish, the poverty . . . and Her Majesty's frustration at finding a suitable prime minister.

"You're doing all you—"

At that there came a rapping on the back door of the flat.

"Who could that be? At suppertime?" Edith said. Then she called, "Jenny, could you please see who's calling?"

"No," Wentworth said, dabbing his face with his linen and standing. "I will go." In a louder voice: "Jenny, I will attend to it. You go about your chores."

"Yes, sir."

He strode through the kitchen and down from the first floor to the ground. The mews where the Wentworths lived was decent and generally safe, and it was possible that the visitor was nothing more than a grindler, hoping for food. But London was London, and this was hardly Mayfair; it could be a lurker with criminal designs. Hence, his attending to the caller.

Wentworth approached the back door, undid the dead bolt, and lifted the bar. He pulled the door open.

The empty alley greeted him.

Curious. He stepped outside. No one.

But ten yards away, something small sat on the cobblestones where the alley-way turned a corner. The evening was foggy, as often at this hour, and he could make out only a shape about eight inches in length. The color was gray, but so was the hue of almost everything here at this time of night in this bleak month.

"Hallo?" he called.

No response save for his own echoing voice.

Wentworth squinted through the mist. Curious. The object seemed to be a purse. Who could possibly have dropped it here?

He looked around him once more.

"Hallo?"

Jacques LaFleur—the Ripper, Saucy Jacky—waited around the corner from the back door of the flat of Detective Inspector Wentworth. A lovely blade was gripped tightly in his hand. Not a surgeon's knife but a proper one, more than a foot long.

He'd found the man's flat with little difficulty. That morning, approaching noon, Jacques had been across Dorset Street, by Mary Kelly's room, and he had watched the policeman walk from the front door of the flat where he'd created such a beautiful object in blood.

The slim officer, in a tweed suit and no overcoat against the chill, had called over several constables and sent them in different directions. Jacques deemed it best to repair to his flat at that time. He had all he needed, anyway—in his mind an image of the detective inspector who was pursuing him.

Later, sitting at his table in his Somerset Street rooms, surrounded by close to one hundred newspaper and periodical articles about the Whitechapel killings, Jacques had skimmed them quickly, regarding the illustrations only. And soon he'd matched the face he recalled with a name. Erasmus Wentworth. One publication, the *Police News,* gave his address.

Now, he listened carefully and heard the Yarder's footsteps approaching the purse he'd left as bait cautiously.

From Jacques's observation of the goings-on in the inspector's flat that evening, he had noted that there might be several permutations that could unfold. The pretty young servant girl might open the door and see the purse and step forward, hoping it would contain a few pence or shillings, or even a sovereign or two. Or the older woman, who he guessed was the inspector's wife, might do the same.

Slitting their throats and then ripping open bodices to swiftly remove their maternal breasts, or slice their bellies, smooth the one, wrinkled the other, would have been delightful too.

But the outcome he truly hoped for was that which was now unfolding.

The copper himself.

Jacques heard the officer say, "Hm."

He'd be wondering who would have rapped on his door, then dropped a purse. He might be concluding it was revelers in their cups.

From the sound of footsteps grating on the alleyway floor, he was almost to the shadows where the bag lay.

Jacques inhaled a deep breath and tensed his legs, picturing the inspector's terror as he lunged forward, slashing, slashing, slashing, painting a beautiful crimson design upon the scaly cobblestones.

Ah, another pleasing thought: the copper would, of course, not die immediately but would scream for assistance.

And his wife, perhaps the servant girl too, would appear.

They, as well, would contribute to the canvas of blood.

Imagine those news accounts!

The footsteps stopped. He'd be standing over the purse.

Steady yourself. One . . . two . . .

Jacques stepped forward one pace.

And then: "No," came a firm whisper near his ear.

He turned fast, raising the knife.

There, leaning on his cane, was Dr. Richard Adams. An Enfield revolver was in his hand, pointed at Jacques's heart.

The man smiled and lowered the blade.

The doctor led him back into the shadows, away from the alley and toward the street. He whispered, "There's a constable not twenty feet from here. The officers investigating the Whitechapel killings all have a guard. And there is a regular patrol not far, as well. Give me the knife."

Jacques turned it handle first and passed it over.

Hiding behind an evergreen, and obscured by the mist, they could just make out Inspector Wentworth picking up and examining the bag, which was empty. He called "Hallo" once more, and when there was no response turned and walked back to the house.

Adams gestured toward the street with the pistol and said sternly to Jacques, "You'll come with me. Now."

The smell in the small, exceedingly damp room was of fish. The place was shadowy. Electric lighting was becoming popular in London—Dr. Richard Adams had it in his practice and soon would in his home near Grosvenor Square—but this was the East End, and some said service would not come here for ten years. Others said it never would.

The illumination in the warehouse tonight came from an oil lamp, not even gas.

Adams looked outside, then pulled together the burlap curtains and turned back to Jacques LaFleur. He pointed to a chair. The killer sat. Adams noted he was dressed well, the garments pressed and clean. He was in a white shirt and ribbon tie. Beneath his checkered suit was his trademark leather waistcoat.

The door opened and Henry Gladbrook entered. He too eyed Jacques and then turned away, hanging up his own greatcoat. He sat down on an unsteady chair, looked down. Removed a match from a box and slipped it under the short leg.

Jacques said to Gladbrook, "Well, sir, the good doctor here found me. Tracked me down, didn't he? Won't tell me how he did it. But here I am."

Adams, assisted by his cane, hobbled to a bench, dusted it with a kerchief, and then sat. "He was about to eviscerate Inspector Wentworth."

Gladbrook shook his head. "We've been having a rather difficult time because of you, my friend," he said. "You didn't quite follow the plan, now, did you?"

Jacques—Jack the Ripper, Saucy Jacky, Leather Apron—gave a faint shrug.

The plan . . .

One month ago, Gladbrook and Adams found themselves in need of a dangerous man, one not afraid to use a knife to kill. A man with no family, no friends . . . an invisible man.

Discreet enquiries among gaolers led to the fellow before them now. He was in Newgate for murdering a solicitor in London during a robbery. Gladbrook had spoken to him and decided he would suit. A word to the Crown Prosecutor and he was released (on the claim he was wanted in Ireland, and was being handed over to authorities there for political expediency).

And so Jacques LaFleur was set free to help the men on their mission.

Yet the instructions were that the hound was to track and kill one fox and one only.

Mary Ann Nichols.

Gladbrook reminded him of this and added, "But suddenly you vanish, and we open the broadsheets and learn that you decided otherwise, despite having taken our guineas. You went on to slaughter *four* more women."

"No, no, no. Three only. Miss Stride I was interrupted during. Only had time to slice her. Still piqued by that, I must say."

"Are you mocking us?" Gladbrook raged.

"No, sir." Jacques fell silent.

"One killing and the incident would have been noted in the public eye for a day or two and then drifted into obscurity. But four others? What would have been a minor crime has gone on to become the talk of the world!"

Adams asked bluntly, "Answer us! Why did you keep killing?"

"Just what you said, governor," Jacques said, eyeing Gladbrook. "The talk of the world." His eyes blazed. He reached into his pocket and withdrew a number of folded sheaves of paper.

Adams could see they were newspaper clippings.

Lovingly the killer spread them out on a nearby table. "Look! Look at this! They are telling my story! I'm the hero of all of them."

Hero? thought Adams.

The small man, his face indeed weaselly, looked up at the two men fiercely. "I was nothing as a boy in Manchester. And I was nothing coming here. I could work only menial jobs . . . I was even condemned to mundane crimes in the Chapel. Mug-heading, pinching, flying the blue pigeon—stealing roof lead! That murder I was in Newgate for? It was thanks to my clumsiness. I dropped the pistol I was robbing the old barrister with and we both leapt for it. It went off by itself! Lor', there's a twist for you!

"I knew I was smart. I knew I was meant for greatness but nothing ever came my way. It was damned unfair! But when I killed Mary Ann? Why, the very next day I was the king of London."

"And the bloodier the crimes, the more your star shone."

"That's right." His face darkened. "Oh, governors, the truth is I hated the blood, hated the cutting, hated carting back this part and that part. That's why there were gaps—August to September to November. I hated it."

Adams laughed coldly. "And that's why you sent the taunting letters. When interest flagged, and the scribblers moved on to other stories, you stirred the pot."

"Ach, I'm telling you, Doctor, murder's hard work. Unpleasant work. Much easier to write a letter. And, suddenly, guvs, I was on the front page again."

The articles had given Gladbrook and Adams considerable cause for concern. They had spent sleepless nights, many of them, worried that their killer was going to tell all in a subsequent missive. Notably: who was truly behind the killings.

"But even the letters weren't enough," Adams said.

"And so Mary Kelly."

"My Little Heart."

Adams blinked at the appellation, recalling the organ he had taken with him.

"Which is why you butchered her more viciously than the others. To garner bigger headlines."

"That's a fact, governor."

Gladbrook said, "And using the name 'Jack.' And 'Jacky'? We thought you were mad to pick that, so similar to your own. But it's clear now. At least a version of your name was in the public eye."

He nodded that this was on the mark.

"All right, Jacques," Gladbrook said. "What's done is done. But now you *must* retire. You've had your notoriety." Gladbrook scooped up the clippings and handed them back. Then he reached into his coat pocket and handed over an envelope, which contained a steamship ticket. Then a heavy leather purse.

"And here's fifty gold sovereigns."

"Blimey."

"Outside there's a hansom to take you to the dock."

"But—"

"There's gold aplenty in there to buy what you need. You leave now. Jack the Ripper transmogrifies back into Jacques LaFleur tonight. You'll go to France and thence wherever you like. But you are never to return to England."

He looked into the bag. "Well, yes, all right. As you wish." He hefted the bag and pulled on his greatcoat. "I answered your questions. Now you answer me, if you would be so kind."

"And what might the question be?" Adams asked.

"You never told me why you wanted her killed, Mary Ann Nichols. Was it she had a client you didn't want the world to know about?"

Gladbrook looked at Adams. The doctor answered, "Yes, that's what this was about."

Jacques eyed them, one then the other, closely. "Well, you're subtle birds, both of you. I hazard there's more to why she died than some husband being where he shouldn't've been. But the answer's between you and God. Or more likely the devil. Good night to you both now. And thank'ee."

The man left and Gladbrook closed the warehouse door behind him. He poured a whisky for himself and the doctor and both men sat. They heard the horses' hoof-falls and the clack of wheels on cobblestones as the killer departed.

Gladbrook said, "So, Doctor, thank God you found him. It appears our plan worked."

After the killing of Mary Ann Nichols and Jacques's rogue descent into murder, the two men, desperate to locate him, came up with a scheme to infiltrate Scotland Yard and discover what the police had learned. They would combine that with what they themselves knew about the real "Ripper." This they hoped would provide sufficient insights so they might track down their renegade killer.

And so Gladbrook, taking his cue from the Conan Doyle novel, suggested that Adams offer his services as a "medical detective" to assist the police.

They knew full well, for instance, LaFleur's appearance, his cologne, the restaurants he frequented, his clothing, and the tobacco he favored.

Working with Inspector Wentworth, Adams learned other facts. He could tell from their posture in repose, and the smell of the garments, that the four later victims had been chloroformed before they were murdered. He also noted from the rent blouse he had examined, as well as the photographs, that both a particular type of knife and a surgical saw had been employed—though the killer was not, as the police surgeon had concluded, a medical man.

And at the Mary Kelly murder, he had observed that there were blood and bits of skin beneath the victim's fingernails. This would not be hers, but his, for she would have collected the crimson stains fighting with him to save herself as he pressed the chloroformed rag over her mouth. (Adams had used his kerchief on the pretense of examining the wound in her palm to remove some samples of the killer's blood and flesh.) After leaving Mary's room and returning to his laboratory, he had tested the blood and skin and learned something about Jacques they had not known. He suffered from the great pox—syphilis. Adams deduced this from large amounts of mercury, the treatment of choice for the disease.

So he and Gladbrook had gone their separate ways, started making the rounds of East End chemists and medical clinics, enquiring about a man who fit the description of the killer, had purchased chloroform and certain surgical implements, and who was being treated for pox.

It was Adams who landed the trout, narrowing the search to Aldgate High Street and, eventually, to shadowy, grim Somerset Street. Ironically, Adams now reflected, it was a news vendor who sent Adams toward Somerset, where a charwoman pointed out his flat. Just as Adams arrived at the place, however, Jacques had stepped outside. The doctor could not, certainly, summon a constable, so he'd pursued the killer discreetly—directly to Inspector Wentworth's town house, where the killer was prepared to murder the inspector himself, and possibly his wife and maid as well.

"And Wentworth suspects nothing?" Gladbrook asked.

"I'm sure not. He believed I was truly trying to help . . . and he was genuinely impressed by my powers of deduction, if you will, in locating the chemist who sold Jack the preserving fluid."

The "discovery" of the chemist, which led to the warehouse on Anthony Street (and the flat on Barker's Row), was a magician's illusion. The real chemist, Owen Merry, had been impersonated by a hulking associate of Gladbrook's, who sent Adams and the inspector to the warehouse where the Fitzgerald's Preserving Fluid had been "delivered" (that is, set there earlier in the day by Gladbrook's man). Wentworth would mark down Jack the Ripper's absence to unfortunate timing, but was nonetheless impressed by Adams's contribution and convinced of his authenticity and value.

"And you will now proceed as we thought?" Gladbrook asked.

"Indeed. I think it's a wise course."

Adams would continue to assist Inspector Wentworth by providing insights and interpretations of the evidence to point the finger of guilt toward one of the suspects already in the sights of Scotland Yard and the City Police. There were several that seemed likely—though, of course, as both Adams and Gladbrook knew, they were completely innocent.

Would that person ever be found guilty? The British system of justice was as sophisticated as any in the world, but it was not infallible. Perhaps, yes, someone would hang for the killings. Or maybe the mystery would remain unsolved for, who could say, a hundred years or more, at which time some investigator, or even some author, might take a fancy to the ancient case and would himself, or herself, try to solve the riddle.

A rap sounded on the door and Gladbrook called, "Enter."

In walked Gladbrook's aide, the muscular Cockney who had impersonated Merry the chemist. He took his hat off, revealing his largely bald scalp, perfectly round with a few renegade hairs.

" 'S done, sir." He handed the bag of sovereigns and the steamship ticket to Gladbrook.

"Potter's Field?"

"Yessir. 'E's six feet down. Unmarked grave. 'E'll never be found on this earth."

This had been Jacques LaFleur's fate from the start. He would have died, murdered by this large man, right after Mary Ann Nichols's murder, had he not vanished. Adams felt no guilt for the man's death; he would have hanged for the solicitor's murder in any event.

Gladbrook fished into the bag and dug out three sovereigns. Handed them over.

"Blimey, sir. Thank you." The man tapped his huge pate, as might a soldier, which he had been, turned on his heels and left.

The men each drained their whisky.

Gladbrook asked, "When are you going to Osborne House?"

"Sunday."

"Please cable me what you learn."

"I will do."

The men rose. Gladbrook donned his top hat and overcoat. They left, stepping onto a foggy pavement. Gladbrook locked the door. He fished a cigar from his case and cut and lit it. "It has worked out to our advantage but, make no mistake, this has been a sad, sordid matter," he muttered.

"A matter of blood, you might say." Adams turned his collar up against the damp chill and, relying on his cane, started off down the street.

THREE

Sunday, 11 November, 2 P.M.

Osborne House, on the Isle of Wight, was the country estate that the royal family most favored.

Located in East Cowes, the Italian Renaissance structure—complete with two Belvedere towers—had been designed largely by Prince Albert himself, consort, husband of Victoria. The other designer, and the builder, was Thomas Cubitt, whose firm also had constructed portions of Buckingham Palace.

Dr. Richard Adams now eyed the splendid edifice from his seat in a brougham, as the horses slowed to a stop. The carriage was comfortable enough, though the uneven ground had toyed cruelly with his war-wounded hip. He now descended stiffly to the ground and, relying on his cane more than he normally would, followed a doorman into the house and thence to a sitting room on the first floor. The view overlooked the gardens in which Victoria and Albert's children had grown vegetables, which they "sold" to their father and later cooked up themselves in the kitchen in Swiss Cottage, not far away on the grounds.

A butler appeared with a tea service and Adams took a cup. As he left, the man said, "The princess will be here shortly, sir."

"Thank you."

The princess . . .

Victoria's granddaughter: Ducal Highness Princess Viktoria Alix Helena Luise Beatrice of Hesse and by Rhine, known throughout the empire as Alix.

It was this innocent child—sixteen years of age—who was the reason, albeit unknowingly, for the death of Mary Ann Nichols—and, Adams now knew, to his shame, the other four unfortunates.

I hazard there's more to why she died than some husband being where he shouldn't've been. But the answer's between you and God. Or more likely the devil . . .

In August the girl had been injured in an equestrian fall and suffered a cut in her thigh.

For most people, such an accident would not have had serious, much less life-threatening, consequences.

But the princess was not like others; she suffered from the Royal Disease.

The malady, known to doctors as hemophilia, was a rare but horrific scourge, in which a flaw in the blood prevents clotting. Even the most minor injuries can result in the victim's bleeding to death quickly. The informal name, "Royal Disease," arose because Queen Victoria carried the proclivity for this condition in her blood and passed it down to her heirs. Hemophilia is a condition that affects the male descendants most seriously (Princess Alix's uncle Leopold died at thirty, after having suffered a minor fall, and the girl's own brother, Frederick, died when two years old—a fall once more), but women can suffer as well. And while the princess was not bleeding in the unstoppable gush that killed her uncle, the seepage from her wounded leg would, sooner or later, take her life if not stanched.

The queen's aide, John Ashton, summoned Gladbrook with instructions to do whatever was necessary to save the girl.

Gladbrook had, in turn, called upon Adams in his chambers.

The suave man of court had implored, "Doctor, we need your assistance as a matter of highest concern to the Crown."

"Yes, of course, sir. How may I assist?"

He had described the princess's imperiled state.

"Yes, I'm aware, from the press, of her riding accident. But I did not know she suffered a bleeding wound."

"It is being kept quiet. The Court physician feels she can survive two weeks at best." After a pause, the man continued, "We of course pray for the child's recovery, for her sake, and for those close to her, her grandmother in particular."

Everyone knew that Her Majesty had never fully recovered from the death of her beloved husband, Prince Albert, nor of their daughter, Princess Alice,

Alix's mother. Victoria also still mourned Leopold's death and that of her infant grandson, Frittie, Alix's brother.

To lose the charming and vivacious Alix would be a catastrophe to the queen.

"But," Gladbrook had added, lowering his voice, though they were alone in the doctor's quarters, "her survival is important for a broader reason. For the Empire itself to thrive, it is vital that England form allegiances with other countries on the Continent. Treaties pale in comparison to the more durable bond of marriage."

Princess Victoria had married Frederick III of Germany; Prince Albert Edward had married Princess Alexandra of Denmark, and Alix's mother, Princess Alice, had married into the Hessian Duchy, now a part of Germany.

"The princess must survive so that she might marry into a royal family, ensuring that that country's fate is entwined with that of Mother England. Now, to my mission here, Doctor. We have heard of your work and it is in that capacity that we seek your help."

Adams was indeed, as Gladbrook had told Detective Inspector Wentworth, one of the most preeminent physicians in England, though not, as stated, for his Sherlock Holmesian skills at deduction. No, he was renowned for research into diseases of the blood and internal organs. He had indeed studied hemophilia and was working to determine what the flaw contained in Victorian blood might be and, once identified, how it might be neutralized.

Gladbrook had said, "I've heard of this treatment you are performing. Transfusions."

Adams had pioneered the practice—taking blood from a healthy individual and injecting it into the veins of an ill patient who had lost blood from wound or lesion.

There was one obstacle to this treatment, however, deriving from the nature of blood itself. The crimson elixir that flowed through one person's veins might be of a different sort than that flowing through another's. In order for a transfusion to work, the blood from the donor had to match the blood of the recipient. Without this compatibility, the introduction of a donor's blood would be fatal. At present it was possible, before a transfusion, to combine two persons' blood samples on an examination slide and, by observing the resulting mixture under a microscope, determine if the donor and recipient were compatible or not, though this required a painstaking process of comparing perhaps hundreds of samples of blood. Sometimes a match was never found.

Yes, in theory transfusions could save a life under some circumstances, routine surgery or war wounds, for instance. However, with hemophilia, there was an additional—indeed, insurmountable—impediment to the treatment. Adams had told Gladbrook, "Even if we find a donor whose blood is in the same category as that of the princess's, to counteract the bleeding I will need gallons of compatible blood: indeed, *all* of the donor's blood. In future years, I will be, I hope, able to isolate a reagent to cause the blood to clot. But at present, no. I need pure blood and in sufficient quantity so that a donor would not survive."

"Ah," the advisor had said. "Then we are presented with a difficult decision."

Adams had required a moment to grasp what the man was saying. "No. No! We are presented with no decision at all. I am a man of medicine. I cannot do what you are asking."

"This is to save the life of a royal and, perhaps, to preserve the Crown itself."

"That does not matter. I have my oath. I cannot take one life, even to save another. That's the province of God."

Gladbrook had sat back in his chair, lit a cigar, and said, "Let me pose you this, Doctor. Say two patients are brought to your surgery simultaneously, both in extremis. There is only you attending. You have the time and medicine to save only one. By choosing the cooper over the baker, the lady over the lord, the hansom driver over the charwoman, are you not killing the other?"

"That's a fatuous argument."

"I think not, Doctor. Every decision we make in life could have lethal consequences. Soldiers on the battlefield know this. Fishermen. Train engineers. Midwives. You as a man of medicine know this as well."

"Still, I cannot do it. I am sorry. And the queen would never condone it."

Gladbrook had leaned forward and said fervently, "Her Majesty will never know. Nor anyone else, save for the few it is necessary to inform."

Adams had blustered, "Well, it is impossible. We'll speak no more of it."

"Then, Doctor," Gladbrook had said, in a low and chillingly calm voice, "I'll find another surgeon, fill his purse with sovereigns, and tell him to cut away and pump the girl full of another's blood."

"No one other than I can perform this procedure."

"Nonetheless, I assure you, I *will* find someone else if you refuse to help us."

Adams, horrified at the thought of what Gladbrook was proposing, had fallen silent.

Gladbrook had gripped his arm. "Please, sir. We need you, the Palace needs you."

Adams had whispered, "But who will the donor be?"

Gladbrook had considered this question for a moment. Then his eyes had narrowed. "My illustration a moment ago? The cooper or the baker, the lord or lady? Now I would posit that the patients you had to choose between were . . . a princess and a whore."

Adams closed his eyes and uttered a simple prayer: God forgive me.

The doctor had then hurried to an infirmary in the East End, run by nuns, who tended to, among others, many prostitutes in the area. Adams, with a vial of the princess's blood in a satchel, had set up at a table in the infirmary and taken samples of the ladies' blood to check for compatibility—provided, of course, that they showed no symptoms of the pox.

Some categories of blood, the doctor had found, were common. Some were rare. As if God were excoriating those involved in the matter, Princess Alix's blood fell into an exceedingly rare category, and for a time Adams despaired of finding a donor who was compatible. But finally a match was made.

Mary Ann Nichols.

Jacques was released from prison, given his chore, and set loose. He tracked Mary Ann, murdered the woman, drained her blood into jars, and, at Adams's instruction, savaged the body and spread the viscera about so that the authorities would not notice that there was a paucity of blood on the ground.

That had been, for Adams, the worst day of his life, mitigated, though it was, by the fact that within hours of the treatment the princess's bleeding stopped and she began her trek to recovery.

The "matter of blood" should have ended there—a bittersweet accomplishment that he would spend the rest of his life trying to forget. But it did not. Because Jacques LaFleur decided to become Jack the Ripper and postpone his retirement, so that he might bask in the perverse glory afforded him by the hyenas of Fleet Street.

Now, sitting in the grand Osborne House, the doctor closed his eyes and, once again, begged God's forgiveness. Adams was quite aware that He chose not to respond.

A moment later the doctor was conscious of footsteps approaching. He now set down his teacup, which he had not once brought to his lips, and rose.

"Dr. Adams!" a girl's voice called.

He found himself looking into the bright eyes of a pretty teenage girl, dressed in a simple white frock, a blue bow in her hair.

"Your Highness." The doctor bowed as he greeted her.

"Doctor," she chided in a tone of good nature, "I always insist you call me Alix."

Adams smiled. "And *I* always hide behind courtly protocol. It is hardly in my nature, Your Highness, to break with a thousand-year tradition."

He greeted the princess's lady-in-waiting, a solid girl, not much older, with raven-black hair. She curtseyed demurely.

He then said, "Now to the point, Your Highness. Please tell me how you are feeling."

She described herself as quite healthy, no light-headedness, no other symptoms. The girl had not worn stockings and she lifted her hem to reveal the site of her wound, which had healed completely. Even the scar was minimal.

He felt her forehead, listened to her heart, and examined her eyes.

"Have you suffered any other incidents resulting in cuts or abrasions?"

"No. I've been infinitely careful, as you have insisted."

Adams still did not know if the transfusion had cured the hemophilia or merely stanched the blood flow in that one instance, with the girl's own flawed blood once again flowing through her veins. The scientist in him would have liked to know more. But this was not a patient to experiment upon.

He put his instruments back into his kit. "I pronounce you healthy as a filly at Ascot."

"You are a miracle worker, Doctor. My grandmother has told me you are to be invited for an audience. She wishes to thank you in person."

Adams had heard the same. He was not looking forward to receiving whatever commendation Her Majesty would confer upon him; that would exponentially increase his guilt. He dared not, however, refuse to attend.

"I shall be honored."

The princess added, "And you will stay for supper this evening? Oh, I do hope so. Father is here."

"I will pay my respects to the Grand Duke, but I am afraid I must be getting back to London. I have patients awaiting my attendance."

"Even on Sunday?"

"Illness observes no holy day."

"Of course, I understand, though I shall be disappointed."

"It has been a pleasure treating you, Your Highness, but I do hope I never have the chance to see you again . . . in a *professional* capacity."

The girl laughed. Then her rosy lips curled into a pout. "But, Doctor, you must understand that I shan't let you leave until you do my bidding."

He bowed and kissed her hand. "You are quite the charming—and formidable—young woman . . . *Alix*." The girl's face bloomed. The doctor added, "I have no doubt that you will someday have the world at your command."

EPILOGUE

The London Daily Mirror, 26 November 1894

PRINCESS ALIX AND TSAR NICHOLAS OF RUSSIA WED

NUPTIALS BRING HOPE TO AN EMPIRE IN MOURNING
Her Majesty's Granddaughter
HENCEFORTH TO BE KNOWN AS
Alexandra Feodorovna Romanova

It was a joyous occasion today at the Winter Palace in St. Petersburg as newly crowned Tsar Nicholas II, Nikolai Alexandrovich Romanov, and Princess Victoria Alix Helena Luise Beatrice, the beloved granddaughter of Her Royal Majesty Queen Victoria, were wed before the Palace priest at just before one o'clock this afternoon.

The wedding did much to dim the sorrow that has pervaded Russia, and the world, since the tragic and untimely death of Nicholas's father, Tsar Alexander III, at the age of 49.

It was the tsar's decision to move forward the ceremony, originally scheduled for the spring of next year, to today, which is the birthday of his mother, the empress dowager.

Following the marriage, our beloved princess is to be known as Alexandra Feodorovna Romanova, Empress Consort of all the Russias.

As the wedding was celebrated during the official period of mourning following Tsar Alexander's death, there was no reception and the married couple forwent a honeymoon.

Countrymen throughout the realm rejoice in this holy union, tightening, as it does, the bond between these two glorious empires, and wish the couple a long and fruitful life together.

Crowned heads from throughout England and the Continent were present at the union, among them Her Royal Highness the Queen of the United Kingdom and Empress of India; the Prince and Princess of Wales; the Duke and Duchess of York; the Empress Dowager of all the Russias, Grand Duchess Xenia Alexandrovna, Grand Duke Alexander Mikhailovich, and many other distinguished guests.

A STUDY IN TERROR

Ellery Queen

This long novella is a major departure for the two Brooklyn cousins who collaborated under the pseudonym Ellery Queen, Frederic Dannay (born Daniel Nathan) (1905–1982) and Manfred Bennington Lee (born Emanuel Benjamin Lepofsky) (1905–1971). Virtually all their novels and short stories were set in contemporary New York and featured Ellery Queen, their much-loved amateur detective. In what remains a brilliant marketing decision, they gave their series character the same name as their byline, reasoning that if readers forgot the name of the author or the name of the character, they might remember the other. It worked, as Ellery Queen is counted among the handful of the best-known names in the history of mystery fiction.

A Study in Terror deviates from their other work in that the majority of it is set in the nineteenth century, bringing Jack the Ripper face-to-face with Sherlock Holmes in a story within a story. Queen is present in the framing sections of the book, introducing and analyzing a manuscript recounting the Holmes–Ripper case. These before-and-after sections, incidentally, were entirely written by Lee and Dannay, while the main section, featuring Holmes, was largely written by Paul W. Fairman (1916–1977), albeit anonymously, with input from Lee and Dannay.

The central story is a novelization of a very good British film with the same title, released in October 1965 by Compton Films; the US release date was nearly a year later, in August 1966, and was at one time titled *Fog*. James Hill directed the original; the story and screenplay were by Donald and Derek Ford. It starred John Neville as Sherlock Holmes, Donald Houston as Dr. Watson, and Robert Morley as Mycroft Holmes; it also starred John Fraser, Anthony Quayle, and Judi Dench. A different murderer than the film villain was named in the novella.

A Study in Terror was first published as a paperback original by Lancer (New York, 1966); it was retitled *Sherlock Holmes versus Jack the Ripper* when it was published in England (London, Victor Gollancz, 1967).

Ellery Begins

Ellery brooded.

For a reasonable time.

After which he got up from his typewriter, seized ten pages of doomed copy, and tore them into four ragged sections.

He scowled at the silent typewriter. The machine leered back.

The phone rang, and he jumped for it as if it were a life-preserver.

"Don't snarl at *me*," said a hurt voice with undertones of anguish. "I'm having fun, per orders."

"Dad! Did I snap at you? I'm in a plot bind. How's Bermuda?"

"Sunshine, blue water, and more damn sand than you can shake a billy at. I want to come *home*."

"No," Ellery said firmly. "The trip cost me a bundle, and I'm going to get my money's worth."

Inspector Queen's sigh was eloquent. "You always were a dictator where I'm concerned. What am I, a basket case?"

"You're overworked."

"Maybe I could arrange a rebate?" Inspector Queen suggested hopefully.

"Your orders are to rest and relax—forget everything."

"Okay, okay. There's a hot horseshoe game going on across from my cabana. Maybe I can horn in."

"Do that, Dad. I'll phone tomorrow for the score."

Ellery hung up and glared at the typewriter. The problem remained. He circled the table warily and began to pace.

Providentially, the doorbell rang.

"Leave them on the table," Ellery called. "Take the money."

The visitor disobeyed. Feet crossed the foyer and entered the scene of the great man's agony. Ellery grunted. "You? I thought it was the boy with the delicatessen."

Grant Ames III, with the aplomb of the privileged bore—a bore with millions—aimed his perfect Brooks Brothers toward the bar. There he exchanged the large manila envelope he was carrying for a bottle of scotch and a glass. "I came to make a delivery, too," Ames announced. "Something a hell of a lot more important than pastrami," and sat down on the sofa. "You stock pretty good scotch, Ellery."

"I'm glad you like it. Take the bottle with you. I'm working."

"But I claim the prerogative of a fan. I devour every one of your stories."

"Borrowed from unscrupulous friends," Ellery growled.

"That," Grant said, pouring, "is unkind. You'll apologize when you know my mission."

"What mission?"

"A delivery. Weren't you listening?"

"Of what?"

"That envelope. By the gin."

Ellery turned in that direction. Grant waved him back. "I insist on filling you in first, Maestro."

The doorbell rang again. This time it was the sandwiches. Ellery stamped into the foyer and returned with his mouth full.

"Why don't you go to work, Grant? Get a job in one of your father's frozen-food plants. Or become a pea-picker. Anything, but get out of my hair. I've got work to do, I tell you."

"Don't change the subject," Grant III said. "You wouldn't have a kosher pickle there, would you? I'm crazy about kosher pickles."

Ellery offered him a slice of pickle and collapsed in his chair. "All right, damn it. Let's get it over with. Fill me in on what?"

"The background. Yesterday afternoon there was a do up in Westchester. I attended."

"A do," Ellery said, looking envious.

"Swimming. A little tennis. That sort of thing. Not many on the scene."

"Most people have the bad habit of working on weekday afternoons."

"You can't make me feel guilty with that kind of drivel," said the playboy. "I'm doing you a service. I acquired the envelope mysteriously, and I bring it to your door as instructed."

"As instructed by whom?" Ellery had still not glanced at the envelope.

"I haven't any idea. When I made my escape, I found it lying on the seat of my Jag. Someone had written on the envelope, 'Please deliver to Ellery Queen.' The way I figure it, it's someone who holds you in too much awe to make the personal approach. And who's aware of our deathless friendship."

"Sounds dreary. Look, Grant, is this something you've made up? I'm damned if I'm going to play games with you at a time like this. I've got that demon deadline breathing down my neck. Go diddle around with one of your playgirls, will you?"

"The envelope." Grant came up like an athlete and went and got it and brought it back. "Here. Duly delivered. From hand to hand. Do with it what you will."

"What am I supposed to do with it?" asked Ellery sourly.

"No idea. It's a manuscript. Handwritten. Looks quite old. Read it, I suppose."

"Then you've examined it?"

"I felt it my duty. It might have been poison-pen stuff. Even pornography. Your sensibilities, old buddy. I had to consider them."

Ellery was studying the inscription with grudging curiosity. "Written by a woman."

"I found the contents quite harmless, however," Grant went on, nursing his glass. "Harmless, but remarkable."

"A standard envelope," Ellery muttered. "Sized to accommodate eight-and-a-half by eleven sheets."

"I swear, Ellery, you have the soul of a bookkeeper. Aren't you going to open it?"

Ellery undid the clasp and pulled out a cardboard-backed notebook with the word *Journal* printed on it in a large, old-fashioned script.

"Well," he said. "It does look old."

Grant regarded him with a sly smile as Ellery opened the ledger, or notebook, studied the first page with widening eyes, turned over, read, turned over again, read again.

"My God," he said. "This purports to be an adventure of Sherlock Holmes in the original manuscript, handwritten by Dr. Watson!"

"Would you say it's authentic?"

Ellery's silvery eyes glittered. "You've read it, you say?"

"I couldn't resist."

"Are you familiar with Watson's style?"

"I," Grant said, admiring the color of the scotch in his glass, "am an *aficionado*. Sherlock Holmes, Ellery Queen, Eddie Poe. Yes, I'd say it's authentic."

"You authenticate easily, my friend." Ellery glanced at his typewriter with a frown; it seemed far away.

"I thought you'd be excited."

"I would if this were on the level. But an unknown Holmes story!" He riffled through the pages. "And, what's more, from the look of it, a novel. A lost novel!" He shook his head.

"You don't believe it."

"I stopped believing in Santa Claus at the age of three, Grant. You, you were born with Santa Claus in your mouth."

"Then you think it's a forgery."

"I don't think anything yet. But the odds that it is are astronomical."

"Why would anyone go to all this trouble?"

"For the same reason people climb mountains. For the hell of it."

"The least you can do is read the first chapter."

"Grant, I don't have the time!"

"For a new Sherlock Holmes novel?" Back at the bar Ames poured himself another scotch. "I'll sit here quietly guzzling and wait." He went back to the sofa and crossed his long legs comfortably.

"Damn you." For a long moment Ellery glared at the notebook. Then he sighed, sounding remarkably like his father, and settled back and began to read.

From the Journal of John Watson, M.D.

CHAPTER I

The Surgeon's-Kit

"You are quite right, Watson. The Ripper may well be a woman."

It was a crisp morning in the fall of the year 1888. I was no longer residing permanently at No. 221B, Baker Street. Having married, and thus become weighted with the responsibility of providing for a wife—a most delightful responsibility—I had gone into practice. Thus, the intimate relationship with my friend Mr. Sherlock Holmes had dwindled to occasional encounters.

On Holmes's side, these consisted of what he mistakenly termed "impositions upon your hospitality," when he required my services as an assistant or a confidant. "You have such a patient ear, my dear fellow," he would say, a preamble which always brought me pleasure, because it meant that I might again be privileged to share in the danger and excitement of another chase. Thus, the thread of my friendship with the great detective remained intact.

My wife, the most understanding of women, accepted this situation like Griselda. Those who have been so constant to my inadequate accounts of Mr. Sherlock Holmes's cases of detection will remember her as Mary Morstan, whom I providentially met while I was involved, with Holmes, in the case I have entitled *The Sign of Four*. As devoted a wife as any man could boast, she had patiently left me to my own devices on too many long evenings, whilst I perused my notes on Holmes's old cases.

One morning at breakfast, Mary said, "This letter is from Aunt Agatha."

I laid down my newspaper. "From Cornwall?"

"Yes, the poor dear. Spinsterhood has made her life a lonely one. Now her doctor has ordered her to bed."

"Nothing serious, I trust."

"She gave no such indication. But she is in her late seventies, and one never knows."

"Is she completely alone?"

"No. She has Beth, my old nanny, with her, and a man to tend the premises."

"A visit from her favourite niece would certainly do her more good than all the medicine in the world."

"The letter does include an invitation—a plea, really—but I hesitated . . ."

"I think you should go, Mary. A fortnight in Cornwall would benefit you also. You have been a little pale lately."

This statement of mine was entirely sincere; but another thought, a far darker one, coloured it. I venture to say that, upon that morning in 1888, every responsible man in London would have sent his wife, or sister, or sweetheart, away, had the opportunity presented itself. This, for a single, all-encompassing reason. Jack the Ripper prowled the night streets and dark alleys of the city.

Although our quiet home in Paddington was distant in many ways from the Whitechapel haunts of the maniac, who could be certain? Logic went by the boards where the dreadful monster was concerned.

Mary was thoughtfully folding the envelope. "I don't like to leave you here alone, John."

"I assure you I'll be quite all right."

"But a change would do you good, too, and there seems to be a lull in your practise."

"Are you suggesting that I accompany you?"

Mary laughed. "Good heavens, no! Cornwall would bore you to tears. Rather that you pack a bag and visit your friend Sherlock Holmes. You have a standing invitation at Baker Street, as well I know."

I am afraid my objections were feeble. Her suggestion was a most alluring one. So, with Mary off to Cornwall and arrangements relative to my practise quickly made, the transition was achieved; to Holmes's satisfaction, I flatter myself in saying, as well as to my own.

It was surprising how easily we fell into the well-remembered routine. Even though I knew I could never again be satisfied with the old life, my renewed proximity to Holmes was delightful. Which brings me, in somewhat circuitous fashion, back to Holmes's remark out of the blue. He went on, "The possibility of a female monster cannot by any means be ignored."

It was the same old cryptic business, and I must confess that I was slightly annoyed. "Holmes! In the name of all that's holy, I gave no indication whatever that such a thought was passing through my mind."

Holmes smiled, enjoying the game. "Ah, but confess, Watson. It was."

"Very well. But——"

"And you are quite wrong in saying that you gave no indication of your trend of thought."

"But I was sitting here quietly—motionless, in fact!—reading my *Times*."

"Your eyes and your head were far from motionless, Watson. As you read, your eyes were trained on the extreme left-hand column of the newspaper, that which contains an account of Jack the Ripper's latest atrocity. After a time, you turned your gaze away from the story, frowning in anger. The thought that such a monster should be able to roam London's streets with impunity was clearly evident."

"That is quite true."

"Then, my dear fellow, your eyes, seeking a resting-place, fell upon that copy of the *Strand Magazine* lying beside your chair. It happens to be open to an advertisement in which Beldell's is offering ladies' evening gowns at what they purport to be a bargain-price. One of the gowns in the advertisement is displayed upon a model. Instantly, your expression changed; it became reflective. An idea had dawned upon you. The expression persisted as you raised your head and re-directed your gaze towards the portrait of her Majesty which hangs beside the fireplace. After a moment, your expression cleared, and you nodded to yourself. You had become satisfied with the idea that had come to you. At which point, I agreed. The Ripper could well be a female."

"But, Holmes——"

"Come, now, Watson. Your retirement from the lists has dulled your perceptions."

"But when I glanced at the *Strand* advertisement, I could have had any of a dozen thoughts!"

"I disagree. Your mind was totally occupied with the story of the Ripper, and surely the advertisement concerning ladies' evening gowns was too far afield from your ordinary interests to divert your thoughts. Therefore, the idea that came to you had to be adjunct to your ponderings upon the monster. You verified this by raising your eyes to the Queen's portrait upon the wall."

"May I ask how that indicated my thought?" asked I, tartly.

"Watson! You certainly saw neither the model nor our gracious Queen as suspects. Therefore, you were scrutinising them as women."

"Granted," I retorted, "but would I not have been more likely to regard them as victims?"

"In that case, your expression would have reflected compassion, rather than that of a bloodhound come suddenly upon the scent."

I was forced to confess defeat. "Holmes, again you destroy yourself by your own volubility."

Holmes's heavy brows drew together. "I do not follow."

"Imagine what an image you would create were you to refuse all explanation of your amazing deductions!"

"But at what expense," said he, drily, "to your melodramatic accounts of my trifling adventures."

I threw up my hands in surrender; and Holmes, who rarely indulged in more than a smile, on this occasion echoed my hearty laughter.

"So long as the subject of Jack the Ripper has arisen," said I, "allow me a further question. Why have you not interested yourself in the grisly affair, Holmes? If for no other reason, it would be a signal service to the people of London."

Holmes's long, thin fingers made an impatient gesture. "I have been busy. As you know, I returned from the Continent only recently, where the mayor of a certain city retained me to solve a most curious riddle. Knowing your turn of mind, I presume you would call it *The Case of the Legless Cyclist*. One day I shall give you the details for your files."

"I shall be delighted to get them! But you *are* back in London, Holmes, and this monster is terrorising the city. I should think you would feel obligated——"

Holmes scowled. "I am obligated to no one."

"Pray do not misunderstand me——"

"I'm sorry, my dear Watson, but you should know me well enough to assume my total indifference towards such a case."

"At the risk of appearing more dense than most of my neighbours——"

"Consider! When given a choice, have I not always sought out problems of an intellectual character? Have I not always been drawn to adversaries of stature? Jack the Ripper, indeed! What possible challenge could this demented oaf present? A slavering cretin roaming the streets after dark, striking at random."

"He has baffled the London Police."

"I venture to suggest that that may reflect the short-comings of Scotland Yard rather than any particular cleverness on the part of the Ripper."

"But still——"

"The thing will end soon enough. I daresay that one of these nights Lestrade will trip over the Ripper while the maniac is in the process of committing a murder, and thus bring him triumphantly to book."

Holmes was chronically annoyed with Scotland Yard for not measuring up to his own stern efficiency; for all his genius, he could be childishly obstinate on such occasions. But further comment from me was cut off by the ringing of the downstairs bell. There was a slight delay; then we heard Mrs. Hudson ascending, and it was with astonishment that I observed her entrance. She was carrying a brown parcel and a pail of water, and she wore an expression of sheer fright.

Holmes burst out laughing for the second time that morning. "It's quite all right, Mrs. Hudson. The package appears harmless enough. I'm sure we shall not need the water."

Mrs. Hudson breathed a sigh of relief. "If you say so, Mr. Holmes. But since that last experience, I was taking no chances."

"And your alertness is to be commended," said Holmes, as he took the parcel. After his long-suffering landlady left, he added, "Just recently, Mrs. Hudson brought me a parcel. It was in connection with an unpleasant little affair I brought to a satisfactory conclusion, and it was sent by a vengeful gentleman who under-estimated the keenness of my hearing. The ticking of the mechanism was quite audible to me, and I called for a pail of water. The incident gave Mrs. Hudson a turn from which she has still not recovered."

"I don't wonder!"

"But what have we here? Hmmm. Approximately fifteen inches by six. Four inches thick. Neatly wrapped in ordinary brown paper. Post-mark, Whitechapel. The name and address written by a woman, I should hazard, who seldom puts pen to paper."

"That seems quite likely, from the clumsy scrawl. And that is certainly done in a woman's hand."

"Then we agree, Watson. Excellent! Shall we delve deeper?"

"By all means!"

The arrival of the parcel had aroused his interest, not to mention mine; his deep-set grey eyes grew bright when he removed the wrappings and drew forth a flat leather case. He held it up for my inspection. "Well, now. What do you make of this, Watson?"

"It is a surgeon's instrument-case."

"And who would be better qualified to know? Would you not say also that it is expensive?"

"Yes. The leather is of superb quality. And the workmanship is exquisite."

Holmes set the case upon the table. He opened it, and we fell silent. It was a standard set of instruments, each fitting snugly into its appropriate niche in the crimson-velvet lining of the case. One niche was empty.

"Which instrument is missing, Watson?"

"The large scalpel."

"The post-mortem knife," said Holmes, nodding and whipping out his lens. "And now, what does this case tell us?" As he examined the case and its contents closely, he went on. "To begin with the obvious, these instruments belonged to a medical man who came upon hard times."

Obliged, as usual, to confess my blindness, I said, "I am afraid that is more obvious to you than to me."

Preoccupied with his inspection, Holmes replied absently, "If you should fall victim to misfortune, Watson, which would be the last of your possessions to reach the pawn-broker's shop?"

"My medical instruments, of course. But——"

"Precisely."

"Wherein do you perceive that this case was pledged?"

"There is double proof. Observe, just there, through my lens."

I peered at the spot he indicated. "A white smudge."

"Silver-polish. No surgeon would cleanse his instruments with such a substance. These have been treated like common cutlery by someone concerned only with their appearance."

"Now that you point it out, Holmes, I must agree. And what is your second proof?"

"These chalk-marks along the spine of the case. They are almost worn away, but if you will examine them closely, you will see that they constitute a number. Such a number as a pawn-broker would chalk upon a pledged article. Obviously, the counterpart of the number upon the pawn-ticket."

I felt the choler rising to my face. It was all too evident to me now.

"Then the kit was stolen!" I exclaimed. "Stolen from some surgeon, and disposed of, for a pittance, in a pawn-shop!" My readers will forgive my indignation, I am sure; it was difficult for me to accept the alternative—that the practitioner would have parted with the instruments of a noble calling under even the most grievous circumstances.

Holmes, however, soon disillusioned me. "I fear, my dear Watson," said he, quite cheerfully, "that you do not perceive the finer aspects of the evidence. Pawn-brokers are a canny breed. It is part of their stock-in-trade not only to appraise the articles brought to them for pledge, but the persons offering them as well.

Had the broker who dispensed his *largesse* for this surgical-case entertained the slightest suspicion that it had been stolen, he would not have displayed it in his shop-window, as of course you observe he has done."

"As of course I do not!" said I, testily. "How can you possibly know that the case has been displayed in a window?"

"Look closely," said Holmes. "The case lay open in a place exposed to the sun; does not the faded velvet on the inner surface of the lid tell us that? Moreover, the pronounced character of the fading marks the time-span as an appreciable one. Surely this adds up to a shop-window?"

I could only nod. As always, when Holmes explained his astonishing observations, they appeared child's-play.

"It is a pity," said I, "that we do not know where the pawn-shop lies. This curious gift might merit a visit to its source."

"Perhaps in good time, Watson," said Holmes, with a dry chuckle. "The pawn-shop in question is well off the beaten track. It faces south, on a narrow street. The broker's business is not flourishing. Also, he is of foreign extraction. Surely you see that?"

"I see nothing of the sort!" said I, nettled again.

"To the contrary," said he, placing his finger-tips together and regarding me kindly, "you see everything, my dear Watson; what you fail to do is to observe. Let us take my conclusions in order. These instruments were not snatched up by any of the numerous medical students in the City of London, which would assuredly have been the case had the shop lain on a well-travelled thoroughfare. Hence my remark that it lies off the beaten track."

"But must it lie on the south side of a narrow street?"

"Note the location of the bleached area. It runs neatly along the uppermost edge of the velvet lining, not elsewhere. Therefore, the sun touched the open case only at its zenith, when its rays were not obstructed by the buildings on the opposite side of the street. Thus the pawn-shop stands on the south side of a narrow street."

"And your identification of the pawn-broker as of foreign extraction?"

"Observe the numeral *seven* in the chalked pledge-mark on the spine. There is a short cross-mark on the ascender. Only a foreigner crosses his sevens in such a fashion."

I felt, as usual, like the fifth-form school-boy who had forgotten the words to the national anthem. "Holmes, Holmes," said I, shaking my head, "I shall never cease to marvel——"

But he was not listening. Again, he had stooped over the case, inserting his tweezers beneath the velvet lining. It gave way, and he peeled it off.

"Aha! What have we here? An attempt at concealment?"

"Concealment? Of what? Stains? Scratches?"

He pointed a long, thin finger. "That."

"Why, it's a coat of arms!"

"One with which I confess I am not familiar. Therefore, Watson, be kind enough to hand down my copy of *Burke's Peerage*."

He continued to study the crest as I moved dutifully towards the book-shelves, murmuring to himself. "Stamped into the leather of the case. The surface is still in excellent condition." He came erect. "A clew to the character of the man who owned the case."

"He was careful with his possessions, perhaps?"

"Perhaps. But I was referring to——"

He broke off. I had handed him the Burke, and he leafed swiftly through the pages. "Ah, here we have it!" After a quick scrutiny, Holmes closed the book, laid it on the table, and dropped into a chair. He stared intently into space with his piercing eyes.

I could contain my patience no longer. "The crest, Holmes! Whose is it?"

"I beg your pardon, Watson," said Holmes, coming to with a start. "Shires. Kenneth Osbourne, the Duke of Shires."

The name was well-known to me, as indeed to all England. "An illustrious line."

Holmes nodded absently. "The estates, unless I mistake, lie in Devonshire, hard by the moors, among hunting-lands well-regarded by noble sportsmen. The manor house—it is more of a feudal castle in appearance—is some four hundred years old, a classic example of Gothic architecture. I know little of the Shires history, beyond the patent fact that the name has never been connected with the world of crime."

"So, Holmes," said I, "we are back to the original question."

"Indeed we are."

"Which is: this surgeon's-case—why was it sent to you?"

"A provocative question."

"Perhaps an explanatory letter was delayed."

"You may well have hit upon the answer, Watson," said Holmes. "Therefore, I suggest we give the sender a little time, let us say until"—he paused to reach for his well-worn Bradshaw's, that admirable guide to British rail movements—"until ten-thirty to-morrow morning. If an explanation is not then forthcoming, we shall repair to Paddington Station and board the Devonshire express."

"For what reason, Holmes?"

"For two reasons. A short journey across the English countryside, with its changing colours at this time of year, should greatly refresh two stodgy Londoners."

"And the other?"

The austere face broke into the most curious smile. "In all justice," said my friend Holmes, "the Duke of Shires should have his property returned to him, should he not?" And he sprang to his feet and seized his violin.

"Wait, Holmes!" said I. "There is something in this you have not told me."

"No, no, my dear Watson," said he, drawing his bow briskly across the strings. "It is simply a feeling I have, that we are about to embark upon deep waters."

Ellery Continues

Ellery raised his eyes from the manuscript. Grant Ames III was at the scotch again.

"You will be cut down eventually," Ellery said, "by a pickled liver."

"Killjoy," Ames said. "But at the moment I feel myself a part of history, son. An actor under the Great Proscenium."

"Drinking himself to death?"

"Bluenose. I'm talking of the manuscript. In the year 1888 Sherlock Holmes received a mysterious surgeon's kit. He trained his marvelous talents on it and began one of his marvelous adventures. Three-quarters of a century later, another package is delivered to another famous detective."

"What's your point?" grumbled Ellery, visibly torn between Dr. Watson's manuscript and the empty typewriter.

"All that remains to complete the historic re-run is to train the modern talent on the modern adventure. Proceed, my dear Ellery. I'll function as Watson."

Ellery squirmed.

"Of course, you may challenge my *bona fides*. In substantiation, I point out that I have followed the Master's career faithfully."

That pierced the fog. Ellery studied his guest distastefully. "Really? All right, wise guy. Quote: 'It was in the spring of the year 1894 and all London was interested, and the fashionable world dismayed, by the murder of the——'?"

"'——Honourable Ronald Adair.' Unquote," said Ames promptly. "*The Adventure of the Empty House*, from *The Return of Sherlock Holmes*."

"Quote: 'She had drawn a little gleaming revolver and emptied barrel after barrel into——'"

"'——Milverton's body, the muzzle within two feet of his shirt-front.' Unquote. *The Adventure of Charles Augustus Milverton*."

"You scintillate, Watson! Quote: 'These are the trodden, but not the downtrodden. These are the lowly, but never the low.'"

"Unquote." The playboy yawned. "Your efforts to trap me are childish, my dear Ellery. You quoted yourself, from *The Player on the Other Side*."

Ellery scowled at him. The fellow was not all overstuffed blondes and expensive scotch. "*Touché, touché*. Now let's see—I'm sure I can stick you——"

"I'm sure you can if you stall long enough, but that's exactly what I'm not going to let you do. Go into your act, Mr. Queen. You've read the first chapter of the manuscript. If you don't come up with some Queenian deductions, I'll never borrow a book of yours again."

"All I can tell you at the moment is that the hand-writing purporting to be Watson's is precise, firm, and a little crabbed."

"You don't sound like Holmes to me, old buddy. The question is, *is* it Watson's? Is the manuscript the McCoy? Come, come, Queen! Apply your powers."

"Oh, shut up," Ellery said, and he went on reading.

CHAPTER II

The Castle on the Moor

In his latter life, as I have recorded elsewhere, my friend Sherlock Holmes retired from the feverish pace of London to keep bees, of all things, on the South Downs. He thus terminated his career with no regret whatever, turning to that husbandman's activity with the same single-mindedness that had enabled him to track down so many of the world's cleverest criminals.

But at the time Jack the Ripper stalked London's streets and by-ways, Holmes was a whole-hearted creature of urban life. His every faculty was keyed to the uncertainties of London's dawns and dusks. The sinister stench of a Soho alley could set his nostrils a-quiver, whilst the scent of spring stirring a rural countryside might well put him a-dozing.

It was therefore with surprise and pleasure that I witnessed his interest in the passing scene as the express hurtled us towards Devonshire that morning. He gazed through the window with a concentrated air, then suddenly straightened his thin shoulders.

"Ah, Watson! The sharp air of approaching winter. It is invigorating."

I for one found it not so at the moment, an atrocious cigar between the teeth of a dour old Scot, who had boarded with us, befouling the compartment. But Holmes seemed not to notice the reek. Outside, the leaves were turning, and flashes of autumnal colour streamed past.

"This England, Watson. This other Eden, demi-Paradise."

I recognised the near-quotation and was doubly surprised. I knew, certainly, of the sentimental streak in my friend, but he rarely allowed it to show through the fabric of his scientific nature. Yet, pride of birth-right in the Briton is a national trait, and Holmes had not escaped it.

As our journey neared its destination, his cheerful mien vanished; he became pensive. We were on the moors, those broad stretches of mire and morass that cling like a great scab to England's face. As if Nature insisted upon a proper setting, the sun had vanished behind thick cloud-banks, and we seemed to have been plunged into a place of eternal twilight.

We soon found ourselves upon the platform of a small country station, where Holmes thrust his hands deep into his pockets, his deep-set eyes kindled, as they so often did when he was beset by a problem.

"Do you recall the affair of the Baskervilles, Watson, and the curse that darkened their lives?"

"Well do I!"

"We are not far from their holdings. But of course we go in the opposite direction."

"And just as well. That hound of Hell still haunts my dreams."

I was puzzled. Ordinarily, when Holmes was involved in a case, he viewed his surroundings single-mindedly, sharply aware of a bruised twig while remaining oblivious of the landscape in which it lay. At such times, reminiscence was no part of it. Now he stirred restlessly, as though he regretted having allowed impulse to send him upon our journey.

"Watson," said he, "let us arrange for the rental of a dog-cart, and get this business over with."

The pony we procured no doubt had relations among the ones that ran wild on the moors, but the little beast was tractable enough, and it clipped steadily away at the road between the village and the Shires land-hold.

After a time, the turrets of Shires Castle came into view, adding their tone of melancholy to the scene.

"The game-preserves are beyond," said Holmes. "The Duke has a variegated terrain." He scanned the country before us and added, "I doubt, Watson, that we shall find a jolly, red-cheeked host in that forbidding pile."

"Why do you say that?"

"People of long blood-lines tend to reflect the colour of their surroundings. You will recall that there was not a single cheerful face at Baskerville Hall."

I did not dispute this, my attention being fixed upon the scowling grey of Shires Castle. It had once been complete with moat and draw-bridge. However, more modern generations had come to depend for defence of life and limb upon the local constabulary. The moat had been filled in, and the bridge-chains had not creaked for many a year.

We were ushered into a cold and cavernous drawing-room by a butler who took our names like Charon checking our passage across the Styx. I soon learned that Holmes's prediction had been accurate. The Duke of Shires was as icily forbidding a man as ever I had met.

He was of slight stature and gave the impression of being phthisical. It was an illusion. Upon closer inspection I saw a well-blooded face, and I sensed a wiry strength in his frail-appearing body.

The Duke did not invite us to be seated. Instead, he stated abruptly, "You were fortunate in finding me here. Another hour, and I should have been on my way to London. I spend little time here in the country. What is your business?"

Holmes's tone in no way reflected the ill-manners of the nobleman. "We will intrude upon your time no longer than is necessary, your Grace. We came merely to bring you this."

He proffered the surgeon's-kit, which we had wrapped in plain brown paper and secured with sealing-wax.

"What is it?" said the Duke, not stirring.

"I suggest, your Grace," replied Holmes, "that you open it and discover for yourself."

With a frown, the Duke of Shires stripped off the wrappings. "Where did you get this?"

"I regret that I must first ask your Grace to identify it as your property."

"I have never seen it before. What earthly reason had you for bringing it to me?" The Duke had raised the lid and was staring at the instruments with what certainly appeared to be genuine bewilderment.

"If you will draw down the lining, you will find our reason imprinted upon the leather underneath."

The Duke followed Holmes's suggestion, still frowning. I was watching closely as he stared at the coat of arms, and it was my turn to feel bewilderment. His expression changed. The palest of smiles touched his thin lips, his eyes brightened, and he regarded the case with a look I can only describe as one of intense satisfaction, almost of triumph. Then, as quickly, the look vanished.

I glanced at Holmes in search of some explanation, knowing that he would not have missed the nobleman's reaction. But the sharp eyes were hooded, the familiar face a mask. "I am sure your Grace's question is now answered," said Holmes.

"Of course," replied the Duke in casual tones, as though brushing the matter aside as of no consequence. "The case does not belong to me."

"Then perhaps your Grace could direct us to the owner?"

"My son, I presume. It no doubt belonged to Michael."

"It came from a London pawn-shop."

The Duke's lips curled in a cruel sneer. "I do not doubt it."

"Then if you will give us your son's address——"

"The son I refer to, Mr. Holmes, is *dead*. My younger, sir."

Holmes spoke gently. "I am indeed sorry to hear that, your Grace. Did he succumb to an illness?"

"A very great illness. He has been *dead* for six months."

The emphasis put by the nobleman upon the word "dead" struck me as odd. "Was your son a physician?" I inquired.

"He studied for the profession, but he failed at it, as he failed at everything. Then he *died*."

Again that strange emphasis. I glanced at Holmes, but he seemed more interested in the ponderous furnishings of the vaulted room, his glance darting here and there, his thin, muscular hands clasped behind his back.

The Duke of Shires held forth the case. "As this is not my property, sir, I return it to you. And now, if you will excuse me, I must prepare for my journey."

I was puzzled by Holmes's behaviour. He had accepted the Duke's cavalier treatment without rancour. Holmes was not in the habit of allowing people to walk over him with hob-nail boots. His bow was deferential as he said, "We shall detain you no longer, your Grace."

The Duke's rude behaviour was consistent. He made no move to reach for the bell-rope that would have summoned the butler. Thus, we were compelled to find our way out as best we could, under his stare.

This proved a stroke of good fortune. We were crossing the baronial hall towards the outer portal, when two persons appeared through a side-entrance, a man and a child.

In contrast to the Duke, they did not seem at all hostile.

The child, a girl of nine or ten years of age, smiled as brightly as her little pallid face would permit. The man, like the Duke, was of slender build. His quick, liquid eyes, although they questioned, were merely curious. His dark resemblance to the Duke of Shires left room for but one conclusion. This was the other son.

It did not seem to me that their arrival was particularly startling, but it appeared to disconcert my friend Holmes. He came to a jerky halt, and the surgeon's-kit that he was carrying fell to the floor with a clatter of steel against stone that echoed through the great hall.

"How clumsy of me!" he exclaimed, and then proceeded to be even clumsier by blocking me off as I attempted to retrieve the instruments.

The man, with a smile, sprang into the breach. "Allow me, sir," said he, and went to his knees.

The child reacted almost as quickly. "Let me help you, Papa."

The man's smile glowed. "So you shall, my dear. We'll help the gentleman together. You may hand me the instruments. But carefully, lest you cut yourself."

We watched in silence as the little girl handed the shining implements to her father, one by one. His affection for her was touchingly apparent, his dark eyes hardly bearing to leave her as he swiftly returned the instruments to their proper niches.

When the business was finished, the man arose. But the little girl continued to scan the flag-stones upon which we stood. "The last one, Papa. Where did it go?"

"It appears to have been missing, dearest. I don't think it fell from the case." He glanced questioningly at Holmes, who came out of the brown study into which he contrived to have fallen.

"Indeed it was missing, sir. Thank you, and pardon my clumsiness."

"No harm done. I trust the instruments were not damaged." He handed the case to Holmes, who took it with a smile.

"Have I, perchance, the honour of addressing Lord Carfax?"

"Yes," the dark man said, pleasantly. "This is my daughter, Deborah."

"Allow me to present my colleague, Dr. Watson; I am Sherlock Holmes."

The name seemed to impress Lord Carfax; his eyes widened in surprise. "Dr. Watson," he murmured in acknowledgement, but his eyes remained on Holmes. "And you, sir—I am honoured indeed. I have read of your exploits."

"Your Lordship is too kind," replied Holmes.

Deborah's eyes sparkled. She curtsied and said, "I am honoured to meet you, too, sirs." She spoke with a sweetness that was touching. Lord Carfax looked on proudly. Yet I sensed a sadness in his manner.

"Deborah," said he, gravely, "you must mark this as an event in your life, the day you met two famous gentlemen."

"Indeed I shall, Papa," replied the little girl, solemnly dutiful. She had heard of neither of us, I was quite certain.

Holmes concluded the amenities by saying, "We called, your Lordship, to return this case to the Duke of Shires, whom I believed to be its rightful owner."

"And you discovered that you were in error."

"Quite. His Grace thought that it had possibly belonged to your deceased brother, Michael Osbourne."

"Deceased?" It was more of a tired comment than a question.

"That was what we were given to understand."

Sadness appeared clearly in Lord Carfax's face. "That may or may not be true. My father, Mr. Holmes, is a stern and unforgiving man, which you no doubt surmised. To him, the good name of Osbourne stands above all else. Keeping the Shires escutcheon free of blemish is a passion with him. When he disowned my younger brother some six months ago, he pronounced Michael dead." He paused to sigh. "I fear Michael will remain dead, so far as Father is concerned, even though he may still live."

"Are you yourself aware," asked Holmes, "whether your brother is alive or dead?"

Lord Carfax frowned, looking remarkably like the Duke. When he spoke, I thought I detected evasiveness in his voice. "Let me say, sir, that I have no actual proof of his death."

"I see," replied Holmes. Then he looked down at Deborah Osbourne and smiled. The little girl came forward and put her hand into his.

"I like you very much, sir," said she, gravely.

It was a charming moment. Holmes appeared embarrassed by this open-hearted confession. Her small hand remained in his as he said, "Granted, Lord Carfax, that your father is an unbending man. Still, to disown a son! A decision such as that is not made lightly. Your brother's transgression must indeed have been a serious one."

"Michael married against my father's wishes." Lord Carfax shrugged his shoulders. "I am not in the habit, Mr. Holmes, of discussing my family's affairs with strangers, but"—and he touched his daughter's shining head—"Deborah is my barometer of character." I thought his Lordship was going to ask what Holmes's interest in Michael Osbourne was based upon, but he did not.

Holmes, too, appeared to have expected such a question. When it did not come, he extended the surgical-case. "Perhaps you would like to have this, your Lordship."

Lord Carfax took the case with a silent bow.

"And now—our train will not wait, I fear—we must be off." Holmes looked down from his great height. "Good-bye, Deborah. Meeting you is the most agreeable thing that has happened to Dr. Watson and me in a very long time."

"I hope you will come again, sir," replied the child. "It gets so lonely here when Papa is away."

Holmes said little as we drove back to the village. He scarcely replied to my comments, and it was not until we were flying back towards London that he invited conversation. His lean features set in that abstracted look I knew so well, he said, "An interesting man, Watson."

"Perhaps," I replied, tartly. "But also as repulsive a one as ever I care to meet. It is men of his calibre—they are few, thank heaven!—who stain the reputation of the British nobility."

My indignation amused Holmes. "I was referring to *filius* rather than *pater*."

"The son? I was touched by Lord Carfax's evident love for his daughter, of course——"

"But you felt he was too informative?"

"That was exactly my impression, Holmes, although I don't see how you became aware of it. I did not enter into the conversation."

"Your face is like a mirror, my dear Watson," said he.

"Even he admitted that he talked too freely about his family's personal affairs."

"But did he? Let us assume him, first, to be a stupid man. In that case he becomes a loving father with an overly-large oral cavity."

"But if we assume him, with more difficulty, to be not stupid at all?"

"Then he created precisely the image he wished to, which I incline to believe. He knew me by name and reputation, and you, Watson. I strongly doubt that he accepted us as mere Good Samaritans, come all this way to restore an old surgeon's-kit to its rightful owner."

"Should that necessarily loose his tongue?"

"My dear fellow, he told us nothing that I did not already know, or could not have discovered with ease in the files of any London daily."

"Then what was it that he did not reveal?"

"Whether his brother Michael is dead or alive. Whether he is in contact with his brother."

"I assumed, from what he said, that he does not know."

"That, Watson, may have been what he wished you to assume." Before I could reply, Holmes went on. "As it happens, I did not go to Shires uninformed. Kenneth Osbourne, the lineal Duke, had two sons. Michael, the younger, of course inherited no title. Whether or not this instilled jealousy in him I do not know, but he so conducted himself thenceforward as to earn the sobriquet, from the journalists of London, of The Wild One. You spoke of his father's brutal sternness, Watson. To the contrary, the record reveals the Duke as having been amazingly lenient with his younger son. The boy finally tried his father's patience too far when he married a woman of the oldest profession; in fine, a prostitute."

"I begin to see," muttered I. "Out of spite, or hatred, to besmirch the title he could not inherit."

"Perhaps," said Holmes. "In any case, it would have been difficult for the Duke to assume otherwise."

"I did not know," said I, humbly.

"It is human, my dear Watson, to side with the under-dog. But it is wise to discover beforehand exactly who the under-dog is. In the case of the Duke, I grant that he is a difficult man, but he bears a cross."

I replied, with some despair, "Then I suppose my evaluation of Lord Carfax is faulty, also."

"I do not know, Watson. We have very little data. However, he did fail on two counts."

"I was not aware of it."

"Nor was he."

My mind was centred upon a broader prospect. "Holmes," said I, "this whole affair is curiously unsatisfactory. Surely this journey was not motivated by a simple desire on your part to restore lost property?"

He gazed out the carriage-window. "The surgeon's-kit was delivered to our door. I doubt we were mistaken for a lost-and-found bureau."

"But by whom was it sent?"

"By someone who wished us to have it."

"Then we can only wait."

"Watson, to say that I smell a devious purpose here is no doubt fanciful. But the stench is strong. Perhaps you will get your wish."

"My wish?"

"I believe you recently suggested that I give the Yard some assistance in the case of Jack the Ripper."

"Holmes——!"

"Of course there is no evidence to connect the Ripper with the surgeon's-kit. But the post-mortem knife is missing."

"The implication has not escaped me. Why, this very night it may be plunged into the body of some unfortunate!"

"A possibility, Watson. The removal of the scalpel may have been symbolical, a subtle allusion to the fiendish stalker."

"Why did the sender not come forward?"

"There could be any number of reasons. I should put fear high on the list. In time, I think, we shall know the truth."

Holmes lapsed into the preoccupation I knew so well. Further probing on my part, I knew, would have been useless. I sat back and stared gloomily out the window as the train sped towards Paddington.

Ellery Tries

Ellery looked up from the notebook.

Grant Ames, finishing his nth drink, asked eagerly, "Well?"

Ellery got up and went to a bookshelf, frowning. He took a book down and searched for something while Grant waited. He returned the book to the shelf and came back.

"Christianson's."

Grant looked blank.

"According to the reference there, Christianson's was a well-known stationery manufacturer of the period. Their watermark is on the paper of the notebook."

"That does it, then!"

"Not necessarily. Anyway, there's no point in trying to authenticate the manuscript. If someone's trying to sell it to me, I'm not buying. If it's genuine, I can't afford it. If it's a phony——"

"I don't think that was the idea, old boy."

"Then what was the idea?"

"How should I know? I suppose someone wants you to read it."

Ellery pulled his nose fretfully. "You're sure it was put into your car at that party?"

"Had to be."

"And it was addressed by a woman. How many women were there?"

Grant counted on his fingers. "Four."

"Any bookworms? Collectors? Librarians? Little old ladies smelling of lavender sachet and must?"

"Hell, no. Four slick young chicks trying to look seductive. After a husband. Frankly, Ellery, I can't conceive one of them knowing Sherlock Holmes from Aristophanes. But with your kooky talents, you could stalk the culprit in an afternoon."

"Look, Grant, any other time and I'd play the game. But I told you. I'm in one of my periodic binds. I simply haven't the time."

"Then it ends here, Maestro? For God's sake, man, what are you, a hack? Here I toss a delicious mystery into your lap——"

"And I," said Ellery, firmly placing the notebook in Grant Ames's lap, "toss it right back to you. I have a suggestion. *You* rush out, glass in hand, and track down your lady joker."

"I might at that," whined the millionaire.

"Fine. Let me know."

"The manuscript didn't grip you?"

"Of course it does." Reluctantly, Ellery picked up the journal and riffled through it.

"That's my old buddy!" Ames rose. "Why don't I leave it here? After all, it is addressed to you. I could report back at intervals——"

"Make it long intervals."

"Mine host. All right, I'll bother you as little as I can."

"Less, if possible. And now will you beat it, Grant? I'm serious."

"What you are, friend, is grim. No fun at all." Ames turned in the doorway. "Oh, by the way, order some more scotch. You've run out."

When he was alone again, Ellery stood indecisively. Finally he put the notebook down on the sofa and went to his desk. He stared at the keys. The keys stared back. He shifted in his swivel chair; his bottom was itching. He pulled the chair closer. He pulled his nose again.

The notebook lay quietly on the sofa.

Ellery ran a sheet of blank paper into the machine. He raised his hands, flexed his fingers, thought, and began to type.

He typed rapidly, stopped, and read what he had written:

"The Lord," said Nikki, *"choves a leerful giver."*

"All *right*!" said Ellery. "Just one more chapter!"

He jumped up and ran over to the sofa and grabbed the notebook and opened it and began to devour Chapter III.

CHAPTER III

Whitechapel

"By the way, Holmes, whatever became of Wiggins?" I asked the question late the following morning in the rooms at Baker Street.

We had had a buffet supper the previous evening at the station after our return from Shires Castle, whereupon Holmes had said, "The young American pianist, Benton, plays at Albert Hall tonight. I recommend him highly, Watson."

"I was not aware that the States had produced any great pianoforte talents."

Holmes had laughed. "Come, come, my dear fellow! Let the Americans go. It has been more than a century now, and they have been doing quite well over there."

"You wish me to accompany you? I should be delighted."

"I was suggesting the concert for your evening. I have a few investigations in mind which are better made at night."

"In that case, I prefer the easy-chair by the fire and one of your fascinating books."

"I recommend one I recently acquired, *Uncle Tom's Cabin,* by an American lady named Stowe. A lugubrious work, meant to stir the nation to correct a great injustice. It was, I believe, one of the causes of the War Between the States. Well, I must be off. Perhaps I shall join you in a night-cap later."

Holmes, however, returned very late, after I was abed. He did not awaken me, so that our next meeting was at breakfast. I hoped for an account of his night's work, but none was forthcoming. Nor did he appear to be in haste to get on with things, lounging lazily in his mouse-coloured dressing-gown over his tea and clouding the room with heavy exhalations from his beloved clay pipe.

Came a sudden clatter upon the stairs, and there rushed into the room a dozen of the dirtiest, most ragged urchins in all London. They were Holmes's incredible band of street Arabs, whom he called variously "the Baker Street division of the detective police force," his "unofficial force," and "the Baker Street irregulars."

" 'Tention!" snapped Holmes; and the urchins struggled into a ragged line and presented their begrimed little faces in what they evidently took to be a military posture.

"Now, have you found it?"

"Yes, sir, we 'ave," replied one of the band.

"It was me, sir!" cut in another eagerly as he grinned, showing gaps where three teeth were wanting.

"Very good," said Holmes, sternly, "but we work as a unit. No individual glory, men. One for all and all for one."

"Yes, *sir*," came the chorus.

"The report?"

"It's in Whitechapel."

"Ah!"

"On Great Heapton Street, near the pass-over. The street is narrow there, sir."

"Very good," said Holmes again. "Here is your pay. Now be off with you."

He gave each urchin a shining shilling. They clattered happily away, as they had come, and we soon heard their shrill young voices from below.

Now Holmes knocked the dottle from his pipe. "Wiggins? Oh, he did very well. Joined her Majesty's forces. My last note from him was post-marked Africa."

"He was a sharp youngster, as I recall."

"So are they all. And London's supply of the little beggars never diminishes. But I have an inquiry to make. Let us be off."

It took no feat of intellect to predict our destination. So I was not surprised when we stood before a pawn-shop window on Great Heapton, in Whitechapel. The street, as Holmes had deduced and the urchins confirmed, was narrow, with high buildings on the side opposite the shop. When we arrived, the sun was just cutting a line across the glass, the inscription upon which read: *Joseph Beck— Loans.*

Holmes pointed to the display in the window. "The kit sat there, Watson. Do you see where the sun strikes?"

I could only nod my head. Accustomed though I was to the unerring keenness of his judgements, the proof never ceased to amaze me.

Inside the shop, we were greeted by a pudgy man of middle-age whose moustaches were heavily waxed and drilled into military points. Joseph Beck was the archetype of German tradesmen, and his efforts to produce a Prussian effect were ludicrous.

"May I be of service, sirs?" His English was thickly accented.

I presume, in that neighbourhood, we were a cut above his usual run of clients; possibly he hoped to acquire a pledge of high value. He actually clicked his heels and came to attention.

"A friend," said Holmes, "recently made me a gift, a surgeon's-case purchased in your shop."

Herr Beck's protuberant little eyes turned sly. "Yes?"

"But one of the instruments was missing from the case. I should like to complete the set. Do you have some surgical instruments from which I might select the missing one?"

"I am afraid, sir, I cannot help you." The pawn-broker was clearly disappointed.

"Do you recall the set I refer to, the transaction?"

"*Ach,* yes, sir. It took place a week ago, and I get very few such articles. But the set was complete when the woman redeemed it and carried it away. Did she tell you one instrument was missing?"

"I do not recall," Holmes said, in an off-hand manner. "The point is that you cannot help me now."

"I am sorry, sir. I have no surgical instruments of any description."

Holmes pretended petulance. "All the way down here for nothing! You have caused me great inconvenience, Beck."

The man looked astonished. "You are being unreasonable, sir. I do not see how I am responsible for what occurred after the case left my shop."

Holmes shrugged his shoulders. "I suppose not," said he, carelessly. "But it is a nuisance. I came a long distance."

"But, sir, if you had inquired of the poor creature who redeemed the set——"

"The poor creature? I don't understand."

The severity of Holmes's tone frightened the man. With the tradesman's instinct to please, he hastened to apologise. "Forgive me, sir. My heart went out to the woman. In fact, I let her have the case at a too generous price. Her terribly disfigured face has haunted me."

"Ah," murmured Holmes. "I see." He was turning away in clever disappointment when his hawk's-face brightened. "A thought occurs to me. The man who originally pledged the case—if I could get in touch with him . . ."

"I doubt it, sir. It was some time ago."

"How long?"

"I would have to consult my ledger."

Frowning, he produced a ledger from underneath the counter and thumbed through it. "Here it is. Why, it has been almost four months. How time flies!"

"Quite," agreed Holmes, drily. "You have the name and address of the man?"

"It was not a man, sir. It was a lady."

Holmes and I glanced at each other. "I see," said Holmes. "Well, even after four months, it might still be worth an effort. What is her name, pray?"

The pawn-broker peered at his ledger. "Young. Miss Sally Young."

"Her address?"

"The Montague Street Hostel."

"Odd place of residence," I ventured.

"Yes, *mein Herr*. It is in the heart of Whitechapel. A dangerous place these days."

"Indeed it is. Good-day to you," said Holmes, civilly. "You have been most accommodating."

As we walked away from the pawn-shop, Holmes laughed softly. "A type who must be adroitly handled, this Joseph Beck. One can lead him great distances, but he cannot be pushed an inch."

"I thought he coöperated handsomely."

"Indeed he did. But the least odour of officialdom in our inquiry and we should not have pried the time of day out of him."

"Your theory that the scalpel was removed as a symbolical gesture, Holmes, has been proved correct."

"Perhaps, though the fact is of no great value. But now, a visit to the Montague

Street Hostel and Miss Sally Young seems in order. I'm sure you have formed opinions as to the stations of the two females we are seeking?"

"Of course. The one who pawned the set was clearly in straitened financial circumstances."

"A possibility, Watson, though far from a certainty."

"If not, why did she pledge the set?"

"I am inclined to think it was a service she rendered a second party. Someone who was unable or did not care to appear personally at the pawn-shop. A surgeon's-kit is hardly an article one would expect to find a lady owning. And as to the woman who redeemed the pledge?"

"We know nothing of her except that she sustained some injury to the face. Perhaps she is a victim of the Ripper, who escaped death at his hands?"

"Capital, Watson! An admirable hypothesis. However, the point that struck me involves something a little different. You will remember that Herr Beck referred to the one who redeemed the case as a *woman,* while he spoke in a more respectful tone of the pledger as a *lady.* Hence, we are safe in assuming that Miss Sally Young is a person to command some respect."

"Of course, Holmes. The implications, I am frank to admit, escaped me."

"The redeemer is no doubt of a lower order. She could well be a prostitute. Certainly this neighbourhood abounds with such unfortunates."

Montague Street lay at no great distance; it was less than a twenty-minute walk from the pawn-shop. It proved to be a short thoroughfare connecting Purdy Court and Olmstead Circus, the latter being well-known as a refuge for London's swarms of beggars. We turned into Montague Street and had progressed only a few steps when Holmes halted. "Aha! What have we here?"

My glance followed his to a sign over an archway of ancient stone, displaying a single word, *Mortuary.* I do not see myself as especially sensitive, but as I gazed into the murky depths of the tunnel-like entrance, the same depression of spirit came over me that I had experienced at first sight of the Shires castle.

"This is no hostel, Holmes," said I. "Unless a sanctuary for the dead can be called such!"

"Let us suspend judgement until we investigate," replied he; and he pushed open a creaking door that led into a cobbled courtyard.

"There is the smell of death here, without a doubt," said I.

"And very recent death, Watson. Else why should our friend Lestrade be on the premises?"

Two men stood in conversation at the far side of the courtyard, and Holmes had identified the one of them more quickly than I. It was indeed Inspector Lestrade of Scotland Yard, even leaner and more ferret-like than I recalled him.

Lestrade turned at the tramp of our footsteps. An expression of surprise came over his face. "Mr. 'Olmes! What are you doing here?"

"How good to see you, Lestrade!" exclaimed Holmes, with a warm smile. "It is heartening to find Scotland Yard dutifully following where crime leads."

"You needn't be sarcastic," grumbled Lestrade.

"Nerves, man? Something seems to have you by the short hairs."

"If you don't know what it is, you didn't read the paper this morning," said Lestrade, shortly.

"As a matter of fact, I did not."

The police officer turned to acknowledge my presence. "Dr. Watson. It has been a long time since our paths crossed."

"Far too long, Inspector Lestrade. You are well, I trust?"

"A bit of lumbago now and again. I'll survive." Then he added darkly, "At least until I see this Whitechapel maniac dragged to the gallows."

"The Ripper again?" asked Holmes, sharply.

"The very same. The fifth attack, Mr. 'Olmes. You have, of course, read about him, although I haven't heard of you coming 'round to offer your services."

Holmes did not parry the thrust. Instead, his eyes flicked in my direction. "We draw closer, Watson."

"What was that?" exclaimed Lestrade.

"The fifth, you said? No doubt you mean the fifth *official* murder?"

"Official or not, 'Olmes——"

"What I meant was that you cannot be sure. You have found the bodies of five of the Ripper's victims. But others may have been dismembered and thoroughly disposed of."

"A cheerful thought," muttered Lestrade.

"This 'fifth' victim. I should like to view the body."

"Inside. Oh, this is Dr. Murray. He is in charge here."

Dr. Murray was a cadaverous man, with a death-like complection, and a poised manner which impressed me favourably. His attitude reflected the inner resignation one often finds in those who deal intimately with the dead. He acknowledged Lestrade's introduction with a bow, and said, "I do officiate here, but I had rather posterity remembered me as director of the hostel next door. It affords greater opportunity for service. The poor wretches who come here are beyond aid."

"Let's get on with it," interrupted Lestrade, and conducted us through a door. A strong carbolic-acid odour greeted us, an odour I had grown to know too well in her Majesty's Indian service.

The room into which we were shown demonstrated how little is ever done to confer dignity upon the dead. It was less a room than a long, wide passage-way, each inch of whose walls and ceiling was tastelessly whitewashed. One entire side consisted of a raised platform, upon which rude wooden tables jutted out at intervals. Fully half the tables were occupied by sheeted, still figures; but Lestrade led us to the far end.

There, another platform stood, with its table and sheeted morsel of humanity. This platform was slightly higher, and so placed that a sign, *The Corpse for To-day*, might well have seemed appropriate.

"Annie Chapman," said Lestrade, morosely. "The latest victim of our butcher." With that, he drew back the sheet.

Holmes was the most objective of men where crime was concerned, but a grim pity invaded his face. And I must confess that I—accustomed to death both in the bed and upon the battlefield—was sickened. The girl had been slaughtered like an animal.

To my amazement, I saw what appeared to be disappointment supplant the pity upon Holmes's face. "The face is not scarred," he murmured, as if in complaint.

"The Ripper does not mutilate the faces of his victims," said Lestrade. "He confines his attentions to the more private parts of the body."

Holmes had turned cold and analytical. He could now have been regarding a specimen in a dissection-room. He touched my arm. "Note the skill of this unholy work, Watson. It verifies what we have read in the journals. The fiend does not cut at random."

Inspector Lestrade was scowling. "There is certainly nothing skilful in that slash across the abdomen, 'Olmes. The Ripper used a butcher's cleaver for that one."

"Before the abdomen was dissected, possibly with a surgeon's scalpel," muttered Holmes.

Lestrade shrugged his shoulders. "That second blow, the one to the heart. It was done by a cleaver, also."

"The left breast was removed with consummate skill, Lestrade," said I, with a shudder.

"The Ripper's surgery varies. Its skill seems to depend upon the time that is available to him. In some cases there has been scarcely any, cases in which he was interrupted in his devil's work."

"I am compelled to alter certain superficial ideas I had formed." Holmes appeared to be speaking to himself rather than to us. "A madman, certainly. But a clever one. Perhaps a brilliant one."

"Then you admit, Mr. 'Olmes, that the Yard is contending with no blundering idiot?"

"Most assuredly, Lestrade. And I shall be happy to give you whatever aid my limited powers allow."

This widened Lestrade's eyes. He had never before heard Holmes deprecate his own talents. The policeman searched for a suitable rejoinder, but apparently such was his astonishment that he could find none.

He recovered sufficiently, however, to voice his standard plaint. "And if you are lucky enough to apprehend the fiend——"

"I seek no credit, Lestrade," said Holmes. "Rest assured, the Yard shall reap the glory." He paused, then added, gloomily, "If there is any." He turned to Dr. Murray. "I wonder if we may be permitted to inspect your hostel, Doctor?"

Dr. Murray bowed. "I should be honoured, Mr. Holmes."

At that moment a door opened, and a pathetic figure appeared. There was much about the shuffling creature to pity, but I was struck first by the total vacancy in his eyes. The expressionless features, the sagging, partially-open mouth, bespoke an idiot. The man shuffled forward and stepped upon the platform. He cast a look of empty inquiry at Dr. Murray, who smiled as one smiles at a child.

"Ah, Pierre. You may cover the body."

A spark of eagerness appeared on that vacuous countenance. I could not help thinking of a faithful dog given a chore by a kindly master. Then Dr. Murray gestured, and we moved away from the platform.

"I'll be off," said Lestrade, sniffing wrinkle-nosed at the carbolic. "If there is any information you require, Mr. 'Olmes," said he, politely, "do not hesitate to call upon me."

"Thank you, Lestrade," said Holmes, with equal courtesy. The two detectives had evidently decided to call a truce until the morbid affair could be resolved—the first such truce between them, I might add, that ever I was aware of.

As we quitted the charnel-house, I glanced back and saw Pierre smoothing the sheet carefully over the body of Annie Chapman. Holmes, I noted, also glanced in the simpleton's direction, and something kindled in his grey eyes.

CHAPTER IV

Dr. Murray's Hostel

"One does what one can," said Dr. Murray, a few moments later, "but, in a city of the size of London, it is a little like trying to sweep back the sea with a broom. A sea of destitution and despair."

We had left the morgue, and crossed a flag-stoned inner courtyard. He ushered us through another door, and into a shabby but more cheerful atmosphere. The hostel was very old. It had been built originally as a stable, a long, low, stone building with the places for the stalls still clearly marked. Again, buckets of whitewash had been used, but the eternal odour of the carbolic was here mingled with a slightly less disagreeable effluvium of medicines, steaming vegetable stew, and unbathed bodies. As the building extended onward in railway fashion, the stalls had been fashioned into larger units, double and sometimes triple their original size, and put to appropriate uses. Black-lettered cards identified them variously as dormitories for women and for men. There was a dispensary, and a clinical waiting-room with stone benches. Ahead of us, a sign read: *This Way to Chapel and Dining-Hall.*

Curtains had been drawn across the entrance to the women's dormitory, but that of the men stood open, and several sorry-looking derelicts slept upon the iron cots.

In the clinical area, three patients awaited attention, while the dispensary was occupied by a huge, brutish man who looked freshly come from sweeping a chimney. He was seated, a sullen scowl upon his face. His eyes were fastened upon a pretty young lady ministering to him. One of his vast feet rested upon a low stool; the young lady had just finished bandaging it. She came up from her knees and brushed a lock of dark hair back from her forehead.

"He cut it badly upon a shard of broken glass," she told Dr. Murray. The doctor stooped to inspect the bandage, giving the brute's foot no less attention than it would have received in any Harley Street surgery. He straightened and spoke kindly.

"You must come back to-morrow and have the dressing changed, my friend. Be sure, now."

The oaf was entirely without gratitude. "I can't put my boot on. 'Ow am I goin' to get about?"

He spoke as though the doctor were responsible, with such surliness that I could not restrain myself. "If you had stayed sober, my good man, perhaps you could have avoided the broken glass."

"'Ere now, guv'ner!" says he, bold as brass. "A man's got to 'ave a pint once in a while!"

"I doubt if you've ever held yourself to a pint."

"Please wait here a few moments," interposed Dr. Murray, "I'll have Pierre bring you a stick. We keep a small stock for emergencies."

Turning to the young lady, he went on, "Sally, these gentlemen are Mr. Sherlock Holmes and his colleague, Dr. Watson. Gentlemen, this is Miss Sally Young, my niece and good right arm. I don't know what the hostel would be without her."

Sally Young extended a slim hand to each of us in turn. "I am honoured," said she, cool and self-possessed. "I have heard both names before. But I never expected to meet such famous personages."

"You are too kind," murmured Holmes.

Her tact in including me, a mere shadow to Sherlock Holmes, was gracious, and I bowed.

Said Dr. Murray, "I'll get the stick myself, Sally. Will you conduct Mr. Holmes and Dr. Watson the rest of the way? Perhaps they would like to see the chapel and the kitchen."

"Certainly. This way, please."

Dr. Murray hurried away in the direction of the morgue, and we followed Miss Young. But only for a short distance. Before we reached the door, Holmes said abruptly, "Our time is limited, Miss Young. Perhaps the tour can be finished during another visit. We are here to-day for professional reasons."

The girl seemed not to be surprised. "I understand, Mr. Holmes. Is there something I can do?"

"Perhaps there is. Some time ago you pledged a certain article in a pawn-shop on Great Heapton Street. Do you recall?"

With no hesitation whatever, she replied, "Of course. It was not so long ago as that."

"Would you object to telling us how you came by the case, and why you pledged it?"

"Not at all. It belonged to Pierre."

I thought this startling news, but Holmes did not move a muscle. "The poor fellow who has lost his wits."

"A pitiful case," said the girl.

"A hopeless one, I venture to say," said Holmes. "We met him a few minutes ago. Could you enlighten us as to his background?"

"We know nothing about him prior to his arrival here. But that arrival, I must say, was dramatic. I came through the morgue late one night, and found him standing beside one of the corpses."

"Doing what, Miss Young?"

"He was doing nothing whatever, merely standing by the body in the confused state you must surely have noticed. I approached him and brought him to my uncle. He has been here ever since. The police were evidently not seeking him, for Inspector Lestrade has shown no interest in him whatever."

My opinion of Miss Sally Young went higher. Here was courage indeed. A girl who could walk at night about a charnel-house, see a gargoyle figure such as Pierre's standing over one of the corpses, and not flee in terror!

"That's hardly a criterion," began Holmes, and stopped.

"I beg your pardon, sir?"

"A random thought, Miss Young. Please proceed."

"We came to the opinion that some-one had guided Pierre to the hostel and left him, as unwed mothers leave their infants at the door of a sanctuary. Dr. Murray examined him, and found that he had once sustained a terrible injury, as if he had been brutally beaten. The wounds about his head had healed, but nothing could be done to dispel the mists that had permanently settled over his brain. He has proved to be harmless, and he is so pathetically eager to help about the place that he has made his own berth. We of course would not dream of sending him back into a world with which he cannot cope."

"And the surgeon's-kit?"

"He had a bundle with him, containing wearing apparel. The kit was buried in their midst, the only thing of value he possessed."

"What did he tell you of himself?"

"Nothing. He speaks only with effort, single words which are hardly intelligible."

"But his name—Pierre?"

She laughed, an attractive touch of colour coming into her cheeks. "I took the liberty of baptising him. What clothing he carried bore French labels. And there was a coloured handkerchief with French script interwoven in the cloth. Thus, and for no other reason, I began calling him Pierre, although I feel sure he is not French."

"How did you happen to pawn the case?" asked Holmes.

"That came about quite simply. As I have told you, Pierre brought virtually nothing with him, and our funds at the hostel are severely allocated. We were in no position to outfit Pierre properly. So I thought of the surgical-case. It was clearly of value, and he could have no need of it. I explained to him what I proposed, and to my surprise he nodded violently." She paused here to laugh. "The only difficulty was in getting him to accept the proceeds. He wanted to put it into the general fund of the hostel."

"Then he is still capable of emotion. At least of gratitude."

"Indeed he is," replied Sally Young, warmly. "And now perhaps, sir, you will answer a question of mine. Why are you interested in the surgeon's-kit?"

"It was sent to me by an unknown person."

Her eyes widened. "Then someone redeemed it!"

"Yes. Have you any idea who that person might have been?"

"Not in the least." After a thoughtful pause, she said, "There does not necessarily have to be a connection. I mean, some-one could have come upon the case and redeemed it as a bargain."

"One of the instruments was missing when it reached me."

"That is odd! I wonder what could have happened to it."

"The set was complete when you pledged it?"

"Indeed it was."

"Thank you, Miss Young."

At that moment the door before us opened; a man came through. And, although Lord Carfax was perhaps not the last person I expected to see, he was certainly not the first.

"Your Lordship," exclaimed Holmes. "Our paths cross again."

Lord Carfax was as surprised as I. Indeed, he seemed utterly discomposed. It was Sally Young who broke the silence. "Your Lordship has met these gentlemen?"

"We had that privilege only yesterday," said Holmes. "At the Duke of Shires's residence."

Lord Carfax found his voice. "Mr. Holmes refers to my father's country-home." Then, turning back to Holmes, he said, "This is a far more likely place for me to be than for you gentlemen. I spend a good deal of my time here."

"Lord Carfax is our angel from Heaven," said Sally Young, rapturously. "He has given of his money and of his time so generously, that the hostel is as much his as ours. It could hardly exist without him."

Lord Carfax flushed. "You make too much of it, my dear."

She laid an affectionate hand upon his arm; her eyes were very bright. Then the glow faded; her whole manner changed. "Lord Carfax. There is another one. Have you heard?"

He nodded, sombrely. "I wonder if it will ever end! Mr. Holmes, are you by any chance applying your talents to the hunt for the Ripper?"

"We shall see what develops," said Holmes, abruptly. "We have taken up enough of your time, Miss Young. I trust that we shall meet again."

With that we bowed and departed, going out through the silent morgue, that was now deserted except for the dead.

Night had fallen, and the street-lamps of Whitechapel dotted the lonely thoroughfares, deepening rather than banishing the shadows.

I drew up my collar. "I don't mind saying, Holmes, that a good fire and a cup of hot tea——"

"On guard, Watson!" cried Holmes, his reactions far sharper than my own; and an instant later we were fighting for our lives. Three toughs had leapt out of the darkness of a courtyard and were upon us.

I saw the flash of a knife-blade as one of them shouted, "You two take the big cove!" Thus I was left with the third thug, but he was quite enough, armed as he was with a glittering weapon. The savagery of his attack left no doubt as to his intentions. I whirled to meet his attack not an instant too soon. But my stick slipped from my grasp, and I would have gone down with the brute's blade in my flesh if he had not slipped in his eagerness to get at me. He fell forward, pawing the air, and I acted from instinct, bringing my knee upwards. A welcome bolt of pain shot up my thigh as my knee-cap connected with my assailant's face. He bellowed in pain and staggered back, blood spouting from his nose.

Holmes had retained his stick and his wits. From the corner of my eye I witnessed his first defensive move. Using the stick as a sword, he thrust straight and true at the nearest man's abdomen. The ferrule sank deep, bringing a scream of agony from the man and sending him down, clutching at his belly.

That was all I saw, because my assailant was up and at me again. I got my fingers around the wrist of his knife-arm and veered the blade off its course towards my throat. Then we were locked together, struggling desperately. We went to the cobble-stones in a frantic sprawl. He was a big man, strongly-muscled, and even though I strained against his arm with every ounce of my strength, the blade moved closer to my throat.

I was in the act of consigning my soul to its Maker when a thud of Holmes's stick glazed the eyes of my would-be murderer and pitched him over my head. With an effort I heaved off the weight of the man's body, and struggled to my knees. At that moment there was a cry of rage and pain from one of Holmes's assailants. One of them cried, "Come on, Butch! These blokes are a bit thick!" and, with that, my attacker was snatched to his feet, the trio ran off into the shadows, and disappeared.

Holmes was kneeling beside me. "Watson! Are you all right? Did that knife get into you?"

"Not so much as a scratch, Holmes," I assured him.

"If you'd been hurt, I should never have forgiven myself."

"Are *you* all right, old chap?"

"Except for a bruised shin." Helping me to my feet, Holmes added grimly, "I am an idiot. An attack was the last thing I anticipated. The aspects of this case change swiftly."

"Don't blame yourself. How could you possibly have known?"

"It is my business to know."

"You were alert enough to beat them at their own game, when every advantage was on their side."

But Holmes would not be comforted. "I am slow, slow, Watson," said he. "Come, we shall find a hansom and get you home to that fire and a hot tea."

A cab hove in sight and picked us up. When we were rattling back towards Baker Street, Holmes said, "It would be interesting to know who sent them."

"Obviously, someone who wishes us dead," was my retort.

"But our ill-wisher, whoever he is, appears to have used poor judgement in selecting his emissaries. He should have chosen cooler heads. Their enthusiasm for the job impaired their efficiency."

"Our good fortune, Holmes."

"They achieved one goal, at least. If there was any doubt before, they have wedded me irrevocably to this case." Holmes's tone was grim indeed, and we rode the remainder of the journey in silence. It was not until we were seated before the fire with steaming cups of Mrs. Hudson's tea that he spoke again.

"After I left you yesterday, Watson, I corroborated a few small points. Did you know that a nude—a quite good work, by the way—by one Kenneth Osbourne, hangs in the National Gallery?"

"Kenneth Osbourne, did you say?" I exclaimed.

"The Duke of Shires."

Ellery Succeeds

He had typed steadily through the night; dawn found him blinking, stubbled, and famished.

Ellery went into the kitchen and opened the refrigerator and brought out a bottle of milk and the three sandwiches he had failed to eat the previous afternoon. He wolfed them down, drained what was left of the milk, wiped his mouth, yawned, stretched, and went to the phone.

"Morning, Dad. Who won?"

"Who won what?" Inspector Queen asked querulously, from Bermuda.

"The horseshoe game."

"Oh, that. They rang in some stacked shoes on me. How's the weather in New York? Lousy, I hope."

"The weather?" Ellery glanced at the window, but the Venetian blinds were closed. "To tell you the truth, Dad, I don't know. I worked all night."

"And you sent me down here for a rest! Son, why don't you join me?"

"I can't. It's not only this book I've got to finish, but Grant Ames dropped in yesterday. He drank me dry and left a package."

"Oh?" said the Inspector, coming to life. "What kind of package?"

Ellery told him.

The old man snorted. "Of all the baloney. Some-body's pulling a funny on you. Did you read it?"

"A few chapters. I must say it's pretty well done. Fascinating, in fact. But then—out of nowhere—lightning struck, and I got back to my typewriter. How do you plan to spend your day, Dad?"

"Frying myself on that damned beach. Ellery, I'm so bored I'm beginning to chew my nails. Son, *won't* you let me come home?"

"Not a chance," said Ellery. "You fry. Tell you what. How would you like to read an unpublished Sherlock Holmes?"

Inspector Queen's voice took on a cunning note. "Say, that's an idea. I'll call the airline and book a stray seat—I can be in New York in no time——"

"Nothing doing. I'll mail the manuscript down to you."

"To hell with the manuscript!" howled his father.

"So long, Daddy," said Ellery. "Don't forget to wear your dark glasses on the beach. And you eat everything they put on your plate."

He hung up hastily, not a second too soon.

He peered at the clock. It had the same bloodshot look as the typewriter.

He went into his bathroom, took a shower, and came back in his pajamas. The first thing he did in his study was to yank the telephone jack out of the wall socket. The second thing he did was to seize Dr. Watson's journal.

It will put me to sleep, he said to himself cunningly.

CHAPTER V

The Diogenes Club

The following morning I awoke to find Holmes up and pacing. Making no reference whatever to the previous night's misadventure, he said, "Watson, I wonder if you would inscribe a few notes for me."

"I should be happy to."

"I apologise for demeaning you to the role of amanuensis, but I have a special reason for wishing the details of this case to be put down in orderly fashion."

"A special reason?"

"Very. If your time is free, we shall call this afternoon upon my brother Mycroft, at his club. A consultation may bear us fruit. In certain ways, you know, Mycroft's analytical talents are superior to mine."

"I am aware of the high respect in which you hold him."

"Of course, his is what you might call a sedentary ability, in that he detests moving about. If a street-chair were ever invented to transport one from office to home and back again, Mycroft would be its first purchaser."

"I do recall that he is a man of rigid routine."

"Thus, he tends to reduce all riddles, human or otherwise, to chess-board dimensions. This is far too restrictive for my taste, but his methods are often quite stimulating, in the broader analysis."

Holmes rubbed his hands together. "And now, let us list our actors. Not necessarily in the order of their importance, we have, first, the Duke of Shires . . .'"

Holmes re-capitulated for an hour, whilst I took notes. Then he prowled the rooms whilst I re-arranged my notes into some semblance of order. When I had finished, I handed him the following résumé. It contained information of which I had no previous knowledge, data that Holmes had gathered over-night:

The Duke of Shires (Kenneth Osbourne)

Present holder of title and lands dating back to 1420. The twentieth descendant of the line. The Duke lives quietly, dividing his time between his estates and a town-house on Berkeley Square, where he pursues a painter's career. He sired two sons by a wife now ten years deceased. He has never re-married.

Lord Carfax (Richard Osbourne)

Elder son of Kenneth. Lineal inheritor of the dukedom. He sired one daughter, Deborah. But tragedy struck when his wife perished upon the delivery-table. The child is cared for by a governess at the Devonshire estate. The bond of affection between father and daughter is strong. Lord Carfax exhibits deep humanitarian tendencies. He gives generously of both his money and his time to the Montague Street Hostel in London, a sanctuary for indigents.

Michael Osbourne

Second son of Kenneth. A source of shame and sorrow to his father. Michael, according to testimony, bitterly resented his inferior position as a second son and non-inheritor, and embarked upon a profligate life. Bent, it is said, upon disgracing the title beyond his reach, he is also reported to have married a woman of the streets, apparently for no other reason than to further that misguided end. This reprehensible act is purported to have taken place while he was a medical student in Paris. He was expelled from the Sorbonne shortly thereafter. His fate thenceforward, and his present address, are unknown.

Joseph Beck

A pawn-broker with a shop on Great Heapton Street. Of doubtful importance, on the basis of data at hand.

Dr. Murray

A dedicated M.D. who superintends the Montague Street morgue, and devotes himself to the adjoining hostel he himself created.

Sally Young

The niece of Dr. Murray. She gives her full time to the hostel. A devoted nurse and social-worker, it was she who pledged the surgeon's-kit at Beck's pawn-shop. When questioned, she gave information freely, and appeared to hold nothing in reserve.

Pierre

A seemingly harmless imbecile taken in at the hostel, where he performs menial tasks. The surgeon's-case was found among his possessions, and pledged by Miss Young for his benefit. He appears to have come from France.

The Scar-faced Woman
Unidentified.

Holmes ran through the résumé with a dissatisfied frown. "If this accomplishes nothing else," said he, "it shows us what a little way we have come, and how far we have still to go. It does not list the victims, who under-score our need for haste. There have been five known butcheries, and any delay on our part will no doubt add to the list. So if you will clothe yourself, Watson, we shall flag a hansom and be off to the Diogenes Club."

Holmes sat deep in thought as we rattled over the cobble-stones, but I risked disturbing him for something that came suddenly to mind.

"Holmes," said I, "as we were leaving the Duke of Shires's estate, you mentioned that Lord Carfax had failed on two counts. I think I have become aware of one of them."

"Indeed?"

"It occurs to me that he made no inquiry as to how you had come by the surgical-case. It therefore seems logical that he already knew."

"Excellent, Watson."

"In the light of the omission, are we justified in assuming that it was he who sent it to you?"

"We have at least a right to suspect that he knows who did."

"Then perhaps Lord Carfax is our key to the identity of the scar-faced woman."

"Entirely possible, Watson. However, recognising a key as such, and turning it, can be two different matters entirely."

"I must confess that his Lordship's second lapse has escaped me."

"You will recall that, in Lord Carfax's presence, I dropped the case and spilled its contents onto the floor? And that he courteously picked up the instruments?"

"Yes?"

"But perhaps you failed to note the practised skill with which he replaced them, each to its proper niche, with no hesitation whatever."

"Why, of course!"

"And, now that you recall this, what additional information does it give you concerning his Lordship?"

"That, even though he professes no surgical knowledge or experience, he is quite familiar with the tools of surgery."

"Precisely. A fact that we must place in our mental file for future reference. But here we are, Watson, and Mycroft awaits us."

The Diogenes Club! I remembered it well, even though I had entered its hushed precincts but once. That had been upon the occasion when Mycroft had shifted to his more active brother's shoulders the curious affair of the Greek Interpreter, which case I had the honour and satisfaction of recording for the pleasure of Holmes's not inconsiderable body of admirers.

The Diogenes Club was formed by, and for the benefit of, men who chose to seek solitude in the heart of the clamourous city. It is a luxurious place, with easy-chairs, excellent food, and all the other appurtenances of creature-comfort. The rules are geared to the Club's basic purpose, and are strictly enforced; rules devised to discourage, nay, to forbid, all sociability. Talking, save in the Stranger's Room—into which we were soundlessly ushered—is forbidden. In fact, it is forbidden any member to take the slightest notice of any other. A tale is told— apocryphal, I am sure—of a member succumbing to a heart-attack in his chair and being found to have expired only when a fellow-member noticed that the *Times* propped before the poor man was three days old.

Mycroft Holmes awaited us in the Stranger's Room, having taken time off, I was later informed, from his government post, around the corner in Whitehall. This, I might add, was an unheard-of interruption of his fixed habits.

Still, neither of the brothers, upon meeting, seemed in any haste to get to the business at hand. Mycroft, a large, comfortable man with thick grey hair and heavy features, bore little resemblance to his younger brother. He extended his hand, and exclaimed, "Sherlock! You're looking fit. Bouncing all over England and the Continent appears to agree with you." Shifting the meaty hand to me, Mycroft said, "Dr. Watson. I had heard that you escaped from Sherlock's clutch into matrimony. Surely Sherlock has not re-captured you?"

"I am most happily married," I assured him. "My wife is visiting an aunt at the moment."

"And Sherlock's long arm reaches out instantly!"

Mycroft's smile was warm. For an unsocial man, he had a curious talent for making one feel at ease. He had met us at the door, and now he moved towards the bow-window looking out upon one of London's busiest streets. We followed, and the brothers stood side by side, surveying the passing scene.

"Sherlock," said Mycroft, "I have not been in this room since your last visit, but the faces outside never change. From the look of that street, it could have been yesterday."

"Yet," murmured Sherlock, "it has changed. Old intrigues have died, new ones have been born."

Mycroft pointed. "Those two fellows at the kerb. Are they involved in some dire plot?"

"Do you mean the lamp-lighter and the book-keeper?"

"The very men."

"I'd say not. The lamp-lighter is consoling the book-keeper for being recently sacked."

"I agree. The book-keeper will no doubt find a berth, but he will lose it speedily and find himself again on the street."

I was compelled to interrupt. "Come, come," said I, and heard myself repeating my old objections. "This is too much!"

"Watson, Watson," chided Mycroft, "after all those years with Sherlock, I should not expect such myopia from you. Even from this distance, surely you observe the smears of ink, both black and red, upon the first man's fingers? Just as surely, the occupational mark of the book-keeper?"

"Observe also," added Holmes the younger, "the ink-blot upon his collar, where he touched pen to linen, and the unpressed condition of his otherwise quite respectable suit."

"From which is it too difficult, my dear Watson," interposed Mycroft, with a kindliness that irritated me, "to project the man's slovenliness to his work, and thus conjure up an irate employer?"

"An employer not only irate but unforgiving," said Sherlock, "as evidenced by the newspaper in the book-keeper's jacket-pocket, opened to the *Situations* column. Hence, he is unemployed."

"But you said he would find a berth!" said I, testily, to Mycroft. "If the fellow is so inefficient, why should a new employer consider him?"

"Most would not, but many of the entries in the newspaper are marked, clearly for investigation. Such energy in seeking a new situation must eventually be rewarded."

I threw up my hands. "I concede, as usual! But the other man's being a lamp-lighter—surely that is sheer surmise on your part?"

"A little more technical," my friend Holmes admitted. "But observe the spot that is worn shiny on his inner right sleeve, extending upwards above the cuff."

"An unfailing mark of the lamp-lighter," said Mycroft.

"In extending his pole to reach the gas-globe with his flame," explained Sherlock, "he rubs the lower end of the pole against that portion of his sleeve again and again. Really elementary, Watson."

Before I could retort, Holmes's mood changed, and he turned from the window with a frown. "I wish our present problem were as easily solved. That is why we are here, Mycroft."

"Give me the details," replied his brother, with a smile. "My afternoon must not be entirely lost."

Twenty minutes later, ensconced in easy-chairs in the Stranger's Room, we sat in silence. It was broken by Mycroft. "Your picture is well-delineated, Sherlock, so far as it goes. But surely you are capable of solving the riddle yourself."

"I have no doubt of that, but there is little time. Preventing further outrages is urgent. Two minds are better than one. You might well discern a point that would save me a precious day or two of searching."

"Then let us see precisely what you have. Or, rather, precisely what you do not have. Your pieces are far from complete."

"Of course."

"Yet you have touched a sensitive spot somewhere, as witness the swift and murderous attack upon you and Watson. Unless you wish to ascribe it to coincidence?"

"I do not!"

"Nor I." Mycroft tugged at an ear. "Of course, it is no cerebral feat to identify the mysterious Pierre by his true name."

"Certainly not," replied Holmes. "He is the Duke of Shires's second son, Michael."

"As to Michael's grievous injuries, the father may be unaware of them. But Lord Carfax certainly knows of Michael's presence at the hostel, and beyond doubt recognised his younger brother."

"I am quite aware," said Holmes, "that Lord Carfax has not been entirely candid."

"He interests me. The philanthropic cloak is an admirable disguise for devilry. Lord Carfax could well have been responsible for Michael's delivery into Dr. Murray's care."

"Also," said Holmes, grimly, "for his injuries."

"Possibly. But you must find the other pieces, Sherlock."

"Time, Mycroft, time! That is my problem. I must identify, quickly, the right thread in this skein, and seize upon it."

"I think you must somehow force Carfax's hand."

I broke in. "May I ask a question?"

"By all means, Watson. We had no intention of excluding you."

"I can be of little help, but certainly identifying Jack the Ripper is our first concern. Therefore I ask, do you believe we have met the murderer? Is the Ripper one of the people with whom we have come in contact?"

Sherlock Holmes smiled. "Do you have a candidate for that dubious honour, Watson?"

"If I were compelled to make a selection, I should name the imbecile. But I must confess that I missed badly in not postulating him as Michael Osbourne."

"On which grounds do you condemn him?"

"Nothing tangible, I fear. But I cannot forget the *tableau* I witnessed as we were leaving the Montague Street morgue. Dr. Murray, you will recall, commanded 'Pierre' to cover the unfortunate's corpse. There was nothing conclusive in his action, but his manner made my flesh fairly crawl. He seemed entranced by the mutilated cadaver. In smoothing out the sheet, his hands ran lovingly over the cold flesh. He appeared to be enamoured of the butchery."

There was a pause during which the brothers evaluated my contribution. Then Mycroft said, gravely, "You have made a most pertinent point, Watson. I would only say that it is difficult, as you are aware, to interpret the actions generated by a damaged mentality. However, your instinctive revulsion may be worth more than all the logic we can muster."

"The observation is certainly to be considered," remarked Sherlock.

I gathered the impression, however, that neither put any great stock in my statement; that they were merely being kind.

Mycroft came ponderously to his feet. "You must gather more facts, Sherlock."

His brother clenched his hands.

It had occurred to me that this entire episode with Mycroft was not at all like the sure-footed, self-confident Sherlock Holmes I had known. I was puzzling the matter when Mycroft, speaking quietly, said, "I believe I know the source of your confusion, Sherlock. You must banish it. You have become subjective in regard to this case."

"I fail to comprehend," Holmes said, a trifle coldly.

"Five of the most heinous murders of the century, and perhaps more to come. If you had entered the case sooner, you might have prevented some of these. That is what gnaws at you. The acid of guilt can dull the keenest intellect."

Holmes had no rebuttal. He shook his head impatiently, and said, "Come, Watson, the game is afoot. We stalk a savage beast."

"And a cunning one," said Mycroft, in clear warning. Then he said, "Sherlock, you seek a scar-faced woman. Also, one of the key-pieces that is missing, the ill-reputed wife of Michael Osbourne. What does that suggest?"

Holmes fixed his brother with an angry eye. "You must indeed feel that I have lost my faculties, Mycroft! It of course suggests that they are one and the same."

On that note, we left the Diogenes Club.

Ellery's Nemesis Investigates

The apartment bell was a carved rosebud set in ivory leaves. Grant Ames jabbed it, and the result was a girl wearing poisonous-green lounging pajamas.

"Hello, Madge. I happened to be in the neighborhood, so here I am."

She glowed. That thinly patrician male face reminded her of a very big dollar sign. "And so you thought you'd drop in?" she said, making it sound like Einstein's first formulation of the Theory; and she threw the door so wide it cracked against the wall.

Grant moved warily forward. "Nice little nest you've got here."

"It's just an ordinary career gal's efficiency apartment. I combed the East Side, absolutely combed it. And finally found this. It's sickeningly expensive, but of course one wouldn't dare live anywhere but Upper East."

"I didn't know you'd gone in for a career."

"Oh, definitely. I'm a consultant. You drink scotch, don't you?"

It behooved a legman to follow through, Grant thought. He asked brightly, "And with whom do you consult?"

"The public relations people at the factory."

"The one your father owns, of course."

"Of course."

Madge Short was a daughter of Short's Shapel Shoes, but with three brothers and two sisters to share the eventual loot. She wagged her pert red head as she extended a scotch-and.

"And the factory is located——?"

"In Iowa."

"You commute?"

"Silly! There's a Park Avenue office."

"You surprise me, dear heart. I see you in a different role."

"As a bride?" Two outstanding young breasts lifted the poisonous green like votive offerings.

"God, no," Grant said hurriedly. "I visualize you somewhere in the literary field."

"You've got to be kidding!"

Grant had checked the room. There were no books in sight—no magazines, either—but that wasn't necessarily conclusive.

"I see you as reading a great deal, chickie. A bit of a bookworm, so to speak."

"In this day and age? Wherever would one get the *time?*"

"Oh, one wedges it in here and there."

"I do read some. *Sex and the Single——*"

"I'm a detective bug myself. Father Brown. Bishop Cushing." He watched narrowly for her reaction. It was like watching for a pink piglet to react.

"I like them, too."

"With a smattering," Grant went on cunningly, "of the philosophers—Burton, Sherlock Holmes."

"One of the men at that party, he's an expert on men." Doubt was beginning to creep in. Grant quickly changed his tactics.

"That blue bikini you wore. Was it ever sharp."

"I'm so glad you liked it, dahling. How about another scotch?"

"No, thanks," Grant said, getting up. "Time goes bucketing by, and—well, there you are." She was hopeless.

He collapsed behind the wheel of the Jag.

How did those fellows do it? Holmes? Even Queen?

Something was pressing against Ellery's nose, smothering him. He awoke and discovered that it was the journal with which he had gone to bed. He yawned, dropped it on the floor, and sat up groggily, elbows on knees. The journal now lay between his feet, so he doubled up, head between his hands.

And began to read, southward.

CHAPTER VI

I Stalk the Ripper

The following morning, I must say, Holmes infuriated me.

When I awoke, he was up and clothed. I instantly saw, from the reddened condition of his eyes, that he had slept little; indeed, I suspected that he had been out all night. But I made no inquiry.

To my gratification, he was of a mind to talk, rather than to sink into one of his reticent moods, out of which little more than cryptic sounds ever emerged.

"Watson," said he, without preliminary, "there is a notorious public-house in Whitechapel."

"There are many."

"True, but the one to which I refer, The Angel and Crown, abuses even the riotous pleasures tendered by that district. It is situated in the heart of the Ripper's prowling-grounds, and three of the murdered prostitutes were seen on the premises shortly before their deaths. I mean to give sharp attention to The Angel and Crown. To-night I shall indulge in a little carousing there."

"Capital, Holmes! If I may confine myself to ale——"

"Not you, my dear Watson. I still shudder at how close to death I have already led you."

"See here, Holmes——"

"My mind is made up," replied he, firmly. "I have no intention of confronting your good wife, upon her return, with the dismal news that her husband's body may be found in the morgue."

"I thought I gave a good account of myself!" said I, heatedly.

"You did, certainly. Without you I might myself well be occupying a pallet in Dr. Murray's establishment. That is no justification, however, for risking your safety a second time. Perhaps whilst I am absent to-day—I have much to do—your practise could do with a little attention."

"It is going along quite nicely, thank you. I have a working arrangement with a most able locum tenens."

"Then might I suggest a concert, or a good book?"

"I am quite capable of occupying my time fruitfully," said I, coldly.

"Indeed you are, Watson," said he. "Well, I must be off! Expect me when you see me. I promise I shall put you abreast of affairs upon my return."

With that he darted out, leaving me to steam at a temperature only a little below that of Mrs. Hudson's tea.

My determination to defy Holmes did not form at once; but, before my morning repast was finished, it was clearly shaped. I passed the day reading a curious monograph from Holmes's book-shelf on the possible use of bees in murder-intrigues, both by causing them to contaminate their honey, and by training them to attack a victim in a swarm. The work was anonymous, but I recognised the concise style of Holmes in the writing. Then, as darkness fell, I planned my night's foray.

I would arrive at The Angel and Crown in the guise of a lecherous man-about-town, sure that I would not stand out, as many of London's more hardened *habitués* made a practise of frequenting such places. I therefore hurried home and donned evening attire. Capping my regalia with top-hat and opera cape, I surveyed myself in the glass, and found that I cut a more dashing figure than I had dared hope. Slipping a loaded revolver into my pocket, I went out into the street, hailed a hansom, and gave The Angel and Crown as my destination.

Holmes had not yet arrived.

It was a horrible place. The long, low-ceilinged public-room was thick with eye-smarting fumes from the many oil-lamps. Clouds of tobacco smoke hung in the air, like storm-warnings. And the crude tables were crowded by as motley a collection of humanity as ever I had encountered. Evil-faced Lascars on leave from the freighters that choke the Thames; inscrutable Orientals; Swedes, and Africans, and seedy-looking Europeans; not to mention the many varieties of native Britons—all bent upon supping off the flesh-pots of the world's largest city.

The flesh-pots were dubiously spiced with females of all ages and conditions. Most were pitiful in their physical deterioration. Only a few were attractive, younger ones who had just set foot upon the downward path.

It was one of these latter who approached me after I had found a table, had ordered a pint of stout, and sat surveying the reckless scene. She was a pretty little thing, but the wicked light in her eye, and her hard manner, indelibly marked her.

"'Ullo, luv. Buy a gel a gin-an'-bitters?"

I was about to decline the honour, but a brutish-looking waiter standing by cried, "Gin-an'-bitters for the lady!" and ploughed towards the bar. The man was no doubt paid on the basis of the liquor the girls wheedled from their marks.

The wench dropped into the chair opposite me and laid her rather dirty hand upon mine. I withdrew mine quickly. This brought an uncertain smile to her painted lips, but her voice was cajoling as she said, "Shy, ducks? No need to be."

"I merely dropped in for a quick pint," said I. The adventure no longer seemed so alluring.

"Sure, luv. All the toffs drop in for quick pints. Then they just 'appen to find out what else we 'ave for sale."

The waiter returned, slopped down the gin-and-tonic, and fumbled among the coins I had laid upon the table. I was sure he appropriated several pence too many, but I did not make an issue of it.

"Me name's Polly, luv. What's yers?"

"Hawkins," said I, quickly. "Sam Hawkins."

"'Awkins, is it?" she laughed. "Well, it's a bit of a change from Smythe. Yer 'eart'd bleed at 'ow many bloody Smythes come 'round."

My reply, if indeed I had any, was cut down by an outburst in another part of the room. A dark-visaged sailor of gorilla proportions gave out a roar of rage and upset a table in his zeal to get at another patron who appeared to have offended him, a Chinese of insignificant stature. For a moment it seemed likely that the Oriental would be killed, so ferocious was the sailor's aspect.

But then another man interposed himself. He was thick-browed, with a heavy neck, and shoulders and arms like trees, although he did not match the angry sailor's proportions. The Oriental's unexpected defender smashed his fist into the sailor's solar plexus. It was a mighty blow, and the sailor's gasp could be heard all over the room as he doubled over in agony. Again the smaller man measured the giant, and again he delivered a blow, this time to the brute's jaw. The sailor's head snapped back; his eyes glazed; and, as he collapsed, his assailant was ready with a hunched shoulder, and caught the man's body like a sack of meal. His load balanced, the victor made calmly for the door, lugging the unconscious mariner as though he weighed no more than a child. He opened the door and hurled the man into the street.

"That's Max Klein," said my doxy in awe. "Strong as a bloody ox, 'e is. Max just bought this place. 'E's owned it for about a four-month, an' 'e don't allow no bloke to get kilt in it, 'e don't."

The performance had been impressive indeed; but, at that moment, something else drew my attention. The door through which Klein had flung the sailor had scarcely closed when it was put to use by a new customer, one whom I thought I recognised. I peered through the haze to make sure my identification was correct. There was no doubt. It was Joseph Beck, the pawn-broker, moving towards a table. I made a mental note to report this fact to Holmes, and then I turned back to Polly.

"I got a nice room, luv," said she, in a seductive tone.

"I fear I'm not interested, Madam," said I, as kindly as I could.

"Madam, 'e says!" cried she, with indignation. "I ain't *that* old, guv'ner. I'm young enough, I promise yer. Young *an'* clean. You 'ave nothin' to fear from me."

"But there must be someone *you* fear, Polly," said I, observing her closely.

"Me? I don't go ter 'urt nobody."

"I mean the Ripper."

A whining note leaped into her voice. "Yer just tryin' to scare me! Well, I ain't afraid." She took a gulp of her drink, eyes darting here and there. They came to focus on a point over my shoulder, and I realised that they had been directed that way during most of our conversation. I turned my head, and beheld as vicious-looking a creature as the imagination could have conjured.

He was incredibly filthy, and he had a hideous knife-scar across one cheek. This twisted his mouth in a permanent leer, and the damaged flesh around his left eye added further to his frightful aspect. I have never seen such malevolence in a human face.

" 'E got Annie, the Ripper did," Polly whispered. " 'E gouged the poor thing up good—Annie wot never 'urt a soul."

I turned back to her. "That brute there, with the knife-scar?"

" 'Oo knows?" Then she cried, "Wot's he 'ave to go and do those things for? Wot's the fun in shovin' a blade into a poor gel's belly, an' cuttin' off 'er breast an' all?"

He was the man.

Explaining my absolute certainty is difficult. In earlier life I indulged for a time in gambling, as a young man will, and there is a feeling that comes over one on certain occasions that is not founded in reason. Instinct, a sixth sense—call it what you will—it comes, and it is impossible to ignore it.

Such a feeling came over me as I studied the creature behind us; his gaze was fixed upon the girl who sat with me, and I could see the foul slaver at the corners of his contorted mouth.

But what to do?

"Polly," I asked, quietly, "did you ever see that man before?"

"Me, ducks? Not ever! Narsty-lookin' cove, ain't 'e?" Then, with the insta-bility that characterises the loose woman, Polly's mood changed. Her natural recklessness, possibly re-inforced by too many drinks, came to the fore. She suddenly raised her glass.

" 'Ere's luck, luv. If yer don't want me lily-white body, yer don't. But yer a good bloke, and I wish yer the best."

"Thank you."

"A gel's got t'make a livin', so I'll be off. Another night, maybe?"

"Perhaps."

She arose from the table, and moved away, flaunting her hips. I watched her, anticipating that she would approach another table for another solicitation. But she did not. Instead, she scanned the room, and then moved swiftly towards the door. She had found the pickings poor that night in The Angel and Crown, I thought, and was going to resort to the streets. I had scarcely begun to feel relief when the repulsive creature beyond my shoulder jumped up and set out after her. My alarm may be imagined. I could think of no other course than to touch the weapon in my pocket for reassurance, and follow the man to the street.

I was beset by a momentary blindness, having to adjust my eyesight to the darkness after the glare of the public-room. When my eyes focussed, fortunately, the man was still within my view. He was skulking along, close by the wall, at the end of the street.

I was now certain that I was embarked upon a perilous course. He was the Ripper, and he was stalking the girl who had endeavoured to entice me to her room, and there was only I between her and a hideous death. I gripped my revolver convulsively.

I followed, treading on the balls of my feet like a Red Indian of the American plains. He turned the corner; and, fearful both of losing him and of finding him, I hurried after.

I rounded the corner, panting, and peered cautiously ahead. There was only one gas-lamp, which made my survey doubly difficult. I strained my eyes. But my quarry had disappeared.

Apprehension seized me. Perhaps the fiend had already dragged the poor girl into an areaway and was slashing the life from her young body. If only I had had the foresight to bring a pocket lantern! I ran forward into darkness, the profound silence of the street broken only by the sounds of my footsteps.

There was enough light to warn me that the street narrowed at the other end, coming down to a passage-way. It was into this that I plunged, my heart in my mouth at what I might find.

Suddenly I heard a choked cry. I had collided with something soft. A fear-stricken voice babbled, "Mercy! Oh, pray, 'ave mercy!"

It was Polly, who had been pressed against the wall in the darkness. In fear that her cries might frighten the Ripper away, I clapped my hand over her mouth and whispered into her ear.

"It's all right, Polly. You are in no danger. I am the gentleman you sat with. I followed you——"

I was struck from behind by a sudden, enormous weight, and knocked back, staggering, along the passage. But my brain still functioned. I had been out-witted by the cunning devil I had followed from The Angel and Crown. He had crept into some shadow and allowed me to pass him. Now, enraged at the prospect of being deprived of his prey, he was attacking like a jungle beast.

I answered in kind, fighting desperately, trying to pull the revolver from my pocket. It should have been in my hand; but, during my stint in her Majesty's Indian service, I had served as a surgeon, not a soldier; I had no training in hand-to-hand fighting.

I was therefore no match for the monster with whom I had come to grips. I went down under his onslaught, gratefully aware that the girl had fled. I felt his powerful hands upon my throat, and I flailed out desperately with my free arm as I struggled still to clear the weapon from my pocket.

To my stupefaction, a familiar voice growled, "Now let us see what manner of beast I have flushed!" Even before a bull's-eye lantern flashed, I became aware of my blunder. The evil-appearing creature seated behind me in the pub had been Holmes—in disguise!

"Watson!" He was as astonished as I.

"Holmes! Good heavens, man! Had I managed to get my revolver out, I might have shot you!"

"And a good thing, too," grumbled he. "Watson, you can write me down an ass." He lifted his lithe body from me and grasped my hand to help me to my feet. Even then, knowing he was my old friend, I could only marvel at the cleverness of his disguise, so different did he appear.

We had no time for further recriminations. As Holmes was pulling me erect, a scream rent the night. His hand released me instantly, and down I tumbled again. An oath erupted from his throat, one of the very few outbursts of profanity I have ever heard from him.

"I've been outdone!" he cried; and he went streaking away into the night.

As I scrambled to my feet, the female cries of terror and pain increased in volume. Suddenly they were cut off; and the sounds of a second pair of running feet were added to those of Holmes.

I must confess that I showed to little advantage in the affair. I had once been the middle-weight boxing champion of my regiment, but those days were in the long-ago, and I leaned against the brick wall, fighting nausea and dizziness. At that moment, I should not have been able to respond had our gracious Queen herself been screaming for aid.

The vertigo passed; the world righted itself; I moved shakily back, as I had come, groping my way along through the silence that had ominously fallen. I had re-traced my steps some two hundred paces, when a quiet voice stopped me.

"Here, Watson."

I turned to my left and discovered a break in the wall.

Again, Holmes's voice: "I dropped my lantern. Will you be so kind as to search for it, Watson?"

His quiet tone was doubly chilling, in that it concealed an agonised inner struggle. I knew Holmes; he was shaken to the core.

Good fortune attended my search for the lantern. I took a single step, and bumped it with my foot. I relighted it, and staggered back from one of the most horrible scenes that has ever met my eyes.

Holmes was on his knees, back bowed, head lowered, a picture of despair.

"I have failed, Watson. I should be brought to the dock for criminal stupidity."

I scarcely heard him, stunned as I was by the bloody sight that confronted me. Jack the Ripper had vented his obscene madness upon poor Polly. Her clothing had been torn from her body, baring fully half of it to view. A great, ragged slash had opened her abdomen, and its torn and mutilated contents were exposed like those of a butchered animal. A second savage thrust had severed her left breast almost from her body. The terrible scene swam before my eyes.

"But he had so little time! How——?"

But Holmes came alive; he sprang to his feet. "Come, Watson! Follow me!"

So abruptly did he launch himself from the area-way towards the street that I was left behind. I called upon the reserve of strength each man possesses in moments of emergency, and ran, pell-mell, after him. He was well in the forefront all the way, but I did not lose him; and, when I again came close, I found him thundering upon the door of Joseph Beck's pawn-shop.

"Beck!" Holmes shouted. "Come out! I demand that you come out this instant!" His fists smote again and again upon the panel. "Open this door, or I shall smash it in!"

A rectangle of light appeared overhead. A window opened; a head was thrust out. Joseph Beck cried, "Are you mad? Who are you?"

The light from the lamp in his hand revealed a red-tasselled night-cap and a high-necked night-dress.

Holmes stood back and bellowed up at him. "Sir, I am Sherlock Holmes, and if you do not come down immediately I shall climb this wall and drag you out by your hair!"

Beck was, understandably, shaken. Holmes was still in his disguise; and to be roused out of sleep, and find such a hideous figure banging at his door in the dead of night, was certainly not an experience for which the life of a tradesman had prepared the pawn-broker.

I sought to help. "Herr Beck! You remember me, do you not?"

He gaped down at me. "You are one of the two gentlemen——?"

"And, despite his appearance, this is the other, Mr. Sherlock Holmes, I promise you."

The pawn-broker hesitated; but then he said, "Very well; I shall come down."

Holmes paced with impatient strides until the light appeared in the shop, and the street-door opened.

"Step out here, Beck!" commanded Holmes, in a deadly voice; and, fearfully, the German obeyed. My friend's powerful hand darted out, and the man shrank back, but he was too slow. Holmes tore open the front of his night-dress, revealing a bare chest pimpled with the chill.

"What are you doing, sir?" quavered the tradesman. "I do not understand."

"Be silent!" said Holmes, harshly; and in the light of Beck's lamp he examined the pawn-broker's chest minutely. "Where did you go, Joseph Beck, after you left The Angel and Crown?" asked Holmes, releasing his grasp.

"Where did I go? I came home to bed!" Reassured by Holmes's milder tone, Beck was now hostile.

"Yes," replied Holmes, thoughtfully, "it appears that you did. Go back to bed, sir. I am sorry if I have frightened you."

With this, Holmes turned unceremoniously away, and I followed. I looked back as we reached the corner, to see Herr Beck still standing before his shop. Holding the lamp high above his head, he appeared for all the world like a night-shirted caricature of that noble statue, Liberty Enlightening the World, presented to the United States by the people of France, the great, hollow, bronze figure that now stands in the harbour at New York City.

We returned to the scene of the butchery, to find that the body of poor Polly had been discovered. An army of the morbidly curious choked the entrance to the street, whilst the lanterns of officialdom illuminated the darkness beyond.

Holmes gazed grimly at the scene, hands thrust deep into his pockets. "There is no point in identifying ourselves, Watson," said he, in a mutter. "It would only make for profitless conversation with Lestrade."

It did not surprise me that Holmes preferred not to reveal our part in that night's terrible affair. It was not merely that he had his methods; in this circumstance, his self-esteem was involved, and it had suffered a grievous blow.

"Let's slip away, Watson," said he, bitterly, "like the addle-brained idiots we have become."

CHAPTER VII

The Slayer of Hogs

"What you failed to see, Watson, was the cloaked figure of Joseph Beck leaving the pub, just as the girl gave evidence of her intention to go elsewhere. You had eyes only for me."

It was dismally evident to me that I had been the culprit, not he, but there was no hint of this in his voice. I attempted to assess the blame, but he cut short my apologies. "No, no," said he, "it was my stupidity that let the monster slip through our fingers, not yours."

Chin on breast, Holmes went on. "When I emerged from the pub, the girl was just turning the corner. Beck was nowhere in sight, and I could only assume either that he had made off in the other direction, or was crouched in one of the dark doorways nearby. I chose the latter assumption. I followed the girl around the corner and heard approaching footsteps, catching a glimpse of a caped man entering behind us. Not dreaming that it was you—your figure and Beck's do not greatly differ, I fear, Watson—I took the skulker to be our pawn-broker. I hid myself in turn, and you passed me. Then I heard the cries, and I thought I had stalked the Ripper successfully. Whereupon I attacked, and discovered my unforgiveable error."

We had finished our morning tea, and Holmes was pacing his quarters at Baker Street in a fury. I followed his movements sadly, wishing I possessed the power to erase the whole incident from the slate, not only for Polly's sake, but for my friend's peace of mind.

"Then," continued Holmes, savagely, "whilst we were preoccupied with our blunders, the Ripper struck. The arrogance of this fiend!" cried he. "The contempt, the utter self-confidence, with which he perpetrates his outrages! Believe me, Watson, I shall lay the monster by the heels if it is the last act of my life!"

"It would appear," said I, trying to divert his bitter thoughts, "that Joseph Beck has been exonerated, at least of last night's murder."

"Quite so. Beck could not possibly have reached his quarters, cleansed himself of the blood, undressed, and donned night-clothes before we were upon him." Holmes seized his cherry-wood, and his Persian slipper, then cast them down in disgust. "Watson," said he, "all we accomplished last night was to eliminate one suspect from amongst London's millions. At such a rate, we shall succeed in spotting our quarry some time during the next century!"

I could find nothing to say in refutation. But then Holmes suddenly threw back his spare shoulders and directed a steely glance at me. "But enough of this, Watson! We shall imitate the Phoenix. Get dressed. We are going to pay another visit to Dr. Murray's mortuary."

Within the hour, we stood before the Montague Street portal to that gloomy establishment. Holmes glanced up and down the shabby thoroughfare.

"Watson," said he, "I should like a more detailed picture of this neighbourhood. Whilst I venture inside, will you be good enough to scout the near streets?"

Eager to atone for my bungling of the previous night, I readily agreed.

"When you have finished, you will no doubt find me in the hostel." Holmes disappeared through the morgue gate.

I found that the vicinity of Montague Street possessed no common commercial establishments. The further side was occupied by a row of warehouses that presented locked entrances and no signs of life.

But when I turned the corner, I came upon a more active scene. I saw a green-grocer's stall, where a house-wife haggled with the proprietor over the price of a cabbage. The shop next door housed a tobacconist's. Just beyond, there stood a small, evil-looking public-house with a weathered replica of a hansom cab above the door.

My attention was soon drawn to an open entranceway on the street's near side. A great squealing emanated therefrom. It sounded as if a battalion of pigs was being slaughtered. As it turned out, this was precisely the case. I entered through an ancient stone archway, came out into a courtyard, and found myself in an abattoir. Four lean, live hogs were penned in one corner; the butcher, a grossly-muscled youth in a bloody leather apron, was in the act of dragging a fifth toward a suspended hook. In a callous manner, he hoisted the animal, and chained its hind legs to the hook. A rusted pulley creaked as he hauled on the rope. He tied a swift knot, and the hog squealed and thrashed as if it knew its fate.

As I watched in disgust, the butcher's boy took up a long knife and, without a qualm, plunged it into the hog's throat. The sounds gurgled away, and the boy stepped back to avoid the gout of dark blood. Then, he walked carelessly into the red pool, and slashed the animal's throat open. Whereupon the knife swept down, opening the animal from tail to jowls.

It was not the butchery, however, that made me look away. My glance was drawn to what appeared to me even more horrible—the sight of the idiot, the creature whom both Sherlock Holmes and his brother Mycroft had identified as Michael Osbourne. He was crouched in one corner of the abattoir, oblivious of all else but the butcher's work. The operation seemed to fascinate him. His eyes drank in the bloody carcase of the animal in a manner that I can only describe as obscene.

His preliminary work done, the butcher's boy stepped back and favoured me with a smile.

"Lookin' for a bit o' pork, guv'ner?"

"No, thank you! I was strolling by——"

"An' you heard the squealin'. Yer has to be a stranger, guv'ner, else you would not o' bothered. The neighbourhood's used to their ruddy noise." He turned cheerfully to Michael Osbourne. "Ain't that right, dummy?"

The imbecile smiled, and nodded.

"The dummy's the on'y one that keeps me comp'ny. I'd be fair lonesome 'thout him."

"Your work is certainly not carried on under the most cleanly conditions," said I, distastefully.

"Clean-ly, says 'e," chuckled the boy. "Guv'ner, folk 'ereabouts 've got a fat lot more to turn their stomachs than a little dirt on their pork—bloody right they 'ave!" He winked. "The gels, 'specially. They're too busy o' nights keepin' their own 'ides in one piece."

"You refer to the Ripper?"

"That I do, guv, that I do. 'E's keepin' the tarts nervy o' late."

"Did you know the girl who was murdered last night?"

"I did. Passed 'er two-and-six t'other night for a quick whack, I did. Poor little tart didn't 'ave 'er rent, and I'm that gen'rous, I 'ates to see a gel trampin' the ruddy streets in the fog fer want o' a bed."

Some instinct made me pursue the tasteless conversation. "Have you any idea as to the identity of the Ripper?"

"Lord love yer, guv. 'E might just be yer own lordship, now, mightn't 'e? Yer got to admit, 'e's prob'ly a toff, don't yer?"

"Why do you say that?"

"Well, now, let's look at it this way. I'm at 'ome with blood in my perfession, cozy with it, yer might say, and so I 'ave to think that way, right?"

"What are you driving at?" "Guv, the way that Ripper carves 'em up, 'e's just got to get smeary. But nobody's never seen a smeared-up bloke runnin' from one o' those murders, now, 'ave they?"

"I believe not," said I, rather startled.

"An' why not, guv'ner? 'Cause a toff wearin' a opry cloak over 'is duds could cover up the bloody res-ee-doo, so ter speak! Wouldn' yer say? Well, I 'ave ter get back to this carcase."

I fled the stench and gore of the place. But I took an image with me, that of Michael Osbourne squatting in his corner, laving the slaughter with watering eyes. No matter what Holmes had said, the misshapen wreck of humanity remained my principal suspect.

I circumviated the square and made my entrance into the morgue through the Montague Street gate, the adjacent premises fixed in mind. The morgue was untenanted, save for the dead. Traversing its narrow length, I paused near the raised table that was reserved for unwilling guests. A white-sheeted form lay there. I contemplated it for a few moments; then, moved by pity, I drew the sheet back from the face.

Her sufferings past, Polly's marble features reflected acceptance of whatever she had found beyond the pale. I do not rate myself a sentimental man, but I do believe that there is a dignity in death, however it comes. Nor am I deeply religious. Still, I breathed a small prayer for the salvation of this unhappy child's spirit. Then I went away.

I found Holmes in the dining-hall of the hostel, in company with Lord Carfax and Miss Sally Young. The latter gave me a smile of welcome. "Dr. Watson, may I fetch you a cup of tea?"

I declined with thanks, and Holmes spoke crisply. "You arrive fortuitously, Watson. Lord Carfax is about to tender some information." His Lordship looked a trifle dubious. "You may speak before my colleague in complete confidence, your Lordship."

"Very well. As I was about to relate, Mr. Holmes, Michael left London for Paris some two years ago. I expected him to live a licentious life in that most licentious of cities, but I strove to keep in touch with him, nonetheless; and I was both surprised and gratified to learn that he had entered the Sorbonne to study medicine. We maintained a correspondence, and I became optimistic as to his future. He appeared to have turned a new leaf." At this point, his Lordship's eyes lowered, and a great sadness came over his sensitive face. "But then, disaster struck. I was stunned to learn that Michael had married a woman of the streets."

"Did you meet her, my lord?"

"Never, Mr. Holmes! I frankly admit that I had little stomach for a face-to-face encounter. It is true, however, that I would have confronted the woman, had the opportunity arisen."

"How, then, do you know she was a prostitute? Your brother would hardly have included such an item in his bill of particulars when he informed you of his marriage."

"My brother did not inform me. I received the information in a letter from one of his fellow-students, a person I had never met, but whose written word reflected an earnest interest in Michael's welfare. This gentleman acquainted me with Angela Osbourne's calling, and suggested that, if I had my brother's future at heart, I should leave for Paris immediately and try to repair his fortunes before they were irretrievably destroyed."

"You informed your father of this communication?"

"Indeed I did not!" said Lord Carfax, sharply. "Unhappily, my correspondent saw to that. He had dispatched two letters, in the event one should be ignored, I suppose."

"How did your father react?"

"You need hardly ask that question, Mr. Holmes."

"The Duke did not reserve judgement until proof was forthcoming?"

"He did not. The letter was too patently truthful; I did not doubt it myself. As for my father, it was in perfect consonance with what he had always expected of Michael." Lord Carfax paused, pain invading his face. "I shall not soon forget the renunciation. I suspected that Father had also received a letter, and I rushed to his town-house. He was at his easel when I arrived; as I entered the studio, his model drew a robe over her nudity, and my father laid down his brush and surveyed me calmly. He said, 'Richard, what brings you here at this time of day?'

"I saw the tell-tale envelope with the French stamp lying by his palette, and I pointed to it. 'That, your Grace. I presume it is from Paris.'

"'You are correct.' He picked up the envelope, but did not remove its contents. 'It is inappropriate. It should have been edged in black.'

"'I do not understand you,' I replied.

"He laid the letter down, coldly. 'Should not all announcements of death be thus marked? So far as I am concerned, Richard, this letter informs me of Michael's demise. In my heart, the service has already been read, and the body is in the earth.'

"His terrible words stunned me. But, knowing that argument was futile, I left."

"You made no effort to reach Michael?" asked Holmes.

"I did not, sir. To me, he was beyond salvation. Some two months later, however, I received an anonymous note, saying that I would find something of interest if I made a visit to this hostel. I did so. I do not have to tell you what I found."

"The note. Did you preserve it, your Lordship?"

"No."

"A pity."

Lord Carfax appeared to be struggling with a natural reticence. Finally, he burst out, "Mr. Holmes, I cannot express to you my shock at finding Michael in his present condition, the victim of an attack so savage that it had turned him into what you have seen—a misshapen creature with but the merest fragment of his reason left."

"How did you proceed, if I may ask?"

Lord Carfax shrugged his shoulders. "The hostel seemed as good a place as any for him. So that part of the problem was solved."

Miss Sally Young had been sitting in amazed silence, her eyes never leaving his Lordship's face. Lord Carfax took cognizance of this. With a sad smile, he said, "I trust you will forgive me, my dear, for not setting the case before you earlier. But it seemed unnecessary—indeed, imprudent. I wished Michael to remain here; and, in truth, I was not eager to confess his identity to you and your uncle."

"I understand," said the girl, quietly. "You were entitled to keep your secret, my lord, if for no other reason than that your support of the hostel has been so generous."

The nobleman seemed embarrassed. "I should have contributed to the maintenance of the hostel in any event, my dear. However, I do not deny that Michael's refuge here enhanced my interest. So perhaps my motives have been as selfish as they have been eleemosynary."

Holmes had been studying Lord Carfax keenly as the story unfolded.

"You made no further efforts in your brother's behalf?"

"One," replied his Lordship. "I communicated with the Paris police, as well as with Scotland Yard, inquiring if their records bore any report of an attack such as my brother had suffered. Their records did not reveal one."

"So you left it there?"

"Yes!" cried the harassed nobleman. "And why not?"

"The felons might have been brought to justice."

"By what method? Michael had become a hopeless idiot. I doubt if he would have been able to recognise his assailants. Even could he have done so, his testimony in a criminal proceeding would have been valueless."

"I see," said Holmes, gravely; but I perceived that he was far from satisfied. "And as to his wife, Angela Osbourne?"

"I never found her."

"Did you not suspect that she wrote the anonymous note?"

"I assumed that she did."

Holmes came to his feet. "I wish to thank your Lordship for being so candid under the difficult circumstances."

This brought a bleak smile. "I assure you, sir, that it has not been through choice. I have no doubt that you would have come by the information through other channels. Now, perhaps, you can let the matter rest."

"Hardly, I fear."

Lord Carfax's face became intense. "I tell you, upon my honour, sir, that Michael has had nothing to do with the horrible murders that have convulsed London!"

"You reassure me," replied Holmes, "and I promise your Lordship that I will do my utmost to spare you further suffering."

Lord Carfax bowed, and said nothing more.

With that, we took our leave. But as we went out of the hostel, I could see only Michael Osbourne, crouched in that filthy abattoir, enchanted by the blood.

Ellery's Legman Reports

Grant Ames III lay on Ellery's sofa balancing the glass on his chest, exhausted. "I went forth an eager beaver. I return a wreck."

"From only two interviews?"

"A party is one thing—you can escape behind a patio plant. But alone, trapped inside four walls . . ."

Ellery, still in pajamas, crouched over his typewriter and scratched the foundations of a magnificent beard. He typed four more words and stopped.

"The interviews bore no fruit?"

"Two gardensful, one decked in spring green, the other in autumnal purple. But with price tags on the goodies."

"Marriage might be your salvation."

The idler shuddered. "If masochism is one of your vices, old buddy, we'll discuss it. But later, when I get my strength back."

"You're sure neither put the journal in your car?"

"Madge Short thinks Sherlock is some kind of new hair-do. And Katherine Lambert—Kat's not a bad kitten from the neck down. She paints, you know. Re-did a loft in the Village. Very intense. The coiled-spring type. You sit there waiting to get the broken end in your eye."

"They may have put you on," Ellery said brutally. "You wouldn't be hard to fool."

"I satisfied myself," Grant said with dignity. "I asked subtle questions. Deep. Searching."

"Such as?"

"Such as, 'Kat, did you put a manuscript addressed to Ellery Queen into the seat of my car at Lita's bash the other day?' "

"And she replied?"

Grant shrugged. "It came in the form of a counter-question—'Who's Ellery Queen?' "

"Have I asked you to leave lately?"

"Let's be kind to each other, friend." Grant paused to drink deeply. "I'm not reporting total failure. I've merely cut the field in half. I shall go doggedly forward. Beyond the Bronx lies New Rochelle."

"Who lives there?"

"Rachel Hager. Third on my list. And then there's Pagan Kelly, a Bennington chick whom you can find in almost any picket line whose protest is silly."

"Two suspects," Ellery said. "But don't rush into it. Go off somewhere and ponder your attack."

"You mean you want me to dawdle?"

"Isn't that what you do best? But not in my apartment. I've got to get this story finished."

"Did you finish the journal?" the playboy asked, not stirring.

"I'm busy with my own mystery."

"Have you gone far enough to spot the killer?"

"Brother," Ellery said, "I haven't spotted the murderer in my own story yet."

"Then I'll leave you to your labors. Oh. Suppose we never find out who sent you the manuscript?"

"I think I'd manage to survive."

"Where did you get your reputation?" the young man asked nastily. He left.

Ellery's brain dangled, like a foot that has fallen asleep. The typewriter keys looked a thousand yards away. Vagrant thoughts began to creep into the vacuum. How was Dad getting along in Bermuda? What were the latest sales figures on his last book? He did not have to ask himself who had sent the manuscript by way of Grant Ames III. He already knew the answer to that. So, by a natural process, he began to wonder about the identity of Sherlock Holmes's visitor from Paris (he had peeked ahead).

After a short battle, which he lost, he went into the bedroom. He plucked Dr. Watson's journal from the floor, where he had left it, and stretched out on his bed to read on.

CHAPTER VIII

A Visitor from Paris

The ensuing days were most trying. In all our association, I had never seen Holmes so restless, and so difficult to get along with.

After our interview with Lord Carfax, Holmes ceased to communicate with me. My overtures were ignored. It then occurred to me that I had intruded further into this case than into any of the investigations I had shared with him. In the light of the chaos I had managed to create, my chastisement seemed just. So I retreated into my customary rôle of bystander, and awaited developments.

They were slow in coming. Holmes had turned, like the Ripper, into a creature of the night. He vanished from Baker Street each evening, to return at dawn and spend the day in brooding silence. I kept to my own room, knowing that solitude was essential to him at such times. His violin wailed at intervals. When I could stand its scratching no longer, I took myself off into the welcome hubbub of London's streets.

On the third morning, however, I was appalled at his appearance.

"Holmes! In God's name!" I cried. "What has happened to you?"

There was an ugly purple contusion below his right temple. The left sleeve of his jacket had been ripped away, and a gashed wrist had no doubt bled copiously. He walked with a limp, and he was as begrimed as any of the street Arabs he so often sent on mysterious missions.

"A dispute in a dark by-way, Watson."

"Let me attend to those wounds!"

I snatched my satchel from my room and returned. Grimly he displayed the bloody knuckles of his right fist. "I attempted to lure our enemy into the open, Watson. I succeeded." Pressing Holmes into a chair, I began my examination. "I succeeded, but I failed."

"You take perilous risks."

"The assassins, two of them, rose to my bait."

"The same ones who attacked us?"

"Yes. My purpose was to lay one of them by the heels, but my revolver jammed—of all the accursed luck!—and both got away."

"Pray relax, Holmes. Lie back. Close your eyes. Perhaps I should give you a sedative."

He made an impatient gesture. "These scratches are nothing. It is my failure that pains me. So near and yet so far. Had I been able to hold one of those scoundrels, I should have gotten the name of his employer soon enough, I warrant you."

"Is it your feeling that these brutes are perpetrating the butcheries?"

"Good heavens, no! They are wholesome, healthy bruisers beside the depraved creature we seek." Holmes stirred nervously. "Another, Watson, a blood-thirsty tiger loose in the jungle of London."

The dread name came into my head. "Professor Moriarty?"

"Moriarty is not involved in this. I have checked his activities, and his whereabouts. He is occupied elsewhere. No, it is not the Professor. I am certain our man is one of four."

"To which four do you refer?"

Holmes shrugged his shoulders. "What does it matter so long as I am unable to put my hands upon him?"

The physical strain had begun to wear on him. Holmes lay back in the chair and gazed, heavy-lidded, at the ceiling. But the fatigue did not extend to his mental faculties.

"This 'tiger' you refer to," said I. "What does it profit him to go about killing luckless prostitutes?"

"The affair is far more tangled than that, Watson. There are several dark threads that twist and turn in this maze."

"That repulsive simpleton at the hostel," I muttered.

Holmes's smile was humourless. "I fear, my dear Watson, that you have your finger upon the wrong thread."

"I cannot believe that Michael Osbourne is in no way involved!"

"Involved, yes. But——"

He did not finish, because at that moment the bell sounded below. Mrs. Hudson was soon opening the door. Holmes said, "I have been expecting a visitor; he is prompt. Pray remain, Watson. My jacket, if you please. I must not look like a street-brawler who has dropped in for medical treatment."

By the time he had gotten into the garment and lighted his pipe, Mrs. Hudson was ushering a tall, blond, good-looking chap into our parlour. I estimated him to be in his mid-thirties. He was assuredly a man of breeding; except for a single startled glance, he made no reference to Holmes's battered appearance.

"Ah," said Holmes. "Mr. Timothy Wentworth, I believe. You are welcome, sir. Take the seat by the fire. The air is damp and chill this morning. This is my friend and colleague, Dr. Watson."

Mr. Timothy Wentworth bowed acknowledgement, and took the proffered chair. "Your name is famous, sir," said he, "as is that of Dr. Watson. I am honoured to make your acquaintance. But I have a busy schedule in Paris, and I tore myself away only because of my regard for a friend, Michael Osbourne. I have been utterly mystified by his unheralded disappearance from Paris. If I can do anything to help Michael, I shall consider the Channel crossing well worth the inconvenience."

"A most admirable loyalty," said Holmes. "Perhaps we can enlighten each other, Mr. Went-worth. If you will tell us what you know about Michael's sojourn in Paris, I shall pick up for you the end of his story."

"Very well. I met Michael some two years ago, when we enrolled together at the Sorbonne. I think I was attracted to him because we were opposites. I am myself somewhat retiring; indeed, my friends consider me shy. On the other hand, Michael was possessed of a fiery spirit, sometimes gay, sometimes bordering upon the violent, when he felt that he had been put upon. He never left the least doubt as to his opinion on any subject; however, by making allowances for each other's short-comings, we got on well together. Michael was very good for me."

"And you for him, sir, I've no doubt," said Holmes. "But, tell me. What did you learn of his personal life?"

"We were candid with each other. I quickly learned that he was second son to a British nobleman."

"Was he embittered by the misfortune of second birth?"

Mr. Timothy Wentworth frowned as he considered his answer. "I should have to say yes, and yet no. Michael had a tendency to break out, one might say, to go wild. His breeding and background forbade such behaviour, and caused a guilt to arise within him. He needed to palliate that guilt, and his position as second son was something against which to revolt, and thus justify his wildness." Our young guest stopped self-consciously. "I'm putting it badly, I fear."

"To the contrary," Holmes assured him, "you express yourself with admirable clarity. And I may assume, may I not, that Michael harboured no bitterness against either his father or his elder brother?"

"I am sure he did not. But I can also understand the contrary opinion of the Duke of Shires. I see the Duke as a man of proud, even haughty, spirit, preoccupied with the honour of his name."

"You see him exactly as he is. But pray go on."

"Well, then there came Michael's alliance with that woman." Timothy Wentworth's distaste was apparent in his tone. "Michael met her in some Pigalle rat's-nest. He told me about her the following day. I thought nothing of it, considering it a mere dalliance. But I now see Michael's withdrawal from our friendship as dating from that time. It was slow when measured in hours and days, but swift enough as I look back upon it—from the time he told me of the meeting, to the morning he packed his clothes in our digs, and told me that he had married the woman."

I interjected a comment. "You must have been shocked, sir."

"Shocked is hardly the term. I was stunned. When I found words with which to remonstrate, he snarled at me to mind my own affairs, and left." Here, a deep regret appeared in the young man's honest, blue eyes. "It was the termination of our friendship."

"You did not see him again?" murmured Holmes.

"I tried, and did see him briefly on two other occasions. Word of that sort of thing, of course, cannot be kept secret—a short time later, Michael was dropped from the Sorbonne. When I heard this, I made a point of seeking him out. I found him living in an unspeakable sty on the Left Bank. He was alone, but I presume his wife was living there with him. He was half-drunk, and received me with hostility—a different man by far from the one I had known. I could not even begin to reach him, so I placed some money upon the table and left. A fortnight later, I met him in the street, near the Sorbonne. His appearance cut me to the quick. It was as if a lost soul had returned to gaze wistfully upon the opportunities he had thrown away. His defiance remained, however. When I attempted to accost him, he snarled at me and slunk away."

"I gather, then, that you have never laid eyes upon his wife?"

"No, but there were rumours concerning her. It was whispered about that the woman had a confederate, a man with whom she had consorted both before and after her marriage. I have no certain knowledge of that, however." He paused, as though pondering the tragic fate of his friend. Then he raised his head and spoke with more spirit. "I believe that Michael was somehow put upon in that disastrous marriage, that in no way did he deliberately seek to bring shame upon his illustrious name."

"And I believe," said Holmes, "that I can reassure you on that point. Michael's kit of surgical instruments has recently come into my possession, and I discovered upon examining it that he had carefully covered the emblazoned coat of arms it bore with a piece of velvet cloth."

Timothy Wentworth's eyes widened. "He was forced to dispose of his instruments?"

"The point I wish to make," continued Holmes, "is that this very act of concealing the insignia indicates not only shame, but an effort to protect the name he has been accused of seeking to disgrace."

"It is intolerable that his father will not believe that. But now, sir, I have told you all I know, and I am eager to hear what you have to tell me."

Holmes was markedly reluctant to reply. He arose from his chair and took a quick turn across the room. Then he stopped. "There is nothing you can do for Michael, sir," said he.

Wentworth seemed ready to spring up. "But we made a bargain!"

"Michael, some time after you last saw him, suffered an accident. At present he is little more than mindless flesh, Mr. Wentworth. He remembers nothing of his past, and his memory will probably never return. But he is being well cared-for. As I have said, there is nothing you can do for him, and in suggesting that you do not see him I am attempting to spare you further distress."

Timothy Wentworth turned his frown upon the floor, considering Holmes's advice. I was glad when he sighed, and said, "Very well, Mr. Holmes, then it is over." Wentworth came to his feet and extended his hand. "But if there is anything I can ever do, sir, please get in touch with me."

"You may depend upon it."

After the young man left, Holmes stood in silence, gazing from the window at our departing visitor. When he spoke, it was in so low a voice that I could scarcely catch his words. "The more grievous our faults, Watson, the closer a true friend clings."

"What was that, Holmes?"

"A passing thought."

"Well, I must say that young Wentworth's account changes my opinion of Michael Osbourne."

Holmes returned to the fire to stab a restless poker at the log. "But I am sure you realise that his hearsay was of far more significance than his fact."

"I confess I do not follow you."

"The rumour that the woman, Michael's wife, had a male accomplice throws additional light upon the problem. Now, who could this man be, Watson, other than our elusive missing link? Our tiger who set assassins upon us?"

"But how did he know?"

"Ah, yes. How did he discover that I was on his trail before I knew it myself? I think we shall make another call upon the Duke of Shires, at his town-house in Berkeley Square."

We were not destined, however, to make that visit. At that moment the bell again rang downstairs, and we heard Mrs. Hudson again answer the door. A great clatter followed; the caller had rushed past our landlady and was taking the stairs two at a time. Our door burst open, and there he stood, a thin and pimple-faced youth with a great air of defiance about him. His manner was such that my hand moved automatically towards a fire-iron.

"W'ich o' you gents is Mr. Sherlock 'Olmes?"

"I, my lad," answered Holmes; and the youth extended a parcel wrapped in brown paper. "This 'ere's to be given to yer, then."

Holmes took the parcel and opened it with no ceremony.

"The missing scalpel!" cried I.

Holmes had no chance to reply. The messenger had bolted, and Holmes whirled about. "Wait!" he shouted. "I must speak with you! You shall not be harmed!"

But the boy was gone. Holmes rushed from the room. I hastened to the window, and beheld the youth fleeing down the street as though all the devils of Hell were after him, Sherlock Holmes swiftly in his wake.

Ellery's Legman Legs It Again

"Rachel?"

She looked back over her shoulder. "Grant! Grant Ames!"

"Just thought I'd drop in," said the playboy.

"So sweet of you!"

Rachel Hager wore a pair of blue jeans and a tight sweater. She had long legs and a slim body, but there were plenty of curves. Her mouth was full and wide, and her eyes were an odd off-brown, and her nose was pugged. She looked like a madonna who had run into a door.

This pleasing paradox did not escape Grant Ames III. She didn't look like this the other day, he thought, and pointed to what she had been doing in the backyard.

"I didn't know you grew roses."

Her laugh revealed the most beautiful buck teeth. "I try. Heavens, how I try. But my thumb stays its natural color. What brings you into the wilds of New Rochelle?" She slipped off her gloves and lifted a strand of hair off her forehead. The shade was mouse brown, but Grant was sure that, bottled, it would have lined them up at the cosmetic counters.

"Just driving by. Hardly got a chance to say hello at Lita's the other day."

"I was there by accident. I couldn't stay around."

"I noticed you didn't swim."

"Why, Grant! Such a nice compliment. Most girls are noticed when they do. How about the patio? I'll bring you a drink. Scotch, isn't it?"

"At times, but at the moment I could do with a frosty iced tea."

"Really? I'll be right back."

When she returned, Grant watched her cross her long legs in a lawn chair too low to be comfortable. For some reason he was stirred. "Lovely garden."

That enchanting buck-toothed laugh again. "You should see it after the kids leave."

"The kids?"

"From the orphanage. We bring a group over once a week, and it's *wild*. They do respect the roses, though. One little girl just sits and stares. Yesterday I gave her an ice cream cone and it melted all over her hand. It was that Mammoth Tropicana over there. She tried to kiss it."

"I didn't know you worked with children." As a matter of cold fact, Grant had not had the least idea what Rachel did, and until now had not cared a whit.

"I'm sure I get more out of it than they do. I'm working on my Master's now, and I have time to spare. I was thinking of the Peace Corps. But there's so much to do right here in the U.S.—in town, in fact."

"You're gorgeous," Grant unbelievingly heard himself mutter.

The girl looked up quickly, not sure she had heard him right. "What on earth are you talking about?"

"I was trying to remember how many times I've seen you. The first was at Snow Mountain, wasn't it?"

"I think it was."

"Jilly Hart introduced us."

"I remember because I broke my ankle that trip. But how can *you* possibly remember? With your harem?"

"I'm not entirely irresponsible," said Grant stuffily.

"I mean, why should you? Me? You've never shown——"

"Would you do me a favor, Rachel?"

"What?" asked Rachel suspiciously.

"Go back and do what you were doing when I got here. Dig at your roses. I want to sit here and look at you."

"Is this your latest line?"

"It's very strange," he mumbled.

"Grant. What did you come here for?"

"What?"

"I said, what did you come here for?"

"Damned if I can remember."

"I'll bet you can," the girl said, a little grimly. "Try."

"Let me see. Oh! To ask if you'd put a brown manila envelope on the seat of my Jag at Lita's. But the hell with that. What kind of fertilizer do you use?"

Rachel squatted. Grant had visions of *Vogue*. "I have no formula. I just keep mixing. Grant, what's the matter with you?"

He looked down at the lovely brown hand on his arm.

My God! It's happened!

"If I come back at seven, will you have a frock on?" he asked.

She looked at him with a dawning light. "Of course, Grant," she said softly.

"And you won't mind my showing you off here and there?"

The hand squeezed. "You darling."

"Ellery, I've found her, I've found her!" Grant Ames III babbled over the telephone.

"Found whom?"

"The Woman!"

"Who put the envelope in your car?" Ellery said in a peculiar voice.

"Who put what?" said Grant.

"The envelope. The journal."

"Oh." There was a silence. "You know what, Ellery?"

"No. What?"

"I didn't find out."

Ellery went back to Dr. Watson, shrugging.

CHAPTER IX

The Lair of the Ripper

I could do nothing but wait. Infected by Holmes's fever of impatience, trying to occupy the hours, I assessed the situation, endeavouring to apply the methods I had so long witnessed Holmes employ.

His identification of the Ripper as one of four men came in for its share of my ponderings, you may be sure, but I was confused by other elements of the puzzle—Mycroft's assertion that, as yet, his brother did not have all the pieces, and Holmes's yearning to come to grips with the "tiger" prowling London's by-ways. If the Ripper was one of four persons whom Holmes had already met, where did the "tiger" fit in? And why was it necessary to locate him before the Ripper could be brought to book?

Elation would have been mine, had I known that at that moment I myself held the key. But I was blind to both the key and its significance; and, when this knowledge did come to me, it brought only humiliation.

Thus I fretted away the hours with but a single break in the monotony. This occurred when a note was delivered to Baker Street by a smartly-uniformed page-boy. "Sir, a message from Mr. Mycroft Holmes to Mr. Sherlock Holmes."

"Mr. Holmes is absent at the moment," said I. "You may leave the note."

After I had dismissed the page, I examined the note. It was in a sealed envelope, from the Foreign Office. The Foreign Office was where Mycroft had his being.

My fingers were itching to tear the flap, but of course I did not. I pocketed the missive and went on with my pacing. The hours passed, with no sign of Holmes. At times, I went to the window and watched the fog that was settling in over London. As twilight fell, I remarked to myself what a fortuitous night this would be for the Ripper.

This had evidently occurred to the maniac also. Quite dramatically, upon the heels of my thought, there came a message from Holmes, delivered by an urchin. I tore it open with trembling fingers as the boy waited.

My dear Watson:

You will give this boy a half-crown for his trouble, and meet me post-haste at the Montague Street morgue.

Sherlock Holmes.

The urchin, a bright-faced lad, had never before received such a handsome *pourboire*, I am certain. In my relief, I gave him a crown.

In no time at all I was in a hansom, urging the cab-man on through the thickening pea-soup that befogged the streets. Fortunately, the jehu had the instincts of a homing-pigeon. In a remarkably short time he said, "The right-'and door, guv'ner. Walk strite on and watch yer nose, or yer'll bang into the ruddy gite."

I found the gate with some groping, went in, and through the court, and found Holmes by the raised table in the mortuary.

"Still another, Watson," was his portentous greeting.

Dr. Murray and the imbecile were also present. Murray stood silently by the table, but Michael-Pierre cringed by the wall, naked fear upon his face.

As Murray remained motionless, Holmes frowned. Said he, sharply, "Dr. Murray, you do not question Dr. Watson's stomach for it?"

"No, no," replied Murray, and drew back the sheet.

But my stomach was tested, nonetheless. It was the most incredible job of butchery on a human body that the sane mind could conceive. With demented skill the Ripper had gone berserk. In decency, I refrain from setting down the details, save for my gasp, "The missing breast, Holmes!"

"This time," responded Holmes, grimly, "our mad-man took away a trophy."

I could endure it no longer; I stepped down from the platform. Holmes followed. "In God's name, Holmes," cried I, "the beast must be stopped!"

"You are in good company with that prayer, Watson."

"Has Scotland Yard been of any aid to you?"

"Rather, Watson," replied he, sombrely, "have I been of any aid to Scotland Yard? Very little, I fear."

We took our leave of Murray and the imbecile. In the swirling fog of the street, I shuddered. "That wreck who was once Michael Osbourne . . . Is it my fancy, Holmes, or did he crouch there for all the world like Murray's faithful hound, expecting a kick for some transgression?"

"Or," replied Holmes, "like a faithful hound sensing his master's horror and seeking to share it. You are obsessed with Michael Osbourne, Watson."

"Perhaps I am." I forced my mind to turn back. "Holmes, were you able to apprehend the messenger who took to his heels?"

"I clung to his trail for several blocks, but he knew London's labyrinths as well as I. I lost him."

"And you spent the rest of the day how, may I ask?"

"A portion of it in the Bow Street Library, attempting to devise a pattern from a hypothetical projection of the madman's brain."

He began walking slowly through the fog-bank, I by his side. "Where are we going, Holmes?"

"To a particular section of Whitechapel. I laid out the pattern, Watson, a positioning of all the known Ripper murders, super-imposed upon a map of the area which they cover. I spent several hours studying it. I am convinced that the Ripper works from a central location, a room, or a flat, a sanctuary from which he ventures forth and to which he returns."

"You propose to search?"

"Yes. We shall see if shoe-leather will reward us where the arm-chair has failed."

"In this fog it will take leg-work indeed."

"True, but we have certain advantages on our side. For example, I have made it a point to question the witnesses."

This startled me. "Holmes! I did not know there were any."

"Of a sort, Watson, of a sort. On several occasions, the Ripper has worked perilously close to detection. In fact, I suspect that he deliberately arranges his murders in that fashion, out of contempt and bravado. You will recall our brush with him."

"Well do I!"

"At any rate, I have decided, from the sounds of his retreating footsteps, that he moves from the perimeter of a circle towards its centre. It is within the centre of that circle that we shall search."

Thus we plunged, that fog-choked night, towards the cesspools of Whitechapel into which the human sewage from the great city drained. Holmes moved with a sure-footedness that bespoke his familiarity with those malodorous depths. We were silent, save when Holmes paused to inquire, "By the way, Watson, I trust you thought to drop a revolver into your pocket."

"It was the last thing I did before I left to join you."

"I, too, am armed."

We ventured first into what proved to be an opium-den. Struggling for breath in the foul fumes, I followed as Holmes moved down the line of bunks, where the addicted victims lay wrapped in their shabby dreams. Holmes paused here and there for a closer inspection. To some he spoke a word; at times, he received a word in return. When we left, he appeared to have garnered nothing of value.

From there we invaded a series of low public-houses, where we were greeted for the most part by sullen silence. Here, also, Holmes spoke *sotto voce* with certain of the individuals we came upon, in such a manner that I was sure he was acquainted with some of them. On occasion, a coin or two passed from his hand into a filthy palm. But always we moved on.

We had left the third dive, more evil than the others, when I could contain myself no longer.

"Holmes, the Ripper is not a cause. He is a result."

"A result, Watson?"

"Of such corrupt places as these."

Holmes shrugged his shoulders.

"Does it not stir you to indignation?"

"I would of course welcome a sweeping change, Watson. Perchance in some future, enlightened time, it will come about. In the meanwhile, I am a realist. Utopia is a luxury upon which I have no time to dream."

Before I could reply, he pushed open another door, and we found ourselves in a brothel. The reek of cheap scent almost staggered me. The room into which we entered was a parlour, with half a dozen partially-naked females seated about in lewd poses as they awaited whoever might emerge from the fog.

Quite candidly, I kept shifting my eyes from the inviting smiles and lascivious gestures that greeted us on all sides. Holmes rose to the occasion with his usual equanimity. Giving his attention to one of the girls, a pale, pretty little thing who sat clad in nothing but a carelessly open robe, he said, "Good-evening, Jenny."

"Evenin', Mr. 'Olmes."

"That address I gave you, of the doctor. Did you visit him?"

"That I did, sir. 'E gave me a clean bill o' 'ealth, 'e did."

A beaded curtain parted and a fat madame with eyes like raisins stood regarding us. "What brings you out on a night like this, Mr. Holmes?"

"I am sure you know, Leona."

Her face turned sulky. "Why do you think my girls are off the streets? I don't want to lose any of them!"

A plump, over-painted creature spoke angrily. "H'it's a bloody shyme, h'it is——a poor gel gettin' pushed by bobbies all the time."

Another commented, "Better than a bloody blade in yer gut, dearie."

"Almost 'ad me a gent, h'I did, wot lives at the Pacquin. 'E was a-goin' up the stairs, all w'ite tie an' cape, 'e was, an' 'e stops w'en 'e sees me. Then this bobby shoves 'is dish outa the fog. ' 'Ere now, dearie,' says 'e. 'Off to yer crib. This is no night to be about.' " The girl spat viciously upon the floor.

Holmes's voice was even as he said, "The gentleman fled, I presume?"

"Up t' 'is room, w'ere else? But not a-takin' me with 'im!"

"An odd place for a gentleman to live, would you not say?"

The girl wiped her mouth with the back of her hand. " 'E can live w'ere 'e pleases, blarst 'is eyes!"

Holmes was already moving towards the door. As he passed me, he whispered, "Come, Watson. Hurry, hurry!"

Back in the fog, he gripped my hand and pulled me recklessly forward. "We have him, Watson! I'm certain of it! Visits—questions—a dropped comment—and we come upon the trail of a fiend who can do many things. But making himself invisible is not one of them!"

Sheer exultancy rang out from every word as Holmes dragged me after him. A few moments later I found myself stumbling up a flight of narrow stairs against a wooden wall.

The exertion of the chase had taxed even Holmes's superb stamina; and, as we climbed, he gasped out his words. "This Pacquin is a sordid rooming-house, Watson. Whitechapel abounds with them. Fortunately, I was familiar with the name."

I glanced upwards, and saw that we were approaching a partly-open door. We reached the top of the stairs, and Holmes hurled himself inside. I staggered after him.

"What accursed luck!" cried he. "Some-one has been here before us!"

Not in all our days together had I seen Holmes present such an image of bitter frustration. He loomed in the middle of a small, shabbily-furnished room, revolver in hand, grey eyes a-blaze.

"If this was the lair of the Ripper," cried I, "he has fled."

"And for good, no doubt of that!"

"Perhaps Lestrade was also on his trail."

"I wager not! Lestrade is off bumbling through some alley."

The room had been well-torn up in the Ripper's haste to get away. As I sought words to ease Holmes's disappointment, he grimly took my arm. "If you doubt that the maniac operates from this den, Watson, look there."

I followed his pointing finger, and saw it. The grisly trophy—the breast missing from the corpse in the Montague Street morgue.

I have seen violence and death enough, but this was worse. There was no heat here, no anger; only dank horror, and my stomach revolted against it.

"I must leave, Holmes. I shall wait for you below."

"There is no point in my remaining, either. What is to be seen here is to be seen quickly. Our quarry is far too cunning to leave the slightest clew behind."

At that moment, possibly because my mind sought a diversion, I remembered the message. "By the way, Holmes, a messenger brought a note to Baker Street this afternoon from your brother Mycroft. In the excitement, I forgot." I handed him the envelope forth-with, and he tore it open.

If I expected his thanks, I was disappointed. After reading the missive, Holmes raised cold eyes. "Would you care to hear what Mycroft writes?"

"Indeed I would."

"The note reads: 'Dear Sherlock: A bit of information has come to me, in a way I shall explain later, which will be of value to you. A man named Max Klein is the proprietor of a Whitechapel sink named The Angel and Crown. Klein, however, purchased the place only recently; some four months ago, in fact, Your brother, Mycroft.' "

I was too confounded to suspect which way the wind lay. I give myself that grace, at least, because so much more can be explained only by admitting to an abysmal stupidity. At any rate, I blurted forth, "Oh, yes, Holmes. I was aware of that. I got the information from the girl with whom I talked during my visit to The Angel and Crown."

"Did you indeed?" asked Holmes, dangerously.

"A redoubtable fellow, this Klein. It occurred to me that it had not taken him long to impress his personality upon the place."

Holmes exploded, raising his fists. "Great God in Heaven! I wade knee-deep in idiots!"

The wind I had not suspected struck me with its blast. My mouth dropped open. I managed feebly to say, "Holmes, I do not understand."

"Then there is no hope for you, Watson! First, you garner the exact information that would have enabled me to solve this case, and you blithely keep it to yourself. Then, you forget to give me the note containing that same vital fact. Watson! Watson! Whose side are you on?"

If I had been confused before, I was now completely at sea. No protest was possible; and defiance, defence of my self-esteem, was out of the question.

But Holmes was never a man to belabour a point. "The Angel and Crown, Watson!" cried he, leaping towards the door. "No, to the morgue first! We shall present that devil with a sample of his own handiwork!"

Ellery Hears from the Past

The doorbell rang.

Ellery slammed down the journal. It was undoubtedly that alcoholic blotter again. He debated answering, glanced guiltily at his typewriter, and went out into the foyer and opened the door.

It was not Grant Ames, but a Western Union messenger. Ellery scribbled his name and read the unsigned telegram.

WILL YOU FOR BLANK'S SAKE PLUG IN YOUR TELEPHONE QUESTION MARK AM GOING STIR CRAZY EXCLAMATION POINT

"No answer," Ellery said. He tipped the messenger and went straightway to obey the Inspector's order.

Muttering to himself, he also plugged in his shaver and plowed its snarling head through his beard. As long as he keeps phoning, he thought, he's still in Bermuda. If I can browbeat him into just one more week . . .

The revitalized phone rang. Ellery snapped the shaver off and answered. Good old Dad.

But it was not good old Dad. It was the quavering voice of an old lady. A very old lady.

"Mr. Queen?"

"Yes?"

"I have been expecting to hear from you."

"I must apologize," Ellery said. "I planned to call on you, but Dr. Watson's manuscript caught me at a most awkward time. I'm up to my ears in a manuscript of my own."

"I'm so sorry."

"I'm the one who's sorry, believe me."

"Then you have not had the time to read it?"

"On the contrary, it was a temptation I couldn't resist, deadline or not. I've had to ration myself, though. I still have two chapters to go."

"Perhaps, Mr. Queen, with your time so limited, I'd best wait until you have completed your own work."

"No—please. My problems there are solved. And I've looked forward to this chat."

The cultured old voice chuckled. "I needn't mention that my advance order for your new mystery has been placed, as always. Or would you consider that deliberate flattery? I hope not!"

"You're very kind."

There was something under the quiet, precise diction, the restraint, the discipline, something Ellery felt sure of, possibly because he had been expecting it —a tension, as if the old lady were almost to the snapping point.

"Were you at all troubled as to the authenticity of the manuscript, Mr. Queen?"

"At first, frankly, when Grant brought me the manuscript, I thought it a forgery. I soon changed my mind."

"You must have thought my mode of delivery eccentric."

"Not after reading the opening chapter," Ellery said. "I understood completely."

The old voice trembled. "Mr. Queen, *he did not do it. He was not the Ripper!*"

Ellery tried to soothe her distress. "It's been so many years. Does it really matter any longer?"

"It does, it does! Injustice always matters. Time changes many things, but not that."

Ellery reminded her that he had not yet finished the manuscript.

"But you know, I feel that you know."

"I'm aware in which direction the finger's pointing."

"And keeps pointing, to the end. But it is not true, Mr. Queen! Sherlock Holmes was wrong for once. Dr. Watson was not to blame. He merely recorded the case as it unfolded—as Mr. Holmes dictated. But Mr. Holmes failed, and did a great injustice."

"But the manuscript was never published——"

"That makes no genuine difference, Mr. Queen. The verdict was known, the stain indelibly imprinted."

"But what can I do? No one can change yesterday."

"The manuscript is all I have, sir! The manuscript and that abominable lie! Sherlock Holmes was not infallible. Who is? God reserves infallibility for Himself alone. The truth must be hidden in the manuscript somewhere, Mr. Queen. I am pleading with you to find it."

"I'll do my best."

"Thank you, young man. Thank you so very much."

With the connection safely broken, Ellery slammed down the phone and glared at it. It was a miserable invention. He was a nice guy who did good works and was kind to his father, and now this.

He was inclined to wish a pox on the head of John Watson, M.D., and all adoring Boswells (where was his?); but then he sighed, remembering the old lady's trembling voice, and sat down with Watson's manuscript again.

CHAPTER X

The Tiger of The Angel and Crown

"I earnestly hope, my dear fellow, that you will accept my apology."

These words from Holmes were the most welcome I had ever received. We were back in the street, pushing along through the fog, as there were no hansoms cruising Whitechapel that night.

"You were totally justified, Holmes."

"To the contrary. I displayed a childish petulance that ill becomes a grown man. Blaming others for one's own mistakes is indefensible. The information, which you so readily extracted from the girl Polly, I should have had the intelligence to come by long ago. You actually proved an ability to do my work far better than I have done it myself."

All of which was specious; but Holmes's praise salved my pride, nonetheless.

"I cannot accept the accolade, Holmes," I protested. "It did not occur to me that Klein was indicated as your missing link."

"That," said Holmes, still over-generous, "was because you neglected to turn your perceptions in the proper direction. We were looking for a strong man, a man brutal and remorseless. Klein, from what you told me, filled that bill; also, from what I myself observed in the pub. Others in Whitechapel would qualify as equally vicious, although it is true that the other bit of information points directly to Klein."

"His recent purchase of the pub? When you explain, it becomes quite simple."

"What happened is now predictable, with only the smallest percentage in favour of error. Klein saw an opportunity in the person of Michael Osbourne. Both Michael and, beyond all doubt, the prostitute Angela, of whom Michael became enamoured, were weak individuals, easily controlled by this cruelly dominating man. It was Klein who engineered the infamous marriage that ruined Michael Osbourne."

"But to what purpose?"

"Blackmail, Watson! The plan failed when Michael stood upon his better nature and refused his coöperation. The plot was saved by Klein only through sheer luck, I am certain. Thus he was able to extort enough money to buy The Angel and Crown, and has no doubt further feathered his noisome nest since."

"But so much is still unanswered, Holmes. Michael—reduced to a state of imbecility. His wife, Angela—whom, I remind you, we have yet to locate—hideously scarred."

"In good time, Watson, in good time."

My confusion was the more compounded by Holmes's tone of confidence.

"Their present plight, you may be sure, is the result of Klein's rage at being thwarted by Michael's refusal to be a party to the blackmail scheme. No doubt it was Klein who administered that brutal beating to Michael which brought on his imbecility. How Angela became disfigured is not so evident, but I suggest that she went to Michael's defence."

At this moment, we walked out of the fog into a pocket of visibility, and saw the gate to the mortuary. I shuddered. "And now, Holmes, you plan to transport the body of that poor girl to The Angel and Crown?"

"Hardly, Watson," said he, absently.

"But you mentioned confronting Klein with his handiwork."

"That we shall do, I promise you."

Shaking my head, I followed Holmes through the mortuary into the hostel, where we found Dr. Murray ministering to the blackened eye of a man who had probably imbibed violence with his pint in some pub.

"Is Michael Osbourne on the premises?" demanded Holmes.

Dr. Murray was haggard. Over-work, and the thankless task of caring for the uncared-for, were taking their toll. Said he, "A short time ago, I would not have recognised that name——"

"Please," interrupted Holmes. "Time is paramount, Dr. Murray. I must take him away with us."

"To-night? Now?"

"There have been certain developments, Doctor. Before dawn, the Ripper will have been run to earth. The account must be settled with the beast responsible for Whitechapel's blood-bath."

Dr. Murray was as bewildered as I. "I do not understand. Do you mean, sir, that the Ripper is a creature of an even greater villain?"

"In a sense. Have you seen Inspector Lestrade lately?"

"He was here an hour ago. He is undoubtedly out in the fog somewhere."

"Tell him, should he return, to follow me to The Angel and Crown."

"But why are you taking Michael Osbourne with you?"

"To confront his wife," said Holmes, impatiently. "Where is he, man? We waste precious time!"

"You will find him in the small room off this end of the mortuary. That is where he sleeps."

We found the imbecile there, and Holmes shook him gently awake. "Angela is waiting for you," said he.

There was no flicker of understanding in the vacant eyes; but, with the trust of a child, he accompanied us into the fog. It was now so thick that we depended completely upon Holmes's hound-like senses to keep us on our course. And, so sinister was the atmosphere of London that night, I half-expected to feel the bite of a blade between my ribs at any moment.

But my curiosity was strong. I ventured a query. "Holmes, I assume that you expect to find Angela Osbourne at The Angel and Crown."

"I am certain of it."

"But what purpose is served by facing her with Michael?"

"The woman may be reluctant to speak. There will be a certain shock-value in suddenly confronting her with her husband."

"I see," said I, although I did not, quite; and lapsed back into silence.

At last there was the sound of a hand tapping upon wood, and I heard Holmes say, "This is it, Watson. Now we search."

A faintly-glowing window indicated that it was a domicile of some sort. Said I, "Was that the front door you tapped upon?"

"It was, but we must find another. I wish to reach the upper rooms unseen."

We pawed along the wall and around a corner. Then a breeze stirred the fog, thinning it.

Holmes had thought to borrow a dark lantern during our visit to the hostel, although he had not used it during our journey. It might well have brought us to the unwelcome attention of foot-pads. It now served us in good stead, outlining a rear door, apparently used for the delivery of beer-kegs and spirits. Holmes pushed the panel open and reached inside. "The hasp has been recently broken," said he; and we went through stealthily.

We were in a store-room. I could hear the muffled noise from the public-room, but it appeared that our presence had gone undetected. Holmes quickly found a laddered ascent to the upper storey. We climbed it with caution, crept through a trap-door, and found ourselves at the end of a dimly-lit corridor.

"Wait here with Michael," whispered Holmes. He soon returned. "Come!"

We followed him to a closed door; a line of light shone upon our boot-tips.

Holmes pressed us back against the wall and tapped upon the panel. There was quick movement inside. The door opened, and a female voice queried, "Tommy?"

Holmes's hand was in like a snake and locked over a shadowed face. "Do not scream, Madam," said he, in a commanding whisper. "We mean you no harm. But we must speak to you."

Holmes warily relaxed the pressure of his hand. The woman's voice asked, "Who are you?" in understandable fear.

"I am Sherlock Holmes. I have brought your husband."

I heard a gasp. "You have brought Michael—here? In God's name, why?"

"It was the prudent thing to do."

Holmes entered the room and nodded to me to follow. Grasping Michael's arm, I did so.

Two oil-lamps were burning, and in their light I saw a woman, wearing a veil whose gauzy texture did not quite conceal a hideous scar. It was undoubtedly Angela Osbourne.

At the sight of the imbecile—her husband—she grasped the arms of the chair in which she sat, and half-arose. But then she sank back and sat with the rigidity of a corpse, her hands gripped together.

"He does not recognise me," she murmured in despair.

Michael Osbourne stood silently by me, regarding her with his empty eyes.

"As well you know, Madam," said Holmes. "But the time is short. You must speak. We know that Klein is responsible for both your husband's condition and your disfigurement. Tell me about the interlude in Paris."

The woman wrung her hands. "I will not waste time making excuses for myself, sir. There are none. As you can perhaps see, I am not like those poor girls downstairs who fell into their shameful calling through poverty and ignorance. I am what I have become because of that beast, Max Klein.

"You wish to know about Paris. I went there because Max had arranged an assignation for me with a wealthy French merchant. Whilst this was taking place, I met Michael Osbourne, and he was taken with me. Believe me, sir, I had no intention of shaming him; but when Max Klein arrived in Paris, he saw an opportunity to use the smitten youth for his own ends. Our marriage was the first step in his plan, and he compelled me to use my wiles. Michael and I were married, despite my tearful protestations to Max.

"Then, with Michael safely in his clutch, Max sprang his trap. It was the most blatant blackmail, Mr. Holmes. He would acquaint the Duke of Shires with the facts, said he, and threaten to reveal his son's wife for what I was, parading me before all the world, unless his Grace paid."

"But this never came about," said Holmes, eyes gleaming.

"No. Michael had more spine than Max had anticipated. He threatened to kill Max, even made the attempt. It was a dreadful scene! Michael stood no chance before Max's brute strength. He felled Michael with a blow. But then Max's temper, his sheer savagery of nature, seized him, and he administered the terrible beating that resulted in Michael's present condition. Indeed, the beating would have ended in Michael's death, had I not intervened. Whereupon Max plucked a knife from the table, and rendered me as you see. His rage left him in the nick of time, averting a double murder."

"His beating of Michael and mutilation of you did not make him abandon his plan?"

"No, Mr. Holmes. Had it done so, I am sure Max would have left us in Paris. Instead, using the considerable sum of money he took from Michael, he brought us back to Whitechapel and purchased this public-house."

"That money was not gained through blackmail, then?"

"No. The Duke of Shires was generous with Michael until he disowned him. Max stripped Michael of every penny he had. Then he imprisoned us here, in The Angel and Crown, plotting, no doubt, to go on with whatever infamous plan he had in mind."

"You said he brought you *back* to Whitechapel, Mrs. Osbourne," said Holmes. "Is this Klein's habitat?"

"Oh, yes, he was born here. He knows its every street and alley. He is greatly feared in this district. There are few who dare cross him."

"What was his plan? Do you know?"

"Blackmail, I am sure. But something happened to balk him; I never discovered what it was. Then Max came to me one morning, fiercely elated. He said that his fortune was made, that he needed Michael no longer, and planned to murder him. I pleaded with him. Perhaps I was able to touch off a spark of humanity in his heart; in any case, he humoured me, as he put it, and delivered Michael to Dr. Murray's hostel, knowing his memory was gone."

"The good fortune that elated Klein, Mrs. Osbourne. What was its nature?"

"I never learned. I did ask him if the Duke of Shires had agreed to pay him a large sum of money. He slapped me and told me to mind my affairs."

"Since that time you have been a prisoner in this place?"

"A willing one, Mr. Holmes. Max has forbidden me to leave this room, it is true, but my mutilated face is my true gaoler." The woman bowed her veiled head. "That is all I can tell you, sir."

"Not quite, Madam!"

"What else?" said she, head rising.

"There is the matter of the surgeon's-case. Also, of an unsigned note informing Lord Carfax of his brother Michael's whereabouts."

"I have no idea, sir——" she began.

"Pray do not evade me, Madam. I must know everything."

"There seems to be no way of keeping a secret from you!" cried Angela Osbourne. "What are you, man or devil? If Max were to get wind of this, he would surely kill me!"

"We are your friends, Madam. He will not hear it from us. How did you discover that the case had been pledged with Joseph Beck?"

"I have a friend. He comes here at the risk of his life, to talk to me and do my errands."

"No doubt the 'Tommy' you expected when I knocked upon your door?"

"Please do not involve him, Mr. Holmes, I beg of you!"

"I see no reason to involve him. But I wish to know more about him."

"Tommy helps out at times at the Montague Street Hostel."

"You sent him there originally?"

"Yes, for news of Michael. After Max delivered him to the hostel, I slipped out one night, at great risk to myself, and posted the note you refer to. I felt I owed Michael at least that. I was sure Max would never find out, because I could see no way in which Lord Carfax might trace us, with Michael's memory gone."

"And the surgeon's-case?"

"Tommy overheard Sally Young discuss with Dr. Murray the possibility of pawning it. It occurred to me that it might be a means of interesting you to turn your talents, Mr. Holmes, to the apprehension of Jack the Ripper. Again I slipped out, redeemed the case, and posted it to you."

"Removing the post-mortem scalpel was deliberate?"

"Yes. I was sure you would understand. Then, when I heard no word of your entrance into the case, I became desperate, and I sent the missing scalpel to you."

Holmes leaned forward, his hawk's-face keen. *Madam, when did you decide that Max Klein is the Ripper?*

Angela Osbourne put her hands to her veil, and moaned. "Oh, I don't know, I don't know!"

"What made you decide he was the monster?" asked Holmes, inexorably.

"The nature of the crimes! I can conceive of no one save Max as being capable of such atrocities. His maniacal temper. His dreadful rages . . ."

We were not destined to hear any more from Angela Osbourne. The door burst open, and Max Klein sprang into the room. His face was contorted by an unholy passion that he was just able, it appeared, to hold in leash. He had a cocked pistol in his hand.

"If either of you moves so much as a finger," cried he, "I'll blow you both to Hell!"

There could be little doubt that he meant it.

Ellery's Legman's Last Bow

The doorbell rang.

Ellery ignored it.

It rang again.

He kept reading.

A third time.

He finished the chapter.

When he finally got there, his caller had given up and left. But he had slipped a telegram under the foyer door.

BOSOM FRIEND DASH WHILE HUNTING A THORN YOUR LEGMAN FOUND A ROSE STOP HE WILL HUNT NO MORE STOP HER NAME IS RACHEL HAGER BUT A NAME CANNOT DO JUSTICE TO HER STOP SHE WENT TO THAT PARTY ONLY BECAUSE I WAS THERE COMMA A FACT THAT POPS MY BUTTONS STOP LAWFUL WEDLOCK IS NEXT STOP STOP WE PLAN CHILDREN STOP OUR JOINT LOVE TO YOU STOP

GRANT

"Thank God I'm shed of *him*," said Ellery, aloud, and went back to Sherlock Holmes.

CHAPTER XI

Holocaust

I think that Holmes would have braved Klein's pistol, were it not that the proprietor of The Angel and Crown was immediately followed into Mrs. Osbourne's room by a man whom I recognised as one of the thugs who had attacked Holmes and me. Under the muzzles of two weapons, Holmes perforce held himself in check.

Max Klein's rage became evil satisfaction.

"Tie them up," snarled he, to his confederate. "And the man who tries to resist gets a bullet through his head."

The thug tore the cords from the window-drapes and swiftly lashed Holmes's hands behind his back, whilst I stood helplessly by. He thereupon treated me in like manner, going even further under Klein's command.

"Shove our good doctor into that chair and lash his ankles to its legs." Why Klein should have considered me a greater threat than Holmes, I did not understand. What courage I possess is thoroughly tempered, I fear, with a great desire to live out the years allotted me by the Almighty.

As his creature did his bidding, Klein turned on Holmes. "Did you think you could walk into my place undetected, Mr. Holmes?"

Replied Holmes, quietly, "I am curious to know how our entrance was discovered."

Klein laughed, a brutal sound. "One of my men had to roll some empty kegs out. Not spectacular, I grant you, Mr. Holmes. But I've got you just the same."

"Getting me, as you phrase it," said Holmes, "and keeping me, Klein, may be a steed of a different colour."

It was evident to me that Holmes was attempting to gain time. But it was to no avail. Klein surveyed my bonds, found them to his liking, and said, "You will come with me, Mr. Holmes. I shall deal with you in private. And if you expect help from below, you will be disappointed. I have cleared the place; it is closed and locked."

The thug indicated Angela Osbourne with a worried glance. "Is it safe leavin' this cull with 'er? She might loose 'im."

"She would not dare," Klein laughed again. "Not if she knows what's good for her. She still values her miserable life."

This proved depressingly true. After Holmes and Michael Osbourne were dragged away, Angela Osbourne was impervious to all persuasion. I spoke with as urgent eloquence as I could command, but she only stared at me in despair, moaning, "Oh, I dare not, I dare not."

Thus passed several of the longest minutes of my life, as I struggled against my bonds, telling myself that Holmes would yet save the day.

Then came the most dreadful moment of all.

The door opened.

The chair in which I sat trussed was so situated that, when I heard the panel swing inwards, I was unable to see who stood there. Angela Osbourne, however, sat in view of the doorway. I could only look in her direction for a clew.

She arose from her chair. Somehow the veil slipped aside, and I saw that hideously-scarred face clearly. Every fibre of my being shrank at the unspeakable mutilation which Klein had visited upon her; but it was made even more repulsive by the wild expression with which she regarded the intruder in the doorway. Then she spoke. "The Ripper! Oh, God in Heaven! It is Jack the Ripper!"

I confess with shame that my first reaction was relief. The man advanced within my sight, and when I beheld the slim, aristocratic figure, clad in top-hat, perfectly-fitting evening-clothes, and opera cape, I cried thankfully, "Lord Carfax! You have come providentially!"

The ghastly truth dawned upon me an instant later, when I espied the glittering knife in his hand. He glanced my way, but only for a moment, and with no sign of recognition. And I beheld the madness in that noble face, a hungry, wild-beast's urge to destroy.

Angela Osbourne was incapable of further outcry. She sat in frozen terror as the lordly Ripper rushed upon her and in a trice tore away her upper clothing. She could only mumble a prayer before Lord Carfax plunged the weapon into her uncovered breast. His clumsy efforts at dissection are best not described; suffice it to say that they did not approach the skill of his earlier mutilations, undoubtedly because he felt pressed for time.

As the body of Angela Osbourne fell to the floor in a welter of blood, the madman seized upon one of the oil-lamps and extinguished the flame. Unscrewing the wick-holder, he proceeded to pour out the oil. His intent was all too clear. Around the room he dashed, like some demon out of Hell, leaving oil in his wake; and then out into the corridor, from whence he returned soon with an empty lamp, which he flung to the floor in a shower of glass.

And then he seized the other lamp, and with it ignited the pool of oil at his feet.

Strangely, he did not flee; even at that worst moment of my life, I wondered why. As it developed, his maniacal ego proved my salvation and his destruction. As the flames mounted, following the river of oil into the corridor, he rushed at me. I closed my eyes and consigned my soul to its Maker. To my stupefaction, instead of slaying me, he slashed my bonds.

With dilated eyes, he hauled me upright and dragged me through the flames towards the nearest window. I sought to struggle with him, but with his maniac's strength he threw me savagely against the window, and the glass shattered.

It was then that he uttered the cry that has echoed through my nightmares ever since.

"Carry the message, Dr. Watson!" he screamed. "Tell them that Lord Carfax is Jack the Ripper!"

With that, he thrust me through the window. Flames had caught my clothing; and I remember that, ludicrously, I slapped at them as I fell the one storey to the street. Then there was a stunning impact with the stones below, I thought I heard running footsteps, and unconsciousness mercifully gripped me.

I knew no more.

CHAPTER XII

The End of Jack the Ripper

The first face I beheld was that of Rudyard, the friend who had taken over my practice as locum tenens. I was in my room at Baker Street.

"A near thing, Watson," said he, as he felt my pulse.

Awareness came flooding back to me. "How long have I slept, Rudyard?"

"Some twelve hours. I gave you a sedative when they carried you here."

"My condition?"

"A most salutary one, under the circumstances. A broken ankle; a sprained wrist; burns no doubt painful, but superficial."

"Holmes. Where is he? Has he been——?"

Rudyard gestured. There was Holmes, seated grave-faced, at the opposite side of my bed. He was pale, but appeared otherwise unharmed. Thankfulness welled up in me.

"Well, I must be off," said Rudyard. To Holmes he said, "See that he doesn't talk too long, Mr. Holmes."

Rudyard departed, saying that he would be back to dress my burns, and warning me again not to tax my strength. But, even through my pain and discomfort, I could not restrain my curiosity. Holmes, I fear, was in no better case, despite his concern for my condition. So I soon found myself relating what had occurred in poor Angela Osbourne's room after Klein had forced him from it.

Holmes nodded, but I could see that he was struggling with a decision. Finally, he said to me, "I fear, old friend, that we have gone through our last adventure together."

"Why do you say that?" asked I, overwhelmed with dismay.

"Because your good wife will never again entrust your welfare to my bungling hands."

"Holmes!" cried I. "I am not a child!"

He shook his head. "You must go back to sleep."

"You know that cannot be until you tell me how you managed to escape from Klein. In a dream, after my sedation, I saw your mangled remains . . ."

I shuddered, and he placed his hand upon mine in a rare display of affection. "My opportunity arose when the staircase burst into flames," said Holmes. "Klein had glutted himself with gloating over me, and he was just raising his weapon when the flames swept down. He and his henchman died in the fire as the structure went up like tinder. The Angel and Crown is now a roofless ruin."

"But you, Holmes! How——?"

Holmes smiled, and shrugged his shoulders. "There was never a doubt but that I could slip my bonds," said he. "You know my dexterity. All that lacked was the chance, and the fire provided it. Unhappily, I was unable to save Michael Osbourne. He seemed to welcome death, poor fellow, and resisted my efforts to drag him out; indeed, he threw himself into the flames, and I was compelled to abandon his body to save my life."

"A blessing in disguise," I muttered. "And that infamous beast, Jack the Ripper?"

Holmes's grey eyes were clouded with sadness; his thoughts appeared to be elsewhere. "Lord Carfax died also. And also from choice, I am certain, like his brother."

"Naturally. He preferred death by fiery immolation to the hangman's noose."

Holmes seemed elsewhere still. In the gravest of voices, he murmured, "Watson, let us respect the decision of an honourable man."

"Honourable man! Surely you are jesting? Oh, I see. You refer to his lucid moments. And the Duke of Shires?"

Holmes's chin was sunken upon his chest. "I am a bearer of dire news about the Duke, too. He has taken his life."

"I see. He could not bear the awful revelation of his first son's crimes. How did you learn this, Holmes?"

"I proceeded directly from the fire to his Berkeley Square residence. Lestrade accompanied me. We were too late. He had already had the news of Lord Carfax. Whereupon he had fallen upon the sword he kept concealed in his stick."

"A true nobleman's death!"

I fancied Holmes nodded; it was the merest inclination of his head. He seemed deeply depressed.

"An unsatisfactory case, Watson, most unsatisfactory," said he. And he fell silent.

I sensed his wish to conclude the conversation, but I would not have it so. I had forgotten all about my broken ankle and the pain of my burns.

"I do not see why, Holmes. The Ripper is dead."

"Yes," said he. "Really, Watson, you must rest now." He made as if to rise.

"I cannot rest," said I, artfully, "until all the pieces are in place." He sank back with resignation. "Even I am able to follow the sequence of those last events that lead up to the fire. The maniacal Ripper, functioning from behind his philanthropic façade as Lord Carfax, did not know the identity or the whereabouts of Angela Osbourne or Max Klein. Am I correct?"

Holmes did not reply.

"When you found his lair," I pressed on, "I am sure you knew also who he was?"

Here Holmes nodded.

"Then we went to the hostel, and although we did not see him there, he saw and heard us—that, or he came shortly thereafter and learned of The Angel and Crown from Dr. Murray, who would have had no reason to withhold the information. Lord Carfax followed us and discovered the beer-keg entrance, as we did."

"Lord Carfax preceded us," said Holmes, abruptly. "You will recall that we found the hasp recently broken."

"Amended. He must have been able to move through the foggy streets more surely than we. No doubt we interrupted his stalking of Angela Osbourne, who was slated to be his next victim. He must have been lying in wait in a corridor-doorway whilst we entered Mrs. Osbourne's room."

Holmes did not contest this.

"Then, realising you had run him to earth, he determined to conclude his infamous career in the blaze of mad defiance that his monstrous ego dictated. His final words to me were, 'Carry the message, Dr. Watson! Tell them that Lord Carfax is Jack the Ripper!' Only an egomaniac would have said that."

Holmes came to his feet with finality. "At any rate, Watson, Jack the Ripper will prowl no more. And now we have defied your doctor's orders long enough. I insist that you sleep."

With that, he left me.

Ellery Visits the Past

Ellery put the Watson manuscript down thoughtfully. He barely heard the click of the lock and the opening and closing of the front door.

He looked up to find his father standing in the study doorway.

"Dad!"

"Hi, son," said the Inspector with a defiant grin. "I just couldn't stand it down there anymore. So here I am."

"Welcome home."

"Then you're not sore?"

"You stayed longer than I expected."

The Inspector came in, scaled his hat to the sofa, and turned to regard his son with relief. It soon became concern.

"You look like hell. What's wrong, Ellery?"

Ellery did not reply.

"How do I look?" asked his father cunningly.

"A damsite better than when I packed you off."

"You're sure *you're* all right?"

"I'm fine."

"Don't give me that. Is your story still sour?"

"No, it's going fine. Everything's fine."

But the old man was not satisfied. He sat down on the sofa and crossed his legs and said, "Tell me all about it."

Ellery shrugged. "I should never have been born the son of a cop. All right, something's happened. An interlocking of events, past and present. The loosening of an old knot."

"Talk English."

"Grant Ames dropped in on me."

"You told me that."

"I got sucked into the manuscript. One thing led to another. And here I am."

"I don't get it."

Ellery sighed. "I suppose I'll have to tell you all about it."

And he talked for a long time.

"And that's where it stands, Dad. She believes absolutely in his innocence. She's nursed it all her life. I suppose she didn't know what to do about it until, in her old age, she suddenly got this inspiration to drag me into it. Inspiration!"

"What are you going to do?"

"I'd just made up my mind to pay her a visit when you walked in on me."

"I should think so!" Inspector Queen got up and took the journal from Ellery's hand. "The way I see it, son, you've got absolutely no choice. After all, she's asked for it."

Ellery got to his feet. "Why don't you read the manuscript while I'm gone?"

"That's just what I'm going to do."

He drove north into Westchester, taking Route 22 until he came to Somers. He passed the wooden elephant at the main intersection, a reminder that Barnum & Bailey's Circus had once wintered there. In Putnam County he thought of the Revolutionary heroes, hoping they were all in a hero's heaven somewhere.

But these were surface thoughts. In depth he was thinking of the old lady he would find at the end of his journey. They were not pleasant thoughts.

He finally turned in at a trim little cottage with a doll's-house drive, got out, and reluctantly went up to the front door. It opened to his knock immediately, as if she had been lying in wait for him. He had half wished she would not be at home.

"Deborah Osbourne Spain," he said, looking down at her. "Hello."

She was very old, of course; she must be in her late 80s, according to his calculations. The manuscript had not given her age on the day Holmes and Watson visited Shires Castle, except in approximate figures. She could be 90.

Like so many very old ladies, especially the tiny plumpish ones, there was a slightly withered-apple look to her, with the bloom still touching her cheeks. Her bosom was large for her size, and fallen, as if tired of its weight. Only her eyes were young. They were bright, and direct, and they twinkled in spite of themselves.

"Do come in, Mr. Queen."

"Could you make it Ellery, Mrs. Spain?"

"It is something I have never quite become accustomed to," she said, ushering him into a cozy little parlor, as mid-Victorian as Victoria's bustle, Ellery thought. It was like stepping into 19th Century England. "I mean, the American habit of instant familiarity. However—take that Morris chair, Ellery—if you wish."

"I wish." He sat down and looked about. "I see you've kept the faith."

She seated herself in a ducal chair, in which she looked lost. "What else does an ancient Englishwoman have?" she asked with a faint smile. "I know—I sound disgustingly Anglophilic. But it's so difficult to get away from one's beginnings. Actually, I'm quite comfortable here. And a visit to New Rochelle once in a while to see Rachel's roses rounds out my existence."

"Rachel *was* the one."

"Oh, yes. At my request."

"Miss Hager is related to you how, exactly?"

"My granddaughter. Shall we have tea?"

"Not just now, if you don't mind, Mrs. Spain," said Ellery. "I'm too chockful of questions. But first." He sat on the edge of the chair, avoiding the lace antimacassar. "You saw him. You met them both. Holmes. Watson. How I envy you!"

Deborah Osbourne Spain's eyes looked far into the past. "It was so very long ago. But of course I remember them. Mr. Holmes's glance, sharp as a sword. And so reserved. When I put my hand in his, I'm sure it disconcerted him. But he was very sweet. They were both such gentlemen. That above all. In those days, Ellery, being a gentleman was important. Of course, I was a little girl, and I recall them as giants, towering to the sky. As I suppose they were, in a way."

"May I ask how you came by the manuscript?"

"After Dr. Watson wrote it, the journal was turned over by Mr. Holmes to the Osbourne estate. It became the responsibility of the estate's solicitor, bless him! He was so faithful to my interests. Then, after I was grown, and shortly before he died, he told me about the manuscript. I begged for it, and he sent it to me. His name was Dobbs, Alfred Dobbs. I think of him so often."

"Why did you wait so long, Mrs. Spain, before doing what you did?"

"Please. Everyone calls me Grandma Deborah. Won't you?"

"Grandma Deborah it shall be."

"I don't know why I waited so long," the old lady said. "The idea of asking an expert to verify my conviction never crystallized in my mind, although I am sure it has been there for a long time. Lately, a feeling that there is a need to hurry has come over me. How much longer can I live? And I should like to die in peace."

The implicit plea moved Ellery to her aid. "Your decision to send me the manuscript came from the manuscript itself, I take it?"

"Yes. Afterwards, Mr. Ames confided in Rachel about the hunt you sent him on."

"Grant's searching accomplished an end, though not the one I expected," Ellery smiled.

"Bless him! Bless them both. I know he gave you no help, Ellery. I also knew you would find me, just as Mr. Holmes had no difficulty in tracing the owner of the surgeon's kit. But I'm still curious as to how you did it."

"It was elementary, Grandma Deborah. It was obvious from the first that the sender had some personal interest in the case. So I put a call through to a friend of mine, a genealogist. He had no trouble tracing you from Shires Castle, as a child, to the custody of the San Francisco branch of the family. I had the names of Grant's four young ladies, and I was sure one of the names would pop up somewhere. From your marriage to Barney Spain in 1906 my expert got to the marriage of your daughter. And, lo and behold, the man your daughter married was named Hager. Q.E.D." His smile became a look of concern. "You're tired. We can put this off for another time."

"Oh, no! I'm fine." The young eyes pleaded. "He was a wonderful man, my father. Kind, gentle. He was not a monster. He was not!"

"You're sure you don't want to lie down?"

"No, no. Not until you've told me . . ."

"Then lie back in your chair, Grandma. Relax. And I'll talk."

Ellery took the withered old hand in his, and he talked against the ticking of the grandfather clock in the corner, its pendulum, like a mechanical finger, wiping the seconds off the face of time.

The little frail hand in Ellery's squeezed at irregular intervals. Then it stopped squeezing, and lay in Ellery's hand like an autumn leaf.

After a while, there was a movement of the portieres at the archway to the parlor, and a middle-aged woman appeared, wearing a white housedress.

"She's fallen asleep," Ellery whispered.

He carefully laid the old hand on her breast and tiptoed from the room.

The woman accompanied him to the door. "I'm Susan Bates. I take care of her. She falls asleep like that more and more."

Ellery nodded and left the cottage and got into his car and drove back to Manhattan, feeling very tired himself. Even old.

The Ripper Case Journal—Final Note
January 12, 1908

Holmes vexes me. I confess, because he was out of England for an extended period, that I took it upon myself, against his wish, to put my notes for the Jack the Ripper case into narrative form. Twenty years have now passed. For nine of these, a new heir, a distant relation, has borne the Shires title. One, I might add, who spends but a fraction of his time in England, and cares little for either the title or its illustrious history.

I had come to feel, however, that it was high time the world was informed of the truth about the Ripper case, which held an equally illustrious place—if that is the word!—in the history of crime, and about Holmes's struggle to end the monster's bloody reign in Whitechapel.

On Holmes's return from abroad, I broached this to him, expressing myself in the most persuasive terms I could muster. But he is adamant in his refusal.

"No, no, Watson, let the bones lie mouldering. The world would be no richer from the publication of the story."

"But, Holmes! All this work——"

"I am sorry, Watson. But that is my last word in the matter."

"Then," said I, with ill-concealed annoyance, "allow me to present you with the manuscript. Perhaps you will find use for the paper as pipe-lighters."

"I am honoured, Watson, and touched," said he, most cheerfully. "In return, allow me to present you with the details of a little matter I have just brought to a successful conclusion. You may apply it to your undeniable *flair* for melodrama, and submit it to your publishers without delay. It has to do with a South American sailing-man, who came very close to duping a European financial syndicate with a 'genuine' roc's egg. Perhaps *The Case of the Peruvian Sinbad* will in some measure assuage your disappointment."

And thus, matters now stand.

Ellery Explains

Ellery's arrival was timely. Inspector Queen had just finished reading Dr. Watson's Ripper manuscript, and he was staring at the journal with marked dissatisfaction. He turned his stare on Ellery.

"Just as well it wasn't published. Holmes was right."

"I thought so, too." Ellery went to the bar. "Damn Grant! I forgot to order scotch."

"How did it turn out?"

"Better than I expected."

"Then you lied like a gentleman. Good for you."

"I didn't lie."

"What?"

"I didn't lie. I told her the truth."

"Then," said Inspector Queen coldly, "you're a rat-fink. Deborah Osbourne loved and believed in her father. She also believes in you. Your mind is certainly crooked enough to have twisted the truth a little."

"I didn't have to twist the truth."

"Why not? Tell me that! A little old lady——"

"Because, Dad," said Ellery, sinking into his swivel chair, "Lord Carfax wasn't Jack the Ripper. A lie wasn't necessary. Deborah's father was no monster. She was right about him all along. She knew it, I knew it——"

"But——"

"And so did Sherlock Holmes."

There was a silence of great length while *pater* tried to catch up with *filius* and failed.

"But it's all down here, Ellery!" protested the Inspector.

"Yes, it is."

"Richard Osbourne, this Lord Carfax, caught with the knife in his hand, butchering his last victim—why, Watson was an eyewitness!—wrote it all down!"

"Your point is, I take it, that Watson was an able reporter?"

"I'd say so. He also knew the evidence of his own eyes!"

Ellery got up and went over to his father, picked up the journal, and returned to his chair. "Watson was also human. He was oversubjective. He saw what Holmes wanted him to see. He reported what Holmes told him."

"Are you saying that Holmes was pulling a fast one?"

"You're damned right I am. The devious thing is that in this case every word from his lips was gospel. It's what he didn't say that counts."

"All *right*. What was it that he didn't say?"

"He didn't at any time, for instance, call Jack the Ripper by the name of Richard Osbourne or Lord Carfax."

"You're quibbling," snorted the Inspector.

Ellery riffled through the old journal. "Dad, didn't you spot the inconsistencies in the case? Certainly you weren't satisfied with the blackmail bit?"

"The blackmail? Let me see . . ."

"It went like this. Max Klein saw an opportunity for blackmail by conniving a marriage between Michael Osbourne and Angela, a prostitute. Considering the Duke of Shires's pride of name, that made sense from Klein's viewpoint. But it didn't work. The marriage became public knowledge."

"But Klein admitted to Angela that the plan had failed."

"Not exactly. He told her, after he'd brought the couple back to London, that the marriage was no longer important as a basis for blackmail. He'd found a better gimmick. Klein lost all interest in Michael and Angela after he discovered this new weapon, obviously a better one than the marriage."

"But the manuscript never said——"

"Dad, who was Klein? What was he? Holmes was aware from the start of his importance, even before the man was identified—when he was Holmes's missing link. And when Holmes confronted Angela, he pried a vital piece of information out of her. To quote her on the subject of Klein: 'Oh, yes, he was born here. He knows its every street and alley. He is greatly feared in this district. There are few who would dare cross him.'"

"So?"

"So what was the great secret Klein had discovered?"

"*The identity of Jack the Ripper*," said the Inspector slowly. "A man like that, who had an intimate knowledge of Whitechapel and its people——"

"Of course, Dad. That's what it had to be. And with the knowledge of the Ripper's identity Klein got rich blackmailing——"

"Lord Carfax."

"No. You'll recall that Lord Carfax was trying desperately to locate Klein and Angela. Blackmailers confront their victims."

"Maybe Carfax knew all the time."

"Then why didn't he strike earlier? Because he only learned that night at the morgue that Klein and Angela were at The Angel and Crown!"

"But Carfax struck at Angela, not Klein."

"Further proof that he was not the blackmail victim. He mistakenly saw his brother's wife as the evil force in the Osbourne disaster. That's why he killed her."

"But none of that is enough to base——"

"Then let's find some more. Let's follow Holmes and Watson that last night. You already know what *appeared* to happen. Let's see what really did. In the first place, there were two men on the trail of the Ripper that night—Sherlock Holmes *and* Lord Carfax. I'm sure Carfax already had his suspicions."

"What indication is there that Carfax was on the Ripper's trail?"

"I'm glad you asked that question," Ellery said sententiously. "Acting on the tip he'd picked up in Madame Leona's whorehouse, Holmes set out on the last leg of his search. He and Watson arrived at the room in the Pacquin——"

"And Holmes said, 'If this was the lair of the Ripper, he has fled.'"

"Holmes didn't say that, Watson did. Holmes cried, 'Someone has been here before us!' There's a world of difference in the two statements. One was the observation of a romantic. The other, Holmes's, of a man trained to read a scene with photographic accuracy."

"You have a point," the older Queen admitted.

"A vital one. But there are others."

"That both Holmes and Lord Carfax found the lair of Jack the Ripper at practically the same time?"

"Also that Carfax saw Holmes and Watson arrive at the Pacquin. He waited outside and followed them to the morgue. It had to be that way."

"Why?"

"In order for Carfax to act as he did, he needed two items of information—the identity of the Ripper, which he got at the Pacquin, and the place where he could find Angela and Klein, which he overheard at the morgue."

Inspector Queen got up and retrieved the journal. He searched and read: "'And that infamous beast, Jack the Ripper?' Watson asked Holmes that question. Holmes answered, 'Lord Carfax died also——'"

"Hold it," Ellery said. "None of this out-of-context business. Give me all of it."

"Quote: 'Holmes's grey eyes were clouded with sadness; his thoughts appeared to be elsewhere. "Lord Carfax died also. And also from choice, I am certain, like his brother."'"

"That's better. Now tell me, would Sherlock Holmes be sad over the death of Jack the Ripper?"

Inspector Queen shook his head and read on. "'Naturally. He no doubt preferred death by fiery immolation to the hangman's noose.'"

"Watson's words, not Holmes's. What Holmes then said was, 'Let us respect the decision of an honourable man.'"

"To which Watson replied, 'Honourable man! Surely you are jesting? Oh, I see. You refer to his lucid moments. And the Duke of Shires?'"

"Watson drew an unwarranted inference from what Holmes had said. Let's quote Holmes again: 'I proceeded directly from the fire to his'—meaning the

Duke's—'Berkeley Square residence . . . He had already had the news of Lord Carfax. Whereupon he had fallen upon the sword he kept concealed in his stick.'"

"And Watson exclaimed, 'A true nobleman's death!'"

"Again Watson was fooled by his own preconceptions and his misunderstanding of Holmes's deliberate indirection. Look, Dad. When Holmes reached the Duke of Shires's townhouse, he found the Duke dead. But 'he (the Duke) had already had the news of Lord Carfax.' I ask you, how could the Duke have 'already had the news of Lord Carfax'? The implication is clear that the Duke had been at his Pacquin lair, where Lord Carfax confronted him, after which he went home and killed himself."

"Because the Duke was the Ripper! And his son, knowing it, took the blame on himself to save his father's reputation!"

"Now you've got it," said Ellery gently. "Remember again what Carfax said to Watson—to spread the word that *he* was Jack the Ripper. He wanted to make dead sure that the guilt fell on his shoulders, not his father's."

"Then Holmes was right," murmured Inspector Queen. "He didn't want to give Lord Carfax's sacrifice away."

"And Deborah's faith in her father has been vindicated after three-quarters of a century."

"I'll be damned!"

Ellery took Dr. Watson's journal from his father's hand again and opened it to the "Final Note."

"'The Case of the Peruvian Sinbad,'" he muttered. "Something about a roc's egg . . ." His eyes glinted. "Dad, do you suppose Holmes could have been pulling Watson's leg about that one, too?"

Red Jack —
An Inspiration

G. I. JACK

A *Four Horsemen Story*

Loren D. Estleman

In addition to being one of America's most beloved writers of western fiction, Loren D. Estleman (1952–) is one of the most versatile authors in the widely defined genre of the mystery, producing novels and stories about Sherlock Holmes; seven Detroit crime novels, each set in a different decade; five novels about Peter Macklin, a hit man; novels based on real-life criminals; and numerous short stories across the literary spectrum.

Nevertheless, among his more than seventy published books, it is Estleman's twenty-five novels about Detroit private investigator Amos Walker for which he is best known. Beginning with *Motor City Blue* (1980), this hard-boiled series has been praised by fans as diverse as Harlan Coben, Steve Forbes, John D. MacDonald, John Lescroart, and the Amazing Kreskin. As one of the most honored writers in America, Estleman was given the Eye, the lifetime achievement award, by the Private Eye Writers of America, who also have given him four Shamus Awards.

He has been nominated for a National Book Award for his historical western novel *The High Rocks* (1979) and an Edgar Award for his Detroit crime novel *Whiskey River* (1990), while winning twenty additional national writing awards, notably the Owen Wister Award for Outstanding Contributions to the American West, the highest honor given by the Western Writers of America; *True West* magazine readers named him America's Best Living Fiction Writer in 2007.

"G.I. Jack" was written especially for this collection and has never previously been published.

Burke said, "What's with Mac? I offered to set him up with a redhead that rooms with a blonde I got my eye on and he said it was no-go."

The detective first grade was addressing his superior, Lieutenant Max Zagreb. They were at 1300 Beaubien, Detroit Police Headquarters, in the fourth year of the Second World War. Detective Third Grade McReary was dimly visible in a far corner reading by the light of a gooseneck lamp.

Just like Lincoln, Zagreb thought. He said, "He's got ambition. He's studying for the sergeant's exam."

"What for? The higher you go, the less people you got to blame stuff on."

"Do yourself a favor. Cancel the date and spend the evening with your wife for a change."

"She'd just think I was up to something."

Zagreb found McReary immersed to his eyebrows in books piled on the desk of an officer currently ducking sniper fire on Iwo Jima. The lieutenant slid the volume off the top of a stack, a fifty-year-old chronicle of murders in both hemispheres. A puff of desiccated paper came out when he cracked it open, making him sneeze. He snapped it shut.

"You know they're not going to ask you this shit on the test. Burke and Hare? Them dumb Doras in the brass'll think it's an insurance firm."

McReary, the bottom face on the totem pole of Detroit's fabled Four Horsemen (the Detroit Racket Squad, to the uninitiated), slid his fedora back from his prematurely bald head. "Once you get started, it's hard to stop. I know the Michigan Penal Code back to front; I can ace that, but they're always looking for more. Most of these old criminal cases were cracked. If I can get a handle on how it was done, I stand to nail the orals."

"Just so long as it don't get in the way of the job. We got a line on a truckload of Australian kangaroo meat that Frankie Orr's looking to pass off as South American beef docking down in Wyandotte, tonight or tomorrow night. My money says it jumps on the side of a rationing violation." He smiled. "Jumps, get it?"

Under ordinary circumstances the junior member of the squad would chuckle at his superior's joke. He grunted only, absorbed deeply in the Crippen poisoning case.

The telephone jangled on yet another vacant desk. It was Lieutenant Osprey with Homicide.

"Yeah, Ox," Zagreb said.

"The name's Oswald. I got a streetwalker carved up like a side of beef I ain't seen since before rationing."

"Since when is a hooker murder a Racket Squad deal?"

"Look, I'm shorthanded since D-Day. If you like I can tell the papers she slept with Goering. We can recant on page eight."

"Something tells me I'm not getting the full story. Oh, right: I'm talking to Ox Osprey, the cop who pled the Fifth seventeen times during the McHenry grand trial."

"So I sprang a small-time bootlegger in return for a case of good Canadian for my tenth anniversary. The head of the review board shot golf with Frankie Orr the day he suspended me. It was Orr's liquor." The homicide lieutenant dropped his voice to a whisper. Zagreb had to press the receiver tightly to his ear to catch the words.

"Listen, we got the button tight on this one. She's number three. All killed the same way: throat slit, stomach cut open, and her guts dumped alongside the body. I need the manpower before the press jumps in and takes page one away from Patton's Third Army."

"Enlighten me on how three dead hookers outscore a thousand of our boys in Europe."

"The press is sick of troop movements and how MacArthur takes his shrimp tempura. You know how they like to get their hands into a sex murder up to their elbows."

Zagreb took down the particulars, depressed the plunger, and called Sergeant Canal's home number. That month the most intimidating member of the squad was living in an apartment on Michigan Avenue directly above a barbershop whose phones never seemed to stop ringing. He owed his cheap rent to a landlord who made the very good case that a little bookmaking on the side compensated for most of his clientele taking their haircuts free courtesy of the U.S. military.

"We got a name to go with the latest stiff?" he shouted above the jangling.

The lieutenant looked at his notes. "Bette Kowalski." He spelled it. "Ox's witnesses says she pronounced it 'Betty,' like Bette Davis."

"Yeah, she was clear about that."

"You *knew* her?"

"Not in the biblical sense, if that's any of your goddamn business, Lieutenant, sir. Since she's dead, I can tell you she was a firehose of information, depending on what we had in the kitty. We dumped over three warehouses of tires, gasoline, and fresh eggs on her word alone."

"Firehoses have to be connected somewhere."

"It ain't exactly a trade secret. We could've turned him over a couple of dozen times, only we'd have spent the rest of the war finding out who took his place and how he operates. Plenty of time to crank him up to the Milan pen once we run Old Glory up Schicklgruber's ass."

"You're saying Frankie Orr's added pimping to his repertoire?"

"I don't know what that is, but if it's buying tail on the street, Frankie's the man to see." Canal cleared his throat; an operation similar to coal sliding down a chute. "I ain't saying this because I need the sleep. We need to corral these bats in broad daylight."

Zagreb had something intelligent in reply; but just then a horse came in at thirty-to-one and the noise level on Canal's end made conversation impossible.

For formality's sake, the entire squad convened in the Wayne County Morgue to get a look at the only real evidence in any case of homicide: the victim's body naked in a pull-out tray, clay-pale except for the blue-black smile the last person she'd known had carved under her jawbone and the black cotton cross-stitches the medical examiner had used to close the incisions he'd made to examine her entrails. She'd been basted together like a made-to-order outfit for a first fitting, and from the extent of the repair work the damage had been more than substantial. She looked very young. As many stiffs as Zagreb had seen, he never got over how the brutal act of murder returned even the most jaded victims to innocence.

"You okay?" he asked McReary. "You look a little green."

"It's the iodoform, L.T. Ma bought it by the gallon during the influenza scare in '19 and doused us all by the day."

"Garlic, me," Canal said. "I ain't just sure if the old lady meant it for the ague or vampires."

Lieutenant Osprey tipped back a flask, exposing the tender flesh under a jaw cut with a miter. He didn't offer to share it with the others. "What I think?

He paid his girls on the installment plan, she preferred cash-and-carry. She beefed, he cut."

"I saw a seal blow 'Anchors Aweigh' on horns in the circus. I guess he thought that was thinking, too." Burke, who had a phobia against promotion, never missed a chance to take a shot at rank, with the single exception of Lieutenant Max Zagreb.

That party fired another question at Osprey just as his neck began to redden. "What about the others?"

A dilapidated notebook came out. "One colored, semi-pro, the other first-generation Albanian with a solicitation record as long as Errol Flynn's dick. Three nights apart, a little over six weeks ago."

"Why the dry spell, you figure?"

"I don't know, but it's a break: The press might not make the connection after all this time, but we got to sew this one up before he puts another notch on his belt."

"He's on a cycle."

They looked at McReary, whose face had begun to show some normal color. "Some of these mass murderers go by phases of the moon or the Zodiac or the anniversary of their mothers' death. If we can nail it down, and study the behavior of known killers, we might narrow the field of suspects."

"What the hell's Dick Tracy Junior flapping his gums about?" Osprey demanded.

Zagreb smiled patiently. "He's cramming for the sergeant's exam, picking over the lush and fascinating history of crime; got it on the brain."

"No kidding. I got my first promotion by doing my damn job."

"And got busted drinking Frankie Orr's booze," Burke said.

Osprey swung his way, fists bunched at his sides. Zagreb, standing in for the League of Nations, distracted him by pressing for more details.

The other scowled, but uncrumpled his notebook and paged back, seesawing his arm as he tried to make out his own weeks-old scrawl. The first victim, Charlotte Adams, had been discovered flayed open in an alley off Grand River in the wee hours by a beat cop. A derelict found her colleague, Maria Zogu, in a trash bin behind the Albanian restaurant where she scooped up most of her clientele. Eyewitness descriptions of companions they were with when last seen were scattered and useless.

"Canal says Kowalski pounded the pavement for Frankie Orr. What about the others?"

"Indies, by all accounts. Say, maybe there's something in that. He's nailed down the steelhaulers', garbage-collectors', and launderers' unions across three counties. Maybe he's moving in on the sex trade, making an example of the holdouts."

"Then why Kowalski? She worked for him."

"She wanted out."

"Listen to the quiz kid," Burke said. "Got an answer for everything except how to close a case on his own."

Osprey wheeled on him. "You want to mix it up, Detective, there's an empty tray right next door."

Zagreb said, "Let's leave the fighting to the boys in uniform and see where it happened."

Bette Kowalski had shared a third-floor walk-up on Erskine with a girl who said she worked a drill-press at the Chrysler tank plant. Zagreb was inclined to believe her: She was a pudding-face brunette who bore no resemblance at all to Rosie the Riveter. None of the swing-shift queens he'd known did.

"I worked days," she said. "That way we only had to have the one bed. That's where I found her." She pointed at a gaunt iron-framed veteran with bare springs. "I got rid of the mattress, but I'm sleeping on the couch anyway. I told the landlady I'm moving out first chance I get." She hugged herself, although the room was stuffy.

"Both doors locked, hall and street," Osprey added. "Let him in, probably. All part of the job."

Zagreb flicked his gaze at Canal, who nodded and touched the girl's arm, steering her into a corner to ask innocuous questions out of earshot of the rest of the conversation.

"She must've been a mess," Zagreb told the man from Homicide.

"If we found her on the riverfront, I'd've thought she got washed up after getting chopped up by the propeller of the mail boat. Working behind closed doors, without interruption, the son of a bitch had all the time in the world."

McReary said, "Ah!"

Osprey turned his head. "You said what?"

"Just, 'Ah!' "

"We'll pay Frankie a visit," Zagreb said, glancing sideways at the detective third grade.

"You need me for that?" Osprey asked.

He knew the prospect of spending time in the same room with Orr wouldn't appeal to the man who'd accepted a case of his liquor. "We're used to him, Ox. We'll take it from here."

The other was so relieved he forgot to take issue with the nickname.

"Spill it," Zagreb said. They were sitting in the 1940 Chrysler the department had issued the squad before the auto industry turned its attention from Air-Flow transmissions to airplanes, Burke at his station behind the wheel, the lieutenant beside him.

McReary, sharing the backseat with Canal, blushed. "Just a hunch, when you said what Ox said about the perp having more time to finish the job because he and the victim were indoors. It reminded me of something I just read. Don't know why I didn't make the connection before: prostitutes cut up and left to be found, the last the worst of all because it was done in a private apartment."

"Drop the other shoe, Baldy," Burke said. "Some of us only squeaked through high school by sitting next to the smartest kid in class."

"The Whitechapel murders, London, En-gland, fall of 1888."

He glanced around at the faces turned his way, brows lifted. "Any takers?"

"I seen a movie or two," Canal said. "Just what we needed. Didn't have enough on the burner with saboteurs, rioters, and the black market, no sir. Let's throw in Jack the Ripper Junior, just to ice the cake." He crumpled his soggy cigar into a ball and threw it out the open window.

*

The Negro who opened the door of Frankie Orr's forty-room house in Grosse Pointe said his employer was out.

"Where'd he be, then, Jeeves?" Canal asked. "We been to his suite in the Book-Cadillac. That butler said try here. I rolled boxcars that looked less alike."

"I can't tell you apart either," said the man, without irony. "If the police can't find him, I certainly can't."

A female voice called out behind him, sounding slightly soused. "Tell 'em to try the yacht club. They can scrape him off the hull with the barnacles."

"Who was that?" asked McReary, when the paneled door shut in their faces.

"Mrs. Orr," Zagreb said. "She must've caught him squeezing one of his other tomatoes."

"Well, at least we won't be burning off gas the boys need on Okinawa." Burke turned toward the Chrysler.

The Grosse Pointe Yacht Club was just a few blocks away, a structure of Venetian design, complete with Gothic arches and a soaring bell tower, built directly into Lake St. Clair. They parked in a sandy lot off Vernier and entered the office, where a salty manager informed them Mr. Orr's boat could be found in slip nine.

The boat in the slip was a converted Great War minesweeper with *Gloria* painted on the stern. McReary said, "I thought his wife's name was Estelle."

"Gloria was his gun girl during Prohibition," Zagreb said. "She reinforced a handbag with steel so it didn't sag when he saw a cop and slipped her his rod."

"What happened to her?"

"Making flack jackets for the Air Corps last I heard. Ahoy the boat!"

A man dressed as a deckhand, in canvas trousers and a striped jersey with the sleeves rolled up past his swollen biceps, came to the rail carrying a Tommy gun. "Scram, bo."

Burke shielded his eyes. "That you, Rocks? I thought the warden had you working the jute mill in Jackson."

"Still would be, if Mr. Orr didn't spring me legal." The machine gun lowered. "Sorry, Detective. I thought you was somebody else."

"I usually am. This is my lieutenant, Max Zagreb. You can call him Lieutenant. We're here to palaver, not pinch."

Rocks gestured with the Tommy and the Horsemen climbed a rope ladder. The boat swayed when their weight hit the deck. "She don't draw much water," Zagreb said.

"Mr. Orr replaced the brass with aluminum. Put in four Rolls Royce engines so he could outrun the Coast Guard with a thousand gallons of Old Log Cabin in the hull."

"Rocks left out the part about me giving up running contraband after Repeal." The new voice belonged to a slender man whose black hair gleamed at the temples under the sweatband of a yachting cap with an anchor embroidered on it in gold thread. He wore a double-breasted blazer, white duck trousers, gum soles, and a silk ascot tucked into the open collar of his shirt.

"Throat sore, Frankie?" Zagreb snatched the weapon from the deckhand and thrust it at Burke, who took it. "Ever hear of the Sullivan Act?"

Orr said, "Rocks is in the naval reserve. He's licensed to carry it in case we run into a U-boat."

Canal grinned around a fresh cigar. "G'wan with you. The service don't take ex-cons."

"They're less picky in the merchant marines. Let's go in the saloon."

"Salon," corrected Rocks. "You told me to remind you, boss."

"It's Captain when we're on the water. Go swab the deck or something while I speak with these gentlemen."

They descended a gangway into a wide cabin containing a chrome bar and an evenly tanned blonde standing behind it in a white sharkskin swimsuit. "Cocktail?"

The visitors ordered bourbon all around except for McReary, who asked for a Vernor's. She mixed, served, and exited the cabin when Orr jerked his chin toward the gangway. Zagreb caught Burke admiring the creamy band of untanned skin where fabric met flesh. "Down, boy." He stirred his glass with a finger and sucked it. "Trouble at home, skipper?"

Orr frowned. "I guess you seen Estelle. She's got a private dick watching the hotel, so I have to smuggle in my hobbies in a dinghy on the Canadian side of the lake."

Canal said, "Try keeping your dinghy at home."

The lieutenant said, "You're mellowing. In the old days you'd drop a snooper out in the middle tied to a Chevy short block."

"Not that I ever done anything like that, but the agency's run by a retired police inspector. You cops hang together a lot tighter than the Purple Gang ever did."

"We're like the Masons that way. Hear what happened to Bette Kowalski?"

"I don't know no one by that name."

Zagreb wobbled good bourbon around his mouth and swallowed. "It gets old: You play dumb, we get tough, you call your mouthpiece ship-to-shore, we stuff you in a torpedo tube and blow you to Windsor. Why not take it easy on our lumbago and you can play hockey some other time?"

"The *Gloria*'s a minesweeper, not a destroyer. She ain't got torpedo tubes. Okay, okay," Orr said, when Canal set down his glass and started his way. "I just want you to understand I don't run whores. The Kowalski dame kept her ear to the ground and told me when one of my joints had to stand for a raid. It gave me time to sacrifice a couple of slot machines and keep my best dealers out of the can."

Zagreb said, "She was your department pipeline?"

"Double agent." Canal spat a soggy piece of tobacco into an ice bucket. "You're saying my snitch was two-timing me with the mob and the whole damn Vice Squad?"

"Not the whole squad; just Sergeant Coopersmith. He pinched her in front of God and everybody whenever he wanted scuttlebutt from the street, and after she made bail she slipped me what she overheard at headquarters. I never paid for nothing else, and if she put out for Coop or didn't, she never said boo either way.

"So you can see I had as much to lose as anybody when she opened her door to that butcher," he finished.

"Not as much as her." McReary's straw gurgled. He got rid of the ginger ale bottle. "When'd you see her last?"

"The night before her roommate found her gutted like a goose. I asked her wasn't it about time the cops swept her off the street again and she said, 'Right after I do my part for the boys in the service.'"

"What'd she mean by that?" Zagreb asked.

Capped teeth flashed white in the gangster's olive-hued face. "I'm just guessing, but I don't think she was planning to serve coffee and doughnuts at the USO."

Zagreb studied him over his half-raised drink. "On the level, she took a serviceman back to her room that night?"

"Bette made Kate Smith look like Tokyo Rose. She bought bonds, donated to the scrap drive, and offered a discount every time she sat under the apple tree with a G.I."

"Thanks, Frankie," the lieutenant said. "Just to show our heart's in the right place, we'll forget about that shipment of kangaroo meat on its way to Wyandotte. We'll even thrown in whatever you got stashed in their pouches."

Orr flushed high on his cheekbones. "How the hell—? Oh," he said, resuming his customary calm. "I hope you boys don't bury her on Zug Island with the other unclaimed stiffs. That was a doozy of a going-away present she gave you."

Back on deck, Burke returned the Thompson to Rocks. "Next time take the safety off, mug. Them underwater Krauts never put theirs on."

Back at 1300, Burke poured two fingers of Four Roses into a Dixie cup. "I ain't George M. Cohan, but nobody's going to sell me one of our troops is slashing hookers."

McReary gave up on the book he was studying. "One of the theories about the Ripper was he served in India or Afghanistan. Hand-to-hand combat can do things to a man."

Canal said, "Seems to me we paid this bill off last July during the riots. Two nutcase killers in one year?"

McReary said, "This is different. That screwball Kilroy thought he was helping the war effort by slicing up ration-stamp hoarders. He only wore a uniform to get in the door."

"I'd buy that this time around, too. The Quartermaster's Corps has got too much on its hands to keep track of what happens to its laundry."

The lieutenant was restless. He'd tried sitting and straddling a number of vacant chairs like Goldilocks and wound up pacing the squad room chain-smoking Chesterfields. "We're wasting time trying to talk ourselves out of thinking he's a G.I. when we ought to be considering what if he is. Ox told us it'd been six weeks since the first two killings. Don't that suggest something?"

"He's on a cycle, like I said," McReary reminded him. "We just got to—" He looked up, color flooding his face.

Zagreb nodded. "Basic training's six weeks. Suppose he threw himself a little call-up party, or enlisted before the investigation turned on him. Now he's out on leave."

Canal, fogging the outside air with one of his nickel stogies, slid off the windowsill. Plaster fell from the ceiling when his clodhoppers hit the floor. "We need a date on that second killing, then call the War Department to see who signed up in any of the services during the next month."

"Six weeks," Zagreb said, "to be sure. You take it."

"Give that to the kid, Zag. He's good on the horn."

"He's better with girls his age. Mac, you're going back to talk to the roommate, and if you come out without a line on just what uniform Bette's last john had on, you got about as much chance of making sergeant as Sad Sack."

"But she said she didn't see anything."

"That's what she thinks. We need to narrow the suspects to one branch of the service. If this son of a bitch ships out before we ID him, he'll be spilling civilian blood all over Europe and the Philippines."

The roommate's name was Jill Wheeler. Her landlady told McReary she was working, but that she usually returned home just after the five o'clock whistle.

Waiting for her at the bus stop on the corner, he caught himself humming "The Five O'Clock Whistle Never Blew." He liked jive music okay, but the way the lyrics wormed their way into his brain shoved out everything important.

She alighted behind a stout woman in a babushka and woolen topcoat that made his own skin prickle in the heat, a dead duck swinging by its neck in one fist; Polish-populated Hamtramck was still the best place to procure quality poultry under rationing. By contrast, Jill Wheeler looked as fresh as Deanna Durbin. Her round face with its clear complexion, black hair cut in a bob, brimmed hat, summer dress, and chunky heels made a refreshing change from the world represented by her dead roommate.

She stopped before the man touching his hat, gripping her handbag tightly. "I know you."

He introduced himself, steeling himself for the back-and-forth: "One or two more questions."

"I've told you everything I know."

"Just for the record, miss."

With that behind them, he escorted her back to her room. There, with the door left open to appease the landlady, she assured him repeatedly she knew nothing about Bette Kowalski's last rendezvous. (She actually used the word; he suspected she'd sat through *Algiers* at least twice.) At length he turned toward the door, putting on his hat. Taking it off in a young lady's presence to expose his bare scalp had been a major contribution to the cause of justice. "If you remember anything else, please call me at headquarters. Daniel J. McReary, Detective Third Grade."

"I can't think what that would be. All I know is she said she hoped she'd make some dogface wag its tail."

He paused in the midst of smoothing the brim. "When'd she say that?"

"I don't know; just before I left for my shift, I suppose. Yes, I was on my way out the door. Is it important?"

"Probably not. But thank you." Lieutenant Zagreb had told him again and again never to let a witness know she'd put you on to something good. "Otherwise they'll start making things up just to get you to pat 'em on the head."

The fog didn't roll, didn't creep; the poets who wrote that had never visited London in the autumn. It spread like sludge from the harbor, yellow as piss and soggy as a snotrag, so thick round your ankles you swore you'd stepped into a bucket of dead squid. On the cobblestone streets, sound carried through it as across a lake; the poets were dead wrong about that as well, claiming it muffled noise when in fact Big Ben's iron bell rang from a mile down the Thames fit to burst your eardrums.

Example: the squeak of a hinge, and a gush of tinny music, cut short abruptly by the clap of a door shutting against it, then the sole of a shoe scraping the pavement, sounding as close as if it were his own, but sharper; a narrow heel attached to a small foot, a fact confirmed by a puff of cheap scent. A woman, and one who doused herself, advertising her availability like a cat in heat. He felt blood rising to his face; but he suppressed his rage, or more accurately channeled it toward the business at hand. He stepped from the doorway neighboring the public-house, the fumes of ale and vomit and urine mingling with the fog as he passed the hellish place, fixing his gaze on snatches of tawdry satin and dyed feathers glimpsed between wisps of mist, but relying as fully on smell and sound; groping, as he closed the distance, for the handle of the knife on his belt. . . .

McReary started awake. Having found Zagreb absent, he'd sat at the desk he'd commandeered for his studies to wait, and didn't know he'd drifted off until the squad room door closed, shaking him out of his dream.

"You're an angel when you sleep." The lieutenant sat on a corner of the desk unoccupied by books and hung a cigarette on his lower lip. "You know, studying all night every night's no good if you doze off during the test."

"Sorry, L.T. I got something from the roommate."

"Too soon. Probably just a bladder infection."

"What? Oh." He blushed. "Does the ribbing stop when I make sergeant?"

"Not unless we bring in a kid younger than you. What'd you get?"

"Just something that came out when I'd finished asking questions." He told him what Jill Wheeler had said.

"Sure you heard her right?"

"Sure I'm sure. Think it's anything?"

Canal came in just then and read their faces. "We take Berlin?"

"Close. The Kowalski dame as much as told her roommate her john was a dogface."

"That's army, ain't it?"

"I think so. Don't Burke have a brother or something in the army?"

"Brother-in-law," said Burke, entering. "Dumb as a box of Lux. He's a cinch to make general."

"Ship out yet?"

"I wish. Dumb cluck's still parking on my couch."

"Ring him up."

The detective snatched up a candlestick phone and dialed. "Me, Sadie. Roy in? Imagine that. Put him on. No, I'm not looking to bust his butt, just ask him a question. Well, sure I have. Didn't I ask him just this morning when's he going to start paying rent?" He pressed the mouthpiece to his chest. "I tell you, if I hadn't knocked her up—Roy?" He leaned forward. "You ever hear anyone in basic call a guy with the navy or marines a dogface?" He listened. "Okay." He pegged the earpiece. "Sailors are gobs, marines leathernecks or jarheads. Dogfaces are army buck privates. Always."

"Gimme that phone." Zagreb asked the long-distance operator for the War Department. While he was waiting, McReary said, "L.T., what's it mean when a cop dreams he's a perp?"

"It means he's got the makings of a good detective."

The news from Washington was disheartening at first. During the six weeks following the murder of Maria Zogu, the second victim, one hundred sixty-six men were recruited into the army from the Detroit area. Many phone calls later determined the following:

Thirty-four with the paratroopers had been shipped overseas directly after basic training, that service having suffered heavy casualties during the push toward Germany.

Twenty-three were discharged for unfitness or insubordination.

Sixteen of those were tracked down and their movements accounted for the night Bette Ko-walski was murdered.

The remaining seven were interviewed and eliminated as likely suspects.

Three died during training, one from incaution during a drill involving live rounds, one from cerebral hemorrhage after a brawl in the PX, one from Spanish influenza.

Eighteen soldiers who'd been exposed to the stricken man were in quarantine at the time of the last murder.

The squad tabled six who supplied sound alibis for at least one of the first two killings.

Little by little, with help from Osprey's Homicide detail, the uniform division, and reserves, most of the eighty-plus men left fell away, leaving just four; a handy number for the Four Horsemen to interview separately.

"What we got?" Zagreb asked when they reunited at 1300.

Canal passed an unlit cigar under his nose and made the same face the others usually made when he lit one. "My guy's eighteen going on eleven. Tried every whistle-stop between here and his hometown in Texas before he found a recruiting sergeant blind enough to accept the date of birth he gave. He's a shrimp. Bette had muscles on her muscles from pounding the pavement and smacking around deadbeats. She'd've took him three falls out of three."

Burke said, "Mine took a swing at me when I told him what I was looking into. I knocked him flat, frisked him and the dump he lives in. If he's our guy, he sure cleans up after himself. He's in holding downstairs."

"We'll take turns," Zagreb said. "Mac?"

McReary got out his notebook. "Lives in Dearborn. With his mother, the landlord says. Both out; she cooks in the bomber plant in Willow Run, gets off at midnight. My guess is he's sowing some oats before he ships out. The landlord wouldn't let me check out the apartment. Should we get a warrant?"

"Not yet." Zagreb looked at his watch. "Twenty to twelve. We'll try schmoozing Mom when she comes home."

"What about yours, Zag?" Canal asked.

"Halfway to Honolulu on a troop ship. If we turn anything up on a search warrant we can tip off the M.P.s, though I'd sure hate to dump it in somebody else's lap."

Burke grinned at McReary. "Slap on the Old Spice, Junior. If you can Romeo a jane like Bette's roomie, the old lady on Dearborn's a fish in a barrel."

"Mrs. Corbett?" Zagreb took off his hat.

"Miss. I went back to my maiden name after my husband left me. For a tramp," she added, pinching her nostrils.

The woman who'd opened the door had a slight middle-aged spread, but was still attractive. A lock of strawberry-blonde hair had strayed from the red bandanna she wore tied around her head. The lieutenant had to admit she resembled Rosie the Riveter, even if her skills with a stove surpassed those with a jackhammer. She smelled not unpleasantly of hot grease.

After the pleasantries, she let the squad into a tidy living room with a fake fireplace above which hung a period photograph in a matted frame of a man in his thirties who parted his hair in the middle and wore a trim moustache.

"My great-great uncle Boston," she said. "He's the man who shot John Wilkes Booth."

Zagreb nodded. "Good for him. Lincoln's my favorite president."

As the others took seats on slightly worn mohair cushions, their lieutenant went through all the motions, assuring their hostess that her son wasn't in trouble, just that they wanted to speak with him in connection with an investigation.

"Leonard should be back any time," she said. "He's to report for duty at eight A.M. By this time next week he'll be in England. I'm hoping he'll find the time to visit family. His great-great-great uncle was born there." The cheerful glitter in her pale-brown eyes fell short of dissembling the concern behind them.

McReary noted it. "He's your only child?"

"Yes."

"Then I'm sure he'll be especially careful."

"You're very kind."

Burke, not kind, asked if she knew where Leonard was on the night of the date Bette Ko-walski was killed.

"Was it a weeknight?"

"Wednesday." Zagreb cut his eyes Burke's way, registering disapproval.

"I wouldn't know, then. I'd have been at work. He may have stayed home, or he may have gone out for a beer with friends. That's what he went out for tonight: He's throwing himself a sort of going-away party." Once again concern clouded the glitter in her eyes.

Canal fumbled at the pocket containing his cigars, but refrained from taking one out. "Could we see his room?"

"Oh, I don't know. He's a very private person. He won't even let me go in to clean."

"We won't disturb anything." McReary looked sincere.

"I'm afraid he keeps it locked."

"No problem, ma'am." Canal took out a small leather case, displaying a collection of picks and skeleton keys.

The room was upstairs, with a yellow tin sign tacked to the door reading:

FIRING RANGE
AUTHORIZED PERSONNEL ONLY

Mrs. Corbett's smile was nervous. "Leonard's little joke. He bought it in the army surplus store. He's always bringing home odd bits."

Five minutes, three keys, and two picks later, the sergeant got off his knees and twisted the knob. Artfully the four men arranged themselves between the woman and the door and drew their revolvers, shielding the maneuver from her line of sight with their bodies. They sprang in single-file and spread out inside the room; holstered their weapons when it proved to be unoccupied.

"Holy—"

"—Mackerel," Zagreb interrupted Burke.

It was a small room with a single bed, a writing table, and a wooden chair. A Class-A army uniform in an open dry cleaner's bag hung in a closet without a door. A metal bookrack beside the desk contained rows of worn books: *The Lodger, The Curse of Mitre Square,* several titled *Jack the Ripper.* A corkboard mounted above the table was plastered with black-and-white and sepia photographs, most of them clipped from newspapers and magazines, showing narrow cobblestone alleys, a stately building captioned New Scotland Yard, and shots taken from dozens of angles of obviously dead women, some of them naked, exposing ghastly slashes imperfectly stitched.

Mrs. Corbett gasped in the hallway. Zagreb jerked his chin at Canal, standing nearest the door. He eased it shut and leaned his back against it.

"I've seen these," McReary said. "There's Annie Chapman, Catherine Eddowes, Elizabeth Stride." He indicated the grisliest image of all, a skilled artist's sketch. "Mary Kelly, the Ripper's last known victim. Ring a bell?"

"He cut up Bette Kowalski the same way," Canal said.

A black satchel, like the kind doctors carried, stood open on the table. It was old and cracked. Zagreb reached inside and began taking out the contents: stethoscope, glass medicine bottles, scalpels, a gadget resembling a brace-and-bit; what some people called a hand drill. He held up the last item. "You're the big reader, Mac. This looks like it belongs in a carpenter's tool box."

"Trepan." McReary paled. "They don't make 'em anymore. Forensic surgeons used it to bore holes in skulls, looking for bullets and such. It's an autopsy kit, L.T."

"None of these scalpels looks big enough for the murder weapon."

"There should be a post-mortem knife in the bag." The detective third grade spread his hands a foot apart. "About yea long. The experts figured that's what the Ripper used."

Zagreb rummaged further, then picked up the bag and dumped it upside-down onto the table. No such instrument made its appearance.

Mrs. Corbett had no idea where her son had gone to celebrate his last night as a civilian. Zagreb borrowed her phone and described Leonard Corbett from a recent photo supplied by his agitated mother, showing a bland-faced young man in his uniform. Minutes later they were driving with the two-way radio turned up full blast.

"Any cars in the vicinity of Woodward and Parsons," crackled the dispatcher's voice. "Suspect seen near the Paradise Theatre. Consider him armed and extremely dangerous."

"That place draws almost as many hookers as jazz buffs," Zagreb said.

Burke flipped on the siren and hit the gas.

The street in front of the popular swing club was a sea of department vehicles, marked and unmarked. Spotting a uniformed officer on the sidewalk holding his side arm, Zagreb rolled down the window and flashed his shield.

The patrolman skipped the preliminaries. "Someone just ducked down that alley." He pointed with his weapon.

They left the Chrysler at the curb. At the lieutenant's instructions, McReary and Canal circled the building on the corner to come in from the other end. Zagreb and Burke gave them two minutes, then entered from the Woodward Avenue side. All four had their weapons out.

Crossing a dark doorway, McReary glimpsed a movement in the shadows. He touched Burke's arm. Burke nodded and leveled his revolver on the doorway as his partner entered. The deep passage was black as a shroud. He felt for the door. A hinge squeaked and it swung open at his touch.

A long hallway with a checkerboard floor showed barely in the dim light of a wall sconce. The far end was in deep shadow. He crept forward.

The man at the far end of the hall came to a locked door. He turned and pressed his back to it, holding his breath. Three yards away, visible in the lighted section, a man with a gun was approaching, wearing a dark suit and a light-colored hat. He himself was secure in the blackness, as if he were enveloped in thick fog. The man creeping his way wore shoes appropriate to someone who habitually carried a gun, but he could hear the slight squish of the rubber soles as he advanced, smell the crisp odor of spice-based aftershave. That was another advantage, his heightened senses. But he would have to move fast and strike surely; this was no tart, her brains dulled by liquor and the plague her kind had brought upon itself.

Closer now. He could almost reach out and touch the man. He drew the knife from his belt and sprang. . . .

Suddenly the shadow at the end of the hall coagulated into something blacker, a distinct shape dressed all in dark clothing. Fabric rustled; the light behind McReary drew a bright line down a length of steel. He raised his piece and fired. Something stung his wrist, something hot splashed onto his hand. An evil stench of singed cloth filled his nostrils; the muzzle flare had set the man's coat on fire.

He kept jerking the trigger, emptying the chamber. Something heavy piled into him. Automatically he threw his arms around it, supporting the dead man entirely.

It was only after he let go and the man slid into a heap at his feet that he realized his wrist was bleeding.

Daniel J. McReary entered the squad room. From habit he reached for his sidearm, intending to lay it on the desk still stacked with books, then remembered. Pending the results of the routine shooting investigation, he'd been relieved of his weapon and assigned to desk duty.

He brightened when Lieutenant Zagreb came in. Flicking the hand belonging to the bandaged wrist at the book on top of the stack, he said, "I've been reading."

"What else is new?"

"It's about the Lincoln assassination. I got interested after Mrs. Corbett told us she was related to the man who killed John Wilkes Booth. This Boston Corbett was a piece of work: born in England under Queen Victoria, with all that entails. He was so mortified after going to bed with a prostitute he castrated himself."

Burke, cleaning his revolver at a nearby desk, dropped it on the blotter. "Holy—"

"Shit," Canal finished. "A thing like that can make a man surly."

"Do tell." McReary opened the book to the page he'd marked. "Says here twenty years after he shot Booth they stuck him in a loony bin for pulling a gun in the Kansas House of Representatives, but he escaped in 1888 and was never heard from since. That's the year the Ripper killings took place. What are the odds Corbett went back home and—?"

"You think Leonard knew about that?" Burke picked up his revolver and blew through the barrel.

"You should write a book," Zagreb said.

"Not me. I'm through with 'em." He slammed the volume shut and tossed it aside.

The lieutenant lifted his eyebrows. "You failed the sergeant's exam?"

"I fell asleep."

AUTHOR'S NOTE: *I wish to thank my friend Dale L. Walker for the Boston Corbett/ Jack the Ripper theory.*

~

THE LEGACY

R. L. Stevens

R. L. Stevens is one of numerous pseudonyms of the short story writer Edward Dentinger Hoch (1930–2008), who also wrote as Irwin Booth, Anthony Circus, Stephen Dentinger, Pat McMahon, Ellery Queen, and Mr. X. He wrote five novels, beginning with *The Shattered Raven* (1969), which was set at the Edgar Awards banquet and featured many thinly disguised real-life mystery writers. *The Blue Movie Murders* (1972), another novel, was written under the Queen pseudonym. His other three novels combined science fiction and mystery. Set in the twenty-first century, they featured Carl Crader and Earl Jazine, a pair of detectives working for the Computer Investigation Bureau who were known as the "Computer Cops."

While his novels did not enjoy much success, Hoch was perhaps the most inventive and prolific practitioner of the pure detective story during the past half century. While never hailed as a great stylist, his mystery fiction presented old-fashioned puzzles in clear, no-nonsense prose that rarely took a false step and proved to be consistently satisfying. He produced more than nine hundred stories in his career, approximately half of them published in *Ellery Queen's Mystery Magazine*, beginning in 1962. In May 1973, Hoch started a remarkable run of publishing at least one story in every issue of *EQMM* until his death thirty-five years later—and beyond, as he had already delivered additional stories.

"The Legacy" was first published in the August 1972 issue of *Ellery Queen's Mystery Magazine*.

> *"You might call it ... a mission in life ... passed on to each new generation by the preceding one ..."*

The old place looked more deteriorated than it had on my last visit, perhaps reflecting the condition of its occupant. For certainly Uncle Alpha was crumbling as surely as the stone pillars that held up the faded front porch.

The nurse, all starched and breathless, met me at the front door. "He's kept me running today," she said. "He'll be glad to see you."

"How does he feel?"

She arched an eyebrow. "Since two months ago? I think you'll find he's failed considerably. This isn't the place for him, Mr. Cayhill. He belongs in a nursing home."

I glanced sideways at her. "You mean under psychiatric care."

"I didn't say that. He's quite rational much of the time."

"Thank you, Miss Murray. I'll speak to you about it later."

I left her at the door and entered his room. If I'd expected to find Uncle Alpha in bed, or sitting in the great old rocking chair he used as a throne, I was disappointed. He was on his feet, shuffling through some papers with his arthritic old fingers. He turned as I entered and motioned me to a chair by the bed.

Alpha Cayhill was my father's older brother and with the passing years he had become my only living relative. He was a wealthy man who'd made a fortune in real estate, had divorced his first wife years ago, and had never remarried. Now, in his mid-seventies, he'd been struck down with a variety of afflictions that confined him to his house and were sapping his strength. I knew, as I had known for the past year, that any one of my bimonthly visits could be the last.

For some reason Uncle Alpha had taken a liking to me and had begun to look forward to my visits. Now, turning toward me, he said, "I thought you would never come, Charles. You've been neglecting an old man."

"You're not that old, Uncle Alpha."

"Old enough, Charles. Old enough. Here, help me over to my chair."

"Have you been out of the house at all? The weather's fine."

"I don't get out anymore. The old legs are only good for a few steps at a time."

"That's too bad. Do you have everything you need? Does Nurse Murray take good care of you?"

"Oh, she's all right," the old man admitted grudgingly. "She's nice to look at, anyway . . ." His voice trailed off and he seemed deep in thought. Finally he lifted his eyes to meet mine. "Charles, we must have a talk."

"Certainly, Uncle. Anytime you want."

"No, no, not anytime. Now, right now."

I glanced at my watch. Although my evening was free I was reluctant to spend it listening to my uncle's rambling reminiscences of better days. "Really, Uncle Alpha, I must be—"

"Our family has a legacy, Charles, a legacy to be passed from one generation to the next. This is something I've never told you before. In fact, I've never breathed it to a living soul."

"A legacy?" I was not so well off that I could walk out on talk of money. "Don't you have a will?"

"It is not that sort of legacy. It is, rather, a legacy of deeds."

"Deeds? You mean—actions?"

There was something lurking in his eyes. It could have been madness or cunning, but it was there. "If it has something to do with a political action group, Uncle, I'm afraid I don't have time for it. My business keeps me pretty well tied down, you know."

"It's nothing like that," the old man assured me. A sly smile played about the corners of his mouth. "What would you say if I were to tell you I had killed somebody?"

"Killed? You mean in the war?"

He smiled. "Charles, there is so much to tell you, so much to prepare you for. You are the only one I have, so the legacy of the family must pass down to you. Whatever you make of it—a blessing or a curse—is up to you to continue."

All I could say was, "I don't understand you. What's all this about killing someone?"

"Help me over to the bookcase. I have something to show you."

He needed a hand now, because his legs were wobbly. After two heart attacks it was an effort for him to stay on his feet. I pressed my arm around his thin shoulder and guided him to the bookcase. He took down a red-leather album and clutched it to his chest. When I offered to carry it for him he hugged it even tighter.

"What is it, Uncle?"

"You might call it our family tree. Your legacy, Charles." He opened the album from the back and I saw at once that it was filled with neatly clipped newspaper accounts. Of murders.

"What is this?"

"A mission in life, Charles. Passed on to each new generation by the preceding one. I have no son, so the legacy must be given to you."

His eyes were glowing now, and I wondered if he might be feverish. "You mean all these killings? Are you telling me you had something to do with them?"

"I killed them, Charles. I killed them all, just as our family has for more than four generations."

I was staring at the headline on one article. It was from a Boston newspaper of a decade ago, and it read: *Cambridge Woman Believed Latest Strangler Victim.* My eyes scanned the account with growing apprehension, and finally I lowered the album to say, "But this is about those Boston murders—the Boston Strangler."

"Yes."

"The man who killed them—didn't he confess?"

"He could only have killed two. I killed the rest."

His voice was so calm in contrast with the fire in his eyes that it took a moment before the chill started down my back. I had almost believed him, and perhaps believing would have been preferable to the knowledge that Uncle Alpha had finally succumbed to his wild imaginings. "I don't believe that, Uncle. You couldn't have done anything as brutal. The Boston killings, as I remember them, were the acts of a sex criminal."

"Yes," he said simply.

"But you would have been in your mid-sixties then."

"Nevertheless, I killed them. I killed them because our family's legacy had passed down to me. And that is the legacy I now pass on to you."

"Uncle—"

"No, no, let me go on!" He flipped forward a few pages in the album. "Perhaps you wonder who it was that revealed this family secret to me. I lived in London for a time in the early nineteen-fifties, you'll remember, and it was there I met my wife's uncle. It was he who instructed me."

"Instructed? You mean he killed women, too?"

Uncle Alpha nodded. "Unfortunately, he was later apprehended by the police and put to death. His name was John Christie."

"Uncle Alpha, are you telling me that John Christie, the British mass murderer, instructed you in the killing of women?"

"Of course. How else would I have known? Our methods were different, of course. He generally used gas, while I almost always strangled my victims. But then John Christie's own mentor—a cousin back in America—used an ax."

My mind could not grasp his words. The man was mad, totally and completely mad, and I only wanted a way out before his madness engulfed me, too. "Don't tell me John Christie's cousin was Lizzie Borden," I said, trying to make a joke of it.

"No, he was the much more successful Axeman of New Orleans, who killed a number of people—mainly Italian grocers and their wives—between 1911 and 1919. The Axeman violated the legacy by killing men as well as women, but he could be excused. John Christie told me he was mad."

"I see," I muttered, not knowing what else to say.

"Before the Axeman, of course, there was his father. He was the most famous of us all."

"His father?"

"Jack the Ripper."

"Uncle—"

"You don't believe me? Is that it? But look—here are all the clippings!"

He turned to the front of the album and I stared at the yellowed pages from *The Penny Illustrated Paper* and *The Times* and the *Reynolds News* and the *Daily Telegraph*. Words like "Ripper" and "Whitechapel" leaped out at me. "You've collected these all your life?" I asked, dazed.

"My predecessors began the collection. I have only added my part. I estimate the family has killed fifty-five women in the past hundred years, with several men thrown in for good measure. All the crimes were not reported, of course."

I got unsteadily to my feet. "I must be going, Uncle. I have a business engagement."

"But we've only begun to talk! There's so much more to discuss! Your choice of weapon, for instance. The Ripper used a knife, of course, but there's something to be said for the other methods—the ax or gas or my own method, strangulation."

"We'll talk again, Uncle. I really must be going now."

"If you must." He leaned toward me. "Oh, you realize this is absolutely secret. I wouldn't want a word of it getting around."

"Of course not," I assured him, grim-faced. We shook hands and I left.

Nurse Murray was waiting downstairs. "Well! That was a short visit!"

I nodded. "I'm afraid what you've been saying about his mental condition is no exaggeration. He needs care, and I'll have to see that he gets it. As soon as possible."

Nurse Murray nodded.

"He has terrible delusions. I'm afraid he'll have to be put away somewhere," I added.

The nurse held the door open for me. "Do something soon. He's not getting any better."

But I did not do anything soon. Or not soon enough. Three days later a detective named Yates was waiting at my office when I returned from lunch.

"Your uncle is Alpha Cayhill?"

"That's correct."

"I'm afraid I have bad news for you, Mr. Cayhill. We found his body this morning. He died of a heart attack sometime during the night."

"A heart—"

The detective nodded and hurried on. "Apparently he surprised a burglar in his home and the shock was too much for his heart. The nurse who cared for him, Miss Murray, was killed by the burglar."

"Miss Murray? Dead?"

"I'm afraid so. A horrible crime. Perhaps your uncle was trying to rescue her when his heart gave out."

I sank into my chair. "My God! Do you have any idea who did it?"

"None whatever. We're still searching the house for clues." He cleared his throat. "We understand you are Mr. Cayhill's only living relative. You'll be handling the funeral arrangements?"

"Of course."

The detective nodded. "I'll be going, then. Sorry I had to bring you such bad news."

"Tell me one thing. How was Nurse Murray killed?"

The detective frowned. "How? She was strangled."

"The events I have recounted occurred in the early 1970s. You might wonder, my son, why I am telling you all this now, some twenty-five years later. If you would be so good as to hand me that red-leather album from the bookcase . . ."

JACK'S LITTLE FRIEND

Ramsey Campbell

As is true of so many of the greatest horror writers of the twentieth century, John Ramsey Campbell (1946–) was heavily influenced by the work of H. P. Lovecraft, publishing three short story collections in a similar style before producing his first novel, *The Doll Who Ate His Mother* (1976; revised edition 1985). Today, he is commonly described by critics and fellow writers as the greatest stylist of the contemporary horror genre, and was named Britain's most respected living horror writer by the *Oxford Companion to English Literature*.

Born in Liverpool, he set many of his novels and stories there and in the fictional city of Brichester in the same region. In 1977, he wrote the novelizations of three films as Carl Dreadstone (a house name under which three additional novels were written by others), successfully bringing a pulpy style that evoked the classic films (*The Bride of Frankenstein, Dracula's Daughter,* and *The Wolfman*). Among the best of his later novels are *The Face That Must Die* (1979), *Incarnate* (1983), *Ancient Images* (1989), *Midnight Sun* (1990), and *The Grin of the Dark* (2008). Among the many awards Campbell has received are multiple World Fantasy nominations and wins, including a 2015 Lifetime Achievement Award, many British Fantasy Society nominations and wins, and a Bram Stoker Lifetime Achievement Award, as well as other Stoker nominations and awards. He has been named the Lifetime President of the British Fantasy Society and was given the Living Legend Award of the International Horror Guild in 2007.

While much of his work is explicitly violent, Campbell's use of metaphor, symbolism, and imagery allows a poetic tone to suffuse his prose, suggesting horrors that remain in the memory long after the initial shock of a starkly brutal occurrence has passed.

"Jack's Little Friend" was first published in *Jack the Knife*, edited by Michel Parry (St. Albans, UK, Mayflower, 1975).

It's afternoon when you find the box. You're in the marshes on the verge of the Thames below London. Perhaps you live in the area, perhaps you're visiting, on business or on holiday. You've been walking. You've passed a power station and its expressionless metallic chord, you've skirted a flat placid field of cows above which black smoke pumps from factory chimneys. Now reeds smear your legs with mud, and you might be proposing to turn back when you see a corner of metal protruding from the bearded mud.

You make your way toward it, squelching. It looks chewed by time, and you wonder how long it's been there. Perhaps it was dumped here recently; perhaps it was thrown out by the river; possibly the Thames, belabouring and dragging the mud, uncovered the box. As the water has built the box a niche of mud so it has washed the lid, and you can make out dates scratched on the metal. They are almost a century old. It's the dates that provoke your curiosity, and perhaps also a gesture against the dull landscape. You stoop and pick up the box, which frees itself with a gasp of mud.

Although it's only a foot square the box is heavier than you anticipated. You skid and regain your balance. You wouldn't be surprised if the box were made of lead. If anyone had thrown it in the river they would certainly have expected it to stay sunk. You wonder why they would have bothered to carry it to the river or to the marshes for disposal. It isn't distinguished, except by the dates carved on the lid by an illiterate or clumsy hand—just a plain box of heavy gray metal. You read the dates:

31/8/1888
8/9/1888
30/9/1888
9/11/1888

There seems to be no pattern. It's as if someone had been trying to work one out. But what kind of calculation would be resolved by throwing away a metal box? Bewildered though you are, that's how you read the clues. What was happening in 1888? You think you read somewhere that expeditions were returning from Egypt around that date. Have you discovered an abandoned archaeological find? There's one way to know. But your fingers slip off the box, which in any case is no doubt locked beneath its coat of mud, and the marsh is seeping into your shoes; so you leave off your attempts to open the lid and stumble away, carrying the box.

By the time you reach the road your excitement has drained somewhat. After all, someone could have scratched the dates on the lid last week; it could even be an understated practical joke. You don't want to take a heavy box all the way home only to prise from its depths a piece of paper saying APRIL FOOL. So you leave the box in the grass at the side of the road and search until you find a metal bar. Sorry if I'm aborting the future of archaeology, you think, and begin to lever at the box.

But even now it's not as easy as you thought. You've wedged the box and can devote all your energy to shifting the lid, but it's fighting you. Once it yields an inch or two and then snaps shut again. It's as if it were being held shut, like the shell of a clam. A car passes on the other side of the road and you begin to give in to a sense of absurdity, to the sight of yourself struggling to jimmy open an old box. You begin to feel like a tourist's glimpse. Another car, on your side this time, and dust sweeps into your face. You blink and weep and cough violently, for the dust seems to have been scooped into your mouth. Then the sensation of dry crawling in your mouth recedes, and only the skin beneath your tongue feels rough. You wipe your eyes and return to the box. And then you drop the bar, for the box is wide open.

And it's empty. The interior is as dull as the exterior. There's nothing, except on the bottom a thin glistening coat of what looks like saliva but must be marsh water. You slam the lid. You memorize the dates and walk away, rolling your tongue around the floor of your mouth, which still feels thick, and grinning wryly. Perhaps the hitch-hiker or whoever finds the box will conceive a use for it.

That night you're walking along a long dim street toward a woman. She seems to be backing away, and you can't see her face. Suddenly, as you rush toward her, her body opens like an anemone. You plunge deep into the wet red fronds.

The dream hoods your brain for days. Perhaps it's the pressure of work or of worry, but you find yourself becoming obsessive. In crowds you halt, thinking of the dates on the box. You've consulted such books as you have access to, but they didn't help. You stare at the asymmetrical faces of the crowd. Smoke rises from their mouths or their jaws work as they drive forward, pulled along by their set eyes. Imagine asking them to help. They wouldn't have touched the box, they would have shuffled on by, scattering their waste paper and condoms. You shake your head to dislodge the crawling thoughts. You aren't usually so misanthropic. You'll have to find out what those dates mean. Obviously your brain won't give you much peace until you do.

So you ask your friend, the one who knows something about history. And your friend says, "That's easy. They're the dates of Jack the Ripper," and tells you that the five murders everyone accepts as the Ripper's work were committed on those dates. You can't help smiling, because you've just had a flash of clarity: of course you must have recognized the dates subconsciously from having read them somewhere, and the recognition was the source of your dream. Then your friend says, "Why are you interested?"

You're about to answer, but your tongue sticks to the floor of your mouth for a moment, like the lid of the box. In that moment you think: why should your friend want to know anyway? They've no right to know, they aren't entitled to a fee for the consultation. You found the box, you'll conduct the inquiry. "I must have read the dates somewhere," you say. "They've been going round in my head and I couldn't remember why."

On the way home you play a game with yourself. No, that bus shelter's no good, too open. Yes, he could hide in that alley, there would be hardly any light where it bends in the middle. You stop, because the skin beneath your tongue is rough and sore, and hinders your thoughts. You explore the softness beneath your tongue with your finger, and as you do so the inflammation seems to draw into itself and spare you.

Later you ponder Jack the Ripper. You've read about him, but when you leaf through your knowledge you realize you're not so well informed. How did he become the Ripper? Why did he stop? But you know that these questions are only your speculations about the box, disguised.

It's inconvenient to go back to find the box, but you manage to clear yourself the time. When you do you think at first you've missed the place where you left the box. Eventually you find the bar, but the box has gone. Perhaps someone kicked it into the hedges. You search among the cramped roots and trapped crisp-bags until your mouth feels scraped dry. You could tell the local police, but then you would have to explain your interest, and they would take the credit for themselves. You don't need the box. Tomorrow you'll begin to research.

And so you do, though it's not as easy as you expected. Everyone's fascinated by the Ripper these days, and the library books are popular. You even have to buy a paperback of one of them, glancing sideways as you do so at the people browsing through the book. The sunlight glares in the cracks and pores and fleshy bags of their faces, giving them a sheen like wet wax: wax animated by simple morbid fascination. You shudder and hurry away. At least you have a reason, but these others haven't risen above the level of the mob that gloated squirming over reports of the Ripper's latest killing. You know how the police of the time must have felt.

You read the books. You spread them across the table, comparing accounts. You're not to be trapped into taking the first one you read as definitive. Your friends, and perhaps your spouse or lover as well, joke and gently rebuke you about your singlemindedness. No doubt they talk about it when you're not there. Let them. Most people seem content to relive, or elaborate, the second-hand. Not you.

You read. 31/8/1888: throat cut twice, head nearly severed, disembowelled twice. 8/9/1888: handkerchief wrapped around almost severed neck, womb missing, intestines cast over shoulder, relatively little blood in the yard where the corpse was found. 30/9/1888: two women, one with windpipe severed; the other, less than an hour later, with right eye damaged, earlobe cut off, intestines over shoulder, kidney and entrails missing. 9/11/1888: throat cut, ears and nose missing, also liver, and a mass of flesh and organs on the bedside table. There's a photograph of her in one book. You stare at it for a moment, then you slam the book and stare at your hands.

But your hands are less real than your thoughts. You think of the Ripper, cutting and feeling his way through the corpses, taking more time and going into more detail with each murder. The last one took two hours, the books tell you. A question is beginning to insist on an answer. What was he looking for?

You aren't sleeping well. You stare at the lights that prick your eyeballs behind your lids and theorize until you topple wakefully into sleep. Sometimes you seem almost to have found a pattern, and you gasp in crowds or with friends. They glance at you and you meet their gaze coldly. They wouldn't be capable of your thoughts, and you certainly don't intend to let them hinder you. But even as their dull gaze falls away you realize that you've lost the inspiration, if indeed it were one.

So you confine yourself to your home. You're glad to have an excuse to do so, for recently you've been growing hypersensitive. When you're outside and the sunlight intensifies it's as though someone were pumping up an already white-hot furnace, and the night settles around you like water about a gasping fish. So you draw the curtains and read the books again.

The more you read the stranger it seems. You feel you could understand the man if a missing crucial detail were supplied. What can you make of his macabre tenderness in wrapping a handkerchief around the sliced throat of Annie Chapman, his second victim? A numbed denial of his authorship of the crime, perhaps? If there were relatively little blood in the yard, then surely the blood must have soaked into the Ripper's clothes, but in that case how could he have walked home in broad daylight? Did he cut the windpipe of Elizabeth Stride because he was interrupted before he was able to do more, or because she had seen too much for him simply to leave her and seek a victim elsewhere? An hour later, was it his frustration that led him to mutilate Catherine Eddowes more extensively and inventively than her predecessors? And why did he wait almost twice as long as hitherto before committing his final murder, that of Mary Kelly, and the most detailed? Was this the exercise of a powerful will, and did the frustration build up to an unprecedented climax? But what frustration? What was he looking for?

You turn to the photograph of Mary Kelly again, and this time you're able to examine it dispassionately. Not that the Victorian camera was able to be particularly explicit. In fact, the picture looks like a piece of early adolescent pornography on a wall, an amateur blob for a face and a gaping darkness between the legs. You suck your tongue, whose underside feels rough and dry.

You read the Ripper's letters. The adolescent wit of the rhymes often gives way to the childish illiteracy of some of the letters. You can understand his feelings of superiority to the victims and to the police; they were undoubtedly at least as contemptible as the people you know. But that doesn't explain the regression of the letters, as if his mind were flinching back as far as possible from his actions. That's probably a common trait of psychopaths, you think: an attempt to reject the part of them that commits the crimes.

Your mind is still frowning. You read through the murders again. First murder, nothing removed. Second, the womb stolen. Third, kidney and entrails stolen. A portion of kidney which had been preserved in spirits was sent to the police, with a note saying that the writer had eaten the rest. Fourth, the liver removed and the ears and nose, but the womb and a three-month-old foetus untouched. Why? To state the hunger which motivated the killings, presumably, but what hunger was that? If cannibalism, surely he would never have controlled himself sufficiently to preserve a portion of his food with which to taunt the police? If not, what worse reality was he disguising from the police, and perhaps from himself, as cannibalism?

You swallow the saliva that's pooling under your tongue and try to grasp your theories. It's as if the hunger spat out the kidney. Not literally, of course. But it certainly seems as if the Ripper had been trying to sate his hunger by varying the delicacies, as if it were a temperamental pet. Surely the death of Mary Kelly couldn't have satisfied it for good, though.

Then you remember the box. If he had externalized the hunger as something other than himself, could his mind have persuaded him that the hunger was alive independent of him and might be trapped? Could he have used one of the portions of Mary Kelly as a lure? Would that have seemed a solution in the grotesque algebra of his mind? Might he have convinced himself that he had locked away his hunger in time, and having scratched the dates on the box to confirm his calculations have thrown it in the river? Perhaps the kidney had been the first attempted lure, insufficiently tempting. And then—well, he could hardly have returned to a normal life, if indeed he had left one, but he might have turned to the socially acceptable destruction of alcoholism and died unknown.

The more you consider your theory the more impressive it becomes. Perhaps you can write it up as an article and sell it somewhere. Of course you'll need to pursue your research first. You feel happy in a detached unreal way, and you even go to your companion willingly for the first time in, now you think about it, a long while. But you feel apart from the moist dilation of flesh and the hard dagger thrust, and are glad when it's over. There's something at the back of your mind you need to coax forward. When you've dealt with that you'll be able to concentrate on other things.

You walk toward her. The light is flickering and the walls wobble like a fair-ground corridor. As you approach her, her dress peels apart and her body splits open. From within the gap trails a web toward which you're drawn. At the center of the web hangs a piece of raw meat.

Your cry wakes you but not your companion. Her body feels like burning rubber against you, and you flinch away. After a minute you get out of bed. You can't stand the sensation, and you want to shake off the dream. You stare from the window; the darkness is paling, and a bird sings tentatively. Suddenly you gasp. You'll write that article now, because you've realized what you need. You can't hope to describe the Ripper or even to meet a psychopath for background. But there's one piece of first-hand research you can do that will help you to understand the Ripper. You don't know why you didn't read your dream that way at once.

Next day you begin searching. You read all the cards you can find in shop windows. They aren't as numerous or as obvious as you expected. You don't want to find yourself actually applying for a course of French lessons. You suppose there are magazines that would help you but you're not sure where to find them. At last, as the streets become grimmer, you notice a group of young men reading cards in a shop window. They nudge each other and point to several of the cards, then they confer and hurry toward a phone box. You're sure this time.

You choose one called Marie, because that was what Mary Kelly used to call herself. No particular reason, but the parallel seems promising. When you telephone her she sounds dubious. She asks what you want and you say, "Nothing special. Just the usual." Your voice may be disturbing her, because your tongue is sticking somehow to the floor of your mouth, which feels swollen and obstructive. She's silent for a moment, then she says, "All right. Come up in twenty minutes," and tells you where she is.

You hadn't realized it would be as swift as that. Probably it's a good thing, because if you had to wait much longer your unease might find you excuses for staying away. You emerge from the phone box and the sunlight thuds against your head. Your mouth is dry, and the flesh beneath your tongue is twitching as if an insect has lodged there. It must be the heat and the tension. You walk slowly toward your rendezvous, which is only a few streets away. You walk through a maze of alleys to keep in the shade. On either side of you empty clothes flap, children shout, and barks run along a chain of dogs.

You reach your destination on time. It's in a street of drab shops: a boarded betting shop, a window full of cardigans and wool, a Chinese take-away. The room you want is above the latter. You skid on trodden chips and shielding your face from the eyes of the queue next door, ring the bell.

As you stare at the new orange paint on the door you wonder what you're going to say. You have some idea and surely enough money, but will she respond to that? You understand some prostitutes refuse to talk rather than act. You can hardly explain your interest in the Ripper. You're still wondering when she opens the door.

She must be in her thirties, but her face has aged like an orange and she's tried to fill in the wrinkles, probably while waiting for you. Her eyelashes are like unwashed black paintbrushes. But she smiles slightly, as if unsure whether you want her to, and then sticks out her tongue at a head craning from next door. "You rang before," she says, and you nod.

The door slams behind you. Your hand reaches blindly for the latch; you can still leave, she'll never be able to pursue you. Beneath your tongue a pulse is going wild. If you don't go through with this now, it will be more difficult next time, and you'll never be rid of the Ripper or of your dreams. You follow her upstairs.

Seeing her from below you find it easy to forget her smile. Her red dress pulls up and her knickers, covered with whorls of colour like the eye of a peacock's tail, alternately bulge and crease. The hint of guilt you were beginning to feel retreats: her job is to be on show, an object, you need have no compunction. Then you're at the top of the stairs and in her room.

There are thick red curtains, mauve walls, a crimson bed and telephone, a color TV, a card from Ibiza and one from Rhyl. Behind a partition you can see pans and knives hanging on hooks in the kitchen area. Then your gaze is wrenched back to her as she says, "Go on then, tell me your name, you know mine."

Of course you don't. You're not so stupid as to suppose she would display her real name in the window. You shake your head and try to smile. But the garish thick colors of the room are beginning to weigh on you, and the trapped heat makes your mouth feel dry, so that the smile comes out soured.

"Never mind, you don't have to," she says. "What do you want? Want me to wear anything?"

Now you have to speak or the encounter will turn into a grotesque misunderstanding. But your tongue feels as if it's glued down, while beneath it the flesh is throbbing painfully. You can feel your face prickling and reddening, and rotted in the discomfort behind your teeth a frustrated disgust with the whole situation is growing.

"Are you shy? There's no need to be," she says. "If you were really shy, you wouldn't have come at all, would you?" She stares into the mute struggle within your eyes and smiling tentatively again, says, "Can't you talk?"

Yes, you can talk, it's only a temporary obstruction. And when you shift it you'll tell her that you've come to use her, because that's what she's for. An object, that's what she's made herself. Inside that crust of makeup there's nothing. No wonder the Ripper sought them out. You don't need compassion in a slaughterhouse. You try to control your raw tongue, but only the throbbing beneath it moves.

"I'm sorry, I'm only upsetting you. Never mind, love," she says. "Nerves are terrible, I know. You sit down and I'll get you a drink."

And that's when you have to act, because your mouth is filling with saliva as if a dam had burst, and your tongue's still straining to raise itself, and the turgid colors have insinuated themselves into your head like migraine, and tendrils of uneasiness are streaming up from your clogged mouth and matting your brain, and at the core of all this there's a writhing disgust and fury that this woman should presume to patronize you. You don't care if you never understand the Ripper so long as you can smash your way out of this trap. You move toward the door, but at the same time your hand is beckoning her, it seems quite independent of you. You haven't reached the door when she's in front of you, her mouth open and saying, "What?" And you do the only thing that seems, in your blind violent frustration, available to you.

You spit into her open mouth.

For a moment you feel free. Your mouth is clean and your tongue can move as you want it to. The colors have retreated, and she's just a well-meaning rather sad woman using her talents as best she can. Then you realize what you've done. Now your tongue's free you don't know what to say. You think perhaps you could explain that you sneezed. Perhaps she'll accept that, if you apologize. But by this time she's already begun to scream.

You were so nearly right most of the time. You realized that the stolen portions of Mary Kelly might have been placed in the box as a lure. If only you'd appreciated the implications of this: that the other mutilations were by no means the act of a maniac, but the attempts of a gradually less sane man to conceal the atrocities of what possessed him. Who knows, perhaps it had come from Egypt. He couldn't have been sure of its existence even when he lured it into the box. Perhaps you'll be luckier, if that's luck, although now you can only stand paralyzed as the woman screams and screams and falls inertly to the floor, and blood begins to seep from her abdomen. Perhaps you'll be able to catch it as it emerges, or at least to see your little friend.

∼

THE STRIPPER

H. H. Holmes

H. H. Holmes is one of the pseudonyms of William Anthony Parker White (1911–1968), a prolific writer of mystery novels and short stories, as well as science fiction and supernatural short stories. His better-known pseudonym is Anthony Boucher (rhymes with "voucher"). Although he had numerous accomplishments in various fields of writing, it is for his work in the mystery world that White is best known.

Under the pseudonym H. H. Holmes, an infamous nineteenth-century serial killer, White wrote two novels about Sister Ursula, a nun, the first of which, *Nine Times Nine* (1940), was voted the ninth-best locked-room mystery of all time in a poll of fellow writers and critics; the second, *Rocket to the Morgue* (1942), was selected as a Haycraft-Queen Cornerstone.

As Boucher, White wrote well-regarded fair-play detective novels, the first of which was *The Case of the Seven of Calvary* (1937). It featured Dr. John Ashwin, a professor of Sanskrit, who solves a series of bizarre murders from his armchair. He wrote four novels about Fergus O'Breen, the one-man detective agency who handles mainly Hollywood cases brought to him by his older sister, Maureen, who had the responsibility of raising him. O'Breen's first appearance was in *The Case of the Crumpled Knave* (1939), which deals with the murder of an elderly inventor whose anti-gas weapon could be of incalculable importance during wartime. O'Breen also appeared in *The Case of the Baker Street Irregulars* (1940), *The Case of the Solid Key* (1941), and *The Case of the Seven Sneezes* (1942). Boucher also wrote a series of short stories featuring Nick Noble, a disgraced former policeman turned wino who sits in a cheap bar and solves complex crimes brought to him by a policeman friend.

"The Stripper" was first published in the May 1945 issue of *Ellery Queen's Mystery Magazine*.

He was called Jack the Stripper because the only witness who had seen him and lived (J. F. Flugelbach, 1463 N. Edgemont) had described the glint of moonlight on bare skin. The nickname was inevitable.

Mr. Flugelbach had stumbled upon the fourth of the murders, the one in the grounds of City College. He had not seen enough to be of any help to the police; but at least he had furnished a name for the killer heretofore known by such routine cognomens as "butcher," "werewolf," and "vampire."

The murders in themselves were enough to make a newspaper's fortune. They were frequent, bloody, and pointless, since neither theft nor rape was attempted. The murderer was no specialist, like the original Jack, but rather an eclectic, like

Kürten the Düsseldorf Monster, who struck when the mood was on him and disregarded age and sex. This indiscriminate taste made better copy; the menace threatened not merely a certain class of unfortunates but every reader.

It was the nudity, however, and the nickname evolved from it, that made the cause truly celebrated. Feature writers dug up all the legends of naked murderers— Courvoisier of London, Durrant of San Francisco, Wallace of Liverpool, Borden of Fall River—and printed them as sober fact, explaining at length the advantages of avoiding the evidence of bloodstains.

When he read this explanation, he always smiled. It was plausible, but irrelevant. The real reason for nakedness was simply that it felt better that way. When the color of things began to change, his first impulse was to get rid of his clothing. He supposed that psychoanalysts could find some atavistic reason for that.

He felt the cold air on his naked body. He had never noticed that before. Noiselessly he pushed the door open and tiptoed into the study. His hand did not waver as he raised the knife.

The Stripper case was Lieutenant Marshall's baby, and he was going nuts. His condition was not helped by the constant allusions of his colleagues to the fact that his wife had once been a stripper of a more pleasurable variety. Six murders in three months, without a single profitable lead, had reduced him to a state where a lesser man might have gibbered, and sometimes he thought it would be simpler to be a lesser man.

He barked into phones nowadays. He hardly apologized when he realized that his caller was Sister Ursula, that surprising nun who had once planned to be a policewoman and who had extricated him from several extraordinary cases. But that was just it; those had been extraordinary, freak locked-room problems, while this was the horrible epitome of ordinary, clueless, plotless murder. There was no room in the Stripper case for the talents of Sister Ursula.

He was in a hurry and her sentences hardly penetrated his mind until he caught the word "Stripper." Then he said sharply, "So? Backtrack please, Sister. I'm afraid I wasn't listening."

"He says," her quiet voice repeated, "that he thinks he knows who the Stripper is, but he hasn't enough proof. He'd like to talk to the police about it; and since he knows I know you, he asked me to arrange it, so that you wouldn't think him just a crank."

"Which," said Marshall, "he probably is. But to please you, Sister . . . What did you say his name is?"

"Flecker. Harvey Flecker. Professor of Latin at the University."

Marshall caught his breath. "Coincidence," he said flatly. "I'm on my way to see him now."

"Oh. Then he did get in touch with you himself?"

"Not with me," said Marshall. "With the Stripper."

"God rest his soul . . ." Sister Ursula murmured.

"So. I'm on my way now. If you could meet me there and bring his letter—"

"Lieutenant, I know our order is a singularly liberal one, but still I doubt if Reverend Mother—"

"You're a material witness," Marshall said authoritatively. "I'll send a car for you. And don't forget the letter."

Sister Ursula hung up and sighed. She had liked Professor Flecker, both for his scholarly wit and for his quiet kindliness. He was the only man who could hold his agnostic own with Father Pearson in disputatious sophistry, and he was also the man who had helped keep the Order's soup-kitchen open at the depth of the depression.

She took up her breviary and began to read the office for the dead while she waited for the car.

"It is obvious," Professor Lowe enunciated, "that the Stripper is one of the three of us."

Hugo Ellis said, "Speak for yourself." His voice cracked a little, and he seemed even younger than he looked.

Professor de' Cassis said nothing. His huge hunchback body crouched in the corner and he mourned his friend.

"So?" said Lieutenant Marshall. "Go on, Professor."

"It was by pure chance," Professor Lowe continued, his lean face alight with logical satisfaction, "that the back door was latched last night. We have been leaving it unfastened for Mrs. Carey since she lost her key; but Flecker must have forgotten that fact and inadvertently reverted to habit. Ingress by the front door was impossible, since it was not only secured by a spring lock but also bolted from within. None of the windows shows any sign of external tampering. The murderer presumably counted upon the back door to make plausible the entrance of an intruder; but Flecker had accidentally secured it, and that accident," he concluded impressively, "will strap the Tripper."

Hugo Ellis laughed, and then looked ashamed of himself.

Marshall laughed too. "Setting aside the Spoonerism, Professor, your statement of the conditions is flawless. This house was locked tight as a drum. Yes, the Stripper is one of the three of you." It wasn't amusing when Marshall said it.

Professor de' Cassis raised his despondent head. "But why?" His voice was guttural. "Why?"

Hugo Ellis said, "Why? With a madman?"

Professor Lowe lifted one finger as though emphasizing a point in a lecture. "Ah, but is this a madman's crime? There is the point. When the Stripper kills a stranger, yes, he is mad. When he kills a man with whom he lives . . . may he not be applying the technique of his madness to the purpose of his sanity?"

"It's an idea," Marshall admitted. "I can see where there's going to be some advantage in having a psychologist among the witnesses. But there's another witness I'm even more anxious to—" His face lit up as Sergeant Raglan came in. "She's here, Rags?"

"Yeah," said Raglan. "It's the sister. Holy smoke, Loot, does this mean this is gonna be another screwy one?"

Marshall had said *she* and Raglan had said *the sister*. These facts may serve as sufficient characterization of Sister Felicitas, who had accompanied her. They were always a pair, yet always spoken of in the singular. Now Sister Felicitas dozed in the corner where the hunchback crouched, and Marshall read and reread the letter which seemed like the posthumous utterance of the Stripper's latest victim:

> *My dear Sister:*
>
> *I have reason to fear that someone close to me is Jack the Stripper.*
>
> *You know me, I trust, too well to think me a sensationalist striving to be a star witness. I have grounds for what I say. This individual, whom I shall for the moment call "Quasimodo" for reasons that might particularly appeal to you, first betrayed himself when I noticed a fleck of blood behind his ear—a trifle, but suggestive. Since then I have religiously observed his comings and goings, and found curious coincidences between the absence of Quasimodo and the presence elsewhere of the Stripper.*
>
> *I have not a conclusive body of evidence, but I believe that I do have sufficient to bring to the attention of the authorities. I have heard you mention a Lieutenant Marshall who is a close friend of yours. If you will recommend me to him as a man whose word is to be taken seriously, I shall be deeply obliged.*
>
> *I may, of course, be making a fool of myself with my suspicions of Quasimodo, which is why I refrain from giving you his real name. But every man must do what is possible to rid this city a negotio perambulante in tenebris.*
>
> *Yours respectfully,*
> *Harvey Flecker.*

"He didn't have much to go on, did he?" Marshall observed. "But he was right. God help him. And he may have known more than he cared to trust to a letter. He must have slipped somehow and let Quasimodo see his suspicions. . . . What does that last phrase mean?"

"Lieutenant! And you an Oxford man!" exclaimed Sister Ursula.

"I can translate it. But what's its connotation?"

"It's from St. Jerome's Vulgate of the ninetieth psalm. The Douay version translates it literally: *of the business that walketh about in the dark;* but that doesn't convey the full horror of that nameless prowling *negotium*. It's one of the most terrible phrases I know, and perfect for the Stripper."

"Flecker was a Catholic?"

"No, he was a resolute agnostic, though I have always had hopes that Thomist philosophy would lead him into the Church. I almost think he refrained because his conversion would have left nothing to argue with Father Pearson about. But he was an excellent Church Latinist and knew the liturgy better than most Catholics."

"Do you understand what he means by Quasimodo?"

"I don't know. Allusiveness was typical of Professor Flecker; he delighted in British crossword puzzles, if you see what I mean. But I think I could guess more readily if he had not said that it might particularly appeal to me . . ."

"So? I can see at least two possibilities—"

"But before we try to decode the Professor's message, Lieutenant, tell me what you have learned here. All I know is that the poor man is dead, may he rest in peace."

Marshall told her. Four university teachers lived in this ancient (for Southern California) two-story house near the Campus. Mrs. Carey came in every day to clean for them and prepare dinner. When she arrived this morning at nine, Lowe and de' Cassis were eating breakfast and Hugo Ellis, the youngest of the group, was out mowing the lawn. They were not concerned over Flecker's absence. He often worked in the study till all hours and sometimes fell asleep there.

Mrs. Carey went about her work. Today was Tuesday, the day for changing the beds and getting the laundry ready. When she had finished that task, she dusted the living room and went on to the study.

The police did not yet have her story of the discovery. Her scream had summoned the others, who had at once called the police and, sensibly, canceled their classes and waited. When the police arrived, Mrs. Carey was still hysterical. The doctor had quieted her with a hypodermic, from which she had not yet revived.

Professor Flecker had had his throat cut and (Marshall skipped over this hastily) suffered certain other butcheries characteristic of the Stripper. The knife, an ordinary kitchen-knife, had been left by the body as usual. He had died instantly, at approximately one in the morning, when each of the other three men claimed to be asleep.

More evidence than that of the locked doors proved that the Stripper was an inmate of the house. He had kept his feet clear of the blood which bespattered the study, but he had still left a trail of small drops which revealed themselves to the minute police inspection—blood which had bathed his body and dripped off as he left his crime.

This trail led upstairs and into the bathroom, where it stopped. There were traces of watered blood in the bathtub and on one of the towels—Flecker's own.

"Towel?" said Sister Ursula. "But you said Mrs. Carey had made up the laundry bundle."

"She sends out only sheets and such—does the towels herself."

"Oh." The nun sounded disappointed.

"I know how you feel, Sister. You'd welcome a discrepancy anywhere, even in the laundry list. But that's the sum of our evidence. Three suspects, all with opportunity, none with an alibi. Absolutely even distribution of suspicion, and our only guidepost is the word *Quasimodo*. Do you know any of these three men?"

"I have never met them, Lieutenant, but feel as though I knew them rather well from Professor Flecker's descriptions."

"Good. Let's see what you can reconstruct. First, Ruggiero de' Cassis, professor of mathematics, formerly of the University of Turin, voluntary exile since the early days of Fascism."

Sister Ursula said slowly, "He admired de' Cassis, not only for his first-rate mind, but because he seemed to have adjusted himself so satisfactorily to life despite his deformity. I remember he said once, 'De' Cassis has never known a woman, yet every day he looks on Beauty bare.'"

"On Beauty . . . ? Oh yes. Millay. *Euclid alone* . . . All right. Now Marvin Lowe, professor of psychology, native of Ohio, and from what I've seen of him a prime pedant. According to Flecker . . . ?"

"I think Professor Lowe amused him. He used to tell us the latest Spoonerisms; he swore that flocks of students graduated from the University believing that modern psychology rested on the researches of two men named Frung and Jeud. Once Lowe said that his favorite book was Max Beerbohm's *Happy Hypocrite*; Professor Flecker insisted that was because it was the only one he could be sure of pronouncing correctly."

"But as a man?"

"He never said much about Lowe personally; I don't think they were intimate. But I do recall his saying, 'Lowe, like all psychologists, is the physician of Greek proverb.'"

"Who was told to heal himself? Makes sense. That speech mannerism certainly points to something a psychiatrist could have fun with. All right. How about Hugo Ellis, instructor in mathematics, native of Los Angeles?"

"Mr. Ellis was a child prodigy, you know. Extraordinary mathematical feats. But he outgrew them, I almost think deliberately. He made himself into a normal young man. Now he is, I gather, a reasonably good young instructor—just run of the mill. An adult with the brilliance which he had as a child might be a great man. Professor Flecker turned the French proverb around to fit him: 'If youth could, if age knew . . .'"

"So. There they are. And which," Marshall asked, "is Quasimodo?"

"Quasimodo . . ." Sister Ursula repeated the word, and other words seemed to follow it automatically. "*Quasimodo geniti infantes . . .*" She paused and shuddered.

"What's the matter?" "I think," she said softly, "I know. But like Professor Flecker, I fear making a fool of myself—and worse, I fear damning an innocent man. . . . Lieutenant, may I look through this house with you?"

He sat there staring at the other two and at the policeman watching them. The body was no longer in the next room, but the blood was. He had never before revisited the scene of the crime; that notion was the nonsense of legend. For that matter he had never known his victim.

He let his mind go back to last night. Only recently had he been willing to do this. At first it was something that must be kept apart, divided from his normal personality. But he was intelligent enough to realize the danger of that. It could produce a seriously schizoid personality. He might go mad. Better to attain complete integration, and that could be accomplished only by frank self-recognition.

It must be terrible to be mad.

"Well, where to first?" asked Marshall.

"I want to see the bedrooms," said Sister Ursula. "I want to see if Mrs. Carey changed the sheets."

"You doubt her story? But she's completely out of the—All right. Come on."

Lieutenant Marshall identified each room for her as they entered it. Harvey Flecker's bedroom by no means consorted with the neatness of his mind. It was a welter of papers and notes and hefty German works on Latin philology and puzzle books by Torquemada and Caliban and early missals and codices from the University library. The bed had been changed and the clean upper sheet was turned back. Harvey Flecker would never soil it.

Professor de' Cassis's room was in sharp contrast—a chaste monastic cubicle. His books—chiefly professional works, with a sampling of Leopardi and Carducci and other Italian poets and an Italian translation of Thomas à Kempis—were neatly stacked in a case, and his papers were out of sight. The only ornaments in the room were a crucifix and a framed picture of a family group, in clothes of 1920.

Hugo Ellis's room was defiantly, almost parodistically the room of a normal, healthy college man, even to the University banner over the bed. He had carefully avoided both Flecker's chaos and de' Cassis's austerity; there was a precisely calculated normal litter of pipes and letters and pulp magazines. The pin-up girls seemed to be carrying normality too far, and Sister Ursula averted her eyes.

Each room had a clean upper sheet.

Professor Lowe's room would have seemed as normal as Ellis's, if less spectacularly so, if it were not for the inordinate quantity of books. Shelves covered all wall space that was not taken by door, window, or bed. Psychology, psychiatry, and criminology predominated; but there was a selection of poetry, humor, fiction for any mood.

Marshall took down William Roughead's *Twelve Scots Trials* and said, "Lucky devil! I've never so much as seen a copy of this before." He smiled at the argumentative pencilings in the margins. Then as he went to replace it, he saw through the gap that there was a second row of books behind. Paperbacks. He took one out and put it back hastily. "You wouldn't want to see that, Sister. But it might fit into that case we were proposing about repressions and word-distortions."

Sister Ursula seemed not to heed him. She was standing by the bed and said, "Come here."

Marshall came and looked at the freshly made bed.

Sister Ursula passed her hand over the mended but clean lower sheet. "Do you see?"

"See what?"

"The answer," she said.

Marshall frowned. "Look, Sister—"

"Lieutenant, your wife is one of the most efficient housekeepers I've ever known. I thought she had, to some extent, indoctrinated you. Think. Try to think with Leona's mind."

Marshall thought. Then his eyes narrowed and he said, "So . . ."

"It is fortunate," Sister Ursula said, "that the Order of Martha of Bethany specializes in housework."

Marshall went out and called downstairs. "Raglan! See if the laundry's been picked up from the back porch."

The Sergeant's voice came back. "It's gone, Loot. I thought there wasn't no harm—"

"Then get on the phone quick and tell them to hold it."

"But what laundry, Loot?"

Marshall muttered. Then he turned to Sister Ursula. "The men won't know of course, but we'll find a bill somewhere. Anyway, we won't need that till the preliminary hearing. We've got enough now to settle Quasimodo."

He heard the Lieutenant's question and repressed a startled gesture. He had not thought of that. But even if they traced the laundry, it would be valueless as evidence without Mrs. Carey's testimony . . .

He saw at once what had to be done.

They had taken Mrs. Carey to the guest room, that small downstairs bedroom near the kitchen which must have been a maid's room when this was a large family house. There were still police posted outside the house, but only Raglan and the Lieutenant inside.

It was so simple. His mind, he told himself, had never been functioning more clearly. No nonsense about stripping this time; this was not for pleasure. Just be careful to avoid those crimson jets. . . .

The Sergeant wanted to know where he thought he was going. He told him.

Raglan grinned. "You should've raised your hand. A teacher like you ought to know that."

He went to the back porch toilet, opened and closed its door without going in. Then he went to the kitchen and took the second-best knife. The best had been used last night.

It would not take a minute. Then he would be safe and later when the body was found what could they prove? The others had been out of the room too.

But as he touched the knife it began to happen. Something came from the blade up his arm and into his head. He was in a hurry, there was no time—but holding the knife, the color of things began to change.

He was half-naked when Marshall found him.

Sister Ursula leaned against the jamb of the kitchen door. She felt sick. Marshall and Raglan were both strong men, but they needed help to subdue him. His face was contorted into an unrecognizable mask like a demon from a Japanese tragedy. She clutched the crucifix of the rosary that hung at her waist and murmured a prayer to the Archangel Michael. For it was not the physical strength of the man that frightened her, nor the glint of his knife, but the pure quality of incarnate evil that radiated from him and made the doctrine of possession a real terror.

As she finished her prayer, Marshall's fist connected with his jaw and he crumpled. So did Sister Ursula.

"I don't know what you think of me," Sister Ursula said as Marshall drove her home. (Sister Felicitas was dozing in the backseat.) "I'm afraid I couldn't ever have been a policewoman after all."

"You'll do," Marshall said. "And if you feel better now, I'd like to run over it with you. I've got to get my brilliant deductions straight for the press."

"The fresh air feels good. Go ahead."

"I've got the sheet business down pat, I think. In ordinary middle-class households you don't change both sheets every week; Leona never does, I remembered.

You put on a clean upper sheet, and the old upper becomes the lower. The other three bedrooms each had one clean sheet—the upper. His had two—upper and lower; therefore his upper sheet had been stained in some unusual way and had to be changed. The hasty bath, probably in the dark, had been careless, and there was some blood left to stain the sheet. Mrs. Carey wouldn't have thought anything of it at the time because she hadn't found the body yet. Right?"

"Perfect, Lieutenant."

"So. But now about Quasimodo . . . I still don't get it. He's the one it *couldn't* apply to. Either of the others—"

"Yes?"

"Well, who is Quasimodo? He's the Hunchback of Notre Dame. So it could mean the deformed de' Cassis. Who wrote Quasimodo? Victor Hugo. So it could be Hugo Ellis. But it wasn't either; and how in heaven's name could it mean Professor Lowe?"

"Remember, Lieutenant: Professor Flecker said this was an allusion that might particularly appeal to me. Now I am hardly noted for my devotion to the anticlerical prejudices of Hugo's *Notre-Dame de Paris*. What is the common meeting-ground of my interests and Professor Flecker's?"

"Church liturgy?" Marshall ventured.

"And why was your Quasimodo so named? Because he was born—or found or christened, I forget which—on the Sunday after Easter. Many Sundays, as you may know, are often referred to by the first word of their introits, the beginning of the proper of the Mass. As the fourth Sunday in Lent is called *Laetare* Sunday, or the third in Advent *Gaudete* Sunday. So the Sunday after Easter is known as *Quasimodo* Sunday, from its introit *Quasimodo geniti infantes* . . . 'As new-born babes.'"

"But I still don't see—"

"The Sunday after Easter," said Sister Ursula, "is more usually referred to as *Low* Sunday."

"Oh," said Marshall. After a moment he added reflectively, "*The Happy Hypocrite* . . ."

"You see that too? Beerbohm's story is about a man who assumes a mask of virtue to conceal his depravity. A schizoid allegory. I wonder if Professor Lowe dreamed that he might find the same happy ending."

Marshall drove on a bit in silence. Then he said, "He said a strange thing while you were out."

"I feel as though he were already dead," said Sister Ursula. "I want to say, 'God rest his soul.' We should have a special office for the souls of the mad."

"That cues into my story. The boys were taking him away and I said to Rags, 'Well, this is once the insanity plea justifies itself. He'll never see the gas chamber.' And he turned on me—he'd quieted down by then—and said, 'Nonsense, sir! Do you think I would cast doubt on my sanity merely to save my life?'"

"Mercy," said Sister Ursula. At first Marshall thought it was just an exclamation. Then he looked at her face and saw that she was not talking to him.

~

THE RIPPER EXPERIENCE

Daniel Stashower

Blending fictional characters, real-life people, historical events, and original storytelling is no small task, but Daniel Meyer Stashower (1960–) has managed it with great success. His novels and short stories have featured Sherlock Holmes, Harry Houdini, and others from different eras.

After winning a Raymond Chandler Fulbright Fellowship in Detective Fiction to work at Oxford University for a year, Stashower produced his first novel, *The Adventure of the Ectoplasmic Man* (1985), which featured Sherlock Holmes and Harry Houdini, the fictional mystery blending with the author's real-life fascination with magic and conjuring; it was nominated for an Edgar Award for Best First Novel. Houdini became a favorite protagonist and appeared in several of Stashower's subsequent novels: *The Dime Museum Murders* (1999), *The Floating Lady Murder* (2000), and *The Houdini Specter* (2001).

Although established as a writer of excellent mystery fiction, mainly historical novels set in the years preceding World War I, Stashower has enjoyed even greater success in recent years with his nonfiction works. He has continued to focus on the nineteenth and early twentieth centuries, writing *Teller of Tales: The Life of Arthur Conan Doyle* (1999), for which he won his first Edgar. He followed this with additional critically acclaimed works on a variety of subjects, including such highly readable tomes as *The Beautiful Cigar Girl: Mary Rogers, Edgar Allan Poe, and the Invention of Murder* (2006), which narrates the true story of the brutal murder on which Poe based his second C. Auguste Dupin story, "The Mystery of Marie Roget," and the Edgar-winning *The Hour of Peril: The Secret Plot to Murder Lincoln Before the Civil War* (2013), which recounts the Pinkertons' tireless efforts to thwart an assassination plot during Lincoln's journey to Washington, a plan that could have divided the nation forever.

"The Ripper Experience" was written especially for this collection and has never previously been published.

"*I'm Jack the Ripper,*" Jayson said. He picked up a cinnamon latte. "How's that? Or maybe just *I'm Jack.*"

I was running late that morning. "Sorry," I said, "there was a—"

He waved it off. "No worries. We're trying to come up with something for the T-shirt."

Martha, one of the new content coordinators, looked up from her notes. "*I'm Jack the Ripper,*" she said. "Have you picked a font?"

"Nightbird. Bold. With blood drips and maybe that knife-slash effect? See how it looks."

"Nightbird." Martha wrote it down. "Are we done?"

"No, I'm not sure I like it." Jayson leaned forward and drummed his fingers on the conference table. "*Got Jack?* No, that's terrible. *I'm with the Ripper.* With a bloody arrow pointing to the person next to you. God, that's even worse." He glanced over as I set down my heavy canvas courier bag. "Annie? You got anything?"

I slipped into my chair. *"Fear the Ripper."*

Jayson shook his head. He was drumming with both hands now, nervous about the day ahead. "*Keep on Slashin'.* No, don't write that down. *Keep Calm and Fear Jack.* No. Terrible. *My Grandmother Was Murdered in Whitechapel and All I Got Was This Lousy T-shirt.*" He pushed back from the table and stood up. "This is hopeless. Annie—you decide."

"Keep it simple," I said. "Like always. Exhibition logo on the back; title on the front. *Saucy Jack: The Ripper Experience.*"

Jayson gave a tight nod and pointed at Martha's note pad. "Write it down."

People are clueless about museum exhibitions. Your average visitor—we call them "guests"—has no idea what it takes to mount a full-scale installation, or even a smaller traveling show. They think you just slap a few things on the wall and print up the tickets. There's no respect for the process, no awareness of what happens behind the scenes. Let me tell you, it doesn't happen overnight. There are a hell of a lot of moving parts. We have a lighting specialist. We have an audio guy. We have a videographer. We have a team of designers and fabricators. We have consultants to oversee the accessibility and educational compliance, especially with the interactives. And if you don't have interactives—the hands-on stuff—you're dead in the water. Trust me on this.

All of it takes money. We'd already spent months writing proposals, applying for grants, and pulling together a sales pitch for Museum-Expo. We had charts to estimate the average dwell time, a mock-up of traffic flow, and bullet points for the STEM-compliant educational benefits. That's Science, Technology, Engineering, and Mathematics. If all went to plan, most of our funding would come from educational foundations, so we had to check all the boxes. But Jayson also wanted to hit the critical-thinking initiatives, which meant an extra layer of classroom handouts and study guides. That's why we needed Arthur Furman, and that's where our troubles began.

"You know Furman?" Jayson had asked, when the name was first mentioned. He must have seen my face fall.

"By reputation, mostly. He was at Western U. When I was an Associate. He's not a nice man."

"Gwen wants him," Jayson said. Gwen Halstram, from the Beckworth Foundation, the biggest of our big-fish donors. "She says he's a 'real scholar.'"

"He's a prick," I began. "He—"

"We have to make nice," Jayson said. "We need this."

He was right. We'd been planning the meeting for weeks, checking the details and polishing the pitch. Jayson and I made a point of getting in early, with coffee and Voodoo donuts. It's a Portland thing. We'd also covered the conference table with fun little party favors, to set the tone. There were little truncheons and police whistles, notepads with the outline of a skulking Jack the Ripper, and letter openers in the shape of a Victorian clasp knife. Everything had Jayson's logo on it. Jayson Straight Exhibition Design.

The walls were covered with Ripper material. Photos, sketches, and maps. Newspaper headlines and *Police Gazette* mock-ups. Wanted posters and book jackets. A facsimile of the "Dear Boss" letter. And those grainy, ghoulish photos of the victims. I'd tried to pin those up in a far corner, so people could look away if they wanted, but Jayson insisted on putting them front and center. "Grist for the mill," he said.

There was also a large gallery of pop culture stuff. The cover of a dime novel, with a blonde in a clingy dress cowering in the Ripper's shadow. A poster from the 1959 movie ("This lady of the night has taken her last walk!"). A panel from "Gotham by Gaslight," with the Ripper squaring off against Batman. We even had an old *Life with Archie* comic, with a frightened Betty peering up at a shadowy, cane-wielding figure. I kid you not. More grist for the mill.

My name is Annie Chapman, which is pretty messed up, when you think about it. Annie Chapman also happens to be the name of one of the Ripper's victims from 1888—the second of the "Canonical Five," as they're known. I even look a little like her, if the records are accurate. Blue eyes, wavy brown hair, a little over five feet tall. I'm not related as far as I know, but I still have a hard time looking at the mortuary photo.

Some people think that's why Jayson hired me, because of the name. Actually, I came on as a research assistant during *Justice for All: The American Legal Experience*. I thought it would be short-term—I needed a job with benefits—but that was eleven years ago. I soon found that I liked working for Jayson. Loved it, in fact.

We had fourteen chairs around the conference table, and six more people would be joining on speakerphones. We'd been having weekly conference calls for six or seven weeks by then, but Jayson wanted a three-day summit at the studio to hammer out the final details before we went into production. He called it a "design charrette." He loved that phrase.

Most of us had been together since *Cursed* and we knew what we were doing. You may have seen that one. *Cursed: Unraveling the Mysteries of King Tut's Tomb*. We built a full-scale replica of the burial chamber, with antechambers where you could design your own burial masks and scarabs.

Our team also did *Forty Whacks: The Lizzie Borden Experience*. That was our big hit. It had all the usual bells and whistles—historical overview, newspaper coverage from 1892, pop culture impact—but the centerpiece was a forensic module of the murder scene. We had fiberglass mannequins of Abby and Andrew Borden with realistic stage blood oozing from their wounds. The guests got to run spatter tests and vote on whether Lizzie did it or not. CSI: Fall River.

But that was four years earlier. Frankly, our next two exhibitions hadn't performed all that well. *Great Powers: The Inside Story of the United Nations* just didn't pull the crowds and *Mayflower: Journey to the New World* drew some backlash from the Native American Council. I'm not going to lie to you. We needed a hit.

The Ripper seemed like a natural, picking up where Lizzie left off. But we'd made some mistakes the first time around. There'd been complaints about the "Whack-a-Skull" booth. The science was good, but looking back on it now, we might have framed it a little differently. Long story short, some of our donors got skittish. That's how we got saddled with Arthur Furman. He was supposed to keep us in line.

Arthur had written a book on the Ripper, some dry-as-dust accounting of how the murders were "contextualized" in the Victorian press. He was a media studies professor at Western U and he was already old when I knew him there. Tall, a little stooped, high forehead, wire-rimmed glasses. The only distinctive thing about him was his facial hair. He had this weird Franz Josef thing going on—a huge, bushy moustache that curled away from his nose and merged into a thick pair of sideburns. I suppose it was striking, if you're into that sort of thing. Which I'm not.

I did my best on that first morning. I took charge of Arthur while the rest of the team drifted in and took their places around the conference table. I got him a coffee and walked him through the material I'd pinned up on the walls. If a particular item passed muster, he'd give a little grunt. If it didn't, he'd let out an exaggerated sigh—a weary scholar among dullards—and make a note on his legal pad.

We made it halfway around the room before he got to a rare old book called *The Whitechapel Murders*. I'd pinned up a color Xerox of the cover, in a loose grouping of "penny dreadfuls" from the period. I wasn't surprised that it caught his eye. *The Whitechapel Murders: Or the Mysteries of the East End* was a hell of a coup for us. The writing is awful but it's a "high spot" collectible. It came out in 1888, while the Ripper was still on the prowl. The cover shows a bearded, scowling Jack slinking away, knife in hand, while his latest victim lies in a pool of spreading blood. A wanted poster is visible in the background, listing the names of the victims and offering a £500 reward. The printing is crude and pulpy, but somehow that makes it all the more menacing. You can just about see the light fading in the dying woman's eyes. I could, anyway.

Arthur must have stared at it for a good five minutes. "Where did you get this?" he asked. He was clearly put out at finding such a treasure in the hands of the Philistines.

"It's extraordinary, isn't it?" I pointed at the gas lamp in the foreground. "I love the way the artist managed to—"

"Where did you get it?" No time for small talk, apparently.

"From the Horowitz Collection at Kent State."

"You mean to say you have the actual novella? The Purkess edition?"

"It's on its way. It'll be here on Wednesday."

"You can't be serious." He gave a wild glance around the room, as if searching for a grown-up. "The Horowitz archive doesn't lend materials, not even to me. They wouldn't just—"

"I spoke to Dr. Horowitz personally," I said. "He was utterly charming."

Arthur studied my face. I could just about see the gears turning behind his eyes. "This is a variant I'd never seen before. It's exceedingly rare. It should be in a museum."

"It will be," I said. "We're designing a museum exhibition."

He snorted. "That's not what I meant. I meant a *real* museum."

Our goals for that first morning were modest. We gave an overview of the seven rooms that would make up the exhibit and sketched out some details for the "Hall of Suspects" module. To be fair, Arthur was reasonably civil for an hour or so. He put up a bit of a fuss over Walter Sickert and James Maybrick, but he passed over Thomas Neill Cream with a magnanimous wave of the hand. "We all know that Dr. Cream didn't do it," he said. "That absurd story of his confession from the scaffold just doesn't hold water. But the man was a murderer, pure and simple. He just wasn't *our* murderer."

Jayson and I exchanged a look. This was promising. I made a checkmark next to Dr. Cream's name. Jayson closed the manila file and lifted the next one from the pile in front of him. "Who's next?" he began. "Ah, Prince Albert Victor, Duke of Clarence and Avondale, eldest son of the Prince of Wales, and grandson of Queen Victoria. Prince Albert is said to have—"

"Absolutely not," Arthur said. "Not a chance."

"I'm sorry?" Jayson's tone suggested that he might have misheard.

"He doesn't belong," Arthur said. "It's a discredited theory. It wasn't even mentioned in print until 1962."

"That doesn't prove anything," said Ajay, one of our researchers. "It could have been hushed up. Isn't he the one that got caught at a brothel? Wasn't that covered up, too?"

Arthur rounded on him. "There's no evidence, only hearsay. And even if that business could be proven, it wouldn't make him guilty of the Ripper killings. He had a strong alibi for each murder."

"But he's part of the Ripper legend," Jayson said. "Just like Dr. Cream and James Maybrick. Right?"

"This is different," Arthur insisted. "The whole royal-Masonic conspiracy theory is a sham. It's just bad scholarship. We must hold ourselves to a higher standard."

"I appreciate that it's controversial," Jayson began, "but it's also—"

"Even Joseph Gorman washed his hands of it," Arthur continued, putting on a head of steam now. "Even Gorman said it was a hoax. And it was largely his doing in the first place!"

Jayson laid his palms flat on the table and took a slow breath. "But it's part of the whole—the whole fabric of the thing. The narrative. People have heard this story. They'd heard that a member of the royal family was involved somehow. They may not remember the name, they may not know the details, but they've read something about it. Or they saw it in a movie. And if we don't have it in our Hall of Suspects, it will leave a big hole. People will grouse. *What about the royal guy? Where was the royal guy?* And then they'll go on Yelp and give us two stars. *It was good, but they forgot the royal guy.*" Jayson pushed back from the table and folded his arms. "We can have a text panel that explains the whole story. All the holes; all the flaws. But we have to include it."

Arthur narrowed his eyes and stroked his bushy whiskers. "I was brought here to uphold a certain standard. I believe that's why Ms. Halstram asked me to come aboard. To instill a sense of academic rigor."

Jayson closed the manila folder on Prince Albert Victor. "We'll put a pin in it. For now."

Arthur scribbled something on his pad. "We'll see," he said. "It's all a question of knowing where to draw the line."

That afternoon we went out back onto the construction floor to see where the autopsies would be done. The fabrication crew was pulling together a full-scale surgical amphitheater, with all the Victorian trimmings. We'd drawn up plans for a gas-lit chamber lined with tiers of horseshoe benches, rising from floor to ceiling. The benches would give the guests a full view of the solid wooden operating table at the center of the room and a long shelf of fearsome-looking surgical instruments—forceps, tenacula, saws, and trocars. Below the table there would be a tin tray filled with sawdust, for catching debris. Smaller workstations would be lined up at the far edge, with an assortment of cork-stoppered vials and Bunsen burners. That's where the guests would do the hands-on work.

Originally we wanted to stage a science module at the crime scene. We mapped out a realistic Victorian alleyway, complete with gaslight and cobblestones, and some swirling fog from a glycol machine. The guests would actually see the body where it fell, and we'd do forensic exercises right there at the scene. But we had to scrap it in the end. We couldn't make it wheelchair-friendly.

In some ways, the autopsy theater was better. The plan was to have the guests come in on timed tickets. White screens would obscure the table. When the benches were full, a short video would play on the screens. We'd have actors portraying Thomas Bond, the medical examiner, and Chief Inspector Frederick Abberline. They'd come in shaking their heads and wringing their hands because another body had been discovered in the East End. We hadn't decided which one it would be yet—possibly Elizabeth Stride, since there were opportunities to do soil analysis and bruise patterns, but Catherine Eddowes gave us a better shot at blood spatter work.

"Bond and Abberline will do the necessary exposition," Jayson explained. "They'll have some back and forth, describing the injuries and laying out the tests and procedures. All the while, we'll be raising the tension on what's hidden behind the screens. We'll do close-ups of Abberline's face, looking a little green when Bond raises the sheet. Bond will say that he's never seen such an atrocity— something like that. Finally, when we've laid it all out just right, Bond will turn to the benches and speak directly to the guests." Jayson flipped through his notes, looking for the exact wording. *Time is of the essence. You have your notebooks; you have your tools. I will be here to guide you. Can you help us catch the killer?* He pointed to the autopsy table. "And then the screens will lift away on pulleys to reveal the body, prepped for the procedure. If we play it right, the crowd will absolutely lose it. They'll go nuts." Jayson grinned and closed his notebook. "What do you think?"

Kristina, our graphics chief, started clapping madly. Others joined in. "I love it, Jayson," Kristina said. "It'll be a huge draw. Bigger than *Cursed,* even."

"I'll find some spooky music," said Gunter, the sound engineer. "Something on a harmonium, high and tinkly."

"And we'll have street noises in the background," Ajay said. "Footsteps. Wooden cab wheels rolling by."

It went on like this for five or ten minutes, everyone chiming in with suggestions. It was the happiest I'd seen Jayson look in months.

And then Arthur had to have his say. He'd been standing apart from the rest of us, sniffing at an especially vicious-looking skull saw. "Do you mean to say that there's going to be a body on this table? An actual body?"

Jayson's smile faded. "Of course not. We'll use a dummy."

"A realistic-looking dummy?"

"Fairly realistic."

Arthur nodded primly. "And when you say 'prepped for the procedure,' what does that mean? Exactly?"

Jayson chose his words carefully. "It means the body will have been transported from the crime scene and readied for Dr. Bond's examination, according to the practices of the time."

"By which you mean an incision along the sternum. With the skin pulled back to expose the internal organs."

"Well . . . yes, according to the practices of the time."

"And you'll have people crowding around to look at it? To poke around inside the body cavity?"

"No, Arthur, no one will touch it. We'll have it sealed off. In Plexiglas, probably."

"It'll have to be non-reflective," said Ajay. "Otherwise you'll get glare from the camera flashes."

Jayson continued as if he hadn't heard. "They'll just be observing the body, Arthur. They'll take note of the bruise patterns—or the pooled blood, whatever. They won't touch the body. They'll just observe."

I jumped in, trying to turn the page. "What happens next? After they observe the body?"

"They'll take their findings to the work-stations," Jayson said quickly. "They'll run an experiment. We'll have a touch screen at each kiosk, with a clip of Dr. Bond guiding them through the steps. They'll press a button that corresponds to the findings they recorded in their notebooks. When they finish, a clip of Inspector Abberline will pop up. He'll say either 'Well done,' or 'Back to the drawing board,' depending on whether they got the right results or not."

Arthur wasn't buying it. "It's utterly nightmarish," he said. "Like one of those midnight creep shows."

"Of course it's a creep show," I said, a little more sharply than I intended. "It's not as if these women lived happily ever after."

"But it's too graphic," Arthur said. "Too gory."

"Did you ever get a chance to see *Cursed*?" I asked. "Our exhibition on King Tut?"

Arthur shook his head.

"We had an interactive where the guests pulled out a brain with an iron hook. Through the nostrils, just like the ancient Egyptians did. Excerebration. Nobody ever complained. You can get away with a little gore, Arthur, as long as there's educational content."

Our production facility, Hawkswood Studios, sprawls out over more than one hundred thousand square feet, with a design center at the front and an enormous fabrication space at the back. We have woodshops, metal presses, electronics labs, recording booths, and custom paint benches. We can take a concept from a scribble on a cocktail napkin and turn out five to eight tons of exhibit material, all crated up and ready to ship out to museums across the world. On any given day the main floor might be set for the Battle of Argonne Forest, complete with scrub wire and foxholes, and the next it could be the House of the Tragic Poet in Pompeii. It's an exciting place to work.

But we're in the middle of nowhere. In the evenings, when we have out-of-towners in for a charrette, we literally have to make our own fun. That night some of the crew guys had done up the sound stage as a 1970s disco, with pulsing lights and throbbing music. There was even a glitter ball hanging from a sound boom and a cardboard stand-up of John Travolta, finger pointing to the sky.

I found Jayson at the bar with a Grey Goose and tonic, looking worried. "There's going to be trouble, Annie," he said.

I didn't have to ask what he meant. Arthur was perched on a folding chair at the far side of the room, wincing theatrically as somebody turned up the volume on Gloria Gaynor.

"He might come around," I said.

"I hope so." He lifted his glass and pressed it to his forehead. "We need this to happen," he said, closing his eyes. "We really do."

I helped myself to a glass of Shiraz. "We've been on the skids before, Jayson."

"Not like this," he said.

"What's he drinking?"

"Scotch and soda. Heavy on the Scotch."

"Shall I try talking to him?"

"Please, Annie. See what you can do. Turn on the charm."

I mixed a strong Scotch and soda and set off across the dance floor. I should probably mention that Jayson wasn't asking me to bat my eyelashes at Arthur Furman. He wasn't asking me to use my feminine wiles. The very idea would have embarrassed him. The fact is that I'm a good twenty years older than Jayson, and he has a quaint notion that people above the age of fifty speak a secret language. He still talks about the cover letter I sent him with my résumé all those years ago, which I'd typed on an IBM Selectric. He once told Mags that he wanted to put my flip phone on *Antiques Roadshow*. Mags, I should probably also mention, is my wife. That's another reason Jayson wouldn't have asked me to go all "come hither" with Arthur. I'm not wired up that way. Which is not to say that I'm without charm. Or so I'm told.

I sat down next to Arthur, who accepted the drink with a curt nod. I leaned in, straining to be heard over the Bee Gees. "I didn't especially care for this music the first time around," I said. "You?"

He shrugged.

"Come on," I said. "It's quieter in the back." He shrugged again and followed me back to the half-built surgical amphitheater on the construction floor. We took a seat on the horseshoe benches. "Listen," I began, "I've been thinking about what you said. About the medical examination being too gory."

"I'm thinking of the children," he said. "Somebody has to." God, he was a prick.

"Do you have children, Arthur? I can't recall."

"Never married," he said. "Not that it's any concern of yours."

"No," I said. "You're right. But what if we put up a parental advisory? We could let parents and educators make up their own minds."

He swirled his drink. "They'd see it anyway, wouldn't they? All the rooms are connected."

"No. People go where we tell them to go. We put colored arrows on the floor. It's how we manage the traffic flow. You'll follow the blue arrows if you want to see the autopsy. Follow the red arrows if you don't."

He grunted. "That won't work."

"We do it all the time," I said. "During peak periods some museums have to speed up the dwell time. They change the arrows so people will bypass one or two rooms. It couldn't be simpler. Believe me, I can make them go anywhere I want."

He took a noisy swig of his drink. "Even if that were the case, I'm not sure I would trust the average educator to make an informed decision."

"Oh, come on. That's a bit—"

"Look," he said sharply, "I just don't see why this is necessary. Not just the so-called forensic module. Any of it. You've gathered a few good resources, you're obviously a very capable researcher, but I can't see what's to be gained by this so-called Ripper Experience. I simply don't hold with the idea of history as entertainment."

"Museums have to turn a profit, Arthur. Just like universities."

"Sometimes it's just a matter of making better choices. Making cuts. Trimming the fat."

"I remember," I said.

He looked at me strangely. "What?"

I set down my wine glass. "I'm just saying that Jack the Ripper is a cultural phenomenon. For better or worse. Always has been. You know this as well as anyone."

He sighed. "That doesn't mean we should turn it into a piece of dinner theater. You said it yourself. Jack the Ripper murdered five women—"

"At least five," I said.

"All right, if we must. At least five. So let's not romanticize it. In my day we were more concerned with—"

"In my day? Did you just say that?"

"Well, it's true. You people are just profiteering."

"Seriously? People have been turning a profit on these murders since the beginning. Even before the blood had dried. That book you're so eager to see? *The Whitechapel Murders*? It came out in 1888! The bodies were still dropping!"

He gave a tight smile. "My interest is in simple data. Microjournalism as a mirror of national identity. I wouldn't expect you to understand."

My fingers tightened on the stem of my wine glass. "I'm just saying—my point is that we're not the first to exploit the public's interest in the Ripper. Not by any stretch of the imagination."

"I'll grant you that. Perhaps these things are cyclical. But there's no academic rigor here. It's just cheap titillation. That's where you went wrong."

"One has to bait the hook, Arthur. Forgive me, but it's true."

"We'll see." He rattled the ice in his glass. "I need another drink." He peered into the dim corridor behind us. "Which way is it?"

"Follow the blue arrows."

He stood up, a little unsteady. "Blue arrows?"

"We use the same system here as in the museums. Arrows on the floor." I watched as he wandered off toward the bar. "See?" I called after him. "I can make you go anywhere I want."

His answer came back from the shadows. "We'll see."

It was late when I left Hawkswood, but I stopped at the hospice anyway. They say she no longer knows if I'm there or not, but I can't imagine that I'd ever skip a day. I sat for a few minutes in the chair by the bed and listened to the hum and clank of the machines, the tinny buzz of the respirator. I took a copy of *Mansfield Park* from my bag and read to her for half an hour. At midnight I changed the pad and put some Vaseline on her lips. Her eyes were open, staring. You could just about see the light fading. "What are we gonna do?" I said. "What are we gonna do, kiddo?"

I was late again the next morning. Jayson looked grim.

"I'm sorry," I began. "There was a—"

"I need to talk to you." He led me over to the coffee and donuts. "We've got trouble," he said in a low voice. "Funding trouble."

"The Beckworth Foundation?"

He nodded. "I got a call from Gwen Halstram. She says she's concerned about the direction we're taking."

I glanced across the room. Arthur hadn't arrived yet. "Did she give any specifics?"

"She said something about 'academic rigor.' She used that phrase twice. And she wondered if perhaps these resources might be put to better use by the academic community. She used those words exactly."

I looked over at the wall where the cover of *The Whitechapel Murders* should have been hanging. He'd taken it down. "This is incredible, Jayson. He's stabbing us in the back and taking souvenirs. Who does that remind you of?"

"Except the Ripper would have looked us in the eye." Jayson rubbed the bridge of his nose.

"So what are we supposed to do?"

He shrugged. "We try to change his mind." He took a sip of his cinnamon latte. "We need this one, Annie. We can't have another washout. We'd have to shut it all down. I'd be out on my ass. I don't know where I'd find another—" He caught himself. "Sorry, Annie. Here I am worrying about—how *is* Mags, by the way?" My face must have gone dark because he looked away quickly. "Sorry, I didn't mean—"

"No," I said, "it's fine. She's fine. No change. So what's the plan? How do we bring Arthur around?"

"We'll show him the really tedious stuff. We bore him to death." A grin spread across his face. "He'll love it."

We spent the entire morning going over educational impact reports. We reviewed translation data and accessibility protocols over lunch. In the afternoon we walked through models and programing data for the legacy room, with information kiosks to demonstrate how the techniques pioneered during the Jack the Ripper investigation carried forward to the forensics and behavioral sciences of today. It was deeply conventional, documents-in-glass-cases stuff.

It seemed to be working. "You've done some solid work here," Arthur admitted. He was standing in front of a seventy-inch classroom smartboard, where a painstakingly educational video called 'A Heritage of Science' was playing on continuous loop. "With a little work, we might be able to salvage something worthwhile out of this. We might even—"

And that's when the ghost of Jack the Ripper appeared.

It started with a dimming of the lights. Next, a high, cackling laugh rose up from below. The image on the smartboard flickered away, and a blood-streaked message bubbled up in its place:

I've had a grand rest, Boss.
Now it's back to work for Saucy Jack!

"What the hell?" Arthur gaped the screen. "What are you playing at?"

But it wasn't over. We heard a sharp scream as a sudden blast of vapor shot up behind us. When the mist cleared, Jack the Ripper stood at the center of the room. It was a thing of beauty, really. We'd built a wax and fiberboard figure about nine feet tall, loosely modeled on Ivor Novello in *The Lodger,* the Hitchcock movie, with a heavy cloak and a thick muffler obscuring the lower half of its face. The eyes glowed yellow and a gnarled, claw-like hand thrust forward with a glinting knife, blood dripping from the blade. There was also a halo of question marks circling the head on fairy wire. It was not subtle.

"What the *hell* are you people—?"

But whatever Arthur was going to say was drowned out by fresh screams and a second blast of vapor. By the time mist cleared, Jack had been lowered out of sight.

Ajay and Gunter burst out of the control room, slapping each other on the back. "Did you see that?" Ajay shouted. "He's magnificent! Glowing eyes! They'll jump out of their skins! They'll crap their—"

"Guys," Jayson said, "I thought we agreed that we'd put a pin in Jack's ghost for today."

Ajay and Gunter heard the anger in Jayson's voice. "Sorry," Gunter said. "We couldn't resist. We had it all queued up and it just seemed too perfect!"

Arthur's face had gone very still. "What the fuck was that?" he asked quietly.

Jayson went into spin mode. "We were thinking that the legacy room might be a bit dry—a bit dry for some people, anyway. We wanted to send the crowds out the door with something memorable, so they'd tell their friends. What better than the ghost of Jack the Ripper? As if the Ripper's spirit were haunting the exhibition?"

"And it would control the dwell time," I said. "We'd have it on a fifteen-minute cycle, to send them out the door."

"Give them a good scare," Jayson added. "So they'll tell their friends."

"A scare," Arthur repeated, shaking his head. "So you actually have a trapdoor over here?"

"It's a star trap, like in a theater," Gunter explained, pointing at the faint hinges visible on the floor. "When the smoke cannon goes off, we raise Jack up on a pressure-lift."

"But only a couple of museums have trap rooms," Ajay said. "So we're figuring out how to get the same effect with optics. Convex lenses and fog projectors, like a hologram."

Arthur looked me square in the face. Whatever glimmers of reason I'd seen earlier were gone. "I've seen enough," he said.

"Arthur—"

But he was already walking away. "A line has to be drawn," he said.

That night the crew guys had done up the sound stage as a Belle Époque café, with music by Edith Piaf and Charles Aznavour piped in. Gunter handed everyone a black beret as they came through the door.

Arthur didn't take a beret. Instead, he went straight to the bar and pounded down a Scotch and soda.

"I'm surprised he's still here," Jayson said gloomily.

"It'll be in his contract," I said. "He's very careful about contracts, as I recall."

Arthur got a second drink and carried it out the door.

"It doesn't look good," Jayson said.

"Let's give it a few minutes," I said. "Maybe there's still something I can do."

By the time I went looking for him, Arthur had found his way back to the benches by the autopsy table. I handed him another drink and took a seat beside him. "You've come to reason with me," he said.

"I shouldn't have to. You're being deliberately obstreperous."

"I'm not."

"I don't see why you have such a problem with us. We're no different from a magic lantern show in the eighteenth century. We engage people's imaginations; get them interested in the subject. Some of them will work their way upstream to the source material. That's how it works. You might even say it's a mirror of national identity."

His ears pricked up at this. "I know you, don't I? Before this?"

"I was at Western U. College of Arts."

He waved a hand, as if batting a mosquito. "I wasn't responsible for that."

"No. Cuts had to be made. Fat had to be trimmed."

"Anyway, it was a long time ago."

"And yet here we are again. Perhaps these things are cyclical."

He shook his head. "You seem like an intelligent person. But there are standards that must be upheld. Ms. Halstram entrusted me with—"

"A lot of these people will lose their livelihoods. Their benefits."

He batted his hand again. "There are always jobs for young people. As for you, you could come back to academe."

"Simple as that?"

He wobbled to his feet. "Come see me," he said. "When *The Whitechapel Murders* arrives. We'll talk." He peered behind him. "Blue arrows, yes?"

I nodded. "Unless somebody changed it."

Six and half months later, *Saucy Jack: The Ripper Experience* opened at the Franklin Institute in Philadelphia. We were booked there for eight months, followed by a six-month run at the Denver Museum of Nature and Science and a full year at the Discovery Cube in Orange County. Queries were already coming in from abroad. If the numbers held up, the show would tour for eight or nine years.

We pulled out all the stops for the preview party in Philadelphia. The serving staff dressed as London bobbies. We had specialty cocktails, including a "Bloody Mary Jane Kelly" and a "Saucy Jack and Coke." We set up a photo booth so you could put your face on a "Ghastly Murderer Still at Large" poster.

Jayson was beaming as he climbed on top of the autopsy table and delivered his welcoming remarks. He gave extravagant thanks to the sponsors and led a round of applause for several of the private donors in the room. Just as he appeared to be wrapping up, the lights suddenly dimmed and the ghost of Jack the Ripper sprang up at the center of the room. There were screams, there were gasps, but mostly there was applause. We put on a hell of a show.

Afterward, Jayson found me lingering in a far corner of the legacy room. Behind me was a small, black-edged plaque with the words "In Memory of a Valued Colleague" engraved across the top. It featured a small photo of Arthur Furman and an impressive listing of his many accomplishments and publications. It finished on the line: "We dedicate this exhibition to his memory."

Jayson handed me a glass of "Bloody Bordeaux."

"He'd have hated this, I suppose," he said.

"No question about it." I glanced at the photo. Arthur appeared to be passing a kidney stone. It was the least disagreeable one we could find.

"But I can't help feeling grateful to him, the bastard."

I took a sip of wine.

"I mean, I thought it was all over that night. After the accident. Especially when we lost the Beckworth money."

"It looked bad," I admitted. My eyes went to a small press clipping beside the plaque. *Noted Scholar Dies in Fall.* That had been one of the more restrained headlines. Most of the coverage took a "Jack the Ripper Strikes Again" angle. The press kept the story going for days, and one could hardly blame them. Arthur had fallen through the trap door in the legacy room. We found him lying dead at the feet of the Ripper statue. One of the paramedics told the press he'd heard high, cackling laughter at the scene. "It was creepy," he'd said. "Like the statue came to life. Like a movie."

Jayson sighed and leaned against a display case. "Does it ever—it still bothers me," he said. "I still don't see how it happened."

"He was drunk," I answered. "He got lost and fell through the star trap. We've been over this a million times."

"I know, I know—but still. All he had to do was follow the arrows. And why was the trap open?"

"It was an accident. We wouldn't be here otherwise. God knows the police were thorough."

Jayson finished his drink. He was drinking quite a lot these days. We both were. "I still feel guilty. Because in the end, it was the best thing that could have happened. For us, I mean. All the publicity about the so-called curse of Jack the Ripper. The donors came out of the woodwork."

"And everybody wants to see the killer statue," I said. "Everybody wants to see the ghost of Jack the Ripper."

"So he was right, in the end. We're just one of those midnight creep shows."

I looked away. "So what if we are?" I said. "It's all a question of knowing where to draw the line."

~

THE TREASURE OF JACK THE RIPPER

Edward D. Hoch

Readers have been of several minds when it comes to deciding which of the series characters created by Edward Dentinger Hoch (1930–2008) is their favorite. He created numerous protagonists, including Nick Velvet, the thief who steals only innately worthless objects (the first story was "The Theft of the Clouded Tiger," 1966); Captain Leopold, the tough but sensitive violent-crime specialist whose most famous case is told in the Edgar-winning "The Oblong Room" (1967), in which he investigates a murder with bizarre religious overtones on a college campus; Dr. Sam Hawthorne, who specializes in solving locked-room and other impossible crimes and made his first appearance in 1974 in "The Problem of the Covered Bridge"; Jeffrey Rand, a British cryptographer-detective; and Ben Snow, an apparently law-abiding drifter in the American West of the late nineteenth and early twentieth centuries around whom the legend has grown that he is actually Billy the Kid.

Perhaps the most bizarre (and compelling) of all Hoch's characters is Simon Ark, who claims to have been a Coptic priest in ancient Egypt two thousand years ago and has been battling evil ever since. He purports to be immortal, but so is the "Ultimate Evil," with whose avatars he is confronted. Ark was the protagonist of Hoch's first published story, "Village of the Dead" (1955), in which the entire population of a village commits suicide by leaping off a cliff, perhaps at the suggestion of a powerful religious leader. The story preceded the mass suicide of nine hundred nine members of the Peoples Temple of Jim Jones in Jonestown, Guyana, in 1978.

"The Treasure of Jack the Ripper" was first published in the October 1978 issue of *Ellery Queen's Mystery Magazine*.

Before recounting the remarkable events surrounding the search for the lost treasure of Jack the Ripper, it might be well to say a few words about my friend and occasional companion, Simon Ark. It was Simon who brought the affair to a satisfying conclusion, as he has so many other times in the twenty-two years I've known him.

I was a young newspaper reporter when I first met Simon Ark back in the mid-fifties. I'd been sent to a remote western town to report on an apparent mass suicide. Simon was there, too, looking tall and imposing and very old. He told me later that he was nearly two thousand years old, that he'd been a Coptic priest in Egypt, and now was doomed to roam the world like some Flying Dutchman or Wandering Jew, undying, seeking a final confrontation with Satan and all that was evil on this earth.

Did I believe any of that?

Frankly, no. Not at first, anyway. I married a wonderful girl named Shelly Constance and moved from a career in journalism to one in publishing. When Simon Ark reappeared in my life, as he kept doing at irregular intervals, I was an editor at Neptune Books. Whether I believed his story or not, I realized his vast knowledge of the occult and the mystic arts could be put to good use. He wrote a book and I published it. This was, after all, the era when every mystic had a book to publish.

In recent years Simon and I drifted apart. I was a middle-aged editor no longer quite up to the sudden journeys to Egypt or Poland or London that used to fascinate me in the old days. And for all I knew, Simon himself might have died of old age. Because I never really believed all that business about Simon being two thousand years old, did I?

It had been fully five years since our last adventure together when suddenly he was back, on the other end of the telephone, acting as if he'd seen me not ten minutes earlier.

"Hello, my friend."

"Simon! Is that really you?"

"Are you free for lunch?"

"Of course! But what—"

"I could not pass through New York without telephoning my publisher now, could I?" I knew his face would have that familiar sly smile as he said it.

I arranged to meet him at one o'clock at a steakhouse near my office. It had a small back room where customers could talk or drink away the afternoon without interruption, and I often took my authors there to iron out some sticky point in their plots or in our contracts.

"You look the same," I told Simon, meaning every word of it. His large body and worn but vigorous face reminded me of our first meeting twenty-two years earlier.

"You are looking good, too, my friend. Putting on a little weight, though. How is Shelly?"

"She's fine. Away visiting her mother in Florida at the moment."

"Ah, then you're alone?"

"Yes," I admitted reluctantly.

"Come to England with me," he said suddenly.

It was the sort of spur-of-the-moment suggestion I would have relished in the old days. "I can't, Simon. I have my work."

"We shall have some high old times, as we did in the old days."

"Still chasing the Devil?"

"Yes. It is an eternal quest." His face had gone solemn at my question. "Satanism has become a new fad among many young people."

"I've been reading about the resurgence of witch cults in England. Is that what you're after?"

He shook his head. "Something far more evil, my friend." The old eyes flashed with a familiar fire. "The treasure of the late Jack the Ripper."

"At least you admit that he's dead. Every once in a while someone tries to prove he's still alive. But I never heard of any treasure."

"I have a communication from a man in London named Ceritus Vats. A collector of esoterica. He feels my presence is needed to forestall a murder. And to find a treasure."

I thought about it. I still had a week's vacation coming, and June was a slow time in publishing. The autumn books were already in various stages of production, the concern of other people, and I wouldn't have to finalize our spring list for months yet. Shelly would be at her mother's place another week. There was no real reason why I couldn't go, except common sense.

And I'd never let that stop me before.

If Simon Ark was going to find a treasure belonging to Jack the Ripper, I wanted to be along for the show.

I phoned Shelly in Florida to tell her what was up. She'd always had mixed feelings about Simon Ark, and I knew she was far from delighted to have him back in our lives. But she didn't argue about the trip. She only said, "Be careful," and then, "I'll see you next week."

At ten o'clock the following night Simon and I were airborne over the Atlantic. It had been a bumpy takeoff from Kennedy, in the midst of an early summer rainstorm, but the flight quickly settled down to a smooth uneventful crossing. "What have you been doing with yourself these past five years?" I asked Simon.

He smiled. "Five years is merely a weekend to me, my friend. A pause, a rest from the search. As a matter of fact, I was studying at an Irish abbey for part of the time. I had only just returned to America when Ceritus Vats got in touch with me."

"What sort of man is Vats? And how did he know where to reach you? I've never known your address in all these years, except for the brief times you stayed with Shelly and me."

"Ceritus Vats is a bookseller, among other things. He operates from a little shop off Hammersmith Road in London. He knows my wants in certain fields, and he knows an address where I may be reached."

"You mentioned esoterica. The mystic arts, I suppose."

"In this case, yes, though he deals in a wide range of books and maps. Anything old or rare."

I was prepared to meet a man who went with his name, but Ceritus Vats was a surprise. Our first afternoon in London was misty with a damp June rain, but the shop of Ceritus Vats was warm and brightly lit. He was a short handsome gentleman with white hair, who moved between the stacks of old books with a nimbleness born of long experience. Though the shop had the traditional hodgepodge look of a good secondhand bookstore, I never doubted that he could lay his hand on any title in the place at a moment's notice.

"So good to see you again, Simon," he said with a smile. "And it's a pleasure to meet you, sir."

I shook his hand and sat down. "I noticed a few of our Neptune Books have drifted across the sea to England."

"Quite a few, actually. Neptune is a fine American house."

Simon cleared his throat, anxious to get down to business. "You can speak freely in front of my friend here. He's shared many adventures with me."

Vats glanced at me a bit uncertainly, then replied, "Very well. Of course you're familiar with Jack the Ripper and his crimes."

"I am," Simon said. "Unfortunately I was not in London at the time, or I might have brought the criminal to justice."

I was used to this sort of talk from Simon, and apparently Vats was, too. He hurried on. "Nowadays the killing of five prostitutes on the streets of London would hardly attract all that fuss."

"Perhaps it would," Simon said. "If done in the manner of the Ripper's killings."

"You mean the mutilations?"

"And the letters to the newspapers. He was nothing if not a showman."

Ceritus Vats leaned back in his chair. "Suppose I told you I have evidence that the Ripper was neither a madman nor a sex fiend, but only a coldly calculating killer whose motive was financial gain?"

"I'd find that difficult to believe," Simon said.

"And suppose I could *name* the Ripper?"

"Do so, by all means!"

"Recently a remarkable document—a handwritten journal—was offered to dealers in rare books and esoterica, like myself. Its author purports to be none other than Jack the Ripper himself. In this journal he explains the motive for his crimes and reveals his identity. I must say that the handwriting compares favorably with that in reproductions of the Ripper's newspaper letters."

"Who is offering this journal?"

"A great-granddaughter of the man who wrote it. Her name is Glenda Coxe. His was Raymond Slackly."

"I've never heard of Slackly," Simon admitted. "Nor the woman either, for that matter."

"According to the journal, Raymond Slackly was a small-time thief. He'd once knifed a man in a brawl, but he admits to no other prior violence. Sometime in the mid-1880s he teamed up with another thief named Hogarth, a smarter criminal who expanded both their horizons. After a number of profitable robberies they heard about the heist of a lifetime.

"It seems that 1887 was Queen Victoria's Jubilee year, the fiftieth anniversary of her coronation. To celebrate the event a merchant named Felix Rhineman collected contributions for the crafting of a solid gold lion encrusted with fifty diamonds. It was to be a surprise gift to Victoria from London's merchants, presented during the summer Jubilee week. Only a few people knew of it in advance, but unfortunately one of them let something slip in a pub. Hogarth and Slackly learned of the golden lion and managed to steal it on the eve of the presentation. The matter was hushed up to avoid embarrassment and Queen Victoria never knew of it."

"Do you believe all this?" I asked with an editor's natural skepticism. "That sort of thing went out with the Maltese Falcon!"

Ceritus Vats merely smiled. "It's possible your Mr. Hammett got his idea from **legends** about the golden lion. Certainly I demand proof for such a story—but the map is proof of a sort."

"What about Jack the Ripper?" Simon pressed on. The lines of his face were deep and his eyes were veiled.

"Hogarth and Slackly were afraid to offer the lion for sale once they'd stolen it. And they possessed neither the knowledge nor the equipment to melt it down. They decided Hogarth would bury the treasure in a safe place for five years, at which time they would then take the lion abroad and sell it."

"Where was it buried?"

Vats shook his head. "Hogarth never told Slackly. He claimed that Slackly drank too much and had a loose tongue. But Slackly insisted he draw a map of the location, in the event he was arrested for some other crime. Hogarth agreed to draw a map in five parts and to leave one part with each of five London streetwalkers. They were paid to keep it, with more money promised in five years' time. Only Hogarth and Slackly had lists of the prostitutes' names."

"An unlikely story," Simon remarked.

"But is it? For the money, and the promise of more money, these women could be depended on. The parts of the map would remain safe. Hogarth seemed certain they wouldn't be lost or misplaced. And even if one of the women died or disappeared, Hogarth himself still knew the location of the treasure. The trouble is, Hogarth died—he was killed in a pub brawl the following year. Slackly was left with five names and nothing more. According to the journal, he tracked the women down over a period of months but each one refused to give him her portion of the map—he hadn't the money that was promised. So he was forced to kill them, all five, using the mutilations and his letters to the press to hide the true motive."

"Is there any evidence besides the handwriting?" Simon asked.

"The journal is curiously reticent about the specific details of the killings— almost as if Slackly himself could no longer face the memory of them. But he does say he strangled the women before using his knife. Donald Rumbelow's recent book on the Ripper confirms that at least four of the victims were probably strangled first."

"Could I examine this journal?"

Vats shook his head. "I was allowed to read portions in the presence of Glenda Coxe, but she would not let me keep it."

"And the map?"

"That's the strangest part of all. Once Slackly retrieved it and put the pieces together, he found he couldn't read it. That's why he wrote the journal, leaving the map for his heirs."

"I assume Miss Coxe can't read it either, or she'd hardly offer it for sale."

"Correct. She feels the journal and the map themselves are of great value, even if the treasure is never located."

"And certainly they are valuable, if the story is true."

"Can you help me, Simon?" Vats asked.

"Just what sort of help do you need? You asked me to forestall a murder."

Vats nodded sadly. "My own. It is depressing to reach this stage in one's life and realize that a colleague would actually kill you for financial gain."

"And this colleague is—?"

"Martin Rood, an antiquarian bookseller and dealer in esoterica like myself. We've been friendly rivals for years."

"Miss Coxe showed him the journal, too?"

"Yes, indeed. She wanted us to bid against each other and she has succeeded admirably."

"Has Rood actually threatened your life?"

"Yes. Last week we held a joint meeting with Miss Coxe. When I topped his bid he stormed out, saying if I cheated him out of the journal and map he'd see me in Hades. He was not jesting."

"But perhaps he's cooled down by now."

"No. On the morning I cabled you I received a package at my shop here. It was an old leather-bound book with no indication of who'd sent it. When I opened the cover I saw the book had been hollowed out—to make room for a live black widow spider."

"My God!" I breathed.

But Simon did not take it so seriously. "Hardly a serious attempt to kill you, Ceritus, or the book would have contained a bomb rather than a spider. Still, it's a bit unpleasant. You think Rood sent it?"

"Who else? The book was an old regimental history of little value. I almost think I'd seen it on his shelves."

"Have you spoken to him since then?"

"I tried to phone him, but he's always out."

"Perhaps a visit to Mr. Rood is in order," Simon decided. "Meanwhile, is it possible that Miss Glenda Coxe has shown this journal to other dealers?"

"I doubt it. Both Rood and I made strong bids for it."

"And the map? Did she allow you to inspect that as well?"

"No. Only the buyer gets to see the map, though she's described it to us as a circle of dots with a horseshoe of dots inside."

Simon Ark lifted his head. "Is that so? And she was unable to identify it?"

"So she says. Do you know—"

"Just a thought. I'll withhold comment for the present."

"Can you speak to Rood, Simon? Somehow get him off my back so I can close this deal for the journal?"

"I can speak to him. But the police could have spoken to him, too. Why didn't you simply call them and tell them about the spider?"

"If the police got wind of this Ripper connection they'd surely confiscate the journal *and* the map. The newspapers would get the story and no one would make a penny out of it!"

"I suppose the monetary factor is important to you."

"Of course it's important. I'm not in this business for my health, Simon! And neither is Rood. This is my chance to acquire the find of a lifetime!"

"Have you and Rood considered sharing it?"

"Share? With him? Never!"

There seemed little more to be said. Simon and I left Vats with a promise to do what we could. But I detected in my friend a depression that our long journey had come to this. "I have known Ceritus for years," he said finally, breaking the gloomy silence, "but I never realized the full extent of his greed. Rood resorts to spiders in hollowed-out books, and Ceritus resorts to me. I am to be the weapon to gain his ends."

"Do you really believe this business about Jack the Ripper's buried treasure?"

"Perhaps this solution is no more fantastic than the original crimes were. However, it leaves one fact unaccounted for: if the Ripper was a sane and rational man bent only on finding that buried lion, why did he find it necessary to mutilate his victims after strangling them?"

"He was crazy and this whole business is crazy, if you ask me. Let's forget it and catch the next plane back to New York."

"I think first a few words with Martin Rood are called for. Then perhaps we will leave."

Rood's Rare Books occupied a shop on Bays-water Road, opposite Kensington Gardens. In its cluttered shelves and haphazard piles of books it was much like Vats's shop, but the lighting was dimmer and the odor a bit mustier. And Martin Rood, when he appeared, looked very much like the sort of person who would send black widow spiders in hollowed-out books. He was as tall as Simon, but much thinner, with sunken cheeks and a pale skin that gave him something of a cadaverous appearance.

"What may I help you with today?" he asked. "We have some fine leather-bound volumes of Sir Walter Scott, just purchased from an estate."

"I'm more in the market for regimental histories," Simon remarked. "Perhaps something on the Black Widows."

"Black Widows?" Rood seemed puzzled. "I don't believe I know that regiment."

"Strange. Ceritus Vats thought you could help me."

At the mention of Vats's name, the bookdealer's whole manner changed. I could see the veins in his temples beginning to throb as he said, "I have no dealings with Vats! I know nothing of the lies he may have told you!"

"They concern a certain Miss Glenda Coxe and a handwritten journal dating from the last century."

"Miss Coxe has contacted me, yes. I believe the entire matter to be a hoax. If Vats wishes to spend his money on it, so be it!"

"You didn't mail him a spider in a book?"

"A spider? In a book? What a quaint idea!"

Simon and I exchanged glances. Either Vats or Rood was a consummate liar. And maybe it didn't much matter which one. But then Simon said something which surprised me. "I'm quite interested in Miss Coxe's journal myself. I'd like to make a purchase offer on it."

"You? Who'd you say you were?"

"The name is Simon Ark."

"American?"

"Most recently."

"You don't exactly sound American."

"I'm a mixture," Simon answered with a smile. "Now about this journal—"

"You can't really believe in it? Jack the Ripper and all that?"

"But if it's true, the journal could be worth a fortune."

Rood considered. "How to prove it?"

"Dig up the golden lion. That should prove it."

"Yes, I suppose so."

Simon turned to me. "Come along, my friend."

"Where are you going?" Rood asked.

"To see Miss Coxe, of course. To put in my bid on Jack the Ripper's map."

Simon's performance may have galvanized Rood into some sort of action. We were only a block away from the shop when I turned to see him lowering the sunshade on his front window and putting out the lights. "Looks as if he's decided to close early," I remarked. "Maybe he wants to beat you to Miss Coxe's place."

"Or else he's planning another little surprise for Ceritus. In any event, I think it's time we called on Miss Coxe. She obviously holds the key to this entire matter."

Glenda Coxe was a psychologist doing basic research in animal behavior at a university laboratory located in London's East End. We found it without much difficulty, and after being announced we were greeted by a cool young woman wearing a white lab coat. Her dark hair was pulled up in a knot at the back of her head, and I had the impression that she might be far prettier if she allowed her hair to hang free. It took me a moment to remember that this was, supposedly, the great-granddaughter of Jack the Ripper.

"Gentlemen, I hope it won't take too long. I'm timing an experiment with some rats." Her voice was cool and dispassionate, like the rest of her.

"In a maze, no doubt," Simon said.

"What?"

"The rats are in a maze."

"Yes, they are. But I'm sure you didn't want to talk about rats."

"As a matter of fact, we came to talk about this journal which has suddenly come to light. And a map, I believe."

"That's correct. Do you wish to purchase them?"

"Could we sit down?" Simon asked, indicating some chairs in one corner. When we were seated he continued, "You realize that this journal of yours could be immensely valuable if it's what you say it is."

"My dear man, I don't say it's anything at all! Perhaps it was a novel my great-grandfather was attempting to compose. I am simply offering it for sale."

"I see. Then you don't believe you're a descendant of Jack the Ripper?"

"I ceased speculating on it long ago. My uncle—" She stopped.

"Your uncle?"

"I was going to say that my uncle does enough speculating for both of us. But that needn't concern you."

"Your uncle believes the journal to be authentic?"

"He does. It's become an obsession with him."

"I'd like to meet him," Simon said.

"That would accomplish nothing."

"Something puzzles me about this whole business, Miss Coxe. When you found this journal, why didn't you take it to the newspapers—or even to a book publisher? Why offer it surreptitiously to a couple of old booksellers?"

"Frankly, I wanted to get rid of the thing. And I didn't want to be plastered across the papers as the great-granddaughter of Jack the Ripper. You must understand that."

"I'd still like to meet your uncle."

"Meet him if you wish, Mr. Ark. But I repeat, it will accomplish nothing."

She gave us his address and then retreated into her laboratory. I decided she wasn't sorry to see us go. Perhaps to her we represented the stigma of publicity she'd tried so hard to avoid.

Or was she trying to avoid it? "Simon, the thought occurs to me that this whole charade might be nothing more than a giant publicity stunt for a new book about Jack the Ripper."

He smiled at me. "British publishers go about things a bit differently from you New Yorkers. I hardly think she's after publicity. At this point we must accept what she tells us at face value."

"And later?"

"After we've met her uncle we might draw other conclusions."

As we drove away we noticed Glenda Coxe leaving through a rear door of the lab. Like Martin Rood, she too was closing early.

Meeting her uncle involved driving to Greenwich, where the Coxe home was located within sight of the Observatory. "Virtually a longitude zero," Simon remarked as we pulled up in front of a red stone house that had obviously seen better days.

His name was Nesbett Coxe and like the house he had seen better days. Somehow he reminded me of a cross between the two bookdealers, Rood and Vats. He moved slowly, with glasses worn low on his nose so he could peer over them. His hair was thin and he looked unwell, though he couldn't have been more than fifty years old. "Oh, yes," he said. "Simon Ark. My niece warned me you were on your way. It's about the Ripper business, what?"

Simon nodded as we followed him through the downstairs rooms. A woman's touch was obvious here and there, but it did little to alleviate the general gloom. "Do you and your niece live here alone?" Simon asked.

"That's right. Wife left me ten years ago. I'm Glenda's guardian for another three years, till she reaches thirty. Her granddad didn't think women matured till thirty." He thought about it and remarked glumly, "I suppose then she'll toss me out and sell the house. That'll be all the thanks I get for bringing her up and putting her through the university."

"Then her grandfather had money? He would have been the son of his man Slackly?"

Nesbett Coxe allowed an evil grin to form on his lips. "I know what you're thinking. But the money didn't come from Slackly's criminal activities—and especially not from Queen Victoria's golden lion. Slackly didn't have a son but a daughter—and she married Herbert Coxe, my father. He was something of a department-store tycoon, with a chain of shops in Liverpool and Bristol and York. Finally opened one in London, but that was his ruin. He couldn't compete with the big boys. Still, there was enough left for me to take care of Glenda when her folks died in a fire."

"Your brother?"

He nodded. "House burned down one night when Glenda was twelve. She lost everything, including her parents. Came to live with me after that. My father was still alive and he left all his money in trust for her till she reached thirty. He felt it would make up for the loss of her parents."

"And this journal?"

"I never knew about it till Glenda showed it to me a few months ago. The map was with it—five little pieces of parchment stitched together, and marked with red dots in a strange sort of ink."

"I'd be most interested in seeing that map," Simon told him.

"That would be impossible unless Glenda approved. This is all hers— the journal and the map, you understand. If it was mine I'd be out selling it to the *News of the World* for a fancy figure."

I was thinking that was why she'd said it would do us no good to see her uncle. Glenda was in complete charge.

He puttered around the house, offered us tea, and finally announced that he had work to do upstairs. That was as close as we came to seeing the mysterious map.

On the way back to London I asked Simon what he thought about it. "Are we in the midst of a hoax, or a feud, or a swindle, or a great historical discovery, or what?"

"I'm not quite sure, my friend. There are several ways of looking at it, and none of them is satisfactory."

Things grew even more puzzling the following morning. Ceritus Vats phoned our hotel quite early to announce that he was being questioned by the police. Glenda Coxe's uncle Nesbett had been murdered the previous night, apparently during an attempted robbery at his home.

The officer investigating the case was Inspector Flaver, a bustling middle-aged man who came right to the point. "So your name is Simon Ark and you're a friend to Mr. Vats. Is that any reason why I should talk to you?"

Simon's last encounter with Scotland Yard had been much too long ago to be meaningful to this man. Nevertheless, Simon told him, "I once helped Inspector Ashly in the matter of some Satanists and an arrow murder. I expect it was before your time."

"Yes, I remember Ashly." He relaxed a bit. "What do you know about this killing?"

"Far less than you at the moment. How did it happen?"

"The niece, Miss Glenda Coxe, who lives with the deceased, was working late at a research laboratory. She returned home around midnight and found him shot to death on the steps going down to the side door. The door itself had been forced open. It looks as if a burglar tried the place, not knowing anyone was home, and Coxe surprised him."

"It looks a great deal like that," Simon agreed. "Does Miss Coxe have an alibi—witnesses who saw her at work?"

"Oh, certainly. You can't suspect her of killing her own uncle, can you?"

"It happens," Simon said. "About what time did the crime occur?"

"About nine, we figure."

"Just getting dark then, this time of year."

Inspector Flaver nodded. "We figure there were no lights on yet. That's why the burglar thought the house was empty. There's a tall hedge on that side, which screens the door from the neighbors."

"They heard no shot?"

"Not a thing. But, you know, they had the telly going."

"I'd like to see Miss Coxe," Simon said.

"She's just finishing her statement. Wait here."

Glenda Coxe appeared about ten minutes later, looking tired and a bit bedraggled. When Simon Ark attempted to speak to her she held up a hand in protest. "I've been up all night. I've told the police everything I know. Please let me pass."

"Ceritus Vats is being questioned. Did you give the police his name?"

"They asked why anyone would try to burgle our house. I had to mention the journal I'd offered both Vats and Rood."

"Is Rood being questioned, too?"

"I assume so. Now please let me pass."

"Miss Coxe, you must have checked to see if the journal and map were stolen. Were they?"

She hesitated a moment and then answered. "They're both safe. I believe the thief was frightened away after shooting my uncle."

"Miss Coxe, I must see that map at once," Simon insisted.

"That's impossible."

"You don't seem to understand your position at present. If the journal and the map are shown to be frauds, this whole business could be viewed as a plot to kill your uncle from the very beginning. You present the journal to two rival bookdealers known for their interest in esoterica. One of them is sent a black widow spider, apparently by the other—though I'm sure such creatures are easy to come by in your research labs. When you have the rivalry and tension between the dealers at a fever pitch, someone breaks into your house and kills your uncle. The dealers are suspected, while you seem to have an alibi. And with your uncle dead you don't have to wait three more years to come into your inheritance."

Her eyes flashed with a cold fury. "Who could concoct such a fantastic plot?"

"A psychologist, Miss Coxe. A psychologist who spends her working days sending rats through mazes."

That stopped her. She gnawed at her bottom lip and asked quietly, "What good would it do you to see the map?"

"The description given me, of a circle of dots with a horseshoe of dots within, reminded me of something. I might know the place where the treasure is buried."

"*You* might know it, when my great-grandfather didn't? When neither my uncle nor I could make anything out of it?"

"This man Hogarth would hardly leave a neatly labeled map in the hands of streetwalkers who were virtual strangers to him. Still, I repeat that I may know the place. You must decide quickly, Miss Coxe. Murder has made this a very serious business."

She hesitated only a moment. "Very well, come with me."

As we followed her in our rented car, I said, "Simon, even if the map and the journal are genuine, that doesn't prove she didn't kill her uncle."

"I know, my friend. But it gives us an opportunity to see this fabled map."

There was no arguing with his logic, so I didn't try. When we reached the house in Greenwich once more, I parked behind her little red car and we followed her inside.

She went at once to a small wall safe and extracted a metal box. Opening it, she took out a faded notebook. "There, gentlemen—the journal of Jack the Ripper. Just as I found it in a trunk in my father's attic."

"At the moment I'm more interested in the map."

She unrolled a small piece of parchment and placed it on the table before us. As described, it consisted of five separate pieces which had been stitched together. The whole thing had a diameter of perhaps eight inches. On it, marked in red ink, was a circle of thirty dots, with an inner horseshoe of five more pairs of dots, and a larger dot near the center. At the top of the map, directly opposite the open end of the horseshoe, was an X.

"Just as I suspected!" Simon announced triumphantly.

"What is it?"

"A simplified diagram of the rocks at Stonehenge. That's where you'll find Jack the Ripper's lost treasure—if there is a treasure."

Simon telephoned Inspector Flaver and told him we planned to dig at Stonehenge for buried treasure. He suggested the inspector meet us there, accompanied by the two bookdealers, Vats and Rood. Then he hung up before the questions started coming.

"How can you be sure it's Stonehenge?" I asked.

"Around 1887 it wouldn't have been uncommon for people to be digging in the area, searching for artifacts of the past. It's only in more recent times that the government has taken steps to preserve and protect these ancient monuments. For Hogarth it would have been the perfect hiding place for his stolen lion."

"But his partner Slackly couldn't read the map even after he recovered its five parts."

"Exactly. He wasn't familiar with Stonehenge and the dots would have meant nothing to him."

The drive to the Salisbury Plain took nearly two hours from London, but when we arrived I spotted the inspector and the two bookdealers at once. Stonehenge seemed alive with police that day, guarding against possible trouble from a nearby rock concert.

"All right," Flaver said, "we came. This had better be worthwhile."

"It will be," Simon assured him.

We took the tunnel from the parking area, beneath the highway to Stonehenge. The place was filled with summer tourists and a group of youths from the rock concert who were carrying on a sort of chanting ceremony. "They imagine they're Druids," Inspector Flaver explained, "though of course these stones were here long before the Druids came."

We passed through the great stone archways, which somehow seemed smaller with all the people about. Then Simon consulted the stitched-together parchment once more and paced off a distance to the point that seemed to correspond roughly with the spot on the map where the X was drawn.

"It's far enough beyond the actual monument, so we can dig here," Simon said. "I trust you brought a shovel, Inspector."

"We have one in the car," he admitted.

Finally it was Martin Rood who insisted on starting the digging. "If it's there I want to find it," he said.

Vats tried to pull the shovel from him, but Inspector Flaver intervened. "If you find anything at all, I'm taking it. If there's any truth to Miss Coxe's story, it's the property of the British government."

But after twenty minutes Rood threw down the shovel. "Nothing here," he said, obviously disappointed.

"Perhaps a bit to the left," Simon suggested, consulting the map again. Ceritus Vats took over the digging for a time while the rest of us watched. Some tourists had drifted over, but Flaver's orders to the police on guard kept them away.

After another half-hour's digging Vats gave up, too. "If it was ever here, it's gone."

"He would have buried it deeper," Simon speculated, "because of all the digging in the area. He wouldn't have wanted it uncovered by accident."

I jumped into the hole and took up the shovel. We were only down about four feet and Simon's reasoning seemed sound to me. If the treasure was here at all, it would be deeper.

As I plunged the shovel into the earth for the third time I hit something solid. "It could be just a rock," I cautioned, stooping to scoop the dirt away by hand.

But it wasn't a rock. It was something hard and heavy, wrapped in burlap sacking that had partly disintegrated with the passage of time. I unwrapped it and held it high, brushing the clinging dirt from its glistening surface.

"The treasure of Jack the Ripper!" Ceritus Vats said in a voice touched with awe. And indeed it seemed a treasure—a striding lion all in gold, with fifty glistening diamonds set into the body at regular intervals.

Only Simon seemed unimpressed. He took the lion in both hands and hefted it. "The journal said solid gold. I could tell by the ease with which you lifted it that this isn't solid gold. A gold statue of this size would weigh nearly a hundred pounds. And those diamonds are fakes as well."

Vats could not believe it. "But—but something like that could never be presented to the queen!"

"Exactly—which leads us to believe it was never meant for Queen Victoria. That merchant, Felix Rhineman, collected the money, had a cheap statue gold-plated and encrusted with imitation diamonds, then dropped word at a place where thieves like Hogarth and Slackly would hear of it. There was no danger from his standpoint. Even if they discovered after the robbery that the statue was a fake, they could hardly report it to the police."

"And Rhineman kept the money he collected," I said. "He made a handsome profit and Queen Victoria never really lost anything."

Simon Ark nodded. "The only losers were those five women who carried parts of Hogarth's map."

"Why did Slackly have to kill them, Simon? Especially the way he did?"

Simon Ark took out the parchment map and held it to the light. "This is not the usual parchment, my friend, made from the skin of a sheep or goat. Slackly mutilated their bodies after strangling them *so the missing pieces of flesh would go unnoticed.* You see, Hogarth paid those poor women to let him tattoo the five parts of his map on their skin."

After that Simon walked for a long time with Inspector Flaver. Then Simon and I departed, leaving Ceritus and his rival Rood with Glenda Coxe and the inspector.

"But who killed Nesbett Coxe?" I asked on the drive back. "You never solved it, Simon!"

"My friend, I am not a detective, much as you would like to make me one. I am merely a wanderer, searching the world for evil. At times I find it in unlikely places. At times I find it in the eyes of a twelve-year-old child grown to adulthood."

"You mean—?"

"The story of the Ripper's treasure was either true or false. On the basis of what we found here, we concluded it was true, to the best of Raymond Slackly's knowledge when he wrote the journal. But if the journal is true, we must believe that Glenda Coxe found it where she said—in her father's attic trunk. Now her uncle told us yesterday that her house burned down when she was twelve. She lost everything, including her parents. Therefore her discovery of Slackly's journal and the map must have come *before* that fire!"

"Perhaps," I was willing to grant.

"Not perhaps, but certainly! And can you imagine the effect this discovery would have on a child of that impressionable age? Her great-grandfather—the most terrible murderer in London's history! We know it had an effect on her, because she kept it a secret all these years till now."

But I shook my head. "There's a flaw in your reasoning, Simon. Suppose she found the journal some time before the fire, as you say. It would still have burned up, unless she deliberately removed it from the house before the fire."

"Exactly, my friend."

"You mean she burned down her own house? Killed her own—?"

"And now resurrected the journal to kill again, in such a way that Vats or Rood would be blamed for it. She needed two suspects, in case one of them could prove an alibi for last night. Remember that back door to her laboratory? An easy way out, and back in, while her coworkers thought she never left the building."

"And you told all this to Inspector Flaver?"

"I did. The proof is up to him. I believe he'll start with the fire fifteen years ago."

"And the map, Simon?"

"I think it will go into Scotland Yard's files, along with the journal. Someday, perhaps, when there is not already enough horror in the world, it can be revealed."

We drove on toward London, and that was the last I ever heard of the treasure of Jack the Ripper.

∿

THE HANDS OF MR. OTTERMOLE

Thomas Burke

Although anyone remotely familiar with the Jack the Ripper murders is fully aware that the weapon of choice was a knife, the killings inspired other writers to produce works about serial killers who may have used different weapons. One such story is "The Hands of Mr. Ottermole" by Sydney Thomas Burke (1886–1945), which was voted the best detective short story of all time in 1949 by Ellery Queen and a panel of eleven other mystery writers.

Burke was born in the London suburb of Clapham, but when he was only a few months old his father died and he was sent to the East End to live with his uncle until the age of ten, when he was put into a home for respectable middle-class children without means. He sold his first story, "The Bellamy Diamonds," when he was fifteen. His first book, *Nights in Town: A London Autobiography,* was published in 1915, soon followed by the landmark volume *Limehouse Nights* (1916), a collection of stories that had originally been published in the magazines *The English Review, Colour,* and *The New Witness.* This volume of romantic but violent stories of the Chinese district of London was enormously popular, but, though largely praised by critics, there were objections to the depictions of interracial relationships, opium use, and other "depravities."

Several of the stories in *Limehouse Nights* served as the basis for films, most notably D. W. Griffith's *Broken Blossoms* (1919), based on "The Chink and the Child." It starred one of America's most beloved actresses, Lillian Gish, as the daughter of a sadistic prizefighter, and Richard Barthelmess as a kind Chinese youth. Charlie Chaplin based his silent movie *A Dog's Life* (1918) on material from the book.

"The Hands of Mr. Ottermole" was first published in the author's collection *The Pleasantries of Old Quong* (London, Constable, 1931); it was published in the United States as *A Tea-Shop in Limehouse* (Boston, Little, Brown, 1931).

At six o'clock of a January evening Mr. Whybrow was walking home through the cobweb alleys of London's East End. He had left the golden clamor of the great High Street to which the tram had brought him from the river and his daily work, and was now in the chessboard of byways that is called Mallon End. None of the rush and gleam of the High Street trickled into these byways. A few paces south—a flood tide of life, foaming and beating. Here—only slow-shuffling figures and muffled pulses. He was in the sink of London, the last refuge of European vagrants.

As though in tune with the street's spirit, he too walked slowly, with head down. It seemed that he was pondering some pressing trouble, but he was not. He had no trouble. He was walking slowly because he had been on his feet all day, and he was bent in abstraction because he was wondering whether the Missis would have herrings for his tea, or haddock; and he was trying to decide which would be the more tasty on a night like this. A wretched night it was, of damp and mist, and the mist wandered into his throat and his eyes, and the damp had settled on pavement and roadway, and where the sparse lamplight fell it sent up a greasy sparkle that chilled one to look at. By contrast it made his speculations more agreeable, and made him ready for that tea—whether herring or haddock. His eye turned from the glum bricks that made his horizon, and went forward half a mile. He saw a gas-lit kitchen, a flamy fire, and a spread tea table. There was toast in the hearth and a singing kettle on the side and a piquant effusion of herrings, or maybe of haddock, or perhaps sausages. The vision gave his aching feet a throb of energy. He shook imperceptible damp from his shoulders, and hastened towards its reality.

But Mr. Whybrow wasn't going to get any tea that evening—or any other evening. Mr. Whybrow was going to die. Somewhere within a hundred yards of him another man was walking; a man much like Mr. Whybrow and much like any other man, but without the only quality that enables mankind to live peaceably together and not as madmen in a jungle. A man with a dead heart eating into itself and bringing forth the foul organisms that arise from death and corruption. And that thing in man's shape, on a whim or a settled idea—one cannot know—had said within himself that Mr. Whybrow should never taste another herring. Not that Mr. Whybrow had injured him. Not that he had any dislike of Mr. Whybrow. Indeed, he knew nothing of him save as a familiar figure about the streets. But, moved by a force that had taken possession of his empty cells, he had picked on Mr. Whybrow with that blind choice that makes us pick one restaurant table that has nothing to mark it from four or five other tables, or one apple from a dish of half a dozen equal apples; or that drives Nature to send a cyclone upon one corner of this planet, and destroy five hundred lives in that corner, and leave another five hundred in the same corner unharmed. So this man had picked on Mr. Whybrow, as he might have picked on you or me, had we been within his daily observation; and even now he was creeping through the blue-toned streets, nursing his large white hands, moving ever closer to Mr. Whybrow's tea table, and so closer to Mr. Whybrow himself.

He wasn't, this man, a bad man. Indeed, he had many of the social and amiable qualities, and passed as a respectable man, as most successful criminals do. But the thought had come into his moldering mind that he would like to murder somebody, and, as he held no fear of God or man, he was going to do it, and would then go home to *his* tea. I don't say that flippantly, but as a statement of fact. Strange as it may seem to the humane, murderers must and do sit down to meals after a murder. There is no reason why they shouldn't, and many reasons why they should. For one thing, they need to keep their physical and mental vitality at full beat for the business of covering their crime. For another, the strain of their effort makes them hungry, and satisfaction at the accomplishment of a desired thing brings a feeling of relaxation towards human pleasures. It is accepted among non-murderers that the murderer is always overcome by fear for his safety and horror at his act; but this type is rare. His own safety is, of course, his immediate concern, but vanity is a marked quality of most murderers, and that, together with the thrill of conquest, makes him confident that he can secure it, and when he has restored his strength with food he goes about securing it as a young hostess goes about the arranging of her first big dinner—a little anxious, but no more. Criminologists and detectives tell us that *every* murderer, however intelligent or cunning, always makes one slip in his tactics—one little slip that brings the affair home to him. But that is only half true. It is true only of the murderers who are caught. Scores of murderers are not caught: therefore scores of murderers do not make any mistake at all. This man didn't.

As for horror or remorse, prison chaplains, doctors, and lawyers have told us that of murderers they have interviewed under condemnation and the shadow of death, only one here and there has expressed any contrition for his act, or shown any sign of mental misery. Most of them display only exasperation at having been caught when so many have gone undiscovered, or indignation at being condemned for a perfectly reasonable act. However normal and humane they may have been before the murder, they are utterly without conscience after it. For what is conscience? Simply a polite nickname for superstition, which is a polite nickname for fear. Those who associate remorse with murder are, no doubt, basing their ideas on the world legend of the remorse of Cain, or are projecting their own frail minds into the mind of the murderer, and getting false reactions. Peaceable folk cannot hope to make contact with this mind, for they are not merely different in mental type from the murderer: they are different in their personal chemistry and construction. Some men can and do kill, not one man, but two or three, and go calmly about their daily affairs. Other men could not, under the most agonizing provocation, bring themselves even to wound. It is men of this sort who imagine the murderer in torments of remorse and fear of the law, whereas he is actually sitting down to his tea.

The man with the large white hands was as ready for his tea as Mr. Whybrow was, but he had something to do before he went to it. When he had done that something, and made no mistake about it, he would be even more ready for it, and would go to it as comfortably as he went to it the day before, when his hands were stainless.

Walk on, then, Mr. Whybrow, walk on; and as you walk, look your last upon the familiar features of your nightly journey. Follow your jack-o'-lantern tea table. Look well upon its warmth and color and kindness; feed your eyes with it, and tease your nose with its gentle domestic odors; for you will never sit down to it. Within ten minutes' pacing of you a pursuing phantom has spoken in his heart, and you are doomed. There you go—you and phantom—two nebulous dabs of mortality, moving through green air along pavements of powder blue, the one to kill, the other to be killed. Walk on. Don't annoy your burning feet by hurrying, for the more slowly you walk, the longer you will breathe the green air of this January dusk, and see the dreamy lamplight and the little shops, and hear the agreeable commerce of the London crowd and the haunting pathos of the street organ. These things are dear to you, Mr. Whybrow. You don't know it now, but in fifteen minutes you will have two seconds to realize how inexpressibly dear they are.

Walk on, then, across this crazy chessboard. You are in Lagos Street now, among the tents of the wanderers of Eastern Europe. A minute or so, and you are in Loyal Lane, among the lodging houses that shelter the useless and the beaten of London's camp followers. The lane holds the smell of them, and its soft darkness seems heavy with the wail of the futile. But you are not sensitive to impalpable things, and you plod through it, unseeing, as you do every evening, and come to Blean Street, and plod through that. From basement to sky rise the tenements of an alien colony. Their windows slot the ebony of their walls with lemon. Behind those windows strange life is moving, dressed with forms that are not of London or of England, yet, in essence, the same agreeable life that you have been living, and tonight will live no more. From high above you comes a voice crooning *The Song of Katta.* Through a window you see a family keeping a religious rite. Through another you see a woman pouring out tea for her husband. You see a man mending a pair of boots; a mother bathing her baby. You have seen all these things before, and never noticed them. You do not notice them now, but if you knew that you were never going to see them again, you would notice them. You never *will* see them again, not because your life has run its natural course, but because a man whom you have often passed in the street has at his own solitary pleasure decided to usurp the awful authority of nature, and destroy you. So perhaps it's as well that you don't notice them, for your part in them is ended. No more for you these pretty moments of our earthly travail: only one moment of terror, and then a plunging darkness.

Closer to you this shadow of massacre moves, and now he is twenty yards behind you. You can hear his footfall, but you do not turn your head. You are familiar with footfalls. You are in London, in the easy security of your daily territory, and footfalls behind you, your instinct tells you, are no more than a message of human company.

But can't you hear something in those footfalls—something that goes with a widdershins beat? Something that says: *Look out, look out. Beware, beware.* Can't you hear the very syllables of *mur-der-er, mur-der-er*? No; there is nothing in footfalls. They are neutral. The foot of villainy falls with the same quiet note as the foot of honesty. But those footfalls, Mr. Whybrow, are bearing on to you a pair of hands, and there *is* something in hands. Behind you that pair of hands is even now stretching its muscles in preparation for your end. Every minute of your days you have been seeing human hands. Have you ever realized the sheer horror of hands—those appendages that are a symbol for our moments of trust and affection and salutation? Have you thought of the sickening potentialities that lie within the scope of that five-tentacled member? No, you never have; for all the human hands that you have seen have been stretched to you in kindness or fellowship. Yet, though the eyes can hate, and the lips can sting, it is only that dangling member that can gather the accumulated essence of evil, and electrify it into currents of destruction. Satan may enter into man by many doors, but in the hands alone can he find the servants of his will.

Another minute, Mr. Whybrow, and you will know all about the horror of human hands.

You are nearly home now. You have turned into your street—Caspar Street— and you are in the center of the chessboard. You can see the front window of your little four-roomed house. The street is dark, and its three lamps give only a smut of light that is more confusing than darkness. It is dark—empty, too. Nobody about; no lights in the front parlors of the houses, for the families are at tea in their kitchens; and only a random glow in a few upper rooms occupied by lodgers. Nobody about but you and your following companion, and you don't notice him. You see him so often that he is never seen. Even if you turned your head and saw him, you would only say "Good evening" to him, and walk on. A suggestion that he was a possible murderer would not even make you laugh. It would be too silly.

And now you are at your gate. And now you have found your door key. And now you are in, and hanging up your hat and coat. The Missis has just called a greeting from the kitchen, whose smell is an echo of that greeting (herrings!) and you have answered it, when the door shakes under a sharp knock.

Go away, Mr. Whybrow. Go away from that door. Don't touch it. Get right away from it. Get out of the house. Run with the Missis to the back garden, and over the fence. Or call the neighbors. But don't touch that door. Don't, Mr. Whybrow, don't open . . .

Mr. Whybrow opened the door.

That was the beginning of what became known as London's Strangling Horrors. Horrors they were called because they were something more than murders: they were motiveless, and there was an air of black magic about them. Each murder was committed at a time when the street where the bodies were found was empty of any perceptible or possible murderer. There would be an empty alley. There would be a policeman at its end. He would turn his back on the empty alley for less than a minute. Then he would look round and run into the night with news of another strangling. And in any direction he looked nobody to be seen and no report to be had of anybody being seen. Or he would be on duty in a long-quiet street, and suddenly be called to a house of dead people whom a few seconds earlier he had seen alive. And, again, whichever way he looked nobody to be seen; and although police whistles put an immediate cordon around the area, and searched all houses, no possible murderer to be found.

The first news of the murder of Mr. and Mrs. Whybrow was brought by the station sergeant. He had been walking through Caspar Street on his way to the station for duty, when he noticed the open door of No. 98. Glancing in, he saw by the gaslight of the passage a motionless body on the floor. After a second look he blew his whistle, and when the constables answered him he took one to join him in a search of the house, and sent others to watch all neighboring streets, and make inquiries at adjoining houses. But neither in the house nor in the streets was anything found to indicate the murderer. Neighbors on either side, and opposite, were questioned, but they had seen nobody about, and had heard nothing. One had heard Mr. Whybrow come home—the scrape of his latchkey in the door was so regular an evening sound, he said, that you could set your watch by it for half past six—but he had heard nothing more than the sound of the opening door until the sergeant's whistle. Nobody had been seen to enter the house or leave it, by front or back, and the necks of the dead people carried no fingerprints or other traces. A nephew was called in to go over the house, but he could find nothing missing; and anyway his uncle possessed nothing worth stealing. The little money in the house was untouched, and there were no signs of any disturbance of the property, or even of struggle. No signs of anything but brutal and wanton murder.

Mr. Whybrow was known to neighbors and workmates as a quiet, likeable, home-loving man; such a man as could not have any enemies. But, then, murdered men seldom have. A relentless enemy who hates a man to the point of wanting to hurt him seldom wants to murder him, since to do that puts him beyond suffering. So the police were left with an impossible situation: no clue to the murderer and no motive for the murders; only the fact that they had been done.

The first news of the affair sent a tremor through London generally, and an electric thrill through all Mallon End. Here was a murder of two inoffensive people, not for gain and not for revenge; and the murderer, to whom, apparently, killing was a casual impulse, was at large. He had left no traces, and, provided he had no companions, there seemed no reason why he should not remain at large. Any clear-headed man who stands alone, and has no fear of God or man, can, if he chooses, hold a city, even a nation, in subjection; but your everyday criminal is seldom clear-headed, and dislikes being lonely. He needs, if not the support of confederates, at least somebody to talk to; his vanity needs the satisfaction of perceiving at first hand the effect of his work. For this he will frequent bars and coffee shops and other public places. Then, sooner or later, in a glow of comradeship, he will utter the one word too much; and the nark, who is everywhere, has an easy job.

But though the doss houses and saloons and other places were "combed" and set with watchers, and it was made known by whispers that good money and protection were assured to those with information, nothing attaching to the Whybrow case could be found. The murderer clearly had no friends and kept no company. Known men of this type were called up and questioned, but each was able to give a good account of himself; and in a few days the police were at a dead end. Against the constant public jibe that the thing had been done almost under their noses, they became restive, and for four days each man of the force was working his daily beat under a strain. On the fifth day they became still more restive.

It was the season of annual teas and entertainments for the children of the Sunday Schools, and on an evening of fog, when London was a world of groping phantoms, a small girl, in the bravery of best Sunday frock and shoes, shining face and new-washed hair, set out from Logan Passage for St. Michael's Parish Hall. She never got there. She was not actually dead until half past six, but she was as good as dead from the moment she left her mother's door. Somebody like a man, pacing the street from which the Passage led, saw her come out; and from that moment she was dead. Through the fog somebody's large white hands reached after her, and in fifteen minutes they were about her.

At half past six a whistle screamed trouble, and those answering it found the body of little Nellie Vrinoff in a warehouse entry in Minnow Street. The sergeant was first among them, and he posted his men to useful points, ordering them here and there in the tart tones of repressed rage, and berating the officer whose beat the street was. "I saw you, Magson, at the end of the lane. What were you up to there? You were there ten minutes before you turned." Magson began an explanation about keeping an eye on a suspicious-looking character at that end, but the sergeant cut him short: "Suspicious characters be damned. You don't want to look for suspicious characters. You want to look for *murderers.* Messing about . . . and then this happens right where you ought to be. Now think what they'll say."

With the speed of ill news came the crowd, pale and perturbed; and on the story that the unknown monster had appeared again, and this time to a child, their faces streaked the fog with spots of hate and horror. But then came the ambulance and more police, and swiftly they broke up the crowd; and as it broke the sergeant's thought was thickened into words, and from all sides came low murmurs of "Right under their noses." Later inquiries showed that four people of the district, above suspicion, had passed that entry at intervals of seconds before the murder, and seen nothing and heard nothing. None of them had passed the child alive or seen her dead. None of them had seen anybody in the street except themselves. Again the police were left with no motive and with no clue.

And now the district, as you will remember, was given over, not to panic, for the London public never yields to that, but to apprehension and dismay. If these things were happening in their familiar streets, then anything might happen. Wherever people met—in the streets, the markets and the shops—they debated the one topic. Women took to bolting their windows and doors at the first fall of dusk. They kept their children closely under their eye. They did their shopping before dark, and watched anxiously, while pretending they weren't watching, for the return of their husbands from work. Under the Cockney's semi-humorous resignation to disaster they hid an hourly foreboding. By the whim of one man with a pair of hands the structure and tenor of their daily life were shaken, as they always can be shaken by any man contemptuous of humanity and fearless of its laws. They began to realize that the pillars that supported the peaceable society in which they lived were mere straws that anybody could snap; that laws were powerful only so long as they were obeyed; that the police were potent only so long as they were feared. By the power of his hands this one man had made a whole community do something new: he had made it think, and had left it gasping at the obvious.

And then, while it was yet gasping under his first two strokes, he made his third. Conscious of the horror that his hands had created, and hungry as an actor who has once tasted the thrill of the multitude, he made fresh advertisement of his presence; and on Wednesday morning, three days after the murder of the child, the papers carried to the breakfast tables of England the story of a still more shocking outrage.

At 9:32 on Tuesday night a constable was on duty in Jarnigan Road, and at that time spoke to a fellow officer named Petersen at the top of Clemming Street. He had seen this officer walk down that street. He could swear that the street was empty at that time, except for a lame bootblack whom he knew by sight, and who passed him and entered a tenement on the side opposite that on which his fellow officer was walking. He had the habit, as all constables had just then, of looking constantly behind him and around him, whichever way he was walking, and he was certain that the street was empty. He passed his sergeant at 9:33, saluted him, and answered his inquiry for anything seen. He reported that he had seen nothing, and passed on. His beat ended at a short distance from Clemming Street, and, having paced it, he turned and came again at 9:34 to the top of the street. He had scarcely reached it before he heard the hoarse voice of the sergeant: "Gregory! You there? Quick. Here's another. My God, it's Petersen! Garotted. Quick, call 'em up!"

That was the third of the Strangling Horrors, of which there were to be a fourth and a fifth; and the five horrors were to pass into the unknown and unknowable. That is, unknown as far as authority and the public were concerned. The identity of the murderer *was* known, but to two men only. One was the murderer himself; the other was a young journalist.

This young man, who was covering the affairs for his paper, the *Daily Torch*, was no smarter than the other zealous newspapermen who were hanging about these byways in the hope of a sudden story. But he was patient, and he hung a little closer to the case than the other fellows, and by continually staring at it he at last raised the figure of the murderer like a genie from the stones on which he had stood to do his murders.

After the first few days the men had given up any attempt at exclusive stories, for there were none to be had. They met regularly at the police station, and what little information there was they shared. The officials were agreeable to them, but no more. The sergeant discussed with them the details of each murder; suggested possible explanations of the man's methods; recalled from the past those cases that had some similarity; and on the matter of motive reminded them of the motiveless Neill Cream and the wanton John Williams, and hinted that work was being done which would soon bring the business to an end; but about that work he would not say a word. The Inspector, too, was gracefully garrulous on the thesis of Murder, but whenever one of the party edged the talk towards what was being done in this immediate matter, he glided past it. Whatever the officials knew, they were not giving it to newspapermen. The business had fallen heavily upon them, and only by a capture made by their own efforts could they rehabilitate themselves in official and public esteem. Scotland Yard, of course, was at work, and had all the station's material; but the station's hope was that they themselves would have the honor of settling the affair; and however useful the coöperation of the Press might be in other cases, they did not want to risk a defeat by a premature disclosure of their theories and plans.

So the sergeant talked at large, and propounded one interesting theory after another, all of which the newspapermen had thought of themselves.

The young man soon gave up these morning lectures on the Philosophy of Crime, and took to wandering about the streets and making bright stories out of the effect of the murders on the normal life of the people. A melancholy job made more melancholy by the district. The littered roadways, the crestfallen houses, the bleared windows—all held the acid misery that evokes no sympathy: the misery of the frustrated poet. The misery was the creation of the aliens, who were living in this makeshift fashion because they had no settled homes, and would neither take the trouble to make a home where they *could* settle, nor get on with their wandering.

There was little to be picked up. All he saw and heard were indignant faces, and wild conjectures of the murderer's identity and of the secret of his trick of appearing and disappearing unseen. Since a policeman himself had fallen a victim, denunciations of the force had ceased, and the unknown was now invested with a cloak of legend. Men eyed other men, as though thinking: It might be *him*. It might be *him*. They were no longer looking for a man who had the air of a Madame Tussaud murderer; they were looking for a man, or perhaps some harridan woman, who had done these particular murders. Their thoughts ran mainly on the foreign set. Such ruffianism could scarcely belong to England, nor could the bewildering cleverness of the thing. So they turned to Roumanian gipsies and Turkish carpet sellers. There, clearly, would be found the "warm" spot. These Eastern fellows—they knew all sorts of tricks, and they had no real religion—nothing to hold them within bounds. Sailors returning from those parts had told tales of conjurors who made themselves invisible; and there were tales of Egyptian and Arab potions that were used for abysmally queer purposes. Perhaps it *was* possible to them; you never knew. They were so slick and cunning, and they had such gliding movements; no Englishman could melt away as they could. Almost certainly the murderer would be found to be one of that sort—with some dark trick of his own—and just because they were sure that he *was* a magician, they felt that it was useless to look for him. He was a power, able to hold them in subjection and to hold himself untouchable. Superstition, which so easily cracks the frail shell of reason, had got into them. He could do anything he chose: he would never be discovered. These two points they settled, and they went about the streets in a mood of resentful fatalism.

They talked of their ideas to the journalist in half tones, looking right and left, as though HE might overhear them and visit them. And though all the district was thinking of him and ready to pounce upon him, yet, so strongly had he worked upon them, that if any man in the street—say, a small man of commonplace features and form—had cried "*I* am the Monster!" would their stifled fury have broken into flood and have borne him down and engulfed him? Or would they not suddenly have seen something unearthly in that everyday face and figure, something unearthly in his everyday boots, something unearthly about his hat, something that marked him as one whom none of their weapons could alarm or pierce? And would they not momentarily have fallen back from this devil, as the devil fell back from the Cross made by the sword of Faust, and so have given him time to escape? I do not know; but so fixed was their belief in his invincibility that it is at least likely that they would have made this hesitation, had such an occasion arisen. But it never did. Today this commonplace fellow, his murder lust sated, is seen and observed among them as he was seen and observed all the time; but because nobody dreamed, or now dreams, that he was what he was, they observed him then, and observe him now, as people observe a lamppost.

Almost was their belief in his invincibility justified; for, five days after the murder of the policeman Petersen, when the experience and inspiration of the whole detective force of London were turned towards his identification and capture, he made his fourth and fifth strokes.

At nine o'clock that evening, the young newspaperman, who hung about every night until his paper was away, was strolling along Richards Lane. Richards Lane is a narrow street, partly a stall market, and partly residential. The young man was in the residential section, which carries on one side small working class cottages, and on the other the wall of a railway goods yard. The great wall hung a blanket of shadow over the lane, and the shadow and the cadaverous outline of the now deserted market stalls gave it the appearance of a living lane that had been turned to frost in the moment between breath and death. The very lamps, that elsewhere were nimbuses of gold, had here the rigidity of gems. The journalist, feeling this message of frozen eternity, was telling himself that he was tired of the whole thing, when in one stroke the frost was broken. In the moment between one pace and another silence and darkness were racked by a high scream and through the scream a voice: "Help! help! *He's here!*"

Before he could think what movement to make, the lane came to life. As though its invisible populace had been waiting on that cry, the door of every cottage was flung open, and from them and from the alleys poured shadowy figures bent in question mark form. For a second or so they stood as rigid as the lamps; then a police whistle gave them direction, and the flock of shadows sloped up the street. The journalist followed them, and others followed him. From the main street and from surrounding streets they came, some risen from unfinished suppers, some disturbed in their ease of slippers and shirt sleeves, some stumbling on infirm limbs, and some upright, and armed with pokers or the tools of their trade. Here and there above the wavering cloud of heads moved the bold helmets of policemen. In one dim mass they surged upon a cottage whose doorway was marked by the sergeant and two constables; and voices of those behind urged them on with "Get in! Find him! Run round the back! Over the wall!" and those in front cried: "Keep back! Keep back!"

And now the fury of a mob held in thrall by unknown peril broke loose. He was here—on the spot. Surely this time he *could not* escape. All minds were bent upon the cottage; all energies thrust towards its doors and windows and roof; all thought was turned upon one unknown man and his extermination. So that no one man saw any other man. No man saw the narrow, packed lane and the mass of struggling shadows, and all forgot to look among themselves for the monster who never lingered upon his victims. All forgot, indeed, that they, by their mass crusade of vengeance, were affording him the perfect hiding place. They saw only the house, and they heard only the rending of woodwork and the smash of glass at back and front, and the police giving orders or crying with the chase; and they pressed on.

But they found no murderer. All they found was news of murder and a glimpse of the ambulance, and for their fury there was no other object than the police themselves, who fought against this hampering of their work.

The journalist managed to struggle through to the cottage door, and to get the story from the constable stationed there. The cottage was the home of a pensioned sailor and his wife and daughter. They had been at supper, and at first it appeared that some noxious gas had smitten all three in mid-action. The daughter lay dead on the hearthrug, with a piece of bread and butter in her hand. The father had fallen sideways from his chair, leaving on his plate a filled spoon of rice pudding. The mother lay half under the table, her lap filled with the pieces of a broken cup and splashes of cocoa. But in three seconds the idea of gas was dismissed. One glance at their necks showed that this was the Strangler again; and the police stood and looked at the room and momentarily shared the fatalism of the public. They were helpless.

This was his fourth visit, making seven murders in all. He was to do, as you know, one more—and to do it that night; and then he was to pass into history as the unknown London horror, and return to the decent life that he had always led, remembering little of what he had done, and worried not at all by the memory. Why did he stop? Impossible to say. Why did he begin? Impossible again. It just happened like that; and if he thinks at all of those days and nights, I surmise that he thinks of them as we think of foolish or dirty little sins that we committed in childhood. We say that they were not really sins, because we were not then consciously ourselves: we had not come to realization; and we look back at that foolish little creature that we once were, and forgive him because he didn't know. So, I think, with this man.

There are plenty like him. Eugene Aram, after the murder of Daniel Clarke, lived a quiet, contented life for fourteen years, unhaunted by his crime and unshaken in his self-esteem. Dr. Crippen murdered his wife, and then lived pleasantly with his mistress in the house under whose floor he had buried the wife. Constance Kent, found Not Guilty of the murder of her young brother, led a peaceful life for five years before she confessed. George Joseph Smith and William Palmer lived amiably among their fellows untroubled by fear or by remorse for their poisoning and drownings. Charles Peace, at the time he made his one unfortunate essay, had settled down into a respectable citizen with an interest in antiques. It happened that, after a lapse of time, these men were discovered, but more murderers than we guess are living decent lives today, and will die in decency, undiscovered and unsuspected. As this man will.

But he had a narrow escape, and it was perhaps this narrow escape that brought him to a stop. The escape was due to an error of judgment on the part of the journalist.

As soon as he had the full story of the affair, which took some time, he spent fifteen minutes on the telephone sending the story through, and at the end of the fifteen minutes, when the stimulus of the business had left him, he felt physically tired and mentally dishevelled. He was not yet free to go home; the paper would not go away for another hour; so he turned into a bar for a drink and some sandwiches.

It was then, when he had dismissed the whole business from his mind, and was looking about the bar and admiring the landlord's taste in watch chains and his air of domination, and was thinking that the landlord of a well-conducted tavern had a more comfortable life than a newspaperman, that his mind received from nowhere a spark of light. He was not thinking about the Strangling Horrors; his mind was on his sandwich. As a public-house sandwich, it was a curiosity. The bread had been thinly cut, it was buttered, and the ham was not two months stale; it was ham as it should be. His mind turned to the inventor of this refreshment, the Earl of Sandwich, and then to George the Fourth, and then to the Georges, and to the legend of that George who was worried to know how the apple got into the apple dumpling. He wondered whether George would have been equally puzzled to know how the ham got into the ham sandwich, and how long it would have been before it occurred to him that the ham could not have got there unless somebody had put it there. He got up to order another sandwich, and in that moment a little active corner of his mind settled the affair. If there was ham in his sandwich, somebody must have put it there. If seven people had been murdered, somebody must have been there to murder them. There was no aeroplane or automobile that would go into a man's pocket; therefore that somebody must have escaped either by running away or standing still; and again therefore—

He was visualizing the front-page story that his paper would carry if his theory were correct, and if—a matter of conjecture—his editor had the necessary nerve to make a bold stroke, when a cry of "Time, gentlemen, please! All out!" reminded him of the hour. He got up and went out into a world of mist, broken by the ragged discs of roadside puddles and the streaming lightning of motorbuses. He was certain that he had *the* story, but, even if it were proved, he was doubtful whether the policy of his paper would permit him to print it. It had one great fault. It was truth, but it was impossible truth. It rocked the foundations of everything that newspaper readers believed and that newspaper editors helped them to believe. They might believe that Turkish carpet sellers had the gift of making themselves invisible. They would not believe this.

As it happened, they were not asked to, for the story was never written. As his paper had by now gone away, and as he was nourished by his refreshment and stimulated by his theory, he thought he might put in an extra half hour by testing that theory. So he began to look about for the man he had in mind—a man with white hair, and large white hands; otherwise an everyday figure whom nobody would look twice at. He wanted to spring his idea on this man without warning, and he was going to place himself within reach of a man armored in legends of dreadfulness and grue. This might appear to be an act of supreme courage—that one man, with no hope of immediate outside support, should place himself at the mercy of one who was holding a whole parish in terror. But it wasn't. He didn't think about the risk. He didn't think about his duty to his employers or loyalty to his paper. He was moved simply by an instinct to follow a story to its end.

He walked slowly from the tavern and crossed into Fingal Street, making for Deever Market, where he had hope of finding his man. But his journey was shortened. At the corner of Lotus Street he saw him—or a man who looked like him. This street was poorly lit, and he could see little of the man: but he *could* see white hands. For some twenty paces he stalked him; then drew level with him; and at a point where the arch of a railway crossed the street, he saw that this was his man. He approached him with the current conversational phrase of the district: "Well, seen anything of the murderer?" The man stopped to look sharply at him; then, satisfied that the journalist was not the murderer, said:

"Eh? No, nor's anybody else, curse it. Doubt if they ever will."

"I don't know. I've been thinking about them, and I've got an idea."

"So?"

"Yes. Came to me all of a sudden. Quarter of an hour ago. And I'd felt that we'd all been blind. It's been staring us in the face."

The man turned again to look at him, and the look and the movement held suspicion of this man who seemed to know so much. "Oh? Has it? Well, why not give us the benefit of it?"

"I'm going to." They walked level, and were nearly at the end of the little street where it meets Deever Market, when the journalist turned casually to the man. He put a finger on his arm. "Yes, it seems to me quite simple now. But there's still one point I don't understand. One little thing I'd like to clear up. I mean the motive. Now, as man to man, tell me, Sergeant Ottermole, just *why* did you kill all those inoffensive people?"

The sergeant stopped, and the journalist stopped. There was just enough light from the sky, which held the reflected light of the continent of London, to give him a sight of the sergeant's face, and the sergeant's face was turned to him with a wide smile of such urbanity and charm that the journalist's eyes were frozen as they met it. The smile stayed for some seconds. Then said the sergeant: "Well, to tell you the truth, Mr. Newspaperman, I don't know. I really don't know. In fact, I've been worried about it myself. But I've got an idea—just like you. Everybody knows that we can't control the workings of our minds. Don't they? Ideas come into our minds without asking. But everybody's supposed to be able to control his body. Why? Eh? We get our minds from Lord-knows-where—from people who were dead hundreds of years before we were born. Mayn't we get our bodies in the same way? Our faces—our legs—our heads—they aren't completely ours. We don't make 'em. They come to us. And couldn't ideas come into our bodies like ideas come into our minds? Eh? Can't ideas live in nerve and muscle as well as in brain? Couldn't it be that parts of our bodies aren't really us, and couldn't ideas come into those parts all of a sudden, like ideas come into—into"—he shot his arms out, showing the great white gloved hands and hairy wrists; shot them out so swiftly to the journalist's throat that his eyes never saw them—"into *my hands*!"

Saucy Jack —
Timeless

YOURS TRULY, JACK THE RIPPER

Robert Bloch

As an enthusiastic reader of *Weird Tales,* the most successful pulp magazine in the science fiction and horror genres, Robert Albert Bloch (1917–1994) especially liked the work of H. P. Lovecraft and began a correspondence with him. Lovecraft encouraged Bloch's writing ambitions, resulting in two of his stories being sold to *Weird Tales* at the age of seventeen, beginning a successful and prolific writing career.

Bloch wrote hundreds of short stories and twenty novels, the most famous being *Psycho* (1959), which was memorably filmed by Alfred Hitchcock. While his early work was virtually a pastiche of Lovecraft, he went on to develop his own style. Much of his work was exceptionally dark, gory, and violent for its time, but a plethora of his short fiction has elements of humor—often relying on a pun or wordplay in the last line. A famously warm, friendly, and humorous man in real life, he defended himself against charges of being a macabre writer by saying that he wasn't that way at all. "Why, I have the heart of a small boy," he said. "It's in a jar, on my desk." He commonly created a short story by inventing a good pun for the last line, then writing a narrative to accompany it.

One of the first stories that brought him renown was "Yours Truly, Jack the Ripper," published in 1943. It was adapted for a radio series titled *The Kate Smith Hour* (1944), starring Laird Cregar; again the following year on *Stay Tuned for Terror*; and for an episode of the television series *Thriller* that starred Boris Karloff in 1961. Bloch returned to Red Jack several times, writing a sequel to "Yours Truly, Jack the Ripper" titled "A Toy for Juliette" (1967); an original *Star Trek* episode titled "Wolf in the Fold" (1967); a short story inspired by the Ripper murders, "A Most Unusual Murder" (1976); and a full-length novel, *The Night of the Ripper* (1984), which featured appearances by such prominent Victorians as Arthur Conan Doyle, George Bernard Shaw, Oscar Wilde, and the Elephant Man.

"Yours Truly, Jack the Ripper" was first published in the July 1943 issue of *Weird Tales* magazine; it was first collected in *Yours Truly, Jack the Ripper* by Robert Bloch (New York, Belmont Books, 1962).

I

I looked at the stage Englishman. He looked at me.

"Sir Guy Hollis?" I asked.

"Indeed. Have I the pleasure of addressing John Carmody, the psychiatrist?"

I nodded. My eyes swept over the figure of my distinguished visitor. Tall, lean, sandy-haired—with the traditional tufted mustache. And the tweeds. I suspected a monocle concealed in a vest pocket, and wondered if he'd left his umbrella in the outer office.

But more than that, I wondered what the devil had impelled Sir Guy Hollis of the British Embassy to seek out a total stranger here in Chicago.

Sir Guy didn't help matters any as he sat down. He cleared his throat, glanced around nervously, tapped his pipe against the side of the desk. Then he opened his mouth.

"Mr. Carmody," he said, "have you ever heard of—Jack the Ripper?"

"The murderer?" I asked.

"Exactly. The greatest monster of them all. Worse than Springheel Jack or Crippen. Jack the Ripper. Red Jack."

"I've heard of him," I said.

"Do you know his history?"

"I don't think we'll get anyplace swapping old wives' tales about famous crimes of history."

He took a deep breath.

"This is no old wives' tale. It's a matter of life or death."

He was so wrapped up in his obsession he even talked that way. Well—I was willing to listen. We psychiatrists get paid for listening.

"Go ahead," I told him. "Let's have the story."

Sir Guy lit a cigarette and began to talk.

"London, 1888," he began. "Late summer and early fall. That was the time. Out of nowhere came the shadowy figure of Jack the Ripper—a stalking shadow with a knife, prowling through London's East End. Haunting the squalid dives of Whitechapel, Spitalfields. Where he came from no one knew. But he brought death. Death in a knife.

"Six times that knife descended to slash the throats and bodies of London's women. Drabs and alley sluts. August 7th was the date of the first butchery. They found her body lying there with thirty-nine stab wounds. A ghastly murder. On August 31st, another victim. The press became interested. The slum inhabitants were more deeply interested still.

"Who was this unknown killer who prowled in their midst and struck at will in the deserted alleyways of night-town? And what was more important—when would he strike again?

"September 8th was the date. Scotland Yard assigned special deputies. Rumors ran rampant. The atrocious nature of the slayings was the subject for shocking speculation.

"The killer used a knife—expertly. He cut throats and removed—certain portions—of the bodies after death. He chose victims and settings with a fiendish deliberation. No one saw him or heard him. But watchmen making their gray rounds in the dawn would stumble across the hacked and horrid thing that was the Ripper's handiwork.

"Who was he? What was he? A mad surgeon? A butcher? An insane scientist? A pathological degenerate escaped from an asylum? A deranged nobleman? A member of the London police?"

"Then the poem appeared in the newspaper. The anonymous poem, designed to put a stop to speculations—but which only aroused public interest to a further frenzy. A mocking little stanza:

I'm not a butcher, I'm not a Yid
Nor yet a foreign skipper,
But I'm your own true loving friend,
Yours truly—Jack the Ripper.

"And on September 30th, two more throats were slashed open. There was silence, then, in London for a time. Silence, and a nameless fear. When would Red Jack strike again? They waited through October. Every figment of fog concealed his phantom presence. Concealed it well—for nothing was learned of the Ripper's identity, or his purpose. The drabs of London shivered in the raw wind of early November. Shivered, and were thankful for the coming of each morning's sun.

"November 9th. They found her in her room. She lay there very quietly, limbs neatly arranged. And beside her, with equal neatness, were laid her breasts and heart. The Ripper had outdone himself in execution.

"Then, panic. But needless panic. For though press, police, and populace alike waited in sick dread, Jack the Ripper did not strike again.

"Months passed. A year. The immediate interest died, but not the memory. They said Jack had skipped to America. That he had committed suicide. They said—and they wrote. They've written ever since. Theories, hypotheses, arguments, treatises. But to this day no one knows who Jack the Ripper was. Or why he killed. Or why he stopped killing."

Sir Guy was silent. Obviously he expected some comment from me.

"You tell the story well," I remarked. "Though with a slight emotional bias."

"I suppose you want to know why I'm interested?" he snapped.

"Yes. That's exactly what I'd like to know."

"Because," said Sir Guy Hollis, "I am on the trail of Jack the Ripper now. I think he's here—in Chicago!"

"Say that again."

"Jack the Ripper is alive, in Chicago, and I'm out to find him."

He wasn't smiling. It wasn't a joke.

"See here," I said. "What was the date of these murders?"

"August to November, 1888."

"1888? But if Jack the Ripper was an able-bodied man in 1888, he'd surely be dead today! Why look, man—if he were merely born in that year, he'd be fifty-seven years old today!"

"Would he?" smiled Sir Guy Hollis. "Or should I say, 'Would she?' Because Jack the Ripper may have been a woman. Or any number of things."

"Sir Guy," I said. "You came to the right person when you looked me up. You definitely need the services of a psychiatrist."

"Perhaps. Tell me, Mr. Carmody, do you think I'm crazy?"

I looked at him and shrugged. But I had to give him a truthful answer.

"Frankly—no."

"Then you might listen to the reasons I believe Jack the Ripper is alive today."

"I might."

"I've studied these cases for thirty years. Been over the actual ground. Talked to officials. Talked to friends and acquaintances of the poor drabs who were killed. Visited with men and women in the neighborhood. Collected an entire library of material touching on Jack the Ripper. Studied all the wild theories or crazy notions.

"I learned a little. Not much, but a little. I won't bore you with my conclusions. But there was another branch of inquiry that yielded more fruitful return. I have studied unsolved crimes. Murders.

"I could show you clippings from the papers of half the world's greatest cities. San Francisco. Shanghai. Calcutta. Omsk. Paris. Berlin. Pretoria. Cairo. Milan. Adelaide.

"The trail is there, the pattern. Unsolved crimes. Slashed throats of women. With the peculiar disfigurations and removals. Yes, I've followed the trail of blood. From New York westward across the continent. Then to the Pacific. From there to Africa. During the World War of 1914–18 it was Europe. After that, South America. And since 1930, the United States again. Eighty-seven such murders—and to the trained criminologist, all bear the stigma of the Ripper's handiwork.

"Recently there were the so-called Cleveland torso slayings. Remember? A shocking series. And finally, two recent deaths in Chicago. Within the past six months. One out on South Dearborn. The other somewhere up on Halsted. Same type of crime, same technique. I tell you, there are unmistakable indications in all these affairs—indications of the work of Jack the Ripper!"

"A very tight theory," I said. I'll not question your evidence at all, or the deductions you draw. You're the criminologist, and I'll take your word for it. Just one thing remains to be explained. A minor point, perhaps, but worth mentioning."

"And what is that?" asked Sir Guy.

"Just how could a man of, let us say, eighty-five years, commit these crimes? For if Jack the Ripper was around thirty in 1888 and lived, he'd be eighty-five today."

"*Suppose he didn't get any older?*" whispered Sir Guy.

"What's that?"

"Suppose Jack the Ripper didn't grow old? Suppose he is still a young man today?

"It's a crazy theory, I grant you," he said. "All the theories about the Ripper are crazy. The idea that he was a doctor. Or a maniac. Or a woman. The reasons advanced for such beliefs are flimsy enough. There's nothing to go by. So why should my notion be any worse?"

"Because people grow older," I reasoned with him. "Doctors, maniacs, and women alike."

"What about—*sorcerers?*"

"Sorcerers?"

"Necromancers. Wizards. Practicers of Black Magic?"

"What's the point?"

"I studied," said Sir Guy. "I studied everything. After a while I began to study the dates of the murders. The pattern those dates formed. The rhythm. The solar, lunar, stellar rhythm. The sidereal aspect. The astrological significance.

"Suppose Jack the Ripper didn't murder for murder's sake alone? Suppose he wanted to make—a sacrifice?"

"What kind of a sacrifice?"

Sir Guy shrugged. "It is said that if you offer blood to the dark gods they grant boons. Yes, if a blood offering is made at the proper time—when the moon and the stars are right—and with the proper ceremonies—they grant boons. Boons of youth. Eternal youth."

"But that's nonsense!"

"No. That's—Jack the Ripper."

I stood up. "A most interesting theory," I told him. "But why do you come here and tell it to me? I'm not an authority on witchcraft. I'm not a police official or criminologist. I'm a practicing psychiatrist. What's the connection?"

Sir Guy smiled.

"You are interested, then?"

"Well, yes. There must be some point."

"There is. But I wished to be assured of your interest first. Now I can tell you my plan."

"And just what is that plan?"

Sir Guy gave me a long look.

"John Carmody," he said, "you and I are going to capture Jack the Ripper."

2

That's the way it happened. I've given the gist of that first interview in all its intricate and somewhat boring detail, because I think it's important. It helps to throw some light on Sir Guy's character and attitude. And in view of what happened after that—

But I'm coming to those matters.

Sir Guy's thought was simple. It wasn't even a thought. Just a hunch.

"You know the people here," he told me. "I've inquired. That's why I came to you as the ideal man for my purpose. You number amongst your acquaintances many writers, painters, poets. The so-called intelligentsia. The lunatic fringe from the near north side.

"For certain reasons—never mind what they are—my clues lead me to infer that Jack the Ripper is a member of that element. He chooses to pose as an eccentric. I've a feeling that with you to take me around and introduce me to your set, I might hit upon the right person."

"It's all right with me," I said. "But just how are you going to look for him? As you say, he might be anybody, anywhere. And you have no idea what he looks like. He might be young or old. Jack the Ripper—a Jack of all trades? Rich man, poor man, beggar man, thief, doctor, lawyer—how will you know?"

"We shall see." Sir Guy sighed heavily. "But I must find him. At once."

"Why the hurry?"

Sir Guy sighed again. "Because in two days he will kill again."

"Are you sure?"

"Sure as the stars. I've plotted this chart, you see. All of the murders correspond to certain astrological rhythm patterns. If, as I suspect, he makes a blood sacrifice to renew his youth, he must murder within two days. Notice the pattern of his first crimes in London. August 7th. Then August 31st. September 8th. September 30th. November 9th. Intervals of twenty-four days, nine days, twenty-two days— he killed two this time—and then forty days. Of course there were crimes in between. There had to be. But they weren't discovered and pinned on him.

"At any rate, I've worked out a pattern for him, based on all my data. And I say that within the next two days he kills. So I must seek him out, somehow, before then."

"And I'm still asking you what you want me to do."

"Take me out," said Sir Guy. "Introduce me to your friends. Take me to parties."

"But where do I begin? As far as I know, my artistic friends, despite their eccentricities, are all normal people."

"So is the Ripper. Perfectly normal. Except on certain nights." Again that far-away look in Sir Guy's eyes. "Then he becomes an ageless pathological monster, crouching to kill."

"All right," I said. "All right. I'll take you."

We made our plans. And that evening I took him over to Lester Baston's studio.

As we ascended to the penthouse roof in the elevator I took the opportunity to warn Sir Guy.

"Baston's a real screwball," I cautioned him. "So are his guests. Be prepared for anything and everything."

"I am." Sir Guy Hollis was perfectly serious. He put his hand in his trousers pocket and pulled out a gun.

"What the—" I began.

"If I see him I'll be ready," Sir Guy said. He didn't smile, either.

"But you can't go running around at a party with a loaded revolver in your pocket, man!"

"Don't worry, I won't behave foolishly."

I wondered. Sir Guy Hollis was not, to my way of thinking, a normal man.

We stepped out of the elevator, went toward Baston's apartment door.

"By the way," I murmured, "just how do you wish to be introduced? Shall I tell them who you are and what you are looking for?"

"I don't care. Perhaps it would be best to be frank."

"But don't you think that the Ripper—if by some miracle he or she is present— will immediately get the wind up and take cover?"

"I think the shock of the announcement that I am hunting the Ripper would provoke some kind of betraying gesture on his part," said Sir Guy.

"It's a fine theory. But I warn you, you're going to be in for a lot of ribbing. This is a wild bunch."

Sir Guy smiled.

"I'm ready," he announced. "I have a little plan of my own. Don't be shocked at anything I do."

I nodded and knocked on the door.

Baston opened it and poured out into the hall. His eyes were as red as the maraschino cherries in his Manhattan. He teetered back and forth regarding us very gravely. He squinted at my square-cut homburg hat and Sir Guy's mustache.

"Aha," he intoned. "The Walrus and the Carpenter."

I introduced Sir Guy.

"Welcome," said Baston, gesturing us inside with over-elaborate courtesy. He stumbled after us into the garish parlor.

I stared at the crowd that moved restlessly through the fog of cigarette smoke.

It was the shank of the evening for this mob. Every hand held a drink. Every face held a slightly hectic flush. Over in one corner the piano was going full blast, but the imperious strains of the *March* from *The Love for Three Oranges* couldn't drown out the profanity from the crap-game in the other corner.

Prokofieff had no chance against African polo, and one set of ivories rattled louder than the other.

Sir Guy got a monocle-full right away. He saw LaVerne Gonnister, the poetess, hit Hymie Kralik in the eye. He saw Hymie sit down on the floor and cry until Dick Pool accidentally stepped on his stomach as he walked through to the dining room for a drink.

He heard Nadia Vilinoff, the commercial artist, tell Johnny Odcutt that she thought his tattooing was in dreadful taste, and he saw Barclay Melton crawl under the dining room table with Johnny Odcutt's wife.

His zoological observations might have continued indefinitely if Lester Baston hadn't stepped to the center of the room and called for silence by dropping a vase on the floor.

"We have distinguished visitors in our midst," bawled Lester, waving his empty glass in our direction. "None other than the Walrus and the Carpenter. The Walrus is Sir Guy Hollis, a something-or-other from the British Embassy. The Carpenter, as you all know, is our own John Carmody, the prominent dispenser of libido liniment."

He turned and grabbed Sir Guy by the arm, dragging him to the middle of the carpet. For a moment I thought Hollis might object, but a quick wink reassured me. He was prepared for this.

"It is our custom, Sir Guy," said Baston, loudly, "to subject our new friends to a little cross-examination. Just a little formality at these very formal gatherings, you understand. Are you prepared to answer questions?"

Sir Guy nodded and grinned.

"Very well," Baston muttered. "Friends—I give you this bundle from Britain. Your witness."

Then the ribbing started. I meant to listen, but at that moment Lydia Dare saw me and dragged me off into the vestibule for one of those Darling-I-waited-for-your-call-all-day routines.

By the time I got rid of her and went back, the impromptu quiz session was in full swing. From the attitude of the crowd, I gathered that Sir Guy was doing all right for himself.

Then Baston himself interjected a question that upset the apple-cart.

"And what, may I ask, brings you to our midst tonight? What is your mission, oh Walrus?"

"I'm looking for Jack the Ripper."

Nobody laughed.

Perhaps it struck them all the way it did me. I glanced at my neighbors and began to *wonder*.

LaVerne Gonnister. Hymie Kralik. Harmless. Dick Pool, Nadia Vilinoff. Johnny Odcutt and his wife. Barclay Melton. Lydia Dare. All harmless.

But what a forced smile on Dick Pool's face! And that sly, self-conscious smirk that Barclay Melton wore!

Oh, it was absurd, I grant you. But for the first time I saw these people in a new light. I wondered about their lives—their secret lives beyond the scenes of parties.

How many of them were playing a part, concealing something?

Who here would worship Hecate and grant that horrid goddess the dark boon of blood?

Even Lester Baston might be masquerading.

The mood was upon us all, for a moment. I saw questions flicker in the circle of eyes around the room.

Sir Guy stood there, and I could swear he was fully conscious of the situation he'd created, and enjoyed it.

I wondered idly just what was *really* wrong with him. Why he had this odd fixation concerning Jack the Ripper. Maybe he was hiding secrets, too. . . .

Baston, as usual, broke the mood. He burlesqued it.

"The Walrus isn't kidding, friends," he said. He slapped Sir Guy on the back and put his arm around him as he orated. "Our English cousin is really on the trail of the fabulous Jack the Ripper. You all remember Jack the Ripper, I presume? Quite a cut-up in the old days, as I recall. Really had some ripping good times when he went out on a tear.

"The Walrus has some idea that the Ripper is still alive, probably prowling around Chicago with a Boy Scout knife. In fact"—Baston paused impressively and shot it out in a rasping stage whisper—"in fact, he has reason to believe that Jack the Ripper might even be right here in our midst tonight."

There was the expected reaction of giggles and grins. Baston eyed Lydia Dare reprovingly. "You girls needn't laugh," he smirked. "Jack the Ripper might be a woman, too, you know. Sort of a Jill the Ripper."

"You mean you actually suspect one of us?" shrieked LaVerne Gonnister, simpering up to Sir Guy. "But that Jack the Ripper person disappeared ages ago, didn't he? In 1888?"

"Aha!" interrupted Baston. "How do you know so much about it, young lady? Sounds suspicious. Watch her, Sir Guy—she may not be as young as she appears. These lady poets have dark pasts."

The tension was gone, the mood was shattered, and the whole thing was beginning to degenerate into a trivial party joke. The man who had played the *March* was eyeing the piano with a *scherzo* gleam in his eye that augured ill for Prokofieff. Lydia Dare was glancing at the kitchen, waiting to make a break for another drink.

Then Baston caught it.

"Guess what?" he yelled. "The Walrus has a gun."

His embracing arm had slipped and encountered the hard outline of the gun in Sir Guy's pocket. He snatched it out before Hollis had the opportunity to protest.

I stared hard at Sir Guy, wondering if this thing had carried far enough. But he flicked a wink my way and I remembered he had told me not to be alarmed.

So I waited as Baston broached a drunken inspiration.

"Let's play fair with our friend the Walrus," he cried. "He came all the way from England to our party on this mission. If none of you is willing to confess, I suggest we give him a chance to find out—the hard way."

"What's up?" asked Johnny Odcutt.

"I'll turn out the lights for one minute. Sir Guy can stand here with his gun. If anyone in this room is the Ripper he can either run for it or take the opportunity to—well, eradicate his pursuer. Fair enough?"

It was even sillier than it sounds, but it caught the popular fancy. Sir Guy's protests went unheard in the ensuing babble. And before I could stride over and put in my two cents' worth, Lester Baston had reached the light switch.

"Don't anybody move," he announced, with fake solemnity. "For one minute we will remain in darkness—perhaps at the mercy of a killer. At the end of that time, I'll turn up the lights again and look for bodies. Choose your partners, ladies and gentlemen."

The lights went out.

Somebody giggled.

I heard footsteps in the darkness. Mutterings.

A hand brushed my face.

The watch on my wrist ticked violently. But even louder, rising above it, I heard another thumping. The beating of my heart.

Absurd. Standing in the dark with a group of tipsy fools. And yet there was real terror lurking here, rustling through the velvet blackness.

Jack the Ripper prowled in darkness like this. And Jack the Ripper had a knife. Jack the Ripper had a madman's brain and a madman's purpose.

But Jack the Ripper was dead, dead and dust these many years—by every human law.

Only there are no human laws when you feel yourself in the darkness, when the darkness hides and protects and the outer mask slips off your face and you feel something welling up within you, a brooding shapeless purpose that is brother to the blackness.

Sir Guy Hollis shrieked.

There was a grisly thud.

Baston put the lights on.

Everybody screamed.

Sir Guy Hollis lay sprawled on the floor in the center of the room. The gun was still clutched in his hand.

I glanced at the faces, marveling at the variety of expressions human beings can assume when confronting horror.

All the faces were present in the circle. Nobody had fled. And yet Sir Guy Hollis lay there.

LaVerne Gonnister was wailing and hiding her face.

"All right."

Sir Guy rolled over and jumped to his feet. He was smiling.

"Just an experiment, eh? If Jack the Ripper *were* among those present, and thought I had been murdered, he would have betrayed himself in some way when the lights went on and he saw me lying there.

"I am convinced of your individual and collective innocence. Just a gentle spoof, my friends."

Hollis stared at the goggling Baston and the rest of them crowding in behind him.

"Shall we leave, John?" he called to me. "It's getting late, I think."

Turning, he headed for the closet. I followed him. Nobody said a word.

It was a pretty dull party after that.

3

I met Sir Guy the following evening as we agreed, on the corner of 29th and South Halsted.

After what had happened the night before, I was prepared for almost anything. But Sir Guy seemed matter-of-fact enough as he stood huddled against a grimy doorway and waited for me to appear.

"Boo!" I said, jumping out suddenly. He smiled. Only the betraying gesture of his left hand indicated that he'd instinctively reached for his gun when I startled him.

"All ready for our wild-goose chase?" I asked.

"Yes." He nodded. "I'm glad that you agreed to meet me without asking questions," he told me. "It shows you trust my judgment." He took my arm and edged me along the street slowly.

"It's foggy tonight, John," said Sir Guy Hollis. "Like London."

I nodded.

"Cold, too, for November."

I nodded again and half-shivered my agreement.

"Curious," mused Sir Guy. "London fog and November. The place and the time of the Ripper murders."

I grinned through darkness. "Let me remind you, Sir Guy, that this isn't London, but Chicago. And it isn't November, 1888. It's over fifty years later."

Sir Guy returned my grin, but without mirth. "I'm not so sure, at that," he murmured. "Look about you. Those tangled alleys and twisted streets. They're like the East End. Mitre Square. And surely they are as ancient as fifty years, at least."

"You're in the black neighborhood of South Clark Street," I said shortly. "And why you dragged me down here I still don't know."

"It's a hunch," Sir Guy admitted. "Just a hunch on my part, John. I want to wander around down here. There's the same geographical conformation in these streets as in those courts where the Ripper roamed and slew. That's where we'll find him, John. Not in the bright lights, but down here in the darkness. The darkness where he waits and crouches."

"Isn't that why you brought a gun?" I asked. I was unable to keep a trace of sarcastic nervousness from my voice. All this talk, this incessant obsession with Jack the Ripper, got on my nerves more than I cared to admit.

"We may need a gun," said Sir Guy, gravely. "After all, tonight is the appointed night."

I sighed. We wandered on through the foggy, deserted streets. Here and there a dim light burned above a gin-mill doorway. Otherwise, all was darkness and shadow. Deep, gaping alleyways loomed as we proceeded down a slanting side-street.

We crawled through that fog, alone and silent, like two tiny maggots floundering within a shroud.

"Can't you see there's not a soul around these streets?" I said.

"He's bound to come," said Sir Guy. "He'll be drawn here. This is what I've been looking for. A *genius loci*. An evil spot that attracts evil. Always, when he slays, it's the slums.

"You see, that must be one of his weaknesses. He has a fascination for squalor. Besides, the women he needs for sacrifice are more easily found in the dives and stewpots of a great city."

"Well, let's go into one of the dives or stewpots," I suggested. "I'm cold. Need a drink. This damned fog gets into your bones. You Britishers can stand it, but I like warmth and dry heat."

We emerged from our side street and stood upon the threshold of an alley.

Through the white clouds of mist ahead, I discerned a dim blue light, a naked bulb dangling from a beer sign above an alley tavern.

"Let's take a chance," I said. "I'm beginning to shiver."

"Lead the way," said Sir Guy. I led him down the alley passage. We halted before the door of the dive.

"What are you waiting for?" he asked.

"Just looking in," I told him. "This is a rough neighborhood, Sir Guy. Never know what you're liable to run into. And I'd prefer we didn't get into the wrong company. Some of these places resent white customers."

"Good idea, John."

I finished my inspection through the doorway. "Looks deserted," I murmured. "Let's try it."

We entered a dingy bar. A feeble light flickered above the counter and railing, but failed to penetrate the further gloom of the back booths.

A gigantic black lolled across the bar. He scarcely stirred as we came in, but his eyes flicked open quite suddenly and I knew he noted our presence and was judging us.

"Evening," I said.

He took his time before replying. Still sizing us up. Then, he grinned.

"Evening, gents. What's your pleasure?"

"Gin," I said. "Two gins. It's a cold night."

"That's right, gents."

He poured, I paid, and took the glasses over to one of the booths. We wasted no time in emptying them.

I went over to the bar and got the bottle. Sir Guy and I poured ourselves another drink. The big man went back into his doze, with one wary eye half-open against any sudden activity.

The clock over the bar ticked on. The wind was rising outside, tearing the shroud of fog to ragged shreds. Sir Guy and I sat in the warm booth and drank our gin.

He began to talk, and the shadows crept up about us to listen.

He rambled a great deal. He went over everything he'd said in the office when I met him, just as though I hadn't heard it before. The poor devils with obsessions are like that.

I listened very patiently. I poured Sir Guy another drink. And another.

But the liquor only made him more talkative. How he did run on! About ritual killings and prolonging the life unnaturally—the whole fantastic tale came out again. And of course, he maintained his unyielding conviction that the Ripper was abroad tonight.

I suppose I was guilty of goading him.

"Very well," I said, unable to keep the impatience from my voice. "Let us say that your theory is correct—even though we must overlook every natural law and swallow a lot of superstition to give it any credence.

"But let us say, for the sake of argument, that you are right. Jack the Ripper was a man who discovered how to prolong his own life through making human sacrifices. He did travel around the world as you believe. He is in Chicago now and he is planning to kill. In other words, let us suppose that everything you claim is gospel truth. So what?"

"What do you mean, 'so what?'" said Sir Guy.

"I mean—so what?" I answered. "If all this is true, it still doesn't prove that by sitting down in a dingy gin-mill on the South Side, Jack the Ripper is going to walk in here and let you kill him, or turn him over to the police. And come to think of it, I don't even know now just what you intend to *do* with him if you ever did find him."

Sir Guy gulped his gin. "I'd capture the bloody swine," he said. "Capture him and turn him over to the government, together with all the papers and documentary evidence I've collected against him over a period of many years. I've spent a fortune investigating this affair, I tell you, a fortune! His capture will mean the solution of hundreds of unsolved crimes, of that I am convinced."

In vino veritas. Or was all this babbling the result of too much gin? It didn't matter. Sir Guy Hollis had another. I sat there and wondered what to do with him. The man was rapidly working up to a climax of hysterical drunkenness.

"That's enough," I said, putting out my hand as Sir Guy reached for the half-emptied bottle again. "Let's call a cab and get out of here. It's getting late and it doesn't look as though your elusive friend is going to put in his appearance. Tomorrow, if I were you, I'd plan to turn all those papers and documents over to the F.B.I. If you're so convinced of the truth of your theory, they are competent to make a very thorough investigation, and find your man."

"No." Sir Guy was drunkenly obstinate. "No cab."

"But let's get out of here anyway," I said, glancing at my watch. "It's past midnight."

He sighed, shrugged, and rose unsteadily. As he started for the door, he tugged the gun free from his pocket.

"Here, give me that!" I whispered. "You can't walk around the street brandishing that thing."

I took the gun and slipped it inside my coat. Then I got hold of his right arm and steered him out of the door. The black man didn't look up as we departed.

We stood shivering in the alleyway. The fog had increased. I couldn't see either end of the alley from where we stood. It was cold. Damp. Dark. Fog or no fog, a little wind was whispering secrets to the shadows at our backs.

Sir Guy, despite his incapacity, still stared apprehensively at the alley, as though he expected to see a figure approaching.

Disgust got the better of me.

"Childish foolishness," I snorted. "Jack the Ripper, indeed! I call this carrying a hobby too far."

"Hobby?" He faced me. Through the fog I could see his distorted face. "You call this a hobby?"

"Well, what is it?" I grumbled. "Just why else are you so interested in tracking down this mythical killer?"

My arm held his. But his stare held me.

"In London," he whispered. "In 1888 . . . one of those nameless drabs the Ripper slew . . . was my mother."

"What?"

"Later I was recognized by my father, and legitimatized. We swore to give our lives to find the Ripper. My father was the first to search. He died in Hollywood in 1926—on the trail of the Ripper. They said he was stabbed by an unknown assailant in a brawl. But I knew who the assailant was.

"So I've taken up his work, do you see, John? I've carried on. And I will carry on until I do find him and kill him with my own hands."

I believed him then. He wouldn't give up. He wasn't just a drunken babbler anymore. He was as fanatical, as determined, as relentless as the Ripper himself.

Tomorrow he'd be sober. He'd continue the search. Perhaps he'd turn those papers over to the F.B.I. Sooner or later, with such persistence—and with his motive—he'd be successful. I'd always known he had a motive.

"Let's go," I said, steering him down the alley.

"Wait a minute," said Sir Guy. "Give me back my gun." He lurched a little. "I'd feel better with the gun on me."

He pressed me into the dark shadows of a little recess.

I tried to shrug him off, but he was insistent.

"Let me carry the gun, now, John," he mumbled.

"All right," I said.

I reached into my coat, brought my hand out.

"But that's not a gun," he protested. "That's a knife."

"I know."

I bore down on him swiftly.

"John!" he screamed.

"Never mind the 'John,' " I whispered, raising the knife. "Just call me . . . Jack."

A TOY FOR JULIETTE

Robert Bloch

Although he is best known for his novel *Psycho* (1959), Robert Albert Bloch (1917–1994) has also enjoyed great success with his short story "Yours Truly, Jack the Ripper" (1943), which has been anthologized relentlessly, as well as serving as the inspiration for numerous radio programs, television dramas, and countless plagiarisms.

The story resonated so powerfully for Harlan Ellison when he was preparing his anthology *Dangerous Visions* (1967) that he made contact with Bloch and asked him for a sequel. One of the most (justly) lauded anthologies ever published, this giant collection of speculative fiction contained original work by many of the greatest names in the history of science fiction, every story edited and introduced (frequently at great length) by Ellison.

The challenge hurled at Bloch was to write a Jack the Ripper story set in the future. It was a logical suggestion, based on the premise of "Yours Truly, Jack the Ripper," and Bloch succeeded with a story every bit the equal of its predecessor.

The story, so to speak, doesn't end there. Inspired by "A Toy for Juliette," Ellison asked Bloch if he would grant permission for him to write a sequel to the sequel. "The image of a creature of Whitechapel fog and filth," Ellison wrote in *Dangerous Visions*, "the dark figure of Leather Apron, skulking through a sterile and automated city of the future, was an anachronism that fascinated me." The story that follows "A Toy for Juliette" in this collection, then, is Ellison's sequel to this sequel.

"A Toy for Juliette" was first published in *Dangerous Visions*, edited by Harlan Ellison (Garden City, NY, Doubleday, 1967).

Juliette entered her bedroom, smiling, and a thousand Juliettes smiled back at her. For all the walls were paneled with mirrors, and the ceiling was set with inlaid panes that reflected her image.

Wherever she glanced she could see the blonde curls framing the sensitive features of a face that was a radiant amalgam of both child and angel; a striking contrast to the rich, ripe revelation of her body in the filmy robe.

But Juliette wasn't smiling at herself. She smiled because she knew that Grandfather was back, and he'd brought her another toy. In just a few moments it would be decontaminated and delivered, and she wanted to be ready.

Juliette turned the ring on her finger and the mirrors dimmed. Another turn would darken the room entirely; a twist in the opposite direction would bring them blazing into brilliance. It was all a matter of choice—but then, that was the secret of life. To choose, for pleasure.

And what was her pleasure tonight?

Juliette advanced to one of the mirror panels and passed her hand before it. The glass slid to one side, revealing the niche behind it; the coffin-shaped opening in the solid rock, with the boot and thumbscrews set at the proper heights.

For a moment she hesitated; she hadn't played *that* game in years. Another time, perhaps. Juliette waved her hand and the mirror moved to cover the opening again.

She wandered along the row of panels, gesturing as she walked, pausing to inspect what was behind each mirror in turn. Here was the rack, there the stocks with the barbed whips resting against the dark-stained wood. And here was the dissecting table, hundreds of years old, with its quaint instruments; behind the next panel, the electrical prods and wires that produced such weird grimaces and contortions of agony, to say nothing of screams. Of course the screams didn't matter in a soundproofed room.

Juliette moved to the side wall and waved her hand again; the obedient glass slid away and she stared at a plaything she'd almost forgotten. It was one of the first things Grandfather had ever given her, and it was very old, almost like a mummy case. What had he called it? The Iron Maiden of Nuremberg, that was it—with the sharpened steel spikes set inside the lid. You chained a man inside, and you turned the little crank that closed the lid, ever so slowly, and the spikes pierced the wrists and the elbows, the ankles and the knees, the groin and the eyes. You had to be careful not to get excited and turn too quickly, or you'd spoil the fun.

Grandfather had shown her how it worked, the first time he brought her a real *live* toy. But then, Grandfather had shown her everything. He'd taught her all she knew, for he was very wise. He'd even given her her name—Juliette—from one of the old-fashioned printed books he'd discovered by the philosopher De Sade.

Grandfather had brought the books from the Past, just as he'd brought the playthings for her. He was the only one who had access to the Past, because he owned the Traveler.

The Traveler was a very ingenious mechanism, capable of attaining vibrational frequencies which freed it from the time-bind. At rest, it was just a big square boxlike shape, the size of a small room. But when Grandfather took over the controls and the oscillation started, the box would blur and disappear. It was still there, Grandfather said—at least the *matrix* remained as a fixed point in space and time—but anything or anyone within the square could move freely into the Past to wherever the controls were programed. Of course they would be invisible when they arrived, but that was actually an advantage, particularly when it came to finding things and bringing them back. Grandfather had brought back some very interesting objects from almost mythical places—the great library of Alexandria, the Pyramid of Cheops, the Kremlin, the Vatican, Fort Knox—all the storehouses of treasure and knowledge which existed thousands of years ago. He liked to go to *that* part of the Past, the period before the thermonuclear wars and the robotic ages, and collect things. Of course books and jewels and metals were useless, except to an antiquarian, but Grandfather was a romanticist and loved the olden times.

It was strange to think of him owning the Traveler, but of course he hadn't actually created it. Juliette's father was really the one who built it, and Grandfather took possession of it after her father died. Juliette suspected Grandfather had killed her father and mother when she was just a baby, but she could never be sure. Not that it mattered; Grandfather was always very good to her, and besides, soon he would die and she'd own the Traveler herself.

They used to joke about it frequently. "I've made you into a monster," he'd say. "And someday you'll end up destroying me. After which, of course, you'll go on to destroy the entire world—or what little remains of it."

"Aren't you afraid?" she'd tease.

"Certainly not. That's my dream—the destruction of everything. An end to all this sterile decadence. Do you realize that at one time there were more than three billion inhabitants on this planet? And now, less than three thousand! Less than three thousand, shut up inside these Domes, prisoners of themselves and sealed away forever, thanks to the sins of the fathers who poisoned not only the outside world but outer space by meddling with the atomic order of the universe. Humanity is virtually extinct already; you will merely hasten the finale."

"But couldn't we all go back to another time, in the Traveler?" she asked.

"Back to *what* time? The continuum is changeless; one event leads memorably to another, all links in a chain which binds us to the present and its inevitable end in destruction. We'd have temporary individual survival, yes, but to no purpose. And none of us are fitted to survive in a more primitive environment. So let us stay here and take what pleasure we can from the moment. *My* pleasure is to be the sole user and possessor of the Traveler. And yours, Juliette—"

Grandfather laughed then. They both laughed, because they knew what *her* pleasure was.

Juliette killed her first toy when she was eleven—a little boy. It had been brought to her as a special gift from Grandfather, from somewhere in the Past, for elementary sex play. But it wouldn't cooperate, and she lost her temper and beat it to death with a steel rod. So Grandfather brought her an older toy, with brown skin, and it cooperated very well, but in the end she tired of it and one day when it was sleeping in her bed she tied it down and found a knife.

Experimenting a little before it died, Juliette discovered new sources of pleasure, and of course Grandfather found out. That's when he'd christened her "Juliette"; he seemed to approve most highly, and from then on he brought her the playthings she kept behind the mirrors in her bedroom. And on his restless rovings into the Past he brought her new toys.

Being invisible, he could find them for her almost anywhere on his travels—all he did was to use a stunner and transport them when he returned. Of course each toy had to be very carefully decontaminated; the Past was teeming with strange micro-organisms. But once the toys were properly antiseptic they were turned over to Juliette for her pleasure, and during the past seven years she had enjoyed herself.

It was always delicious, this moment of anticipation before a new toy arrived. What would it be like? Grandfather was most considerate; mainly, he made sure that the toys he brought her could speak and understand Anglish—or "English," as they used to call it in the Past. Verbal communication was often important, particularly if Juliette wanted to follow the precepts of the philosopher De Sade and enjoy some form of sex relation before going on to keener pleasures.

But there was still the guessing beforehand. Would this toy be young or old, wild or tame, male or female? She'd had all kinds, and every possible combination. Sometimes she kept them alive for days before tiring of them—or before the subtleties of which she was capable caused them to expire. At other times she wanted it to happen quickly; tonight, for example, she knew she could be soothed only by the most primitive and direct action.

Once Juliette realized this, she stopped playing with her mirror panels and went directly to the big bed. She pulled back the coverlet, groped under the pillow until she felt it. Yes, it was still there—the big knife with the long, cruel blade. She knew what she would do now: take the toy to bed with her and then, at precisely the proper moment, combine her pleasures. If she could time her knife thrust—

She shivered with anticipation, then with impatience.

What kind of toy would it be? She remembered the suave, cool one—Benjamin Bathurst was his name, an English diplomat from the time of what Grandfather called the Napoleonic Wars. Oh, he'd been suave and cool enough, until she beguiled him with her body, into the bed. And there'd been that American aviatrix from slightly later on in the Past, and once, as a very special treat, the entire crew of a sailing vessel called the *Marie Celeste*. They had lasted for *weeks*!

Strangely enough, she'd even read about some of her toys afterwards. Because when Grandfather approached them with his stunner and brought them here, they disappeared forever from the Past, and if they were in any way known or important in their time, such disappearances were noted. And some of Grand-father's books had accounts of the "mysterious vanishing" which took place and was, of course, never explained. How delicious it all was!

Juliette patted the pillow back into place and slid the knife under it. She couldn't wait, now; what was delaying things?

She forced herself to move to a vent and depress the sprayer, shedding her robe as the perfumed mist bathed her body. It was the final allurement—but why didn't her toy arrive?

Suddenly Grandfather's voice came over the auditor.

"I'm sending you a little surprise, dearest."

That's what he always said; it was part of the game.

Juliette depressed the communicator-toggle. "Don't tease," she begged. "Tell me what it's like."

"An Englishman. Late Victorian Era. Very prim and proper, by the looks of him."

"Young? Handsome?"

"Passable." Grandfather chuckled. "Your appetites betray you, dearest."

"Who is it—someone from the books?"

"I wouldn't know the name. We found no identification during the decontam-ination. But from his dress and manner, and the little black bag he carried when I discovered him so early in the morning, I'd judge him to be a physician returning from an emergency call."

Juliette knew about "physicians" from her reading, of course; just as she knew what "Victorian" meant. Somehow the combination seemed exactly right.

"Prim and proper?" She giggled. "Then I'm afraid it's due for a shock."

Grandfather laughed. "You have something in mind, I take it."

"Yes."

"Can I watch?"

"Please—not this time."

"Very well."

"Don't be mad, darling. I love you."

Juliette switched off. Just in time, too, because the door was opening and the toy came in.

She stared at it, realizing that Grandfather had told the truth. The toy was a male of thirty-odd years, attractive but by no means handsome. It couldn't be, in that dark garb and those ridiculous side whiskers. There was something almost depressingly refined and mannered about it, an air of embarrassed repression.

And of course, when it caught sight of Juliette in her revealing robe, and the bed surrounded by mirrors, it actually began to *blush*.

That reaction won Juliette completely. A blushing Victorian, with the build of a bull—and unaware that this was the slaughterhouse!

It was so amusing she couldn't restrain herself; she moved forward at once and put her arms around it.

"Who—who are you? Where am I?"

The usual questions, voiced in the usual way. Ordinarily, Juliette would have amused herself by parrying with answers designed to tantalize and titillate her victim. But tonight she felt an urgency which only increased as she embraced the toy and pressed it back toward the waiting bed.

The toy began to breathe heavily, responding. But it was still bewildered. "Tell me—I don't understand. Am I alive? Or is this heaven?"

Juliette's robe fell open as she lay back. "You're alive, darling," she murmured. "Wonderfully alive." She laughed as she began to prove the statement. "But closer to heaven than you think."

And to prove *that* statement, her free hand slid under the pillow and groped for the waiting knife.

But the knife wasn't there anymore. Somehow it had already found its way into the toy's hand. And the toy wasn't prim and proper any longer, its face was something glimpsed in nightmare. Just a glimpse, before the blinding blur of the knife blade, as it came down, again and again and again—

The room, of course, was soundproof, and there was plenty of time. They didn't discover what was left of Juliette's body for several days.

Back in London, after the final mysterious murder in the early morning hours, they never did find Jack the Ripper. . . .

AFTERWORD:

A number of years have passed since I sat down at the typewriter one gloomy winter day and wrote "Yours Truly, Jack the Ripper" for magazine publication. The magazine in which it appeared gave up its ghost, and interest in ghosts, a long time ago. But somehow my little story seems to have survived. It has since pursued me in reprint, collections, anthologies, foreign translations, radio broadcasts, and television.

So when the editor of this anthology proposed that I do a story and suggested, "What about Jack the Ripper in the future?" I was capable of only one response.

You've just read it.

THE PROWLER IN THE CITY AT THE EDGE OF THE WORLD

Harlan Ellison

In addition to being a prodigiously prolific short story writer, essayist, critic, novelist, screenwriter, and teleplay writer, Harlan Jay Ellison (1934–) is perhaps the most honored author of speculative fiction who has ever lived. He has won ten Hugo Awards (for best science fiction or fantasy work); four Nebula Awards, including the Grand Master for lifetime achievement (presented by the Science Fiction and Fantasy Writers of America); five Bram Stoker Awards, including one for lifetime achievement (given by the Horror Writers Association); eighteen Locus Awards (presented by the preeminent fan magazine in the speculative fiction field); and two Edgar Awards from the Mystery Writers of America. He is the only writer ever to win the Writers Guild of America award for Most Outstanding Teleplay four times.

Ellison was born in Cleveland, Ohio. After taking jobs in widely diverse fields in various parts of the country (performer in minstrel shows, tuna fisherman, crop picker, short-order cook, dynamite truck driver, taxi driver, lithographer, book salesman, department store floor walker, door-to-door brush salesman, stand-up comedian, and actor), he settled in New York to pursue a writing career before permanently moving to Southern California more than five decades ago.

"The Prowler in the City at the Edge of the World" was first published in *Dangerous Visions* (Garden City, NY, Doubleday, 1967), edited by Ellison, one of the most lauded and successful anthologies of the twentieth century.

First there was the City, never night. Tin and reflective, walls of antiseptic metal like an immense autoclave. Pure and dust-free, so silent that even the whirling innards of its heart and mind were sheathed from notice. The city was self-contained, and footfalls echoed up and around—flat slapped notes of an exotic leather-footed instrument. Sounds that reverberated back to the maker like yodels thrown out across mountain valleys. Sounds made by humbled inhabitants whose lives were as ordered, as sanitary, as metallic as the city they had caused to hold them bosom-tight against the years. The city was a complex artery, the people were the blood that flowed icily through the artery. They were a gestalt with one another, forming a unified whole. It was a city shining in permanence, eternal in concept, flinging itself up in a formed and molded statement of exaltation; most modern of all modern structures, conceived as the pluperfect residence for the perfect people. The final end-result of all sociological blueprints aimed at Utopia. Living space, it had been called, and so, doomed to *live* they were, in that Erewhon of graphed respectability and cleanliness.

Never night.

Never shadowed.

. . . a shadow.

A blot moving against the aluminum cleanliness. The movement of rags and bits of clinging earth from graves sealed ages before. A shape.

He touched a gunmetal-gray wall in passing: the imprint of dusty fingers. A twisted shadow moving through antiseptically pure streets, and they become—with his passing—black alleys from another time.

Vaguely, he knew what had happened. Not specifically, not with particulars, but he was strong, and he was able to get away without the eggshell-thin walls of his mind caving in. There was no place in this shining structure to secrete himself, a place to think, but he had to have time. He slowed his walk, seeing no one. Somehow—inexplicably—he felt . . . safe? Yes, safe. For the first time in a very long time.

A few minutes before, he had been standing in the narrow passageway outside No. 13 Miller's Court. It had been 6:15 in the morning. London had been quiet as he paused in the passageway of M'Carthy's Rents, in that fetid, urine-redolent corridor where the whores of Spitalfields took their clients. A few minutes before, the foetus in its bath of formaldehyde tightly-stoppered in a glass bottle inside his Gladstone bag, he had paused to drink in the thick fog, before taking the circuitous route back to Toynbee Hall. That had been a few minutes before. Then, suddenly, he was in another place and it was no longer 6:15 of a chill November morning in 1888.

He had looked up as light flooded him in that other place. It had been soot silent in Spitalfields, but suddenly, without any sense of having moved or having *been* moved, he was flooded with light. And when he looked up he was in that other place. Paused now, only a few minutes after the transfer, he leaned against the bright wall of the city, and recalled the light. From a thousand mirrors. In the walls, in the ceiling. A bedroom with a girl in it. A lovely girl. Not like Black Mary Kelly or Dark Annie Chapman or Kate Eddowes or any of the other pathetic scum he had been forced to attend . . .

A lovely girl. Blonde, wholesome, until she had opened her robe and turned into the same sort of slut he had been compelled to use in his work in Whitechapel . . .

A sybarite, a creature of pleasures, a Juliette she had said, before he used the big-bladed knife on her. He had found the knife under the pillow, on the bed to which she had led him—how shameful, unresisting had he been, all confused, clutching his black bag with all the tremors of a child, he who had moved through the London night like oil, moved where he wished, accomplished his ends unchecked eight times, now led toward sin by another, merely another of the tarts, taking advantage of him while he tried to distinguish what had happened to him and where he was, how shameful—and he had used it on her.

That had only been minutes before, though he had worked very efficiently on her.

The knife had been rather unusual. The blade had seemed to be two wafer-thin sheets of metal with a pulsing, glowing *something* between. A kind of sparking, such as might be produced by a Van de Graaff generator. But that was patently ridiculous. It had no wires attached to it, no bus bars, nothing to produce even the crudest electrical discharge. He had thrust the knife into the Gladstone bag, where now it lay beside the scalpels and the spool of catgut and the racked vials in their leather cases, and the foetus in its bottle. Mary Jane Kelly's foetus.

He had worked efficiently, but swiftly, and had laid her out almost exactly in the same fashion as Kate Eddowes: the throat slashed completely through from ear-to-ear, the torso laid open down between the breasts to the vagina, the intestines pulled out and draped over the right shoulder, a piece of the intestines being detached and placed between the left arm and the body. The liver had been punctured with the point of the knife, with a vertical cut slitting the left lobe of the liver. (He had been surprised to find the liver showed none of the signs of cirrhosis so prevalent in these Spitalfields tarts, who drank incessantly to rid themselves of the burden of living the dreary lives they moved through grotesquely. In fact, this one seemed totally unlike the others, even if she had been more brazen in her sexual overtures. And that knife under the bed pillow . . .) He had severed the vena cava leading to the heart. Then he had gone to work on the face.

He had thought of removing the left kidney again, as he had Kate Eddowes's. He smiled to himself as he conjured up the expression that must have been on the face of Mr. George Lusk, chairman of the Whitechapel Vigilance Committee, when he received the cardboard box in the mail. The box containing Miss Eddowes's kidney, and the letter, impiously misspelled:

From hell, Mr. Lusk, sir, I send you half the kidne I took from one woman, prasarved it for you, tother piece I fried and ate it; was very nice. I may send you the bloody knif that took it out if you only wate while longer. Catch me when you can, Mr. Lusk.

He had wanted to sign *that* one "Yours Truly, Jack the Ripper" or even Spring-Heeled Jack or maybe Leather Apron, whichever had tickled his fancy, but a sense of style had stopped him. To go too far was to defeat his own purposes. It may even have been too much to suggest to Mr. Lusk that he had eaten the kidney. How hideous. True, he *had* smelled it . . .

This blonde girl, this Juliette with the knife under her pillow. She was the ninth. He leaned against the smooth steel wall without break or seam, and he rubbed his eyes. When would he be able to stop? When would they realize, when would they get his message, a message so clear, written in blood, that only the blindness of their own cupidity forced them to misunderstand! Would he be compelled to decimate the endless regiments of Spitalfields sluts to make them understand? Would he be forced to run the cobbles ankle-deep in black blood before they sensed what he was saying, and were impelled to make reforms?

But as he took his blood-soaked hands from his eyes, he realized what he must have sensed all along: he was no longer in Whitechapel. This was not Miller's Court, nor anywhere in Spitalfields. It might not even be London. But how could *that* be?

Had God taken him?

Had he died, in a senseless instant between the anatomy lesson of Mary Jane Kelly (that filth, she had actually *kissed* him!) and the bedroom disembowelment of this Juliette? Had Heaven finally called him to his reward for the work he had done?

The Reverend Mr. Barnett would love to know about this. But then, he'd have loved to know about it *all*. But "Bloody Jack" wasn't about to tell. Let the reforms come as the Reverend and his wife wished for them, and let them think their pamphleteering had done it, instead of the scalpels of Jack.

If he was dead, would his work be finished? He smiled to himself. If Heaven had taken him, then it must be that the work *was* finished. Successfully. But if *that* was so, then who was this Juliette who now lay spread out moist and cooling in the bedroom of a thousand mirrors? And in that instant he felt fear.

What if even God misinterpreted what he had done?

As the good folk of Queen Victoria's London had misinterpreted. As Sir Charles Warren had misinterpreted. What if God believed the superficial and ignored the *real* reason? But no! Ludicrous. If anyone would understand, it was the good God who had sent him the message that told him to set things a-right.

God loved him, as he loved God, and God would know.

But he felt fear, in that moment.

Because who was the girl he had just carved?

"She was my granddaughter, Juliette," said a voice immediately beside him.

His head refused to move, to turn that few inches to see who spoke. The Gladstone was beside him, resting on the smooth and reflective surface of the street. He could not get to a knife before he was taken. At last they had caught up with Jack. He began to shiver uncontrollably.

"No need to be afraid," the voice said. It was a warm and succoring voice. An older man. He shook as with an ague. But he turned to look. It was a kindly old man with a gentle smile. Who spoke again, without moving his lips. "No one can hurt you. How do you do?"

The man from 1888 sank slowly to his knees. "Forgive me. Dear God, I did not know." The old man's laughter rose inside the head of the man on his knees. It rose like a beam of sunlight moving across a Whitechapel alleyway, from noon to one o'clock, rising and illuminating the gray bricks of soot-coated walls. It rose, and illuminated his mind.

"I'm not God. Marvelous idea, but no, I'm not God. Would you like to meet God? I'm sure we can find one of the artists who would mold one for you. Is it important? No, I can see it isn't. What a strange mind you have. You neither believe nor doubt. How can you contain both concepts at once . . . would you like me to straighten some of your brain-patterns? No. I see, you're afraid. Well, let it be for the nonce. We'll do it another time."

He grabbed the kneeling man and drew him erect.

"You're covered with blood. Have to get you cleaned up. There's an ablute near here. Incidentally, I was very impressed with the way you handled Juliette. You're the first, you know. No, how could you know? In any case, you *are* the first to deal her as good as she gave. You would have been amused at what she did to Kaspar Hauser. Squeezed part of his brain and then sent him back, let him live out part of his life and then—the little twit—she made me bring him back a second time and used a knife on him. Same knife you took, I believe. Then sent him back to his own time. Marvelous mystery. In all the tapes on unsolved phenomena. But she was much sloppier than you. She had a great verve in her amusements, but very little *éclat*. Except with Judge Crater; there she was—" He paused, and laughed lightly. "I'm an old man and I ramble on like a muskrat. You want to get cleaned up and shown around, I know. And *then* we can talk."

"I just wanted you to know I was satisfied with the way you disposed of her. In a way, I'll miss the little twit. She was such a good fuck."

The old man picked up the Gladstone bag and, holding the man spattered with blood, he moved off down the clean and shimmering street. "You *wanted* her killed?" the man from 1888 asked, unbelieving.

The old man nodded, but his lips never moved. "Of course. Otherwise why bring her Jack the Ripper?"

Oh my dear God, he thought, *I'm in Hell. And I'm entered as Jack.*

"No, my boy, no no no. You're not in Hell at all. You're in the future. For you the future, for me the world of now. You came from 1888 and you're now in"—he stopped, silently speaking for an instant, as though computing apples in terms of dollars, then resumed—"3077. It's a fine world, filled with happy times, and we're glad to have you with us. Come along now, and you'll wash."

In the ablutatorium, the late Juliette's grandfather changed his head. "I really despise it," he informed the man from 1888, grabbing fingerfuls of his cheeks and stretching the flabby skin like elastic. "But Juliette insisted. I was willing to humor her, if indeed that was what it took to get her to lie down. But what with toys from the past, and changing my head every time I wanted her to fuck me, it was trying; very trying."

He stepped into one of the many identically shaped booths set flush into the walls. The tambour door rolled down and there was a soft *chukk* sound, almost chitinous. The tambour door rolled up and the late Juliette's grandfather, now six years younger than the man from 1888, stepped out, stark naked and wearing a new head. "The body is fine, replaced last year," he said, examining the genitals and a mole on his right shoulder. The man from 1888 looked away. This was Hell and God hated him.

"Well, don't just *stand* there, Jack." Juliette's grandfather smiled. "Hit one of those booths and get your ablutions."

"That isn't my name," said the man from 1888 very softly, as though he had been whipped.

"It'll do, it'll do . . . now go get washed."

Jack approached one of the booths. It was a light green in color, but changed to mauve as he stopped in front of it. "Will it—"

"It will only *clean* you, what are you afraid of?"

"I don't want to be changed."

Juliette's grandfather did not laugh. "That's a mistake," he said cryptically. He made a peremptory motion with his hand and the man from 1888 entered the booth, which promptly revolved in its niche, sank into the floor and made a hearty *zeeeezzzz* sound. When it rose and revolved and opened, Jack stumbled out, looking terribly confused. His long sideburns had been neatly trimmed, his beard stubble had been removed, his hair was three shades lighter and was now parted on the left side, rather than in the middle. He still wore the same long dark coat trimmed with astrakhan, dark suit with white collar and black necktie (in which was fastened a horseshoe stickpin) but now the garments seemed new, unsoiled of course, possibly synthetics built to look like his former garments.

"Now!" Juliette's grandfather said. "Isn't that much better? A good cleansing always sets one's mind to rights." And he stepped into another booth from which he issued in a moment wearing a soft paper jumper that fitted from neck to feet without a break. He moved toward the door.

"Where are we going?" the man from 1888 asked the younger grandfather beside him.

"I want you to meet someone," said Juliette's grandfather, and Jack realized that he was moving his lips now. He decided not to comment on it. There had to be a reason.

"I'll walk you there, if you promise not to make gurgling sounds at the city. It's a nice city, but I live here, and frankly, tourism is boring." Jack did not reply. Grandfather took it for acceptance of the terms.

They walked. Jack became overpowered by the sheer *weight* of the city. It was obviously extensive, massive, and terribly clean. It was his dream for Whitechapel come true. He asked about slums, about doss houses. The grandfather shook his head. "Long gone."

So it had come to pass. The reforms for which he had pledged his immortal soul, they had come to pass. He swung the Gladstone and walked jauntily. But after a few minutes his pace sagged once more: there was no one to be seen in the streets.

Just shining clean buildings and streets that ran off in aimless directions and came to unexpected stops as though the builders had decided people might vanish at one point and reappear someplace else, so why bother making a road from one point to the other.

The ground was metal, the sky seemed metallic, the buildings loomed on all sides, featureless explorations of planed space by insensitive metal. The man from 1888 felt terribly alone, as though every act he had performed had led inevitably to his alienation from the very people he had sought to aid.

When he had come to Toynbee Hall, and the Reverend Mr. Barnett had opened his eyes to the slum horrors of Spitalfields, he had vowed to help in any way he could. It had seemed as simple as faith in the Lord, what to do, after a few months in the sinkholes of Whitechapel. The sluts, of what use were they? No more use than the disease germs that had infected these very same whores. So he had set forth as Jack, to perform the will of God and raise the poor dregs who inhabited the East End of London. That Lord Warren, the Metropolitan Police Commissioner, and his Queen, and all the rest thought him a mad doctor, or an amok butcher, or a beast in human form did not distress him. He knew he would remain anonymous through all time, but that the good works he had set in motion would proceed to their wonderful conclusion.

The destruction of the most hideous slum area the country had ever known, and the opening of Victorian eyes. But all the time *had* passed, and now he was here, in a world where slums apparently did not exist, a sterile Utopia that was the personification of the Reverend Mr. Barnett's dreams—but it didn't seem . . . *right*.

This grandfather, with his young head.

Silence in the empty streets.

The girl, Juliette, and her strange hobby.

The lack of concern at her death.

The grandfather's expectation that he, Jack, *would* kill her. And now his friendliness.

Where were they going?

[Around them, the City. As they walked, the grandfather paid no attention, and Jack watched but did not understand. But this was what they saw as they walked:

[Thirteen hundred beams of light, one foot wide and seven molecules thick, erupted from almost-invisible slits in the metal streets, fanned out and washed the surfaces of the buildings; they altered hue to a vague blue and washed down the surfaces of the buildings; they bent and covered all open surfaces, bent at right angles, then bent again, and again, like origami paper figures; they altered hue a second time, soft gold, and penetrated the surfaces of the buildings, expanding and contracting in solid waves, washing the inner surfaces; they withdrew rapidly into the sidewalks; the entire process had taken twelve seconds.

[Night fell over a sixteen-block area of the City. It descended in a solid pillar and was quite sharp-edged, ending at the street corners. From within the area of darkness came the distinct sounds of crickets, marsh frogs belching, night birds, soft breezes in trees, and faint music of unidentifiable instruments.

[Panes of frosted light appeared suspended freely in the air, overhead. A wavery insubstantial quality began to assault the topmost levels of a great structure directly in front of the light-panes. As the panes moved slowly down through the air, the building became indistinct, turned into motes of light, and floated upward. As the panes reached the pavement, the building had been completely dematerialized. The panes shifted color to a deep orange, and began moving upward again. As they moved, a new structure began to form where the previous building had stood, drawing—it seemed—motes of light from the air and forming them into a cohesive whole that became, as the panes ceased their upward movement, a new building. The light-panes winked out of existence.

[The sound of a bumblebee was heard for several seconds. Then it ceased.

[A crowd of people in rubber garments hurried out of a gray pulsing hole in the air, patted the pavement at their feet, then rushed off around a corner, from where emanated the sound of prolonged coughing. Then silence returned.

[A drop of water, thick as quicksilver, plummeted to the pavement, struck, rebounded, rose several inches, then evaporated into a crimson smear in the shape of a whale's tooth, which settled to the pavement and lay still.

[Two blocks of buildings sank into the pavement and the metal covering was smooth and unbroken, save for a metal tree whose trunk was silver and slim, topped by a ball of foliage constructed of golden fibers that radiated brightly in a perfect circle. There was no sound.

[The late Juliette's grandfather and the man from 1888 continued walking.]

"Where are we going?"

"To van Cleef's. We don't usually walk; oh, sometimes; but it isn't as much pleasure as it used to be. I'm doing this primarily for you. Are you enjoying yourself?"

"It's . . . unusual."

"Not much like Spitalfields, is it? But I rather like it back there, at that time. I have the only Traveler, did you know? The only one ever made. Juliette's father constructed it, my son. I had to kill him to get it. He was thoroughly unreasonable about it, really. It was a casual thing for him. He was the last of the tinkerers, and he might just as easily have given it to me. But I suppose he was being cranky. That was why I had you carve up my granddaughter. She would have gotten around to me almost any time now. Bored, just silly bored is what she was—"

The gardenia took shape in the air in front of them, and turned into the face of a woman with long white hair. "Hernon, we can't wait much longer!" She was annoyed.

Juliette's grandfather grew livid. "You scum bitch! I *told* you pace. But no, you just couldn't, could you? Jump jump jump, that's all you ever do. Well, now it'll only be feddels less, that's all. Feddels, damn you! I set it for pace, I was *working* pace, and *you* . . . !"

His hand came up and moss grew instantly toward the face. The face vanished, and a moment later the gardenia reappeared a few feet away. The moss shriveled and Hernon, Juliette's grandfather, dropped his hand, as though weary of the woman's stupidity. A rose, a water lily, a hyacinth, a pair of phlox, a wild celandine, and a bull thistle appeared near the gardenia. As each turned into the face of a different person, Jack stepped back, frightened.

All the faces turned to the one that had been the bull thistle. "Cheat! Rotten bastard!" they screamed at the thin white face that had been the bull thistle. The gardenia-woman's eyes bulged from her face, the deep purple eye-shadow that completely surrounded the eyeball making her look like a deranged animal peering out of a cave. "Turd!" she shrieked at the bull thistle-man. "We all agreed, we all said and agreed; you *had* to formz a thistle, didn't you, scut! Well, now you'll see . . ."

She addressed herself instantly to the others. "Formz now! To hell with waiting, pace fuck! Now!"

"No, dammit!" Hernon shouted. "We were going to *paaaaace!*" But it was too late. Centering in on the bull thistle-man, the air roiled thickly like silt at a river-bottom, and the air blackened as a spiral began with the now terrified face of the bull thistle-man and exploded whirling outward, enveloping Jack and Hernon and all the flower-people and the City and suddenly it was night in Spitalfields and the man from 1888 was *in* 1888, with his Gladstone bag in his hand, and a woman approaching down the street toward him, shrouded in the London fog.

(There were eight additional nodules in Jack's brain.)

The woman was about forty, weary and not too clean. She wore a dark dress of rough material that reached down to her boots. Over the skirt was fastened a white apron that was stained and wrinkled. The bulbed sleeves ended midway up her wrists and the bodice of the dress was buttoned close around her throat. She wore a kerchief tied at the neck, and a hat that looked like a wide-brimmed skimmer with a raised crown. There was a pathetic little flower of unidentifiable origin in the band of the hat. She carried a beaded handbag of capacious size, hanging from a wrist-loop.

Her step slowed as she saw him standing there, deep in the shadows. Saw him was hardly accurate: sensed him.

He stepped out and bowed slightly from the waist. "Fair evenin' to ye, Miss. Care for a pint?"

Her features—sunk in misery of a kind known only to women who have taken in numberless shafts of male blood-gorged flesh—rearranged themselves. "Coo, sir, I thought was 'im for true. Old Leather Apron hisself. Gawdamighty, you give me a scare." She tried to smile. It was a rictus. There were bright spots in her cheeks from sickness and too much gin. Her voice was ragged, a broken-edged instrument barely workable.

"Just a solicitor caught out without comp'ny," Jack assured her. "And pleased to buy a handsome lady a pint of stout for a few hours' companionship."

She stepped toward him and linked arms. "Emily Matthewes, sir, an' pleased to go with you. It's a fearsome chill night, and with Slippery Jack abroad not safe for a respectin' woman such's m'self."

They moved off down Thrawl Street, past the doss houses where this drab might flop later, if she could obtain a few coppers from this neat-dressed stranger with the dark eyes.

He turned right onto Commercial Street, and just abreast of a stinking alley almost to Flower & Dean Street, he nudged her sharply side-wise. She went into the alley, and thinking he meant to steal a smooth hand up under her petticoats, she settled back against the wall and opened her legs, starting to lift the skirt around her waist. But Jack had hold of the kerchief and, locking his fingers tightly, he twisted, cutting off her breath. Her cheeks ballooned, and by a vagary of light from a gas standard in the street he could see her eyes go from hazel to a dead-leaf brown in an instant. Her expression was one of terror, naturally, but commingled with it was a deep sadness, at having lost the pint, at having not been able to make her doss for the night, at having had the usual Emily Matthewes bad luck to run afoul this night of the one man who would ill-use her favors. It was a consummate sadness at the inevitability of her fate.

I come to you out of the night.
The night that sent me down
all the minutes of our lives
to this instant.
From this time forward, men will
wonder what happened
at this instant. They will silently
hunger to go back, to come to my
instant with you and see my face
and know my name and perhaps
not even try to stop me, for
then I would not be who I am,
but only someone who tried
and failed. Ah.

For you and me it becomes history
that will lure men always;
but they will never understand
why we both suffered, Emily;
they will never truly understand
why each of us died so terribly.

A film came over her eyes, and as her breath husked out in wheezing, pleading tremors, his free hand went into the pocket of the greatcoat. He had known he would need it, when they were walking, and he had already invaded the Gladstone bag. Now his hand went into the pocket and came up with the scalpel.

"Emily . . ." softly.

Then he sliced her.

Neatly, angling the point of the scalpel into the soft flesh behind and under her left ear. *Sternocleidomastoideus.* Driving it in to the gentle crunch of cartilage giving way. Then, grasping the instrument tightly, tipping it down and drawing it across the width of the throat, following the line of the firm jaw. *Glandula submandibularis.* The blood poured out over his hands, ran thickly at first and then burst spattering past him, reaching the far wall of the alley. Up his sleeves, soaking his white cuffs. She made a watery rattle and sank limply in his grasp, his fingers still twisted tight in her kerchief; black abrasions where he had scored the flesh. He continued the cut up past the point of the jaw's end, and sliced into the lobe of the ear. He lowered her to the filthy paving. She lay crumpled, and he straightened her. Then he cut away the garments, laying her naked belly open to the wan and flickering light of the gas standard in the street. Her belly was bloated. He started the primary cut in the hollow of her throat. *Glandula thyreoidea.* His hand was sure as he drew a thin black line of blood down and down, between the breasts. *Sternum.* Cutting a deep cross in the hole of her navel. Something vaguely yellow oozed up. *Plica umbilicalis medialis.* Down over the rounded hump of the belly, biting more deeply, withdrawing for a neat incision. *Mesenterium dorsale commune.* Down to the matted-with-sweat roundness of her privates. Harder here. *Vesica urinaria.* And finally, to the end, *vagina.*

Filth hole.

Foul-smelling die red lust pit wet hole of sluts.

And in his head, succubi. And in his head, eyes watching. And in his head, minds impinging. And in his head titillation

for a gardenia
  a water lily
  a rose
  a hyacinth
  a pair of phlox
  a wild celandine
and a dark flower with petals of obsidian, a stamen of onyx, pistils of anthracite, and the mind of Hernon, who was the late Juliette's grandfather.

They watched the entire horror of the mad anatomy lesson. They watched him nick the eyelids. They watched him remove the heart. They watched him slice out the fallopian tubes. They watched him squeeze, till it ruptured, the "ginny" kidney. They watched him slice off the sections of breast till they were nothing but shapeless mounds of bloody meat, and arrange them, one mound each on a still-staring, wide-open, nicked-eyelid eye. They watched.

They watched and they drank from the deep troubled pool of his mind. They sucked deeply at the moist quivering core of his id. And they delighted:

Oh God how Delicious look at that It looks like the uneaten rind of a Pizza or look at That It looks like lumaconi *oh god IIIIIwonder what it would be like to Tasteit!*

See how smooth the steel.

He hates them all, every one of them, something about a girl, a venereal disease, fear of his God, Christ, the Reverend Mr. Barnett, he . . . he wants to fuck the reverend's wife!

Social reform can only be brought about by concerted effort of a devoted few. Social reform is a justifiable end, condoning any expedient short of decimation of over fifty percent of the people who will be served by the reforms. The best social reformers are the most audacious. He believes it! How lovely!

You pack of vampires, you filth, you scum, you . . .

He senses us!

Damn him! Damn you, Hernon, you drew off too deeply, he knows we're here, that's disgusting, what's the sense now? I'm withdrawing!

Come back, you'll end the formz . . .

. . . back they plunged in the spiral as it spiraled back in upon itself and the darkness of the night of 1888 withdrew. The spiral drew in and in and locked at its most infinitesimal point, at the charred and blackened face of the man who had been the bull thistle. He was quite dead. His eyeholes had been burned out; charred wreckage lay where intelligence had lived. They had used him as a focus.

The man from 1888 came back to himself instantly, with a full and eidetic memory of what he had just experienced. It had not been a vision, or a dream, or a delusion, or a product of his mind. It had happened. They had sent him back, erased his mind of the transfer into the future, of Juliette, of everything after the moment outside No. 13 Miller's Court. And they had set him to work pleasuring them, while they drained off his feelings, his emotions, and his unconscious thoughts; while they battened and gorged themselves with the most private sensations. Most of which, till this moment—in a strange feedback—he had not even known he possessed. As his mind plunged on from one revelation to the next, he felt himself growing ill. At one concept his mind tried to pull back and plunge him into darkness rather than confront it. But the barriers were down, they had opened new patterns and he could read it all, remember it all. *Stinking sex hole, sluts, they have to die.* No, that wasn't the way he thought of women, any women, no matter how low or common. He was a gentleman, and women were to be respected. *She had given him the clap. He remembered.* The shame and the endless fear till he had gone to his physician father and confessed it. The look on the man's face. He remembered it all. The way his father had tended him, the way he would have tended a plague victim. It had never been the same between them again. He had tried for the cloth. *Social reform hahahaha.* All delusion. He had been a mountebank, a clown . . . and worse. He had slaughtered for something in which not even he believed. They left his mind wide open, and his thoughts stumbled . . . raced further and further toward the thought of

EXPLOSION!IN!HIS!MIND!

He fell face forward on the smooth and polished metal pavement, but he never touched. Something arrested his fall, and he hung suspended, bent over at the waist like a ridiculous Punch divested of strings or manipulation from above. A whiff of something invisible, and he was in full possession of his senses almost before they had left him. His mind was forced to look at it:

He wants to fuck the Reverend Mr. Barnett's wife.

Henrietta, with her pious petition to Queen Victoria—"Madam, we, the women of East London, feel horror at the dreadful sins that have been lately committed in our midst . . ."—asking for the capture of himself, of Jack, whom she would never, not *ever* suspect was residing right there with her and the Reverend in Toynbee Hall. The thought was laid as naked as her body in the secret dreams he had never remembered upon awakening. All of it, they had left him with opened doors, with unbounded horizons, and he saw himself for what he was.

A psychopath, a butcher, a lecher, a hypocrite, a clown.

"You did this to me! Why did you do this?"

Frenzy cloaked his words. The flower-faces became the solidified hedonists who had taken him back to 1888 on that senseless voyage of slaughter.

Van Cleef, the gardenia-woman, sneered. "Why do you think, you ridiculous bumpkin? (Bumpkin, is that the right colloquialism, Hernon? I'm so uncertain in the mid-dialects.) When you'd done in Juliette, Hernon wanted to send you back. But why should he? He owed us at least three formz, and you did passing well for one of them."

Jack shouted at them till the cords stood out in his throat. "Was it necessary, this last one? Was it important to do it, to help my reforms . . . was it?"

Hernon laughed. "Of course not."

Jack sank to his knees. The City let him do it. "Oh God, oh God almighty, I've done what I've done . . . I'm covered with blood . . . and for *nothing,* for *nothing* . . ."

Cashio, who had been one of the phlox, seemed puzzled. "Why is he concerned about *this* one, if the others don't bother him?"

Nosy Verlag, who had been a wild celandine, said sharply. "They do, all of them do. Probe him, you'll see."

Cashio's eyes rolled up in his head an instant, then rolled down and refocused—Jack felt a quicksilver shudder in his mind and it was gone—and he said lackadaisically, "Mm-hmm."

Jack fumbled with the latch of the Gladstone. He opened the bag and pulled out the foetus in the bottle. Mary Jane Kelly's unborn child, from November 9th, 1888. He held it in front of his face a moment, then dashed it to the metal pavement. It never struck. It vanished a fraction of an inch from the clean, sterile surface of the City's street.

"What marvelous loathing!" exulted Rose, who had been a rose.

"Hernon," said van Cleef, "he's centering on you. He begins to blame you for all of this."

Hernon was laughing (without moving his lips) as Jack pulled Juliette's electrical scalpel from the Gladstone and lunged. Jack's words were incoherent, but what he was saying, as he struck, was: "I'll show you what filth you are! I'll show you you can't do this kind of thing! I'll teach you! You'll die, all of you!" This is what he was saying, but it came out as one long sustained bray of revenge, frustration, hatred, and directed frenzy.

Hernon was still laughing as Jack drove the whisper-thin blade with its shimmering current into his chest. Almost without manipulation on Jack's part, the blade circumscribed a perfect 360° hole that charred and shriveled, exposing Hernon's pulsing heart and wet organs. He had time to shriek with confusion before he received Jack's second thrust, a direct lunge that severed the heart from its attachments. *Vena cava superior. Aorta. Arteria pulmonalis. Bronchus principalis.*

The heart flopped forward and a spreading wedge of blood under tremendous pressure ejaculated, spraying Jack with such force that it knocked his hat from his head and blinded him. His face was now a dripping black-red collage of features and blood.

Hernon followed his heart, and fell forward, into Jack's arms. Then the flower-people screamed as one, vanished, and Hernon's body slipped from Jack's hands to wink out of existence an instant before it struck at Jack's feet. The walls around him were clean, unspotted, sterile, metallic, uncaring.

He stood in the street, holding the bloody knife.

"Now!" he screamed, holding the knife aloft. "Now it begins!"

If the city heard, it made no indication, but

[Pressure accelerated in temporal linkages.

[A section of shining wall on the building eighty miles away changed from silver to rust.

[In the freezer chambers, two hundred gelatin caps were fed into a ready trough.

[The weathermaker spoke softly to itself, accepted data and instantly constructed an intangible mnemonic circuit.]

and in the shining eternal city where night only fell when the inhabitants had need of night and called specifically for night . . .

Night fell. With no warning save: *"Now!"*

In the City of sterile loveliness a creature of filth and decaying flesh prowled. In the last City of the world, a City on the edge of the world, where the ones who had devised their own paradise lived, the prowler made his home in shadows. Slipping from darkness to darkness with eyes that saw only movement, he roamed in search of a partner to dance his deadly rigadoon.

He found the first woman as she materialized beside a small waterfall that flowed out of empty air and dropped its shimmering, tinkling moisture into an azure cube of nameless material. He found her and drove the living blade into the back of her neck. Then he sliced out the eyeballs and put them into her open hands.

He found the second woman in one of the towers, making love to a very old man who gasped and wheezed and clutched his heart as the young woman forced him to passion. She was killing him as Jack killed her. He drove the living blade into the lower rounded surface of her belly, piercing her sex organs as she rode astride the old man. She decamped blood and viscous fluids over the prostrate body of the old man, who also died, for Jack's blade had severed the penis within the young woman. She fell forward across the old man and Jack left them that way, joined in the final embrace.

He found a man and throttled him with his bare hands, even as the man tried to dematerialize. Then Jack recognized him as one of the phlox, and made neat incisions in the face, into which he inserted the man's genitals.

He found another woman as she was singing a gentle song about eggs to a group of children. He opened her throat and severed the strings hanging inside. He let the vocal cords drop onto her chest. But he did not touch the children, who watched it all avidly. He liked children.

He prowled through the unending night making a grotesque collection of hearts, which he cut out of one, three, nine people. And when he had a dozen, he took them and laid them as road markers on one of the wide boulevards that never were used by vehicles, for the people of this City had no need of vehicles.

Oddly, the City did not clean up the hearts. Nor were the people vanishing any longer. He was able to move with relative impunity, hiding only when he saw large groups that might be searching for him. But *something* was happening in the City. (Once, he heard the peculiar sound of metal grating on metal, the *skrikkk* of plastic cutting into plastic—and he instinctively knew it was the sound of a machine malfunctioning.)

He found a woman bathing, and tied her up with strips of his own garments, and cut off her legs at the knees and left her still sitting up in the swirling crimson bath, screaming as she bled away her life. The legs he took with him.

When he found a man hurrying to get out of the night, he pounced on him, cut his throat and sawed off the arms. He replaced the arms with the bath-woman's legs.

And it went on and on, for a time that had no measure. He was showing them what evil could produce. He was showing them their immorality was silly beside his own.

But one thing finally told him he was winning. As he lurked in an antiseptically pure space between two low aluminum-cubes, he heard a voice that came from above him and around him and even from inside him. It was a public announcement, broadcast by whatever mental communications system the people of the City on the edge of the World used.

OUR CITY IS PART OF US. WE ARE PART OF OUR CITY. IT RESPONDS TO OUR MINDS AND WE CONTROL IT. THE GESTALT THAT WE HAVE BECOME IS THREATENED. WE HAVE AN ALIEN FORCE WITHIN THE CITY AND WE ARE GEARING TO LOCATE IT. BUT THE MIND OF THIS MAN IS STRONG. IT IS BREAKING DOWN THE FUNCTIONS OF THE CITY. THIS ENDLESS NIGHT IS AN EXAMPLE. WE MUST ALL CON-CENTRATE. WE MUST ALL CONSCIOUSLY FOCUS OUR THOUGHTS TO MAINTAINING THE CITY. THIS THREAT IS OF THE FIRST ORDER. IF OUR CITY DIES, WE DIE.

It was not an announcement in those terms, though that was how Jack interpreted it. The message was much longer and much more complex, but that was what it meant, and he knew he was winning. He was destroying them. Social reform was laughable, they had said.

He would show them.

And so he continued with his lunatic pogrom. He butchered and slaughtered and carved them wherever he found them, and they could not vanish and they could not escape and they could not stop him. The collection of hearts grew to fifty and seventy and then a hundred.

He grew bored with hearts and began cutting out their brains. The collection grew.

For numberless days it went on, and from time to time in the clean, scented autoclave of the City, he could hear the sounds of screaming. His hands were always sticky.

Then he found van Cleef, and leaped from hiding in the darkness to bring her down. He raised the living blade to drive it into her breast, but she

van   ished

He got to his feet and looked around. Van Cleef reappeared ten feet from him. He lunged for her and again she was gone. To reappear ten feet away. Finally, when he had struck at her half a dozen times and she had escaped him each time, he stood panting, arms at sides, looking at her.

And she looked back at him with disinterest.

"You no longer amuse us," she said, moving her lips.

Amuse? His mind whirled down into a place far darker than any he had known before, and through the murk of his blood-lust he began to realize. It had all been for their amusement. They had *let* him do it. They had given him the run of the City, and he had capered and gibbered for them.

Evil? He had never even suspected the horizons of that word. He went for her, but she disappeared with finality.

He was left standing there as the daylight returned. As the City cleaned up the mess, took the butchered bodies and did with them what it had to do. In the freezer chambers the gelatin caps were returned to their niches, no more inhabitants of the City need be thawed to provide Jack the Ripper with utensils for his amusement of the sybarites. His work was truly finished.

He stood there in the empty street. A street that would *always* be empty to him. The people of the City had all along been able to escape him, and now they would. He was finally and completely the clown they had shown him to be. He was not evil, he was pathetic.

He tried to use the living blade on himself, but it dissolved into motes of light and wafted away on a breeze that had blown up for just that purpose.

Alone, he stood there staring at the victorious cleanliness of this Utopia. With their talents they would keep him alive, possibly alive forever, immortal in the possible expectation of needing him for amusement again someday. He was stripped to raw essentials in a mind that was no longer anything more than jelly matter. To go madder and madder, and never to know peace or end or sleep.

He stood there, a creature of dirt and alleys, in a world as pure as the first breath of a baby.

"My name isn't Jack," he said softly. But they would never know his real name. Nor would they care. *"My name isn't Jack!"* he said loudly. No one heard.

"MY NAME ISN'T JACK, AND I'VE BEEN BAD, VERY BAD, I'M AN EVIL PERSON BUT MY NAME ISN'T JACK!" he screamed, and screamed, and screamed again, walking aimlessly down an empty street, in plain view, no longer forced to prowl. A stranger in the City.

~

GENTLEMAN OF THE SHADE

Harry Turtledove

Because his editor insisted that no one would believe his real name was Harry Norman Turtledove (1949–), the author's first novels, *Wereblood* (1979) and *Werenight* (1979), were published under the pseudonym Eric G. Iverson, a name he continued to use until 1985, after which he used his own name for dozens of novels and short stories.

Working in several subgenres of speculative fiction, including science fiction, fantasy, historical fiction, and alternate history, Turtledove is a prolific author, with about one hundred fifty short stories and nearly one hundred novels to his credit, many of the novels being gathered in series. Among his most successful are Videssos (1987–2005), including a cycle of novels that imagines a Byzantine Empire in which one of Julius Caesar's legions exists in a land in which the rules of magic apply to normal life. His Darkness series (1999–2004) also employs the premise of magic existing but is set mainly against a background of global war in medieval Europe. Magic also exists in the War Between the Provinces trilogy (2000–2002), based on the American Civil War but with the positions of the North and South reversed.

Turtledove has received too many honors to count, including three Hugo nominations (winning for best novella in 1994 with "Down in the Bottomlands") and two Nebula nominations; he has been named the guest of honor at more than thirty science fiction and fantasy conventions.

"Gentleman of the Shade" was first published in *Ripper!*, edited by Gardner Dozois and Susan Casper (New York, Tom Doherty Associates, 1988).

The gas flame flickered ever so slightly within its mantle of pearly glass as Hignett opened the door to fetch us in our port and cheeses. All five of us were in the lounge that Friday evening, an uncommon occasion in the annals of the Sanguine Club and one calling therefore for a measure of celebration.

As always, the cheeses went untouched, yet Hignett will insist on setting them out; as well reverse the phases of the moon as expect an English butler to change his habits. But some of us quite favour port, I among them. I have great relish for the fashion in which it makes the sweet blood sing through my veins.

Bowing, Hignett took his leave of us. I poured the tawny port with my own hand. For the toast to the Queen, all of us raised glasses to our lips, as is but fitting. Then, following our custom, we toasted the Club as well, after which those of us who care not for such drink may in honour decline further potations.

Yet whether or not we imbibe, the company of our own kind is precious to us, for we are so few even in London, the greatest city the world has known. Thus it was that we all paid close heed when young Martin said, "I saw in the streets last evening one I reckon will make a sixth for us."

"By Jove!" said Titus. He is the eldest of us, and swears that oath from force of habit. "How long has it been since you joined us, Martin, dear chap?"

"Myself?" Martin rubbed the mustache he has lately taken to wearing. "I don't recollect, exactly. It has been some goodish while, hasn't it?"

"Six!" I exclaimed, suddenly finding new significance in the number. "Then two of us can be away and still leave enough for the whist table!"

Amidst general laughter, Titus said, "Ah, Jerome, this unwholesome passion of yours for the pasteboards does truly make me believe you to have Hoyle's blood in you."

"Surely not, after so long," I replied, which occasioned fresh mirth. I sighed in mock heaviness. "Ah, well, I fear me even so we may go without a game as often as not. But tell me more of the new one, Martin, so as to permit me to indulge my idle fancy."

"You will understand I was upon my own occasions, and so not able to make proper enquiry of him," Martin said, "but there can be little doubt of the matter. Like calls to like, as we all know."

"He noted you, then?" Arnold asked, rising to refill his goblet.

"Oh, I should certainly think so. He stared at me for some moments before proceeding down Buck's Row."

"Buck's Row, is it?" said Titus with an indulgent chuckle. "Out chasing the Whitechapel tarts again like a proper young buck, were you?"

"No denying they're easy to come by there," Martin returned. In that he was, of course, not in error. Every one of us in the Club, I am certain, has resorted to the unfortunate "widows" of Whitechapel to slake his lusts when no finer opportunity presented itself.

"A pity you did not think to have him join you, so you could hunt together," remarked Arnold.

The shadow of a frown passed across Martin's countenance. "I had intended to do so, my friend, yet something, I know not what, stayed my hand. I felt somehow the invitation would be unwelcome to him."

"Indeed!" Titus rumbled indignantly. "If this individual spurns the friendship of an honoured member" ("You honour me, sir," Martin broke in. "Not at all, sir," our Senior replied, before resuming:) "—an honoured member, as I say, of what is, if I may speak with pardonable pride, perhaps the most exclusive club in London, why then, this individual appears to me to be no gentleman, and hence not an appropriate aspirant for membership under any circumstances."

Norton had not taken part in the discussion up to this time, contenting himself with sitting close to the fire and observing the play of the flames. As always when he did choose to speak, his words were to the point. "Nonsense, Titus," he said. "Martin put it well: like calls to like."

"You think we shall encounter him again, then, under circumstances more apt to let us judge his suitability?"

"I am certain of it," Norton replied, nor in the end did he prove mistaken. I often think him the wisest of us all.

The evening passed most pleasantly, as do all our weekly gatherings. Our practice is to meet until midnight, and then to adjourn to seek the less cerebral pleasures the night affords. By the end of August, the sun does not rise until near on five of the clock, granting us no small opportunity to do as we would under the comforting blanket of night.

For myself, I chose to wander the Whitechapel streets. Past midnight, many London districts lay quiet as the crypt. Not so Whitechapel, which like so much of the dissolute East End of the city knows night from day no more than good from evil. The narrow winding streets that change their names from block to block have always their share of traffic. I sought them for that, as I have many times before, but also, I will not deny, in the hope that I might encounter the personage whom Martin had previously met.

That I did not: I supposed him to have sated himself the night before, and so to be in no need of such peregrinations now—here again, as events transpired, I was not in error. Yet this produced in me only the mildest of disappointments for, as I have said, I had other reasons for frequenting Whitechapel.

The clocks were just striking two when I saw coming toward me down Flower and Dean Street a likely-seeming wench. Most of the few lamps such a small, dingy lane merits were long since out, so she was nearly upon me before realizing I was there. She drew back in startlement, fearing, I suppose, me to be some footpad, but then decided from my topper, clawhammer, and brocaded waistcoat that such was not the case.

"Begging your pardon, guvnor," she said, smiling now, "but you did give me 'arf a turn, springing from the shadows like that." She smelled of sweat and beer and sausage.

I bowed myself nearly double, saying, "It is I who must apologize to you, my dear, for frightening so lovely a creature." This is the way the game is played, as it has been from time immemorial.

"Don't you talk posh, now!" she exclaimed. She put her hands on her hips, looking saucily up at me. She was a fine strong trollop, with rounded haunches and a shelflike bosom that she thrust my way; plainly she profited better from her whoring than so many of the skinny lasses who peddle their wares in Whitechapel. Her voice turned crooning, coaxing. "Only sixpence, sir, for a night to remember always."

Her price was more than that of the usual Whitechapel tart, but had I been other than I, I daresay I should have found her worth the difference. As it was, I hesitated only long enough to find the proper coin and press it into her hand. She peered down through the gloom to ensure I had not cheated her, then pressed her warm, firm body against me. "What's your pleasure, love?" she murmured in my ear, her tongue teasing at it between words.

When I led her to a wall in deeper darkness, she gave forth a tiny sigh, having I supposed hoped to ply her trade at leisure in a bed. She hiked up her skirts willingly enough, though, and her mouth sought mine with practiced art. Her hands fumbled at my trouser buttons while my teeth nibbled her lower lip.

"'Ave a care," she protested, twisting in my embrace. "I'd not like for you to make me bleed." Then she sighed again, a sound different from that which had gone before, and stood stockstill and silent as one made into a statue. Her skirts rustled to the ground once more. I bent my head to her white neck and began to feed.

Were it not for the amnesic and anaesthetic agent contained within our spittle, I do not doubt that humans should have hounded us vampires to extinction a long age ago. Even as is, they remain uneasily aware of our existence, though less so, I own to my relief, in this teeming faceless metropolis of London where no one knows his neighbour, or cares to, than in the hidden faraway mountains and valleys whence our kind sprang and where folk memory and fear run back for ever.

When I had drunk my fill, I passed my tongue over the twin wounds I had inflicted, whereupon they healed with the same rapidity as does my own flesh. The whore stirred then. What her dreams were I cannot say, but they must have been sweet, for she declared roundly, "Ah, sir, you can do me any time, and for free if you're hard up." Greater praise can no courtesan give. She seemed not a whit perplexed at the absence of any spunk of mine dribbling down her fat thighs; doubtless she had coupled with another recently enough beforehand so as not to miss it.

She entreated me for another round, but I begged off, claiming adequate satisfaction, as was indeed the case. We went our separate ways, each well pleased with the other.

She had just turned down Osborn Street towards Christ Church and I was about to enter on Commercial Street when I spied one who had to be he whom Martin had previously encountered. His jaunty stride and erect carriage proclaimed him recently to have fed, and fed well, yet somehow I found myself also aware of Titus's stricture, delivered sight unseen, that here was no gentleman. I could find no concrete reason for this feeling, and was about to dismiss it as a vagary of my own when he also became aware of my presence.

His grin was mirthless; while his cold eyes still held me, he slowly ran his tongue over his lips, as if to say he was fain to drink from my veins. My shock and revulsion must have appeared on my features, for his smile grew wider yet. He bowed so perfectly as to make perfection itself a mockery, then disappeared.

I know not how else to put it. We have of course sometimes the ability briefly to cloud a mere man's mind, but I had never thought, never imagined the occasion could arise, to turn this power upon my own kind. Only the trick's surprise, I think, lent it success, but success, at least a moment's worth, it undeniably had. By the time I recovered full use of my faculties, the crass japester was gone.

I felt angry enough, nearly, to go in pursuit of him. Yet the sun would rise at five, and my flat lay in Knightsbridge, no small distance away. Reluctantly I turned my step toward the Aldgate Station. As well I did; the train was late, and morning twilight was already painting the eastern horizon with bright colors when I neared home.

The streets by then were filling with the legions of waggons London requires for her daily revictualing. Newsboys stood on every corner hawking their papers. I spent a penny and tucked one away for later reading, time having grown too short for me to linger.

My landlady is of blessedly incurious nature; so long as the rent is promptly paid and an appearance of quiet and order maintained, she does not wonder at one of her tenants not being seen abroad by day. All of us of the Sanguine Club have digs of this sort: another advantage of the metropolis over lesser towns, where folk of such mercenary nature are in shorter supply. Did they not exist, we should be reduced to squalid, hole-and-corner ways of sheltering ourselves from the sun, ways in ill accord with the style we find pleasing once night has fallen.

The setting of the sun having restored my vitality, I glanced through the paper I had purchased before. The headlines screamed of a particularly grisly murder done in Whitechapel in the small hours of the previous day. Being who and what I am, such does not easily oppress me, but the details of the killing—for the paper proved to be of the lurid sort—did give me more than momentary pause.

I soon dismissed them from my mind, however, being engaged in going up and down in the city in search of profit. Men with whom I deal often enough for them to note my nocturnal habit ask no more questions on it than my landlady, seeing therein the chance to mulct me by virtue of my ignorance of the day's events. At times they even find their efforts crowned with success, but, if I may be excused for boasting, infrequently. I have matched myself against their kind too long now to be easily fooled. Most of the losses I suffer are self-inflicted.

I could be, I suppose, a Croesus or a Crassus, but to what end? The truly rich become conspicuous by virtue of their wealth, and such prominence is a luxury, perhaps the one luxury, I cannot afford. My road to safety lies in drawing no attention to myself.

At the next gathering of the Club, that being Friday the seventh, only four of us were in attendance, Martin having either business similar to mine or the need to replenish himself at one of the multitudinous springs of life abounding in the city. By then the Whitechapel slaying was old news, and occasioned no conversation: none of us, full of the wisdom long years bring though we are, yet saw the danger from that direction.

We spoke instead of the new one. I added the tale of my brief encounter to what Martin had related at the previous meeting, and found I was not the only one to have seen the subject of our discussion. So also had Titus and Norton, both in the East End.

Neither appeared to have formed a favourable impression of the newcomer, though as was true with Martin and myself, neither had passed words with him. Said our Senior, "He may eventually make a sixth for us, but no denying he has a rougher manner than do those whose good company now serves to warm these rooms."

Norton being Norton was more plain-spoken: "Like calls to like, as I said last week, and I wish it didn't."

Of those present, only Arnold had not yet set eyes on the stranger. He now enquired, "What in him engenders such aversion?"

To that none of the rest of us could easily reply, the more so as nothing substantial backed our hesitancy. At last Norton said, "He strikes me as the sort who, were he hungry, would feed on Hignett."

"On our own servant? I should sooner starve!"

"So should we all, Arnold, so should we all," Titus said soothingly, for the shock in our fellow's voice was quite apparent. Norton and I gave our vigorous agreement. Some things are not done.

We decided it more prudent for a time not to seek out the newcomer. If he showed any greater desire than heretofore for intercourse with us, he could without undue difficulty contrive to make his path cross one of ours. If not, loss of his society seemed a hardship under which we could bear up with equanimity.

Having settled that, as we thought, to our satisfaction, we adjourned at my urging to cards, over which we passed the balance of the meeting, Arnold and I losing three guineas each to Norton and Titus. There are mortals, and not a few of them too, with better card sense than Arnold's. Once we broke up, I hunted in Mayfair with good enough luck and went home.

Upon arising on the evening of the eighth, my first concern was a paper, as I had not purchased one before retiring and as the newsboys were crying them with a fervour warning that something of which I should not be ignorant had passed during the hours of my undead sleep. And so it proved: at some time near 5:30 that morning, about when I was going up to bed, the Whitechapel killer had slain again, as hideously as before, the very least of his atrocities being the cutting of his victim's throat so savagely as almost to sever her head from her body.

Every one of the entrepreneurs with whom I had dealings that evening mentioned of his own accord the murders. An awful fascination lay beneath their ejaculations of horror. I had no trouble understanding it. A madman who kills once is frightening, but one who kills twice is far more than doubly so, the second slaying portending who could say how many more to come.

This fear, not surprisingly, was all the worse among those whom the killer had marked for his own. Few tarts walked the streets the next several evenings, and such as did often went in pairs to afford themselves at least what pitiful protection numbers gave. I had a lean time of it, in which misfortune, as I learned at the next meeting of the Club, I was not alone. For the first time in some years we had not even a quorum, three of our five being absent, presumably in search of sustenance. The gathering, if by that name I may dignify an occasion on which only Arnold and I were present, was the worst I remember, and ended early, something hitherto unknown among us. Nor did my business affairs prosper in the nights that followed. I have seldom known a less pleasant period.

At length, despite our resolutions to the contrary, I felt compelled to visit the new one's haunts in the East End. I suspect I was not the first of us driven to this step. Twelve hundred drabs walk the brown-fogged streets of Whitechapel, and hunger works in them no less than in me. Fear of the knife that may come fades to insignificance when set against the rumbling of the belly that never leaves.

I did then eventually manage to gain nourishment, but only after a search long and inconvenient enough to leave me rather out of temper despite my success. Not to put too fine a point on it, I should have chosen another time to make the acquaintance of our new associate. The choice proved not to be mine to make: he hailed me as I was walking toward St. Mary's Station on Whitechapel Road.

Something in the timbre of his voice spoke to me, though I had not heard it before; even as I turned, I knew who he was. He hurried up to me and pumped my hand. We must have made a curious spectacle for those few people who witnessed our meeting. Like all members of the Sanguine Club, I dress to suit my station; moreover, formal attire with its stark blacks and whites fits my temperament, and I have been told I look well in it.

My new companion, by contrast, wore a checked suit of cut and pattern so bold as to be more appropriate for the comedic stage than even for a swell in the streets of Whitechapel. Of his tie I will say nothing save that it made the suit stodgy by comparison. His boots were patent-leather, with mother-of-pearl buttons. On his head perched a low-crowned billycock hat as evil as the rest of the rig.

I should not have been surprised to smell on his breath whisky or more likely gin (the favoured drink of Whitechapel), but must confess I could not. "Hullo, old chap," he said, his accent exactly what one would expect from the clothes. "You must be one o' the toffs I've seen now and again. The name's Jack, and pleased t'meetcher."

Still a bit nonplussed at such heartiness where before he had kept his distance, I rather coolly returned my own name.

"Pleased t'meetcher," he said again, as if once were not enough. Now that he stood close by, I had the chance to study him as well as his villainous apparel. He was taller than I, and younger seeming (though among us, I know, this is of smaller signification than is the case with mankind), with greasy side-whiskers like, you will I pray forgive me, a pimp's.

Having repeated himself, he appeared to have shot his conversational bolt, for he stood waiting for some response from me. "Do you by any chance play whist?" I asked, lacking any better query.

He threw back his head and laughed loud and long. "Blimey, no! I've better games than that, yes I do." He set a finger by the side of his nose and winked with a familiarity he had no right to assume.

"What are those?" I asked, seeing he expected it of me. In truth I heartily wished the encounter over. We have long made it a point to extend the privileges of the Sanguine Club to all our kind in London, but despite ancient custom I would willingly have withheld them from this Jack, whose vulgarity disbarred him from our class.

This thought must have been plain on my face, as he laughed again, less good-naturedly than before. "Why, the ones wiv dear Pollie and Annie, of course."

The names so casually thrown out meant nothing to me for a moment. When at last I did make the connection, I took it to be no more than a joke of taste similar to the rest of his character. "Claiming yourself to be Leather Apron, sir, or whatever else the papers call that killer, is not a jest I find amusing."

"Jest, is it?" He drew himself up, offended. "I wasn't jokin' wiv yer. Ah, Annie, she screamed once, but too late." His eyes lit in, I saw, fond memory. That more than anything else convinced me he spoke the truth.

I wished then the sign of the cross were not forbidden me. Still, I fought to believe my fear mistaken. "You cannot mean that!" I cried. "The second killing, by all accounts, was done in broad daylight, and—" I forbore to state the obvious, that none of our kind may endure Old Sol.

"Oh, it were daylight, right enough, but the sun not up. I 'ad just time to do 'er proper, then nip into my 'idin' place on 'Anbury Street. The bobbies, they never found me," he added with scorn in his voice for the earnest bumbling humans who sought to track him down. However much I found the thought repugnant, I saw he was truly one of us in that, his sentiment differing perhaps in degree from our own, but not in kind.

I observed also once more the relish with which he spoke of the slaying, and of his hairsbreadth escape from destruction; the sun is a greater danger to us than ever Scotland Yard will be. Still, we of the Sanguine Club have survived and flourished as we have in London by making it a point never to draw undue attention to ourselves. Being helpless by day, we are hideously vulnerable should a determined foe ever set himself against us. I said as much to Jack, most vehemently, but saw at once I was making no impression upon him.

"Aren't you the toffee-nose, now?" he said. "I didn't ask for no by-your-leave, and don't need one of you neither. You bloody fool, they're only people, and I'll deal wiv 'em just as I please. Go on; tell me you've not done likewise."

To that I could make no immediate reply. I have fed innumerable times from victims who would have recoiled in loathing if in full possession of their senses. Nor am I myself guiltless of killing; few if any among us are. Yet with reflection, I think I may say I have never slain wantonly, for the mere sport of it. Such conduct must inevitably debase one who employs it, and in Jack I could not help noting the signs of that defilement. Having no regard for our prey, he would end with the same emptiness of feeling for his fellows (a process I thought already well advanced, by his rudeness toward me) and for himself. I have seen madness so many times among humanity, but never thought to detect it in one of my own.

All this is, however, as I say, the product of rumination considerably after the fact. At the time I found myself so very unnerved as to fasten on utter trivialities as if they were matters of great importance. I asked, then, not that he give over his cruel sport, but rather where he had come by the apron that gave him his sobriquet in the newspapers.

He answered without hesitation: "Across the lane from where I done the first one is Barber's 'Orse Slaughter 'Ouse—I filched it there, just after I 'ad me bit o' fun. Fancy the fools thinkin' it 'as some meanin' to it." His amusement confirmed what I had already marked, that he found humanity so far beneath him that it existed but for him to do with as he wished.

Again I expostulated with him, urging him to turn from his course of slaughter.

"Bloody 'ell I will," he said coarsely. "Oo's to make me, any road? The bobbies? They couldn't catch the clap in an 'ore-house."

At last I began to grow angry myself, rather than merely appalled, as I had been up to this point. "If necessary, my associates and I shall prevent you. If you risked only yourself, I would say do as you please and be damned to you, but your antics threaten all of us, for if by some mischance you are captured, you expose not only your own presence alone but reveal that of your kind as well. We have been comfortable in London for long years; we should not care to have to abandon it suddenly and seek to establish ourselves elsewhere on short notice."

I saw this warning, at least, hit home; Jack might despise mankind, but could scarcely ignore the threat his fellows might pose to him. "You've no right to order me about so," he said sullenly, his hands curling into fists.

"The right to self-preservation knows no bounds," I returned. "I am willing to let what is done stay done; we can hardly, after all, yield you up to the constabulary without showing them also what you are. But no more, Jack. You will have us to reckon with if you kill again."

For an instant I thought he would strike me, such was the ferocity suffusing his features. I resolved he should not relish the attempt if he made it. But he did not, contenting himself instead with turning his back and wordlessly taking himself off in the rudest fashion imaginable. I went on to the station and then to my home.

At the next meeting of the Club I discovered I had not been the only one to encounter Jack and hear his boasts. So also had Norton, who, I was pleased to learn, had issued a warning near identical to mine. If anything, he was blunter than I; Norton, as I have remarked, is not given to mincing words. Our actions met with general approbation, Martin being the only one to express serious doubt at what we had done.

As the youngest among us (he has been a member fewer than two hundred years), Martin is, I fear, rather more given than the rest of us to the passing intellectual vagaries of the mass of humanity, and has lately been much taken with what they call psychology. He said, "Perhaps this Jack acts as he does because he has been deprived of the company of his own kind, and would be more inclined toward sociability in the world as a whole if his day-to-day existence included commerce with his fellows."

This I found a dubious proposition; having met Jack, I thought him vicious to the core, and not likely to reform merely through the good agency of the Club. Norton confined himself to a single snort, but the fashion in which he rolled his eyes was eloquent.

Titus and Arnold, however, with less acquaintance of the newcomer, eagerly embraced Martin's suggestion: the prospect of adding another to our number after so long proved irresistible to them. After some little argument, I began to wonder myself if I had not been too harsh a judge of Jack, nor did Norton protest overmuch when it was decided to tender an invitation to the Club to him for the following Friday, that is to say 21 September.

I remarked on Norton's reticence as we broke up, and was rewarded with a glance redolent of cynicism. "They'll find out," he said, and vanished into the night.

It was with a curious mingling of anticipation and apprehension that I entered the premises of the Club for our next meeting, an exhilarating mixture whose like I had not known since the bad nights when all of mankind was superstitious enough to make our kind's every moment a risk. Titus was there before me, his features communicating the same excitement I felt. At that I knew surprise afresh, Titus having seen everything under the moon: he derives his name, after all, from that of the Roman Augustus in whose reign he was born.

"He'll come?" I asked.

"So Martin tells me," replied our Senior.

And indeed it was not long before good Hignett appeared at the lounge door to announce the arrival of our guest. Being the perfect butler, he breathes discretion no less than air, yet I could hear no hint of approval in his voice. What tone he would have taken had he known more of Jack I can only imagine. Even now his eye lingered doubtfully on the newcomer, whose garments were as gaudy as the ones in which I had first met him, and which contrasted most strikingly with the sober raiment we of the Sanguine Club commonly prefer.

After leaving the port and the inevitable cheeses, Hignett retired to grant us our privacy. We spent some moments taking the measure of the stranger in our midst, while he, I should think, likewise took ours. He addressed us first, commenting, "What a grim lot o' sobersides y'are."

"Your plumage is certainly brighter than ours, but beneath it we are much the same," said Martin, still proceeding along the lines he had proposed at our previous session.

"Oh, balls," Jack retorted; he still behaved as though on the Whitechapel streets rather than in one of the more refined salons London boasts. Norton and I exchanged a knowing glance. Titus's raised eyebrow was eloquent as a shout.

Martin, however, remained as yet undaunted, and persisted, "But we are. The differences between you and us, whatever they may be, are as nothing when set against the difference between the lot of us on the one hand and those among whom we dwell on the other."

"Why ape 'em so, then?" asked Jack, dismissing with a sneer our crystal and plate, and overstuffed chintz chairs in which we sat, our carpets and our paneling of carved and polished oak, our gaslight which yields an illumination more like that of the sun (or so say those who can compare the two) than any previously created, in short all the amenities that serve to make the Sanguine Club the pleasant haven it is. His scorn at last made an impression upon Martin, who knew not how to respond.

"Why should we not like our comforts, sir?" Titus, as I have found in the course of our long association, is rarely at a loss for words. He continued, "We have been in straitened circumstances more often than I can readily recall, and more than I for one should care to. Let me remind you, no one compels you to share in this against your will."

"An' a good thing, too—I'd sooner drink 'orseblood from Barber's, I would, than 'ave a digs like this. Blimey, next you'll be joinin' the bleedin' Church o' Hengland."

"Now you see here!" Arnold, half-rising from his seat in anger, spoke for all of us. Horseblood is an expedient upon which I have not had to rely since the Black Death five and a half centuries ago made men both too scarce and too wary to be easily approached. To this night I shudder at the memory of the taste, as do all those of us whom mischance has at one time or another reduced to such a condition. I almost found it more shocking than the notion of entering a church.

Yet Jack displayed no remorse, which indeed, as should by this point be apparent, played no part in his character. "Get on!" he said. "You might as well be people your own selves, way you carry on. They ain't but our cattle, and don't deserve better from us than they give their beasts."

"If what Jerome and Norton say is true, you give them rather worse than that," Titus said.

Jack's grin was broad and insolent. "Aye, well, we all have our sports. I like making 'em die monstrous well, better even than feeding off 'em." He drew from his belt a long sharp blade, and lowered his eyes so as to study the gleaming, polished steel. Did our reflections appear in mirrors, I should have said he was examining his features in the metal.

"But you must not act so," Titus expostulated. "Can you not grasp that your slayings endanger not you alone, but all of us? These cattle, as you call them, possess the ability to turn upon their predators and hunt us down. They must never suspect themselves to be prey."

"You talk like this bugger 'ere," said Jack, pointing in my direction. "I were wrong, guvnor, an' own it—it's not men the lot of yez are, it's so many old women. An' as for Jack, 'e does as 'e pleases, an' any as don't fancy it can go play wiv themselves for all 'e cares."

"Several of us have warned you of the consequences of persisting in your folly," said Titus in a voice like that of a magistrate passing sentence. "Let me say now that you may consider that warning to come from the Sanguine Club as a whole." He looked from one of us to the next, and found no dissent to his pronouncement, even Martin by this time having come to realize our now unwelcome guest was not amenable to reason.

"You try an' stop me and I'll give yer what Pollie an' Annie got," Jack shouted in a perfect transport of fury, brandishing the weapon with which he had so brutally let the life from the two poor jades. We were, however, many to his one, and not taken by surprise as had been his earlier victims. Norton seized the knife that sat among Hignett's despised cheeses. Of the rest of us, several, myself included, carried blades of our own, if not so vicious as the one Jack bore.

Balked thus even of exciting terror, Jack foully cursed us all and fled, being as I suspected too great a coward to attack without the odds all in his favour. He slammed the door behind him with violence to make my goblet of port spring from the end table where it sat and hurtle to the floor. Only the quickness of my kind enabled me to save it from destruction and thus earn, though he would never know of it, Hignett's gratitude.

The crash of Jack's abrupt departure was still ringing in our ears when Martin most graciously turned to me and said, "You and Norton appear to have been correct; my apologies for doubting you."

"We shall have to watch him," Titus said. "I fear he will pay no heed to our advice."

"We shall also have to keep watch over Whitechapel as a whole, from this time forth," Arnold said. "He may escape our close surveillance, yet be deterred by observing our vigilance throughout the district."

"We must make the attempt, commencing this very night," Titus declared, again with no disagreement. "That is a mad dog loose on the streets of London, mad enough, I fear, to enable even the purblind humans of Scotland Yard eventually to run him to earth."

"Which will also endanger us," I put in.

"Precisely. If, however, we prevent his slaying again, the hue and cry over this pair of killings will eventually subside. As we are all gathered here now, let us agree on a rotation that will permit at least three of us to patrol Whitechapel each night, and" (here Titus paused to utter a heavy sigh) "all of us on our Fridays. Preservation here must take precedence over sociability."

There was some grumbling at that, but not much; one thing our years confer upon us is the ability to see what must be done. Hignett evinced signs of distress when we summoned him from downstairs long before the time usually appointed, and more upon being informed we should not be reconvening for some indefinite period. Not even the promise that his pay would continue heartened him to any great extent; he had grown used to our routine, and naturally resented any interruption thereof.

Having decided to patron Whitechapel, we walked west along the south bank of the Thames past the Tower of London and the edifice that will upon its completion be known as Tower Bridge (and which would, were it complete, offer us more convenient access to the northeastern part of the city) to London Bridge and up Gracechurch Street to Fenchurch Street and Whitechapel. Once there, we separated, to cover as much ground as our limited numbers permitted.

Jack had by this time gained a considerable lead upon us; we could but hope he had worked no mischief while we were coming to the decision to pursue him. Yet the evening was still relatively young, and both of his previous atrocities had taken place in later hours, the second, indeed, so close to sunrise as to seem to me to display a heedlessness to danger suitable only to a lunatic among our kind.

I prowled the lanes near Spitalfields Market, not far from where I had first set eyes on Jack after supping off the young whore, as I have already related. I should not have been sorry to encounter her there once more, since, I having in a manner of speaking made her acquaintance, she would not have shied from my approach, as did several ladies of the evening, and I was, if not yet ravenous, certainly growing hungry.

It must have been nearing three when I spied Jack in Crispin Street, between Dorset and Brushfield. He was coming up behind a tart when I hailed him; they both turned at the sound of my voice. "Ah, cousin Jack, how are you these days?" I called cheerily, pretending not to have noticed her. In my most solicitous tones I continued, "The pox troubles you less, I hope?"

"Piss off!" he snarled. The damage to his cause, however, was done, for the whore speedily took herself elsewhere. He shook his fist at me. "You'll pay for that, you bugger. I only wanted a bit of a taste from 'er."

"Starve," I said coldly, our enmity now open and undisguised. Would that keeping him from his prey might have forced that fate upon him, but we do not perish so easily. Still, the hunger for blood grows maddening if long unsatisfied, and I realized his suffering hardly less than he the twin effusions of gore he had visited upon Whitechapel.

He slunk away; I followed. He employed all the tricks of our kind to throw me off his track. Against a man they would surely have succeeded, but I was ready for them and am in any case no man, though here I found myself in the curious position of defending humanity against one of my own kind gone bad. He failed to escape me. Indeed, as we went down Old Montague Street, Arnold fell in with us, and he and I kept double vigil on Jack till the sky began to grow light.

The weakness of our plan then became apparent, for Arnold and I found ourselves compelled to withdraw to our own domiciles in distant parts of the city to protect ourselves against the imminent arrival of the sun, while Jack, who evidently quartered himself in or around Whitechapel, was at liberty to carry out whatever outrage he could for some little while before finding it necessary to seek shelter. A similar period of freedom would be his after every sunset, as we would have to travel from our homes to the East End and locate him afresh each night. Still, I reflected as I made my way out of the slums towards Knightsbridge, in the early hours of the evening people swarmed through the streets, making the privacy and leisure required for his crimes hard to come by. That gave me some small reason, at least, to hope.

Yet I must confess that when nightfall restored my vitality I departed from my flat with no little trepidation, fearing to learn of some new work of savagery during the morning twilight. The newsboys were, however, using other means to cry their papers, and I knew relief. The concern of getting through each night was new to me, and rather invigorating; it granted a bit of insight into the sort of existence mortals must lead.

That was not one of the nights assigned me to wander through Whitechapel, nor on my next couple of tours of duty there did I set eyes on Jack. The newspapers made no mention of fresh East End horrors, though, so the Sanguine Club was performing as well as Titus could have wished.

Our Senior, however, greeted me with grim and troubled countenance as we met on Fenchurch Street early in the evening of the twenty-seventh, preparatory to our nightly Whitechapel vigil. He drew from his waistcoat pocket an envelope which he handed to me, saying, "The scoundrel grows bolder. I stopped by the Club briefly last night to pay my respects to Hignett, and found this waiting there for us."

The note the envelope contained was to the point, viz.: "You dear chums aren't as clever as you think. You won't catch me if I don't want that. And remember, you haven't found my address but I know where this place is. Give me trouble— not that you really can—and the peelers will too. Yours, Jack the Ripper."

"The Ripper, is it?" My lip curled at the grotesque sobriquet, and also at the tone of the missive and the threat it conveyed. Titus perfectly understood my sentiments, having no doubt worked through during the course of the previous night the thought process now mine.

He said, "We shall have to consider harsher measures than we have contemplated up to this point. A menace to the Club is a menace to us all, individually and severally."

I nodded my affirmation. Yet to suppress Jack we had first to find him, which proved less easy than heretofore. Norton and I met in the morning twilight of the twenty-eighth at St. Mary's Station without either one of us having set eyes on him. "He may be staying indoors for fear of our response to his note," I said, having first informed Norton of the letter's contents.

My dour colleague gloomily shook his head. "He fears nothing, else he would not have sent it in the first place." Norton paused a while in silent thought—an attitude not uncommon for him—then continued, "My guess is, he is merely deciding what new atrocity to use to draw attention to himself." I did not care for this conclusion but, in view of Jack's already demonstrated proclivities, hardly found myself in position to contradict it.

The night of Saturday the twenty-ninth found me in the East End once more. (Most of the previous evening, when under happier circumstances the Sanguine Club would have met, I spent beating down a most stubborn man over the price of a shipment of copra, and was sorely tempted to sink teeth into his neck afterwards to repay him for the vexation and delay he caused me. I had not thought the transaction would take above an hour, but the wretch haggled over every farthing. Titus was most annoyed at my failure to join our prearranged patrol, and I counted myself fortunate that Jack again absented himself as well.)

Early in the evening I thought I caught a glimpse of Jack by London Hospital as I was coming down Mount Street from Whitechapel Road, but though I hastened up and down Oxford Street, and Philpot and Turner which come off it, I could find no certain trace. Full of vague misgivings, I turned west onto Commercial Road.

Midnight passed, and I still had no idea of my quarry's whereabouts. I had by chance encountered both Martin and Arnold, who shared the night with me, and learned of their equal lack of success. "I believe he must still be in hiding, in the hope of waiting us out," Arnold said.

"If so, I replied, "he is in yet another way a fool. Does he think us mortals, to grow bored after days or weeks and let down our guard?"

The answer to that soon became all too clear. At one or so a great outcry arose on Berner Street, scarcely an hundred yards from Commercial Road where I had walked but a short while before. As soon as I heard the words "Leather Apron," I knew Jack had chosen to strike again in defiance not only in human London, but also of the Sanguine Club, and also that he had succeeded in evading us, making good the boast in his recent note.

I started to rush toward the scene of this latest crime, but had not gone far before I checked myself. I reasoned that Jack could scarcely strike again in or close to such a crowd, if that was his desire, but would take advantage of the confusion this murder engendered, and of the natural attraction of the constabulary in the area to it. It was Norton's reasoning that made me fear Jack would not be content with a single slaying, but might well look at once for a fresh victim to demonstrate everyone's impotence in bringing him to heel.

My instinct proved accurate, yet I was unfortunately not in time to prevent Jack's next gruesome crime; that I came so close only served to frustrate me more thoroughly than abject failure would have done. I was trotting west along Fenchurch Street, about to turn down Jewry Street to go past the Fenchurch Street Station, as the hour approached twenty of two, when suddenly there came to my nose the thick rich scent of fresh-spilled blood.

Being who I am, that savoury aroma draws me irresistibly, and I am by the nature of things more sensitive to it by far than is a man, or even, I should say, a hound. Normally it would have afforded me only pleasure, but now I felt alarm as well, realizing that the large quantity required to produce the odour in the intensity with which I perceived it could only have come from the sort of wounds Jack delighted in producing.

I followed my nose up Mitre Street to a courtyard off the roadway, where, as I had feared, lay the body of a woman. Despite the sweetness of the blood-tang rising intoxicatingly from her and from the great pool of gore on the paving, I confess with shame to drawing back in horror, for not only had she been eviscerated, but her throat was slashed, her features mutilated almost beyond identity, and part of one earlobe nearly severed from her head.

I had time to learn no more than that, or to feed past the briefest sampling, for I heard coming up Mitre Street the firm, uncompromising tread likely in that part of the city to belong only to a bobby, footpads and whores being more circumspect and men of good conscience in short supply. I withdrew from the court, thankful for my ability to move with silence and not to draw the eye if I did not wish it. Hardly a minute later, the blast of a police whistle pierced the night as humanity discovered this latest piece of Jack's handiwork.

As I once more walked Mitre Street, I discovered the odour of blood to be diminishing less rapidly than I should have expected. Looking down, I discovered a drop on the pavement. I stooped to taste of it; I could not doubt its likeness to that which I had just tried. A bit further along the street was another. I hastened down this track, hoping also to discover one of my fellows to lend me assistance in overpowering Jack. As if in answer to my wish, up came Martin from a side street, drawn like me by the pull of blood. Together we hastened after Jack.

The drippings from his hand or knife soon ceased, yet the alluring aroma still lingering in the air granted us a trail we could have followed blindfolded. I wondered how Jack hoped to escape pursuers of our sort, but soon found he knew the East End better than did Martin or myself, and was able to turn that knowledge to his advantage.

On Goldstone Street, in front of the common stairs leading to Nos. 108 to 119, stood a public sink. It was full of water, water which my nose at once informed me to be tinctured with blood: here Jack had paused to rinse from his hands the traces of his recent deeds. Martin found also a bit of bloodstained black cloth similar to that of a garment the latest unfortunate victim had worn.

At the base of the sink, close by the piece of fabric, lay a lump of chalk. I picked it up and tossed it in the air idly once or twice, then, thinking back on Jewry Street where I had been when first I detected Jack's newest abomination, was seized by inspiration. The Jews of London form a grouping larger than we of the Sanguine Club, yet hardly less despised than we would become were Jack's insanity finally to expose our identity to the general populace. How better, thought I, to distract suspicion from us than by casting it upon others themselves in low repute? Above the sink, then, I chalked, "The Jewes are the men who will not be blamed for nothing," a message ambiguous enough, or so I hoped, to excite attention without offering any definite information. And when Martin would have removed the bloodstained cloth, I prevailed on him to replace it, to draw the eyes and thoughts of the constabulary to my scrawled note.

Martin and I attempted to resume our pursuit, but unsuccessfully. In washing himself and, I believe, cleansing his blade on the rag from his victim's apron, he removed the lingering effluvium by which we had followed him, and forced us to rely once more on chance to bring us into proximity to him. Chance did not prove kind, even when we separated in order to cover more ground than would have been possible in tandem. Just as he had bragged, Jack had slain again (and slain twice!), eluding all attempts to stay his hand.

I was mightily cast down in spirit as I travelled homeward in the morning twilight. Nor did the clamour in the papers the next evening and during the nights that followed serve to assuage my anxiety. "Revolting and mysterious," "horrible," and "ghastly" were among the epithets they applied to the slayings; "Whitechapel horrors," shrieked *The Illustrated Police News*. It was, however, a subhead in that same paper which truly gave me cause for concern: it spoke of the latest "victim of the Whitechapel Fiend," a designation whose aptness I knew only too well, and one which I could only hope would not be literally construed.

Titus must also have seen that paper and drawn the same conclusion as had I. When I came to myself on the evening of the second I found in my postbox a note in his classic hand. "Henceforward we must all fare forth nightly," he wrote, "to prevent a repetition of these latest acts of depravity. We owe this duty not only to ourselves but to our flock, lest they suffer flaying rather than the judicious shearing we administer."

Put so, the plea was impossible to withstand. All of us prowled the sordid streets of Whitechapel the next few nights, and encountered one another frequently. Of Jack, however, we found no sign; once more he chose to hide himself in his lair. Yet none of us, now, was reassured on that account, and when he did briefly sally forth he worked as much mischief, almost, without spilling a drop of blood as he had with his knife.

We failed to apprehend him in his forays, but their results soon became apparent. The lunatic, it transpired, had not merely written to us of the Sanguine Club, but also, in his arrogance, to the papers and the police! They, with wisdom unusual in humans, had suppressed his earliest missive, sent around the same time as the one to us, perhaps being uncertain as to its authenticity, but he sent another note after the horrid morning of the thirtieth, boasting of what he termed his "Double Event." As the police had not yet announced the murders, not even men could doubt its genuineness.

Once more the press went mad, filled with lurid rehashes and speculations, some claiming the Ripper (for so he had styled himself also in his public letters) to be a man seeking to stamp out the vice of prostitution (presumably by extirpating those who plied the trade), others taking varying psychological tacks which intrigued our faddish Martin with their crackbrained ingenuity and left the rest of us sourly amused, still others alleging Jack a deranged *shochet*.

"Your work takes credit there, Jerome," Titus remarked to me as we chanced upon each other one evening not far from the place where Jack's last victim had died. "A madman of a ritual slaughterer fits the particulars of the case well."

"The Jews always make convenient scapegoats," I replied.

"How true," Titus murmured, and again I was reminded of the Caesar for whom he had been named.

Other, darker conjectures also saw print, though, ones I could not view without trepidation. For those Jack himself was responsible, due to a bit of sport he had had with the police after his second killing: after slaying Annie Chapman, he had torn two rings from her fingers and set them with some pennies and a pair of new-minted farthings at her feet. This he had wasted time to do, I thought with a frisson of dread, as the sun was on the point of rising and ending his amusements for ever! It naturally brought to mind black, sorcerous rituals of unknown but doubtless vile purpose, and thoughts of sorcery and of matters in any way unmundane were the last things I desired to see inculcated in the folk of London.

I did my best to set aside my worries. For all Jack's dark skill, murder no longer came easy in Whitechapel. Aside from us of the Sanguine Club, the constabulary increased their patrols in the district, while a certain Mr. George Lusk established a Whitechapel Vigilance Committee whose membership also went back and forth through the area.

Neither constables nor Committee members, I noted during my own wanderings, refrained from enjoying the occasional streetwalker, but the women themselves took more pleasure from those encounters than they should have from a meeting with Jack. The same also holds true for the whores we of the Club engaged. As I have previously noted, the wounds we inflicted healed quickly, the only aftereffect being perhaps a temporary lassitude if one of us feed over-deep because of unusual hunger.

Jack may have taken a hiatus from slaughter, but remained intent on baiting those who so futilely pursued him. October was not yet a week old when he showed his scorn for the Whitechapel Vigilance Committee by means of a macabre gift to its founder: he sent Mr. Lusk, in a neatly wrapped cardboard box, half the kidney of his latest victim, with a mocking note enclosed.

"He will be the ruin of us all," I said gloomily to Martin upon the papers' disclosure of this new ghoulery. "Would you had never set eyes on him."

"With that I cannot take issue," replied my colleague, "yet this lapse, however revolting humans may find it—and I confess," he added with a fastidious shudder, "to being repelled myself at the prospect of eating a piece from a woman's kidney—however revolting, I say, it does not add to any fears directed toward us, for none of our kind would do such a deed, not even Jack, I should say."

"One never knows, where he is concerned," I said, and Martin's only response was a glum nod.

As October wore on, more letters came to the papers and police, each one setting off a flurry of alarm. Some of these may indeed have been written by Jack; others, I suspect, sprang from the pens of men hardly less mad than he, and fully as eager for notoriety. Men have so little time to make their mark that such activity is in them at least faintly comprehensible, but for Jack, with years beyond limit before him, I offer no explanation past simple viciousness. In his instance, that was more than adequate.

Still, despite sensations such as I have described, the month progressed with fresh slayings. Once I dashed a couple of furlongs down Old Montague Street into Bakers Row, drawn as on the night of the Double Event by the scent of blood, but discovered only a stabbed man of middle years with his pockets turned out: a matter in which the police were certain to take an interest, but not one, I was confident, that concerned me.

My business affairs suffered somewhat during this period, but not to any irreparable extent; at bottom they were sound, and not liable to sudden disruption. I thought I would miss the weekly society of the Sanguine Club to a greater degree than proved to be the case. The truth is that we of the Club saw more of one another in our wanderings through Whitechapel than we had at our meetings.

October passed into November, the nights growing longer but less pleasant, being now more liable to chill and to wet fogs. These minor discomforts aside, winter long has been our kind's favourite season of the year, especially since coming to this northern latitude where around the December solstice we may be out and about seventeen hours of the twenty-four, and fifteen even in the mid-autumnal times to which my narrative now has come. Yet with Jack abroad, the increased period of darkness seemed this year no boon, as I was only capable of viewing it as a greater opportunity for him to sally forth on another murderous jaunt.

On the evening of the eighth, then, I reached Whitechapel before the clocks struck five. By the time they chimed for six, I had already encountered in the narrow, gridless streets Norton, Arnold, and Titus. We tipped our hats each to the other as we passed. I saw Martin for the first time that night shortly after six. We were complete, as ready as we might be should the chance present itself.

The night gave at the outset no reason for supposing it likely to prove different from any other. I wandered up toward Bishopsgate Station, having learned that the whore who was Jack's latest victim had been released from there not long before her last, fatal encounter. "Ta-ta, old cock, I'll see you again soon!" she had called drunkenly to the gaoler, a prediction that, unfortunately for her, was quickly proven inaccurate.

Wherever Jack prowled, if indeed he was on the loose at that hour, I found no trace of him. Seeing that so many prostitutes passed through the station, I made it a point to hang about: Jack might well seek in those environs an easy target. Whores indeed I saw in plenty thereabouts but, as I say, no sign of Jack. When the clocks struck twelve, ushering in a new day, I gave it up and went to hunt elsewhere.

Walking down Dorset Street near 12:30, I heard a woman with an Irish lilt to her voice singing in a room on one of the courtyards there. I paused a moment to listen; such good spirits are rarely to be found in bleak Whitechapel. Then I continued east, going by London Hospital and the Jews' Cemetery, my route in fact passing the opening of Buck's Row onto Brady Street, close to the site of Jack's first killing.

That area proved no more profitable than had been my prior wanderings of the night: no more profitable, indeed, than the whole of the past five weeks' exertions on the part of the Sanguine Club. True, I am more patient than a man, but even patience such as mine desires some reward, some hint that it is not employed in pursuit of an *ignis fatuus*. As I lacked any such hint, it was with downcast mien that I turned my steps westward once more.

My nostrils began to twitch before I had any conscious awareness of the fact. I was on Wentworth Street between Commercial and Goulston, when at last my head went suddenly up and back, as I have seen a wolf's do on taking a scent. Blood was in the air, and had been for some little while. Yet like a wolf which scents its prey at a distance, I had to cast about to find the precise source of the odour.

In this search I was unsurprised to encounter Norton, who was coming down Flower and Dean Street toward Commercial. His features bore the same abstracted set I knew appeared on my own. "Odd sort of trail," he said without preamble, as is his way.

"It is." I tested the air again. "The source lies north of us still, I am certain, but more precise than that I cannot be. It is not like the spoor I took from Jack's last pleasantry."

"A *man* could have followed that, from what you said of it," Norton snorted, and though he spoke in jest I do not think him far wrong. He continued, "Let us hunt together."

I agreed at once, and we proceeded side by side up Commercial (which in the dark and quiet of the small hours belied its name) to a corner where, after deliberation, we turned west onto White Street rather than east onto Fashion. Well that we did, for hurrying in our direction from Bishopsgate came Titus. His strides, unlike our own, had nothing of doubt to them. Being our Senior, he is well supplied with hunters' lore.

"Well met!" he cried on recognizing us. "This way! We have him, unless I miss my guess!" Practically at a run, he swept us north along Crispin Street to Dorset, the very ground I had patrolled not long before.

The scent trail was stronger now, but remained curiously diffuse. "How do you track with such confidence?" I asked.

"That is much blood, escaping but slowly to the outside air," Titus replied. "I think our quarry has taken his atrocious games indoors, in hopes of thwarting us. He has been—you will, I pray, pardon the play on words—too sanguine in his expectations."

His proposed explanation so precisely fit the spoor we were following that I felt within me the surge of hope I recently described as lacking. A much-battered signboard on the street read "Miller's Court"; it was the one from which I had earlier heard song. A light burned in Number 13. From that door, too, welled the scent which had drawn us; now that we had come so close, its source could not be mistaken.

As our tacit leader, Titus grasped the doorknob, Norton and I standing behind him to prevent Jack from bursting past and fleeing. Jack evidently had anticipated no disturbances, for the door was not locked. On Titus's opening it, the blood smell came forth as strongly as ever I have known it, save only on the battlefield.

The scene I glimpsed over Titus's shoulder will remain with me through all my nights. Our approach had taken Jack unawares, he being so intent on his pleasure that the world beyond the squalid little room was of no import to him. A picture-nail in his hand, he stared at us in frozen shock from his place by the wall.

Both my eyes and nose, though, drew me away from him to the naked flesh on the bed. I use that appellative in preference to body, for with leisure at his disposal Jack gained the opportunity to exercise his twisted ingenuity to a far greater and more grisly extent than he had on the streets of Whitechapel. The chamber more closely resembled an abbatoir than a lodging.

By her skin, such of it as was not covered with blood, the poor wretch whose abode this presumably had been was younger than the previous objects of his depravity. Whether she was fairer as well I cannot say, as he had repeatedly slashed her face and sliced off her nose and ears and set them on a bedside table. The only relief for her was that she could have known none of this, as her throat was cut; it gaped at me like a second, speechless mouth.

Nor had Jack contented himself with working those mutilations. Along with her nose and ears on that table lay her heart, her kidneys (another offering, perhaps, to George Lusk), and her breasts, his gory handprints upon them. He had gutted her as well.

Not even those horrors were the worst. When we interrupted him, Jack was engaged in hanging bits of the woman's flesh on the wall, as if they were engravings the effect of whose placement he was examining.

The tableau that held us all could not have endured above a few seconds. Jack first recovered the power of motion, and waved in invitation to the blood-drenched sheets. "Plenty there for the lot o' yez," said he, grinning.

So overpowering was the aroma hanging in the room that my tongue of itself ran across my lips, and my head swung toward that scarlet swamp. So, I saw, did Titus's. Norton, fortunately, was made of sterner stuff, and was not taken by surprise when Jack tried to spring past us. Their grapple recalled to our senses the Senior and myself, and I seized Jack's wrist as he tried to take hold of his already much-used knife, which, had it found one of our hearts, could have slain us as certainly as if we were mortal.

In point of fact, Jack did score Norton's arm with the blade before Titus rapped his hand against the floor and sent the weapon skittering away. Norton cursed at the pain of the cut, but only for a moment, as it healed almost at once. The struggle, being three against one, did not last long after that. Having subdued Jack and stuffed a silk handkerchief in his mouth to prevent his crying out, we dragged him from the dingy cubicle out into Mitre Court.

Just then, likely drawn by the fresh outpouring of the blood scent from the newly opened door of Number 13, into the court rushed Martin, and the stout fellow had with him a length of rope for use in the event that Jack should be captured, an eventuality for which he, perhaps inspirited by youthful optimism, was more prepared than were we his elders. We quickly trussed our quarry and hauled him away to obtain more certain privacy in which to decide his fate.

We were coming out of Mitre Court onto Dorset Street when I exclaimed, "The knife!"

"What of it? Let it be," Titus said. Norton grunted in agreement.

On most occasions, the one's experience and the other's sagacity would have been plenty to persuade me to accede to their wishes, but everything connected with Jack, it seemed, was out of the ordinary. I shook my head, saying, "That blade has fleshed itself in you, Norton. Men in laboratories are all too clever these days; who knows what examination of the weapon might reveal to them?"

Martin supported me, and my other two colleagues saw the force of my concern: why stop Jack if we gave ourselves away through the mute testimony of the knife? I dashed into Number 13 once more, found the blade, and tucked it into the waistband of my trousers. I found coherent thought in that blood-charged atmosphere next to impossible, but realized it would be wise to screen the horrid and pathetic corpse on the bed from view. Accordingly, I shut the door and dragged up a heavy bureau to secure it, only then realizing I was still inside myself.

Feeling very much a fool, I climbed to the top of the chest of drawers, broke out a pane of glass, and awkwardly scrambled down outside. I hurried to catch up to my comrades, who were conveying Jack along Commercial Street. As he was most unwilling, this would have attracted undue attention from passersby, save that we do not draw men's notice unless we wish it.

We turned off onto Thrawl Street and there, in the shelter of a recessed doorway, held a low-voiced discussion. "He must perish; there is no help for it," Martin declared. To this statement none of us dissented. Jack glared mute hatred at us all.

"How then?" said I. I drew forth Jack's own knife. "Shall I drive this into his breast now, and put an end to it?" The plan had a certain poetic aptness I found appealing.

Martin nodded approvingly, but Titus, to my surprise, demurred. He explained, "Had I not observed this latest outrage, Jerome, I should have no complaint. But having seen it, my judgement is that the punishment you propose errs in the excessive mercy it would grant."

"What then?" I cast about for some harsher fate, but arrived only at the obvious. "Shall we leave him, bound, for the sun to find?" I have never seen the effects of sunlight on the flesh of our kind, of course; had I been in position to observe it, I should not now be able to report our conversation. Yet instinctively we know what we risk. It is said to be spectacularly pyrotechnic.

Jack's writhings increased when he heard my proposal. He had dared the sun to kill for his own satisfaction, but showed no relish for facing it without choice. Our Senior coldly stared down at him. "You deserve worse."

"So he does," Norton said. "However much the sun may pain him, it will only be for a little while. He ought instead to have eternity to contemplate his failings."

"How do you propose to accomplish that?" asked Martin. "Shall we store him away in the basement of the Sanguine Club? Watch him as we will, one day he may effect his escape and endanger us all over again."

"I'd not intended that," replied Norton.

"What then?" Titus and I demanded together.

"I say we take him to the Tower Bridge now building, and brick him up in one of its towers. Then every evening he will awaken to feel the traffic pounding close by, yet be powerless to free himself from his little crypt. He will get rather hungry, bye and bye."

The image evoked by Norton's words made the small hairs prickle up at the nape of my neck. To remain for ever in a tiny, black, airless chamber, to feel hunger grow and grow, and not to be able even to perish . . . were he not already mad, such incarceration would speedily render Jack so.

"Ah, most fitting indeed," Titus said in admiration. Martin and I both nodded; Norton's ingenuity was a fitting match for that which Jack had displayed. Lifting the miscreant, we set off for the bridge, which lay only a couple of furlongs to the south of us. Our untiring strength served us well as we bore Jack thither. His constant struggles might have exhausted a party of men, or at the least persuaded them to knock him over the head.

Although we draw little notice from mortals when we do not wish it, the night watchman spied our approach and turned his lantern on us. " 'Ere, wot's this?" he cried, seeing Jack's helpless figure in our arms.

We were, however, prepared for this eventuality. Martin sprang forward, to sink his teeth into the watchman's hand. At once the fellow, under the influence of our comrade's spittle, grew calm and quiet. Titus, Norton, and I pressed onto the unfinished span of the bridge and into its northern tower, Martin staying behind to murmur in the watchman's ear and guide his dreams so he should remember nothing out of the ordinary.

The other three of us fell to with a will. The bricklayers had left the tools of their trade when they went home for the night. "Do you suppose they will notice their labour is farther advanced than when they left it?" I asked, slapping a brick into place.

Titus brought up a fresh hod of mortar. "I doubt they will complain of it, if they should," he said, with the slightest hint of chuckle in his voice, and I could not argue with him in that.

Norton paused a moment from his labour to stir Jack with his foot. "Nor will this one complain, not while the sun's in the sky. And by the time it sets tomorrow, they'll have built well past him." He was right in that; already the tower stood higher than the nearby Tower of London from which the bridge derives its name. Norton continued, "After that, he can shout as he pleases, and think on what he's done to merit his new home."

Soon, what with our unstinting effort, Jack's receptacle was ready to receive him. We lifted him high, set him aside, and bricked him up. I thought I heard him whimpering behind his gag, but he made no sound loud enough to penetrate the masonry surrounding him. That was also massive enough to keep him from forcing his way out, bound as he was, while the cement joining the bricks remained unset. He would eventually succeed in scraping through the ropes that held him, but not before daybreak . . . and the next night would be too late.

"There," said Norton when we had finished, "is a job well done."

Nodding, we went back to reclaim Martin, who left off charming the night watchman. That worthy stirred as he came back to himself. He touched his grizzled forelock. "You chaps 'ave a good evenin' now," he said respectfully as we walked past him. We were none too soon, for the sky had already begun to pale toward morning.

"Well, my comrades, I shall see you this evening," Titus said as we prepared to go our separate ways. I am embarrassed to confess that I, along with the rest of us, stared at him in some puzzlement over the import of his words. Had we not just vanquished Jack? Seeing our confusion, he burst out laughing: "Have you forgotten, friends, it will be Club night?" As a matter of fact, we had, having given the day of the week but scant regard in our unceasing pursuit of Jack.

On boarding my train at St. Mary's Station, I found myself in the same car as Arnold, who as luck would have it had spent the entire night in the eastern portion of Whitechapel, which accounted for his nose failing to catch the spoor that led the rest of us to Jack; he had entered the train at Whitechapel Station, half a mile east of my own boarding point. He fortunately took in good part my heckling over his absence.

After so long away, our return to the comforts of the Sanguine Club proved doubly delightful, and stout Hignett's welcome flattering in the extreme. Almost I found myself tempted to try eating cheese for his sake, no matter that it should render me ill, our kind not being suited to digest it.

Despite the desire I and, no doubt, the rest of us felt to take the opportunity to begin to return to order our interrupted affairs, all of us were present that evening to symbolize the formal renewal of our weekly fellowship. We drank to the Queen and to the Club, and also all drank again to an unusual third toast proposed by Titus: "To the eternal restoration of our security!" Indeed, at that we raised a cheer and flung our goblets into the fireplace. A merrier gathering of the Club I cannot recall.

And yet now, in afterthought, I wonder how permanent our settlement of these past months' horrors shall prove. I was not yet in London when Peter of Colechurch erected Old London Bridge seven centuries ago, but recall well the massive reconstruction undertaken by Charles Lebelye, as that was but a hundred thirty years gone by; and there are still men alive who remember the building of New London Bridge in its place by John Rennie, Jr., from the plans of his father six decades ago.

Who can be certain Tower Bridge will not someday have a similar fate befall it, and release Jack once more into the world, madder and more savage even than before? As the French say, "*Tout passe, tout casse, tout lasse*"—everything passes, everything perishes, everything palls. We of the Sanguine Club, to whom the proverb does not apply, know its truth better than most. Still, even by our standards, Jack surely will not find freedom soon. If and when he should, that, I daresay, will be time for our concern.

~

THE ADVENTURE OF THE GRINDER'S WHISTLE

Howard Waldrop

(Writing as Edward Malone)

The off-center science fiction author Howard Waldrop (1946–) has an unusual history with Jack the Ripper. To celebrate (an odd locution, when one thing and another is considered) the centennial of the Ripper murders of 1888, an anthology of stories about Red Jack was planned for publication. Invited to participate, Waldrop began work on "The Tale of the Fierce Bad Gentleman," which described the meeting of Jack the Ripper and Beatrix Potter—a combination that might not have occurred to others. The publication deadline, however, was too imminent, and the story couldn't be completed in time, so Waldrop's tale was never written. Ironically, the publication was delayed, but by then it was too late to restart the writing process.

Best known as a short story writer, Waldrop has published twelve collections, beginning with *Howard Who?* (1986); the most recent volume of tales is *Horse of a Different Color: Stories* (2013). His most familiar work is "The Ugly Chickens," about the extinction of the dodo, which won the 1981 Nebula and World Fantasy Awards for best short story; it also was nominated for a Hugo, a Locus, and a Balrog Award.

"The Adventure of the Grinder's Whistle" was planned for an anthology of stories by fictional authors (Gene Wolfe, for example, wrote a story that was bylined David Copperfield) that was never completed. It was first published in *Chacal* 2 (Spring 1977); it was first collected in book form in *Night of the Cooters: More Neat Stories* by Howard Waldrop (Kansas City, MO, Ursus Imprints, and Shingletown, CA, Mark V. Ziesing, 1990).

Author's Foreword: *Retelling events which happened when one was seven years of age, from a vantage point eighty-six years removed, is a dangerous undertaking. Events blur and change in the mind, and one summer or fall, one neighborhood and another, this vista and that bit of scenery become confused.*

I confess this is normally so. There is one singular event in my life which has never, and will never, lose its sharp edges. Of that, I am sure. Those which came later, the adventure with Professor Challenger in Maple White Land, the aftermath of the comet, and with the earth needle, were surely excitement enough for any man's life. That I was privileged, during the last war, to write the history of His Majesty's part in the development of the fission bomb was an additional boon which time gave me.

My part in the affair of which I write was small, and will not detain the reader for very long. My agent has insisted that I commit this memory to print. I am, I believe, giving an account which has not been told before.

A few words of explanation. I came to London with my mother soon after the death of my father in the late summer of 1888. We were living with my aunt's family, and I was very happy at the time since I was held out of school for that fall term. How I fell in with the rough gang to be described is not important. It involved several fistfights, most of which I won, and an initiation which, if my widowed mother had ever known about, would have assured that I had been returned to the halls of academe forthwith.

Let us go back, then, to the era of fog and gaslights. . . .

It was a foggy night, and we were following around behind the lamplighter and turning off the gas.

Jenkins, our leader, was a gangly lad of fifteen. He towered far over me, as he did the others, all except for Neddie, who was a big lug, if ever there were one.

We'd sneak behind the lampman, old Mr. Soakes. Very quiet-like, Jenkins would lift one of the younger of us (sometimes myself or Aubrey) up and we'd twist off the supply and all be gone giggling and laughing down the alleyways.

(I sometimes came home those days with traces of soot behind my ears I'd failed to clean off, and would suffer my mother's reproofs.)

We were having to be very careful for constables. What with the Ripper murders and all, they'd doubled the force in our district.

My mother and I had a discussion about that, too. One which I'd won by shocking her Calvinistic upbringing. She said I wasn't to go out at night because the Ripper was about. I told her that no one who wasn't a lady of easy virtue had anything to worry about from the fiend.

Us fellows had had talks about the Ripper. He was the topic of conversation in London, even in our circles, which were none too high. Some of us thought he was a fine-dressed gentleman who came down to Whitechapel to work his way with the ladies. Some thought him a butcher gone mad, or to be like old Sweeney Todd, the Demon Barber of Fleet Street some years ago. Jack Leatherapron, people were calling him, and we could envision him all covered in blood from head to foot, carrying off the heart of his victim. Others supposed he was one of the mad Russian socialists who lived all together in the big house over in Seldon Row West, out killing capitalists. He was sure starting at the bottom of the money ladder if he were, we agreed.

"Well," said Jenkins that night, after we'd put out the twelfth light and had to cut through fences because old Soakes had seen us and given the alarm. We'd heard some bobby-whistles and club-thumping a few minutes later, but by then we were holed up in the basement where we held our meetings.

"Well what, then?" asked Neddie, all out of breath. "The coppers have put the kibosh on the fun tonight. They'll be looking for us, sure."

"Let's go filch from the pruneseller in the Square," said Aubrey, who was older than me, but even shorter.

"Aw, who wants prunes?" asked Neddie.

Toldo Wigmore, who read a lot but didn't say much, grunted.

"What is it, Toldo?" asked Jenkins, all attention.

"I's just thinkin' 'pon what we kin do tomorrer," said Toldo. He hitched up the leg of his knicker and scratched. "We could all go out to Maxon Heath and see the new steam combine-tractor. It's just in from Americker."

"Capital idea!" I said, and they all looked at me, expectant. "But you can't. I re—" and you must remember I wanted to be one of the gang, so I couldn't let on that I read, yet. My mother'd taught me to read before I was five, she was being somewhat of a progressive. So I caught my slip in time. "I mean, my mom told me it was stolen early this morning."

"Was not!" yelled Toldo. "Leastwise, I ain't seen that in no newspapers. Yer mother's lying!"

Before the fight could start, there was somewhat of a noise upstairs, and Jenkins went to see what it was. He came bounding downstairs with a whoop in a few seconds. "Line up, men!" he hollers, all official like a sergeant major.

We hopped to and stood before him in the basement.

"We've been hired by a gentleman," he said. We gave a ragged cheer. I joined in, though I'd only heard about working from one of the boys who'd been in the gang longer.

"Alright, you newer members," said Jenkins, pacing back and forth before us, looking especially hard at Aubrey and myself. "You're to remember that we do anything within reason for the gentleman, and when we're paid off, half the money is to go to the club funds."

I didn't like that very well. I knew that meant Jenkins would end up with most of my money before this was over. And they'd told me about looking for tarbarrels all one night once, down at the quays and such. I didn't look to have a very pleasant night ahead of me.

"All right," says Jenkins. "Let's go!"

We ran, whooping and hollering and raising a commotion through the streets and alleys, and got two more boys on the way. Our yelling caught in our throats, though, when we saw the bobbies and their lanterns ahead of us in the fog.

We got very respectable. A sergeant of police stopped us. He was wearing his slicker and his hardpot hat with the shield on it. It was the first bobby I'd really seen up close. He had a great thick mustache. I was very impressed.

"Here, boys," he said, spreading his arms like a railcrossing signal. "You can't come through here. There's been a foul deed perpetrated."

"I'll bet it's the Ripper!" said Toldo, out of the corner of his mouth.

Jenkins became very respectful-looking, and took off his cap. "We've been sent for by that gentleman over there, sergeant," he said, pointing into the fog.

"He sent for you, did he?" asked the policeman. "Just a mo'." He walked to a plainclothes-dressed man and spoke to him. The fellow looked us over from under his bowler hat and said something to the sergeant. There were others moving around in the fog like ghosts. I couldn't see what had happened, but there was a great knot of police standing toward one of the building corners.

"All right, you boys," said the sergeant, returning. "Stand about out of the way. And don't you touch nothing."

"Fine, sir," said Jenkins. "We sha'n't."

We moved to the building wall opposite the gathering of policemen. Jenkins kept us all quiet and in line.

There was a bluff-looking man with a mustache standing with the bobbies. He didn't look like any policeman to me. He held one of his shoulders just a little higher than the other, and was talking with two of the plainclothes detectives.

"Would you look at thart," said Toldo, to me, and pointed.

There was a man crawling around on the paving of the street.

"Is he hurt?" I asked Jenkins. "Maybe he's the one that's hurt?"

"Naw. That's the man who hired us," said the leader. "That's . . ."

"Step over here a moment, Watson, and have a look at this," said the man on the ground, peering toward the knot of policemen.

"Of course, Holmes," said the man with the off-shoulder. We were quite near them, so I heard all this.

The man on all fours moved around until he got the gaslight shining before him.

"This Ripper business is ghastly, what?" said the bluff man.

"What do you make of these?" asked Holmes, getting to one knee above the cobbles.

Watson peered at the uneven pavings. I couldn't see what they were looking at.

"Faint scratches of some sort," he said.

"Quite right, Watson, quite right." Holmes dropped to the ground again and looked left and right.

"Whatever are you doing, Holmes?" asked the other.

"Be a good fellow and see if Lestrade needs any help. I should imagine your bedside manner could calm the woman," said Mr. Holmes.

For the first time I noticed there was a woman among the police. She seemed to be talking, and I heard some whimpers from the crowd. It may have been her, but the fog muffled voices so I couldn't tell.

Two of the plainclothesmen came toward Watson as he got up. As they left the group of constables, I saw a lumpy greatcoat lying on the street. Someone had thrown it over a body, for a great pool of blood was drying around it. I nudged Aubrey and he poked Toldo and Toldo jabbed Jenkins, but Jenkins just nodded his head wisely.

That's why he's the leader.

"Dr. Daniels agrees with you, Dr. Watson. However, it remains to be seen what will come out at the inquest. I'm not entirely convinced at all. Not at all," said the plainclothesman in the bowler hat.

"What do you propose is happening, Le-strade?" asked Holmes, getting up from the street and wiping his hands.

"Certainly no mad Jack Ripper is committing these deeds. I refuse to believe a man to be capable of such violence."

"You may be right, there, Lestrade," said Holmes, but I don't think the policeman was paying any attention. He seemed to be waiting to be asked something.

"Well," asked Dr. Watson. "What's your explanation, Inspector?"

"Suicide," said Lestrade, with a note of triumph.

"*Suicide?*" asked Watson.

Toldo started to giggle, but Jenkins silenced him with a foot in the ankle.

"Certainly," said the plainclothesman. "These unfortunate women of the streets, in remorse for having sunk to such a low level, drink themselves senseless, stumble to some doorway here in Whitechapel, and do themselves in with repeated jabs of large knives. It's all very simple."

"So is the inspector," whispered Toldo.

"But, Lestrade, what becomes of the murder weapon?" asked Watson.

"With their last ounce of strength, they fling the knives away from themselves. I'm sure my men's search of the rooftops and curbs will reveal the instrument of suicide." The inspector put his hands in his vest pockets and rocked back and forth on his heels.

"Very interesting, Inspector," said Holmes. "Might I now interview the woman you have there? I have certain questions of my own."

"Certainly, Mr. Holmes. Though she claims to have heard this non-existent Leather Apron. She's frightened, like the rest of the inhabitants of the district, by the newspaper headlines and the penny-dreadfuls. She'll not be of any use to you if it's the truth you're after."

And, to this day, I'll swear I heard Mr. Holmes say this to Inspector Lestrade. He said: "Often, in the search for truth, the frightened have more to offer than the brave."

A P.C. had finished taking down notes from the woman, and brought her toward us. She looked shabby-respectable, like someone's great-auntie fallen on bad times.

"She manages the doss house across the way," said Lestrade to Mr. Holmes, under his breath.

The woman was holding her head in her hands and moaning.

"Oh, it was 'orrible, 'orrible!" she said.

"Madame," said Holmes. "Though I quite realize you are in distress, there are certain things I must ask you."

"Oh, it was 'orrible!" she said, as if Holmes were not there. Someone brought her some brandy from a house down the way. She drank at it and seemed to calm down. Holmes stood patiently, watching until she had finished. He was a tall man, with a nose like a beak. He reminded me of a heron, except that he had bright eyes, like a cat's. They caught glints from the gaslamps and police lanterns as I watched. My knicker leg was working free of the sock and I bent to rebutton it. I didn't hear the woman when she first started talking again.

". . . way she was screaming. Like the devil himself was after her. And he was, too. Him with his satanic whistle. He . . ."

"Whistle? Whistle, did you say?" asked Mr. Holmes, all rushing. "What type of whistle? Any melody?"

"No, no tune to it, at all. That's what made it so eerie. That, an 'im sharpenin' 'is knives again and again, over and over . . ."

"A sound like, say, someone using a large whetstone? Like scissors-grinder?" asked Holmes, all nervous-like.

"That's it! That's it exactly!" said the old woman.

"Just as I thought!" yelled Mr. Holmes. "Watson, you have your revolver?"

"Yes, Holmes, of course. What is it?"

"No time, Watson. The game's afoot."

Jenkins snapped to, with a call of "Attention!" This made the police and some of the bystanders jump.

"Ah," said Holmes. "Jenkins."

"Baker Street Irregulars reporting for duty, Mr. Holmes."

"Good," said Holmes. "Then I shan't worry about needing reinforcements from the Yard.

"Inspector," said Holmes, turning to Le-strade. "If I remember correctly, the lowest road to be reached from here, by . . . say, a coach and four . . . is Bremick Road. Do . . ."

I spoke before the Inspector. "The lowest place is near the drain into the river, Mr. Holmes." I stumbled, then continued. "In the alleyways across from the pier. Though a coach-and-four would have to take several short streets between here and there."

"Good!" said Holmes. "Bright lad." He turned again to Lestrade. "Meet me, then, at Bremick Road with five armed men as soon as you're done here. Come, Watson! Irregulars, ho!"

"But where?" asked Lestrade, as we hurried away.

"The Irregulars will lead you," yelled Mr. Holmes, as we ran into the thickening fog.

It made me proud.

We all ran so fast I was winded quickly. But it was Doctor Watson who began to slow after we had run twenty blocks. "Dammit, Holmes," he yelled. "I'm afraid I can't keep this up much longer. The jezail bullet in my shoulder, you know?"

"Quite alright," said Mr. Holmes, bending low to the cobbles as he had every hundred feet or so since we left the police. "The fog is thickening. I propose the Ripper will come with it. We're quite close enough already. I've lost the trail some time back. I must station the Irregulars and flush out our Cheeky Jack."

We rushed onto the Road. Holmes surveyed about him through the fog. "Station yourself there, Watson, with your revolver handy. You—" He pointed to me.

"Malone," said I.

"Malone, keep watch with Dr. Watson. Be his ears and eyes if he needs them."

He turned, motioned to Jenkins and the others, then faced back to Watson.

"When the Ripper comes, Watson, and he surely shall, you must aim for the glasses."

"His glasses? Whatever do you mean, Holmes? What? How will I know the Ripper when he comes?"

"You'll know him well enough, Watson. He'll be whistling and sharpening his knives."

"But Holmes!" said Watson, frustrated.

"He shall come from that alley, and you'll know him, Watson. Be a steady fellow." And then he was gone with the other members of the gang into the roiling fog.

"But, Holmes . . ." said Dr. Watson, into the mist.

I was shivering with excitement and the cold.

Dr. Watson turned to me. "What the devil did Holmes mean I must aim for his glasses? And how does he know where the Ripper will come from? And why with the fog?"

"I—I'm sure I don't know," I said to him.

"Oh . . . oh. Pardon me, lad," he said. "I'm quite sure you don't." He had the air of someone distracted. He was a large man himself, and his greatcoat made him seem all the larger. He had a reddish mustache, blockish features, and reminded me of an uncle of mine on my father's side.

"There's danger here, er . . . Malone," he said. "We must wait quietly and make no noise. You're up to danger, aren't you?"

"Yes, sir," I said, very resolutely, though my heart was in my throat.

Though there was a light cold breeze off the River, the fog grew thicker than it had been all evening. I stood in place and trembled.

We had been waiting about ten minutes, I guess, when we both thought we heard something. Was that a whistle? My skin went as gooseflesh. Coming face-to-face with Jack the Ripper would not be as much fun as I had once imagined. Doctor Watson cocked his head and gripped his Webley revolver more tightly. Little beads of moisture were collecting on his hand and dripping down his coatfront. I was becoming soaked through, and my teeth began to chatter.

Then the sound came to us again. It was like the old lady said, a high, keening tuneless whistle. I looked toward the fog in the alleyway across from us, the place Mr. Holmes said the Ripper would come from. I could barely see the buildings to each side.

Doctor Watson regripped his pistol. The tuneless whistle came, now soft, now loud, as if the Ripper were moving to and fro across the alley, perhaps checking doorways for victims. I could see him in my mind: a huge formless man, all covered with gore from head to heel, eating the liver . . .

I jumped as Doctor Watson brushed my arm.

The sound was coming toward us.

It was then I heard the sound with it, as must have the doctor. A sharp clicking sound. I had heard sounds like it, but much smaller, when on vacation at Blackpool with my mother and father.

I could only liken it to the opening and closing of the claws of a giant crab.

I saw Doctor Watson take aim along his revolver barrel where the alleyway entered the thoroughfare. Then the mists thickened, and all across the street was lost to view. He lowered his pistol and stepped into the roadway from our hiding place. I went out with him. My heart wasn't in it.

The noises came louder. The eerie whistle sent shivers along my damp spine. The tenor of the clicking grew and changed; they now sounded exactly as if someone were sharpening a large knife again and again. What a sound . . .

I started to wet my pants but held back.

I could see now why those poor women the Ripper killed must have frozen in their tracks when they heard him coming, while he bore down on them and perpetrated his outrages.

The fog roiled. The whistling grew louder. A shape moved at the edge of the alleyway, and the whistling and whetting fairly screamed toward us.

Doctor Watson braced his legs, swung his barrel in line with the shape.

He fired twice, the discharges lighting his face and arm pure white. He couldn't have missed, that close.

Like a juggernaut of doom, the Ripper came down at us. He was immense. I couldn't see anything distinct, but sensed something *big*, like in a nightmare, coming for me. He was whistling louder, sharpening his knife like a demon as he charged across the alley for me and the doctor.

A voice on the rooftop behind us yelled, "The glasses, Watson! *The glasses!*"

At the same time, I saw a glint of light above the ground, reflected from the gaslight down the way, as the Ripper came for me.

So did Doctor Watson. He emptied his Webley at it.

There was a loud shrill whistle and a scream, and the Ripper slowed his movement. A few seconds later, the sound of whetting died away in the fog.

"Good show, Watson," said Mr. Holmes, climbing down from the rooftop. "Well done, old man."

Through the fog, I heard police whistles, pounding of feet and nightsticks, and the yells of the Irregulars coming toward us.

I *had* wet my pants.

"You mean to tell me, Holmes," Watson said loudly as the detective examined the silent machinery with Lestrade and the constables, "that you were watching all the time! Why, we might have been killed!"

"Things were well in hand, Watson. If you failed to shoot out the pressure glasses on the combine machine, I was prepared to jump from the rooftop and engage the hand brake, there." He pointed to the operating levers of the steam behemoth.

"What a ghastly machine," remarked Lestrade. "Five murders, by this?"

"Wrong, Lestrade," said Holmes, examining the tractor. "The Ripper still stalks Whitechapel. This steam combine is responsible only for the death of the streetwalker tonight."

"Whatever put you on to it, Mr. Holmes?" asked Lestrade.

"The marks in the street, and the mutilations of the body," said the detective, lighting a pipe with a match struck against the boiler of the tractor. "That, and the comment of the witness to the whistle and continuous sharpening of the knives. Whistles suggest steam, continuous motion suggests machinery. Steam-driven machinery, simply.

"Deduction tells us," he continued after a puff, "that the farmers who thought the machine stolen had not properly extinguished the boiler fires. They only banked them. Something in the valves failed, probably due to humidity in the fogs. The steam combine trundled itself away. It followed the lowest courses into London. The valve must have closed in the evening, banking the fires once more. At nightfall, the return of the fog opened the valve once more. The unfortunate woman happened in its way. She was either too drunk or too frightened to move, and was caught up in the rakes."

"How dreadful," said Lestrade.

"Eventually," said Mr. Sherlock Holmes, "the steam machine would have run into the Thames. And this Jack Leatherapron, at least, would disappear from the face of London."

"But what of the real Ripper?" asked Le-strade.

"Your superintendent has already engaged the services of Doctor Doyle, Lestrade," said Holmes. "I sha'n't be needed.

"Jenkins," said Holmes, turning to us. "Your Irregulars behaved admirably, especially young Malone, there." He winked at me with his bright eyes like glass. "I wouldn't mind having to depend upon him in a fight." Holmes handed Jenkins coins. "Your usual pay, plus a bonus. Now, perhaps you'd better get out of Lestrade's way."

We took off then, back to Baker Street, hollering. There Jenkins divided up the money. Then I had to tell them how it was a dozen times or more. By morning, we were laughing. Near dawn, the whole thing seemed miles away, and comical, and already we were calling it Jack the Reaper.

They never did notice my pants.

SAGITTARIUS

Ray Russell

Although a notably literary writer of gothic horror fiction, Ray Russell (1924–1999) has had involvement with some rather cheesy motion pictures. His most famous literary work is the short story "Sardonicus," described by Stephen King as "perhaps the finest example of the modern gothic ever written." The story was first published in *Playboy* in January 1961 and collected in *Sardonicus and Other Stories* later in the same year. It is about a man whose face is frozen in a perpetually sardonic grin due to a traumatic psychological episode. Also in 1961, Russell adapted it as a screenplay for William Castle; the film was released as *Mr. Sardonicus* (1961). It anchored the trilogy *Unholy Trinity* (1967), which also included "Sagittarius" and "Sanguinarius," a fictionalized version of the life of the "Blood Countess," Elizabeth Bathory.

Russell also cowrote (with Robert Dillon) the screenplay for Roger Corman's *X* (1963), later titled *X: The Man with the X-Ray Eyes*, about a scientist who develops eye drops that give him X-ray vision but with horrific consequences. It starred Ray Milland, who also starred in *Premature Burial* (1962), a film written by Charles Beaumont and Russell, based on Edgar Allan Poe's story "The Premature Burial." Russell was the solo screenwriter for William Castle's *Zotz!* (1962), about a professor who acquires an ancient coin that gives him three powers: to inflict pain, to slow down time, and to kill. Russell was the fiction editor of *Playboy* in the 1960s and received the World Fantasy Award in 1991 for lifetime achievement.

"Sagittarius" was originally published in *Playboy* in March 1962. It was first collected in book form in its expanded version in *Unholy Trinity* (New York, Bantam, 1967).

I

The Century Club

"If Mr. Hyde had sired a son," said Lord Terry, "do you realize that the loathsome child could be alive at this moment?"

It was a humid summer evening, but he and his guest, Rolfe Hunt, were cool and crisp. They were sitting in the quiet sanctuary of the Century Club (so named, say wags, because its members all appear to be close to that age) and, over their drinks, had been talking about vampires and related monsters, about ghost stories and other dark tales of happenings real and imagined, and had been recounting some of their favorites. Hunt had been drinking martinis, but Lord Terry—The Earl Terrence Glencannon, rather—was a courtly old gentleman who considered the martini one of the major barbarities of the Twentieth Century. He would take only the finest, driest sherry before dinner, and he was now sipping his third glass. The conversation had touched upon the series of mutilation-killings that were currently shocking the city, and then upon such classic mutilators as Bluebeard and Jack the Ripper, and then upon murder and evil in general; upon certain works of fiction, such as *The Turn of the Screw* and its alleged ambiguities, *Dracula*, the short play *A Night at an Inn,* the German silent film *Nosferatu,* some stories of Blackwood, Coppard, Machen, Montague James, Le Fanu, Poe, and finally upon *The Strange Case of Dr. Jekyll and Mr. Hyde,* which had led the Earl to make his remark about Hyde's hypothetical son.

"How do you arrive at that, sir?" Hunt asked, with perhaps too much deference, but after all, to old Lord Terry, Hunt must have seemed a damp fledgling for all his thirty-five years, and the younger man could not presume too much heartiness simply because the Earl had known Hunt's father in the old days back in London. Lord Terry entertained few guests now, and it was a keen privilege to be sitting with him in his club—"The closest thing to an English club I could find in this beastly New York of yours," he once had granted, grudgingly.

Now, he was deftly evading Hunt's question by tearing a long, narrow ribbon from the evening paper and twisting it into that topological curiosity, the Möbius strip. "Fascinating," he smiled, running his finger along the little toy. "A surface with only one side. We speak of 'split personalities'—schizophrenes, Jekyll-and-Hyde, and whatnot—as if such persons were cleanly divided, marked off, with lines running down their centers. Actually, they're more like this Möbius strip—they *appear* to have two sides, but you soon discover that what you thought was the upper side turns out to be the under side as well. The two sides are one, strangely twisting and merging. You can never be sure which side you're looking at, or exactly where one side becomes the other . . . I'm sorry, did you ask me something?"

"I merely wondered," said Hunt, "how you happened to arrive at that interesting notion of yours: that Mr. Hyde's son—if Hyde had been a real person and if he had fathered a son—might be alive today?"

"Ah," Lord Terry said, putting aside the strip of paper. "Yes. Well, it's simple, really. We must first make a great leap of concession and, for sake of argument, look upon Bobbie Stevenson's story not as a story but as though it were firmly based in *fact.*"

It certainly was a great leap, but Hunt nodded.

"So much for that. Now, the story makes no reference to specific years—it uses that eighteen-followed-by-a-dash business which writers were so fond of in those days, I've never understood why—but we *do* know it was published in 1886. So, still making concessions for sake of argument, mind you, we might say Edward Hyde was 'born' in that year—but born a full-grown man, a creature capable of reproducing himself. We know, from the story, that Hyde spent his time in pursuit of carnal pleasures so gross that the good Dr. Jekyll was pale with shame at the remembrance of them. Surely one result of those pleasures might have been a child, born to some poor Soho wretch, and thrust nameless upon the world? Such a child, born in '86 or '87, would be in his seventies today. So you see it's quite possible."

He drained his glass. "And think of this now: whereas all other human creatures are compounded of both good and evil, Edward Hyde stood alone in the roster of mankind. For he was the first—and, let us hope, the last—human being who was *totally* evil. Consider his son. He is the offspring of one parent who, like all of us, was part good and part evil (the mother) and of one parent who was *all* evil (the father, Hyde). The son, then (to work it out arithmetically, if that is possible in a question of human factors), is three-quarters pure evil, with only a single thin flickering quarter of good in him. We might even weight the dice, as it were, and suggest that his mother, being most likely a drunken drab of extreme moral looseness, was hardly a person to bequeath upon her heir a strong full quarter of good—perhaps only an eighth, or a sixteenth. Not to put too fine a point on it, Hyde's son—if he is alive—is the second-most evil person who has ever lived; and—since his father is dead—*the* most evil person on the face of the earth today!" Lord Terry stood up. "Shall we go in to dinner?" he said.

The dining room was inhabited by men in several stages of advanced decrepitude, and still-handsome Lord Terry seemed, in contrast, rather young. His bearing, his tall, straight body, clear eye, ruddy face, and unruly shock of thick white hair made him a vital figure among a room full of near-ghosts. The heavy concentration of senility acted as a depressant on Hunt's spirits, and Lord Terry seemed to sense this, for he said, as they sat down, "Waiting room. The whole place is one vast waiting room, full of played-out chaps waiting for the last train. They tell you age has its compensations. Don't believe it. It's ghastly."

Lord Terry recommended the red snapper soup with sherry, the Dover sole, the Green Goddess salad. "Named after a play, you know, *The Green Goddess,* George Arliss made quite a success in it, long before your time." He scribbled their choices on the card and handed it to the hovering waiter, also ordering another martini for Hunt and a fourth sherry for himself. "Yes," he said, his eye fixed on some long-ago stage, "used to go to the theatre quite a lot in the old days. They put on jolly good shows then. Not all this rot . . ." He focused on Hunt. "But I mustn't be boorish—you're somehow involved in the theatre yourself, I believe you said?"

Hunt told him he was writing a series of theatrical histories, that his histories of the English and Italian theatres had already been published and that currently he was working on the French.

"Ah," the old man said. "Splendid. Will you mention Sellig?"

Hunt confessed that the name was new to him.

Lord Terry sighed. "Such is fame. A French actor. All the rage in Paris at one time. His name was spoken in the same breath with Mounet-Sully's, and some even considered him the new Lemaître. Bernhardt nagged Sardou into writing a play for him, they say, though I don't know if he ever did. Rostand left an unfinished play, *Don Juan's Last Night, La Dernière Nuit de Don Juan,* which some say was written expressly for Sellig, but Sellig never played it."

"Why not?"

Lord Terry shrugged. "Curious fellow. Very—what would you say—pristine, very dedicated to the highest theatrical art, classic stuff like Corneille and Racine, you know. The very highest. Wouldn't even do Hugo or Dumas. And yet he became a name not even a theatrical historian is familiar with."

"You must make me familiar with it," Hunt said, as the drinks arrived.

Lord Terry swallowed a white lozenge he took from a slim gold box. "Pills," he said. "In our youth we sow wild oats; in our dotage we reap pills." He replaced the box in his weskit pocket. "Yes, I'll tell you about Sellig, if you like. I knew him very well."

II

The Dangers of Charm

We were both of an age (said Lord Terry), very young, twenty-three or four, and Paris in those days was a grand place to be young in. The Eiffel Tower was a youngster then, too, our age exactly, for this was still the first decade of the century, you see. Gauguin had been dead only six years, Lautrec only eight, and although that Parisian Orpheus, Jacques Offenbach, had died almost thirty years before, his music and his gay spirit still ruled the city, and jolly *parisiennes* still danced the can-can with bare derrières to the rhythm of his *Galop Infernal*. The air was heady with a wonderful mixture of *ancien régime* elegance (the days of which were numbered and which would soon be dispelled forever by the War) combined with a forward-looking curiosity and excitement about the new century. Best of both worlds, you might say. The year, to be exact about it, was 1909.

It's easy to remember because in that very year both Coquelin brothers—the actors, you know—died. The elder, more famous brother, Constant-Benoît, who created the role of Cyrano, died first, and the younger, Alexandre Honoré, died scarcely a fortnight later. Here's a curious tidbit about Coquelin's Cyrano which you may want to use in your book: he played the first act wearing a long false nose, the second act with a shorter nose, and at the end of the play, wore no false nose at all—the really odd thing being that the audience never noticed it! Sir Cedric told me that just before he died. Hardwicke, you know. Where was I? Oh, yes. It was through a friend of the Coquelin family—a minor *comédien* named César Baudouin—that I first came to know Paris and, consequently, Sébastien Sellig.

He was appearing at the Théâtre Français, in Racine's *Britannicus*. He played the young Nero. And he played him with such style and fervor and godlike grace that one could *feel* the audience's sympathies being drawn toward Nero as to a magnet. I saw him afterward, in his dressing room, where he was removing his make-up. César introduced us.

He was a man of surpassing beauty: a face like the Apollo Belvedere, with classic features, a tumble of black curls, large brown eyes, and sensuous lips. I did not compliment him on his good looks, of course, for the world had only recently become unsafe for even the most innocent admiration between men, Oscar Wilde having died in Paris just nine years before. I did compliment him on his performance, and on the rush of sympathy which I've already remarked.

"Thank you," he said, in English, which he spoke very well. "It was unfortunate."

"Unfortunate?"

"The audience's sympathies should have remained with Britannicus. By drawing them to myself—quite inadvertently, I assure you—I upset the balance, reversed Racine's intentions, and thoroughly destroyed the play."

"But," observed César lightly, "you achieved a personal triumph."

"Yes," said Sellig. "At irreparable cost. It will not happen again, dear César, you may be sure of that. Next time I play Nero, I shall do so without violating Racine."

César, being a professional, took exception. "You can't be blamed for your charm, Sébastien," he insisted.

Sellig wiped off the last streak of paint from his face and began to draw on his street clothes. "An actor who cannot control his charm," he said, "is like an actor who cannot control his voice or his limbs. He is worthless." Then he smiled, charmingly. "But we mustn't talk shop in front of your friend. So very rude. Come, I shall take you to an enchanting little place for supper."

It was a small, dark place called L'Oubliette. The three of us ate an enormous and very good omelette, with crusty bread and a bottle of white wine. Sellig talked of the differences between France's classic poetic dramatist, Racine, and England's, Shakespeare. "Racine is like"—he lifted the bottle and refilled our glasses—"well, he is like a very fine vintage white. Delicate, serene, cool, subtle. So subtle that the excellence is not immediately enjoyed by uninitiated palates. Time is required, familiarity, a return and another return and yet another."

As an Englishman, I was prepared to defend our bard, so I asked, a little belligerently: "And Shakespeare?"

"Ah, Shakespeare!" smiled Sellig. "*Passionel, tumultueux!* He is like a mulled red, hot and bubbling from the fire, dark and rich with biting spices and sweet honey! The senses are smitten, one is overwhelmed, one becomes drunk, one reels, one spins . . . it can be a most agreeable sensation."

He drank from his glass. "Think of tonight's play. It depicts the first atrocity in a life of atrocities. It ends as Nero murders his brother. Later, he was to murder his mother, two wives, a trusted tutor, close friends, and untold thousands of Christians who died horribly in his arenas. But we see none of this. If Shakespeare had written the play, it would have *begun* with the death of Britannicus. It would then have shown us each new outrage, the entire chronicle of Nero's decline and fall and ignoble end. *Enfin*, it would have been *Macbeth*."

I had heard of a little club where the girls danced in shockingly indecorous costumes, and I was eager to go. César allowed himself to be persuaded to take me there, and I invited Sellig to accompany us. He declined, pleading fatigue and a heavy day ahead of him. "Then perhaps," I said, "you will come with us tomorrow evening? It may not tempt a gentleman of your lofty theatrical tastes, but I'm determined to see a show at this Grand Guignol which César has told me of. Quite bloody and outrageous, I understand—rather like Shakespeare." Sellig laughed at my little joke. "Will you come? Or perhaps you have a performance . . ."

"I do have a performance," he said, "so I cannot join you until later. Suppose we plan to meet there, in the foyer, directly after the last curtain?"

"Will you be there in time?" I asked. "The Guignol shows are short, I hear."

"I will be there," said Sellig, and we parted.

III

Stage of Torture

Le Théâtre du Grand Guignol, as you probably know, had been established just a dozen or so years before, in 1896, on the Rue Chaptal, in a tiny building that had once been a chapel. Father Didon, a Dominican, had preached there, and in the many incarnations the building was to go through in later years it was to retain its churchly appearance. Right up to the date of its demolition in 1962, I'm told, it remained exactly as it had always been: quaint, small, huddled inconspicuously in a cobble-stone nook at the end of a Montmartre alley; inside, black-raftered, with gothic tracery writhing along the portals and fleurs-de-lis on the walls, with carved cherubs and a pair of seven-foot angels—dim with the patina of a century—smiling benignly down on the less than three hundred seats and loges . . . which, you know, looked not like conventional seats and loges but like church pews and confessionals. After the good Father Didon was no longer active, his chapel became the shop of a dealer specializing in religious art; still later, it was transformed into a studio for the academic painter, Rochegrosse; and so on, until, in '96, a man named Méténier—who had formerly been secretary to a *commissaire de police*—rechristened it the Théâtre du Grand Guignol and made of it the famous carnival of horror. Méténier died the following year, aptly enough, and Max Maurey took it over. I met Maurey briefly—he was still operating the theatre in 1909, the year of my little story.

The subject matter of the Guignol plays seldom varied. Their single acts were filled with girls being thrown into lighthouse lamps . . . faces singed by vitriol or pressed forcibly down upon red hot stoves . . . naked ladies nailed to crosses and carved up by gypsies . . . a variety of surgical operations . . . mad old crones who put out the eyes of young maidens with knitting needles . . . chunks of flesh ripped from victims' necks by men with hooks for hands . . . bodies dissolved in acid baths . . . hands chopped off; also arms, legs, heads . . . women raped and strangled . . . all done in a hyper-realistic manner with ingenious trick props and the Guignol's own secretly formulated blood—a thick, suety, red gruel which was actually capable of congealing before your eyes and which was kept continually hot in a big cauldron backstage.

Some actors—but especially actresses—made spectacular careers at the Guignol. You may know of Maxa? She was after my time, actually, but she was supposed to have been a beautiful woman, generously endowed by Nature, and they say it was impossible to find one square inch of her lovely body that had not received some variety of stage violence in one play or another. The legend is that she died ten thousand times, in sixty separate and distinct ways, each more hideous than the last; and that she writhed in the assaults of brutal rapine on no less than three thousand theatrical occasions. For the remainder of her life she could not speak above a whisper: the years of screaming had torn her throat to shreds.

At any rate, the evening following my first meeting with Sellig, César and I were seated in this unique little theatre with two young ladies we had escorted there; they were uncommonly pretty but uncommonly common—in point of fact, they were barely on the safe side of respectability's border, being inhabitants of that peculiar demimonde, that shadow world where several professions—actress, model, barmaid, bawd—mingle and merge and overlap and often coexist. But we were young, César and I, and this was, after all, Paris. Their names, they told us, were Clothilde and Mathilde—and I was never quite sure which was which. Soon after our arrival, the lights dimmed and the Guignol curtain was raised.

The first offering on the programme was a dull, shrill little boudoir farce that concerned itself with broken corset laces and men hiding under the bed and popping out of closets. It seemed to amuse our feminine companions well enough, but the applause in the house was desultory, I thought, a mere form . . . this fluttering nonsense was not what the patrons had come for, was not the sort of fare on which the Guignol had built its reputation. It was an hors d'oeuvre. The entrée followed.

It was called, if memory serves, *La Septième Porte*, and was nothing more than an opportunity for Bluebeard—played by an actor wearing an elaborately ugly make-up—to open six of his legendary seven doors for his new young wife (displaying, among other things, realistically mouldering cadavers and a torture chamber in full operation). Remaining faithful to the legend, Bluebeard warns his wife never to open the seventh door. Left alone on stage, she of course cannot resist the tug of curiosity—she opens the door, letting loose a shackled swarm of shrieking, livid, rag-bedecked but not entirely unattractive harpies, whose white bodies, through their shredded clothing, are crisscrossed with crimson welts. They tell her they are Bluebeard's ex-wives, kept perpetually in a pitch-dark dungeon, in a state near to starvation, and periodically tortured by the vilest means imaginable. Why? the new wife asks. Bluebeard enters, a black whip in his hand. For the sin of curiosity, he replies—they, like you, could not resist the lure of the seventh door! The other wives chain the girl to them, and cringing under the crack of Bluebeard's whip, they crawl back into the darkness of the dungeon. Bluebeard locks the seventh door and soliloquizes: Diogenes had an easy task, to find an honest man; but my travail is tenfold—for where is she, does she live, the wife who does not pry and snoop, who does not pilfer her husband's pockets, steam open his letters, and when he is late returning home, demand to know what wench he has been tumbling?

The lights had been dimming slowly until now only Bluebeard was illuminated, and at this point he turned to the audience and addressed the women therein. "*Mesdames et Mademoiselles!*" he declaimed. "*Écoute! En garde! Voici la septième porte*—Hear me! Beware! Behold the seventh door!" By a stage trick the door was transformed into a mirror. The curtain fell to riotous applause.

Recounted badly, *La Septième Porte* seems a trumpery entertainment, a mere excuse for scenes of horror—and so it was. But there was a strength, a power to the portrayal of Bluebeard; that ugly devil up there on the shabby little stage was like an icy flame, and when he'd turned to the house and delivered that closing line, there had been such force of personality, such demonic zeal, such hatred and scorn, such monumental threat, that I could feel my young companion shrink against me and shudder.

"Come, come, *ma petite*," I said, "it's only a play."

"*Je le déteste,*" she said.

"You detest him? Who, Bluebeard?"

"Laval."

My French was sketchy at that time, and her English almost nonexistent, but as we made our slow way up the aisle, I managed to glean that the actor's name was Laval, and that she had at one time had some offstage congress with him, congress of an intimate nature, I gathered. I could not help asking *why*, since she disliked him so. (I was naïf then, you see, and knew little of women;

it was somewhat later in life I learned that many of them find evil and even ugliness irresistible.) In answer to my question, she only shrugged and delivered a platitude: "*Les affaires sont les affaires*—Business is business."

Sellig was waiting for us in the foyer. His height, and his great beauty of face, made him stand out. Our two pretty companions took to him at once, for his attractive exterior was supplemented by waves of charm.

"Did you enjoy the programme?" he asked of me.

I did not know exactly what to reply. "Enjoy? . . . Let us say I found it fascinating, M'sieu' Sellig."

"It did not strike you as tawdry? Cheap? Vulgar?"

"All those, yes. But at the same time, exciting, as sometimes only the tawdry, the cheap, the vulgar can be."

"You may be right. I have not watched a Guignol production for several years. Although, surely, the acting . . ."

We were entering a carriage, all five of us. I said, "The acting was unbelievably bad—with one exception."

"Really? And the exception?"

"The actor who played Bluebeard in a piece called *La Septième Porte*. His name is—" I turned to my companion again.

"Laval," she said, and the sound became a viscous thing.

"Ah yes," said Sellig. "Laval. The name is not entirely unknown to me. Shall we go to Maxime's?"

We did, and experienced a most enjoyable evening. Sellig's fame and personal magnetism won us the best table and the most efficient service. He told a variety of amusing—but never coarse—anecdotes about theatrical life, and did so without committing that all-too-common actor's offense of dominating the conversation. One anecdote concerned the theatre we had just left:

"I suppose César has told the story of the Guignol doctor. No? Ah then, it seems that at one point it was thought a capital idea to hire a house physician— to tend to swooning patrons and so on, you know. This was done, but it was unsuccessful. On the first night of the physician's tour of duty, a male spectator found one particular bit of stage torture too much for him, and he fainted. The house physician was summoned. He could not be found. Finally, the ushers revived the unconscious man without benefit of medical assistance, and naturally they apologized profusely and explained they had not been able to find the doctor. 'I know,' the man said, rather sheepishly, '*I am the doctor.*'"

At the end of the evening, César and I escorted our respective (but not precisely respectable) ladies to their dwellings, where more pleasure was found. Sellig went home alone. I felt sorry for him, and there was a moment when it crossed my mind that perhaps he was one of those men who have no need of women— the theatrical profession is thickly inhabited by such men—but César privately assured me that Sellig had a mistress, a lovely and gracious widow named Lise, for Sellig's tastes were exceedingly refined and his image unblemished by descents into the dimly lit world of the sporting house. My own tastes, though acute, were not so elevated, and thus I enjoyed myself immensely that night.

Ignorance, they say, is bliss. I did not know that my ardent companion's warmth would turn unalterably cold in the space of a single night.

IV

Face of Evil

The *commissaire de police* had never seen anything like it. He spoke poor English, but I was able to glean his meaning without too much difficulty. "It is how you say . . ."

"Horrible?"

"*Ah, oui, mais . . . étrange, incroyable . . .*"

"Unique?"

"*Si! Uniquement monstrueux! Uniquement dégoûtant!*"

Uniquely disgusting. Yes, it was that. It was that, certainly.

"The manner, M'sieu' . . . the method . . . the—"

"Mutilation."

"*Oui, la mutilation . . . est irrégulière, anormale . . .*"

We were in the morgue—not that newish Medico-Legal Institute of the University on the banks of the Seine, but the *old* morgue, that wretched, ugly place on the quai de l'Archevêché. She—Clothilde, my *petite amie* of the previous night—had been foully murdered; killed with knives; her prettiness destroyed; her very womanhood destroyed, extracted bloodily but with surgical precision. I stood in the morgue with the *commissaire,* César, Sellig, and the other girl, Mathilde. Covering the corpse with its anonymous sheet, the *commissaire* said, "It resembles, does it not, the work of your English killer . . . Jacques?"

"Jack," I said. "Jack the Ripper."

"*Ah oui.*" He looked down upon the covered body. "*Mais pourquoi?*"

"Yes," I said hoarsely. "Why indeed? . . ."

"*La cause . . . la raison . . . le motif,*" he said; and then delivered himself of a small, eloquent, Gallic shrug. "*Inconnu.*"

Motive unknown. He had stated it succinctly. A girl of the streets, a *fille de joie,* struck down, mutilated, her femaleness cancelled out. Who did it? *Inconnu.* And why? *Inconnu.*

"*Merci, messieurs, mademoiselle . . .*" The *commissaire* thanked us and we left the cold repository of Paris's unclaimed dead. All four of us—it had been "all five of us" just the night before—were strained, silent. The girl Mathilde was weeping. We, the men, felt not grief exactly—how could we, for one we had known so briefly, so imperfectly?—but a kind of embarrassment. Perhaps that is the most common reaction produced by the presence of death: embarrassment. Death is a kind of nakedness, a kind of indecency, a kind of *faux pas.* Unless we have known the dead person well enough to experience true loss, or unless we have wronged the dead person enough to experience guilt, the only emotion we can experience is embarrassment. I must confess my own embarrassment was tinged with guilt. It was I, you see, who had used her, such a short time before. And now she would never be used again. Her warm lips were cold; her knowing fingers, still; her cajoling voice, silent; the very stronghold and temple of her treasure was destroyed.

In the street, I felt I had to make some utterance. "To think," I said, "that her last evening was spent at the Guignol!"

Sellig smiled sympathetically. "My friend," he said, "the Grand Guignol is not only a shabby little theatre in Montmartre alley. This"—his gesture took in the world—"this is the Grandest Guignol of all."

I nodded. He placed a hand on my shoulder. "Do not be too much alone," he advised me. "Come to the Théâtre tonight. We are playing *Cinna.*"

"Thank you," I said. "But I have a strange urge to revisit the Guignol . . ."

César seemed shocked or puzzled, but Sellig understood. "Yes," he said, "that is perhaps a good thought." We parted—Sellig to his rooms, César with the weeping girl, I to my hotel.

I have an odd infirmity—perhaps it is not so odd, and perhaps it is no infirmity at all—but great shock or disappointment or despair do not rob me of sleep as they rob the sleep of others. On the contrary, they rob me of energy, they drug me, they send me into the merciful solace of sleep like a powerful anodyne. And so, that afternoon, I slept. But it was a sleep invaded by dreams . . . dreams of gross torture and mutilation, of blood, and of the dead Clothilde—alive again for the duration of a nap—repeating over and over again a single statement.

I awoke covered with perspiration, and with that statement gone just beyond the reach of my mind. Try as I did, I could not recall it. I dashed cold water in my face to clear my head, and although I had no appetite, I rang for service and had some food brought me in my suite. Then, the theatre hour approaching, I dressed and made my way toward Montmartre and the rue Chaptal.

The Guignol's *chef-d'oeuvre* that evening was a bit of white supremacy propaganda called *Chinoiserie.* ("The yellow menace" was just beginning to become a popular prejudice.) A white girl played by a buxom but ungifted actress was sold as a slave to a lecherous Chinese mandarin, and after being duly ravished by him and established as his most favored concubine, fell into the clutches of the beautiful but jealous Chinese woman who had hitherto occupied that honored post. The Woman Scorned, taking advantage of the temporary absence of her lord, seized the opportunity to strip her rival naked and subject her to the first installment of The Death of a Thousand Slices, when her plans were thwarted by the appearance of a handsome French lieutenant who freed the white girl and offered her the chance to turn the tables on the Asian witch. The liberated victim, after first frightening her tormentress with threats of the Thousand Slices, proved a credit to her race by contenting herself with a plume. Although I had been told that *l'épisode du chatouillement*—the tickling scene—was famed far and wide, going on for several minutes of shrieking hysterics until the tickled lady writhed herself out of her clothing, I left before its conclusion. The piece was unbearably boring, though it was no worse than the previous evening's offering. The reason for its tediousness was simple: Laval did not appear in the play. On my way out of the theatre, I inquired of an usher about the actor's absence. "Ah, the great Laval," he said, with shuddering admiration. "It is his—do you say 'night away'?"

"Night off . . ."

"*Oui.* His night off. He appears on alternate nights, *M'sieu'* . . ."

Feeling somehow cheated, I decided to return the following night. I did so; in fact, I made it a point to visit the Guignol every night that week on which Laval was playing. I saw him in several little plays—shockers in which he starred as the monsters of history and legend—and in each, his art was lit by black fire and was the more admirable since he did not rely upon a succession of fantastic make-ups—

in each, he wore the *same* grotesque make-up (save for the false facial hair) he had worn as Bluebeard; I assumed it was his trademark. The plays—which were of his own authorship, I discovered—included *L'Inquisiteur,* in which he played Torquemada, the merciless heretic-burner (convincing flames on the stage) and *L'Empoisonneur,* in which he played the insane, incestuous Cesare Borgia. There were many more, among them a contemporary story, *L'Éventreur,* in which he played the currently notorious Jack the Ripper, knifing pretty young harlots with extreme realism until the stage was scarlet with sham blood. In this, there was one of those typically Lavalesque flashes, an infernally inspired *cri de coeur,* when The Ripper, remorseful, sunken in shame, enraged at his destiny, surfeited with killings but unable to stop, tore a rhymed couplet from the bottom of his soul and flung it like a live thing into the house:

La vie est un corridor noir
D'impuissance et de désespoir!

That's not very much in English—"Life is a black corridor of impotence and despair"—but in the original, and when hurled with the ferocity of Laval, it was Kean's Hamlet, Irving's Macbeth, Salvini's Othello, all fused into a single theatrical moment.

And, in that moment, there was another fusion—a fusion, in my own mind, of two voices. One was that of the *commissaire de police*—"It resembles, does it not, the work of your English killer . . . Jacques?" The other was the voice of the dead Clothilde, repeating a phrase she had first uttered in life, and then, after her death, in that fugitive dream—*"Je le déteste."*

As the curtain fell, to tumultuous applause, I sent my card backstage, thus informing Laval that *"un admirateur"* wished to buy him a drink. Might we meet at L'Oubliette? The response was long in coming, insultingly long, but at last it did come and it was affirmative. I left at once for L'Oubliette.

Forty minutes later, after I had consumed half a bottle of red wine, Laval entered. The waitress brought him to my table and we shook hands.

I was shocked, for, as I looked into his face, I immediately realized that Laval never wore evil make-up on the Guignol stage.

He had no need of it.

V

An Intimate Knowledge of Horrors

Looking about, Laval said, "L'Oubliette," and sat down. "The filthy place is aptly named. Do you know what an *oubliette* is, M'sieu'?"

"No," I said; "I wish my French were as excellent as your English."

"But surely you know our word, *oublier*?"

"My French-English lexicon," I replied, "says it means 'to forget, to omit, to leave.'"

He nodded. "That is correct. In the old days, a variety of secret dungeon was called an *oubliette.* It was subterranean. It had no door, no window. It could be entered only by way of a trapdoor at the top. The trapdoor was too high to reach, even by climbing, since the walls sloped in the wrong direction and were eternally thick with slime. There was no bed, no chair, no table, no light, and very little air. Prisoners were dropped down into such dungeons to be—literally—forgotten. They seldom left alive. Infrequently, when a prisoner was fortunate enough to be freed by a change in administration, he was found to have become blind—from years in the dark. And almost always, of course, insane."

"You have an intimate knowledge of horrors, Monsieur Laval," I said.

He shrugged. *"C'est mon métier."*

"Will you drink red wine?"

"Since you are paying, I will drink whisky," he said; adding, "if they have it here."

They did, an excellent Scotch and quite expensive. I decided to join him. He downed the first portion as soon as it was poured—not waiting for even a perfunctory toast—and instantly demanded another. This, too, he flung down his throat in one movement, smacking his bestial lips. I could not help thinking how much more graphic than our "he drinks like a fish" or "like a drainpipe" is the equivalent French figure of speech: "He drinks like a hole."

"Now then, M'sieu' . . . Pendragon? . . ."

"Glencannon."

"Yes. You wished to speak with me."

I nodded.

"Speak," he said, gesturing to the barmaid for another drink.

"Why," I began, "I'm afraid I have nothing in particular to say, except that I admire your acting . . ."

"Many people do."

What a graceless boor, I told myself, but I continued: "Rightfully so, Monsieur Laval. I am new to Paris, but I have seen much theatre here these past few weeks, and to my mind yours is a towering talent, in the front rank of contemporary *artistes,* perhaps second only to—"

"Eh? Second?" He swallowed the fresh drink and looked up at me, his unwholesome eyes flaming. "Second to—whom, would you say?"

"I was going to say Sellig."

Laval laughed. It was not a warming sound. His face grew uglier. "Sellig! Indeed. Sellig, the handsome. Sellig, the classicist. Sellig, the noble. *Bah!*"

I was growing uncomfortable. "Come, sir," I said, "surely you are not being fair . . ."

"Fair. That is oh so important to you English, is it not? Well, let me tell you, M'sieu' Whatever-your-name-is—the lofty strutting of the mounte-bank Sellig makes me sick! What he can do, fools can do. Who cannot pompously declaim the cold, measured alexandrines of Racine and Corneille and Molière? Stop any schoolboy on the street and ask him to recite a bit of *Phèdre* or *Tartuffe* and he will oblige you, in that same stately classroom drone Sellig employs. Do not speak to me of this Sellig. He is a fraud; *worse*—he is a bore."

"He is also," I said, "my friend."

"A sorry comment on your taste."

"And yet it is a taste that can also appreciate you."

"To some, champagne and seltzer water taste the same."

"You know, sir, you are really quite rude."

"True."

"You must have few friends."

"Wrong. I have none."

"But that is distressing! Surely—"

He interrupted. "There is a verse of the late Rostand's. Perhaps you know it. '*A force de vous voir vous faire des amis . . .*' et cetera?"

"My French is poor."

"You need not remind me. I will give you a rough translation. 'Seeing the sort of friends you others have in tow, I cry with joy: send me another foe!'"

"And yet," I said, persisting, "all men need friends . . ."

Laval's eyes glittered like dark gems. "I am no ordinary man," he said. "I was born under the sign of Sagittarius. Perhaps you know nothing of astrology? Or, if you do, perhaps you think of Sagittarius as merely the innocuous sign of the Archer? Remember, then, just who that archer is—not a simple bear or bull or crab or pair of fish, not a man, not a creature at all, but a very unnatural creature half human, half bestial. Sagittarius: the Man-Beast. And I tell you this, M'sieu' . . ." He dispatched the whisky in one gulp and banged the empty glass on the table to attract the attention of the barmaid. "I tell you this," he repeated. "So potent was the star under which I was born, that I have done what no one in the world has done—nor ever *can* do!"

The sentence was like a hot iron, searing my brain. I was to meet it once again before I left Paris. But now, sitting across the table from the mad—for he indeed seemed mad—Laval, I said, softly, "And what is it you have done, Monsieur?"

He chuckled nastily. "That," he said, "is a professional secret."

I tried another approach. "Monsieur Laval . . ."

"Yes?"

"I believe we have a mutual friend."

"Who may that be?"

"A lady."

"Oh? And her name?"

"She calls herself Clothilde. I do not know her last name."

"Then I gather she is not, after all, a lady."

I shrugged. "Do you know her?"

"I know many women," he said; and his face clouding with bitterness, he added, "Do you find that surprising—with this face?"

"Not at all. But you have not answered my question."

"I may know your Mam'selle Clothilde; I cannot be certain. May I have another drink?"

"To be sure." I signalled the waitress, and turned again to Laval. "She told me she knew you in her—professional capacity."

"It may be so. I do not clot my mind with memories of such women." The waitress poured out another portion of Scotch and Laval downed it. "Why do you ask?"

"For two reasons. First, because she told me she detested you."

"It is a common complaint. And the second reason?"

"Because she is dead."

"Ah?"

"Murdered. Mutilated. Obscenely disfigured."

"*Quel dommage.*"

"It is not a situation to be met with a platitude, Monsieur!"

Laval smiled. It made him look like a lizard. "Is it not? How must I meet it, then? With tears? With a clucking of the tongue? With a beating of my breast and a rending of my garments? Come, M'sieu' . . . she was a woman of the streets . . . I scarcely knew her, if indeed I knew her at all . . ."

"Why did she detest you?" I suddenly demanded.

"Oh, my dear sir! If I knew the answers to such questions, I would be clairvoyant. Because I have the face of a Notre Dame gargoyle, perhaps. Because she did not like the way I combed my hair. Because I left her too small a fee. Who knows? I assure you, her detestation does not perturb me in the slightest."

"To speak plainly, you relish it."

"Yes. Yes, I relish it."

"Do you also relish"—I toyed with my glass—"blood, freshly spilt?"

He looked at me blankly for a moment. Then he threw back his head and roared with amusement. "I see," he said at last. "I understand now. You suspect I murdered this trollop?"

"She is dead, sir. It ill becomes you to malign her."

"This *lady,* then. You really think I killed her?"

"I accuse you of nothing, Monsieur Laval. But . . ."

"But?"

"But it strikes me as a distinct possibility."

He smiled again. "How interesting. How very, very interesting. Because she detested me?"

"That is one reason."

He pushed his glass to one side. "I will be frank with you, M'sieu'. Yes, I knew Clothilde, briefly. Yes, it is true she loathed me. She found me disgusting. But can you not guess why?"

I shook my head. Laval leaned forward and spoke more softly. "You and I, M'sieu', we are men of the world. . . . and surely you can understand that there are things . . . certain little things . . . that an imaginative man might require of such a woman? Things which—if she were overly fastidious—she might find objectionable?" Still again, he smiled. "I assure you, her detestation of me had no other ground than that. She was a silly little *bourgeoise.* She had no flair for her profession. She was easily shocked." Conspiratorially, he added: "Shall I be more specific?"

"That will not be necessary." I caught the eye of the waitress and paid her. To Laval, I said, "I must not detain you further, Monsieur."

"Oh, am I being sent off?" he said, mockingly, rising. "Thank you for the whisky, M'sieu'. It was excellent." And, laughing hideously, he left.

VI

The Monster

I felt shaken, almost faint, and experienced a sudden desire to talk to someone. Hoping Sellig was playing that night at the Théâtre Français, I took a carriage there and was told he could probably be found at his rooms. My informant mentioned an address to my driver, and before long, Sébastien seemed pleasantly surprised at the appearance of his announced guest.

Sellig's rooms were tastefully appointed. The drapes were tall, classic folds of deep blue. A few good pictures hung on the walls, the chairs were roomy and comfortable, and the mingled fragrances of tobacco and book leather gave the air a decidedly masculine musk. Over a small spirit lamp, Sellig was preparing a simple ragout. As he stood in his shirt sleeves, stirring the food, I talked.

"You said, the other evening, that the name Laval was not unknown to you."

"That gentleman seems to hold you fascinated," he observed.

"Is it an unhealthy fascination, would you say?" I asked, candidly.

Sellig laughed. "Well, he is not exactly an appealing personage."

"Then you do know him?"

"In a sense. I have never seen him perform, however."

"He is enormously talented. He dominates the stage. There are only two actors in Paris who can transfix an audience in that manner."

"The other is . . . ?"

"You."

"Ah. Thank you. And yet, you do not equate me with Laval?"

Quickly, I assured him: "No, not at all. In everything but that one quality you and he are utterly different. Diametrically opposed."

"I am glad of that."

"Have you known him long?" I asked.

"Laval? Yes. For quite some time."

"He is not 'an appealing personage,' you said just now. Would you say he is . . . morally reprehensible?"

Sellig turned to me. "I would be violating a strict confidence if I told you any more than this: if he is morally corrupt (and I am not saying that he is), he is not reprehensible. If he is evil, then he was evil even in his mother's womb."

A popular song came to my mind, and I said, lightly, "More to be pitied than censured?"

Sellig received this remark seriously. "Yes," he said. "Yes, that is the point precisely. 'The sins of the father . . .'" But then he broke off and served the ragout.

As he ate, I—who had no appetite—spoke of my troubled mind and general depression.

"Perhaps it is not good for you to stay alone tonight," he said. "Would you like to sleep here? There is an extra bedroom."

"It would inconvenience you . . ."

"Not at all. I should be glad of the company."

I agreed to stay, for I was not looking forward to my lonely hotel suite, and not long after that we retired to our rooms. I fell asleep almost at once, but woke in a sweat about three in the morning. I arose, wrapped myself in one of Sel-lig's robes, and walked into the library for a book that might send me off to sleep again.

Sellig's collection of books was extensive, although heavily overbalanced by plays, volumes of theatrical criticism, biographies of actors, and so forth, a high percentage of them in En-glish. I chose none of these: instead, I took down a weighty tome of French history. Its pedantic style and small type, as well as my imperfect command of the language, would combine to form the needed sedative. I took the book to bed with me.

My grasp of written French being somewhat firmer than my grasp of the conversational variety, I managed to labor through most of the first chapter before I began to turn the leaves in search of a more interesting section. It was quite by accident that my eyes fell upon a passage that seemed to thrust itself up from the page and stamp itself upon my brain. Though but a single sentence, I felt stunned by it. In a fever of curiosity, I read the other matter on that page, then turned back and read from an earlier point. I read in that volume for about ten minutes, or so I thought, but when I finished and looked up at the clock, I realized that I had read for over an hour. What I had read had numbed and shaken me.

I have never been a superstitious man. I have never believed in the existence of ghosts, or vampires, or other undead creatures out of lurid legend. They make excellent entertainment, but never before that shattering hour had I accepted them as anything more than entertainment. But as I sat in that bed, the book in my hands, the city outside silent, I had reason to feel as if a hand from some sub-zero hell had reached up and laid itself—oh, very gently—upon my heart. A shudder ran through my body. I looked down again at the book.

The pages I had read told of a monster—a real monster who had lived in France centuries before. The Marquis de Sade, in comparison, was a mischievous schoolboy. This was a man of high birth and high aspirations, a marshal of France who at the peak of his power had been the richest noble in all of Europe and who had fought side by side with Joan of Arc, but who had later fallen into such depths of degeneracy that he had been tried and sentenced to the stake by a shocked legislature. In a search for immortality, a yearning to avoid death, he had carried out disgusting experiments on the living bodies of youths and maidens and little children. Seven or eight hundred had died in the laboratory of his castle, died howling in pain and insanity, the victims of a "science" that was more like the unholy rites of the Black Mass. "The accused," read one of the charges at his trial, "has taken innocent boys and girls, and inhumanly butchered, killed, dismembered, burned, and otherwise tortured them, and the said accused has immolated the bodies of the said innocents to devils, invoked and sacrificed to evil spirits, and has foully committed sin with young boys and in other ways lusted against nature after young girls, while they were alive or sometimes dead or even sometimes during their death throes." Another charge spoke of "the hand, the eyes, and the heart of one of these said children, with its blood in a glass vase . . ." And yet this madman, this miscreant monster, had offered no resistance when arrested, had felt justified for his actions, had said proudly and defiantly under the legislated torture: "*So potent was the star under which I was born that I have done what no one in the world has done nor ever can do.*"

His name was Gilles de Laval, Baron de Rais, and he became known for all time and to all the world, of course, as Bluebeard.

I was out of bed in an instant, and found myself pounding like a madman on the door of Sellig's bedroom. When there was no response, I opened the door and went in. He was not in his bed. Behind me, I heard another door open. I turned.

Sellig was coming out of yet another room, hardly more than a closet: behind him, just before he closed the door and locked it, I caught a glimpse of bottles and glass trays—I remember surmising, in that instant, that perhaps he was a devotee of the new art of photography, but I had no wish to dwell further on this, for I was bursting with what I wanted to say. "Sébastien!" I cried. "I must tell you something . . ."

"What are you doing up at this hour, my friend?"

". . . Something incredible . . . terrifying . . ." (It did not occur to me to echo his question.)

"But you are distraught. Here, sit down . . . let me fetch you some cognac . . ."

The words tumbled out of me pell-mell, and I could see they made very little sense to Sellig. He wore the expression of one confronted by a lunatic. His eyes remained fixed on my face, as if he were alert for the first sign of total disintegration and the cognac he had placed in my hand.

Sellig spoke. "Let me see if I understand you," he began. "You met Laval this evening . . . and he said something about his star, and the accomplishment of something no other man has ever accomplished . . . and just now, in this book, you find the same statement attributed to Bluebeard . . . and, from this, you are trying to tell me that Laval . . ."

I nodded. "I know it sounds mad . . ."

"It does."

". . . But consider, Sébastien: the names, first of all, are identical—Bluebeard's name was Gilles de *Laval*. In the shadow of the stake, he boasted of doing what no man had ever done, of succeeding at his ambition . . . and are you aware of the nature of his ambition? To live forever! It was to that end that he butchered hundreds of innocents, trying to wrest the very riddle of life from their bodies!"

"But you say he was burned at the stake . . ."

"No! *Sentenced* to be burned! In return for not revoking the confessions he made under torture, he was granted the mercy of strangulation before burning . . ."

"Even so—"

"Listen to me! His relatives were allowed to remove his strangled body from the pyre before the flames reached it! That is a historical fact! They took it away—so they *said*!—to inter it in a Carmelite church in the vicinity. But don't you see what they really did?"

"No . . ."

"Don't you see, Sébastien, that this monster had found the key to eternal life, and had instructed his helots to revive his strangled body by use of those same loathsome arts he had practised? Don't you see that he went on living? That he lives still? That he tortures and murders still? That even when his hands are not drenched in human blood, they are drenched in the mock blood of the Guignol? That the actor Laval and the Laval of old are one and the same?"

Sellig looked at me strangely. It infuriated me. "I am not mad!" I said. I rose and screamed at him: "*Don't you understand?*"

And then—what with the lack of food, and the wine I had drunk with Laval, and the cognac, and the tremulous state of my nerves—the room began to tilt, then shrink, then spin, then burst into a star-shower, and I dimly saw Sellig reach out for me as I fell forward into blackness.

VII

A Transparent Cryptogram

The bedroom was full of noonday sunlight when I awoke. It lacerated my eyes. I turned away from it and saw someone sitting next to the bed. My eyes focussed, not without difficulty, and I realized it was a woman—a woman of exceptional beauty. Before I could speak, she said, "My name is Madame Pelletier. I am Sébastien's friend. He has asked me to care for you. You were ill last night."

"You must be . . . Lise . . ."

She nodded. "Can you sit up now?"

"I think so."

"Then you must take a little bouillon."

At the mention of food, I was instantly very hungry. Madame Pelletier helped me sit up, propped pillows at my back and began to feed me broth with a spoon. At first, I resisted this, but upon discovering that my trembling hand would not support the weight of the spoon, I surrendered to her ministrations.

Soon, I asked, "And where is Sébastien now?"

"At the Théâtre. A rehearsal of *Oedipe*." With a faintly deprecatory inflection, she added, "Voltaire's."

I smiled at this, and said, "Your theatrical tastes are as pristine as Sébastien's."

She smiled in return. "It was not always so, perhaps. But when one knows a man like Sébastien, a man dedicated, noble, with impeccable taste and living a life beyond reproach . . . one climbs up to his level, or tries to."

"You esteem him highly."

"I love him, M'sieu'."

I had not forgotten my revelation of the night before. True, it seemed less credible in daylight, but it continued to stick in my mind like a burr. I asked myself what I should do with my fantastic theory. Blurt it out to this charming lady and have her think me demented? Take it to the *commissaire* and have him think me the same? Try to place it again before Sébastien, in more orderly fashion, and solicit his aid? I decided on the last course, and informed my lovely nurse that I felt well enough to leave. She protested; I assured her my strength was restored; and at last she left the bedroom and allowed me to dress. I did so quickly, and left the Sellig rooms immediately thereafter.

By this time, they knew me at the Théâtre Français, and I was allowed to stand in the wings while the Voltaire tragedy was being rehearsed. When the scene was finished, I sought out Sellig, drew him aside, and spoke to him, phrasing my suspicions with more calm than I had before.

"My dear friend," he said, "I flatter myself that my imagination is broad and ranging, that my mind is open, that I can give credence to many wonders at which other men might scoff. But *this*—"

"I know, I know," I said hastily, "and I do not profess to believe it entirely myself—but it is a clue, if nothing more, to Laval's character; a solution, perhaps, to a living puzzle . . ."

Sellig was a patient man. "Very well. I will have a bit of time after this rehearsal and before tonight's performance. Come back later and we will . . ." His voice trailed off. "And we will talk, at least. I do not know what else we can do."

I agreed to leave. I went directly to the Guignol, even though I knew that, being midafternoon, it would not be open. Arriving there, I found an elderly functionary, asked if Monsieur Laval was inside, perhaps rehearsing, and was told there was no one in the theatre. Then, after pressing a banknote into the old man's hand, I persuaded him to give me Laval's address. He did, and I immediately hailed a passing carriage.

As it carried me away from Montmartre, I tried to govern my thoughts. Why was I seeking out Laval? What would I say to him once I had found him? Would I point a finger at him and dramatically accuse him of being Gilles de Laval, Baron de Rais, a man of the Fifteenth Century? He would laugh at me, and have me committed as a madman. I still had not decided on a plan of attack when the carriage stopped, and the driver opened the door and said, "We are here, M'sieu'."

I stepped out, paid him, and looked at the place to which I had been taken. Dumbfounded, I turned to the driver and said, "But this is not—"

"It is the address M'sieu' gave me." He was correct. It was. I thanked him and the carriage drove off. My mind churning, I entered the building.

It was the same one which contained Sellig's rooms. Summoning the concierge, I asked the number of Laval's apartments. He told me no such person lived there. I described Laval. He nodded and said, "Ah. The ugly one. Yes, he lives here, but his name is not Laval. It is De Retz."

Rayx, Rays, Retz, Rais—according to the history book, they were different spellings of the same name. "And the number of his suite?" I asked, impatiently.

"Oh, he shares a suite," he said. "He shares a suite with M'sieu' Sellig . . ."

I masked my astonishment and ran up the stairs, growing more angry with each step. To think that Sébastien had concealed this from me! Why? For what reason? And yet Laval had not shared the apartment the night before . . . What did it mean?

Etiquette discarded, I did not knock but threw open the door and burst in. "Laval!" I shouted. "Laval, I know you are here! You cannot hide from me!"

There was no answer. I stalked furiously through the rooms. They were empty. "Madame?" I called. "Madame Pelletier?" And then, standing in Sellig's bedroom, I saw that the place had been ransacked. Drawers of chiffoniers had been pulled out and relieved of their contents. It appeared very much as if the occupant had taken sudden flight.

Then I remembered the little room or closet I had seen Sellig leaving in the small hours. Going to it, I turned the knob and found it locked. Desperation and anger flooded my arms with strength, and yelling unseemly oaths, I broke into the room.

It was chaos.

The glass phials and demijohns had been smashed into shards, as if someone had flailed methodically among them with a cane. What purpose they had served was now a mystery. Perhaps a chemist could have analyzed certain residues among the debris, but I could not. Yet, somehow, these ruins did not seem, as I had first assumed, equipment for the development of photographic plates.

Again, supernatural awe turned me cold. Was this the dread laboratory of Bluebeard? Had these bottles and jars contained human blood and vital organs? In this Paris apartment, with Sellig as his conscripted assistant, had Laval distilled, out of death itself, the inmost secrets of life?

Quaking, I backed out of the little room, and in so doing, displaced a corner of one of the blue draperies. Odd things flicker through one's mind in the direst of circumstances—for some reason, I remembered having once heard that blue is sometimes a mortuary color used in covering the coffins of young persons . . . and also that it is a symbol of eternity and human immortality . . . blue coffins . . . blue drapes . . . Bluebeard . . .

I looked down at the displaced drape and saw something that was to delay my return to London, to involve me with the police for many days until they would finally judge me innocent and release me. On the floor at my feet, only half hidden by the blue drapes, was the naked, butchered, dead body of Madame Pelletier.

I think I screamed. I know I must have dashed from those rooms like a possessed thing. I cannot remember my flight, nor the hailing of any carriage, but I do know I returned to the Théâtre Français, a babbling, incoherent maniac who demanded that the rehearsal be stopped, who insisted upon seeing Sébastien Sellig.

The manager finally succeeded in breaking through the wall of my hysteria. He said only one thing, but that one thing served as the cohesive substance that made everything fall into place in an instant.

"He is not here, M'sieu'," he said. "It is very odd . . . he has never missed a rehearsal or a performance before today . . . he was here earlier, but now . . . an understudy has taken his place . . . I hope nothing has happened to him . . . but M'sieu' Sellig, believe me, is not to be found."

I stumbled out into the street, my brain a kaleidoscope. I thought of that little laboratory . . . and of those two utterly opposite men, the sublime Sellig and the depraved Laval, living in the same suite . . . I thought of Sagittarius, the Man-Beast . . . I thought of the phrase "The sins of the fathers," and of a banal tune, "More to be Pitied than Censured." . . . I realized now why Laval was absent from the Guignol on certain nights, the very nights Sellig appeared at the Théâtre Français . . . I heard my own voice, on that first night, inviting Sellig to accompany us to the Guignol: "Will you come? Or perhaps you have a performance?" And Sellig's answer: "I do háve a performance" (yes, but *where?*) . . . I heard Sellig's voice in other scraps: *I have not watched a Guignol performance for several years; I have never seen Laval perform* . . .

Of course not! How could he, when he and Laval . . .

I accosted a gendarme, seized his lapels, and roared into his astonished face: "Don't you see? How is it possible I overlooked it? It is so absurdly simple! It is the crudest . . . the most childish . . . the most transparent of cryptograms!"

"*What* is, M'sieu'?" he demanded.

I laughed—or wept. "*Sellig!*" I cried. "One has only to spell it backward!"

VIII

Over the Precipice

The dining room of the Century Club was now almost deserted. Lord Terry was sipping a brandy with his coffee. He had refused dessert, but Hunt had not, and he was dispatching the last forkful of a particularly rich *baba au rhum*. His host produced from his pocket a massive, ornate case—of the same design as his pill box—and offered Hunt a cigar. It was deep brown, slender, fragrant, marvelously fresh. "The wizard has his wand," said Lord Terry, "the priest his censer, the king his sceptre, the soldier his sword, the policeman his nightstick, the orchestra conductor his baton. I have these. I suppose your generation would speak of phallic symbolism."

"We might," Hunt answered, smiling; "but we would also accept a cigar." He did, and a waiter appeared from nowhere to light them for the two men.

Through the first festoons of smoke, Hunt said, "You tell a grand story, sir."

"Story," the Earl repeated. "By that, you imply I have told a—whopper?"

"An extremely entertaining whopper."

He shrugged. "Very well. Let it stand as that and nothing more." He drew reflectively on his cigar.

"Come, Lord Terry," Hunt said. "Laval and Sellig were one man? The son of Edward Hyde? Starring at the Guignol in his evil personality and then, after a drink of his father's famous potion in that little laboratory, transforming himself into the blameless classicist of the Théâtre Français?"

"Exactly, my boy. And a murderer, besides, at least the Laval part of him; a murderer who felt I was drawing too close to the truth, and so fled Paris, never to be heard from again."

"Fled where?"

"Who knows? To New York, perhaps, where he still lives the double life of a respectable man in constant fear of involuntarily becoming a monster in public (Jekyll came to that pass in the story), and who must periodically imbibe his father's formula simply to remain a man . . . and who sometimes fails. Think of it! Even now, somewhere, in this very city, this very *club,* the inhuman Man-Beast, blood still steaming on his hands, may be drinking off the draught that will transform him into a gentleman of spotless reputation! A gentleman who, when dominant, loathes the dormant evil half of his personality—just as that evil half, when *it* is dominant, loathes the respectable gentleman! I am not insisting he is still alive, you understand, but that is precisely the way it was in Paris, back in the early Nineteen Hundreds."

Hunt smiled. "You don't expect me to believe you, sir, surely?"

"If I have given you a pleasant hour," Lord Terry replied, "I am content. I do not ask you to accept my story as truth. But I do inquire of you: why *not* accept it? Why couldn't it be the truth?"

"He is teasing me, of course," Hunt told himself, "luring me on to another precipice of the plot, like any seasoned storyteller. And part of his art is the dead seriousness of his tone and face."

"Why couldn't it?" Lord Terry repeated.

Hunt was determined not to be led into pitfalls, so he did not trot out lengthy rebuttals and protestations about the fantastic and antinatural "facts" of the tale—he was sure the Earl had arguments woven of the best casuistry to meet and vanquish anything he might have said. So he simply conceded: "It could be true, I suppose."

But a second later, not able to resist, he added, "The—story—does have one very large flaw."

"Flaw? Rubbish. What flaw?"

"It seems to me you've tried to have the best of both worlds, sir, tried to tell two stories in one, and they don't really meld. Let's say, for the sake of argument, that I am prepared to accept as fact the notion that Gilles de Rais was not burned at the stake, that he not only escaped death but managed to live for centuries, thanks to his unholy experiments. All well and good. Let's say that he was indeed the Guignol actor known as Laval. Still well, still good. But you've made him something else—something he could not possibly be. The son of Dr. Henry Jekyll, or rather, of Jekyll's alter ego, Edward Hyde. In my trade, we would say your story 'needs work.' We would ask you to make up your mind—was Laval the son of Edward Hyde, or was he a person centuries older than his own father? He could not be both."

Lord Terry nodded. "Oh, I see," he said. "Yes, I should have made myself clearer. No, I do not doubt for a moment that Laval and Sellig were one and the same person and that person the natural son of Edward Hyde. I think the facts support that. The Bluebeard business is, as you say, quite impossible. It was a figment of my disturbed mind, nothing more. Sellig could not have been Gilles."

"Then—"

"You or I might take a saint as our idol, might we not, or a great statesman—Churchill, Roosevelt—or possibly a literary or musical or scientific genius. At any rate, some lofty benefactor of immaculate prestige. But the son of Hyde? Would he not be drawn to and fascinated by history's great figures of evil? Might he not liken himself to Bluebeard? Might he not assume his name? Might he not envelop himself in symbolic blue draperies? Might he not delight in portraying his idol upon the Guignol stage? Might it not please his fiendish irony to saddle even his 'good' self with a disguised form of Gilles's name, and to exert such influence over that good self that even as the noble Sellig he could wallow in the personality of, say, a Nero? Of *course* he was not actually Bluebeard. It was adulation and aping, my dear sir, identification and a touch of madness. In short, it was hero worship, pure and simple."

He had led Hunt to the precipice, after all, and the younger man had neatly tumbled over the edge.

"There is something else," Lord Terry said presently. "Something I have been saving for the last. I did not wish to inundate you with too much all at once. You say I've tried to tell two stories. But it may be—it just possibly may be—that I have not two but three stories here."

"Three?"

"Yes, in a way. It's just supposition, of course, a theory, and I have no evidence at all, other than circumstantial evidence, a certain remarkable juxtaposition of time and events that is a bit too pat to be coincidence . . ."

He treated himself to an abnormally long draw on his cigar, letting Hunt and the syntax hang in the air; then he started a new sentence: "Laval's father, Edward Hyde, may have left his mark on history in a manner much more real than the pages of a supposedly fictional work by Stevenson. Certain criminal deeds that are matters of police record may have been his doing. I think they were. Killings that took place between 1885 and 1891 in London, Paris, Moscow, Texas, New York, Nicaragua, and perhaps a few other places, by an unknown, unapprehended monster about whom speculation varies greatly but generally agrees on one point: the high probability that he was a medical man. Hyde, of course, was a medical man; or rather, Jekyll was; the same thing, really.

"What I'm suggesting, you see, is that Laval was—is?—not only the son of Hyde but the son of the fiend who has been supposed an Englishman, a Frenchman, an Algerian, a Polish Jew, a Russian, and an American; whose supposed true names include George Chapman, Severin Klosowski, Neill Cream, Sir William Gull, Aleksandr Pedachenko, Ameer Ben Ali, and even Queen Victoria's grandson, Eddy, Prince Albert Victor Christian Edward. His sobriquets are also legion: Frenchy, El Destripador, L'Éventreur, The Whitechapel Butcher, and, most popularly—"

Hunt snatched the words from his mouth: "Jack the Ripper."

IX

The Suspension of Disbelief

"Exactly," said Lord Terry. "The Ripper's killings, without exception, resembled the later Paris murders, and also the earlier massacres of Bluebeard's, in that they were obsessively sexual and resulted in 'wounds of a nature too shocking to be described,' as the London *Times* put it. The Bluebeard comparison is not exclusive with me—a Chicago doctor named Kiernan arrived at it independently and put it forth at the time of the Whitechapel murders. And the current series of perverted butcheries here in New York are, of course, of that same stripe. Incidently, may I call your attention to the sound of Jekyll's name? Trivial, of course, but it would have been characteristic of that scoundrel Hyde to tell one of his victims his name was Jekyll, which she might have taken as 'jackal' and later gasped out in her last fits, you know. We've placed Hyde's 'birth' at 1886 for no better reason than because the Stevenson story was published in that year . . . but if the story is based in truth, then it is a telling of events that took place before the publication date, perhaps very shortly before. Yes, there is a distinct possibility that Jack the Ripper was Mr. Hyde."

Hunt toyed with the dregs of his coffee. "Excuse me, Lord Terry," he said, "but another flaw has opened up."

"Truth cannot be flawed, my boy."

"Truth cannot, no." This time, it was Hunt who stalled. He signalled the waiter for hot coffee, elaborately added sugar and cream, stirred longly and thoughtfully. Then he said, "Jack the Ripper's crimes were committed, you say, between the years 1885 and 1891?"

"According to the best authorities, yes."

"But, sir," Hunt said, smiling deferentially all the while, "in Stevenson's story, published in 1886, Hyde *died*. He therefore could not have committed those crimes that took place after 1886."

Lord Terry spread his arms expansively. "Oh, my dear boy," he said, "when I suggest that the story was based in truth, I do not mean to imply that it was a newspaper report, a dreary list of dates and statistics. For one thing, many small items, such as names and addresses, were surely changed for obvious reasons (Soho for Whitechapel, perhaps). For another thing, Stevenson was a consummate craftsman, not a police blotter. The unfinished, so-called realistic story is stylish today, but in Stevenson's time a teller of tales had to bring a story to a satisfying and definite conclusion, like a symphony. No, no, I'm afraid I can't allow you even a technical point."

"If names were fabricated, what about that Jekyll-jackal business?"

"Quite right—I retract the Jekyll-jackal business. Trivial anyway."

Hunt persisted. "Was Hyde's nationality a fabrication of Stevenson's, too, then?"

"No, I'm inclined to believe he was actually English . . ."

"Ah! But Laval and Sellig—"

"Were French? Oh, I rather think not. Both spoke English like natives, you know. And Laval drank Scotch whisky like water—which I've never seen a Frenchman do. Also, he mistook my name for Pendragon—a grand old English name out of Arthurian legend, not the sort of name that would spring readily to French lips, I shouldn't think. No, I'm sure they—he—were compatriots of mine."

"What was he—they—doing in France?"

"For the matter of that, what was I? But if you really need reasons over and above the mundane, you might consider the remote possibility that he was using an assumed nationality as a disguise, a shield from the police. That's not *too* fanciful for you, I hope? Although this may be: might not a man obsessed with worship of Gilles de Rais, a man who tried to emulate his evil idol in all things, also put on his idol's nation and language like a magic cloak? But I shan't defend the story any further." He looked at his gold pocket watch, the size of a small potato and nearly as thick. "Too late, for one thing. Time for long-winded old codgers to be in their beds."

It was dismissal. He was, after all, an earl, and accustomed to calling the tune. Hunt hoped, however, that he hadn't offended him. As they walked slowly to the cloakroom to redeem Hunt's hat, the Earl's guest thought about truth and fiction and Byron's remark that the first was stranger than the second. He thought, too, about that element so essential to the reception of a strange tale whether it be true or false—the element of believability, at least the suspension of disbelief. Lord Terry had held him spellbound with his story, then had covered his tracks and filled in the chinks in his armor pretty well. If Hunt were disposed to be indulgent and generous, he could believe—or suspend disbelief—in the notion that Hyde was an actual person, that he was the maniac killer known as Jack the Ripper, even that he had sired a son who'd lived and died under the names of Laval and Sellig around the turn of the century, in a glamorous Paris that exists now only in memories and stories. All that was comfortably remote. But it was the other idea of Lord Terry's—that Hyde's son might still be alive today—that strained Hunt's credulity, shattered the pleasant spell, and somewhat spoiled the story for him. By any logical standard, it was the easiest of all to believe, granted the other premise; but belief does not depend upon logic, it is a delicate and fragile flower that draws nourishment from intuition and instinct and hunch. There was something about this latter half of the Twentieth Century—with its sports cars and television and nuclear bombs and cold wars—that just did not jibe with the flamboyant alchemy, the mysterious powders, the exotic elixirs, the bubbling, old-fashioned retorts and demijohns of Dr. Jekyll's and Mr. Hyde's. The thought of Laval, a monster "three-quarters pure evil, with only a single thin flickering quarter of good in him," alive now, perhaps in New York, perhaps the perpetrator of the current revolting crimes; the thought of him rushing desperately through crowded Manhattan streets to some secret laboratory, mixing his arcane chemicals and drinking off the churning, smoking draught that would transform him into the eminently acceptable Sellig—no, that was the last straw. It was the one silly thing that destroyed the whole story for Hunt. He expressed these feelings, cordially and respectfully, to Lord Terry.

The Earl chuckled good naturedly. "My story still—needs work?"

Hunt's hat was on and he stood at the door, ready to leave his host and allow him to go upstairs to bed. "Yes," he said, "just a little."

"I will take that under advisement," Lord Terry said. Then, his eyes glinting with mischief, he added, "As for those old-fashioned demijohns and other outmoded paraphernalia, however—modern science has made many bulky pieces of apparatus remarkably compact. The transistor radio and whatnot, you know. To keep my amateur standing as a raconteur, I must continue to insist that my story is true—except for one necessary alteration. Good night, my boy. It was pleasant to see you."

"Good night, sir. And thanks again for your kindness."

Outside, the humidity had been dispelled, and the air, though warm, was dry and clear. The sky was cloudless and dense with the stars of summer. From among them, Hunt picked out the eleven stars that form the constellation Sagittarius. The newspapers were announcing the appearance of another mutilated corpse, discovered in an alley only a few hours before. Reading the headlines, Hunt recalled a certain utterance—"*This . . . is the Grandest Guignol of all.*" And another—"*La vie est un corridor noir/D'impuissance et de désespoir.*" He bought a paper and hailed a taxi.

It was in the taxi, three blocks away from the club, that he suddenly "saw" the trivial, habitual action that had accompanied Lord Terry's closing remark about modern compactness. The old man had reached into his pocket for that little gold case and had casually taken a pill.

∼

THE DEMON SPELL

Hume Nisbet

The multitalented James Hume Nisbet (1849–1923) acted at the Theatre Royal in Melbourne, studied art at the National Gallery and South Kensington Museum, and wrote forty-six novels, as well as volumes of poetry and short stories.

Born in Scotland, he went to Melbourne at sixteen, then traveled extensively in Australia, New Zealand, and the South Seas before returning to Great Britain. An associate of John Ruskin, he exhibited at the Royal Scottish Academy but found little success with his oils and watercolors, so turned to writing.

About half of Nisbet's novels are set in Australia and the South Seas and appeal to a popular taste, with subjects ranging from swashbucklers to romance to crime. He was evidently much-influenced by H. Rider Haggard, with such lost-race adventures as *The Great Secret* (1895), in which an island of the dead is discovered, and *The Empire Makers* (1900), in which another lost race is found in South Africa. Nine of his novels involve fantasy, the genre in which he is best known, including *The Jolly Roger* (1891), with mass hypnotism a key element of the plot, and *Valdmar the Viking* (1893), in which a reincarnated Greek man is able to revive his lost love from the deep ice of the North Pole. The title story of *The Haunted Station and Other Stories* (1894) is a frequently reprinted ghost story.

"The Demon Spell" was first published in *The Haunted Station and Other Stories* (London, F. V. White, 1894).

It was about the time when spiritualism was all the craze in England, and no party was reckoned complete without a spirit-rapping séance being included amongst the other entertainments.

One night I had been invited to the house of a friend, who was a great believer in the manifestations from the unseen world, and who had asked for my special edification a well-known trance medium. "A pretty as well as a heaven-gifted girl whom you will be sure to like, I know," he said as he asked me.

I did not believe much in the return of spirits, yet, thinking to be amused, consented to attend at the hour appointed. At that time I had just returned from a long sojourn abroad, and was in a very delicate state of health, easily impressed by outward influences, and nervous to a most extraordinary extent.

To the hour appointed I found myself at my friend's house and was then introduced to the sitters who had assembled to witness the phenomena. Some were strangers like myself to the rules of the table, others who were adepts took their places at once in the order to which they had in former meetings attended. The trance medium had not yet arrived, and while waiting upon her coming we sat down and opened the séance with a hymn.

We had just finished the second verse when the door opened and the medium glided in, and took her place on a vacant seat by my side, joining with the others in the last verse, after which we all sat motionless with our hands resting upon the table, waiting upon the first manifestation from the unseen world.

Now, although I thought all this performance very ridiculous, there was something in the silence and the dim light, for the gas had been turned low down, and the room seemed filled with shadows; something about the fragile figure at my side, with her drooping head, which thrilled me with a curious sense of fear and icy horror such as I had never felt before.

I am not by nature imaginative or inclined to superstition, but, from the moment that young girl had entered the room, I felt as if a hand had been laid upon my heart, a cold iron hand, that was compressing it, and causing it to stop throbbing. My sense of hearing also had grown more acute and sensitive, so that the beating of the watch in my vest pocket sounded like the thumping of a quartz-crushing machine, and the measured breathing of those about me as loud and nerve-disturbing as the snorting of a steam engine.

Only when I turned to look upon the trance medium did I become soothed; then it seemed as if a cold air wave had passed through my brain, subduing, for the time being, those awful sounds.

"She is possessed," whispered my host on the other side of me. "Wait, and she will speak presently, and tell us whom we have got beside us."

As we sat and waited the table had moved several times under our hands, while knockings at intervals took place in the table and all round the room, a most weird and blood-curdling, yet ridiculous performance, which made me feel half inclined to run out with fear, and half inclined to sit still and laugh; on the whole, I think, however, that horror had the more complete possession of me.

Presently she raised her head and laid her hand upon mine, beginning to speak in a strange, monotonous, far-away voice, "This is my first visit since I passed from earth-life, and *you* have called me here."

I shivered as her hand touched mine, but had no strength to withdraw it from her light, soft grasp.

"I am what you would call a lost soul; that is, I am in the lowest sphere. Last week I was in the body, but met my death down Whitechapel way. I was what you call an unfortunate, aye, unfortunate enough. Shall I tell you how it happened?"

The medium's eyes were closed, and whether it was my distorted imagination or not, she appeared to have grown older and decidedly debauched-looking since she sat down, or rather as if a light, filmy mask of degrading and soddened vice had replaced the former delicate features.

No one spoke, and the trance medium continued:

"I had been out all that day and without any luck or food, so that I was dragging my wearied body along through the slush and mud, for it had been wet all day, and I was drenched to the skin, and miserable, ah, ten thousand times more wretched than I am now, for the earth is a far worse hell for such as I than our hell here.

"I had importuned several passers-by as I went along that night, but none of them spoke to me, for work had been scarce all this winter, and I suppose I did not look so tempting as I have been; only once a man answered me, a dark-faced, middle-sized man, with a soft voice, and much better dressed than my usual companions.

"He asked me where I was going, and then left me, putting a coin into my hand, for which I thanked him. Being just in time for the last public-house, I hurried up, but on going to the bar and looking at my hand, I found it to be a curious foreign coin, with outlandish figures on it, which the landlord would not take, so I went out again to the dark fog and rain without my drink after all.

"There was no use going any further that night. I turned up the court where my lodgings were, intending to go home and get a sleep, since I could get no food, when I felt something touch me softly from behind like as if someone had caught hold of my shawl; then I stopped and turned about to see who it was.

"I was alone, and with no one near me, nothing but fog and the half-light from the court lamp. Yet I felt as if something had got hold of me, though I could not see what it was, and that it was gathering about me.

"I tried to scream out, but could not, as this unseen grasp closed upon my throat and choked me, and then I fell down and for a moment forgot everything.

"Next moment I woke up, outside my own poor mutilated body, and stood watching the fell work going on—as you see it now."

Yes, I saw it all as the medium ceased speaking, a mangled corpse lying on a muddy pavement, and a demoniac, dark, pock-marked face bending over it, with the lean claws outspread, and the dense fog instead of a body, like the half-formed incarnation of muscles.

"That is what did it, and you will know it again," she said, "I have come for you to find it."

"Is he an Englishman?" I gasped, as the vision faded away and the room once more became definite.

"It is neither man nor woman, but it lives as I do, it is with me now and may be with you tonight, still if you will have me instead of it, I can keep it back, only you must wish for *me* with all your might."

The séance was now becoming too horrible, and by general consent our host turned up the gas, and then I saw for the first time the medium, now relieved from her evil possession, a beautiful girl of about nineteen, with I think the most glorious brown eyes I had ever before looked into.

"Do you believe what you have been speaking about?" I asked her as we were sitting talking together.

"What was that?"

"About the murdered woman."

"I don't know anything at all, only that I have been sitting at the table. I never know what my trances are."

Was she speaking the truth? Her dark eyes looked truth, so that I could not doubt her.

That night when I went to my lodgings I must confess that it was some time before I could make up my mind to go to bed. I was decidedly upset and nervous, and wished that I had never gone to this spirit meeting, making a mental vow, as I threw off my clothes and hastily got into bed, that it was the last unholy gathering I would ever attend.

For the first time in my life I could not put out the gas, I felt as if the room was filled with ghosts, or as if this pair of ghastly spectres, the murderer and his victim, had accompanied me home, and were at that moment disputing the possession of me, so instead, I pulled the bedclothes over my head, it being a cold night, and went that fashion off to sleep.

Twelve o'clock! and the anniversary of the day that Christ was born. Yes, I heard it striking from the street spire and counted the strokes, slowly tolled out, listening to the echoes from other steeples, after this one had ceased, as I lay awake in that gas-lit room, feeling as if I was not alone this Christmas morn.

Thus, while I was trying to think what had made me wake so suddenly, I seemed to hear a far off echo cry "Come to me." At the same time the bedclothes were slowly pulled from the bed, and left in a confused mass on the floor.

"Is that you, Polly?" I cried, remembering the spirit séance, and the name by which the spirit had announced herself when she took possession.

Three distinct knocks resounded on the bedpost at my ear, the signal for "Yes."

"Can you speak to me?"

"Yes," an echo rather than a voice replied, while I felt my flesh creeping, yet strove to be brave.

"Can I see you?"

"No!"

"Feel you?"

Instantly the feeling of a light cold hand touched my brow and passed over my face.

"In God's name, what do you want?"

"To save the girl I was *in* tonight. *It* is after her and will kill her if you do not come quickly."

In an instant I was out of the bed, and tumbling my clothes on any way, horrified through it all, yet feeling as if Polly were helping me to dress. There was a Kandian dagger on my table which I had brought from Ceylon, an old dagger which I had bought for its antiquity and design, and this I snatched up as I left the room, with that light unseen hand leading me out of the house and along the deserted snow-covered streets.

I did not know where the trance medium lived, but I followed where that light grasp led me, through the wild, blinding snow-drift, round corners and through shortcuts, with my head down and the flakes falling thickly about me, until at last I arrived at a silent square and in front of a house, which by some instinct, I knew that I must enter.

Over by the other side of the street I saw a man standing looking up to a dimly-lighted window, but I could not see him very distinctly and I did not pay much attention to him at the time, but rushed instead up the front steps and into the house, that unseen hand still pulling me forward.

How that door opened, or if it did open I could not say, only know that I got in, as we get into places in a dream, and up the inner stairs, I passed into a bedroom where the light was burning dimly.

It was her bedroom, and she was struggling in the thug-like grasp of those same demon claws, with that demoniac face close to hers, and the rest of it drifting away to nothingness.

I saw it all at a glance, her half-naked form, with the disarranged bedclothes, as the uniformed demon of muscles clutched that delicate throat, and then I was at it like a fury with my Kandian dagger, slashing crossways at those cruel claws and that evil face, while blood streaks followed the course of my knife, making ugly stains, until at last it ceased struggling and disappeared like a horrid nightmare, as the half-strangled girl, now released from that fell grip, woke up the house with her screams, while from her relaxing hand dropped a strange coin, which I took possession of.

Thus I left her, feeling that my work was done, going downstairs as I had come up, without impediment or even seemingly, in the slightest degree, attracting the attention of the other inmates of the house, who rushed in their night-dresses towards the bedroom from whence the screams were issuing.

Into the street again, with that coin in one hand and my dagger in the other I rushed, and then I remembered the man whom I had seen looking up at the window. Was he there still? Yes, but on the ground in a confused black mass amongst the white snow as if he had been struck down.

I went over to where he lay and looked at him. Was he dead? Yes. I turned him round and saw that his throat was gashed from ear to ear, and all over his face—the same dark, pallid, pock-marked evil face, and claw-like hands, I saw the dark slashes of my Kandian dagger, while the soft white snow around him was stained with crimson life pools, and as I looked I heard the clock strike one, while from the distance sounded the chant of the coming waits. Then I turned and fled blindly into the darkness.

MY SHADOW IS THE FOG

Charles L. Grant

As Mount Judge, Pennsylvania, was to John Updike in his Harry "Rabbit" Angstrom novels, so was Oxrun Station, Connecticut, to Charles Lewis Grant (1942–2006) in his novels of quiet horror. The prolific Grant, who wrote more than forty novels under the pseudonyms Geoffrey Marsh, Lionel Fenn, Simon Lake, Felicia Andrews, Steven Charles, and Deborah Lewis, as well as thirty under his own name, produced twelve books (eight novels and four collections of novellas) set in that quiet suburban town.

Unlike many contemporary writers of horror fiction, Grant eschewed the ultraviolence that filled the pages of Clive Barker's books and the writers who followed with graphic descriptions of torture, beheadings, eviscerations, and the like, soon echoed in such movie series as Halloween and Friday the 13th.

Instead, like Shirley Jackson, Algernon Blackwood, and others who preferred the more subtle depiction of terror engendered by the unseen, Grant appreciated the notion that the anticipation of a terrible act is often far more chilling than descriptions of gore, body parts, and overtly depraved behavior. As both a joke and an homage to the great Universal horror movies, Grant wrote three books that featured a vampire count (*The Soft Whisper of the Dead,* 1982), a wolfman (*The Dark Cry of the Moon,* 1985), and a mummy (*The Long Night of the Grave,* 1986), and placed them in Oxrun Station. Grant also was noted for editing an outstanding series of anthologies, Shadows (1978–1991).

"My Shadow Is the Fog" was first published in *Ripper!*, edited by Gardner Dozois and Susan Casper (New York, Tom Doherty Associates, 1988).

The wind was strong that day. I remember that much. It was strong. And it was cool.

The fog wasn't there.

Not at first; not until later.

But there were whitecaps on the bay and great masses of white clouds and a distant white haze that veiled the low hump of South End from the beach where I sat and threw handfuls of pebbles into the dark water. The chair that I used was of the folding kind, and the coat that I wore was barely enough to keep me warm, though it was still September and the walk from my room had put a mirror of nervous sweat along the ridge of my brow.

I had arrived just after noon, and stopped in front of a low deserted building whose function I've never learned, not in all the years it's waited for me, doors nailed shut and windows shut with nailed planks. Facing the water was a wide platform—a loading dock, I think—raised above the beach and walled with concrete. I have no idea what was beneath it; I only knew that I was higher by at least a yard than the land around me, and it was a chore to climb up there, to hoist myself from the stony beach to the battered wooden flooring with its whorls and sighs and scrabblings of blown sand.

No one who saw me paid me any heed. I was, after all, only another old man come to take in what there was of a pale, waning sun. Nothing special, nothing different. A face scraped with the chisel of too many decades living, hair the colour of old straw thinned in useless harvest, shoulders slightly rounded. My hands were gloveless, my feet in lightweight boots, and the cardigan I wore under the caped black coat was one I've had for what seems like a hundred years.

I remember the wind, and the bay, and the feel of Whitstable at my back, aged enough I suppose to rightfully want a bit of peace at the end. I don't really know. I never asked, and people never told me.

But damnit, I do remember the wind, and I remember sitting in the death of the summer sun most of the afternoon throwing pebbles into the water and nearly falling out of my chair when I heard someone say, "Hello."

I looked over, looked down, and there was a little girl with short brown hair and a short tartan skirt blowing about her legs snug in white tights. A red sweater a size too large, hanging to the middle of her thighs, billowing and slapping when the wind slipped beneath. She smiled at me, her eyes squinting from the sun's glare.

"Hello," I said.

"Are you waiting for him, then?" she asked, her head slightly tilted to one side.

"I don't know," I answered with a smile. "Am I?"

"You look as if you are."

My smile widened. "Then I suppose I am."

She turned to face the bay, one hand to the side of her red-cheeked face to protect it from the wind. "I don't think he's coming."

"Oh?"

"Oh no, I don't think so. May I throw one of your stones, please?"

I handed one over—it was round, sea-smooth, mottled, and dry. Without a word of thanks, she raised her arm, sighted, and threw it as hard as she could. It didn't go very far, barely past the first waves, but it was far enough to make her giggle and ask if she could do it again.

"Your hands will get dirty," I said in gentle admonition as I handed another one over. "Your mother will be angry."

"No, she won't," the girl said. "She never gets mad at me."

I raised an eyebrow. "Never?"

She threw the second stone, a bit farther than the first. "No."

A gust made me close my eyes, and when they opened again she was staring closely at me, like a bird trying to decide if I was part of the chain that provided it with meals at the end of a spring shower.

I waited for her to say something.

A gull cried overhead.

At last she shrugged and jumped down to the beach, walking very carefully over the stones to the edge of the water. Though the waves here were quite low because of the wood-and-rock breakwaters spaced along the shore, I wanted to call a caution to her. Instead, I only watched, marvelling at the way she kept her balance while the wind kicked at her skirt, at the loose ends of her sweater, and lifted her hair until she turned a youthful gorgon.

She pointed then to the eastern horizon and, without turning around, called, "Do you know France is over there?"

"I do," I called back, cupping a hand to the side of my mouth.

"Do you know a lot, then?"

I smiled. "I used to," I said. "I don't remember it all now."

"Pity," she said. Just like that—pity.

"I suppose it is."

"He doesn't always remember either," she said, not sadly. "He's terribly old, you know." She looked at me, an odd look, and I wondered if she was comparing my age with her friend's. "Terribly old. Sometimes, when he's lost, I think he doesn't remember me at all." The look changed then, from odd to almost sly. "Do you remember?"

I was getting weary of shouting, but she showed no inclination to turn around, and I didn't have the strength to climb down beside her.

"This man," I said then. "Who is he? Is he from around here?"

She nodded. "Yes. But you're not, are you? You talk funny."

I had to smile. "You're right. I'm not. I'm from a long way away."

I had to smile, because I wasn't sure.

"America," she decided, and nodded once to agree with herself. "I could tell. I'm good at telling things like that, I'm almost always right." Then she looked at me over her shoulder and gave me the brightest, most loving smile I had ever seen. "He's a cleaner, you see."

I wasn't sure I heard her properly and shook my head. She lifted her hands in a sigh and came back to me, leaned on the top of the wall and repeated herself, her tone telling me frankly that I should have known that.

"I see," I said. "And just what does he clean?"

"Everything, I guess. For goodness' sake, don't you remember anything?"

I frowned. Her cheerfulness was gone now, replaced by the impatience a child has for one like me, who has nothing but patience left and no way to use it. I didn't care for her company anymore. I was like that, a dubious privilege of old age—judgements that come and go like the nightmares that warn me just how much longer I have to live, how much more I have to endure before I can have peace. They aren't premonitions, I don't believe in things like that, but it's why I returned to Whitstable—an old town and an old man, waiting for someone to decide what should be done with them before they turn into embarrassments for the future.

But I do remember the wind, and the sun, and the matter-of-fact way she looked at me again, then walked to the near breakwater and climbed it, looked back at me and grinned before walking out to the end.

It was narrow.

It couldn't have been more than a foot or so wide, and there she was, out at the tip and balanced on one leg.

I was so stunned I couldn't move, and I didn't dare breathe lest she lose her balance and fall.

Fool, I thought; you stupid little fool, you'll kill yourself out there.

She laughed. Her arms spread wide, her fingers spread to the wind, and she glanced over her shoulder and called something to me. I couldn't hear. My ears were stoppered in anticipation of her falling screams. She called again, and spun around, and I found myself rising, though my legs were too weak to carry me fast enough, my voice too weak to call out for help, for someone to stop her. I looked frantically behind me but there was no one in the parking lot beside the pub where I'd had an early lunch, no one in the narrow streets, no one in the windows. My arms flapped uselessly at my sides, my mouth opened, closed, opened again, and when I reached the breakwater's edge I kept stepping forward, stepping back, a fearful dance of indecision that soon dropped me to my knees.

The wind brought the clouds, hid the sun, and I watched her little game, gasping, until she tired of it and came back as easily as if she were walking a wide pavement. I leaned forward anxiously, one hand thumping against my chest to force my lungs to work, the other reaching out as if to help her.

"Can you do that?" she said when she reached me at last. "It's not very hard."

I rolled and staggered to my feet and backed away from her. My chair had toppled over and I fumbled for it, with it, cursed it until I could set it right again and drop into it, panting.

"Who are you?" I asked, wiping my mouth, brushing back my hair.

"Delia," she said. "Delia Travers."

I looked away from her, into the sun.

"Who are *you*?" she asked quickly.

"Jack," I said finally. "Jack Light." My voice sounded hoarse, and distant, certainly not my own, so I cleared my throat and gave my name again. And as I waited for a response, and for my heart to calm and my lungs to take air without burning inside, I glanced at her from the corner of my vision.

And blinked because suddenly I thought I knew who she was. I had seen her before.

But only in fog.

She giggled.

I looked at her sharply.

"The cleaner's name is Jack," she said.

"Yes," I said slowly. "I know." And frowned because I wasn't sure I was right.

She nodded, crossed her arms on the top of the wall and tucked her chin on one wrist. "That's two Jacks I know," she said. "Do you know two Jacks?"

I shook my head.

For a moment the sun again pulled a cloud over its face, and the beach grew too cold for me to endure. As I fumbled into a pair of worn black gloves, I thought of leaving, of heading for the pub where I could go downstairs, to the back corner, and drink myself to nightfall. I could think just as easily in there, with the warmth and the chatter and the laughter all about me, certainly more easily than I could out here, in the cold and the wind-silence, where the waves slanted away from me as if they knew who I was.

Footsteps on the stones, then.

The girl turned as I did, to watch a quartet of young people walking awkwardly toward the water, holding each other, laughing in each other's shoulders, glancing at us once and grinning as if to include us in their fun. Delia waved shyly; I nodded and looked away.

I didn't want to watch them.

There was too much noise, too much life, and I didn't like the way the little girl kept watching me not watching them. Her expression was knowing, and finally it was sly again, and I couldn't help wishing her friend would come along and take her away.

She made me nervous.

I didn't know why.

But when the laughter and squealing grew, I watched the young people anyway, and squinted so hard there were tears in my eyes. A hand brushed hard over my face, and I looked away from the setting sun. Time to go, I told myself; you'll catch your death if you wait.

"Do you know," the girl said suddenly, turning her back on the others, "that Jack is even older than you?"

"Is that possible?" I said, smiling.

"Oh yes. He's older than everybody!"

She grunted and puffed her way to the top of the wall and sat crosslegged, her back to the drop, rocking on her bottom. "Did you know what he did when he was a man?"

"No," I said, curiously uneasy because I thought I knew and didn't much care for the way she'd put the question.

Old men, you see, aren't men at all; they're relics in museums, ghosts that walk the earth to remind real men of what they would become, because once they got there they never would remember.

The sun dropped to the horizon; the warmth and wind died. The bay was empty, South End gone in a twilight shadow, and there was only one of the young people left on the beach. A woman, kneeling at water's edge and poking at something with a pale stick.

The girl hunched her shoulders and leaned forward, her secret obviously not for anyone but me. "He killed people." Then she looked side to side, up to the clouds, back to my face. "He really did. He was *horrid*."

And she crossed her eyes and laughed.

The young woman looked up, startled, and returned to her prodding.

I pushed out of the chair and walked over to the girl, stiffly, in anger. I crouched in front of her and pulled off my left glove. She stopped laughing when she saw my hand thrust at her face.

"Do you see that?" I said.

She nodded, slowly.

It was an old hand, liver spots and high veins and the knuckles more prominent than the fingers they started.

The wind pushed at my back, pushed hair into my eyes, and I used my free hand to balance me on the platform.

"A hand can kill, little girl," I said grimly, softly, holding her gaze with mine and pleased at the fear I saw there at last. "A hand with a gun, a knife, a razor, a club . . . it can kill, and it isn't something to laugh at. Not now. Not ever. A hand kills. Do you understand me?" I took a breath; she didn't speak. "It is horrible, to kill. I don't care how young you are, child, it's not right to laugh."

My hand trembled, from the cold, from my anger, and I watched it trace a pattern in front of her eyes before I jammed it back into its glove and dropped the rest of the way to my knees.

The girl blinked, wiped a hand over her eyes, and blinked again. "I'm sorry, Jack," she whispered, and looked over her shoulder. "I'm sorry," she said again, and ran over to the woman, knelt beside her and watched her until the two of them were laughing, sharing a secret and once in a while glancing over at me.

I felt the fool.

And I felt a stirring. A remembering. As intangible as the fog that now drifted in behind me. I hadn't noticed it before, sneaking and ducking behind the swells, filling the hollows, waiting until the wind died and the sun died before climbing into the twilight. Touching the back of my neck like the kiss of an old friend, curling around my throat like the caress of an old lover.

When I looked to my left, the village was gone, grey in its place and shimmering blotches of light where the pub's windows ought to be, echoes of footsteps and the muffled cough of an engine.

Delia and the young woman were nearly invisible when I looked back; all I could see was the red sweater, all I could hear was the laughing—soft, and low, and a comfort to my ears, so much so that I managed to climb down to the stones without embarrassing myself by falling.

I straightened.

The fog deepened, and I took a deep breath.

The fog held me, and I swayed, and spread my fingers to catch it.

Spread them. And flexed them. Felt the strength return, and the knowing.

And the light was nearly gone when Delia came back and took my hand.

"Jack," she said. "I have a new friend."

I nodded.

"Do you remember?"

It was only a few seconds before I nodded again.

She gave a small cry and threw her arms around me, hugged me, pressed her cheek to me, burrowed into me then looked up to show me the tears filling her eyes. "I didn't think you would," she said.

I didn't always want to.

That was something she couldn't understand, could never understand—that it took more than a wishing to make a dream come true, that it took more than a wanting to make a friend come to stay, to save you from dying when dying should have been.

"I'm so glad you're back," she whispered. "To meet my new friend."

The wind had been strong that day, strong and cool.

I remember that much.

As I remember the look on the young woman's face, the same look on all their faces when they see me and wonder and wonder at my smile, and the odd little girl standing at my side, and the way I hold out my hand to help her to her feet.

"Good evening," I said politely. I remember that; I always do.

Delia stirs and wriggles with the impatience of her kind.
"The fog is bad tonight," I said further. "Come with me, I'll show you home."
And she followed. They always do.
Into the fog.
Into the dark.
Where I remember all the rest.
And Delia hands me the knife.

~

BY FLOWER AND DEAN STREET

Patrice Chaplin

Patrice Chaplin (1940–) is an internationally renowned playwright and author with more than thirty-five books and plays to her credit. One of her most notable works is *Siesta: A Supernatural Love Story* (1979), in which a young woman in Spain wakes up blood-soaked and bruised but with no memory of the past few days. When she has flashbacks, she begins to think she might have killed someone. It was made into a 1987 film starring Ellen Barkin, Gabriel Byrne, Jodie Foster, Martin Sheen, and Isabella Rossellini.

Among her other works are her first novel, *A Lonely Diet* (1970), the autobiographical *Albany Park: A Story of Bohemian Adventure and Obsessive Love* (1986), *Into the Darkness Laughing: The Story of Jeanne Hébuterne, Modigliani's Last Mistress* (1990), *Night Fishing: An Urban Tale* (1992), and *Hidden Star: Oona O'Neill Chaplin: A Memoir* (1995); Patrice Chaplin was once married to one of Charlie Chaplin's sons, Michael.

Several of Chaplin's plays, documentaries, and short stories have been adapted for radio. The short story "Night in Paris" has been translated into many languages, and her stage play *From the Balcony,* a joint commission by London's National Theatre in conjunction with BBC Radio 3, was performed at the Cottesloe Theatre. Her journalistic pieces have been published in numerous newspapers and magazines, including *The Guardian*, *The Sunday Times*, *Marie Claire*, *The Jewish Chronicle*, *The Daily Mail*, and *The London Magazine*.

"By Flower and Dean Street" was first published in *By Flower and Dean Street & The Love Apple* by Patrice Chaplin (London, Duckworth, 1976).

I

The London sky was pale and hard and glistened like an ice rink. At the end of a long wintry front garden stood a narrow three-storey house with dry dignified trees on either side. Everything was still. The two lower floors were brightly lit and at some windows curtains weren't drawn. Light from the street lamp didn't reach the garden because rough overgrown shrubs with dead honeysuckle tangling through them ganged together just inside the railings, and small ones, spiky, treacherous, hid by the gate. A child's new tricycle lay on its side across the path, its handlebars poking into the cracked earth of the flower border. A wind shook the trees. Then everything was still again.

A light went off on the first floor. The front door opened, and a man and woman walked quickly along the path. "Damn the child!" the man said and swung the tricycle away across the lawn and into a shed while the woman went on to the gate, the gravel spitting under her tall elegant shoes. She waited on the pavement, her black fur coat sleek around her, and the light of the street lamp shone on her face, pale and beautiful, as she turned and shouted, "Daniel! We're late." From the road, the house no longer looked isolated—there were other houses nearby, a church hung over the garden shed, cars lined the kerb.

Daniel ran to the gate, out of breath, and, knowing the plants well, jumped to avoid them. But sly, undercover, they were waiting somewhere else, and he tripped and swore.

"I'll pull them up tomorrow, Connie," he promised.

He closed the gate. It squeaked open immediately and they got into the car.

"Why doesn't he put it away I wonder? Does he want to get it pinched?"

"Perhaps he does." She laughed. "I think he's bored with it already and daren't admit it."

He started the engine, and then turned and kissed her. "I didn't give you this in front of the children." He took a small black case from his pocket. "I wanted to wait until we were alone. A little extra present."

She opened the case. Glittering on a nest of black satin was a small diamond brooch shaped like a heart. Still smiling, she said, "Oh. Oh, it's lovely, Daniel. Really lovely." She was all the more touched as once again he'd given her something she would never use. She never wore brooches—thought they were for elderly women. It would join the bottles of scent, kid gloves, jewelled powder compacts, which were aging elegantly in her bedroom. "But why a heart?"

He squeezed her hand. The car moved forward, and she undid the fur and pinned the heart to her dress.

Silence came back into the long wintry garden and the narrow house looked lonely again.

It was Connie's thirtieth birthday.

2

The restaurant was well known for its intimate atmosphere, its roast beef, its blazing log-fire and the difficulty of getting a table.

They sat with two friends by the fire as the waiter cleared the empty Beaujolais bottle and glasses and brought the champagne. Jane had black bright eyes. She was full of energy, and she considered herself Connie's best friend. She pushed back her long shining hair and started on her third portion of fresh figs.

"Can't get enough of them," she said, and seeing Daniel laughing at her, wriggled athletically. She could never keep still.

Her husband, Mark, was quiet and withdrawn and had pale, powdery skin like a moth.

Daniel raised his glass. "Happy Birthday, and thank you for ten marvellous years."

"They haven't all been marvellous," said Connie. "What about when I couldn't cook? You can't have forgotten that. Are you drunk? It got better when I learned to open tins." She laughed, and her teeth were slightly protruding; but even that,

Jane thought, seemed attractive on Connie. "Before that, poor man! The burnt dinners, undercooked dinners, non-existent dinners he had to come home to."

"You're exaggerating," said Mark mournfully. "I've had some very good dinners at your place." He always seemed tired except when he talked about his work.

"They were usually burnt and undercooked at the same time," murmured Connie.

"It's lovely," said Jane, flinging her hair back into the eyes of a passing waiter and nearly toppling his tray. She shivered towards the next table. "I haven't had champagne for ages."

Her black plain dress, its material, its style, seemed only to emphasise her flat chest. "It's as much as I can do to get Mark to remember my birthday, let alone celebrate." She looked at Connie's bosom, generously revealed by the cut-out in the bodice of her dark-red dress, and she had to admit that in spite of nursing four children, it was still shapely. Jane gulped some champagne. "That's a super brooch."

The cut-out was shaped like a diamond; and Mark, eyeing more than the brooch, said, "Diamonds are definitely the evening's motif." Something like light came back into his eyes.

"The frock was meant to be modest," Daniel told him. "But the long sleeves and high neck obviously got too much for the designer, so he ripped it open at the most telling point."

"You need something super when you get into your thirties," said Connie. "Thirty! Definitely the end. No more silly girlish indulgences—eh, Papa?" She pulled Daniel's ear. "Can't blame my mistakes on immaturity." Her voice was husky.

"Will you have any more kids?" asked Jane. "God, that sounds awful. I didn't mean they're a mistake."

"When David's at school, perhaps. I'd like one more baby. I'd like really to enjoy it, lavish attention on it." Her eyes were warm, caressing, as she smiled. Connie looked at people as though she cared for them; she'd been well-loved. She twisted the glass round, and the champagne splashed about and fizzed, and Jane noticed that even her hands were rounded and in proportion. "I had the others in such a rush. There was so much to do. I couldn't give them enough time."

"I'm certainly not having any more," said Jane defiantly, and she looked at Daniel, for some reason, as though he'd contradict her.

He didn't. "It's the only solution," he said firmly. "They're easy to build, economical, hygienic—they're sensible."

"What's he on about?" asked Jane. "Not tower blocks again?"

"They suck up the drifting surplus overnight. You can cram fifty families in the space you would use for one. They might not be pretty," he added sharply, as though Mark had opposed him, "but how pretty is half a million with nowhere to live?"

"He's going grey," said Jane.

"Who?" asked Connie.

"Daniel. And his stomach! It's a hazard."

"You ought to see the ones the Council get. You'd soon forget your preoccupation with saving cornices and low-timbered roofs."

Mark didn't answer. His cheeks full of unchewed food, he looked like a hamster.

"Pansies. That whole group are pansies, Mark. What do they know about housing women and kids?"

"How d'you mean, a hazard?" asked Connie.

"Well, it sticks out," said Jane.

Connie looked at Daniel's stomach. "You mean someone might bump into it?" she giggled.

"No. It's a health hazard. Men over a certain age should watch it. I'd stop giving him puddings."

"You might say the hospital dominates the heath. You might say it should have been spread across, rather than up—but it saved space, for crissake, Mark. It's economical."

Mark still didn't answer. Then he remembered the forgotten food and started chewing.

"Do you know you can see it from wherever you are on the heath?" said Jane disingenuously. "Even in the woody bits."

Not quite sure of her tone, Daniel looked at her, his dark eyes, with their yellow lights, unblinking.

"I mean, wherever you are in Hampstead you just never forget that hospital."

"People need clean, hygienic blocks," he said swiftly and refilled the glasses. "Anyway, Mark, how's Golders Green's next best thing to a Regency terrace working out?"

Connie nudged him.

"It's not!" snapped Jane.

"The builders are no good," said Mark gently. "Very expensive, unreliable—"

"And who's to blame for that?" asked Jane. "Who chose them?" Smiling, Mark pointed at himself.

"Change them," said Daniel.

He started to answer, but Jane said: "It's been unlucky from the start, that scheme. He did the drawings and spec. in his spare time. Then he found he'd put the drawings back to front. They'd all have been peeing in the front garden."

Daniel looked sympathetically at the younger man and thought of a way to change the subject, so that Jane would keep out of it. "There's another council meeting Friday. I'm proposing new flats for that old station site near—"

"Oh no," said Jane flatly. "Don't get him involved in any more work. I hardly—"

"—Camden Town. I think we should use a local architect. You'll have to do some provisional drawings." His decisive tone dropped under Jane's high howl and gave Mark confidence to reply, softly, "I'll have to think about it."

"I hardly ever see him as it is." Jane bounced up and down in her chair.

"Have some more figs," said Daniel.

Mark suddenly looked crushed by fatigue. Jane took his energy, absorbed it and shone even brighter, spoke even louder, her smiles thrusting, her eyes jabbing, leaving him shrunken and uninteresting at the tail end of everyone's conversation. She took the glow from everything except Connie. She even took it away from the brass ornaments round the fire.

Almost before Daniel looked in his direction, the waiter was beside him and another bottle was whisked to the table.

"It may be unimaginative, even ugly," said Daniel. "No. Not ugly, I'd call it uncompromising. It serves a damn useful purpose. It's a million times more efficient than that old Victorian one."

"Efficient?" cried Jane. "Hell. It took me half an hour just to find the X-ray department. There's no signs anywhere. Even the nurses don't know where anything is. I walked miles. It's like a city."

"When I look back on my twentieth birthday—help!" said Connie. "I thought leaving your teens was the end of the world. I cried. D'you remember, Daniel? I've led a very sheltered life, when I think about it."

"It's been uneventful compared with everyone else's," said Jane, and she stared at Daniel. "I mean, it's been so smooth. Married straight from boarding school—"

"Well, so were you," said Mark.

"No. It's different. I mean—" For a moment she looked sad, and as her eyes were pointing at the empty plate Daniel was going to suggest yet another helping of figs, when she said suddenly, "I'm going to teach full-time. I've decided. The money's not worth it doing just mornings."

"Oh no," said Daniel. "That means you'll be even fitter, your cheeks will be even rosier. You're already the healthiest mum in N.W.3. Do you know that?" He leaned towards her, playfully. She turned scarlet. "You'll put us all to shame." He straightened back into his chair.

"I'll give them isometrics and more running," she said breathlessly. "Running's what they need."

Mark pointed over Daniel's shoulder and Daniel turned round quickly.

"What?" He frowned, seeing nothing sensational.

"Through the windows, across the road—one of the most beautiful houses in London. Keats House. Late eighteenth century. Surrounded by gardens. Don't you just long to tear it down and build one of your nice gleaming tower blocks?"

Daniel stared at him—at his long floppy face which strain and living with Jane had made already old, at his blue, harmless eyes, his woman's mouth—and he said, "I'd really love you for the new project. If you can get it. I'll certainly push you. We need an architect with taste."

"Yes but—" Jane exploded.

"You'll get a good fee," he added quickly, not quite looking at Jane.

"How much?" she asked.

He shrugged. "Double, treble what—"

"We'll think about it," she decided. "I need a new fridge."

"No more for me." Mark put his hand over his glass and tried not to yawn.

"Don't you ever get bored, Connie? Honestly?" asked Jane.

Connie, surprised, shook her head.

"You look all right, though. I don't know how you do it with four kids and that big house. What's your secret? Vitamin E?"

Connie laughed, and the way she looked at Daniel suggested he had a lot to do with it.

Mark was saying, "With the prices of everything now you can't afford them."

"Can't afford what?" asked Jane.

"Kids."

"Well, you're not having any more, so don't start worrying your head about affording them." Her long teeth gleamed as she smiled at Connie. "He can't even cope with one."

"We've enough difficulty with one," Mark was saying.

"But you've put your money into the cottage and you've had some rather exclusive holidays," said Daniel.

"Jane likes to feel free."

"Free!" Jane crossed her eyes.

Daniel put his glass down and his hand dropped out of sight. Suddenly Connie looked flushed—pleased. Daniel's eyes were hot as he watched her.

Aroused, Jane could only wriggle wildly. Connie shivered a little, as though with anticipation. Nobody saw it, except Jane.

"Is that beauty spot by your eye real?" she asked fiercely.

"I hope so," murmured Connie, her mind not really on what Jane was saying.

"Mark, d'you hear that? Mark!" she cried; and a waiter crept up, wondering how to deal with this obtrusive customer without upsetting her host, whom he cherished for his demeanour, his reckless appetite, and his bank balance. He offered her more champagne, naively thinking that that would shut her up. After several of her more spectacular sounds, she dragged Mark's attention from out of whatever private grey crevice it had been hiding in. "Yes?" he sighed.

"D'you know that Connie's beauty spot is real? I always thought it was false."

"Is it?" he replied. Nothing much of what his wife said ever got through to him.

"I like this place better than the one we went to on Connie's last birthday. It's more intimate."

Mark's empty expression suggested that it was too intimate for him with her at the same table. Her remarks whizzed wall to wall like a ball on a squash court. Her "Oh goshes" and "How terrifics" became part of other people's conversations. Her shriek, as the third bottle was uncorked, had everyone frozen.

"Daniel gave me a velvet dress—you know, one of those lovely new Ossie Clark ones—as well as this brooch." Connie lowered her voice dramatically, hoping she'd follow her example. "The children gave me an electric mixer."

"I thought you'd already got a mixer."

"Not an electric one."

Connie reached across for the ashtray. For a moment Jane smelt the light, flowery perfume Connie always used—it echoed persuasively in her clothes, in her bedroom, in rooms she visited; it was a part of Connie, and Jane, who had never smelt it on anyone else, had secretly hung her nose over perfume testers in chemists all over the place but had never been able to track it down. It reminded her of summer. For some reason she felt silly, shy of asking Connie its name.

"You don't go out much," she accused her. "You must get fed up staying in. I know *I* would."

"I don't think about it."

"Staying in makes one dull."

Connie, with a little smile, said: "Well, I have so much to do." She looked sideways at Daniel. "I mean by the time I've got the children to bed and David's nappies soaked and we've had dinner and I've washed up and scrubbed the sink and cut the grapefruits ready for breakfast, I don't feel like going out." In spite of her tone, the little smile was still there.

Jane, unaware that she was being teased, said: "You lay breakfast the night before? Sounds like a boarding house."

Connie almost laughed. "Well, I have to," she managed to say, "or I'd never get the children's handkerchiefs ironed for school and Daniel's"—she nudged him under the table—"-overcoat brushed properly."

"Poor thing! Everyone thinks you're awfully domesticated—I mean, homely—but I never realised you thought like this about it. I'll show you some shortcuts. And we could do an evening class together once or twice a week. What about squash?"

Daniel's mouth twitched, and Connie, who was shaking with the effort not to laugh, stared hard at the table. Then she thought of her house, of sitting by the fire, and she could see no reason why she should ever leave it.

The headwaiter padded over and gave his panda's smile. Behind his back his hand made signals, and a tray of sweets was brought to the table. "On the house, sir. And would you like me to keep this table for Wednesday, sir? Or would you rather have the corner?"

"I'm not certain it will be Wednesday. It depends when my clients arrive."

"I'll keep the table for an hour, sir?"

Daniel said decisively: "Yes, keep it. My secretary will cancel if necessary. Friday week I'd like a table for six."

"Very good, Mr. Stein. Very good, sir."

"I'm handling the Bryant case. The old man's flying over from the States. We're in court ten days," he told Mark.

"How will it go?" asked Mark.

"Oh, we'll win," he said lightly.

"You must hate it when Daniel's out in the evenings," said Jane.

"Usually he's only out when he's doing the free advice evenings, but now because of the flat project and—"

"You must hate it."

"I don't mind being on my own. I quite like it."

"If your husband's a Labour councillor, you can forget your cosy evenings round the fire talking about squash," said Daniel. "A Conservative councillor—well that's another thing." He winked at Mark.

"Get an au pair," said Jane.

"Don't want one," said Connie.

"You'd be much freer," said Jane ferociously.

"Where you read rights for the Left, I read houses for the middle-class at lower cost. Why should—"

Jane snorted, and the sound terrified a man at the next table. "Enough of this," she said, getting up. "You can discuss all this anytime. Come on." She took Connie's arm. "We've got a special birthday surprise."

3

Jane's surprise was a crowded nightclub in the West End, and they sat near the floorshow watching six girls, dressed as tigers, slither through a jungle number.

Their breasts were bare, their eyes bored. Any interest they might have unearthed in Mark was quelled immediately by the music, which was so loud he had to cover his ears. Jane alone managed to shout above it. "This isn't the surprise." The music got louder, the girls spun faster, the lights cut out—Mark looked as though he'd have to be carried out. During the polite applause a spotlight picked out the Master of Ceremonies as he swished onto the floor.

"And now what we've all been waiting for. He's taken them by storm in Paris, thrilled them in Berlin, and now, on his first-ever visit to London, we have the exclusive pleasure of bringing to you, the Magician from Hungary, the Greatest Magician in the World, Danchenko!"

Jane cried: "He's supposed to be terrific."

The lights changed colour several times as he came on in a cloud of white doves, produced a doubtful rabbit from a black hat and juggled a hoop, a ball and a skittle successfully. A pink chiffon scarf gave birth to multicoloured chiffon scarves.

"It's not feasible to have the bloody thing spread all over London," said Daniel. "What d'you want? A fleet of taxis to take patients from haemotology to X-ray?"

"I just said it spoils the view," murmured Mark.

Drums rolled, doves disappeared, the magician climbed onto a small dais, and Mark fell asleep.

"He used to be a councillor before he became articulate—"

"Wake up, Mark!" Jane hissed. She passed him his drink.

"I'm not asleep, for Godsake."

The magician was thin, dramatic; and he could have been any age. The MC stretched up and blindfolded him with three thick scarves.

". . . No. I've never actually heard Lewis talk," said Daniel. "He grunts. When he belches they mistake it for a protest and call point of order. Jenkins is the only tricky one. But I'll push it through."

"Not once, not twice, but three times for Danchenko! Now I will touch any object you choose and Danchenko will identify it." The MC moved swiftly among the tables with his black tails whipping from side to side—he looked like a snake. "What am I touching now, Maestro?"

"Now you have a handkerchief. It is a woman's handkerchief. Not new. Into it has flowed many tears, but the handkerchief will now stay dry. The cause of the tears is over."

"You'll have a free hand, Mark."

"I've got a lot on."

"You'll do it," said Jane happily. "You'll fit it in. I want to get out of Europe this summer."

"What am I touching?"

"A glass."

"And now?"

"Another glass."

Laughter. "You can't fool Danchenko," said the MC.

"Come out to the lavatory, Mark, and I'll give you a dozen reasons why you should."

Jane, waving her watch, jumped up and down, among the crowd all vying for attention. The MC, dismayed by her flapping hair and digging fingers, had no choice, and the watch was forced into his hand. He just stopped her holding up his arm by doing it himself.

"Now, Danchenko."

"A wristwatch with a thin strap. I feel it is too tight."

Jane's mouth hung open.

"The wearer of this watch has a strong wrist. The pulse is often very fast but strong. The person does much running. The arm sometimes waves strenuously, but not goodbye to a lover she no longer has use for, nor again to warn a lover she likes that her husband is home." Laughter. "She is playing tennis." Loud applause and the MC escaped over to the other side of the room.

"I can't Wednesday," said Daniel. "The Lord Mayor's having a thing at the Goldsmith's Hall. Have a stab at the drawings and—"

"Did you hear that?" asked Jane.

"Terrific," said Daniel.

"And what am I holding here, Maestro?"

"You are touching a bald head."

Laughter.

"It's all done by code," Daniel told Jane. "Or he can see."

"Well, he couldn't see my strap was too tight. Still, it's not the only thing tight around here. Wake up, Mark. Pull yourself together."

"A glass," said Danchenko.

"What's in the glass?" shouted a man in the audience.

"Give him something of yours, Daniel. Give him—" Jane looked at his coat, then at Connie. "Give him her brooch. Go on, Dan."

He stiffened. He'd made rather a point of always being called Daniel.

"Amber liquid. It won't be there long." Men around the table cheered. The magician leaned forward. Suddenly his blindfolded eyes seemed to peer into the audience. In a low menacing voice, he said: "The glass forever emptying, forever refilling. A sorrow is being swilled away. A hardening liver can be more sorrowful, my friend. Take an old magic man's advice."

During the shocked silence, Daniel was heard to say, "Isn't there a bar or something? Let's go and discuss it properly. The girls are all right. They're having fun."

"Too near the mark, Maestro," someone bellowed.

The magician chuckled.

"His laugh isn't the funniest thing in the world," said Jane. She looked at Daniel—at his mouth, firm and decisive, at his yellow eyes, penetrating, steady— and she looked so hard she nearly missed the next bit and Connie nudged her. The MC was holding his hand up in the air.

"And now?"

"Do not think you are touching nothing, my friend. The air is not empty but full of vibrations."

Daniel held out Connie's brooch, but the MC, attracted to a nail-file at the next table, turned his back and was about to reach for it, when Jane, grabbing the brooch, swung it like lightning in front of the almost victorious nail-file and dumped it unceremoniously onto the MC's outstretched hand. She'd won too many relay races to let her side be ignored, and the MC, startled by her, was obliged to hold it up and say: "And now?"

The magician shuddered. Perhaps it was his black, flowing clothes that made the action so terrifying. Conversation died, forgotten. Jane still tipped the champagne bottle against her glass. All around were objects, held out, held up, dangling, foolish. Only the cigarette smoke carried on drifting up, unafraid.

"A heart," and he smiled—a long cavernous smile that made his face look like a Halloween lantern. Then the audience started to move, to mutter. A man at the next table leaned across to Jane. The MC, disconcerted, tried to hand the brooch back. The noise grew, and through it the magician said quietly: "A heart. It will not be gashed or cut or crushed but taken whole and still beating from the body."

Stunned, Connie turned to Daniel. He was talking to Mark. No longer believing what she'd heard, she said, "Did you hear that?"

"What?" asked Mark.

She grabbed Jane. "Did you hear it?" Then she saw a woman at the next table looking at her. She'd heard it. She was appalled.

"He said something about a heart," said Jane.

"'It will not be cut or . . .' He said that," said Connie. Jane looked at her, startled.

"I didn't hear that. Come on, Maestro. It's her birthday," she shouted.

The magician had taken his blindfold off and the MC was gliding onto the floor. The drums rolled, people clapped; but the atmosphere in the club was not as festive as it had been.

The magician walked slowly forward and pointed a long finger at a man at the back. "Bring me that glass, my friend."

Amid a few calls and whistles ("Watch it or he'll turn you into a rabbit"), the man went self-consciously up to Danchenko and gave him the glass.

Danchenko said softly: "What the magician touches brings luck. And now a small thing." He peered into the audience, and here and there an object was held out to him. "An ear-ring? No, not an ear-ring." He bent towards a middle-aged fat woman and chuckled. "Beware your ear hears too much gossip. A cackling woman and a crowing hen bring no luck to cock or hen."

"He's got that wrong," murmured Jane. She was staring at Daniel again. "Hasn't he?" She squirmed long and luxuriously. It seemed to relieve something. He looked away.

The magician's black-rimmed eyes swung over the room, searching. They flicked onto Connie, and flicked away; but it was she he chose. The long finger pointed unquestionably at her. "And now bring me the heart."

"Go on," said Jane, excited.

"How did he know who it belonged to?" asked Daniel.

"He must have seen Jane give it back," said Mark.

Connie got up and walked to the centre of the floor, her soft dark hair blue in the strange light. The magician held the heart for a moment, and then said, "A clean cut of the knife. Beware the reformer."

Connie stared at him. Then she turned and went back to her place. She was still moving gracefully.

The magician did a complicated trick, during which he turned red, and then green. There was smoke, the doves flew round, the glass and the heart disappeared, and Connie thought, "How did he know the brooch was mine?"

As though encouraged by the half-light, Jane's leg shifted so close to Daniel it must almost have been touching him.

Daniel was looking at Mark. "Will you do it?"

It was after four as they walked along a deserted road to the car. Daniel, though short-legged and pudgy, moved with surprising agility and had more speed even than Jane.

"The baby-sitter had better stay the night—what's left of it," said Connie. "It was fun, but I didn't like his laugh."

"He's a fake," said Daniel.

"He is not, Dan!" Jane pranced up and down like a horse.

Seeing her husband's expression, Connie said, "*Daniel* doesn't believe in the super-natural."

"When will you get the drawings in?" Daniel asked Mark.

"End of the week," said Jane. "He got my watch strap being tight."

"Law of averages," said Daniel. "He certainly isn't Hungarian."

"What are you muttering about?" Jane asked Mark. "Yes, you'll have time. I'll let you off the hour with the kid each night and you'll have a clear run. Poor old Connie. Beating hearts and beware informers."

"*Reformers*," said Mark.

"Hardly a birthday greeting," she said. "Anyway, how do you know? You were asleep most of the time. At least Dan doesn't fall asleep." Her voice was slurred.

"Yes, what was all that about?" asked Mark. "I thought I heard him say something about cutting things out from a body."

"I didn't hear that," said Daniel. "I'm sure he didn't say that."

"He did," said Connie. "Everyone was making such a noise. I wonder what it means."

"Nothing to worry about," said Jane. "Probably an abortion."

Connie shuddered.

"And what about your departing and approaching lovers?" said Daniel.

"Huh!" Jane flushed. She had, unknown to the men, but known to Connie, just trifled with a lean young tennis player. "I wonder where we'll go on Connie's next birthday."

Connie was aware of the street without looking at it. It was narrow, ordinary, its buildings vague, except for a lighted shop-front here and there, and at the end Regent's Street brimming with light. Suddenly it all changed. The lights didn't look right. The corner of the street moved, and the tailor's shop was something else. She stopped, and blinked; but when she opened her eyes the street was all right again.

"Forgotten something?" Daniel asked.

"Too much to drink."

4

Connie's kitchen was large, and its long harsh lights made the red-and-black tiled floor jump and dazzle, with all the impact of a migraine attack. The rugs were away at the cleaners. When they were there the kitchen was cosy. Old, useless things on their various journeys from other parts of the house to the dustcart had congregated there and stayed. There was a dilapidated rocking-chair that squealed if touched, an ancient mangle with nonsensical legs, an enormous radiogram, its insides long since gone; and these things, like aged and stubborn relatives, had their place and refused to move or be humiliated by the rest of the kitchen, which gleamed and was impeccably the latest thing.

Connie, dressed in long striped socks, slippers and a short skirt, was sweeping the floor. Her green-and-white striped sweater emphasised her body and the hazel-green of her eyes. She bent to pick up a crust and saw, beneath the table, other things that had a way of gathering there—the forbidden toys.

"Daniel!" she shouted. "Tell the horrors to come down and take their stuff up to the playroom. I keep telling them." She waited optimistically for a reply, and then, when there wasn't one, went to the door and shouted, "Right! I'm throwing them out."

"Coming, Mum," called the child least likely to come.

Daniel wasn't fooled and shouted from his study, "Adam! Do what your mother tells you."

Connie shoved her mending-basket and the heap of clothes to be ironed further along the wooden table and wiped the new space with kitchen paper. She fetched a plate piled with raw meat from the fridge; and as she did so Daniel came in and put down his coffee cup, a screwdriver, a door-handle, and the space was gone. "I'll propose Mark for the new scheme if I can get it through." The heap of ironing overflowed onto the floor. "We're voting tonight."

Connie kicked the fridge-door shut and hurried across with the heavy plate. "Move all that," she said, eyeing the screwdriver.

"I want to talk to him. He'd be good, you know. But I must do it somewhere where she can't possibly be, or he'll never get a word in."

"Male sauna," and she pushed the plate to the end of the table and got a chopping board from the drawer.

The overhead light started whirring, and like an answering mating call the pipes started rattling. At the other side of the kitchen the fridge did its bobbing-and-shaking dance.

"Pub," he said. "Tomorrow lunchtime."

"But he doesn't want to do it."

"We'll go round the corner to the Crown. Lamb's Conduit Street's too crowded."

Connie found a recipe book and put on her big shiny apron. The fridge slowed down, and there was sudden silence.

Daniel pressed himself against her back and stroked her breast. "He gets quite soppy about the changing face of London. I don't know if he's got illusions or just rather commonplace scruples."

"He's sensitive."

"He'll grow out of it." He left her breast alone and ate a hunk of cheese. "She's not always as bad as the other night. She seems to get louder when she's with you, for some reason. He's quite worn out by her. No wonder people think he's dull."

"She's a good friend, Daniel. Her heart's in the right place."

She went over to the other side of the kitchen, over to the long sink unit with its jangling jungle of metal implements, tricks and time-savers, and picked out her sharpest knife.

Daniel checked his watch with the electric clock. "Yes, I'll get him to the pub."

"I wish you'd get them to take their stuff upstairs. I wait on them hand and foot."

"I've told you. You've devalued a mother's best weapon. No television."

"Threats are no good. I—"

"Of course they're no good," he shouted. "You never carry them out. Just take the plug out." He ate a tomato and looked at the collection Connie had put by the door. "The sight of Dolly Deirdre in the dustbin now . . ."

In the twitching strip-lighting, Connie's face was flawless, serene. Its only signs of age were small lines at the corners of her eyes—upward, optimistic lines. Her eyes, beautiful in shape and colour, had a rare combination of elusiveness and good humour. Her eyes were all you really noticed, some people said; and that was lucky, they added, because her looks were so ordinary.

"It would really be one up, you know, if I could get Mark to do it."

Upstairs the battle of the television channels raged, and the losers gave the action a last twist by screeching. It brought Daniel up there in a flash and the plug was pulled out.

Connie cut the meat.

"Adam's getting smug," said Daniel coming back. "The answer is two television sets, Dad," he mimicked. "Why should I watch crap?"

She smiled and shifted the cut-off fat to one side.

"What's it going to be?" he asked, looking over her shoulder.

"Steak and kidney pie."

"Plenty of crust."

"Jane says you're getting horribly fat." She went on cutting.

"Has he done his homework, by the way?" he asked, and rushed out.

The meat was tough suddenly.

Upstairs, her eldest son discovered that his father's idea of hard work did not match his.

The meat became fleshy, knotty. It seeped bloodily. She cut again, and blood spurted out, ran over her hands, spread blackly over the chopping board. She put the knife down carefully and backed away, trying to wipe her hands on the slippery apron. Then the meat looked all right again. She stared at it. The blood seemed less. She turned and walked slowly across the kitchen. The red polished floor was blinding.

Daniel was in the living-room putting papers in his briefcase.

"Darling, would you cut the meat for me?"

He looked up, surprised. "But I'm just off. Use a sharper knife. You all right?"

She nodded.

"You look quite pale." He kissed her quickly and hurried to the front door. "Ring Jane, will you, and go on to her about exotic holidays. Three weeks in India. No, that's too cheap. Safari. That's it. She'd enjoy that. Back about midnight— if Jenkins doesn't stir the idiots up too much."

When he'd gone, she crept back into the kitchen. Upstairs, children splashed in the bath. Timidly, she approached the meat. It looked like stewing steak. She started cutting again.

It was curious, that change in the meat, she thought. For a moment it had looked alive.

5

It was almost dark as Jane and Connie, both carrying Sainsbury bags piled high with food, stood on the corner of Willoughby Road near the heath.

"I'm fed up with Mark," said Jane, putting down her carrier. "He shuts himself up in his room and works every evening. What life do I get? I'm sure he doesn't have to work so much. The kid and me are important as well. You must get fed up with Daniel being out so much."

"Well, I'd rather he was home, but there's a lot happening on the council at the moment. Have you talked to Mark about it?"

"Of course. He just retreats even further. And now Daniel's waving this new project under his nose. I don't know what to think. I don't know whether we should do it or not. I'd like the money." She hopped from foot to foot and banged her big fur mittens together. "Anyway, I'm off with you-know-who tonight. I'll say I'm with you, so please back me up."

Connie hesitated, and then said reluctantly: "Well, all right. What if he rings?"

"He won't. Haven't you ever wanted a change?"

"Well, I suppose there've been men I've thought attractive, yes, but it's never gone further than that. I suppose its because I'm O.K. with Daniel."

"You still feel the same about each other sexually after ten years? I don't believe it."

"No, it's not the same. It's better, if anything. But it goes in cycles. Sometimes for days we hardly notice each other."

"You're lucky." Jane was envious but open about it. "Still, Daniel's put on weight. I told him so. Doesn't he do any sports? I thought he said he was good at athletics."

"He doesn't have time."

"His eyes really look at you, don't they? That's what makes him attractive. Mark goes round as though he's blanketed in thick fog. Still, I must be off, if I'm going to—you know."

"Jane, have you ever had something happen to you where things you're looking at change shape . . . texture . . . just for a moment?"

Jane laughed. "Frequently—if I've drunk a bit too much."

"I'm serious."

"Then, no."

"I can't tell if it's the things or my perceptions. It's happened the past few days."

"Tiredness. Eyestrain. Anyway, I must go."

Connie walked home. The dark streets seemed too empty. There were people about—a long way off. The wind blew the trees and she heard footsteps behind her, a man's footsteps, getting nearer. Nervously she walked faster, but the other person was catching up. When he was almost up to her she gasped, and swiftly crossed the road. The man gave her a quick, surprised look and carried on walking. At the end of the road he went into his house, and Connie, her heart still thumping, felt rather silly.

The next day Connie was sprawled in the huge padded chair, watching television. Her eyes were half-closed and she looked fluffy and full of curves like a big cat. A book lay open at her feet, and beside her the electric fire, full on, sent its never-dying flames leaping up the tin grate; the coals twinkled rhythmically. The curtains weren't drawn. Outside, the trees, taller than anything around them, stretched up into the clear night sky. A breeze flapped around them. They creaked and the smaller branches jabbed against the roof.

The programme faded, and on came the adverts, blaring and bold, tumbling over each other like bad clowns. Connie stretched luxuriously, and then lay back again. She'd endure the adverts—anything rather than move.

The programme began again, but her eyes suddenly flicked over to the window. Seeing only trees they returned, rather carefully, to the television. Then she jerked up and listened. There should be a sound. She looked at the round polished table, at the hi-fi, at all the familiar things in her living room, but they didn't seem familiar anymore. The trees stiffened, alert, waiting, and high up a stronger breeze prowled through their branches. What was the sound she expected to hear? The television audience laughed. She sprang out of the chair and turned round. The front door, she could see, was closed. She switched off the set and, after the loud audience laughter, the house was too quiet. She didn't like the trees, the way their hard silent trunks filled the window, so she drew the curtains and stood still, scarcely breathing. There was a sharp noise in the kitchen—but it was just the fridge getting ready for its next dance. Things around her only looked recognisable when she examined each one and murmured its name. Sweating slightly and out of breath, her heart tumbling inside her, she forced herself back into the plump black chair. She turned down the fire, and the flames were obliged to twitch over coals reduced to a mere glow. She picked up the book and opened it, and put her slippers on. Her mouth was dry. She looked at the page. She looked at the clock, then at her watch. She looked into space. She looked at the clock again.

From the window, the garden seemed too long. She couldn't see the road, she realised, because the shrubs were too high. The swing didn't look harmless. The little stubbly plants she liked had disappeared. She let go the curtain. She sighed: breathing wasn't easy.

She'd go to the kitchen and make some tea. Purposefully she crossed the living room but stopped at the edge of the hallway. The staircase looked menacing. For the first time, her own house frightened her. The front door, bristling with old locks and bolts, disused and rusty, gave no security. The panels of frosted glass seemed particularly frail. She put the chain on quickly, and then remembered the back door and sped down to the kitchen to make sure it was locked.

Everything was too bright here. Alone on the dazzling floor she was exposed. She hurried back to the shadows and the dubious security of the hallway, and for some time she stood, her back pressed to the wall, alert, listening for the sound she wanted. She could almost hear it now. Then she remembered Daniel. Weak with relief, she reached across for the phone and dialled his number.

"Hello, darling." Her voice sounded too loud. "I wondered how you're getting on."

"All right, Catkin. Is it anything special?"

"I wondered when you were coming back."

"I told you. I'm not sure. Are you all right?"

"I'm feeling a bit shaky."

"Maybe you're getting flu."

"I'm worried about that chain."

"What chain?"

"The chain on the bloody door."

"Connie!"

"It's all right. It's all right. But the kitchen locks aren't any good. They're rusty. Any—"

"Connie. I've got to go back to the meeting. I'm holding everyone up. Look, you sound as though you're getting a touch of something. Have a scotch, a strong one, and go to bed." He hung up.

She poured (she was not an accustomed drinker) what she considered a strong one. It tasted vile. She went upstairs and looked at her sleeping children. Listening to them breathe made her feel better.

Coming down the stairs she saw something—something on the wall, on the curving wall of the stairway. It was a huge shadow of a man. Terrified, she turned round. There was only the stairs and the boxes on the landing. She looked at the shadow. It *looked* like a man and his arm was raised high above his head. She'd never seen the shadow before.

She walked down to the phone, her legs tingling and stiff, and as her shadow passed into the other it looked as though the arm was about to strike her.

She called Jane.

"So you've heard the news?" Jane said immediately.

"No, Jane. Look, I'm—"

"Daniel's proposed him for the scheme, and—"

"Look, Jane. I'm feeling a bit wobbly. I don't know what it is. I've got a feeling that—"

"Yes?"

"—that someone's trying to get in."

Jane gave an animal shriek. "Let's hope it's someone nice."

"Jane," she said hesitantly. "Could you come round?"

"Oh, Connie. I can't. There's no one with the kid. Mark's out. Go to a neighbour."

"They're a long way away."

"Don't be ridiculous."

"Well, they seem a long way. I've got to go down that long garden and through the gate—"

"Hop over a wall."

Connie, hurt, didn't say anything. Jane said, "No, really. Go over the wall. It doesn't sound like you."

"I've been feeling a bit odd for days."

"Pregnant. You're pregnant again. You know that awful early stage."

Connie sat down, dazed with relief. "That's it. That's why the meat looked funny."

"Get yourself a big drink and watch television. Get your mind off it. We'll see you Thursday. So long, kid."

Then she heard the sound she had been expecting. It seemed to come from a long long way away. It was the sound of heavy, wooden wheels and a child's squeaky voice shouting, *"Watercresses!"*

Something woke her. She lay, not breathing, wondering what the noise had been. Without turning in the bed, she knew she was alone. A muffled noise downstairs coming from the hallway, the noise of someone trying to get in. She jolted up. "Cor." The expression lingered in her mind, even after she heard Daniel's voice call, "Connie, open the door."

She was so relieved, she half fell on the stairs in the rush to get to him. The door jammed; she'd forgotten the chain. Dithering, she took it off and clung to him and "Cor!" clung to her mind and she couldn't get rid of it.

"All right, Catkin." He comforted her. "What's happened?"

She shook her head.

He sat her gently on the stairs. "Why did you have the chain on?"

She looked at him, at his dark eyes, at his black sleek hair, at his pallor, at his firm mouth, at all those things she loved. Then she remembered the shadow.

Without looking, she pointed above her head, upwards at the curving landing. He stiffened.

"The shadow," she whispered.

He frowned at her, and then darting up the stairs, "Shadow? Shadow? What shadow?" He was tired, on edge. She came up behind him.

"There," and she pointed at the thick, looming shape.

He looked at it as though he was in an art gallery viewing pictures way beyond his comprehension. He frowned, blinked, bent sideways. "It's always been there, Connie," was all he could find to say about it.

"It hasn't."

"For Godsake!"

"I haven't seen it." She was nearly crying.

"Anyway, what about it?"

"Ssh!" indicating the children. "Can't you see?" she whispered.

He turned and looked at her.

"It's—it's a man, isn't it?" she said.

"No, Connie, it isn't a man. It's a meaningless shape caused by the landing." He turned and looked upwards, searching.

"But he's holding his arm up. Can't you see that?"

"That's a box. That long box up there. Jutting out." He ran up four stairs, pushed the box up so it rested against the wall and the menacing arm disappeared. "It must have fallen down."

"Oh," she murmured. "I am sorry." The shadow was now nothing more than a big blob.

"It must have fallen yesterday when I was getting my old case notes out," he explained patiently. "It stuck out and caused that shape. It's five to one. Now let's get some sleep. Please."

The next night she sat in the kitchen sewing her daughter's dress. The electric clock thumped out the minutes and a chicken soup bubbled on the stove. It was full of home-grown herbs and smelt delicious. Connie bit through the thread, put the dress gently on the table and went up to the curving stairway. She looked at the shadow. It was exactly as it had been before he moved the box. A man loomed up, his arm raised and somehow she knew, before she even turned, that the long box would be up against the wall and not jutting out.

6

On Thursday evening they sat at the oval table in Connie's small dining room. There were long white candles, white roses, a crisp white table cloth. They'd just enjoyed, or said they had, Connie's first attempt at home-made cannellonis in Neapolitan sauce. The frozen beans had been excellent. The dinner was to celebrate Mark getting the Camden Town flat project and there were three bottles of claret on the sideboard.

Connie was wearing the scarlet velvet dress Daniel had bought for her birthday, and her shoulder-length hair was pinned up in a chignon. She didn't wear the diamond brooch and nobody mentioned it. Jane, who again wore her prim black frock, said she was impressed with the way Connie looked and she kept nudging Mark. "Doesn't she look old-fashioned?"

Exhaustion had already got a foothold on his evening and he sighed "Yes. Yes." His wife was getting loud again, but at least it wasn't in public.

"Everyone should have a deep freeze," said Jane.

"Nonsense," Mark replied, his voice high and cracking. "They're just a fad. You've survived all this time without one."

"That's no reason for not having one. I want one. Why shouldn't I have one?" Her eyes gleamed maliciously. "You have what you want. What about that twelve-function calculator you got last month? You can work perfectly well without it but I didn't stop you having it."

"It seems amazing people ever got by without refrigerators," said Daniel and scooped up the last beans.

"Think," said Jane, looking at his fleshy chin and the suggestion of others under it.

He grinned and cut a huge lump of bread.

She poked her tongue out and then turned to Connie. "I'm saving up for a deep freeze. I don't know whether to get a really big one, like you've got, or an upright one."

Mark gave her a baleful glance. "There's no room."

"There will be, Mark. There will be," and her staccato laugh made him fear for his twelve-function calculator and all his other luxuries.

"I'm thinking of placing the flats round a central space area," Mark said, rather awkwardly.

"How will you fill the space?" asked Daniel.

"I wasn't thinking of filling it."

"Christine across the road from me has just got a washing-up machine," said Jane. "It's the only thing for that job."

"Only for large families," said Daniel.

"Rubbish! For any family. Why not? Though why she needs one, when she's got an au pair, I don't know."

"I was thinking of having just grass," said Mark.

Daniel shrugged and looked at the sideboard. "You'll have trouble getting grass past Jenkins. He wants a shopping precinct included in the scheme."

"But there's shops all round—"

"A modern shopping precinct, split-level. Where's the chocolate, Connie?"

"You know Christine. Her husband's in advertising. She wears loads of make-up even first thing in the morning. Mark's seen her before seven with eyelashes on."

Connie's youngest boy, David, came running into the room, a baby's bottle hanging by its teat from between his teeth.

"Go to bed, angel," Connie said softly.

"Want lilly juice."

"Bed!" roared Daniel and the child tottered off.

"What's lilly juice?" asked Jane.

"Gripe water." Connie laughed. "He'll never grow up."

"The kid's the same about—"

"Would you support me?" Mark asked suddenly. "I mean—what do *you* think?"

"Sure," Daniel said rather absently.

"You see, it would be a play area. I'll show you the new drawings."

"The drawings should be simple. Straight up and down."

"No, there's no problem about—"

"Pass your glass, Jane, Connie. Try this one—. . ."

"It's not twenty pound a night," said Mark.

The candles had gone right down, and wax dripped over the holders and hung suspended in obscene, horrid shapes. Connie stared at them.

"It is," Jane insisted.

"On the *wagon-lit,* she means," said Daniel; and he opened another bottle.

Connie was leaning, elbow on the table, head resting in her hand, precariously. Her eyes were unseeing and the exact purpose of the evening was no longer clear.

"For two," said Mark.

"Twenty pound a night," shouted Jane.

Connie heard, quite clearly, another voice say, "*It's fourpence a night for the doss house, Liz. Otherwise it's the casual ward.*"

"It's ten pound each, stupid," said Jane.

The other, a rough, deep Cockney voice, said, "*If you go in the casual ward, you've got to stay there two days.*"

"You don't want to try Flower and Dean Street?" Connie said and her head lurched off her hand. She jerked it up again.

"What?" asked Daniel.

"In Buck Row it's mixed. You can sleep two to a bed," and Connie giggled.

They all stared at her. "Are you all right?" Jane asked.

Connie, suddenly bewildered, tried to laugh. "Of course I'm all right."

"Well, what's all this two-to-a-bed?" asked Jane.

Connie tried to laugh again. "Just a joke." She poured some wine and her fork fell on the floor. A vague sense of her position as hostess came back to her and she said to Mark, in a loud voice, "Congratulations!"

They were staring at her. Then Jane said firmly, "It's a hell of a price for one night," and drew the men's attention off Connie. "I'd rather sit up. Wouldn't you? Except of course if you've got the kids with you. Then no price would be too high."

"The other night she put the chain on the door," Daniel told Mark, quietly.

"Well, that's not such a bad idea," he murmured.

"No. That's not what I mean."

"I don't even sleep in a *wagon-lit*," said Jane. "It's either too hot or too cold. It's always noisy."

"We've lived here for over ten years," said Daniel. "She loves this house. It was my mother's house."

Connie gulped her wine and poured some more. Her way of drinking became unfamiliar. It was out of control, angular.

"Half the time the back door isn't locked even when she goes out," Daniel said. "We've got nothing to steal, after all." He looked at Connie, who was swaying a bit, and winced.

"It may be her nerves," muttered Mark. That was a complaint he was familiar with.

Jane pounced on "nerves." She knew all about "nerves." "It is not her nerves. Anyone can see she's pregnant."

The men looked at Jane, astounded. She'd got their attention and she meant to keep it. "Women go through funny changes at the beginning of pregnancies."

"But she's not been like this before," Daniel said, timidly.

"Every pregnancy is different, Daniel. She'll be all right after the twelfth week. Anyway, she wanted another one."

Connie was poised between the desire to pour her next drink and oblivion. She stroked her thigh in an inviting way, then looked down sharply.

"What have you dropped?" asked Jane.

"I touched my dress. It felt rough. Then I look down. I see velvet." She hiccoughed.

"They're lovely flowers," said Jane brightly.

"Daniel got them for me. He gets me such lovely presents." She emphasised the "lovely" and giggled.

Daniel clapped a hand over her glass. "That's enough."

"I wish Mark would," said Jane. "Get presents I mean." She hooted with laughter.

Connie started singing, at first hesitantly.

"Oh, they say I killed a man, so they said.
Oh, they say I killed a man, so they said.
For I hit him on the 'ead

With a bloody great lump of lead
Damn 'is eyes.
Oh they put me—"

"Shut up!" said Daniel.

Jane took her arm. "What about a bit of air? Come on."

Connie wouldn't move. There was a different expression on her face. She looked—lewd. "Pass the bottle, love," she said to Mark.

"Time to go," said Mark, waving his eyebrows at Jane. "We'll walk back. It's a fresh night."

Connie bawled,

"Oh they put me into quod
All for killing of that sod."

Daniel, aghast, said, "Shut up!"

"They did so 'elp me Gawd
Damn their eyes."

Embarrassed, Jane tried to join in, but she didn't know the words.

Connie slumped onto the table, knocking her glass over.

"She did want another one," Jane said again.

Connie murmured, "Another new bonnet, pretty one. It cost a sovereign. That's not a bloody sovereign, you bugger. It's a church farthing. You polished it up."

Mark, hoping to save Daniel further embarrassment, got their coats and waited in the hallway. Daniel opened the front door.

"Just have a pee," and Jane ran upstairs.

Mark hesitated, and then said, "Could I see you before the planning permission meeting? I'd like to get the idea across to—"

Daniel shook his head abruptly. "I doubt if I'll make the meeting. I've got the Bryant case all this week and I'm eager to get that derelict area near Lisson Grove used properly. They're talking about building some damn silly composition football pitch."

Connie started singing again.

"She's got quite a voice," said Jane, adjusting her dress.

Daniel almost shoved them out and then hurried back to the dining room.

"Come on. Bed!"

"Why should I go with you?" She waved a finger at him. "You've got me mixed up."

Connie lay dizzily in bed, a cold flannel on her forehead, a glass of Alka Seltzer fizzing murderously beside her. She was talking into the phone, and every word had to be dragged up with great effort. David ran round and round the room.

"I'm sorry about last night, Jane. Was I awful?"

"Pretty drunk."

"I can't remember a thing. Daniel's furious. I spilt wine all over the cloth. He had to do everything—this morning. I couldn't move."

"Have you been sick?"

"Not yet. Anyway, say sorry to Mark. It's not something I'll do again, believe me."

"I wouldn't. You're just not yourself when you're like that. It's like being with a different person."

7

Spring was early and Connie moved David's toys onto the lawn and started preparing her flower borders and vegetable patch. She hadn't seen Jane for some days and she arrived unexpectedly as Connie was running round the garden with David.

"How've you been?" Jane asked.

"Fine."

They sat on the grass.

"It's such a good day I thought I'd go on the heath."

"I hope it doesn't go cold again. It'll kill everything."

"I've just had another set-to with Mark. I want a deep freeze and a hi-fi. He says we can only have a deep freeze. He's astonishing. He's not really mean, just careful, and there's no reason for it, especially now he's got the new thing from Daniel. You must come to dinner with us. Daniel's amazing the speed he gets things done." After a pause she asked, "Done any more take-offs of the Good Old Days lately?"

Connie shivered.

"I know Daniel didn't go much on the coarse bits, but Mark was terribly impressed. I mean, you knew it all through. Where did you learn it?"

"I don't know," she said quietly.

"You couldn't have heard it at boarding school—though on the other hand boarding school is probably just the place you would."

"That must be it."

"What would you do about the hi-fi? I feel like just going and getting one."

"Well, do." Connie was preoccupied.

"Don't you and Daniel ever have rows?"

She shook her head without thinking.

"You don't belong in Hampstead. With a marriage like yours you ought to be living in Golders Green."

Connie, wearing her latest dress, yellow, short and backless, stood at the sink. The sound of voices talking and shouting, police whistles, and feet running, started up among the clatter of plates and noise of running water.

"*No one came out of Buck's Row.*"

"*Some sneaky yid who wouldn't pay for his fun.*"

"*She cut up nasty.*"

"*Come quickly for gawd's sake. It's something horrible.*"

She turned off the tap and, almost collapsing, held on to the sink. Around her there were only the ordinary noises of the kitchen. A plate was broken.

"Aren't you cold?" asked Daniel, suddenly behind her. "It's a very appealing number, but I don't want strawberries and cream getting cold." He patted her bare back. "Back when I can, Catkin."

"Don't go!"

"Oh, Connie."

"Please don't go. I can't stand it."

"What, dear?"

And then she turned round and he saw her face. The fluorescent strip-light had whited out all colour from it.

"Connie!"

"Being alone. I can't stand it."

In a responsible tone he said, "Now look here. You were alone Sunday night and perfectly all right. I've got to do my stint at the Neighbourhood Law Centre. I can't just not go."

"Not tonight. Please not tonight." She started crying.

"You'll wake the children! Oh, Connie, I'm sorry." He touched her cheek. "Come on, old girl." He had no idea how to cope with the situation and he was badly alarmed. "You'll be all right. You've got to do some pulling together. Now I'll only—"

She shrieked, "Someone is trying to kill me!"

She stood, quite still, appalled at what she'd said.

"Now stop it! Stop it!" he said, anticipating a storm of hysterics. "Stop it!"

She didn't move or speak. Slightly reassured, he pulled over a chair and sat her in it. He gave her a drink of water. When she did speak her voice was calm.

"That shadow came back and you wouldn't see it. It came back even though you moved the box. I showed you but you wouldn't see."

"The shadow didn't change," he said.

"You said the box made that arm."

"I moved the bloody box."

"The arm came back. It's there now."

Exasperated, he said, "I'm going to phone Jane."

Jane looked at the shadow and laughed loudly. "It's—it's—I don't know what it is. It's like the blotting paper test they do for your personality. Everyone interprets it differently."

"But how do you see it?" asked Daniel.

"A cloud. Oh, I don't know." He was standing close to her, and she was suddenly embarrassed.

"Well, Jane, would you say it looked like a man with his arm raised?"

She hopped up and down, her body in a turmoil. She almost touched him. "Yes, it could be. Yes, now you come to mention it."

Downstairs, Connie waited, sullen.

Jane held Connie's hand as they sat in the kitchen. She'd just cooked some dinner but Connie wouldn't touch it. Jane nudged her. "Come on. Eat up."

The meat looked more meaty than it should. It was sinuous, knotty. Nauseated, Connie pushed the plate away.

"You're all right," said Jane. "I mean, you've got everything."

Then Connie heard the sound again. In the distance the child's voice cried, "*Watercresses. Four bunches a penny.*"

She looked almost slyly at Jane. Jane hadn't heard it.

"You've got a bloke who's nuts about you, a super house, good health, lovely kids that you wanted. This is no time to crack up."

Daniel came into the kitchen.

"You're early," said Jane brightly.

"I came back." He took his coat off and looked at Jane, like a conspirator. Connie was staring at the pepper pot. They watched her for some time. She didn't blink.

"Eat up, love," said Jane.

It echoed in Connie's mind. "*Eat up, love, or you'll never go to heaven. Along came Jack and then there were seven.*"

"She won't touch meat," said Daniel.

"Then she is pregnant." Jane was triumphant.

"No. She isn't." He sighed, and sat at the table and took Connie's other hand. "I'm getting an au pair because I think some of this—a lot of this—is strain."

Connie shook her head.

"It can suddenly hit you. You go for years doing the same thing day after day and one day—bang!"

Jane nodded energetically.

"It isn't that." Her voice was toneless and depressed.

"Well, for Godsake what is it?" he shouted.

"Oh do leave me alone. It's just my nerves." She shivered and near to tears said, "Please leave me alone."

Offended, he got up and went out of the kitchen.

Connie's eyes filled with tears and she lit a cigarette, her hands trembling. Jane, who had never seen her like this, was astonished.

"Come on. It's not like you. What's wrong? What is it?"

"I don't know. I mean—it's voices." She sighed deeply. "They say things I've never heard. Everything changes, just for a moment."

For once, Jane could think of nothing to say. She'd just realised Connie was nuts.

"I don't even smell like me." She wiped the tears off her cheeks. "I have a bath every day, yet sometimes I *stink*." She emphasised the word and looked at Jane.

Jane remembered the perfume, the lovely summery perfume, and was secretly pleased. Then the moment passed, and she asked, quite kindly, "What of?"

"Sweat. Nasty sweat. And other things. Sperm. Stale sperm." Her voice was pale, resigned.

"What d'you do then?"

"I wash again."

"Well, use something. A deodorant. No, not a deodorant. Something stronger. An anti-perspirant. You know, one of those you spray on. They last for hours and they've got a nice smell." She shrieked with laughter. "Help! We sound like a TV ad." Connie smiled. "And shave your armpits. If you're in a nervous state, your sweat does smell. So remember—shave."

Baffled, his world a hurting, inexplicable mess, Daniel arranged to meet Mark in a local pub after work. Mark as usual looked tired, but not as tired as Daniel. They stood at the bar, and Mark, having turned to make sure he wouldn't be overheard—an eccentric precaution considering his small voice—mumbled, "Is there anything else?"

"What?"

"Anything apart from being alone in the house that worries her?"

"Water."

"Water?"

"Kids in the bath. The other night David—she was washing his hair—came up from under the water and she got a funny feeling he was drowned. She said for a moment he looked dead. Damned job calming her. She won't let them near the pond at the top of the heath. It's only two inches deep, for Godsake. She hears things. Said this morning she thinks she's possessed."

"You don't think she could be a—schizophrenic?"

"Is persecution conflict—I mean mania—a part of schizophrenia?"

"Does she have hallucinations? That's the decisive symptom with schizophrenia." He was dimly trying to visualise the shelf of tatty psychiatric paperbacks he'd collected a month after marrying Jane. "Withdrawal from reality."

"Happens to everyone at some time or other," said Daniel. He was equally authoritative. "Three out of four women go in the bin at least once in their lives." He swallowed his beer quickly. "The figures may be inaccurate, but you know what I mean."

Mark nodded. "Change of life."

"For heavensake! Connie's a bit young for that."

"No. I mean, it disturbs them."

"First it was the doors, then the windows. I've had bars and grilles put all over the place. Damned job explaining to the kids. It takes a quarter of an hour to lock up at night. Then, sod it, she gets out of bed on some pretext and checks it all. Now it's the children and water."

"Symptoms of anxiety change." Mark looked at the ceiling. "You treat one thing. There's another. The cause, you see, doesn't change."

"You're talking about an anxiety—" He paused, fumbling for the name.

"Neurosis?"

"That'll do. Neurosis. Not schizophrenia."

"Jane says Connie's worried about smells."

"Smells?"

"Body odours." Shyly, Mark took a long drink and plunged into the delicate question of underarms and sperm.

"She really said that?"

"The schizophrenia possibility aside, I would have bet it was a—" A long silence, and then Mark dredged up, "phobic illness, if it wasn't for this revulsion to the smell of semen. That's important. It indicates sexual—uh—problems." He'd just read a thick book on sexual aberrations. He knew all about that.

"She never has had. I mean—"

"They're deep-rooted. Is her father alive?"

"Why yes. What's that got to do with it?"

"A transference—uh—state is difficult to . . . It could be a transference state."

Daniel urgently tried to think of an equally illuminating possibility. Mark definitely had the grip on all the good ones. He was deciding between nervous breakdown and premenstrual blues when Mark said, his voice croaking with pleasure, "Guilt."

"Sounds more like transference to me."

Mark looked at him out of the corner of his eye. "Actually, I'm not that sure what transference is."

"No. Well, I'm not absolutely certain about that one."

"I mean, I know it's what a lot of people go to an analyst for. But guilt is quite common. It causes all sorts of—traumas."

"Yep. Yep."

"I've got a suggestion, a tentative one. It could be suppressed nymphomania."

"*Re*pressed nymphomania, you mean. The trouble is it could be anything. There's so many damn things they get. Care for a short?"

Meanwhile, Connie, her hair pinned up, sat in the hot scented bathwater shaving her armpits.

They came back from the pub, slightly drunk, and Mark came in for a last scotch and another look at the patient. Whatever they'd been expecting, Connie morbidly gazing at the shadow or overchecking the window locks, they were not prepared for what they did see. Connie stood in the hallway, by the telephone. She was naked, wet, and blood oozed down her left breast and spilt onto the carpet—the patch by her feet was already scarlet. For a moment it seemed to Daniel there was blood everywhere.

"Doctor," said Mark, and leaving him to tend to the blood he rang the GP.

"The blood wouldn't stop. It wouldn't stop. There was lots of blood." She was getting hysterical.

"What were you doing?" Daniel was frantic.

"Shaving. The water's all pink. I couldn't stop the blood."

He put a cold flannel under her arm, wrapped her in his coat while Mark located the brandy and three glasses. By the time the GP arrived the blood had stopped, but she was shaking violently and unable to speak.

The GP was puzzled. Although the cut was fairly deep, it wasn't serious enough to cause such shock. He gave her two injections, one for tetanus, helped her to swallow a glucose drink, disinfected the cut and covered it with gauze. Then he took Daniel to one side. "She's overshocked."

"There was a lot of blood."

"Well, there's bound to be if you cut yourself in the bath. The hot water makes the tiniest cut bleed like the devil." He turned and looked at her, yawning and pale on the sofa, and said: "The cut's nothing, but I think a night in hospital might be the thing, just to get her over this—shock."

There was a dark blue light overhead and Connie, wearing a white hospital nightgown, lay on her bed in the general ward. It was night, but women, some of them dressed, were wandering about or sitting on each other's beds talking quietly. Among their words were others and Connie heard a voice distinctly say, *"She's in the casual ward off Thrawl Street."*

Another voice said, *"You've got to stay the forty-eight hours. It's the law. She's gone to her sister."*

"Which one?"

"You know. Across the river. They've been hop-picking."

"Where's the money, then?"

"Drunk it, haven't they? She was drunk as a lord."

"Here's tuppence, but not for rum. You look real poorly, Liz."

A patient came up to Connie's bed and asked, "What are you here for?"

"My kids were drowned when the pleasure steamer went down. I lost my old man."

"You don't sound English."

"I'm Swedish."

"You're the worse for drink," said another voice.

9

The next morning was dark and sodden. The windows and frosted-glass partition in the roof rattled with uneven bickering rain which, discovering the occasional hesitant slates, worried at them, nagged at them, until finally it dribbled between them. A patch in the corner of the ceiling started to darken and bulge.

They kept the hot white lights on and everybody, sick and well, turned a disturbing greenish colour. All around there was a powerful smell of wet rubber raincoats. Connie woke up feeling quite different. She felt all right. A young house doctor, his drenched hair sticking up in spikes, took her pulse and ordered commonplace drugs. She wanted to go. The depression was gone.

When Jane came to take her home at midday she was so full of energy, she said, "Let's go and have a marvellous lunch. Let's go shopping. Let's walk across the heath."

"Are you mad?" Jane's hand flew to her mouth. "I mean, it's pouring with rain."

"Oh, rain's lovely. It's soothing."

Discomfited, Jane shifted from foot to foot. Then the old, how-to-handle-the-insane adage came to her rescue. Humour them.

"Well, all right. Let's." Her enthusiasm seemed false even to someone accustomed to her noise.

Connie took Jane's arm affectionately. "It's really nice of you to come and get me."

"Well, I needed a day off." Her voice was gruff.

"Is David O.K.?"

"Fine. My mother's there—will be there for some time. Much to Mark's dismay."

"That cut was an exorcism. All the horrors leaked out of it." She laughed.

Jane's expression was far from humourous. "Well, don't rush things." Mark had thrown another derangement into the ring—manic depression—and Jane felt he might have a point.

The summer leaves, swollen with rain, hung motionless like huge furry tongues. They made Jane feel quite disturbed and she was glad to get off the heath. They turned into the narrow streets leading to the top of Hampstead. Jane was talking about hi-fis and washing-up machines. She'd just got a deep freeze, and a washing-up machine was the new idol and new excuse for battle with Mark. "Happened to call in at his bank on the way to get you and what do you think I find? There's two thousand quid in there. I'm not letting it rot while I spend half the day standing at the sink."

Connie looked down. "That's funny. The street's cobbled."

"A lot are." Jane eyed her suspiciously.

For a moment Connie felt badly shaken. Then she looked up—up into the grim sky—and said, "Yes, a washing-up machine sounds a good thing but you still have to spend time loading it." She took a noisy breath. "Perhaps they should invent a machine for that."

Obsessive, Jane decided.

The next street-corner was high up on a slope and there was a conspicuous shop, oddly shaped, painted black, that sold pottery. Connie could see a big floral jug in the window. Then it wasn't there. The shop wasn't there. It was nighttime. Nearby, men were singing drunkenly. She could hear a horse and cart coming along behind her. She screamed. "There's a horse and cart behind me."

Jane's voice cut in. "Of course there's a horse and cart."

Connie whirled round and the nighttime was gone. Coming up the splashy slope was a rag and bone man with his horse.

"I hope you've not come out too soon," said Jane. "You've gone a horrible colour."

"It's probably the blood I lost. I'm all right." She started talking quickly. "We'll go to the new French place. We'll have lots of wine and garlic bread. I'd love onion soup, a steak—"

By the time she got to Heath Street her heart had stopped jumping and her colour was back. She walked effortlessly, enjoying the rain, and feeling good. People passing looked as though they thought her pretty, but she didn't feel quite as good as she had felt earlier. There was a shadow on her.

Connie and Jane sat on the sofa, and Daniel, undecided, paced between the armchair and piano stool on the other side of the room. He passed two floor cushions, almost sat on the straight-backed chair in the corner but ended up for the third time at the drinks cabinet where he poured another large soothing whisky. Jane's hair was tied in a ponytail. Two racquets waited by the door. The bourgeois ordinariness of the room emphasised the barred windows, and Daniel, looking miserable, drew the curtains. It was a cold evening, the fire was on and Connie, watching the twinkling, twitching, flitting flames, said: "I know it can't go on, Daniel. But don't you see, I say things I can't possibly have heard."

"What do the voices sound like? Are they talking *to* you?" asked Jane.

Daniel left the room.

"No. They're just going on around me." She spoke steadily. "They sound normal until I realise what they're saying. No one I know speaks like that."

"Is it like hearing them on a telephone?"

"More like a radio. They suddenly tune in, and then they're gone. Sometimes they're faint, but mostly they're just like you and me talking now. Do you know anything about possession, Jane?"

"I do," said Daniel, back in the room. "It doesn't exist." He stared at Jane's thick white socks and went out again.

"That song I sang the night you came to dinner. How could I have known it?"

Jane, thinking back over that evening, said, "Do you know Flower and Dean Street?"

Connie shook her head. She looked pale again.

"You said something about Flower and Dean Street. I remember the name."

Connie, not aware she'd said anything, looked even paler.

"I've never heard of it," said Jane.

They sat in silence.

"It was about the time of my birthday," Connie said slowly. "It all began then. It was something about that magician."

"Oh, don't be ridiculous," said Jane rudely. "I admit he got my watch strap being tight but—well, he also got lovers departing and approaching, didn't he?" She jigged her knees up and down. "I suppose if you start tampering with all that magic stuff things could—get out of control, mixed up, all those vibrations flying about. Still I don't really believe it, any of it. You probably knew a Flower and Dean Street when you were a kid."

"Probably," Connie lied.

"It's a nice name." She crossed to the bookcase, picked out the A–Z and turned to the index. "It's here." She crouched on the floor and her brown finger traced a squared map for some moments before she found it. "It's a little street. It's in Whitechapel in the East End."

"I've never been to the East End."

"Perhaps when you were a kid . . ."

"Living in Brighton? Unlikely."

Jane shivered. "It seems extraordinary. It's probably a coincidence. Still . . ."

"Do you believe me, Jane?"

"I don't know."

"Well, I know," said Daniel, hurrying back to the whisky bottle. "People say extraordinary things, do extraordinary things, clairvoyance, E.S.P., what you will. Yet when they're put to the test, the result is very ordinary. Nothing. It's not possible, so it doesn't exist."

"Its not existing doesn't mean it isn't possible," said Jane hotly. "Fucking rationalist!" she said, as he went out.

"I'm going to find out what's happening to me and why," said Connie bluntly.

"You'd better keep it from him. Balding, fat go-getter."

They sat close together in Jivanjee Natraj's waiting room. It was very plush, and Jane whispered: "The supernatural's on his side." He appeared stealthily in the doorway, an exceptionally tall, thin brown man, dressed in a well-cut grey suit. He bowed slightly but didn't speak, and Jane burst out laughing. Connie, giggly, embarrassed, followed him into his consulting room, where, still without speaking, he took her hands, covered the palms with blue marking-ink and pressed them flat onto some paper. He touched her shoulder lightly and she followed him into a colourful cloakroom where he indicated a sink and she washed her hands. Back in his room he sat behind his enormous imitation Regency desk and pointed to a chair opposite. She sat down, which made her lower than him by about a foot. He put a pair of horn-rimmed spectacles on, and studied the imprints of her palms. "Date of birth?" His voice, though soft, seemed to echo, and what he said stayed in the room.

She told him.

"You have an exceptionally good life with your husband. I see you are a good wife. Your life is tranquil, but you have an appetite for adventure."

She looked surprised.

"In books." He laughed. "I see you like reading. The distinguished wife of a famous politician came to me yesterday. Like you, she is a good wife. Her eminent husband has many problems, but I am able to solve them. I help the Prime Minister of India. I help many people." He pushed across a huge leather-bound book of press cuttings. "Look. There is what the Prime Minister says about me. And here, the famous actor, celebrated all over the world—see what he says. I advise him on the roles he should accept." He looked at the cutting hungrily. "And here—see what they say about me in California."

"Quite fantastic," she said and snapped the book shut. "Will I have any children?"

He laughed uproariously. "You are participating in a trick, dear lady. You know you have four." He looked back at the print. "Your husband is very kind to you, most kind. He is well-suited to you."

"Will I have any more children?"

Slightly uneasy, he looked out the window. "That is up to you, my dear lady. You have a decision to make soon. Please do not look so alarmed. It's about education. You have boy child, no?"

She nodded.

"You have your way about education, but you have to fight. Remember my advice and it will give you strength. You have a rosy future." He smiled and his yellow teeth were stained and crooked. The smile gave his dignified face the crafty aspect of a jackal. "That will be seven pounds."

She paid him and turned to go. His expression changed. He stared very hard and thoughtfully at her as she went to the door.

"What crap!" She imitated his voice. "You have rosy future. You have boy child, no?" She laughed. "What shall I do now?"

"Try another one."

And they felt quite safe about trying another one.

10

Connie's bedroom was spacious and calm and reflected her serenity, her need for order. Daniel's personality didn't exist there at all. Rich blue curtains tumbled luxuriously onto the white wall-to-wall carpet. There was a full-length gilt-edged looking-glass. The lights were low except the one above the dressing table, where she sat, making up her face.

She mascaraed her lashes quickly, and then without thinking picked up an eyebrow pencil and emphasised her eyebrows. She unscrewed an unused rouge-pot and flooded her cheeks with colour. She painted her mouth. Dissatisfied, she searched for a darker lipstick. She picked up the pencil again and gave the eyebrows sensational arches. On impulse she enlarged her beauty spot. She packed her face with white powder, combed her hair so that it hung over one eye and gave Daniel the fright of his life. She seemed hardly aware of what she was doing.

"Cab, Connie."

He managed not to say anything but silently repeated over and over the GP's number as though it was some mind-saving mantra. They walked to the gate, and he opened the door of the cab.

"Give my best to Jane."

She got in and he shut the door. Loudly, she told the driver the name of a local cinema. Before they reached the corner she turned to wave, but Daniel had already disappeared.

As the cab turned left by the heath, she leaned forward and said, "Take me instead to Flower and Dean Street, E.1."

The cab throbbed at the corner of Fashion Street, while she walked up and down Flower and Dean Street. It was dark and cold and she had no feeling of recognition or anything else. Half the buildings had been pulled down. There was no one about. It was depressing.

She got back in the cab, and the driver said: "Looking for anything special?"

"No."

"It's all changed round here. All been torn down."

"What was here before?"

"Houses."

"Are any of the old parts still left?"

"I should think so. You ought to ask at the library."

On Saturday evenings Connie and Daniel usually went to the home of Baxter, one of Daniel's colleagues on the council, and the routine was to have a drink and play mahjong. The following Saturday was Baxter's birthday and there were more people and more to drink. Daniel, his heart sinking, kept close to Connie; but she stayed sober, her make-up muted—she even seemed to enjoy herself. It gave him confidence to attend, as he'd hoped to, a meeting to try to pry the Lisson Grove derelict area out of the hands of the mad composition footballers.

At a quarter to twelve, Baxter came out with Connie to find her a taxi. He was older than Daniel, officious, hearty, with a loud voice and a clipped moustache.

"Dannyboy's a bit of a bounder with this Lisson Grove thing. He'll get his way. Wants half London torn down and his new hygienic—hey, cabbie!" He waved both arms.

"He likes getting things done," she said loyally. "Thanks for a lovely evening. Come to us next week."

"Thanks, love, I will."

The cab stopped, and he gave her address. He was just about to open the door when she said, "*Give us some money.*"

Taken aback, he fumbled in his pocket. "Will a pound do?" Then he laughed. She was having a joke.

"*No, it will not do.*"

His smile died. If it was a joke, he didn't find it funny. "Now come on, Connie—"

"*Come on, you bugger. Give us some more.*" She leaned sensually against the taxi and in the street light her face was coarse. "*Give us all you've got, big boy.*" She prodded him. "*All of it.*" She hiccoughed and giggled.

He pushed the pound into her hand, forced her into the cab, slammed the door and walked away fast.

Connie was preparing the Sunday lunch when the phone rang. Wiping her hands on her apron, she ran up to the hallway and answered it.

Baxter said, "How are you?"

"How are you, Baxter? Isn't it a gorgeous day? It's spring again."

"Terrific."

"D'you want Daniel?"

"No. Is he there?"

"He's in the garden, pulling up the shrubs by the gate. People keep tripping up. I'll call him."

"No. Look, Connie. I'm an old friend and I'm going to say something straight. Straight, anyway, is the only way to say it. Lay off the bottle. You can't take it."

"But I hardly had anything."

"I know. That's what's been worrying me until I remembered the ladies who carry gin in scent bottles. Lay off it, flower. It doesn't suit you. It isn't nice." When she didn't answer, he said, "D'you remember getting into the cab?"

"It's a bit hazy."

"I bet it is. You were as tight as a tick."

"Was I?" Her heart pounding, she sat on the stairs.

"You made me look a damn fool in front of the cabbie. You behaved just like a tart."

Overcome, she put the phone down. David ran up with his bottle, then stopped and stared at her, worried.

"It's all right. It's all right," she murmured. Then she grabbed him and held him to her, tightly.

II

Feeling rather silly, Jane and Connie sat in the kitchen of a small untidy house in the suburbs, while a little homely woman bustled about making tea.

"Is it a reading for both of you?"

"No. Only my friend," said Jane. She dug Connie under the table and indicated her wedding-ring. Connie took it off.

"Well, I charge fifteen shillings a reading—or should I say seventy-five pence as it is in the new money? Is that all right? I've had to put my prices up a bit, I'm afraid."

"That's all right," said Connie.

The woman beamed at her. "Well, we'll get straight on, shall we? You don't look too well," she said kindly. "But I won't ask you any questions. Do you want your friend here, or would you prefer to be alone? She can sit in the living room. There's a good fire."

"I'd rather she was here."

The woman pulled up a chair and sat facing Connie, their knees almost touching, and instead of peering into the tea leaves, as Connie had expected, she reached out, took Connie's hands in hers and then gently let them go. Her eyes were shut, as she settled back in her chair.

She shivered. "Is it a cold day? I feel quite shivery suddenly. I expect you've come a long way."

"Quite a long way," Jane said brusquely.

"How did you get my name, dear? I only ask because I don't advertise, and I like to know how people come to me." She spoke normally, but her eyes were still shut.

"From a girl who works with my friend—a teacher," said Connie softly.

Jane looked at Connie as though to say, "You're giving yourself away."

"People come to me from all over. I don't see many people anymore as a rule, because I'm retired." Connie, prepared for another failure, relaxed back in her chair. Then the woman said, "But I thought I should see you. You probably wonder why I keep going on like this, but it's as though I want to get away from that shivery feeling. I think that's how you've been feeling lately. You keep doing things, going out, talking, you feel—oh, if I could only get back to the way it was before."

"Yes."

The woman's eyes were shut tight behind the thick pebble-glasses and she looked mottled, closed in like a tortoise.

"Are you afraid of gas lamps, dear? I know it sounds a silly question, but that's what I'm getting, so I have to ask you."

"No."

"Well, watch out for it, dear. I'm getting a lot of children here, oh, ever so many. Are they all yours? There's nine. No. You're too young. They don't have such big families as they used to. That's a funny thing to say, but I had to say it. Does it mean anything to you?"

"No."

"There's a gentleman here, older than you. A father perhaps. Are you married? I have to ask. Otherwise what I say next is going to sound rather rude."

Ignoring Jane's passionate signs she said, "Yes, I am married," and she felt in her pocket for the ring.

"Well, I don't think I can really ask you anyway, because the question seems more for an older woman."

"Please ask me."

"Someone's asking how many half-pennies you got from the last bloke. It's funny, because half-pennies aren't used anymore. It's funny as well because when I told you the price I said it in shillings, even though I've got so used to the new money I hardly ever make a mistake." She spoke quickly, as though embarrassed. "I feel you're running, but whether it's *from* someone or *to* them I can't see.

You've not been well lately. It's not your body, more your—nerves. Have you been in hospital?"

Connie shook her head, forgetting completely the night she'd spent the month before.

"Have you got a dog? Well, I can see someone offering you one. You're not connected with the theatre, are you? I don't mean as an actress, more in the wardrobe department."

"No."

"I see a lot of costumes. Old-fashioned dresses and shawls and boots and bonnets. Perhaps you're going to get a job," she said brightly. "Do you wear gloves? No? I've got this older gentleman again. He's, oh—I get a feeling of irritation. If he gets a bit short with you, you mustn't mind. He's worried, but he doesn't know what to do. Is he a lot older than you?"

"Thirteen years."

"Then he's not this gentleman I'm getting now, because this one's more your age. I see blackness all round this one. He comes out in the night. Does he work at night?"

"Her husband often goes out at night," Jane cut in.

"I get a feeling of dissatisfaction. Is that your husband?"

"It might be."

"Terrible dissatisfaction. Frustration. I think it's more this younger man. A job not finished. Does that mean anything to you?"

Connie shook her head.

"He doesn't wish you well, dear. I wish I could say he does."

"Who is he?"

"He's too vague for me to see him. He's smart. Well turned out. He's a long way off."

"Do I know him?"

"You have known him. Just once."

The kitchen was suddenly very depressing. The woman stopped talking. Even Jane was still.

Then the woman said, making an effort to be cheerful, "I get children going to school. I get only three. There should be four. One's not well and stays at home."

"He's too young to go to school."

"I think he should go to school. It would be better for him. Even a little nursery school."

"Why?"

The woman seemed to hesitate, then she looked directly at Connie. "When you're not too well, dear, it upsets him. I want to sing a song. Oh, it's ever such an old one." She looked at her lap. "It's even before my time.

"A smart and stylish girl you see,
Belle of good society;
Not too strict, but rather free
Yet as right as right can be.
Never forward, never bold
Not too hot and not too cold.

But the very thing I'm told
That in your arms you'll like to hold.
Ta-ra-ra-Boom-de-ay.

"My voice isn't very tuneful. You must excuse me. Does it mean anything to you?"

"No."

"You haven't said anything about her future," said Jane.

"Well, I can only see a little way ahead with anyone." She looked at the window. "Anyway, it looks as though it's brightened up a bit."

They were both awake and staring into the dark.

"Connie," he whispered.

"Yes. I can't sleep either."

"I think we should go away, right away this summer. What about Spain? I could take my holiday earlier."

"That would be lovely. But what about the summer-house for the back garden? You won't have the money for both."

"I'll do that next year. Have you taken the pills the quack gave you?"

"Yes."

"I'm sure you haven't. I wish you would. You're still depressed. They're supposed to be anti-depressants."

"I'd like David to go to nursery school."

"What?"

"I think he'd enjoy it."

"Well—I—I'm not keen. No, Connie. We'll have to think about that."

They lay silent again. She felt she was almost asleep at last when he suddenly turned and got on top of her and started kissing her, passionately. She didn't like it. The feeling got worse the more excited he got. She tried to sit up. She looked round her in the dark. She didn't know quite where she was. The moment of alarm passed and she closed her eyes and relaxed. A different expression came into her face—lewd, cunning—and she murmured something sexually provocative, something a prostitute might say, something she couldn't have known. Daniel froze, then slapped her face hard.

Slowly he got off her and fumbled his way back to his place in the bed. They lay as before—separate, sleepless. Then she reached out and touched his hand and said, "I'm sorry. I don't know what came over me. It felt different. I didn't know where I was." She tried to laugh.

He didn't respond. She lay still, tears streaming down her face.

12

Six weeks after Connie cut her armpit, she had to go back to the doctor for a second tetanus injection and what he called a check-up. Daniel had been phoning him non-stop. Jane came with her.

The waiting room—it was also his drawing room—was lived-in and pleasant, with enormous sagging brown chairs like old dogs humped in front of the fire. There were only tattered magazines on knitting and housecraft, so Jane opened the bookcase.

"Do they go in for medical books! *The Aberrations of*—Can't pronounce it. Ah! This looks interesting. Crime. My God! The pictures. Ugh! 'Her head had been nearly severed from her body, the womb and two thirds of the—'"

"Shut up!"

"'Had been pulled from her and left lying over her shoulder and—'"

"Will you shut up, you bitch!"

Jane looked up. "Oh, I'm sorry. Christ! Is it upsetting you? I just thought—"

"I've got to get some new shoes." Her voice was shrill. "I want some red ones with—" Her foot tipped up. She stared at it.

Jane flopped onto a massive hairy chair, and its brown arms sank inwards and hugged her. She seemed quite unable not to read aloud. "Lobe of her right ear missing? What could he have wanted that for? No one knew who he was, you know."

"I don't want to hear, goddamn you, Jane!" Connie looked grey and drawn.

"He used to creep up behind them—Good God! They mention Flower and Dean Street." Jane whipped over a page. "Help! He did two in one night. Elizabeth Stride. Throat cut. No mutilation. Possibly because he'd been interrupted by a hawker arriving with his horse and cart." She leapt up, leaving the chair lopsided. "Ah, here's an interesting one."

"What does it say about that horse-and-cart one?"

"This girl's much more interesting. It took six hours in the mortuary to get her looking like a human—"

"Go back to the other one!" Connie's voice, low and desperate, was hardly recognisable.

Jane, resentful at being dragged away from an attractive victim, took a long time finding the page. "Elizabeth Stride. Married in 1869 to a carpenter. Came from Sweden. In 1878, the pleasure steamer *Princess Alice* sank in the Thames and her husband and two of her nine children were drowned. She ended up in Flower and Dean Street, notorious for prostitutes, and was frequently arrested for being drunk. It doesn't say much."

Connie murmured, "Drowned . . . drowned."

"Now with this other girl—"

"Go back to Elizabeth Stride. What about her death?"

"Just throat cut in Berners Street, 30th September, 1888. A hawker found her body at one A.M. . . . His horse shied with fright and probably disturbed the murderer, who disappeared as if by some black magic before he could do anything worse. He had the desire, if that's the right word, to remove bits of the body. A labourer said he saw her with a man shortly before she died and the man said, 'You'd say anything but your prayers.' She was holding some grapes in her right hand and sweetmeats in the left."

"A dissatisfied gentleman," Connie said quietly.

"Where are you going? Hey, Connie."

Connie was on the pavement by the time Jane caught up with her. "What about your appointment? He needs, I mean wants, to see you. I'm sorry if I

upset you. Heavens, you're a dreadful colour." Connie seemed drained of blood—
she could hardly walk. "You are upset. I wouldn't have thought that would
upset you."

Connie insisted that Jane should go with her to Whitechapel; and Jane, although
she said she thought it perverse, agreed. They took the 253 bus from Camden
Town; it was a grey heavy afternoon and in that light Jane realised how Connie
had changed. The laughter-lines at the corners of her eyes were wrinkles; her hair
was lank; she no longer smelt of the summery perfume.

"God, you've lost weight," said Jane.

Connie's face was washed out, the beauty spot glaring. She'd tried to go back
to the clairvoyant in the suburbs, but when the woman knew who it was she said
she'd definitely retired, most definitely. Connie had asked quickly, "The man who
didn't wish me well. Does he want to kill me?" And she had replied: "I didn't get
kill as much as steal."

They trailed around the streets that had once been trailed around by the
Ripper's victims, and Jane, who was carrying her long bag full of racquets, asked,
"Do you feel anything?"

Connie shook her head.

Jane stopped and took her arm. "You've got to admit it's daft. We've done
Flower and Dean Street twice, Berners Square three times." She started giggling.
"I mean, if anyone knew what we'd been doing they'd lock us up."

She laughed so much that Connie started too, and a man nearby stopped and
stared at them.

"Perhaps he's the Ripper," said Jane, and they doubled up, helpless with
laughter.

13

The summer seemed full of heavy grey afternoons. One Sunday towards the end of
July, Mark, Daniel, and Connie sat by a tennis court watching Jane play. The club
tournament—today the women's finals and Jane was winning. She was brown
and lean, and she looked cooler than anyone around her, even the spectators.
Connie watched Daniel watching her legs. It seemed to Connie that people had
always noticed Jane's flat chest—*only* noticed her flat chest—but now suddenly it
was her thighs. Her thighs were riveting. She put a hand on his arm, but he took
no notice and went on watching Jane.

After the match silver cups were distributed, and everyone drank lemonade and
escaped from the exhausting heat outside into the stuffy cool of the clubhouse.
Kids whizzed round the long tables piled with sandwiches and lurid cakes. Jane
pushed up to Daniel, showed him her cup and waited foolishly for his approval.
Mark elbowed his way through the crowds towards her, said Congratulations,
and was ignored. He attempted to kiss her, but someone got in the way.

"It's got to go back to have my name engraved on it. I got the doubles as well."
She seemed weak with victory.

"It's a nice shape," said Daniel. "How does it feel to win?"

"Terrific," and she hugged the cup.

As Connie was pouring lemonade for the children, she noticed Daniel in a corner, standing close to Jane, and it seemed to her that as they talked they were looking into each other's eyes.

The next morning, early, Jane came swinging up the path. Connie, wearing a bikini, was tidying the kitchen, and when she saw her, she bent down fast and hoped to creep to the stairs without being seen. She did not want to talk to Jane. It was another grey thick day and she was deeply depressed.

Too late. Jane's voice clattered into the kitchen. "What are you doing?"

"Picking up something."

"Can you have the kid tonight?"

They stood silently looking at each other. Without her racquet Jane looked vaguely unsatisfactory.

"Is Daniel in?"

Connie shook her head. Another silence.

"I just wondered if he could sort out a point of law for me. It's about HP," she said breathlessly. "I'm getting the washing-up machine on HP. It's the only way to get it. Mark makes Scrooge look like the Gulbenkian Foundation." She started talking faster and louder. She hopped left-leg, right-leg, with an occasional yelp—she seemed much more her usual self.

"I'm going to track down that magician."

"Oh no, Connie, don't! Don't be a fool. I mean, nothing's happened. I mean, the voices don't warn you of anything. Mark says it'll just wear off—vanish like poltergeists do. Anyway, I wouldn't go near a magician. There's a theory that the Ripper *was* a magician. He had to do five murders—the number five formed a pentagram—and then he'd be immune from discovery. He never was discovered . . . Mark and I are going through a real wobbler. We fought all night. At least I did. He won't. He locked himself in the kitchen. I've taken the key away. If he's not careful I'll take myself away. God, you're lucky you've never had anything awful in your life."

"Will you help me find the magician?"

"No. I've got too much on my mind. I've got my own problems. Concentrate on what you've got going for you. I think Mark and I are—finished. I've got that feeling."

Connie stared out thoughtfully at the grey day.

Connie went back to the nightclub. A fire door was open and the beam of afternoon light showed up the whirling dust and made the red plush chairs and little pink table-lights tawdry. The owner, tired and irritable, stood smoking a cigar and watching a chorus girls' audition. Connie, standing beside him, had finished her story and was waiting for a reply.

"Danchenko? Danchenko? He's not here."

"Do you know where I can find him?"

"Why d'you want him? D'you want to book him?" He turned and looked at her.

"Yes. No."

The man shrugged, and looked back at the girls. "He's probably in New York."

At the second theatrical agency a secretary said, "He's not Hungarian. He comes from Tottenham. I can't give you his address, but he's appearing at the Spread Eagle in Barking."

Seeing Connie's reaction, she added, "It's his slack season."

That evening Connie got the children to bed early and made chilled cucumber soup, cheese soufflé and a crisp salad. She put on her yellow backless dress and her new platform shoes and served dinner in their rarely used dining room. The sideboard was full of flowers from the garden. There were long candles in elegant holders and iced white wine.

As Daniel and Connie ate, they looked at each other from time to time but didn't once speak.

14

Connie was walking with David along a main road by the heath when a car slowed down beside them. She turned, and Daniel said, "Get in."

He drove to the nursery and they sat and watched as David knocked on the door and then turned and waved, smiling happily. They waved back.

"It can't go on," he said.

She stared ahead.

"Bye, Mummy," David called.

"It's not been right for weeks. We haven't made love, we haven't—"

"Well, you don't want to—"

"Nor do you. Not in your heart of hearts. We just avoid each other all the time—"

"You don't love me, Daniel."

After a pause, he said, "I do. Anyway, we've been together a long time."

"What's that supposed to mean? I'm not tired of *you*."

"Look, love." He put his arm round her. "I was put off the night you—well, you remember. I know I'll get over it. I'll certainly try. But you'll have to try. I think you should have analysis."

"All right," she sighed. "All right. All right. Maybe I *am* nuts. I decided I must be the day we watched Jane play. I got terribly jealous. It was the way you were looking at her."

"Oh, for heavensake, Jane!" He laughed.

"I got quite upset. I thought you were having an affair."

He squeezed her to him. "Well, let's you and me have a pact. You go to analysis and I won't look at Jane's thighs. O.K.?"

"Yes. I've never realised she had such lovely thighs."

He stroked her hair, persuasively, and suddenly she grabbed his hand and kissed it.

"It's a lovely morning," he said softly. "You go and have a long walk on the heath. Enjoy it."

Suddenly, marvellously happy, she walked across the heath in the sweet morning. The light was golden. A crocodile of schoolchildren moved noisily along a path to her left, a bumpy path that converged with hers by the lake. Today was the height of summer, with the heath over-ripe, full of scents and buzzings, the trees blowsy. Connie looked serene again. She moved at the same speed as the gnashing, swaying crocodile, its chattering so loud and shrill that it was impossible to distinguish anything, and they arrived at the lake together.

For a moment they muddled up. Schoolchildren tried to pass Connie. She bumped into one, apologised and hurried to get ahead of them. Dazzled with sun, she stepped behind the old men with their fishing tackle and sandwiches, and the crocodile wound round, squeezed past the men and followed her. Among the shrill voices—were other shrill voices.

"Murder! Murder! He's done it again."

Connie stopped.

"He's ripped her properly."

The crocodile nudged up behind her. She ran, right to the top of the hill and over it, and flopped exhausted onto a bench. Below her, London was spread out misty and silent. She could see right across the river.

The crocodile came over the top of the hill and the children's voices rose up, again tinny and confused. Then she heard, *"Ripped out one kidney, whole. Ate it for his breakfast."*

She jumped up and ran screaming down the hill.

The pub in Barking was brightly lit and had a very different atmosphere and clientele from the nightclub. Throughout the magician's act, the audience laughed uproariously. Instead of an MC an old woman, with a cracked voice, shuffled round touching objects.

"What am I touching?"

"A glass."

"And now?"

"Another glass."

"You can't fool Danchenko. And what am I holding now?"

"You are touching a bald head."

The audience screamed with laughter.

"A glass."

"What's in the glass?"

"Amber liquid. It won't be there long."

"And now?"

"A looking-glass."

"Wrong!" yelled the audience.

"Well, you know what I mean." Caught off his guard, his accent was not the usual approximation to mid-European but a more familiar strain that came from no farther than Tottenham.

The old woman held her hand up as high as she could, but her bent body, stiff with rheumatism, deprived the action of drama, and the magician's response, sonorous, melodramatic—"Do not think you are touching nothing my friend. The air is not empty but full of vibrations"—made the audience roll about with laughter.

"She can't reach, Danchenko."

"Want a bunk up, luv?"

The old woman lowered her arm and scuttled off into a corner. Danchenko, probably deciding that the supernatural stuff was getting nowhere with this audience, took off his blindfold and looked straight at Connie. "He will not come like a thief in the night. And that means something to someone over there." He circled a long finger and chose a woman at the back of the room. "*She* knows what it means." And he added, addressing a fat woman by the bar, "No, lady. He's not under your bed."

Wild laughter.

"Happy birthday to Alf behind the bar. Seventy today."

People cheered.

The magician looked at Connie. "Now what have we here? The ideal couple? Ah, but only half of it tonight."

"Her better half's gone off," shouted a man nearby, and before the laughter entirely stopped, Danchenko said:

"And where's your heart this time, doomed lady? Not on your sleeve."

"Go on. Make us laugh, Danchenko. Make us happy," yelled the audience.

"Some people are too happy, my friends," he said maliciously, his eyes still on Connie. "Some people are *too pure* of heart." He accented the "pure" and made it sound horrible. Then, rubbing his hands, he smiled round at the audience, and the smile, the most chilling thing so far, had quite the opposite effect to making them happy. The room was quiet as he took off his wizard's hat and gave it to the old woman. He leaned forward. "Make sure you fill it up. Then Danchenko will show you a trick or two."

As she took it round, Danchenko shouted abuse. "Come on, you stingy swine. You miser. Your silver's in your other pocket. That's not enough, lady. I may be a magician but I can't live on air."

The magician changed his clothes in the publican's cramped office on the first floor. A single naked light-bulb hanging from the middle of the ceiling showed up the peeling walls, the dust, the damp, the disorder. It seemed even to accentuate the smell—which was a mixture of stale beer, gin, fish, and other less nice, less definable things. A cat had been sick on the soggy matting.

Connie, nervous but in control, knocked and went in without waiting for an answer. Danchenko, his thin body existing easily in the small space between a cluttered desk and a pile of beer crates, was taking off his make-up in front of a cracked mirror.

He twisted round, and they looked at each other, their eyes solemn in the gloomy room. Abruptly, he turned back to the mirror. He was not pleased to see her. His face changed with every layer he peeled off. He looked young, and then old and sinister, and then strangely naive. He stripped off the sides of his nose and wiped out his eyebrows; for a moment he looked like a professional tango-dancer from the '30s. Removing his wig, he revealed a head of black sleek hair, which he patted over with Brylcreem.

"Why call me doomed?" she asked.

"I have nothing for you. The show's over." The Hungarian accent was gone. He straightened up and seemed much taller than he did on the stage.

"Why doomed?" she asked angrily, and the desperation of the past months took away all fear.

"We are all doomed."

"Why me?" she asked swiftly.

"Why me? Why me? Why not you?" he said in a sing-song voice. "Why shouldn't anything happen to you? Why should you have everything?" He slithered out from between the desk and the crates and closed his black case.

"But I'm going to die."

"Why shouldn't you die? People die violently every day. Excuse me!" and carrying the case he slid past her and into the passage-way with all the ease and slipperiness of an eel.

She ran after him. From behind he looked young, sleek. "It's my life!" she shouted.

He turned and said, scathingly, "Why would *your* life belong to you?" He opened the exit door and turned left in the street.

Again she followed him. "I'll run away. I'll hide. I'll stay in. I'll go abroad. I'll—"

He shook his head as he opened the door of the public bar. "Whatever you do won't make any difference. It'll happen when you least expect it."

He went in. The door swung shut.

Fleetingly, she saw him through the window leaning against the bar, a pint of beer in front of him. He looked malevolent.

15

It was a cold November night, and the station was ill-lit; but Daniel and Connie with Jane, Mark, and several other friends were in high spirits and slightly drunk. They were waiting at the end of a short platform for the infrequent local train to take them back to London. The station was old-fashioned, neglected. A woman said to Mark, "Some of these stations are early Victorian."

"I love this line," he replied mournfully. "I hope they don't close it. They're always threatening to."

"You've got that wrong," said Jane. She hopped about and smiled at Connie. "Soon be your birthday. Where shall we go? Soho?"

"It's what I've given the last two months of my life to do," said Daniel. "Tear down those old blocks. They're ugly. Of no historical value. Rip 'em up. Get rid of the squalor."

"All at once?" asked Baxter.

"A clean cut of the knife . . ."

Connie shivered.

Jane hopped more energetically. "Connie, I'm dying for a pee."

"It's nice to see old Connie again," said Baxter, thinking it was the last thing he wanted. She'd changed drastically. He'd decided it must be the booze. "Where've you been hiding yourself?"

"Oh, I don't go out much. We don't entertain." She looked cautiously at Daniel.

"You could hardly miss this evening," he said. "Daniel's victorious assault on big bogey itself."

"Terrific darling!" Connie kissed him, but he didn't respond. He was looking at Jane.

"Come with me, Connie," she said.

"The train's due in four minutes," said Mark.

"Maybe it is, but you'll have a splashy patch on the platform."

Connie moved close to Daniel, which put her under the light. Baxter decided her face was too pale. For an instant he thought of the terminal ward at the local hospital. He'd have to have a word with old Daniel about this.

Something made Connie look up, and she gasped.

"Why, it's a gas lamp," said Baxter, pleased. "You don't often see those."

"Oh, these little stations often have them," said Mark.

Connie moved out of the light, and her face, Baxter admitted with slight disappointment, was all right again.

"Isn't there a loo on the train?" asked the woman.

"No there is not," snapped Jane. "It's all that beer I've put back. I can't hold it. Come on," and grabbing Connie she ran squealing to the waiting-room.

"Have one for me," shouted Baxter.

It was locked up.

"Blast!" Jane scuttled to the ticket office. The collector was lolling by the entrance looking up the road.

"Where is it—the lav?"

"It's out of order. Best go to the pub, love."

"Where? Where?"

"Just over there," and he pointed up the street.

Jane and Connie started running.

"Can't hold it since I had the kid. A pint of bitter and I'm up all night."

Making a strange growling noise, she dashed into the pub; and Connie was about to follow, when a group of people plunged out and sped towards the station. A train was approaching.

Connie waited on the corner, her black fur coat sleek around her and the light of the street lamp on her. She wasn't as beautiful as a year ago, but she was still appealing. The street—modern, suburban, with lighted shop-fronts further along—seemed deserted. She walked up and down, and then lounged on one leg and looked up idly at the sky.

Footsteps came up behind her. She froze. They were quite distinct on the stone-slab pavement. She began to walk fast in the direction she was facing, away from the station. The footsteps got faster. She started running. She could see a pub on the next corner. She could hear singing. Enormously relieved, she ran towards it. Though it was a cold night, a knot of people were standing outside drinking, and for some reason they stared at Connie. She looked at them. They didn't seem quite right. Their clothes were strange . . . She started running again, her hair falling forward over her eyes. She lost a shoe and looked down. The street was cobbled.

Gasping for breath, her chest aching, her legs numb, she stumbled on. She nearly fell. The footsteps, definite and slow, came right up behind her and stopped. In the distance, "*That in your arms you'd like to hold. Ta-ra-ra Boom-de-ay.*"

She turned, just slightly, and saw a shadow on the wall. She knew the shadow well. Then a man's voice—soft, educated—said, "*Now, my dear. You'd say any-thing but your prayers.*"

THE FINAL STONE

William F. Nolan

The evidently tireless William Francis Nolan (1928–) has written dozens of novels, short stories, teleplays, motion pictures, poems, biographies, and nonfiction studies in a variety of genres, including horror, science fiction, mystery, and dark fantasy, most famously, perhaps, the landmark science fiction novel *Logan's Run* (1967, coauthored with George Clayton Johnson); he also wrote the novel sequels *Logan's World* (1977) and *Logan's Search* (1980). His classic postapocalyptic tale "Small World" (1957) was recently adapted into comics form in *Evil Jester Presents* 1 (2013).

Among his screenwriting work are the 1975 television movie *Trilogy of Terror* (cowritten with Richard Matheson) and 1976's adaptation *Burnt Offerings* (based on the novel by Robert Marasco), which starred Karen Black and Bette Davis. Other television writing credits include episodes of *One Step Beyond*, *Wanted: Dead or Alive*, and several ABC and NBC Movie of the Week features.

Nolan has also written biographies of Dashiell Hammett, Steve McQueen, John Huston, Barney Oldfield, and Ernest Hemingway, among others.

Nolan has received numerous lifetime achievement awards, including Living Legend in Dark Fantasy from the International Horror Guild in 2002, Author Emeritus from the Science Fiction and Fantasy Writers of America in 2006, the Lifetime Achievement Award from the Horror Writers Association in 2010, and the World Horror Society's Grand Master Award in 2015.

"The Final Stone" was first published in *Cutting Edge: Brave New Horror Stories*, edited by Dennis Etchison (Garden City, NY, Doubleday, 1986).

They were from Indianapolis. Newly married. Dave and *stirring, flexing muscle, feeling power now . . . anger . . . a sudden driving thirst for* Alice Williamson, both in their late twenties, both excited about their trip to the West Coast. This would be their last night in Arizona. Tomorrow they planned to be in Palm Springs. To visit Dave's sister. But only one of them would make it to California. Dave, not Alice. *with the scalpel glittering*

Alice would die before midnight, her throat slashed cleanly across. *glittering, raised against the moon*

"Wait till you see what's here," Dave told her. "Gonna just be fantastic."

They were pulling their used Camaro into the parking lot at a tourist site in Lake Havasu City, Arizona. He wouldn't tell her where they were. It was late. The lot was wide and dark, with only two other cars parked there, one a service vehicle.

"What is this place?" Alice was tired and hungry. *hungry*

"You'll find out. Once you see it, you'll never forget it. That's what they say."

"I just want to eat," she said. *the blade eating flesh, drinking*

"First we'll have a look at it, then we'll eat," said Dave, *them getting out of the car, walking toward the gate* smiling at her, giving her a hug.

The tall iron gate, black pebbled iron, led into a picture-perfect Tudor Village. A bit of Olde England rising up from raw Arizona desert. A winged dragon looked down at them from the top of the gate.

"That's ugly," said Alice.

"It's historic," Dave told her. "That's the official Heraldic Dragon from the City of London."

"Is *that* what all this is—some sort of replica of London?"

"Much more than that. Heck, Ally, this was all built *around* it, to give it the proper atmosphere."

"I'm in no mood for atmosphere," she said. "We've been driving all day and I don't feel like playing games. I want to know what you—"

Dave cut into the flow of her words: "There it is!"

They both stared at it. Ten thousand tons of fitted stone. Over nine hundred feet of arched granite spanning the dark waters of the Colorado River. Tall and massive and magnificent.

"Christ!" murmured Dave. "Doesn't it just knock you out?" Imagine—all the way from England, from the Thames River . . . the by-God-for-real London Bridge!"

"It *is* amazing," Alice admitted. She smiled, kissed him on the cheek. "And I'm glad you didn't tell me . . . that you kept it for a surprise."

glittering cold steel

They moved along the concrete walkway beneath the Bridge, staring upward at the giant gray-black structure. Dave said: "When the British tore it down they numbered all the stones so our people would know where each one went. Thousands of stones. Like a jigsaw puzzle. Took three years to build it all over again here in Arizona." He gestured around them. "All this was just open desert when they started. After the Bridge was finished they diverted a section of the Colorado River to run under it. And built the village."

"Why did the British give us their bridge?"

"They were putting up a better one," said Dave. "But, hey, they didn't *give* this one to us. The guy that had it built here paid nearly two and a half million for it. Plus the cost of shipping all the stones over. Some rich guy named McCulloch. Died since then, I think."

dead death dead dead death

"Well, we've seen it," said Alice. "Let's eat now. C'mon, I'm really starving."

"You don't want to *walk* on it?"

"Maybe after we eat," said Alice. *going inside the restaurant now . . . will wait . . . she's perfect . . . white throat, blue vein pulsing under the chin . . . long graceful neck . . .*

They ate at the City of London Arms in the Village. Late. Last couple in for dinner that evening. Last meal served.

"You folks should have come earlier," the waitress told them. "Lots of excitement here today, putting in the final stone. I mean, with the Bridge dedication and all."

"I thought it was dedicated in 1971," said Dave.

"Oh, it was. But there was this *one* stone missing. Everyone figured it had been lost on the trip over. But they found it last month in London. Had fallen into the water when they were taking the Bridge apart. Today, it got fitted back where it belonged." She smiled brightly. "So London Bridge is *really* complete now!"

Alice set her empty wineglass on the tablecloth. "All this Bridge talk is beginning to *bore* me," she said. "I need another drink."

"You've had enough," said Dave.

"Hell I have!" To the waitress: "Bring us another bottle of wine."

"Sorry, but we're closing, I'm not allowed to—"

"I *said* bring another!"

"And she said they're closing," snapped Dave. "Let's go."

They paid the check, left. The doors were locked behind them.

The City of London Arms sign blinked off as they moved down the restaurant steps. *to me to me*

"You'll feel better when we get back to the motel," Dave said.

"I feel fine. Let's go walk on London Bridge. That's what you wanted, isn't it?"

"Now now, Ally," he said. "We can do that tomorrow, before we leave. Drive over from the motel."

"*You* go to the damn motel," she said tightly. "*I'm* walking on the damn Bridge!"

He stared at her. "You're *drunk*!"

She giggled. "So what? Can't drunk people walk on the damn Bridge?"

"Come on," said Dave, taking her arm. "We're going to the car."

"You go to the car," she snapped, pulling away. "I'm gonna walk on the damn Bridge."

"Fine," said Dave. "Then you can get a *taxi* to the motel."

And, dark-faced with anger, he walked away from her, back to their car. Got in. Drove off.

alone now for me . . . just for me

Alice Williamson walked toward London Bridge through the massed tree shadows along the dark river pathway. She reached the foot of the wide gray-granite Bridge steps, looked up.

At a tall figure in black. Slouch hat, dark cloak, boots.

She was looking at death.

She stumbled back, turned, poised to run—but the figure moved, glided, flowed *mine now mine* down the granite steps with horrific speed.

And the scalpel glitter-danced against the moon.

Two days later.

Evening, with the tour boat empty, heading for its home dock, Angie Shepherd at the wheel. Angie was the boat's owner. She lived beside the river, had all her life. Knew its currents, its moods, under moon and sun, knew it intimately. Thompson Bay . . . Copper Canyon . . . Cattail Cove . . . Red Rock . . . Black Meadow . . . Topock Gorge. Knew its eagles and hawks and mallards, its mud turtles and great horned owls. Knew the sound of its waters in calm and in storm.

Her home was a tall, weathered-wood building that once served as a general store. She lived alone here. Made a living with her boat, running scenic tours along the Colorado. Age twenty-eight. Never married, and no plans in that area.

Angie docked the boat, secured it, entered the tall wooden building she called Riverhouse. She fussed in the small kitchen, taking some wine, bread, and cheese out to the dock. It was late; the night was ripe with river sounds and the heart-pulse of crickets.

She sat at the dock's edge, legs dangling in the cool water. Nibbled cheese. Listened to a night bird crying over the river.

Something bumped her foot in the dark water. Something heavy, sodden. Drifting in the slow night current.

Something called Alice Williamson.

Dan Gregory had no clues to the murder. The husband was a logical suspect (most murders are family-connected), but Gregory knew that Dave Williamson was not guilty. You develop an instinct about people, and he knew Williamson was no wife-killer. For one thing, the man's grief was deep and genuine; he seemed totally shattered by the murder—blamed himself, bitterly, for deserting Alice in the Village.

Gregory was tipped back in his desk chair, an unlit Marlboro in his mouth. (He was trying to give up smoking.) Williamson slouched in the office chair in front of him, looking broken and defeated. "Your wife was drunk, you had an argument. You got pissed and drove off. Happens to people all the time. Don't blame yourself for this."

"But if I'd stayed there, been there when—"

"Then you'd probably *both* be dead," said Gregory. "You go back to the motel, take those pills the doc gave you and get some sleep. Then head for Palm Springs. We'll contact you at your sister's if we come up with anything."

Williamson left the office. Gregory talked to Angie Shepherd next, about finding the body. She was shaken, but cooperative.

"I've never seen anyone dead before," she told him.

"No family funerals?"

"Sure. A couple. But I'd never walk past the open caskets. I didn't want to have to see people I'd love . . . *that* way." She shrugged. "In your business I guess you see a lot of death."

"Not actually," said Gregory. "Your average Highway Patrol officer sees more of it in a month than I have in ten years. You don't get many murders in a town this size."

"That how long you've been Chief of Police here, ten years?"

"Nope. Just over a year. Used to be a police lieutenant in Phoenix. Moved up to this job." He raised an eyebrow at her. "How come you being a local, you don't know how long I've been Chief?"

"I never follow politics—*especially* small-town politics. Sorry about that." And she smiled.

Gregory was a square-faced man in his thirties with hard, ice-blue eyes, offset by a quick, warm way of grinning. Had never married; most women bored him. But he liked Angie. And the attraction was mutual.

Alice Williamson's death had launched a relationship.

＊

In August, four months after the first murder, there were two more. Both women. Both with throats cut. Both found along the banks of the Colorado. One at Pilot Rock, the other near Whipple Bay.

Dan Gregory had no reason to believe the two August "River Killings" (as the local paper had dubbed them) had been committed near London Bridge. He told a reporter that the killer might be a transient, passing through the area, killing at random. The murders lacked motive; the three victims had nothing in common beyond being female. Maybe the murderer, suggested Gregory, was just someone who hates women.

The press had a field day. "Madman on Loose" . . . "Woman-Hating Killer Haunts Area" . . . "Chief of Police Admits No Clues to River Killings."

Reading the stories, Gregory muttered softly: "Assholes!"

Early September. A classroom at Lake Havasu City High School. Senior English. Lyn Esterly was finishing a lecture on William Faulkner's *Light in August*.

". . . therefore, Joe Christmas became the victim of his own twisted personality. He truly believed he was cursed by an outlaw strain of blood, a white man branded black by a racially bigoted society. Your assignment is to write a five-hundred-word essay on his inner conflicts."

After she'd dismissed the class, Lyn phoned her best friend, Angie Shepherd, for lunch. They had met when Lyn had almost drowned swimming near Castle Rock. Angie had saved her life.

"You're not running the boat today, and I need to talk to you, okay?"

"Sure . . . okay," agreed Angie. "Meet you in town. Tom's all right?"

"Tom's it is."

Trader Tom's was a seafood restaurant, specializing in fresh shrimp, an improbable business establishment in the middle of the Arizona desert. Angie, "the primitive," adored fresh shrimp, which had been introduced to her by Lyn, the "city animal," their joke names for one another.

Over broiled shrimp and sole amandine they relaxed into a familiar discussion: "I'll never be able to understand how you can live out there all alone on the river," said Lyn. "It's positively *spooky*—especially with a woman-killer running loose. Aren't you afraid?"

"No. I keep a gun with me in the house, and I know how to use it."

"*I'd* be terrified."

"That's because you're a victim of your own imagination," said Angie, dipping a huge shrimp into Tom's special Cajun sauce. "You and your fascination with murder."

"Lots of people are true-crime buffs," said Lyn. "In fact that's why I wanted to talk to you today. It's about the River Killings."

"You've got a theory about 'em, right?"

"This one's pretty wild."

"Aren't they all?" Angie smiled, unpeeling another shrimp. "I'm listening."

"The first murder, the Williamson woman, that one took place on the third of April."

"So?"

"The second murder was on the seventh of August, the third on the thirty-first. All three dates are a perfect match."

"For what?"

"For a series of killings, seven in all, committed in 1888 by Jack the Ripper. His first three were on exact matching dates."

Angie paused, a shrimp halfway to her mouth. "Wow! Okay . . . you *did* say wild."

"And there's more. Alice Williamson, we know, was attacked near London Bridge—which is where the Ripper finally disappeared in 1888. They had him trapped there, but the fog was really thick that night and when they closed in on him from both ends of the Bridge he just . . . vanished. And he was never seen or heard of again."

"Are you telling me that some nut is out there in the dark near London Bridge trying to duplicate the original Ripper murders? Is that your theory?"

"That's it."

"But why *now*? What triggered the pattern?"

"I'm working on that angle." Lyn's eyes were intense. "I'm telling you this today for a vitally important reason."

"I'm still listening."

"You've become very friendly with Chief Gregory. He'll listen to you. He must be told that the fourth murder will take place *tonight,* the eighth of September, before midnight."

"But I . . ."

"You've got to warn him to post extra men near the Bridge tonight. And he should be there himself."

"Because of your theory?"

"Of course! Because of my theory."

Angie slowly shook her head. "Dan would think I was around the bend. He's a realist. He'd laugh at me."

"Isn't it *worth* being laughed at to save a life?" Lyn's eyes burned at her. "Honest, Angie, if you don't convince Gregory that I'm making sense, that I'm onto a real pattern here, then another woman is going to get her throat slashed open near London Bridge tonight."

Angie pushed her plate away. "You sure do know how to spoil a terrific lunch."

That afternoon, back at Riverhouse, Angie tried to make sense of Lyn's theory. The fact that these murders had fallen on the same dates as three murders a century earlier was interesting and curious, but not enough to set a hard-minded man like Gregory in motion.

It was crazy, but still Lyn *might* be onto something.

At least she could phone Dan and suggest dinner in the Village. She could tell him what Lyn said—and then he *would* be there in the area, just in case something happened.

Dan said yes, they'd meet at the City of London Arms.

When Angie left for the Village that night she carried a pearl-handled .32-caliber automatic in her purse.

If. Just if.

Dan was late. On the phone he'd mentioned a meeting with the City Council, so maybe that was it. The Village was quiet, nearly empty of tourists.

Angie waited, seated on a park bench near the restaurant, nervous in spite of herself, thinking that *alone, her back to the trees, thick shadow trees, vulnerable* maybe she should wait inside, at the bar.

A tall figure, moving toward her. Behind her.

A thick-fingered hand reaching out for her. She flinched back eyes wide, fingers closing on the automatic inside her open purse.

"Didn't mean to scare you."

It was Dan. His grin made her relax. "I've . . . been a little nervous today."

"Over what?"

"Something Lyn Esterly told me." She took his arm. "I'll tell you all about it at dinner."

lost her . . . can't with him

And they went inside.

". . . so what do you think?" Angie asked. They were having an after-dinner drink. The booths around them were silent, unoccupied.

"I think your friend's imagination is working overtime."

Angie frowned. "I knew you'd say something like that."

Dan leaned forward, taking her hand. "You don't really believe there's going to be another murder in this area tonight just because *she* says so, do you?"

"No, I guess I don't really believe that."

And she guessed she didn't.

But . . .

There! Walking idly on the Bridge, looking down at the water, alone, young woman alone . . . her throat naked, skin naked and long-necked . . . open to me . . . blade sharp sharp . . . soft throat

A dark pulsing glide onto the Bridge, a swift reaching out, a small choked cry of shocked horror, a sudden drawn-across half-moon of bright crimson—and the body falling . . . falling into deep Colorado waters.

Although Dan Gregory was a skeptic, he was not a fool. He ordered the entire Village area closed to tourists and began a thorough search.

Which proved rewarding.

An object was found on the Bridge, wedged into an aperture between two stones below one of the main arches: a surgeon's scalpel with fresh blood on it. And with blackened stains on the handle and blade.

It was confirmed that the fresh blood matched that of the latest victim. The dark stains proved to be dried blood. But they did not match the blood types of the other three murder victims. It was old blood. Very old.

Lab tests revealed that the bloodstains had remained on the scalpel for approximately one hundred years.

Dating back to the 1880s.

"Are you Angela Shepherd?"

A quiet Sunday morning along the river. Angie was repairing a water-damaged section of dock, briskly hammering in fresh nails, and had not heard the woman walk up behind her. She put down the claw hammer, stood, pushing back her hair. "Yes, I'm Angie Shepherd. Who are you?"

"Lenore Harper. I'm a journalist."

"What paper?"

"Free-lance. Could we talk?"

Angie gestured toward the house. Lenore was tall, trim-bodied, with penetrating green eyes.

"Want a Coke?" asked Angie. "Afraid it's all I've got. I wasn't expecting company."

"No, I'm fine," said Lenore, seating herself on the living-room couch and removing a small notepad from her purse.

"You're doing a story on the River Killings, right?"

Lenore nodded. "But I'm going after something different. That's why I came to you."

"Why me?"

"Well . . . you discovered the first body."

Angie sat down in a chair opposite the couch, ran a hand through her hair. "I didn't *discover* anything. When the body drifted downriver against the dock I happened to be there. That's all there is to it."

"Where you shocked . . . frightened?"

"Sickened is a better word. I don't enjoy seeing people with their throats cut."

"Of course. I understand, but . . ."

Angie stood up. "Look, there's really nothing more I can tell you. If you want facts on the case, talk to Chief Gregory at the police department."

"I'm more interested in ideas, emotions—in personal reactions to these killings. I'd like to know *your* ideas. *Your* theories."

"If you want to talk theory, go see Lyn Esterly. She's got some original ideas on the case. Lyn's a true-crime buff. She'll probably be anxious to help you."

"Sounds like a good lead. Where can I find her?"

"Lake Havasu High. She teaches English there."

"Great." Lenore put away her notepad, then shook Angie's hand. "You've been very kind. Appreciate your talking to me."

"No problem."

Angie looked deeply into Lenore Harper's green eyes. Something about her I like, she thought. Maybe I've made a new friend. Well . . . "Good luck with your story," she said.

Lenore's talk with Lyn Esterly bore colorful results. The following day's paper carried "an exclusive feature interview" by Lenore Harper:

"Is River Killer Another Jack the Ripper?" the headline asked. Then, below it, a subheading: "Havasu High Teacher Traces Century-Old Murder Pattern."

According to the story, if the killer continued to follow the original Ripper's pattern, he would strike again on the thirtieth of September. And not once, but twice. On the night of September 30, 1888, Jack the Ripper butchered *two* women in London's Whitechapel district—victims #5 and #6. Would these gruesome double murders be repeated here in Lake Havasu?

The story ended with a large question mark.

Angie, on the phone to Lyn: "Maybe I did the wrong thing, sending her to see you."

"Why? I like her. She really *listened* to me."

"I just get the feeling that her story makes you ... well, a kind of target."

"I doubt that."

"The killer knows all about you now. Even your picture was there in the paper. He knows that you're doing all this special research, that you worked out the whole copycat-Ripper idea ..."

"So what? I can't catch him. That's up to the police. He's not going to bother with me. Getting my theory into print was important. Now that his sick little game has been exposed, maybe he'll quit. Might not be fun for him anymore. These weirdos are like that. Angie, it could all be over."

"So you're not sore at me for sending her to you?"

"Are you kidding? For once, someone has taken a theory of mine seriously enough to print it. Makes all this work mean something. Hell, I'm a celebrity now."

"That's what worries me."

And their conversation ended.

Angie had been correct in her hunch regarding Lenore Harper: the two women *did* become friends. As a free-lance journalist, Lenore had roved the world, while Angie had spent her entire life in Arizona. Europe seemed, to her, exotic and impossibly far away. She was fascinated with Lenore's tales of global travel and of her childhood and early schooling in London.

On the night of September 30, Lyn Esterly turned down Angie's invitation to spend the evening at Riverhouse.

"I'm into something *new*, something really exciting on this Ripper thing," Lyn told her. "But I need to do more research. If what I think is true, then a lot of people are going to be surprised."

"God," sighed Angie, "how you love being mysterious!"

"Guilty as charged," admitted Lyn. "Anyhow, I'll feel a lot safer working at the library in the middle of town than being out there on that desolate river with you."

"Dan's taking your ideas seriously," Angie told her. "He's still got the Village closed to tourists—and he's bringing in extra men tonight in case you're right about the possibility of a double murder."

"I *want* to be wrong, Angie, honest to God I do. Maybe this creep has been scared off by all the publicity. Maybe tonight will prove that—but to be on the safe side, if I were you, I'd spend the night in town ... not alone out there in that damn haunted castle of yours!"

"Okay, you've made your point. I'll take in a movie, then meet Dan later. Ought to be safe enough with the Chief of Police, eh?"

"Absolutely. And by tomorrow I may have a big surprise for you. This is like a puzzle that's finally coming together. It's exciting!"

"Call me in the morning?"

"That's a promise."

And they rang off.

Ten P.M. Lyn working alone in the reference room on the second floor of the city library. The building had been closed to the public for two hours. Even the staff had gone. But, as a teacher, Lyn had special privileges. And her own key.

A heavy night silence. Just the shuffling sound of her books and the faint scratch of her ballpoint pen, her own soft breathing.

When the outside door to the parking lot clicked open on the floor below her, Lyn didn't hear it.

The Ripper glided upward, a dark spider-shape on the stairs, *and she's there waiting to meet me, heart pumping blood for the blade* reached the second floor, moved down the silent hallway to the reference room, *pumping crimson* pushed open the door. *pumping*

To her. Behind her. Soundless.

Lyn's head was jerked violently back.

Death in her eyes—and the blade at her throat.

A single, swift movement.

pumping

And after this one, another before midnight.

Sherry, twenty-three, a graduate student from Chicago on vacation. Staying with a girlfriend. Out for a six-pack of Heineken, a quart of nonfat, and a Hershey's Big Bar.

She left the 7-Eleven with her bag of groceries, walked to her car parked behind the building. Somebody was in the backseat, but Sherry didn't know that.

She got in, fished for the ignition key in her purse, and heard a sliding, rustling sound behind her. Twisted in sudden breathless panic.

Ripper.

Angie did not attend Lyn Esterly's funeral. She refused to see Dan or Lenore, canceled her tours, stocked her boat with food, and took it far upriver, living like a wounded animal. She allowed the river itself to soothe and comfort her, not speaking to anyone, drifting into tiny coves and inlets . . .

Until the wounds began to heal. Until she had regained sufficient emotional strength to return to Lake Havasu City.

She phoned Dan: "I'm back."

"I've been trying to trace you. Even ran a copter upriver, but I guess you didn't want to be found."

"I was all right."

"I *know* that, Angie. I wasn't worried about you. Especially after we caught him. That was what I wanted to find you for, to tell you the news. We *got* the bastard!"

"The River Killer?"

"Yeah. Calls himself 'Bloody Jack.' Says that he's the ghost of the Ripper."

"But how did you . . . ?"

"We spotted this guy prowling near the Bridge. 'Bout a week ago. He'd been living in a shack by the river, up near Mesquite Campground. One of my men followed him there. Walked right in and made the arrest."

"And he admitted he was the killer?"

"Bragged about it! Couldn't wait to get his picture in the papers."

"Dan . . . are you *sure* he's the right man?"

"Hell, we've got a ton of evidence. We found several weapons in the shack, including surgical knives. *Three* scalpels. And he had the newspaper stories on each of his murders tacked to the wall. He'd slashed the faces of all the women, their pictures, I mean. Deep knife cuts in each news photo."

"That's . . . *sick*," said Angie.

"And we have a witness who saw him go into that 7-Eleven on the night of the double murder—where the college girl was killed. He's the one, all right. A real psycho."

"Can I see you tonight? I *need* to be with you, Dan."

"I need you just as much. Meet you soon as I've finished here at the office. And, hey . . ."

"Yes?"

"I've *missed* you."

That night they made love in the moonlight, with the silken whisper of the river as erotic accompaniment. Lying naked in bed, side by side, they listened to the night crickets and touched each other gently, as if to make certain all of this was real for both of them.

"Murder is an awful way to meet somebody," said Angie, leaning close to him, her eyes shining in the darkness. "But I'm glad I met you. I never thought I could."

"Could what?"

"Find someone to love. To *really* love."

"Well, you've found me," he said quietly. "And *I've* found you."

She giggled. "You're . . ."

"I know." He grinned. "You do that to me."

And they made love again.

And the Colorado rippled its languorous night waters.

And from the dark woods a tall figure watched them.

It wasn't over.

Another month passed.

With the self-confessed killer in jail, the English Village and Bridge site were once again open to tourists.

Angie had not seen Lenore for several weeks and was anxious to tell her about the marriage plans she and Dan had made. She wanted Lenore to be her maid of honor at the wedding.

They met for a celebration dinner at the City of London Arms in the Village. But the mood was all wrong.

Angie noticed that Lenore's responses were brief, muted. She ate slowly, picking at her food.

"You don't seem all that thrilled to see me getting married," said Angie.

"Oh, but I *am*. Truly. And I know I've been a wet blanket. I'm sorry."

"What's wrong?"

"I just . . . don't think it's over."

"What are you talking about?"

"The Ripper thing. The killings."

Angie stared at her. "But they've *got* him. He's in jail right now. Dan is convinced that he . . ."

"He's not the one." Lenore said it flatly, softly. "I just *know* he's not the one."

"You're nuts! All the evidence . . ."

". . . is circumstantial. Oh, I'm sure this kook *thinks* he's the Ripper—but where is the *real* proof: blood samples . . . fingerprints . . . the actual murder weapons?"

"You're paranoid, Lenore! I had some doubts too, in the beginning, but Dan's a good cop. He's done his job. The killer's locked up."

Lenore's green eyes flashed. "Look, I asked you to meet me down here in the Village tonight for a reason—and it had nothing to do with your wedding." She drew in her breath. "I just didn't want to face this alone."

"Face what?"

"The fear. It's November the ninth. *Tonight* is the ninth!"

"So?"

"The date of the Ripper's seventh murder—back in 1888." Her tone was strained. "If that man in jail really *is* the Ripper, then nothing will happen here tonight. But . . . if he *isn't* . . ."

"My God, you're really scared. One of *us* could become his seventh victim."

"Look," said Angie. "It's like they say to pilots after a crash. You've got to go right back up or you'll never fly again. Well, it's time for you to do some flying tonight."

"I don't understand."

"You can't let yourself get spooked by what isn't real. And this fear of yours just isn't *real*, Lenore. There's no killer in the Village tonight. And, to prove it, I'm going to walk you to that damn Bridge."

Lenore grew visibly pale. "No . . . no, that's . . . No, I won't go."

"Yes, you will." Angie nodded. She motioned for the check. Lenore stared at her numbly.

Outside, in the late-night darkness, the Village was once more empty of tourists. The last of them had gone—and the wide parking lot was quiet and deserted beyond the gate.

"We're insane to be doing this," Lenore said. Her mouth was tightly set. "Why should *I* do this?"

"To prove that irrational fear must be faced and overcome. You're my friend now—my best friend—and I won't let you give in to irrationality."

"Okay, okay . . . if I agree to walk to the Bridge, then can we get the hell out of here?"

"Agreed."

And they began to walk.

moving toward the Bridge . . . mine now, mine

"I've been poking through Lyn's research papers," Lenore said, "and I think I know what her big surprise would have been."

"Tell me."

"Most scholars now agree on the true identity of the Ripper."

"Yes. A London doctor, a surgeon. Jonathan Bascum."

"Well, Lyn Esterly didn't believe he was the Ripper. And after what I've seen of her research, neither do I."

"Then who *was* he?" asked Angie.

"Jonathan had a twin sister, Jessica. She helped the poor in that area. They practically sainted her—called her 'the Angel of Whitechapel.'"

"I've heard of her."

"Did you know she was as medically skilled as her brother?"

"... That Jonathan allowed her to use his medical books? Taught her. Jessica turned out to be a better surgeon than he was. And she *used* her medical knowledge in Whitechapel."

The stimulation of what she was revealing to Angie seemed to quell much of the fear in Lenore. Her voice was animated.

keep moving . . . closer

"No *licensed* doctors would practice among the poor in that area. No money to be made. So she doctored these people. All illegal, of course. And, at first, it seemed she *was* a kind of saint, working among the destitute. Until her compulsion asserted itself."

"Compulsion?"

"To kill. Between April third and November ninth, 1888, she butchered seven women—and yet, to this day, historians claim her *brother* was responsible for the murders."

Angie was amazed. "Are you telling me that the Angel of Whitechapel was really Jack the Ripper?"

"That was Lyn's conclusion," said Lenore. "And, when you think of it, why not? It explains how the Ripper always seemed to *vanish* after a kill. Why was it that no one ever *saw* him leave Whitechapel? Because 'he' was Jessica Bascum. She could move freely through the area without arousing suspicion. No one ever saw the Ripper's face . . . no one who *lived,* that is. To throw off the police, she sent notes to them signed 'Jack.' It was a *woman* they chased onto the Bridge that night in 1888."

Lenore seemed unaware that they were approaching the Bridge now. It loomed ahead of them, a dark, stretched mass of waiting stone.

closer

"Lyn had been tracing the Bascum family history," explained Lenore. "Jessica gave birth to a daughter in 1888, the same year she vanished on the Bridge. The line continued through her granddaughter, born in 1915, and her great-granddaughter, born in 1940. The last Bascum daughter was born in 1960."

"Which means she'd be in her mid-twenties today," said Angie.

"That's right." Lenore nodded. "Like you. *You're* in your mid-twenties, Angie."

Angie's eyes flashed. She stopped walking. The line of her jaw tightened.

Bitch!

"Suppose she was drawn here," said Lenore, "to London Bridge. Where her great-great-grandmother vanished a century ago. And suppose that, with the completion of the Bridge, with the placement of that final missing stone in April, Jessica's spirit entered her great-great-granddaughter. Suppose the six killings in the Lake Havasu area were done by *her*—that it was her cosmic destiny to commit them."

"Are you saying that you think *I* am a Bascum?" Angie asked softly. They continued to walk toward the Bridge.

"I don't *think* anything. I have the facts."

"And just what might those be?" Angie's voice was tense.

"Lyn was very close to solving the Ripper case. When she researched the Bascum family history in England she traced some of the descendants here to America. She *knew.*"

"Knew what, Lenore?" Her eyes glittered. "You *do* believe that I'm a Bascum." Harshly: "*Don't* you?"

"No." Lenore shook her head. "I know you're not." She looked intently at Angie. "Because *I* am."

They had reached the steps leading up to the main part of the Bridge. In numb horror, Angie watched Lenore slide back a panel in one of the large granite blocks and remove the Ripper's hat, greatcoat, and cape. And the medical bag.

"This came down to me from the family. It was *her* surgical bag—the same one she used in Whitechapel. I'd put it away—until April, when they placed the final stone." Her eyes sparked. "When I touched the stone I felt *her* . . . Jessica's soul flowed into *me,* became part of me. And I knew what I had to do."

She removed a glittering scalpel, held it up. The blade flashed in the reflected light of the lamps on the Bridge. Lenore's smile was satanic. "This is for you!"

Angie's heart trip-hammered; she was staring, trancelike, into the eyes of the killer. Suddenly she pivoted, began running.

Down the lonely, shadow-haunted, brick-and-cobblestone streets, under the tall antique lamps, past the clustered Tudor buildings of Old London.

And the Ripper followed. Relentlessly. Confident of a seventh kill.

she'll taste the blade

Angie circled the main square, ran between buildings to find a narrow, dimly lit alleyway that led her to the rear section of the City of London Arms. Phone inside. Call Dan!

Picking up a rock from the alley, she smashed a rear window, climbed inside, began running through the dark interior, searching for a phone. One here somewhere . . . somewhere . . .

The Ripper followed her inside.

Phone! Angie fumbled in her purse, finding change for the call. She also found . . .

The pearl-handled .32 automatic—the weapon she'd been carrying for months, totally forgotten in her panic.

Now she could fight back. She knew how to use a gun.

She inserted the coins, got Dan's number at headquarters. Ringing . . . ringing . . . "Lake Havasu City Police Department."

"Dan . . . Chief Gregory . . . Emergency!"

"I'll get him on the line."

"Hurry!"

A pause. Angie's heart, hammering.

"This is Gregory. Who's . . . ?"

"Dan!" she broke in. "It's Angie. The Ripper's *here*, trying to kill me!"

"Where are you?"

A dry buzzing. The line was dead.

A clean, down-slicing move with the scalpel had severed the phone cord.

die now . . . time to die

Angie turned to face the killer.

And triggered the automatic.

At close range, a .32-caliber bullet smashed into Lenore Bascum's flesh. She staggered back, falling to one knee on the polished wood floor of the restaurant, blood flowing from the wound.

Angie ran back to the smashed window, crawled through it, moved quickly down the alley. A rise of ground led up to the parking lot. Her car was there.

She reached it, sobbing to herself, inserted the key.

A shadow flowed across the shining car body. Two blood-spattered hands closed around Angie's throat.

The Ripper's eyes were coals of green fire, burning into Angie. She tore at the clawed fingers, pounded her right fist into the demented face. But the hands tightened. Darkness swept through Angie's brain; she was blacking out.

die, bitch

She was dying.

Did she hear a siren? Was it real, or in her mind?

A second siren joined the first. Filling the night darkness.

bleeding . . . my blood . . . wrong, all wrong . . .

A dozen police cars roared into the lot, tires sliding on the night-damp tarmac. Dan!

The Ripper's hands dropped away from Angie's throat. The tall figure turned, ran for the Bridge.

And was trapped there.

Police were closing in from both sides of the vast structure.

Angie and Dan were at the Bridge. "How did you know where to find me?"

"Silent alarm. Feeds right into headquarters. When you broke the window, the alarm was set off. I figured that's where you were."

"She's hit," Angie told him. "I shot her. She's dying."

In the middle of the span the Ripper fell to one knee. Then, a mortally wounded animal, she slipped over the side and plunged into the dark river beneath the Bridge.

Lights blazed on the water, picking out her body. She was sinking, unable to stay afloat. Blood gouted from her open mouth. "Damn you!" she screamed. "Damn all of you!"

She was gone.

The waters rippled over her grave.

Angie was convulsively gripping the automatic, the pearl handle cold against her fingers.

Cold.

THE GATECRASHER

R. Chetwynd-Hayes

Known in the United Kingdom as "Britain's Prince of Chill," Ronald Henry Glynn Chetwynd-Hayes (1919–2001) was born in Isleworth, West London. He left school at the age of fourteen, working in a variety of menial jobs, including as an extra in crowd scenes in British war films, before serving in the British Army in World War II.

He began his writing career with a science fiction novel, *The Man from the Bomb* (1959), after which he sold a supernatural romance, *The Dark Man* (1964), which has had several film options. He sold his first horror story, "The Thing," to Herbert van Thal for *The Seventh Pan Book of Horror Stories* (1966). Having noticed a great number of horror titles on the shelves of a bookseller, Chetwynd-Hayes wrote his own collection of horror stories and submitted it to two publishers simultaneously, embarrassing himself when both accepted it.

Becoming a highly prolific writer of short stories in the genre, with more than two hundred published, he was given the Lifetime Achievement Award by both the Horror Writers Association in 1988 and the British Fantasy Society in 1989. Four of his stories were adapted for the film *From Beyond the Grave* (1974), and three others for *The Monster Club* (1981). His story "Housebound" (1968) was the basis for an episode of *Rod Serling's Night Gallery* titled "Something in the Woodwork" (1973).

"The Gatecrasher" was first published in the author's short story collection *The Unbidden* (London, Tandem, 1971).

Someone said, "Let's hold a seance," and someone else said, "Let's," and five minutes later they were all seated round a table. There was a lot of giggling, and any amount of playing footsie under the table, and it is possible that the entire idea might have collapsed if it had not been for Edward Charlton.

He was a tall, thin youth, with a hungry intense expression that is often peculiar to young men who embrace some burning cause. He had long-fingered hands that were never still, and his ears, which were rather large, stuck out like miniature wings.

"I say." No one paid much attention, so he raised his voice, "I say, let's treat the matter seriously."

This had not been the original intention, and everyone looked at him with astonishment.

"I mean to say," he cleared his throat, "if one is going to do this kind of thing, one should do it properly."

Normally he would have been laughed down, but they were in his flat, and good manners, or what passed for good manners in that company, demanded the host be given some freedom in his choice of entertainment.

"What do we do?" asked a blonde girl.

"We all hold hands." He waited for the ribald comments to die down, then went on. "So as to form an unbroken circle. Yes, and I'll turn all the lights out except the table lamp."

They sat in the semi-gloom holding hands, and the occasional giggle was more an expression of uneasiness than one of merriment. Edward felt more confident now the lighting had been subdued, and his voice was stronger.

"You must empty your minds," he instructed.

"That won't be difficult for some of us," a voice remarked.

"Then," Edward went on, "we must concentrate all our powers on the spirit world."

The young man cursed when a feeble wit asked: "Whisky or gin?" but nobody bothered to laugh.

"Now concentrate," Edward ordered.

They all obeyed him in their different ways, but an undisciplined mind is like a wild stallion when subjected to restraint. Under Edward's continual bombardment of whispered "Concentrate"s, several minds tried to chain thought, but mental pictures manifested in the void, and the senses would not be muted. Hand could feel hand; ears heard the sound of breathing; eyes saw the shaded table lamp; smell sipped at a whiff of perfume; and imagination was never idle.

"Is there anyone here?" asked Edward in a stage whisper.

"Only us chickens," the humorous one could not help himself, and now several voices ordered him to belt up.

"If anyone is there, come in," Edward invited, "don't be afraid—come in."

There was an ungrateful silence; the blonde girl shivered and tightened her grip on her neighbor's hand. Presently the shiver ran round the entire circle, passed from hand to hand, up arms, down legs, leaving behind a paralyzing coldness. Consciousness fled, and was replaced by dreams.

Edward walked in the footsteps of a tall man; a great towering figure dressed in a black coat and matching broad-brimmed hat. The man stopped, then turned, and Edward looked upon the lean dark face, the deep sunken eyes, the jutting beak of a nose; the coat fell open, revealing a row of knives stuck in a black belt. He heard the distant sound of carriage wheels, and tasted the bitter fog.

The room was like an ice chamber; the table lamp dimmed down to an orange glimmer, and the room was full of fog, and all around him he could hear the moans of his companions. Slowly the fog lifted, rose to the ceiling and gradually dispersed, and the coldness went as the lamp grew brighter. Edward looked at the faces of his companions with astonishment that gradually merged into horror. It was as though they had all gone to sleep with their eyes open. The blonde girl had fallen back in her chair and was moaning as though in great pain; one young man had his face twisted up into a snarling grimace; another was opening and closing his hands while staring with unseeing eyes at the overmantel mirror. Edward whispered, "Stop messing about," but without much conviction; then he rose, went over to the wall switch and flooded the room with light. They all returned to the land of the living shortly afterwards.

The mass exodus began some five minutes later; no one said much, but eyes accused Edward of some unspeakable crime; a violation, an act of indecency, an unpardonable breach of human behavior that was beyond normal reproach.

The last man to go out the front door looked back at Edward with scornful, but at the same time, fearful eyes.

"I wouldn't be you, brother," he said, "not for all the tea in China."

He slammed the door, and Edward was left alone.

His bed stood on a dais situated in the center of the far wall of his sitting room; during the day it was surrounded by a curtain, but at night he drew this back and by raising his head could see the entire room. As he lay on the bed and put out his hand to turn off the bedside lamp, the fear came to him, and he wondered, in that revealing moment, why it had not come before.

The fear was at first without form. It was just black, unreasoning terror, and he shrank back against his pillow and tried to see beyond the circle of light cast by his lamp. Then he knew. He was afraid of the dark. He lay awake all that night with the light on.

The next day was spent in anticipation of the night which must follow, and when he finally put his key into the lock and opened his front door there was a sense of fearful expectancy. But his flat was empty, was almost irritatingly normal, and he experienced a strange feeling of disappointment. As he ate a solitary meal before the artificial electric log fire, and later tried to read a book, his mind circled the canker of fear, like a bird flying round a snake. He toyed with the idea of going out; perhaps staying the night at a hotel. But this fear took him to the borderline of insanity. If he were to leave the flat, he would be haunted by the knowledge it was empty; his imagination would picture what was moving among his furniture; if his body slept, then surely his soul would return here and bring back some macabre memory to the waking brain.

He did not intend to fall asleep, but he had been awake the entire previous night, and unconsciousness smothered him unawares so he did not hear the book fall from his lax fingers. The icy cold woke him. The limb-freezing, hair-raising chill, and the wild thumping of his heart. He choked, cleared the bitter bile from his throat, gripped the arms of his chair, cried out like a frightened child as his sitting room door opened, then closed with a resounding slam. The overhead electric lamp trembled slightly, then began to swing to and fro, making a pattern of light circles dance a mad reel across the room. He looked up at the swaying lamp, and, as though it had been caught out in some childish prank, it suddenly became still; his gaze moved across the ceiling and travelled down to the overmantel mirror, then stopped. A man's face was staring at him out of the mirror.

A face that was long, lean, and dark. The sunken eyes, glittering pools of darkness, stared down at the shrinking figure and betrayed no emotion. Indeed, the entire face was a blank mask; the eyes moved, studied the room with the same unreasoning stare, then looked down again. The thin lips parted, and Edward read the soundless word.

"Come."

Like a sleepwalker, he rose and walked to the mirror.

*

Greek Street mumbled in the half sleep that falls upon Soho in the small hours. The after-theatre crowds had long since finished their late dinner and gone home; now only the night-club revellers, or more likely, seekers of esoteric entertainment, still moved like maundering snails along the pavement, glancing hopefully into darkened doorways, or looking upwards at lighted windows.

The girl came upon Edward suddenly. She materialized out of a shop doorway and gripped his arm, while gazing up at him with an air of one who has just stumbled upon an old and extremely dear friend.

"Hullo, darling, how nice to see you again."

One blue-painted lid closed in an expressive wink, and that part of Edward's brain that still worked took in the words, the expression, and the wink, then came to a decision.

"Let's start walking, darling." The full red lips scarcely parted, and the blue eyes were never still. "You never know when a bloody copper is going to poke his nose round the corner."

"Let's walk," said Edward in a flat voice.

She took his arm, and together they walked along the pavement. The girl gave Edward a calculating sideways glance. "Like to come to my place, darling? Five quid and no hurry."

"I would like you to come to my place," said Edward.

"How far?" Now there was a hint of suspicion in her voice.

"Off the Edgware Road."

"Rather a long way. Have to make it worth my while."

"Shall we say thirty pounds?" Edward suggested.

Next time the girl spoke her voice sounded like a cash register.

"You a pussy, dear?"

"A pussy?"

"Yes, pussy—cat—do you go in for the rough stuff? If you do, count me out. I've got me other clients to think about. In any case I'd want more than thirty pounds."

Edward chuckled and the girl frowned. "Nothing like that. Just your company."

She relaxed. "All right then. Ten pound down in the taxi, and the rest when we say goodbye. O.K.?"

"O.K.," said Edward.

He opened his front door and, after turning on the hall light, stood aside for her to enter. Despite the carefully applied makeup, tell-tale lines marred her face, and the muscles under her chin sagged slightly; the brash metallic blonde hair was brittle, while her calves were plump and streaked with extended veins. He helped her take off the light blue coat, noting with cold detachment the short, sleeveless, and very low-cut black dress. He then guided her through the sitting room door and she gasped with pretended, or perhaps genuine, delight at the cosy surroundings.

"You are nice and comfy." She wriggled her bottom and the action made her suddenly grotesque, and a mirthless grin parted his lips. "Do you think I could have a little drinkie?"

"Of course." He walked over to the sideboard. "Whisky all right?"

"Luvely." She rubbed her well-corseted stomach. "Nothing like a drop of the hard stuff to turn me on."

He poured a generous helping of whisky into two glasses, then carried them over to the sofa where she sprawled, displaying a large amount of not particularly appetizing leg. She gulped down the neat spirit with experienced ease, then glanced suggestively over one shoulder.

"I see you've got everything handy. Curtains and all. This is quite a treat after my place, and you know how to treat a girl. I always like dealing with gentlemen. At one time I had an extensive refined clientele, if you follow me. No riff-raff. But times are hard now, what with the Squeeze, and the Wolfenden Report, and all. Thank you, darling, perhaps I will have another. Tell me, have you anything special in mind?"

Edward's eyes were cold, devoid of expression.

"Yes," he said, "something very special."

"Well," she shrugged, "with one or two of these inside me, perhaps I won't mind. But I'll have to put my fee up." She suddenly shivered. "Strike a light, it's bloody cold in here."

He backed slowly to the window bay; an alcove lined with dark red curtains, and so masked with shadow the outward edge of a small mahogany table could only just be seen. With his eyes still fixed upon her face, Edward walked slowly backwards until he was stopped by the table; he reached back with his right hand and took something from the table. Slowly he bought it out and the overhead lamp reflected its light on the steel blade. The woman, her wits dulled with whisky, giggled softly.

"Oh no, dear, not knives. I mean, there's a limit . . ."

Edward came out from the window bay, the knife clasped firmly in his right hand, and behind him strode a second figure. A tall, dark man, with a bitter lean face, his eyes masked by the shadow of his broad-brimmed hat; together they crept forward, the tall man's hands resting on Edward's shoulders. Their legs worked in unison. Breast to back, thighs to buttocks, legs to legs; the tall man's chin rested on Edward's head, and while his face was white, devoid of emotion, the stranger's lips were parted in a joyous, anticipatory smile, his eyes gleamed with unholy joy, and his hands pressed down on his partner's shoulders, steering him . . .

"Gawd," the woman was sober now, and half rose from the sofa, "not two of you . . . ?"

The tall man's eyes willed her to silence, forced her back onto the sofa, where she lay like a plump broken doll with a wide open mouth and glazed eyes. The four-legged, two-headed monster now stood over her; the two pairs of eyes, one cold, blue, dead fish, the other black, glittering, stared down. Then the tall man raised his hand, and Edward raised his knife. The stranger's thin lips moved, and from between the tightly clenched teeth came one hissing word.

"Now."

Edward's hand flashed down—then up, then down, then up, then down, until the gleaming knife blade was an unbroken streak of red blotched silver light.

There was blood everywhere, but no body.

Once the curtains had been pulled back and the early morning light flooded the room, his eyes refused to be deceived. There was a dark ominous stain covering the sofa and most of the surrounding carpet. In some places the stains were lighter in color, as though they had been scrubbed in a futile effort to remove them. His suit hung in front of the electric fire, shrunken and creased; it was still damp, and although it had clearly been washed, ugly dark stains darkened the coat front and trousers. His grey waistcoat was like a screwed-up house flannel, and his shirt was missing. He went up close to the overmantel mirror until his reflection filled it.

"Why?"

There was blood in his hair. His face and body had been washed, but the subconscious, or whatever had controlled his body during the dark hours, had not considered shampoo.

"How?"

That one was easy. In the bathroom he found a clean carving knife with a bloodstained towel next to it; the subconscious had not bothered to empty the bath either. The water was pink, red-rimmed, and foul; his missing shirt floated on the surface like the upturned belly of a dead fish.

"Where?"

That was indeed the master question. Where was the body that had given forth such a profusion of blood? He stumbled from room to room, searched the six-by-eight kitchen, even looked under the bed, opened cupboards; it took him a full five minutes to summon courage to open the blanket chest, but he did not find a body. His terror became flecked with anger, and he glared at the mirror.

"Where?" he hissed the word, "where did you hide it?" and instantly there came to him a thought. Maybe the victim had not died, but had managed to escape. If so, why had not the police paid him a visit long since? He went out onto the landing, examined the banisters, stair carpet, even the hall door. There was no sign of blood.

He was about to open the front door when he realized he was still dressed in pyjamas, and the sound of the postman mounting the steps made him scurry back to his top-floor flat. He dressed quickly, then like an unhappy ghost went out to haunt the city.

He walked all day. The sunlight burnt up the hours like a fire devouring the last frail barricade, and night was sending forth its first dark spears when sheer weariness forced him to come to rest, and enter a workman's cafe. The table at which he sat was situated by a mirror; a long, oblong frame with its surface misty with steam, flyblown, and in some places the quick-silver had become blurred, but it still cast a reflection.

His coffee had grown cold, and the food on his plate congealed when that familiar face looked at him out of the mirror. He tried not to look into the eyes; made one futile effort to rise from his chair, then the great coldness froze him, and slowly his head came up, and then round.

The thin lips moved, and Edward did not have to read the word.

She was young this time, and walked with pathetic bravado along the pavement, swinging her cheap green handbag with childlike abandon, and recklessly eyeing the men who passed.

The tall young man with a white drawn face stepped out of the shadows, and the girl slowed her pace, and looked back over one shoulder.

"You a nosy?"

Her voice had a north-country accent, and her grey eyes, in that pitifully young, grossly over-made-up face, were hard. Like chips of grey flint.

"If you mean, am I a policeman, the answer is no."

"Oh, la-de-la," she relaxed and moved towards him, her hips swinging in what she considered to be a seductive walk. "Are you lonely, then? Looking for a friend, then?"

"I could be."

"You look as if you need one."

She eyed him up and down with some distaste. "You're not down on yer luck, are you? I mean, you've got some of the ready? I mean, I don't do it for peanuts."

The young man smiled and took out his pocketbook. The girl's eyes widened when she saw the thick wad of banknotes, and her smile flashed on like a neon sign.

"Oh, well," she patted her Elizabeth Taylor hairdo, "looks as if this is my lucky night."

The young man nodded gravely. "It is indeed."

For the first time the girl betrayed signs of embarrassment.

"Look, have you got a car? Or maybe a place nearby? You see I haven't been in Fogsville long, and me landlady ain't a regular, if you get my meaning. She won't stand for anything."

"I was going to suggest you come back to my place. It's not very far."

She took his arm and he looked down at the bright red finger-nails; the hand was small, plump, and not over clean; her false eyelashes were long, and stuck out like black spikes.

"We'll get a taxi," he said.

The flat looked like a well-furnished slaughter house. There was blood everywhere; the bedclothes were sopping wet, again there had been a futile effort at washing; the old stains on the carpet were overlaid with fresh ones; blurred red fingerprints stood out on the pale blue emulsion paint on one wall; there were even red spots on the ceiling. Another ruined suit; hung before the electric fire.

Edward stood against the door and surveyed the macabre scene with curious detachment. He was shocked to find his feeling of terrified disgust was less strong than yesterday. It was as though his senses were numb; his brain seemed to have absorbed its full capacity of horror, and now was willing to view the outrageous rationally. Terror, black dread, still smarting under the first healing skin, but it was just bearable. Tomorrow—next time—the pain would be less, and one day, perhaps when the room was a red cavern, and he paced a squelching carpet, there would be a strange peace that comes with normality.

For the second time—was it only the second time?—there was no body. At least almost no body. In the bathroom he caught a glimpse of his white, unshaven face; three long scratches curved down over one cheek. Three red lines that scarcely broke the skin, save in one place, just a little to the left of his mouth. A small fragment was embedded in the flesh. He pulled it out and stared down at that sliver of fingernail; it still retained traces of bright red lacquer, and the horror flared up, burnt away the healed scab, and gave him a brief moment of sanity.

"I must confess," he shouted the words, ran into his tiny hall and screamed his defiance. "I'll give myself up. I'll make them lock me away."

The tall figure came out of the kitchen and moved towards him. The deep sunken eyes glared their awful anger from under the broad-brimmed hat, and the lips were stretched back in a mirthless grin.

"Never again," Edward was whispering now, a harsh madman's whisper, "I'll bring the police up here. I'll let them see it all . . ."

He stopped short as the gaunt head slowly moved from side to side. The voice spoke and his ears heard the word it uttered.

"Mine."

"I'm not yours. Not—not—not . . ."

The words came slowly, with great effort.

"Life—I—now—walk—in—daylight."

The teeth parted and he saw the black nothingness beyond. Then the laughter came, hollow, punctuated by silent pauses, like a faulty radio.

"Ha—ha—ha . . ."

He covered his ears with shaking hands, but the laughter echoed round the limitless caverns of his skull; then the figure was gone, and the laughter was his. Hollow, madman's laughter, that the walls absorbed, the very air contained, and whose vibrations still throbbed long after he had sunk to the floor in merciful oblivion.

The days passed and became weeks. In the world outside questions were being asked, but without great concern, for no mutilated bodies had been found and there were many reasons why a prostitute might find it good policy to disappear.

But one person was perturbed, but for a different reason. Mr. Hulbert Jeffries stood on the landing outside Edward's flat and gently pressed the bell push. He waited for a few moments, then pressed again. He heard a door open, then footsteps; a slow hesitant tread. A voice, muffled by the closed door, came to him; a tired, frightened voice.

"Who is it?"

"The chap from downstairs." Hulbert was irritated by all this security. In his world a fellow never spoke from behind a closed door; in fact if he had any sense, he would never lock his door in the first place. There was no telling who you might lock out. "Can I have a word with you?"

For a while it seemed as if his request was going to be ignored, then the door reluctantly opened, and Hulbert gasped when he saw the skeleton face, the sunken eyes that flickered with a baleful light, and almost abandoned his self-imposed mission. Then he remembered what had prompted that mission, and hardened his heart.

"Sorry to bother you, 'specially if you're feeling under the weather, but I had to speak with you."

He paused, waiting for encouragement, but those awful eyes just stared at him, so he swallowed hastily and continued.

"I hope you'll take this in the right spirit, but I wondered if you would quieten things down a bit. I mean when you entertain your lady friends. I know a certain amount of noise is unavoidable, but there is a limit . . ."

Again he waited for some response; an excuse, even possibly an explanation, however feeble. But the bloodless lips only moved and muttered something that sounded like "Sorry," and the door began to slowly close.

"Here, wait a minute!" Hulbert's normally placid disposition became ruffled. "That's not the only thing. There's all that hammering, and if you must throw things, and spill stuff over the floor, for Pete's sake mop up the mess. I've got bloody great patches all over my ceiling."

The door jerked back, and a bony-fingered hand shot out and gripped Hulbert's shirt front; a hollow voice croaked:

"What patches?"

"Watch it, Matey." Hulbert gripped the slender wrist and wrenched his shirt free. "You're asking for a punch-up. The patches on my ceiling. It's beginning to look like the map of the world before we lost the empire. You must have knocked a couple of barrels of red port over to make a mess like that." He sniffed suddenly. "What the hell is that bloody stink?"

The door was slammed in his face, and he was left pounding out his rage upon its unresponsive panels. After a while he went back to his own apartment muttering angrily to himself.

He looked up at his disfigured ceiling. The dark red stains were deeper towards the center; even as he watched, one swelled into a scarlet globule, it elongated, its tip became detached, then fell to a tabletop with a minute splash. Another red, glistening driblet yo-yoed down as Hulbert reached for his telephone.

Edward was ripping up his fitted carpet, an easy task, for most of the tacks had been removed, and those that remained slid out of their holes at the first pressure. He rolled back the carpet, tore at the underfelt, and stared at the bare boards. They bore many bruises, made by a hammer wielded by an inexperienced hand; they were also blood-stained, and in some places not quite flat, like the lid of a suitcase that has been forced down on a too full interior. Edward stood up as the tall man entered the room.

"Is this the end?"

"I fear so." The tall man bowed his head gravely. "And it is to be regretted that our fruitful association has to terminate. But," he smiled, or rather bared his teeth, "the vessel is, in more respects than one, full, and indeed, overflowing."

Fear had long since died, now only curiosity remained; an unsated lust for forbidden knowledge.

"What now?"

The lean cheeks were now tinted with color, the lips full and red, the eyes bright with fully-charged life.

"Now I am replete, and the wheel has turned a full circle—almost. You alone can seal the circle, give me the power to walk abroad. Eighty years ago I suspected the truth, now I know. I too called forth a shade from the dark lands, and I gave him the seven sacrifices that are necessary, plus the ultimate."

"Your master," Edward asked, "he still walks the earth?"

The eyes sparkled, and the deep voice took on a joyous tone.

"He walks, they all walk, for we are legion. We sit in high places and fan discord until the guns begin to boom, and the bayonets flash. Your lovely wars are a feast, a banquet that charges us for twenty or thirty years. Once past the first barrier there is no reason why any of us should starve."

"What is the ultimate?" Edward knew the answer but he wanted the tall man to tell him. The strong, deep voice went on.

"It is important that the seven initial sacrifices be dispatched in a special way. You were an apt pupil, although at first your tiresome conscience wanted to cover up. That futile scrubbing and washing. But," he glanced round at the blood-spotted, in some places, blood-coated, room, "you grew out of that in time."

He pulled his greatcoat open and lovingly selected a long bladed knife; when he looked up his smile was gentle, his voice soft, comforting.

"How said Brutus on the Plains of Philippi?"

Edward looked into those shining eyes and knew he must follow the path of knowledge to the end—and beyond.

"Hold then my sword, and turn away thy face, while I do run upon it."

"That," whispered the tall man, "is the ultimate."

Edward moved forward and the knife came up; the blade quivered, then was still. The lean face turned and looked back over one shoulder.

"Grip my shoulders and thrust forward. You helped me to come here, it is only right that I should assist you to go there."

Edward gripped the powerful shoulders, then pulled with all his strength. The pain was cold fire that paralyzed his body; he sank to the floor and watched his lifeblood pouring out over the bare floor-boards.

"Have patience," the tall man whispered, then threw wide his arms in a triumphant gesture. "Have patience; you have all eternity."

They tore up the floor-boards and took away the bits and pieces. The room was stripped; the bed went to the flames, the furniture was dispersed, the wallpaper removed, but they left the over-mantel mirror.

Time had no meaning, and perhaps a year passed before a new tenant took up residence in the flat; perhaps two, even five. But one evening that which had been Edward Charlton looked out of the mirror and saw that a new bed stood on the dais, a fresh carpet covered the floor, and unfamiliar furniture cluttered the room.

Night darkened the window, then the sun painted a golden bar across the carpet, and existence became a panorama of light and darkness; lamps that went on, then off, the murmur of far-off voices; the void waiting to be filled.

Tenants came, then departed, fashions changed, furniture became bizarre, strange contraptions entered the flat, but the overmantel, now a priceless antique, remained.

Young people dressed in outlandish clothes gathered before whatever had replaced Edward's electric fire; they danced, made love, ate, drank, and finally became bored. Suddenly the words rang out, a clarion call that brought Edward floating to the mirror; he gazed out at the crowded room.

A young man with pink hair and a spotty face asked: "What did you say?"

A girl's voice, young, fresh, impatient, repeated the long-awaited call.

"Let's hold a seance."

A PUNISHMENT TO FIT THE CRIMES

Richard A. Gordon

Trying to follow the names used by Richard Alexander Steuart Gordon (1947–2009) on his various works is a complex maze indeed. His first story, "A Light in the Sky" (1965), was released as by Richard A. Gordon, but the hilarious Doctor series was being published with another author's pseudonymous byline of Richard Gordon. To avoid confusion, he was asked to switch it and chose Alex Stuart, but again, fears of confusion with another author's pseudonymous historical novels, issued as by Alex Stuart, forced a change, so he adopted Alex R. Stuart and, finally, Stuart Gordon, under which name most of his novels were published.

The Scottish-born author wrote mainly science fiction in his early career, notably *Time Story* (1972), in which a criminal attempts to escape capture via time travel; the five novels in the Bikers series about motorcycle gangs of monsters that terrorize Great Britain: *The Bikers* (1971), *The Outlaws* (1972), *The Last Trip* (1972), *The Bike from Hell* (1973), and *The Devils' Rider* (1973); three dystopian novels set in a postapocalyptic world: *One-Eye* (1973), *Two-Eyes* (1974), and *Three-Eyes* (1975); and *Fire in the Abyss* (1983), another time-travel novel in which a sixteenth-century sailor travels to a doomed twentieth century where he is incarcerated after an attempt to learn useful secrets from the past. Many of Gordon's fictional works rely on historical facts to give verisimilitude to his created stories. Later in his career, he wrote travel guides to Scotland and books about paranormal occurrences, myths, legends, and miracles.

"A Punishment to Fit the Crimes" was first published in *The Fiend in You*, edited by Charles Beaumont (New York, Ballantine, 1962).

"Oyez! Oyez! The court is now in session!" chanted the red-robed figure with ritual solemnity in the nearly empty chamber. He was powerfully built, handsome, and lithe in his movements before the shadowed dock except that he favored one leg ever so slightly. His judicial wig, perfectly expressive of the dignity of his person and position, stood just a little away from his forehead as if displaced by a pair of short, unobtrusive horns, which, as a matter of fact, it was.

"This court will hear no plea of innocent," he continued, "and will render no verdict of not guilty. However, the Accused is an Englishman and must have a trial. I am the prosecutor; I am the judge; and I am the jury. I will pronounce sentence and carry it out in due course. It would be inappropriate for me to say, 'May God have mercy on his soul.'

"Before I proceed to the calling of the first witness, I should like to comment on the promptness and dispatch with which the prisoner has been brought to the bar. The crimes of which he is accused were committed a mere seventy-odd years ago, and, of course, he has been in our possession for even less time than that. Nevertheless, his processing has been completed; those who were accessories after the fact are in our hands; and there is no need to extradite any of the witnesses against him because they too are in our jurisdiction. We take pride in the fact that no one in any way connected with this case has escaped us. The whole affair is much more neatly tied up than usual, and we are ready to proceed.

"I call the first witness." The dim shape of a woman appeared in the box. "You have been chosen from among many who have knowledge of these crimes and whose testimony would be essentially the same as yours. We will not waste our time on the others; the weight of your evidence will be multiplied by the number of those whose stories can differ from yours only in their names and ages. Our case rests on you; you know what is required of you and can imagine the consequences if it is not forthcoming.

"Doyousolemnlysweartotellthetruththe-wholetruthandnothingbutthetruth, so help you?"

"I do."

"Your name, calling, and address?"

"My name was Annie Chapman. My trade was streetwalker, and I plied that trade in the stinking, teeming alleys of the lowest part of London. My price was what I could get—a few farthings, sixpence, perhaps a shilling. I had no fixed address.

"Annie Chapman—even now, more than seventy years later, my name is remembered. It is true that in life I was ragged and filthy, diseased, drunken, always hungry, always cold, often abused. It is true that I was scorned by the respectable women of the neighborhood, mocked by their children, and cheated by their men, but how many of them are remembered after seventy years? You see, on the night of September Eighth, 1888, in Hanbury Street, Whitechapel, when I was forty-seven years old, the Defendant slit my throat, sliced open my abdomen, and made off with one of my ovaries and three brass rings. By killing me, he made me immortal."

The handsome face of the prosecutor took on a reflective look. He raised his hand, and the shade of Annie Chapman fell silent.

"Why did you do it?" he asked. "We understand the Accused; in our preparation for his trial, we learned what there is to know about him—who he was, why he chose to commit the crimes he did in the way he did, and the reason he suddenly retired after his career of carnage and terror, unidentified and unexplained. We understand him, but we do not understand you. You—Emma Smith and Martha Tabram, Mary Nichols and Annie Chapman, Long Liz Stride and Catherine Eddowes and Mary Jane Kelly—all of you who paid him for immortality in the transient coin of passing gratification, you are here for reasons unconnected with *his* crimes. We have examined the mind of the murderer, but we cannot fathom the minds of the victims. Whitechapel and the whole East End of London were in panic as he struck again and again, always in the same area, always at the same women. Didn't you feel it? Why did you continue to walk the streets at night alone, courting the coppers of all men and the steel of one? Speak for them all, witness; why did you do it?"

"It was our life," said Annie Chapman simply. "It was our life, and like farmers on the flank of Vesuvius, we had to live it or die; we lived it, and we died.

"We bear him no grudge. Poor fellow, he did himself more harm than he did us. It was over for us in a moment—a mere slash of a knife across our throats, and after that, if he chose to indulge himself on our bodies, why it was no more than he had paid to do, paid like the countless others before him. It was the way we made our living."

"The witness will confine herself to the questions I ask and not venture into matters of opinion or forgiveness. Forgiveness is not the business of this court," interrupted the prosecutor severely. "I understand the Defendant stole from you certain items of value?"

"Nothing of value, sir, only some brass rings and my life. And what was life? The autopsy surgeon who finished what the Defendant had started said that my body showed signs of great deprivation, that I was badly fed, that I was bruised. The night I was killed, I was turned out into the deadly dark streets from a common lodging house for lack of fourpence to pay for my bed. Yes, I bear him no grudge; he was just part of a foolish destiny which was misread for me in a cracked teacup."

"Explain, please."

"Once I was an honest wife living in Windsor with a respectable husband, a coachman who was dull but good, good but very dull. I was a romantic—aging, searching, unfulfilled. A gypsy read my fortune in the tea leaves and saw—need I say it?—a tall dark man who would change my life. One day, a tall dark man did appear, and I left my short, fair, good husband and went away with him—I, a woman of forty-two, no beauty, but a fine figure of a woman, aging and discontented— I went with him, searching for romance like a green girl. It was not long before he left me. He changed my life; that much of the gypsy's prophecy was true.

"For a time, my husband, the coachman, dull but very good, sent me ten shillings a week, but then he died. I was left to sell my body in courtyards and arcades for miserable farthings; I had already sold my soul for the fraudulent romance of a gypsy charlatan.

"For it was the promise of romance that made me leave the humdrum of Windsor for the lodging houses of Thawl Street and Dorset Street and the lanes and alleys of Spitalfields and Whitechapel. The gypsy never promised fame; she never told me that seventy years after my death people would still know my name and wonder about what had happened to me. I believed in romance; I would never have believed in immortality.

"Romance! When I was lucky I went drunken to a filthy bed and awoke with coppers for rum at the Ringers or the Five Bells. Rum was my only friend and my dearest enemy. Oh, I pursued romance to the bitter end, the very depths! I wore three brass rings as if they were gold, and I sang sad songs in a cracked voice and wept at their false sentiment—'It was only a violet I plucked from Mother's grave . . .'"

"Spare us, please," said the figure in red. "You may be excused. We will attend to you later." And the woman who had been Annie Chapman faded from the box.

"We rest our case," intoned the prosecutor as he ascended to the bench and assumed the role of judge. "We have proved beyond doubt what was already known beyond doubt: the Defendant murdered Annie Chapman and the others, women unknown to him, in a manner calculated to terrify a whole city and to horrify succeeding generations. Despite our reputation, it is neither our function nor our desire to reward evil. If the Defendant wishes to make a statement before we pass sentence, he may do so."

From the darkness of the dock rose a face so ravaged by an unspeakable disease as to be unrecognizable as an individual or, indeed, even as a human being.

"Why am I here? Why am I made to stand this mockery of a trial? Hell I expect, but why am I singled out for special punishment? I did not escape retribution on earth; I have been punished humanly and inhumanly. I plead that my debt has been paid. I do not demand justice; I beg for mercy."

The judge laughed. "We deal only in justice here. However, if you think you can soften our heart, proceed."

"Let me go back then. Let me speak to you from the damnation which was mine before my death. Let me prove that my punishment on earth was crueler than any which you might devise in Hell. Let me show that my debt has been paid so that I may share in the general damnation of all sinners rather than suffer alone a particular fate which will again make me a stranger to mankind."

"You may go back," said the judge. "Return to the years that intervened between the death of Mary Jane Kelly and your own. Speak to us from there."

From the dock, the voice, echoing back through the years, was dull with puzzlement and pain, but in its very dullness, fear and horror screamed in imprisoned agony as the halting words asked questions of a fugitive self that was afraid to answer them.

"Where am I? Why am I here? The iron bars at my window are artfully wrought in the fanciful shapes of flowers that do not grow, of birds that neither fly nor sing, and of animals that do not leap nor love nor, indeed, live. The bars are gilded, but they are still iron and still bars. The locks on my door, they say, are to keep out the terrors and affrights of the world, but they also keep *me* in. My gaolers are called nurse, companion, mother, but they are still gaolers. They say that I am ill, but I am a prisoner. Though my bonds be of the softest silk, they are as of the strongest steel; I am a prisoner.

"I do not know how it happened. There are no mirrors in my cell wherein I can divine the reason for my being here. It is buried in the barren wastes of my mind, and I spend my days frantically digging, frantically tearing at the bleeding soil of an injured brain hoping to find the answer and fearing what I might find. I dare not succeed, and I dare not fail, and I am lost in the nothingness between.

"It was my hands that sinned, not I. I look at my hands and marvel that they are still unstained by the crimes which they, not I, committed, and which I cannot now remember. Even now as I speak, my words seem strange to me, the product of my hands, of another and alien personality.

"Who am I? Once I was free. I remember I walked in the world beyond this cell as John S——, Fellow of the Royal College of Surgeons, respected and loved, healing the sick and mourning the dead. And I remember that I was also young Saucy Jackie, Gentleman, and only slightly—only youthfully—wicked. Once there was gaiety and wine and the friendship of men and the love of women. I remember the strengths and lusts of youth, the high-life of the West End and the low-life of the East—the oat-sowing evenings which began in the glittering salons of Mayfair and ended stupidly in silly, drunken, sordid commerce with pitiful drabs in the squalid alleys of Whitechapel and Spitalfields.

"There was a time when my mother did not weep for her son, and when the gilded iron at my window formed a mere decorative grate, a bar to intrusion instead of to escape. There was a time when I was a single, unfragmented being, when my hands did not make my mind shudder and flee into the darkness, the most miserable victim of my own unremembered crimes.

"They say that I am ill. It is true; I am ill. But the dread and revulsion I see in the eyes of my attendants are not caused by the loathsome disease which rots my body and turns my brain to corruption. I am ill and horrible to look at, but that does not explain why I am denied a razor to shave my beard and a knife to cut my food. Do they fear that I might commit some small crime against myself? Or can it be that they would guard against some horrid abomination to themselves?

"I am ill, but that is not why I am a prisoner; that is not why the doctor comes, a smiling executioner, speaking to me as if he were a man and I were a man like him, smiling and exchanging false encouragements with my gaolers, smiling and lying, smiling and hating the obvious wealth that has bought him and his silence and his smiles.

"Perhaps he will come soon, bearing his gift of sleep, of sleep in a bottle, of sleep without dreams. Once, I remember, sleep came as a friend, but now there are dreams which have robbed me of my freedom and have made my hands the enemies of my mind. Now there are dreams, and I awake feeling my guilt but without the memory of my crimes.

"So here am I with my bars and my locks and my dreams. Here am I, knowing that I might be saved if I remember, knowing that I might be lost if I remember. I *must* remember! The only thing worse than remembering is not remembering. Who am I? Where am I? Why am I here? If I could remember, perhaps I could repent. I *must* remember! A crime out of mind is a crime out of conscience. I *must* repent! For in repentance is the salvation of the soul, and my mind and body are already damned.

"I must remember. The dreams—the fog in Whitechapel, always the same—myself, nameless and faceless in the fog, always the same—but each night a different cowering figure—each night the flash of my knife in the fog—and then—AND THEN! . . ."

The tormented voice stopped abruptly and then started again on a note of despair: "Where am I? Why am I here? The iron bars at my window are artfully wrought in the fanciful shapes . . ."

The judge broke the spell. He had been listening intently. Now he clapped his hands with a sharp report which shut off the dismal flow of words from the dock.

"Come back through the years and hear my sentence; return and hear your doom! The punishment meted out to you on earth by your mother for love and your attendants for gain is indeed as just and as cruel as any we could devise here. For their sins, I condemn your mother, your physician, your nurses and companions, all of whom are in our power, to relive their roles throughout eternity; I condemn the one to despair and grief and the others to hatred and fear for all time.

"As for you, John S——, Surgeon, alias Saucy Jackie, alias Jack the Ripper, I sentence you to the care of those who protected you in life from the justice of men; I sentence you to that barred room until the end of time, to the fear of your own hands and mind and past forever.

"ALL HOPE ABANDON, YE WHO ENTER HERE!"

~

FROM HELL AGAIN

Gregory Frost

As an author of science fiction, fantasy, and horror, Gregory Frost (1951–) has been nominated for numerous awards, most notably for his novelette "Madonna of the Maquiladora" (2002), which received nominations for the Nebula, the Hugo, the James Tiptree, Jr., and the Theodore Sturgeon Memorial Awards. The historical thriller *Fitcher's Brides* (2002), a tale of Bluebeard reimagined as a combination ghost story and Gothic horror novel, was a finalist for both the World Fantasy and International Horror Guild Awards for Best Novel.

Other novels by Frost include *Lyrec* (1984), about Lyrec and Borregad— two interdimensional travelers who set out to hunt down and kill a giant creature named Miradomon who destroys whole worlds; *Táin* (1986) and its sequel *Rem-scela* (1988), which retell the Irish epic *Táin Bó Cuailnge*— the stories of Cú Chulainn, the hero of Ulster who at the age of eighteen single-handedly defended his people against the invading army of the sorcerous queen Maeve; and *The Pure Cold Light* (1993), a futuristic tale in which a rebel journalist discovers a conspiracy that threatens the basis of human civilization. He has also produced a short story collection, *Attack of the Jazz Giants* (2005).

Frost has served as an expert researcher for episodes of television programs on the Discovery Channel and the Learning Channel. He also is the director of the fiction writing workshop at Swarthmore College.

"From Hell Again" was first published in *Ripper!*, edited by Gardner Dozois and Susan Casper (New York, Tom Doherty Associates, 1988).

He pulled lightly upon the oars, stroke upon stroke, and his boat skimmed the black water of the Thames. Mayhew was a dredger and this his work, but no commission had ever been so strange. He pondered what it could all mean and how it had come to be. In his Peter boat, shallow-bottomed and easy to row, he often forgot himself entirely. Sometimes he sang or hummed a tune. Sometimes his thoughts just strayed, to happier times before his wife had taken to drink and run away, when his daughter had lived with him. But now she was back after all, and things would be better again . . . with this commission.

He remembered Demming. Two nights before, coming out of the fog in a frock coat, a tall toff's hat and shadow for a face, Demming had appeared upon the quay as Mayhew tied up his boat. Gaslight glinted off the gold of Demming's walking stick. He asked after Patrick Mayhew, and feigned surprise when he learned who he was speaking to. "You've a reputation as a dredger," Demming told him. And Demming knew how lean the summer was—so lean that no sane man could have denied his offer: a job of dredging with five hundred guineas paid in advance and a promise of an impossible five hundred more if it proved successful. "Tomorrow night then," Demming said, "I'll meet you here at two." Mayhew remembered how his footsteps faded in the fog but the sound of the stick tapping went on and on.

It seemed to echo in the slap of the water against his squared bow.

The second meeting. Demming had given him the heavy purse as promised. He hadn't needed to count it to know how much it must contain. But in the interim the questions filled with worry had come to plague him, and these had to be cleared up. "This is criminal, what you want me to do," he said over the purse. "Not at all," Demming replied. "It's dredgework that you've done a thousand times before." "Will I need a net or grappling hooks? What is it you want me to find?" Demming paused before answering. His face was plainly visible now in the light of Mayhew's lantern: a long, proud face, pouchy under the eyes, perhaps from drink. A clean-shaven face, a powdered face. "Hooks or nets is a matter for you—I can't say. What you seek is a body. However, the corpse itself hardly concerns me. The man—for it is a man, Mr. Mayhew—stole from me a watch, a family heirloom that is irreplaceable. The mischief that befell him is of no concern. If you find money on him, you may keep it, but you may *not* turn him in to the police for any finder's fee. I'm paying you quite enough to discourage that. Nor are you to mention him to anyone. Anyone at all." Mayhew thought he understood this: "You kill the fella?" he asked. But Demming hardly balked. "That is none of your business, either. You perform your dredgework, stick to that, and we will get on just fine." This left him believing that Demming had killed a man without knowing that the man carried the stolen watch on his person. An odd oversight, but not an impossible scenario to envision. And it was not much of a crime to refrain from turning the corpse in, not enough of one to overcome a small fortune.

Mayhew listened for a moment to a drunk shouting, somewhere out in the dark, near the passing quay.

Last night on the river. With the half-built Tower Bridge a mangled horror hanging over him, he secured his weighted nets to the boat, then unshipped the oars and began the long, exhausting process. Lights on the ships at dock winked at him. He dragged and hauled nets, dragged and hauled again. His black-tarred sou'wester coat kept the sodden nets from soaking him, but made him sweat twice as hard at the oars so there was hardly a difference. As dawn came up, he called it quits with three shillings worth of coal dredged up but nary a sign of a body.

Then the happiest moment of all in this whole adventure took place. Returning to his house, he found his daughter, Louise, on the stoop. She had come back to him out of the depths of the East End. He listened to the whole sordid story, forgiving her for her sins before he even heard them. She had lived as a whore for nearly a year, keeping with a man in Castle Alley. He had been cruel to her, but she feared, as most of the whores did, the one the papers called "the Ripper," and her hateful prosser was at least protection against that. Soon enough she had turned to drink—ironically, to the same Dutch gin that her mother had loved. She cried as she spoke, and Mayhew held her close; she was his little girl again.

He felt the weight of the money in the pocket of his coat, and he dreamed of their new life. Soon he would quit the river, carry his daughter away from the squalor of Lambeth. They would take a country house, a small estate—just as soon as he found the body, and the watch.

With renewed vigor at the thought of success, he put his back to it, and the Peter boat skimmed the water like a skater across ice.

At three he was under the Tower Bridge once more, his weighted nets dragging, catching. Ship lights gleamed like will-o'-the-wisps along the banks. The first haul produced a piece of a hansom wheel and an intact lantern, also from a carriage, and Mayhew wondered if an entire cab could lie beneath him in the black depths. The lamp was worth some money to him, and it was a curious enough proposition that he dropped his nets there again to see if he would collect more fragments from a hansom. As he rowed vigorously, the nets caught again, this time holding like an anchor. He tried, but couldn't pull them free. Taking one of his grappling hooks, he stood, removed his coat, and tossed the hook out behind his boat so that it would sink beyond the nets. Down and down the rope played out, until the hook touched bottom. Then he retrieved it, slowly, letting it drag along. The hook, too, caught on something, and Mayhew pulled on that for all he was worth. He strained till his pulse was throbbing in his head. The hook tore free suddenly, sent him sprawling back into the wet bottom of his boat. He reeled in the hook. It brought up a large broken slab of wood caught on one of the spikes. When he tried the nets, he found them freed as well, and drew them in as fast as he could.

The nets brought up more broken wood and what looked to be a piece of iron rail of the sort that might garnish a driver's platform. Then there *was* a hansom on the river bottom, as unbelievable as that seemed. He sat back in wonder at how such a thing could happen, and looked right up at his answer—at the jutting promontory of the Tower Bridge. As Mayhew imagined what happened, the water behind his boat erupted in a release of bubbles. He scrambled to the rear in time to see a body flung up onto the surface of the Thames, bob there for a moment, then sink out of sight. Hastily, he grabbed his nets and flung them out where the water still rippled. Then he rotated the oars into the water and rowed hard, nearly lifting himself onto his feet. The nets took on weight and dragged. He shipped the oars quickly and started drawing the nets in hand over fist, soaking himself but too single-minded in his purpose to stop and put on the slick sou'wester.

The nets and their tangled capture bumped against the boat. Mayhew grabbed hold and pulled the whole mess in at once. The body rolled beneath the ropes, the head flopped back, and death stared up at Patrick Mayhew.

The man had been in the water much longer than Mayhew had supposed, long enough for the skin to have sloughed away from the sludge-covered bones in most places, to leave a wet, glistening visage, a moulage of mud. As much as a year, Mayhew guessed, pulling back. He had hauled corpses in every horrible state of decay imaginable, most of them obscenely bloated. This eyeless figure ought to have been insignificant by comparison, but it now sent a wave of terror shooting like an electrical discharge through Mayhew. He found himself pressed against the side, gripping one oar as if to crush it. This unreasoned fear lasted only moments and then passed like a breeze continuing on downstream. Mayhew had a vision of the people on the ships at dock waking from their sleep, lifting taut faces from pints of ale, as the cadaverous wind rolled by. He wanted nothing more than to grab the nets and fling this body back into the blackness of the Thames; but he had a purpose here, and he was not finished.

He inched his way to the remains. The body wore a cloak and, beneath this, the remains of a coat, vest and tie. Mayhew tore the cloak apart when he lifted it—the material shredded with the weight of muck to support. He dug his fingers through the slime and drew back the black coat—which looked to have been a fashionable dinner jacket—to get at the vest. At first he thought there was no watch, because the chain, covered with weedy slime, was as dark as the material. As he shifted the corpse, something in the watch pocket gleamed, and he moved the lantern nearer, then reached in and drew out the watch. Where every other part of the corpse was caked or colored from its long stay in the water, the watch case glistened as if it had been polished that morning. Mayhew turned it over, disbelieving that it could be in such condition, but the other side was as shiny and unblemished. He could make out distinctly the smoothly molded ridges of the case and the stylized face of a Gorgon in a raised circle, even in the lantern light. He stood, and the body rolled slightly. One arm was suddenly flung out. The knuckles clacked against the side; the sharp, blackened fingers began to curl up slowly. He could bear the thing no longer. He stuffed the watch into his pocket, knelt down, grabbing the netting, and heaved the body over the side. When it did not sink right away, he grabbed a short boat hook and stabbed out, shoving the body under the surface. The hook must have caught on the corpse's coat because, when he tried to draw it back in, it snagged, tipping Mayhew off-balance. He twisted around and the hook caught on the edge of the boat. All of his weight went on it as he turned, and the hook snapped. The spot was cursed. In a panic, Mayhew threw down the broken pole, sat and began hauling on the oars as hard as he could, desperate to escape that haunted place. Never had the Thames carried any fear for him before this, but now, even with the body back where it belonged, he could not get rid of the apprehension that had crawled into his boat with the corpse. It was as if the fear had slithered off and condensed into the muck on his clothes, at his feet. His shoulders ached and his lungs burned at the effort, but Mayhew did not slacken his pace until he was in sight of his dock. He left hooks and nets in the boat, threw the tarp hastily over everything, and set off, almost at a dead run, for home.

Louise was awake, and he could not hide his uneasiness from her. He had told her of the job, of Demming, and of what he suspected. Now he showed her the watch as he described in trembling detail his encounter with the submerged carriage and the passenger he had released, for that was how he interpreted the events. They sat at the small dinner table, Louise in her nightclothes and a shawl, Mayhew still dressed in his checked shirt and smelling of the river, the watch on display between them. Louise marvelled at the etched Gorgon on the case. She reached out and picked up the watch, which Mayhew, in his loathing of it, was unable to do. He wanted to tell her to put it down, but also wanted to see inside it. Louise pressed the winding stem and the case popped open. She opened the lid. Mayhew dragged the lamp closer.

The face of the watch amazed him; whatever he had anticipated, this certainly was not it. The watch dial, a simple dial, took up the lower quarter of the face. Around it, the gold had been etched beautifully with trumpet swirls and leaves. Above and to each side of the dial were two oval insets. These contained small photos that appeared to have been stuffed in; one of them was loose along one edge, and Mayhew peeled it down to find a painted design like a piece of foreign calligraphy underneath. The photos themselves were the only parts of the watch that showed damage from being in the river. They had gone dark and gray, and the best that Mayhew and his daughter could make out was that one of the photos was of a woman's face. The features were too vague to hint at more than that. In the top of the watch, filling that quarter, was a circle the same size as the dial below, and containing another etched Gorgon ringed by snakes. Mayhew noticed now that the face was not quite human in that it had two eyes to each side of the nasal fissures where a nose ought to have been. And the teeth came to points, bared, like two rows of daggers. He closed the case to ascertain that the other Gorgon mirrored this image, and it did. He raised his eyes to Louise. She smiled at him, apparently unaffected by the horrible aspects he saw in the watch.

"Let me see something, papa," she said as she spun the watch towards herself. She sprang open the case again, then lightly ran one fingertip around the edge of the Medusa circle. About three-quarters of the way around, she stopped and pressed with her thumb, and the circle popped up. Louise stared with momentary shock, then began to laugh. "Oh, look at this," and she held the watch out to him.

The Medusa circle had hidden a small painting. For a moment, Mayhew did not comprehend the picture, but then he understood and did not know whether to laugh or be disgusted. The painting showed a grinning priest seated on a small padded stool while a demon knelt, its mouth and one claw clamped around his marrowbone. The demon's body was a dark green, rough with warts, and it had a second lewd face on its arse, yellow teeth and red eyes. That second face finally tipped the scales for Mayhew. "Don't laugh," he ordered Louise, "it's blasphemous. What sort of a gentleman would own a watch like that?"

"You'd be surprised as to what 'gentlemen' carry on them."

"I don't want to know. I found what's wanted and I'll give it away like I'm supposed to, nor do anything but."

"I wonder if it still runs," Louise mused. She closed the case, then began winding the stem. The watch started to tick after a moment, loud and precise.

"Put it down!" Mayhew spluttered. "The man was in the water well onto a *year* by the look of him. There wasn't a part of him that the water hadn't rotted at, and here's his watch that runs like it come from a shop this morning. By what Providence can such a thing be?"

Louise put the watch down. "I don't have an idea. But there it is. Maybe that's as why he wants it back, your Mr. Demming. Maybe he's got the most special watch in the world."

"Maybe so. I don't care nor I get my money, but you leave it be. I'm tired from rowing for my life, so let's get us some sleep, and today I'll take him his watch and buy you something real fine." His head swam for a moment as he stood. He shuffled off and laid down on his small bed, listening to Louise climb into hers, listening to the watch ticking on the table across the room.

The rhythmic ticking washed over him as he fell asleep and followed him down into the landscape of dream. He found himself walking through a darkened Aldgate Street. Gaslight created bubbles of clarity along the murky avenue, which contained shops that he did not recognize, many of them canted forward, looming over him, others stretching high above. Soon, he walked along Whitechapel Road. People began to appear in the pools of flickering light, their faces as distorted as the buildings. They watched him pass; most were grinning like the priest in the little painting, and their sharpened teeth held all of his attention. The rest of their features escaped him. He hastened on, found himself in a darkened lane. Someone spoke close by, and he turned to see Louise's face. At first she was the forlorn child on the doorstep but as she came to him her features distorted, her hair writhing as if alive. He stared into her eyes and found them empty, two great holes through which he could see some other place where the sky was shot through with stars. The ticking of the watch sounded like a scrabbling rat.

A weight in his hand tugged at his awareness like a child pulling on his arm. He looked down, found a huge knife there, a strange knife that looked like an immense carpenter's file. Again he faced Louise, and this time he found the features of her face fallen away, revealing muscle and bone, teeth like daggers. Her mouth hung open and he could see more of that other place between the ivory points. Her jaw clacked shut, the bared grin horrible. "Take me *here*," she said softly. Her fleshless hand slid down across his trousers. He was becoming aroused by his own daughter. The knife pulled at him, begging to be put to use. "*Open the gate,*" a cold voice said. Could it have been him? "You don't want to do that, or the coppers will find us," Louise said. "*Open the gate, let them through,*" the voice insisted harshly. He turned, and Louise was a skeleton poised before that other place, which now poured through the alley, suffusing every shadow with a reddish glow. Someone moved into it, and he saw Demming there, behind the living skeleton, looking accusatorily at him. Demming reached out, saying, "Give it to me," and the skeleton begged, "Papa, don't." Demming scowled and slapped the bones aside. They shattered and went tumbling; some clattered on the stones, others landed in the altered shadows without a sound and dropped into the star-shot void. "The watch," Demming demanded. With a scabrous, warty hand, he opened his cloak to attach the gold fob, which now ran from Mayhew to him. The swirling stars played in the shadows beneath his coat, too. "Papa," Louise called. "Papa." The ticking of the watch beat at his brain. He squeezed shut his eyes and tried to cover his ears.

When he opened his eyes, he was standing near the door. Pressed between him and the wall, Louise had her palms up under his jaw as if trying to push him aside. Mayhew backed away. He saw that her nightgown was torn, purple marks on her throat. "Did I—?" he tried to ask. Tears spilled from her eyes. Mayhew could not look at her. He had known other dredgers, other men, who actually boasted of having coupled with their daughters; and once, in a pub years earlier, he had struck a man who grabbed hold of Louise. That *he* had almost done this awful thing, that the desire might live inside him as it did in those other monsters— he could hardly stand to think on it. He went and sat on his bed. Louise covered herself with her shawl and came to sit beside him.

"Papa," she said, "I ain't like that, no matter what you think. I ain't a whore for you, nor anymore for anyone else. I wish I'd never told you none of it." He tried to reply, to explain, but beyond her shoulder he saw the lamp on the table and, beside it, the recovered watch. The watch had run down and stopped.

Demming lived in St. James's, a neighborhood far more fashionable than Mayhew's. Both the dredger and his daughter went along to Demming's house; he feared that if he left her home she would not be there when he got back. She had accepted his apology and his explanation, but he could tell that she did not truly believe any of it.

A black iron sign hung on the wall beside the door: Walter A. Demming, Doctor of Neuroses. A servant answered their knock and escorted them directly to a second-floor office. There was a single desk to one side of the room, and behind it a case containing skulls of humans and related mammals. A glass jar on the desk held for viewing a model of the brain. Mayhew went to the case and saw, on the shelf below the prominent skulls, a display of medical tools, most of them scalpels and probes. He understood only that these were tools for cutting into people. Behind him the door opened, and Demming, all in tweed, swept in.

"I dared not hope that it was you, Mr. Mayhew. With all I said to you, I maintained doubts. I—" He broke off, staring darkly at Louise.

"My daughter," Mayhew interjected by way of an introduction. He did not care for the intensity of Demming's stare.

The doctor blinked and placed a look of humor upon himself. "Of course," he said. "You have it?"

Louise reached in and removed the watch from her coat, placing it on the table. Her father had been unable to touch it, even in daylight.

Demming barely restrained himself from leaping on the watch, though from his expression he might as easily have intended to crush it as to gather it up. He seemed to forget that the dredger and his daughter still occupied the room with him; his loftier demeanor vanished, and he wrung his trembling hands and mumbled under his breath. His eyes rolled back and for a moment he struck the pose of a man lost in prayer. Mayhew noticed how dark Demming's eyelids were. Then the doctor opened the drawer of the desk and withdrew a velvet purse identical to the first one that he had given Mayhew. "You have done me an inestimable service," he said, while staring once more at Louise, this time with what might have been trepidation. "I shan't forget it." He pulled the handkerchief from his breast pocket and began rubbing at the watch case, harder than if merely polishing it.

"The watch," said Mayhew slowly, dismayed, "you sure it's the right one?" He took the purse.

"There is no doubt of that. There could be no other watch like this. And now, regrettably, I'm late for my appointments at Bethlem Hospital, so I will have to ask you to go, and take my appreciation from the money."

"Of course," Mayhew replied, goaded into recalling the class distinctions at work here. He tucked the purse away, took Louise's arm, and led her out. The liveried servant waited at the top of the stairs and showed them out onto the quiet, tree-lined sidewalk.

They walked down through the park to Birdcage Walk without a word traded between them. With Parliament in sight, Louise could no longer stand the silence. "He was a very impressive man, weren't he?" she asked.

Mayhew drew up short and turned her to him. "Don't you ever mention him again. Not to me, not to anyone. It's done, I'm paid, and I choose to forget everything, just like he wants. You do the same, girl."

"Papa—"

"No, damn you! Never!" He let go the moment she struggled, and watched her run ahead. She did not understand what he was trying to say. He lacked any real understanding of it himself. Perhaps the nightmare was still distorting his reason, and his hatred of Demming was due to the foul memory that he carried all too near the surface. He believed that, for reasons he could not explain, he had come in contact with something monstrous, something unholy and well beyond his comprehension. The best thing he could do, he thought, was to forget it all, to bury the memory as he had buried the corpse by tossing it back into the water. This had now been done. He hastened after his daughter, to explain the way he saw things.

Returning home, he found that Louise had not gone there. She had run off to cry, he tried to assure himself. Later she would come back and he would apologize. Later. Suddenly very weary, Mayhew lay down to sleep.

When he awoke, it was past six and still Louise had not appeared. Mayhew began to worry, but anger soon tinged his concern. This was how things had gone with her before, the last time she ran away. He suspected that she might have fled back to the East End this time, too. If whoring was all she was good for, then to Hell with her; a daughter of his should be made of better stuff than that. "This time I can't forgive her," he announced to the empty room, and buried his own loneliness beneath anger. He might have made something of her, but he saw now that she would only waste his money on drink, attracting the same filth that combed the East End. He knew he had not been rough—he hadn't hit her, and he hadn't even been yelling at her, not really. He cursed her for being like her mother, cursed her mother for everything in the world that wasn't right. He dug into his pocket, felt the weight of the coins. Well, at least something was right in the world—at least he had money enough for a long time to come. A country squire, what a great man he would become. Maybe he would marry a fine woman and raise another daughter, one of distinction this time. He went and fetched the other purse, then sat down at his table and counted his way to sleep. He awoke before dawn and took a stroll, smoking a cigarette to ward off the dampness. On Webber Row he stopped into the Frog and Peach for a pint. The few patrons were all huddled in one smoky corner and whispering excitedly. Mayhew sat up on a stool and asked the man who drew his pint what was going on.

"Well, it'll be in the papers by noon, I suppose."

"What will?"

"That the Ripper's back. Killed him a woman last night in Whitechapel, just like before."

Mayhew set down his pint. "Where? Where'd it happen?"

"Castle Alley's the street as is being given. Here, where you going?"

Running at breakneck speed, past fruit vendors, fish vendors, beggars, and drunkards, Mayhew dashed headlong across London Bridge and into the East

End. The visions of the day before tinged everything he saw with evil. Louise, turning from woman to carcass to bone, and in the background, Demming, always Demming. Now he forgave her, now he whined her name and begged God to forgive him for all the hateful things he had thought about her; it was really only her mother he condemned, and it always had been. Onto Whitechapel Road, shoving desperately through a line of people who waited in their own desperation outside a casual ward house to get a bed for the night. He skirted other such lines, except once to get directions to the street. The backstreets were narrower, and clogged with carts, wagons, and horses. He ran past row houses, and the wide wooden gates of pungent stable yards, then at last into the cramped corridor of Castle Alley. Wagons and carts lined one side of the road. The smell here was much worse than that by the stables. Halfway along, three policemen stood on drier stones, on small islands in the excremental sea. Mayhew grabbed onto one of them, babbling his questions between breaths. The other two pulled him off and shoved him up against a wall with a nightstick under his jaw. Mayhew began to cry. The policemen looked at one another, embarrassed to be sharing this. The one with the nightstick eased back and said "What's the matter, then? She your strumpet?"

"Strumpet?" Mayhew rubbed at one eye.

"Yeah, you know old 'Claypipe'?"

"You was a customer, then," suggested one of the others in the hope of lightening the mood. "Must a' been a good piece to set a man weepin'."

"I—what was the name of the woman killed?"

"Alice McKenzie. She's known round here as 'Claypipe Alice.' What, did you think it was somebody you knew?"

He nodded, wiped at his face with both hands and tried to regain some equanimity. "My daughter. I heard that there'd been another murder—the Ripper."

"Oh, there's been that, right enough. His handiwork, all right. Through the throat, 'e got her, just like before. Found her between two vans, right up there." He pointed. The third policeman, silent till now, moved forward, close to Mayhew, and said, "So, you heard about a killing and you decided that it was your daughter got done. Gawd, people do go on, don't they?" He shared a laugh with the other two.

Mayhew's hand trembled and he shoved it into his pocket. He dared not tell them about Demming, about what he suspected, about his dream. They would jail him for his part in it all, he was certain. "My daughter, she lives on this street. Her name's Louise—Louise Mayhew."

He sought for their recognition and got more than he wanted. One of them became beet red and turned away as if to scrutinize the alley. The policeman who had questioned him said flatly, "Number twenty-three." He stepped back, rubbing his thumbs against his fingertips. None of them would meet his eyes now. They stepped from the walk and clomped off toward where the body had been found. Murder they could live with, but the father of a whore—the notion even that whores had families—was something they could not allow for.

Mayhew sniffled and moved quickly on to twenty-three. Not until he had his hand raised to knock, did he hesitate, turning away suddenly in indecision, pressing again to the wall. What was he going to say to her now that she was alive? His thoughts had been for a dead girl. Anything he said to her here would only shame her. If he left her alone, she might come home again; but if he left her alone . . . His wild thoughts collected like bees, and he realized for the first time what he was thinking: Demming was Jack the Ripper. How could this be coincidence—Castle Alley of all the winding corridors in the East End? Somehow, some poor bastard had discovered this—had discovered that a gold watch helped him, or made him do it, or something that Mayhew couldn't even guess at—and Demming had been unable to continue without it. That hateful watch, everything was tied to that watch; and he had retrieved it. He started back out of the grimy street, ignoring the odd glances of the police.

He wandered distractedly most of the day. Mayhew was not a man of action, nor a particularly skilled thinker. All he knew were nets and grappling hooks and the cold waters of the Thames. But he had to do something—Demming was going to kill Louise, of that much he was certain.

A drizzling rain rustled the leaves in St. James's Park and made the air smell of earth and decay. Prostitutes of a much higher class strolled by under umbrellas. One murmured to him as he passed. He kept his left arm pressed against his body to keep the item in his sleeve from slipping out. It had been a short boat hook not two days earlier; Mayhew had used a rasp file to sharpen the broken point into a needle. When a policeman appeared ahead, he ducked instinctively from sight, but in the rain Mayhew hardly looked different from anyone else in the park.

He reached Demming's street and, as he drew near the house, he saw the door open and a figure come out. The figure—a man dressed as if for a party—walked purposefully past him. Mayhew made a quick glance to determine that the man was not Demming. He glimpsed a pale, sweaty face and round, glassy eyes beneath the brim of a tall silk hat. Demming's door thumped shut. The street was silent, no one else about.

Mayhew went up to the door and rapped the knocker. A few moments passed before the door opened a crack and one eye stared out at him. It was Demming himself. The door opened wide, and the doctor stood cavalierly before him. "Well, this is a surprise. Come to hobnob, Mr. Mayhew?"

"You're Jack the Ripper."

Demming spluttered a surprised laugh. "Am I?" He was about to go on but paused to look past Mayhew, out into the gaslit street where Mayhew could hear footsteps. "Why don't you come in and tell me about it?" Demming let him in, then led him perfunctorily up the stairs into the same office they had stood in the day before. A chair now sat before the desk, as if he had been expected. The leather was warm, and Mayhew recalled the visitor who had passed him. "Now," said Demming, "I've done a great deal of work with lunatic delusions. Why don't you tell me yours and let's see what I can do to help." He opened a box on the desk and with a steady hand took out a cigar, closing the box without offering one to Mayhew. He leaned back against the desk, his ankles crossed. "How am I the—the infamous Ripper?"

Mayhew raised his head to meet Demming's conciliatory stare and said simply, "The watch."

For a fraction of a second, Demming faltered. If Mayhew had not been staring hard at him, he would have missed the twinge. Then Demming laughed and replied, "Mr. Mayhew, you are either drunk or mad. If the former, I advise you to go home and sleep it off; if the latter, you must accompany me to Bethlem this very evening." He moved around the desk and leaned for emphasis on the blotter, his cigar still unlit between his fingers.

Mayhew could only shake his head. He had entertained doubts till now, moments all the way here from Lambeth when he drew up short, thinking himself insane, his notions absurd at best. But he did not need to be a specialist in "lunatic delusions" to see that the doctor was lying, and prodding him to reveal what he knew in order to determine how he should be dealt with.

"You killed Alice McKenzie last night. But you were looking for Louise."

"Absurd, sir. I was at the theatre and a dinner party last night. A Gilbert and Sullivan musical. I went nowhere near your lovely daughter."

"You're lying."

"How many witnesses will be needed, Mr. Mayhew, to prove it?"

"The watch, then. Somehow the watch let you do it. When Louise wound it, I went to sleep, and you were in the dream—"

"You let her wind it?" The facade was gone: first the doctor showed fearful amazement; then his eyes narrowed with determination. He drew open a drawer and pulled out a pistol, aimed it at Mayhew, who pressed back into the creaking chair as if to escape. "You saw some things, but you haven't all the facts. Still, your zeal might be enough to set the police on me, and we can't have that, not when we're so close."

"Close to what?"

"To opening the gates, to giving me some peace. What do you do on the river, Mayhew, spend hours just sitting and thinking?" He said this with an air of humor, a hint of admiration. "I'll tell you, then—as a reward of sorts.

"I've spent much of my life studying the diseases that can afflict the mind, Mr. Mayhew, while you rowed aimlessly about the Thames. I had begun working with hypnosis to treat patients. I found in a few of them a curiously recurring set of images amidst their twisted fantasies—images of other worlds and their concomitant demons, much of which sounded like the reflections of some barbaric priest upon his drug-induced 'journeys.' Among those patients caged in Bethlem Hospital, I found one who was susceptible both to hypnosis and to this uncanny tapestry of images. I used a rather unusual watch to put him in a trance where he could describe his demons. It's Swiss, it was a . . . I once thought it was a gift. Have you ever heard the name Cagliostro? No, of course not. He was a sorcerer who followed in the footsteps of Mesmer, in Paris. The Catholics claimed all sorts of satanic things about him—even that he had feasted with the dead. The man who gave me that watch told me that it had reputedly been fashioned for Cagliostro by a corpse through the practice of necromancy, subsequently had fallen into the hands of Eliphas Levi, another infamous villain, and had passed to my acquaintance after Levi's death in '75. A *corpse*—we joked about it. Such a wild, absurd tale. And I—I wore the watch, here, in my vest. For years I wore it with not so much as a hint of its . . . God, of its power. It took a madman to do that.

"What I expected, I can hardly remember. Of course I had him stay here rather than at 'Bedlam.' Outwardly, he was passive and I felt sure he would be safe. It wasn't until the third murder that I discovered the—the connection. The watch turned up missing, you see, and while searching I found that my patient was not in his room. I did not find him that night. But early the next morning—I could not sleep—I discovered him unconscious in his bed. He had climbed in the second-floor window, which still lay open. He was wearing one of my suits, and his face, his chin and nose, had warts on it that I could not remember him having. The watch was in his—my—breast pocket. It was not ticking. I picked it up without waking him, to take it, and turned the stem just a little, casually, thoughtlessly. With a cry of absolute agony, my patient snapped bolt upright. I dropped the watch and he lay back down.

"Later that day I put him in a trance and got from him a story that I then found hard to believe. He said that the watch had spoken to him in his trance state, that it took control of him, that the fantastic demons of his dreams could not compare with the real ones inhabiting the watch. They were making him perform terrible crimes. Here it was, then: I had unleashed Jack the Ripper upon the East End. Worse, he had worn my clothes and used *my* surgical knife. I considered returning him to the hospital but I decided against this, mostly out of fear that someone else might discover what I now knew. I finally resolved to keep the watch from him while trying to cure him of his delusion. These were only East End trollops he had used in his aborted rituals—the world could do without a few of them—but I had never wanted this to happen, never. I do not know if he wrote any of the letters that the police collected.

"You will already know that I failed. He disappeared and with him went my watch. To this day I have no idea how he escaped. My suspicion is that one of my staff unknowingly wound the watch. I sought him everywhere, discreetly of course, but had no luck. Then, after the last one, the woman Mary Kelly, he returned here. I hardly recognized him. His eyes were shot with blood, and the warts had grown in clusters across his cheek. I feared that he might actually be leprous. His mind had gone, and he babbled out that he had been moments away from completing some task, from bringing the demons of his dreams into the real world, when some other spirit, as of reason, took hold of him—which I presume means that the watch had stopped. He saw what horrors he had wrought under the demons' influence and he tried to destroy the watch in Mary Kelly's hearth. It revealed the extent of its power then, and instead of being destroyed, it erupted with some terrible energy. I still believed that this was all some dark corner of his mind, with no anchor in reality. Only later did I discover that some of the things on the grate in Mary Kelly's house had actually melted, that some unaccountable force had been unleashed. At the time, as I said, I dealt only with him. He had been burned rather severely on one arm. His mind collapsed finally even as I injected him with a soporific, careful not to touch him directly. The things he said afterwards made no sense whatsoever. I could no longer keep him here, and I dared never return him to 'Bedlam.' "

"You killed him."

"In point of fact he was still alive when I pushed the rented hansom off the Tower Bridge. Your river murdered him, not I."

Mayhew shook his head at this rationalization. "Then why dredge him up when he was safely put down? And that devil's own watch," he said, but the realization dawned on him even as he asked it. "You can't mean to try again?"

Demming twisted the pistol away in his sharp gesture. "I've no choice now. Those vile things of his madness have come creeping into my own dreams. Oh, faint at first, very vague; but in the past few months I haven't dared to sleep without morphine. I would never have sought you out, except that the fiends even managed to crawl through *that* barrier. God knows what they really are. The painting in the watch hardly begins to suggest . . . Mr. Mayhew, they're like worms burrowing into your brain, eating their way right through it. If you fail them, deny them, the excrutiation they can induce—Cagliostro died in a madman's anguish, in prison, and I know—I know why."

After a moment, he went on more calmly. "I knew I was going insane. All they wanted—all they *demanded*—was that I retrieve the watch and continue what had begun. For any chance at peace, I hired you, I found another at Bethlem, and I set him to it just like before."

"The watch," Mayhew said, "the fella I passed coming in here—he's got it."

"You don't think *I'd* carve her up. What if she looked at me, what if the image of my face were caught in her retina for the photographers to find? Let them have some other face to identify in the dead woman's gaze."

"But why my Louise?"

"It's the damned watch, don't you see? You let her handle it, and it lives by these murders. I tried to clean all traces of her off the damned thing—you saw me do that! But the demons—their energy, their substance, must have drunk of her life in just those few moments. I'm sorry. It knows her."

"How will you kill me, Mr. Demming? That's a gun, not the Thames, you got there."

Demming looked down at his hand. "Yes," he said in sad agreement. At that moment, Mayhew flung his short spear across the desk. It smashed an inkwell on its way, throwing blackness across Demming's face, a wide gash of shadow. The point entered him below his neck and Mayhew leaped up and shoved it with all his might. Demming sprawled back, slammed into the glass cabinet of skulls, shattering it, then fell forward across the desk. Mayhew stole the gun from his twitching fingers, then made himself withdraw the boat hook from Demming. The doctor flailed briefly, then lay on his side, gasping. Underneath him, spurting blood pooled and mixed with the ink on the desk.

Mayhew did not wait to see if the doctor died. His concern was with the monster already out and prowling the night.

He ran to Pall Mall and hailed a cab, giving the driver one of his gold coins in advance for the fastest ride to Whitechapel the man could manage. The delighted driver asked no questions, and his coach skidded every turn on two wheels, plunging through the rainy night.

No one was guarding Castle Alley; the police knew well that the Ripper did not work so regularly and never returned to the exact same location. Not before tonight.

Mayhew leapt from the coach, twisting his ankle on the ordure-slick stones. He ignored the pain and ran into the narrow street. At the other end of it, walking steadily, stiffly on, was the well-dressed man he had met outside Demming's. Mayhew slowed up, his heart and mind racing, then started ahead on the same side of the road. Twenty-three lay directly between them. He increased his pace to ensure that the Ripper did not reach it before him. With every step, he considered what to do and how to do it.

Steam rose from the sidewalk, a stench of decay. Mayhew hurriedly removed his heavy black sou'wester and balled it up around his arm. The approaching man still seemed to take no notice of him. They were close enough together now that Mayhew could see the droplets of rain on the brim of the top hat, the point of a crooked nose, the whites of shadowed eyes that continued to stare straight at number twenty-three.

The Ripper noticed him only at the last moment. Mayhew saw the face twist with hateful recognition. The Ripper's hand drew from a coat pocket a huge knife—the one that had appeared in his dream. The Ripper raised the knife and lunged at the same instant that Mayhew jumped forward and rammed his wrapped hand into the Ripper's chest. Demming's pistol made four thumping noises, quieter than if he'd knocked on a door. The Ripper stumbled back a step, staring down at himself, then up at the acrid smoke curling out from the coat. Part of his face held onto the evil scowl, but one corner of his mouth turned up as if in a grin. "Just like that," he said. He giggled, then fell over on his side. His head cracked loudly against the cobblestones and the gold watch skittered out on its length of chain, as if trying to escape into the gutter.

Mayhew looked at the body for some time before he realized that he did not see the knife. He started to bend down to search and sensed an odd coldness in his back. Reaching up, he encountered the hilt of the knife projecting acutely above his shoulder. Bracing, he pulled it free. Strange, he thought, that there was no pain. He knew he did not want to be found outside Louise's door like this; he wanted her to come home of her own volition. And she would, he pledged, she would.

The Thames was vague behind the ceaseless drizzle. Each easy pull on the oars made Mayhew grind his teeth. His shirt, under the shiny tarred coat, was soaked in blood. He had grown tired and cold, almost as cold as the burden he carried wound about in his weighted nets. He could see the dull shine of the watch where he had tied it securely to the nets. The Tower Bridge loomed out of the rain like some great broken limb, making Mayhew think of bones rather than iron. He guessed that this was the spot more or less where he had discovered the watch. He shipped the oars and crawled back to the body. Listlessly, he took the gun, the blade, and tossed them over the side. In the coach that had carried him and his "drunken" companion to Lambeth, he had looked over at the face and wondered who the man was, what he had been. Now he no longer cared.

With the last of his energy, he grabbed onto his nets and dragged the body up over the lip of his boat and let it slide gently into the Thames. The ripples of its passing spread out across the water, disrupting all of those from the rain. Finally accepting exhaustion, Mayhew slumped back and closed his eyes, envisioning the two bodies rotting together in the coach on the bottom, the watch and the evil it contained buried in muck for all time. The tide was going out. Mayhew let it take hold of him. Slowly, he drifted beneath the jagged overhang of the bridge, cutting off the rain. He blinked the drops away like tears as the darkness crawled up him.

AN AWARENESS OF ANGELS

Karl Edward Wagner

Beginning his career as a writer of sword and sorcery novels in the tradition of Robert E. Howard's Conan series by creating a similar hero in Kane, the Mystic Swordsman, Karl Edward Wagner (1945–1994) is said to have revitalized the genre by imbuing his character with intelligence and humor—scarce characteristics in most barbarians.

It was common for Kane, one of the most important and memorable antiheroes in fantasy fiction, to encounter supernatural adversaries, leading Wagner eventually to move his career into the horror genre. In addition to being an award-winning author (he won the World Fantasy Award in 1983 for his vampire/reincarnation novella "Beyond Any Measure" and three British Fantasy Awards for his short stories), he was a successful editor who collected (and published) single-author collections of stories by Manly Wade Wellman, Hugh Cave, and E. Hoffmann Price, and edited fifteen volumes of *The Year's Best Horror Stories* (1980–1994).

Wagner was deeply involved with Howard's work, both as an inspiration and as a champion. He edited three volumes of Conan stories, restoring the work to the form in which it was originally published; wrote a full-length pastiche of Conan titled *The Road of Kings* (1979); wrote a novel featuring a different Howard character, Bran Mak Morn, *Legion from the Shadows* (1976); and wrote an unproduced screenplay for *Conan III*.

"An Awareness of Angels" was originally published in *Ripper!*, edited by Gardner Dozois and Susan Casper (New York, Tom Doherty Associates, 1988).

He surrendered so meekly. It was over so quietly. It was anticlimactic.

Sheriff Jimmy Stringer certainly thought so. "Please." And there were tears quavering his voice, but his hand with the .357 was steady. "Please. Just try something. Please try something."

But the killer just stood there placidly in the glare of their lights, blood-smeared surgical gloves raised in surrender.

In the back of his van they could see the peppermint-stripe body of the fourteen-year-old hooker, horribly mutilated and neatly laid out on a shower curtain. Another few minutes, and all would be bundled up tidily—destined shortly thereafter for a shallow grave in some pine-and-scrub wasteland, or perhaps a drop from a bridge with a few cinder blocks for company. Like the other eleven they had so far been able to find.

"Please. Do it," begged Stringer. One of the eleven had been an undercover policewoman, and it had been Stringer's idea. "Come on. Try something."

But already there were uniformed bodies crowding into the light. Handcuffs flashed and clacked, and someone began reading the kid his rights.

"Steady on there, Jimmy. You're not Clint Eastwood." Dr. Nathan Hodgson's grip on his shoulder was casual, but surprisingly strong.

His own hand suddenly shaking, Stringer slowly lowered his Smith & Wesson, gently dropped its hammer, and returned the revolver to the holster at his side. His belt was a notch tighter now, needed one more. He'd lost fifteen of his two hundred pounds during the long investigation, despite a six-pack every night to help him sleep.

More sirens were curdling the night, and camera flashes made grotesque strobe effects with the flashing lights of police and emergency vehicles. They'd already shoved the killer—the suspect—into one of the county cars.

Stringer let out a shuddering breath and faced the forensic psychiatrist. Dr. Hodgson looked too much like a television evangelist for his liking, but Stringer had to admit they'd never have nailed this punk tonight without the shrink's help. *Modus operandi* was about as useful as 20-20 hindsight: Hodgson had been able to study the patterns and to predict where the psycho most likely would strike again. Like hunting a rabbit with beagles: wait till it runs around by you again—then, *bang*.

"Suppose now that we caught this little piece of shit, you'll do your best to prove he's crazy, and all he needs is some tender loving care for a couple months."

Stringer's freckled face was sweaty, and he looked ready to hit someone. "Darn it, Nate! They'll just turn the fucker loose and call him a responsible member of society. Let him kill and kill again!"

Dr. Hodgson showed no offense. "If he's guilty, then he'll pay the penalty. I don't make the laws."

An old excuse, but works every time. Stringer tried to spit, found his mouth too dry. The bright flashes of light hurt his eyes. Like kicking over a long-dead dog on the side of the road. Just a bunch of wriggling lumps, all bustling about a black Chevy van and the vivisected thing in its belly. Lonely piece of two-lane blacktop, an old country road orphaned by the new lake. Old farm fields overrun with cedar and briar and a couple years' growth of pine and sumac. Probably a good place to hunt rabbits. He had half a beer in his car.

"Neither do I," Stringer said heavily. "I just try to enforce them."

Right off the TV reruns, but he was too tired to be clever. He hoped some asshole deputy hadn't used his beercan for an ashtry.

His name was Matthew Norbrook, and he wanted to make a full confession. So they'd only found a dozen? He'd show them where to look for the rest. If he could remember them all. The ones in this end of the state. Would they like to know about the others? Maybe the ones in other states?

Too easy, and they weren't taking chances on blowing this case due to some technicality. The judge ordered a psychiatric examination for the next morning.

Dr. Nathan Hodgson was in charge.

There were four of them in the observation room, watching through the two-way mirror as Dr. Hodgson conducted his examination. Morton Bowers was the court-appointed defense attorney—a gangling black cleanly dressed in an off-the-rack mill outlet suit that didn't really fit him. Cora Steinman was the local D.A., and her businesswoman's power suit fit her very well indeed. Dr. something Gottlieb—Stringer hadn't remembered her first name—was wearing a shapeless white lab coat, and alternated between scribbling notes and fooling with the video recording equipment. Stringer was wearing his uniform for a change—none too neat, and that wasn't a change—partly to show that this was official business, but mainly to remind these people that he was in charge here, at least for now. A further reminder, two of Stringer's deputies were standing just outside in the hallway. In charge for now: the state boys would be crowding in soon, and probably the FBI next.

Stringer sipped on his coffee. It reminded him of watching some bad daytime drama on the big projection TV they had in the bar at the new Trucker's Heaven off I-40—actually their sign read "Haven," but try to tell that to anyone. Stringer wished for a smoke, but they'd all jumped on his case when he'd earlier pulled out a pack. It had all been boring thus far: preliminaries and legal technicalities. Stringer supposed it all served some purpose.

Trouble was, you could be damn sure that the purpose was to make certain this murdering little pervert got off scot-free. Stringer just wished they'd leave him alone in a room with the filthy creep—two-way mirrors or not. He might be pushing fifty, but . . .

"Before we go any farther," Norbrook was saying, "I want it perfectly understood that I consider myself to be entirely sane."

He was wearing orange county jail coveralls—Dr. Hodgson had insisted that they remove the handcuffs—but he still managed the attitude of having kindly granted this interview. His manner was condescending, his speech pedantic to the point of arrogance.

Some bright little college punk, Stringer judged—probably high on drugs most of the time. About thirty, and tall, dark and handsome, just like they say. He'd have no problem picking up girls: Let's climb into my van and snort a little coke. Here, try on this gag while I get out my knives. Stringer knotted his heavy fists and glared at that TV-star nose and smiling mouth of toothpaste-ad teeth.

"Are you sometimes concerned that other people might not think that you are entirely sane?" Dr. Hodgson asked him.

The psychiatrist was wearing a three-piece suit that probably cost more than Stringer's pick-up truck. He was almost twice the age of the suspect—of his patient—but had the distinguished good looks and grey-at-the-temples pompadour that seemed to turn on women from teeny-boppers to golden-agers. Stringer had heard enough gossip to know that Hodgson was sure no fairy, and maybe there was a dent or two in the old Hippocratic oath back up north that had made the doc content to relocate here in a rural southern county.

Norbrook's smile was supercilious. "Please, Dr. . . . Hodgson, is it? We can dispense with the how-do-you-feel-about-that routine. My concern is that the story I propose to tell may at first sound completely mad. That's why I asked for this interview. I had hoped that a psychiatrist might have the intelligence to listen without preconception or ignorant incredulity. All Sheriff Andy of Mayberry and his redneck deputies here seem capable of understanding is a body count, and that rather limits them to their ten fingers."

Stringer dreamed of sharing Norbrook's ten fingers with a sturdy brick. Afterward they'd slip into those surgical gloves just like Jell-O going into a fancy mould.

"This story you want to tell me must seem very important to you," Dr. Hodgson said.

"Important to the entire human race," Norbrook said levelly. "That's why I decided to surrender when I might have escaped through the brush. I didn't want to risk the chance that a bullet would preserve their secrets."

"Their secrets?"

"All right. I'm perfectly aware that you're fully prepared to dismiss everything I'm about to tell you as paranoid fantasy. And I'm perfectly aware that paranoid schizophrenics have no doubt sat here in this same chair and offered this same protest. All I ask is that you listen with an open mind. If I weren't able to furnish proof of what I'm about to tell you, I'd never have permitted myself to be captured. Agreed?"

"Suppose you begin at the beginning."

"It began a hundred years ago. No, to be precise, it began before history—perhaps at the dawn of the human race. But my part of the story begins a century ago in London.

"My great-grandfather was Jack the Ripper."

Norbrook paused to study the effect of his words.

Hodgson listened imperturbably. He never made notes during an interview; it was intrusive, and it was simpler just to play back the tape.

Stringer muttered, "Bullshit!"—and crumpled his coffee cup.

"I suppose," continued Norbrook, "that many people will say that madness is inherited."

"Is that how you sometimes feel?" Hodgson asked.

"My great-grandfather wasn't mad, you see—and that's the crux of it all."

Norbrook settled back in his chair, smiling with the air of an Agatha Christie detective explaining a locked-room murder.

"My great-grandfather—his identity has defied discovery all these years, although I intend to reveal it in good time—was a brilliant experimental surgeon of his day. Because of his research, some would have condemned him as a vivisectionist."

"Can you tell me how all of this was revealed to you?"

"Not through voices no one else can hear," Norbrook snorted. "Please, doctor. Listen and don't interrupt with your obvious ploys. My great-grandfather kept an extensive journal, made careful notes of all of his experiments.

"You see, those prostitutes—those creatures—that he killed. Their deaths were not the random murders of a deranged fiend. On the contrary, they were experimental subjects for my great-grandfather's early researches. The mutilation of their corpses was primarily a smokescreen to disguise the real purpose for their deaths. It was better that the public know him as Jack the Ripper, a murderous sex-fiend, rather than as a dedicated scientist whose researches were destined to expose an unsuspected malignancy as deadly to humanity as any plague bacillus."

Norbrook leaned forward in his chair—his face tense with the enormity of his disclosure.

"You must understand. They aren't *human*."

"Prostitutes, do you mean—or women in general?"

"Damn you! Don't mock me!"

Stringer started to head for the door, but Norbrook remained seated.

"Not all women," he continued. "Not all prostitutes. But *some* of them. And they're more likely by far to be hookers or those one-night-stand easy lays anyone can pick up in singles bars. Liberated women! I'm certain that *they* engineered this so-called sexual revolution."

"They?"

"Yes, *they*. The proverbial *they*. The legendary *they*. They really are in legend, you know."

"I'm not certain if I follow entirely. Could you perhaps . . . ?"

"Who was Adam's first wife?"

"Eve, I suppose."

"*Wrong.*" Norbrook levelled a finger. "It was Lilith, so the legend goes. Lilith—a lamia, a night creature—Adam's mate before the creation of Eve, the first woman. Lilith was the mother of Cain, who slew Abel, the first child born of two human parents. It was the offspring of Lilith that introduced the taint of murder and violence into the blood of mankind."

"Do you consider yourself a Creationist, Mr. Norbrook?"

Norbrook laughed. "Far from it. I'm afraid I'm not your textbook religious nut, Dr. Hodgson. I said we were speaking of legends—but there must be a basis for any legend, a core of truth imperfectly interpreted by the minds of those who have experienced it.

"There's a common thread that runs through legends of all cultures. What were angels really? Why are they generally portrayed as feminine? Why was mankind warned to beware of receiving angels unawares? Why are witches usually seen as women? Why was mankind told not to suffer a witch to live? Why were the saints tormented by visions of sexual lust by demonic temptresses? What is the origin of the succubus—a female demon who copulates with sleeping men?"

"Do you sometimes feel threatened by women?"

"I've already told you. They aren't human."

Norbrook leaned back in his chair and studied the psychiatrist's face. Hodgson's expression was impassively attentive.

"Not *all* women, of course," Norbrook proceeded. "Only a certain small percentage of them. I'm aware of how this must sound to you, but consider this with an open mind.

"Suppose that throughout history a separate intelligent race has existed alongside mankind. Its origin is uncertain: parallel evolution, extraterrestrial, supernatural entities—as you will. What is important is that such a race does exist—a race that is parasitic, inimical, and undetectable. Rather, *was* undetectable until my great-grandfather discovered their existence.

"They are virtually identical to the human female. Almost always they are physically attractive, and always their sexual appetites are insatiable. They become prostitutes not for monetary gain, but out of sexual craving. With today's permissive society, many of them choose instead the role of a hot-to-trot pickup: two beers in a singles bar, and it's off to the ball. Call them fast or easy or nymphos—but they won't be the ones complaining about it on your couch, doctor."

Dr. Hodgson shifted himself in his chair. "Why do you think these women are so sexually promiscuous?"

"The answer is obvious. Their race is self-sterile. Think of them as some sort of hybrid, and you'll understand—a hybrid of human form and alien intelligence. To reproduce they require human sperm, and constant inseminations are required before the right conditions for fertilization are met. It's the same as with other hybrids. Fortunately for us, reproduction is difficult for them, or they'd have reduced humanity to mere breeding stock long ago.

"They use mankind as cuckoos do other birds, placing their eggs in nests of other species to be nurtured at the expense of natural hatchlings. This is the truth behind the numerous legends of changlings—human-appearing infants exchanged in the crib for natural offspring, and the human infant carried away by malevolent elves or fairies. Remember that elves and fairies are more often objects of fear in the older traditions, rather than the cutesy cartoon creatures of today. It's hardly coincidence that elves and fairies are usually thought of as feminine."

"This is a fucking waste of time!" Stringer muttered—then responded: "Beg pardon, ladies," to Dr. Gottlieb's angry "Shh!"

To Stringer's disgust, Dr. Hodgson seemed to be taking it all in. "Why do you think they only take the shape of women?"

"We've considered that," Norbrook said. "Possibly for some reason only the female body is suited for their requirements. Another reason might be a genetic one: only female offspring can be produced."

"When you say 'we' do you sometimes feel that there are others who have these same thoughts as you do?"

"All right, I didn't really expect you to accept what I've told you as fact. I asked you to keep an open mind, and I ask that you continue to do so. I am able to prove what I'm telling you.

"By 'we' I mean my great-grandfather and those of our family who have pursued his original research."

"Could you tell me a little more about what you mean by research?"

"My great-grandfather made his initial discovery quite by accident—literally. A prostitute who had been run over by a carriage was brought into his surgery. She was terribly injured; her pelvis was crushed, and she was unconscious from skull injuries. Her lower abdomen had been laid open, and he worked immediately to try to stop the profuse bleeding there. To his dismay, his patient regained consciousness during the surgery. His assistant hastened to administer more ether, but too late. The woman died screaming under the knife, although considering the extent of her injuries, she could hardly have noticed the scalpel.

"Her uterus had been ruptured, and it was here that my great-grandfather was at work at the moment of her death. His efforts there continued with renewed energy, although by now his surgical exploration was clearly more in the nature of an autopsy. When his assistant set aside the ether and rejoined him, my great-grandfather described a sort of lesion which he characterized as 'an amoeboid pustulance' that had briefly appeared under his blade at the moment of her death agony. The lesion had then vanished in the welter of blood—rather like an oyster slipping from the fork and into the tomato sauce, to use his expression—and subsequent diligent dissection could reveal no trace of it. His assistant had seen nothing, and my great-grandfather was forced to attribute it all to nervous hallucination.

"He might have dismissed the incident, had not he been witness to a railway smash-up while on holiday. Among the first to rush to the aid of the victims, he entered the wreckage of a second-class carriage where a woman lay screaming. Shards of glass had virtually eviscerated her, and as he tried to staunch the bleeding with her petticoats, he again saw a glimpse of a sort of ill-defined purulent mass sliding through the ruin of her perineum just at the instant of her final convulsion. He sought after it, but found no further trace—these were hardly ideal conditions—until other rescuers drew him to the aid of other victims. Later he conducted a careful autopsy of the woman without success. It was then that he learned the victim had been a notorious prostitute.

"Despite my great-grandfather's devotion to medical research, he was a man of firm religious convictions. In deliberating over what he had twice seen, he considered at first that he had witnessed physical evidence of the human soul, liberated in the instant of death. I won't bore you with details of the paths he followed with his initial experiments to establish this theory; they are all recorded in his journals. It soon became evident that this transient mass—this entity—manifested itself only at the moment of violent death.

"Prostitutes seemed natural subjects for his research. They were easily led into clandestine surroundings; they served no good purpose in the world; they were sinful corrupters of virtue—undeserving of mercy. Moreover, that in both cases when he had witnessed the phenomenon the victims had been prostitutes was a circumstance not lost upon my great-grandfather—or Jack the Ripper as he was soon to be known.

"He was unsuccessful in most of his experiments, but he put it down to imprecise technique and the need for haste. Fortunately for him, not all of his subjects were discovered. Mary Ann Nichols was his first near success, then nothing until Catherine Eddowes. With Mary Jane Kelly he had time to perform his task carefully, and afterward he was able to formulate a new theory.

"It wasn't the human soul that he had glimpsed. It was a corporeal manifestation of evil—a possession, if you prefer—living within the flesh of sinful harlots. It was an incarnation of Satan's power taken seed within woman—woman, who brought about mankind's fall from Grace—for the purpose of corrupting innocence through the lure of wanton flesh. This malignant entity became fleetingly visible only at the instant of death through sexual agony—rather like rats fleeing a sinking ship, or vermin deserting a corpse."

Norbrook paused and seemed to want to catch his breath. "I use my great-grandfather's idiom, of course. We've long since abandoned that Victorian frame of reference."

Dr. Hodgson glanced toward the two-way mirror and adjusted his tie. "How did you happen to come into possession of this journal?"

"My great-grandfather feared discovery. As quickly as discretion allowed, he emigrated to the United States. Here, he changed his name and established a small practice in New York. By then he had become more selective with his experimental subjects—and more cautious about the disposal of their remains.

"He was, of course, a married man—Jack the Ripper was, after all, a dedicated researcher and not a deranged misogynist—and his son, my grandfather, grew up to assist him in his experiments. After my great-grandfather's death shortly before the First World War, my grandfather returned to England in order to serve as an army field surgeon in France. The hostilities furnished ample opportunity for his research, as well as a cover for any outrage that may have occurred. Blame it on the Hun.

"It was my grandfather's opinion that the phenomenon was of an ectoplasmic nature, and he attempted to study it as being a sort of electrical force. He married an American nurse at the close of the war and returned to New York, where my father was born. By now, my grandfather's researches had drifted entirely into the realm of spiritualism, and his journals, preserved alongside my great-grandfather's, are worth reading only as curiosa. He died at the height of the Depression—mustard gas had damaged his lungs—discredited by peers and remembered as a harmless crank.

"It was intended that my father should follow the family tradition, as they say. He was working his way through medical school at the time of Pearl Harbour. During his college days, his pro-Nazi sentiments had made him unpopular with some of his class-mates, but like many other Americans he was quick to enlist once bombs and tanks replaced political rhetoric. His B-17 was shot down over France early on, and he spent the remainder of the war in various prison camps. After the fall of Berlin, my father was detained for some time by the Russians, who had liberated the small prison camp where he was assisting in the hospital. There was talk of collaboration and atrocities, but the official story was that the Russians had grabbed him up along with all the other German scientists engaged in research there. My father was a minor Cold War hero when the Russians finally released him.

"He left the Army and resettled in Southern California, where he married my mother and spent his remaining reclusive years on her father's citrus farm. His manner was that of a hunted fugitive, and he had a great fear of strangers—eccentricities the locals attributed to the horrors of German and Russian prison camps. His journals recounting his wartime experiences, fragmentary as they are, show that he had good reason to feel hunted. By the time I was born, a decade after the war, there were rumours of newly declassified documents that linked my father to certain deplorable experiments regarding tests for racial purity—performed under his direction. I'm afraid my father was rather obsessed with the concept of Aryan superiority, and his research was vitiated by this sort of tunnel-vision. It was about the time they got Eichmann when they found him hanging in the orange grove. They ruled it suicide, although there was talk of Nazi-hunters. I know better.

"So did my mother. She sold the farm, bundled me up and left for Oregon. I heard that afterward the whole place was burned to the ground. My mother never told me how much she knew. She hardly had the chance: I ran off to San Francisco early in my teens to join the Haight-Ashbury scene. When I hitched my way home five years later, I found that my mother had been murdered during a burglary. There was insurance money and a trust fund—enough for college and a medical education, though they threw me out after my third year. Her lawyers had a few personal items as well, held in trust for my return. My great-grandfather's Bible didn't interest me, until I untied the cord and found the microfiche of the journals tucked into a hollow within.

"I suppose they got the originals and didn't concern themselves with me. In any event, I covered my tracks, got a formal education. Living on the streets for five years had taught me how to survive. In time I duplicated their experiments, avoided all the blind alleys their preconceptions had led them down, formed conclusions of my own.

"It's amazing just how really easy it is these days to pick up a woman and take her to a place of privacy—and I assure you that they all came willingly. After the first it was obvious that the subjects had to *want* to be fucked. No, kidnapping was counter-productive, although I had to establish a few baselines first. They're all the same wherever you go, and I should know. Over the past few years I've killed them all across the country—a few here, a few there, keep on moving. In all this time I've been able to establish positive proof in about one case out of twenty."

"Proof?"

"Portable VCRs are a wonderful invention. No messy delays with developing film, and if you draw a blank, just record over it on the next experiment. You have to have the camera exactly right: the alien presence—shall we consider it an inhuman ovum?—exudes from the uterus only in the instant of violent death, then dissipates through intracellular spaces within the dead tissue. I've come to the conclusion that this inhuman ovum is a sentient entity on some level, seeking to escape dissolution at the moment of death. Or is it trying to escape detection? I wonder."

"There were videocassettes found in your van."

"Useless tapes. I've put the essential tapes in a safe place along with the microfiches."

"A safe place?"

"I've already told my attorney how to find them. The judge tried to appoint a woman attorney to defend me, you know, but I saw the danger there."

"You say you allowed yourself to be captured. Wasn't some part of you frightened?"

"I have the proof to expose them. My forebears lacked the courage of their misguided convictions. Personal safety aside, I feel that I have a duty to the human race."

"Do you see yourself as handing this trust on to your son?"

"I have no children, if that's what you mean. Knowing what I do, I find the idea of inseminating any woman totally abhorrent."

"Tell what you remember most about your mother?"

Norbrook stood up abruptly. "I said no psychiatric games, Dr. Hodgson. I've told you all I need to in order to establish my sanity and motives. That's all a part of legal and medical record now. I think this interview is terminated."

The door opened as Norbrook arose. He turned, with cold dignity permitted the deputies to cuff his wrists.

Stringer stopped the psychiatrist as he followed the others into the hallway. The sheriff scowled after Norbrook, as his deputies led him away to the car.

"Well, Doc—what do you think?"

"You heard it all, didn't you?"

Stringer dug out a cigarette. "Craziest line of bullshit I ever listened to. Guess he figures he can plead insanity if he makes up a load of crap like that."

Dr. Hodgson shook his head. "Oh, Matthew Norbrook's insane—no doubt about it. He's a classic paranoid schizophrenic: well-ordered delusional system, grandiosity, feelings of superiority, sense of being persecuted, belief that his actions are done in the name of a higher purpose. On an insanity scale of one to three, I'd have to rate him as four-plus. He'll easily be found innocent by reason of insanity."

"Damn!" Stringer muttered, watching Norbrook enter the elevator.

"The good news, at least from the patient's point of view," Hodgson went on, "is that paranoid schizophrenia so easily responds to treatment. Why, with the right medication and some expert counseling, Matthew Norbrook will probably be out of the hospital and living a normal life in less than a year."

Stringer's hand shook as he drew on the cigarette. "It isn't *justice*, Nate!"

"Perhaps not, Jimmy, but it's the way the law works. And look at it this way— the dead don't care whether their murderer is executed or cured. Norbrook may yet live to make a valuable contribution to society. Give me one of those, will you?"

Stringer hadn't known the doctor smoked. "The dead don't care," he repeated.

"Thanks, Jimmy." Hodgson shook out a Marlboro. "I know how you must feel. I saw a little of what was on that one videocassette—the one where he tortured that poor policewoman, Sherri Wilson. Hard to believe she could have remained conscious through it all. Guess it was the cocaine he used on her. Must have really been tough on you, since you talked her into posing as a hooker to try to trap him. It's understandable that you're feeling a lot of guilt about it. If you'd like to come around and talk about it sometime . . ."

Hodgson was handing back the cigarettes, but already Stringer had turned his back and walked off without another word.

Cora Steinman, the district attorney, stepped out from the doorway of the observation room. She watched the elevator doors close behind Stringer.

"I hope you know what you're doing," she said finally.

Dr. Hodgson crushed his unsmoked cigarette into the sand of a hallway ashcan. "I know my man."

From the parking lot, the report of the short-barreled .357 echoed like cannon-fire against the clinic walls.

"Morton, you've taken care of the journals?" Hodgson asked.

The black defense attorney collected his briefcase. "I took care of *everything*. His collection of evidence is now a couple books on Jack the Ripper, a bunch of S&M porno, and a couple snuff films."

"Then it's just a matter of the tape from the interview."

"I think there's been a malfunction in the equipment," Dr. Gottlieb decided.

"It pays to be thorough," Steinman observed.

A deputy flung open the stairway door. He was out of breath. "Norbrook tried to escape. Had a knife hidden on him. Jimmy had to shoot."

"I'll get the emergency tray!" Dr. Hodgson said quickly.

"Hell, Doc." The deputy paused for another breath. "Just get a hose. Most of the sucker's head is spread across your parking lot."

"I'll get the tray anyway," Hodgson told him.

He said to the others as the deputy left: "Must keep up appearances."

"Why," Steinman wondered, as they walked together toward the elevator, "why do you suppose he was so convinced that we only exist as females?"

Dr. Hodgson shrugged. "Just a male chauvinist *human*."

A MOST UNUSUAL MURDER

Robert Bloch

Robert Albert Bloch (1917–1994) began his writing career in the horror genre, being heavily influenced by H. P. Lovecraft. It was with the story "Yours Truly, Jack the Ripper" (1943) that his own style is first in evidence, combining terror, murder, and violence with humor. During his long and extremely prolific career, he continued to write tales of terror and dark fantasy, but he also became drawn to the mystery and suspense genre, most famously with *Psycho* (1959).

In addition to three short stories, a novel, and a teleplay about Jack the Ripper, Bloch frequently wrote about other serial killers much like Red Jack but set in contemporary times. His first novel, *The Scarf* (1947), featured the first-person account of a multiple murderer, and most of his subsequent novels, as well as many of his more than four hundred short stories, were devoted to examinations of violence in society, generally in the form of a single individual who wreaks atrocities on others. Other novels that illustrate that compelling scenario include *Spiderweb* (1954), *The Kidnaper* (1954), *The Will to Kill* (1954), *Shooting Star* (1958), *The Dead Beat* (1960), *Firebug* (1961), *The Couch* (1962), *Terror* (1962), and *The Night of the Ripper* (1984). When Bloch reread *The Scarf*, his first novel, twenty years later, he was astonished at how much the perception of his protagonist had changed: "I wrote him as a villain—today he emerges as an antihero."

"A Most Unusual Murder" was first published in the March 1976 issue of *Ellery Queen's Mystery Magazine*; it was first collected in *Out of the Mouths of Graves* (New York, Mysterious Press, 1979).

> *It all started outside an especially curious curiosity shop in London's Saxe-Coburg Square . . . and ended in a shabby lodging at 17 Dorcas Lane, the two friends drawn there by a famous mystery and themselves becoming part of the terrible legend . . .*

Only the dead know Brooklyn.

Thomas Wolfe said that, and he's dead now, so he ought to know.

London, of course, is a different story.

At least that's the way Hilary Kane thought of it. Not as a story, perhaps, but rather as an old-fashioned, outsize picaresque novel in which every street was a chapter crammed with characters and incidents of its own. Each block a page, each structure a separate paragraph unto itself within the sprawling, tangled plot—such was Hilary Kane's concept of the city, and he knew it well.

Over the years he strolled the pavements, reading the city sentence by sentence until every line was familiar; he'd learned London by heart.

And that's why he was so startled when, one bleak afternoon late in November, he discovered the shop in Saxe-Coburg Square.

"I'll be damned!" he said.

"Probably." Lester Woods, his companion, took the edge off the affirmation with an indulgent smile. "What's the problem?"

"This." Kane gestured toward the tiny window of the establishment nestled inconspicuously between two residential relics of Victoria's day.

"An antique place." Woods nodded. "At the rate they're springing up there must be at least one for every tourist in London."

"But not here." Kane frowned. "I happen to have come by this way less than a week ago, and I'd swear there was no shop in the Square."

"Then it must have opened since." The two men moved up to the entrance, glancing through the display window in passing.

Kane's frown deepened. "You call this new? Look at the dust on those goblets."

"Playing detective again, eh?" Woods shook his head. "Trouble with you, Hilary, is that you have too many hobbies." He glanced across the Square as a chill wind heralded the coming of twilight. "Getting late—we'd better move along."

"Not until I find out about this."

Kane was already opening the door and Woods sighed. "The game is afoot, I suppose. All right, let's get it over with."

The shop-bell tinkled and the two men stepped inside. The door closed, the tinkling stopped, and they stood in the shadows and the silence.

But one of the shadows was not silent. It rose from behind the single counter in the small space before the rear wall.

"Good afternoon, gentlemen," said the shadow. And switched on an overhead light. It cast a dim nimbus over the countertop and gave dimension to the shadow, revealing the substance of a diminutive figure with an unremarkable face beneath a balding brow.

Kane addressed the proprietor. "Mind if we have a look?"

"Is there any special area of interest?" The proprietor gestured toward the shelves lining the wall behind them. "Books, maps, china, crystal?"

"Not really," Kane said. "It's just that I'm always curious about a new shop of this sort—"

The proprietor shook his head. "Begging your pardon, but it's hardly new."

Woods glanced at his friend with a barely suppressed smile, but Kane ignored him.

"Odd," Kane said. "I've never noticed this place before."

"Quite so. I've been in business a good many years, but this *is* a new location."

Now it was Kane's turn to glance quickly at Woods, and his smile was not suppressed. But Woods was already eyeing the artifacts on display, and after a moment Kane began his own inspection.

Peering at the shelving beneath the glass counter, he made a rapid inventory. He noted a boudoir lamp with a beaded fringe, a lavaliere, a tray of pearly buttons, a durbar souvenir programme, and a framed and inscribed photograph of Matilda Alice Victoria Wood *aka* Bella Delmare *aka* Marie Lloyd. There was a miscellany of old jewelry, hunting-watches, pewter mugs, napkin rings, a toy bank in the shape of a miniature Crystal Palace, and a display poster of a formidably mustachioed Lord Kitchener with his gloved finger extended in a gesture of imperious command.

It was, he decided, the mixture as before. Nothing unusual, and most of it—like the Kitchener poster—not even properly antique but merely outmoded. Those fans on the bottom shelf, for example, and the silk toppers, the opera glasses, the black bag in the far corner covered with what was once called "American cloth."

Something about the phrase caused Kane to stoop and make a closer inspection. *American cloth.* Dusty now, but once shiny, like the tarnished silver nameplate identifying its owner. He read the inscription.

J. Ridley, M.D.

Kane looked up, striving to conceal his sudden surge of excitement.

Impossible! It couldn't be—and yet it was. Keeping his voice and gesture carefully casual, he indicated the bag to the proprietor.

"A medical kit?"

"Yes, I imagine so."

"Might I ask where you acquired it?"

The little man shrugged. "Hard to remember. In this line one picks up the odd item here and there over the years."

"Might I have a look at it, please?"

The elderly proprietor lifted the bag to the countertop. Woods stared at it, puzzled, but Kane ignored him, his gaze intent on the nameplate below the lock. "Would you mind opening it?" he said.

"I'm afraid I don't have a key."

Kane reached out and pressed the lock; it was rusted, but firmly fixed. Frowning, he lifted the bag and shook it gently.

Something jiggled inside, and as he heard the click of metal against metal his elation peaked. Somehow he suppressed it as he spoke.

"How much are you asking?"

The proprietor was equally emotionless. "Not for sale."

"But—"

"Sorry, sir. It's against my policy to dispose of blind items. And since there's no telling what's inside—"

"Look, it's only an old medical bag. I hardly imagine it contains the Crown jewels."

In the background Woods snickered, but the proprietor ignored him. "Granted," he said. "But one can't be certain of the contents." Now the little man lifted the bag and once again there was a clicking sound. "Coins, perhaps."

"Probably just surgical instruments," Kane said impatiently. "Why don't you force the lock and settle the matter?"

"Oh, I couldn't do that. It would destroy its value."

"What value?" Kane's guard was down now; he knew he'd made a tactical error but he couldn't help himself.

The proprietor smiled. "I told you the bag is not for sale."

"Everything has its price."

Kane's statement was a challenge, and the proprietor's smile broadened as he met it. "One hundred pounds."

"A hundred pounds for *that*?" Woods grinned—then gaped at Kane's response.

"Done and done."

"But, sir—"

For answer Kane drew out his wallet and extracted five twenty-pound notes. Placing them on the countertop, he lifted the bag and moved toward the door. Woods followed hastily, turning to close the door behind him.

The proprietor gestured. "Wait—come back—"

But Kane was already hurrying down the street, clutching the black bag under his arm.

He was still clutching it half an hour later as Woods moved with him into the spacious study of Kane's flat overlooking the verdant vista of Cadogan Square. Dappled splotches of sunlight reflected from the gleaming oilcloth as Kane set the bag on the table and wiped away the dust. He smiled at Woods.

"Looks a bit better now, don't you think?"

"I don't think anything." Woods shook his head. "A hundred pounds for an old medical kit—"

"A *very* old medical kit," said Kane. "Dates back to the Eighties, if I'm not mistaken."

"Even so, I hardly see—"

"Of course you wouldn't! I doubt if anyone besides myself would attach much significance to the name of J. Ridley, M.D."

"Never heard of him."

"That's understandable." Kane smiled. "He preferred to call himself Jack the Ripper."

"Jack the Ripper?"

"Surely you know the case. Whitechapel, 1888—the savage slaying and mutilation of prostitutes by a cunning mass-murderer who taunted the police—a shadow, stalking his prey in the streets."

Woods frowned. "But he was never caught, was he? Not even identified."

"In that you're mistaken. No murderer has been identified quite as frequently as Red Jack. At the time of the crimes and over the years since, a score of suspects were named. A prime candidate was the Pole, Klosowski, alias George Chapman, who killed several wives—but poison was his method and gain his motive, whereas the Ripper's victims were all penniless prostitutes who died under the knife. Another convicted murderer, Neill Cream, even openly proclaimed he was the Ripper—"

"Wouldn't that be the answer, then?"

Kane shrugged. "Unfortunately, Cream happened to be in America at the time of the Ripper murders. Egomania prompted his false confession." He shook his head. "Then there was John Pizer, a bookbinder known by the nickname of 'Leather Apron'—he was actually arrested, but quickly cleared and released. Some think the killings were the work of a Russian called Konovalov who also went by the name of Pedachenko and worked as a barber's surgeon; supposedly he was a Tsarist secret agent who perpetrated the slayings to discredit the British police."

"Sounds pretty far-fetched if you ask me."

"Exactly." Kane smiled. "But there are other candidates, equally improbable. Montague John Druitt for one, a barrister of unsound mind who drowned himself in the Thames shortly after the last Ripper murder. Unfortunately, it has been established that he was living in Bournemouth, and on the days before and after the final slaying he was there, playing cricket. Then there was the Duke of Clarence—"

"Who?"

"Queen Victoria's grandson in direct line of succession to the throne."

"Surely you're not serious?"

"No, but others are. It has been asserted that Clarence was a known deviate who suffered from insanity as the result of venereal infection, and that his death in 1892 was actually due to the ravages of his disease."

"But that doesn't prove him to be the Ripper."

"Quite so. It hardly seems possible that he could write the letters filled with American slang and crude errors in grammar and spelling which the Ripper sent to the authorities; letters containing information which could be known only by the murderer and the police. More to the point, Clarence was in Scotland at the time of one of the killings and at Sandringham when others took place. And there are equally firm reasons for exonerating suggested suspects close to him—his friend James Stephen and his physician, Sir William Gull."

"You've really studied up on this," Woods murmured. "I'd no idea you were so keen on it."

"And for good reason. I wasn't about to make a fool of myself by advancing an untenable notion. I don't believe the Ripper was a seaman, as some surmise, for there's not a scintilla of evidence to back the theory. Nor do I think the Ripper was a slaughterhouse worker, a midwife, a man disguised as a woman, or a London bobby. And I doubt the very existence of a mysterious physician named Dr. Stanley, out to avenge himself against the woman who had infected him, or his son."

"But there do seem to be a great number of medical men amongst the suspects," Woods said.

"Right you are, and for good reason. Consider the nature of the crimes— the swift and skillful removal of vital organs, accomplished in the darkness of the streets under constant danger of imminent discovery. All this implies the discipline of someone versed in anatomy, someone with the cool nerves of a practising surgeon. Then too there's the matter of escaping detection. The Ripper obviously knew the alleys and byways of the East End so thoroughly that he could slip through police cordons and patrols without discovery. But if seen, who would have a better alibi than a respectable physician, carrying a medical bag on an emergency call late at night?

"With that in mind, I set about my search, examining the rolls of London Hospital in Whitechapel Road. I went over the names of physicians and surgeons listed in the Medical Registry for that period."

"All of them?"

"It wasn't necessary. I knew what I was looking for—a surgeon who lived and practised in the immediate Whitechapel area. Whenever possible, I followed up with a further investigation of my suspects' histories—researching hospital and clinic affiliations, even hobbies and background activities from medical journals, press reports, and family records. Of course, all this takes a great deal of time and patience. I must have been tilting at this windmill for a good five years before I found my man."

Woods glanced at the nameplate on the bag. "J. Ridley, M.D.?"

"John Ridley. *Jack,* to his friends—if he had any." Kane paused, thoughtful. "But that's just the point. Ridley appears to have had no friends, and no family. An orphan, he received his degree from Edinburgh in 1878, ten years before the date of the murders. He set up private practise here in London, but there is no office address listed. Nor is there any further information to be found concerning him; it's as though he took particular care to suppress every detail of his personal and private life. This, of course, is what roused my suspicions. For an entire decade J. Ridley lived and practised in the East End without a single mention of his name anywhere in print, except for his Registry listing. And after 1888, even *that* disappeared."

"Suppose he died?"

"There's no obituary on record."

Woods shrugged. "Perhaps he moved, emigrated, took sick, abandoned practise?"

"Then why the secrecy? Why conceal his whereabouts? Don't you see—it's the very lack of such ordinary details which leads me to suspect the extraordinary."

"But that's not evidence. There's no proof that your Dr. Ridley was the Ripper."

"That's why this is so important." Kane indicated the bag on the tabletop. "If we knew its history, where it came from—"

As he spoke, Kane reached down and picked up a brass letter-opener from the table, then moved to the bag.

"Wait." Woods put a restraining hand on Kane's shoulder. "That may not be necessary."

"What do you mean?"

"I think the shopkeeper was lying. He knew what the bag contains—he had to, or else why did he fix such a ridiculous price? He never dreamed you'd take him up on it, of course. But there's no need for you to force the lock any more than there was for him to do so. My guess is that he has a key."

"You're right." Kane set the letter-opener down. "I should have realized, if I'd taken the time to consider his reluctance. He must have the key." He lifted the shiny bag and turned. "Come along—let's get back to him before the shop closes. And this time we won't be put off by any excuses."

Dusk had descended as Kane and his companion hastened through the streets, and darkness was creeping across the deserted silence of Saxe-Coburg Square when they arrived.

They halted then, staring into the shadows, seeking the spot where the shop nestled between the residences looming on either side. The shadows were deeper here and they moved closer, only to stare again at the empty gap between the two buildings.

The shop was gone.

Woods blinked, then turned and gestured to Kane. "But we were here—we saw it—"

Kane didn't reply. He was staring at the dusty, rubble-strewn surface of the space between the structures; at the weeds which sprouted from the bare ground beneath. A chill night wind echoed through the emptiness. Kane stooped and sifted a pinch of dust between his fingers. The dust was cold, like the wind that whirled the fine grains from his hand and blew them away into the darkness.

"What happened?" Woods was murmuring. "Could we both have dreamed—"

Kane stood erect, facing his friend. "This isn't a dream," he said, gripping the black bag.

"Then what's the answer?"

"I don't know." Kane frowned thoughtfully. "But there's only one place where we can possibly find it."

"Where?"

"The 1888 Medical Registry lists the address of John Ridley as Number 17 Dorcas Lane."

The cab which brought them to Dorcas Lane could not enter its narrow accessway. The dim alley beyond was silent and empty, but Kane plunged into it without hesitation, moving along the dark passage between solid rows of grimy brick. Treading over the cobblestone, it seemed to Woods that he was being led into another era, yet Kane's progress was swift and unfaltering.

"You've been here before?" Woods said.

"Of course." Kane halted before the unlighted entrance to Number 17, then knocked.

The door opened—not fully, but just enough to permit the figure behind it to peer out at them. Both glance and greeting were guarded.

"Whatcher want?"

Kane stepped into the fan of light from the partial opening. "Good evening. Remember me?"

"Yes." The door opened wider and Woods could see the squat shadow of the middle-aged woman who nodded up at his companion. "Yer the one what rented the back vacancy last Bank 'oliday, ain'tcher?"

"Right. I was wondering if I might have it again."

"I dunno." The woman glanced at Woods.

"Only for a few hours." Kane reached for his wallet. "My friend and I have a business matter to discuss."

"Business, eh?" Woods felt the unflattering appraisal of the landlady's beady eyes. "Cost you a fiver."

"Here you are."

A hand extended to grasp the note. Then the door opened fully, revealing the dingy hall and the stairs beyond.

"Mind the steps now," the landlady said.

The stairs were steep and the woman was puffing as they reached the upper landing. She led them along the creaking corridor to the door at the rear, fumbling for the keys in her apron.

"'Ere we are."

The door opened on musty darkness, scarcely dispelled by the faint illumination of the overhead fixture as she switched it on. The landlady nodded at Kane. "I don't rent this for lodgings no more—it ain't properly made up."

"Quite all right." Kane smiled, his hand on the door.

"If there's anything you'll be needing, best tell me now. I've got to run over to the neighbor for a bit—she's been took ill."

"I'm sure we'll manage." Kane closed the door, then listened for a moment as the landlady's footsteps receded down the hall.

"Well," he said. "What do you think?"

Woods surveyed the shabby room with its single window framed by yellowing curtains. He noted the faded carpet with its pattern well nigh worn away, the marred and chipped surfaces of the massive old bureau and heavy morris-chair, the brass bed covered with a much-mended spread, the ancient gas-log in the fireplace framed by a cracked marble mantelpiece, and the equally-cracked washstand fixture in the corner.

"I think you're out of your mind," Woods said. "Did I understand correctly that you've been here before?"

"Exactly. I came several months ago, as soon as I found the address in the Registry. I wanted a look around."

Woods wrinkled his nose. "More to smell than there is to see."

"Use your imagination, man! Doesn't it mean anything to you that you're in the very room once occupied by Jack the Ripper?"

Woods shook his head. "There must be a dozen rooms to let in this old barn. What makes you think this is the right one?"

"The Registry entry specified 'rear.' And there are no rear accommodations downstairs—that's where the kitchen is located. So this had to be the place."

Kane gestured. "Think of it—you may be looking at the very sink where the Ripper washed away the traces of his butchery, the bed in which he slept after his dark deeds were performed! Who knows what sights this room has seen and heard—the voice crying out in a tormented nightmare—"

"Come off it, Hilary!" Woods grimaced impatiently. "It's one thing to use your imagination, but quite another to let your imagination use you."

"Look." Kane pointed to the far corner of the room. "Do you see those indentations in the carpet? I noticed them when I examined this room on my previous visit. What do they suggest to you?"

Woods peered dutifully at the worn surface of the carpet, noting the four round, evenly spaced marks. "Must have been another piece of furniture in that corner. Something heavy, I'd say."

"But what sort of furniture?"

"Well—" Woods considered. "Judging from the space, it wasn't a sofa or chair. Could have been a cabinet, perhaps a large desk—"

"Exactly. A rolltop desk. Every doctor had one in those days." Kane sighed. "I'd give a pretty penny to know what became of that item. It might have held the answer to all our questions."

"After all these years? Not bloody likely." Woods glanced away. "Didn't find anything else, did you?"

"I'm afraid not. As you say, it's been a long time since the Ripper stayed here."

"I didn't say that." Woods shook his head. "You may be right about the desk. And no doubt the Medical Registry gives a correct address. But all it means is that this room may once have been rented by a Dr. John Ridley. You've already inspected it once—why bother to come back?"

"Because now I have this." Kane placed the black bag on the bed. "And this." He produced a pocket-knife.

"You intend to force the lock after all?"

"In the absence of a key I have no alternative." Kane wedged the blade under the metal guard and began to pry upwards. "It's important that the bag be opened here. Something it contains may very well be associated with this room. If we recognize the connection we might have an additional clue, a conclusive link—"

The lock snapped.

As the bag sprang open, the two men stared down at its contents—the jumble of vials and pillboxes, the clumsy old-style stethoscope, the probes and tweezers, the roll of gauze. And, resting atop it, the scalpel with the steel-tipped surface encrusted with brownish stains.

They were still staring as the door opened quietly behind them and the balding, elderly little man entered the room.

"I see my guess is correct, gentlemen. You too have read the Medical Registry." He nodded. "I was hoping I'd find you here."

Kane frowned. "What do you want?"

"I'm afraid I must trouble you for my bag."

"But it's my property now—I bought it."

The little man sighed. "Yes, and I was a fool to permit it. I thought putting on that price would dissuade you. How was I to know you were a collector like myself?"

"Collector?"

"Of curiosa pertaining to murder." The little man smiled. "A pity you cannot see some of the memorabilia I've acquired. Not the commonplace items associated with your so-called Black Museum in Scotland Yard, but true rarities with historical significance." He gestured. "The silver jar in which the notorious French sorceress, La Voisin, kept her poisonous ointments, the actual dirks which dispatched the unfortunate nephews of Richard III in the Tower—yes, even the poker responsible for the atrocious demise of Edward II at Berkeley Castle on the night of September 21st, 1327. I had quite a bit of trouble locating it until I realized the date was reckoned according to the old Julian calendar."

Kane frowned impatiently. "Who are you? What happened to that shop of yours?"

"My name would mean nothing to you. As for the shop, let us say that it exists spatially and temporally as I do—when and where necessary for my purposes. By your current and limited understanding, you might call it a sort of time-machine."

Woods shook his head. "You're not making sense."

"Ah, but I am, and very good sense too. How else do you think I could pursue my interests so successfully unless I were free to travel in time? It is my particular pleasure to return to certain eras in this primitive past of yours, visiting the scenes of famous and infamous crimes and locating trophies for my collection.

"The shop, of course, is just something I used as a blind for this particular mission. It's gone now, and I shall be going too, just as soon as I retrieve my property. It happens to be the souvenir of a most unusual murder."

"You see?" Kane nodded at Woods. "I told you this bag belonged to the Ripper!"

"Not so," said the little man. "I already have the Ripper's murder weapon, which I retrieved directly after the slaying of his final victim on November 9th, 1888. And I can assure you that your Dr. Ridley was not Jack the Ripper but merely and simply an eccentric surgeon—" As he spoke, he edged toward the bed.

"No you don't!" Kane turned to intercept him, but he was already reaching for the bag. "Let go of that!" Kane shouted.

The little man tried to pull away, but Kane's hand swooped down frantically into the open bag and clawed. Then it rose, gripping the scalpel.

The little man yanked the bag away. Clutching it, he retreated as Kane bore down upon him furiously.

"Stop!" Woods cried. Hurling himself forward, he stepped between the two men, directly into the orbit of the descending blade.

There was a gurgle, then a thud, as he fell.

The scalpel clattered to the floor, slipping from Kane's nerveless fingers and coming to rest in the spreading crimson stain.

The little man stooped and picked up the scalpel. "Thank you," he said softly. "You have given me what I came for." He dropped the weapon into the bag.

Then he shimmered. Shimmered—and disappeared.

But Woods's body didn't disappear. Kane stared down at it—at the throat ripped open from ear to ear.

He was still staring when they came and took him away.

The trial, of course, was a sensation. It wasn't so much the crazy story Kane told as the fact that nobody could ever find the fatal weapon.

It was a most unusual murder . . .

JACK THE RIPPER IN HELL

Stephen Hunter

A perennial presence on the bestseller list, Stephen Hunter (1946–) has enjoyed enormous success with his contemporary thrillers, beginning with *The Master Sniper* (1980) and continuing for an additional twenty novels. Several of his most popular books feature Bob "the Nailer" Swagger, a Marine sniper given the sobriquet for his extraordinary skill with a rifle. There are nine books in the Bob Lee Swagger series, beginning with *Point of Impact* (1993), on which the 2007 film *Shooter* was based, with Mark Wahlberg in the starring role.

While producing a string of bestselling novels, Hunter also worked as the film critic for *The Baltimore Sun* and *The Washington Post,* winning a Pulitzer Prize for criticism in 2003.

Against the wishes of his agent, editor, and publisher, Hunter abandoned his trademark action-based thrillers in 2015 with a period novel, *I, Ripper,* which also went to the top of bestseller lists. It is a tour de force in which the gas-lit Victorian era is convincingly evoked in chapters that alternate between pages from Jack the Ripper's diary and the memoirs of a cocky young journalist whose fame and fortune rest on his coverage of the East End atrocities for the *Star,* an ambitious little afternoon newspaper competing with fifty others for the attention of a public ravenous for news of the vicious killer.

The editor of *I, Ripper* decided that one chapter of the manuscript was inappropriate for inclusion in the novel. Although there is a great deal of wit and humor in the dialogue of the book, it is a suspense novel, and the consensus appears to have been that the out-and-out humor of "Jack the Ripper in Hell" carried with it the wrong tone. It appears here for the first time.

I found myself, rather suddenly, at the front door of a great hall of the sort that dominates and has dominated the English countryside for hundreds of years. This was itself an astonishment; as a skeptic of long-standing, I had expected nothing but nothingness and more nothingness, an eternity of nothingness. It sounded rather keen, actually. But no, there I was, before this large house.

It had lots of windows, gables, walls, chimneys, bushes, gardens, nooks, crannies, stables, ponds, crests, crowns, the usual muckety-muck that the tiny percentage of druids, dwarves, and fools bred to rule have always occupied. Forthwith, the imposing door was opened by a snooty footman in livery, from his slippers to his pouffy periwinkle, complete-to-obviously-insincere beauty mark upon his powdered face, his splendid red-silk tunic over ruffles and flourishes, his tight pantaloons, his white silk stockings and his buckled slippers. He was a bit fat, however, and his gracefulness was somewhat undercut by the ample size of his ass.

"Hell?" I inquired.

"Indeed," he said. "You are expected."

"Why, of course I am!" I replied.

He led me through the great house and of course it was lit by candle, not gas, its rooms were spacious, if jammed with bric-a-brac, damask hangings depicting long-forgotten hunting triumphs, dead animal heads from same, intricate furniture with much refined carving upon it, wood chiseled to flower and beast and texture of great ingenuity, and everywhere porcelain figurines of dubious taste. Far be it from me to criticize hell, but most country houses are assembled with better wit. They needed to redecorate the place!

In several rooms, it appeared that formal balls were being held. In one, I saw, sweating profusely, the emperor Napoleon dancing an Irish jig. I waited for the music to stop but it never did and he danced and danced, though his face radiated embarrassment and discomfort.

"He got his," I said to the servant, who was too imperious to notice me.

We climbed a grand stairway, went through a room where a man I believe to be Attila the Hun, or possibly Genghis Khan, was attempting to needlepoint a lovely thrush onto a stiff cloth brace but couldn't quite get the hang of it, much to the chagrin of his instructress, a small, sanctimonious English lass of about eight.

"You are not paying attention," she rebuked him sternly. "It's five *then* three."

He too was getting his, unto eternity, and I could read the suffering from his tragic eyes.

Finally, I found myself in what I took to be the Head Man's office. He was there, too, though not what I expected. This being eternally 1755 or whatever, horns and tails and blazing red faces were definitely recherché. Instead our Dear Boss sat daintily cross-legged at his desk, behind a feather quill, attending to paperwork in great swirly penmanship, itself a specimen of ruffles and flourishes. He, too, had a periwinkle (perhaps hiding the stubs of horns?), a blue silk tunic over the usual frothy folds, powder on his face (hiding the red complexion, it being hell and all) with a completely ridiculous beauty mark. Everywhere that there wasn't blue silk there was white lace. He eventually laid down his quill, and took a snuff break, forcing some appalling brown and sugary substance up his left nostril. He had a nice sneeze, very satisfying, and then turned to face me.

"Dr. Ripper, I presume?"

"That is I, sir. And you are He, of many names but eternal malice, are you not?"

"I am indeed, sir."

"Interesting place you have here," I said. "I thought it would be more sulfurous fires and screaming as hot irons were applied."

"That's all in the cellar. We can arrange it for you, if you are so interested."

"If there are other options, perhaps we should discuss them."

"That is the point. I like to chat with new boys and discuss what lies ahead. It's just better that way, I've found."

"I think it's quite responsible of you," I said.

"One tries," he said.

At this point, he reached inside his tunic and emerged with a pince-nez which he wedged onto the bridge of his nose. He turned, retrieved the document upon which he had been laboring, and seemed to read its truth.

"Five, I see," he said. "Rather brutally, too, I'm afraid. I do so hate messes."

"If you examine carefully," I said, "you'll note that the so-called 'messiness' was all achieved post-mortem. It looked far worse than it was. Only one, which I deeply regret, suffered, when strangulation became necessary. Mistakes do happen. For the others it was a swift blur, perhaps a sting or pinch, and then they went away. In all cases, wherever they ended up, it was a better place than they'd been."

"Allowing that you speak the truth as you see it, I must point out that that is your diagnosis of the situation. They, and I have discussed this with them quite thoroughly, none of them had any eagerness to leave the place they were. It was not the best place, to be sure, and none were 'happy' in the way that a wealthy young woman with a brilliant fiancé and an unlimited wardrobe budget might be happy, but none was so at ends that she would have chosen death over life."

"Well said. However, by my way of thinking it was necessary to achieve certain ends which were of paramount importance to me. I weighed their needs against mine and found my case more convincing. Banal, sir, I am sure, but banality is the commonplace of murder, is it not?"

"Quite so. The dreary tales I hear of why so and so had the absolute right to tup so and so. It's the worst part of the job, but one must do what one must do."

"I hope that you appreciate that. I will not stoop to the argument that they did not matter. Of course they mattered, to self and loved ones and, in the abstract, to the conventions of society which cannot formally accept the insignificance of any individual, even if every battle, flood, fire and shipwreck proves how meaningless the individual is. Thus, considered objectively, it's hard to argue that my crimes in any way but the formally legalistic would be considered a sin. Am I not right in suspecting your interest here is sin, not legal finding?"

"You are, sir, indeed. My profession is sin, my expertise is sin."

"Then again, allow me another tangent."

"Please continue."

"You have people here who have killed in the millions. I didn't see him but I guess Tamerlane is here."

"He is. Downstairs. We don't like to show new boys what we had to do with that chap. Quite horrifying. Involves broken glass on an endless stairway to heaven. He bleeds out, screaming, then awakens to do it all over again. Forever. Oh, well, it was his choice."

"And Alexander the Great."

"The cities *that* one put to sword. Appalling. Hundreds of thousands, all totally innocent. He's on a cross. If it was good enough for my friend Jesus, it's good enough for him."

"My point exactly. So far beyond me."

"Yes, but you, sir, are self-aware. Tamerlane and Alexander never thought they were sinning. You knew you were sinning. So in a certain way, your five weigh more heavily than their millions."

"I take your point. However, sir, it does seem to me that simply sticking me on a skewer and rotating me over coals for a million years is rather beneath you. It is clear from your surroundings that you are a man of taste and discrimination. I might have done with fewer porcelain collies, but that's another issue altogether. Surely you have subtler stratagems in mind for so bold and profligate a brute as me than the old up-the-arse and onto-the-fire routine. I would be so disappointed."

"You flatter me, sir, and, alas, it is true that one aspect of hell the various religious fellows have never quite comprehended is the importance of flattery. I, after all, invented flattery. It is one of the most basic of sins, and the one sure road to my cellar, more specifically the skewer/flambe wing of the cellar."

"That is justice," I said.

"But flattery applied to me, as is yours? I do so enjoy it! Oh, yes, goody goody! Most are too terrified. They beg and mewl. It's so unfortunate and it does them no good at all. I find your sangfroid truly amusing, to repay flattery with flattery. Jack knew his knife but when it came time to pay up, he could try to outtalk *der teufel selbst.*"

"I have always been the chatty sort, sir. I have a gift for jibber-jabber."

He leaned back. "This is the fun part of the job. Coming up with just the right thing for a true bad boy."

"Napoleon doing a million years of jigs was quite a stroke, if I may say so."

"Yes, I rather thought so. Now . . . What for Jack? Hmm, your vanities would seem to be a positively gargantuan sense of self-entitlement, which causes you to do monstrous things."

"It is true. I must get my way and when I do not, there is hell to pay. Well, not this hell, but a sort of earthbound hell, one might say."

"Among the reasons you believe you are so entitled is that you consider yourself a man of taste, of erudition, of intellect, a superior being in all matters."

"Alas, it's true."

"It's amazing, by the way, how much higher the intelligence of those under my rule than those under His. I'm sure it's blissful Up There, but how could it not be with just dumb clucks and fat hens and the like. The parties must be such a bore."

"Perhaps, if I may, a suggestion," I said.

"Yes, yes, do go ahead. I'm all ears."

"A fitting sentence would be to turn my taste against me. Force me to read doggerel and bromide forever. An eternity spent with Bunyan in the various lands of the *Pilgrim's* godawful *Progress* would be quite severe."

"Yes, I see the point, but fear you are lying to the devil. Bunyan, though no Shakespeare and no Marlowe, was at the same time not without talent. Though rather drear from a philosophical sense, the *Progress* shows vision, passion, and exquisite language. Could you have made up a phrase as apt as 'slough of despond'?"

"I fear not, sir."

"Yes, I must aim lower, by far. But you have shown the way. I do like to invite participation. It seems so damned democratic, doesn't it?"

"Three cheers for democracy," I said.

"Yes. Anyhow, whom for Jack the Ripper? Hawthorne. Frightful and dull. Alas, a genius. Disapproved of puritans, which was his saving grace. Do you like the sea?"

"I abhor the sea."

"Then perhaps another American, Melville, who writes endlessly of whale hunting."

"I must say, that sounds rather interesting."

"Yes, yes, it is. I mean to punish you and would only reward you. It will not do. Hmm, I wonder—oh yes, yes, I have it!"

"Oh, God," I said. "Please . . . Not Dickens."

"Ha ha ha," he laughed. "Worse than Dickens. In fact, Dickens despised him, that's how bad he was."

I saw in a second about whom it was he was disquisitioning. Talk about a slough of despond! That is where I was to be sent for an eternity far longer than one involving flame, penetration, and roasting haunches.

"Please, sir," I said.

"'It was a dark and stormy night,'" the Devil chortled, amused by himself.

"I beg you, sir. You reduce me to tears!"

"Ha ha ha. Jack the Ripper, in hell, reading the collected works of Edward Bulwer-Lytton, forever. 'It was a dark and stormy night; the rain fell in torrents—except at occasional intervals, when it was checked by a violent gust of wind which swept up the streets (for it is in London that our scene lies) rattling along the housetops and fiercely agitating the scanty flame of the lamps that struggled the darkness'!"

"I beseech thee!"

"Beseech away, Dr. Ripper. It's so deliciously low! Trite, banal, utterly without interest, and yet it goes on and on and on. No wonder he's in heaven!"

"Even," I was reduced to pleading, "the operas?"

"*Especially* the operas," sayeth the Devil.

～

PERMISSIONS ACKNOWLEDGMENTS

David Abrahamsen. "Victims in the Night" by David Abrahamsen, copyright © 1992 by David Abrahamsen. Originally published in *Murder and Madness: The Secret Life of Jack the Ripper* (Donald I. Fine, 1992). Reprinted by permission of Dutton, an imprint of Penguin Publishing Group, a division of Penguin Random House LLC.

Boris Akunin. "The Decorator" by Boris Akunin, copyright © 1999 by Boris Akunin. Originally published in Russian as "Dekorator" in *Osobye Porucheniya* (Zakharov Publishers, 1999). This English translation originally published by Weidenfeld & Nicolson, London, in 2007, and subsequently published by Random House, a division of Penguin Random House LLC, New York, in 2008. Translation copyright © 2007 by Andrew Bromfield. Reprinted by permission of the author.

Scott Baker. "The Sins of the Fathers" by Scott Baker, copyright © 1988. Originally published in *Ripper!*, edited by Gardner Dozois and Susan Casper (Tom Doherty Associates, 1988). Reprinted by permission of the author.

Theodora Benson. "In the Fourth Ward" by Theodora Benson, copyright © 1930 by Theodora Benson. Reprinted by permission of the Estate of Theodora Benson and A. M. Heath & Co. Ltd.

Robert Bloch. "A Most Unusual Murder" by Robert Bloch, copyright © 1976 by *Ellery Queen's Mystery Magazine*, copyright renewed 1978 by Robert Bloch. Originally published in *Ellery Queen's Mystery Magazine* (March 1976). Reprinted by permission of the Estate of Robert Bloch and Richard Henshaw Group LLC.

Robert Bloch. "A Toy for Juliette" by Robert Bloch, copyright © 1967 by Harlan Ellison. Originally published in *Dangerous Visions*, edited by Harlan Ellison (Doubleday, 1967). Reprinted by permission of the Estate of Robert Bloch and Richard Henshaw Group LLC.

Robert Bloch. "Yours Truly, Jack the Ripper" by Robert Bloch, copyright © 1943 by *Weird Tales*, copyright renewed 1971 by Robert Bloch. Originally published in *Weird Tales* (July 1943). Reprinted by permission of the Estate of Robert Bloch and Richard Henshaw Group LLC.

Anthony Boucher. "A Kind of Madness" by Anthony Boucher, copyright © 1972, renewed. Originally published in *Ellery Queen's Mystery Magazine* (August 1972). Reprinted by permission of Curtis Brown, Ltd.

Ramsey Campbell. "Jack's Little Friend" by Ramsey Campbell, copyright © 1975 by Ramsey Campbell. Originally published in *Jack the Knife*, edited by Michel Parry (Mayflower, 1975). Reprinted by permission of the author.

Susan Casper. "Spring-Fingered Jack" by Susan Casper, copyright © 1983 by Susan Casper. Originally published in *Fears*, edited by Charles L. Grant (Berkley, 1983). Reprinted by permission of the author.

Patrice Chaplin. "By Flower and Dean Street" by Patrice Chaplin, copyright © 1976 by Patrice Chaplin. Originally published in *By Flower and Dean Street & The Love Apple* (Duckworth, 1976). Reprinted by permission of Christopher Sinclair-Stevenson.

R. Chetwynd-Hayes. "The Gatecrasher" by R. Chetwynd-Hayes, copyright © 1971 by R. Chetwynd-Hayes. Originally published in *The Unbidden* (Tandem, 1971). Reprinted by permission of the Estate of R. Chetwynd-Hayes.

Jeffery Deaver. "A Matter of Blood" by Jeffery Deaver, copyright © 2016 by Gunner Publications LLC. Used by permission of the author.